CHARLES DICKENS

Four Great Novels

·PARRAGON·

This edition published and distributed by
Parragon Book Service Ltd in 1995
Unit 13-17 Avonbridge Trading Estate
Atlantic Road
Avonmouth
Bristol BS11 9QD

Produced by Magpie Books Ltd, London

ISBN 0 75251 355 9

A copy of the British Library Cataloguing in Publication Data is available from the British Library.

Printed in Great Britain.

Oliver Twist

Chapter I

Treats of the Place where Oliver Twist was Born, and of the Circumstances attending his Birth

AMONG other public buildings in a certain town, which for many reasons it will be prudent to refrain from mentioning, and to which I will assign no fictitious name, there is one anciently common to most towns, great or small: to wit, a workhouse; and in this workhouse was born; on a day and date which I need not trouble myself to repeat, inasmuch as it can be of no possible consequence to the reader, in this stage of the business at all events; the item of mortality whose name is prefixed to the head of this chapter.

For a long time after it was ushered into this world of sorrow and trouble, by the parish surgeon, it remained a matter of considerable doubt whether the child would survive to bear any name at all; in which case it is somewhat more than probable that these memoirs would never have appeared; or, if they had, that being comprised within a couple of pages, they would have possessed the inestimable merit of being the most concise and faithful specimen of biography, extant in the literature of any age or country.

Although I am not disposed to maintain that the being born in a workhouse, is in itself the most fortunate and enviable circumstance that can possibly befall a human being, I do mean to say that in this particular instance, it was the best thing for Oliver Twist that could by possibility have occurred. The fact is, that there was considerable difficulty in inducing Oliver to take upon himself the office of respiration, – a troublesome practice, but one which custom has rendered necessary to our easy existence; and for some time he lay gasping on a little flock mattress, rather unequally poised between this world and the next: the balance being decidedly in favour of the latter. Now, if, during this brief period, Oliver had been surrounded by careful grandmothers, anxious aunts, experienced nurses, and doctors of profound wisdom, he would most inevitably and indubitably have been killed in no time. There being nobody by, however, but a pauper old woman, who was rendered rather misty by an unwonted allowance of beer; and a parish surgeon who did such matters by contract; Oliver and Nature fought out the point between them. The result was, that, after a few struggles, Oliver breathed, sneezed, and proceeded to advertise to the inmates of the workhouse the fact of a new burden having been imposed upon the parish, by setting up as loud a cry as could reasonably have been expected from a male infant who had not been possessed of that very useful appendage, a voice, for a much longer space of time than three minutes and a quarter.

As Oliver gave this first proof of the free and proper action of his lungs, the patchwork coverlet which was carelessly flung over the iron bedstead, rustled; the pale face of a young woman was raised feebly from the pillow; and a faint voice imperfectly articulated the words, "Let me see the child, and die."

The surgeon had been sitting with his face turned towards the fire: giving the palms of his hands a warm and a rub alternately. As the young woman spoke, he rose, and advancing to the bed's head, said, with more kindness than might have been expected of him:

"Oh, you must not talk about dying yet."

"Lor bless her dear heart, no!" interposed the nurse, hastily depositing in her pocket a green glass bottle, the contents of which she had been tasting in a corner with evident satisfaction. "Lor bless her dear heart, when she has lived as long as I have, sir, and had thirteen children of her own, and all on 'em dead except two, and them in the wurkus with me, she'll know better than to take on in that way, bless her dear heart! Think what it is to be a mother, there's a dear young lamb, do."

Apparently this consolatory perspective of a mother's prospects failed in producing its due effect. The patient shook her head, and stretched out her hand towards the child.

The surgeon deposited it in her arms. She imprinted her cold white lips passionately on its forehead; passed her hands over her face; gazed wildly round; shuddered; fell back – and died. They chafed her breast, hands, and temples; but the blood had stopped for ever. They talked of hope and comfort. They had been strangers too long.

"It's all over, Mrs Thingummy!" said the surgeon at last.

"Ah, poor dear, so it is!" said the nurse, picking up the cork of the green bottle, which had fallen out on the pillow, as she stooped to take up the child. "Poor dear!"

"You needn't mind sending up to me, if the child cries, nurse," said the surgeon, putting on his gloves with great deliberation. "It's very likely it *will* be troublesome. Give it a little gruel if it is." He put on his hat, and, pausing by the bed-side on his way to the door, added, "She was a good-looking girl, too; where did she come from?"

"She was brought here last night," replied the old woman, "by the overseer's order. She was found lying in the street. She had walked some distance, for her shoes were worn to pieces; but where she came from, or where she was going to, nobody knows."

The surgeon leaned over the body, and raised the left hand. "The old story," he said, shaking his head: "no wedding-ring, I see. Ah! Good night!"

The medical gentleman walked away to dinner; and the nurse, having once more applied herself to the green bottle, sat down on a low chair before the fire, and proceeded to dress the infant.

What an excellent example of the power of dress, young Oliver Twist was! Wrapped in the blanket which had hitherto formed his only covering, he might have been the child of a nobleman or a beggar; it would have been hard for the haughtiest stranger to have assigned him his proper station in society. But now that he was enveloped in the old calico robes which had grown yellow in the same service, he was badged and ticketed, and fell into his place at once – a parish child – the orphan of a workhouse – the humble, half-starved drudge – to be cuffed and buffeted through the world – despised by all, and pitied by none.

Oliver cried lustily. If he could have known that he was an orphan, left to the tender mercies of churchwardens and overseers, perhaps he would have cried the louder.

Chapter II

Treats of Oliver Twist's Growth, Education, and Board

For the next eight or ten months, Oliver was the victim of a systematic course of treachery and deception. He was brought up by hand. The hungry and destitute situation of the infant orphan was duly reported by the workhouse authorities to the parish authorities. The parish authorities inquired with dignity of the workhouse authorities, whether there was no female then domiciled in "the house" who was in a situation to impart to Oliver Twist, the consolation and nourishment of which he stood in need. The workhouse authorities replied with humility, that there was not. Upon this, the parish authorities magnanimously and humanely resolved, that Oliver should be "farmed," or, in other words, that he should be despatched to a branch-workhouse some three miles off, where twenty or thirty other juvenile offenders against the poor-laws, rolled about the floor all day, without the inconvenience of too much food or too much clothing, under the parental superintendence of an elderly female, who received the culprits at and for the consideration of sevenpence-halfpenny per small head per week. Sevenpence-halfpenny's worth per week is a good round diet for a child; a great deal may be got for sevenpence-halfpenny, quite enough to overload its stomach, and make it uncomfortable. The elderly female was a woman of wisdom and experience; she knew what was good for children; and she had a very accurate perception of what was good for herself. So, she appropriated the greater part of the weekly stipend to her own use, and consigned the rising parochial generation to even a shorter allowance than was originally provided for them. Thereby finding in the lowest depth a deeper still; and proving herself a very great experimental philosopher.

Everybody knows the story of another experimental philosopher who had a great theory about a horse being able to live without eating, and who demonstrated it so well, that he got his own horse down to a straw a day, and would unquestionably have rendered him a very spirited and rampacious animal on nothing at all, if he had not died, four-and-twenty hours before he was to have had his first comfortable bait of air. Unfortunately for the experimental philosophy of the female to whose protecting care Oliver Twist was delivered over, a similar result usually attended the operation of *her* system; for at the very moment when a child had contrived to exist upon the smallest possible portion of the weakest possible food, it did perversely happen in eight and a half cases out of ten, either that it sickened from want and cold, or fell into the fire from neglect, or got half-smothered by accident; in any one of which cases, the miserable little being was usually summoned into another world, and there gathered to the fathers it had never known in this.

Occasionally, when there was some more than usually interesting inquest upon a parish child who had been overlooked in turning up a bedstead, or inadvertently scalded to death when there happened to be a washing – though the latter accident was very scarce, anything approaching to a washing being of rare occurrence in the farm – the jury would take it into their heads to ask troublesome questions, or the parishioners would rebelliously affix their signatures to a remonstrance. But these impertinences were speedily checked by the evidence of the surgeon, and the testimony of the beadle; the former of whom had always opened the body and found nothing inside (which was very probable indeed), and the latter of whom invariably swore whatever the parish wanted; which was very self-devotional. Besides, the board made periodical pilgrimages to the farm, and always sent the beadle the day before, to say they were going. The children were neat and clean to behold, when *they* went; and what more would the people have!

It cannot be expected that this system of farming would produce any very extraordinary or luxuriant crop. Oliver Twist's ninth birth-day found him a pale thin child, somewhat diminutive in stature, and decidedly small in circumference. But nature or inheritance had implanted a good sturdy spirit in Oliver's breast. It had had plenty of room to expand, thanks to the spare diet of the establishment; and perhaps to this circumstance may be attributed his having any ninth birth-day at all. Be this as it may, however, it *was* his ninth birth-day; and he was keeping it in the coal-cellar with a select party of two other young gentlemen, who, after participating with him in a sound thrashing, had been locked up for atrociously presuming to be hungry, when Mrs Mann, the good lady of the house, was unexpectedly startled by the apparition of Mr Bumble, the beadle, striving to undo the wicket of the garden-gate.

"Goodness gracious! Is that you, Mr Bumble, sir?" said Mrs Mann, thrusting her head out of the window in well-affected ecstasies of joy. "(Susan, take Oliver and them two brats up stairs, and wash 'em directly.) My heart alive! Mr Bumble, how glad I am to see you, sure-ly!"

Now, Mr Bumble was a fat man, and a choleric; so, instead of responding to this open-hearted salutation in a kindred spirit, he gave the little wicket a tremendous shake, and then bestowed upon it a kick which could have emanated from no leg but a beadle's.

"Lor, only think," said Mrs Mann, running out, – for the three boys had been removed by this time, – "only think of that! That I should have forgotten that the gate was bolted on the inside, on account of them dear children! Walk in, sir; walk in, pray, Mr Bumble, do, sir."

Although this invitation was accompanied with a curtsey that might have softened the heart of a churchwarden, it by no means mollified the beadle.

"Do you think this respectful or proper conduct, Mrs Mann," inquired Mr Bumble, grasping his cane, "to keep the parish officers a waiting at your garden-gate, when they come here upon porochial business connected with the porochial orphans? Are you aweer, Mrs Mann, that you are, as I may say, a porochial delegate, and a stipendiary?"

"I'm sure, Mr Bumble, that I was only a telling one or two of the dear children as is so fond of you, that it was you a coming," replied Mrs Mann with great humility.

Mr Bumble had a great idea of his oratorical powers and his importance. He had displayed the one, and vindicated the other. He relaxed.

"Well, well, Mrs Mann," he replied in a calmer tone; "it may be as you say; it may be. Lead the way in, Mrs Mann, for I come on business, and have something to say."

Mrs Mann ushered the beadle into a small parlour with a brick floor; placed a seat for him; and officiously deposited his cocked hat and cane on the table before him. Mr Bumble wiped from his forehead the perspiration which his walk had engendered, glanced complacently at the cocked hat, and smiled. Yes, he smiled. Beadles are but men; and Mr Bumble smiled.

"Now don't you be offended at what I'm a going to say," observed Mrs Mann, with captivating sweetness. "You've had a long walk, you know, or I wouldn't mention it. Now, will you take a little drop of somethink, Mr Bumble?"

"Not a drop. Not a drop," said Mr Bumble, waving his right hand in a dignified, but placid manner.

"I think you will," said Mrs Mann, who had noticed the tone of the refusal, and the gesture that had accompanied it. "Just a leetle drop, with a little cold water, and a lump of sugar."

Mr Bumble coughed.

"Now, just a leetle drop," said Mrs Mann persuasively.

"What is it?" inquired the beadle.

"Why, it's what I'm obliged to keep a little of in the house to put into the blessed infants" Daffy, when they ain't well, Mr Bumble," replied Mrs Mann as she opened a corner cupboard, and took down a bottle and glass. "It's gin. I'll not deceive you, Mr B. It's gin."

"Do you give the children Daffy, Mrs Mann?" inquired Bumble, following with his eyes the interesting process of mixing.

"Ah, bless 'em, that I do, dear as it is," replied the nurse. "I couldn't see 'em suffer before my very eyes, you know, sir."

"No;" said Mr Bumble approvingly; "no, you could not. You are a humane woman, Mrs Mann." (Here she set down the glass.) "I shall take a early opportunity of mentioning it to the board, Mrs Mann." (He drew it towards him.) "You feel as a mother, Mrs Mann." (He stirred the gin-and-water.) "I – I drink your health with cheerfulness, Mrs Mann;" and he swallowed half of it.

"And now about business," said the beadle, taking out a leathern pocket-book. "The child that was half-baptized Oliver Twist, is nine year old to-day."

"Bless him!" interposed Mrs Mann, inflaming her left eye with the corner of her apron.

"And notwithstanding a offered reward of ten pound, which was afterwards increased to twenty pound. Notwithstanding the most superlative, and, I may say, supernat"ral exertions on the part of this parish," said Bumble, "we have never been able to discover who is his father, or what was his mother's settlement, name, or condition."

Mrs Mann raised her hands in astonishment; but added, after a moment's reflection, "How comes he to have any name at all, then?"

The beadle drew himself up with great pride, and said, "I inwented it."

"You, Mr Bumble!"

"I, Mrs Mann. We name our fondlings in alphabetical order. The last was a S, – Swubble, I named him. This was a T, – Twist, I named *him*. The next one as comes will be Unwin, and the next Vilkins. I have got names ready made to the end of the alphabet, and all the way through it again, when we come to Z."

"Why, you're quite a literary character, sir!" said Mrs Mann.

"Well, well," said the beadle, evidently gratified with the compliment; "perhaps I may be. Perhaps I may be, Mrs Mann." He finished the gin-and-water, and added, "Oliver being now too old to remain here, the board have determined to have him back into the house. I have come out myself to take him there. So let me see him at once."

"I'll fetch him directly," said Mrs Mann, leaving the room for that purpose. Oliver, having had by this time as much of the outer coat of dirt which encrusted his face and hands, removed, as could be scrubbed off in one washing, was led into the room by his benevolent protectress.

"Make a bow to the gentleman, Oliver," said Mrs Mann.

Oliver made a bow, which was divided between the beadle on the chair, and the cocked-hat on the table.

"Will you go along with me, Oliver?" said Mr Bumble, in a majestic voice.

Oliver was about to say that he would go along with anybody with great readiness, when, glancing upward, he caught sight of Mrs Mann, who had got behind the beadle's chair, and was shaking her fist at him with a furious countenance. He took the hint at once, for the fist had been too often impressed upon his body not to be deeply impressed upon his recollection.

"Will *she* go with me?" inquired poor Oliver.

"No, she can't," replied Mr Bumble. "But she'll come and see you sometimes."

This was no very great consolation to the child. Young as he was, however, he had sense enough to make a feint of feeling great regret at going away. It was no very difficult matter for the boy to call tears into his eyes. Hunger and recent ill-usage are great assistants if you want to cry; and Oliver cried very naturally indeed. Mrs Mann gave him a thousand embraces, and, what Oliver wanted a great deal more, a piece of bread and butter, lest he should seem too hungry when he got to the workhouse. With the slice of bread in his hand, and the little brown-cloth parish cap on his head, Oliver was then led away by Mr Bumble from the wretched home where one kind word or look had never lighted the gloom of his infant years. And yet he burst into an agony of childish grief, as the cottage-gate closed after him. Wretched as were the little companions in misery he was leaving behind, they were the only friends he had ever known; and a sense of his loneliness in the great wide world, sank into the child's heart for the first time.

Mr Bumble walked on with long strides; little Oliver, firmly grasping his gold-laced cuff, trotted beside him, inquiring at the end of every quarter of a mile whether they were "nearly there." To these interrogations Mr Bumble returned very brief and snappish replies; for the temporary blandness which gin-and-water awakens in some bosoms had by this time evaporated; and he was once again a beadle.

Oliver had not been within the walls of the workhouse a quarter of an hour, and had scarcely completed the demolition of a second slice of bread, when Mr Bumble, who had handed him over to the care of an old woman, returned; and, telling him it was a board night, informed him that the board had said he was to appear before it forthwith.

Not having a very clearly defined notion of what a live board was, Oliver was rather astounded by this intelligence, and was not quite certain whether he ought to laugh or cry. He had no time to think about the matter, however; for Mr Bumble gave him a tap on the head, with his cane, to wake him up: and another on the back to make him lively: and bidding him follow, conducted him into a large white-washed room, where eight or ten fat gentlemen were sitting round a table. At the top of the table, seated in an armchair rather higher than the rest, was a particularly fat gentleman with a very round, red face.

"Bow to the board," said Bumble. Oliver brushed away two or three tears that were lingering in his eyes; and seeing no board but the table, fortunately bowed to that.

"What's your name, boy?" said the gentleman in the high chair.

Oliver was frightened at the sight of so many gentlemen, which made him tremble: and the beadle gave him another tap behind, which made him cry. These two causes made him answer in a very low and hesitating voice; whereupon a gentleman in a white waistcoat said he was a fool. Which was a capital way of raising his spirits, and putting him quite at his ease.

"Boy," said the gentleman in the high chair, "listen to me. You know you're an orphan, I suppose?"

"What's that, sir?" inquired poor Oliver.

"The boy *is* a fool – I thought he was," said the gentleman in the white waistcoat.

"Hush!" said the gentleman who had spoken first. "You know you've got no father or mother, and that you were brought up by the parish, don't you?

"Yes, sir," replied Oliver, weeping bitterly.

"What are you crying for?" inquired the gentleman in the white waistcoat. And to be sure it was very extraordinary. What *could* the boy be crying for?

"I hope you say your prayers every night," said another gentleman in a gruff voice; "and pray for the people who feed you, and take care of you – like a Christian."

"Yes, sir," stammered the boy. The gentleman who spoke last was unconsciously right. It would have been *very* like a Christian, and a marvellously good Christian, too, if Oliver had prayed for the people who fed and took care of *him*. But he hadn't, because nobody had taught him.

"Well! You have come here to be educated, and taught a useful trade," said the red-faced gentleman in the high chair.

"So you'll begin to pick oakum to-morrow morning at six o'clock," added the surly one in the white waistcoat.

For the combination of both these blessings in the one simple process of picking oakum, Oliver bowed low by the direction of the beadle, and was then hurried away to a large ward: where, on a rough, hard bed, he sobbed himself to sleep. What a noble illustration of the tender laws of England! They let the paupers go to sleep!

Poor Oliver! He little thought, as he lay sleeping in happy unconsciousness of all around him, that the board had that very day arrived at a decision which would exercise the most material influence over all his future fortunes. But they had. And this was it:

The members of this board were very sage, deep, philosophical men; and when they came to turn their attention to the workhouse, they found out at once, what ordinary folks would never have discovered – the poor people liked it! It was a regular place of public entertainment for the poorer classes; a tavern where there was nothing to pay; a public breakfast, dinner, tea, and supper all the year round; a brick and mortar elysium, where it was all play and no work. "Oho!" said the board, looking very knowing; "we are the fellows to set this to rights; we'll stop it all, in no time." So, they established the rule, that all poor people should have the alternative (for they would compel nobody, not they), of being starved by a gradual process in the house, or by a quick one out of it. With this view, they contracted with the water-works to lay on an unlimited supply of water; and with a corn-factor to supply periodically small quantities of oatmeal; and issued three meals of thin gruel a day, with an onion twice a week, and half a roll on Sundays. They made a great many other wise and humane regulations, having reference to the ladies, which it is not necessary to repeat; kindly undertook to divorce poor married people, in consequence of the great expense of a suit in Doctors" Commons; and, instead of compelling a man to support his family, as they had theretofore done, took his family away from him, and made him a bachelor! There is no saying how many applicants for relief, under these last two heads, might have started up in all classes of society, if it had not been coupled with the workhouse; but the board were long-headed men, and had provided for this difficulty. The relief was inseparable from the workhouse and the gruel; and that frightened people.

For the first six months after Oliver Twist was removed, the system was in full operation. It was rather expensive at first, in consequence of the increase in the undertaker's bill, and the necessity of taking in the clothes of all the paupers, which fluttered loosely on their wasted, shrunken forms, after a week or two's gruel. But the number of workhouse inmates got thin as well as the paupers; and the board were in ecstasies.

The room in which the boys were fed, was a large stone hall, with a copper at one end: out of which the master, dressed in an apron for the purpose, and assisted by one or two women, ladled the gruel at meal-times. Of this festive composition each boy had one porringer, and no more – except on occasions of great public rejoicing, when he had two ounces and a quarter of bread besides. The bowls never wanted washing. The boys polished them with their spoons till they shone again; and when they had performed this operation (which never took very long, the spoons being nearly as large as the bowls), they would sit staring at the copper, with such eager eyes, as if they could have devoured the very bricks of which it was composed; employing themselves, meanwhile, in sucking their fingers most assiduously, with the view of catching up any stray splashes of gruel that might have been cast thereon. Boys have generally excellent appetites. Oliver Twist and his companions suffered the tortures of slow starvation for three months: at last they got so voracious and wild with hunger, that one boy, who was tall for his age, and hadn't been used to that sort of thing (for his father had kept a small cook-shop), hinted darkly to his companions, that unless he had another basin of gruel *per diem*, he was afraid he might some night happen to eat the boy who slept next him, who happened to be a weakly youth of tender age. He had a wild, hungry eye; and they implicitly believed him. A council was held; lots were cast who should walk up to the master after supper that evening, and ask for more; and it fell to Oliver Twist.

The evening arrived; the boys took their places. The master, in his cook's uniform, stationed himself at the copper; his pauper assistants ranged themselves behind him; the gruel was served out; and a long grace was said over the short commons. The gruel disappeared; the boys whispered each other, and winked at Oliver; while his next neighbours nudged him. Child as he was, he was desperate with hunger, and reckless with misery. He rose from the table; and advancing to the master, basin and spoon in hand, said: somewhat alarmed at his own temerity:

"Please, sir, I want some more."

The master was a fat, healthy man; but he turned very pale. He gazed in stupefied astonishment on the small rebel for some seconds, and then clung for support to the copper. The assistants were paralysed with wonder; the boys with fear.

"What!" said the master at length, in a faint voice.

"Please, sir," replied Oliver, "I want some more."

The master aimed a blow at Oliver's head with the ladle; pinioned him in his arms; and shrieked aloud for the beadle.

The board were sitting in solemn conclave, when Mr Bumble rushed into the room in great excitement, and addressing the gentleman in the high chair, said.

"Mr Limbkins, I beg your pardon, sir! Oliver Twist has asked for more!"

There was a general start. Horror was depicted on every countenance.

"For *more!*" said Mr Limbkins. "Compose yourself, Bumble, and answer me distinctly. Do I understand that he asked for more, after he had eaten the supper allotted by the dietary?"

"He did, sir," replied Bumble.

"That boy will be hung," said the gentleman in the white waistcoat. "I know that boy will be hung."

Nobody controverted the prophetic gentleman's opinion. An animated discussion took place. Oliver was ordered into instant confinement; and a bill was next morning pasted on the outside of the gate, offering a reward of five pounds to anybody who would take Oliver Twist off the hands of the parish. In other words, five pounds and Oliver Twist were offered to any man or woman who wanted an apprentice to any trade, business, or calling.

"I never was more convinced of anything in my life," said the gentleman in the white waistcoat, as he knocked at the gate and read the bill next morning: "I never was more convinced of anything in my life, than I am that that boy will come to be hung."

As I purpose to show in the sequel whether the white-waistcoated gentleman was right or not, I should perhaps mar the interest of this narrative (supposing it to possess any at all), if I ventured to hint just yet, whether the life of Oliver Twist had this violent termination or no.

Chapter III

Relates how Oliver Twist was very near getting a Place, which would not have been a Sinecure

For a week after the commission of the impious and profane offence of asking for more, Oliver remained a close prisoner in the dark and solitary room to which he had been consigned by the wisdom and mercy of the board. It appears, at first sight, not unreasonable to suppose, that, if he had entertained a becoming feeling of respect for the prediction of the gentleman in the white waistcoat, he would have established that sage individual's prophetic character, once and for ever, by tying one end of his pocket-handkerchief to a hook in the wall, and attaching himself to the other. To the performance of this feat, however, there was one obstacle: namely, that pocket-handkerchiefs being decided articles of luxury, had been, for all future times and ages, removed from the noses of paupers by the express order of the board, in council assembled; solemnly given and pronounced under their hands and seals. There was a still greater obstacle in Oliver's youth and childishness. He only cried bitterly all day; and, when the long, dismal night came on, spread his little hands before his eyes to shut out the darkness, and crouching in the corner, tried to sleep: ever and anon waking with a start and tremble, and drawing himself closer and closer to the wall, as if to feel even its cold hard surface were a protection in the gloom and loneliness which surrounded him.

Let it not be supposed by the enemies of "the system," that, during the period of his solitary incarceration. Oliver was denied the benefit of exercise, the pleasure of society, or the advantages of religious consolation. As for exercise, it was nice cold weather, and he was allowed to perform his ablutions every morning under the pump, in a stone yard, in the presence of Mr Bumble, who prevented his catching cold, and caused a tingling sensation to pervade his frame, by repeated applications of the cane. As for society, he was carried every other day into the hall where the boys dined, and there sociably flogged as a public warning and example. And so far from being denied the advantages of religious consolation, he was kicked into the same apartment every evening at prayer-time, and there permitted to listen to, and console his mind with, a general supplication of the boys, containing a special clause, therein inserted by authority of the board, in which they entreated to be made good, virtuous, contented, and obedient, and to be guarded from the sins and vices of Oliver Twist: whom the supplication distinctly set forth to be under the exclusive patronage and protection of the powers of wickedness, and an article direct from the manufactory of the very Devil himself.

It chanced one morning, while Oliver's affairs were in this auspicious and comfortable state, that Mr Gamfield, chimney-sweep, went his way down the High Street, deeply cogitating in his mind his ways and means of paying certain arrears of rent, for which his landlord had become rather pressing. Mr Gamfield's most sanguine estimate of his finances could not raise them within full five pounds of the desired amount; and, in a species of arithmetical desperation, he was alternately cudgelling his brains and his donkey, when, passing the workhouse, his eyes encountered the bill on the gate.

"Wo – o!" said Mr Gamfield to the donkey.

The donkey was in a state of profound abstraction: wondering, probably, whether he was destined to be regaled with a cabbage-stalk or two when he had disposed of the two sacks of soot with which the little cart was laden; so, without noticing the word of command, he jogged onward.

Mr Gamfield growled a fierce imprecation on the donkey generally, but more particularly on his eyes; and, running after him, bestowed a blow on his head, which would inevitably have beaten in any skull but a donkey's. Then, catching hold of the bridle, he gave his jaw a sharp wrench, by way of gentle reminder that he was not his own master; and by these means turned him round. He then gave him another blow on the head, just to stun him till he came back again. Having completed these arrangements, he walked up to the gate, to read the bill.

The gentleman with the white waistcoat was standing at the gate with his hands behind him, after having delivered himself of some profound sentiments in the board-room. Having witnessed the little dispute between Mr Gamfield and the donkey, he smiled joyously when that person came up to read the bill, for he saw at once that Mr Gamfield was exactly the sort of master Oliver Twist wanted. Mr Gamfield smiled, too, as he perused the document; for five pounds was just the sum he had been wishing for;

and, as to the boy with which it was encumbered, Mr Gamfield, knowing what the dietary of the workhouse was, well knew he would be a nice small pattern, just the very thing for register stoves. So, he spelt the bill through again, from beginning to end; and then, touching his fur cap in token of humility, accosted the gentleman in the white waistcoat.

"This here boy, sir, wot the parish wants to 'prentis," said Mr Gamfield.

"Ay, my man," said the gentleman in the white waistcoat, with a condescending smile. "What of him?"

"If the parish vould like him to learn a right pleasant trade, in a good 'spectable chimbley-sweepin" business," said Mr Gamfield, "I wants a 'prentis, and I am ready to take him."

"Walk in," said the gentleman in the white waistcoat. Mr Gamfield having lingered behind, to give the donkey another blow on the head, and another wrench of the jaw, as a caution not to run away in his absence, followed the gentleman with the white waistcoat into the room where Oliver had first seen him.

"It's a nasty trade," said Mr Limbkins, when Gamfield had again stated his wish.

"Young boys have been smothered in chimneys before now," said another gentleman.

"That's acause they damped the straw afore they lit it in the chimbley to make 'em come down agin," said Gamfield; "that's all smoke, and no blaze; vereas smoke ain't o' no use at all in making a boy come down, for it only sinds him to sleep, and that's wot he likes. Boys is wery obstinit, and wery lazy, gen'lmen, and there's nothink like a good hot blaze to make 'em come down vith a run. It's humane too, gen'lmen, acause, even if they've stuck in the chimbley, roasting their feet makes 'em struggle to hextricate theirselves."

The gentleman in the white waistcoat appeared very much amused by this explanation; but his mirth was speedily checked by a look from Mr Limbkins. The board then proceeded to converse among themselves for a few minutes, but in so low a tone, that the words "saving of expenditure," "looked well in the accounts," "have a printed report published," were alone audible. These only chanced to be heard, indeed, on account of their being very frequently repeated with great emphasis.

At length the whispering ceased; and the members of the board, having resumed their seats and their solemnity, Mr Limbkins said:

"We have considered your proposition, and we don't approve of it."

"Not at all," said the gentleman in the white waistcoat.

"Decidedly not," added the other members.

As Mr Gamfield did happen to labour under the slight imputation of having bruised three or four boys to death already, it occurred to him that the board had, perhaps, in some unaccountable freak, taken it into their heads that this extraneous circumstance ought to influence their proceedings. It was very unlike their general mode of doing business, if they had; but still, as he had no particular wish to revive the rumour, he twisted his cap in his hands, and walked slowly from the table.

"So you won't let me have him, gen'lmen?" said Mr Gamfield, pausing near the door.

"No," replied Mr Limbkins; "at least, as it's a nasty business, we think you ought to take something less than the premium we offered."

Mr Gamfield's countenance brightened, as, with a quick step, he returned to the table, and said,

"What'll you give, gen'lmen? Come! Don't be too hard on a poor man. What'll you give?"

"I should say, three pound ten was plenty," said Mr Limbkins.

"Ten shillings too much," said the gentleman in the white waistcoat.

"Come!" said Gamfield: "say four pound, gen'lmen. Say four pound, and you've got rid on him for good and all. There!"

"Three pound ten," repeated Mr Limbkins, firmly.

"Come! I'll split the difference, gen'lmen," urged Gamfield. "Three pound fifteen."

"Not a farthing more," was the firm reply of Mr Limbkins.

"You're desperate hard upon me, gen'lmen," said Gamfield, wavering.

"Pooh! pooh! nonsense!" said the gentleman in the white waistcoat. "He'd be cheap with nothing at all, as a premium. Take him, you silly fellow! He's just the boy for you. He wants the stick, now and then: it'll do him good; and his board needn't come very expensive, for he hasn't been over-fed since he was born. Ha! ha! ha!"

Mr Gamfield gave an arch look at the faces round the table, and, observing a smile on all of them, gradually broke into a smile himself. The bargain was made. Mr Bumble was at once instructed that Oliver Twist and his indentures were to be conveyed before the magistrate, for signature and approval, that very afternoon.

In pursuance of this determination, little Oliver, to his excessive astonishment, was released from bondage, and ordered to put himself into a clean shirt. He had hardly achieved this very unusual gymnastic performance, when Mr Bumble brought him, with his own hands, a basin of gruel, and the holiday allowance of two ounces and a quarter of bread. At this tremendous sight, Oliver began to cry very piteously: thinking, not unnaturally, that the board must have determined to kill him for some useful purpose, or they never would have begun to fatten him up in that way.

"Don't make your eyes red, Oliver, but eat your food and be thankful," said Mr Bumble, in a tone of impressive pomposity. "You're a going to be made a 'prentice of, Oliver."

"A 'prentice, sir!" said the child, trembling.

"Yes, Oliver," said Mr Bumble. "The kind and blessed gentlemen which is so many parents to you, Oliver, when you have none of your own: are a going to "prentice you: and to set you up in life, and make a man of you: although the expense to the parish is three pound ten! – three pound ten, Oliver! – seventy shillins – one hundred and forty sixpences! – and all for a naughty orphan which nobody can't love."

As Mr Bumble paused to take breath, after delivering this address in an awful voice, the tears rolled down the poor child's face, and he sobbed bitterly.

"Come," said Mr Bumble, somewhat less pompously, for it was gratifying to his feelings to observe the effect his eloquence had produced; "Come,

Oliver! Wipe your eyes with the cuffs of your jacket, and don't cry into your gruel; that's a very foolish action, Oliver." It certainly was, for there was quite enough water in it already.

On their way to the magistrate, Mr Bumble instructed Oliver that all he would have to do, would be to look very happy, and say, when the gentleman asked him if he wanted to be apprenticed, that he should like it very much indeed; both of which injunctions Oliver promised to obey: the rather as Mr Bumble threw in a gentle hint, that if he failed in either particular, there was no telling what would be done to him. When they arrived at the office, he was shut up in a little room by himself, and admonished by Mr Bumble to stay there, until he came back to fetch him.

There the boy remained, with a palpitating heart, for half an hour. At the expiration of which time Mr Bumble thrust in his head, unadorned with the cocked hat, and said aloud:

"Now, Oliver, my dear, come to the gentleman." As Mr Bumble said this, he put on a grim and threatening look, and added, in a low voice, "Mind what I told you, you young rascal!"

Oliver stared innocently in Mr Bumble's face at this somewhat contradictory style of address; but that gentleman prevented his offering any remark thereupon, by leading him at once into an adjoining room: the door of which was open. It was a large room, with a great window. Behind a desk, sat two old gentlemen with powdered heads: one of whom was reading the newspaper; while the other was perusing, with the aid of a pair of tortoise-shell spectacles, a small piece of parchment which lay before him. Mr Limbkins was standing in front of the desk on one side; and Mr Gamfield, with a partially washed face, on the other; while two or three bluff-looking men, in top-boots, were lounging about.

The old gentleman with the spectacles gradually dozed off, over the little bit of parchment; and there was a short pause, after Oliver had been stationed by Mr Bumble in front of the desk.

"This is the boy, your worship," said Mr Bumble.

The old gentleman who was reading the newspaper raised his head for a moment, and pulled the other old gentleman by the sleeve; whereupon, the last-mentioned old gentleman woke up.

"Oh, is this the boy?" said the old gentleman.

"This is him, sir," replied Mr Bumble. "Bow to the magistrate, my dear."

Oliver roused himself, and made his best obeisance. He had been wondering, with his eyes fixed on the magistrates" powder, whether all boards were born with that white stuff on their heads, and were boards from thenceforth on that account.

"Well," said the old gentleman, "I suppose he's fond of chimney-sweeping?"

"He doats on it, your worship," replied Bumble; giving Oliver a sly pinch, to intimate that he had better not say he didn't.

"And he *will* be a sweep, will he?" inquired the old gentleman.

"If we was to bind him to any other trade to-morrow, he'd run away simultaneous, your worship," replied Bumble.

"And this man that's to be his master – you, sir – you'll treat him well, and feed him, and do all that sort of thing, will you?" said the old gentleman.

"When I says I will, I means I will," replied Mr Gamfield doggedly.

"You're a rough speaker, my friend, but you look an honest, open-hearted man," said the old gentleman: turning his spectacles in the direction of the candidate for Oliver's premium, whose villanous countenance was a regular stamped receipt for cruelty. But the magistrate was half blind and half childish, so he couldn't reasonably be expected to discern what other people did.

"I hope I am, sir," said Mr Gamfield, with an ugly leer.

"I have no doubt you are, my friend," replied the old gentleman: fixing his spectacles more firmly on his nose, and looking about him for the inkstand.

It was the critical moment of Oliver's fate. If the inkstand had been where the old gentleman thought it was, he would have dipped his pen into it, and signed the indentures, and Oliver would have been straightway hurried off. But, as it chanced to be immediately under his nose, it followed, as a matter of course, that he looked all over his desk for it, without finding it; and happening in the course of his search to look straight before him, his gaze encountered the pale and terrified face of Oliver Twist: who despite all the admonitory looks and pinches of Bumble, was regarding the repulsive countenance of his future master, with a mingled expression of horror and fear, too palpable to be mistaken, even by a half-blind magistrate.

The old gentleman stopped, laid down his pen, and looked from Oliver to Mr Limbkins; who attempted to take snuff with a cheerful and unconcerned aspect.

"My boy!" said the old gentleman, leaning over the desk. Oliver started at the sound. He might be excused for doing so: for the words were kindly said; and strange sounds frighten one. He trembled violently, and burst into tears.

"My boy!" said the old gentleman, "you look pale and alarmed. What is the matter?"

"Stand a little away from him, Beadle," said the other magistrate: laying aside the paper, and leaning forward with an expression of interest. "Now, boy, tell us what's the matter: don't be afraid."

Oliver fell on his knees, and clasping his hands together, prayed that they would order him back to the dark room – that they would starve him – beat him – kill him if they pleased – rather than send him away with that dreadful man.

"Well!" said Mr Bumble, raising his hands and eyes with most impressive solemnity, "Well! of all the artful and designing orphans that ever I see, Oliver, you are one of the most bare-facedest."

"Hold your tongue, Beadle," said the second old gentleman, when Mr Bumble had given vent to this compound adjective.

"I beg your worship's pardon," said Mr Bumble, incredulous of his having heard aright. "Did your worship speak to me?"

"Yes. Hold your tongue."

Mr Bumble was stupefied with astonishment. A beadle ordered to hold his tongue! A moral revolution!

The old gentleman in the tortoise-shell spectacles looked at his companion, he nodded significantly.

"We refuse to sanction these indentures," said the old gentleman: tossing aside the piece of parchment as he spoke.

"I hope," stammered Mr Limbkins: "I hope the magistrates will not form the opinion that the authorities have been guilty of any improper conduct, on the unsupported testimony of a mere child."

"The magistrates are not called upon to pronounce any opinion on the matter," said the second old gentleman sharply. "Take the boy back to the workhouse, and treat him kindly. He seems to want it."

That same evening, the gentleman in the white waistcoat most positively and decidedly affirmed, not only that Oliver would be hung, but that he would be drawn and quartered into the bargain. Mr Bumble shook his head with gloomy mystery, and said he wished he might come to good; where-unto Mr Gamfield replied, that he wished he might come to him; which, although he agreed with the beadle in most matters, would seem to be a wish of a totally opposite description.

The next morning, the public were once more informed that Oliver Twist was again To Let, and that five pounds would be paid to anybody who would take possession of him.

Chapter IV

Oliver, being offered another Place, makes his first Entry into Public Life

In great families, when an advantageous place cannot be obtained, either in possession, reversion, remainder, or expectancy, for the young man who is growing up, it is a very general custom to send him to sea. The board, in imitation of so wise and salutary an example, took counsel together on the expediency of shipping off Oliver Twist, in some small trading vessel bound to a good unhealthy port. This suggested itself as the very best thing that could possibly be done with him: the probability being, that the skipper would flog him to death, in a playful mood, some day after dinner, or would knock his brains out with an iron bar; both pastimes being, as is pretty generally known, very favourite and common recreations among gentlemen of that class. The more the case presented itself to the board, in this point of view, the more manifold the advantages of the step appeared; so, they came to the conclusion that the only way of providing for Oliver effectually, was to send him to sea without delay.

Mr Bumble had been despatched to make various preliminary inquiries, with the view of finding out some captain or other who wanted a cabin-boy without any friends; and was returning to the workhouse to communicate the result of his mission; when he encountered at the gate, no less a person than Mr Sowerberry, the parochial undertaker.

Mr Sowerberry was a tall, gaunt, large-jointed man, attired in a suit of threadbare black, with darned cotton stockings of the same colour, and shoes to answer. His features were not naturally intended to wear a smiling aspect, but he was in general rather given to professional jocosity. His step was elastic, and his face betokened inward pleasantry, as he advanced to Mr Bumble, and shook him cordially by the hand.

"I have taken the measure of the two women that died last night, Mr Bumble," said the undertaker.

"You'll make your fortune, Mr Sowerberry," said the beadle, as he thrust his thumb and forefinger into the proffered snuff-box of the undertaker: which was an ingenious little model of a patent coffin. "I say you'll make your fortune, Mr Sowerberry," repeated Mr Bumble, tapping the undertaker on the shoulder, in a friendly manner, with his cane.

"Think so?" said the undertaker in a tone which half admitted and half disputed the probability of the event. "The prices allowed by the board are very small, Mr Bumble."

"So are the coffins," replied the beadle: with precisely as near an approach to a laugh as a great official ought to indulge in.

Mr Sowerberry was much tickled at this: as of course he ought to be; and laughed a long time without cessation. "Well, well, Mr Bumble," he said at length, "there's no denying that, since the new system of feeding has come in, the coffins are something narrower and more shallow than they used to be; but we must have some profit, Mr Bumble. Well-seasoned timber is an expensive article, sir; and all the iron handles come, by canal, from Birmingham."

"Well, well," said Mr Bumble, "every trade has its drawbacks. A fair profit is, of course, allowable."

"Of course, of course," replied the undertaker; "and if I don't get a profit upon this or that particular article, why, I make it up in the long-run, you see – he! he! he!"

"Just so," said Mr Bumble.

"Though I must say," continued the undertaker, resuming the current of observations which the beadle had interrupted: "though I must say, Mr Bumble, that I have to contend against one very great disadvantage: which is, that all the stout people go off the quickest. The people who have been better off, and have paid rates for many years, are the first to sink when they come into the house; and let me tell you, Mr Bumble, that three or four inches over one's calculation makes a great hole in one's profits; especially when one has a family to provide for, sir."

As Mr Sowerberry said this, with the becoming indignation of an ill-used man; and as Mr Bumble felt that it rather tended to convey a reflection on the honour of the parish; the latter gentleman thought it advisable to change the subject. Oliver Twist being uppermost in his mind, he made him his theme.

"By the bye," said Mr Bumble, "you don't know anybody who wants a boy, do you? A porochial "prentis, who is at present a deadweight; a millstone, as I may say; round the porochial throat? Liberal terms, Mr Sowerberry, liberal terms!" As Mr Bumble spoke, he raised his cane to the bill above him, and gave three distinct raps upon the words "five pounds:" which were printed thereon in Roman capitals of gigantic size.

"Gadso!" said the undertaker: taking Mr Bumble by the gilt-edged lappel of his official coat; "that's just the very thing I wanted to speak to you about. You know – dear me, what a very elegant button this is, Mr Bumble! I never noticed it before."

"Yes, I think it is rather pretty," said the beadle, glancing proudly downwards at the large brass buttons which embellished his coat. "The die is the same as the porochial seal – the Good Samaritan healing the sick and bruised man. The board presented it to me on New-year's morning, Mr Sowerberry. I put it on, I remember, for the first time, to attend the inquest on that reduced tradesman, who died in a doorway at midnight."

"I recollect," said the undertaker. "The jury brought it in, "Died from exposure to the cold, and want of the common necessaries of life," didn't they?"

Mr Bumble nodded.

"And they made it a special verdict, I think," said the undertaker, "by adding some words to the effect, that if the relieving officer had –"

"Tush! Foolery!" interposed the beadle. "If the board attended to all the nonsense that ignorant jurymen talk, they'd have enough to do."

"Very true," said the undertaker; "they would indeed."

"Juries," said Mr Bumble, grasping his cane tightly, as was his wont when working into a passion: "juries is ineddicated, vulgar, grovelling wretches."

"So they are," said the undertaker.

"They haven't no more philosophy nor political economy about 'em than that," said the beadle, snapping his fingers contemptuously.

"No more they have," acquiesced the undertaker.

"I despise 'em," said the beadle, growing very red in the face.

"So do I," rejoined the undertaker.

"And I only wish we'd a jury of the independent sort, in the house for a week or two," said the beadle; "the rules and regulations of the board would soon bring their spirit down for 'em."

"Let 'em alone for that," replied the undertaker. So saying, he smiled, approvingly: to calm the rising wrath of the indignant parish officer.

Mr Bumble lifted off his cocked hat; took a handkerchief from the inside of the crown; wiped from his forehead the perspiration which his rage had engendered; fixed the cocked hat on again; and, turning to the undertaker, said in a calmer voice:

"Well; what about the boy?"

"Oh!" replied the undertaker; "why, you know, Mr Bumble, I pay a good deal towards the poor's rates."

"Hem!" said Mr Bumble. "Well?"

"Well," replied the undertaker, "I was thinking that if I pay so much towards 'em, I've a right to get as much out of 'em as I can, Mr Bumble; and so – and so – I think I'll take the boy myself."

Mr Bumble grasped the undertaker by the arm, and led him into the building. Mr Sowerberry was closeted with the board for five minutes; and it was arranged that Oliver should go to him that evening "upon liking" – a phrase which means, in the case of a parish apprentice, that if the master find, upon a short trial, that he can get enough work out of a boy without putting too much food into him, he shall have him for a term of years, to do what he likes with.

When little Oliver was taken before "the gentlemen" that evening; and informed that he was to go, that night, as general house-lad to a coffin-maker's; and that if he complained of his situation, or ever came back to the parish again, he would be sent to sea, there to be drowned, or knocked on the head, as the case might be, he evinced so little emotion, that they by common consent pronounced him a hardened young rascal, and ordered Mr Bumble to remove him forthwith.

Now, although it was very natural that the board, of all people in the world, should feel in a great state of virtuous astonishment and horror at the smallest tokens of want of feeling on the part of anybody, they were rather out, in this particular instance. The simple fact was, that Oliver, instead of possessing too little feeling, possessed rather too much; and was in a fair way of being reduced, for life, to a state of brutal stupidity and sullenness by the ill usage he had received. He heard the news of his destination, in perfect silence; and, having had his luggage put into his hand – which was not very difficult to carry, inasmuch as it was all comprised within the limits of a brown paper parcel, about half a foot square by three inches deep – he pulled his cap over his eyes; and once more attaching himself to Mr Bumble's coat cuff, was led away by that dignitary to a new scene of suffering.

For some time, Mr Bumble drew Oliver along, without notice or remark; for the beadle carried his head very erect, as a beadle always should: and, it being a windy day, little Oliver was completely enshrouded by the skirts of Mr Bumble's coat as they blew open, and disclosed to great advantage his flapped waistcoat and drab plush knee-breeches. As they drew near to their destination, however, Mr Bumble thought it expedient to look down, and see that the boy was in good order for inspection by his new master: which he accordingly did, with a fit and becoming air of gracious patronage.

"Oliver!" said Mr Bumble.

"Yes, sir," replied Oliver, in a low, tremulous voice.

"Pull that cap off your eyes, and hold up your head, sir."

Although Oliver did as he was desired, at once; and passed the back of his unoccupied hand briskly across his eyes, he left a tear in them when he looked up at his conductor. As Mr Bumble gazed sternly upon him, it rolled down his cheek. It was followed by another, and another. The child made a strong effort, but it was an unsuccessful one. Withdrawing his other hand from Mr Bumble's, he covered his face with both; and wept until the tears sprung out from between his chin and bony fingers.

"Well!" exclaimed Mr Bumble, stopping short, and darting at his little charge a look of intense malignity. "Well! Of *all* the ungratefullest, and worst-disposed boys as ever I see, Oliver, you are the –"

"No, no, sir," sobbed Oliver, clinging to the hand which held the well-known cane; "no, no, sir; I will be good indeed; indeed, indeed I will, sir! I am a very little boy, sir; and it is so – so –"

"So what?" inquired Mr Bumble in amazement.

"So lonely, sir! So very lonely!" cried the child. "Everybody hates me.

Oh! sir, don't, don't pray be cross to me!" The child beat his hand upon his heart; and looked in his companion's face, with tears of real agony.

Mr Bumble regarded Oliver's piteous and helpless look, with some astonishment, for a few seconds; hemmed three or four times in a husky manner; and, after muttering something about "that troublesome cough," bade Oliver dry his eyes and be a good boy. Then once more taking his hand, he walked on with him in silence.

The undertaker, who had just put up the shutters of his shop, was making some entries in his day-book by the light of a most appropriate dismal candle, when Mr Bumble entered.

"Aha!" said the undertaker: looking up from the book, and pausing in the middle of a word; "is that you, Bumble?"

"No one else, Mr Sowerberry," replied the beadle. "Here! I've brought the boy." Oliver made a bow.

"Oh! that's the boy, is it?" said the undertaker: raising the candle above his head, to get a better view of Oliver. "Mrs Sowerberry, will you have the goodness to come here a moment, my dear?"

Mrs Sowerberry emerged from a little room behind the shop, and presented the form of a short, thin, squeezed-up woman, with a vixenish countenance.

"My dear," said Mr Sowerberry, deferentially, "this is the boy from the workhouse that I told you of." Oliver bowed again.

"Dear me!" said the undertaker's wife, "he's very small."

"Why, he *is* rather small," replied Mr Bumble: looking at Oliver as if it were his fault that he was no bigger; "he *is* small. There's no denying it. But he'll grow, Mrs Sowerberry – he'll grow."

"Ah! I dare say he will," replied the lady pettishly, "on our victuals and our drink. I see no saving in parish children, not I; for they always cost more to keep, than they're worth. However, men always think they know best. There! Get down stairs, little bag o" bones." With this, the undertaker's wife opened a side door, and pushed Oliver down a steep flight of stairs into a stone cell, damp and dark: forming the ante-room to the coal-cellar, and denominated "kitchen:" wherein sat a slatternly girl, in shoes down at heel, and blue worsted stockings very much out of repair.

"Here, Charlotte," said Mrs Sowerberry, who had followed Oliver down, "give this boy some of the cold bits that were put by for Trip. He hasn't come home since the morning, so he may go without 'em. I dare say the boy isn't too dainty to eat 'em, – are you, boy?"

Oliver, whose eyes had glistened at the mention of meat, and who was trembling with eagerness to devour it, replied in the negative; and a plateful of coarse broken victuals was set before him.

I wish some well-fed philosopher, whose meat and drink turn to gall within him; whose blood is ice, whose heart is iron; could have seen Oliver Twist clutching at the dainty viands that the dog had neglected. I wish he could have witnessed the horrible avidity with which Oliver tore the bits asunder with all the ferocity of famine. There is only one thing I should like better; and that would be to see the Philosopher making the same sort of meal himself, with the same relish.

"Well," said the undertaker's wife, when Oliver had finished his supper: which she had regarded in silent horror, and with fearful auguries of his future appetite: "have you done?"

There being nothing eatable within his reach, Oliver replied in the affirmative.

"Then come with me," said Mrs Sowerberry: taking up a dim and dirty lamp, and leading the way up stairs; "your bed's under the counter. You don't mind sleeping among the coffins, I suppose? But it doesn't much matter whether you do or don't, for you can't sleep anywhere else. Come; don't keep me here all night!"

Oliver lingered no longer, but meekly followed his new mistress.

Chapter V

Oliver mingles with new Associates. Going to a Funeral for the first Time, he forms an unfavourable Notion of his Master's Business

OLIVER, being left to himself in the undertaker's shop, set the lamp down on a workman's bench, and gazed timidly about him with a feeling of awe and dread, which many people a good deal older than he, will be at no loss to understand. An unfinished coffin on black tressels, which stood in the middle of the shop, looked so gloomy and death-like that a cold tremble came over him, every time his eyes wandered in the direction of the dismal object: from which he almost expected to see some frightful form slowly rear its head, to drive him mad with terror. Against the wall were ranged, in regular array, a long row of elm boards cut into the same shape: looking in the dim light, like high-shouldered ghosts with their hands in their breeches-pockets. Coffin-plates, elm-chips, bright-headed nails, and shreds of black cloth, lay scattered on the floor; and the wall behind the counter was ornamented with a lively representation of two mutes in very stiff neckcloths, on duty at a large private door, with a hearse drawn by four black steeds, approaching in the distance. The shop was close and hot. The atmosphere seemed tainted with the smell of coffins. The recess beneath the counter in which his flock mattress was thrust, looked like a grave.

Nor were these the only dismal feelings which depressed Oliver. He was alone in a strange place; and we all know how chilled and desolate the best of us will sometimes feel in such a situation. The boy had no friends to care for, or to care for him. The regret of no recent separation was fresh in his mind; the absence of no loved and well-remembered face sank heavily into his heart. But his heart *was* heavy, notwithstanding; and he wished, as he crept into his narrow bed, that that were his coffin, and that he could be lain in a calm and lasting sleep in the church-yard ground, with the tall grass waving gently above his head, and the sound of the old deep bell to soothe him in his sleep.

Oliver was awakened in the morning, by a loud kicking at the outside of the shop-door: which, before he could huddle on his clothes, was repeated, in an angry and impetuous manner, about twenty-five times. When he began to undo the chain, the legs desisted, and a voice began.

"Open the door, will yer?" cried the voice which belonged to the legs which had kicked at the door.

"I will, directly, sir," replied Oliver: undoing the chain, and turning the key.

"I suppose yer the new boy, ain't yer?" said the voice through the key-hole.

"Yes, sir," replied Oliver.

"How old are yer?" inquired the voice.

"Ten, sir," replied Oliver.

"Then I'll whop yer when I get in," said the voice; "you just see if I don't, that's all, my work"us brat!" and having made this obliging promise, the voice began to whistle.

Oliver had been too often subjected to the process to which the very expressive monosyllable just recorded bears reference, to entertain the smallest doubt that the owner of the voice, whoever he might be, would redeem his pledge, most honourably. He drew back the bolts with a trembling hand, and opened the door.

For a second or two, Oliver glanced up the street, and down the street, and over the way: impressed with the belief that the unknown, who had addressed him through the keyhole, had walked a few paces off, to warm himself; for nobody did he see but a big charity-boy, sitting on a post in front of the house, eating a slice of bread and butter: which he cut into wedges, the size of his mouth, with a clasp knife, and then consumed with great dexterity.

"I beg your pardon, sir," said Oliver at length: seeing that no other visitor made his appearance; "did you knock?"

"I kicked," replied the charity-boy.

"Did you want a coffin, sir?" inquired Oliver, innocently.

At this the charity-boy looked monstrous fierce; and said that Oliver would want one before long, if he cut jokes with his superiors in that way.

"Yer don't know who I am, I suppose, Work"us?" said the charity-boy, in continuation: descending from the top of the post, meanwhile, with edifying gravity.

"No, sir," rejoined Oliver.

"I'm Mister Noah Claypole," said the charity-boy, "and you're under me. Take down the shutters, yer idle young ruffian!" With this, Mr Claypole administered a kick to Oliver, and entered the shop with a dignified air, which did him great credit. It is difficult for a large-headed, small-eyed youth, of lumbering make and heavy countenance, to look dignified under any circumstances; but it is more especially so, when superadded to these personal attractions are a red nose and yellow smalls.

Oliver, having taken down the shutters, and broken a pane of glass in his efforts to stagger away beneath the weight of the first one to a small court at the side of the house in which they were kept during the day, was graciously assisted by Noah: who having consoled him with the assurance that "he'd catch it," condescended to help him. Mr Sowerberry came down soon after.

Shortly afterwards, Mrs Sowerberry appeared. Oliver having "caught it," in fulfilment of Noah's prediction, followed that young gentleman down the stairs to breakfast.

"Come near the fire, Noah," said Charlotte. "I saved a nice little bit of bacon for you from master's breakfast. Oliver, shut that door at Mister Noah's back, and take them bits that I've put out on the cover of the bread-pan. There's your tea; take it away to that box, and drink it there, and make haste, for they'll want you to mind the shop. D'ye hear?"

"D'ye hear, Work'us?" said Noah Claypole.

"Lor, Noah!" said Charlotte, "what a rum creature you are! Why don't you let the boy alone?"

"Let him alone!" said Noah. "Why everybody lets him alone enough, for the matter of that. Neither his father nor his mother will ever interfere with him. All his relations let him have his own way pretty well. Eh, Charlotte? He! he! he!"

"Oh, you queer soul!" said Charlotte, bursting into a hearty laugh, in which she was joined by Noah; after which they both looked scornfully at poor Oliver Twist, as he sat shivering on the box in the coldest corner of the room, and ate the stale pieces which had been specially reserved for him.

Noah was a charity-boy, but not a workhouse orphan. No chance-child was he, for he could trace his genealogy all the way back to his parents, who lived hard by; his mother being a washerwoman, and his father a drunken soldier, discharged with a wooden leg, and a diurnal pension of twopence-halfpenny and an unstateable fraction. The shop-boys in the neighbourhood had long been in the habit of branding Noah, in the public streets, with the ignominious epithets of "leathers," "charity," and the like; and Noah had borne them without reply. But, now that fortune had cast in his way a nameless orphan, at whom even the meanest could point the finger of scorn, he retorted on him with interest. This affords charming food for contemplation. It shows us what a beautiful thing human nature may be made to be; and how impartially the same amiable qualities are developed in the finest lord and the dirtiest charity-boy.

Oliver had been sojourning at the undertaker's some three weeks or a month. Mr and Mrs Sowerberry – the shop being shut up – were taking their supper in the little back-parlour, when Mr Sowerberry, after several deferential glances at his wife, said,

"My dear –" He was going to say more; but, Mrs Sowerberry looking up, with a peculiarly unpropitious aspect, he stopped short.

"Well," said Mrs Sowerberry, sharply.

"Nothing, my dear, nothing," said Mr Sowerberry.

"Ugh, you brute!" said Mrs Sowerberry.

"Not at all, my dear," said Mr Sowerberry humbly. "I thought you didn't want to hear, my dear. I was only going to say –"

"Oh, don't tell me what you were going to say," interposed Mrs Sowerberry. "I am nobody; don't consult me, pray. *I* don't want to intrude upon your secrets." As Mrs Sowerberry said this, she gave an hysterical laugh, which threatened violent consequences.

"But, my dear," said Sowerberry, "I want to ask your advice."

"No, no, don't ask mine," replied Mrs Sowerberry, in an affecting manner: "ask somebody else's." Here, there was another hysterical laugh, which frightened Mr Sowerberry very much. This is a very common and much-approved matrimonial course of treatment, which is often very effective. It at once reduced Mr Sowerberry to begging, as a special favour, to be allowed to say what Mrs Sowerberry was most curious to hear. After a short altercation of less than three quarters of an hour's duration, the permission was most graciously conceded.

"It's only about young Twist, my dear," said Mr Sowerberry. "A very-good-looking boy, that, my dear."

"He need be, for he eats enough," observed the lady.

"There's an expression of melancholy in his face, my dear," resumed Mr Sowerberry, "which is very interesting. He would make a delightful mute, my love."

Mrs Sowerberry looked up with an expression of considerable wonderment. Mr Sowerberry remarked it; and, without allowing time for any observation on the good lady's part, proceeded.

"I don't mean a regular mute to attend grown-up people, my dear, but only for children's practice. It would be very new to have a mute in proportion, my dear. You may depend upon it, it would have a superb effect."

Mrs Sowerberry, who had a good deal of taste in the undertaking way, was much struck by the novelty of this idea; but, as it would have been compromising her dignity to have said so, under existing circumstances, she merely inquired, with much sharpness, why such an obvious suggestion had not presented itself to her husband's mind before? Mr Sowerberry rightly construed this, as an acquiescence in his proposition; it was speedily determined, therefore, that Oliver should be at once initiated into the mysteries of the trade; and, with this view, that he should accompany his master on the very next occasion of his services being required.

The occasion was not long in coming. Half an hour after breakfast next morning, Mr Bumble entered the shop; and supporting his cane against the counter, drew forth his large leathern pocket-book: from which he selected a small scrap of paper, which he handed over to Sowerberry.

"Aha!" said the undertaker, glancing over it with a lively countenance; "an order for a coffin, eh?"

"For a coffin first, and a porochial funeral afterwards," replied Mr Bumble, fastening the strap of the leathern pocket-book: which, like himself, was very corpulent.

"Bayton," said the undertaker, looking from the scrap of paper to Mr Bumble. "I never heard the name before."

Bumble shook his head, as he replied, "Obstinate people, Mr Sowerberry; very obstinate. Proud, too, I'm afraid, sir."

"Proud, eh?" exclaimed Mr Sowerberry with a sneer. "Come, that's too much."

"Oh, it's sickening," replied the beadle. "Antimonial, Mr Sowerberry!"

"So it is," acquiesced the undertaker.

"We only heard of the family the night before last," said the beadle; "and we shouldn't have known anything about them, then, only a woman who lodges in the same house made an application to the porochial committee for them to send the porochial surgeon to see a woman as was very bad. He had gone out to dinner; but his "prentice (which is a very clever lad) sent 'em some medicine in a blacking-bottle, off-hand."

"Ah, there's promptness," said the undertaker.

"Promptness, indeed!" replied the beadle. "But what's the consequence; what's the ungrateful behaviour of these rebels, sir? Why, the husband sends back word that the medicine won't suit his wife's complaint, and so she shan't take it – says she shan't take it, sir! Good, strong, wholesome medicine, as was given with great success to two Irish labourers and a coalheaver, only a week before – sent 'em for nothing, with a blackin"-bottle in, – and he sends back word that she shan't take it, sir!"

As the atrocity presented itself to Mr Bumble's mind in full force, he struck the counter sharply with his cane, and became flushed with indignation.

"Well," said the undertaker, "I ne – ver – did –"

"Never did, sir!" ejaculated the beadle. "No, nor nobody never did; but, now she's dead, we've got to bury her; and that's the direction; and the sooner it's done, the better."

Thus saying, Mr Bumble put on his cocked hat wrong side first, in a fever of parochial excitement; and flounced out of the shop.

"Why, he was so angry, Oliver, that he forgot even to ask after you!" said Mr Sowerberry, looking after the beadle as he strode down the street.

"Yes, sir," replied Oliver, who had carefully kept himself out of sight, during the interview; and who was shaking from head to foot at the mere recollection of the sound of Mr Bumble's voice. He needn't have taken the trouble to shrink from Mr Bumble's glance, however; for that functionary, on whom the prediction of the gentleman in the white waistcoat had made a very strong impression, thought that now the undertaker had got Oliver upon trial the subject was better avoided, until such time as he should be firmly bound for seven years, and all danger of his being returned upon the hands of the parish should be thus effectually and legally overcome.

"Well," said Mr Sowerberry, taking up his hat, "the sooner this job is done, the better. Noah, look after the shop. Oliver, put on your cap, and come with me." Oliver obeyed, and followed his master on his professional mission.

They walked on, for some time, through the most crowded and densely inhabited part of the town; and then, striking down a narrow street more dirty and miserable than any they had yet passed through, paused to look for the house which was the object of their search. The houses on either side were high and large, but very old, and tenanted by people of the poorest class: as their neglected appearance would have sufficiently denoted, without the concurrent testimony afforded by the squalid looks of the few men and women who, with folded arms and bodies half doubled, occasionally skulked along. A great many of the tenements had shop-fronts; but these were fast closed, and mouldering away; only the upper rooms being inhabited. Some houses which had become insecure from age and decay, were prevented from falling into the street, by huge beams of wood reared against the walls, and firmly planted in the road; but even these crazy dens seemed to have been selected as the nightly haunts of some houseless wretches, for many of the rough boards which supplied the place of door and window, were wrenched from their positions to afford an aperture wide enough for the passage of a human body. The kennel was stagnant and filthy. The very rats, which here and there lay putrefying in its rottenness, were hideous with famine.

There was neither knocker nor bell-handle at the open door where Oliver and his master stopped; so, groping his way cautiously through the dark passage, and bidding Oliver keep close to him and not be afraid, the undertaker mounted to the top of the first flight of stairs. Stumbling against a door on the landing, he rapped at it with his knuckles.

It was opened by a young girl of thirteen or fourteen. The undertaker at once saw enough of what the room contained, to know it was the apartment to which he had been directed. He stepped in; Oliver followed him.

There was no fire in the room; but a man was crouching, mechanically, over the empty stove. An old woman, too, had drawn a low stool to the cold hearth, and was sitting beside him. There were some ragged children in another corner; and in a small recess, opposite the door, there lay upon the ground, something covered with an old blanket. Oliver shuddered as he cast his eyes towards the place, and crept involuntarily closer to his master; for though it was covered up, the boy felt that it was a corpse.

The man's face was thin and very pale; his hair and beard were grizzly; his eyes were bloodshot. The old woman's face was wrinkled; her two remaining teeth protruded over her under lip; and her eyes were bright and piercing. Oliver was afraid to look at either her or the man. They seemed so like the rats he had seen outside.

"Nobody shall go near her," said the man, starting fiercely up, as the undertaker approached the recess. "Keep back! Damn you, keep back, if you've a life to lose!"

"Nonsense, my good man," said the undertaker, who was pretty well used to misery in all its shapes. "Nonsense!"

"I tell you," said the man: clenching his hands, and stamping furiously on the floor, – "I tell you I won't have her put into the ground. She couldn't rest there. The worms would worry her – not eat her – she is so worn away."

The undertaker offered no reply to this raving; but producing a tape from his pocket, knelt down for a moment by the side of the body.

"Ah!" said the man: bursting into tears, and sinking on his knees at the feet of the dead woman; "kneel down, kneel down – kneel round her, every one of you, and mark my words! I say she was starved to death. I never knew how bad she was, till the fever came upon her; and then her bones were starting through the skin. There was neither fire nor candle; she died in the dark – in the dark! She couldn't even see her children's faces, though we heard her gasping out their names. I begged for her in the streets: and they sent me to prison. When I came back, she was dying; and all the blood in my heart has dried up, for they starved her to death. I swear it before the God that saw it! They starved her!" He twined his hands in his hair; and, with a loud scream, rolled grovelling upon the floor: his eyes fixed, and the foam covering his lips.

The terrified children cried bitterly; but the old woman, who had hitherto remained as quiet as if she had been wholly deaf to all that passed, menaced them into silence. Having unloosed the cravat of the man who still remained extended on the ground, she tottered towards the undertaker.

"She was my daughter," said the old woman, nodding her head in the direction of the corpse; and speaking with an idiotic leer, more ghastly than even the presence of death in such a place. "Lord, Lord! Well, it *is* strange that I who gave birth to her, and was a woman then, should be alive and merry now, and she lying there: so cold and stiff! Lord, Lord! – to think of it; it's as good as a play – as good as a play!"

As the wretched creature mumbled and chuckled in her hideous merriment, the undertaker turned to go away.

"Stop, stop!" said the old woman in a loud whisper. "Will she be buried to-morrow, or next day, or to-night? I laid her out; and I must walk, you know. Send me a large cloak: a good warm one: for it is bitter cold. We should have cake and wine, too, before we go! Never mind; send some bread – only a loaf of bread and a cup of water. Shall we have some bread, dear?" she said eagerly: catching at the undertaker's coat, as he once more moved towards the door.

"Yes, yes," said the undertaker, "of course. Anything you like!" He disengaged himself from the old woman's grasp; and, drawing Oliver after him, hurried away.

The next day, (the family having been meanwhile relieved with a half-quartern loaf and a piece of cheese, left with them by Mr Bumble himself,) Oliver and his master returned to the miserable abode; where Mr Bumble had already arrived, accompanied by four men from the workhouse, who were to act as bearers. An old black cloak had been thrown over the rags of the old woman and the man; and the bare coffin having been screwed down, was hoisted on the shoulders of the bearers, and carried into the street.

"Now, you must put your best leg foremost, old lady!" whispered Sowerberry in the old woman's ear; "we are rather late; and it won't do, to keep the clergyman waiting. Move on, my men, – as quick as you like!"

Thus directed, the bearers trotted on under their light burden; and the two mourners kept as near them, as they could. Mr Bumble and Sowerberry walked at a good smart pace in front; and Oliver, whose legs were not so long as his master's, ran by the side.

There was not so great a necessity for hurrying as Mr Sowerberry had anticipated, however; for when they reached the obscure corner of the churchyard in which the nettles grew, and where the parish graves were made, the clergyman had not arrived; and the clerk, who was sitting by the vestry-room fire, seemed to think it by no means improbable that it might be an hour or so, before he came. So, they put the bier on the brink of the grave; and the two mourners waited patiently in the damp clay, with a cold rain drizzling down, while the ragged boys whom the spectacle had attracted into the churchyard played a noisy game at hide-and-seek among the tombstones, or varied their amusements by jumping backwards and forwards over the coffin. Mr Sowerberry and Bumble, being personal friends of the clerk, sat by the fire with him, and read the paper.

At length, after a lapse of something more than an hour, Mr Bumble, and Sowerberry, and the clerk, were seen running towards the grave. Immediately afterwards, the clergyman appeared: putting on his surplice as he came along. Mr Bumble then thrashed a boy or two, to keep up appearances; and the reverend gentleman, having read as much of the burial service as could be compressed into four minutes, gave his surplice to the clerk, and walked away again.

"Now, Bill!" said Sowerberry to the grave-digger. "Fill up!"

It was no very difficult task; for the grave was so full, that the uppermost coffin was within a few feet of the surface. The grave-digger shovelled in the earth; stamped it loosely down with his feet: shouldered his spade; and walked off, followed by the boys, who murmured very loud complaints at the fun being over so soon.

"Come, my good fellow!" said Bumble, tapping the man on the back. "They want to shut up the yard."

The man, who had never once moved, since he had taken his station by the grave side, started, raised his head, stared at the person who had addressed him, walked forward for a few paces; and fell down in a swoon. The crazy old woman was too much occupied in bewailing the loss of her cloak (which the undertaker had taken off), to pay him any attention; so they threw a can of cold water over him; and when he came to, saw him safely out of the churchyard, locked the gate, and departed on their different ways.

"Well, Oliver," said Sowerberry, as they walked home, "how do you like it?"

"Pretty well, thank you, sir," replied Oliver, with considerable hesitation. "Not very much, sir."

"Ah, you'll get used to it in time, Oliver," said Sowerberry. "Nothing when you *are* used to it, my boy."

Oliver wondered, in his own mind, whether it had taken a very long time to get Mr Sowerberry used to it. But he thought it better not to ask the question; and walked back to the shop; thinking over all he had seen and heard.

Chapter VI

Oliver, being goaded by the Taunts of Noah, rouses into Action, and rather astonishes him

THE month's trial over, Oliver was formally apprenticed. It was a nice sickly season just at this time. In commercial phrase, coffins were looking up; and, in the course of a few weeks, Oliver acquired a great deal of experience. The success of Mr Sowerberry's ingenious speculation, exceeded even his most sanguine hopes. The oldest inhabitants recollected no period at which measles had been so prevalent, or so fatal to infant existence; and many were the mournful processions which little Oliver headed, in a hat-band reaching down to his knees, to the indescribable admiration and emotion of all the mothers in the town. As Oliver accompanied his master in most of his adult expeditions, too, in order that he might acquire that equanimity of demeanour and full command of nerve which are essential to a finished undertaker, he had many opportunities of observing the beautiful resignation and fortitude with which some strong-minded people bear their trials and losses.

For instance; when Sowerberry had an order for the burial of some rich old lady or gentleman, who was surrounded by a great number of nephews and nieces, who had been perfectly inconsolable during the previous illness, and whose grief had been wholly irrepressible even on the most public occasions, they would be as happy among themselves as need be – quite cheerful and contended – conversing together with as much freedom and gaiety, as if nothing whatever had happened to disturb them. Husbands, too, bore the loss of their wives with the most heroic calmness. Wives, again, put on weeds for their husbands, as if, so far from grieving in the garb of sorrow, they had made up their minds to render it as becoming and attractive as possible. It was observable, too, that ladies and gentlemen who were in passions of anguish during the ceremony of interment, recovered almost as soon as they reached home, and became quite composed before the tea-drinking was over. All this was very pleasant and improving to see; and Oliver beheld it with great admiration.

That Oliver Twist was moved to resignation by the example of these good people, I cannot, although I am his biographer, undertake to affirm with any degree of confidence; but I can most distinctly say, that for many months he continued meekly to submit to the domination and ill-treatment of Noah Claypole: who used him far worse than before, now that his jealousy was roused by seeing the new boy promoted to the black stick and hat-band, while he, the old one, remained stationary in the muffin-cap and leathers. Charlotte treated him ill, because Noah did; and Mrs Sowerberry was his decided enemy, because Mr Sowerberry was disposed to be his friend; so, between these three on one side, and a glut of funerals on the other, Oliver was not altogether as comfortable as the hungry pig was, when he was shut up, by mistake, in the grain department of a brewery.

And now, I come to a very important passage in Oliver's history; for I have to record an act, slight and un-important perhaps in appearance, but which indirectly produced a material change in all his future prospects and proceedings.

One day, Oliver and Noah had descended into the kitchen at the usual dinner-hour, to banquet upon a small joint of mutton – a pound and a half of the worst end of the neck – when Charlotte being called out of the way, there ensued a brief interval of time, which Noah Claypole, being hungry and vicious, considered he could not possibly devote to a worthier purpose than aggravating and tantalising young Oliver Twist.

Intent upon this innocent amusement, Noah put his feet on the table-cloth; and pulled Oliver's hair; and twitched his ears; and expressed his opinion that he was a "sneak;" and furthermore announced his intention of coming to see him hanged, whenever that desirable event should take place; and entered upon various other topics of petty annoyance, like a malicious and ill-conditioned charity-boy as he was. But, none of these taunts producing the desired effect of making Oliver cry, Noah attempted to be more facetious still; and in this attempt, did what many small wits, with far greater reputations than Noah, sometimes do to this day, when they want to be funny. He got rather personal.

"Work'us," said Noah, "how's your mother?"

"She's dead," replied Oliver; "don't you say anything about her to me!"

Oliver's colour rose as he said this; he breathed quickly; and there was a curious working of the mouth and nostrils, which Mr Claypole thought must be the immediate precursor of a violent fit of crying. Under this impression he returned to the charge.

"What did she die of, Work'us?" said Noah.

"Of a broken heart, some of our old nurses told me," replied Oliver: more as if he were talking to himself, than answering Noah. "I think I know what it must be to die of that!"

"Tol de rol lol lol, right fol lairy, Work'us," said Noah, as a tear rolled down Oliver's cheek. "What's set you a snivelling now?"

"Not *you*," replied Oliver, hastily brushing the tear away. "Don't think it."

"Oh, not me, eh!" sneered Noah.

"No, not you," replied Oliver, sharply. "There; that's enough. Don't say anything more to me about her; you'd better not!"

"Better not!" exclaimed Noah. "Well! Better not! Work'us, don't be impudent. *Your* mother, too! She was a nice 'un, she was. Oh, Lor!" And here, Noah nodded his head expressively; and curled up as much of his small red nose as muscular action could collect together, for the occasion.

"Yer know, Work'us," continued Noah, emboldened by Oliver's silence, and speaking in a jeering tone of affected pity: of all tones the most annoying: "Yer know, Work'us, it can't be helped now; and of course yer couldn't help it then; and I'm very sorry for it; and I'm sure we all are, and pity yer very much. But yer must know, Work'us, yer mother was a regular right-down bad 'un."

"What did you say?" inquired Oliver, looking up very quickly.

"A regular right-down bad 'un, Work'us," replied Noah, coolly. "And it's a great deal better, Work'us, that she died when she did, or else she'd have been hard labouring in Bridewell, or transported, or hung; which is more likely than either, isn't it?

Crimson with fury, Oliver started up, overthrew the chair and table; seized Noah by the throat; shook him, in the violence of his rage, till his teeth chattered in his head; and, collecting his whole force into one heavy blow, felled him to the ground.

A minute ago, the boy had looked the quiet, mild, dejected creature that harsh treatment had made him. But his spirit was roused at last; the cruel insult to his dead mother had set his blood on fire. His breast heaved; his attitude was erect; his eye bright and vivid; his whole person changed, as he stood glaring over the cowardly tormentor who now lay crouching at his feet; and defied him with an energy he had never known before.

"He'll murder me!" blubbered Noah. "Charlotte! missis! Here's the new boy a murdering of me! Help! help! Oliver's gone mad! Char – lotte!"

Noah's shouts were responded to, by a loud scream from Charlotte, and a louder from Mrs Sowerberry; the former of whom rushed into the kitchen by a side-door, while the latter paused on the staircase till she was quite certain that it was consistent with the preservation of human life, to come further down.

"Oh, you little wretch!" screamed Charlotte: seizing Oliver with her utmost force, which was about equal to that of a moderately strong man in particularly good training, "Oh, you little un-grate-ful, mur-de-rous, hor-rid villain!" And between every syllable, Charlotte gave Oliver a blow with all her might: accompanying it with a scream, for the benefit of society.

Charlotte's fist was by no means a light one; but, lest it should not be effectual in calming Oliver's wrath, Mrs Sowerberry plunged into the kitchen, and assisted to hold him with one hand, while she scratched his face with the other. In this favourable position of affairs, Noah rose from the ground, and pommelled him behind.

This was rather too violent exercise to last long. When they were all wearied out, and could tear and beat no longer, they dragged Oliver, struggling and shouting, but nothing daunted, into the dust-cellar, and there locked him up. This being done, Mrs Sowerberry sunk into a chair, and burst into tears.

"Bless her, she's going off!" said Charlotte. "A glass of water, Noah, dear. Make haste!"

"Oh! Charlotte," said Mrs Sowerberry; speaking as well as she could, through a deficiency of breath, and a sufficiency of cold water, which Noah had poured over her head and shoulders. "Oh! Charlotte, what a mercy we have not all been murdered in our beds!"

"Ah! mercy indeed, ma'am," was the reply. "I only hope this 'll teach master not to have any more of these dreadful creaturs, that are born to be murderers and robbers from their very cradle. Poor Noah! He was all but killed, ma'am, when I come in."

"Poor fellow!" said Mrs Sowerberry: looking piteously on the charity-boy.

Noah, whose top waistcoat-button might have been somewhere on a level with the crown of Oliver's head, rubbed his eyes with the inside of his wrists while this commiseration was bestowed upon him, and performed some affecting tears and sniffs.

"What's to be done!" exclaimed Mrs Sowerberry. "Your master's not at home; there's not a man in the house, and he'll kick that door down in ten minutes." Oliver's vigorous plunges against the bit of timber in question, rendered this occurrence highly probable.

"Dear, dear! I don't know, ma'am," said Charlotte, "unless we send for the police-officers."

"Or the millingtary," suggested Mr Claypole.

"No, no," said Mrs Sowerberry: bethinking herself of Oliver's old friend. "Run to Mr Bumble, Noah, and tell him to come here directly, and not to lose a minute; never mind your cap! Make haste! You can hold a knife to that black eye, as you run along. It'll keep the swelling down."

Noah stopped to make no reply, but started off at his fullest speed; and very much it astonished the people who were out walking, to see a charity-boy tearing through the streets pell-mell, with no cap on his head, and a clasp-knife at his eye.

Chapter VII

Oliver continues refractory

NOAH Claypole ran along the streets at his swiftest pace, and paused not once for breath, until he reached the workhouse-gate. Having rested here, for a minute or so, to collect a good burst of sobs and an imposing show of tears and terror, he knocked loudly at the wicket; and presented such a rueful face to the aged pauper who opened it, that even he, who saw nothing but rueful faces about him at the best of times, started back in astonishment.

"Why, what's the matter with the boy!" said the old pauper.

"Mr Bumble! Mr Bumble!" cried Noah, with well affected dismay: and in tones so loud and agitated, that they not only caught the ear of Mr Bumble himself, who happened to be hard by, but alarmed him so much that he rushed into the yard without his cocked hat, – which is a very curious and remarkable circumstance: as showing that even a beadle, acted upon by a sudden and powerful impulse, may be afflicted with a momentary visitation of loss of self-possession, and forgetfulness of personal dignity.

"Oh, Mr Bumble, sir!" said Noah: "Oliver, sir, – Oliver has –"

"What? What?" interposed Mr Bumble: with a gleam of pleasure in his metallic eyes. "Not run away; he hasn't run away, has he, Noah?"

"No, sir, no. Not run away, sir, but he's turned wicious," replied Noah. "He tried to murder me, sir; and then he tried to murder Charlotte; and then missis. Oh! what dreadful pain it is! Such agony, please, sir!" And here, Noah writhed and twisted his body into an extensive variety of eel-like positions; thereby giving Mr Bumble to understand that, from the violent and sanguinary onset of Oliver Twist, he had sustained severe internal injury and damage, from which he was at that moment suffering the acutest torture.

When Noah saw that the intelligence he communicated perfectly paralysed Mr Bumble, he imparted additional effect thereunto, by bewailing his dreadful wounds ten times louder than before; and when he observed a gentleman in a white waistcoat crossing the yard, he was more tragic in his lamentations than ever: rightly conceiving it highly expedient to attract the notice, and rouse the indignation, of the gentleman aforesaid.

The gentleman's notice was very soon attracted; for he had not walked three paces, when he turned angrily round, and inquired what that young cur was howling for, and why Mr Bumble did not favour him with something which would render the series of vocular exclamations so designated, an involuntary process?

"It's a poor boy from the free-school, sir," replied Mr Bumble, "who has been nearly murdered – all but murdered, sir, – by young Twist."

"By Jove!" exclaimed the gentleman in the white waistcoat, stopping short. "I knew it! I felt a strange presentiment from the very first, that that audacious young savage would come to be hung!"

"He has likewise attempted, sir, to murder the female servant," said Mr Bumble, with a face of ashy paleness.

"And his missis," interposed Mr Claypole.

"And his master, too, I think you said, Noah?" added Mr Bumble.

"No! he's out, or he would have murdered him," replied Noah. "He said he wanted to."

"Ah! Said he wanted to, did he, my boy?" inquired the gentleman in the white waistcoat.

"Yes, sir," replied Noah. "And please, sir, missis wants to know whether Mr Bumble can spare time to step up there, directly, and flog him – 'cause master's out."

"Certainly, my boy; certainly," said the gentleman in the white waistcoat: smiling benignly, and patting Noah's head, which was about three inches higher than his own. "You're a good boy – a very good boy. Here's a penny for you. Bumble, just step up to Sowerberry's with your cane, and see what's best to be done. Don't spare him, Bumble."

"No, I will not, sir," replied the beadle: adjusting the wax-end which was twisted round the bottom of his cane, for purpose of parochial flagellation.

"Tell Sowerberry not to spare him either. They'll never do anything with him, without stripes and bruises," said the gentleman in the white waistcoat.

"I'll take care, sir," replied the beadle. And the cocked hat and cane having been, by this time, adjusted to their owner's satisfaction, Mr Bumble and Noah Claypole betook themselves with all speed to the undertaker's shop.

Here the position of affairs had not at all improved. Sowerberry had not yet returned, and Oliver continued to kick, with undiminished vigour, at the cellar-door. The accounts of his ferocity, as related by Mrs Sowerberry and Charlotte, were of so startling a nature, that Mr Bumble judged it prudent to parley, before opening the door. With this view he gave a kick at the outside, by way of prelude; and, then, applying his mouth to the keyhole, said, in a deep and impressive tone:

"Oliver!"

"Come; you let me out!" replied Oliver, from the inside.

"Do you know this here voice, Oliver?" said Mr Bumble.

"Yes," replied Oliver.

"Ain't you afraid of it, sir? Ain't you a-trembling while I speak, sir?" said Mr Bumble.

"No!" replied Oliver, boldly.

An answer so different from the one he had expected to elicit, and was in the habit of receiving, staggered Mr Bumble not a little. He stepped back from the keyhole; drew himself up to his full height; and looked from one to another of the three by-standers, in mute astonishment.

"Oh, you know, Mr Bumble, he must be mad," said Mrs Sowerberry. "No boy in half his senses could venture to speak so to you."

"It's not Madness, ma"am," replied Mr Bumble, after a few moments of deep meditation. "It's Meat."

"What?" exclaimed Mrs Sowerberry.

"Meat, ma"am, meat," replied Bumble, with stern emphasis. "You've over-fed him, ma"am. You've raised a artificial soul and spirit in him, ma"am, unbecoming a person of his condition: as the board, Mrs Sowerberry, who are practical philosophers, will tell you. What have paupers to do with soul or spirit? It's quite enough that we let 'em have live bodies. If you had kept the boy on gruel, ma"am, this would never have happened."

"Dear, dear!" ejaculated Mrs Sowerberry, piously raising her eyes to the kitchen ceiling: "this comes of being liberal!"

The liberality of Mrs Sowerberry to Oliver, had consisted in a profuse bestowal upon him of all the dirty odds and ends which nobody else would eat; so there was a great deal of meekness and self-devotion in her voluntarily remaining under Mr Bumble's heavy accusation. Of which, to do her justice, she was wholly innocent, in thought, word, or deed.

"Ah!" said Mr Bumble, when the lady brought her eyes down to earth again; " the only thing that can be done now, that I know of, is to leave him in the cellar for a day or so, till he's a little starved down; and then to take him out, and keep him on gruel all through his apprenticeship. He comes of a bad family. Excitable natures, Mrs Sowerberry! Both the nurse and doctor said, that that mother of his made her way here, against difficulties and pain that would have killed any well-disposed woman, weeks before."

At this point of Mr Bumble's discourse, Oliver, just hearing enough to know that some new allusion was being made to his mother, recommenced kicking, with a violence that rendered every other sound inaudible. Sowerberry returned at this juncture. Oliver's offence having been explained to him, with such exaggerations as the ladies thought best calculated to rouse his ire, he unlocked the cellar-door in a twinkling, and dragged his rebellious apprentice out, by the collar.

Oliver's clothes had been torn in the beating he had received; his face was bruised and scratched; and his hair scattered over his forehead. The angry flush had not disappeared, however; and when he was pulled out of his prison, he scowled boldly on Noah, and looked quite undismayed.

"Now, you are a nice young fellow, ain't you?" said Sowerberry; giving Oliver a shake, and a box on the ear.

"He called my mother names," replied Oliver.

"Well, and what if he did, you little ungrateful wretch?" said Mrs Sowerberry. "She deserved what he said, and worse."

"She didn't," said Oliver.

"She did," said Mrs Sowerberry.

"It's a lie!" said Oliver.

Mrs Sowerberry burst into a flood of tears.

This flood of tears left Mr Sowerberry no alternative. If he had hesitated for one instant to punish Oliver most severely, it must be quite clear to every experienced reader that he would have been, according to all precedents in disputes of matrimony established, a brute, an unnatural husband, an insulting creature, a base imitation of a man, and various other agreeable characters too numerous for recital within the limits of this chapter. To do him justice, he was, as far as his power went – it was not very extensive – kindly disposed towards the boy; perhaps, because it was his interest to be so; perhaps, because his wife disliked him. The flood of tears, however, left him no resource; so he at once gave him a drubbing, which satisfied even Mrs Sowerberry herself, and rendered Mr Bumble's subsequent application of the parochial cane, rather unnecessary. For the rest of the day, he was shut up in the back kitchen, in company with a pump and a slice of bread; and, at night, Mrs Sowerberry, after making various remarks outside the door, by no means complimentary to the memory of his mother, looked into the room, and, amidst the jeers and pointings of Noah and Charlotte, ordered him up stairs to his dismal bed.

It was not until he was left alone in the silence and stillness of the gloomy workshop of the undertaker, that Oliver gave way to the feelings which the day's treatment may be supposed likely to have awakened in a mere child. He had listened to their taunts with a look of contempt; he had borne the lash without a cry: for he felt that pride swelling in his heart which would have kept down a shriek to the last, though they had roasted him alive. But now, when there were none to see or hear him, he fell upon his knees on the floor; and, hiding his face in his hands, wept such tears as, God send for the credit of our nature, few so young may ever have cause to pour out before him!

For a long time, Oliver remained motionless in this attitude. The candle was burning low in the socket when he rose to his feet. Having gazed cautiously round him, and listened intently, he gently undid the fastenings of the door, and looked abroad.

It was a cold, dark night. The stars seemed, to the boy's eyes, farther from the earth than he had ever seen them before; there was no wind; and the sombre shadows thrown by the trees upon the ground, looked sepulchral and death-like, from being so still. He softly reclosed the door. Having availed himself of the expiring light of the candle to tie up in a handkerchief the few articles of wearing apparel he had, sat himself down upon a bench, to wait for morning.

With the first ray of light that struggled through the crevices in the shutters, Oliver arose, and again unbarred the door. One timid look around – one moment's pause of hesitation – he had closed it behind him, and was in the open street.

He looked to the right and to the left, uncertain whither to fly. He remembered to have seen the waggons, as they went out, toiling up the hill. He took the same route; and arriving at a footpath across the fields: which he knew, after some distance, led out again into the road: struck into it, and walked quickly on.

Along this same footpath, Oliver well remembered he had trotted beside Mr Bumble, when he first carried him to the workhouse from the farm. His way lay directly in front of the cottage. His heart beat quickly when he bethought himself of this; and he half resolved to turn back. He had come a long way though, and should lose a great deal of time by doing so. Besides, it was so early that there was very little fear of his being seen; so he walked on.

He reached the house. There was no appearance of its inmates stirring at that early hour. Oliver stopped, and peeped into the garden. A child was weeding one of the little beds; as he stopped, he raised his pale face and disclosed the features of one of his former companions. Oliver felt glad to see him, before he went; for, though younger than himself, he had been his little friend and playmate. They had been beaten and starved, and shut up together, many and many a time.

"Hush, Dick!" said Oliver, as the boy ran to the gate, and thrust his thin arm between the rails to greet him. "Is any one up?"

"Nobody but me," replied the child.

"You mustn't say you saw me, Dick," said Oliver. "I am running away. They beat and ill-use me, Dick; and I am going to seek my fortune, some long way off. I don't know where. How pale you are!"

"I heard the doctor tell them I was dying," replied the child with a faint smile. "I am very glad to see you, dear; but don't stop, don't stop!"

"Yes, yes, I will, to say good-b'ye to you," replied Oliver. "I shall see you again, Dick. I know I shall! You will be well and happy!"

"I hope so," replied the child. "After I am dead, but not before. I know the doctor must be right, Oliver, because I dream so much of Heaven, and Angels, and kind faces that I never see when I am awake. Kiss me," said the child, climbing up the low gate, and flinging his little arms round Oliver's neck. "Good-b'ye, dear! God bless you!"

The blessing was from a young child's lips, but it was the first that Oliver had ever heard invoked upon his head; and through the struggles and sufferings, and troubles and changes, of his after life, he never once forgot it.

Chapter VIII

Oliver walks to London. He encounters on the Road a Strange sort of young Gentleman

OLIVER reached the stile at which the by-path terminated; and once more gained the high-road. It was eight o'clock now. Though he was nearly five miles away from the town, he ran, and hid behind the hedges, by turns, till noon: fearing that he might be pursued and overtaken. Then he sat down to rest by the side of the milestone, and began to think, for the first time, where he had better go and try to live.

The stone by which he was seated, bore, in large characters, an intimation that it was just seventy miles from that spot to London. The name awakened a new train of ideas in the boy's mind. London! – that great large place! – nobody – not even Mr Bumble – could ever find him there! He had often heard the old men in the workhouse, too, say that no lad of spirit need want in London; and that there were ways of living in that vast city, which those who had been bred up in country parts had no idea of. It was the very place for a homeless boy, who must die in the streets unless some one helped him. As these things passed through his thoughts, he jumped upon his feet, and again walked forward.

He had diminished the distance between himself and London by full four miles more, before he recollected how much he must undergo ere he could hope to reach his place of destination. As this consideration forced itself upon him, he slackened his pace a little, and meditated upon his means of getting there. He had a crust of bread, a coarse shirt, and two pairs of stockings, in his bundle. He had a penny too – a gift of Sowerberry's after some funeral in which he had acquitted himself more than ordinarily well – in his pocket. "A clean shirt," thought Oliver, "is a very comfortable thing; and so are two pairs of darned stockings; and so is a penny; but they are small helps to a sixty-five miles" walk in winter time." But Oliver's thoughts, like those of most other people, although they were extremely ready and active to point out his difficulties, were wholly at a loss to suggest any feasible mode of surmounting them; so, after a good deal of thinking to no particular purpose, he changed his little bundle over to the other shoulder, and trudged on.

Oliver walked twenty miles that day; and all that time tasted nothing but the crust of dry bread, and a few draughts of water, which he begged at the cottage-doors by the roadside. When the night came, he turned into a meadow; and, creeping close under a hay-rick, determined to lie there, till morning. He felt frightened at first, for the wind moaned dismally over the empty fields: and he was cold and hungry, and more alone than he had ever felt before. Being very tired with his walk, however, he soon fell asleep and forgot his troubles.

He felt cold and stiff, when he got up next morning, and so hungry that he was obliged to exchange the penny for a small loaf, in the very first village through which he passed. He had walked no more than twelve miles, when night closed in again. His feet were sore, and his legs so weak that they trembled beneath him. Another night passed in the bleak damp air, made him worse; when he set forward on his journey next morning, he could hardly crawl along.

He waited at the bottom of a steep hill till a stage-coach came up, and then begged of the outside passengers; but there were very few who took any notice of him: and even those told him to wait till they got to the top of the hill, and then let them see how far he could run for a halfpenny. Poor Oliver tried to keep up with the coach a little way, but was unable to do it, by reason of his fatigue and sore feet. When the outsides saw this, they put their halfpence back into their pockets again, declaring that he was an idle young dog, and didn't deserve anything; and the coach rattled away and left only a cloud of dust behind.

In some villages, large painted boards were fixed up: warning all persons who begged within the district, that they would be sent to jail. This frightened Oliver very much, and made him glad to get out of those villages with all possible expedition. In others, he would stand about the inn-yards, and look mournfully at every one who passed: a proceeding which generally terminated in the landlady's ordering one of the post-boys who were lounging about, to drive that strange boy out of the place, for she was sure he had come to steal something. If he begged at a farmer's house, ten to one but they threatened to set the dog on him; and when he showed his nose in a shop, they talked about the beadle – which brought Oliver's heart into his mouth, – very often the only thing he had there, for many hours together.

In fact, if it had not been for a good-hearted turnpike-man, and a benevolent old lady, Oliver's troubles would have been shortened by the very same process which had put an end to his mother's; in other words, he would most assuredly have fallen dead upon the king's highway. But the turnpike-man gave him a meal of bread and cheese; and the old lady, who had a shipwrecked grandson wandering barefoot in some distant part of the earth, took pity upon the poor orphan, and gave him what little she could afford – and more – with such kind and gentle words, and such tears of sympathy and compassion, that they sank deeper into Oliver's soul, than all the sufferings he had ever undergone.

Early on the seventh morning after he had left his native place, Oliver limped slowly into the little town of Barnet. The window-shutters were closed; the street was empty; not a soul had awakened to the business of the day. The sun was rising in all its splendid beauty; but the light only served to show the boy his own lonesomeness and desolation, as he sat, with bleeding feet and covered with dust, upon a door-step.

By degrees, the shutters were opened; the window-blinds were drawn up; and people began passing to and fro. Some few stopped to gaze at Oliver for a moment or two, or turned round to stare at him as they hurried by; but none relieved him, or troubled themselves to inquire how he came there. He had no heart to beg. And there he sat.

He had been crouching on the step for some time: wondering at the great number of public-houses (every other house in Barnet was a tavern, large or small), gazing listlessly at the coaches as they passed through, and thinking how strange it seemed that they could do, with ease, in a few hours, what it had taken him a whole week of courage and determination beyond his years to accomplish: when he was roused by observing that a boy, who had passed him carelessly some minutes before, had returned, and was now surveying him most earnestly from the opposite side of the way. He took little heed of this at first; but the boy remained in the same attitude of close observation so long, that Oliver raised his head, and returned his steady look. Upon this, the boy crossed over; and, walking close up to Oliver, said,

"Hullo, my covey! What's the row?"

The boy who addressed this inquiry to the young wayfarer, was about his own age: but one of the queerest looking boys that Oliver had ever seen. He was a snub-nosed, flat-browed, common-faced boy enough; and as dirty a juvenile as one would wish to see; but he had about him all the airs and manners of a man. He was short of his age: with rather bow-legs, and little, sharp, ugly eyes. His hat was stuck on the top of his head so lightly, that it threatened to fall off every moment – and would have done so, very often, if the wearer had not had a knack of every now and then giving his head a sudden twitch, which brought it back to its old place again. He wore a man's coat, which reached nearly to his heels. He had turned the cuffs back, half-way up his arm, to get his hands out of the sleeves: apparently with the ultimate view of thrusting them into the pockets of his corduroy trousers; for there he kept them. He was, altogether, as roystering and swaggering a young gentleman as ever stood four feet six, or something less, in his bluchers.

"Hullo, my covey! What's the row?" said this strange young gentleman to Oliver.

"I am very hungry and tired," replied Oliver: the tears standing in his eyes as he spoke. "I have walked a long way. I have been walking these seven days."

"Walking for sivin days!" said the young gentleman. "Oh, I see. Beak's order, eh? But," he added, noticing Oliver's look of surprise, "I suppose you don't know what a beak is, my flash com-pan-i-on."

Oliver mildly replied, that he had always heard a bird's mouth described by the term in question.

"My eyes, how green!" exclaimed the young gentleman. "Why, a beak's a madgst'rate; and when you walk by a beak's order, it's not straight forerd, but always a going up, and nivir a coming down agin. Was you never on the mill?"

"What mill?" inquired Oliver.

"What mill! Why, *the* mill – the mill as takes up so little room that it'll work inside a Stone Jug; and always goes better when the wind's low with people, than when it's high; acos then they can't get workmen. But come," said the young gentleman; "you want grub, and you shall have it. I'm at low-water-mark myself – only one bob and a magpie; but, *as* far *as* it goes, I'll fork out and stump. Up with you on your pins. There! Now then! Morrice!"

Assisting Oliver to rise, the young gentleman took him to an adjacent chandler's shop, where he purchased a sufficiency of ready-dressed ham and a half-quartern loaf, or, as he himself expressed it, "a fourpenny bran!" the ham being kept clean and preserved from dust, by the ingenious expedient of making a hole in the loaf by pulling out a portion of the crumb, and stuffing it therein. Taking the bread under his arm, the young gentleman turned into a small public-house, and led the way to a tap-room in the rear of the premises. Here, a pot of beer was brought in, by direction of the mysterious youth; and Oliver, falling to, at his new friend's bidding, made a long and hearty meal, during the progress of which, the strange boy eyed him from time to time with great attention.

"Going to London?" said the strange boy, when Oliver had at length concluded.

"Yes."

"Got any lodgings?"

"No."

"Money?"

"No."

The strange boy whistled; and put his arms into his pockets as far as the big coat sleeves would let them go.

"Do you live in London?" inquired Oliver.

"Yes. I do, when I'm at home," replied the boy. "I suppose you want some place to sleep in to-night, don't you?"

"I do, indeed," answered Oliver. "I have not slept under a roof since I left the country."

"Don't fret your eyelids on that score," said the young gentleman. "I've got to be in London to-night; and I know a "spectable old genelman as lives there, wot'll give you lodgings for nothink, and never ask for the change – that is, if any genelman he knows interduces you. And don't he know me? Oh, no! Not in the least! By no means. Certainly not!"

The young gentleman smiled, as if to intimate that the latter fragments of discourse were playfully ironical; and finished the beer as he did so.

This unexpected offer of shelter was too tempting to be resisted; especially as it was immediately followed up, by the assurance that the old gentleman referred to, would doubtless provide Oliver with a comfortable place, without loss of time. This led to a more friendly and confidential dialogue; from which Oliver discovered that his friend's name was Jack Dawkins, and that he was a peculiar pet and *protégé* of the elderly gentleman before mentioned.

Mr Dawkins's appearance did not say a vast deal in favour of the comforts which his patron's interest obtained for those whom he took under his protection; but, as he had a rather flighty and dissolute mode of conversing, and furthermore avowed that among his intimate friends he was better known by the *sobriquet* of "The artful Dodger," Oliver concluded that, being of a dissipated and careless turn, the moral precepts of his benefactor had hitherto been thrown away upon him. Under this impression, he secretly resolved to cultivate the good opinion of the old gentleman as quickly as possible; and, if he found the Dodger incorrigible, as he more than half suspected he should, to decline the honour of his farther acquaintance.

As John Dawkins objected to their entering London before nightfall, it was nearly eleven o'clock when they reached the turnpike at Islington. They crossed from the Angel into St. John's Road; struck down the small street which terminates at Sadler's Wells Theatre; through Exmouth Street and Coppice Row; down the little court by the side of the workhouse; across the classic ground which once bore the name of Hockley-in-the-Hole; thence into Little Saffron Hill; and so into Saffron Hill the Great: along which the Dodger scudded at a rapid pace, directing Oliver to follow close at his heels.

Although Oliver had enough to occupy his attention in keeping sight of his leader, he could not help bestowing a few hasty glances on either side of the way, as he passed along. A dirtier or more wretched place he had never seen. The street was very narrow and muddy, and the air was impregnated with filthy odours. There were a good many small shops; but the only stock in trade appeared to be heaps of children, who, even at that time of night, were crawling in and out at the doors, or screaming from the inside. The sole places that seemed to prosper amid the general blight of the place, were the public-houses; and in them, the lowest orders of Irish were wrangling with might and main. Covered ways and yards, which here and there diverged from the main street, disclosed little knots of houses, where drunken men and women were positively wallowing in filth; and from several of the door-ways, great ill-looking fellows were cautiously emerging, bound, to all appearance, on no very well-disposed or harmless errands.

Oliver was just considering whether he hadn't better run away, when they reached the bottom of the hill. His conductor, catching him by the arm, pushed open the door of a house near Field Lane; and, drawing him into the passage, closed it behind them.

"Now, then!" cried a voice from below, in reply to a whistle from the Dodger.

"Plummy and slam!" was the reply.

This seemed to be some watchword or signal that all was right; for the light of a feeble candle gleamed on the wall at the remote end of the passage; and a man's face peeped out, from where a balustrade of the old kitchen staircase had been broken away.

"There's two on you," said the man, thrusting the candle farther out, and shading his eyes with his hand. "Who's the t'other one?"

"A new pal," replied Jack Dawkins, pulling Oliver forward.

"Where did he come from?"

"Greenland. Is Fagin up stairs?"

"Yes, he's a sortin' the wipes. Up with you!" The candle was drawn back, and the face disappeared.

Oliver, groping his way with one hand, and having the other firmly grasped by his companion, ascended with much difficulty the dark and broken stairs: which his conductor mounted with an ease and expedition that showed he was well acquainted with them. He threw open the door of a back-room, and drew Oliver in after him.

The walls and ceiling of the room were perfectly black with age and dirt. There was a deal table before the fire: upon which were a candle, stuck in a ginger-beer bottle, two or three pewter pots, a loaf and butter, and a plate. In a frying-pan, which was on the fire, and which was secured to the mantelshelf by a string, some sausages were cooking; and standing over them, with a toasting-fork in his hand, was a very old shrivelled Jew, whose villanous-looking and repulsive face was obscured by a quantity of matted red hair. He was dressed in a greasy flannel gown, with his throat bare; and seemed to be dividing his attention between the frying-pan and a clothes-horse, over which a great number of silk handkerchiefs were hanging. Several rough beds made of old sacks, were huddled side by side on the floor. Seated round the table were four or five boys, none older than the Dodger, smoking long clay pipes, and drinking spirits with the air of middle-aged men. These all crowded about their associate as he whispered a few words to the Jew; and then turned round and grinned at Oliver. So did the Jew himself, toasting-fork in hand.

"This is him, Fagin," said Jack Dawkins; "my friend Oliver Twist."

The Jew grinned; and, making a low obeisance to Oliver, took him by the hand, and hoped he should have the honour of his intimate acquaintance. Upon this, the young gentlemen with the pipes came round him, and shook both his hands very hard – especially the one in which he held his little bundle. One young gentleman was very anxious to hang up his cap for him; and another was so obliging as to put his hands in his pockets, in order that, as he was very tired, he might not have the trouble of emptying them, himself, when he went to bed. These civilities would probably have been extended much farther, but for a liberal exercise of the Jew's toasting-fork on the heads and shoulders of the affectionate youths who offered them.

"We are very glad to see you, Oliver, very," said the Jew. "Dodger, take off the sausages; and draw a tub near the fire for Oliver. Ah, you're a-staring at the pocket-handkerchiefs! eh, my dear! There are a good many of 'em, ain't there? We've just looked 'em out, ready for the wash; that's all, Oliver; that's all. Ha! ha! ha!"

The latter part of this speech, was hailed by a boisterous shout from all the hopeful pupils of the merry old gentleman. In the midst of which, they went to supper.

Oliver ate his share, and the Jew then mixed him a glass of hot gin and water: telling him he must drink it off directly, because another gentleman wanted the tumbler. Oliver did as he was desired. Immediately afterwards he felt himself gently lifted on to one of the sacks; and then he sunk into a deep sleep.

Chapter IX

Containing further Particulars concerning the pleasant old Gentleman and his hopeful Pupils

It was late next morning when Oliver awoke, from a sound, long sleep. There was no other person in the room but the old Jew, who was boiling some coffee in a saucepan for breakfast, and whistling softly to himself as he stirred it round and round, with an iron spoon. He would stop every now and then to listen when there was the least noise below: and when he had satisfied himself, he would go on, whistling and stirring again, as before.

Although Oliver had roused himself from sleep, he was not thoroughly awake. There is a drowsy state, between sleeping and waking, when you dream more in five minutes with your eyes half open, and yourself half conscious of everything that is passing around you, than you would in five nights with your eyes fast closed, and your senses wrapt in perfect unconsciousness. At such times, a mortal knows just enough of what his mind is doing, to form some glimmering conception of its mighty powers, its bounding from earth and spurning time and space, when freed from the restraint of its corporeal associate.

Oliver was precisely in this condition. He saw the Jew with his half-closed eyes; heard his low whistling; and recognised the sound of the spoon grating against the saucepan's sides; and yet the self-same senses were mentally engaged, at the same time, in busy action with almost everybody he had ever known.

When the coffee was done, the Jew drew the saucepan to the hob. Standing, then, in an irresolute attitude for a few minutes as if he did not well know how to employ himself, he turned round and looked at Oliver, and called him by his name. He did not answer, and was to all appearance asleep.

After satisfying himself upon this head, the Jew stepped gently to the door: which he fastened. He then drew forth: as it seemed to Oliver, from some trap in the floor: a small box, which he placed carefully on the table. His eyes glistened as he raised the lid, and looked in. Dragging an old chair to the table, he sat down; and took from it a magnificent gold watch, sparkling with jewels.

"Aha!" said the Jew, shrugging up his shoulders, and distorting every feature with a hideous grin. "Clever dogs! Clever dogs! Staunch to the last! Never told the old parson where they were. Never peached upon old Fagin! And why should they? It wouldn't have loosened the knot, or kept the drop up, a minute longer. No, no, no! Fine fellows! Fine fellows!"

With these, and other muttered reflections of the like nature, the Jew once more deposited the watch in its place of safety. At least half a dozen more were severally drawn forth from the same box, and surveyed with equal pleasure; besides rings, brooches, bracelets, and other articles of jewellery, of such magnificent materials, and costly workmanship, that Oliver had no idea, even of their names.

Having replaced these trinkets, the Jew took out another: so small that it lay in the palm of his hand. There seemed to be some very minute inscription on it; for the Jew laid it flat upon the table, and, shading it with his hand, pored over it, long and earnestly. At length he put it down, as if despairing of success; and, leaning back in his chair muttered:

"What a fine thing capital punishment is! Dead men never repent; dead men never bring awkward stories to light. Ah, it's a fine thing for the trade! Five of 'em strung up in a row, and none left to play booty, or turn white-livered!"

As the Jew uttered these words, his bright dark eyes, which had been staring vacantly before him, fell on Oliver's face; the boy's eyes were fixed on his in mute curiosity; and although the recognition was only for an instant – for the briefest space of time that can possibly be conceived – it was enough to show the old man that he had been observed. He closed the lid of the box with a loud crash; and, laying his hand on a bread knife which was on the table, started furiously up. He trembled very much though; for, even in his terror, Oliver could see that the knife quivered in the air.

"What's that?" said the Jew. "What do you watch me for? Why are you awake? What have you seen? Speak out, boy! Quick – quick! for your life!"

"I wasn't able to sleep any longer, sir," replied Oliver meekly. "I am very sorry if I have disturbed you, sir."

"You were not awake an hour ago?" said the Jew, scowling fiercely on the boy.

"No! No, indeed!" replied Oliver.

"Are you sure?" cried the Jew: with a still fiercer look than before: and a threatening attitude.

"Upon my word I was not, sir," replied Oliver, earnestly. "I was not, indeed, sir."

"Tush, tush, my dear!" said the Jew, abruptly resuming his old manner, and playing with the knife a little, before he laid it down; as if to induce the belief that he had caught it up, in mere sport. "Of course I know that, my dear. I only tried to frighten you. You're a brave boy. Ha! ha! you're a brave boy, Oliver!" The Jew rubbed his hands with a chuckle, but glanced uneasily at the box, notwithstanding.

"Did you see any of these pretty things, my dear?" said the Jew, laying his hand upon it after a short pause.

"Yes, sir," replied Oliver.

"Ah!" said the Jew, turning rather pale. "They – they're mine, Oliver; my little property. All I have to live upon, in my old age. The folks call me a miser, my dear. Only a miser; that's all."

Oliver thought the old gentleman must be a decided miser to live in such a dirty place, with so many watches; but, thinking that perhaps his fondness for the Dodger and the other boys, cost him a good deal of money, he only cast a deferential look at the Jew, and asked if he might get up.

"Certainly, my dear, certainly," replied the old gentleman. "Stay. There's a pitcher of water in the corner by the door. Bring it here; and I'll give you a basin to wash in, my dear."

Oliver got up; walked across the room; and stooped for an instant to raise the pitcher. When he turned his head, the box was gone.

He had scarcely washed himself, and made everything tidy, by emptying the basin out of the window, agreeably to the Jew's directions, when the Dodger returned: accompanied by a very sprightly young friend, whom Oliver had seen smoking on the previous night, and who was now formally introduced to him as Charley Bates. The four sat down, to breakfast, on the coffee, and some hot rolls and ham which the Dodger had brought home in the crown of his hat.

"Well," said the Jew, glancing slyly at Oliver, and addressing himself to the Dodger, "I hope you've been at work this morning, my dears?"

"Hard," replied the Dodger.

"As Nails," added Charley Bates.

"Good boys, good boys!" said the Jew. "What have *you* got, Dodger?"

"A couple of pocket-books," replied that young gentleman.

"Lined?" inquired the Jew, with eagerness.

"Pretty well," replied the Dodger, producing two pocket-books; one green, and the other red.

"Not so heavy as they might be," said the Jew, after looking at the insides carefully; "but very neat and nicely made. Ingenious workman, ain't he, Oliver?"

"Very, indeed, sir," said Oliver. At which Mr Charles Bates laughed uproariously; very much to the amazement of Oliver, who saw nothing to laugh at, in anything that had passed.

"And what have you got, my dear?" said Fagin to Charley Bates.

"Wipes," replied Master Bates; at the same time producing four pocket-handkerchiefs.

"Well," said the Jew, inspecting them closely; "they're very good ones, very. You haven't marked them well, though, Charley; so the marks shall be picked out with a needle, and we'll teach Oliver how to do it. Shall us, Oliver, eh? Ha! ha! ha!"

"If you please, sir," said Oliver.

"You'd like to be able to make pocket-handkerchiefs as easy as Charley Bates, wouldn't you, my dear?" said the Jew.

"Very much, indeed, if you'll teach me, sir," replied Oliver.

Master Bates saw something so exquisitely ludicrous in this reply, that he burst into another laugh; which laugh, meeting the coffee he was drinking, and carrying it down some wrong channel, very nearly terminated in his premature suffocation.

"He is so jolly green!" said Charley when he recovered, as an apology to the company for his unpolite behaviour.

The Dodger said nothing, but he smoothed Oliver's hair over his eyes, and said he'd know better, by-and-bye; upon which the old gentleman, observing Oliver's colour mounting, changed the subject by asking whether there had been much of a crowd at the execution that morning? This made him wonder more and more; for it was plain from the replies of the two boys that they had both been there; and Oliver naturally wondered how they could possibly have found time to be so very industrious.

When the breakfast was cleared away, the merry old gentleman and the two boys played at a very curious and uncommon game, which was performed in this way. The merry old gentleman, placing a snuff-box in one pocket of his trousers, a note-case in the other, and a watch in his waistcoat pocket, with a guard-chain round his neck, and sticking a mock diamond pin in his shirt: buttoned his coat tight round him, and putting his spectacle-case and handkerchief in his pockets, trotted up and down the room with a stick, in imitation of the manner in which old gentlemen walk about the streets any hour in the day. Sometimes he stopped at the fire-place, and sometimes at the door, making believe that he was staring with all his might into shop-windows. At such times, he would look constantly round him, for fear of thieves, and would keep slapping all his pockets in turn, to see that he hadn't lost anything, in such a very funny and natural manner, that Oliver laughed till the tears ran down his face. All this time, the two boys followed him closely about: getting out of his sight, so nimbly, every time he turned round, that it was impossible to follow their motions. At last, the Dodger trod upon his toes, or ran upon his boot accidentally, while Charley Bates stumbled up against him behind; and in that one moment they took from him, with the most extraordinary rapidity, snuff-box, note-case, watch-guard, chain, shirt-pin, pocket-handkerchief, even the spectacle-case. If the old gentleman felt a hand in any one of his pockets, he cried out where it was; and then the game began all over again.

When this game had been played a great many times, a couple of young ladies called to see the young gentlemen; one of whom was named Bet, and the other Nancy. They wore a good deal of hair, not very neatly turned up behind, and were rather untidy about the shoes and stockings. They were not exactly pretty, perhaps; but they had a great deal of colour in their faces, and looked quite stout and hearty. Being remarkably free and agreeable in their manners, Oliver thought them very nice girls indeed. As there is no doubt they were.

These visitors stopped a long time. Spirits were produced, in consequence of one of the young ladies complaining of a coldness in her inside; and the conversation took a very convivial and improving turn. At length, Charley Bates expressed his opinion that it was time to pad the hoof. This, it occurred to Oliver, must be French for going out; for, directly afterwards, the Dodger, and Charley, and the two young ladies, went away together, having been kindly furnished by the amiable old Jew with money to spend.

"There, my dear," said Fagin. "That's a pleasant life, isn't it? They have gone out for the day."

"Have they done work, sir?" inquired Oliver.

"Yes, " said the Jew; "that is, unless they should unexpectedly come across any, when they are out; and they won't neglect it, if they do, my dear, depend upon it. Make 'em your models, my dear. Make 'em your models," tapping the fireshovel on the hearth to add force to his words; "do everything they bid you, and take their advice in all matters – especially the Dodger's, my dear. He'll be a great man himself, and will make you one too, if you take pattern by him. – Is my handkerchief hanging out of my pocket, my dear?" said the Jew, stopping short.

"Yes, sir," said Oliver.

"See if you can take it out, without my feeling it: as you saw them do, when we were at play this morning."

Oliver held up the bottom of the pocket with one hand, as he had seen the Dodger hold it, and drew the handkerchief lightly out of it with the other.

"Is it gone?" cried the Jew.

"Here it is, sir," said Oliver, showing it in his hand.

"You're a clever boy, my dear," said the playful old gentleman, patting Oliver on the head approvingly. "I never saw a sharper lad. Here's a shilling for you. If you go on, in this way, you'll be the greatest man of the time. And now come here, and I'll show you how to take the marks out of the handkerchiefs."

Oliver wondered what picking the old gentleman's pocket in play, had to do with his chances of being a great man. But, thinking that the Jew, being so much his senior, must know best, he followed him quietly to the table, and was soon deeply involved in his new study.

Chapter X

Oliver becomes better acquainted with the Characters of his new Associates; and purchases Experience at a High Price. Being a short, but very important Chapter, in this History

For many days, Oliver remained in the Jew's room, picking the marks out of the pocket-handkerchiefs, (of which a great number were brought home,) and sometimes taking part in the game already described: which the two boys and the Jew played, regularly, every morning. At length, he began to languish for fresh air, and took many occasions of earnestly entreating the old gentleman to allow him to go out to work, with his two companions.

Oliver was rendered the more anxious to be actively employed, by what he had seen of the stern morality of the old gentleman's character. Whenever the Dodger or Charley Bates came home at night, empty-handed, he would expatiate with great vehemence on the misery of idle and lazy habits; and would enforce upon them the necessity of an active life, by sending them supperless to bed. One one occasion, indeed, he even went so far as to knock them both down a flight of stairs; but this was carrying out his virtuous precepts to an unusual extent.

At length, one morning, Oliver obtained the permission he had so eagerly sought. There had been no handkerchiefs to work upon, for two or three days, and the dinners had been rather meagre. Perhaps these were reasons for the old gentleman's giving his assent; but, whether they were or no, he told Oliver he might go, and placed him under the joint guardianship of Charley Bates, and his friend the Dodger.

The three boys sallied out; the Dodger with his coat-sleeves tucked up, and his hat cocked, as usual; Master Bates sauntering along with his hands in his pockets; and Oliver between them, wondering where they were going, and what branch of manufacture he would be instructed in, first.

The pace at which they went, was such a very lazy, ill-looking saunter, that Oliver soon began to think his companions were going to deceive the old gentleman, by not going to work at all. The Dodger had a vicious propensity, too, of pulling the caps from the heads of small boys and tossing them down areas; while Charley Bates exhibited some very loose notions concerning the rights of property, by pilfering divers apples and onions from the stalls at the kennel sides, and thrusting them into pockets which were so surprisingly capacious, that they seemed to undermine his whole suit of clothes in every direction. These things looked so bad, that Oliver was on the point of declaring his intention of seeking his way back, in the best way he could; when his thoughts were suddenly directed into another channel, by a very mysterious change of behaviour on the part of the Dodger.

They were just emerging from a narrow court not far from the open square in Clerkenwell, which is yet called, by some strange perversion of terms, "The Green:" when the Dodger made a sudden stop; and, laying his finger on his lip, drew his companions back again, with the greatest caution and circumspection.

"What's the matter?" demanded Oliver.

"Hush!" replied the Dodger. "Do you see that old cove at the book-stall?"

"The old gentleman over the way?" said Oliver. "Yes, I see him."

"He'll do," said the Dodger.

"A prime plant," observed Master Charley Bates.

Oliver looked from one to the other, with the greatest surprise; but he was not permitted to make any inquiries; for the two boys walked stealthily across the road, and slunk close behind the old gentleman towards whom his attention had been directed. Oliver walked a few paces after them; and, not knowing whether to advance or retire, stood looking on in silent amazement.

The old gentleman was a very respectable-looking personage, with a powdered head and gold spectacles. He was dressed in a bottle-green coat with a black velvet collar; wore white trousers; and carried a smart bamboo cane under his arm. He had taken up a book from the stall, and there he stood, reading away, as hard as if he were in his elbow-chair, in his own study. It is very possible that he fancied himself there, indeed; for it was plain, from his abstraction, that he saw not the book-stall, nor the street, nor the boys, nor, in short, anything but the book itself: which he was reading straight through: turning over the leaf when he got to the bottom of a page, beginning at the top line of the next one, and going regularly on, with the greatest interest and eagerness.

What was Oliver's horror and alarm as he stood a few paces off, looking on with his eyelids as wide open as they would possibly go, to see the Dodger plunge his hand into the old gentleman's pocket, and draw from thence a handkerchief! To see him hand the same to Charley Bates; and finally to behold them, both, running away round the corner at full speed.

In an instant the whole mystery of the handkerchiefs, and the watches, and the jewels, and the Jew, rushed upon the boy's mind. He stood, for a moment, with the blood so tingling through all his veins from terror, that he felt as if he were in a burning fire; then, confused and frightened, he took to his heels; and, not knowing what he did, made off as fast as he could lay his feet to the ground.

This was all done in a minute's space. In the very instant when Oliver began to run, the old gentleman, putting his hand to his pocket, and missing his handkerchief, turned sharp round. Seeing the boy scudding away at such a rapid pace, he very naturally concluded him to be the depredator; and, shouting "Stop thief!" with all his might, made off after him, book in hand.

But the old gentleman was not the only person who raised the hue-and-cry. The Dodger and Master Bates, unwilling to attract public attention by running down the open street, had merely retired into the very first doorway round the corner. They no sooner heard the cry, and saw Oliver running, than, guessing exactly how the matter stood, they issued forth with great promptitude; and, shouting "Stop thief!" too, joined in the pursuit like good citizens.

Although Oliver had been brought up by philosophers, he was not theoretically acquainted with the beautiful axiom that self-preservation is the first law of nature. If he had been, perhaps he would have been prepared for this. Not being prepared, however, it alarmed him the more; so away he went like the wind, with the old gentleman and the two boys roaring and shouting behind him.

"Stop thief! Stop thief!" There is a magic in the sound. The tradesman leaves his counter, and the carman his waggon; the butcher throws down his tray; the baker his basket; the milkman his pail; the errand-boy his parcels; the school-boy his marbles; the paviour his pickaxe; the child his battledore. Away they run, pell-mell, helter-skelter, slap-dash: tearing, yelling, screaming, knocking down the passengers as they turn the corners, rousing up the dogs, and astonishing the fowls: and streets, squares, and courts, re-echo with the sound.

"Stop thief! Stop thief!" The cry is taken up by a hundred voices, and the crowd accumulate at every turning. Away they fly, splashing through the mud, and rattling along the pavements: up go the windows, out run the people, onward bear the mob, a whole audience desert Punch in the very thickest of the plot, and, joining the rushing throng, swell the shout, and lend fresh vigour to the cry, "Stop thief! Stop thief!"

"Stop thief! Stop thief!" There is a passion *for hunting something* deeply implanted in the human breast. One wretched breathless child, panting with exhaustion; terror in his looks; agony in his eyes; large drops of perspiration streaming down his face; strains every nerve to make head upon his pursuers; and as they follow on his track, and gain upon him every instant, they hail his decreasing strength with still louder shouts, and whoop and scream with joy. "Stop thief!" Ay, stop him for God's sake, were it only in mercy!

Stopped at last! A clever blow. He is down upon the pavement; and the crowd eagerly gather round him: each new comer, jostling and struggling with the others to catch a glimpse. "Stand aside!" "Give him a little air!" "Nonsense! he don't deserve it." "Where's the gentleman?" "Here he is, coming down the street." "Make room there for the gentleman!" "Is this the boy, sir!" "Yes."

Oliver lay, covered with mud and dust, and bleeding from the mouth, looking wildly round upon the heap of faces that surrounded him, when the old gentleman was officiously dragged and pushed into the circle by the foremost of the pursuers.

"Yes," said the gentleman, "I am afraid it is the boy."

"Afraid!" murmured the crowd. "That's a good "un!"

"Poor fellow!" said the gentleman, "he has hurt himself."

"*I* did that, sir," said a great lubberly fellow, stepping forward; "and preciously I cut my knuckle agin" his mouth. *I* stopped him, sir."

The fellow touched his hat with a grin, expecting something for his pains; but, the old gentleman, eyeing him with an expression of dislike, looked anxiously round, as if he contemplated running away himself: which it is very possible he might have attempted to do, and thus have afforded another chase, had not a police officer (who is generally the last person to arrive in such cases) at that moment made his way through the crowd, and seized Oliver by the collar.

"Come, get up," said the man, roughly.

"It wasn't me indeed, sir. Indeed, indeed, it was two other boys," said Oliver, clasping his hands passionately, and looking round. "They are here somewhere."

"Oh no, they ain't," said the officer. He meant this to be ironical, but it was true besides; for the Dodger and Charley Bates had fled off down the first convenient court they came to. "Come, get up!"

"Don't hurt him," said the old gentleman, compassionately.

"Oh no, I won't hurt him," replied the officer, tearing his jacket half off his back, in proof thereof. "Come, I know you; it won't do. Will you stand upon your legs, you young devil?"

Oliver, who could hardly stand, made a shift to raise himself on his feet, and was at once lugged along the streets by the jacket-collar, at a rapid pace. The gentleman walked on with them by the officer's side; and as many of the crowd as could achieve the feat, got a little a-head, and stared back at Oliver from time to time. The boys shouted in triumph; and on they went.

Chapter XI

Treats of Mr Fang the Police Magistrate; and furnishes a slight Specimen of his Mode of administering Justice

The offence had been committed within the district, and indeed in the immediate neighbourhood of, a very notorious metropolitan police office. The crowd had only the satisfaction of accompanying Oliver through two or three streets, and down a place called Mutton Hill, when he was led beneath a low archway, and up a dirty court, into this dispensary of summary justice, by the backway. It was a small paved yard into which they turned; and here they encountered a stout man with a bunch of whiskers on his face, and a bunch of keys in his hand.

"What's the matter now?" said the man carelessly.

"A young fogle-hunter," replied the man who had Oliver in charge.

"Are you the party that's been robbed, sir?" inquired the man with the keys.

"Yes, I am," replied the old gentleman; "but I am not sure that this boy actually took the handkerchief. I – I would rather not press the case."

"Must go before the magistrate now, sir," replied the man. "His worship will be disengaged in half a minute. Now, young gallows!"

This was an invitation for Oliver to enter through a door which he unlocked as he spoke, and which led into a stone cell. Here he was searched; and nothing being found upon him, locked up.

This cell was in shape and size something like an area cellar, only not so light. It was most intolerably dirty; for it was Monday morning; and it had been tenanted by six drunken people, who had been locked up, elsewhere, since Saturday night. But this is little. In our station-houses, men and women are every night confined on the most trivial *charges* – the word is worth noting – in dungeons, compared with which, those in Newgate, occupied by the most atrocious felons, tried, found guilty, and under sentence of death, are palaces. Let any one who doubts this, compare the two.

The old gentleman looked almost as rueful as Oliver when the key grated in the lock. He turned with a sigh to the book, which had been the innocent cause of all this disturbance.

"There is something in that boy's face," said the old gentleman to himself as he walked slowly away, tapping his chin with the cover of the book, in a thoughtful manner; "something that touches and interests me. *Can* he be innocent? He looked like. – By the bye," exclaimed the old gentleman, halting very abruptly, and staring up into the sky, "Bless my soul! Where have I seen something like that look before?"

After musing for some minutes, the old gentleman walked, with the same meditative face, into a back ante-room opening from the yard; and there, retiring into a corner, called up before his mind's eye a vast amphitheatre of faces over which a dusky curtain had hung for many years. "No," said the old gentleman, shaking his head; "it must be imagination."

He wandered over them again. He had called them into view, and it was not easy to replace the shroud that had so long concealed them. There were the faces of friends, and foes, and of many that had been almost strangers peering intrusively from the crowd; there were the faces of young and blooming girls that were now old women; there were faces that the grave had changed and closed upon, but which the mind, superior to its power, still dressed in their old freshness and beauty, calling back the lustre of the eyes, the brightness of the smile, the beaming of the soul through its mask of clay, and whispering of beauty beyond the tomb, changed but to be heightened, and taken from earth only to be set up as a light, to shed a soft and gentle glow upon the path to Heaven.

But the old gentleman could recall no one countenance of which Oliver's features bore a trace. So, he heaved a sigh over the recollections he had awakened; and being, happily for himself, an absent old gentleman, buried them again in the pages of the musty book.

He was roused by a touch on the shoulder, and a request from the man with the keys to follow him into the office. He closed his book hastily; and was at once ushered into the imposing presence of the renowned Mr Fang.

The office was a front parlour, with a panelled wall. Mr Fang sat behind a bar, at the upper end; and on one side the door was a sort of wooden pen in which poor little Oliver was already deposited: trembling very much at the awfulness of the scene.

Mr Fang was a lean, long-backed, stiff-necked, middle-sized man, with no great quantity of hair, and what he had, growing on the back and sides of his head. His face was stern, and much flushed. If he were really not in the habit of drinking rather more than was exactly good for him, he might have brought an action against his countenance for libel, and have recovered heavy damages.

The old gentleman bowed respectfully; and advancing to the magistrate's desk, said, suiting the action to the word, "That is my name and address, sir." He then withdrew a pace or two; and, with another polite and gentlemanly inclination of the head, waited to be questioned.

Now, it so happened that Mr Fang was at that moment perusing a leading article in a newspaper of the morning, adverting to some recent decision of his, and commending him, for the three hundred and fiftieth time, to the special and particular notice of the Secretary of State for the Home Department. He was out of temper; and he looked up with an angry scowl.

"Who are you?" said Mr Fang.

The old gentleman pointed, with some surprise, to his card.

"Officer!" said Mr Fang, tossing the card contemptuously away with the newspaper. "Who is this fellow?"

"My name, sir," said the old gentleman, speaking *like* a gentleman, "my name, sir, is Brownlow. Permit me to inquire the name of the magistrate who offers a gratuitous and unprovoked insult to a respectable person, under the protection of the bench." Saying this, Mr Brownlow looked round the office as if in search of some person who would afford him the required information.

"Officer!" said Mr Fang, throwing the paper on one side, "what's this fellow charged with?"

"He's not charged at all, your worship," replied the officer. "He appears against the boy, your worship."

His worship knew this perfectly well; but it was a good annoyance, and a safe one.

"Appears against the boy, does he?" said Fang, surveying Mr Brownlow contemptuously from head to foot. "Swear him!"

"Before I am sworn, I must beg to say one word," said Mr Brownlow: "and that is, that I really never, without actual experience, could have believed –"

"Hold your tongue, sir!" said Mr Fang, peremptorily.

"I will not, sir!" replied the old gentleman.

"Hold your tongue this instant, or I'll have you turned out of the office!" said Mr Fang. "You're an insolent, impertinent fellow. How dare you bully a magistrate!"

"What!" exclaimed the old gentleman, reddening.

"Swear this person!" said Fang to the clerk. "I'll not hear another word. Swear him."

Mr Brownlow's indignation was greatly roused; but reflecting perhaps, that he might only injure the boy by giving vent to it, he suppressed his feelings and submitted to be sworn at once.

"Now," said Fang, "What's the charge against this boy? What have you got to say, sir?"

"I was standing at a bookstall –" Mr Brownlow began.

"Hold your tongue, sir," said Mr Fang. "Policeman! Where's the policeman? Here, swear this policeman. Now, policeman, what is this?"

The policeman, with becoming humility, related how he had taken the charge; how he had searched Oliver, and found nothing on his person; and how that was all he knew about it.

"Are there any witnesses?" inquired Mr Fang.

"None, your worship," replied the policeman.

Mr Fang sat silent for some minutes, and then, turning round to the prosecutor, said in a towering passion.

"Do you mean to state what your complaint against this boy is, man, or do you not? You have been sworn. Now, if you stand there, refusing to give evidence, I'll punish you for disrespect to the bench; I will, by – "

By what, or by whom, nobody knows, for the clerk and jailor coughed very loud, just at the right moment; and the former dropped a heavy book upon the floor, thus preventing the word from being heard – accidentally, of course.

With many interruptions, and repeated insults, Mr Brownlow contrived to state his case; observing that, in the surprise of the moment, he had run after the boy because he saw him running away; and expressing his hope that, if the magistrate should believe him, although not actually the thief, to be connected with thieves, he would deal as leniently with him as justice would allow.

"He has been hurt already," said the old gentleman in conclusion. "And I fear," he added, with great energy, looking towards the bar, "I really fear that he is ill."

"Oh! yes, I dare say!" said Mr Fang, with a sneer. "Come, none of your tricks here, you young vagabond; they won't do. What's your name?"

Oliver tried to reply, but his tongue failed him. He was deadly pale; and the whole place seemed turning round and round.

"What's your name, you hardened scoundrel?" demanded Mr Fang. "Officer, what's his name?"

This was addressed to a bluff old fellow, in a striped waistcoat, who was standing by the bar. He bent over Oliver, and repeated the inquiry; but finding him really incapable of understanding the question; and knowing that his not replying would only infuriate the magistrate the more, and add to the severity of his sentence; he hazarded a guess.

"He says his name's Tom White, your worship," said this kind-hearted thief-taker.

"Oh, he won't speak out, won't he?" said Fang. "Very well, very well. Where does he live?"

"Where he can, your worship," replied the officer; again pretending to receive Oliver's answer.

"Has he any parents?" inquired Mr Fang.

"He says they died in his infancy, your worship," replied the officer: hazarding the usual reply.

At this point of the inquiry, Oliver raised his head; and, looking round with imploring eyes, murmured a feeble prayer for a draught of water.

"Stuff and nonsense!" said Mr Fang: "don't try to make a fool of me."

"I think he really is ill, your worship," remonstrated the officer.

"I know better," said Mr Fang.

"Take care of him, officer," said the old gentleman, raising his hands instinctively; "he'll fall down."

"Stand away, officer," cried Fang; "let him, if he likes."

Oliver availed himself of the kind permission, and fell to the floor in a fainting fit. The men in the office looked at each other, but no one dared to stir.

"I knew he was shamming," said Fang, as if this were incontestable proof of the fact. "Let him lie there; he'll soon be tired of that."

"How do you propose to deal with the case, sir?" inquired the clerk in a low voice.

"Summarily," replied Mr Fang. "He stands committed for three months – hard labour of course. Clear the office."

The door was opened for this purpose, and a couple of men were preparing to carry the insensible boy to his cell; when an elderly man of decent but poor appearance, clad in an old suit of black, rushed hastily into the office, and advanced towards the bench.

"Stop, stop! Don't take him away! For Heaven's sake stop a moment!" cried the new-comer, breathless with haste.

Although the presiding Genii in such an office as this, exercise a summary and arbitrary power over the liberties, the good name, the character, almost the lives, of Her Majesty's subjects, especially of the poorer class; and although, within such walls, enough fantastic tricks are daily played to make the angels blind with weeping; they are closed to the public, save through the medium of the daily press.* Mr Fang was consequently not a little indignant to see an unbidden guest enter in such irreverent disorder.

"What is this? Who is this? Turn this man out. Clear the office!" cried Mr Fang.

"I *will* speak," cried the man; "I will not be turned out. I saw it all. I keep the book-stall. I demand to be sworn. I will not be put down. Mr Fang, you must hear me. You must not refuse, sir."

The man was right. His manner was determined; and the matter was growing rather too serious to be hushed up.

"Swear the man," growled Mr Fang, with a very ill grace. "Now, man, what have you got to say?"

"This," said the man: "I saw three boys: two others and the prisoner here: loitering on the opposite side of the way, when this gentleman was reading. The robbery was committed by another boy. I saw it done; and I saw that this boy was perfectly amazed and stupefied by it." Having by this time recovered a little breath, the worthy book-stall keeper proceeded to relate, in a more coherent manner, the exact circumstances of the robbery.

"Why didn't you come here before?" said Fang, after a pause.

"I hadn't a soul to mind the shop," replied the man. "Everybody who could have helped me, had joined in the pursuit. I could get nobody till five minutes ago; and I've run here all the way."

"The prosecutor was reading, was he?" inquired Fang, after another pause.

"Yes," replied the man. "The very book he has in his hand."

"Oh, that book, eh?" said Fang. "Is it paid for?"

"No, it is not," replied the man, with a smile.

"Dear me, I forgot all about it!" exclaimed the absent old gentleman, innocently.

"A nice person to prefer a charge against a poor boy!" said Fang, with a comical effort to look humane. "I consider, sir, that you have obtained possession of that book, under very suspicious and disreputable circumstances; and you may think yourself very fortunate that the owner of the property declines to prosecute. Let this be a lesson to you, my man, or the law will overtake you yet. The boy is discharged. Clear the office."

"D—n me!" cried the old gentleman, bursting out with the rage he had kept down so long, "d—n me! I'll –"

"Clear the office!" said the magistrate. "Officers, do you hear? Clear the office!"

The mandate was obeyed; and the indignant Mr Brownlow was conveyed

* Or were virtually, then.

out, with the book in one hand, and the bamboo cane in the other: in a perfect phrenzy of rage and defiance. He reached the yard; and his passion vanished in a moment. Little Oliver Twist lay on his back on the pavement, with his shirt unbuttoned, and his temples bathed with water; his face a deadly white; and a cold tremble convulsing his whole frame.

"Poor boy, poor boy!" said Mr Brownlow, bending over him. "Call a coach, somebody, pray. Directly!"

A coach was obtained, and Oliver, having been carefully laid on one seat, the old gentleman got in and sat himself on the other.

"May I accompany you?" said the book-stall keeper, looking in.

"Bless me, yes, my dear sir," said Mr Brownlow quickly. "I forgot you. Dear, dear! I have this unhappy book still! Jump in. Poor fellow! There's no time to lose."

The book-stall keeper got into the coach; and away they drove.

Chapter XII

In which Oliver is taken better Care of than he ever was before. And in which the Narrative reverts to the merry old Gentleman and his youthful Friends

THE coach rattled away, over nearly the same ground as that which Oliver had traversed when he first entered London in company with the Dodger, and, turning a different way when it reached the Angel at Islington, stopped at length before a neat house, in a quiet shady street near Pentonville. Here, a bed was prepared, without loss of time, in which Mr Brownlow saw his young charge carefully and comfortably deposited; and here, he was tended with a kindness and solicitude that knew no bounds.

But, for many days, Oliver remained insensible to all the goodness of his new friends. The sun rose and sank, and rose and sank again, and many times after that; and still the boy lay stretched on his uneasy bed, dwindling away beneath the dry and wasting heat of fever. The worm does not his work more surely on the dead body, than does this slow creeping fire upon the living frame.

Weak, and thin, and pallid, he awoke at last from what seemed to have been a long and troubled dream. Feebly raising himself in the bed, with his head resting on his trembling arm, he looked anxiously around.

"What room is this? Where have I been brought to?" said Oliver. "This is not the place I went to sleep in."

He uttered these words in a feeble voice, being very faint and weak; but they were overheard at once. The curtain at the bed's head was hastily drawn back, and a motherly old lady, very neatly and precisely dressed, rose as she undrew it, from an arm-chair close by, in which she had been sitting at needle-work.

"Hush, my dear," said the old lady softly. "You must be very quiet, or you will be ill again; and you have been very bad, – as bad as bad could be, pretty nigh. Lie down again; there's a dear!" With those words, the old lady very gently placed Oliver's head upon the pillow; and, smoothing back his hair from his forehead, looked so kindly and lovingly in his face, that he could not help placing his little withered hand in hers, and drawing it round his neck.

"Save us!" said the old lady, with tears in her eyes, "What a grateful little dear it is. Pretty creetur! What would his mother feel if she had sat by him as I have, and could see him now!"

"Perhaps she does see me," whispered Oliver, folding his hands together; "perhaps she has sat by me. I almost feel as if she had."

"That was the fever, my dear," said the old lady mildly.

"I suppose it was," replied Oliver, "because heaven is a long way off; and they are too happy there, to come down to the bedside of a poor boy. But if she knew I was ill, she must have pitied me, even there; for she was very ill herself before she died. She can't know anything about me though," added Oliver after a moment's silence. "If she had seen me hurt, it would have made her sorrowful; and her face has always looked sweet and happy, when I have dreamed of her."

The old lady made no reply to this; but wiping her eyes first, and her spectacles, which lay on the counterpane, afterwards, as if they were part and parcel of those features, brought some cool stuff for Oliver to drink; and then, patting him on the cheek, told him he must lie very quiet, or he would be ill again.

So, Oliver kept very still; partly because he was anxious to obey the kind old lady in all things; and partly, to tell the truth, because he was completely exhausted with what he had already said. He soon fell into a gentle doze, from which he was awakened by the light of a candle: which, being brought near the bed, showed him a gentleman with a very large and loud-ticking gold watch in his hand, who felt his pulse, and said he was a great deal better.

"You *are* a great deal better, are you not, my dear?" said the gentleman.

"Yes, thank you, sir," replied Oliver.

"Yes, I know you are," said the gentleman: "You're hungry too, an't you?"

"No, sir," answered Oliver.

"Hem!" said the gentleman. "No, I know you're not. He is not hungry, Mrs Bedwin," said the gentleman: looking very wise.

The old lady made a respectful inclination of the head, which seemed to say that she thought the doctor was a very clever man. The doctor appeared much of the same opinion himself.

"You feel sleepy, don't you, my dear?" said the doctor.

"No, sir," replied Oliver.

"No," said the doctor, with a very shrewd and satisfied look. "You're not sleepy. Nor thirsty. Are you?"

"Yes, sir, rather thirsty," answered Oliver.

"Just as I expected, Mrs Bedwin," said the doctor. "It's very natural that he should be thirsty. You may give him a little tea, ma'am, and some dry toast without any butter. Don't keep him too warm, ma'am; but be careful that you don't let him be too cold; will you have the goodness?"

The old lady dropped a curtsey. The doctor, after tasting the cool stuff, and expressing a qualified approval of it, hurried away: his boots creaking in a very important and wealthy manner as he went down stairs.

Oliver dozed off again, soon after this; when he awoke, it was nearly twelve o'clock. The old lady tenderly bade him good-night shortly afterwards, and left him in charge of a fat old woman who had just come: bringing with her, in a little bundle, a small Prayer Book and a large nightcap. Putting the latter on her head and the former on the table, the old woman, after telling Oliver that she had come to sit up with him, drew her chair close to the fire and went off into a series of short naps, chequered at frequent intervals with sundry tumblings forward, and divers moans and chokings. These, however, had no worse effect than causing her to rub her nose very hard, and then fall asleep again.

And thus the night crept slowly on. Oliver lay awake for some time, counting the little circles of light which the reflection of the rushlight-shade threw upon the ceiling; or tracing with his languid eyes the intricate pattern of the paper on the wall. The darkness and the deep stillness of the room were very solemn; as they brought into the boy's mind the thought that death had been hovering there, for many days and nights, and might yet fill it with the gloom and dread of his awful presence, he turned his face upon the pillow, and fervently prayed to Heaven.

Gradually, he fell into that deep tranquil sleep which ease from recent suffering alone imparts; that calm and peaceful rest which it is pain to wake from. Who, if this were death, would be roused again to all the struggles and turmoils of life; to all its cares for the present; its anxieties for the future; more than all, its weary recollections of the past!

It had been bright day, for hours, when Oliver opened his eyes; he felt cheerful and happy. The crisis of the disease was safely past. He belonged to the world again.

In three days" time he was able to sit in an easy-chair, well propped up with pillows; and, as he was still too weak to walk, Mrs Bedwin had him carried down stairs into the little housekeeper's room, which belonged to her. Having him set, here, by the fireside, the good old lady sat herself down too; and, being in a state of considerable delight at seeing him so much better, forthwith began to cry most violently.

"Never mind me, my dear," said the old lady. "I'm only having a regular good cry. There; it's all over now; and I'm quite comfortable."

"You're very, very kind to me, ma'am," said Oliver.

"Well, never you mind that, my dear," said the old lady; "that's got nothing to do with your broth; and it's full time you had it; for the doctor says Mr Brownlow may come in to see you this morning; and we must get up our best looks, because the better we look, the more he'll be pleased." And with this, the old lady applied herself to warming up, in a little saucepan, a basin full of broth: strong enough, Oliver thought, to furnish an ample dinner, when reduced to the regulation strength, for three hundred and fifty paupers, at the lowest computation.

"Are you fond of pictures, dear?" inquired the old lady, seeing that Oliver had fixed his eyes, most intently, on a portrait which hung against the wall; just opposite his chair.

"I don't quite know, ma'am," said Oliver, without taking his eyes from the canvas; "I have seen so few, that I hardly know. What a beautiful, mild face that lady's is!"

"Ah!" said the old lady, "painters always make ladies out prettier than they are, or they wouldn't get any custom, child. The man that invented the machine for taking likenesses might have known *that* would never succeed; it's a deal too honest. A deal," said the old lady, laughing very heartily at her own acuteness.

"Is – is that a likeness, ma'am?" said Oliver.

"Yes," said the old lady, looking up for a moment from the broth: "that's a portrait."

"Whose, ma'am?" asked Oliver.

"Why, really, my dear, I don't know," answered the old lady in a good-humoured manner. "It's not a likeness of anybody that you or I know, I expect. It seems to strike your fancy, dear."

"It is so very pretty," replied Oliver.

"Why, sure you're not afraid of it?" said the old lady: observing, in great surprise, the look of awe with which the child regarded the painting.

"Oh no, no," returned Oliver quickly; "but the eyes look so sorrowful; and where I sit, they seem fixed upon me. It makes my heart beat," added Oliver in a low voice, "as if it was alive, and wanted to speak to me, but couldn't."

"Lord save us!" exclaimed the old lady, starting; "don't talk in that way, child. You're weak and nervous after your illness. Let me wheel your chair round to the other side; and then you won't see it. There!" said the old lady, suiting the action to the word; "you don't see it now, at all events."

Oliver *did* see it in his mind's eye as distinctly as if he had not altered his position; but he thought it better not to worry the kind old lady; so he smiled gently when she looked at him; and Mrs Bedwin, satisfied that he felt more comfortable, salted and broke bits of toasted bread into the broth, with all the bustle befitting so solemn a preparation. Oliver got through it with extraordinary expedition. He had scarcely swallowed the last spoonful, when there came a soft rap at the door. "Come in," said the old lady; and in walked Mr Brownlow.

Now, the old gentleman came in as brisk as need be; but, he had no sooner raised his spectacles on his forehead, and thrust his hands behind the skirts of his dressing-gown to take a good long look at Oliver, than his countenance underwent a very great variety of odd contortions. Oliver looked very worn and shadowy from sickness, and made an ineffectual attempt to stand up, out of respect to his benefactor, which terminated in his sinking back into the chair again; and the fact is, if the truth must be told, that Mr Brownlow's heart, being large enough for any six ordinary old gentlemen of humane disposition, forced a supply of tears into his eyes, by some hydraulic process which we are not sufficiently philosophical to be in a condition to explain.

"Poor boy, poor boy!" said Mr Brownlow, clearing his throat. "I'm rather hoarse this morning, Mrs Bedwin. I'm afraid I have caught cold."

"I hope not, sir," said Mrs Bedwin. "Everything you have had, has been well aired, sir."

"I don't know, Bedwin. I don't know," said Mr Brownlow; "I rather think I had a damp napkin at dinner-time yesterday; but never mind that. How do you feel, my dear?"

"Very happy, sir," replied Oliver. "And very grateful indeed, sir, for your goodness to me."

"Good boy," said Mr Brownlow, stoutly. "Have you given him any nourishment, Bedwin? Any slops, eh?"

"He has just had a basin of beautiful strong broth, sir," replied Mrs Bedwin: drawing herself up slightly, and laying a strong emphasis on the last word: to intimate that between slops, and broth well compounded, there existed no affinity or connexion whatsoever.

"Ugh!" said Mr Brownlow, with a slight shudder; "a couple of glasses of port wine would have done him a great deal more good. Wouldn't they, Tom White, eh?"

"My name is Oliver, sir," replied the little invalid: with a look of a great astonishment.

"Oliver," said Mr Brownlow; "Oliver what? Oliver White, eh?"

"No, sir, Twist, Oliver Twist."

"Queer name!" said the old gentleman. "What made you tell the magistrate your name was White?"

"I never told him so, sir," returned Oliver in amazement.

This sounded so like a falsehood, that the old gentleman looked somewhat sternly in Oliver's face. It was impossible to doubt him; there was truth in every one of its thin and sharpened lineaments.

"Some mistake," said Mr Brownlow. But, although his motive for looking steadily at Oliver no longer existed, the old idea of the resemblance between his features and some familiar face came upon him so strongly, that he could not withdraw his gaze.

"I hope you are not angry with me, sir?" said Oliver, raising his eyes beseechingly.

"No, no," replied the old gentleman. "Why! what's this? Bedwin, look there!"

As he spoke, he pointed hastily to the picture above Oliver's head, and then to the boy's face. There was its living copy. The eyes, the head, the mouth; every feature was the same. The expression was, for the instant, so precisely alike, that the minutest line seemed copied with startling accuracy!

Oliver knew not the cause of this sudden exclamation; for, not being strong enough to bear the start it gave him, he fainted away. A weakness on his part, which affords the narrative an opportunity of relieving the reader from suspense, in behalf of the two young pupils of the Merry Old Gentleman; and of recording –

That when the Dodger, and his accomplished friend Master Bates, joined in the hue-and-cry which was raised at Oliver's heels, in consequence of their executing an illegal conveyance of Mr Brownlow's personal property, as has been already described, they were actuated by a very laudable and becoming regard for themselves; and forasmuch as the freedom of the subject and the liberty of the individual are among the first and proudest boasts of a true-hearted Englishman, so, I need hardly beg the reader to observe, that this action should tend to exalt them in the opinion of all public and patriotic men, in almost as great a degree as this strong proof of their anxiety for their own preservation and safety goes to corroborate and confirm the little code of laws which certain profound and sound-judging philosophers have laid down as the mainsprings of all Nature's deeds and actions: the said philosophers very wisely reducing the good lady's proceedings to matters of maxim and theory: and, by a very neat and pretty compliment to her exalted wisdom and understanding, putting entirely out of sight any considerations of heart, or generous impulse and feeling. For, these are matters totally beneath a female who is acknowledged by universal admission to be far above the numerous little foibles and weaknesses of her sex.

If I wanted any further proof of the strictly philosophical nature of the conduct of these young gentlemen in their very delicate predicament, I should at once find it in the fact (also recorded in a foregoing part of this narrative), of their quitting the pursuit, when the general attention was fixed upon Oliver; and making immediately for their home by the shortest possible cut. Although I do not mean to assert that it is usually the practice of renowned and learned sages, to shorten the road to any great conclusion (their course indeed being rather to lengthen the distance, by various circumlocutions and discursive staggerings, like unto those in which drunken men under the pressure of a too mighty flow of ideas, are prone to indulge); still, I do mean to say, and do say distinctly, that it is the invariable practice of many mighty philosophers, in carrying out their theories, to evince great wisdom and foresight in providing against every possible contingency which can be supposed at all likely to affect themselves. Thus, to do a great right, you may do a little wrong; and you may take any means which the end to be attained will justify; the amount of the right, or the amount of the wrong, or indeed the distinction between the two, being left entirely to the philosopher concerned, to be settled and determined by his clear, comprehensive, and impartial view of his own particular case.

It was not until the two boys had scoured, with great rapidity, through a most intricate maze of narrow streets and courts, that they ventured to halt beneath a low and dark archway. Having remained silent here, just long enough to recover breath to speak, Master Bates uttered an exclamation of amusement and delight; and, bursting into an uncontrollable fit of laughter, flung himself upon a door-step, and rolled thereon in a transport of mirth.

"What's the matter?" inquired the Dodger.

"Ha! ha! ha!" roared Charley Bates.

"Hold your noise," remonstrated the Dodger, looking cautiously round. "Do you want to be grabbed, stupid?"

"I can't help it," said Charley, "I can't help it! To see him splitting away at that pace, and cutting round the corners, and knocking up again the posts, and starting on again as if he was made of iron as well as them, and me with the wipe in my pocket, singing out arter him – oh, my eye!" The vivid imagination of Master Bates, presented the scene before him in too strong colours. As he arrived at this apostrophe, he again rolled upon the door-step, and laughed louder than before.

"What'll Fagin say?" inquired the Dodger; taking advantage of the next interval of breathlessness on the part of his friend to propound the question.

"What?" repeated Charley Bates.

"Ah, what?" said the Dodger.

"Why, what should he say?" inquired Charley: stopping rather suddenly in his merriment; for the Dodger's manner was impressive. "What should he say?"

Mr Dawkins whistled for a couple of minutes; then, taking off his hat, scratched his head, and nodded thrice.

"What do you mean?" said Charley.

"Toor rul lol loo, gammon and spinnage, the frog he wouldn't, and high cockolorum," said the Dodger: with a slight sneer on his intellectual countenance.

This was explanatory, but not satisfactory. Master Bates felt it so; and again said, "What do you mean?"

The Dodger made no reply; but putting his hat on again, and gathering the skirts of his long-tailed coat under his arm, thrust his tongue into his cheek, slapped the bridge of his nose some half-dozen times in a familiar but expressive manner, and turning on his heel, slunk down the court. Master Bates followed, with a thoughtful countenance.

The noise of footsteps on the creaking stairs, a few minutes after the occurrence of this conversation, roused the merry old gentleman as he sat over the fire with a saveloy and a small loaf in his left hand; a pocket-knife in his right; and a pewter pot on the trivet. There was a rascally smile on his white face as he turned round, and, looking sharply out from under his thick red eyebrows, bent his ear towards the door, and listened.

"Why, how's this?" muttered the Jew, changing countenance; "only two of 'em? Where's the third? They can't have got into trouble. Hark!"

The footsteps approached nearer; they reached the landing. The door was slowly opened; and the Dodger and Charley Bates entered, closing it behind them.

Chapter XIII

Some new Acquaintances are introduced to the intelligent Reader, connected with whom, various pleasant Matters are related, appertaining to this History

"Where's Oliver?" said the Jew, rising with a menacing look. "Where's the boy?"

The young thieves eyed their preceptor as if they were alarmed at his violence; and looked uneasily at each other. But they made no reply.

"What's become of the boy?" said the Jew, seizing the Dodger tightly by the collar, and threatening him with horrid imprecations. "Speak out, or I'll throttle you!"

Mr Fagin looked so very much in earnest, that Charley Bates, who deemed it prudent in all cases to be on the safe side, and who conceived it by no means improbable that it might be his turn to be throttled second, dropped upon his knees, and raised a loud, well-sustained, and continuous roar – something between a mad bull and a speaking trumpet.

"Will you speak?" thundered the Jew: shaking the Dodger so much that his keeping in the big coat at all, seemed perfectly miraculous.

"Why, the traps have got him, and that's all about it," said the Dodger, sullenly. "Come, let go o'me, will you!" And, swinging himself, at one jerk, clean out of the big coat, which he left in the Jew's hands, the Dodger snatched up the toasting fork, and made a pass at the merry old gentleman's waistcoat; which, if it had taken effect, would have let a little more merriment out, than could have been easily replaced.

The Jew stepped back in this emergency, with more agility than could have been anticipated in a man of his apparent decrepitude; and, seizing up the pot, prepared to hurl it at his assailant's head. But Charley Bates, at this moment, calling his attention by a perfectly terrific howl, he suddenly altered its destination, and flung it full at that young gentleman.

"Why, what the blazes is in the wind now!" growled a deep voice. "Who pitched that 'ere at me? It's well it's the beer, and not the pot, as hit me, or I'd have settled somebody. I might have know'd, as nobody but an infernal, rich, plundering, thundering old Jew could afford to throw away any drink but water – and not that, unless he done the River Company every quarter. Wot's it all about, Fagin? D—me, if my neck-handkercher an't lined with beer! Come in, you sneaking warmint; wot are you stopping outside for, as if you was ashamed of your master! Come in!"

The man who growled out these words, was a stoutly-built fellow of about five-and-thirty, in a black velveteen coat, very soiled drab breeches, lace-up half boots, and grey cotton stockings, which inclosed a bulky pair of legs, with large swelling calves; – the kind of legs, which in such costume, always look in an unfinished and incomplete state without a set of fetters to garnish them. He had a brown hat on his head, and a dirty belcher handkerchief round his neck: with the long frayed ends of which he smeared the beer from his face as he spoke. He disclosed, when he had done so, a broad heavy countenance with a beard of three days' growth, and two scowling eyes; one of which displayed various parti-coloured symptoms of having been recently damaged by a blow.

"Come in, d'ye hear?" growled this engaging ruffian.

A white shaggy dog, with his face scratched and torn in twenty different places, skulked into the room.

"Why didn't you come in afore?" said the man. "You're getting too proud to own me afore company, are you? Lie down!"

This command was accompanied with a kick, which sent the animal to the other end of the room. He appeared well used to it, however; for he coiled himself up in a corner very quietly, without uttering a sound, and winking his very ill-looking eyes twenty times in a minute, appeared to occupy himself in taking a survey of the apartment.

"What are you up to? Ill-treating the boys, you covetous, avaricious, in-sa-ti-a-ble old fence?" said the man, seating himself deliberately. "I wonder they don't murder you! *I* would if I was them. If I'd been your 'prentice, I'd have done it long ago, and – no, I couldn't have sold you afterwards, for you're fit for nothing but keeping as a curiosity of ugliness in a glass bottle, and I suppose they don't blow glass bottles large enough."

"Hush! hush! Mr Sikes," said the Jew, trembling; "don't speak so loud."

"None of your mistering," replied the ruffian; "you always mean mischief when you come that. You know my name: out with it! I shan't disgrace it when the time comes."

"Well, well, then – Bill Sikes," said the Jew, with abject humility. "You seem out of humour, Bill."

"Perhaps I am," replied Sikes; "I should think *you* was rather out of sorts too, unless you mean as little harm when you throw pewter pots about, as you do when you blab and –"

"Are you mad?" said the Jew, catching the man by the sleeve, and pointing towards the boys.

Mr Sikes contented himself with tying an imaginary knot under his left ear, and jerking his head over on the right shoulder; a piece of dumb show which the Jew appeared to understand perfectly. He then, in cant terms, with which his whole conversation was plentifully besprinkled, but which would be quite unintelligible if they were recorded here, demanded a glass of liquor.

"And mind you don't poison it," said Mr Sikes, laying his hat upon the table.

This was said in jest; but if the speaker could have seen the evil leer with which the Jew bit his pale lip as he turned round to the cupboard, he might have thought the caution not wholly unnecessary, or the wish (at all events) to improve upon the distiller's ingenuity not very far from the old gentleman's merry heart.

After swallowing two or three glasses of spirits, Mr Sikes condescended to take some notice of the young gentlemen; which gracious act led to a conversation, in which the cause and manner of Oliver's capture were circumstantially detailed, with such alterations and improvements on the truth, as to the Dodger appeared most advisable under the circumstances.

"I'm afraid," said the Jew, "that he may say something which will get us into trouble."

"That's very likely," returned Sikes with a malicious grin. "You're blowed upon, Fagin."

"And I'm afraid, you see," added the Jew, speaking as if he had not noticed the interruption; and regarding the other closely as he did so, – "I'm afraid that, if the game was up with us, it might be up with a good many more, and that it would come out rather worse for you than it would for me, my dear."

The man started, and turned round upon the Jew. But the old gentleman's shoulders were shrugged up to his ears; and his eyes were vacantly staring on the opposite wall.

There was a long pause. Every member of the respectable coterie appeared plunged in his own reflections; not excepting the dog, who by a certain malicious licking of his lips seemed to be meditating an attack upon the legs of the first gentleman or lady he might encounter in the streets when he went out.

"Somebody must find out wot's been done at the office," said Mr Sikes in a much lower tone than he had taken since he came in.

The Jew nodded assent.

"If he hasn't peached, and is committed, there's no fear till he comes out again," said Mr Sikes, "and then he must be taken care on. You must get hold of him somehow."

Again the Jew nodded.

The prudence of this line of action, indeed, was obvious; but unfortunately, there was one very strong objection to its being adopted. This was, that the Dodger, and Charley Bates, and Fagin, and Mr William Sikes, happened, one and all, to entertain a violent and deeply-rooted antipathy to going near a police-office on any ground or pretext whatever.

How long they might have sat and looked at each other, in a state of uncertainty not the most pleasant of its kind, it is difficult to guess. It is not necessary to make any guesses on the subject, however; for the sudden entrance of the two young ladies whom Oliver had seen on a former occasion, caused the conversation to flow afresh.

"The very thing!" said the Jew. "Bet will go; won't you, my dear?"

"Wheres?" inquired the young lady.

"Only just up to the office, my dear," said the Jew coaxingly.

It is due to the young lady to say that she did not positively affirm that she would not, but that she merely expressed an emphatic and earnest desire to be "blessed" if she would; a polite and delicate evasion of the request, which shows the young lady to have been possessed of that natural good breeding which cannot bear to inflict upon a fellow-creature the pain of a direct and pointed refusal.

The Jew's countenance fell. He turned from this young lady, who was gaily, not to say gorgeously attired, in a red gown, green boots, and yellow curl-papers, to the other female.

"Nancy, my dear," said the Jew in a soothing manner, "what do *you* say?"

"That it won't do; so it's no use a-trying it on, Fagin," replied Nancy.

"What do you mean by that?" said Mr Sikes, looking up in a surly manner.

"What I say, Bill," replied the lady collectedly.

"Why, you're just the very person for it," reasoned Mr Sikes: "nobody about here knows anything of you."

"And as I don't want 'em to, neither," replied Nancy in the same composed manner, "it's rather more no than yes with me, Bill."

"She'll go, Fagin," said Sikes.

"No, she won't, Fagin," said Nancy.

"Yes she will, Fagin," said Sikes.

And Mr Sikes was right. By dint of alternate threats, promises, and bribes, the lady in question was ultimately prevailed upon to undertake the commission. She was not, indeed, withheld by the same considerations as her agreeable friend; for, having recently removed into the neighbourhood of Field Lane from the remote but genteel suburb of Ratcliffe, she was not under the same apprehension of being recognised by any of her numerous acquaintance.

Accordingly, with a clean white apron tied over her gown, and her curl-papers tucked up under a straw bonnet, – both articles of dress being provided from the Jew's inexhaustible stock, – Miss Nancy prepared to issue forth on her errand.

"Stop a minute, my dear," said the Jew, producing a little covered basket. "Carry that in one hand. It looks more respectable, my dear."

"Give her a door-key to carry in her t"other one, Fagin," said Sikes; "it looks real and genivine like."

"Yes, yes, my dear, so it does," said the Jew, hanging a large street-door key on the forefinger of the young lady's right hand. "There; very good! Very good indeed, my dear!" said the Jew, rubbing his hands.

"Oh, my brother! My poor, dear, sweet, innocent little brother!" exclaimed Nancy, bursting into tears, and wringing the little basket and the street-door key in an agony of distress. "What has become of him! Where have they taken him to! Oh, dó have pity, and tell me what's been done with the dear boy, gentlemen; do, gentlemen, if you please, gentlemen!"

Having uttered these words in a most lamentable and heart-broken tone to the immeasurable delight of her hearers, Miss Nancy paused, winked to the company, nodded smilingly round, and disappeared.

"Ah! she's a clever girl, my dears," said the Jew, turning round to his young friends, and shaking his head gravely, as if in mute admonition to them to follow the bright example they had just beheld.

"She's a honour to her sex," said Mr Sikes, filling his glass, and smiting the table with his enormous fist. "Here's her health, and wishing they was all like her!"

While these, and many other encomiums, were being passed on the accomplished Nancy, that young lady made the best of her way to the police-office; whither, notwithstanding a little natural timidity consequent upon walking through the streets alone and unprotected, she arrived in perfect safety shortly afterwards.

Entering by the back way, she tapped softly with the key at one of the cell-doors, and listened. There was no sound within: so she coughed and listened again. Still there was no reply: so she spoke.

"Nolly, dear?" murmured Nancy in a gentle voice; "Nolly?"

There was nobody inside but a miserable shoeless criminal, who had been taken up for playing the flute, and who, the offence against society having been clearly proved, had been very properly committed by Mr Fang to the House of Correction for one month; with the appropriate and amusing remark that since he had so much breath to spare, it would be more wholesomely expended on the treadmill than in a musical instrument.

He made no answer: being occupied in mentally bewailing the loss of the flute, which had been confiscated for the use of the county; so Nancy passed on to the next cell, and knocked there.

"Well!" cried a faint and feeble voice.

"Is there a little boy here?" inquired Nancy, with a preliminary sob.

"No," replied the voice; "God forbid."

This was a vagrant of sixty-five, who was going to prison for *not* playing the flute; or, in other words, for begging in the streets, and doing nothing for his livelihood. In the next cell, was another man, who was going to the same prison for hawking tin saucepans without a license; thereby doing something for his living, in defiance of the Stamp-office.

But, as neither of these criminals answered to the name of Oliver, or knew anything about him, Nancy made straight up to the bluff officer in the striped waistcoat; and with the most piteous wailings and lamentations, rendered more piteous by a prompt and efficient use of the street-door key and the little basket, demanded her own dear brother.

"*I* haven't got him, my dear," said the old man.

"Where is he?" screamed Nancy, in a distracted manner.

"Why, the gentleman's got him," replied the officer.

"What gentleman? Oh, gracious heavens! What gentleman?" exclaimed Nancy.

In reply to this incoherent question, the old man informed the deeply affected sister that Oliver had been taken ill in the office, and discharged in consequence of a witness having proved the robbery to have been committed by another boy, not in custody; and that the prosecutor had carried him away, in an insensible condition, to his own residence: of and concerning which, all the informant knew was, that it was somewhere at Pentonville, he having heard that word mentioned in the directions to the coachman.

In a dreadful state of doubt and uncertainty, the agonised young woman staggered to the gate, and then, exchanging her faltering walk for a swift run, returned by the most devious and complicated route she could think of, to the domicile of the Jew.

Mr Bill Sikes no sooner heard the account of the expedition delivered, than he very hastily called up the white dog, and, putting on his hat, expeditiously departed: without devoting any time to the formality of wishing the company good morning.

"We must know where he is, my dears; he must be found," said the Jew greatly excited. "Charley, do nothing but skulk about, till you bring home some news of him! Nancy, my dear, I must have him found. I trust to you, my dear, – to you and the Artful for everything! Stay, stay," added the Jew, unlocking a drawer with a shaking hand; "there's money, my dears. I shall shut up this shop to-night. You'll know where to find me! Don't stop here a minute. Not an instant, my dears!"

With these words, he pushed them from the room: and carefully double-locking and barring the door behind them, drew from its place of concealment the box which he had unintentionally disclosed to Oliver. Then, he hastily proceeded to dispose the watches and jewellery beneath his clothing.

A rap at the door startled him in this occupation. "Who's there?" he cried in a shrill tone.

"Me!" replied the voice of the Dodger, through the key-hole.

"What now?" cried the Jew impatiently.

"Is he to be kidnapped to the other ken, Nancy says?" inquired the Dodger.

"Yes," replied the Jew, "wherever she lays hands on him. Find him, find him out, that's all! I shall know what to do next; never fear."

The boy murmured a reply of intelligence; and hurried down stairs after his companions.

"He has not peached so far," said the Jew as he pursued his occupation. "If he means to blab us among his new friends, we may stop his mouth yet."

Chapter XIV

Comprising further Particulars of Oliver's Stay at Mr Brownlow's. With the remarkable Prediction which one Mr Grimwig uttered concerning him, when he went out on an Errand

OLIVER soon recovering from the fainting-fit into which Mr Brownlow's abrupt exclamation had thrown him, the subject of the picture was carefully avoided, both by the old gentleman and Mrs Bedwin, in the conversation that ensued: which indeed bore no reference to Oliver's history or prospects, but was confined to such topics as might amuse without exciting him. He was still too weak to get up to breakfast; but, when he came down into the housekeeper's room next day, his first act was to cast an eager glance at the wall, in the hope of again looking on the face of the beautiful lady. His expectations were disappointed, however, for the picture had been removed.

"Ah!" said the housekeeper, watching the direction of Oliver's eyes. "It is gone, you see."

"I see it is, ma'am," replied Oliver. "Why have they taken it away?"

"It has been taken down, child, because Mr Brownlow said, that as it seemed to worry you, perhaps it might prevent your getting well, you know," rejoined the old lady.

"Oh, no, indeed. It didn't worry me, ma'am," said Oliver. "I liked to see it. I quite loved it."

"Well, well!" said the old lady, good-humouredly; "you get well as fast as ever you can, dear, and it shall be hung up again. There! I promise you that! Now, let us talk about something else."

This was all the information Oliver would obtain about the picture at that time. As the old lady had been so kind to him in his illness, he endeavoured to think no more of the subject just then; so he listened attentively to a great many stories she told him, about an amiable and handsome daughter of hers, who was married to an amiable and handsome man, and lived in the country; and about a son, who was clerk to a merchant in the West Indies;

and who was, also, such a good young man, and wrote such dutiful letters home four times a-year, that it brought the tears into her eyes to talk about them. When the old lady had expatiated, a long time, on the excellences of her children, and the merits of her kind good husband besides, who had been dead and gone, poor dear soul! just six-and-twenty years, it was time to have tea. After tea she began to teach Oliver cribbage: which he learnt as quickly as she could teach: and at which game they played, with great interest and gravity, until it was time for the invalid to have some warm wine and water, with a slice of dry toast, and then to go cosily to bed.

They were happy days, those of Oliver's recovery. Everything was so quiet, and neat, and orderly; everybody was kind and gentle; that after the noise and turbulence in the midst of which he had always lived, it seemed like Heaven itself. He was no sooner strong enough to put his clothes on, properly, than Mr Brownlow caused a complete new suit, and a new cap, and a new pair of shoes, to be provided for him. As Oliver was told that he might do what he liked with the old clothes, he gave them to a servant who had been very kind to him, and asked her to sell them to a Jew, and keep the money for herself. This she very readily did; and, as Oliver looked out of the parlour window, and saw the Jew roll them up in his bag and walk away, he felt quite delighted to think that they were safely gone, and that there was now no possible danger of his ever being able to wear them again. They were sad rags, to tell the truth; and Oliver had never had a new suit before.

One evening, about a week after the affair of the picture, as he was sitting talking to Mrs Bedwin, there came a message down from Mr Brownlow, that if Oliver Twist felt pretty well, he should like to see him in his study, and talk to him a little while.

"Bless us, and save us! Wash your hands, and let me part your hair nicely for you, child," said Mrs Bedwin. "Dear heart alive! If we had known he would have asked for you, we would have put you a clean collar on, and made you as smart as sixpence!"

Oliver did as the old lady bade him; and, although she lamented grievously, meanwhile, that there was not even time to crimp the little frill that bordered his shirt-collar; he looked so delicate and handsome, despite that important personal advantage, that she went so far as to say: looking at him with great complacency from head to foot, that she really didn't think it would have been possible, on the longest notice, to have made much difference in him for the better.

Thus encouraged, Oliver tapped at the study door. On Mr Brownlow calling to him to come in, he found himself in a little back room, quite full of books, with a window, looking into some pleasant little gardens. There was a table drawn up before the window, at which Mr Brownlow was seated reading. When he saw Oliver, he pushed the book away from him, and told him to come near the table, and sit down. Oliver complied; marvelling where the people could be found to read such a great number of books as seemed to be written to make the world wiser. Which is still a marvel to more experienced people than Oliver Twist, every day of their lives.

"There are a good many books, are there not, my boy?" said Mr

Brownlow, observing the curiosity with which Oliver surveyed the shelves that reached from the floor to the ceiling.

"A great number, sir," replied Oliver. "I never saw so many."

"You shall read them, if you behave well," said the old gentleman kindly; "and you will like that, better than looking at the outsides, – that is, in some cases; because there *are* books of which the backs and covers are by far the best parts."

"I suppose they are those heavy ones, sir," said Oliver, pointing to some large quartos, with a good deal of gilding about the binding.

"Not always those," said the old gentleman, patting Oliver on the head, and smiling as he did so; "there are other equally heavy ones, though of a much smaller size. How should you like to grow up a clever man, and write books, eh?"

"I think I would rather read them, sir," replied Oliver.

"What! wouldn't you like to be a book-writer?" said the old gentleman.

Oliver considered a little while; and at last said, he should think it would be a much better thing to be a book-seller; upon which the old gentleman laughed heartily, and declared he had said a very good thing. Which Oliver felt glad to have done, though he by no means knew what it was.

"Well, well," said the old gentleman, composing his features. "Don't be afraid! We won't make an author of you, while there's an honest trade to be learnt, or brick-making to turn to."

"Thank you, sir," said Oliver. At the earnest manner of his reply, the old gentleman laughed again; and said something about a curious instinct, which Oliver, not understanding, paid no very great attention to.

"Now," said Mr Brownlow, speaking if possible in a kinder, but at the same time in a much more serious manner, than Oliver had ever known him assume yet, "I want you to pay great attention, my boy, to what I am going to say. I shall talk to you without any reserve; because I am sure you are as well able to understand me, as many older persons would be."

"Oh, don't tell me you are going to send me away, sir, pray!" exclaimed Oliver, alarmed at the serious tone of the old gentleman's commencement! "Don't turn me out of doors to wander in the streets again. Let me stay here, and be a servant. Don't send me back to the wretched place I came from. Have mercy upon a poor boy, sir!"

"My dear child," said the old gentleman, moved by the warmth of Oliver's sudden appeal; "you need not be afraid of my deserting you, unless you give me cause."

"I never, never will, sir," interposed Oliver.

"I hope not," rejoined the old gentleman. "I do not think you ever will. I have been deceived, before, in the objects whom I have endeavoured to benefit, but I feel strongly disposed to trust you, nevertheless; and I am more interested in your behalf than I can well account for, even to myself. The persons on whom I have bestowed my dearest love, lie deep in their graves; but, although the happiness and delight of my life lie buried there too, I have not made a coffin of my heart, and sealed it up, for ever, on my best affections. Deep affliction has but strengthened and refined them."

As the old gentleman said this in a low voice: more to himself than to his companion: and as he remained silent for a short time afterwards: Oliver sat quite still.

"Well, well!" said the old gentleman at length, in a more cheerful tone, "I only say this, because you have a young heart; and knowing that I have suffered great pain and sorrow, you will be more careful, perhaps, not to wound me again. You say you are an orphan, without a friend in the world; all the inquiries I have been able to make, confirm the statement. Let me hear your story; where you come from; who brought you up; and how you got into the company in which I found you. Speak the truth, and you shall not be friendless while I live."

Oliver's sobs checked his utterance for some minutes; when he was on the point of beginning to relate how he had been brought up at the farm, and carried to the workhouse by Mr Bumble, a peculiarly impatient little double-knock was heard at the street-door: and the servant, running up stairs, announced Mr Grimwig.

"Is he coming up?" inquired Mr Brownlow.

"Yes, sir," replied the servant. "He asked if there were any muffins in the house; and, when I told him yes, he said he had come to tea."

Mr Brownlow smiled; and, turning to Oliver, said that Mr Grimwig was an old friend of his, and he must not mind his being a little rough in his manners; for he was a worthy creature at bottom, as he had reason to know.

"Shall I go down stairs, sir?" inquired Oliver.

"No," replied Mr Brownlow, "I would rather you remained here."

At this moment, there walked into the room: supporting himself by a thick stick: a stout old gentleman, rather lame in one leg, who was dressed in a blue coat, striped waistcoat, nankeen breeches and gaiters, and a broad-brimmed white hat, with the sides turned up with green. A very small-plaited shirt frill stuck out from his waistcoat; and a very long steel watch-chain, with nothing but a key at the end, dangled loosely below it. The ends of his white neckerchief were twisted into a ball about the size of an orange; the variety of shapes into which his countenance was twisted, defy description. He had a manner of screwing his head on one side when he spoke; and of looking out of the corners of his eyes at the same time: which irresistibly reminded the beholder of a parrot. In this attitude, he fixed himself, the moment he made his appearance; and, holding out a small piece of orange-peel at arm's length, exclaimed, in a growling, discontented voice.

"Look here! do you see this! Isn't it a most wonderful and extraordinary thing that I can't call at a man's house but I find a piece of this poor surgeon's-friend on the staircase? I've been lamed with orange-peel once, and I know orange-peel will be my death at last. It will, sir: orange-peel will be my death, or I'll be content to eat my own head, sir!"

This was the handsome offer with which Mr Grimwig backed and confirmed nearly every assertion he made; and it was the more singular in his case, because, even admitting for the sake of argument, the possibility of scientific improvements being ever brought to that pass which will enable a gentleman to eat his own head in the event of his being so disposed, Mr Grimwig's head was such a particularly large one, that the most sanguine man alive could hardly entertain a hope of being able to get through it at a sitting – to put entirely out of the question, a very thick coating of powder.

"I'll eat my head, sir," repeated Mr Grimwig, striking his stick upon the ground. "Hallo! what's that!" looking at Oliver, and retreating a pace or two.

"This is young Oliver Twist, whom we were speaking about," said Mr Brownlow.

Oliver bowed.

"You don't mean to say that's the boy who had the fever, I hope?" said Mr Grimwig, recoiling a little more. "Wait, a minute! Don't speak! Stop –" continued Mr Grimwig, abruptly, losing all dread of the fever in his triumph at the discovery; "that's the boy who had the orange! If that's not the boy, sir, who had the orange, and threw this bit of peel upon the staircase, I'll eat my head, and his too."

"No, no, he has not had one," said Mr Brownlow, laughing. "Come! Put down your hat; and speak to my young friend."

"I feel strongly on this subject, sir," said the irritable old gentleman, drawing off his gloves. "There's always more or less orange-peel on the pavement in our street; and I *know* it's put there by the surgeon's boy at the corner. A young woman stumbled over a bit last night, and fell against my garden-railings; directly she got up I saw her look towards his infernal red lamp with the pantomime-light. "Don't go to him," I called out of the window, "he's an assassin! A man-trap!" So he is. If he is not –" Here the irascible old gentleman gave a great knock on the ground with his stick; which was always understood, by his friends, to imply the customary offer, whenever it was not expressed in words. Then, still keeping his stick in his hand, he sat down; and, opening a double eye-glass, which he wore attached to a broad black riband, took a view of Oliver: who, seeing that he was the object of inspection, coloured, and bowed again.

"That's the boy, is it?" said Mr Grimwig, at length.

"That is the boy," replied Mr Brownlow.

"How are you, boy?" said Mr Grimwig.

"A great deal better, thank you, sir," replied Oliver.

Mr Brownlow, seeming to apprehend that his singular friend was about to say something disagreeable, asked Oliver to step down stairs and tell Mrs Bedwin they were ready for tea; which, as he did not half like the visitor's manner, he was very happy to do.

"He is a nice-looking boy, is he not?" inquired Mr Brownlow.

"I don't know," replied Mr Grimwig, pettishly.

"Don't know?"

"No. I don't know. I never see any difference in boys. I only know two sorts of boys. Mealy boys, and beef-faced boys."

"And which is Oliver?"

"Mealy. I know a friend who has a beef-faced boy; a fine boy, they call him; with a round head, and red cheeks, and glaring eyes; a horrid boy; with a body and limbs that appear to be swelling out of the seams of his blue clothes; with the voice of a pilot, and the appetite of a wolf. I know him! The wretch!"

"Come," said Mr Brownlow, "these are not the characteristics of young Oliver Twist; so he needn't excite your wrath."

"They are not," replied Mr Grimwig. "He may have worse."

Here, Mr Brownlow coughed impatiently; which appeared to afford Mr Grimwig the most exquisite delight.

"He may have worse, I say," repeated Mr Grimwig. "Where does he come from? Who is he? What is he? He has had a fever. What of that? Fevers are not peculiar to good people; are they? Bad people have fevers sometimes; haven't they, eh? I knew a man who was hung in Jamaica for murdering his master. He had had a fever six times; he wasn't recommended to mercy on that account. Pooh! nonsense!"

Now, the fact was, that in the inmost recesses of his own heart, Mr Grimwig was strongly disposed to admit that Oliver's appearance and manner were unusually prepossessing; but he had a strong appetite for contradiction, sharpened on this occasion by the finding of the orange-peel; and, inwardly determining that no man should dictate to him whether a boy was well-looking or not, he had resolved, from the first, to oppose his friend. When Mr Brownlow admitted that on no one point of inquiry could he yet return a satisfactory answer; and that he had postponed any investigation into Oliver's previous history until he thought the boy was strong enough to bear it; Mr Grimwig chuckled maliciously. And he demanded, with a sneer, whether the housekeeper was in the habit of counting the plate at night; because, if she didn't find a table-spoon or two missing some sunshiny morning, why, he would be content to – and so forth.

All this, Mr Brownlow, although himself somewhat of an impetuous gentleman: knowing his friend's peculiarities, bore with great good humour; as Mr Grimwig, at tea, was graciously pleased to express his entire approval of the muffins, matters went on very smoothly; and Oliver, who made one of the party, began to feel more at his ease than he had yet done in the fierce old gentleman's presence.

"And when are you going to hear a full, true, and particular account of the life and adventures of Oliver Twist?" asked Grimwig of Mr Brownlow, at the conclusion of the meal: looking sideways at Oliver, as he resumed the subject.

"To-morrow morning," replied Mr Brownlow. "I would rather he was alone with me at the time. Come up to me to-morrow morning at ten o'clock, my dear."

"Yes, sir," replied Oliver. He answered with some hesitation, because he was confused by Mr Grimwig's looking so hard at him.

"I'll tell you what," whispered that gentleman to Mr Brownlow; "he won't come up to you to-morrow morning. I saw him hesitate. He is deceiving you, my good friend."

"I'll swear he is not," replied Mr Brownlow, warmly.

"If he is not," said Mr Grimwig, "I'll –" and down went the stick.

"I'll answer for that boy's truth with my life!" said Mr Brownlow, knocking the table.

"And I for his falsehood with my head!" rejoined Mr Grimwig, knocking the table also.

"We shall see," said Mr Brownlow, checking his rising anger.

"We will," replied Mr Grimwig, with a provoking smile; "we will."

As fate would have it, Mrs Bedwin chanced to bring in, at this moment, a small parcel of books, which Mr Brownlow had that morning purchased of the identical bookstall-keeper, who has already figured in this history; having laid them on the table, she prepared to leave the room.

"Stop the boy, Mrs Bedwin!" said Mr Brownlow; "there is something to go back."

"He has gone, sir," replied Mrs Bedwin.

"Call after him," said Mr Brownlow; "it's particular. He is a poor man, and they are not paid for. There are some books to be taken back, too."

The street door was opened. Oliver ran one way; and the girl ran another; and Mrs Bedwin stood on the step and screamed for the boy; but there was no boy in sight. Oliver and the girl returned, in a breathless state, to report that there were no tidings of him.

"Dear me, I am very sorry for that," exclaimed Mr Brownlow; "I particularly wished those books to be returned tonight."

"Send Oliver with them," said Mr Grimwig, with an ironical smile; "he will be sure to deliver them safely, you know."

"Yes; do let me take them, if you please, sir," said Oliver. "I'll run all the way, sir."

The old gentleman was just going to say that Oliver should not go out on any account; when a most malicious cough from Mr Grimwig determined him that he should; and that, by his prompt discharge of the commission, he should prove to him the injustice of his suspicions: on this head at least: at once.

"You *shall* go, my dear," said the old gentleman. "The books are on a chair by my table. Fetch them down."

Oliver, delighted to be of use, brought down the books under his arm in a great bustle; and waited, cap in hand, to hear what message he was to take.

"You are to say," said Mr Brownlow, glancing steadily at Grimwig; "you are to say that you have brought those books back; and that you have come to pay the four pound ten I owe him. This is a five-pound note, so you will have to bring me back, ten shillings change."

"I won't be ten minutes, sir," replied Oliver, eagerly. Having buttoned up the bank-note in his jacket pocket, and placed the books carefully under his arm, he made a respectful bow, and left the room. Mrs Bedwin followed him to the street-door, giving him many directions about the nearest way, and the name of the bookseller, and the name of the street: all of which Oliver said he clearly understood. Having superadded many injunctions to be sure and not take cold, the old lady at length permitted him to depart.

"Bless his sweet face!" said the old lady, looking after him. "I can't bear, somehow, to let him go out of my sight."

At this moment, Oliver looked gaily round, and nodded before he turned the corner. The old lady smilingly returned his salution, and, closing the door, went back, to her own room.

"Let me see; he'll be back in twenty minutes, at the longest," said Mr Brownlow, pulling out his watch, and placing it on the table. "It will be dark by that time."

"Oh! you really expect him to come back, do you?" inquired Mr Grimwig.

"Don't you?" asked Mr Brownlow, smiling.

The spirit of contradiction was strong in Mr Grimwig's breast, at the moment; and it was rendered stronger by his friend's confident smile.

"No," he said, smiting the table with his fist, "I do not. The boy has a new suit of clothes on his back, a set of valuable books under his arm, and a five-pound note in his pocket. He'll join his old friends the thieves, and laugh at you. If ever that boy returns to this house, sir, I'll eat my head."

With these words he drew his chair closer to the table; and there the two friends sat, in silent expectation, with the watch between them.

It is worthy of remark, as illustrating the importance we attach to our own judgments, and the pride with which we put forth our most rash and hasty conclusions, that, although Mr Grimwig was not by any means a bad-hearted man, and though he would have been unfeignedly sorry to see his respected friend duped and deceived, he really did most earnestly and strongly hope at that moment, that Oliver Twist might not come back.

It grew so dark, that the figures on the dial-plate were scarcely discernible; but there the two old gentlemen continued to sit, in silence, with the watch between them.

Chapter XV

Showing how very fond of Oliver Twist, the merry old Jew and Miss Nancy were

In the obscure parlour of a low public-house, in the filthiest part of Little Saffron Hill; a dark and gloomy den, where a flaring gas-light burnt all day in the winter-time; and where no ray of sun ever shone in the summer: there sat, brooding over a little pewter measure and a small glass, strongly impregnated with the smell of liquor, a man in a velveteen coat, drab shorts, half boots and stockings, whom even by that dim light no experienced agent of police would have hesitated to recognise as Mr William Sikes. At his feet, sat a white-coated, red-eyed dog; who occupied himself, alternately, in winking at his master with both eyes at the same time; and in licking a large, fresh cut on one side of his mouth, which appeared to be the result of some recent conflict.

"Keep quiet, you warmint! Keep quiet!" said Mr Sikes, suddenly breaking silence. Whether his meditations were so intense as to be disturbed by the dog's winking, or whether his feelings were so wrought upon by his reflections that they required all the relief derivable from kicking an unoffending animal to allay them, is matter for argument and consideration. Whatever was the cause, the effect was a kick and a curse, bestowed upon the dog simultaneously.

Dogs are not generally apt to revenge injuries inflicted upon them by their masters; but Mr Sikes's dog, having faults of temper in common with his owner, and labouring, perhaps, at this moment, under a powerful sense of injury, made no more ado but at once fixed his teeth in one of the half-boots. Having given it a hearty shake, he retired, growling, under a form; just escaping the pewter measure which Mr Sikes levelled at his head.

"You would, would you?" said Sikes, seizing the poker in one hand, and deliberately opening with the other a large clasp knife, which he drew from his pocket. "Come here, you born devil! Come here! D'ye hear?"

The dog no doubt heard; because Mr Sikes spoke in the very harshest key of a very harsh voice; but, appearing to entertain some unaccountable objection to having his throat cut, he remained where he was, and growled more fiercely than before: at the same time grasping the end of the poker between his teeth, and biting at it like a wild beast.

This resistance only infuriated Mr Sikes the more; who, dropping on his knees, began to assail the animal most furiously. The dog jumped from right to left, and from left to right: snapping, growling, and barking; the man thrust and swore, and struck and blasphemed; and the struggle was reaching a most critical point for one or other; when, the door suddenly opening, the dog darted out: leaving Bill Sikes with the poker and the clasp-knife in his hands.

There must always be two parties to a quarrel, says the old adage. Mr Sikes, being disappointed of the dog's participation, at once transferred his share in the quarrel to the new-comer.

"What the devil do you come in between me and my dog for?" said Sikes, with a fierce gesture.

"I didn't know, my dear, I didn't know," replied Fagin, humbly; for the Jew was the new-comer.

"Didn't know, you white-livered thief!" growled Sikes. "Couldn't you hear the noise?"

"Not a sound of it, as I'm a living man, Bill," replied the Jew.

"Oh no! You hear nothing, you don't," retorted Sikes with a fierce sneer. "Sneaking in and out, so as nobody hears how you come or go! I wish you had been the dog, Fagin, half a minute ago."

"Why?" inquired the Jew with a forced smile.

"'Cause the government, as cares for the lives of such men as you, as haven't half the pluck of curs, lets a man kill a dog how he likes," replied Sikes, shutting up the knife with a very expressive look; "that's why."

The Jew rubbed his hands; and, sitting down at the table, affected to laugh at the pleasantry of his friend. He was obviously very ill at ease, however.

"Grin away," said Sikes, replacing the poker, and surveying him with savage contempt; "grin away. You'll never have the laugh at me, though, unless it's behind a night-cap. I've got the upper hand over you, Fagin; and, d—me, I'll keep it. There! If I go, you go; so take care of me."

"Well, well, my dear," said the Jew, "I know all that; we – we – have a mutual interest, Bill, – a mutual interest."

"Humph," said Sikes, as if he thought the interest lay rather more on the Jew's side than on his. "Well, what have you got to say to me?"

"It's all passed safe through the melting-pot," replied Fagin, "and this is your share. It's rather more than it ought to be, my dear; but as I know you'll do me a good turn another time, and –"

"Stow that gammon," interposed the robber, impatiently. "Where is it? Hand over!"

"Yes, yes, Bill; give me time, give me time," replied the Jew, soothingly. "Here it is! All safe!" As he spoke, he drew forth an old cotton handkerchief from his breast and untying a large knot in one corner, produced a small brown-paper packet. Sikes, snatching it from him, hastily opened it; and proceeded to count the sovereigns it contained.

"This is all, is it?" inquired Sikes.

"All," replied the Jew.

"You haven't opened the parcel and swallowed one or two as you come along, have you?" inquired Sikes, suspiciously. "Don't put on an injured look at the question; you've done it many a time. Jerk the tinkler."

These words, in plain English, conveyed an injunction to ring the bell. It was answered by another Jew: younger than Fagin, but nearly as vile and repulsive in appearance.

Bill Sikes merely pointed to the empty measure. The Jew, perfectly understanding the hint, retired to fill it: previously exchanging a remarkable look with Fagin, who raised his eyes for an instant, as if in expectation of it, and shook his head in reply; so slightly that the action would have been almost imperceptible to an observant third person. It was lost upon Sikes, who was stooping at the moment to tie the boot-lace which the dog had torn. Possibly, if he had observed the brief interchange of signals, he might have thought that it boded no good to him.

"Is anybody here, Barney?" inquired Fagin; speaking, now that Sikes was looking on, without raising his eyes from the ground.

"Dot a shoul," replied Barney; whose words: whether they came from the heart or not: made their way through the nose.

"Nobody?" inquired Fagin, in a tone of surprise: which perhaps might mean that Barney was at liberty to tell the truth.

"Dobody but Biss Dadsy," replied Barney.

"Nancy!" exclaimed Sikes. "Where? Strike me blind, if I don't honour that 'ere girl, for her native talents."

"She's bid havid a plate of boiled beef id the bar," replied Barney.

"Send her here," said Sikes, pouring out a glass of liquor. "Send her here."

Barney looked timidly at Fagin, as if for permission; the Jew remaining silent, and not lifting his eyes from the ground, he retired; and presently returned, ushering in Nancy; who was decorated with the bonnet, apron, basket, and street-door key, complete.

"You are on the scent, are you, Nancy?" inquired Sikes, proffering the glass.

"Yes, I am, Bill," replied the young lady, disposing of its contents; "and tired enough of it I am, too. The young brat's been ill and confined to the crib; and –"

"Ah, Nancy, dear!" said Fagin, looking up.

Now, whether a peculiar contraction of the Jew's red eyebrows, and a half-closing of his deeply-set eyes, warned Miss Nancy that she was disposed to be too communicative, is not a matter of much importance. The fact is all we need care for here; and the fact is, that she suddenly checked herself, and with several gracious smiles upon Mr Sikes, turned the conversation to other matters. In about ten minutes" time, Mr Fagin was seized with a fit of coughing; upon which Nancy pulled her shawl over her shoulders, and declared it was time to go. Mr Sikes, finding that he was walking a short part of her way himself, expressed his intention of accompanying her; they went away together, followed, at a little distance, by the dog, who slunk out of a back-yard as soon as his master was out of sight.

The Jew thrust his head out of the room door when Sikes had left it; looked after him as he walked up the dark passage; shook his clenched fist; muttered a deep curse; and then, with a horrible grin, re-seated himself at the table; where he was soon deeply absorbed in the interesting pages of the Hue-and-Cry.

Meanwhile, Oliver Twist, little dreaming that he was within so very short a distance of the merry old gentleman, was on his way to the book-stall. When he got into Clerkenwell, he accidentally turned down a bye-street which was not exactly in his way; but not discovering his mistake until he had got half-way down it, and knowing it must lead in the right direction, he did not think it worth while to turn back; and so marched on, as quickly as he could, with the books under his arm.

He was walking along, thinking how happy and contented he ought to feel; and how much he would give for only one look at poor little Dick, who, starved and beaten, might be weeping bitterly at that very moment; when he was startled by a young woman screaming out very loud, "Oh, my dear brother!" And he had hardly looked up, to see what the matter was, when he was stopped by having a pair of arms thrown tight round his neck.

"Don't," cried Oliver, struggling. "Let go of me. Who is it? What are you stopping me for?"

The only reply to this, was a great number of loud lamentations from the young woman who had embraced him; and who had a little basket and a street-door key in her hand.

"Oh my gracious!" said the young woman, "I've found him! Oh! Oliver! Oliver! Oh you naughty boy, to make me suffer sich distress on your account! Come home, dear, come. Oh, I've found him. Thank gracious goodness heavins, I've found him!" With these incoherent exclamations, the young woman burst into another fit of crying, and got so dreadfully hysterical, that a couple of women who came up at the moment asked a butcher's boy with a shiny head of hair anointed with suet, who was also looking on, whether he didn't think he had better run for the doctor. To which, the butcher's boy: who appeared of a lounging, not to say indolent disposition: replied, that he thought not.

"Oh, no, no, never mind," said the young woman, grasping Oliver's hand; "I'm better now. Come home directly, you cruel boy! Come!"

"What's the matter, ma"am?" inquired one of the women.

"Oh, ma"am," replied the young woman, "he ran away, near a month ago, from his parents, who are hard-working and respectable people; and went and joined a set of thieves and bad characters; and almost broke his mother's heart."

"Young wretch!" said one woman.

"Go home, do, you little brute," said the other.

"I am not," replied Oliver, greatly alarmed. "I don't know her. I haven't any sister, or father and mother either. I'm an orphan; I live at Pentonville."

"Only hear him, how he braves it out!" cried the young woman.

"Why, it's Nancy!" exclaimed Oliver; who now saw her face for the first time; and started back, in irrepressible astonishment.

"You see he knows me!" cried Nancy, appealing to the bystanders. "He can't help himself. Make him come home, there's good people, or he'll kill his dear mother and father, and break my heart!"

"What the devil's this?" said a man, bursting out of a beer-shop, with a white dog at his heels; "young Oliver! Come home to your poor mother, you young dog! Come home directly."

"I don't belong to them. I don't know them. Help! help!" cried Oliver, struggling in the man's powerful grasp.

"Help!" repeated the man. "Yes; I'll help you, you young rascal! What books are these? You've been a stealing 'em, have you? Give 'em here." With these words, the man tore the volumes from his grasp, and struck him on the head.

"That's right!" cried a looker-on, from a garret-window. "That's the only way of bringing him to his senses!"

"To be sure!" cried a sleepy-faced carpenter, casting an approving look at the garret-window.

"It'll do him good!" said the two women.

"And he shall have it, too!" rejoined the man, administering another blow, and seizing Oliver by the collar. "Come on, you young villain! Here, Bull's-eye, mind him, boy! Mind him!"

Weak with recent illness; stupefied by the blows and the suddenness of the attack; terrified by the fierce growling of the dog, and the brutality of the man; overpowered by the conviction of the bystanders that he really was the hardened little wretch he was described to be; what could one poor child do! Darkness had set in; it was a low neighbourhood; no help was near; resistance was useless. In another moment, he was dragged into a labyrinth of dark narrow courts, and was forced along them at a pace which rendered the few cries he dared to give utterance to, unintelligible. It was of little moment, indeed, whether they were intelligible or no; for there was nobody to care for them, had they been ever so plain.

* * *

The gas-lamps were lighted; Mrs Bedwin was waiting anxiously at the open door; the servant had run up the street twenty times to see if there were any traces of Oliver; and still the two old gentlemen sat, perseveringly, in the dark parlour, with the watch between them.

Chapter XVI

Relates what became of Oliver Twist, after he had been claimed by Nancy

THE narrow streets and courts, at length, terminated in a large open space; scattered about which, were pens for beasts, and other indications of a cattle-market. Sikes slackened his pace when they reached this spot: the girl being quite unable to support any longer, the rapid rate at which they had hitherto walked. Turning to Oliver, he roughly commanded him to take hold of Nancy's hand.

"Do you hear?" growled Sikes, as Oliver hesitated, and looked round.

They were in a dark corner, quite out of the track of passengers. Oliver saw, but too plainly, that resistance would be of no avail. He held out his hand, which Nancy clasped tight in hers.

"Give me the other," said Sikes, seizing Oliver's unoccupied hand. "Here, Bull's-eye!"

The dog looked up, and growled.

"See here, boy!" said Sikes, putting his other hand to Oliver's throat; "if he speaks ever so soft a word, hold him! D'ye mind!"

The dog growled again; and licking his lips, eyed Oliver as if he were anxious to attach himself to his windpipe without delay.

"He's as willing as a Christian, strike me blind if he isn't!" said Sikes, regarding the animal with a kind of grim and ferocious approval. "Now, you know what you've got to expect, master, so call as quick as you like; the dog will soon stop that game. Get on, young 'un!"

Bull's-eye wagged his tail in acknowledgement of this unusually endearing form of speech; and, giving vent to another admonitory growl for the benefit of Oliver, led the way onward.

It was Smithfield that they were crossing, although it might have been Grosvenor Square, for anything Oliver knew to the contrary. The night was dark and foggy. The lights in the shops could scarcely struggle through the heavy mist, which thickened every moment and shrouded the streets and houses in gloom; rendering the strange place still stranger in Oliver's eyes; and making his uncertainty the more dismal and depressing.

They had hurried on a few paces, when a deep church-bell struck the hour. With its first stroke, his two conductors stopped, and turned their heads in the direction whence the sound proceeded.

"Eight o'clock, Bill," said Nancy, when the bell ceased.

"What's the good of telling me that; I can hear it, can't I!" replied Sikes.

"I wonder whether *they* can hear it," said Nancy.

"Of course they can," replied Sikes. "It was Bartlemy time when I was shopped; and there warn't a penny trumpet in the fair, as I couldn't hear the squeaking on. Arter I was locked up for the night, the row and din outside made the thundering old jail so silent, that I could almost have beat my brains out against the iron plates of the door."

"Poor fellows!" said Nancy, who still had her face turned towards the quarter in which the bell had sounded. "Oh, Bill, such fine young chaps as them!"

"Yes; that's all you women think of," answered Sikes. "Fine young chaps! Well, they're as good as dead, so it don't much matter."

With this consolation, Mr Sikes appeared to repress a rising tendency to jealousy, and, clasping Oliver's wrist more firmly, told him to step out again.

"Wait a minute!" said the girl: "I wouldn't hurry by, if it was you that was coming out to be hung, the next time eight o'clock struck, Bill. I'd walk round and round the place till I dropped, if the snow was on the ground, and I hadn't a shawl to cover me."

"And what good would that do?" inquired the unsentimental Mr Sikes. "Unless you could pitch over a file and twenty yards of good stout rope, you might as well be walking fifty mile off, or not walking at all, for all the good it would do me. Come on, and don't stand preaching there."

The girl burst into a laugh; drew her shawl more closely round her; and they walked away. But Oliver felt her hand tremble, and, looking up in her face as they passed a gas-lamp, saw that it had turned a deadly white.

They walked on, by little-frequented and dirty ways, for a full half-hour: meeting very few people, and those appearing from their looks to hold much the same position in society as Mr Sikes himself. At length they turned into a very filthy narrow street, nearly full of old-clothes shops; the dog running forward, as if conscious that there was no further occasion for his keeping on guard, stopped before the door of a shop that was closed and apparently untenanted; the house was in a ruinous condition, and on the door was nailed a board, intimating that it was to let: which looked as if it had hung there for many years.

"All right," cried Sikes, glancing cautiously about.

Nancy stooped below the shutters, and Oliver heard the sound of a bell. They crossed to the opposite side of the street, and stood for a few moments under a lamp. A noise, as if a sash window were gently raised, was heard; and soon afterwards the door softly opened. Mr Sikes then seized the terrified boy by the collar with very little ceremony; and all three were quickly inside the house.

The passage was perfectly dark. They waited, while the person who had let them in, chained and barred the door.

"Anybody here?" inquired Sikes.

"No," replied a voice, which Oliver thought he had heard before.

"Is the old "un here?" asked the robber.

"Yes," replied the voice; "and precious down in the mouth he has been. Won't he be glad to see you? Oh, no!"

The style of this reply, as well as the voice which delivered it, seemed familiar to Oliver's ears: but it was impossible to distinguish even the form of the speaker in the darkness.

"Let's have a glim," said Sikes, "or we shall go breaking our necks, or treading on the dog. Look after your legs if you do!"

"Stand still a moment, and I'll get you one," replied the voice. The receding footsteps of the speaker were heard; and, in another minute, the form of Mr John Dawkins, otherwise the artful Dodger, appeared. He bore in his right hand a tallow candle stuck in the end of a cleft stick.

The young gentleman did not stop to bestow any other mark of recognition upon Oliver than a humorous grin; but turning away, beckoned the visitors to follow him down a flight of stairs. They crossed an empty kitchen; and, opening the door of a low earthy-smelling room, which seemed to have been built in a small back-yard, were received with a shout of laughter.

"Oh, my wig, my wig!" cried Master Charles Bates, from whose lungs the laughter had proceeded; "here he is! oh, cry, here he is! Oh, Fagin, look at him! Fagin, do look at him! I can't bear it; it is such a jolly game, I can't bear it. Hold me, somebody, while I laugh it out."

With this irrepressible ebullition of mirth, Master Bates laid himself flat on the floor: and kicked convulsively for five minutes, in an ecstasy of facetious joy. Then jumping to his feet, he snatched the cleft stick from the Dodger; and, advancing to Oliver, viewed him round and round; while the Jew, taking off his nightcap, made a great number of low bows to the bewildered boy. The Artful, meantime, who was of a rather saturnine disposition, and seldom gave way to merriment when it interfered with business, rifled Oliver's pockets with steady assiduity.

"Look at his togs, Fagin!" said Charley, putting the light so close to his new jacket as nearly to set him on fire. "Look at his togs! Superfine cloth, and the heavy swell cut! Oh, my eye, what a game! And his books, too! Nothing but a gentleman, Fagin!"

"Delighted to see you looking so well, my dear," said the Jew, bowing with mock humility. "The Artful shall give you another suit, my dear, for fear you should spoil that Sunday one. Why didn't you write, my dear, and say you were coming? We'd have got something warm for supper."

At this, Master Bates roared again: so loud, that Fagin himself relaxed, and even the Dodger smiled; but as the Artful drew forth the five-pound note at that instant, it is doubtful whether the sally or the discovery awakened his merriment.

"Hallo! what's that?" inquired Sikes, stepping forward as the Jew seized the note. "That's mine, Fagin."

"No, no, my dear," said the Jew. "Mine, Bill, mine. You shall have the books."

"If that ain't mine!" said Bill Sikes, putting on his hat with a determined air; "mine and Nancy's, that is; I'll take the boy back again."

The Jew started. Oliver started too, though from a very different cause; for he hoped that the dispute might really end in his being taken back.

"Come! Hand over, will you?" said Sikes.

"This is hardly fair, Bill; hardly fair, is it, Nancy?" inquired the Jew.

"Fair, or not fair," retorted Sikes, "hand over, I tell you! Do you think Nancy and me has got nothing else to do with our precious time but to spend it in scouting arter and kidnapping, every young boy as gets grabbed through you? Give it here, you avaricious old skeleton, give it here!"

With this gentle remonstrance, Mr Sikes plucked the note from between the Jew's finger and thumb; and looking the old man coolly in the face, folded it up small, and tied it in his neckerchief.

"That's for our share of the trouble," said Sikes; "and not half enough, neither. You may keep the books, if you're fond of reading. If you a'n't, sell 'em."

"They're very pretty," said Charley Bates: who, with sundry grimaces, had been affecting to read one of the volumes in question: "beautiful writing, isn't it, Oliver?" At sight of the dismayed look with which Oliver regarded his tormentors, Master Bates, who was blessed with a lively sense of the ludicrous, fell into another ecstasy, more boisterous than the first.

"They belong to the old gentleman," said Oliver, wringing his hands; "to the good, kind, old gentleman who took me into his house, and had me nursed, when I was near dying of the fever. Oh, pray send them back; send him back the books and money. Keep me here all my life long; but pray, pray send them back. He'll think I stole them; the old lady: all of them who were so kind to me: will think I stole them. Oh, do have mercy upon me, and send them back!"

With those words, which were uttered with all the energy of passionate grief, Oliver fell upon his knees at the Jew's feet; and beat his hands together, in perfect desperation.

"The boy's right," remarked Fagin, looking covertly round, and knitting his shaggy eyebrows into a hard knot. "You're right, Oliver, you're right; they *will* think you have stolen 'em. Ha! ha!" chuckled the Jew, rubbing his hands; "it couldn't have happened better, if we had chosen our time!"

"Of course it couldn't," replied Sikes; "I know'd that, directly I see him coming through Clerkenwell, with the books under his arm. It's all right enough. They're soft-hearted psalm-singers, or they wouldn't have taken him in at all; and they'll ask no questions after him, fear they should be obliged to prosecute, and so get him lagged. He's safe enough."

Oliver had looked from one to the other, while these words were being spoken, as if he were bewildered, and could scarcely understand what passed; but when Bill Sikes concluded, he jumped suddenly to his feet, and tore wildly from the room: uttering shrieks for help, which made the bare old house echo to the roof.

"Keep back the dog, Bill!" cried Nancy, springing before the door, and closing it, as the Jew and his two pupils darted out in pursuit. "Keep back the dog; he'll tear the boy to pieces."

"Serve him right!" cried Sikes, struggling to disengage himself from the girl's grasp. "Stand off from me, or I'll split your head against the wall."

"I don't care for that, Bill, I don't care for that," screamed the girl, struggling violently with the man: "the child shan't be torn down by the dog, unless you kill me first."

"Shan't he!" said Sikes, setting his teeth. "I'll soon do that, if you don't keep off."

The housebreaker flung the girl from him to the further end of the room, just as the Jew and the two boys returned, dragging Oliver among them.

"What's the matter here!" said Fagin, looking round.

"The girl's gone mad, I think," replied Sikes, savagely.

"No, she hasn't," said Nancy, pale and breathless from the scuffle; "no, she hasn't, Fagin; don't think it."

"Then keep quiet, will you?" said the Jew, with a threatening look.

"No, I won't do that, neither," replied Nancy, speaking very loud. "Come! What do you think of that?"

Mr Fagin was sufficiently well acquainted with the manners and customs of that particular species of humanity to which Nancy belonged, to feel tolerably certain that it would be rather unsafe to prolong any conversation with her, at present. With the view of diverting the attention of the company, he turned to Oliver.

"So you wanted to get away, my dear, did you?" said the Jew, taking up a jagged and knotted club which lay in a corner of the fireplace; "eh?"

Oliver made no reply. But he watched the Jew's motions, and breathed quickly.

"Wanted to get assistance; called for the police; did you?" sneered the Jew, catching the boy by the arm. "We'll cure you of that, my young master."

The Jew inflicted a smart blow on Oliver's shoulders with the club; and was raising it for a second, when the girl, rushing forward, wrested it from his hand. She flung it into the fire, with a force that brought some of the glowing coals whirling out into the room.

"I won't stand by and see it done, Fagin," cried the girl. "You've got the boy, and what more would you have? – Let him be – let him be – or I shall put that mark on some of you, that will bring me to the gallows before my time."

The girl stamped her foot violently on the floor as she vented this threat; and with her lips compressed, and her hands clenched, looked alternately at the Jew and the other robber; her face quite colourless from the passion of rage into which she had gradually worked herself.

"Why, Nancy!" said the Jew, in a soothing tone, after a pause, during which he and Mr Sikes had stared at one another in a disconcerted manner; "you – you're more clever than ever to-night. Ha! ha! my dear, you are acting beautifully."

"Am I!" said the girl. "Take care I don't overdo it. You will be the worse for it, Fagin, if I do; and so I tell you in good time to keep clear of me."

There is something about a roused woman: especially if she add to all her other strong passions, the fierce impulses of recklessness and despair: which few men like to provoke. The Jew saw that it would be hopeless to affect any further mistake regarding the reality of Miss Nancy's rage; and, shrinking involuntarily back a few paces, cast a glance, half imploring and half cowardly at Sikes: as if to hint that he was the fittest person to pursue the dialogue.

Mr Sikes, thus mutely appealed to; and possibly feeling his personal pride and influence interested in the immediate reduction of Miss Nancy to reason; gave utterance to about a couple of score of curses and threats, the rapid production of which reflected great credit on the fertility of his invention. As they produced no visible effect on the object against whom they were discharged, however, he resorted to more tangible arguments.

"What do you mean by this?" said Sikes; backing the inquiry with a very common imprecation concerning the most beautiful of human features:

which, if it were heard above, only once out of every fifty thousand times that it is uttered below, would render blindness as common a disorder as measles: "what do you mean by it? Burn my body! Do you know who you are, and what you are?"

"Oh, yes, I know all about it," replied the girl, laughing hysterically; and shaking her head from side to side, with a poor assumption of indifference.

"Well, then, keep quiet," rejoined Sikes, with a growl like that he was accustomed to use when addressing his dog, "or I'll quiet you for a good long time to come."

The girl laughed again: even less composedly than before; and, darting a hasty look at Sikes, turned her face aside, and bit her lip till the blood came.

"You're a nice one," added Sikes, as he surveyed her with a contemptuous air, "to take up the humane and genteel side! A pretty subject for the child, as you call him, to make a friend of!"

"God Almighty help me, I am!" cried the girl passionately; "and I wish I had been struck dead in the street, or had changed places with them we passed so near to-night, before I had lent a hand in bringing him here. He's a thief, a liar, a devil, all that's bad, from this night forth. Isn't that enough for the old wretch, without blows?"

"Come, come, Sikes," said the Jew, appealing to him in a remonstratory tone, and motioning towards the boys, who were eagerly attentive to all that passed; "we must have civil words; civil words, Bill."

"Civil words!" cried the girl, whose passion was frightful to see. "Civil words, you villain! Yes, you deserve 'em from me. I thieved for you when I was a child not half as old as this!" pointing to Oliver. "I have been in the same trade, and in the same service, for twelve years since. Don't you know it? Speak out! Don't you know it?"

"Well, well," replied the Jew, with an attempt at pacification; "and, if you have, it's your living!"

"Aye, it is!" returned the girl; not speaking, but pouring out the words in one continuous and vehement scream. "It is my living; and the cold, wet, dirty streets are my home; and you're the wretch that drove me to them long ago, and that'll keep me there, day and night, till I die!"

"I shall do you a mischief!" interposed the Jew, goaded by these reproaches; "a mischief worse than that, if you say much more!"

The girl said nothing more; but, tearing her hair and dress in a transport of passion, made such a rush at the Jew as would probably have left signal marks of her revenge upon him, had not her wrists been seized by Sikes at the right moment; upon which, she made a few ineffectual struggles, and fainted.

"She's all right now," said Sikes, laying her down in a corner. "She's uncommon strong in the arms, when she's up in this way."

The Jew wiped his forehead: and smiled, as if it were a relief to have the disturbance over; but neither he, nor Sikes, nor the dog, nor the boys, seemed to consider it in any other light than a common occurrence incidental to business.

"It's the worst of having to do with women," said the Jew, replacing his club; "but they're clever, and we can't get on, in our line, without 'em. Charley, show Oliver to bed."

"I suppose he'd better not wear his best clothes to-morrow, Fagin, had he?" inquired Charley Bates.

"Certainly not," replied the Jew, reciprocating the grin with which Charley put the question.

Master Bates, apparently much delighted with his commission, took the cleft stick: and led Oliver into an adjacent kitchen, where there were two or three of the beds on which he had slept before; and here, with many uncontrollable bursts of laughter, he produced the identical old suit of clothes which Oliver had so much congratulated himself upon leaving off at Mr Brownlow's; and the accidental display of which, to Fagin, by the Jew who purchased them, had been the very first clue received, of his whereabout.

"Pull off the smart ones," said Charley, "and I'll give 'em to Fagin to take care of. What fun it is!"

Poor Oliver unwillingly complied. Master Bates rolling up the new clothes under his arm, departed from the room, leaving Oliver in the dark, and locking the door behind him.

The noise of Charley's laughter, and the voice of Miss Betsy, who opportunely arrived to throw water over her friend, and perform other feminine offices for the promotion of her recovery, might have kept many people awake under more happy circumstances than those in which Oliver was placed. But he was sick and weary; and he soon fell sound asleep.

Chapter XVII

Oliver's Destiny continuing unpropitious, brings a Great Man to London to injure his Reputation

It is the custom on the stage, in all good murderous melodramas, to present the tragic and the comic scenes, in as regular alternation, as the layers of red and white in a side of streaky bacon. The hero sinks upon his straw bed, weighed down by fetters and misfortunes; in the next scene, his faithful but unconscious squire regales the audience with a comic song. We behold, with throbbing bosoms, the heroine in the grasp of a proud and ruthless baron: her virtue and her life alike in danger, drawing forth her dagger to preserve the one at the cost of the other; and just as our expectations are wrought up to the highest pitch, a whistle is heard, and we are straightway transported to the great hall of the castle: where a grey-headed seneschal sings a funny chorus with a funnier body of vassals, who are free of all sorts of places, from church vaults to palaces, and roam about in company, carolling perpetually.

Such changes appear absurd; but they are not so unnatural as they would seem at first sight. The transitions in real life from well-spread boards to death-beds, and from mourning-weeds to holiday garments, are not a whit less startling; only, there, we are busy actors, instead of passive lookers-on, which makes a vast difference. The actors in the mimic life of the theatre, are blind to violent transitions and abrupt impulses of passion or feeling, which, presented before the eyes of mere spectators, are at once condemned as outrageous and preposterous.

As sudden shiftings of the scene, and rapid changes of time and place, are not only sanctioned in books by long usage, but are by many considered as the great art of authorship: an author's skill in his craft being, by such critics, chiefly estimated with relation to the dilemmas in which he leaves his characters at the end of every chapter: this brief introduction to the present one may perhaps be deemed unnecessary. If so, let it be considered a delicate intimation on the part of the historian that he is going back to the town in which Oliver Twist was born; the reader taking it for granted that there are good and substantial reasons for making the journey, or he would not be invited to proceed upon such an expedition.

Mr Bumble emerged at early morning from the workhouse-gate, and walked with portly carriage and commanding steps, up the High Street. He was in the full bloom and pride of beadlehood; his cocked hat and coat were dazzling in the morning sun; he clutched his cane with the vigorous tenacity of health and power. Mr Bumble always carried his head high; but this morning it was higher than usual. There was an abstraction in his eye, an elevation in his air, which might have warned an observant stranger that thoughts were passing in the beadle's mind, too great for utterance.

Mr Bumble stopped not to converse with the small shopkeepers and others who spoke to him, deferentially, as he passed along. He merely returned their salutations with a wave of his hand, and relaxed not in his dignified pace, until he reached the farm where Mrs Mann tended the infant paupers with parochial care.

"Drat that beadle!" said Mrs Mann, hearing the well-known shaking at the garden-gate. "If it isn't him at this time in the morning! Lauk, Mr Bumble, only think of its being you! Well, dear me, it *is* a pleasure, this is! Come into the parlour, sir, please."

The first sentence was addressed to Susan; and the exclamations of delight were uttered to Mr Bumble: as the good lady unlocked the garden-gate, and showed him, with great attention and respect, into the house.

"Mrs Mann," said Mr Bumble; not sitting upon, or dropping himself into a seat, as any common jackanapes would: but letting himself gradually and slowly down into a chair; "Mrs Mann, ma'am, good morning."

"Well, and good morning to *you*, sir," replied Mrs Mann, with many smiles; "and hoping you find yourself well, sir!"

"So-so, Mrs Mann," replied the beadle. "A porochial life is not a bed of roses, Mrs Mann."

"Ah, that it isn't indeed, Mr Bumble," rejoined the lady. And all the infant paupers might have chorused the rejoinder with great propriety, if they had heard it.

"A porochial life, ma'am," continued Mr Bumble, striking the table with his cane, "is a life of worrit, and vexation, and hardihood; but all public characters, as I may say, must suffer prosecution."

Mrs Mann, not very well knowing what the beadle meant, raised her hands with a look of sympathy, and sighed.

"Ah! You may well sigh, Mrs Mann!" said the beadle.

Finding she had done right, Mrs Mann sighed again: evidently to the satisfaction of the public character: who, repressing a complacent smile by looking sternly at his cocked hat, said,

"Mrs Mann, I am a going to London."

"Lauk, Mr Bumble!" cried Mrs Mann, starting back.

"To London, ma'am," resumed the inflexible beadle, "by coach. I and two paupers, Mrs Mann! A legal action is a coming on, about a settlement; and the board has appointed me – me, Mrs Mann – to depose to the matter before the quarter-sessions at Clerkinwell. And I very much question," added Mr Bumble, drawing himself up, "whether the Clerkinwell Sessions will not find themselves in the wrong box before they have done with me."

"Oh! you mustn't be too hard upon them, sir," said Mrs Mann, coaxingly.

"The Clerkinwell Sessions have brought it upon themselves ma'am," replied Mr Bumble; "and if the Clerkinwell Sessions find that they come off rather worse than they expected, the Clerkinwell Sessions have only themselves to thank."

There was so much determination and depth of purpose about the menacing manner in which Mr Bumble delivered himself of these words, that Mrs Mann appeared quite awed by them. At length she said,

"You're going by coach, sir? I thought it was always usual to send them paupers in carts."

"That's when they're ill, Mrs Mann," said the beadle. "We put the sick paupers into open carts in the rainy weather, to prevent their taking cold."

"Oh!" said Mrs Mann.

"The opposition coach contracts for these two; and takes them cheap," said Mr Bumble. "They are both in a very low state, and we find it would come two pound cheaper to move 'em than to bury 'em – that is, if we can throw 'em upon another parish, which I think we shall be able to do, if they don't die upon the road to spite us. Ha! ha! ha!"

When Mr Bumble had laughed a little while, his eyes again encountered the cocked hat; and he became grave.

"We are forgetting business, ma'am," said the beadle; "here is your porochial stipend for the month."

Mr Bumble produced some silver money rolled up in paper, from his pocket-book; and requested a receipt: which Mrs Mann wrote.

"It's very much blotted, sir," said the farmer of infants; "but it's formal enough, I dare say. Thank you, Mr Bumble, sir, I am very much obliged to you, I'm sure."

Mr Bumble nodded, blandly, in acknowledgment of Mrs Mann's curtsey; and inquired how the children were.

"Bless their dear little hearts!" said Mrs Mann with emotion, "they're as well as can be, the dears! Of course, except the two that died last week. And little Dick."

"Isn't that boy no better?" inquired Mr Bumble.

Mrs Mann shook her head.

"He's a ill-conditioned, wicious, bad-disposed porochial child that," said Mr Bumble angrily. "Where is he?"

"I'll bring him to you in one minute, sir," replied Mrs Mann. "Here, you Dick!"

After some calling, Dick was discovered. Having had his face put under the pump, and dried upon Mrs Mann's gown, he was led into the awful presence of Mr Bumble, the beadle.

The child was pale and thin; his cheeks were sunken; and his eyes large and bright. The scanty parish dress, the livery of his misery, hung loosely on his feeble body; and his young limbs had wasted away, like those of an old man.

Such was the little being who stood trembling beneath Mr Bumble's glance; not daring to lift his eyes from the floor; and dreading even to hear the beadle's voice.

"Can't you look at the gentleman, you obstinate boy?" said Mrs Mann.

The child meekly raised his eyes, and encountered those of Mr Bumble.

"What's the matter with you, porochial Dick?" inquired Mr Bumble, with well-timed jocularity.

"Nothing, sir," replied the child faintly.

"I should think not," said Mrs Mann, who had of course laughed very much at Mr Bumble's humour. "You want for nothing, I'm sure."

"I should like –" faltered the child.

"Heyday!" interposed Mrs Mann, "I suppose you're going to say that you *do* want for something, now? Why, you little wretch –"

"Stop, Mrs Mann, stop!" said the beadle, raising his hand with a show of authority. "Like what, sir, eh?"

"I should like," faltered the child, "if somebody that can write, would put a few words down for me on a piece of paper, and fold it up and seal it, and keep it for me, after I am laid in the ground."

"Why, what does the boy mean?" exclaimed Mr Bumble, on whom the earnest manner and wan aspect of the child had made some impression: accustomed as he was to such things. "What do you mean, sir?"

"I should like," said the child, "to leave my dear love to poor Oliver Twist; and to let him know how often I have sat by myself and cried to think of his wandering about in the dark nights with nobody to help him. And I should like to tell him," said the child, pressing his small hands together, and speaking with great fervour, "that I was glad to die when I was very young; for, perhaps, if I had lived to be a man, and had grown old, my little sister who is in Heaven, might forget me, or be unlike me; and it would be so much happier if we were both children there together."

Mr Bumble surveyed the little speaker, from head to foot, with indescribable astonishment; and, turning to his companion said, "They're all in one story, Mrs Mann. That out-dacious Oliver has demogalized them all!"

"I couldn't have believed it, sir!" said Mrs Mann, holding up her hands, and looking malignantly at Dick. "I never see such a hardened little wretch!"

"Take him away, ma'am!" said Mr Bumble imperiously. "This must be stated to the board, Mrs Mann."

"I hope the gentlemen will understand that it isn't my fault, sir?" said Mrs Mann, whimpering pathetically.

"They shall understand that, ma'am; they shall be acquainted with the true state of the case," said Mr Bumble. "There; take him away, I can't bear the sight on him."

Dick was immediately taken away, and locked up in the coal-cellar. Mr Bumble shortly afterwards took himself off, to prepare for his journey.

At six o'clock next morning, Mr Bumble: having exchanged his cocked hat for a round one, and encased his person in a blue great-coat with a cape to it: took his place on the outside of the coach, accompanied by the criminals whose settlement was disputed; with whom, in due course of time, he arrived in London. He experienced no other crosses on the way, than those which originated in the perverse behaviour of the two paupers, who persisted in shivering, and complaining of the cold, in a manner which, Mr Bumble declared, caused his teeth to chatter in his head, and made him feel quite uncomfortable; although he had a great-coat on.

Having disposed of these evil-minded persons for the night, Mr Bumble sat himself down in the house at which the coach stopped; and took a temperate dinner of steaks, oyster sauce, and porter. Putting a glass of hot gin-and-water on the chimney-piece, he drew his chair to the fire; and, with sundry moral reflections on the too-prevalent sin of discontent and complaining, composed himself to read the paper.

The very first paragraph upon which Mr Bumble's eye rested, was the following advertisement.

"FIVE GUINEAS REWARD.

"Whereas a young boy, named Oliver Twist, absconded, or was enticed, on Thursday evening last, from his home, at Pentonville; and has not since been heard of. The above reward will be paid to any person who will give such information as will lead to the discovery of the said Oliver Twist, or tend to throw any light upon his previous history, in which the advertiser is, for many reasons, warmly interested."

And then followed a full description of Oliver's dress, person, appearance, and disappearance: with the name and address of Mr Brownlow at full length.

Mr Bumble opened his eyes; read the advertisement, slowly and carefully, three several times; and in something more than five minutes was on his way to Pentonville: having actually, in his excitement, left the glass of hot gin-and-water, untasted.

"Is Mr Brownlow at home?" inquired Mr Bumble of the girl who opened the door.

To this inquiry the girl returned the not uncommon, but rather evasive reply of "I don't know; where do you come from?"

Mr Bumble no sooner uttered Oliver's name, in explanation of his errand, than Mrs Bedwin, who had been listening at the parlour door, hastened into the passage in a breathless state.

"Come in, come in," said the old lady: "I knew we should hear of him. Poor dear! I knew we should! I was certain of it. Bless his heart! I said so, all along."

Having said this, the worthy old lady hurried back into the parlour again; and seating herself on a sofa, burst into tears. The girl, who was not quite so susceptible, had run up stairs meanwhile; and now returned with a request that Mr Bumble would follow her immediately: which he did.

He was shown into the little back study, where sat Mr Brownlow and his friend Mr Grimwig, with decanters and glasses before them. The latter gentleman at once burst into the exclamation:

"A beadle! A parish beadle, or I'll eat my head."

"Pray don't interrupt just now," said Mr Brownlow. "Take a seat, will you?"

Mr Bumble sat himself down: quite confounded by the oddity of Mr Grimwig's manner. Mr Brownlow moved the lamp, so as to obtain an uninterrupted view of the Beadle's countenance; and said, with a little impatience,

"Now, sir, you come in consequence of having seen the advertisement?"

"Yes, sir," said Mr Bumble.

"And you *are* a beadle, are you not?" inquired Mr Grimwig.

"I am a porochial beadle, gentlemen," rejoined Mr Bumble, proudly.

"Of course," observed Mr Grimwig aside to his friend, "I knew he was. A beadle all over!"

Mr Brownlow gently shook his head to impose silence on his friend, and resumed:

"Do you know where this poor boy is now?"

"No more than nobody," replied Mr Bumble.

"Well, what *do* you know of him?" inquired the old gentleman. "Speak out, my friend, if you have anything to say. What *do* you know of him?"

"You don't happen to know any good of him, do you?" said Mr Grimwig, caustically; after an attentive perusal of Mr Bumble's features.

Mr Bumble, catching at the inquiry very quickly, shook his head with portentous solemnity.

"You see?" said Mr Grimwig, looking triumphantly at Mr Brownlow.

Mr Brownlow looked apprehensively at Mr Bumble's pursed-up countenance; and requested him to communicate what he knew regarding Oliver, in as few words as possible.

Mr Bumble put down his hat; unbuttoned his coat; folded his arms; inclined his head in a retrospective manner; and, after a few moments" reflection, commenced his story.

It would be tedious if given in the beadle's words: occupying, as it did, some twenty minutes in the telling; but the sum and substance of it was, That Oliver was a foundling, born of low and vicious parents. That he had, from his birth, displayed no better qualities than treachery, ingratitude, and malice. That he had terminated his brief career in the place of his birth, by making a sanguinary and cowardly attack on an unoffending lad, and running away in the night-time from his master's house. In proof of his really being the person he represented himself, Mr Bumble laid upon the table the papers he had brought to town. Folding his arms again, he then awaited Mr Brownlow's observations.

"I fear it is all too true," said the old gentleman sorrowfully, after looking over the papers. "This is not much for your intelligence; but I would gladly have given you treble the money, if it had been favourable to the boy."

It is not improbable that if Mr Bumble had been possessed of this information at an earlier period of the interview, he might have imparted a very different colouring to his little history. It was too late to do it now, however; so he shook his head gravely, and, pocketing the five guineas, withdrew.

Mr Brownlow paced the room to and fro for some minutes; evidently so much disturbed by the beadle's tale, that even Mr Grimwig forbore to vex him further.

At length he stopped, and rang the bell violently.

"Mrs Bedwin," said Mr Brownlow, when the housekeeper appeared; "that boy, Oliver, is an impostor."

"It can't be, sir. It cannot be," said the old lady, energetically.

"I tell you he is," retorted the old gentleman. "What do you mean by can't be? We have just heard a full account of him from his birth; and he has been a thorough-paced little villain, all his life."

"I never will believe it, sir," replied the old lady, firmly. "Never!"

"You old women never believe anything but quack-doctors, and lying story-books," growled Mr Grimwig. "I knew it all along. Why didn't you take my advice in the beginning; you would, if he hadn't had a fever, I suppose, eh? He was interesting, wasn't he? Interesting! Bah!" And Mr Grimwig poked the fire with a flourish.

"He was a dear, grateful, gentle child, sir," retorted Mrs Bedwin, indignantly. "I know what children are, sir; and have done these forty years; and people who can't say the same, shouldn't say anything about them. That's my opinion!"

This was a hard hit at Mr Grimwig, who was a bachelor. As it extorted nothing from that gentleman but a smile, the old lady tossed her head, and smoothed down her apron preparatory to another speech, when she was stopped by Mr Brownlow.

"Silence!" said the old gentleman, feigning an anger he was far from feeling. "Never let me hear the boy's name again. I rang to tell you that. Never. Never, on any pretence, mind! You may leave the room, Mrs Bedwin. Remember! I am in earnest."

There were sad hearts at Mr Brownlow's that night.

Oliver's heart sank within him, when he thought of his good kind friends; it was well for him that he could not know what they had heard, or it might have broken outright.

Chapter XVIII

How Oliver passed his Time, in the improving Society of his reputable Friends

About noon next day, when the Dodger and Master Bates had gone out to pursue their customary avocations, Mr Fagin took the opportunity of reading Oliver a long lecture on the crying sin of ingratitude: of which he clearly demonstrated he had been guilty, to no ordinary extent, in wilfully absenting himself from the society of his anxious friends; and, still more, in endeavouring to escape from them after so much trouble and expense had been incurred in his recovery. Mr Fagin laid great stress on the fact of his having taken Oliver in, and cherished him, when, without his timely aid, he might have perished with hunger; and he related the dismal and affecting history of a young lad whom, in his philanthropy, he had succoured under parallel circumstances, but who, proving unworthy of his confidence and evincing a desire to communicate with the police, had unfortunately come to be hanged at the Old Bailey one morning. Mr Fagin did not seek to conceal his share in the catastrophe, but lamented with tears in his eyes that the wrong-headed and treacherous behaviour of the young person in question, had rendered it necessary that he should become the victim of certain evidence for the crown: which, if it were not precisely true, was indispensably necessary for the safety of him (Mr Fagin) and a few select friends. Mr Fagin concluded by drawing a rather disagreeable picture of the discomforts of hanging, and, with great friendliness and politeness of manner, expressed his anxious hopes that he might never be obliged to submit Oliver Twist to that unpleasant operation.

Little Oliver's blood ran cold, as he listened to the Jew's words, and imperfectly comprehended the dark threats conveyed in them. That it was possible even for justice itself to confound the innocent with the guilty when they were in accidental companionship, he knew already; and that deeply-laid plans for the destruction of inconveniently knowing or over-communicative persons, had been really devised and carried out by the old Jew on more occasions than one, he thought by no means unlikely, when he recollected the general nature of the altercations between that gentleman and Mr Sikes: which seemed to bear reference to some foregone conspiracy of the kind. As he glanced timidly up, and met the Jew's searching look, he felt that his pale face and trembling limbs were neither unnoticed nor unrelished by that wary old gentleman.

The Jew, smiling hideously, patted Oliver on the head, and said, that if he kept himself quiet, and applied himself to business, he saw they would be very good friends yet. Then, taking his hat, and covering himself with an old patched great-coat, he went out, and locked the room-door behind him.

And so Oliver remained all that day, and for the greater part of many subsequent days, seeing nobody, between early morning and midnight, and left during the long hours to commune with his own thoughts. Which, never failing to revert to his kind friends, and the opinion they must long ago have formed of him, were sad indeed.

After the lapse of a week or so, the Jew left the room-door unlocked; and he was at liberty to wander about the house.

It was a very dirty place. The rooms up stairs had great high wooden chimney-pieces and large doors, with panelled walls and cornices to the ceilings; which, although they were black with neglect and dust, were ornamented in various ways. From all these tokens Oliver concluded that a long time ago, before the old Jew was born, it had belonged to better people, and had perhaps been quite gay and handsome: dismal and dreary as it looked now.

Spiders had built their webs in the angles of the walls and ceilings; and sometimes, when Oliver walked softly into a room, the mice would scamper across the floor, and run back terrified to their holes. With these exceptions, there was neither sight nor sound of any living thing; and often, when it grew dark, and he was tired of wandering from room to room, he would crouch in the corner of the passage by the street-door, to be as near living people as he could; and would remain there, listening and counting the hours, until the Jew or the boys returned.

In all the rooms, the mouldering shutters were fast closed: the bars which held them were screwed tight into the wood; the only light which was admitted, stealing its way through round holes at the top: which made the rooms more gloomy, and filled them with strange shadows. There was a back-garret window with rusty bars outside, which had no shutter; and out of this, Oliver often gazed with a melancholy face for hours together; but nothing was to be descried from it but a confused and crowded mass of house-tops, blackened chimneys, and gable-ends. Sometimes, indeed, a grizzly head might be seen, peering over the parapet-wall of a distant house: but it was quickly withdrawn again; and as the window of Oliver's observatory was nailed down, and dimmed with the rain and smoke of years, it was as much as he could do to make out the forms of the different objects beyond, without making any attempt to be seen or heard, – which he had as much chance of being, as if he had lived inside the ball of St Paul's Cathedral.

One afternoon, the Dodger and Master Bates being engaged out that evening, the first-named young gentleman took it into his head to evince some anxiety regarding the decoration of his person (to do him justice, this was by no means an habitual weakness with him); and, with this end and aim, he condescendingly commanded Oliver to assist him in his toilet, straightway.

Oliver was but too glad to make himself useful; too happy to have some faces, however bad, to look upon; too desirous to conciliate those about him when he could honestly do so; to throw any objection in the way of this proposal. So he at once expressed his readiness; and, kneeling on the floor, while the Dodger sat upon the table so that he could take his foot in his lap, he applied himself to a process which Mr Dawkins designated as "japanning his trotter-cases." The phrase, rendered into plain English, signifieth, cleaning his boots.

Whether it was the sense of freedom and independence which a rational animal may be supposed to feel when he sits on a table in an easy attitude smoking a pipe, swinging one leg carelessly to and fro, and having his boots cleaned all the time, without even the past trouble of having taken them off, or the prospective misery of putting them on, to disturb his reflections; or whether it was the goodness of the tobacco that soothed the feelings of the Dodger, or the mildness of the beer that mollified his thoughts; he was evidently tinctured, for the nonce, with a spice of romance and enthusiasm, foreign to his general nature. He looked down on Oliver, with a thoughtful countenance, for a brief space; and then, raising his head, and heaving a gentle sigh, said, half in abstraction, and half to Master Bates:

"What a pity it is he isn't a prig!"

"Ah!" said Master Charles Bates; "he don't know what's good for him."

The Dodger sighed again, and resumed his pipe: as did Charley Bates. They both smoked, for some seconds, in silence.

"I suppose you don't even know what a prig is?" said the Dodger mournfully.

"I think I know that," replied Oliver, looking up. "It's a th– ; you're one, are you not?" inquired Oliver, checking himself.

"I am," replied the Dodger. "I'd scorn to be anything else." Mr Dawkins gave his hat a ferocious cock, after delivering this sentiment, and looked at Master Bates, as if to denote that he would feel obliged by his saying anything to the contrary.

"I am," repeated the Dodger. "So's Charley. So's Fagin. So's Sikes. So's Nancy. So's Bet. So we all are, down to the dog. And he's the downiest one of the lot!"

"And the least given to peaching," added Charley Bates.

"He wouldn't so much as bark in a witness-box, for fear of committing himself; no, not if you tied him up in one, and left him there without wittles for a fortnight," said the Dodger.

"Not a bit of it," observed Charley.

"He's a rum dog. Don't he look fierce at any strange cove that laughs or sings when he's in company!" pursued the Dodger. "Won't he growl at all, when he hears a fiddle playing! And don't he hate other dogs as ain't of his breed! Oh, no!"

"He's an out-and-out Christian," said Charley.

This was merely intended as a tribute to the animal's abilities, but it was an appropriate remark in another sense, if Master Bates had only known it; for there are a good many ladies and gentlemen, claiming to be out-and-out Christians, between whom, and Mr Sikes" dog, there exist strong and singular points of resemblance.

"Well, well," said the Dodger, recurring to the point from which they had strayed: with that mindfulness of his profession which influenced all his proceedings. "This hasn't got anything to do with young Green here."

"No more it has," said Charley. "Why don't you put yourself under Fagin, Oliver?"

"And make your fortun" out of hand?" added the Dodger, with a grin.

"And so be able to retire on your property, and do the gen-teel: as I mean to, in the very next leap-year but four that ever comes, and the forty-second Tuesday in Trinity-week," said Charley Bates.

"I don't like it," rejoined Oliver, timidly; "I wish they would let me go. I – I – would rather go."

"And Fagin would *rather* not!" rejoined Charley.

Oliver knew this too well; but thinking it might be dangerous to express his feelings more openly, he only sighed, and went on with boot-cleaning.

"Go!" exclaimed the Dodger. "Why, where's your spirit? Don't you take any pride out of yourself? Would you go and be dependent on your friends?"

"Oh, blow that!" said Master Bates: drawing two or three silk handkerchiefs from his pocket, and tossing them into a cupboard, "that's too mean; that is."

"*I* couldn't do it," said the Dodger, with an air of haughty disgust.

"You can leave your friends, though," said Oliver with a half smile; "and let them be punished for what you did."

"That," rejoined the Dodger, with a wave of his pipe, "That was all out of consideration for Fagin, 'cause the traps know that we work together, and he might have got into trouble if we hadn't made our lucky; that was the move, wasn't it, Charley?"

Master Bates nodded assent, and would have spoken; but the recollection of Oliver's flight came so suddenly upon him, that the smoke he was inhaling got entangled with a laugh, and went up into his head, and down into his throat: and brought on a fit of coughing and stamping, about five minutes long.

"Look here!" said the Dodger, drawing forth a handful of shillings and half-pence. "Here's a jolly life! What's the odds where it comes from? Here, catch hold; there's plenty more where they were took from. You won't, won't you? Oh, you precious flat!"

"It's naughty, ain't it, Oliver?" inquired Charley Bates. "He'll come to be scragged, won't he?"

"I don't know what that means," replied Oliver.

"Something in this way, old feller," said Charley. As he said it, Master Bates caught up an end of his neckerchief; and, holding it erect in the air, dropped his head on his shoulder, and jerked a curious sound through his teeth: thereby indicating, by a lively pantomimic representation, that scragging and hanging were one and the same thing.

"That's what it means," said Charley. "Look how he stares, Jack! I never did see such prime company as that 'ere boy; he'll be the death of me, I know he will." Master Charles Bates, having laughed heartily again, resumed his pipe with tears in his eyes.

"You've been brought up bad," said the Dodger, surveying his boots with much satisfaction when Oliver had polished them. "Fagin will make something of you, though, or you'll be the first he ever had that turned out unprofitable. You'd better begin at once; for you'll come to the trade long before you think of it; and you're only losing time, Oliver."

Master Bates backed this advice with sundry moral admonitions of his own: which, being exhausted, he and his friend Mr Dawkins launched into a glowing description of the numerous pleasures incidental to the life they led, interspersed with a variety of hints to Oliver that the best thing he could do, would be to secure Fagin's favour without more delay, by the means which they themselves had employed to gain it.

"And always put this in your pipe, Nolly," said the Dodger, as the Jew was heard unlocking the door above, "if you don't take fogles and tickers –"

"What's the good of talking in that way? interposed Master Bates; "he don't know what you mean."

"If you don't take pocket-handkechers and watches," said the Dodger, reducing his conversation to the level of Oliver's capacity, "some other cove will; so that the coves that lose 'em will be all the worse, and you'll be all the worse too, and nobody half a ha'p'orth the better, except the chaps wot gets them – and you've just as good a right to them as they have."

"To be sure, to be sure!" said the Jew, who had entered, unseen by Oliver. "It all lies in a nutshell, my dear; in a nutshell, take the Dodger's word for it. Ha! ha! ha! He understands the catechism of his trade."

The old man rubbed his hands gleefully together, as he corroborated the Dodger's reasoning in these terms; and chuckled with delight at his pupil's proficiency.

The conversation proceeded no farther at this time, for the Jew had returned home accompanied by Miss Betsy, and a gentleman whom Oliver had never seen before, but who was accosted by the Dodger as Tom Chitling; and who, having lingered on the stairs to exchange a few gallantries with the lady, now made his appearance.

Mr Chitling was older in years than the Dodger: having perhaps numbered eighteen winters; but there was a degree of deference in his deportment towards that young gentleman which seemed to indicate that he felt himself conscious of a slight inferiority in point of genius and professional acquirements. He had small twinkling eyes, and a pock-marked face; wore a fur cap, a dark corduroy jacket, greasy fustian trousers, and an apron. His wardrobe was, in truth, rather out of repair; but he excused himself to the company by stating that his "time" was only out an hour before; and that, in consequence of having worn the regimentals for six weeks past, he had not been able to bestow any attention on his private clothes. Mr Chitling added, with strong marks of irritation, that the new way of fumigating clothes up yonder was infernal unconstitutional, for it burnt holes in them, and there was no remedy against the County. The same remark he considered to apply to the regulation mode of cutting the hair: which he held to be decidedly unlawful. Mr Chitling wound up his observations by stating that he had not touched a drop of anything for forty-two mortal long hard-working days; and that he "wished he might be busted if he warn't as dry as a lime-basket."

"Where do you think the gentleman has come from, Oliver?" inquired the Jew, with a grin, as the other boys put a bottle of spirits on the table.

"I – I – don't know, sir," replied Oliver.

"Who's that?" inquired Tom Chitling, casting a contemptuous look at Oliver.

"A young friend of mine, my dear," replied the Jew.

"He's in luck, then," said the young man, with a meaning look at Fagin. "Never mind where I came from, young 'un; you'll find your way there, soon enough, I'll bet a crown!"

At this sally, the boys laughed. After some more jokes on the same subject, they exchanged a few short whispers with Fagin; and withdrew.

After some words apart between the last comer and Fagin, they drew their chairs towards the fire; and the Jew, telling Oliver to come and sit by him, led the conversation to the topics most calculated to interest his hearers. These were, the great advantages of the trade, the proficiency of the Dodger, the amiability of Charley Bates, and the liberality of the Jew himself. At length these subjects displayed signs of being thoroughly exhausted; and Mr Chitling did the same: for the house of correction becomes fatiguing after a week or two. Miss Betsy accordingly withdrew; and left the party to their repose.

From this day, Oliver was seldom left alone; but was placed in almost constant communication with the two boys, who played the old game with the Jew every day: whether for their own improvement or Oliver's, Mr Fagin best knew. At other times the old man would tell them stories of robberies he had committed in his younger days: mixed up with so much that was droll and curious, that Oliver could not help laughing heartily, and showing that he was amused in spite of all his better feelings.

In short, the wily old Jew had the boy in his toils. Having prepared his mind, by solitude and gloom, to prefer any society to the companionship of his own sad thoughts in such a dreary place, he was now slowly instilling into his soul the poison which he hoped would blacken it, and change its hue for ever.

Chapter XIX

In which a notable Plan is discussed and determined on

It was a chill, damp, windy night, when the Jew: buttoning his great-coat tight round his shrivelled body, and pulling the collar up over his ears so as completely to obscure the lower part of his face: emerged from his den. He paused on the step as the door was locked and chained behind him; and having listened while the boys made all secure, and until their retreating footsteps were no longer audible, slunk down the street as quickly as he could.

The house to which Oliver had been conveyed, was in the neighbourhood of Whitechapel. The Jew stopped for an instant at the corner of the street; and, glancing suspiciously round, crossed the road, and struck off in the direction of Spitalfields.

The mud lay thick upon the stones, and a black mist hung over the streets; the rain fell sluggishly down, and everything felt cold and clammy to the touch. It seemed just the night when it befitted such a being as the Jew to be abroad. As he glided stealthily along, creeping beneath the shelter of the walls and doorways, the hideous old man seemed like some loathsome reptile, engendered in the slime and darkness through which he moved: crawling forth, by night, in search of some rich offal for a meal.

He kept on his course, through many winding and narrow ways, until he reached Bethnal Green; then, turning suddenly off to the left, he soon became involved in a maze of the mean and dirty streets which abound in that close and densely-populated quarter.

The Jew was evidently too familiar with the ground he traversed to be at all bewildered, either by the darkness of the night, or the intricacies of the way. He hurried through several alleys and streets, and at length turned into one, lighted only by a single lamp at the farther end. At the door of a house in this street, he knocked; having exchanged a few muttered words with the person who opened it, he walked up stairs.

A dog growled as he touched the handle of a room-door; and a man's voice demanded who was there.

"Only me, Bill; only me, my dear," said the Jew, looking in.

"Bring in your body then," said Sikes. "Lie down, you stupid brute! Don't you know the devil when he's got a great-coat on?"

Apparently, the dog had been somewhat deceived by Mr Fagin's outer garment; for as the Jew unbuttoned it, and threw it over the back of a chair, he retired to the corner from which he had risen: wagging his tail as he went, to show that he was as well satisfied as it was in his nature to be.

"Well!" said Sikes.

"Well, my dear," replied the Jew. – "Ah! Nancy."

The latter recognition was uttered with just enough of embarrassment to imply a doubt of its reception; for Mr Fagin and his young friend had not met, since she had interfered in behalf of Oliver. All doubts upon the subject, if he had any, were speedily removed by the young lady's behaviour. She took her feet off the fender, pushed back her chair, and bade Fagin draw up his, without saying more about it: for it was a cold night, and no mistake.

"It *is* cold, Nancy dear," said the Jew, as he warmed his skinny hands over the fire. "It seems to go right through one," added the old man touching his side.

"It must be a piercer, if it finds its way through *your* heart," said Mr Sikes. "Give him something to drink, Nancy. Burn my body, make haste! It's enough to turn a man ill, to see his lean old carcase shivering in that way, like a ugly ghost just rose from the grave."

Nancy quickly brought a bottle from a cupboard, in which there were many: which, to judge from the diversity of their appearance, were filled with several kinds of liquids. Sikes pouring out a glass of brandy, bade the Jew drink it off.

"Quite enough, quite, thankye, Bill," replied the Jew, putting down the glass after just setting his lips to it.

"What! You're afraid of our getting the better of you, are you?" inquired Sikes, fixing his eyes on the Jew. "Ugh!"

With a hoarse grunt of contempt, Mr Sikes seized the glass, and threw the remainder of its contents into the ashes: as a preparatory ceremony to filling it again for himself: which he did at once.

The Jew glanced round the room, as his companion tossed down the second glassful; not in curiosity, for he had seen it often before; but in a restless and suspicious manner habitual to him. It was a meanly furnished apartment, with nothing but the contents of the closet to induce the belief that its occupier was anything but a working man; and with no more suspicious articles displayed to view than two or three heavy bludgeons which stood in a corner, and a "life-preserver" that hung over the chimney-piece.

"There," said Sikes, smacking his lips. "Now I'm ready."

"For business?" inquired the Jew.

"For business," replied Sikes; "so say what you've got to say."

"About the crib at Chertsey, Bill?" said the Jew, drawing his chair forward, and speaking in a very low voice.

"Yes. Wot about it?" inquired Sikes.

"Ah! you know what I mean, my dear," said the Jew. "He knows what I mean, Nancy; don't he?"

"No, he don't," sneered Mr Sikes. "Or he won't, and that's the same thing. Speak out, and call things by their right names; don't sit there, winking and blinking, and talking to me in hints, as if you warn't the very first that thought about the robbery. Wot d"ye mean?"

"Hush, Bill, hush!" said the Jew, who had in vain attempted to stop this burst of indignation; "somebody will hear us, my dear. Somebody will hear us."

"Let 'em hear!" said Sikes; "I don't care." But as Mr Sikes *did* care, on reflection, he dropped his voice as he said the words, and grew calmer.

"There, there," said the Jew, coaxingly. "It was only my caution, nothing more. Now, my dear, about that crib at Chertsey; when is it to be done, Bill, eh? When is it to be done? Such plate, my dear, such plate!" said the Jew: rubbing his hands, and elevating his eyebrows in a rapture of anticipation.

"Not at all," replied Sikes coldly.

"Not to be done at all!" echoed the Jew, leaning back in his chair.

"No, not at all," rejoined Sikes. "At least it can't be a put-up job, as we expected."

"Then it hasn't been properly gone about," said the Jew, turning pale with anger. "Don't tell me!"

"But I will tell you," retorted Sikes. "Who are you that's not to be told? I tell you that Toby Crackit has been hanging about the place for a fortnight, and he can't get one of the servants into a line."

"Do you mean to tell me, Bill," said the Jew: softening as the other grew heated: "that neither of the two men in the house can be got over?"

"Yes, I do mean to tell you so," replied Sikes. "The old lady has had 'em these twenty year; and if you were to give 'em five hundred pound, they wouldn't be in it."

"But do you mean to say, my dear," remonstrated the Jew, "that the women can't be got over?"

"Not a bit of it," replied Sikes.

"Not by flash Toby Crackit?" said the Jew incredulously. "Think what women are, Bill."

"No; not even by flash Toby Crackit," replied Sikes. "He says he's worn sham whiskers, and a canary waistcoat, the whole blessed time he's been loitering down there, and it's all of no use."

"He should have tried mustachios and a pair of military trousers, my dear," said the Jew.

"So he did," rejoined Sikes, "and they warn't of no more use than the other plant."

The Jew looked blank at this information. After ruminating for some minutes with his chin sunk on his breast, he raised his head and said, with a deep sigh, that if flash Toby Crackit reported aright, he feared the game was up.

"And yet," said the old man, dropping his hands on his knees, "it's a sad thing, my dear, to lose so much when we had set our hearts upon it."

"So it is," said Mr Sikes. "Worse luck!"

A long silence ensued; during which the Jew was plunged in deep thought, with his face wrinkled into an expression of villany perfectly demoniacal. Sikes eyed him furtively from time to time. Nancy, apparently fearful of irritating the housebreaker, sat with her eyes fixed upon the fire, as if she had been deaf to all that passed.

"Fagin," said Sikes, abruptly breaking the stillness that prevailed; "is it worth fifty shiners extra, if it's safely done from the outside?"

"Yes," said the Jew, as suddenly rousing himself.

"Is it a bargain?" inquired Sikes.

"Yes, my dear, yes," rejoined the Jew; his eyes glistening, and every muscle in his face working, with the excitement that the inquiry had awakened.

"Then," said Sikes, thrusting aside the Jew's hand, with some disdain, "let it come off as soon as you like. Toby and me were over the garden-wall the night afore last, sounding the panels of the door and shutters. The crib's barred up at night like a jail; but there's one part we can crack, safe and softly."

"Which is that, Bill?" asked the Jew eagerly.

"Why," whispered Sikes, "as you cross the lawn –"

"Yes?" said the Jew, bending his head forward, with his eyes almost starting out of it.

"Umph!" cried Sikes, stopping short, as the girl, scarcely moving her head, looked suddenly round, and pointed for an instant to the Jew's face. "Never mind which part it is. You can't do it without me, I know; but it's best to be on the safe side when one deals with you."

"As you like, my dear, as you like," replied the Jew. "Is there no help wanted, but yours and Toby's?"

"None," said Sikes. "'Cept a centre-bit and a boy. The first we've both got; the second you must find us."

"A boy!" exclaimed the Jew. "Oh! then it's a panel, eh?"

"Never mind wot it is!" replied Sikes. "I want a boy, and he mustn't be a big un. Lord!" said Mr Sikes, reflectively, "if I'd only got that young boy of Ned, the chimbley-sweeper's! He kept him small on purpose, and let him out by the job. But the father gets lagged; and then the Juvenile Delinquent Society comes, and takes the boy away from a trade where he was arning money, teaches him to read and write, and in time makes a "prentice of him. And so they go on," said Mr Sikes, his wrath rising with the recollection of his wrongs, "so they go on; and, if they'd got money enough (which it's a Providence they haven't,) we shouldn't have half-a-dozen boys left in the whole trade, in a year or two."

"No more we should," acquiesced the Jew, who had been considering during this speech, and had only caught the last sentence. "Bill!"

"What now?" inquired Sikes.

The Jew nodded his head towards Nancy, who was still gazing at the fire; and intimated, by a sign, that he would have her told to leave the room. Sikes shrugged his shoulders impatiently, as if he thought the precaution unnecessary; but complied, nevertheless, by requesting Miss Nancy to fetch him a jug of beer.

"You don't want any beer," said Nancy, folding her arms, and retaining her seat very composedly.

"I tell you I do!" replied Sikes.

"Nonsense," rejoined the girl coolly. "Go on, Fagin. I know what he's going to say, Bill; he needn't mind me."

The Jew still hesitated. Sikes looked from one to the other in some surprise.

"Why, you don't mind the old girl, do you, Fagin?" he asked at length. "You've known her long enough to trust her, or the Devil's in it. She ain't one to blab. Are you, Nancy?"

"*I* should think not!" replied the young lady: drawing her chair up to the table, and putting her elbows upon it.

"No, no, my dear, I know you're not," said the Jew; "but –" and again the old man paused.

"But wot?" inquired Sikes.

"I didn't know whether she mightn't p'r"aps be out of sorts, you know, my dear, as she was the other night," replied the Jew.

At this confession, Miss Nancy burst into a loud laugh; and, swallowing a glass of brandy, shook her head with an air of defiance, and burst into sundry exclamations of "Keep the game a-going!" "Never say die!" and the like. These seemed to have the effect of re-assuring both gentlemen; for the Jew nodded his head with a satisfied air, and resumed his seat: as did Mr Sikes likewise.

"Now, Fagin," said Nancy with a laugh. "Tell Bill at once, about Oliver!"

"Ha! you're a clever one, my dear; the sharpest girl I ever saw!" said the Jew, patting her on the neck. "It *was* about Oliver I was going to speak, sure enough. Ha! ha! ha!"

"What about him?" demanded Sikes.

"He's the boy for you, my dear," replied the Jew in a hoarse whisper; laying his finger on the side of his nose, and grinning frightfully.

"He!" exclaimed Sikes.

"Have him, Bill!" said Nancy. "I would, if I was in your place. He mayn't be so much up, as any of the others; but that's not what you want, if he's only to open a door for you. Depend upon it he's a safe one, Bill."

"I know he is," rejoined Fagin. "He's been in good training these last few weeks, and it's time he began to work for his bread. Besides, the others are all too big."

"Well, he is just the size I want," said Mr Sikes, ruminating.

"And will do everything you want, Bill, my dear," interposed the Jew; "he can't help himself. That is, if you frighten him enough."

"Frighten him!" echoed Sikes. "It'll be no sham frightening, mind you. If there's anything queer about him when we once get into the work; in for a penny, in for a pound. You won't see him alive again, Fagin. Think of that, before you send him. Mark my words!" said the robber, poising a crowbar, which he had drawn from under the bedstead.

"I've thought of it all," said the Jew with energy. "I've – I've had my eye upon him, my dears, close – close. Once let him feel that he is one of us; once fill his mind with the idea that he has been a thief; and he's ours! Ours for his life. Oho! It couldn't have come about better!" The old man crossed his arms upon his breast; and, drawing his head and shoulders into a heap, literally hugged himself for joy.

"Ours!" said Sikes. "Yours, you mean."

"Perhaps I do, my dear," said the Jew, with a shrill chuckle. "Mine, if you like, Bill."

"And wot," said Sikes, scowling fiercely on his agreeable friend, "wot makes you take so much pains about one chalk-faced kid, when you know there are fifty boys snoozing about Common Garden every night, as you might pick and choose from?"

"Because they're of no use to me, my dear," replied the Jew, with some confusion, "not worth the taking. Their looks convict 'em when they get into trouble, and I lose 'em all. With this boy, properly managed, my dears, I could do what I couldn't with twenty of them. Besides," said the Jew, recovering his self-possession, "he has us now if he could only give us leg-bail again; and he *must* be in the same boat with us. Never mind how he came there; it's quite enough for my power over him that he was in a robbery; that's all I want. Now, how much better this is, than being obliged to put the poor leetle boy out of the way – which would be dangerous, and we should lose by it besides."

"When is it to be done?" asked Nancy, stopping some turbulent exclamation on the part of Mr Sikes, expressive of the disgust with which he received Fagin's affectation of humanity.

"Ah, to be sure," said the Jew; "when is it to be done, Bill?"

"I planned with Toby, the night arter to-morrow," rejoined Sikes in a surly voice, "if he heerd nothing from me to the contrairy."

"Good," said the Jew; "there's no moon."

"No," rejoined Sikes.

"It's all arranged about bringing off the swag, is it?" asked the Jew.

Sikes nodded.

"And about –"

"Oh, ah, it's all planned," rejoined Sikes, interrupting him. "Never mind particulars. You'd better bring the boy here to-morrow night. I shall get off the stones an hour arter daybreak. Then you hold your tongue, and keep the melting-pot ready, and that's all you'll have to do."

After some discussion, in which all three took an active part, it was decided that Nancy should repair to the Jew's next evening when the night had set in, and bring Oliver away with her; Fagin craftily observing, that, if he evinced any disinclination to the task, he would be more willing to accompany the girl who had so recently interfered in his behalf, than anybody else. It was also solemnly arranged that poor Oliver should, for the purposes of the contemplated expedition, be unreservedly consigned to the care and custody of Mr William Sikes; and further, that the said Sikes should deal with him as he thought fit; and should not be held responsible by the Jew for any mischance or evil that might befall him, or any punishment with which it might be necessary to visit him: it being understood that, to render the compact in this respect binding, any representations made by Mr Sikes on his return should be required to be confirmed and corroborated, in all important particulars, by the testimony of flash Toby Crackit.

These preliminaries adjusted, Mr Sikes proceeded to drink brandy at a furious rate, and to flourish the crowbar in an alarming manner; yelling forth, at the same time, most unmusical snatches of song, mingled with wild execrations. At length, in a fit of professional enthusiasm, he insisted upon producing his box of housebreaking tools: which he had no sooner stumbled in with, and opened for the purpose of explaining the nature and properties of the various implements it contained, and the peculiar beauties of their construction, than he fell over the box upon the floor, and went to sleep where he fell.

"Good night, Nancy," said the Jew, muffling himself up as before.

"Good night."

Their eyes met, and the Jew scrutinised her, narrowly. There was no flinching about the girl. She was as true and earnest in the matter as Toby Crackit himself could be.

The Jew again bade her good night, and, bestowing a sly kick upon the prostrate form of Mr Sikes while her back was turned, groped down stairs.

"Always the way!" muttered the Jew to himself as he turned homeward. "The worst of these women is, that a very little thing serves to call up some long-forgotten feeling; and the best of them is, that it never lasts. Ha! ha! The man against the child, for a bag of gold!"

Beguiling the time with these pleasant reflections, Mr Fagin wended his way, through mud and mire, to his gloomy abode: where the Dodger was sitting up, impatiently awaiting his return.

"Is Oliver a-bed? I want to speak to him," was his first remark as they descended the stairs.

"Hours ago," replied the Dodger, throwing open a door. "Here he is!"

The boy was lying, fast asleep, on a rude bed upon the floor; so pale with anxiety, and sadness, and the closeness of his prison, that he looked like death; not death as it shows in shroud and coffin, but in the guise it wears when life has just departed; when a young and gentle spirit has, but an instant, fled to Heaven, and the gross air of the world has not had time to breathe upon the changing dust it hallowed.

"Not now," said the Jew, turning softly away. "To-morrow. To-morrow."

Chapter XX

Wherein Oliver is delivered over to Mr William Sikes

When Oliver awoke in the morning, he was a good deal surprised to find that a new pair of shoes, with strong thick soles, had been placed at his bedside; and that his old shoes had been removed. At first, he was pleased with the discovery: hoping that it might be the forerunner of his release; but such thoughts were quickly dispelled, on his sitting down to breakfast along with the Jew, who told him, in a tone and manner which increased his alarm, that he was to be taken to the residence of Bill Sikes that night.

"To – to – stop there, sir?" asked Oliver, anxiously.

"No, no, my dear. Not to stop there," replied the Jew. "We shouldn't like to lose you. Don't be afraid, Oliver, you shall come back to us again. Ha! ha! ha! We won't be so cruel as to send you away, my dear. Oh no, no!"

The old man, who was stooping over the fire toasting a piece of bread, looked round as he bantered Oliver thus; and chuckled as if to show that he knew he would still be very glad to get away if he could.

"I suppose," said the Jew, fixing his eyes on Oliver, "you want to know what you're going to Bill's for – eh, my dear?"

Oliver coloured, involuntarily, to find that the old thief had been reading his thoughts; but boldly said, Yes, he did want to know.

"Why, do you think?" inquired Fagin, parrying the question.

"Indeed I don't know, sir," replied Oliver.

"Bah!" said the Jew, turning away with a disappointed countenance from a close perusal of the boy's face. "Wait till Bill tells you, then."

The Jew seemed much vexed by Oliver's not expressing any greater curiosity on the subject; but the truth is, that, although Oliver felt very anxious, he was too much confused by the earnest cunning of Fagin's looks, and his own speculations, to make any further inquiries just then. He had no other opportunity: for the Jew remained very surly and silent till night: when he prepared to go abroad.

"You may burn a candle," said the Jew, putting one upon the table. "And here's a book for you to read, till they come to fetch you. Good night!"

"Good night!" replied Oliver, softly.

The Jew walked to the door: looking over his shoulder at the boy as he went. Suddenly stopping, he called him by his name.

Oliver looked up; the Jew, pointing to the candle, motioned him to light it. He did so; and, as he placed the candlestick upon the table, saw that the Jew was gazing fixedly at him, with lowering and contracted brows, from the dark end of the room.

"Take heed, Oliver! take heed!" said the old man, shaking his right hand before him in a warning manner. "He's a rough man, and thinks nothing of blood when his own is up. Whatever falls out, say nothing; and do what he bids you. Mind!" Placing a strong emphasis on the last word, he suffered his features gradually to resolve themselves into a ghastly grin, and, nodding his head, left the room.

Oliver leaned his head upon his hand when the old man disappeared, and pondered, with a trembling heart, on the words he had just heard. The more he thought of the Jew's admonition, the more he was at a loss to divine its real purpose and meaning. He could think of no bad object to be attained by sending him to Sikes, which would not be equally well answered by his remaining with Fagin; and after meditating for a long time, concluded that he had been selected to perform some ordinary menial offices for the housebreaker, until another boy, better suited for his purpose, could be engaged. He was too well accustomed to suffering, and had suffered too much where he was, to bewail the prospect of change very severely. He remained lost in thought for some minutes; and then, with a heavy sigh, snuffed the candle, and, taking up the book which the Jew had left with him, began to read.

He turned over the leaves. Carelessly at first; but, lighting on a passage which attracted his attention, he soon became intent upon the volume. It was a history of the lives and trials of great criminals; and the pages were soiled and thumbed with use. Here, he read of dreadful crimes that made the blood run cold; of secret murders that had been committed by the lonely wayside; of bodies hidden from the eye of man in deep pits and wells: which would not keep them down, deep as they were, but had yielded them up at last, after many years, and so maddened the murderers with the sight, that in their horror they had confessed their guilt, and yelled for the gibbet to end their agony. Here, too, he read of men who, lying in their beds at dead of night, had been tempted (so they said) and led on, by their own bad thoughts, to such dreadful bloodshed as it made the flesh creep, and the limbs quail, to think of. The terrible descriptions were so real and vivid, that the sallow pages seemed to turn red with gore; and the words upon them, to be sounded in his ears, as if they were whispered, in hollow murmurs, by the spirits of the dead.

In a paroxysm of fear, the boy closed the book, and thrust it from him. Then, falling upon his knees, he prayed Heaven to spare him from such deeds; and rather to will that he should die at once, than be reserved for crimes, so fearful and appalling. By degrees, he grew more calm, and besought, in a low and broken voice, that he might be rescued from his present dangers; and that if any aid were to be raised up for a poor outcast boy who had never known the love of friends or kindred, it might come to him now, when, desolate and deserted, he stood alone in the midst of wickedness and guilt.

He had concluded his prayer, but still remained with his head buried in his hands, when a rustling noise aroused him.

"What's that!" he cried, starting up, and catching sight of a figure standing by the door. "Who's there?"

"Me. Only me," replied a tremulous voice.

Oliver raised the candle above his head: and looked towards the door. It was Nancy.

"Put down the light," said the girl, turning away her head. "It hurts my eyes."

Oliver saw that she was very pale, and gently inquired if she were ill. The girl threw herself into a chair, with her back towards him: and wrung her hands; but made no reply.

"God forgive me!" she cried after a while, "I never thought of this."

"Has anything happened?" asked Oliver. "Can I help you? I will if I can. I will, indeed."

She rocked herself to and fro; caught her throat; and, uttering a gurgling sound, gasped for breath.

"Nancy!" cried Oliver, "What is it?"

The girl beat her hands upon her knees, and her feet upon the ground; and, suddenly stopping, drew her shawl close round her: and shivered with cold.

Oliver stirred the fire. Drawing her chair close to it, she sat there, for a little time, without speaking; but at length she raised her head, and looked round.

"I don't know what comes over me sometimes," said she, affecting to busy herself in arranging her dress; "it's this damp dirty room, I think. Now, Nolly, dear, are you ready?"

"Am I to go with you?" asked Oliver.

"Yes. I have come from Bill," replied the girl. "You are to go with me."

"What for?" asked Oliver, recoiling.

"What for?" echoed the girl, raising her eyes, and averting them again, the moment they encountered the boy's face. "Oh! For no harm."

"I don't believe it," said Oliver; who had watched her closely.

"Have it your own way," rejoined the girl, affecting to laugh. "For no good, then."

Oliver could see that he had some power over the girl's better feelings, and, for an instant, thought of appealing to her compassion for his helpless state. But, then, the thought darted across his mind that it was barely eleven o'clock; and that many people were still in the streets: of whom surely some might be found to give credence to his tale. As the reflection occured to him, he stepped forward: and said, somewhat hastily, that he was ready.

Neither his brief consideration, nor its purport, was lost on his companion. She eyed him narrowly, while he spoke; and cast upon him a look of intelligence which sufficiently showed that she guessed what had been passing in his thoughts.

"Hush!" said the girl, stooping over him, and pointing to the door as she looked cautiously round. "You can't help yourself. I have tried hard for you, but all to no purpose. You are hedged round and round. If ever you are to get loose from here, this is not the time."

Struck by the energy of her manner, Oliver looked up in her face with great surprise. She seemed to speak the truth; her countenance was white and agitated; and she trembled with very earnestness.

"I have saved you from being ill-used once, and I will again, and I do now," continued the girl aloud; "for those who would have fetched you, if I had not, would have been far more rough than me. I have promised for your being quiet and silent; if you are not, you will only do harm to yourself and me too, and perhaps be my death. See here! I have borne all this for you already, as true as God sees me show it."

She pointed, hastily, to some livid bruises on her neck and arms; and continued, with great rapidity:

"Remember this! And don't let me suffer more for you, just now. If I could help you, I would; but I have not the power. They don't mean to harm you; whatever they make you do, is no fault of yours. Hush! Every word from you is a blow for me. Give me your hand. Make haste! Your hand!"

She caught the hand which Oliver instinctively placed in hers, and, blowing out the light, drew him after her up the stairs. The door was opened, quickly, by some one shrouded in the darkness, and was as quickly closed, when they had passed out. A hackney-cabriolet was in waiting; with the same vehemence which she had exhibited in addressing Oliver, the girl pulled him in with her, and drew the curtains close. The driver wanted no directions, but lashed his horse into full speed, without the delay of an instant.

The girl still held Oliver fast by the hand, and continued to pour into his ear, the warnings and assurances she had already imparted. All was so quick and hurried, that he had scarcely time to recollect where he was, or how he came there, when the carriage stopped at the house to which the Jew's steps had been directed on the previous evening.

For one brief moment, Oliver cast a hurried glance along the empty street, and a cry for help hung upon his lips. But the girl's voice was in his ear, beseeching him in such tones of agony to remember her, that he had not the heart to utter it. While he hesitated, the opportunity was gone; he was already in the house, and the door was shut.

"This way," said the girl, releasing her hold for the first time. "Bill!"

"Hallo!" replied Sikes: appearing at the head of the stairs, with a candle. "Oh! That's the time of day. Come on!"

This was a very strong expression of approbation, an uncommonly hearty welcome, from a person of Mr Sikes's temperament. Nancy, appearing much gratified thereby, saluted him cordially.

"Bull's-eye's gone home with Tom," observed Sikes, as he lighted them up. "He'd have been in the way."

"That's right," rejoined Nancy.

"So you've got the kid," said Sikes, when they had all reached the room: closing the door as he spoke.

"Yes, here he is," replied Nancy.

"Did he come quiet?" inquired Sikes.

"Like a lamb," rejoined Nancy.

"I'm glad to hear it," said Sikes, looking grimly at Oliver; "for the sake of his young carcase: as would otherways have suffered for it. Come here, young un; and let me read you a lectur', which is as well got over at once."

Thus addressing his new pupil, Mr Sikes pulled off Oliver's cap and threw it into a corner; and then, taking him by the shoulder, sat himself down by the table, and stood the boy in front of him.

"Now, first: do you know wot this is?" inquired Sikes, taking up a pocket-pistol which lay on the table.

Oliver replied in the affirmative.

"Well, then, look here," continued Sikes. "This is powder; that 'ere's a bullet; and this is a little bit of a old hat for waddin'."

Oliver murmured his comprehension of the different bodies referred to; and Mr Sikes proceeded to load the pistol, with great nicety and deliberation.

"Now it's loaded," said Mr Sikes, when he had finished.

"Yes, I see it is, sir," replied Oliver.

"Well," said the robber, grasping Oliver's wrist, and putting the barrel so close to his temple that they touched; at which moment the boy could not repress a start; "if you speak a word when you're out o' doors with me, except when I speak to you, that loading will be in your head without notice. So, if you *do* make up your mind to speak without leave, say your prayers first."

Having bestowed a scowl upon the object of this warning, to increase its effect, Mr Sikes continued.

"As near as I know, there isn't anybody as would be asking very partickler arter you, if you *was* disposed of; so I needn't take this devil-and-all of trouble to explain matters to you, if it warn't for your own good. D"ye hear me?"

"The short and the long of what you mean," said Nancy: speaking very emphatically, and slightly frowning at Oliver as if to bespeak his serious attention to her words: "is, that if you're crossed by him in this job you have on hand, you'll prevent his ever telling tales afterwards, by shooting him through the head, and will take your chance of swinging for it, as you do for a great many other things in the way of business, every month of your life."

"That's it!" observed Mr Sikes, approvingly; "women can always put things in fewest words. – Except when it's blowing up; and then they lengthens it out. And now that he's thoroughly up to it, let's have some supper, and get a snooze before starting."

In pursuance of this request, Nancy quickly laid the cloth; disappearing for a few minutes, she presently returned with a pot of porter and a dish of sheep's heads: which gave occasion to several pleasant witticisms on the part of Mr Sikes, founded upon the singular coincidence of "jemmies" being a cant name, common to them, and also to an ingenious implement much used in his profession. Indeed, the worthy gentleman, stimulated perhaps by the immediate prospect of being on active service, was in great spirits and good humour; in proof whereof, it may be here remarked, that he humorously drank all the beer at a draught, and did not utter, on a rough calculation, more than four-score oaths during the whole progress of the meal.

Supper being ended – it may be easily conceived that Oliver had no great appetite for it – Mr Sikes disposed of a couple of glasses of spirits and water, and threw himself on the bed; ordering Nancy, with many imprecations in case of failure, to call him at five precisely. Oliver stretched himself in his clothes, by command of the same authority, on a mattress upon the floor; and the girl, mending the fire, sat before it, in readiness to rouse them at the appointed time.

For a long time Oliver lay awake, thinking it not impossible that Nancy might seek that opportunity of whispering some further advice; but the girl sat brooding over the fire, without moving, save now and then to trim the light. Weary with watching and anxiety, he at length fell asleep.

When he awoke, the table was covered with tea-things, and Sikes was thrusting various articles into the pockets of his great-coat, which hung over the back of a chair. Nancy was busily engaged in preparing breakfast. It was not yet daylight; for the candle was still burning, and it was quite dark outside. A sharp rain, too, was beating against the window-panes; and the sky looked black and cloudy.

"Now, then!" growled Sikes, as Oliver started up; "half-past five! Look sharp, or you'll get no breakfast; for it's late as it is."

Oliver was not long in making his toilet; having taken some breakfast, he replied to a surly inquiry from Sikes, by saying that he was quite ready.

Nancy, scarcely looking at the boy, threw him a handkerchief to tie round his throat; Sikes gave him a large rough cape to button over his shoulders. Thus attired, he gave his hand to the robber, who, merely pausing to show him with a menacing gesture that he had that same pistol in a side-pocket of his great-coat, clasped it firmly in his, and, exchanging a farewell with Nancy, led him away.

Oliver turned, for an instant, when they reached the door, in the hope of meeting a look from the girl. But she had resumed her old seat in front of the fire, and sat, perfectly motionless before it.

Chapter XXI

The Expedition

It was a cheerless morning when they got into the street; blowing and raining hard; and the clouds looking dull and stormy. The night had been very wet: large pools of water had collected in the road: and the kennels were overflowing. There was a faint glimmering of the coming day in the sky; but it rather aggravated than relieved the gloom of the scene: the sombre light only serving to pale that which the street lamps afforded, without shedding any warmer or brighter tints upon the wet housetops, and dreary streets. There appeared to be nobody stirring in that quarter of the town; the windows of the houses were all closely shut; and the streets through which they passed, were noiseless and empty.

By the time they had turned into the Bethnal Green Road, the day had fairly begun to break. Many of the lamps were already extinguished; a few country waggons were slowly toiling on, towards London; now and then, a stage-coach, covered with mud, rattled briskly by: the river bestowing, as he passed, an admonitory lash upon the heavy waggoner who, by keeping on the wrong side of the road, had endangered his arriving at the office a quarter of a minute after his time. The public-houses, with gas-lights burning inside, were already open. By degrees, other shops began to be unclosed, and a few scattered people were met with. Then, came straggling groups of labourers going to their work; then, men and women with fish-baskets on their heads; donkey-carts laden with vegetables; chaise-carts filled with live-stock or whole carcasses of meat; milk-women with pails; an unbroken concourse of people, trudging out with various supplies to the easter suburbs of the town. As they approached the City, the noise and traffic gradually increased;

when they threaded the streets between Shoreditch and Smithfield, it had swelled into a roar of sound and bustle. It was as light as it was likely to be, till night came on again, and the busy morning of half the London population had begun.

Turning down Sun Street and Crown Street, and crossing Finsbury Square, Mr Sikes struck, by way of Chiswell Street, into Barbican: thence into Long Lane, and so into Smithfield; from which latter place arose a tumult of discordant sounds that filled Oliver Twist with amazement.

It was market-morning. The ground was covered, nearly ankle-deep, with filth and mire; a thick steam, perpetually rising from the reeking bodies of the cattle, and mingling with the fog, which seemed to rest upon the chimney-tops, hung heavily above. All the pens in the centre of the large area, and as many temporary pens as could be crowded into the vacant space, were filled with sheep; tied up to posts by the gutter side were long lines of beasts and oxen, three or four deep. Countrymen, butchers, drovers, hawkers, boys, thieves, idlers, and vagabonds of every low grade, were mingled together in a mass; the whistling of drovers, the barking of dogs, the bellowing and plunging of oxen, the bleating of sheep, the grunting and squeaking of pigs, the cries of hawkers, the shouts, oaths, and quarrelling on all sides; the ringing of bells and roar of voices, that issued from every public-house; the crowding, pushing, driving, beating, whooping, and yelling; the hideous and discordant din that resounded from every corner of the market; and the unwashed, unshaven, squalid, and dirty figures constantly running to and fro, and bursting in and out of the throng; rendered it a stunning and bewildering scene, which quite confounded the senses.

Mr Sikes, dragging Oliver after him, elbowed his way through the thickest of the crowd, and bestowed very little attention on the numerous sights and sounds, which so astonished the boy. He nodded, twice or thrice, to a passing friend; and, resisting as many invitations to take a morning dram, pressed steadily onward, until they were clear of the turmoil, and had made their way through Hosier Lane into Holborn.

"Now, young un!" said Sikes, looking up at the clock of St Andrew's Church, "hard upon seven! you must step out. Come, don't lag behind already, Lazylegs!"

Mr Sikes accompanied this speech with a jerk at his little companion's wrist; Oliver, quickening his pace into a kind of trot, between a fast walk and a run, kept up with the rapid strides of the housebreaker as well as he could.

They held their course at this rate, until they had passed Hyde Park corner, and were on their way to Kensington: when Sikes relaxed his pace, until an empty cart which was at some little distance behind, came up. Seeing "Hounslow" written on it, he asked the driver with as much civility as he could assume, if he would give them a lift as far as Isleworth.

"Jump up," said the man. "Is that your boy?"

"Yes; he's my boy," replied Sikes, looking hard at Oliver, and putting his hand abstractedly into the pocket where the pistol was.

"Your father walks rather too quick for you, don't he, my man?" inquired the driver: seeing that Oliver was out of breath.

"Not a bit of it," replied Sikes, interposing. "He's used to it. Here, take hold of my hand, Ned. In with you!"

Thus addressing Oliver, he helped him into the cart; and the driver, pointing to a heap of sacks, told him to lie down there, and rest himself.

As they passed the different mile-stones, Oliver wondered, more and more, where his companion meant to take him. Kensington, Hammersmith, Chiswick, Kew Bridge, Brentford, were all passed; and yet they went on as steadily as if they had only just begun their journey. At length, they came to a public-house called the Coach and Horses: a little way beyond which, another road appeared to turn off. And here, the cart stopped.

Sikes dismounted with great precipitation, holding Oliver by the hand all the while; and lifting him down directly, bestowed a furious look upon him, and rapped the side-pocket with his fist, in a significant manner.

"Good-bye, boy," said the man.

"He's sulky," replied Sikes, giving him a shake; "he's sulky. A young dog! Don't mind him."

"Not I!" rejoined the other, getting into his cart. "It's a fine day, after all." And he drove away.

Sikes waited until he had fairly gone; and then, telling Oliver he might look about him if he wanted, once again led him onward on his journey.

They turned round to the left, a short way past the public-house; and then, taking a right-hand road, walked on for a long time: passing many large gardens and gentlemen's houses on both sides of the way, and stopping for nothing but a little beer, until they reached a town. Here against the wall of a house, Oliver saw written up in pretty large letters, "Hampton." They lingered about, in the fields, for some hours. At length, they came back into the town; and, turning into an old public-house with a defaced sign-board, ordered some dinner by the kitchen fire.

The kitchen was an old, low-roofed room; with a great beam across the middle of the ceiling, and benches, with high backs to them, by the fire; on which were seated several rough men in smock-frocks, drinking and smoking. They took no notice of Oliver; and very little of Sikes; and, as Sikes took very little notice of them, he and his young comrade sat in a corner by themselves, without being much troubled by their company.

They had some cold meat for dinner, and sat so long after it, while Mr Sikes indulged himself with three or four pipes, that Oliver began to feel quite certain they were not going any further. Being much tired with the walk, and getting up so early, he dozed a little at first; then, quite overpowered by fatigue and the fumes of the tobacco, fell asleep.

It was quite dark when he was awakened by a push from Sikes. Rousing himself sufficiently to sit up and look about him, he found that worthy in close fellowship and communication with a labouring man, over a pint of ale.

"So, you're going on to Lower Halliford, are you?" inquired Sikes.

"Yes, I am," replied the man, who seemed a little the worse – or better, as the case might be – for drinking; "and not slow about it neither. My horse hasn't got a load behind him going back, as he had coming up in the mornin'; and he won't be long a-doing of it. Here's luck to him! Ecod! he's a good un!"

"Could you give my boy and me a lift as far as there?" demanded Sikes, pushing the ale towards his new friend.

"If you're going directly, I can," replied the man, looking out of the pot. "Are you going to Halliford?"

"Going on to Shepperton," replied Sikes.

"I'm your man, as far as I go," replied the other. "Is all paid, Becky?"

"Yes, the other gentleman's paid," replied the girl.

"I say!" said the man, with tipsy gravity; "that won't do, you know."

"Why not?" rejoined Sikes. "You're a-going to accommodate us, and wot's to prevent my standing treat for a pint or so, in return?"

The stranger reflected upon this argument, with a very profound face; having done so, he seized Sikes by the hand and declared he was a real good fellow. To which Mr Sikes replied, he was joking; as, if he had been sober, there would have been strong reason to suppose he was.

After the exchange of a few more compliments, they bade the company good night, and went out; the girl gathering up the pots and glasses as they did so, and lounging out to the door, with her hands full, to see the party start.

The horse, whose health had been drunk in his absence, was standing outside: ready harnessed to the cart. Oliver and Sikes got in without any further ceremony; and the man to whom he belonged, having lingered for a minute or two "to bear him up," and to defy the hostler and the world to produce his equal, mounted also. Then, the hostler was told to give the horse his head; and, his head being given him, he made a very unpleasant use of it: tossing it into the air with great disdain, and running into the parlour windows over the way; after performing those feats, and supporting himself for a short time on his hind-legs, he started off at great speed, and rattled out of the town right gallantly.

The night was very dark. A damp mist rose from the river, and the marshy ground about; and spread itself over the dreary fields. It was piercing cold, too; all was gloomy and black. Not a word was spoken; for the driver had grown sleepy; and Sikes was in no mood to lead him into conversation. Oliver sat huddled together, in a corner of the cart; bewildered with alarm and apprehension; and figuring strange objects in the gaunt trees, whose branches waved grimly to and fro, as if in some fantastic joy at the desolation of the scene.

As they passed Sunbury Church, the clock struck seven. There was a light in the ferry-house window opposite: which streamed across the road, and threw into more sombre shadow a dark yew-tree with graves beneath it. There was a dull sound of falling water not far off; and the leaves of the old tree stirred gently in the night wind. It seemed like quiet music for the repose of the dead.

Sunbury was passed through, and they came again into the lonely road. Two or three miles more, and the cart stopped. Sikes alighted, took Oliver by the hand, and they once again walked on.

They turned into no house at Shepperton, as the weary boy had expected; but still kept walking on, in mud and darkness, through gloomy lanes and over cold open wastes, until they came within sight of the lights of a town at no great distance. On looking intently forward, Oliver saw that the water was just below them, and that they were coming to the foot of a bridge.

Sikes kept straight on, until they were close upon the bridge; then turned suddenly down a bank upon the left.

"The water!" thought Oliver, turning sick with fear. "He has brought me to this lonely place to murder me!"

He was about to throw himself on the ground, and make one struggle for his young life, when he saw that they stood before a solitary house: all ruinous and decayed. There was a window on each side of the dilapidated entrance; and one story above; but no light was visible. The house was dark, dismantled: and, to all appearance, uninhabited.

Sikes, with Oliver's hand still in his, softly approached the low porch, and raised the latch. The door yielded to the pressure, and they passed in together.

Chapter XXII

The Burglary

"HALLO!" cried a loud, hoarse voice, as soon as they set foot in the passage.

"Don't make such a row," said Sikes, bolting the door. "Show a glim, Toby."

"Aha! my pal!" cried the same voice. "A glim, Barney, a glim! Show the gentleman in, Barney; wake up first, if convenient."

The speaker appeared to throw a boot-jack, or some such article, at the person he addressed, to rouse him from his slumbers: for the noise of a wooden body, falling violently, was heard; and then an indistinct muttering, as of a man between asleep and awake.

"Do you hear?" cried the same voice. "There's Bill Sikes in the passage with nobody to do the civil to him; and you sleeping there, as if you took laudanum with your meals, and nothing stronger. Are you any fresher now, or do you want the iron candlestick to wake you thoroughly?"

A pair of slipshod feet shuffled, hastily, across the bare floor of the room, as this interrogatory was put; and there issued, from a door on the right hand: first, a feeble candle: and next, the form of the same individual who has been heretofore described as labouring under the infirmity of speaking through his nose, and officiating as waiter at the public-house on Saffron Hill.

"Bister Sikes!" exclaimed Barney, with real or counterfeit joy; "cub id, sir; cub id."

"Here! you get on first," said Sikes, putting Oliver in front of him. "Quicker! or I shall tread upon your heels."

Muttering a curse upon his tardiness, Sikes pushed Oliver before him; and they entered a low dark room with a smoky fire, two or three broken chairs, a table, and a very old couch: on which, with his legs much higher than his head, a man was reposing at full length, smoking a long clay pipe. He was dressed in a smartly-cut snuff-coloured coat, with large brass buttons; an orange neckerchief; a coarse, staring, shawl-pattern waistcoat; and drab breeches. Mr Crackit (for he it was) had no very great quantity of hair, either upon his head or face; but what he had, was of a reddish dye, and tortured into long corkscrew curls, through which he occasionally thrust some very dirty fingers, ornamented with large common rings. He was a trifle above the middle size, and apparently rather weak in the legs; but this circumstance by no means detracted from his own admiration of his top-boots, which he contemplated, in their elevated situation, with lively satisfaction.

"Bill, my boy!" said this figure, turning his head towards the door, "I'm glad to see you. I was almost afraid you'd given it up: in which case I should have made a personal wentur. Hallo!"

Uttering this exclamation in a tone of great surprise, as his eye rested on Oliver, Mr Toby Crackit brought himself into a sitting posture, and demanded who that was.

"The boy. Only the boy!" replied Sikes, drawing a chair towards the fire.

"Wud of Bister Fagin's lads," exclaimed Barney, with a grin.

"Fagin's, eh!" exclaimed Toby, looking at Oliver. "Wot an inwalable boy that'll make, for the old ladies" pockets in chapels! His mug is a fortun" to him."

"There – there's enough of that," interposed Sikes, impatiently; and stooping over his recumbent friend, he whispered a few words in his ear: at which Mr Crackit laughed immensely, and honoured Oliver with a long stare of astonishment.

"Now," said Sikes, as he resumed his seat, "if you'll give us something to eat and drink while we're waiting, you'll put some heart in us; or in me, at all events. Sit down by the fire, younker, and rest yourself; for you'll have to go out with us again to-night, though not very far off."

Oliver looked at Sikes, in mute and timid wonder; and drawing a stool to the fire, sat with his aching head upon his hands, scarcely knowing where he was, or what was passing around him.

"Here," said Toby, as the young Jew placed some fragments of food, and a bottle upon the table, "Success to the crack!" He rose to honour the toast; and, carefully depositing his empty pipe in a corner, advanced to the table, filled a glass with spirits, and drank off its contents. Mr Sikes did the same.

"A drain for the boy," said Toby, half-filling a wine glass. "Down with it, innocence."

"Indeed," said Oliver, looking piteously up into the man's face; "indeed, I –"

"Down with it!" echoed Toby. "Do you think I don't know what's good for you? Tell him to drink it, Bill."

"He had better!" said Sikes, clapping his hand upon his pocket. "Burn my body, if he isn't more trouble than a whole family of Dodgers. Drink it, you perwerse imp; drink it!"

Frightened by the menacing gestures of the two men, Oliver hastily swallowed the contents of the glass, and immediately fell into a violent fit of coughing: which delighted Toby Crackit and Barney, and even drew a smile from the surly Mr Sikes.

This done, and Sikes having satisfied his appetite (Oliver could eat nothing but a small crust of bread which they made him swallow), the two men laid themselves down on chairs for a short nap. Oliver retained his stool by the fire; Barney, wrapped in a blanket, stretched himself on the floor: close outside the fender.

They slept, or appeared to sleep, for some time; nobody stirring but Barney, who rose once or twice to throw coals upon the fire. Oliver fell into a heavy doze: imagining himself straying along the gloomy lanes, or wandering about the dark churchyard, or retracing some one or other of the scenes of the past day: when he was roused by Toby Crackit jumping up and declaring it was half-past one.

In an instant, the other two were on their legs, and all were actively engaged in busy preparation. Sikes and his companion enveloped their necks and chins in large dark shawls, and drew on their great-coats; Barney, opening a cupboard, brought forth several articles, which he hastily crammed into the pockets.

"Barkers for me, Barney," said Toby Crackit.

"Here they are," replied Barney, producing a pair of pistols. "You loaded them yourself."

"All right!" replied Toby, stowing them away. "The persuaders?"

"I've got 'em," replied Sikes.

"Crape, keys, centre-bits, darkies – nothing forgotten?" inquired Toby: fastening a small crowbar to a loop inside the skirt of his coat.

"All right," rejoined his companion. "Bring them bits of timber, Barney. That's the time of day."

With these words, he took a thick stick from Barney's hands, who, having delivered another to Toby, busied himself in fastening on Oliver's cape.

"Now then!" said Sikes, holding out his hand.

Oliver: who was completely stupefied by the unwonted exercise, and the air, and the drink which had been forced upon him: put his hand mechanically into that which Sikes extended for the purpose.

"Take his other hand, Toby," said Sikes. "Look out, Barney."

The man went to the door, and returned to announce that all was quiet. The two robbers issued forth with Oliver between them. Barney, having made all fast, rolled himself up as before, and was soon asleep again.

It was now intensely dark. The fog was much heavier than it had been in the early part of the night; and the atmosphere was so damp, that, although no rain fell, Oliver's hair and eyebrows, within a few minutes after leaving the house, had become stiff with the half-frozen moisture that was floating about. They crossed the bridge, and kept on towards the lights which he had seen before. They were at no great distance off; and, as they walked pretty briskly, they soon arrived at Chertsey.

"Slap through the town," whispered Sikes; "there'll be nobody in the way, to-night, to see us."

Toby acquiesced; and they hurried through the main street of the little town, which at that late hour was wholly deserted. A dim light shone at intervals from some bed-room window; and the hoarse barking of dogs occasionally broke the silence of the night. But there was nobody abroad. They had cleared the town, as the church-bell struck two.

Quickening their pace, they turned up a road upon the left hand. After walking about a quarter of a mile, they stopped before a detached house surrounded by a wall: to the top of which, Toby Crackit, scarcely pausing to take breath, climbed in a twinkling.

"The boy next," said Toby. "Hoist him up; I'll catch hold of him."

Before Oliver had time to look round, Sikes had caught him under the arms; and in three or four seconds he and Toby were lying on the grass on the other side. Sikes followed directly. And they stole cautiously towards the house.

And now, for the first time, Oliver, well-nigh mad with grief and terror, saw that housebreaking and robbery, if not murder, were the objects of the expedition. He clasped his hands together, and involuntarily uttered a subdued exclamation of horror. A mist came before his eyes; the cold sweat stood upon his ashy face; his limbs failed him; and he sank upon his knees.

"Get up!" murmured Sikes, trembling with rage, and drawing the pistol from his pocket; "Get up, or I'll strew your brains upon the grass."

"Oh! for God's sake let me go!" cried Oliver; "let me run away and die in the fields. I will never come near London; never, never! Oh! pray have mercy on me, and do not make me steal. For the love of all the bright Angels that rest in Heaven, have mercy upon me!"

The man to whom this appeal was made, swore a dreadful oath, and had cocked the pistol, when Toby, striking it from his grasp, placed his hand upon the boy's mouth, and dragged him to the house.

"Hush!" cried the man; "it won't answer here. Say another word, and I'll do your business myself with a crack on the head. That makes no noise, and is quite as certain, and more genteel. Here, Bill, wrench the shutter open. He's game enough now, I'll engage. I've seen older hands of his age took the same way, for a minute or two, on a cold night."

Sikes, invoking terrific imprecations upon Fagin's head for sending Oliver on such an errand, plied the crowbar vigorously, but with little noise. After some delay, and some assistance from Toby, the shutter to which he had referred, swung open on its hinges.

It was a little lattice window, about five feet and a half above the ground, at the back of the house: which belonged to a scullery, or small brewing-place, at the end of the passage. The aperture was so small, that the inmates had probably not thought it worth while to defend it more securely; but it was large enough to admit a boy of Oliver's size, nevertheless. A very brief exercise of Mr Sikes's art, sufficed to overcome the fastening of the lattice; and it soon stood wide open also.

"Now listen, you young limb," whispered Sikes, drawing a dark lantern from his pocket, and throwing the glare full on Oliver's face; "I'm a going to put you through there. Take this light; go softly up the steps straight afore you, and along the little hall, to the street door; unfasten it, and let us in."

"There's a bolt at the top, you won't be able to reach," interposed Toby. "Stand upon one of the hall chairs. There are three there, Bill, with a jolly large blue unicorn and gold pitchfork on 'em: which is the old lady's arms."

"Keep quiet, can't you?" replied Sikes, with a threatening look. "The room-door is open, is it?"

"Wide," replied Toby, after peeping in to satisfy himself. "The game of that is, that they always leave it open with a catch, so that the dog, who's got a bed in here, may walk up and down the passage when he feels wakeful. Ha! ha! Barney 'ticed him away to-night. So neat!"

Although Mr Crackit spoke in a scarcely audible whisper, and laughed without noise, Sikes imperiously commanded him to be silent, and to get to work. Toby complied, by first producing his lantern, and placing it on the ground; then by planting himself firmly with his head against the wall beneath the window, and his hands upon his knees, so as to make a step of his back. This was no sooner done, than Sikes, mounting upon him, put Oliver gently through the window with his feet first; and, without leaving hold of his collar, planted him safely on the floor inside.

"Take this lantern," said Sikes, looking into the room. "You see the stairs afore you?"

Oliver, more dead than alive, gasped out, "Yes." Sikes, pointing to the street-door with the pistol-barrel, briefly advised him to take notice that he was within shot all the way; and that if he faltered, he would fall dead that instant.

"It's done in a minute," said Sikes, in the same low whisper. "Directly I leave go of you, do your work. Hark!"

"What's that?" whispered the other man.

They listened intently.

"Nothing," said Sikes, releasing his hold of Oliver. "Now!"

In the short time he had had to collect his senses, the boy had firmly resolved that, whether he died in the attempt or not, he would make one effort to dart up stairs from the hall, and alarm the family. Filled with this idea, he advanced at once, but stealthily.

"Come back!" suddenly cried Sikes aloud. "Back! back!"

Scared by the sudden breaking of the dead stillness of the place, and by a loud cry which followed it, Oliver let his lantern fall, and knew not whether to advance or fly.

The cry was repeated – a light appeared – a vision of two terrified half-dressed men at the top of the stairs swam before his eyes – a flash – a loud noise – a smoke – a crash somewhere, but where he knew not, – and he staggered back.

Sikes had disappeared for an instant; but he was up again, and had him by the collar before the smoke had cleared away. He fired his own pistol after the men, who were already retreating; and dragged the boy up.

"Clasp your arm tighter," said Sikes, as he drew him through the window. "Give me a shawl here. They've hit him. Quick! How the boy bleeds!"

Then came the loud ringing of a bell, mingled with the noise of fire-arms, and the shouts of men, and the sensation of being carried over uneven ground at a rapid pace. And then, the noises grew confused in the distance; and a cold deadly feeling crept over the boy's heart; and he saw or heard no more.

Chapter XXIII

Which contains the Substance of a pleasant Conversation between Mr Bumble and a Lady; and shows that even a Beadle may be susceptible on some Points

THE night was bitter cold. The snow lay on the ground, frozen into a hard thick crust, so that only the heaps that had drifted into by-ways and corners were affected by the sharp wind that howled abroad: which, as if expending increased fury on such prey as it found, caught it savagely up in clouds, and, whirling it into a thousand misty eddies, scattered it in air. Bleak, dark, and piercing cold, it was a night for the well-housed and fed to draw round the bright fire and thank God they were at home; and for the homeless, starving wretch to lay him down and die. Many hunger-worn outcasts close their eyes in our bare streets, at such times, who, let their crimes have been what they may, can hardly open them in a more bitter world.

Such was the aspect of out-of-doors affairs, when Mrs Corney, the matron of the workhouse to which our readers have been already introduced as the birthplace of Oliver Twist, sat herself down before a cheerful fire in her own little room, and glanced, with no small degree of complacency, at a small round table: on which stood a tray of corresponding size, furnished with all necessary materials for the most grateful meal that matrons enjoy. In fact, Mrs Corney was about to solace herself with a cup of tea. As she glanced from the table to the fireplace, where the smallest of all possible kettles was singing a small song in a small voice, her inward satisfaction evidently increased, – so much so, indeed, that Mrs Corney smiled.

"Well!" said the matron, leaning her elbow on the table, and looking reflectively at the fire; "I'm sure we have all on us a great deal to be grateful for! A great deal, if we did but know it. Ah!"

Mrs Corney shook her head mournfully, as if deploring the mental blindness of those paupers who did not know it; and thrusting a silver spoon (private property) into the inmost recesses of a two-ounce tin tea-caddy, proceeded to make the tea.

How slight a thing will disturb the equanimity of our frail minds! The black teapot, being very small and easily filled, ran over while Mrs Corney was moralising; and the water slightly scalded Mrs Corney's hand.

"Drat the pot!" said the worthy matron, setting it down very hastily on the hob; "a little stupid thing, that only holds a couple of cups! What use is it of, to anybody! Except," said Mrs Corney, pausing, "except to a poor desolate creature like me. Oh dear!"

With these words, the matron dropped into her chair, and, once more resting her elbow on the table, thought of her solitary fate. The small teapot, and the single cup, had awakened in her mind sad recollections of Mr Corney (who had not been dead more than five-and-twenty years); and she was overpowered.

"I shall never get another!" said Mrs Corney, pettishly; "I shall never get another – like him."

Whether this remark bore reference to the husband, or the teapot, is uncertain. It might have been the latter; for Mrs Corney looked as it as she spoke; and took it up afterwards. She had just tasted her first cup, when she was disturbed by a soft tap at the room-door.

"Oh, come in with you!" said Mrs Corney, sharply. "Some of the old women dying, I suppose. They always die when I'm at meals. Don't stand there, letting the cold air in, don't. What's amiss now, eh?"

"Nothing, ma'am, nothing," replied a man's voice.

"Dear me!" exclaimed the matron, in a much sweeter tone, "is that Mr Bumble?"

"At your service, ma'am," said Mr Bumble, who had been stopping outside to rub his shoes clean, and to shake the snow off his coat; and who now made his appearance, bearing the cocked hat in one hand and a bundle in the other. "Shall I shut the door, ma'am?"

The lady modestly hesitated to reply, lest there should be any impropriety in holding an interview with Mr Bumble, with closed doors. Mr Bumble taking advantage of the hesitation, and being very cold himself, shut it without permission.

"Hard weather, Mr Bumble," said the matron.

"Hard, indeed, ma'am," replied the beadle. "Anti-porochial weather this, ma'am. We have given away, Mrs Corney, we have given away a matter of twenty quartern loaves and a cheese and a half, this very blessed afternoon; and yet them paupers are not contented."

"Of course not. When would they be, Mr Bumble?" said the matron, sipping her tea.

"When, indeed, ma'am!" rejoined Mr Bumble. "Why here's one man that, in consideration of his wife and large family, has a quartern loaf and a good pound of cheese, full weight. Is he grateful, ma'am? Is he grateful? Not a copper farthing's worth of it! What does he do, ma'am, but ask for a few coals; if it's only a pocket handkerchief full, he says! Coals! What would he do with coals? toast his cheese with 'em, and then come back for more. That's the way with these people, ma'am; give 'em a apron full of coals today, and they'll come back for another, the day after to-morrow, as brazen as alabaster."

The matron expressed her entire concurrence in this intelligible simile; and the beadle went on.

"I never," said Mr Bumble, "see anything like the pitch it's got to. The day afore yesterday, a man – you have been a married woman, ma'am, and I may mention it to you – a man, with hardly a rag upon his back (here Mrs Corney looked at the floor), goes to our overseer's door when he has got company coming to dinner; and says, he must be relieved, Mrs Corney. As he wouldn't go away, and shocked the company very much, our overseer sent him out a pound of potatoes and half a pint of oatmeal. "My heart!" says the ungrateful villain, "what's the use of *this* to me? You might as well give me a pair of iron spectacles!" "Very good," says our overseer, taking 'em away again, "you won't get anything else here." "Then I'll die in the streets!" says the vagrant. "Oh no, you won't," says our overseer."

"Ha! ha! That was very good! So like Mr Grannett, wasn't it?" interposed the matron. "Well, Mr Bumble?"

"Well, ma'am," rejoined the beadle, "he went away; and he *did* die in the streets. There's a obstinate pauper for you!"

"It beats anything I could have believed," observed the matron emphatically. "But don't you think out-of-door relief a very bad thing, any way, Mr Bumble? You're a gentleman of experience, and ought to know. Come."

"Mrs Corney," said the beadle, smiling as men smile who are conscious of superior information, "out-of-door relief, properly managed: properly managed, ma'am: is the porochial safeguard. The great principle of out-of-door relief is, to give the paupers exactly what they don't want; and then they get tired of coming."

"Dear me!" exclaimed Mrs Corney. "Well, that is a good one, too!"

"Yes. Betwixt you and me, ma'am," returned Mr Bumble, "that's the great principle; and that's the reason why, if you look at any cases that get into them owdacious newspapers, you'll always observe that sick families have been relieved with slices of cheese. That's the rule now, Mrs Corney, all over the country. But, however," said the beadle, stopping to unpack his bundle, "these are official secrets, ma'am; not to be spoken of; except, as I may say, among the porochial officers, such as ourselves. This is the port wine, ma'am, that the board ordered for the infirmary; real, fresh, genuine port wine; only out of the cask this forenoon; clear as a bell; and no sediment!"

Having held the first bottle up to the light, and shaken it well to test its excellence, Mr Bumble placed them both on the top of a chest of drawers; folded the handkerchief in which they had been wrapped; put it carefully in his pocket; and took up his hat, as if to go.

"You'll have a very cold walk, Mr Bumble," said the matron.

"It blows, ma'am," replied Mr Bumble, turning up his coat-collar, "enough to cut one's ears off."

The matron looked, from the little kettle, to the beadle, who was moving towards the door; and as the beadle coughed, preparatory to bidding her good night, bashfully inquired whether – whether he wouldn't take a cup of tea?

Mr Bumble instantaneously turned back his collar again; laid his hat and stick upon a chair; and drew another chair up to the table. As he slowly seated himself, he looked at the lady. She fixed her eyes upon the little tea-pot. Mr Bumble coughed again, and slightly smiled.

Mrs Corney rose to get another cup and saucer from the closet. As she sat down, her eyes once again encountered those of the gallant beadle; she coloured, and applied herself to the task of making his tea. Again Mr Bumble coughed, – louder this time than he had coughed yet.

"Sweet? Mr Bumble?" inquired the matron, taking up the sugar-basin.

"Very sweet, indeed, ma'am," replied Mr Bumble. He fixed his eyes on Mrs Corney as he said this; and if ever a beadle looked tender, Mr Bumble was that beadle at that moment.

The tea was made, and handed in silence. Mr Bumble, having spread a handkerchief over his knees to prevent the crumbs from sullying the splendour of his shorts, began to eat and drink; varying these amusements, occasionally, by fetching a deep sigh; which, however, had no injurious effect upon his appetite, but, on the contrary, rather seemed to facilitate his operations in the tea and toast department.

"You have a cat, ma'am, I see," said Mr Bumble, glancing at one who, in the centre of her family, was basking before the fire; "and kittens too, I declare!"

"I am so fond of them, Mr Bumble, you can't think," replied the matron. "They're *so* happy, *so* frolicsome, and *so* cheerful, that they are quite companions for me."

"Very nice animals, ma'am," replied Mr Bumble, approvingly; "so very domestic."

"Oh, yes!" rejoined the matron with enthusiasm; "so fond of their home too, that it's quite a pleasure, I'm sure."

"Mrs Corney, ma'am," said Mr Bumble, slowly, and marking the time with his teaspoon, "I mean to say this, ma'am; that any cat, or kitten, that could live with you, ma'am, and *not* be fond of its home, must be a ass, ma'am."

"Oh, Mr Bumble!" remonstrated Mrs Corney.

"It's of no use disguising facts, ma'am," said Mr Bumble, slowly flourishing the teaspoon with a kind of amorous dignity which made him doubly impressive; "I would drown it myself, with pleasure."

"Then you're a cruel man," said the matron vivaciously, as she held out her hand for the beadle's cup; "and a very hard-hearted man besides."

"Hard-hearted, ma'am?" said Mr Bumble. "Hard?" Mr Bumble resigned his cup without another word; squeezed Mrs Corney's little finger as she took it; and inflicting two open handed slaps upon his laced waistcoat, gave a mighty sigh, and hitched his chair a very little morsel farther from the fire.

It was a round table; and as Mrs Corney and Mr Bumble had been sitting opposite each other, with no great space between them, and fronting the fire, it will be seen that Mr Bumble, in receding from the fire, and still keeping at the table, increased the distance between himself and Mrs Corney; which proceeding, some prudent readers will doubtless be disposed to admire, and to consider an act of great heroism on Mr Bumble's part: he being in some sort tempted by time, place, and opportunity, to give utterance to certain soft nothings, which however well they may become the lips of the light and thoughtless, do seem immeasurably beneath the dignity of judges of the land, members of parliament, ministers of state, lord mayors, and other great public functionaries, but more particularly beneath the stateliness and gravity of a beadle: who (as is well known) should be the sternest and most inflexible among them all.

Whatever were Mr Bumble's intentions, however (and no doubt they were of the best): it unfortunately happened, as has been twice before remarked, that the table was a round one; consequently Mr Bumble, moving his chair by little and little, soon began to diminish the distance between himself and the matron; and, continuing to travel round the outer edge of the circle, brought his chair, in time, close to that in which the matron was seated. Indeed, the two chairs touched; and when they did so, Mr Bumble stopped.

Now, if the matron had moved her chair to the right, she would have been scorched by the fire; and if to the left, she must have fallen into Mr Bumble's arms; so (being a discreet matron, and no doubt foreseeing these consequences at a glance) she remained where she was, and handed Mr Bumble another cup of tea.

"Hard-hearted, Mrs Corney?" said Mr Bumble, stirring his tea, and looking up into the matron's face; "are *you* hard-hearted, Mrs Corney?"

"Dear me!" exclaimed the matron, "what a very curious question from a single man. What can you want to know for, Mr Bumble?"

The beadle drank his tea to the last drop; finished a piece of toast; whisked the crumbs off his knees; wiped his lips; and deliberately kissed the matron.

"Mr Bumble!" cried that discreet lady in a whisper; for the fright was so great, that she had quite lost her voice, "Mr Bumble, I shall scream!" Mr Bumble made no reply; but in a slow and dignified manner, put his arm round the matron's waist.

As the lady had stated her intention of screaming, of course she would have screamed at this additional boldness, but that the exertion was rendered unnecessary by a hasty knocking at the door: which was no sooner heard, than Mr Bumble darted, with much agility, to the wine bottles, and began dusting them with great violence: while the matron sharply demanded who was there. It is worthy of remark, as a curious physical instance of the efficacy of a sudden surprise in counteracting the effects of extreme fear, that her voice had quite recovered all its official asperity.

"If you please, mistress," said a withered old female pauper, hideously ugly: putting her head in at the door, "Old Sally is a-going fast."

"Well, what's that to me?" angrily demanded the matron. "I can't keep her alive, can I?"

"No, no, mistress," replied the old woman, "nobody can; she's far beyond the reach of help. I've seen a many people die; little babes and great strong men; and I know when death's a-coming, well enough. But she's troubled in her mind: and when the fits are not on her, – and that's not often, for she is dying very hard, – she says she has got something to tell, which you must hear. She'll never die quiet till you come, mistress."

At this intelligence, the worthy Mrs Corney muttered a variety of invectives against old women who couldn't even die without purposely annoying their betters; and, muffling herself in a thick shawl which she hastily caught up, briefly requested Mr Bumble to stay till she came back, lest anything particular should occur. Bidding the messenger walk fast, and not be all night hobbling up the stairs, she followed her from the room with a very ill grace, scolding all the way.

Mr Bumble's conduct on being left to himself, was rather inexplicable. He opened the closet, counted the teaspoons, weighed the sugar-tongs, closely inspected a silver milk-pot to ascertain that it was of the genuine metal, and, having satisfied his curiosity on these points, put on his cocked-hat corner-wise, and danced with much gravity four distinct times round the table. Having gone through this very extraordinary performance, he took off the cocked-hat again, and, spreading himself before the fire with his back towards it, seemed to be mentally engaged in taking an exact inventory of the furniture.

Chapter XXIV

Treats of a very poor Subject. But is a short one, and may be found of Importance in this History

It was no unfit messenger of death, who had disturbed the quiet of the matron's room. Her body was bent by age; her limbs trembled with palsy; her face, distorted into a mumbling leer, resembled more the grotesque shaping of some wild pencil, than the work of Nature's hand.

Alas! How few of Nature's faces are left alone to gladden us with their beauty! The cares, and sorrows, and hungerings of the world, change them as they change hearts; and it is only when those passions sleep, and have lost their hold for ever, that the troubled clouds pass off, and leave Heaven's surface clear. It is a common thing for the countenances of the dead, even in that fixed and rigid state, to subside into the long-forgotten expression of sleeping infancy, and settle into the very look of early life; so calm, so peaceful, do they grow again, that those who knew them in their happy childhood, kneel by the coffin's side in awe, and see the Angel even upon earth.

The old crone tottered along the passages, and up the stairs, muttering some indistinct answers to the chidings of her companion; being at length compelled to pause for breath, she gave the light into her hand, and remained behind to follow as she might: while the more nimble superior made her way to the room where the sick woman lay.

It was a bare garret-room, with a dim light burning at the farther end. There was another old woman watching by the bed; the parish apothecary's apprentice was standing by the fire, making a toothpick out of a quill.

"Cold night, Mrs Corney," said this young gentleman, as the matron entered.

"Very cold, indeed, sir," replied the mistress, in her most civil tones, and dropping a curtsey as she spoke.

"You should get better coals out of your contractors," said the apothecary's deputy, breaking a lump on the top of the fire with the rusty poker; "these are not at all the sort of thing for a cold night."

"They're the board's choosing, sir," returned the matron. "The least they could do, would be to keep us pretty warm: for our places are hard enough."

The conversation was here interrupted by a moan from the sick woman.

"Oh!" said the young man, turning his face towards the bed, as if he had previously quite forgotten the patient, "it's all U.P. there, Mrs Corney."

"It is, is it, sir?" asked the matron.

"If she lasts a couple of hours, I shall be surprised," said the apothecary's apprentice, intent upon the toothpick's point. "It's a break-up of the system altogether. Is she dozing, old lady?"

The attendant stooped over the bed, to ascertain; and nodded in the affirmative.

"Then perhaps she'll go off in that way, if you don't make a row," said the young man. "Put the light on the floor. She won't see it there."

The attendant did as she was told: shaking her head meanwhile, to intimate that the woman would not die so easily; having done so, she resumed her seat by the side of the other nurse, who had by this time returned. The mistress, with an expression of impatience, wrapped herself in her shawl, and sat at the foot of the bed.

The apothecary's apprentice, having completed the manufacture of the toothpick, planted himself in front of the fire and made good use of it for ten minutes or so: when apparently growing rather dull, he wished Mrs Corney joy of her job, and took himself off on tiptoe.

When they had sat in silence for some time, the two old women rose from the bed, and crouching over the fire, held out their withered hands to catch the heat. The flame threw a ghastly light on their shrivelled faces, and made their ugliness appear terrible, as, in this position, they began to converse in a low voice.

"Did she say any more, Anny dear, while I was gone?" inquired the messenger.

"Not a word," replied the other. "She plucked and tore at her arms for a little time; but I held her hands, and she soon dropped off. She hasn't much strength in her, so I easily kept her quiet. I ain't so weak for an old woman, although I am on parish allowance; no, no!"

"Did she drink the hot wine the doctor said she was to have?" demanded the first.

"I tried to get it down," rejoined the other. "But her teeth were tight set, and she clenched the mug so hard that it was as much as I could do to get it back again. So *I* drank it; and it did me good!"

Looking cautiously round, to ascertain that they were not overheard, the two hags cowered nearer to the fire, and chuckled heartily.

"I mind the time," said the first speaker, "when she would have done the same, and made rare fun of it afterwards."

"Ay, that she would," rejoined the other; "she had a merry heart. A many, many, beautiful corpses she laid out, as nice and neat as wax-work. My old eyes have seen them – ay, and those old hands touched them too; for I have helped her, scores of times."

Stretching forth her trembling fingers as she spoke, the old creature shook them exultingly before her face, and fumbling in her pocket, brought out an old time-discoloured tin snuffbox, from which she shook a few grains into the outstretched palm of her companion, and a few more into her own. While they were thus employed, the matron, who had been impatiently watching until the dying woman should awaken from her stupor, joined them by the fire, and sharply asked how long she was to wait?

"Not long, mistress," replied the second woman, looking up into her face. "We have none of us long to wait for Death. Patience, patience! He'll be here soon enough for us all."

"Hold your tongue, you doting idiot!" said the matron, sternly. "You, Martha, tell me; has she been in this way before?"

"Often," answered the first woman.

"But will never be again," added the second one; "that is, she'll never wake again but once – and mind, mistress, that won't be for long!"

"Long or short," said the matron, snappishly, "she won't find me here when she does wake; take care, both of you, how you worry me again for nothing. It's no part of my duty to see all the old women in the house die, and I won't – that's more. Mind that, you impudent old harridans. If you make a fool of me again, I'll soon cure you, I warrant you!"

She was bouncing away, when a cry from the two women, who had turned towards the bed, caused her to look round. The patient had raised herself upright, and was stretching her arms towards them.

"Who's that?" she cried, in a hollow voice.

"Hush, hush!" said one of the women, stopping over her. "Lie down, lie down!"

"I'll never lie down again alive!" said the woman, struggling. "I *will* tell her! Come here! Nearer! Let me whisper in your ear."

She clutched the matron by the arm, and forcing her into a chair by the bedside, was about to speak, when looking round, she caught sight of the two old women bending forward in the attitude of eager listeners.

"Turn them away," said the old woman, drowsily; "make haste! make haste!"

The two old crones, chiming in together, began pouring out many piteous lamentations that the poor dear was too far gone to know her best friends; and were uttering sundry protestations that they would never leave her, when the superior pushed them from the room, closed the door, and returned to the bedside. On being excluded, the old ladies changed their tone, and cried through the keyhole that old Sally was drunk; which, indeed, was not unlikely; since, in addition to a moderate dose of opium prescribed by the apothecary, she was labouring under the effects of a final taste of gin-and-water which had been privily administered, in the openness of their hearts, by the worthy old ladies themselves.

"Now listen to me," said the dying woman aloud, as if making a great effort to revive one latent spark of energy. "In this very room – in this very bed – I once nursed a pretty young creetur", that was brought into the house with her feet cut and bruised with walking, and all soiled with dust and blood. She gave birth to a boy, and died. Let me think – what was the year again!"

"Never mind the year," said the impatient auditor; "what about her?"

"Ay," murmured the sick woman, relapsing into her former drowsy state, "what about her? – what about – I know!" she cried, jumping fiercely up: her face flushed, and her eyes starting from her head – "I robbed her, so I did! She wasn't cold – I tell you she wasn't cold, when I stole it!"

"Stole what, for God's sake?" cried the matron, with a gesture as if she would call for help.

"*It!*" replied the woman, laying her hand over the other's mouth. "The only thing she had. She wanted clothes to keep her warm, and food to eat; but she had kept it safe, and had it in her bosom. It was gold, I tell you! Rich gold, that might have saved her life!"

"Gold!" echoed the matron, bending eagerly over the woman as she fell back. "Go on, go on – yes – what of it? Who was the mother? When was it?"

"She charged me to keep it safe," replied the woman with a groan, "and trusted me as the only woman about her. I stole it in my heart when she first showed it me hanging round her neck; and the child's death, perhaps, is on me besides! They would have treated him better, if they had known it all!"

"Known what?" asked the other. "Speak!"

"The boy grew so like his mother," said the woman, rambling on, and not heeding the question, "that I could never forget it when I saw his face. Poor girl! poor girl! She was so young, too! Such a gentle lamb! Wait; there's more to tell. I have not told you all, have I?"

"No, no," replied the matron, inclining her head to catch the words, as they came more faintly from the dying woman. "Be quick, or it may be too late!"

"The mother," said the woman, making a more violent effort than before; "the mother, when the pains of death first came upon her, whispered in my ear that if her baby was born alive, and thrived, the day might come when it would not feel so much disgraced to hear its poor young mother named. "And oh, kind Heaven!" she said, folding her thin hands together, "whether it be boy or girl, raise up some friends for it in this troubled world, and take pity upon a lonely desolate child, abandoned to its mercy!""

"The boy's name?" demanded the matron.

"They *called* him Oliver," replied the woman, feebly. "The gold I stole was –"

"Yes, yes – what?" cried the other.

She was bending eagerly over the woman to hear her reply; but drew back, instinctively, as she once again rose, slowly and stiffly, into a sitting posture; then, clutching the coverlid with both hands, muttered some indistinct sounds in her throat, and fell lifeless on the bed.

* * *

"Stone dead!" said one of the old women, hurrying in as soon as the door was opened.

"And nothing to tell, after all," rejoined the matron, walking carelessly away.

The two crones, to all appearance, too busily occupied in the preparations for their dreadful duties to make any reply, were left alone, hovering about the body.

Chapter XXV

Wherein this History reverts to Mr Fagin and Company

WHILE these things were passing in the country workhouse, Mr Fagin sat in the old den – the same from which Oliver had been removed by the girl – brooding over a dull, smoky fire. He held a pair of bellows upon his knee, with which he had apparently been endeavouring to rouse it into more cheerful action; but he had fallen into deep thought; and with his arms folded on them, and his chin resting on his thumbs, fixed his eyes, abstractedly, on the rusty bars.

At a table behind him sat the Artful Dodger, Master Charles Bates, and Mr Chitling: all intent upon a game of whist; the Artful taking dummy against Master Bates and Mr Chitling. The countenance of the first-named gentleman, peculiarly intelligent at all times, acquired great additional interest from his close observance of the game, and his attentive perusal of Mr Chitling's hand; upon which, from time to time, as occasion served, he bestowed a variety of earnest glances: wisely regulating his own play by the result of his observations upon his neighbour's cards. It being a cold night, the Dodger wore his hat, as, indeed, was often his custom within doors. He also sustained a clay pipe between his teeth, which he only removed for a brief space when he deemed it necessary to apply for refreshment to a quart pot upon the table, which stood ready filled with gin-and-water for the accommodation of the company.

Master Bates was also attentive to the play; but being of a more excitable nature than his accomplished friend, it was observable that he more frequently applied himself to the gin-and-water, and moreover indulged in many jests and irrelevant remarks, all highly unbecoming a scientific rubber. Indeed, the Artful, presuming upon their close attachment, more than once took occasion to reason gravely with his companion upon these improprieties: all of which remonstrances, Master Bates received in extremely good part; merely requesting his friend to be "blowed," or to insert his head in a sack, or replying with some other neatly-turned witticism of a similar kind, the happy application of which, excited considerable admiration in the mind of Mr Chitling. It was remarkable that the latter gentleman and his partner invariably lost; and that the circumstance, so far from angering Master Bates, appeared to afford him the highest amusement, inasmuch as he laughed most uproariously at the end of every deal, and protested that he had never seen such a jolly game in all his born days.

"That's two doubles and the rub," said Mr Chitling, with a very long face, as he drew half-a-crown from his waistcoat-pocket. "I never see such a feller as you, Jack; you win everything. Even when we've good cards, Charley and I can't make nothing of 'em."

Either the matter or the manner of this remark, which was made very ruefully, delighted Charley Bates so much, that his consequent shout of laughter roused the Jew from his reverie, and induced him to inquire what was the matter.

"Matter, Fagin!" cried Charley. "I wish you had watched the play. Tommy Chitling hasn't won a point; and I went partners with him against the Artful and dum."

"Ay, ay!" said the Jew, with a grin, which sufficiently demonstrated that he was at no loss to understand the reason. "Try 'em again, Tom; try 'em again."

"No more of it for me, thankee, Fagin," replied Mr Chitling; "I've had enough. That 'ere Dodger has such a run of luck that there's no standing again" him."

"Ha! ha! my dear," replied the Jew, "you must get up very early in the morning, to win against the Dodger."

"Morning!" said Charley Bates; "you must put your boots on over-night, and have a telescope at each eye, and a opera-glass between your shoulders, if you want to come over *him*."

Mr Dawkins received these handsome compliments with much philosophy, and offered to cut any gentleman in company, for the first picture-card, at a shilling a time. Nobody accepting the challenge, and his pipe being by this time smoked out, he proceeded to amuse himself by sketching a ground-plan of Newgate on the table with the piece of chalk which had served him in lieu of counters; whistling, meantime, with peculiar shrillness.

"How precious dull you are, Tommy!" said the Dodger, stopping short when there had been a long silence; and addressing Mr Chitling. "What do you think he's thinking of, Fagin?"

"How should I know, my dear?" replied the Jew, looking round as he plied the bellows. "About his losses, maybe; or the little retirement in the country that he's just left, eh? Ha! ha! Is that it, my dear?"

"Not a bit of it," replied the Dodger, stopping the subject of discourse as Mr Chitling was about to reply. "What do *you* say, Charley?"

"*I* should say," replied Master Bates, with a grin, "that he was uncommon sweet upon Betsy. See how he's a-blushing! Oh, my eye! here's a merry-go-rounder! Tommy Chitling's in love! Oh, Fagin, Fagin! what a spree!"

Thoroughly overpowered with the notion of Mr Chitling being the victim of the tender passion, Master Bates threw himself back in his chair with such violence, that he lost his balance, and pitched over upon the floor; where (the accident abating nothing of his merriment) he lay at full length until his laugh was over, when he resumed his former position, and began another laugh.

"Never mind him, my dear," said the Jew, winking at Mr Dawkins, and giving Master Bates a reproving tap with the nozzle of the bellows. "Betsy's a fine girl. Stick up to her, Tom. Stick up to her."

"What I mean to say, Fagin," replied Mr Chitling, very red in the face, "is, that that isn't anything to anybody here."

"No more it is," replied the Jew; "Charley will talk. Don't mind him, my dear; don't mind him. Betsy's a fine girl. Do as she bids you, Tom, and you will make your fortune."

"So I *do* do as she bids me," replied Mr Chitling; "I shouldn't have been milled, if it hadn't been for her advice. But it turned out a good job for you; didn't it, Fagin! And what's six weeks of it? It must come, some time or another, and why not in the winter time when you don't want to go out a-walking so much; eh, Fagin?"

"Ah, to be sure, my dear," replied the Jew.

"You wouldn't mind it again, Tom, would you," asked the Dodger, winking upon Charley and the Jew, "if Bet was all right?"

"I mean to say that I shouldn't," replied Tom, angrily. "There, now. Ah! Who'll say as much as that, I should like to know; eh, Fagin?"

"Nobody, my dear," replied the Jew; "not a soul, Tom. I don't know one of 'em that would do it besides you; not one of 'em, my dear."

"I might have got clear off, if I'd split upon her; mightn't I, Fagin?" angrily pursued the poor half-witted dupe. "A word from me would have done it; wouldn't it, Fagin?"

"To be sure it would, my dear," replied the Jew.

"But I didn't blab it; did I, Fagin?" demanded Tom, pouring question upon question with great volubility.

"No, no, to be sure," replied the Jew; "you were too stout-hearted for that. A deal too stout, my dear!"

"Perhaps I was," rejoined Tom, looking round; "and if I was, what's to laugh at, in that; eh, Fagin?"

The Jew, perceiving that Mr Chitling was considerably roused, hastened to assure him that nobody was laughing; and to prove the gravity of the company, appealed to Master Bates, the principal offender. But, unfortunately, Charley, in opening his mouth to reply that he was never more serious in his life, was unable to prevent the escape of such a violent roar, that the abused Mr Chitling, without any preliminary ceremonies, rushed across the room and aimed a blow at the offender; who, being skilful in evading pursuit, ducked to avoid it, and chose his time so well that it lighted on the chest of the merry old gentleman, and caused him to stagger to the wall, where he stood panting for breath, while Mr Chitling looked on in intense dismay. "Hark!" cried the Dodger at this moment, "I heard the tinkler." Catching up the light, he crept softly up stairs.

The bell was rung again, with some impatience, while the party were in darkness. After a short pause, the Dodger reappeared, and whispered Fagin mysteriously.

"What!" cried the Jew, "alone?"

The Dodger nodded in the affirmative, and, shading the flame of the candle with his hand, gave Charley Bates a private intimation, in dumb show, that he had better not be funny just then. Having performed this friendly office, he fixed his eyes on the Jew's face, and awaited his directions.

The old man bit his yellow fingers, and meditated for some seconds; his face working with agitation the while, as if he dreaded something, and feared to know the worst. At length he raised his head.

"Where is he?" he asked.

The Dodger pointed to the floor above, and made a gesture, as if to leave the room.

"Yes," said the Jew, answering the mute inquiry; "bring him down. Hush! Quiet, Charley! Gently, Tom! Scarce, scarce!"

This brief direction to Charley Bates, and his recent antagonist, was softly and immediately obeyed. There was no sound of their whereabout, when the Dodger descended the stairs, bearing the light in his hand, and followed by a man in a coarse smock-frock; who, after casting a hurried glance round the room, pulled off a large wrapper which had concealed the lower portion of his face, and disclosed: all haggard, unwashed, and unshorn: the features of flash Toby Crackit.

"How are you, Faguey?" said this worthy, nodding to the Jew. "Pop that shawl away in my castor, Dodger, so that I may know where to find it when I cut; that's the time of day! You'll be a fine young cracksman afore the old file now."

With these words he pulled up the smock-frock; and, winding it round his middle, drew a chair to the fire, and placed his feet upon the hob.

"See there, Faguey," he said, pointing disconsolately to his top-boots; "not a drop of Day and Martin since you know when; not a bubble of blacking, by Jove! But don't look at me in that way, man. All in good time. I can't talk about business till I've eat and drank; so produce the sustainance, and let's have a quiet fill-out for the first time these three days!"

The Jew motioned to the Dodger to place what eatables there were, upon the table; and, seating himself opposite the housebreaker, waited his leisure.

To judge from appearances, Toby was by no means in a hurry to open the conversation. At first, the Jew contented himself with patiently watching his countenance, as if to gain from its expression some clue to the intelligence he brought; but in vain. He looked tired and worn, but there was the same complacent repose upon his features that they always wore: and through dirt, and beard, and whisker, there still shone, unimpaired, the self-satisfied smirk of flash Toby Crackit. Then, the Jew, in an agony of impatience, watched every morsel he put into his mouth; pacing up and down the room, meanwhile, in irrepressible excitement. It was all of no use. Toby continued to eat with the utmost outward indifference, until he could eat no more; then, ordering the Dodger out, he closed the door, mixed a glass of spirits and water, and composed himself for talking.

"First and foremost, Faguey," said Toby.

"Yes, yes!" interposed the Jew, drawing up his chair.

Mr Crackit stopped to take a draught of spirits and water, and to declare that the gin was excellent; then placing his feet against the low mantelpiece, so as to bring his boots to about the level of his eye, he quietly resumed,

"First and foremost, Faguey," said the housebreaker, "how's Bill?"

"What!" screamed the Jew, starting from his seat.

"Why, you don't mean to say –" began Toby, turning pale.

"Mean!" cried the Jew, stamping furiously on the ground. "Where are they? Sikes and the boy! Where are they? Where have they been? Where are they hiding? Why have they not been here?"

"The crack failed," said Toby, faintly.

"I know it," replied the Jew, tearing a newspaper from his pocket and pointing to it. "What more?"

"They fired and hit the boy. We cut over the fields at the back, with him between us – straight as the crow flies – through hedge and ditch. They gave chase. Damme! the whole country was awake, and the dogs upon us."

"The boy!

"Bill had him on his back, and scudded like the wind. We stopped to take him between us; his head hung down, and he was cold. They were close upon our heels; every man for himself, and each from the gallows! We parted company, and left the youngster lying in a ditch. Alive or dead, that's all I know about him."

The Jew stopped to hear no more; but uttering a loud yell, and twining his hands in his hair, rushed from the room, and from the house.

Chapter XXVI

In which a mysterious Character appears upon the Scene, and many Things, inseparable from this History, are done and performed

THE old man had gained the street corner, before he began to recover the effect of Toby Crackit's intelligence. He had relaxed nothing of his unusual speed; but was still pressing onward, in the same wild and disordered manner, when the sudden dashing past of a carriage: and a boisterous cry from the foot passengers, who saw his danger: drove him back upon the pavement. Avoiding, as much as possible, all the main streets, and skulking only through the byways and alleys, he at length emerged on Snow Hill. Here he walked even faster than before; nor did he linger until he had again turned into a court; when, as if conscious that he was now in his proper element, he fell into his usual shuffling pace, and seemed to breathe more freely.

Near to the spot on which Snow Hill and Holborn Hill meet, there opens, upon the right hand as you come out of the City, a narrow and dismal alley leading to Saffron Hill. In its filthy shops are exposed for sale huge bunches of second-hand silk handkerchiefs, of all sizes and patterns; for here reside the traders who purchase them from pickpockets. Hundreds of these handkerchiefs hang dangling from pegs outside the windows or flaunting from the door-posts; and the shelves, within, are piled with them. Confined as the limits of Field Lane are, it has its barber, its coffee-shop, its beer-shop, and its fried-fish warehouse. It is a commercial colony of itself: the emporium of petty larceny: visited at early morning, and setting-in of dusk, by silent merchants, who traffic in dark back-parlours, and who go as strangely as they come. Here, the clothesman, the shoe-vamper, and the rag-merchant, display their goods, as sign-boards to the petty thief; here, stores of old iron and bones, and heaps of mildewy fragments of woollen-stuff and linen, rust and rot in the grimy cellars.

It was into this place that the Jew turned. He was well known to the sallow denizens of the lane; for such of them as were on the look-out to buy or sell, nodded, familiarly, as he passed along. He replied to their salutations in the same way; but bestowed no closer recognition until he reached the further end of the alley; when he stopped, to address a salesman of small stature, who had squeezed as much of his person into a child's chair as the chair would hold, and was smoking a pipe at his warehouse door.

"Why, the sight of you, Mr Fagin, would cure the hoptalmy!" said this respectable trader, in acknowledgment of the Jew's inquiry after his health.

"The neighbourhood was a little too hot, Lively," said Fagin, elevating his eyebrows, and crossing his hands upon his shoulders.

"Well, I've heerd that complaint of it, once or twice before," replied the trader; "but it soon cools down again; don't you find it so?"

Fagin nodded in the affirmative. Pointing in the direction of Saffron Hill, he inquired whether any one was up yonder to-night.

"At the Cripples?" inquired the man.

The Jew nodded.

"Let me see," pursued the merchant, reflecting. "Yes, there's some half-dozen of 'em gone in, that I knows. I don't think your friend's there."

"Sikes is not, I suppose?" inquired the Jew, with a disappointed countenance.

"*Non istwentus*, as the lawyers say," replied the little man, shaking his head, and looking amazingly sly. "Have you got anything in my line to-night?"

"Nothing to-night," said the Jew, turning away.

"Are you going up to the Cripples, Fagin?" cried the little man, calling after him. "Stop! I don't mind if I have a drop there with you!"

But as the Jew, looking back, waved his hand to intimate that he preferred being alone; and, moreover, as the little man could not very easily disengage himself from the chair; the sign of the Cripples was, for a time, bereft of the advantage of Mr Lively's presence. By the time he had got upon his legs, the Jew had disappeared; so Mr Lively, after ineffectually standing on tiptoe, in the hope of catching sight of him, again forced himself into the little chair, and, exchanging a shake of the head with a lady in the opposite shop, in which doubt and mistrust were plainly mingled, resumed his pipe with a grave demeanour.

The Three Cripples, or rather the Cripples: which was the sign by which the establishment was familiarly known to its patrons: was the public-house in which Mr Sikes and his dog have already figured. Merely making a sign to a man at the bar, Fagin walked straight up stairs, and opening the door of a room, and softly insinuating himself into the chamber, looked anxiously about: shading his eyes with his hand, as if in search of some particular person.

The room was illuminated by two gas-lights; the glare of which was prevented by the barred shutters, and closely-drawn curtains of faded red, from being visible outside. The ceiling was blackened, to prevent its colour from being injured by the flaring of the lamps; and the place was so full of dense tobacco smoke, that at first it was scarcely possible to discern anything more. By degrees, however, as some of it cleared away through the open door, an assemblage of heads, as confused as the noise that greeted the ear, might be made out; and as the eye grew more accustomed to the scene, the spectator gradually became aware of the presence of a numerous company, male and female, crowded round a long table: at the upper end of which, sat a chairman with a hammer of office in his hand; while a professional gentleman, with a bluish nose, and his face tied up for the benefit of a toothache, presided at a jingling piano in a remote corner.

As Fagin stepped softly in, the professional gentleman, running over the keys by way of prelude, occasioned a general cry of order for a song; which, having subsided, a young lady proceeded to entertain the company with a ballad in four verses, between each of which the accompanyist played the melody all through, as loud as he could. When this was over, the chairman gave a sentiment, after which, the professional gentlemen on the chairman's right and left volunteered a duet, and sang it, with great applause.

It was curious to observe some faces which stood out prominently from among the group. There was the chairman himself, (the landlord of the house,) a coarse, rough, heavy built fellow, who, while the songs were proceeding, rolled his eyes hither and thither, and, seeming to give himself up to joviality, had an eye for everything that was done, and an ear for everything that was said – and sharp ones, too. Near him were the singers: receiving, with professional indifference, the compliments of the company, and applying themselves, in turn, to a dozen proffered glasses of spirits and water, tendered by their more boisterous admirers; whose countenances, expressive of almost every vice in almost every grade, irresistibly attracted the attention, by their very repulsiveness. Cunning, ferocity, and drunkenness in all its stages, were there, in their strongest aspects; and women: some with the last lingering tinge of their early freshness almost fading as you looked: others with every mark and stamp of their sex utterly beaten out, and presenting but one loathsome blank of profligacy and crime; some mere girls, others but young women, and none past the prime of life; formed the darkest and saddest portion of this dreary picture.

Fagin, troubled by no grave emotions, looked eagerly from face to face while these proceedings were in progress; but apparently without meeting that of which he was in search. Succeeding, at length, in catching the eye of the man who occupied the chair, he beckoned to him slightly, and left the room, as quietly as he had entered it.

"What can I do for you, Mr Fagin?" inquired the man, as he followed him out to the landing. "Won't you join us? They'll be delighted, every one of 'em."

The Jew shook his head impatiently, and said in a whisper, "Is *he* here?"

"No," replied the man.

"And no news of Barney?" inquired Fagin.

"None," replied the landlord of the Cripples; for it was he. "He won't stir till it's all safe. Depend on it, they're on the scent down there; and that if he moved, he'd blow upon the thing at once. He's all right enough, Barney is, else I should have heard of him. I'll pound it, that Barney's managing properly. Let him alone for that."

"Will *he* be here to-night?" asked the Jew, laying the same emphasis on the pronoun as before.

"Monks, do you mean?" inquired the landlord, hesitating.

"Hush!" said the Jew. "Yes."

"Certain," replied the man, drawing a gold watch from his fob; "I expected him here before now. If you'll wait ten minutes, he'll be –"

"No, no," said the Jew, hastily; as though, however desirous he might be to see the person in question, he was nevertheless relieved by his absence. "Tell him I came here to see him; and that he must come to me to-night. No, say to-morrow. As he is not here, to-morrow will be time enough."

"Good!" said the man. "Nothing more?"

"Not a word now," said the Jew, descending the stairs.

"I say," said the other, looking over the rails, and speaking in a hoarse whisper; "what a time this would be for a sell! I've got Phil Barker here: so drunk, that a boy might take him."

"Aha! But it's not Phil Barker's time," said the Jew, looking up. "Phil has something more to do, before we can afford to part with him; so go back to the company, my dear, and tell them to lead merry lives – *while they last*. Ha! ha! ha!"

The landlord reciprocated the old man's laugh; and returned to his guests. The Jew was no sooner alone, than his countenance resumed its former expression of anxiety and thought. After a brief reflection, he called a hack cabriolet, and bade the man drive towards Bethnal Green. He dismissed him within some quarter of a mile of Mr Sikes's residence, and performed the short remainder of the distance, on foot.

"Now," muttered the Jew, as he knocked at the door, "if there is any deep play here, I shall have it out of you, my girl, cunning as you are."

She was in her room, the woman said. Fagin crept softly up stairs, and entered it without any previous ceremony. The girl was alone; lying with her head upon the table, and her hair straggling over it.

"She has been drinking," thought the Jew, coolly, "or perhaps she is only miserable."

The old man turned to close the door, as he made this reflection; the noise thus occasioned, roused the girl. She eyed his crafty face narrowly, as she inquired whether there was any news, and as she listened to his recital of Toby Crackit's story. When it was concluded, she sank into her former attitude, but spoke not a word. She pushed the candle impatiently away; and once or twice as she feverishly changed her position, shuffled her feet upon the ground; but this was all.

During the silence, the Jew looked restlessly about the room, as if to assure himself that there were no appearances of Sikes having covertly returned. Apparently satisfied with his inspection, he coughed twice or thrice, and made as many efforts to open a conversation; but the girl heeded him no more than if he had been made of stone. At length he made another attempt; and rubbing his hands together, said, in his most conciliatory tone,

"And where should you think Bill was now, my dear?"

The girl moaned out some half intelligible reply, that she could not tell; and seemed, from the smothered noise that escaped her, to be crying.

"And the boy, too," said the Jew, straining his eyes to catch a glimpse of her face. "Poor leetle child! Left in a ditch, Nance; only think!"

"The child," said the girl, suddenly looking up, "is better where he is, than among us; and if no harm comes to Bill from it, I hope he lies dead in the ditch, and that his young bones may rot there."

"What!" cried the Jew, in amazement.

"Ay, I do," returned the girl, meeting his gaze. "I shall be glad to have him away from my eyes, and to know that the worst is over. I can't bear to have him about me. The sight of him turns me against myself, and all of you."

"Pooh!" said the Jew, scornfully. "You're drunk."

"Am I?" cried the girl, bitterly. "It's no fault of yours, if I am not! You'd never have me anything else, if you had your will, except now; – the humour doesn't suit you, doesn't it?"

"No!" rejoined the Jew, furiously. "It does not."

"Change it, then!" responded the girl, with a laugh.

"Change it!" exclaimed the Jew, exasperated beyond all bounds by his companion's unexpected obstinacy, and the vexation of the night, "I WILL change it! Listen to me, you drab. Listen to me, who with six words, can strangle Sikes as surely as if I had his bull's throat between my fingers now. If he comes back, and leaves the boy behind him; if he gets off free, and dead or alive, fails to restore him to me; murder him yourself if you would have him escape Jack Ketch. And do it the moment he sets foot in this room, or mind me, it will be too late!"

"What is all this?" cried the girl involuntarily.

"What is it?" pursued Fagin, mad with rage. "When the boy's worth hundreds of pounds to me, am I to lose what chance threw me in the way of getting safely, through the whims of a drunken gang that I could whistle away the lives of! And me bound, too, to a born devil that only wants the will, and has the power to, to –"

Panting for breath, the old man stammered for a word; and in that instant checked the torrent of his wrath, and changed his whole demeanour. A moment before, his clenched hands had grasped the air; his eyes had dilated; and his face grown livid with passion; but now, he shrunk into a chair, and, cowering together, trembled with the apprehension of having himself disclosed some hidden villany. After a short silence, he ventured to look round at his companion. He appeared somewhat reassured, on beholding her in the same listless attitude from which he had first roused her.

"Nancy, dear!" croaked the Jew, in his usual voice. "Did you mind me, dear?"

"Don't worry me now, Fagin!" replied the girl, raising her head languidly. "If Bill has not done it this time, he will another. He has done many a good job for you, and will do many more when he can; and when he can't he won't; so no more about that."

"Regarding this boy, my dear?" said the Jew, rubbing the palms of his hands nervously together.

"The boy must take his chance with the rest," interrupted Nancy, hastily; "and I say again, I hope he is dead, and out of harm's way, and out of yours, – that is, if Bill comes to no harm. And if Toby got clear off, Bill's pretty sure to be safe; for Bill's worth two of Toby any time."

"And about what I was saying, my dear?" observed the Jew, keeping his glistening eye steadily upon her.

"You must say it all over again, if it's anything you want me to do," rejoined Nancy; "and if it is, you had better wait till to-morrow. You put me up for a minute; but now I'm stupid again."

Fagin put several other questions: all with the same drift of ascertaining whether the girl had profited by his unguarded hints; but, she answered them so readily, and was withal so utterly unmoved by his searching looks, that his original impression of her being more than a trifle in liquor, was confirmed. Nancy, indeed, was not exempt from a failing which was very common among the Jew's female pupils; and in which, in their tenderer years, they were rather encouraged than checked. Her disordered appearance, and a wholesale perfume of Geneva which pervaded the apartment, afforded strong confirmatory evidence of the justice of the Jew's supposition; and when, after indulging in the temporary display of violence above described, she subsided, first into dulness, and afterwards into a compound of feelings: under the influence of which she shed tears one minute, and in the next gave utterance to various exclamations of "Never say die!" and divers calculations as to what might be the amount of the odds so long as a lady or gentleman was happy, Mr Fagin, who had had considerable experience of such matters in his time, saw, with great satisfaction, that she was very far gone indeed.

Having eased his mind by this discovery; and having accomplished his twofold object of imparting to the girl what he had, that night, heard, and of ascertaining, with his own eyes, that Sikes had not returned, Mr Fagin again turned his face homeward: leaving his young friend asleep, with her head upon the table.

It was within an hour of midnight. The weather being dark, and piercing cold, he had no great temptation to loiter. The sharp wind that scoured the streets, seemed to have cleared them of passengers, as of dust and mud, for few people were abroad, and they were to all appearance hastening fast home. It blew from the right quarter for the Jew, however, and straight before it he went: trembling, and shivering, as every fresh gust drove him rudely on his way.

He had reached the corner of his own street, and was already fumbling in his pocket for the door-key, when a dark figure emerged from a projecting entrance which lay in deep shadow, and, crossing the road, glided up to him unperceived.

"Fagin!" whispered a voice close to his ear.

"Ah!" said the Jew, turning quickly round, "is that –"

"Yes!" interrupted the stranger. "I have been lingering here these two hours. Where the devil have you been?"

"On your business, my dear," replied the Jew, glancing uneasily at his companion, and slackening his pace as he spoke. "On your business all night."

"Oh, of course!" said the stranger, with a sneer. "Well; and what's come of it?"

"Nothing good," said the Jew.

"Nothing bad, I hope?" said the stranger, stopping short, and turning a startled look on his companion.

The Jew shook his head, and was about to reply, when the stranger, interrupting him, motioned to the house, before which they had by this time arrived: remarking, that he had better say what he had got to say, under cover: for his blood was chilled with standing about so long, and the wind blew through him.

Fagin looked as if he could have willingly excused himself from taking home a visitor at that unseasonable hour; and, indeed, muttered something about having no fire; but his companion repeating his request in a peremptory manner, he unlocked the door, and requested him to close it softly, while he got a light.

"It's as dark as the grave," said the man, groping forward a few steps. "Make haste!"

"Shut the door," whispered Fagin from the end of the passage. As he spoke, it closed with a loud noise.

"That wasn't my doing," said the other man, feeling his way. "The wind blew it to, or it shut of its own accord: one or the other. Look sharp with the light, or I shall knock my brains out against something in this confounded hole."

Fagin stealthily descended the kitchen stairs. After a short absence, he returned with a lighted candle, and the intelligence that Toby Crackit was asleep in the back room below, and that the boys were in the front one. Beckoning the man to follow him, he led the way up stairs.

"We can say the few words we've got to say in here, my dear," said the Jew, throwing open a door on the first floor; "and as there are holes in the shutters, and we never show lights to our neighbours, we'll set the candle on the stairs. There!"

With those words, the Jew, stooping down, placed the candle on an upper flight of stairs, exactly opposite to the room door. This done, he led the way into the apartment; which was destitute of all moveables save a broken armchair, and an old couch or sofa without covering, which stood behind the door. Upon this piece of furniture, the stranger sat himself with the air of a weary man; and the Jew, drawing up the arm-chair opposite, they sat face to face. It was not quite dark; the door was partially open; and the candle outside, threw a feeble reflection on the opposite wall.

They conversed for some time in whispers. Though nothing of the conversation was distinguishable beyond a few disjointed words here and there, a listener might easily have perceived that Fagin appeared to be defending himself against some remarks of the stranger; and that the latter was in a state of considerable irritation. They might have been talking, thus, for a quarter of an hour or more, when Monks – by which name the Jew had designated the strange man several times in the course of their colloquy – said, raising his voice a little,

"I tell you again, it was badly planned. Why not have kept him here among the rest, and made a sneaking, snivelling pickpocket of him at once?"

"Only hear him!" exclaimed the Jew, shrugging his shoulders.

"Why, do you mean to say you couldn't have done it, if you had chosen?" demanded Monks, sternly. "Haven't you done it, with other boys, scores of times? If you had had patience for a twelvemonth, at most, couldn't you have got him convicted, and sent safely out of the kingdom; perhaps for life?"

"Whose turn would that have served, my dear?" inquired the Jew humbly.

"Mine," replied Monks.

"But not mine," said the Jew, submissively. "He might have become of use to me. When there are two parties to a bargain, it is only reasonable that the interests of both should be consulted; is it, my good friend?"

"What then?" demanded Monks.

"I saw it was not easy to train him to the business," replied the Jew; "he was not like other boys in the same circumstances."

"Curse him, no!" muttered the man, "or he would have been a thief, long ago."

"I had no hold upon him to make him worse," pursued the Jew, anxiously watching the countenance of his companion. "His hand was not in. I had nothing to frighten him with; which we always must have in the beginning, or we labour in vain. What could I do? Send him out with the Dodger and Charley? We had enough of that, at first, my dear; I trembled for us all."

"*That* was not my doing," observed Monks.

"No, no, my dear!" renewed the Jew. "And I don't quarrel with it now; because, if it had never happened, you might never have clapped eyes upon the boy to notice him, and so led to the discovery that it was him you were looking for. Well! I got him back for you by means of the girl; and then *she* begins to favour him."

"Throttle the girl!" said Monks, impatiently.

"Why, we can't afford to do that just now, my dear," replied the Jew, smiling; "and, besides, that sort of thing is not in our way; or, one of these days, I might be glad to have it done. I know what these girls are, Monks, well. As soon as the boy begins to harden, she'll care no more for him, than for a block of wood. You want him made a thief. If he is alive, I can make him one from this time; and if – if –" said the Jew, drawing nearer to the other, – "it's not likely, mind, – but if the worst comes to the worst, and he is dead –"

"It's no fault of mine if he is!" interposed the other man, with a look of terror, and clasping the Jew's arm with trembling hands. "Mind that, Fagin! I had no hand in it. Anything but his death, I told you from the first. I won't shed blood; it's always found out, and haunts a man besides. If they shot him dead, I was not the cause; do you hear me? Fire this infernal den! What's that?"

"What!" cried the Jew, grasping the coward round the body, with both arms, as he sprung to his feet. "Where?"

"Yonder!" replied the man, glaring at the opposite wall. "The shadow! I saw the shadow of a woman, in a cloak and bonnet, pass along the wainscot like a breath!"

The Jew released his hold, and they rushed tumultuously from the room. The candle, wasted by the draught, was standing where it had been placed. It showed them only the empty staircase, and their own white faces. They listened intently: a profound silence reigned throughout the house.

"It's your fancy," said the Jew, taking up the light and turning to his companion.

"I'll swear I saw it!" replied Monks, trembling. "It was bending forward when I saw it first; and when I spoke, it darted away."

The Jew glanced contemptuously at the pale face of his associate, and, telling him he could follow, if he pleased, ascended the stairs. They looked into all the rooms; they were cold, bare, and empty. They descended into the passage, and thence into the cellars below. The green damp hung upon the low walls; the tracks of the snail and slug glistened in the light of the candle; but all was still as death.

"What do you think now?" said the Jew, when they had regained the passage. "Besides ourselves, there's not a creature in the house except Toby and the boys; and they're safe enough. See here!"

As a proof of the fact, the Jew drew forth two keys from his pocket; and explained, that when he first went down stairs, he had locked them in, to prevent any intrusion on the conference.

This accumulated testimony effectually staggered Mr Monks. His protestations had gradually become less and less vehement as they proceeded in their search without making any discovery; and, now, he gave vent to several very grim laughs, and confessed it could only have been his excited imagination. He declined any renewal of the conversation, however, for that night: suddenly remembering that it was past one o'clock. And so the amiable couple parted.

Chapter XXVII

Atones for the Unpoliteness of a former Chapter; which deserted a Lady, most unceremoniously

As it would be, by no means, seemly in a humble author to keep so mighty a personage as a beadle waiting, with his back to the fire, and the skirts of his coat gathered up under his arms, until such time as it might suit his pleasure to relieve him; and as it would still less become his station, or his gallantry to involve in the same neglect a lady on whom that beadle had looked with an eye of tenderness and affection, and in whose ear he had whispered sweet words, which, coming from such a quarter, might well thrill the bosom of maid or matron of whatsoever degree; the historian whose pen traces these words – trusting that he knows his place, and that he entertains a becoming reverence for those upon earth to whom high and important authority is delegated – hastens to pay them that respect which their position demands, and to treat them with all that duteous ceremony which their exalted rank, and (by consequence) great virtues, imperatively claim at his hands. Towards this end, indeed, he had purposed to introduce, in this place, a dissertation touching the divine right of beadles, and elucidative of the position, that a beadle can do no wrong: which could not fail to have been both pleasurable and profitable to the right-minded reader, but which he is unfortunately compelled, by want of time and space, to postpone to some more convenient and fitting opportunity; on the arrival of which, he will be prepared to show, that a beadle properly constituted: that is to say, a parochial beadle, attached to a parochial workhouse, and attending in his official capacity the parochial church: is, in right and virtue of his office, possessed of all the excellences and best qualities of humanity; and that to none of those excellences, can mere companies" beadles, or court-of-law beadles, or even chapel-of-ease beadles (save the last, and they in a very lowly and inferior degree), lay the remotest sustainable claim.

Mr Bumble had re-counted the tea-spoons, re-weighed the sugar-tongs, made a closer inspection of the milk-pot, and ascertained to a nicety the exact condition of the furniture, down to the very horse-hair seats of the chairs; and had repeated each process full half-a-dozen times; before he began to think that it was time for Mrs Corney to return. Thinking begets thinking; as there were no sounds of Mrs Corney's approach, it occurred to Mr Bumble that it would be an innocent and virtuous way of spending the time, if he were further to allay his curiosity by a cursory glance at the interior of Mrs Corney's chest of drawers.

Having listened at the keyhole, to assure himself that nobody was approaching the chamber, Mr Bumble, beginning at the bottom, proceeded to make himself acquainted with the contents of the three long drawers: which, being filled with various garments of good fashion and texture, carefully preserved between two layers of old newspapers, speckled with dried lavender: seemed to yield him exceeding satisfaction. Arriving, in course of time, at the right-hand corner drawer (in which was the key), and beholding therein a small padlocked box, which, being shaken, gave forth a pleasant sound, as of the chinking of coin, Mr Bumble returned with a stately walk to the fireplace; and, resuming his old attitude, said, with a grave and determined air, "I'll do it!" He followed up this remarkable declaration, by shaking his head in a waggish manner for ten minutes, as though he were remonstrating with himself for being such a pleasant dog; and then, he took a view of his legs in profile, with much seeming pleasure and interest.

He was still placidly engaged in this latter survey, when Mrs Corney, hurrying into the room, threw herself, in a breathless state, on a chair by the fireside, and covering her eyes with one hand, placed the other over her heart, and gasped for breath.

"Mrs Corney," said Mr Bumble, stooping over the matron, "what is this, ma'am? Has anything happened, ma'am? Pray answer me; I'm on – on –" Mr Bumble, in his alarm, could not immediately think of the word "tenter-hooks," so he said "broken bottles."

"Oh, Mr Bumble!" cried the lady, "I have been so dreadfully put out!"

"Put out, ma'am!" exclaimed Mr Bumble; "who has dared to – ? I know!" said Mr Bumble, checking himself, with native majesty, "this is them wicious paupers!"

"It's dreadful to think of!" said the lady, shuddering.

"Then *don't* think of it, ma'am," rejoined Mr Bumble.

"I can't help it," whimpered the lady.

"Then take something, ma'am," said Mr Bumble soothingly. "A little of the wine?"

"Not for the world!" replied Mrs Corney. "I couldn't, – oh! The top shelf in the right-hand corner – oh!" Uttering these words, the good lady pointed, distractedly, to the cupboard, and underwent a convulsion from internal spasms. Mr Bumble rushed to the closet; and, snatching a pint green-glass bottle from the shelf thus incoherently indicated, filled a tea-cup with its contents, and held it to the lady's lips.

"I'm better now," said Mrs Corney, falling back, after drinking half of it.

Mr Bumble raised his eyes piously to the ceiling in thankfulness; and, bringing them down again to the brim of the cup, lifted it to his nose.

"Peppermint," exclaimed Mrs Corney, in a faint voice, smiling gently on the beadle as she spoke. "Try it! There's a little – a little something else in it."

Mr Bumble tasted the medicine with a doubtful look; smacked his lips; took another taste; and put the cup down empty.

"It's very comforting," said Mrs Corney.

"Very much so indeed, ma'am," said the beadle. As he spoke, he drew a chair beside the matron, and tenderly inquired what had happened to distress her.

"Nothing," replied Mrs Corney. "I am a foolish, excitable, weak creetur."

"Not weak, ma'am," retorted Mr Bumble, drawing his chair a little closer. "Are you a weak creetur, Mrs Corney?"

"We are all weak creeturs," said Mrs Corney, laying down a general principle.

"So we are," said the beadle.

Nothing was said, on either side, for a minute or two afterwards. By the expiration of that time, Mr Bumble had illustrated the position by removing his left arm from the back of Mrs Corney's chair, where it had previously rested, to Mrs Corney's apron-string, round which it gradually became entwined.

"We are all weak creeturs," said Mr Bumble.

Mrs Corney sighed.

"Don't sigh, Mrs Corney," said Mr Bumble.

"I can't help it," said Mrs Corney. And she sighed again.

"This is a very comfortable room, ma'am," said Mr Bumble, looking round. "Another room, and this, ma'am, would be a complete thing."

"It would be too much for one," murmured the lady.

"But not for two, ma'am," rejoined Mr Bumble, in soft accents. "Eh, Mrs Corney?"

Mrs Corney drooped her head, when the beadle said this; the beadle drooped his, to get a view of Mrs Corney's face. Mrs Corney, with great propriety, turned her head away, and released her hand to get at her pocket-handkerchief; but insensibly replaced it in that of Mr Bumble.

"The board allow you coals, don't they, Mrs Corney?" inquired the beadle, affectionately pressing her hand.

"And candles," replied Mrs Corney, slightly returning the pressure.

"Coals, candles, and house-rent free," said Mr Bumble. "Oh, Mrs Corney, what a Angel you are!"

The lady was not proof against this burst of feeling. She sank into Mr Bumble's arms; and that gentleman in his agitation, imprinted a passionate kiss upon her chaste nose.

"Such porochial perfection!" exclaimed Mr Bumble, rapturously. "You know that Mr Slout is worse to-night, my fascinator?"

"Yes," replied Mrs Corney, bashfully.

"He can't live a week, the doctor says," pursued Mr Bumble. "He is the master of this establishment; his death will cause a wacancy: that wacancy must be filled up. Oh, Mrs Corney, what a prospect this opens! What a opportunity for a jining of hearts and housekeepings!"

Mrs Corney sobbed.

"The little word?" said Mr Bumble, bending over the bashful beauty. "The one little, little, little word, my blessed Corney?"

"Ye – ye – yes!" sighed out the matron.

"One more," pursued the beadle; "compose your darling feelings for only one more. When is it to come off?"

Mrs Corney twice essayed to speak: and twice failed. At length summoning up courage, she threw her arms round Mr Bumble's neck, and said, it might be as soon as ever he pleased, and that he was "a irresistible duck."

Matters being thus amicably and satisfactorily arranged, the contract was solemnly ratified in another teacupful of the peppermint mixture; which was rendered the more necessary, by the flutter and agitation of the lady's spirits. While it was being disposed of, she acquainted Mr Bumble with the old woman's decease.

"Very good," said that gentleman, sipping his peppermint; "I'll call at Sowerberry's as I go home, and tell him to send to-morrow morning. Was it that as frightened you, love?"

"It wasn't anything particular, dear," said the lady, evasively.

"It must have been something, love," urged Mr Bumble. "Won't you tell your own B.?"

"Not now," rejoined the lady; "one of these days. After we're married, dear."

"After we're married!" exclaimed Mr Bumble. "It wasn't any impudence from any of them male paupers as –"

"No, no, love!" interposed the lady, hastily.

"If I thought it was," continued Mr Bumble; "if I thought as any one of 'em had dared to lift his wulgar eyes to that lovely countenance –"

"They wouldn't have dared to do it, love," responded the lady.

"They had better not!" said Mr Bumble, clenching his fist. "Let me see any man, porochial or extra-porochial, as would presume to do it; and I can tell him that he wouldn't do it a second time!"

Unembellished by any violence of gesticulation, this might have seemed no very high compliment to the lady's charms; but, as Mr Bumble accompanied the threat with many warlike gestures, she was much touched with this proof of his devotion, and protested, with great admiration, that he was indeed a dove.

The dove then turned up his coat-collar, and put on his cocked-hat; and, having exchanged a long and affectionate embrace with his future partner, once again braved the cold wind of the night: merely pausing, for a few minutes, in the male paupers" ward, to abuse them a little, with the view of satisfying himself that he could fill the office of workhouse-master with needful acerbity. Assured of his qualifications, Mr Bumble left the building with a light heart, and bright visions of his future promotion: which served to occupy his mind until he reached the shop of the undertaker.

Now, Mr and Mrs Sowerberry having gone out to tea and supper: and Noah Claypole not being at any time disposed to take upon himself a greater amount of physical exertion than is necessary to a convenient performance of the two functions of eating and drinking, the shop was not closed, although it was past the usual hour of shutting-up. Mr Bumble tapped with his cane on the counter several times: but, attracting no attention, and beholding a light shining through the glass-window of the little parlour at the back of the shop, he made bold to peep in and see what was going forward; and when he saw what *was* going forward, he was not a little surprised.

The cloth was laid for supper; the table was covered with bread and butter, plates and glasses; a porter-pot and a wine-bottle. At the upper end of the table, Mr Noah Claypole lolled negligently in an easy-chair, with his legs thrown over one of the arms: an open clasp-knife in one hand, and a mass of buttered bread in the other. Close beside him stood Charlotte, opening oysters from a barrel: which Mr Claypole condescended to swallow, with remarkable avidity. A more than ordinary redness in the region of the young gentleman's nose, and a kind of fixed wink in his right eye, denoted that he was in a slight degree intoxicated; these symptoms were confirmed by the intense relish with which he took his oysters, for which nothing but a strong appreciation of their cooling properties, in cases of internal fever, could have sufficiently accounted.

"Here's a delicious fat one, Noah, dear!" said Charlotte; "try him, do; only this one."

"What a delicious thing is a oyster!" remarked Mr Claypole, after he had swallowed it. "What a pity it is, a number of 'em should ever make you feel uncomfortable; isn't it, Charlotte?"

"It's quite a cruelty," said Charlotte.

"So it is," acquiesced Mr Claypole. "A'nt yer fond of oysters?"

"Not overmuch," replied Charlotte. "I like to see you eat 'em, Noah dear, better than eating 'em myself."

"Lor"!" said Noah, reflectively; "how queer!"

"Have another," said Charlotte. "Here's one with such a beautiful, delicate beard!"

"I can't manage any more," said Noah. "I'm very sorry. Come here, Charlotte, and I'll kiss yer."

"What!" said Mr Bumble, bursting into the room. "Say that again, sir."

Charlotte uttered a scream, and hid her face in her apron. Mr Claypole, without making any further change in his position than suffering his legs to reach the ground, gazed at the beadle in drunken terror.

"Say it again, you wile, owdacious fellow!" said Mr Bumble. "How dare you mention such a thing, sir? And how dare you encourage him, you insolent minx? Kiss her!" exclaimed Mr Bumble, in strong indignation. "Faugh!"

"I didn't mean to do it!" said Noah, blubbering. "She's always a-kissing of me, whether I like it, or not."

"Oh, Noah," cried Charlotte, reproachfully.

"Yer are; yer know yer are!" retorted Noah. "She's always a-doin of it. Mr Bumble, sir; she chucks me under the chin, please, sir; and makes all manner of love!"

"Silence!" cried Mr Bumble, sternly. "Take yourself down stairs, ma'am. Noah, you shut up the shop; say another word till your master comes home, at your peril; and, when he does come home, tell him that Mr Bumble said he was to send a old woman's shell after breakfast tomorrow morning. Do you hear, sir? Kissing!" cried Mr Bumble, holding up his hands. "The sin and wickedness of the lower orders in this porochial district is frightful! If parliament don't take their abominable courses under consideration, this country's ruined, and the character of the peasantry gone for ever!" With these words, the beadle strode, with a lofty and gloomy air, from the undertaker's premises.

And now that we have accompanied him so far on his road home, and have made all necessary preparations for the old woman's funeral, let us set on foot a few inquiries after young Oliver Twist, and ascertain whether he be still lying in the ditch where Toby Crackit left him.

Chapter XXVIII

Looks after Oliver, and proceeds with his Adventures

"Wolves tear your throats!" muttered Sikes, grinding his teeth. "I wish I was among some of you; you'd howl the hoarser for it."

As Sikes growled forth this imprecation, with the most desperate ferocity that his desperate nature was capable of, he rested the body of the wounded boy across his bended knee; and turned his head, for an instant, to look back at his pursuers.

There was little to be made out, in the mist and darkness; but the loud shouting of men vibrated through the air, and the barking of the neighbouring dogs, roused by the sound of the alarm bell, resounded in every direction.

"Stop, you white-livered hound!" cried the robber, shouting after Toby Crackit, who, making the best use of his long legs, was already ahead. "Stop!"

The repetition of the word, brought Toby to a dead stand-still. For he was not quite satisfied that he was beyond the range of pistol-shot; and Sikes was in no mood to be played with.

"Bear a hand with the boy," cried Sikes, beckoning furiously to his confederate. "Come back!"

Toby made a show of returning; but ventured, in a low voice, broken for want of breath, to intimate considerable reluctance as he came slowly along.

"Quicker!" cried Sikes, laying the boy in a dry ditch at his feet, and drawing a pistol from his pocket. "Don't play booty with me."

At this moment the noise grew louder. Sikes, again looking round, could discern that the men who had given chase were already climbing the gate of the field in which he stood; and that a couple of dogs were some paces in advance of them.

"It's all up, Bill!" cried Toby; "drop the kid, and show 'em your heels." With this parting advice, Mr Crackit, preferring the chance of being shot by his friend, to the certainty of being taken by his enemies, fairly turned tail, and darted off at full speed. Sikes clenched his teeth; took one look around; threw over the prostrate form of Oliver, the cape in which he had been hurriedly muffled; ran along the front of the hedge, as if to distract the attention of those behind, from the spot where the boy lay; paused, for a second, before another hedge which met it at right angles; and whirling his pistol high into the air, cleared it at a bound, and was gone.

"Ho, ho, there!" cried a tremulous voice in the rear; "Pincher! Neptune! Come here, come here!"

The dogs, who, in common with their masters, seemed to have no particular relish for the sport in which they were engaged, readily answered to the command. Three men, who had by this time advanced some distance into the field, stopped to take counsel together.

"My advice, or, leastways, I should say, my *orders*, is," said the fattest man of the party, "that we 'mediately go home again."

"I am agreeable to anything which is agreeable to Mr Giles," said a shorter man; who was by no means of a slim figure, and who was very pale in the face, and very polite: as frightened men frequently are.

"I shouldn't wish to appear ill-mannered, gentlemen," said the third, who had called the dogs back, "Mr Giles ought to know."

"Certainly," replied the shorter man; "and whatever Mr Giles says, it isn't our place to contradict him. No, no, I know my sitiwation! Thank my stars, I know my sitiwation." To tell the truth, the little man *did* seem to know his situation, and to know perfectly well that it was by no means a desirable one; for his teeth chattered in his head as he spoke.

"You are afraid, Brittles," said Mr Giles.

"I a'n't," said Brittles.

"You are," said Giles.

"You're a falsehood, Mr Giles," said Brittles.

"You're a lie, Brittles," said Mr Giles.

Now, these four retorts arose from Mr Giles's taunt; and Mr Giles's taunt had arisen from his indignation at having the responsibility of going home again, imposed upon himself under cover of a compliment. The third man brought the dispute to a close, most philosophically.

"I'll tell you what it is, gentlemen," said he, "we're all afraid."

"Speak for yourself, sir," said Mr Giles, who was the palest of the party.

"So I do," replied the man. "It's natural and proper to be afraid, under such circumstances. *I* am."

"So am I," said Brittles; "only there's no call to tell a man he is, so bounceably."

These frank admissions softened Mr Giles, who at once owned that *he* was afraid; upon which, they all three faced about, and ran back again with the completest unanimity, until Mr Giles (who had the shortest wind of the party, and was encumbered with a pitchfork) most handsomely insisted on stopping, to make an apology for his hastiness of speech.

"But it's wonderful," said Mr Giles, when he had explained, "what a man will do, when his blood is up. I should have committed murder – I know *I* should – if we'd caught one of them rascals."

As the other two were impressed with a similar presentiment; and as their blood, like his, had all gone down again; some speculation ensued upon the cause of this sudden change in their temperament.

"I know what it was," said Mr Giles; "it was the gate."

"I shouldn't wonder if it was," exclaimed Brittles, catching at the idea.

"You may depend upon it," said Giles, "that that gate stopped the flow of the excitement. I felt all mine suddenly going away, as I was climbing over it."

By a remarkable coincidence, the other two had been visited with the same unpleasant sensation at that precise moment. It was quite obvious, therefore, that it was the gate; especially as there was no doubt regarding the time at which the change had taken place, because all three remembered that they had come in sight of the robbers at the instant of its occurrence.

This dialogue was held between the two men who had surprised the burglars, and a travelling tinker who had been sleeping in an outhouse, and who had been roused, together with his two mongrel curs, to join in the pursuit. Mr Giles acted in the double capacity of butler and steward to the old lady of the mansion; Brittles was a lad of all-work: who, having entered her service a mere child, was treated as a promising young boy still, though he was something past thirty.

Encouraging each other with such converse as this; but, keeping very close together, notwithstanding, and looking apprehensively round, whenever a fresh gust rattled through the boughs; the three men hurried back to a tree, behind which they had left their lantern, lest its light should inform the thieves in what direction to fire. Catching up the light, they made the best of their way home, at a good round trot; and long after their dusky forms had ceased to be discernible, the light might have been seen twinkling and dancing in the distance, like some exhalation of the damp and gloomy atmosphere through which it was swiftly borne.

The air grew colder, as day came slowly on; and the mist rolled along the ground like a dense cloud of smoke. The grass was wet; the pathways, and low places, were all mire and water; the damp breath of an unwholesome wind went languidly by, with a hollow moaning. Still, Oliver lay motionless and insensible on the spot where Sikes had left him.

Morning drew on apace. The air became more sharp and piercing, as its first dull hue – the death of night, rather than the birth of day – glimmered faintly in the sky. The objects which had looked dim and terrible in the darkness, grew more and more defined, and gradually resolved into their familiar shapes. The rain came down, thick and fast, and pattered noisily among the leafless bushes. But, Oliver felt it not, as it beat against him; for he still lay stretched, helpless and unconscious, on his bed of clay.

At length, a low cry of pain broke the stillness that prevailed; and uttering it, the boy awoke. His left arm, rudely bandaged in a shawl, hung heavy and useless at his side: the bandage was saturated with blood. He was so weak, that he could scarcely raise himself into a sitting posture; when he had done so, he looked feebly round for help, and groaned with pain. Trembling in every joint, from cold and exhaustion, he made an effort to stand upright; but, shuddering from head to foot, fell prostrate on the ground.

After a short return of the stupor in which he had been so long plunged, Oliver: urged by a creeping sickness at his heart, which seemed to warn him that if he lay there, he must surely die: got upon his feet, and essayed to walk. His head was dizzy, and he staggered to and fro like a drunken man. But he kept up, nevertheless, and, with his head drooping languidly on his breast, went stumbling onward, he knew not whither.

And now, hosts of bewildering and confused ideas came crowding on his mind. He seemed to be still walking between Sikes and Crackit, who were angrily disputing – for the very words they said, sounded in his ears; and when he caught his own attention, as it were, by making some violent effort to save himself from falling, he found that he was talking to them. Then, he was alone with Sikes, plodding on as on the previous day; and as shadowy people passed them, he felt the robber's grasp upon his wrist. Suddenly, he started back at the report of fire-arms; there rose into the air, loud cries and shouts; lights gleamed before his eyes; all was noise and tumult, as some unseen hand bore him hurriedly away. Through all these rapid visions, there ran an undefined, uneasy consciousness of pain, which wearied and tormented him incessantly.

Thus he staggered on, creeping, almost mechanically, between the bars of gates, or through hedge-gaps as they came in his way, until he reached a road. Here the rain began to fall so heavily, that it roused him.

He looked about, and saw that at no great distance there was a house, which perhaps he could reach. Pitying his condition, they might have compassion on him; and if they did not, it would be better, he thought, to die near human beings, than in the lonely open fields. He summoned up all his strength for one last trial, and bent his faltering steps towards it.

As he drew nearer to this house, a feeling came over him that he had seen it before. He remembered nothing of its details; but the shape and aspect of the building seemed familiar to him.

That garden wall! On the grass inside, he had fallen on his knees last night, and prayed the two men's mercy. It was the very house they had attempted to rob.

Oliver felt such fear come over him when he recognised the place, that, for the instant, he forgot the agony of his wound, and thought only of flight. Flight! He could scarcely stand: and if he were in full possession of all the best powers of his slight and youthful frame, whither could he fly? He pushed against the garden-gate; it was unlocked, and swung open on its hinges. He tottered across the lawn; climbed the steps; knocked faintly at the door; and, his whole strength failing him, sunk down against one of the pillars of the little portico.

It happened that about this time, Mr Giles, Brittles, and the tinker, were recruiting themselves, after the fatigues and terrors of the night, with tea and sundries, in the kitchen. Not that it was Mr Giles's habit to admit to too great familiarity the humbler servants: towards whom it was rather his wont to deport himself with a lofty affability, which, while it gratified, could not fail to remind them of his superior position in society. But, death, fires, and burglary, make all men equals; so Mr Giles sat with his legs stretched out before the kitchen fender, leaning his left arm on the table, while, with his right, he illustrated a circumstantial and minute account of the robbery, to which his hearers (but especially the cook and housemaid, who were of the party) listened with breathless interest.

"It was about half-past two," said Mr Giles, "or I wouldn't swear that it mightn't have been a little nearer three, when I woke up, and, turning round in my bed, as it might be so," (here Mr Giles turned round in his chair, and pulled the corner of the table-cloth over him to imitate bed-clothes,) "I fancied I heerd a noise."

At this point of the narrative the cook turned pale, and asked the housemaid to shut the door: who asked Brittles, who asked the tinker, who pretended not to hear.

"– Heerd a noise," continued Mr Giles. "I says, at first, "This is illusion;" and was composing myself off to sleep, when I heerd the noise again, distinct."

"What sort of a noise?" asked the cook.

"A kind of a busting noise," replied Mr Giles, looking round him.

"More like the noise of powdering a iron bar on a nutmeg-grater," suggested Brittles.

"It was, when *you* heerd it, sir," rejoined Mr Giles; "but, at this time, it had a busting sound. I turned down the clothes;" continued Giles, rolling back the table-cloth, "sat up in bed; and listened."

The cook and housemaid simultaneously ejaculated "Lor!" and drew their chairs closer together.

"I heerd it now, quite apparent," resumed Mr Giles. ""Somebody," I says, "is forcing of a door, or window; what's to be done? I'll call up that poor lad, Brittles, and save him from being murdered in his bed; or his throat," I says, "may be cut from his right ear to his left, without his ever knowing it.""

Here, all eyes were turned upon Brittles, who fixed his upon the speaker, and stared at him, with his mouth wide open, and his face expressive of the most unmitigated horror.

"I tossed off the clothes," said Giles, throwing away the table-cloth, and looking very hard at the cook and housemaid, "got softly out of bed; drew on a pair of –"

"Ladies present, Mr Giles," murmured the tinker.

"– Of *shoes*, sir," said Giles, turning upon him, and laying great emphasis on the word; "seized the loaded pistol that always goes up stairs with the plate-basket; and walked on tiptoes to his room. "Brittles," I says, when I had woke him, "don't be frightened!""

"So you did," observed Brittles, in a low voice.

""We're dead men, I think, Brittles," I says," continued Giles; ""but don't be frightened.""

"*Was* he frightened?" asked the cook.

"Not a bit of it," replied Mr Giles. "He was as firm – ah! pretty near as firm as I was."

"I should have died at once, I'm sure, if it had been me," observed the housemaid.

"You're a woman," retorted Brittles, plucking up a little.

"Brittles is right," said Mr Giles, nodding his head, approvingly; "from a woman, nothing else was to be expected. We, being men, took a dark lantern that was standing on Brittles's hob, and groped our way down stairs in the pitch dark, – as it might be so."

Mr Giles had risen from his seat, and taken two steps with his eyes shut, to accompany his description with appropriate action, when he started violently, in common with the rest of the company, and hurried back to his chair. The cook and housemaid screamed.

"It was a knock," said Mr Giles, assuming perfect serenity. "Open the door, somebody."

Nobody moved.

"It seems a strange sort of a thing, a knock coming at such a time in the morning," said Mr Giles, surveying the pale faces which surrounded him, and looking very blank himself; "but the door must be opened. Do you hear, somebody?"

Mr Giles, as he spoke, looked at Brittles; but that young man, being naturally modest, probably considered himself nobody, and so held that the inquiry could not have any application to him; at all events, he tendered no reply. Mr Giles directed an appealing glance at the tinker; but he had suddenly fallen asleep. The women were out of the question.

"If Brittles would rather open the door, in the presence of witnesses," said Mr Giles, after a short silence, "I am ready to make one."

"So am I," said the tinker, waking up, as suddenly as he had fallen asleep.

Brittles capitulated on these terms; and the party being somewhat re-assured by the discovery (made on throwing open the shutters) that it was now broad day, took their way up stairs; with the dogs in front. The two women, who were afraid to stay below, brought up the rear. By the advice of Mr Giles, they all talked very loud, to warn any evil-disposed person outside, that they were strong in numbers; and by a master-stroke of policy, originating in the brain of the same ingenious gentleman, the dogs" tails were well pinched, in the hall, to make them bark savagely.

These precautions having been taken, Mr Giles held on fast by the tinker's arm (to prevent his running away, as he pleasantly said), and gave the word of command to open the door. Brittles obeyed; the group, peeping timorously over each other's shoulders, beheld no more formidable object than poor little Oliver Twist, speechless and exhausted, who raised his heavy eyes, and mutely solicited their compassion.

"A boy!" exclaimed Mr Giles, valiantly pushing the tinker into the background. "What's the matter with the – eh? – Why – Brittles – look here – don't you know?"

Brittles, who had got behind the door to open it, no sooner saw Oliver, than he uttered a loud cry. Mr Giles, seizing the boy by one leg and one arm (fortunately not the broken limb) lugged him straight into the hall, and deposited him at full length on the floor thereof.

"Here he is!" bawled Giles, calling, in a state of great excitement, up the staircase; "here's one of the thieves, ma'am! Here's a thief, miss! Wounded, miss! I shot him, miss; and Brittles held the light."

"– In a lantern, miss," cried Brittles, applying one hand to the side of his mouth, so that his voice might travel the better.

The two women-servants ran up stairs to carry the intelligence that Mr Giles had captured a robber; and the tinker busied himself in endeavouring to restore Oliver, lest he should die before he could be hanged. In the midst of all this noise and commotion, there was heard a sweet female voice, which quelled it in an instant.

"Giles!" whispered the voice from the stair-head.

"I'm here, miss," replied Mr Giles. "Don't be frightened, miss; I ain't much injured. He didn't make a very desperate resistance, miss! I was soon too many for him."

"Hush!" replied the young lady; "you frighten my aunt as much as the thieves did. Is the poor creature much hurt?"

"Wounded desperate, miss," replied Giles, with indescribable complacency.

"He looks as if he was a-going, miss," bawled Brittles, in the same manner as before. "Wouldn't you like to come and look at him, miss, in case he should!"

"Hush, pray; there's a good man!" rejoined the lady. "Wait quietly only one instant, while I speak to aunt."

With a footstep as soft and gentle as the voice, the speaker tripped away. She soon returned, with the direction that the wounded person was to be carried, carefully, up stairs to Mr Giles's room; and that Brittles was to saddle the pony and betake himself instantly to Chertsey: from which place, he was to despatch, with all speed, a constable and doctor.

"But won't you take one look at him, first, miss?" asked Mr Giles, with as much pride as if Oliver were some bird of rare plumage, that he had skilfully brought down. "Not one little peep, miss?"

"Not now, for the world," replied the young lady. "Poor fellow! Oh! treat him kindly, Giles, for my sake!"

The old servant looked up at the speaker, as she turned away, with a glance as proud and admiring as if she had been his own child. Then, bending over Oliver, he helped to carry him up stairs, with the care and solicitude of a woman.

Chapter XXIX

Has an introductory Account of the Inmates of the House, to which Oliver resorted

In a handsome room: though its furniture had rather the air of old-fashioned comfort, than of modern elegance: there sat two ladies at a well-spread breakfast-table. Mr Giles, dressed with scrupulous care in a full suit of black, was in attendance upon them. He had taken his station some halfway between the sideboard and the breakfast-table; and, with his body drawn up to its full height, his head thrown back, and inclined the merest trifle on one side, his left leg advanced, and his right hand thrust into his waistcoat, while his left hung down by his side, grasping a waiter, looked like one who laboured under a very agreeable sense of his own merits and importance.

Of the two ladies, one was well advanced in years; but the high-backed oaken chair in which she sat, was not more upright than she. Dressed with the utmost nicety and precision, in a quaint mixture of by-gone costume, with some slight concessions to the prevailing taste, which rather served to point the old style pleasantly than to impair its effect, she sat, in a stately manner, with her hands folded on the table before her. Her eyes (and age had dimmed but little of their brightness) were attentively fixed upon her young companion.

The younger lady was in the lovely bloom and spring-time of womanhood; at the age, when, if ever angels be for God's good purposes enthroned in mortal forms, they may be, without impiety, supposed to abide in such as hers.

She was not past seventeen. Cast in so slight and exquisite a mould; so mild and gentle; so pure and beautiful; that earth seemed not her element, nor its rough creatures her fit companions. The very intelligence that shone in her deep blue eye, and was stamped upon her noble head, seemed scarcely of her age, or of the world; and yet the changing expression of sweetness and good humour, the thousand lights that played about the face, and left no shadow there; above all, the smile, the cheerful, happy smile, were made for Home, and fireside peace and happiness.

She was busily engaged in the little offices of the table. Chancing to raise her eyes as the elder lady was regarding her, she playfully put back her hair, which was simply braided on her forehead; and threw into her beaming look, such an expression of affection and artless loveliness, that blessed spirits might have smiled to look upon her.

"And Brittles has been gone upwards of an hour, has he?" asked the old lady, after a pause.

"An hour and twelve minutes, ma'am," replied Mr Giles, referring to a silver watch, which he drew forth by a black ribbon.

"He is always slow," remarked the old lady.

"Brittles always was a slow boy, ma'am," replied the attendant. And seeing, by-the-by, that Brittles had been a slow boy for upwards of thirty years, there appeared no great probability of his ever being a fast one.

"He gets worse instead of better, I think," said the elder lady.

"It is very inexcusable in him if he stops to play with any other boys," said the young lady, smiling.

Mr Giles was apparently considering the propriety of indulging in a respectful smile himself, when a gig drove up to the garden gate: out of which there jumped a fat gentleman, who ran straight up to the door: and who, getting quickly into the house by some mysterious process, burst into the room, and nearly overtuned Mr Giles and the breakfast-table together.

"I never heard of such a thing!" exclaimed the fat gentleman. "My dear Mrs Maylie – bless my soul – in the silence of night, too – I *never* heard of such a thing!"

With these expressions of condolence, the fat gentleman shook hands with both ladies, and drawing up a chair, inquired how they found themselves.

"You ought to be dead; positively dead with the fright," said the fat gentleman. "Why didn't you send? Bless me, my man should have come in a minute; and so would I; and my assistant would have been delighted; or anybody, I'm sure, under such circumstances. Dear, dear! So unexpected! In the silence of night, too!"

The doctor seemed especially troubled by the fact of the robbery having been unexpected, and attempted in the night-time; as if it were the established custom of gentlemen in the housebreaking way to transact business at noon, and to make an appointment, by post a day or two previous.

"And you, Miss Rose," said the doctor, turning to the young lady, "I –"

"Oh! very much so, indeed," said Rose, interrupting him; "but there is a poor creature up stairs, whom aunt wishes you to see."

"Ah! to be sure," replied the doctor, "so there is. That was your handiwork, Giles, I understand."

Mr Giles, who had been feverishly putting the tea-cups to rights, blushed very red, and said that he had that honour.

"Honour, eh?" said the doctor; "well, I don't know; perhaps it's as honourable to hit a thief in a back kitchen, as to hit your man at twelve paces. Fancy that he fired in the air, and you've fought a duel, Giles."

Mr Giles, who thought this light treatment of the matter an unjust attempt at diminishing his glory, answered respectfully, that it was not for the like of him to judge about that; but he rather thought it was no joke to the opposite party.

"Gad that's true!" said the doctor. "Where is he? Show me the way. I'll look in again, as I come down, Mrs Maylie. That's the little window that he got in at, eh? Well, I couldn't have believed it!"

Talking all the way, he followed Mr Giles up stairs; and while he is going up stairs, the reader may be informed, that Mr Losberne, a surgeon in the neighbourhood, known through a circuit of ten miles round as "the doctor," had grown fat, more from good-humour than from good living: and was as kind and hearty, and withal as eccentric an old bachelor, as will be found in five times that space, by any explorer alive.

The doctor was absent, much longer than either he or the ladies anticipated. A large flat box was fetched out of the gig; and a bed-room bell was rung very often; and the servants ran up and down stairs perpetually; from which tokens it was justly concluded that something important was going on above. At length he returned; and in reply to an anxious inquiry after his patient, looked very mysterious, and closed the door, carefully.

"This is a very extraordinary thing, Mrs Maylie," said the doctor, standing with his back to the door, as if to keep it shut.

"He is not in danger, I hope?" said the old lady.

"Why, that would *not* be an extraordinary thing, under the circumstances," replied the doctor; "though I don't think he is. Have you seen this thief?"

"No," rejoined the old lady.

"Nor heard anything about him?"

"No."

"I beg your pardon, ma'am," interposed Mr Giles; "but I was going to tell you about him when Doctor Losberne came in."

The fact was, that Mr Giles had not, at first, been able to bring his mind to the avowal, that he had only shot a boy. Such commendations had been bestowed upon his bravery, that he could not, for the life of him, help postponing the explanation for a few delicious minutes; during which he had flourished, in the very zenith of a brief reputation of undaunted courage.

"Rose wished to see the man," said Mrs Maylie, "but I wouldn't hear of it."

"Humph!" rejoined the doctor. "There is nothing very alarming in his appearance. Have you any objection to see him in my presence?"

"If it be necessary," replied the old lady, "certainly not."

"Then I think it is necessary," said the doctor; "at all events, I am quite sure that you would deeply regret not having done so, if you postponed it. He is perfectly quiet and comfortable now. Allow me – Miss Rose, will you permit me? Not the slightest fear, I pledge you my honour!"

Chapter XXX

Relates what Oliver's new Visitors thought of him

WITH many loquacious assurances that they would be agreeably surprised in the aspect of the criminal, the doctor drew the young lady's arm through one of his; and offering his disengaged hand to Mrs Maylie, led them, with much ceremony and stateliness, up stairs.

"Now," said the doctor, in a whisper, as he softly turned the handle of a bedroom-door, "let us hear what you think of him. He has not been shaved very recently, but he don't look at all ferocious notwithstanding. Stop, though! Let me first see that he is in visiting order."

Stepping before them, he looked into the room. Motioning them to advance, he closed the door when they had entered; and gently drew back the curtains of the bed. Upon it, in lieu of the dogged, black-visaged ruffian they had expected to behold, there lay a mere child: worn with pain and exhaustion, and sunk into a deep sleep. His wounded arm, bound and splintered up, was crossed upon his breast; his head reclined upon the other arm, which was half hidden by his long hair, as it streamed over the pillow.

The honest gentleman held the curtain in his hand, and looked on for a minute or so, in silence. Whilst he was watching the patient thus, the younger lady glided softly past, and seating herself in a chair by the bedside, gathered Oliver's hair from his face. As she stooped over him, her tears fell upon his forehead.

The boy stirred, and smiled in his sleep, as though these marks of pity and compassion had awakened some pleasant dream of a love and affection he had never known. Thus, a strain of gentle music, or the rippling of water in a silent place, or the odour of a flower, or the mention of a familiar word, will sometimes call up sudden dim remembrances of scenes that never were, in this life; which vanish like a breath; which some brief memory of a happier existence, long gone by, would seem to have awakened; which no voluntary exertion of the mind can ever recall.

"What can this mean?" exclaimed the elder lady. "This poor child can never have been the pupil of robbers!"

"Vice," sighed the surgeon, replacing the curtain, "takes up her abode in many temples; and who can say that a fair outside shall not enshrine her?"

"But at so early an age!" urged Rose.

"My dear young lady," rejoined the surgeon, mournfully shaking his head; "crime, like death, is not confined to the old and withered alone. The youngest and fairest are too often its chosen victims."

"But, can you – oh! can you really believe that this delicate boy has been the voluntary associate of the worst outcasts of society?" said Rose.

The surgeon shook his head, in a manner which intimated that he feared it was very possible; and observing that they might disturb the patient, led the way into an adjoining apartment.

"But even if he has been wicked," pursued Rose, "think how young he is; think that he may never have known a mother's love, or the comfort of a home; that ill-usage and blows, or the want of bread, may have driven him to herd with men who have forced him to guilt. Aunt, dear aunt, for mercy's sake, think of this, before you let them drag this sick child to a prison, which in any case must be the grave of all his chances of amendment. Oh! as you love me, and know that I have never felt the want of parents in your goodness and affection, but that I might have done so, and might have been equally helpless and unprotected with this poor child, have pity upon him before it is too late!"

"My dear love," said the elder lady, as she folded the weeping girl to her bosom, "do you think I would harm a hair of his head?"

"Oh, no!" replied Rose, eagerly.

"No, surely," said the old lady; "my days are drawing to their close; and may mercy be shown to me as I show it to others! What can I do to save him, sir?"

"Let me think, ma'am," said the doctor; "let me think."

Mr Losberne thrust his hands into his pockets, and took several turns up and down the room; often stopping, and balancing himself on his toes, and frowning frightfully. After various exclamations of "I've got it now" and "no, I haven't," and as many renewals of the walking and frowning, he at length made a dead halt, and spoke as follows:

"I think if you give me a full and unlimited commission to bully Giles, and that little boy, Brittles, I can manage it. Giles is a faithful fellow and an old servant, I know; but you can make it up to him in a thousand ways, and reward him for being such a good shot besides. You don't object to that?"

"Unless there is some other way of preserving the child," replied Mrs Maylie.

"There is no other," said the doctor. "No other, take my word for it."

"Then my aunt invests you with full power," said Rose, smiling through her tears; "but pray don't be harder upon the poor fellows than is indispensably necessary."

"You seem to think," retorted the doctor, "that everybody is disposed to be hard-hearted to-day, except yourself, Miss Rose. I only hope, for the sake of the rising male sex generally, that you may be found in as vulnerable and soft-hearted a mood by the first eligible young fellow who appeals to your compassion; and I wish I were a young fellow, that I might avail myself, on the spot, of such a favourable opportunity for doing so, as the present."

"You are as great a boy as poor Brittles himself," returned Rose, blushing.

"Well," said the doctor, laughing heartily, "that is no very difficult matter. But to return to this boy. The great point of our agreement is yet to come. He will wake in an hour or so, I dare say; and although I have told that thick-headed constable-fellow down stairs that he mustn't be moved or spoken to, on peril of his life, I think we may converse with him without danger. Now I make this stipulation – that I shall examine him in your presence, and that, if, from what he says, we judge, and I can show to the satisfaction of your cool reason, that he is a real and thorough bad one (which is more than possible), he shall be left to his fate, without any farther interference on my part, at all events."

"Oh no, aunt!" entreated Rose.

"Oh yes, aunt!" said the doctor. "Is it a bargain?"

"He cannot be hardened in vice," said Rose; "It is impossible."

"Very good," retorted the doctor; "then so much the more reason for acceding to my proposition."

Finally the treaty was entered into; and the parties there-unto sat down to wait, with some impatience, until Oliver should awake.

The patience of the two ladies was destined to undergo a longer trial than Mr Losberne had led them to expect; for hour after hour passed on, and still Oliver slumbered heavily. It was evening, indeed, before the kind-hearted doctor brought them the intelligence, that he was at length sufficiently restored to be spoken to. The boy was very ill, he said, and weak from the loss of blood; but his mind was so troubled with anxiety to disclose something, that he deemed it better to give him the opportunity, than to insist upon his remaining quiet until next morning: which he should otherwise have done.

The conference was a long one. Oliver told them all his simple history, and was often compelled to stop, by pain and want of strength. It was a solemn thing, to hear, in the darkened room, the feeble voice of the sick child recounting a weary catalogue of evils and calamities which hard men had brought upon him. Oh! if when we oppress and grind our fellow-creatures, we bestowed but one thought on the dark evidences of human error, which, like dense and heavy clouds, are rising, slowly it is true, but not less surely, to Heaven, to pour their after-vengeance on our heads; if we heard but one instant, in imagination, the deep testimony of dead men's voices, which no power can stifle, and no pride shut out; where would be the injury and injustice, the suffering, misery, cruelty, and wrong, that each day's life brings with it!

Oliver's pillow was smoothed by gentle hands that night; and loveliness and virtue watched him as he slept. He felt calm and happy, and could have died without a murmur.

The momentous interview was no sooner concluded, and Oliver composed to rest again, than the doctor, after wiping his eyes, and condemning them for being weak all at once, betook himself down stairs to open upon Mr Giles. And finding nobody about the parlours, it occurred to him, that he could perhaps originate the proceedings with better effect in the kitchen; so into the kitchen he went.

There were assembled, in that lower house of the domestic parliament, the women-servants, Mr Brittles, Mr Giles, the tinker (who had received a special invitation to regale himself for the remainder of the day, in consideration of his services), and the constable. The latter gentleman had a large staff, a large head, large features, and large half-boots; and he looked as if he had been taking a proportionate allowance of ale – as indeed he had.

The adventures of the previous night were still under discussion; for Mr Giles was expatiating upon his presence of mind, when the doctor entered; Mr Brittles, with a mug of ale in his hand, was corroborating everything, before his superior said it.

"Sit still!" said the doctor, waving his hand.

"Thank you, sir," said Mr Giles. "Misses wished some ale to be given out, sir; and as I felt no ways inclined for my own little room, sir, and was disposed for company, I am taking mine among 'em here."

Brittles headed a low murmur, by which the ladies and gentlemen generally were understood to express the gratification they derived from Mr Giles's condescension. Mr Giles looked round with a patronising air, as much as to say that so long as they behaved properly, he would never desert them.

"How is the patient to-night, sir?" asked Giles.

"So-so;" returned the doctor. "I am afraid you have got yourself into a scrape there, Mr Giles."

"I hope you don't mean to say, sir," said Mr Giles, trembling, "that he's going to die. If I thought it, I should never be happy again. I wouldn't cut a boy off: no, not even Brittles here: not for all the plate in the county, sir."

"That's not the point," said the doctor, mysteriously. "Mr Giles, are you a Protestant?"

"Yes, sir, I hope so," faltered Mr Giles, who had turned very pale.

"And what are *you*, boy?" said the doctor, turning sharply upon Brittles.

"Lord bless me, sir!" replied Brittles, starting violently: "I'm – the same as Mr Giles, sir."

"Then tell me this," said the doctor, "both of you, both of you! Are you going to take upon yourselves to swear, that that boy up stairs is the boy that was put through the little window last night? Out with it! Come! We are prepared for you!"

The doctor, who was universally considered one of the best-tempered creatures on earth, made this demand in such a dreadful tone of anger, that Giles and Brittles, who were considerably muddled by ale and excitement, stared at each other in a state of stupefaction.

"Pay attention to the reply, constable, will you?" said the doctor, shaking his forefinger with great solemnity of manner, and tapping the bridge of his nose with it, to bespeak the exercise of that worthy's utmost acuteness. "Something may come of this before long."

The constable looked as wise as he could, and took up his staff of office: which had been reclining indolently in the chimney-corner.

"It's a simple question of identity, you will observe," said the doctor.

"That's what it is, sir," replied the constable, coughing with great violence; for he had finished his ale in a hurry, and some of it had gone the wrong way.

"Here's a house broken into," said the doctor, "and a couple of men catch one moment's glimpse of a boy, in the midst of gunpowder-smoke, and in all the distraction of alarm and darkness. Here's a boy comes to that very same house, next morning, and because he happens to have his arm tied up, these men lay violent hands upon him – by doing which, they place his life in great danger – and swear he is the thief. Now, the question is, whether these men are justified by the fact; if not, in what situation do they place themselves?"

The constable nodded profoundly. He said, if that wasn't law, he would be glad to know what was.

"I ask you again," thundered the doctor, "are you, on your solemn oaths, able to identify that boy?"

Brittles looked doubtfully at Mr Giles; Mr Giles looked doubtfully at Brittles; the constable put his hand behind his ear, to catch the reply; the two women and the tinker leaned forward to listen; the doctor glanced keenly round; when a ring was heard at the gate, and at the same moment, the sound of wheels.

"It's the runners!" cried Brittles, to all appearance much relieved.

"The what?" exclaimed the doctor, aghast in his turn.

"The Bow Street officers, sir," replied Brittles, taking up a candle; "me and Mr Giles sent for 'em this morning."

"What?" cried the doctor.

"Yes," replied Brittles; "I sent a message up by the coachman, and I only wonder they weren't here before, sir."

"You did, did you? Then confound your – slow coaches down here; that's all," said the doctor, walking away.

Chapter XXXI

Involves a critical Position

"WHO's that?" inquired Brittles, opening the door a little way, with the chain up, and peeping out, shading the candle with his hand.

"Open the door," replied a man outside; "it's the officers from Bow Street, as was sent to, to-day."

Much comforted by this assurance, Brittles opened the door to its full width, and confronted a portly man in a great-coat; who walked in, without saying anything more, and wiped his shoes on the mat, as coolly as if he lived there.

"Just send somebody out to relieve my mate, will you, young man?" said the officer; "he's in the gig, a-minding the prad. Have you got a coach "us here, that you could put it up in, for five or ten minutes?"

Brittles replying in the affirmative, and pointing out the building, the portly man stepped back to the garden-gate, and helped his companion to put up the gig: while Brittles lighted them, in a state of great admiration. This done, they returned to the house, and, being shown into a parlour, took off their great-coats and hats, and showed like what they were.

The man who had knocked at the door, was a stout personage of middle height, aged about fifty: with shiny black hair, cropped pretty close; half-whiskers, a round face, and sharp eyes. The other was a red-headed, bony man, in top-boots; with a rather ill-favoured countenance, and a turned-up sinister-looking nose.

"Tell your governor that Blathers and Duff is here, will you?" said the stouter man, smoothing down his hair, and laying a pair of handcuffs on the table. "Oh! Good evening, master. Can I have a word or two with you in private, if you please?"

This was addressed to Mr Losberne, who now made his appearance; that gentleman, motioning Brittles to retire, brought in the two ladies, and shut the door.

"This is the lady of the house," said Mr Losberne, motioning towards Mrs Maylie.

Mr Blathers made a bow. Being desired to sit down, he put his hat on the floor, and taking a chair, motioned Duff to do the same. The latter gentleman, who did not appear quite so much accustomed to good society, or quite so much at his ease in it – one of the two – seated himself, after undergoing several muscular affections of the limbs, and forced the head of his stick into his mouth, with some embarrassment.

"Now, with regard to this here robbery, master," said Blathers. "What are the circumstances?"

Mr Losberne, who appeared desirous of gaining time, recounted them at great length, and with much circumlocution. Messrs Blathers and Duff looked very knowing meanwhile, and occasionally exchanged a nod.

"I can't say, for certain, till I see the work, of course," said Blathers;

"but my opinion at once is, – I don't mind committing myself to that extent, – that this wasn't done by a yokel; eh, Duff?"

"Certainly not," replied Duff.

"And, translating the word yokel for the benefit of the ladies, I apprehend your meaning to be, that this attempt was not made by a countryman?" said Mr Losberne, with a smile.

"That's it, master," replied Blathers. "This is all about the robbery, is it?"

"All," replied the doctor.

"Now, what is this, about this here boy that the servants are a-talking on?" said Blathers.

"Nothing at all," replied the doctor. "One of the frightened servants chose to take it into his head, that he had something to do with this attempt to break into the house; but it's nonsense: sheer absurdity."

"Wery easy disposed of, if it is," remarked Duff.

"What he says is quite correct," observed Blathers, nodding his head in a confirmatory way, and playing carelessly with the handcuffs, as if they were a pair of castanets. "Who is the boy? What account does he give of himself? Where did he come from? He didn't drop out of the clouds, did he, master?"

"Of course not," replied the doctor, with a nervous glance at the two ladies. "I know his whole history: but we can talk about that presently. You would like, first, to see the place where the thieves made their attempt, I suppose?"

"Certainly," rejoined Mr Blathers. "We had better inspect the premises first, and examine the servants arterwards. That's the usual way of doing business."

Lights were then procured; and Messrs Blathers and Duff, attended by the native constable, Brittles, Giles, and everybody else in short, went into the little room at the end of the passage and looked out at the window; and afterwards went round by way of the lawn, and looked in at the window; and after that, had a candle handed out to inspect the shutter with; and after that, a lantern to trace the footsteps with; and after that, a pitchfork to poke the bushes with. This done, amidst the breathless interest of all beholders, they came in again; and Mr Giles and Brittles were put through a melodramatic representation of their share in the previous night's adventures: which they performed some six times over: contradicting each other, in not more than one important respect, the first time, and in not more than a dozen the last. This consummation being arrived at, Blathers and Duff cleared the room, and held a long council together, compared with which, for secrecy and solemnity, a consultation of great doctors on the knottiest point in medicine, would be mere child's play.

Meanwhile, the doctor walked up and down the next room in a very uneasy state; and Mrs Maylie and Rose looked on, with anxious faces.

"Upon my word," he said, making a halt, after a great number of very rapid turns, "I hardly know what to do."

"Surely," said Rose, "the poor child's story, faithfully repeated to these men, will be sufficient to exonerate him."

"I doubt it, my dear young lady," said the doctor, shaking his head.

"I don't think it would exonerate him, either with them, or with legal functionaries of a higher grade. What is he, after all, they would say? A run-away. Judged by mere worldly considerations and probabilities, his story is a very doubtful one."

"You believe it, surely?" interrupted Rose.

"*I* believe it, strange as it is; and perhaps I may be an old fool for doing so," rejoined the doctor; "but I don't think it is exactly the tale for a practised police-officer, nevertheless."

"Why not?" demanded Rose.

"Because, my pretty cross-examiner," replied the doctor: "because, viewed with their eyes, there are many ugly points about it; he can only prove the parts that look ill, and none of those that look well. Confound the fellows, they *will* have the why and the wherefore, and will take nothing for granted. On his own showing, you see, he has been the companion of thieves for some time past; he has been carried to a police-office, on a charge of picking a gentleman's pocket; he has been taken away, forcibly, from that gentleman's house, to a place which he cannot describe or point out, and of the situation of which he has not the remotest idea. He is brought down to Chertsey, by men who seem to have taken a violent fancy to him, whether he will or no; and is put through a window to rob a house; and then, just at the very moment when he is going to alarm the inmates, and so do the very thing that would set him all to rights, there rushes into the way, a blundering dog of a half-bred butler, and shoots him! As if on purpose to prevent his doing any good for himself! Don't you see all this?"

"I see it, of course," replied Rose, smiling at the doctor's impetuosity; "but still I do not see anything in it, to criminate the poor child."

"No," replied the doctor; "of course not! Bless the bright eyes of your sex! They never see, whether for good or bad, more than one side of any question; and that is, always, the one which first presents itself to them."

Having given vent to this result of experience, the doctor put his hands into his pockets, and walked up and down the room with even greater rapidity than before.

"The more I think of it," said the doctor, "the more I see that it will occasion endless trouble and difficulty if we put these men in possession of the boy's real story. I am certain it will not be believed; and even if they can do nothing to him in the end, still the dragging it forward, and giving publicity to all the doubts that will be cast upon it, must interfere, materially, with your benevolent plan of rescuing him from misery."

"Oh! what is to be done?" cried Rose. "Dear, dear! why did they send for these people?"

"Why, indeed!" exclaimed Mrs Maylie. "I would not have had them here, for the world."

"All I know is," said Mr Losberne, at last: sitting down with a kind of desperate calmness, "that we must try and carry it off with a bold face. The object is a good one, and that must be our excuse. The boy has strong symptoms of fever upon him, and is in no condition to be talked to any more; that's one comfort. We must make the best of it; and if bad be the best, it is no fault of ours. Come in!"

"Well, master," said Blathers, entering the room followed by his colleague, and making the door fast, before he said any more. "This warn't a put-up thing."

"And what the devil's a put-up thing?" demanded the doctor, impatiently.

"We call it a put-up robbery, ladies," said Blathers, turning to them, as if he pitied their ignorance, but had a contempt for the doctor's, "when the servants is in it."

"Nobody suspected them, in this case," said Mrs Maylie.

"Wery likely not, ma'am," replied Blathers; "but they might have been in it, for all that."

"More likely on that wery account," said Duff.

"We find it was a town hand," said Blathers, continuing his report; "for the style of work is first-rate."

"Wery pretty indeed it is," remarked Duff, in an under tone.

"There was two of 'em in it," continued Blathers; "and they had a boy with 'em; that's plain from the size of the window. That's all to be said at present. We'll see this lad that you've got up stairs at once, if you please."

"Perhaps they will take something to drink first, Mrs Maylie?" said the doctor: his face brightening, as if some new thought had occurred to him.

"Oh! to be sure!" exclaimed Rose, eagerly. "You shall have it immediately, if you will."

"Why, thank you, miss!" said Blathers, drawing his coat-sleeve across his mouth; "it's dry work, this sort of duty. Anythink that's handy, miss; don't put yourself out of the way, on our accounts."

"What shall it be?" asked the doctor, following the young lady to the sideboard.

"A little drop of spirits, master, if it's all the same," replied Blathers. "It's a cold ride from London, ma'am; and I always find that spirits comes home warmer to the feelings."

This interesting communication was addressed to Mrs Maylie, who received it very graciously. While it was being conveyed to her, the doctor slipped out of the room.

"Ah!" said Mr Blathers: not holding his wine-glass by the stem, but grasping the bottom between the thumb and forefinger of his left hand: and placing it in front of his chest; "I have seen a good many pieces of business like this, in my time, ladies."

"That crack down in the back lane at Edmonton, Blathers," said Mr Duff, assisting his colleague's memory.

"That was something in this way, warn't it?" rejoined Mr Blathers; "that was done by Conkey Chickweed, that was."

"You always gave that to him," replied Duff. "It was the Family Pet, I tell you. Conkey hadn't any more to do with it than I had."

"Get out!" retorted Mr Blathers; "I know better. Do you mind that time when Conkey was robbed of is money, though? What a start that was! Better than any novel-book *I* ever see!"

"What was that?" inquired Rose: anxious to encourage any symptoms of good-humour in the unwelcome visitors.

"It was a robbery, miss, that hardly anybody would have been down upon," said Blathers. "This here Conkey Chickweed –"

"Conkey means Nosey, ma'am," interposed Duff.

"Of course the lady knows that, don't she?" demanded Mr Blathers. "Always interrupting, you are, partner! This here Conkey Chickweed, miss, kept a public-house over Battlebridge way, and he had a cellar, where a good many young lords went to see cock-fighting, and badger-drawing, and that; and a wery intellectual manner the sports was conducted in, for I've seen 'em off'en. He warn't one of the family, at that time; and one night he was robbed of three hundred and twenty-seven guineas in a canvas bag, that was stole out of his bedroom in the dead of night, by a tall man with a black patch over his eye, who had concealed himself under the bed, and after committing the robbery, jumped slap out of the window: which was only a story high. He was wery quick about it. But Conkey was quick, too; for he was woke by the noise, and darting out of bed, he fired a blunderbuss arter him, and roused the neighbourhood. They set up a hue-and-cry, directly, and when they came to look about 'em, found that Conkey had hit the robber; for there was traces of blood, all the way to some palings a good distance off; and there they lost 'em. However, he had made off with the blunt; and, consequently, the name of Mr Chickweed, licensed witler, appeared in the Gazette among the other bankrupts; and all manner of benefits and subscriptions, and I don't know what all, was got up for the poor man, who was in a wery low state of mind about his loss, and went up and down the streets, for three or four days, a pulling his hair off in such a desperate manner that many people was afraid he might be going to make away with himself. One day he come up to the office, all in a hurry, and had a private interview with the magistrate, who, after a deal of talk, rings the bell, and orders Jem Spyers in (Jem was a active officer), and tells him to go and assist Mr Chickweed in apprehending the man as robbed his house. "I see him, Spyers," said Chickweed, "pass my house yesterday morning." "Why didn't you up, and collar him!" says Spyers. "I was so struck all of a heap, that you might have fractured my skull with a toothpick," says the poor man; "but we're sure to have him; for between ten and eleven o'clock at night he passed again." Spyers no sooner heard this, than he put some clean linen and a comb, in his pocket, in case he should have to stop a day or two; and away he goes, and sets himself down at one of the public-house windows behind the little red curtain, with his hat on, all ready to bolt out, at a moment's notice. He was smoking his pipe here, late at night, when all of a sudden Chickweed roars out "Here he is! Stop thief! Murder!" Jem Spyers dashes out; and there he sees Chickweed, a-tearing down the street full cry. Away goes Spyers; on goes Chickweed; round turns the people; everybody roars out, "Thieves!" and Chickweed himself keeps on shouting, all the time, like mad. Spyers loses sight of him a minute as he turns a corner; shoots round; sees a little crowd; dives in; "Which is the man?" "D—me!" says Chickweed, "I've lost him again!" It was a remarkable occurrence, but he warn't to be seen nowhere, so they went back to the public-house. Next morning, Spyers took his old place, and looked out, from behind the curtain, for a tall man with a black patch over his eye, till his own two eyes ached again. At last, he couldn't help shutting 'em, to ease 'em a minute; and the very moment he did so, he hears Chickweed a-roaring out, "Here he is!" Off he starts once more, with Chickweed halfway down the street ahead of him; and after twice as long a run as the yesterday's one, the man's lost again! This was done, once or twice more, till one-half the neighbours gave out that Mr Chickweed had been robbed by the devil, who was playing tricks with him arterwards; and the other half, that poor Mr Chickweed had gone mad with grief."

"What did Jem Spyers say?" inquired the doctor: who had returned to the room shortly after the commencement of the story.

"Jem Spyers," resumed the officer, "for a long time said nothing at all, and listened to everything without seeming to, which showed he understood his business. But, one morning, he walked into the bar, and taking out his snuff-box, says, "Chickweed, I've found out who done this here robbery." "Have you?" said Chickweed. "Oh, my dear Spyers, only let me have wengeance, and I shall die contented! Oh, my dear Spyers, where is the villain!" "Come!" said Spyers, offering him a pinch of snuff, "none of that gammon! You did it yourself." So he had; and a good bit of money he had made by it, too; and nobody would never have found it out, if he hadn't been so precious anxious to keep up appearances!" said Mr Blathers, putting down his wineglass, and clinking the handcuffs together.

"Very curious, indeed," observed the doctor. "Now, if you please, you can walk up stairs."

"If *you* please, sir," returned Mr Blathers. Closely following Mr Losberne, the two officers ascended to Oliver's bedroom; Mr Giles preceding the party, with a lighted candle.

Oliver had been dozing; but looked worse, and was more feverish than he had appeared yet. Being assisted by the doctor, he managed to sit up in bed for a minute or so; and looked at the strangers without at all understanding what was going forward – in fact, without seeming to recollect where he was, or what had been passing.

"This," said Mr Losberne, speaking softly, but with great vehemence notwithstanding, "this is the lad, who, being accidentally wounded by a spring-gun in some boyish trespass on Mr What-d"ye-call-him's grounds, at the back here, comes to the house for assistance this morning, and is immediately laid hold of and mal-treated, by that ingenious gentleman with the candle in his hand: who has placed his life in considerable danger, as I can professionally certify."

Messrs Blathers and Duff looked at Mr Giles, as he was thus recommended to their notice. The bewildered butler gazed from them towards Oliver, and from Oliver towards Mr Losberne, with a most ludicrous mixture of fear and perplexity.

"You don't mean to deny that, I suppose?" said the doctor, laying Oliver gently down again.

"It was all done for the – for the best, sir?" answered Giles. "I am sure I thought it was the boy, or I wouldn't have meddled with him. I am not of an inhuman disposition, sir."

"Thought it was what boy?" inquired the senior officer.

"The housebreaker's boy, sir!" replied Giles. "They – they certainly had a boy."

"Well? Do you think so now?" inquired Blathers.

"Think what, now?" replied Giles, looking vacantly at his questioner.

"Think it's the same boy, Stupid-head?" rejoined Blathers, impatiently.

"I don't know; I really don't know," said Giles, with a rueful countenance. "I couldn't swear to him."

"What do you think?" asked Mr Blathers.

"I don't know what to think," replied poor Giles. "I don't think it is the boy: indeed, I'm almost certain that it isn't. You know it can't be."

"Has this man been a-drinking, sir?" inquired Blathers, turning to the doctor.

"What a precious muddle-headed chap you are!" said Duff, addressing Mr Giles, with supreme contempt.

Mr Losberne had been feeling the patient's pulse during this short dialogue; but he now rose from the chair by the bedside, and remarked, that if the officers had any doubts upon the subject, they would perhaps like to step into the next room, and have Brittles before them.

Acting upon this suggestion, they adjourned to a neighbouring apartment, where Mr Brittles, being called in, involved himself and his respected superior in such a wonderful maze of fresh contradictions and impossibilities, as tended to throw no particular light on anything, but the fact of his own strong mystification; except, indeed, his declarations that he shouldn't know the real boy, if he were put before him that instant; that he had only taken Oliver to be he, because Mr Giles had said he was; and that Mr Giles had, five minutes previously, admitted in the kitchen, that he began to be very much afraid he had been a little too hasty.

Among other ingenious surmises, the question was then raised, whether Mr Giles had really hit anybody; and upon examination of the fellow pistol to that which he had fired, it turned out to have no more destructive loading than gunpowder and brown paper: a discovery which made a considerable impression on everybody but the doctor, who had drawn the ball about ten minutes before. Upon no one, however, did it make a greater impression than on Mr Giles himself; who, after labouring, for some hours, under the fear of having mortally wounded a fellow-creature, eagerly caught at this new idea, and favoured it to the utmost. Finally, the officers, without troubling themselves very much about Oliver, left the Chertsey constable in the house, and took up their rest for that night in the town; promising to return next morning.

With the next morning, there came a rumour, that two men and a boy were in the cage at Kingston, who had been apprehended over night under suspicious circumstances; and to Kingston Messrs Blathers and Duff journeyed accordingly. The suspicious circumstances, however, resolving themselves, on investigation, into the one fact, that they had been discovered sleeping under a haystack; which, although a great crime, is only punishable by imprisonment, and is, in the merciful eye of the English law, and its comprehensive love of all the king's subjects, held to be no satisfactory proof, in the absence of all other evidence, that the sleeper, or sleepers, have committed burglary accompanied with violence, and have therefore rendered themselves liable to the punishment of death; Messrs Blathers and Duff came back again, as wise as they went.

In short, after some more examination, and a great deal more conversation, a neighbouring magistrate was readily induced to take the joint bail of Mrs Maylie and Mr Losberne for Oliver's appearance if he should ever be called upon; and Blathers and Duff, being rewarded with a couple of guineas, returned to town with divided opinions on the subject of their expedition: the latter gentleman on a mature consideration of all the circumstances, inclining to the belief that the burglarious attempt had originated with the Family Pet; and the former being equally disposed to concede the full merit of it to the great Mr Conkey Chickweed.

Meanwhile, Oliver gradually throve and prospered under the united care of Mrs Maylie, Rose, and the kind-hearted Mr Losberne. If fervent prayers, gushing from hearts overcharged with gratitude, be heard in heaven – and if they be not, what prayers are! – the blessings which the orphan child called down upon them, sunk into their souls, diffusing peace and happiness.

Chapter XXXII

Of the happy Life Oliver began to lead with his kind Friends

OLIVER's ailings were neither slight nor few. In addition to the pain and delay attendant on a broken limb, his exposure to the wet and cold had brought on fever and ague: which hung about him for many weeks, and reduced him sadly. But, at length, he began, by slow degrees, to get better, and to be able to say sometimes, in a few tearful words, how deeply he felt the goodness of the two sweet ladies, and how ardently he hoped that when he grew strong and well again, he could do something to show his gratitude; only something which would let them see the love and duty with which his breast was full; something, however slight, which would prove to them that their gentle kindness had not been cast away; but that the poor boy whom their charity had rescued from misery, or death, was eager to serve them with his whole heart and soul.

"Poor fellow!" said Rose, when Oliver had been one day feebly endeavouring to utter the words of thankfulness that rose to his pale lips: "you shall have many opportunities of serving us, if you will. We are going into the country, and my aunt intends that you shall accompany us. The quiet place, the pure air, and all the pleasures and beauties of spring, will restore you in a few days. We will employ you in a hundred ways, when you can bear the trouble."

"The trouble!" cried Oliver. "Oh! dear lady, If I could but work for you; if I could only give you pleasure by watering your flowers, or watching your birds, or running up and down the whole day long, to make you happy; what would I give to do it!"

"You shall give nothing at all," said Miss Maylie, smiling; "for, as I told you before, we shall employ you in a hundred ways; and if you only take half the trouble to please us, that you promise now, you will make me very happy indeed."

"Happy, ma'am!" cried Oliver; "how kind of you to say so!"

"You will make me happier than I can tell you," replied the young lady. "To think that my dear good aunt should have been the means of rescuing any one from such sad misery as you have described to us, would be an unspeakable pleasure to me; but to know that the object of her goodness and compassion was sincerely grateful and attached, in consequence, would delight me, more than you can well imagine. Do you understand me?" she inquired, watching Oliver's thoughtful face.

"Oh yes, ma'am, yes!" replied Oliver, eagerly; "but I was thinking that I am ungrateful now."

"To whom?" inquired the young lady.

"To the kind gentleman, and the dear old nurse, who took so much care of me before," rejoined Oliver. "If they knew how happy I am, they would be pleased, I am sure."

"I am sure they would," rejoined Oliver's benefactress; "and Mr Losberne has already been kind enough to promise that when you are well enough to bear the journey, he will carry you to see them."

"Has he, ma'am?" cried Oliver, his face brightening with pleasure. "I don't know what I shall do for joy when I see their kind faces once again!"

In a short time Oliver was sufficiently recovered to undergo the fatigue of this expedition. One morning he and Mr Losberne set out, accordingly, in a little carriage which belonged to Mrs Maylie. When they came to Chertsey Bridge, Oliver turned very pale, and uttered a loud exclamation.

"What's the matter with the boy?" cried the doctor, as usual, all in a bustle. "Do you see anything – hear anything – feel anything – eh?"

"That, sir," cried Oliver, pointing out of the carriage window. "That house!"

"Yes; well, what of it? Stop coachman. Pull up here," cried the doctor. "What of the house, my man; eh?"

"The thieves – the house they took me to!" whispered Oliver.

"The devil it is!" cried the doctor. "Halloa, there! let me out!"

But, before the coachman could dismount from his box, he had tumbled out of the coach, by some means or other; and, running down to the deserted tenement, began kicking at the door like a madman.

"Halloa?" said a little ugly hump-backed man: opening the door so suddenly, that the doctor, from the very impetus of his last kick, nearly fell forward into the passage. "What's the matter here?"

"Matter!" exclaimed the other, collaring him, without a moment's reflection. "A good deal. Robbery is the matter."

"There'll be Murder the matter, too," replied the humpbacked man, coolly, "if you don't take your hands off. Do you hear me?"

"I hear you," said the doctor, giving his captive a hearty shake. "Where's – confound the fellow, what's his rascally name – Sikes; that's it. Where's Sikes, you thief?"

The hump-backed man stared, as if in excess of amazement and indignation; then, twisting himself, dexterously, from the doctor's grasp, growled forth a volley of horrid oaths, and retired into the house. Before he could shut the door, however, the doctor had passed into the parlour, without a word of parley. He looked anxiously round; not an article of furniture; not a vestige of anything, animate or inanimate; not even the position of the cupboards; answered Oliver's description!

"Now!" said the hump-backed man, who had watched him keenly, "what do you mean by coming into my house, in this violent way? Do you want to rob me, or to murder me? Which is it?"

"Did you ever know a man come out to do either, in a chariot and pair, you ridiculous old vampire?" said the irritable doctor.

"What do you want, then?" demanded the hunchback. "Will you take yourself off, before I do you a mischief? Curse you!"

"As soon as I think proper," said Mr Losberne, looking into the other parlour; which, like the first, bore no resemblance whatever to Oliver's account of it. "I shall find you out, some day, my friend."

"Will you?" sneered the ill-favoured cripple. "If you ever want me, I'm here. I haven't lived here mad and all alone, for five-and-twenty years, to be scared by you. You shall pay for this; you shall pay for this." And so saying, the misshapen little demon set up a yell, and danced upon the ground, as if wild with rage.

"Stupid enough, this," muttered the doctor to himself; "the boy must have made a mistake. Here! Put that in your pocket, and shut yourself up again." With these words he flung the hunchback a piece of money, and returned to the carriage

The man followed to the chariot door, uttering the wildest imprecations and curses all the way; but as Mr Losberne turned to speak to the driver, he looked into the carriage, and eyed Oliver for an instant with a glance so sharp and fierce and at the same time so furious and vindictive, that, waking or sleeping, he could not forget it for months afterwards. He continued to utter the most fearful imprecations, until the driver had resumed his seat; and when they were once more on their way, they could see him some distance behind: beating his feet upon the ground, and tearing his hair, in transports of real or pretended rage.

"I am an ass!" said the doctor, after a long silence. "Did you know that before, Oliver?"

"No, sir."

"Then don't forget it another time.

"An ass," said the doctor again, after a further silence of some minutes. "Even if it had been the right place, and the right fellows had been there, what could I have done, single-handed? And if I had had assistance, I see no good that I should have done, except leading to my own exposure, and an unavoidable statement of the manner in which I have hushed up this business. That would have served me right, though. I am always involving myself in some scrape or other, by acting on impulse. It might have done me good."

Now, the fact was that the excellent doctor had never acted upon anything but impulse all through his life, and it was no bad compliment to the nature of the impulses which governed him, that so far from being involved in any peculiar troubles or misfortunes, he had the warmest respect and esteem of all who knew him. If the truth must be told, he was a little out of temper, for a minute or two, at being disappointed in procuring corroborative evidence of Oliver's story, on the very first occasion on which he had a chance of obtaining any. He soon came round again, however; and finding that Oliver's replies to his questions, were still as straightforward and consistent, and still delivered with as much apparent sincerity and truth, as they had ever been, he made up his mind to attach full credence to them, from that time forth.

As Oliver knew the name of the street in which Mr Brownlow resided, they were enabled to drive straight thither. When the coach turned into it, his heart beat so violently, that he could scarcely draw his breath.

"Now, my boy, which house is it?" inquired Mr Losberne.

"That! That!" replied Oliver, pointing eagerly out of the window. "The white house. Oh! make haste! Pray make haste! I feel as if I should die; it makes me tremble so."

"Come, come!" said the good doctor, patting him on the shoulder. "You will see them directly, and they will be overjoyed to find you safe and well."

"Oh! I hope so!" cried Oliver. "They were so good to me; so very, very good to me."

The coach rolled on. It stopped. No; that was the wrong house; the next door. It went on a few paces, and stopped again. Oliver looked up at the windows, with tears of happy expectation coursing down his face.

Alas! the white house was empty and there was a bill in the window. "To Let."

"Knock at the next door," cried Mr Losberne, taking Oliver's arm in his. "What has become of Mr Brownlow, who used to live in the adjoining house, do you know?"

The servant did not know; but would go and inquire. She presently returned, and said, that Mr Brownlow had sold off his goods, and gone to the West Indies, six weeks before. Oliver clasped his hands, and sank feebly backward.

"Has his housekeeper gone, too?" inquired Mr Losberne, after a moment's pause.

"Yes, sir;" replied the servant. "The old gentleman, the housekeeper, and a gentleman who was a friend of Mr Brownlow's, all went together."

"Then turn towards home again," said Mr Losberne to the driver; "and don't stop to bait the horses, till you get out of this confounded London!"

"The book-stall keeper, sir?" said Oliver. "I know the way there. See him, pray, sir! Do see him!"

"My poor boy, this is disappointment enough for one day," said the doctor. "Quite enough for both of us. If we go to the book-stall keeper's, we shall certainly find that he is dead, or has set his house on fire, or run away. No; home again straight!" And in obedience to the doctor's impulse, home they went.

This bitter disappointment caused Oliver much sorrow and grief, even in the midst of his happiness; for he had pleased himself, many times during his illness, with thinking of all that Mr Brownlow and Mrs Bedwin would say to him: and what delight it would be to tell them how many long days and nights he had passed in reflecting on what they had done for him, and in bewailing his cruel separation from them. The hope of eventually clearing himself with them, too, and explaining how he had been forced away, had buoyed him up, and sustained him, under many of his recent trials; and now, the idea that they should have gone so far, and carried with them the belief that he was an impostor and a robber – a belief which might remain uncontradicted to his dying day – was almost more than he could bear.

The circumstance occasioned no alteration, however, in the behaviour of his benefactors. After another fortnight, when the fine warm weather had fairly begun, and every tree and flower was putting forth its young leaves and rich blossoms, they made preparations for quitting the house at Chertsey, for some months. Sending the plate, which had so excited Fagin's cupidity, to the banker's; and leaving Giles and another servant in care of the house, they departed to a cottage at some distance in the country, and took Oliver with them.

Who can describe the pleasure and delight, the peace of mind and soft tranquility, the sickly boy felt in the balmy air, and among the green hills and rich woods, of an inland village! Who can tell how scenes of peace and quietude sink into the minds of pain-worn dwellers in close and noisy places, and carry their own freshness, deep into their jaded hearts! Men who have lived in crowded, pent-up streets, through lives of toil, and who have never wished for change; men, to whom custom has indeed been second nature, and who have come almost to love each brick and stone that formed the narrow boundaries of their daily walks; even they, with the hand of death upon them, have been known to yearn at last for one short glimpse of Nature's face; and, carried far from the scenes of their old pains and pleasures, have seemed to pass at once into a new state of being. Crawling forth, from day to day, to some green sunny spot, they have had such memories wakened up within them by the sight of sky, and hill and plain, and glistening water, that a foretaste of heaven itself has soothed their quick decline, and they have sunk into their tombs, as peacefully as the sun whose setting they watched from their lonely chamber window but a few hours before, faded from their dim and feeble sight! The memories which peaceful country scenes call up, are not of this world, nor of its thoughts and hopes. Their gentle influence may teach us how to weave fresh garlands for the graves of those we loved: may purify our thoughts, and bear down before it old enmity and hatred; but beneath all this, there lingers, in the least reflective mind, a vague and half-formed consciousness of having held such feelings long before, in some remote and distant time, which calls up solemn thoughts of distant times to come, and bends down pride and worldliness beneath it.

It was a lovely spot to which they repaired. Oliver, whose days had been spent among squalid crowds, and in the midst of noise and brawling, seemed to enter on a new existence there. The rose and honeysuckle clung to the cottage walls; the ivy crept round the trunks of the trees; and the garden-flowers perfumed the air with delicious odours. Hard by, was a little churchyard; not crowded with tall unsightly gravestones, but full of humble mounds, covered with fresh turf and moss: beneath which, the old people of the village lay at rest. Oliver often wandered here; and, thinking of the wretched grave in which his mother lay, would sometimes sit him down and sob unseen; but, when he raised his eyes to the deep sky overhead, he would cease to think of her as lying in the ground, and would weep for her, sadly, but without pain.

It was a happy time. The days were peaceful and serene; the nights brought with them neither fear nor care; no languishing in a wretched prison, or associating with wretched men; nothing but pleasant and happy thoughts. Every morning he went to a white-headed old gentleman, who lived near the little church: who taught him to read better, and to write: and who spoke so kindly, and took such pains, that Oliver could never try enough to please him. Then, he would walk with Mrs Maylie and Rose, and hear them talk of books; or perhaps sit near them, in some shady place, and listen whilst the young lady read: which he could have done, until it grew too dark to see the letters. Then, he had his own lesson for the next day to prepare; and at this, he would work hard, in a little room which looked into the garden, till evening came slowly on, when the ladies would walk out again, and he with them: listening with such pleasure to all they said: and so happy if they wanted a flower that he could climb to reach, or had forgotten anything he could run to fetch: that he could never be quick enough about it. When it became quite dark, and they returned home, the young lady would sit down to the piano, and play some pleasant air, or sing, in a low and gentle voice, some old song which it pleased her aunt to hear. There would be no candles lighted at such times as these; and Oliver would sit by one of the windows, listening to the sweet music, in a perfect rapture.

And when Sunday came, how differently the day was spent, from any way in which he had ever spent it yet! and how happily too; like all the other days in that most happy time! There was the little church, in the morning, with the green leaves fluttering at the windows: the birds singing without: and the sweet-smelling air stealing in at the low porch, and filling the homely building with its fragrance. The poor people were so neat and clean, and knelt so reverently in prayer, that it seemed a pleasure, not a tedious duty, their assembling there together; and though the singing might be rude, it was real, and sounded more musical (to Oliver's ears at least) than any he had ever heard in church before. Then, there were the walks as usual, and many calls at the clean houses of the labouring men; and at night, Oliver read a chapter or two from the Bible, which he had been studying all the week, and in the performance of which duty he felt more proud and pleased, than if he had been the clergyman himself.

In the morning, Oliver would be a-foot by six o'clock, roaming the fields, and plundering the hedges, far and wide, for nosegays of wild flowers, with which he would return laden, home; and which it took great care and consideration to arrange, to the best advantage, for the embellishment of the breakfast-table. There was fresh groundsel, too, for Miss Maylie's birds, with which Oliver, who had been studying the subject under the able tuition of the village clerk, would decorate the cages, in the most approved taste. When the birds were made all spruce and smart for the day, there was usually some little commission of charity to execute in the village; or, failing that, there was rare cricket-playing, sometimes, on the green; or, failing that, there was always something to do in the garden, or about the plants, to which Oliver (who had studied this science also, under the same master, who was a gardener by trade,) applied himself with hearty goodwill, until Miss Rose made her appearance: when there were a thousand commendations to be bestowed on all he had done.

So three months glided away; three months which, in the life of the most blessed and favoured of mortals, might have been unmingled happiness, and which, in Oliver's, were true felicity. With the purest and most amiable generosity on one side; and the truest, warmest, soul-felt gratitude on the other; it is no wonder that, by the end of that short time, Oliver Twist had become completely domesticated with the old lady and her niece, and that the fervent attachment of his young and sensitive heart, was repaid by their pride in, and attachment to, himself.

Chapter XXXIII

Wherein the Happiness of Oliver and his Friends, experiences a sudden Check

SPRING flew swiftly by, and summer came. If the village had been beautiful at first it was now in the full glow and luxuriance of its richness. The great trees, which had looked shrunken and bare in the earlier months, had now burst into strong life and health; and stretching forth their green arms over the thirsty ground, converted open and naked spots into choice nooks, where was a deep and pleasant shade from which to look upon the wide prospect, steeped in sunshine, which lay stretched beyond. The earth had donned her mantle of brightest green; and shed her richest perfumes abroad. It was the prime and vigour of the year; all things were glad and flourishing.

Still, the same quiet life went on at the little cottage, and the same cheerful serenity prevailed among its inmates. Oliver had long since grown stout and healthy; but health or sickness made no difference in his warm feelings to those about him, though they do in the feelings of a great many people. He was still the same gentle, attached, affectionate creature that he had been when pain and suffering had wasted his strength, and when he was dependent for every slight attention and comfort on those who tended him.

One beautiful night, they had taken a longer walk than was customary with them: for the day had been unusually warm, and there was a brilliant moon, and a light wind had sprung up, which was unusually refreshing. Rose had been in high spirits, too, and they had walked on, in merry conversation, until they had far exceeded their ordinary bounds. Mrs Maylie being fatigued, they returned more slowly home. The young lady merely throwing off her simple bonnet, sat down to the piano as usual. After running abstractedly over the keys for a few minutes, she fell into a low and very solemn air; and as she played it, they heard a sound as if she were weeping.

"Rose, my dear!" said the elder lady.

Rose made no reply, but played a little quicker, as though the words had roused her from some painful thoughts.

"Rose, my love!" cried Mrs Maylie, rising hastily, and bending over her. "What is this? In tears! My dear child, what distresses you?"

"Nothing, aunt; nothing," replied the young lady. "I don't know what it is; I can't describe it; but I feel –"

"Not ill, my love?" interposed Mrs Maylie.

"No, no! Oh, not ill!" replied Rose: shuddering as though some deadly chillness were passing over her, while she spoke; "I shall be better presently. Close the window, pray!"

Oliver hastened to comply with her request. The young lady, making an effort to recover her cheerfulness, strove to play some livelier tune; but her fingers dropped powerless on the keys. Covering her face with her hands, she sank upon a sofa, and gave vent to the tears which she was now unable to repress.

"My child!" said the elderly lady, folding her arms about her, "I never saw you so before."

"I would not alarm you if I could avoid it," rejoined Rose; "but indeed I have tried very hard, and cannot help this. I fear I *am* ill, aunt."

She was, indeed; for, when candles were brought, they saw that in the very short time which had elapsed since their return home, the hue of her countenance had changed to a marble whiteness. Its expression had lost nothing of its beauty; but it was changed; and there was an anxious, haggard look about the gentle face, which it had never worn before. Another minute, and it was suffused with a crimson flush: and a heavy wildness came over the soft blue eye. Again this disappeared, like the shadow thrown by a passing cloud; and she was once more deadly pale.

Oliver, who watched the old lady anxiously, observed that she was alarmed by these appearances; and so in truth, was he; but seeing that she affected to make light of them, he endeavoured to do the same, and they so far succeeded, that when Rose was persuaded by her aunt to retire for the night, she was in better spirits; and appeared even in better health: assuring them that she felt certain she should rise in the morning, quite well.

"I hope," said Oliver, when Mrs Maylie returned, "that nothing is the matter? She don't look well to-night, but –"

The old lady motioned to him not to speak; and sitting herself down in a dark corner of the room, remained silent for some time. At length, she said, in a trembling voice:

"I hope not, Oliver. I have been very happy with her for some years: too happy, perhaps. It may be time that I should meet with some misfortune; but I hope it is not this."

"What?" inquired Oliver.

"The heavy blow," said the old lady, "of losing the dear girl who has so long been my comfort and happiness."

"Oh! God forbid!" exclaimed Oliver, hastily.

"Amen to that, my child!" said the old lady, wringing her hands.

"Surely there is no danger of anything so dreadful?" said Oliver. "Two hours ago, she was quite well."

"She is very ill now," rejoined Mrs Maylie; "and will be worse, I am sure. My dear, dear Rose! Oh, what should I do without her!"

She gave way to such great grief, that Oliver, suppressing his own emotion, ventured to remonstrate with her; and to beg, earnestly, that, for the sake of the dear young lady herself she would be more calm.

"And consider, ma'am," said Oliver, as the tears forced themselves into his eyes, despite of his efforts to the contrary. "Oh! consider how young and good she is, and what pleasure and comfort she gives to all about her. I am sure – certain – quite certain – that, for your sake, who are so good yourself; and for her own; and for the sake of all she makes so happy; she will not die. Heaven will never let her die so young."

"Hush!" said Mrs Maylie, laying her hand on Oliver's head. "You think like a child, poor boy. But you teach me my duty, notwithstanding. I had forgotten it for a moment, Oliver, but I hope I may be pardoned, for I am old, and have seen enough of illness and death to know the agony of separation from the objects of our love. I have seen enough, too, to know that it is not always the youngest and best who are spared to those that love them; but this should give us comfort in our sorrow; for Heaven is just; and such things teach us, impressively, that there is a brighter world than this; and that the passage to it is speedy. God's will be done! I love her; and He knows how well!"

Oliver was surprised to see that as Mrs Maylie said these words, she checked her lamentations as though by one effort; and drawing herself up as she spoke, became composed and firm. He was still more astonished to find that this firmness lasted; and that, under all the care and watching which ensued, Mrs Maylie was ever ready and collected: performing all the duties which devolved upon her, steadily, and, to all external appearance, even cheerfully. But he was young, and did not know what strong minds are capable of, under trying circumstances. How should he, when their possessors so seldom know themselves?

An anxious night ensued. When morning came, Mrs Maylie's predictions were but too well verified. Rose was in the first stage of a high and dangerous fever.

"We must be active, Oliver, and not give way to useless grief," said Mrs Maylie, laying her finger on her lip, as she looked steadily into his face; "this letter must be sent, with all possible expedition, to Mr Losberne. It must be carried to the market-town: which is not more than four miles off, by the footpath across the fields: and thence dispatched, by an express on horseback, straight to Chertsey. The people at the inn will undertake to do this; and I can trust to you to see it done, I know."

Oliver could make no reply, but looked his anxiety to be gone at once.

"Here is another letter," said Mrs Maylie, pausing to reflect; "but whether to send it now, or wait until I see how Rose goes on, I scarcely know. I would not forward it, unless I feared the worst."

"Is it for Chertsey, too, ma'am?" inquired Oliver: impatient to execute his commission, and holding out his trembling hand for the letter.

"No," replied the old lady, giving it to him mechanically. Oliver glanced at it, and saw that it was directed to Harry Maylie, Esquire, at some great Lord's house in the country; where, he could not make out.

"Shall it go, ma'am?" asked Oliver, looking up, impatiently.

"I think not," replied Mrs Maylie, taking it back. "I will wait until to-morrow."

With these words, she gave Oliver her purse, and he started off, without more delay, at the greatest speed he could muster.

Swiftly he ran across the fields, and down the little lanes which sometimes divided them: now almost hidden by the high corn on either side, and now emerging on an open field, where the mowers and haymakers were busy at their work: nor did he stop once, save now and then, for a few seconds, to recover breath, until he came, in a great heat, and covered with dust, on the little market-place of the market-town.

Here he paused, and looked about for the inn. There were a white bank, and a red brewery, and a yellow town-hall; and in one corner there was a large house, with all the wood about it painted green: before which was the sign of "The George." To this he hastened, as soon as it caught his eye.

He spoke to a postboy who was dozing under the gateway; and who, after hearing what he wanted, referred him to the ostler; who after hearing all he had to say again, referred him to the landlord; who was a tall gentleman in a blue neckcloth, a white hat, drab breeches, and boots with tops to match, leaning against a pump by the stable-door, picking his teeth with a silver toothpick.

This gentleman walked with much deliberation into the bar to make out the bill: which took a long time making out: and after it was ready, and paid, a horse had to be saddled and a man to be dressed, which took up ten good minutes more. Meanwhile Oliver was in such a desperate state of impatience and anxiety, that he felt as if he could have jumped upon the horse himself, and galloped away, full tear, to the next stage. At length, all was ready; and the little parcel having been handed up, with many injunctions and entreaties for its speedy delivery, the man set spurs to his horse, and rattling over the uneven paving of the market-place, was out of the town, and galloping along the turnpike-road, in a couple of minutes.

As it was something to feel certain that assistance was sent for, and that no time had been lost, Oliver hurried up the inn-yard, with a somewhat lighter heart. He was turning out of the gateway when he accidentally stumbled against a tall man wrapped in a cloak, who was at that moment coming out of the inn door.

"Hah!" cried the man, fixing his eyes on Oliver, and suddenly recoiling. "What the devil's this?"

"I beg your pardon, sir," said Oliver; "I was in a great hurry to get home, and didn't see you were coming."

"Death!" muttered the man to himself, glaring at the boy with his large dark eyes. "Who would have thought it! Grind him to ashes! He'd start from a stone coffin, to come in my way!"

"I am sorry," stammered Oliver, confused by the strange man's wild look. "I hope I have not hurt you!"

"Rot you!" murmured the man, in a horrible passion; between his clenched teeth; "if I had only had the courage to say the word, I might have been free of you in a night. Curses on your head, and black death on your heart, you imp! What are you doing here?"

The man shook his fist, as he uttered these words incoherently. He advanced towards Oliver, as if with the intention of aiming a blow at him, but fell violently on the ground: writhing and foaming, in a fit.

Oliver gazed, for a moment, at the struggles of the madman (for such he supposed him to be); and then darted into the house for help. Having seen him safely carried into the hotel, he turned his face homewards, running as fast as he could, to make up for lost time: and recalling with a great deal of astonishment and some fear, the extraordinary behaviour of the person from whom he had just parted.

The circumstance did not dwell in his recollection long, however: for when he reached the cottage, there was enough to occupy his mind, and to drive all considerations of self completely from his memory.

Rose Maylie had rapidly grown worse; before midnight she was delirious. A medical practitioner, who resided on the spot, was in constant attendance upon her; and after first seeing the patient, he had taken Mrs Maylie aside, and pronounced her disorder to be one of a most alarming nature. "In fact," he said, "it would be little short of a miracle, if she recovered."

How often did Oliver start from his bed that night, and stealing out, with noiseless footstep, to the staircase, listen for the slightest sound from the sick chamber! How often did a tremble shake his frame, and cold drops of terror start upon his brow, when a sudden trampling of feet caused him to fear that something too dreadful to think of, had even then occurred! And what had been the fervency of all the prayers he had ever uttered, compared with those he poured forth, now, in the agony and passion of his supplication for the life and health of the gentle creature, who was tottering on the deep grave's verge!

Oh! the suspense, the fearful, acute suspense, of standing idly by while the life of one we dearly love, is trembling in the balance! Oh! the racking thoughts that crowd upon the mind, and make the heart beat violently, and the breath come thick, by the force of the images they conjure up before it; the desperate anxiety *to be doing something* to relieve the pain, or lessen the danger, which we have no power to alleviate; the sinking of soul and spirit, which the sad remembrance of our helplessness produces; what tortures can equal these; what reflections or endeavours can, in the full tide and fever of the time, allay them!

Morning came; and the little cottage was lonely and still. People spoke in whispers; anxious faces appeared at the gate, from time to time; women and children went away in tears. All the livelong day, and for hours after it had grown dark, Oliver paced softly up and down the garden, raising his eyes every instant to the sick chamber, and shuddering to see the darkened window, looking as if death lay stretched inside. Late at night, Mr Losberne arrived. "It is hard," said the good doctor, turning away as he spoke; "so young; so much beloved; but there is very little hope."

Another morning. The sun shone brightly: as brightly as if it looked upon no misery or care; and, with every leaf and flower in full bloom about her: with life, and health, and sounds and sights of joy, surrounding her on every side: the fair young creature lay, wasting fast. Oliver crept away to the old churchyard, and sitting down on one of the green mounds wept and prayed for her, in silence.

There was such peace and beauty in the scene; so much of brightness and mirth in the sunny landscape; such blithesome music in the songs of the summer birds; such freedom in the rapid flight of the rook, careering overhead; so much of life and joyousness in all; that, when the boy raised his aching eyes, and looked about, the thought instinctively occurred to him, that this was not a time for death; that Rose could surely never die when humbler things were all so glad and gay; that graves were for cold and cheerless winter: not for sunlight and fragrance. He almost thought that shrouds were for the old and shrunken; and that they never wrapped the young and graceful form in their ghastly folds.

A knell from the church bell broke harshly on these youthful thoughts. Another! Again! It was tolling for the funeral service. A group of humble mourners entered the gate: wearing white favours; for the corpse was young. They stood uncovered by a grave; and there was a mother – a mother once – among the weeping train. But the sun shone brightly, and the birds sang on.

Oliver turned homeward, thinking on the many kindnesses he had received from the young lady, and wishing that the time could come over again, that he might never cease showing her how grateful and attached he was. He had no cause for self-reproach on the score of neglect, or want of thought, for he had been devoted to her service; and yet a hundred little occasions rose up before him, on which he fancied he might have been more zealous, and more earnest, and wished he had been. We need be careful how we deal with those about us, when every death carries to some small circle of survivors, thoughts of so much omitted, and so little done – of so many things forgotten, and so many more which might have been repaired! There is no remorse so deep as that which is unavailing; if we would be spared its tortures, let us remember this, in time.

When he reached home Mrs Maylie was sitting in the little parlour. Oliver's heart sank at sight of her; for she had never left the bedside of her niece; and he trembled to think what change could have driven her away. He learnt that she had fallen into a deep sleep, from which she would waken, either to recovery and life, or to bid them farewell, and die.

They sat, listening, and afraid to speak, for hours. The untasted meal was removed, with looks which showed that their thoughts were elsewhere, they watched the sun as he sank lower and lower, and, at length, cast over sky and earth those brilliant hues which herald his departure. Their quick ears caught the sound of an approaching footstep. They both involuntarily darted to the door, as Mr Losberne entered.

"What of Rose?" cried the old lady. "Tell me at once! I can bear it; anything but suspense! Oh, tell me! in the name of Heaven!"

"You must compose yourself," said the doctor, supporting her. "Be calm, my dear ma'am, pray."

"Let me go, in God's name! My dear child! She is dead! She is dying!"

"No!" cried the doctor, passionately. "As He is good and merciful, she will live to bless us all, for years to come."

The lady fell upon her knees, and tried to fold her hands together; but the energy which had supported her so long, fled up to Heaven with her first thanksgiving; and she sank into the friendly arms which were extended to receive her.

Chapter XXXIV

Contains some introductory Particulars relative to a young Gentleman who now arrives upon the Scene; and a new Adventure which happened to Oliver

IT was almost too much happiness to bear. Oliver felt stunned and stupefied by the unexpected intelligence; he could not weep, or speak, or rest. He had scarcely the power of understanding anything that had passed, until, after a long ramble in the quiet evening air, a burst of tears came to his relief, and he seemed to awaken, all at once, to a full sense of the joyful change that had occurred, and the almost insupportable load of anguish which had been taken from his breast.

The night was fast closing in, when he returned homeward, laden with flowers which he had culled, with peculiar care, for the adornment of the sick chamber. As he walked briskly along the road, he heard behind him, the noise of some vehicle, approaching at a furious pace. Looking round, he saw that it was a post-chaise, driven at great speed, and as the horses were galloping, and the road was narrow, he stood leaning against a gate until it should have passed him.

As it dashed on, Oliver caught a glimpse of a man in a white nightcap, whose face seemed familiar to him, although his view was so brief that he could not identify the person. In another second or two, the nightcap was thrust out of the chaise-window, and a stentorian voice bellowed to the driver to stop, which he did, as soon as he could pull up his horses. Then, the nightcap once again appeared: and the same voice called Oliver by his name.

"Here!" cried the voice. "Oliver, what's the news? Miss Rose! Master O-li-ver!"

"Is it you, Giles?" cried Oliver, running up to the chaise-door.

Giles popped out his nightcap again, preparatory to making some reply, when he was suddenly pulled back by a young gentleman who occupied the other corner of the chaise, and who eagerly demanded what was the news.

"In a word!" cried the gentleman, "Better or worse?"

"Better – much better!" replied Oliver, hastily.

"Thank Heaven!" exclaimed the gentleman. "You are sure?"

"Quite, sir," replied Oliver. "The change took place only a few hours ago; and Mr Losberne says, that all danger is at an end."

The gentleman said not another word, but, opening the chaise-door, leaped out, and taking Oliver hurriedly by the arm, led him aside.

"You are quite certain? There is no possibility of any mistake on your part, my boy, is there?" demanded the gentleman in a tremulous voice. "Do not deceive me, by awakening hopes that are not to be fulfilled."

"I would not for the world, sir," replied Oliver. "Indeed you may believe me. Mr Losberne's words were, that she would live to bless us all for many years to come. I heard him say so."

The tears stood in Oliver's eyes as he recalled the scene which was the beginning of so much happiness, and the gentleman turned his face away, and remained silent, for some minutes. Oliver thought he heard him sob, more than once; but he feared to interrupt him by any fresh remark – for he could well guess what his feelings were – and so stood apart, feigning to be occupied with his nosegay.

All this time, Mr Giles, with the white nightcap on, had been sitting on the steps of the chaise, supporting an elbow on each knee, and wiping his eyes with a blue cotton pocket-handkerchief dotted with white spots. That the honest fellow had not been feigning emotion, was abundantly demonstrated by the very red eyes with which he regarded the young gentleman, when he turned round and addressed him.

"I think you had better go on to my mother's in the chaise, Giles," said he. "I would rather walk slowly on, so as to gain a little time before I see her. You can say I am coming."

"I beg your pardon, Mr Harry," said Giles: giving a final polish to his ruffled countenance with the handkerchief; "but if you would leave the postboy to say that, I should be very much obliged to you. It wouldn't be proper for the maids to see me in this state, sir; I should never have any more authority with them if they did."

"Well," rejoined Harry Maylie, smiling, "you can do as you like. Let him go on with the luggage, if you wish it, and do you follow with us. Only first exchange that night-cap for some more appropriate covering, or we shall be taken for madmen."

Mr Giles, reminded of his unbecoming costume, snatched off and pocketed his nightcap; and substituted a hat, of grave and sober shape, which he took out of the chaise. This done, the postboy drove off; Giles, Mr Maylie, and Oliver, followed at their leisure.

As they walked along, Oliver glanced from time to time with much interest and curiosity at the new-comer. He seemed about five-and-twenty years of age, and was of the middle height; his countenance was frank and handsome; and his demeanour easy and prepossessing. Notwithstanding the difference between youth and age, he bore so strong a likeness to the old lady, that Oliver would have had no great difficulty in imagining their relationship, if he had not already spoken of her as his mother.

Mrs Maylie was anxiously waiting to receive her son when he reached the cottage. The meeting did not take place without great emotion on both sides.

"Mother!" whispered the young man; "why did you not write before?"

"I did," replied Mrs Maylie; "but, on reflection, I determined to keep back the letter until I had heard Mr Losberne's opinion."

"But why," said the young man, "why run the chance of that occurring which so nearly happened? If Rose had – I cannot utter that word now – if this illness had terminated differently, how could you ever have forgiven yourself! How could I ever have known happiness again!"

"If that *had* been the case, Harry," said Mrs Maylie, "I fear your happiness would have been effectually blighted, and that your arrival here, a day sooner or a day later, would have been of very, very little import."

"And who can wonder if it be so, mother?" rejoined the young man; "or why should I say, *if?* – It is – it is – you know it, mother – you must know it!"

"I know that she deserves the best and purest love the heart of man can offer," said Mrs Maylie; "I know that the devotion and affection of her nature require no ordinary return, but one that shall be deep and lasting. If I did not feel this, and know, besides, that a changed behaviour in one she loved would break her heart, I should not feel my task so difficult of performance, or have to encounter so many struggles in my own bosom, when I take what seems to me to be the strict line of duty."

"This is unkind, mother," said Harry. "Do you still suppose that I am a boy ignorant of my own mind, and mistaking the impulses of my own soul?"

"I think, my dear son," returned Mrs Maylie, laying her hand upon his shoulder, "that youth has many generous impulses which do not last; and that among them are some, which, being gratified, become only the more fleeting, Above all, I think," said the lady, fixing her eyes on her son's face, "that if an enthusiastic, ardent, and ambitious man marry a wife on whose name there is a stain, which, though it originate in no fault of her, may be visited by cold and sordid people upon her, and upon his children also: and, in exact proportion to his success in the world, be cast in his teeth, and made the subject of sneers against him: he may, no matter how generous and good his nature, one day repent of the connexion he formed in early life. And she may have the pain of knowing that he does so."

"Mother," said the young man, impatiently, "he would be a selfish brute, unworthy alike of the name of man and of the woman you describe, who acted thus."

"You think so now, Harry," replied his mother.

"And ever will!" said the young man. "The mental agony I have suffered, during the last two days, wrings from me the avowal to you of a passion which, as you well know, is not one of yesterday, nor one I have lightly formed. On Rose, sweet, gentle girl! my heart is set, as firmly as ever heart of man was set on woman. I have no thought, no view, no hope in life, beyond her; and if you oppose me in this great stake, you take my peace and happiness in your hands, and cast them to the wind. Mother, think better of this, and of me, and do not disregard the happiness of which you seem to think so little."

"Harry," said Mrs Maylie, "it is because I think so much of warm and sensitive hearts, that I would spare them from being wounded. But we have said enough, and more than enough, on this matter, just now."

"Let it rest with Rose, then," interposed Harry. "You will not press these overstrained opinions of yours, so far, as to throw any obstacle in my way?"

"I will not," rejoined Mrs Maylie; "but I would have you consider –"

"I *have* considered!" was the impatient reply; "Mother, I have considered, years and years. I have considered, ever since I have been capable of serious reflection. My feelings remain unchanged, as they ever will; and why should I suffer the pain of a delay in giving them vent, which can be productive of no earthly good? No! Before I leave this place, Rose shall hear me."

"She shall," said Mrs Maylie.

"There is something in your manner, which would almost imply that she will hear me coldly, mother," said the young man.

"Not coldly," rejoined the old lady; "far from it."

"How then?" urged the young man. "She has formed no other attachment?"

"No, indeed," replied his mother; "you have, or I mistake, too strong a hold on her affections already. What I would say," resumed the old lady, stopping her son as he was about to speak, "is this. Before you stake your all on this chance; before you suffer yourself to be carried to the highest point of hope; reflect for a few moments, my dear child, on Rose's history, and consider what effect the knowledge of her doubtful birth may have on her decision: devoted as she is to us, with all the intensity of her noble mind, and with that perfect sacrifice of self which, in all matters, great or trifling, has always been her characteristic."

"What do you mean?"

"That I leave you to discover," replied Mrs Maylie. "I must go back to her. God bless you!"

"I shall see you again to-night?" said the young man, eagerly.

"By and by," replied the lady; "when I leave Rose."

"You will tell her I am here?" said Harry.

"Of course," replied Mrs Maylie.

"And say how anxious I have been, and how much I have suffered, and how I long to see her. You will not refuse to do this, mother?"

"No," said the old lady; "I will tell her all." And pressing her son's hand, affectionately, she hastened from the room.

Mr Losberne and Oliver had remained at another end of the apartment while this hurried conversation was proceeding. The former now held out his hand to Harry Maylie; and hearty salutations were exchanged between them. The doctor then communicated, in reply to multifarious questions from his young friend, a precise account of his patient's situation; which was quite as consolatory and full of promise, as Oliver's statement had encouraged him to hope; and to the whole of which, Mr Giles, who affected to be busy about the luggage, listened with greedy ears.

"Have you shot anything particular, lately, Giles?" inquired the doctor, when he had concluded.

"Nothing particular, sir," replied Mr Giles, colouring up to the eyes.

"Nor catching any thieves, nor identifying any house-breakers?" said the doctor.

"None at all, sir," replied Mr Giles, with much gravity.

"Well," said the doctor, "I am sorry to hear it, because you do that sort of thing admirably. Pray, how is Brittles?"

"The boy is very well, sir," said Mr Giles, recovering his usual tone of patronage; "and sends his respectful duty, sir."

"That's well," said the doctor. "Seeing you here, reminds me, Mr Giles, that on the day before that on which I was called away so hurriedly, I executed, at the request of your good mistress, a small commission in your favour. Just step into this corner a moment, will you?"

Mr Giles walked into the corner with much importance, and some wonder, and was honoured with a short whispering conference with the doctor, on the termination of which, he made a great many bows, and retired with steps of unusual stateliness. The subject matter of this conference was not disclosed in the parlour, but the kitchen was speedily enlightened concerning it; for Mr Giles walked straight thither, and having called for a mug of ale, announced, with an air of majesty, which was highly effective, that it had pleased his mistress, in consideration of his gallant behaviour on the occasion of that attempted robbery, to deposit, in the local savings-bank, the sum of five and twenty pounds, for his sole use and benefit. At this, the two women-servants lifted up their hands and eyes, and supposed that Mr Giles would begin to be quite proud now; whereunto Mr Giles, pulling out his shirt-frill, replied, "No, no;" and that if they observed that he was at all haughty to his inferiors, he would thank them to tell him so. And then he made a great many other remarks, no less illustrative of his humility, which were received with equal favour and applause, and were, withal, as original and as much to the purpose, as the remarks of great men commonly are.

Above stairs, the remainder of the evening passed cheerfully away; for the doctor was in high spirits; and however fatigued or thoughtful Harry Maylie might have been at first, he was not proof against the worthy gentleman's good humour, which displayed itself in a great variety of sallies and professional recollections, and an abundance of small jokes, which struck Oliver as being the drollest things he had ever heard, and caused him to laugh proportionately: to the evident satisfaction of the doctor, who laughed immoderately at himself, and made Harry laugh almost as heartily, by the very force of sympathy. So, they were as pleasant a party as, under the circumstances, they could well have been; and it was late before they retired, with light and thankful hearts, to take that rest of which, after the doubt and suspense they had recently undergone, they stood much in need.

Oliver rose next morning, in better heart, and went about his usual early occupations, with more hope and pleasure than he had known for many days. The birds were once more hung out, to sing, in their old places; and the sweetest wild flowers that could be found, were once more gathered to gladden Rose with their beauty. The melancholy which had seemed to the sad eyes of the anxious boy to hang, for days past, over every object, beautiful as all were, was dispelled by magic. The dew seemed to sparkle more brightly on the green leaves; the air to rustle among them with a sweeter music; and the sky itself to look more blue and bright. Such is the influence which the condition of our own thoughts, exercises, even over the appearance of external objects. Men who look on nature, and their fellow-men, and cry that all is dark and gloomy, are in the right; but the sombre colours are reflections from their own jaundiced eyes and hearts. The real hues are delicate, and need a clearer vision.

It is worthy of remark, and Oliver did not fail to note it at the time, that his morning expeditions were no longer made alone. Harry Maylie, after the very first morning when he met Oliver coming laden home, was seized with such a passion for flowers, and displayed such a taste in their arrangement, as left his young companion far behind. If Oliver were behindhand in these respects, however, he knew where the best were to be found; and morning after morning they scoured the country together, and brought home the fairest that blossomed. The window of the young lady's chamber was opened now; for she loved to feel the rich summer air stream in, and revive her with its freshness; but there always stood in water, just inside the lattice, one particular little bunch, which was made up with great care, every morning. Oliver could not help noticing that the withered flowers were never thrown away, although the little vase was regularly replenished; nor, could he help observing, that whenever the doctor came into the garden, he invariably cast his eyes up to that particular corner, and nodded his head most expressively, as he set forth on his morning's walk. Pending these observations, the days were flying by; and Rose was rapidly recovering.

Nor did Oliver's time hang heavy on his hands, although the young lady had not yet left her chamber, and there were no evening walks, save now and then, for a short distance, with Mrs Maylie. He applied himself, with redoubled assiduity, to the instructions of the white-headed old gentleman, and laboured so hard that his quick progress surprised even himself. It was while he was engaged in this pursuit, that he was greatly startled and distressed by a most unexpected occurrence.

The little room in which he was accustomed to sit, when busy at his books, was on the ground-floor, at the back of the house. It was quite a cottage-room, with a lattice-window: around which were clusters of jessamine and honeysuckle, that crept over the casement, and filled the place with their delicious perfume. It looked into a garden, whence a wicket-gate opened into a small paddock; all beyond, was fine meadow-land and wood. There was no other dwelling near, in that direction; and the prospect it commanded was very extensive.

One beautiful evening, when the first shades of twilight were beginning to settle upon the earth, Oliver sat at this window, intent upon his books. He had been poring over them for some time; and, as the day had been uncommonly sultry, and he had exerted himself a great deal, it is no disparagement to the authors, whoever they may have been, to say that gradually and by slow degrees, he fell asleep.

There is a kind of sleep that steals upon us sometimes, which, while it holds the body prisoner, does not free the mind from a sense of things about it, and enable it to ramble at its pleasure. So far as an overpowering heaviness, a prostration of strength, and an utter inability to control our thoughts or power of motion, can be called sleep, this is it; and yet, we have a consciousness of all that is going on about us, and, if we dream at such a time, words which are really spoken, or sounds which really exist at the moment, accommodate themselves with surprising readiness to our visions, until reality and imagination become so strangely blended that it is afterwards almost matter of impossibility to separate the two. Nor is this, the most striking phenomenon incidental to such a state. It is an undoubted fact, that although our senses of touch and sight be for the time dead, yet our sleeping thoughts, and the visionary scenes that pass before us, will be influenced and materially influenced, by the *mere silent presence* of some external object; which may not have been near us when we closed our eyes: and of whose vicinity we have had no waking consciousness.

Oliver knew, perfectly well, that he was in his own little room; that his books were lying on the table before him; that the sweet air was stirring among the creeping plants outside. And yet he was asleep. Suddenly, the scene changed; the air became close and confined; and he thought, with a glow of terror, that he was in the Jew's house again. There sat the hideous old man, in his accustomed corner, pointing at him, and whispering to another man, with his face averted, who sat beside him.

"Hush, my dear!" he thought he heard the Jew say, "it is he, sure enough. Come away."

"He!" the other man seemed to answer; "could I mistake him, think you? If a crowd of ghosts were to put themselves into his exact shape, and he stood amongst them, there is something that would tell me how to point him out. If you buried him fifty feet deep, and took me across his grave, I fancy I should know, if there wasn't a mark above it, that he lay buried there!"

The man seemed to say this, with such dreadful hatred, that Oliver awoke with the fear, and started up.

Good Heaven! what was that, which sent the blood tingling to his heart, and deprived him of his voice, and of power to move! There – there – at the window – close before him – so close, that he could have almost touched him before he started back: with his eyes peering into the room, and meeting his: there stood the Jew! And beside him, white with rage or fear, or both, were the scowling features of the very man who had accosted him in the inn-yard.

It was but an instant, a glance, a flash, before his eyes; and they were gone. But they had recognised him, and he them; and their look was as firmly impressed upon his memory, as if it had been deeply carved in stone, and set before him from his birth. He stood transfixed for a moment; then, leaping from the window into the garden, called loudly for help.

Chapter XXXV

Containing the unsatisfactory Result of Oliver's Adventure; and a Conversation of some Importance between Harry Maylie and Rose

When the inmates of the house, attracted by Oliver's cries, hurried to the spot from which they proceeded, they found him, pale and agitated, pointing in the direction of the meadows behind the house, and scarcely able to articulate the words, "The Jew! the Jew!"

Mr Giles was at a loss to comprehend what this outcry meant; but Harry Maylie, whose perceptions were something quicker, and who had heard Oliver's history from his mother, understood it at once.

"What direction did he take?" he asked, catching up a heavy stick which was standing in a corner.

"That," replied Oliver, pointing out the course the man had taken; "I missed them in an instant."

"Then, they are in the ditch!" said Harry. "Follow! And keep as near me, as you can." So saying, he sprang over the hedge, and darted off with a speed which rendered it matter of exceeding difficulty for the others to keep near him.

Giles followed as well as he could; and Oliver followed too; and in the course of a minute or two, Mr Losberne, who had been out walking, and just then returned, tumbled over the hedge after them, and picking himself up with more agility than he could have been supposed to possess, struck into the same course at no contemptible speed, shouting all the while, most prodigiously, to know what was the matter.

On they all went; nor stopped they once to breathe, until the leader, striking off into an angle of the field indicated by Oliver, began to search, narrowly, the ditch and hedge adjoining; which afforded time for the remainder of the party to come up; and for Oliver to communicate to Mr Losberne the circumstances that had led to so vigorous a pursuit.

The search was all in vain. There were not even the traces of recent footsteps, to be seen. They stood now, on the summit of a little hill, commanding the open fields in every direction for three or four miles. There was the village in the hollow on the left; but, in order to gain that, after pursuing the track Oliver had pointed out, the men must have made a circuit of open ground, which it was impossible they could have accomplished in so short a time. A thick wood skirted the meadow-land in another direction; but they could not have gained that covert for the same reason.

"It must have been a dream, Oliver," said Harry Maylie.

"Oh no, indeed, sir," replied Oliver, shuddering at the very recollection of the old wretch's countenance; "I saw him too plainly for that. I saw them both, as plainly as I see you now."

"Who was the other?" inquired Harry and Mr Losberne, together.

"The very same man I told you of, who came so suddenly upon me at the inn," said Oliver. "We had our eyes fixed full upon each other; and I could swear to him."

"They took this way?" demanded Harry: "are you sure?"

"As I am that the men were at the window," replied Oliver, pointing down, as he spoke, to the hedge which divided the cottage-garden from the meadow. "The tall man leaped over, just there; and the Jew, running a few paces to the right, crept through that gap."

The two gentlemen watched Oliver's earnest face, as he spoke, and looking from him to each other, seemed to feel satisfied of the accuracy of what he said. Still, in no direction were there any appearances of the trampling of men in hurried flight. The grass was long; but it was trodden down nowhere, save where their own feet had crushed it. The sides and brinks of the ditches were of damp clay; but in no one place could they discern the print of men's shoes, or the slightest mark which would indicate that any feet had pressed the ground for hours before.

"This is strange!" said Harry.

"Strange?" echoed the doctor. "Blathers and Duff, themselves, could make nothing of it."

Notwithstanding the evidently useless nature of their search, they did not desist until the coming on of night rendered its further prosecution hopeless; and even then, they gave it up with reluctance. Giles was despatched to the different ale-houses in the village, furnished with the best description Oliver could give of the appearance and dress of the strangers. Of these, the Jew was, at all events, sufficiently remarkable to be remembered, supposing he had been seen drinking, or loitering about; but Giles returned without any intelligence, calculated to dispel or lessen the mystery.

On the next day, fresh search was made, and the inquiries renewed; but with no better success. On the day following, Oliver and Mr Maylie repaired to the market-town, in the hope of seeing or hearing something of the men there; but this effort was equally fruitless. After a few days, the affair began to be forgotten, as most affairs are, when wonder, having no fresh food to support it, dies away of itself.

Meanwhile, Rose was rapidly recovering. She had left her room: was able to go out; and mixing once more with the family, carried joy into the hearts of all.

But, although this happy change had a visible effect on the little circle; and although cheerful voices and merry laughter were once more heard in the cottage; there was at times, an unwonted restraint upon some there: even upon Rose herself: which Oliver could not fail to remark. Mrs Maylie and her son were often closeted together for a long time; and more than once Rose appeared with traces of tears upon her face. After Mr Losberne had fixed a day for his departure to Chertsey, these symptoms increased; and it became evident that something was in progress which affected the peace of the young lady, and of somebody else besides.

At length, one morning, when Rose was alone in the breakfast-parlour, Harry Maylie entered; and, with some hesitation, begged permission to speak with her for a few moments.

"A few – a very few – will suffice, Rose," said the young man, drawing his chair towards her. "What I shall have to say, has already presented itself to your mind; the most cherished hopes of my heart are not unknown to you, though from my lips you have not yet heard them stated."

Rose had been very pale from the moment of his entrance; but that might have been the effect of her recent illness. She merely bowed; and bending over some plants that stood near, waited in silence for him to proceed.

"I – I – ought to have left here, before," said Harry.

"You should, indeed," replied Rose. "Forgive me for saying so, but I wish you had."

"I was brought here, by the most dreadful and agonising of all apprehensions," said the young man; "the fear of losing the one dear being on whom my every wish and hope are fixed. You had been dying: trembling between earth and heaven. We know that when the young, the beautiful, and good, are visited with sickness, their pure spirits insensibly turn towards their bright home of lasting rest; we know,

Heaven help us! that the best and fairest of our kind, too often fade in blooming."

There were tears in the eyes of the gentle girl, as these words were spoken; and when one fell upon the flower over which she bent, and glistened brightly in its cup, making it more beautiful, it seemed as though the outpouring of her fresh young heart, claimed kindred naturally, with the loveliest things in nature.

"A creature," continued the young man, passionately, "a creature as fair and innocent of guile as one of God's own angels, fluttered between life and death. Oh! who could hope, when the distant world to which she was akin, half opened to her view, that she would return to the sorrow and calamity of this! Rose, Rose, to know that you were passing away like some soft shadow, which a light from above, casts upon the earth; to have no hope that you would be spared to those who linger here; hardly to know a reason why you should be; to feel that you belonged to that bright sphere whither so many of the fairest and the best have winged their early flight; and yet to pray, amid all these consolations, that you might be restored to those who loved you – these were distractions almost too great to bear. They were mine, by day and night; and with them, came such a rushing torrent of fears, and apprehensions, and selfish regrets, lest you should die, and never know how devotedly I loved you, as almost bore down sense and reason in its course. You recovered. Day by day, and almost hour by hour, some drop of health came back, and mingling with the spent and feeble stream of life which circulated languidly within you, swelled it again to a high and rushing tide. I have watched you change almost from death, to life, with eyes that turned blind with their eagerness and deep affection. Do not tell me that you wish I had lost this; for it has softened my heart to all mankind."

"I did not mean that," said Rose, weeping; "I only wish you had left here, that you might have turned to high and noble pursuits again; to pursuits well worthy of you."

"There is no pursuit more worthy of me: more worthy of the highest nature that exists: than the struggle to win such a heart as yours," said the young man, taking her hand. "Rose, my own dear Rose! For years – for years – I have loved you; hoping to win my way to fame, and then come proudly home and tell you it had been pursued only for you to share; thinking, in my day-dreams, how I would remind you, in that happy moment, of the many silent tokens I had given of a boy's attachment, and claim your hand, as in redemption of some old mute contract that had been sealed between us! That time has not arrived; but here, with no fame won, and no young vision realised, I offer you the heart so long your own, and stake my all upon the words with which you greet the offer."

"Your behaviour has ever been kind and noble," said Rose, mastering the emotions by which she was agitated. "As you believe that I am not insensible or ungrateful, so hear my answer."

"It is, that I may endeavour to deserve you; it is, dear Rose?"

"It is," replied Rose, "that you must endeavour to forget me; not as your old and dearly-attached companion, for that would wound me deeply; but, as the object of your love. Look into the world; think how many hearts you would be proud to gain, are there. Confide some other passion to me, if you will; I will be the truest, warmest, and most faithful friend you have."

There was a pause, during which, Rose, who had covered her face with one hand, gave free vent to her tears. Harry still retained the other.

"And your reasons, Rose," he said, at length, in a low voice; "your reasons for this decision?"

"You have a right to know them," rejoined Rose. "You can say nothing to alter my resolution. It is a duty that I must perform. I owe it, alike to others, and to myself."

"To yourself?"

"Yes, Harry. I owe it to myself, that I, a friendless, portionless girl, with a blight upon my name, should not give your friends reason to suspect that I had sordidly yielded to your first passion, and fastened myself, a clog, on all your hopes and projects. I owe it to you and yours, to prevent you from opposing, in the warmth of your generous nature, this great obstacle to your progress in the world."

"If your inclinations chime with your sense of duty – " Harry began.

"They do not," replied Rose, colouring deeply.

"Then you return my love?" said Harry. "Say but that, dear Rose; say but that; and soften the bitterness of this hard disappointment!"

"If I could have done so, without doing heavy wrong to him I loved," rejoined Rose, "I could have – "

"Have received this declaration very differently?" said Harry. "Do not conceal that from me, at least, Rose."

"I could," said Rose. "Stay!" she added, disengaging her hand, "why should we prolong this painful interview? Most painful to me, and yet productive of lasting happiness, notwithstanding; for it *will* be happiness to know that I once held the high place in your regard which I now occupy, and every triumph you achieve in life will animate me with new fortitude and firmness. Farewell, Harry! As we have met to-day, we meet no more; but in other relations than those in which this conversation would have placed us, we may be long and happily entwined; and may every blessing that the prayers of a true and earnest heart can call down from the source of all truth and sincerity, cheer and prosper you!"

"Another word, Rose," said Harry. "Your reason in your own words. From your own lips, let me hear it!"

"The prospect before you," answered Rose, firmly, "is a brilliant one. All the honours to which great talents and powerful connexions can help men in public life, are in store for you. But those connexions are proud; and I will neither mingle with such as may hold in scorn the mother who gave me life; nor bring disgrace or failure on the son of her who has so well supplied that mother's place. In a word," said the young lady, turning away, as her temporary firmness forsook her, "there is a stain upon my name, which the world visits on innocent heads. I will carry it into no blood but my own; and the reproach shall rest alone on me."

"One word more, Rose. Dearest Rose! one more!" cried Harry, throwing himself before her. "If I had been less – less fortunate, the world would call it – if some obscure and peaceful life had been my destiny – if I had been poor, sick, helpless – would you have turned from me then? Or has my probable advancement to riches and honour, given this scruple birth?"

"Do not press me to reply," answered Rose. "The question does not arise, and never will. It is unfair, almost unkind, to urge it."

"If your answer be what I almost dare to hope it is," retorted Harry, "it will shed a gleam of happiness upon my lonely way, and light the path before me. It is not an idle thing to do so much, by the utterance of a few brief words, for one who loves you beyond all else. Oh, Rose! in the name of my ardent and enduring attachment; in the name of all I have suffered for you, and all you doom me to undergo; answer me this one question!"

"Then, if your lot had been differently cast," rejoined Rose; "if you had been even a little, but not so far, above me; if I could have been a help and comfort to you in any humble scene of peace and retirement, and not a blot and drawback in ambitious and distinguished crowds; I should have been spared this trial. I have every reason to be happy, very happy, now; but then, Harry, I own I should have been happier."

Busy recollections of old hopes, cherished as a girl, long ago, crowded into the mind of Rose, while making this avowal; but they brought tears with them, as old hopes will when they come back withered; and they relieved her.

"I cannot help this weakness, and it makes my purpose stronger," said Rose, extending her hand. "I must leave you now, indeed."

"I ask one promise," said Harry. "Once, and only once more, – say within a year, but it may be much sooner, – I may speak to you again on this subject, for the last time."

"Not to press me to alter my right determination," replied Rose, with a melancholy smile; "it will be useless."

"No," said Harry; "to hear you repeat it, if you will – finally repeat it! I will lay at your feet, whatever of station or fortune I may possess; and if you still adhere to your present resolution, will not seek, by word or act, to change it."

"Then let it be so," rejoined Rose; "it is but one pang the more, and by that time I may be enabled to bear it better."

She extended her hand again. But the young man caught her to his bosom; and imprinting one kiss on her beautiful forehead, hurried from the room.

Chapter XXXVI

Is a very short one, and may appear of no great Importance in its Place. But it should be read notwithstanding, as a Sequel to the last, and a Key to one that will follow when its Time arrives

"AND so you are resolved to be my travelling companion this morning; eh?" said the doctor, as Harry Maylie joined him and Oliver at the breakfast-table. "Why, you are not in the same mind or intention two half-hours together!"

"You will tell me a different tale one of these days," said Harry, colouring without any perceptible reason.

"I hope I may have good cause to do so," replied Mr Losberne; "though I confess I don't think I shall. But yesterday morning you had made up your mind, in a great hurry, to stay here, and to accompany your mother, like a dutiful son, to the sea-side. Before noon, you announce that you are going to do me the honour of accompanying me as far as I go, on your road to London. And at night, you urge me, with great mystery, to start before the ladies are stirring; the consequence of which is, that young Oliver here is pinned down to his breakfast when he ought to be ranging the meadows after botanical phenomena of all kinds. Too bad, isn't it, Oliver?"

"I should have been very sorry not to have been at home when you and Mr Maylie went away, sir," rejoined Oliver.

"That's a fine fellow," said the doctor; "you shall come and see me when you return. But, to speak seriously, Harry; has any communication from the great nobs produced this sudden anxiety on your part to be gone?"

"The great nobs," replied Harry, "under which designation, I presume, you include my most stately uncle, have not communicated with me at all, since I have been here; nor, at this time of the year, is it likely that anything would occur to render necessary my immediate attendance among them."

"Well," said the doctor, "you are a queer fellow. But of course they will get you into parliament at the election before Christmas, and these sudden shiftings and changes are no bad preparation for political life. There's something in that. Good training is always desirable, whether the race be for place, cup, or sweepstakes."

Harry Maylie looked as if he could have followed up this short dialogue by one or two remarks that would have staggered the doctor not a little; but he contented himself with saying, "We shall see," and pursued the subject no farther. The post-chaise drove up to the door shortly afterwards; and Giles coming in for the luggage, the good doctor bustled out, to see it packed.

"Oliver," said Harry Maylie, in a low voice, "let me speak a word with you."

Oliver walked into the window-recess to which Mr Maylie beckoned him; much surprised at the mixture of sadness and boisterous spirits, which his whole behaviour displayed.

"You can write well now?" said Harry, laying his hand upon his arm.

"I hope so, sir," replied Oliver.

"I shall not be at home again, perhaps for some time; I wish you would write to me – say once a fortnight: every alternate Monday: to the General Post Office in London. Will you?"

"Oh! certainly, sir; I shall be proud to do it," exclaimed Oliver, greatly delighted with the commission.

"I should like to know how – how my mother and Miss Maylie are," said the young man; "and you can fill up a sheet by telling me what walks you take, and what you talk about, and whether she – they, I mean – seem happy and quite well. You understand me?"

"Oh! quite, sir, quite," replied Oliver.

"I would rather you did not mention it to them," said Harry, hurrying over his words; "because it might make my mother anxious to write to me oftener, and it is a trouble and worry to her. Let it be a secret between you and me; and mind you tell me everything! I depend upon you."

Oliver, quite elated and honoured by a sense of his importance, faithfully promised to be secret and explicit in his communications. Mr Maylie took leave of him, with many assurances of his regard and protection.

The doctor was in the chaise; Giles (who, it had been arranged, should be left behind) held the door open in his hand; and the women-servants were in the garden, looking on. Harry cast one slight glance at the latticed window, and jumped into the carriage.

"Drive on!" he cried, "hard, fast, full gallop! Nothing short of flying will keep pace with me, to-day."

"Holloa!" cried the doctor, letting down the front glass in a great hurry, and shouting to the postillion; "something very short of flying will keep pace with *me*. Do you hear?"

Jingling and clattering, till distance rendered its noise inaudible, and its rapid progress only perceptible to the eye, the vehicle wound its way along the road, almost hidden in a cloud of dust: now wholly disappearing, and now becoming visible again, as intervening objects, or the intricacies of the way, permitted. It was not until even the dusty cloud was no longer to be seen, that the gazers dispersed.

And there was one looker-on, who remained with eyes fixed upon the spot where the carriage had disappeared, long after it was many miles away; for, behind the white curtain which had shrouded her from view when Harry raised his eyes towards the window, sat Rose herself.

"He seems in high spirits and happy," she said, at length. "I feared for a time he might be otherwise. I was mistaken. I am very, very glad."

Tears are signs of gladness as well as grief; but those which coursed down Rose's face, as she sat pensively at the window, still gazing in the same direction, seemed to tell more of sorrow than of joy.

Chapter XXXVII

In which the Reader may perceive a Contrast, not uncommon in matrimonial Cases

Mr Bumble sat in the workhouse parlour, with his eyes moodily fixed on the cheerless grate, whence, as it was summer time, no brighter gleam proceeded, than the reflection of certain sickly rays of the sun, which were sent back from its cold and shining surface. A paper fly-cage dangled from the ceiling, to which he occasionally raised his eyes in gloomy thought; and, as the heedless insects hovered round the gaudy net-work, Mr Bumble would heave a deep sigh, while a more gloomy shadow overspread his countenance. Mr Bumble was meditating; it might be that the insects brought to mind, some painful passage in his own past life.

Nor was Mr Bumble's gloom the only thing calculated to awaken a pleasing melancholy in the bosom of a spectator. There were not wanting other appearances, and those closely connected with his own person, which announced that a great change had taken place in the position of his affairs. The laced coat, and the cocked-hat; where were they? He still wore knee-breeches, and dark cotton stockings on his nether limbs; but they were not *the* breeches. The coat was wide-skirted; and in that respect like *the* coat, but, oh, how different! The mighty cocked-hat was replaced by a modest round one. Mr Bumble was no longer a beadle.

There are some promotions in life, which, independent of the more substantial rewards they offer, acquire peculiar value and dignity from the coats and waistcoats connected with them. A field-marshal has his uniform; a bishop his silk apron; a counsellor his silk gown; a beadle his cocked-hat. Strip the bishop of his apron, or the beadle of his hat and lace; what are they? Men. Mere men. Dignity, and even holiness too, sometimes, are more questions of coat and waistcoat than some people imagine.

Mr Bumble had married Mrs Corney, and was master of the workhouse. Another beadle had come into power. On him the cocked-hat, gold-laced coat, and staff, had all three descended.

"And to-morrow two months it was done!" said Mr Bumble, with a sigh. "It seems a age."

Mr Bumble might have meant that he had concentrated a whole existence of happiness into the short space of eight weeks; but the sigh – there was a vast deal of meaning in the sigh.

"I sold myself," said Mr Bumble, pursuing the same train of reflection, "for six teaspoons, a pair of sugar-tongs, and a milk-pot; with a small quantity of second-hand furniture, and twenty pound in money. I went very reasonable. Cheap, dirt cheap!"

"Cheap!" cried a shrill voice in Mr Bumble's ear: "you would have been dear at any price; and dear enough I paid for you, Lord above knows that!"

Mr Bumble turned, and encountered the face of his interesting consort, who, imperfectly comprehending the few words she had overheard of his complaint, had hazarded the foregoing remark at a venture.

"Mrs Bumble, ma'am!" said Mr Bumble, with sentimental sternness.

"Well!" cried the lady.

"Have the goodness to look at me," said Mr Bumble, fixing his eyes upon her. ("If she stands such a eye as that," said Mr Bumble to himself, "she can stand anything. It is a eye I never knew to fail with paupers. If it fails with her, my power is gone.")

Whether an exceedingly small expansion of eye be sufficient to quell paupers, who, being lightly fed, are in no very high condition; or whether the late Mrs Corney was particularly proof against eagle glances; are matters of opinion. The matter of fact is, that the matron was in no way overpowered by Mr Bumble's scowl, but, on the contrary, treated it with great disdain, and even raised a laugh thereat, which sounded as though it were genuine.

On hearing this most unexpected sound, Mr Bumble looked, first incredulous, and afterwards amazed. He then relapsed into his former state; nor did he rouse himself until his attention was again awakened by the voice of his partner.

"Are you going to sit snoring there, all day?" inquired Mrs Bumble.

"I am going to sit here, as long as I think proper, ma'am," rejoined Mr Bumble; "and although I was *not* snoring, I shall snore, gape, sneeze, laugh, or cry, as the humour strikes me; such being my prerogative."

"*Your* prerogative!" sneered Mrs Bumble, with ineffable contempt.

"I said the word, ma'am," said Mr Bumble. "The prerogative of a man is to command."

"And what's the prerogative of a woman, in the name of Goodness?" cried the relict of Mr Corney deceased.

"To obey, ma'am," thundered Mr Bumble. "Your late unfortunate husband should have taught it you; and then, perhaps, he might have been alive now. I wish he was, poor man!"

Mrs Bumble, seeing at a glance, that the decisive moment had now arrived, and that a blow struck for the mastership on one side or other, must necessarily be final and conclusive, no sooner heard this allusion to the dead and gone, than she dropped into a chair, and with a loud scream that Mr Bumble was a hard-hearted brute, fell into a paroxysm of tears.

But, tears were not the things to find their way to Mr Bumble's soul; his heart was waterproof. Like washable beaver hats that improve with rain, his nerves were rendered stouter and more vigorous, by showers of tears, which, being tokens of weakness, and so far tacit admissions of his own power, pleased and exalted him. He eyed his good lady with looks of great satisfaction, and begged, in an encouraging manner, that she should cry, her hardest: the exercise being looked upon, by the faculty, as strongly conducive to health.

"It opens the lungs, washes the countenance, exercises the eyes, and softens down the temper," said Mr Bumble. "So cry away."

As he discharged himself of this pleasantry, Mr Bumble took his hat from a peg, and putting it on, rather rakishly, on one side, as a man might, who felt he had asserted his superiority in a becoming manner, thrust his hands into his pockets, and sauntered towards the door, with much ease and waggishness depicted in his whole appearance.

Now, Mrs Corney that was, had tried the tears, because they were less troublesome than a manual assault; but, she was quite prepared to make trial of the latter mode of proceeding, as Mr Bumble was not long in discovering.

The first proof he experienced of the fact, was conveyed in a hollow sound, immediately succeeded by the sudden flying off of his hat to the opposite end of the room. This preliminary proceeding laying bare his head, the expert lady, clasping him tightly round the throat with one hand, inflicted a shower of blows (dealt with singular vigour and dexterity) upon it with the other. This done, she created a little variety by scratching his face, and tearing his hair; and, having, by this time, inflicted as much punishment as she deemed necessary for the offence, she pushed him over a chair, which was luckily well situated for the purpose: and defied him to talk about his prerogative again, if he dared.

"Get up!" said Mrs Bumble, in a voice of command. "And take yourself away from here, unless you want me to do something desperate."

Mr Bumble rose with a very rueful countenance: wondering much what something desperate might be. Picking up his hat, he looked towards the door.

"Are you going?" demanded Mrs Bumble.

"Certainly, my dear, certainly," rejoined Mr Bumble, making a quicker motion towards the door. "I didn't intend to – I'm going, my dear! You are so very violent, that really I – "

At this instant, Mrs Bumble stepped hastily forward to replace the carpet, which had been kicked up in the scuffle. Mr Bumble immediately darted out of the room, without bestowing another thought on his unfinished sentence: leaving the late Mrs Corney in full possession of the field.

Mr Bumble was fairly taken by surprise, and fairly beaten. He had a decided propensity for bullying: derived no inconsiderable pleasure from the exercise of petty cruelty; and, consequently, was (it is needless to say) a coward. This is by no means a disparagement to his character; for many official personages, who are held in high respect and admiration, are the victims of similar infirmities. The remark is made, indeed, rather in his favour than otherwise, and with a view of impressing the reader with a just sense of his qualifications for office.

But, the measure of his degradation was not yet full. After making a tour of the house, and thinking, for the first time, that the poor-laws really were too hard on people; and that men who ran away from their wives, leaving them chargeable to the parish, ought, in justice, to be visited with no punishment at all, but rather rewarded as meritorious individuals who had suffered much; Mr Bumble came to a room where some of the female paupers were usually employed in washing the parish linen: whence the sound of voices in conversation, now proceeded.

"Hem!" said Mr Bumble, summoning up all his native dignity. "These women at least shall continue to respect the prerogative. Hallo! hallo there! What do you mean by this noise, you hussies?"

With these words, Mr Bumble opened the door, and walked in with a very fierce and angry manner: which was at once exchanged for a most humiliated and cowering air, as his eyes unexpectedly rested on the form of his lady wife.

"My dear," said Mr Bumble, "I didn't know you were here."

"Didn't know I was here!" repeated Mrs Bumble. "What do *you* do here?"

"I thought they were talking rather too much to be doing their work properly, my dear," replied Mr Bumble: glancing distractedly at a couple of old women at the wash-tub, who were comparing notes of admiration at the workhouse-master's humility.

"*You* thought they were talking too much?" said Mrs Bumble. "What business is it of yours?"

"Why, my dear –" urged Mr Bumble submissively.

"What business is it of yours?" demanded Mrs Bumble, again.

"It's very true, you're matron here, my dear," submitted Mr Bumble; "but I thought you mightn't be in the way just then."

"I'll tell you what, Mr Bumble," returned his lady. "We don't want any of your interference. You're a great deal too fond of poking your nose into things that don't concern you, making everybody in the house laugh, the moment your back is turned, and making yourself look like a fool every hour in the day. Be off; come!"

Mr Bumble, seeing with excruciating feelings, the delight of the two old paupers, who were tittering together most rapturously, hesitated for an instant. Mrs Bumble, whose patience brooked no delay, caught up a bowl of soap-suds, and motioning him towards the door, ordered him instantly to depart, on pain of receiving the contents upon his portly person.

What could Mr Bumble do? He looked dejectedly round, and slunk away; and, as he reached the door, the titterings of the paupers broke into a shrill chuckle of irrepressible delight. It wanted but this. He was degraded in their eyes; he had lost caste and station before the very paupers; he had fallen from all the height and pomp of beadleship, to the lowest depth of the most snubbed hen-peckery.

"All in two months!" said Mr Bumble, filled with dismal thoughts. "Two months! No more than two months ago, I was not only my own master, but everybody else's, so far as the porochial workhouse was concerned, and now! – "

It was too much. Mr Bumble boxed the ears of the boy who opened the gate for him (for he had reached the portal in his reverie); and walked, distractedly, into the street.

He walked up one street, and down another, until exercise had abated the first passion of his grief; and then the revulsion of feeling made him thirsty. He passed a great many public-houses; but, at length paused before one in a by-way, whose parlour, as he gathered from a hasty peep over the blinds, was deserted, save by one solitary customer. It began to rain, heavily, at the moment. This determined him. Mr Bumble stepped in; and ordering something to drink, as he passed the bar, entered the apartment into which he had looked from the street.

The man who was seated there, was tall and dark, and wore a large cloak. He had the air of a stranger; and seemed, by a certain haggardness in his look, as well as by the dusty soils on his dress, to have travelled some distance. He eyed Bumble askance, as he entered, but scarcely deigned to nod his head in acknowledgment of his salutation.

Mr Bumble had quite dignity enough for two: supposing even that the stranger had been more familiar: so he drank his gin-and-water in silence, and read the paper with great show of pomp and circumstance.

It so happened, however: as it will happen very often, when men fall into company under such circumstances: that Mr Bumble felt, every now and then, a powerful inducement, which he could not resist, to steal a look at the stranger: and that whenever he did so, he withdrew his eyes, in some confusion, to find that the stranger was at that moment stealing a look at him. Mr Bumble's awkwardness was enhanced by the very remarkable expression of the stranger's eye, which was keen and bright, but shadowed by a scowl of distrust and suspicion, unlike anything he had ever observed before, and repulsive to behold.

When they had encountered each other's glance several times in this way, the stranger, in a harsh, deep voice, broke silence.

"Were you looking for me," he said, "when you peered in at the window?"

"Not that I am aware of, unless you're Mr – " Here Mr Bumble stopped short; for he was curious to know the stranger's name, and thought in his impatience, he might supply the blank.

"I see you were not," said the stranger; an expression of quiet sarcasm playing about his mouth; "or you would have known my name. You don't know it. I would recommend you not to ask for it."

"I meant no harm, young man," observed Mr Bumble, majestically.

"And have done none," said the stranger.

Another silence succeeded this short dialogue: which was again broken by the stranger.

"I have seen you before, I think?" said he. "You were differently dressed at that time, and I only passed you in the street, but I should know you again. You were beadle here, once; were you not?"

"I was," said Mr Bumble, in some surprise; "porochial beadle."

"Just so," rejoined the other, nodding his head. "It was in that character I saw you. What are you now?"

"Master of the workhouse," rejoined Mr Bumble, slowly and impressively, to check any undue familiarity the stranger might otherwise assume. "Master of the workhouse, young man!"

"You have the same eye to your own interest, that you always had, I doubt not?" resumed the stranger, looking keenly into Mr Bumble's eyes, as he raised them in astonishment at the question. "Don't scruple to answer freely, man. I know you pretty well, you see."

"I suppose, a married man," replied Mr Bumble, shading his eyes with his hand, and surveying the stranger, from head to foot, in evident perplexity, "is not more averse to turning an honest penny when he can, than a single one. Porochial officers are not so well paid that they can afford to refuse any little extra fee, when it comes to them in a civil and proper manner."

The stranger smiled, and nodded his head again: as much as to say, he had not mistaken his man; then rang the bell.

"Fill this glass again," he said, handing Mr Bumble's empty tumbler to the landlord. "Let it be strong and hot. You like it so, I suppose?"

"Not too strong," replied Mr Bumble, with a delicate cough.

"You understand what that means, landlord!" said the stranger, drily.

The host smiled, disappeared, and shortly afterwards returned with a steaming jorum: of which, the first gulp brought the water into Mr Bumble's eyes.

"Now listen to me," said the stranger, after closing the door and window. "I came down to this place, to-day, to find you out; and, by one of those chances which the devil throws in the way of his friends sometimes, you walked into the very room I was sitting in, while you were uppermost in my mind. I want some information from you. I don't ask you to give it for nothing, slight as it is. Put up that, to begin with."

As he spoke, he pushed a couple of sovereigns across the table to his companion, carefully, as though unwilling that the chinking of money should be heard without. When Mr Bumble had scrupulously examined the coins, to see that they were genuine, and had put them up, with much satisfaction, in his waistcoat-pocket, he went on:

"Carry your memory back – let me see – twelve years, last winter."

"It's a long time," said Mr Bumble. "Very good. I've done it."

"The scene, the workhouse."

"Good!"

"And the time, night."

"Yes."

"And the place, the crazy hole, wherever it was, in which miserable drabs brought forth the life and health so often denied to themselves – gave birth to puling children for the parish to rear; and hid their shame, rot 'em, in the grave!"

"The lying-in room, I suppose?" said Mr Bumble, not quite following the stranger's excited description.

"Yes," said the stranger. "A boy was born there."

"A many boys," observed Mr Bumble, shaking his head, despondingly.

"A murrain on the young devils!" cried the stranger; "I speak of one; a meek-looking, pale-faced boy, who was apprenticed down here, to a coffin-maker – I wish he had made his coffin, and screwed his body in it – and who afterwards ran away to London, as it was supposed."

"Why you mean Oliver! Young Twist!" said Mr Bumble; "I remember him, of course. There wasn't a obstinater young rascal –"

"It's not of him I want to hear; I've heard enough of him," said the stranger, stopping Mr Bumble in the outset of a tirade on the subject of poor Oliver's vices. "It's of a woman; the hag that nursed his mother. Where is she?"

"Where is she?" said Mr Bumble, whom the gin-and-water had rendered facetious. "It would be hard to tell. There's no midwifery there, whichever place she's gone to; so I suppose she's out of employment, anyway."

"What do you mean?" demanded the stranger, sternly.

"That she died last winter," rejoined Mr Bumble.

The man looked fixedly at him when he had given this information, and although he did not withdraw his eyes for some time afterwards, his gaze gradually became vacant and abstracted, and he seemed lost in thought. For some time, he appeared doubtful whether he ought to be relieved or disappointed by the intelligence; but at length he breathed more freely; and withdrawing his eyes, observed that it was no great matter. With that he rose, as if to depart.

But Mr Bumble was cunning enough; and he at once saw that an opportunity was opened, for the lucrative disposal of some secret in the possession of his better half. He well remembered the night of old Sally's death, which the occurrences of that day had given him good reason to recollect, as the occasion on which he had proposed to Mrs Corney; and although that lady had never confided to him the disclosure of which she had been the solitary witness, he had heard enough to know that it related to something that had occurred in the old woman's attendance, as workhouse nurse, upon the young mother of Oliver Twist. Hastily calling this circumstance to mind, he informed the stranger, with an air of mystery, that one woman had been closeted with the old harridan shortly before she died; and that she could, as he had reason to believe, throw some light on the subject of his inquiry.

"How can I find her?" said the stranger, thrown off his guard; and plainly showing that all his fears (whatever they were) were aroused afresh by the intelligence.

"Only through me," rejoined Mr Bumble.

"When?" cried the stranger, hastily.

"To-morrow," rejoined Bumble.

"At nine in the evening," said the stranger, producing a scrap of paper, and writing down upon it, an obscure address by the water-side, in characters that betrayed his agitation; "at nine in the evening, bring her to me there. I needn't tell you to be secret. It's your interest."

With these words, he led the way to the door, after stopping to pay for the liquor that had been drunk. Shortly remarking that their roads were different, he departed, without more ceremony than an emphatic repetition of the hour of appointment for the following night.

On glancing at the address, the parochial functionary observed that it contained no name. The stranger had not gone far, so he made after him to ask it.

"What do you want?" cried the man, turning quickly round, as Bumble touched him on the arm. "Following me?"

"Only to ask a question," said the other, pointing to the scrap of paper. "What name am I to ask for?"

"Monks!" rejoined the man; and strode, hastily, away.

Chapter XXXVIII

Containing an Account of what passed Between Mr and Mrs Bumble, and Mr Monks, at their nocturnal interview

It was a dull, close, overcast summer evening. The clouds, which had been threatening all day, spread out in a dense and sluggish mass of vapour, already yielded large drops of rain, and seemed to presage a violent thunder-storm, when Mr and Mrs Bumble, turning out of the main street of the town, directed their course towards a scattered little colony of ruinous houses, distant from it some mile and a-half, or thereabouts, and erected on a low unwholesome swamp, bordering upon the river.

They were both wrapped in old and shabby outer garments, which might, perhaps, serve the double purpose of protecting their persons from the rain, and sheltering them from observation. The husband carried a lantern, from which, however, no light yet shone; and trudged on, a few paces in front, as though – the way being dirty – to give his wife the benefit of treading in his heavy foot-prints. They went on, in profound silence; every now and then, Mr Bumble relaxed his pace, and turned his head as if to make sure that his helpmate was following; then, discovering that she was close at his heels, he mended his rate of walking, and proceeded, at a considerable increase of speed, towards their place of destination.

This was far from being a place of doubtful character; for it had long been known as the residence of none but low ruffians, who, under various pretences of living by their labour, subsisted chiefly on plunder and crime. It was a collection of mere hovels: some, hastily built with loose bricks: others, of old worm-eaten ship-timber: jumbled together without any attempt at order or arrangement, and planted, for the most part, within a few feet of the river's bank. A few leaky boats drawn up on the mud, and made fast to the dwarf wall which skirted it: and here and there an oar or coil of rope: appeared, at first to indicate that the inhabitants of these miserable cottages pursued some avocation on the river; but a glance at the shattered and useless condition of the articles thus displayed, would have led a passer-by, without much difficulty, to the conjecture that they were disposed there, rather for the preservation of appearances, than with any view to their being actually employed.

In the heart of this cluster of huts; and skirting the river, which its upper stories overhung; stood a large building, formerly used as a manufactory of some kind. It had, in its day, probably furnished employment to the inhabitants of the surrounding tenements. But it had long since gone to ruin. The rat, the worm, and the action of the damp, had weakened and rotted the piles on which it stood; and a considerable portion of the building had already sunk down into the water; while the remainder, tottering and bending over the dark stream, seemed to wait a favourable opportunity of following its old companion, and involving itself in the same fate.

It was before this ruinous building that the worthy couple paused, as the first peal of distant thunder reverberated in the air, and the rain commenced pouring violently down.

"The place should be somewhere here," said Bumble, consulting a scrap of paper he held in his hand.

"Halloa there!" cried a voice from above.

Following the sound, Mr Bumble raised his head, and descried a man looking out of a door, breast-high, on the second story.

"Stand still, a minute," cried the voice; "I'll be with you directly." With which the head disappeared, and the door closed.

"Is that the man?" asked Mr Bumble's good lady.

Mr Bumble nodded in the affirmative.

"Then, mind what I told you," said the matron: "and be careful to say as little as you can, or you'll betray us at once."

Mr Bumble, who had eyed the building with very rueful looks, was apparently about to express some doubts relative to the advisability of proceeding any further with the enterprise just then, when he was prevented by the appearance of Monks: who opened a small door, near which they stood, and beckoned them inwards.

"Come in!" he cried impatiently, stamping his foot upon the ground. "Don't keep me here!"

The woman, who had hesitated at first, walked boldly in, without any other invitation. Mr Bumble, who was ashamed or afraid to lag behind, followed: obviously very ill at ease and with scarcely any of that remarkable dignity which was usually his chief characteristic.

"What the devil made you stand lingering there, in the wet?" said Monks, turning round, and addressing Bumble, after he had bolted the door behind them.

"We – we were only cooling ourselves," stammered Bumble, looking apprehensively about him.

"Cooling yourselves!" retorted Monks. "Not all the rain that ever fell, or ever will fall, will put as much of hell's fire out, as a man can carry about with him. You won't cool yourselves so easily; don't think it!"

With this agreeable speech, Monks turned short upon the matron, and bent his gaze upon her, till even she, who was not easily cowed, was fain to withdraw her eyes, and turn them towards the ground.

"This is the woman, is it?" demanded Monks.

"Hem! That is the woman," replied Mr Bumble, mindful of his wife's caution.

"You think women never can keep secrets, I suppose?" said the matron, interposing, and returning, as she spoke, the searching look of Monks.

"I know they will always keep *one* till it's found out," said Monks.

"And what may that be?" asked the matron.

"The loss of their own good name," replied Monks. "So, by the same rule, if a woman's a party to a secret that might hang or transport her, I'm not afraid of her telling it to anybody; not I! Do you understand, mistress?"

"No," rejoined the matron, slightly colouring as she spoke.

"Of course you don't!" said Monks. "How should you?"

Bestowing something half-way between a smile and a frown upon his two companions, and again beckoning them to follow him, the man hastened across the apartment, which was of considerable extent, but low in the roof. He was preparing to ascend a steep staircase, or rather ladder, leading to another floor of warehouses above: when a bright flash of lightning streamed down the aperture, and a peal of thunder followed, which shook the crazy building to its centre.

"Hear it!" he cried, shrinking back. "Hear it! Rolling and crashing on as if it echoed through a thousand caverns where the devils were hiding from it. I hate the sound!"

He remained silent for a few moments; and then, removing his hands suddenly from his face, showed to the unspeakable discomposure of Mr Bumble, that it was much distorted, and discoloured.

"These fits come over me, now and then," said Monks, observing his alarm; "and thunder sometimes brings them on. Don't mind me now; it's all over for this once."

Thus speaking, he led the way up the ladder; and hastily closing the window-shutter of the room into which it led, lowered a lantern which hung at the end of a rope and pulley passed through one of the heavy beams in the ceiling: and which cast a dim light upon an old table and three chairs that were placed beneath it.

"Now," said Monks, when they had all three seated themselves, "the sooner we come to our business, the better for all. The woman knows what it is, does she?"

The question was addressed to Bumble; but his wife anticipated the reply, by intimating that she was perfectly acquainted with it.

"He is right in saying that you were with this hag the night she died; and that she told you something – "

"About the mother of the boy you named," replied the matron interrupting him. "Yes."

"The first question is, of what nature was her communication?" said Monks.

"That's the second," observed the woman with much deliberation. "The first is, what may the communication be worth?"

"Who the devil can tell that, without knowing of what kind it is?" asked Monks.

"Nobody better than you, I am persuaded," answered Mrs Bumble: who did not want for spirit, as her yokefellow could abundantly testify.

"Humph!" said Monks significantly, and with a look of eager inquiry; "there may be money's worth to get, eh?"

"Perhaps there may," was the composed reply.

"Something that was taken from her," said Monks. "Something that she wore. Something that – "

"You had better bid," interrupted Mrs Bumble. "I have heard enough, already, to assure me that you are the man I ought to talk to."

Mr Bumble, who had not yet been admitted by his better half into any greater share of the secret than he had originally possessed, listened to this dialogue with outstretched neck and distended eyes: which he directed towards his wife and Monks, by turns, in undisguised astonishment; increased, if possible, when the latter sternly demanded what sum was required for the disclosure.

"What's it worth to you?" asked the woman, as collectedly as before.

"It may be nothing; it may be twenty pounds," replied Monks. "Speak out, and let me know which."

"Add five pounds to the sum you have named; give me five-and-twenty pounds in gold," said the woman; "and I'll tell you all I know. Not before."

"Five-and-twenty pounds!" exclaimed Monks, drawing back.

"I spoke as plainly as I could," replied Mrs Bumble. "It's not a large sum, either."

"Not a large sum for a paltry secret, that may be nothing when it's told!" cried Monks impatiently; "and which has been lying dead for twelve years past or more!"

"Such matters keep well, and, like good wine, often double their value in course of time," answered the matron, still preserving the resolute indifference she had assumed. "As to lying dead, there are those who will lie dead for twelve thousand years to come, or twelve million, for anything you or I know, who will tell strange tales at last!"

"What if I pay it for nothing?" asked Monks, hesitating.

"You can easily take it away again," replied the matron. "I am but a woman; alone here; and unprotected."

"Not alone, my dear, nor unprotected neither," submitted Mr Bumble, in a voice tremulous with fear: "*I* am here, my dear. And besides," said Mr Bumble, his teeth chattering as he spoke, "Mr Monks is too much of a gentleman to attempt any violence on porochial persons. Mr Monks is aware that I am not a young man, my dear, and also that I am a little run to seed, as I may say; but he has heerd: I say I have no doubt Mr Monks has heerd, my dear: that I am a very determined officer, with very uncommon strength, if I'm once roused. I only want a little rousing; that's all."

As Mr Bumble spoke, he made a melancholy feint of grasping his lantern with fierce determination; and plainly showed, by the alarmed expression of every feature, that he *did* want a little rousing, and not a little, prior to making any very warlike demonstration: unless, indeed, against paupers, or other person or persons trained down for the purpose.

"You are a fool," said Mrs Bumble, in reply; "and had better hold your tongue."

"He had better have cut it out, before he came, if he can't speak in a lower tone," said Monks, grimly. "So! He's your husband, eh?"

"He my husband!" tittered the matron, parrying the question.

"I thought as much, when you came in," rejoined Monks, marking the angy glance which the lady darted at her spouse as she spoke. "So much the better; I have less hesitation in dealing with two people, when I find that there's only one will between them. I'm in earnest. See here!"

He thrust his hand into a side-pocket; and producing a canvas bag, told out twenty-five sovereigns on the table, and pushed them over to the woman.

"Now," he said, "gather them up; and when this cursed peal of thunder, which I feel is coming up to break over the house-top, is gone, let's hear your story."

The thunder, which seemed in fact much nearer, and to shiver and break almost over their heads, having subsided, Monks, raising his face from the table, bent forward to listen to what the woman should say. The faces of the three nearly touched, as the two men leant over the small table in their eagerness to hear, and the woman also leant forward to render her whisper audible. The sickly rays of the suspended lantern falling directly upon them, aggravated the paleness and anxiety of their countenances: which, encircled by the deepest gloom and darkness, looked ghastly in the extreme.

"When this woman, that we called old Sally, died," the matron began, "she and I were alone."

"Was there no one by?" asked Monks, in the same hollow whisper; "no sick wretch or idiot in some other bed? No one who could hear, and might, by possibility, understand?"

"Not a soul," replied the woman; "we were alone. *I* stood alone beside the body when death came over it."

"Good," said Monks, regarding her attentively. "Go on."

"She spoke of a young creature," resumed the matron, "who had brought a child into the world some years before; not merely in the same room, but in the same bed, in which she then lay dying."

"Ay?" said Monks, with quivering lip, and glancing over his shoulder, "Blood! How things come about!"

"The child was the one you named to him last night," said the matron, nodding carelessly towards her husband; "the mother this nurse had robbed."

"In life?" asked Monks.

"In death," replied the woman, with something like a shudder. "She stole from the corpse, when it had hardly turned to one, that which the dead mother had prayed her, with her last breath, to keep for the infant's sake."

"She sold it?" cried Monks, with desperate eagerness; "did she sell it? Where? When? To whom? How long before?"

"As she told me, with great difficulty, that she had done this," said the matron, "she fell back and died."

"Without saying more?" cried Monks, in a voice which, from its very suppression, seemed only the more furious. "It's a lie! I'll not be played with. She said more. I'll tear the life out of you both, but I'll know what it was."

"She didn't utter another word," said the woman, to all appearance unmoved (as Mr Bumble was very far from being) by the strange man's violence; "but she clutched my gown, violently, with one hand, which was partly closed; and when I saw that she was dead, and so removed the hand by force, I found it clasped a scrap of dirty paper."

"Which contained – " interposed Monks, stretching forward.

"Nothing," replied the woman; "it was a pawnbroker's duplicate."

"For what?" demanded Monks.

"In good time I'll tell you," said the woman. "I judge that she had kept the trinket, for some time, in the hope of turning it to better account; and then had pawned it; and had saved or scraped together money to pay the pawnbroker's interest year by year, and prevent its running out; so that if anything came of it, it could still be redeemed. Nothing had come of it; and, as I tell you, she died with the scrap of paper, all worn and tattered, in her hand. The time was out in two days; I thought something might one day come of it too; and so redeemed the pledge."

"Where is it now?" asked Monks quickly.

"*There*," replied the woman. And, as if glad to be relieved of it, she hastily threw upon the table a small kid bag scarcely large enough for a French watch, which Monks pouncing upon, tore open with trembling hands. It contained a little gold locket: in which were two locks of hair, and a plain gold wedding-ring.

"It has the word "Agnes" engraved on the inside," said the woman. "There is a blank left for the surname; and then follows the date; which is within a year before the child was born. I found out that."

"And this is all?" said Monks, after a close and eager scrutiny of the contents of the little packet.

"All," replied the woman.

Mr Bumble drew a long breath, as if he were glad to find that the story was over, and no mention made of taking the five-and-twenty pounds back again; and now he took courage to wipe off the perspiration which had been trickling over his nose, unchecked, during the whole of the previous dialogue.

"I know nothing of the story, beyond what I can guess at," said his wife addressing Monks, after a short silence; "and I want to know nothing; for it's safer not. But I may ask you two questions, may I?"

"You may ask," said Monks, with some show of surprise; "but whether I answer or not is another question."

"– Which makes three," observed Mr Bumble, essaying a stroke of facetiousness.

"Is that what you expected to get from me?" demanded the matron.

"It is," replied Monks. "The other question?"

"What you propose to do with it? Can it be used against me?"

"Never," rejoined Monks; "nor against me either. See here! But don't move a step forward, or your life is not worth a bulrush."

With these words, he suddenly wheeled the table aside, and pulling an iron ring in the boarding, threw back a large trap-door which opened close at Mr Bumble's feet, and caused that gentleman to retire several paces backward, with great precipitation.

"Look down," said Monks, lowering the lantern into the gulf. "Don't fear me. I could have let you down, quietly enough, when you were seated over it, if that had been my game."

Thus encouraged the matron drew near to the brink; and even Mr Bumble himself, impelled by curiosity, ventured to do the same. The turbid water, swollen by the heavy rain, was rushing rapidly on below; and all other sounds were lost in the noise of its plashing and eddying against the green and slimy piles. There had once been a water-mill beneath; the tide foaming and chafing round the few rotten stakes, and fragments of machinery that yet remained, seemed to dart onward, with a new impulse, when freed from the obstacles which had unavailingly attempted to stem its headlong course.

"If you flung a man's body down there, where would it be to-morrow morning?" said Monks, swinging the lantern to and fro in the dark well.

"Twelve miles down the river, and cut to pieces besides," replied Bumble, recoiling at the thought.

Monks drew the little packet from his breast, where he had hurriedly thrust it; and tying it to a leaden weight, which had formed a part of some pulley, and was lying on the floor, dropped it into the stream. It fell straight, and true as a die; clove the water with a scarcely audible splash; and was gone.

The three looking into each other's faces, seemed to breathe more freely.

"There!" said Monks, closing the trap-door, which fell heavily back into its former position. "If the sea ever gives up its dead, as books say it will, it will keep its gold and silver to itself, and that trash among it. We have nothing more to say, and may break up our pleasant party."

"By all means," observed Mr Bumble, with great alacrity.

"You'll keep a quiet tongue in your head, will you?" said Monks, with a threatening look. "I am not afraid of your wife."

"You may depend upon me, young man," answered Mr Bumble, bowing himself gradually towards the ladder, with excessive politeness. "On everybody's account, young man; on my own, you know, Mr Monks."

"I am glad, for your sake, to hear it," remarked Monks. "Light your lantern! And get away from here as fast as you can."

It was fortunate that the conversation terminated at this point, or Mr Bumble, who had bowed himself to within six inches of the ladder, would infallibly have pitched headlong into the room below. He lighted his lantern from that which Monks had detached from the rope, and now carried in his hand; and making no effort to prolong the discourse, descended in silence, followed by his wife. Monks brought up the rear, after pausing on the steps to satisfy himself that there were no other sounds to be heard than the beating of the rain without, and the rushing of the water.

They traversed the lower room, slowly, and with caution; for Monks started at every shadow; and Mr Bumble, holding his lantern a foot above the ground, walked not only with remarkable care, but with a marvellously light step for a gentleman of his figure: looking nervously about him for hidden trap-doors. The gate at which they had entered, was softly unfastened and opened by Monks; merely exchanging a nod with their mysterious acquaintance, the married couple emerged into the wet and darkness outside.

They were no sooner gone, than Monks, who appeared to entertain an invincible repugnance to being left alone, called to a boy who had been hidden somewhere below. Bidding him go first, and bear the light, he returned to the chamber he had just quitted.

Chapter XXXIX

Introduces some respectable Characters with whom the Reader is already acquainted, and shows how Monks and the Jew laid their worthy Heads together

On the evening following that upon which the three worthies mentioned in the last chapter, disposed of their little matter of business as therein narrated, Mr William Sikes, awakening from a nap, drowsily growled forth an inquiry what time of night it was.

The room in which Mr Sikes propounded this question, was not one of those he had tenanted, previous to the Chertsey expedition, although it was in the same quarter of the town, and was situated at no great distance from his former lodgings. It was not, in appearance, so desirable a habitation as his old quarters: being a mean and badly-furnished apartment, of very limited size; lighted only by one small window in the shelving roof, and abutting on a close and dirty lane. Nor were there wanting other indications of the good gentleman's having gone down in the world of late; for a great scarcity of furniture, and total absence of comfort, together with the disappearance of all such small moveables as spare clothes and linen, bespoke a state of extreme poverty; while the meagre and attenuated condition of Mr Sikes himself would have fully confirmed these symptoms, if they had stood in any need of corroboration.

The house-breaker was lying on the bed, wrapped in his white great-coat, by way of dressing-gown, and displaying a set of features in no degree improved by the cadaverous hue of illness, and the addition of a soiled nightcap, and a stiff, black beard of a week's growth. The dog sat at the bedside: now eyeing his master with a wistful look, and now pricking his ears, and uttering a low growl as some noise in the street, or in the lower part of the house, attracted his attention. Seated by the window, busily engaged in patching an old waistcoat which formed a portion of the robber's ordinary dress, was a female: so pale and reduced with watching and privation, that there would have been considerable difficulty in recognising her as the same Nancy who has already figured in this tale, but for the voice in which she replied to Mr Sikes's question.

"Not long gone seven," said the girl. "How do you feel to-night, Bill?"

"As weak as water," replied Mr Sikes, with an imprecation on his eyes and limbs. "Here; lend us a hand, and let me get off this thundering bed anyhow."

Illness had not improved Mr Sikes's temper; for, as the girl raised him up and led him to a chair, he muttered various curses on her awkwardness, and struck her.

"Whining are you?" said Sikes. "Come! Don't stand snivelling there. If you can't do anything better than that, cut off altogether. D"ye hear me?"

"I hear you," replied the girl, turning her face aside, and forcing a laugh. "What fancy have you got in your head now?"

"Oh! you've thought better of it, have you?" growled Sikes, marking the tear which trembled in her eye. "All the better for you, you have."

"Why, you don't mean to say, you'd be hard upon me to-night, Bill," said the girl, laying her hand upon his shoulder.

"No!" cried Mr Sikes. "Why not?"

"Such a number of nights," said the girl, with a touch of woman's tenderness, which communicated something like sweetness of tone, even to her voice: "such a number of nights as I've been patient with you, nursing and caring for you, as if you had been a child: and this the first that I've seen you like yourself; you wouldn't have served me as you did just now, if you'd thought of that, would you? Come, come; say you wouldn't."

"Well, then," rejoined Mr Sikes, "I wouldn't. Why, damme, now, the girl's whining again!"

"It's nothing," said the girl, throwing herself into a chair. "Don't you seem to mind me. It'll soon be over."

"What'll be over?" demanded Mr Sikes in a savage voice. "What foolery are you up to, now, again? Get up and bustle about, and don't come over me with your woman's nonsense."

At any other time, this remonstrance, and the tone in which it was delivered, would have had the desired effect; but the girl being really weak and exhausted, dropped her head over the back of the chair, and fainted, before Mr Sikes could get out a few of the appropriate oaths with which, on similar occasions, he was accustomed to garnish his threats. Not knowing, very well, what to do, in this uncommon emergency; for Miss Nancy's hysterics were usually of that violent kind which the patient fights and struggles out of, without much assistance; Mr Sikes tried a little blasphemy: and finding that mode of treatment wholly ineffectual, called for assistance.

"What's the matter here, my dear?" said Fagin, looking in.

"Lend a hand to the girl, can't you?" replied Sikes impatiently. "Don't stand chattering and grinning at me!"

With an exclamation of surprise, Fagin hastened to the girl's assistance, while Mr John Dawkins (otherwise the Artful Dodger), who had followed his venerable friend into the room, hastily deposited on the floor a bundle with which he was laden; and snatching a bottle from the grasp of Master Charles Bates who came close at his heels, uncorked it in a twinkling with his teeth, and poured a portion of its contents down the patient's throat: previously taking a taste, himself, to prevent mistakes.

"Give her a whiff of fresh air with the bellows, Charley," said Mr Dawkins; "and you slap her hands, Fagin, while Bill undoes the petticuts."

These united restoratives, administered with great energy: especially that department consigned to Master Bates, who appeared to consider his share in the proceedings, a piece of unexampled pleasantry: were not long in producing the desired effect. The girl gradually recovered her senses; and, staggering to a chair by the bedside, hid her face upon the pillow: leaving Mr Sikes to confront the new-comers, in some astonishment at their unlooked-for appearance.

"Why, what evil wind has blowed you here?" he asked Fagin.

"No evil wind at all, my dear, for evil winds blow nobody any good; and I've brought something good with me, that you'll be glad to see. Dodger, my dear, open the bundle; and give Bill the little trifles that we spent all our money on, this morning."

In compliance with Mr Fagin's request, the Artful untied his bundle, which was of large size, and formed of an old table-cloth; and handed the articles it contained, one by one, to Charley Bates: who placed them on the table, with various encomiums on their rarity and excellence.

"Sitch a rabbit pie, Bill," exclaimed that young gentleman, disclosing to view a huge pasty; "sitch delicate creeturs, with sitch tender limbs, Bill, that the wery bones melt in your mouth, and there's no occasion to pick 'em; half a pound of seven and sixpenny green, so precious strong that if you mix it with biling water, it'll go nigh to blow the lid of the tea-pot off; a pound and a-half of moist sugar that the niggers didn't work at all at, afore they got it up to sitch a pitch of goodness, – oh no! Two half-quartern brans; pound of best fresh; piece of double Glo"ster; and, to wind up all, some of the richest sort you ever lushed!"

Uttering this last panegyric, Master Bates produced, from one of his extensive pockets, a full-sized wine-bottle, carefully corked; while Mr Dawkins, at the same instant, poured out a wine-glassful of raw spirits from the bottle he carried: which the invalid tossed down his throat without a moment's hesitation.

"Ah!" said Fagin, rubbing his hands with great satisfaction. "You'll do, Bill; you'll do now."

"Do!" exclaimed Mr Sikes; "I might have been done for, twenty times over, afore you'd have done anything to help me. What do you mean by leaving a man in this state, three weeks and more, you false-hearted wagabond?"

"Only hear him, boys!" said Fagin, shrugging his shoulders. "And us come to bring him all these beau-ti-ful things."

"The things is well enough in their way," observed Mr Sikes: a little soothed as he glanced over the table; "but what have you got to say for yourself, why you should leave me here, down in the mouth, health, blunt, and everything else; and take no more notice of me, all this mortal time, than if I was that 'ere dog? – Drive him down, Charley!"

"I never see such a jolly dog as that," cried Master Bates, doing as he was desired. "Smelling the grub like a old lady a going to market! He'd make his fortun on the stage that dog would, and rewive the drayma besides."

"Hold your din," cried Sikes, as the dog retreated under the bed: still growling angrily. "What have you got to say for yourself, you withered old fence, eh?"

"I was away from London, a week and more, my dear, on a plant," replied the Jew.

"And what about the other fortnight?" demanded Sikes. "What about the other fortnight that you've left me lying here, like a sick rat in his hole?"

"I couldn't help it, Bill. I can't go into a long explanation before company; but I couldn't help it, upon my honour."

"Upon your what?" growled Sikes, with excessive disgust. "Here! Cut me off a piece of that pie, one of you boys, to take the taste of that out of my mouth, or it'll choke me dead."

"Don't be out of temper, my dear," urged Fagin, submissively. "I have never forgot you, Bill; never once."

"No! I'll pound it that you han't," replied Sikes, with a bitter grin. "You've been scheming and plotting away, every hour that I have laid shivering and burning here; and Bill was to do this; and Bill was to do that; and Bill was to do it all, dirt cheap, as soon as he got well: and was quite poor enough for your work. If it hadn't been for the girl, I might have died."

"There now, Bill," remonstrated Fagin, eagerly catching at the word. "If it hadn't been for the girl! Who but poor ould Fagin was the means of your having such a handy girl about you?"

"He says true enough there!" said Nancy, coming hastily forward. "Let him be; let him be."

Nancy's appearance gave a new turn to the conversation; for the boys, receiving a sly wink from the wary old Jew, began to ply her with liquor: of which, however, she took very sparingly; while Fagin, assuming an unusual flow of spirits, gradually brought Mr Sikes into a better temper, by affecting to regard his threats as a little pleasant banter; and, moreover, by laughing very heartily at one or two rough jokes, which, after repeated applications to the spirit-bottle, he condescended to make.

"It's all very well," said Mr Sikes; "but I must have some blunt from you to-night."

"I haven't a piece of coin about me," replied the Jew.

"Then you've got lots at home," retorted Sikes; "and I must have some from there."

"Lots!" cried Fagin, holding up his hands. "I haven't so much as would – "

"I don't know how much you've got, and I dare say you hardly know yourself, as it would take a pretty long time to count it," said Sikes; "but I must have some to-night; and that's flat."

"Well, well," said Fagin, with a sigh, "I'll send the Artful round presently."

"You won't do nothing of the kind," rejoined Mr Sikes. "The Artful's a deal too artful, and would forget to come, or lose his way, or get dodged by traps and so be perwented, or anything for an excuse, if you put him up to it. Nancy shall go to the ken and fetch it, to make all sure; and I'll lie down and have a snooze while she's gone."

After a great deal of haggling and squabbling, Fagin beat down the amount of the required advance from five pounds to three pounds four and sixpence: protesting with many solemn asseverations that that would only leave him eighteenpence to keep house with; Mr Sikes sullenly remarking that if he couldn't get any more he must be content with that, Nancy prepared to accompany him home; while the Dodger and Master Bates put the eatables in the cupboard. The Jew then, taking leave of his affectionate friend, returned homeward, attended by Nancy and the boys: Mr Sikes, meanwhile, flinging himself on the bed, and composing himself to sleep away the time until the young lady's return.

In due course, they arrived at Fagin's abode, where they found Toby Crackit and Mr Chitling intent upon their fifteenth game at cribbage, which it is scarcely necessary to say the latter gentleman lost, and with it, his fifteenth and last sixpence: much to the amusement of his young friends. Mr Crackit, apparently somewhat ashamed at being found relaxing himself with a gentleman so much his inferior in station and mental endowments, yawned, and inquiring after Sikes, took up his hat to go.

"Has nobody been, Toby?" asked Fagin.

"Not a living leg," answered Mr Crackit, pulling up his collar; "it's been as dull as swipes. You ought to stand something handsome, Fagin, to recompense me for keeping house so long. Damme, I'm as flat as a juryman; and should have gone to sleep, as fast as Newgate, if I hadn't had the good natur" to amuse this youngster. Horrid dull, I'm blessed if I an't!"

With these and other ejaculations of the same kind, Mr Toby Crackit swept up his winnings, and crammed them into his waistcoat pocket with a haughty air, as though such small pieces of silver were wholly beneath the consideration of a man of his figure; this done, he swaggered out of the room, with so much elegance and gentility, that Mr Chitling, bestowing numerous admiring glances on his legs and boots till they were out of sight, assured the company that he considered his acquaintance cheap at fifteen sixpences an interview, and that he didn't value his losses the snap of his little finger.

"Wot a rum chap you are, Tom!" said Master Bates, highly amused by this declaration.

"Not a bit of it," replied Mr Chitling. "Am I, Fagin?"

"A very clever fellow, my dear," said Fagin, patting him on the shoulder, and winking to his other pupils.

"And Mr Crackit *is* a heavy swell; an't he, Fagin?" asked Tom.

"No doubt at all of that, my dear."

"And it *is* a creditable thing to have his acquaintance; an't it, Fagin?" pursued Tom.

"Very much so, indeed, my dear. They're only jealous, Tom, because he won't give it to them."

"Ah!" cried Tom, triumphantly, "that's where it is! He has cleaned me out. But I can go and earn some more, when I like; can't I, Fagin?"

"To be sure you can, and the sooner you go the better, Tom; so make up your loss at once, and don't lose any more time. Dodger!

Charley! It's time you were on the lay. Come! It's near ten, and nothing done yet."

In obedience to this hint, the boys, nodding to Nancy, took up their hats, and left the room; the Dodger and his vivacious friend indulging, as they went, in many witticisms at the expense of Mr Chitling; in whose conduct, it is but justice to say, there was nothing very conspicuous or peculiar: inasmuch as there are a great number of spirited young bloods upon town, who pay a much higher price than Mr Chitling for being seen in good society: and a great number of fine gentlemen (composing the good society aforesaid) who establish their reputation upon very much the same footing as flash Toby Crackit.

"Now," said Fagin, when they had left the room, "I'll go and get you that cash, Nancy. This is only the key of a little cupboard where I keep a few odd things the boys get, my dear. I never lock up my money, for I've none to lock up, my dear – ha! ha! ha! – none to lock up. It's a poor trade, Nancy, and no thanks; but I'm fond of seeing the young people about me; and I bear it all, I bear it all. Hush!" he said, hastily concealing the key in his breast; "who's that? Listen!"

The girl, who was sitting at the table with her arms folded appeared in no way interested in the arrival: or to care whether the person, whoever he was, came or went: until the murmur of a man's voice reached her ears. The instant she caught the sound, she tore off her bonnet and shawl, with the rapidity of lightning, and thrust them under the table. The Jew, turning round immediately afterwards, she muttered a complaint of the heat: in a tone of languor that contrasted, very remarkably, with the extreme haste and violence of this action: which, however, had been unobserved by Fagin, who had his back towards her at the time.

"Bah!" he whispered, as though nettled by the interruption; "it's the man I expected before; he's coming down stairs. Not a word about the money while he's here, Nance. He won't stop long. Not ten minutes, my dear."

Laying his skinny forefinger upon his lip, the Jew carried a candle to the door, as a man's step was heard upon the stairs without. He reached it, at the same moment as the visitor, who, coming hastily into the room, was close upon the girl before he observed her.

It was Monks.

"Only one of my young people," said Fagin, observing that Monks drew back, on beholding a stranger. "Don't move, Nancy."

The girl drew closer to the table, and glancing at Monks with an air of careless levity, withdrew her eyes; but as he turned his towards Fagin, she stole another look: so keen and searching, and full of purpose, that if there had been any bystander to observe the change, he could hardly have believed the two looks to have proceeded from the same person.

"Any news?" inquired Fagin.

"Great."

"And – and – good?" asked Fagin, hesitating as though he feared to vex the other man by being too sanguine.

"Not bad, any way," replied Monks with a smile. "I have been prompt enough this time. Let me have a word with you."

The girl drew closer to the table, and made no offer to leave the room, although she could see that Monks was pointing to her. The Jew: perhaps fearing she might say something aloud about the money, if he endeavoured to get rid of her: pointed upward, and took Monks out of the room.

"Not that infernal hole we were in before," she could hear the man say as they went up stairs. Fagin laughed; and making some reply which did not reach her, seemed, by the creaking of the boards, to lead his companion to the second story.

Before the sound of their footsteps had ceased to echo through the house, the girl had slipped off her shoes; and drawing her gown loosely over her head, and muffling her arms in it, stood at the door, listening with breathless interest. The moment the noise ceased, she glided from the room; ascended the stairs with incredible softness and silence; and was lost in the gloom above.

The room remained deserted for a quarter of an hour or more; the girl glided back with the same unearthly tread; and, immediately afterwards, the two men were heard descending. Monks went at once into the street; and the Jew crawled up stairs again for the money. When he returned, the girl was adjusting her shawl and bonnet, as if preparing to be gone.

"Why, Nance," exclaimed the Jew, starting back as he put down the candle, "how pale you are!"

"Pale!" echoed the girl, shading her eyes with her hands, as if to look steadily at him.

"Quite horrible. What have you been doing to yourself?"

"Nothing that I know of, except sitting in this close place for I don't know how long and all," replied the girl carelessly. "Come! Let me get back; that's a dear."

With a sigh for every piece of money, Fagin told the amount into her hand. They parted without more conversation, merely interchanging a "good night."

When the girl got into the open street, she sat down upon a doorstep; and seemed, for a few moments, wholly bewildered and unable to pursue her way. Suddenly she arose; and hurrying on, in a direction quite opposite to that in which Sikes was awaiting her return, quickened her pace, until it gradually resolved into a violent run. After completely exhausting herself, she stopped to take breath: and, as if suddenly recollecting herself, and deploring her inability to do something she was bent upon, wrung her hands, and burst into tears.

It might be that her tears relieved her, or that she felt the full hopelessness of her condition; but she turned back; and hurrying with nearly as great rapidity in the contrary direction: partly to recover lost time, and partly to keep pace with the violent current of her own thoughts: soon reached the dwelling where she had left the house-breaker.

If she betrayed any agitation, when she presented herself to Mr Sikes, he did not observe it; for merely inquiring if she had brought the money, and receiving a reply in the affirmative, he uttered a growl of satisfaction, and replacing his head upon the pillow, resumed the slumbers which her arrival had interrupted.

It was fortunate for her that the possession of money occasioned him so much employment next day in the way of eating and drinking; and withal had so beneficial an effect in smoothing down the asperities of his temper; that he had neither time nor inclination to be very critical upon her behaviour and deportment. That she had all the abstracted and nervous manner of one who is on the eve of some bold and hazardous step, which it has required no common struggle to resolve upon, would have been obvious to the lynx-eyed Fagin, who would most probably have taken the alarm at once; but Mr Sikes lacking the niceties of discrimination, and being troubled with no more subtle misgivings than those which resolve themselves into a dogged roughness of behaviour towards everybody; and being, furthermore, in an unusually amiable condition, as has been already observed; saw nothing unusual in her demeanour, and indeed, troubled himself so little about her, that, had her agitation been far more perceptible than it was, it would have been very unlikely to have awakened his suspicions.

As that day closed in, the girl's excitement increased; and, when night came on, and she sat by, watching until the house-breaker should drink himself asleep, there was an unusual paleness in her cheek, and a fire in her eye, that even Sikes observed with astonishment.

Mr Sikes being weak from the fever, was lying in bed, taking hot water with his gin to render it less inflammatory; and had pushed his glass towards Nancy to be replenished for the third or fourth time, when these symptoms first struck him.

"Why, burn my body!" said the man, raising himself on his hands as he stared the girl in the face. "You look like a corpse come to life again. What's the matter?"

"Matter!" replied the girl. "Nothing. What do you look at me so hard for?"

"What foolery is this?" demanded Sikes, grasping her by the arm, and shaking her roughly. "What is it? What do you mean? What are you thinking of?"

"Of many things, Bill," replied the girl, shivering, and as she did so, pressing her hands upon her eyes. "But, Lord! What odds in that?"

The tone of forced gaiety in which the last words were spoken, seemed to produce a deeper impression on Sikes than the wild and rigid look which had preceded them.

"I tell you wot it is," said Sikes; "if you haven't caught the fever, and got it comin" on, now, there's something more than usual in the wind, and something dangerous too. You're not a-going to –. No, damme! you wouldn't do that!"

"Do what?" asked the girl.

"There ain't," said Sikes, fixing his eyes upon her, and muttering the words to himself; "there ain't a stauncher-hearted gal going, or I'd have cut her throat three months ago. She's got the fever coming on; that's it."

Fortifying himself with this assurance, Sikes drained the glass to the bottom, and then, with many grumbling oaths, called for his physic. The girl jumped up, with great alacrity; poured it quickly out, but with her back towards him; and held the vessel to his lips, while he drank off the contents.

"Now," said the robber, "come and sit aside of me, and put on your own face; or I'll alter it so, that you won't know it again when you *do* want it."

The girl obeyed. Sikes, locking her hand in his, fell back upon the pillow: turning his eyes upon her face. They closed; opened again; closed once more; again opened. He shifted his position restlessly; and, after dozing again, and again, for two or three minutes, and as often springing up with a look of terror, and gazing vacantly about him, was suddenly stricken, as it were, while in the very attitude of rising, into a deep and heavy sleep. The grasp of his hand relaxed; the upraised arm fell languidly by his side; and he lay like one in a profound trance.

"The laudanum has taken effect at last," murmured the girl, as she rose from the bedside. "I may be too late, even now."

She hastily dressed herself in her bonnet and shawl looking fearfully round, from time to time, as if, despite the sleeping draught, she expected every moment to feel the pressure of Sikes's heavy hand upon her shoulder; then, stooping softly over the bed, she kissed the robber's lips; and then opening and closing the room-door with noiseless touch, hurried from the house.

A watchman was crying half-past nine, down a dark passage through which she had to pass, in gaining the main thoroughfare.

"Has it long gone the half-hour?" asked the girl.

"It'll strike the hour in another quarter," said the man: raising his lantern to her face.

"And I cannot get there in less than an hour or more," muttered Nancy: brushing swiftly past him, and gliding rapidly down the street.

Many of the shops were already closing in the back lanes and avenues through which she tracked her way, in making from Spitalfields towards the West-End of London. The clock struck ten, increasing her impatience. She tore along the narrow pavement: elbowing the passengers from side to side; and darting almost under the horses" heads, crossed crowded streets, where clusters of persons were eagerly watching their opportunity to do the like.

"The woman is mad!" said the people, turning to look after her as she rushed away.

When she reached the more wealthy quarter of the town, the streets were comparatively deserted; and here her headlong progress excited a still greater curiosity in the stragglers whom she hurried past. Some quickened their pace behind, as though to see whither she was hastening at such an unusual rate; and a few made head upon her, and looked back, surprised at her undiminished speed; but they fell off one by one; and when she neared her place of destination, she was alone.

It was a family hotel in a quiet but handsome street near Hyde Park. As the brilliant light of the lamp which burnt before its door, guided her to the spot, the clock struck eleven. She had loitered for a few paces as though irresolute, and making up her mind to advance; but the sound determined her, and she stepped into the hall. The porter's seat was vacant. She looked round with an air of incertitude, and advanced towards the stairs.

"Now, young woman!" said a smartly-dressed female, looking out from a door behind her, "who do you want here?"

"A lady who is stopping in this house," answered the girl.

"A lady!" was the reply, accompanied with a scornful look. "What lady?"

"Miss Maylie," said Nancy.

The young woman, who had by this time, noted her appearance, replied only by a look of virtuous disdain; and summoned a man to answer her. To him, Nancy repeated her request.

"What name am I to say?" asked the waiter.

"It's of no use saying any," replied Nancy.

"Nor business?" said the man.

"No, nor that neither," rejoined the girl. "I must see the lady."

"Come!" said the man, pushing her towards the door. "None of this. Take yourself off."

"I shall be carried out, if I go!" said the girl violently; "and I can make that a job that two of you won't like to do. Isn't there anybody here," she said, looking round, "that will see a simple message carried for a poor wretch like me?"

This appeal produced an effect on a good-tempered-faced man-cook, who with some other of the servants was looking on, and who stepped forward to interfere.

"Take it up for her, Joe; can't you?" said this person.

"What's the good?" replied the man. "You don't suppose the young lady will see such as her; do you?"

This allusion to Nancy's doubtful character, raised a vast quantity of chaste wrath in the bosoms of four housemaids, who remarked, with great fervour, that the creature was a disgrace to her sex; and strongly advocated her being thrown, ruthlessly, into the kennel.

"Do what you like with me," said the girl, turning to the men again; "but do what I ask you first, and I ask you to give this message for God Almighty's sake."

The soft-hearted cook added his intercession, and the result was that the man who had first appeared undertook its delivery.

"What's it to be?" said the man, with one foot on the stairs.

"That a young woman earnestly asks to speak to Miss Maylie alone," said Nancy; "and that if the lady will only hear the first word she has to say, she will know whether to hear her business, or to have her turned out of door as an impostor."

"I say," said the man, "you're coming it strong!"

"You give the message," said the girl firmly; "and let me hear the answer."

The man ran up stairs. Nancy remained, pale and almost breathless, listening with quivering lip to the very audible expressions of scorn, of which the chaste housemaids were very prolific; and of which they became still more so, when the man returned, and said the young woman was to walk up stairs.

"It's no good being proper in this world," said the first housemaid.

"Brass can do better than the gold what has stood the fire," said the second.

The third contented herself with wondering "what ladies was made of;" and the fourth took the first in a quartette of "Shameful!" with which the Dianas concluded.

Regardless of all this: for she had weightier matters at heart: Nancy followed the man, with trembling limbs, to a small antechamber, lighted by a lamp from the ceiling. Here he left her, and retired.

Chapter XL

A strange Interview, which is a Sequel to the last Chapter

THE girl's life had been squandered in the streets, and among the most noisome of the stews and dens of London, but there was something of the woman's original nature left in her still; and when she heard a light step approaching the door opposite to that by which she had entered, and thought of the wide contrast which the small room would in another moment contain, she felt burdened with the sense of her own deep shame, and shrunk as though she could scarcely bear the presence of her with whom she had sought this interview.

But struggling with these better feelings was pride, – the vice of the lowest and most debased creatures no less than of the high and self-assured. The miserable companion of thieves and ruffians, the fallen outcast of low haunts, the associate of the scourings of the jails and hulks, living within the shadow of the gallows itself, – even this degraded being felt too proud to betray a feeble gleam of the womanly feeling which she thought a weakness, but which alone connected her with that humanity, of which her wasting life had obliterated so many, many traces when a very child.

She raised her eyes sufficiently to observe that the figure which presented itself was that of a slight and beautiful girl; then, bending them on the ground, she tossed her head with affected carelessness as she said:

"It's a hard matter to get to see you, lady. If I had taken offence, and gone away, as many would have done, you'd have been sorry for it one day, and not without reason either."

"I am very sorry if any one has behaved harshly to you," replied Rose. "Do not think of that. Tell me why you wished to see me. I am the person you inquired for."

The kind tone of this answer, the sweet voice, the gentle manner, the absence of any accent of haughtiness or displeasure, took the girl completely by surprise, and she burst into tears.

"Oh, lady, lady!" she said, clasping her hands passionately before her face, "if there was more like you, there would be fewer like me, – there would – there would!"

"Sit down," said Rose, earnestly. "If you are in poverty or affliction I shall be truly glad to relieve you if I can, – I shall indeed. Sit down."

"Let me stand, lady," said the girl, still weeping, "and do not speak to me so kindly till you know me better. It is growing late. Is – is – that door shut?"

"Yes," said Rose, recoiling a few steps, as if to be nearer assistance in case she should require it. "Why?"

"Because," said the girl, "I am about to put my life, and the lives of others, in your hands. I am the girl that dragged little Oliver back to old Fagin's, on the night he went out from the house in Pentonville."

"You!" said Rose Maylie.

"I, lady!" replied the girl. "I am the infamous creature you have heard of, that lives among the thieves, and that never from the first moment I can recollect my eyes and senses opening on London streets have known any better life, or kinder words than they have given me, so help me God! Do not mind shrinking openly from me, lady. I am younger than you would think, to look at me, but I am well used to it. The poorest women fall back, as I make my way along the crowded pavement."

"What dreadful things are these!" said Rose, involuntarily falling from her strange companion.

"Thank Heaven upon your knees, dear lady," cried the girl, "that you had friends to care for and keep you in your childhood, and that you were never in the midst of cold and hunger, and riot and drunkenness, and – and – something worse than all – as I have been from my cradle. I may use the word, for the alley and the gutter were mine, as they will be my death-bed."

"I pity you!" said Rose, in a broken voice. "It wrings my heart to hear you!"

"Heaven bless you for your goodness!" rejoined the girl. "If you knew what I am sometimes, you would pity me, indeed. But I have stolen away from those who would surely murder me, if they knew I had been here, to tell you what I have overheard. Do you know a man named Monks?"

"No," said Rose.

"He knows you," replied the girl; "and knew you were here, for it was by hearing him tell the place that I found you out."

"I never heard the name," said Rose.

"Then he goes by some other amongst us," rejoined the girl, "which I more than thought before. Some time ago, and soon after Oliver was put into your house on the night of the robbery, I – suspecting this man – listened to a conversation held between him and Fagin in the dark. I found out, from what I heard, that Monks – the man I asked you about, you know – "

"Yes," said Rose, "I understand."

" – That Monks," pursued the girl, "had seen him accidentally with two of our boys on the day we first lost him, and had known him directly to be the same child that he was watching for, though I couldn't make out why. A bargain was struck with Fagin, that if Oliver was got back he should have a certain sum; and he was to have more for making him a thief, which this Monks wanted for some purpose of his own."

"For what purpose?" asked Rose.

"He caught sight of my shadow on the wall as I listened, in the hope of finding out," said the girl; "and there are not many people besides me that could have got out of their way in time to escape discovery. But I did; and I saw him no more till last night."

"And what occurred then?"

"I'll tell you, lady. Last night he came again. Again they went up stairs, and I, wrapping myself up so that my shadow should not betray me, again listened at the door. The first words I heard Monks say were these: "So the only proofs of the boy's identity lie at the bottom of the river, and the old hag that received them from the mother is rotting in her coffin." They laughed, and talked of his success in doing this; and Monks, talking on about the boy, and getting very wild, said that though he had got the young devil's money safely now, he'd rather have had it the other way; for, what a game it would have been to have brought down the boast of the father's will, by driving him through every jail in town, and then hauling him up for some capital felony which Fagin could easily manage, after having made a good profit of him besides."

"What is all this!" said Rose.

"The truth, lady, though it comes from my lips," replied the girl. "Then, he said, with oaths common enough in my ears, but strange to yours, that if he could gratify his hatred by taking the boy's life without bringing his own neck in danger, he would; but, as he couldn't, he'd be upon the watch to meet him at every turn in life; and if he took advantage of his birth and history, he might harm him yet. "In short, Fagin," he says, "Jew as you are, you never laid such snares as I'll contrive for my young brother, Oliver.""

"His brother!" exclaimed Rose.

"Those were his words," said Nancy, glancing uneasily round, as she had scarcely ceased to do, since she began to speak, for a vision of Sikes haunted her perpetually. "And more. When he spoke of you and the other lady, and said it seemed contrived by Heaven, or the devil, against him, that Oliver should come into your hands, he laughed, and said there was some comfort in that too, for how many thousands and hundreds of thousands of pounds would you not give, if you had them, to know who your two-legged spaniel was."

"You do not mean," said Rose, turning very pale, "to tell me that this was said in earnest?"

"He spoke in hard and angry earnest, if a man ever did," replied the girl, shaking her head. "He is an earnest man when his hatred is up. I know many who do worse things; but I'd rather listen to them all a dozen times, than to that Monks once. It is growing late, and I have to reach home without suspicion of having been on such an errand as this. I must get back quickly."

"But what can I do?" said Rose. "To what use can I turn this communication without you? Back! Why do you wish to return to companions you paint in such terrible colours? If you repeat this information to a gentleman whom I can summon in an instant from the next room, you can be consigned to some place of safety without half an hour's delay."

"I wish to go back," said the girl. "I must go back, because – how can I tell such things to an innocent lady like you? – because among the men I have told you of, there is one: the most desperate among them all; that I can't leave; no, not even to be saved from the life I am leading now."

"Your having interfered in this dear boy's behalf before," said Rose; "your coming here, at so great a risk, to tell me what you have heard; your manner, which convinces me of the truth of what you say; your evident contrition, and sense of shame; all lead me to believe that you might be yet reclaimed. Oh!" said the earnest girl, folding her hands as the tears coursed down her face, "do not turn a deaf ear to the entreaties of one of your own sex; the first – the first, I do believe, who ever appealed to you in the voice of pity and compassion. Do hear my words, and let me save you yet, for better things."

"Lady," cried the girl, sinking on her knees, "dear, sweet, angel lady, you *are* the first that ever blessed me with such words as these, and if I had heard them years ago, they might have turned me from a life of sin and sorrow; but it is too late, it is too late!"

"It is never too late," said Rose, "for penitence and atonement."

"It is," cried the girl, writhing in the agony of her mind; "I cannot leave him now! I could not be his death."

"Why should you be?" asked Rose.

"Nothing could save him," cried the girl. "If I told others what I have told you, and led to their being taken, he would be sure to die. He is the boldest, and has been so cruel!"

"Is it possible," cried Rose, "that for such a man as this, you can resign every future hope, and the certainty of immediate rescue? It is madness."

"I don't know what it is," answered the girl; "I only know that it is so, and not with me alone, but with hundreds of others as bad and wretched as myself. I must go back. Whether it is God's wrath for the wrong I have done, I do not know; but I am drawn back to him through every suffering and ill usage; and I should be, I believe, if I knew that I was to die by his hand at last."

"What am I to do?" said Rose. "I should not let you depart from me thus."

"You should, lady, and I know you will," rejoined the girl, rising. "You will not stop my going because I have trusted in your goodness, and forced no promise from you, as I might have done."

"Of what use, then, is the communication you have made?" said Rose. "This mystery must be investigated, or how will its disclosure to me, benefit Oliver, whom you are anxious to serve?"

"You must have some kind gentleman about you that will hear it as a secret, and advise you what to do," rejoined the girl.

"But where can I find you again when it is necessary?" asked Rose. "I do not seek to know where these dreadful people live, but where will you be walking or passing at any settled period from this time?"

"Will you promise me that you will have my secret strictly kept, and come alone, or with the only other person that knows it; and that I shall not be watched or followed?" asked the girl.

"I promise you solemnly," answered Rose.

"Every Sunday night, from eleven until the clock strikes twelve," said the girl without hesitation, "I will walk on London Bridge if I am alive."

"Stay another moment," interposed Rose, as the girl moved hurriedly towards the door. "Think once again on your own condition, and the opportunity you have of escaping from it. You have a claim on me: not only as the voluntary bearer of this intelligence, but as a woman lost almost beyond redemption. Will you return to this gang of robbers, and to this man, when a word can save you? What fascination is it that can take you back, and make you cling to wickedness and misery? Oh! is there no chord in your heart that I can touch! Is there nothing left, to which I can appeal against this terrible infatuation!"

"When ladies as young, and good, and beautiful as you are," replied the girl steadily, "give away your hearts, love will carry you all lengths – even such as you, who have home, friends, other admirers, everything, to fill them. When such as I, who have no certain roof but the coffin-lid, and no friend in sickness or death but the hospital nurse, set our rotten hearts on any man, and let him fill the place that has been a blank through all our wretched lives, who can hope to cure us? Pity us, lady – pity us for having only one feeling of the woman left, and for having that turned, by a heavy judgment, from a comfort and a pride, into a new means of violence and suffering."

"You will," said Rose, after a pause, "take some money from me, which may enable you to live without dishonesty – at all events until we meet again?"

"Not a penny," replied the girl, waving her hand.

"Do not close your heart against all my efforts to help you," said Rose, stepping gently forward. "I wish to serve you indeed."

"You would serve me best, lady," replied the girl, wringing her hands, "if you could take my life at once; for I have felt more grief to think of what I am, to-night, than I ever did before, and it would be something not to die in the hell in which I have lived. God bless you, sweet lady, and send as much happiness on your head as I have brought shame on mine!"

Thus speaking, and sobbing aloud, the unhappy creature turned away; while Rose Maylie, overpowered by this extraordinary interview, which had more the semblance of a rapid dream than an actual occurrence, sank into a chair, and endeavoured to collect her wandering thoughts.

Chapter XLI

Containing fresh Discoveries, and showing that Surprises, like Misfortunes, seldom come alone

HER situation was, indeed, one of no common trial and difficulty. While she felt the most eager and burning desire to penetrate the mystery in which Oliver's history was enveloped, she could not but hold sacred the confidence which the miserable woman with whom she had just conversed, had reposed in her, as a young and guileless girl. Her words and manner had touched Rose Maylie's heart; and, mingled with her love for her young charge, and scarcely less intense in its truth and fervour, was her fond wish to win the outcast back to repentance and hope.

They purposed remaining in London only three days, prior to departing for some weeks to a distant part of the coast. It was now midnight of the first day. What course of action could she determine upon, which could be adopted in eight-and-forty hours? Or how could she postpone the journey without exciting suspicion?

Mr Losberne was with them, and would be for the next two days; but Rose was too well acquainted with the excellent gentleman's impetuosity, and foresaw too clearly the wrath with which, in the first explosion of his indignation, he would regard the instrument of Oliver's re-capture, to trust him with the secret, when her representations in the girl's behalf could be seconded by no experienced person. These were all reasons for the greatest caution and most circumspect behaviour in communicating it to Mrs Maylie, whose first impulse would infallibly be to hold a conference with the worthy doctor on the subject. As to resorting to any legal adviser, even if she had known how to do so, it was scarcely to be thought of, for the same reasons. Once the thought occurred to her of seeking assistance from Harry; but this awakened the recollection of their last parting, and it seemed unworthy of her to call him back, when – the tears rose to her eyes as she pursued this train of reflection – he might have by this time learnt to forget her, and to be happier away.

Disturbed by these different reflections; inclining now to one course and then to another, and again recoiling from all, as each successive consideration presented itself to her mind; Rose passed a sleepless and anxious night. After more communing with herself next day, she arrived at the desperate conclusion of consulting Harry.

"If it be painful to him," she thought, "to come back here, how painful it will be to me! But perhaps he will not come; he may write, or he may come himself, and studiously abstain from meeting me – he did when he went away. I hardly thought he would; but it was better for us both." And here Rose dropped the pen, and turned away, as though the very paper which was to be her messenger should not see her weep.

She had taken up the same pen, and laid it down again fifty times, and had considered and reconsidered the first line of her letter without writing the first word, when Oliver, who had been walking in the streets, with Mr Giles for a body-guard, entered the room in such breathless haste and violent agitation, as seemed to betoken some new cause of alarm.

"What makes you look so flurried?" asked Rose, advancing to meet him.

"I hardly know how; I feel as if I should be choked," replied the boy. "Oh dear! To think that I should see him at last, and you should be able to know that I have told you all the truth!"

"I never thought you had told us anything but the truth," said Rose, soothing him. "But what is this? – of whom do you speak?"

"I have seen the gentleman," replied Oliver, scarcely able to articulate, "the gentleman who was so good to me – Mr Brownlow, that we have so often talked about."

"Where?" asked Rose.

"Getting out of a coach," replied Oliver, shedding tears of delight, "and going into a house. I didn't speak to him – I couldn't speak to him, for he didn't see me, and I trembled so, that I was not able to go up to him. But Giles asked, for me, whether he lived there, and they said he did. Look here," said Oliver, opening a scrap of paper, "here it is; here's where he lives – I'm going there directly! Oh, dear me, dear me! What shall I do when I come to see him and hear him speak again!"

With her attention not a little distracted by these and a great many other incoherent exclamations of joy, Rose read the address, which was Craven Street, in the Strand. She very soon determined upon turning the discovery to account.

"Quick!" she said. "Tell them to fetch a hackney-coach, and be ready to go with me. I will take you there directly, without a minute's loss of time. I will only tell my aunt that we are going out for an hour, and be ready as soon as you are."

Oliver needed no prompting to despatch, and in little more than five minutes they were on their way to Craven Street. When they arrived there, Rose left Oliver in the coach, under pretence of preparing the old gentleman to receive him; and sending up her card by the servant, requested to see Mr Brownlow on very pressing business. The servant soon returned, to beg that she would walk up stairs; and following him into an upper room, Miss Maylie was presented to an elderly gentleman of benevolent appearance, in a bottle-green coat. At no great distance from whom, was seated another old gentleman, in nankeen breeches and gaiters; who did not look particularly benevolent, and who was sitting with his hands clasped on the top of a thick stick, and his chin propped thereupon.

"Dear me," said the gentleman, in the bottle-green coat, hastily rising with great politeness, "I beg your pardon, young lady – I imagined it was some importunate person who – I beg you will excuse me. Be seated, pray."

"Mr Brownlow, I believe, sir?" said Rose, glancing from the other gentleman to the one who had spoken.

"That is my name," said the old gentleman. "This is my friend, Mr Grimwig. Grimwig, will you leave us for a few minutes?"

"I believe," interposed Miss Maylie, "that at this period of our interview, I need not give that gentleman the trouble of going away. If I am correctly informed, he is cognizant of the business on which I wish to speak to you."

Mr Brownlow inclined his head. Mr Grimwig, who had made one very stiff bow, and risen from his chair, made another very stiff bow, and dropped into it again.

"I shall surprise you very much, I have no doubt," said Rose, naturally embarrassed; "but you once showed great benevolence and goodness to a very dear young friend of mine, and I am sure you will take an interest in hearing of him again."

"Indeed!" said Mr Brownlow.

"Oliver Twist you knew him as," replied Rose.

The words no sooner escaped her lips, than Mr Grimwig, who had been affecting to dip into a large book that lay on the table, upset it with a great crash, and falling back in his chair, discharged from his features every expression but one of unmitigated wonder, and indulged in a prolonged and vacant stare; then, as if ashamed of having betrayed so much emotion, he jerked himself, as it were, by a convulsion into his former attitude, and looking out straight before him emitted a long deep whistle, which seemed, at last, not to be discharged on empty air, but to die away in the innermost recesses of his stomach.

Mr Brownlow was no less surprised, although his astonishment was not expressed in the same eccentric manner. He drew his chair nearer to Miss Maylie's, and said,

"Do me the favour, my dear young lady, to leave entirely out of the question that goodness and benevolence of which you speak, and of which nobody else knows anything; and if you have it in your power to produce any evidence which will alter the unfavourable opinion I was once induced to entertain of that poor child, in Heaven's name put me in possession of it."

"A bad one! I'll eat my head if he is not a bad one," growled Mr Grimwig, speaking by some ventriloquial power, without moving a muscle of his face.

"He is a child of a noble nature and a warm heart," said Rose, colouring; "and that Power which has thought fit to try him beyond his years, has planted in his breast affections and feelings which would do honour to many who have numbered his days six times over."

"I'm only sixty-one," said Mr Grimwig, with the same rigid face. "And, as the devil's in it if this Oliver is not twelve years old at least, I don't see the application of that remark."

"Do not heed my friend, Miss Maylie," said Mr Brownlow; "he does not mean what he says."

"Yes, he does," growled Mr Grimwig.

"No, he does not," said Mr Brownlow, obviously rising in wrath as he spoke.

"He'll eat his head, if he doesn't," growled Mr Grimwig.

"He would deserve to have it knocked off, if he does," said Mr Brownlow.

"And he'd uncommonly like to see any man offer to do it," responded Mr Grimwig, knocking his stick upon the floor.

Having gone thus far, the two old gentlemen severally took snuff, and afterwards shook hands, according to their invariable custom.

"Now, Miss Maylie," said Mr Brownlow, "to return to the subject in which your humanity is so much interested. Will you let me know what intelligence you have of this poor child: allowing me to premise that I exhausted every means in my power of discovering him, and that since I have been absent from this country, my first impression that he had imposed upon me, and had been persuaded by his former associates to rob me, has been considerably shaken."

Rose, who had had time to collect her thoughts, at once related, in a few natural words, all that had befallen Oliver since he left Mr Brownlow's house; reserving Nancy's information for that gentleman's private ear, and concluding with the assurance that his only sorrow, for some months past, had been the not being able to meet with his former benefactor and friend.

"Thank God!" said the old gentleman. "This is great happiness to me, great happiness. But you have not told me where he is now, Miss Maylie. You must pardon my finding fault with you, – but why not have brought him?"

"He is waiting in a coach at the door," replied Rose.

"At this door!" cried the old gentleman. With which he hurried out of the room, down the stairs, up the coach-steps, and into the coach, without another word.

When the room-door closed behind him, Mr Grimwig lifted up his head, and converting one of the hind legs of his chair into a pivot, described three distinct circles with the assistance of his stick and the table: sitting in it all the time. After performing this evolution, he rose and limped as fast as he could up and down the room at least a dozen times, and then stopping suddenly before Rose, kissed her without the slightest preface.

"Hush!" he said, as the young lady rose in some alarm at this unusual proceeding. "Don't be afraid. I'm old enough to be your grandfather. You're a sweet girl. I like you. Here they are!"

In fact, as he threw himself at one dexterous dive into his former seat, Mr Brownlow returned, accompanied by Oliver, whom Mr Grimwig received very graciously; and if the gratification of that moment had been the only reward for all her anxiety and care in Oliver's behalf, Rose Maylie would have been well repaid.

"There is somebody else who should not be forgotten, by the by," said Mr Brownlow, ringing the bell. "Send Mrs Bedwin here, if you please."

The old housekeeper answered the summons with all dispatch; and dropping a curtsey at the door, waited for orders.

"Why, you get blinder every day, Bedwin," said Mr Brownlow, rather testily.

"Well, that I do, sir," replied the old lady. "People's eyes, at my time of life, don't improve with age, sir."

"I could have told you that," rejoined Mr Brownlow; "but put on your glasses, and see if you can't find out what you were wanted for, will you?"

The old lady began to rummage in her pocket for her spectacles. But Oliver's patience was not proof against this new trial; and yielding to his first impulse, he sprang into her arms.

"God be good to me!" cried the old lady, embracing him; "it is my innocent boy!"

"My dear old nurse!" cried Oliver.

"He would come back – I knew he would," said the old lady, holding him in her arms. "How well he looks, and how like a gentleman's son he is dressed again! Where have you been, this long, long while? Ah! the same sweet face, but not so pale; the same soft eye, but not so sad. I have never forgotten them or his quiet smile, but have seen them every day, side by side with those of my own dear children, dead and gone since I was a lightsome young creature." Running on thus, and now holding Oliver from her to mark how he had grown, now clasping him to her and passing her fingers fondly through his hair, the good soul laughed and wept upon his neck by turns.

Leaving her and Oliver to compare notes at leisure, Mr Brownlow led the way into another room; and there, heard from Rose a full narration of her interview with Nancy, which occasioned him no little surprise and perplexity. Rose also explained her reasons for not confiding in her friend Mr Losberne in the first instance. The old gentleman considered that she had acted prudently, and readily undertook to hold solemn conference with the worthy doctor himself. To afford him an early opportunity for the execution of this design, it was arranged that he should call at the hotel at eight o'clock that evening, and that in the meantime Mrs Maylie should be cautiously informed of all that had occurred. These preliminaries adjusted, Rose and Oliver returned home.

Rose had by no means overrated the measure of the good doctor's wrath. Nancy's history was no sooner unfolded to him, than he poured forth a shower of mingled threats and execrations; threatened to make her the first victim of the combined ingenuity of Messrs. Blathers and Duff; and actually put on his hat preparatory to sallying forth to obtain the assistance of those worthies. And, doubtless, he would, in this first outbreak, have carried the intention into effect without a moment's consideration of the consequences, if he had not been restrained, in part, by corresponding violence on the side of Mr Brownlow, who was himself of an irascible temperament, and partly by such arguments and representations as seemed best calculated to dissuade him from his hotbrained purpose.

"Then what the devil is to be done?" said the impetuous doctor, when they had rejoined the two ladies. "Are we to pass a vote of thanks to all these vagabonds, male and female, and beg them to accept a hundred pounds, or so, apiece, as a trifling mark of our esteem, and some slight acknowledgment of their kindness to Oliver?"

"Not exactly that," rejoined Mr Brownlow, laughing; "but we must proceed gently and with great care."

"Gentleness and care," exclaimed the doctor. "I'd send them one and all to – "

"Never mind where," interposed Mr Brownlow. "But reflect whether sending them anywhere is likely to attain the object we have in view."

"What object?" asked the doctor.

"Simply, the discovery of Oliver's parentage, and regaining for him the inheritance of which, if this story be true, he has been fraudulently deprived."

"Ah!" said Mr Losberne, cooling himself with his pocket-handkerchief; "I almost forgot that."

"You see," pursued Mr Brownlow; "placing this poor girl entirely out of the question, and supposing it were possible to bring these scoundrels to justice without compromising her safety, what good should we bring about?"

"Hanging a few of them at least, in all probability," suggested the doctor, "and transporting the rest."

"Very good," replied Mr Brownlow smiling; "but no doubt they will bring that about for themselves in the fulness of time, and if we step in to forestall them, it seems to me that we shall be performing a very Quixotic act, in direct opposition to our own interest – or at least to Oliver's, which is the same thing."

"How?" inquired the doctor.

"Thus. It is quite clear that we shall have extreme difficulty in getting to the bottom of this mystery, unless we can bring this man, Monks, upon his knees. That can only be done by stratagem, and by catching him when he is not surrounded by these people. For, suppose he were apprehended, we have no proof against him. He is not even (so far as we know, or as the facts appear to us) concerned with the gang in any of their robberies. If he were not discharged, it is very unlikely that he could receive any further punishment than being committed to prison as a rogue and vagabond; and of course ever afterwards his mouth would be so obstinately closed that he might as well, for our purposes, be deaf, dumb, blind, and an idiot."

"Then," said the doctor impetuously, "I put it to you again, whether you think it reasonable that this promise to the girl should be considered binding; a promise made with the best and kindest intentions, but really – "

"Do not discuss the point, my dear young lady, pray," said Mr Brownlow, interrupting Rose as she was about to speak. "The promise shall be kept. I don't think it will, in the slightest degree, interfere with our proceedings. But, before we can resolve upon any precise course of action, it will be necessary to see the girl; to ascertain from her whether she will point out this Monks, on the understanding that he is to be dealt with by us, and not by the law; or, if she will not, or cannot do that, to procure from her such an account of his haunts and description of his person, as will enable us to identify him. She cannot be seen until next Sunday night; this is Tuesday. I would suggest that in the meantime, we remain perfectly quiet, and keep these matters secret even from Oliver himself."

Although Mr Losberne received with many wry faces a proposal involving a delay of five whole days, he was fain to admit that no better course occurred to him just then; and as both Rose and Mrs Maylie sided very strongly with Mr Brownlow, that gentleman's proposition was carried unanimously.

"I should like," he said, "to call in the aid of my friend Grimwig. He is a strange creature, but a shrewd one, and might prove of material assistance to us; I should say that he was bred a lawyer, and quitted the Bar in disgust because he had only one brief and a motion of course, in twenty years, though whether that is a recommendation or not, you must determine for yourselves."

"I have no objection to your calling in your friend if I may call in mine," said the doctor.

"We must put it to the vote," replied Mr Brownlow, "who may he be?"

"That lady's son, and this young lady's – very old friend," said the doctor, motioning towards Mrs Maylie, and concluding with an expressive glance at her niece.

Rose blushed deeply, but she did not make any audible objection to this motion (possibly she felt in a hopeless minority); and Harry Maylie and Mr Grimwig were accordingly added to the committee.

"We stay in town, of course," said Mrs Maylie, "while there remains the slightest prospect of prosecuting this inquiry with a chance of success. I will spare neither trouble nor expense in behalf of the object in which we are all so deeply interested, and I am content to remain here, if it be for twelve months, so long as you assure me that any hope remains."

"Good!" rejoined Mr Brownlow. "And as I see on the faces about me, a disposition to inquire how it happened that I was not in the way to corroborate Oliver's tale, and had so suddenly left the kingdom, let me stipulate that I shall be asked no questions until such time as I may deem it expedient to forestall them by telling my own story. Believe me, I make this request with good reason, for I might otherwise excite hopes destined never to be realised, and only increase difficulties and disappointments already quite numerous enough. Come! Supper has been announced, and young Oliver, who is all alone in the next room, will have begun to think, by this time, that we have wearied of his company, and entered into some dark conspiracy to thrust him forth upon the world."

With these words, the old gentleman gave his hand to Mrs Maylie, and escorted her into the supper-room. Mr Losberne followed, leading Rose; and the council was, for the present, effectually broken up.

Chapter XLII

An old Acquaintance of Oliver's, exhibiting decided Marks of Genius, becomes a public Character in the Metropolis

UPON the night when Nancy, having lulled Mr Sikes to sleep, hurried on her self-imposed mission to Rose Maylie, there advanced towards London, by the Great North Road, two persons, upon whom it is expedient that this history should bestow some attention.

They were a man and woman; or perhaps they would be better described as a male and female: for the former was one of those long-limbed, knock-kneed, shambling, bony people, to whom it is difficult to assign any precise age, – looking as they do, when they are yet boys, like undergrown men, and when they are almost men, like overgrown boys. The woman was young, but of a robust and hardy make, as she need have been to bear the weight of the heavy bundle which was strapped to her back. Her companion was not encumbered with much luggage, as there merely dangled from a stick which he carried over his shoulder, a small parcel wrapped in a common handkerchief, and apparently light enough. This circumstance, added to the length of his legs, which were of unusual extent, enabled him with much ease to keep some half-dozen paces in advance of his companion, to whom he occasionally turned with an impatient jerk of the head: as if reproaching her tardiness, and urging her to greater exertion.

Thus, they had toiled along the dusty road, taking little heed of any object within sight, save when they stepped aside to allow a wider passage for the mail-coaches which were whirling out of town, until they passed through Highgate archway; when the foremost traveller stopped and called impatiently to his companion.

"Come on, can't yer? What a lazybones yer are, Charlotte."

"It's a heavy load, I can tell you," said the female, coming up, almost breathless with fatigue.

"Heavy! What are yer talking about? What are yer made for?" rejoined the male traveller, changing his own little bundle as he spoke, to the other shoulder. "Oh, there yer are, resting again! Well, if yer ain't enough to tire any body's patience out, I don't know what is!"

"Is it much farther?" asked the woman, resting herself against a bank, and looking up with the perspiration streaming from her face.

"Much farther! Yer as good as there," said the long-legged tramper, pointing out before him. "Look there! Those are the lights of London."

"They're a good two mile off, at least," said the woman despondingly.

"Never mind whether they're two mile off, or twenty," said Noah Claypole; for he it was; "but get up and come on, or I'll kick yer, and so I give yer notice."

As Noah's red nose grew redder with anger, and as he crossed the road while speaking, as if fully prepared to put his threat into execution, the woman rose without any further remark, and trudged onward by side.

"Where do you mean to stop for the night, Noah?" she asked, after they had walked a few hundred yards.

"How should I know?" replied Noah, whose temper had been considerably impaired by walking.

"Near, I hope," said Charlotte.

"No, not near," replied Mr Claypole. "There! Not near; so don't think it."

"Why not?"

"When I tell yer that I don't mean to do a thing, that's enough, without any why or because either," replied Mr Claypole with dignity.

"Well, you needn't be so cross," said his companion.

"A pretty thing it would be, wouldn't it, to go and stop at the very first public-house outside the town, so that Sowerberry, if he come up after us, might poke in his old nose, and have us taken back in a cart with handcuffs on," said Mr Claypole in a jeering tone. "No! I shall go and lose myself among the narrowest streets I can find, and not stop till we come to the very out-of-the-wayest house I can set eyes on. 'Cod, yer may thank yer stars I've got a head; for if we hadn't gone, at first, the wrong road a purpose, and come back across country, yer'd have been locked up hard and fast a week ago, my lady. And serve yer right for being a fool."

"I know I ain't as cunning as you are," replied Charlotte; "but don't put all the blame on me, and say *I* should have been locked up. You would have been if I had been, any way."

"Yer took the money from the till, yer know yer did," said Mr Claypole.

"I took it for you, Noah, dear," rejoined Charlotte.

"Did I keep it?" asked Mr Claypole.

"No; you trusted in me, and let me carry it like a dear, and so you are," said the lady, chucking him under the chin, and drawing her arm through his.

This was indeed the case; but as it was not Mr Claypole's habit to repose a blind and foolish confidence in anybody, it should be observed, in justice to that gentleman, that he had trusted Charlotte to this extent, in order that, if they were pursued, the money might be found on her: which would leave him an opportunity of asserting his innocence of any theft, and would greatly facilitate his chances of escape. Of course, he entered at this juncture, into no explanation of his motives, and they walked on very lovingly together.

In pursuance of this cautious plan, Mr Claypole went on, without halting, until he arrived at the Angel at Islington, where he wisely judged, from the crowd of passengers and number of vehicles, that London began in earnest. Just pausing to observe which appeared the most crowded streets, and consequently the most to be avoided, he crossed into Saint John's Road, and was soon deep in the obscurity of the intricate and dirty ways, which, lying between Gray's Inn Lane and Smithfield, render that part of the town one of the lowest and worst that improvement has left in the midst of London.

Through these streets, Noah Claypole walked, dragging Charlotte after him; now stepping into the kennel to embrace at a glance the whole external character of some small public-house; now jogging on again, as some fancied appearance induced him to believe it too public for his purpose. At length, he stopped in front of one, more humble in appearance and more dirty than any he had yet seen; and, having crossed over and surveyed it from the opposite pavement, graciously announced his intention of putting up there, for the night.

"So give us the bundle," said Noah, unstrapping it from the woman's shoulders, and slinging it over his own; "and don't yer speak, except when yer spoke to. What's the name of the house – t-h-r – three what?"

"Cripples," said Charlotte.

"Three Cripples," repeated Noah, "and a very good sign too. Now, then! Keep close at my heels, and come along." With these injunctions, he pushed the rattling door with his shoulder, and entered the house, followed by his companion.

There was nobody in the bar but a young Jew, who, with his two elbows on the counter, was reading a dirty newspaper. He stared very hard at Noah, and Noah stared very hard at him.

If Noah had been attired in his charity-boy's dress, there might have been some reason for the Jew opening his eyes so wide; but as he had discarded the coat and badge, and wore a short smock-frock over his leathers, there seemed no particular reason for his appearance exciting so much attention in a public-house.

"Is this the Three Cripples?" asked Noah.

"That is the dabe of this ouse," replied the Jew.

"A gentleman we met on the road, coming up from the country, recommended us here," said Noah, nudging Charlotte, perhaps to call her attention to this most ingenious device for attracting respect, and perhaps to warn her to betray no surprise. "We want to sleep here to-night."

"I"b dot certaid you cad," said Barney, who was the attendant sprite; "but I'll idquire."

"Show us the tap, and give us a bit of cold meat and a drop of beer while yer inquiring, will yer?" said Noah.

Barney complied by ushering them into a small back-room, and setting the required viands before them; having done which, he informed the travellers that they could be lodged that night, and left the amiable couple to their refreshment.

Now, this back-room was immediately behind the bar, and some steps lower, so that any person connected with the house, undrawing a small curtain which concealed a single pane of glass fixed in the wall of the last-named apartment, about five feet from its flooring, could not only look down upon any guests in the back-room without any great hazard of being observed (the glass being in a dark angle of the wall, between which and a large upright beam the observer had to thrust himself), but could, by applying his ear to the partition, ascertain with tolerable distinctness, their subject of conversation. The landlord of the house had not withdrawn his eye from this place of espial for five minutes, and Barney had only just returned from making the communication above related, when Fagin, in the course of his evening's business, came into the bar to inquire after some of his young pupils.

"Hush!" said Barney: "stradegers id the next roob."

"Strangers!" repeated the old man in a whisper.

"Ah! Ad rub uds too," added Barney. "Frob the cuttry, but subthig in your way, or I"b bistaked."

Fagin appeared to receive this communication with great interest. Mounting a stool, he cautiously applied his eye to the pane of glass, from which secret post he could see Mr Claypole taking cold beef from the dish, and porter from the pot, and administering homœopathic doses of both to Charlotte, who sat patiently by, eating and drinking at his pleasure.

"Aha!" he whispered, looking round to Barney, "I like that fellow's looks. He'd be of use to us; he knows how to train the girl already. Don't make as much noise as a mouse, my dear, and let me hear 'em talk – let me hear 'em."

He again applied his eye to the glass, and turning his ear to the partition, listened attentively: with a subtle and eager look upon his face, that might have appertained to some old goblin.

"So I mean to be a gentleman," said Mr Claypole, kicking out his legs, and continuing a conversation, the commencement of which Fagin had arrived too late to hear. "No more jolly old coffins, Charlotte, but a gentleman's life for me: and, if yer like yer shall be a lady."

"I should like that well enough, dear," replied Charlotte; "but tills ain't to be emptied every day, and people to get clear off after it."

"Tills be blowed!" said Mr Claypole; "there's more things besides tills to be emptied."

"What do you mean?" asked his companion.

"Pockets, women's ridicules, houses, mail-coaches, banks!" said Mr Claypole, rising with the porter.

"But you can't do all that, dear," said Charlotte.

"I shall look out to get into company with them as can," replied Noah. "They'll be able to make us useful some way or another. Why, you yourself are worth fifty women; I never see such a precious sly and deceitful creetur as yer can be when I let yer."

"Lor, how nice it is to hear you say so!" exclaimed Charlotte, imprinting a kiss upon his ugly face.

"There, that'll do: don't yer be too affectionate, in case I'm cross with yer," said Noah, disengaging himself with great gravity. "I should like to be the captain of some band, and have the whopping of 'em, and follering 'em about, unbeknown to themselves. That would suit me, if there was good profit; and if we could only get in with some gentlemen of this sort, I say it would be cheap at that twenty-pound note you've got, – especially as we don't very well know how to get rid of it ourselves."

After expressing this opinion, Mr Claypole looked into the porter-pot with an aspect of deep wisdom; and having well shaken its contents, nodded condescendingly to Charlotte, and took a draught, wherewith he appeared greatly refreshed. He was meditating another, when the sudden opening of the door, and the appearance of a stranger, interrupted him.

The stranger was Mr Fagin. And very amiable he looked, and a very low bow he made, as he advanced, and setting himself down at the nearest table, ordered something to drink of the grinning Barney.

"A pleasant night, sir, but cool for the time of year," said Fagin, rubbing his hands. "From the country, I see, sir?"

"How do yer see that?" asked Noah Claypole.

"We have not so much dust as that in London," replied Fagin, pointing from Noah's shoes to those of his companion, and from them to the two bundles.

"Yer a sharp feller," said Noah. "Ha! ha! only hear that, Charlotte!"

"Why, one need be sharp in this town, my dear," replied the Jew, sinking his voice to a confidential whisper; "and that's the truth."

Fagin followed up this remark by striking the side of his nose with his right forefinger, – a gesture which Noah attempted to imitate, though not with complete success, in consequence of his own nose not being large enough for the purpose. However, Mr Fagin seemed to interpret the endeavour as expressing a perfect coincidence with his opinion, and put about the liquor which Barney re-appeared with, in a very friendly manner.

"Good stuff that," observed Mr Claypole, smacking his lips.

"Dear!" said Fagin. "A man need be always emptying a till, or a pocket, or a woman's reticule, or a house, or a mail-coach, or a bank, if he drinks it regularly."

Mr Claypole no sooner heard this extract from his own remarks than he fell back in his chair, and looked from the Jew to Charlotte with a countenance of ashy paleness and excessive terror.

"Don't mind me, my dear," said Fagin, drawing his chair closer. "Ha! ha! it was lucky it was only me that heard you by chance. It was very lucky it was only me."

"I didn't take it," stammered Noah, no longer stretching out his legs like an independent gentleman, but coiling them up as well as he could under his chair; "it was all her doing: yer've got it now, Charlotte, yer know yer have."

"No matter who's got it, or who did it, my dear!" replied Fagin, glancing, nevertheless, with a hawk's eye at the girl and the two bundles. "I'm in that way myself, and I like you for it."

"In what way?" asked Mr Claypole, a little recovering.

"In that way of business," rejoined Fagin; "and so are the people of the house. You've hit the right nail upon the head, and are as safe here as you could be. There is not a safer place in all this town than is the Cripples; that is, when I like to make it so. And I have taken a fancy to you and the young woman; so I've said the word, and you may make your minds easy."

Noah Claypole's mind might have been at ease after this assurance, but his body certainly was not; for he shuffled and writhed about, into various uncouth positions: eyeing his new friend meanwhile with mingled fear and suspicion.

"I'll tell you more," said Fagin, after he had reassured the girl, by dint of friendly nods and muttered encouragements. "I have got a friend that I think can gratify your darling wish, and put you in the right way, where you can take whatever department of the business you think will suit you best at first, and be taught all the others."

"Yer speak as if yer were in earnest," replied Noah.

"What advantage would it be to me to be anything else?" inquired Fagin, shrugging his shoulders. "Here! Let me have a word with you outside."

"There's no occasion to trouble ourselves to move," said Noah, getting his legs by gradual degrees abroad again. "She'll take the luggage up stairs the while. Charlotte, see to them bundles!"

This mandate, which had been delivered with great majesty, was obeyed without the slightest demur; and Charlotte made the best of her way off with the packages while Noah held the door open and watched her out.

"She's kept tolerably well under, ain't she?" he asked as he resumed his seat: in the tone of a keeper who has tamed some wild animal.

"Quite perfect," rejoined Fagin, clapping him on the shoulder. "You're a genius, my dear."

"Why, I suppose if I wasn't, I shouldn't be here," replied Noah. "But, I say, she'll be back if yer lose time."

"Now, what do you think?" said Fagin. "If you was to like my friend, could you do better than join him?"

"Is he in a good way of business; that's where it is!" responded Noah, winking one of his little eyes.

"The top of the tree; employs a power of hands; has the very best society in the profession."

"Regular town-maders?" asked Mr Claypole.

"Not a countryman among 'em; and I don't think he'd take you, even on my recommendation, if he didn't run rather short of assistants just now," replied Fagin.

"Should I have to hand over?" said Noah, slapping his breeches-pocket.

"It couldn't possibly be done without," replied Fagin, in a most decided manner.

"Twenty pound, though, – it's a lot of money!"

"Not when it's in a note you can't get rid of," retorted Fagin. "Number and date taken, I suppose? Payment stopped at the Bank? Ah! It's not worth much to him. It'll have to go abroad, and he couldn't sell it for a great deal in the market."

"When could I see him?" asked Noah doubtfully.

"To-morrow morning."

"Where?"

"Here."

"Um!" said Noah. "What's the wages?"

"Live like a gentleman – board lodging, pipes and spirits free – half of all you earn, and half of all the young woman earns," replied Mr Fagin.

Whether Noah Claypole, whose rapacity was none of the least comprehensive, would have acceded even to these glowing terms, had he been a perfectly free agent, is very doubtful; but as he recollected that, in the event of his refusal it was in the power of his new acquaintance to give him up to justice immediately (and more unlikely things had come to pass), he gradually relented, and said he thought that would suit him.

"But, yer see," observed Noah, "as she will be able to do a good deal, I should like to take something very light."

"A little fancy work?" suggested Fagin.

"Ah! something of that sort," replied Noah. "What do you think would suit me now? Something not too trying for the strength, and not very dangerous, you know. That's the sort of thing!"

"I heard you talk of something in the spy way upon the others, my dear," said Fagin. "My friend wants somebody who would do that well, very much."

"Why, I did mention that, and I shouldn't mind turning my hand to it sometimes," rejoined Mr Claypole slowly; "but it wouldn't pay by itself, you know."

"That's true!" observed the Jew, ruminating or pretending to ruminate. "No, it might not."

"What do you think, then?" asked Noah, anxiously regarding him. "Something in the sneaking way, where it was pretty sure work, and not much more risk than being at home."

"What do you think of the old ladies?" asked Fagin. "There's a good deal of money made in snatching their bags and parcels, and running round the corner."

"Don't they holler out a good deal, and scratch sometimes?" asked Noah, shaking his head. "I don't think that would answer my purpose. Ain't there any other line open?"

"Stop!" said Fagin, laying his hand on Noah's knee. "The kinchin lay."

"What's that?" demanded Mr Claypole.

"The kinchins, my dear," said Fagin, "is the young children that's sent on errands by their mother, with sixpences and shillings; and the lay is just to take their money away – they've always got it ready in their hands, – then knock 'em into the kennel, and walk off very slow, as if there were nothing else the matter but a child fallen down and hurt itself. Ha! ha! ha!"

"Ha! ha!" roared Mr Claypole, kicking up his legs in an ecstasy. "Lord, that's the very thing!"

"To be sure it is," replied Fagin; "and you can have a few good beats chalked out in Camden Town, and Battle Bridge, and neighbourhoods like that, where they're always going errands; and you can upset as many kinchins as you want, any hour in the day. Ha! ha! ha!"

With this, Fagin poked Mr Claypole in the side, and they joined in a burst of laughter both long and loud.

"Well, that's all right!" said Noah, when he had recovered himself, and Charlotte had returned. "What time to-morrow shall we say?"

"Will ten do?" asked Fagin, adding, as Mr Claypole nodded assent, "What name shall I tell my good friend?"

"Mr Bolter," replied Noah, who had prepared himself for such an emergency. "Mr Morris Bolter. This is Mrs Bolter."

"Mrs Bolter's humble servant," said Fagin, bowing with grotesque politeness. "I hope I shall know her better very shortly."

"Do you hear the gentleman, Charlotte?" thundered Mr Claypole.

"Yes, Noah, dear!" replied Mrs Bolter, extending her hand.

"She calls me Noah, as a sort of fond way of talking," said Mr Morris Bolter, late Claypole, turning to Fagin. "You understand?"

"Oh yes, I understand – perfectly," replied Fagin, telling the truth for once. "Good night! Good night!"

With many adieus and good wishes, Mr Fagin went his way. Noah

Claypole, bespeaking his good lady's attention, proceeded to enlighten her relative to the arrangement he had made, with all that haughtiness and air of superiority, becoming, not only a member of the sterner sex, but a gentleman who appreciated the dignity of a special appointment on the kinchin lay, in London and its vicinity.

Chapter XLIII

Wherein is shown how the Artful Dodger got into Trouble

"And so it was you that was your own friend, was it?" asked Mr Claypole, otherwise Bolter, when, by virtue of the compact entered into between them, he had removed next day to Fagin's house. "'Cod, I thought as much last night!"

"Every man's his own friend, my dear," replied Fagin, with his most insinuating grin. "He hasn't as good a one as himself anywhere."

"Except sometimes," replied Morris Bolter, assuming the air of a man of the world. "Some people are nobody's enemies but their own, yer know."

"Don't believe that," said Fagin. "When a man's his own enemy, it's only because he's too much his own friend; not because he's careful for everybody but himself. Pooh! pooh! There ain't such a thing in nature."

"There oughtn't to be, if there is," replied Mr Bolter.

"That stands to reason. Some conjurers say that three is the magic number, and some say number seven. It's neither, my friend, neither. It's number one."

"Ha! ha!" cried Mr Bolter. "Number one for ever."

"In a little community like ours, my dear," said Fagin, who felt it necessary to qualify this position, "we have a general number one; that is, you can't consider yourself as number one, without considering me too as the same, and all the other young people."

"Oh, the devil!" exclaimed Mr Bolter.

"You see," pursued Fagin, affecting to disregard this interruption, "we are so mixed up together, and identified in our interest, that it must be so. For instance, it's your object to take care of number one – meaning yourself."

"Certainly," replied Mr Bolter. "Yer about right there."

"Well! You can't take care of yourself, number one, without taking care of me, number one."

"Number two, you mean," said Mr Bolter, who was largely endowed with the quality of selfishness.

"No, I don't!" retorted Fagin. "I'm of the same importance to you, as you are to yourself."

"I say," interrupted Mr Bolter, "yer a very nice man, and I'm very fond of yer; but we ain't quite so thick together, as all that comes to."

"Only think," said Fagin, shrugging his shoulders, and stretching out his hands; "only consider. You've done what's a very pretty thing, and what I love you for doing; but what at the same time would put the cravat round your throat, that's so very easily tied and so very difficult to unloose – in plain English, the halter!"

Mr Bolter put his hand to his neckerchief, as if he felt it inconveniently tight; and murmured an assent, qualified in tone but not in substance.

"The gallows," continued Fagin, "the gallows, my dear, is an ugly finger-post, which points out a very short and sharp turning that has stopped many a bold fellow's career on the broad highway. To keep in the easy road, and keep it at a distance, is object number one with you."

"Of course it is," replied Mr Bolter. "What do yer talk about such things for?"

"Only to show you my meaning clearly," said the Jew, raising his eyebrows. "To be able to do that, you depend upon me. To keep my little business all snug, I depend upon you. The first is your number one, the second my number one. The more you value your number one, the more careful you must be of mine; so we come at last to what I told you at first – that a regard for number one holds us all together, and must do so, unless we would all go to pieces in company."

"That's true," rejoined Mr Bolter, thoughtfully. "Oh! yer a cunning old codger!"

Mr Fagin saw, with delight, that this tribute to his powers was no mere compliment, but that he had really impressed his recruit with a sense of his wily genius, which it was most important that he should entertain in the outset of their acquaintance. To strengthen an impression so desirable and useful, he followed up the blow by acquainting him, in some detail, with the magnitude and extent of his operations; blending truth and fiction together, as best served his purpose; and bringing both to bear, with so much art, that Mr Bolter's respect visibly increased, and became tempered, at the same time, with a degree of wholesome fear, which it was highly desirable to awaken.

"It's this mutual trust we have in each other that consoles me under heavy losses," said Fagin. "My best hand was taken from me, yesterday morning."

"You don't mean to say he died?" cried Mr Bolter.

"No, no," replied Fagin, "not so bad as that. Not quite so bad."

"What, I suppose he was – "

"Wanted," interposed Fagin. "Yes, he was wanted."

"Very particular?" inquired Mr Bolter.

"No," replied Fagin, "not very. He was charged with attempting to pick a pocket, and they found a silver snuffbox on him, – his own, my dear, his own, for he took snuff himself, and was very fond of it. They remanded him till to-day, for they thought they knew the owner. Ah! he was worth fifty boxes, and I'd give the price of as many to have him back. You should have known the Dodger, my dear; you should have known the Dodger."

"Well, but I shall know him, I hope; don't yer think so?" said Mr Bolter.

"I'm doubtful about it," replied Fagin, with a sigh. "If they don't get any fresh evidence, it'll only be a summary conviction, and we shall have him back again after six weeks or so; but, if they do, it's a case of lagging. They know what a clever lad he is; he'll be a lifer. They'll make the Artful nothing less than a lifer."

"What do yer mean by lagging and a lifer?" demanded Mr Bolter. "What's the good of talking in that way to me; why don't yer speak so as I can understand yer?"

Fagin was about to translate these mysterious expressions into the vulgar tongue; and, being interpreted, Mr Bolter would have been informed that they represented that combination of words, "transportation for life," when the dialogue was cut short by the entry of Master Bates, with his hands in his breeches-pockets, and his face twisted into a look of semi-comical woe.

"It's all up, Fagin," said Charley, when he and his new companion had been made known to each other.

"What do you mean?"

"They've found the gentleman as owns the box; two or three more's a coming to "dentify him; and the Artful's booked for a passage out," replied Master Bates. "I must have a full suit of mourning, Fagin, and a hatband, to wisit him in, afore he sets out upon his travels. To think of Jack Dawkins – lummy Jack – the Dodger – the Artful Dodger – going abroad for a common twopenny-halfpenny sneeze-box! I never thought he'd a done it under a gold watch, chain, and seals, at the lowest. Oh, why didn't he rob some rich old gentleman of all his walables, and go out *as* a gentleman, and not like a common prig, without no honour nor glory!"

With this expression of feeling for his unfortunate friend, Master Bates sat himself on the nearest chair with an aspect of chagrin and despondency.

"What do you talk about his having neither honour nor glory for!" exclaimed Fagin, darting an angry look at his pupil. "Wasn't he always top-sawyer among you all! Is there one of you that could touch him or come near him on any scent! Eh?"

"Not one," replied Master Bates, in a voice rendered husky by regret; "not one."

"Then what do you talk of?" replied Fagin angrily; "what are you blubbering for?"

""Cause it isn't on the rec-ord, is it?" said Charley, chafed into perfect defiance of his venerable friend by the current of his regrets; "'cause it can't come out in the "dictment; 'cause nobody will never know half of what he was. How will he stand in the Newgate Calendar? P'raps not be there at all. Oh, my eye, my eye, wot a blow it is!"

"Ha! ha!" cried Fagin extending his right hand, and turning to Mr Bolter in a fit of chuckling which shook him as though he had the palsy; "see what a pride they take in their profession, my dear. Ain't it beautiful?"

Mr Bolter nodded assent; and Fagin, after contemplating the grief of Charley Bates for some seconds with evident satisfaction, stepped up to that young gentleman and patted him on the shoulder.

"Never mind, Charley," said Fagin soothingly; "it'll come out, it'll be sure to come out. They'll all know what a clever fellow he was; he'll show it himself, and not disgrace his old pals and teachers. Think how young he is too! What a distinction, Charley, to be lagged at his time of life!"

"Well, it is a honour that is!" said Charley, a little consoled.

"He shall have all he wants," continued the Jew. "He shall be kept in the Stone Jug, Charley, like a gentleman. Like a gentleman! With his beer every day, and money in his pocket to pitch and toss with, if he can't spend it."

"No, shall he though?" cried Charley Bates.

"Ay, that he shall," replied Fagin, "and we'll have a big-wig, Charley: one that's got the greatest gift of the gab: to carry on his defence; and he shall make a speech for himself too, if he likes; and we'll read it all in the papers – "Artful Dodger – shrieks of laughter – here the court was convulsed" – eh, Charley, eh?"

"Ha! ha!" laughed Master Bates, "what a lark that would be, wouldn't it, Fagin? I say, how the Artful would bother 'em, wouldn't he?"

"Would!" cried Fagin. "He shall – he will!"

"Ah, to be sure, so he will," repeated Charley, rubbing his hands.

"I think I see him now," cried the Jew, bending his eyes upon his pupil.

"So do I," cried Charley Bates. "Ha! ha! ha! so do I. I see it all afore me, upon my soul I do, Fagin. What a game! What a regular game! All the big-wigs trying to look solemn, and Jack Dawkins addressing of 'em as intimate and comfortable as if he was the judge's own son making a speech arter dinner – ha! ha! ha!"

In fact, Mr Fagin had so well humoured his young friend's eccentric disposition, that Master Bates, who had at first been disposed to consider the imprisoned Dodger rather in the light of a victim, now looked upon him as the chief actor in a scene of most uncommon and exquisite humour, and felt quite impatient for the arrival of the time when his old companion should have so favourable an opportunity of displaying his abilities.

"We must know how he gets on to-day, by some handy means or other," said Fagin. "Let me think."

"Shall I go?" asked Charley.

"Not for the world," replied Fagin. "Are you mad, my dear, stark mad, that you'd walk into the very place where – No, Charley, no. One is enough to lose at a time."

"You don't mean to go yourself, I suppose?" said Charley with a humorous leer.

"That wouldn't quite fit," replied Fagin shaking his head.

"Then why don't you send this new cove?" asked Master Bates, laying his hand on Noah's arm. "Nobody knows him."

"Why, if he didn't mind – " observed Fagin.

"Mind!" interposed Charley. "What should *he* have to mind?"

"Really nothing, my dear," said Fagin, turning to Mr Bolter, "really nothing."

"Oh, I dare say about that, yer know," observed Noah, backing towards the door, and shaking his head with a kind of sober alarm. "No, no – none of that. It's not in my department, that ain't."

"Wot department has he got, Fagin?" inquired Master Bates, surveying Noah's lank form with much disgust. "The cutting away when there's anything wrong, and the eating all the wittles when there's everything right; is that his branch?"

"Never mind," retorted Mr Bolter; "and don't yer take liberties with yer superiors, little boy, or yer'll find yerself in the wrong shop."

Master Bates laughed so vehemently at this magnificent threat, that it was some time before Fagin could interpose, and represent to Mr Bolter that he incurred no possible danger in visiting the police-office; that, inasmuch as no account of the little affair in which he had been engaged, nor any description of his person, had yet been forwarded to the metropolis, it was very probable that he was not even suspected of having resorted to it for shelter; and that, if he were properly disguised, it would be as safe a spot for him to visit as any in London, inasmuch as it would be, of all places, the very last, to which he could be supposed likely to resort of his own free will.

Persuaded, in part, by these representations, but overborne in a much greater degree by his fear of Fagin, Mr Bolter at length consented with a very bad grace, to undertake the expedition. By Fagin's directions, he immediately substituted for his own attire, a waggoner's frock, velveteen breeches, and leather legging: all of which articles the Jew had at hand. He was likewise furnished with a felt hat well garnished with turnpike tickets; and a carter's whip. Thus equipped, he was to saunter into the office, as some country fellow from Covent Garden market might be supposed to do for the gratification of his curiosity; and as he was as awkward, ungainly, and raw-boned a fellow as need be, Mr Fagin had no fear but that he would look the part to perfection.

These arrangements completed, he was informed of the necessary signs and tokens by which to recognise the Artful Dodger, and was conveyed by Master Bates through dark and winding ways to within a very short distance of Bow Street. Having described the precise situation of the office, and accompanied it with copious directions how he was to walk straight up the passage, and when he got into the yard take the door up the steps on the right-hand side, and pull off his hat as he went into the room, Charley Bates bade him hurry on alone, and promised to bide his return on the spot of their parting.

Noah Claypole, or Morris Bolter as the reader pleases, punctually followed the directions he had received, which – Master Bates being pretty well acquainted with the locality – were so exact that he was enabled to gain the magisterial presence without asking any question, or meeting with any interruption by the way. He found himself jostled among a crowd of people, chiefly women, who were huddled together in a dirty frowsy room, at the upper end of which was a raised platform railed off from the rest, with a dock for the prisoners on the left hand against the wall, a box for the witnesses in the middle, and a desk for the magistrates on the right; the awful locality last named, being screened off by a partition which concealed the bench from the common gaze, and left the vulgar to imagine (if they could) the full majesty of justice.

There were only a couple of women in the dock, who were nodding to their admiring friends, while the clerk read some depositions to a couple of policemen and a man in plain clothes who leant over the table. A jailer stood reclining against the dock-rail, tapping his nose listlessly with a large key, except when he repressed an undue tendency to conversation among the idlers, by proclaiming silence; or looked sternly up to bid some woman "Take that baby out," when the gravity of justice was disturbed by feeble cries, half-smothered in the mother's shawl, from some meagre infant. The room smelt close and unwholesome; the walls were dirt-discoloured; and the ceiling blackened. There was an old smoky bust over the mantel-shelf, and a dusty clock above the dock – the only thing present, that seemed to go on as it ought; for depravity, or poverty, or an habitual acquaintance with both, had left a taint on all the animate matter, hardly less unpleasant than the thick greasy scum on every inanimate object that frowned upon it.

Noah looked eagerly about him for the Dodger; but although there were several women who would have done very well for that distinguished character's mother or sister, and more than one man who might be supposed to bear a strong resemblance to his father, nobody at all answering the description given him of Mr Dawkins was to be seen. He waited in a state of much suspense and uncertainty until the women, being committed for trial, went flaunting out; and then was quickly relieved by the appearance of another prisoner who he felt at once could be no other than the object of his visit.

It was indeed Mr Dawkins, who, shuffling into the office with the big coat sleeves tucked up as usual, his left hand in his pocket, and his hat in his right hand, preceded the jailer, with a rolling gait altogether indescribable, and, taking his place in the dock, requested in an audible voice to know what he was placed in that 'ere disgraceful sitivation for.

"Hold your tongue, will you?" said the jailer.

"I'm an Englishman, ain't I?" rejoined the Dodger. "Where are my priwileges?"

"You'll get your privileges soon enough," retorted the jailer, "and pepper with 'em."

"We'll see wot the Secretary of State for the Home Affairs has got to say to the beaks, if I don't," replied Mr Dawkins. "Now then! Wot is this here business? I shall thank the madg"strates to dispose of this here little affair, and not to keep me while they read the paper, for I've got an appointment with a gentleman in the City, and as I'm a man of my word an wery punctual in business matters, he'll go away if I ain't there to my time, and then pr"aps there won't be an action for damage against them as kep me away. Oh no, certainly not!"

At this point, the Dodger, with a show of being very particular with a view to proceedings to be had thereafter, desired the jailer to communicate "the names of them two files as was on the bench." Which so tickled the spectators, that they laughed almost as heartily as Master Bates could have done if he had heard the request.

"Silence there!" cried the jailer.

"What is this?" inquired one of the magistrates.

"A pick-pocketing case, your worship."

"Has the boy ever been here before?"

"He ought to have been, a many times," replied the jailer. "He has been pretty well everywhere else. *I* know him well, your worship."

"Oh! you know me, do you?" cried the Artful, making a note of the statement. "Wery good. That's a case of deformation of character, any way."

Here there was another laugh, and another cry of silence.

"Now then, where are the witnesses?'said the clerk.

"Ah! that's right," added the Dodger. "Where are they? I should like to see 'em."

This wish was immediately gratified, for a policeman stepped forward who had seen the prisoner attempt the pocket of an unknown gentleman in a crowd, and indeed take a handkerchief therefrom, which, being a very old one, he deliberately put back again, after trying it on his own countenance. For this reason, he took the Dodger into custody as soon as he could get near him and the said Dodger, being searched, had upon his person a silver snuff-box, with the owner's name engraved upon the lid. This gentleman had been discovered on reference to the Court Guide, and being then and there present, swore that the snuff-box was his, and that he had missed it on the previous day, the moment he had disengaged himself from the crowd before referred to. He had also remarked a young gentleman in the throng, particularly active in making his way about, and that young gentleman was the prisoner before him.

"Have you anything to ask this witness, boy?" said the magistrate.

"I wouldn't abase myself by descending to hold no conversation with him," replied the Dodger.

"Have you anything to say at all?"

"Do you hear his worship ask if you've anything to say?" inquired the jailer, nudging the silent Dodger with his elbow.

"I beg your pardon," said the Dodger, looking up with an air of abstraction. "Did you redress yourself to me, my man?"

"I never see such an out-and-out young wagabond, your worship," observed the officer with a grin. "Do you mean to say anything, you young shaver?"

"No," replied the Dodger, "not here, for this ain't the shop for justice; besides which, my attorney is a-breakfasting this morning with the Wice President of the House of Commons; but I shall have something to say elsewhere, and so will he, and so will a wery numerous and "spectable circle of acquaintance as'll make them beaks wish they'd never been born, or that they'd got their footmen to hang'em up to their own hat-pegs, "afore they let 'em come out this morning to try it on upon me. I'll – "

"There! He's fully committed!" interposed the clerk. "Take him away."

"Come on," said the jailer.

"Oh ah! I'll come on," replied the Dodger, brushing his hat with the palm of his hand. "Ah! (to the Bench) it's no use your looking frightened; I won't show you no mercy, not a ha"porth of it. *You'll* pay for this, my fine fellers. I wouldn't be you for something! I wouldn't go free, now, if you was to fall down on your knees and ask me. Here, carry me off to prison! Take me away!"

With these last words, the Dodger suffered himself to be led off by the collar; threatening, till he got into the yard, to make a parliamentary business of it; and then grinning in the officer's face, with great glee and self-approval.

Having seen him locked up by himself in a little cell, Noah made the best of his way back to where he had left Master Bates. After waiting here some time, he was joined by that young gentleman, who had prudently abstained from showing himself until he had looked carefully abroad from a snug retreat, and ascertained that his new friend had not been followed by any impertinent person.

The two hastened back together, to bear to Mr Fagin the animating news that the Dodger was doing full justice to his bringing-up, and establishing for himself a glorious reputation.

Chapter XLIV

The Time arrives for Nancy to redeem her Pledge to Rose Maylie. She fails

ADEPT as she was, in all the arts of cunning and dissimulation, the girl Nancy could not wholly conceal the effect which the knowledge of the step she had taken wrought upon her mind. She remembered that both the crafty Jew and the brutal Sikes had confided to her schemes, which had been hidden from all others: in full confidence that she was trustworthy and beyond the reach of their suspicion. Vile as those schemes were, desperate as were their originators, and bitter as were her feelings towards Fagin, who had led her, step by step, deeper and deeper down into an abyss of crime and misery, whence was no escape; still, there were times when, even towards him, she felt some relenting, lest her disclosure should bring him within the iron grasp he had so long eluded, and he should fall at last – richly as he merited such a fate – by her hand.

But, these were the mere wanderings of a mind unable wholly to detach itself from old companions and associations, though enabled to fix itself steadily on one object, and resolved not to be turned aside by any consideration. Her fears for Sikes would have been more powerful inducements to recoil while there was yet time; but she had stipulated that her secret should be rigidly kept, she had dropped no clue which could lead to his discovery, she had refused, even for his sake, a refuge from all the guilt and wretchedness that encompassed her – and what more could she do! She was resolved.

Though all her mental struggles terminated in this conclusion, they forced themselves upon her, again and again, and left their traces too. She grew pale and thin, even within a few days. At times, she took no heed of what was passing before her, or no part in conversations where once, she would have been the loudest. At other times, she laughed without merriment, and was noisy without cause or meaning. At others – often within a moment afterwards – she sat silent and dejected, brooding with her head upon her hands, while the very effort by which she roused herself, told, more forcibly than even these indications, that she was ill at ease, and that her thoughts were occupied with matters very different and distant from those in course of discussion by her companions.

It was Sunday night, and the bell of the nearest church struck the hour. Sikes and the Jew were talking, but they paused to listen. The girl looked up from the low seat on which she crouched, and listened too. Eleven.

"An hour this side of midnight," said Sikes, raising the blind to look out and returning to his seat. "Dark and heavy it is too. A good night for business this."

"Ah!" replied Fagin. "What a pity, Bill, my dear, that there's none quite ready to be done."

"You're right for once," replied Sikes gruffly. "It is a pity, for I'm in the humour too."

Fagin sighed, and shook his head despondingly.

"We must make up for lost time when we've got things into a good train. That's all I know," said Sikes.

"That's the way to talk, my dear," replied Fagin, venturing to pat him on the shoulder. "It does me good to hear you."

"Does you good does it!" cried Sikes. "Well, so be it."

"Ha! ha! ha!" laughed Fagin, as if he were relieved by even this concession. "You're like yourself to-night, Bill! Quite like yourself."

"I don't feel like myself when you lay that withered old claw on my shoulder, so take it away," said Sikes casting off the Jew's hand.

"It makes you nervous, Bill, – reminds you of being nabbed, does it?" said Fagin, determined not to be offended.

"Reminds me of being nabbed by the devil," returned Sikes. "There never was another man with such a face as yours, unless it was your father, and I suppose *he* is singeing his grizzled red beard by this time, unless you came straight from the old "un without any father at all betwixt you; which I shouldn't wonder at, a bit."

Fagin offered no reply to this compliment; but, pulling Sikes by the sleeve, pointed his finger towards Nancy, who had taken advantage of the foregoing conversation to put on her bonnet, and was now leaving the room.

"Hallo!" cried Sikes. "Nance. Where's the gal going to at this time of night?"

"Not far."

"What answer's that?" returned Sikes. "Where are you going?"

"I say, not far."

"And I say where?" retorted Sikes. "Do you hear me?"

"I don't know where," replied the girl.

"Then I do," said Sikes, more in the spirit of obstinacy than because he had any real objection to the girl going where she listed. "Nowhere. Sit down."

"I'm not well. I told you that before," rejoined the girl. "I want a breath of air."

"Put your head out of the winder," replied Sikes.

"There's not enough there," said the girl. "I want it in the street."

"Then you won't have it," replied Sikes. With which assurance he rose, locked the door, took the key out, and pulling her bonnet from her head, flung it up to the top of an old press. "There," said the robber. "Now stop quietly where you are, will you?"

"It's not such a matter as a bonnet would keep me," said the girl turning very pale. "What do you mean, Bill? Do you know what you're doing?"

"Know what I'm – Oh!" cried Sikes turning to Fagin, "she's out of her senses, you know, or she daren't talk to me in that way."

"You'll drive me on to something desperate," muttered the girl placing both hands upon her breast, as though to keep down by force some violent outbreak. "Let me go, will you, – this minute – this instant."

"No!" said Sikes.

"Tell him to let me go, Fagin. He had better. It'll be better for him. Do you hear me?" cried Nancy stamping her foot upon the ground.

"Hear you!" repeated Sikes turning round in his chair to confront her. "Aye! And if I hear you for half a minute longer, the dog shall have such a grip on your throat as'll tear some of that screaming voice out. Wot has come over you, you jade! Wot is it?"

"Let me go," said the girl with great earnestness; then sitting herself down on the floor, before the door, she said, "Bill, let me go; you don't know what you are doing. You don't, indeed. For only one hour – do – do!"

"Cut my limbs off one by one!" cried Sikes, seizing her roughly by the arm, "if I don't think the gal's stark raving mad. Get up."

"Not till you let me go – not till you let me go – Never – never!" screamed the girl. Sikes looked on, for a minute, watching his opportunity, and suddenly pinioning her hands dragged her, struggling and wrestling with him by the way, into a small room adjoining, where he sat himself on a bench, and thrusting her into a chair, held her down by force. She struggled and implored by turns until twelve o'clock had struck, and then, wearied and exhausted, ceased to contest the point any further. With a caution, backed by many oaths, to make no more efforts to go out that night, Sikes left her to recover at leisure and rejoined Fagin.

"Whew!" said the housebreaker wiping the perspiration from his face. "Wot a precious strange gal that is!"

"You may say that, Bill," replied Fagin thoughtfully. "You may say that."

"Wot did she take it into her head to go out to-night for, do you think?" asked Sikes. "Come; you should know her better than me. Wot does it mean?"

"Obstinacy; woman's obstinacy, I suppose, my dear."

"Well, I suppose it is," growled Sikes. "I thought I had tamed her, but she's as bad as ever."

"Worse," said Fagin thoughtfully. "I never knew her like this, for such a little cause."

"Nor I," said Sikes. "I think she's got a touch of that fever in her blood yet, and it won't come out – eh?"

"Like enough."

"I'll let her a little blood, without troubling the doctor, if she's took that way again," said Sikes.

Fagin nodded an expressive approval of this mode of treatment.

"She was hanging about me all day, and night too, when I was stretched on my back; and you, like a blackhearted wolf as you are, kept yourself aloof," said Sikes. "We was very poor too, all the time, and I think, one way or other, it's worried and fretted her; and that being shut up here so long has made her restless – eh?"

"That's it, my dear," replied the Jew in a whisper. "Hush!"

As he uttered these words, the girl herself appeared and resumed her former seat. Her eyes were swollen and red; she rocked herself to and fro; tossed her head; and, after a little time, burst out laughing.

"Why, now she's on the other tack!" exclaimed Sikes, turning a look of excessive surprise on his companion.

Fagin nodded to him to take no further notice just then; and, in a few minutes, the girl subsided into her accustomed demeanour. Whispering Sikes that there was no fear of her relapsing, Fagin took up his hat and bade him good-night. He paused when he reached the room-door, and looking round, asked if somebody would light him down the dark stairs.

"Light him down," said Sikes, who was filling his pipe. "It's a pity he should break his neck himself, and disappoint the sight-seers. Show him a light."

Nancy followed the old man down stairs, with a candle. When they reached the passage, he laid his finger on his lip, and drawing close to the girl, said, in a whisper,

"What is it, Nancy, dear?"

"What do you mean?" replied the girl, in the same tone.

"The reason of all this," replied Fagin. "If *he*" – he pointed with his skinny fore-finger up the stairs – "is so hard with you (he's a brute, Nance, a brute-beast), why don't you – "

"Well?" said the girl, as Fagin paused, with his mouth almost touching her ear, and his eyes looking into hers.

"No matter just now. We'll talk of this again. You have a friend in me, Nance; a staunch friend. I have the means at hand, quiet and close. If you want revenge on those that treat you like a dog – like a dog! worse than his dog, for he humours him sometimes – come to me. I say, come to me. He is the mere hound of a day, but you know me of old, Nance."

"I know you well," replied the girl, without manifesting the least emotion. "Good night."

She shrank back, as Fagin offered to lay his hand on hers, but said good night again, in a steady voice, and, answering his parting look with a nod of intelligence, closed the door between them.

Fagin walked towards his own home, intent upon the thoughts that were working within his brain. He had conceived the idea – not from what had just passed, though that had tended to confirm him, but slowly and by degrees – that Nancy, wearied of the housebreaker's brutality, had conceived an attachment for some new friend. Her altered manner, her repeated absences from home alone, her comparative indifference to the interests of the gang for which she had once been so zealous, and, added to these, her desperate impatience to leave home that night at a particular hour, all favoured the supposition, and rendered it, to him at least, almost matter of certainty. The object of this new liking was not among his myrmidons. He would be a valuable acquisition with such an assistant as Nancy, and must (thus Fagin argued) be secured without delay.

There was another, and a darker object, to be gained. Sikes knew too much, and his ruffian taunts had not galled Fagin the less, because the wounds were hidden. The girl must know, well, that if she shook him off, she could never be safe from his fury, and that it would be surely wreaked – to the maiming of limbs, or perhaps the loss of life – on the object of her more recent fancy. "With a little persuasion," thought Fagin, "what more likely than that she would consent to poison him? Women have done such things, and worse, to secure the same object before now. There would be the dangerous villain: the man I hate: gone; another secured in his place;

and my influence over the girl, with a knowledge of this crime to back it, unlimited."

These things passed through the mind of Fagin, during the short time he sat alone, in the housebreaker's room; and with them uppermost in his thoughts, he had taken the opportunity afterwards afforded him, of sounding the girl in the broken hints he threw out at parting. There was no expression of surprise, no assumption of an inability to understand his meaning. The girl clearly comprehended it. Her glance at parting showed *that*.

But perhaps she would recoil from a plot to take the life of Sikes, and that was one of the chief ends to be attained. "How," thought Fagin, as he crept homeward, "can I increase my influence with her? what new power can I acquire?"

Such brains are fertile in expedients. If, without extracting a confession from herself, he laid a watch, discovered the object of her altered regard, and threatened to reveal the whole history to Sikes (of whom she stood in no common fear) unless she entered into his designs, could he not secure her compliance?

"I can," said Fagin, almost aloud. "She durst not refuse me then. Not for her life, not for her life! I have it all. The means are ready, and shall be set to work. I shall have you yet!"

He cast back a dark look, and a threatening motion of the hand, towards the spot where he had left the bolder villain; and went on his way: busying his bony hands in the folds of his tattered garment, which he wrenched tightly in his grasp, as though there were a hated enemy crushed with every motion of his fingers.

Chapter XLV

Noah Claypole is employed by Fagin on a secret Mission

THE old man was up, betimes, next morning, and waited impatiently for the appearance of his new associate, who after a delay that seemed interminable, at length presented himself, and commenced a voracious assault on the breakfast.

"Bolter," said Fagin, drawing up a chair and seating himself opposite Morris Bolter.

"Well, here I am," returned Noah. "What's the matter? Don't yer ask me to do anything till I have done eating. That's a great fault in this place. Yer never get time enough over yer meals."

"You can talk as you eat, can't you?" said Fagin, cursing his dear young friend's greediness from the very bottom of his heart.

"Oh yes, I can talk. I get on better when I talk," said Noah, cutting a monstrous slice of bread. "Where's Charlotte?"

"Out," said Fagin. "I sent her out this morning with the other young woman, because I wanted us to be alone."

"Oh!" said Noah. "I wish yer'd ordered her to make some buttered toast first. Well. Talk away. Yer won't interrupt me."

There seemed, indeed, no great fear of anything interrupting him, as he had evidently sat down with a determination to do a great deal of business.

"You did well yesterday, my dear," said Fagin. "Beautiful! Six shillings and ninepence halfpenny on the very first day! The kinchin lay will be a fortune to you."

"Don't you forget to add three pint-pots and a milk-can," said Mr Bolter.

"No, no, my dear. The pint-pots were great strokes of genius: but the milk-can was a perfect masterpiece."

"Pretty well, I think, for a beginner," remarked Mr Bolter complacently. "The pots I took off airy railings, and the milk-can was standing by itself outside a public-house. I thought it might get rusty with the rain, or catch cold, yer know. Eh? Ha! ha! ha!"

Fagin affected to laugh very heartily; and Mr Bolter having had his laugh out, took a series of large bites, which finished his first hunk of bread and butter, and assisted himself to a second.

"I want you, Bolter," said Fagin, leaning over the table, "to do a piece of work for me, my dear, that needs great care and caution."

"I say," rejoined Bolter, "don't yer go shoving me into danger, or sending me to any more o" yer police-offices. That don't suit me, that don't; and so I tell yer."

"There's not the smallest danger in it – not the very smallest," said the Jew; "it's only to dodge a woman."

"An old woman?" demanded Mr Bolter.

"A young one," replied Fagin.

"I can do that pretty well, I know," said Bolter. "I was a regular cunning sneak when I was at school. What am I to dodge her for? Not to – "

"Not to do anything, but to tell me where she goes, who she sees, and, if possible, what she says; to remember the street, if it is a street, or the house, if it is a house; and to bring me back all the information you can."

"What'll yer give me?" asked Noah, setting down his cup, and looking his employer, eagerly, in the face.

"If you do it well, a pound, my dear. One pound," said Fagin, wishing to interest him in the scent as much as possible. "And that's what I never gave yet, for any job of work where there wasn't valuable consideration to be gained."

"Who is she?" inquired Noah.

"One of us."

"Oh Lor!" cried Noah, curling up his nose. "Yer doubtful of her, are yer?"

"She has found out some new friends, my dear, and I must know who they are," replied Fagin.

"I see," said Noah. "Just to have the pleasure of knowing them, if they're respectable people, eh? Ha! ha! ha! I'm your man."

"I knew you would be," cried Fagin, elated by the success of his proposal.

"Of course, of course," replied Noah. "Where is she? Where am I to wait for her? Where am I to go?"

"All that, my dear, you shall hear from me. I'll point her out at the proper time," said Fagin. "You keep ready, and leave the rest to me."

That night, and the next, and the next again, the spy sat booted and equipped in his carter's dress: ready to turn out at a word from Fagin. Six nights passed – six long weary nights – and on each, Fagin came home with a disappointed face, and briefly intimated that it was not yet time. On the seventh, he returned earlier, and with an exultation he could not conceal. It was Sunday.

"She goes abroad to-night," said Fagin, "and on the right errand, I'm sure; for she has been alone all day, and the man she is afraid of, will not be back much before daybreak. Come with me. Quick!"

Noah started up without saying a word; for the Jew was in a state of such intense excitement that it infected him. They left the house stealthily, and, hurrying through a labyrinth of streets, arrived at length before a public-house, which Noah recognised as the same in which he had slept, on the night of his arrival in London.

It was past eleven o'clock, and the door was closed. It opened softly on its hinges as Fagin gave a low whistle. They entered, without noise; and the door was closed behind them.

Scarcely venturing to whisper, but substituting dumb show for words, Fagin, and the young Jew who had admitted them, pointed out the pane of glass to Noah, and signed to him to climb up and observe the person in the adjoining room.

"Is that the woman?" he asked, scarcely above his breath.

Fagin nodded yes.

"I can't see her face well," whispered Noah. "She is looking down, and the candle is behind her."

"Stay there," whispered Fagin. He signed to Barney, who withdrew. In an instant, the lad entered the room adjoining, and, under pretence of snuffing the candle, moved it in the required position, and, speaking to the girl, caused her to raise her face.

"I see her now," cried the spy.

"Plainly?"

"I should know her among a thousand."

He hastily descended, as the room-door opened, and the girl came out. Fagin drew him behind a small partition which was curtained off, and they held their breaths as she passed within a few feet of their place of concealment, and emerged by the door at which they had entered.

"Hist!" cried the lad who held the door. "Dow."

Noah exchanged a look with Fagin, and darted out.

"To the left," whispered the lad; "take the left had, and keep od the other side."

He did so; and, by the light of the lamps, saw the girl's retreating figure, already at some distance before him. He advanced as near as he considered prudent, and kept on the opposite side of the street, the better to observe her motions. She looked nervously round, twice or thrice, and once stopped to let two men who were following close behind her, pass on. She seemed to gather courage as she advanced, and to walk with a steadier and firmer step. The spy preserved the same relative distance between them, and followed: with his eye upon her.

Chapter XLVI

The Appointment kept

The church clocks chimed three quarters past eleven, as two figures emerged on London Bridge. One, which advanced with a swift and rapid step, was that of a woman who looked eagerly about her as though in quest of some expected object; the other figure was that of a man, who slunk along in the deepest shadow he could find, and, at some distance, accommodated his pace to hers: stopping when she stopped: and as she moved again, creeping stealthily on: but never allowing himself, in the ardour of his pursuit, to gain upon her footsteps. Thus, they crossed the bridge, from the Middlesex to the Surrey shore, when the woman, apparently disappointed in her anxious scrutiny of the foot-passengers, turned back. The movement was sudden; but he who watched her, was not thrown off his guard by it; for, shrinking into one of the recesses which surmount the piers of the bridge, and leaning over the parapet the better to conceal his figure, he suffered her to pass on the opposite pavement. When she was about the same distance in advance as she had been before, he slipped quietly down, and followed her again. At nearly the centre of the bridge, she stopped. The man stopped too.

It was a very dark night. The day had been unfavourable, and at that hour and place there were few people stirring. Such as there were, hurried quickly past: very possibly without seeing but certainly without noticing, either the woman, or the man who kept her in view. Their appearance was not calculated to attract the importunate regards of such of London's destitute population, as chanced to take their way over the bridge that night in search of some cold arch or doorless hovel wherein to lay their heads; they stood there in silence: neither speaking nor spoken to, by any one who passed.

A mist hung over the river, deepening the red glare of the fires that burnt upon the small craft moored off the different wharfs, and rendering darker and more indistinct the mirky buildings on the banks. The old smoke-stained storehouses on either side, rose heavy and dull from the dense mass of roofs and gables, and frowned sternly upon water too black to reflect even their lumbering shapes. The tower of old Saint Saviour's Church, and the spire of Saint Magnus, so long the giant-warders of the ancient bridge, were visible in the gloom; but the forest of shipping below bridge, and the thickly scattered spires of churches above, were nearly all hidden from the sight.

The girl had taken a few restless turns to and fro – closely watched meanwhile by her hidden observer – when the heavy bell of St Paul's tolled for the death of another day. Midnight had come upon the crowded city. The palace, the night-cellar, the jail, the madhouse: the chambers of birth and death, of health and sickness, the rigid face of the corpse and the calm sleep of the child: midnight was upon them all.

The hour had not struck two minutes, when a young lady, accompanied by a grey-haired gentleman, alighted from a hackney-carriage within a short distance of the bridge, and, having dismissed the vehicle, walked straight towards it. They had scarcely set foot upon its pavement, when the girl started, and immediately made towards them.

They walked onward, looking about them with the air of persons who entertained some very slight expectation which had little chance of being realised, when they were suddenly joined by this new associate. They halted with an exclamation of surprise, but suppressed it immediately; for a man in the garments of a countryman came close up – brushed against them, indeed – at that precise moment.

"Not here," said Nancy hurriedly, "I am afraid to speak to you here. Come away – out of the public road – down the steps yonder!"

As she uttered these words, and indicated, with her hand, the direction in which she wished them to proceed, the countryman looked round, and roughly asking what they took up the whole pavement for, passed on.

The steps to which the girl had pointed, were those which, on the Surrey bank, and on the same side of the bridge as Saint Saviour's Church, form a landing-stairs from the river. To this spot, the man bearing the appearance of a countryman, hastened unobserved; and after a moment's survey of the place, he began to descend.

These stairs are a part of the bridge; they consist of three flights. Just below the end of the second, going down, the stone wall on the left terminates in an ornamental pilaster facing towards the Thames. At this point the lower steps widen: so that a person turning that angle of the wall, is necessarily unseen by any others on the stairs who chance to be above him, if only a step. The countryman looked hastily round, when he reached this point; and as there seemed no better place of concealment, and, the tide being out, there was plenty of room, he slipped aside, with his back to the pilaster, and there waited: pretty certain that they would come no lower, and that even if he could not hear what was said, he could follow them again, with safety.

So tardily stole the time in this lonely place, and so eager was the spy to penetrate the motives of an interview so different from what he had been led to expect, that he more than once gave the matter up for lost, and persuaded himself, either that they had stopped far above, or had resorted to some entirely different spot to hold their mysterious conversation. He was on the point of emerging from his hiding-place, and regaining the road above, when he heard the sound of footsteps, and directly afterwards of voices almost close at his ear.

He drew himself straight upright against the wall, and, scarcely breathing, listened attentively.

"This is far enough," said a voice, which was evidently that of the gentleman. "I will not suffer the young lady to go any farther. Many people would have distrusted you too much to have come even so far, but you see I am willing to humour you."

"To humour me!" cried the voice of the girl whom he had followed.

"You're considerate, indeed, sir. To humour me! Well, well, it's no matter."

"Why, for what," said the gentleman in a kinder tone, "for what purpose can you have brought us to this strange place? Why not have let me speak to you, above there, where it is light, and there is something stirring, instead of bringing us to this dark and dismal hole?"

"I told you before," replied Nancy, "that I was afraid to speak to you there. I don't know why it is," said the girl, shuddering, "but I have such a fear and dread upon me to-night that I can hardly stand."

"A fear of what?" asked the gentleman, who seemed to pity her.

"I scarcely know of what," replied the girl. "I wish I did. Horrible thoughts of death, and shrouds with blood upon them, and a fear that has made me burn as if I was on fire, have been upon me all day. I was reading a book to-night, to wile the time away, and the same things came into the print."

"Imagination," said the gentleman, soothing her.

"No imagination," replied the girl in a hoarse voice. "I'll swear I saw "coffin" written in every page of the book in large black letters, – aye, and they carried one close to me, in the streets to-night."

"There is nothing unusual in that," said the gentleman. "They have passed me often."

"*Real ones*," rejoined the girl. "This was not."

There was something so uncommon in her manner, that the flesh of the concealed listener crept as he heard the girl utter these words, and the blood chilled within him. He had never experienced a greater relief than in hearing the sweet voice of the young lady as she begged her to be calm, and not allow herself to become the prey of such fearful fancies.

"Speak to her kindly," said the young lady to her companion. "Poor creature! She seems to need it."

"You haughty religious people would have held their heads up to see me as I am to-night, and preached of flames and vengeance," cried the girl. "Oh, dear lady, why ar'n't those who claim to be God's own folks as gentle and as kind to us poor wretches as you, who, having youth, and beauty, and all that they have lost, might be a little proud instead of so much humbler?"

"Ah!" said the gentleman. "A Turk turns his face, after washing it well, to the East, when he says his prayers; these good people, after giving their faces such a rub against the World as to take the smiles off, turn with no less regularity, to the darkest side of Heaven. Between the Mussulman and the Pharisee, commend me to the first!"

These words appeared to be addressed to the young lady, and were perhaps uttered with the view of affording Nancy time to recover herself. The gentleman, shortly afterwards, addressed himself to her.

"You were not here last Sunday night," he said.

"I couldn't come," replied Nancy; "I was kept by force."

"By whom?"

"Him that I told the young lady of before."

"You were not suspected of holding any communication with anybody on the subject which has brought us here tonight, I hope?" asked the old gentleman.

"No," replied the girl, shaking her head. "It's not very easy for me to leave him unless he knows why; I couldn't have seen the lady when I did, but that I gave him a drink of laudanum before I came away."

"Did he awake before you returned?" inquired the gentleman.

"No; and neither he nor any of them suspect me."

"Good," said the gentleman. "Now listen to me."

"I am ready," replied the girl, as he paused for a moment.

"This young lady," the gentleman began, "has communicated to me, and to some other friends who can be safely trusted, what you told her nearly a fortnight since. I confess to you that I had doubts, at first, whether you were to be implicitly relied upon, but now I firmly believe you are."

"I am," said the girl earnestly.

"I repeat that I firmly believe it. To prove to you that I am disposed to trust you, I tell you without reserve, that we propose to extort the secret, whatever it may be, from the fears of this man Monks. But if – if – " said the gentleman, "he cannot be secured, or, if secured, cannot be acted upon as we wish, you must deliver up the Jew."

"Fagin," cried the girl, recoiling.

"That man must be delivered up by you," said the gentleman.

"I will not do it! I will never do it!" replied the girl. "Devil that he is, and worse than devil as he has been to me, I will never do that."

"You will not?" said the gentleman, who seemed fully prepared for this answer.

"Never!" returned the girl.

"Tell me why?"

"For one reason," rejoined the girl firmly, "for one reason, that the lady knows and will stand by me in, I know she will, for I have her promise; and for this other reason, besides, that, bad life as he had led, I have led a bad life too; there are many of us who have kept the same courses together, and I'll not turn upon them, who might – any of them – have turned upon me, but didn't, bad as they are."

"Then," said the gentleman, quickly, as if this had been the point he had been aiming to attain; "put Monks into my hands, and leave him to me to deal with."

"What if he turns against the others?"

"I promise you that in that case, if the truth is forced from him, there the matter will rest; there must be circumstances in Oliver's little history which it would be painful to drag before the public eye, and if the truth is once elicited, they shall go scot free."

"And if it is not?" suggested the girl.

"Then," pursued the gentleman, "this Fagin shall not be brought to justice without your consent. In such a case I could show you reasons, I think, which would induce you to yield it."

"Have I the lady's promise for that?" asked the girl.

"You have," replied Rose. "My true and faithful pledge."

"Monks would never learn how you knew what you do?" said the girl, after a short pause.

"Never," replied the gentleman. "The intelligence should be so brought to bear upon him, that he could never even guess."

"I have been a liar, and among liars from a little child," said the girl after another interval of silence, "but I will take your words."

After receiving an assurance from both, that she might safely do so, she proceeded in a voice so low that it was often difficult for the listener to discover even the purport of what she said, to describe, by name and situation, the public-house whence she had been followed that night. From the manner in which she occasionally paused, it appeared as if the gentleman were making some hasty notes of the information she communicated. When she had thoroughly explained the localities of the place, the best position from which to watch it without exciting observation, and the night and hour on which Monks was most in the habit of frequenting it, she seemed to consider for a few moments, for the purpose of recalling his features and appearance more forcibly to her recollection.

"He is tall," said the girl, "and a strongly made man, but not stout; he has a lurking walk; and as he walks, constantly looks over his shoulder, first on one side, and then on the other. Don't forget that, for his eyes are sunk in his head so much deeper than any other man's, that you might almost tell him by that alone. His face is dark, like his hair and eyes; and, although he can't be more than six or eight and twenty, withered and haggard. His lips are often discoloured and disfigured with the marks of teeth; for he has desperate fits, and sometimes even bites his hands and covers them with wounds – why did you start?" said the girl, stopping suddenly.

The gentleman replied, in a hurried manner, that he was not conscious of having done so, and begged her to proceed.

"Part of this," said the girl, "I've drawn out from other people at the house I tell you of, for I have only seen him twice, and both times he was covered up in a large cloak. I think that's all I can give you to know him by. Stay though," she added. "Upon his throat: so high that you can see a part of it below his neckerchief when he turns his face: there is – "

"A broad red mark, like a burn or scald?" cried the gentleman.

"How's this?" said the girl. "You know him!"

The young lady uttered a cry of surprise, and for a few moments they were so still that the listener could distinctly hear them breathe.

"I think I do," said the gentleman, breaking silence. "I should by your description. We shall see. Many people are singularly like each other. It may not be the same."

As he expressed himself to this effect, with assumed carelessness, he took a step or two nearer the concealed spy, as the latter could tell from the distinctness with which he heard him mutter, "It must be he!"

"Now," he said, returning: so it seemed by the sound: to the spot where he had stood before, "you have given us most valuable assistance, young woman, and I wish you to be the better for it. What can I do to serve you?"

"Nothing," replied Nancy.

"You will not persist in saying that," rejoined the gentleman, with a voice and emphasis of kindness that might have touched a much harder and more obdurate heart. "Think now. Tell me."

"Nothing, sir," rejoined the girl, weeping. "You can do nothing to help me. I am past all hope, indeed."

"You put yourself beyond its pale," said the gentleman. "The past has been a dreary waste with you, of youthful energies mis-spent, and such priceless treasures lavished, as the Creator bestows but once and never grants again, but, for the future, you may hope. I do not say that it is in our power to offer you peace of heart and mind, for that must come as you seek it; but a quiet asylum, either in England, or, if you fear to remain here, in some foreign country, it is not only within the compass of our ability but our most anxious wish to secure you. Before the dawn of morning, before this river wakes to the first glimpse of daylight, you shall be placed as entirely beyond the reach of your former associates, and leave as utter an absence of all trace behind you, as if you were to disappear from the earth this moment. Come! I would not have you go back to exchange one word with any old companion, or take one look at any old haunt, or breathe the very air which is pestilence and death to you. Quit them all, while there is time and opportunity!"

"She will be persuaded now," cried the young lady. "She hesitates, I am sure."

"I fear not, my dear," said the gentleman.

"No, sir, I do not," replied the girl, after a short struggle. "I am chained to my old life. I loathe and hate it now, but I cannot leave it. I must have gone too far to turn back, – and yet I don't know, for if you had spoken to me so, some time ago, I should have laughed it off. But," she said, looking hastily round, "this fear comes over me again. I must go home."

"Home!" repeated the young lady, with great stress upon the word.

"Home, lady," rejoined the girl. "To such a home as I have raised for myself with the work of my whole life. Let us part. I shall be watched or seen. Go! Go! If I have done you any service, all I ask is, that you leave me, and let me go my way alone."

"It is useless," said the gentleman, with a sigh. "We compromise her safety, perhaps, by staying here. We may have detained her longer than she expected already."

"Yes, yes," urged the girl. "You have."

"What," cried the young lady, "can be the end of this poor creature's life!"

"What!" repeated the girl. "Look before you, lady. Look at that dark water. How many times do you read of such as I who spring into the tide, and leave no living thing, to care for, or bewail them. It may be years hence, or it may be only months, but I shall come to that at last."

"Do not speak thus, pray," returned the young lady, sobbing.

"It will never reach your ears, dear lady, and God forbid such horrors should!" replied the girl. "Good night, good night!"

The gentleman turned away.

"This purse," cried the young lady. "Take it for my sake, that you may have some resource in an hour of need and trouble."

"No!" replied the girl. "I have not done this for money. Let me have that to think of. And yet – give me something that you have worn: I should like to have something – no, no, not a ring – your gloves or handkerchief – anything that I can keep, as having belonged to you, sweet lady. There. Bless you! God bless you. Good night, good night!"

The violent agitation of the girl, and the apprehension of some discovery which would subject her to ill-usage and violence, seemed to determine the gentleman to leave her, as she requested. The sound of retreating footsteps were audible and the voices ceased.

The two figures of the young lady and her companion soon afterwards appeared upon the bridge. They stopped at the summit of the stairs.

"Hark!" cried the young lady, listening. "Did she call! I thought I heard her voice."

"No, my love," replied Mr Brownlow, looking sadly back. "She has not moved, and will not till we are gone."

Rose Maylie lingered, but the old gentleman drew her arm through his, and led her, with gentle force, away. As they disappeared, the girl sunk down nearly at her full length upon one of the stone stairs, and vented the anguish of her heart in bitter tears.

After a time she arose, and with feeble and tottering steps ascended to the street. The astonished listener remained motionless on his post for some minutes afterwards, and having ascertained, with many cautious glances round him, that he was again alone, crept slowly from his hiding-place, and returned, stealthily and in the shade of the wall, in the same manner as he had descended.

Peeping out, more than once, when he reached the top, to make sure that he was unobserved, Noah Claypole darted away at his utmost speed, and made for the Jew's house as fast as his legs would carry him.

Chapter XLVII

Fatal Consequences

It was nearly two hours before day-break; that time which in the autumn of the year, may be truly called the dead of night; when the streets are silent and deserted; when even sounds appear to slumber, and profligacy and riot have staggered home to dream; it was at this still and silent hour, that Fagin sat watching in his old lair, with face so distorted and pale, and eyes so red and bloodshot, that he looked less like a man, than like some hideous phantom moist from the grave, and worried by an evil spirit.

He sat crouching over a cold hearth, wrapped in an old torn coverlet, with his face turned towards a wasting candle that stood upon a table by his side. His right hand was raised to his lips, and as, absorbed in thought, he bit his long black nails, he disclosed among his toothless gums a few such fangs as should have been a dog's or rat's.

Stretched upon a mattress on the floor, lay Noah Claypole, fast asleep. Towards him the old man sometimes directed his eyes for an instant, and then brought them back again to the candle; which with a long-burnt wick drooping almost double, and hot grease falling down in clots upon the table, plainly showed that his thoughts were busy elsewhere.

Indeed they were. Mortification at the overthrow of his notable scheme; hatred of the girl who had dared to palter with strangers; an utter distrust of the sincerity of her refusal to yield him up; bitter disappointment at the loss of his revenge on Sikes: the fear of detection, and ruin, and death; and a fierce and deadly rage kindled by all; these were the passionate considerations which, following close upon each other with rapid and ceaseless whirl, shot through the brain of Fagin, as every evil thought and blackest purpose lay working at his heart.

He sat without changing his attitude in the least, or appearing to take the smallest heed of time, until his quick ear seemed to be attracted by a footstep in the street.

"At last," he muttered, wiping his dry and fevered mouth. "At last!"

The bell rang gently as he spoke. He crept up stairs to the door, and presently returned accompanied by a man muffled to the chin, who carried a bundle under one arm. Sitting down and throwing back his outer coat, the man displayed the burly frame of Sikes.

"There!" he said, laying the bundle on the table. "Take care of that, and do the most you can with it. It's been trouble enough to get; I thought I should have been here, three hours ago."

Fagin laid his hand upon the bundle, and locking it in the cupboard, sat down again without speaking. But he did not take his eyes off the robber, for an instant, during this action; and now that they sat over against each other, face to face, he looked fixedly at him, with his lips quivering so violently, and his face so altered by the emotions which had mastered him, that the housebreaker involuntarily drew back his chair, and surveyed him with a look of real affright.

"Wot now?" cried Sikes. "Wot do you look at a man so for?"

Fagin raised his right hand, and shook his trembling fore-finger in the air; but his passion was so great, that the power of speech was for the moment gone.

"Damme!" said Sikes, feeling in his breast with a look of alarm. "He's gone mad. I must look to myself here."

"No, no," rejoined Fagin, finding his voice. "It's not – you're not the person, Bill. I've no – no fault to find with you."

"Oh, you haven't, haven't you?" said Sikes, looking sternly at him, and ostentatiously passing a pistol into a more convenient pocket. "That's lucky – for one of us. Which one that is, don't matter."

"I've got that to tell you, Bill," said Fagin, drawing his chair nearer, "will make you worse than me."

"Aye?" returned the robber with an incredulous air. "Tell away! Look sharp, or Nance will think I'm lost."

"Lost!" cried Fagin. "She has pretty well settled that, in her own mind, already."

Sikes looked with an aspect of great perplexity into the Jew's face, and reading no satisfactory explanation of the riddle there, clenched his coat collar in his huge hand and shook him soundly.

"Speak, will you!" he said; "or if you don't, it shall be for want of breath. Open your mouth and say wot you've got to say in plain words. Out with it, you thundering old cur, out with it!"

"Suppose that lad that's lying there – " Fagin began.

Sikes turned round to where Noah was sleeping, as if he had not previously observed him. "Well!" he said, resuming his former position.

"Suppose that lad," pursued Fagin, "was to peach – to blow upon us all – first seeking out the right folks for the purpose, and then having a meeting with 'em in the street to paint our likenesses, describe every mark that they might know us by, and the crib where we might be most easily taken. Suppose he was to do all this, and besides to blow upon a plant we've all been in, more or less – of his own fancy; not grabbed, trapped, tried, earwigged by the parson and brought to it on bread and water, – but of his own fancy; to please his own taste; stealing out at nights to find those most interested against us, and peaching to them. Do you hear me?" cried the Jew, his eyes flashing with rage. "Suppose he did all this, what then?"

"What then!" replied Sikes; with a tremendous oath. "If he was left alive till I came, I'd grind his skull under the iron heel of my boot into as many grains as there are hairs upon his head."

"What if *I* did it!" cried Fagin almost in a yell. "*I*, that know so much, and could hang so many besides myself!"

"I don't know," replied Sikes, clenching his teeth and turning white at the mere suggestion. "I'd do something in the jail that "ud get me put in irons; and if I was tried along with you, I'd fall upon you with them in the open court, and beat your brains out afore the people. I should have such strength," muttered the robber, poising his brawny arm, "that I could smash your head as if a loaded waggon had gone over it."

"You would?"

"Would I!" said the housebreaker. "Try me."

"If it was Charley, or the Dodger, or Bet, or – "

"I don't care who," replied Sikes impatiently. "Whoever it was, I'd serve them the same."

Fagin looked hard at the robber; and, motioning him to be silent, stooped over the bed upon the floor, and shook the sleeper to rouse him. Sikes leant forward in his chair: looking on with his hands upon his knees, as if wondering much what all this questioning and preparation was to end in.

"Bolter, Bolter! Poor lad!" said Fagin, looking up with an expression of devilish anticipation, and speaking slowly and with marked emphasis. "He's tired – tired with watching for *her* so long, – watching for *her*, Bill."

"Wot d"ye mean?" asked Sikes, drawing back.

Fagin made no answer, but bending over the sleeper again, hauled him into a sitting posture. When his assumed name had been repeated several times, Noah rubbed his eyes, and, giving a heavy yawn, looked sleepily about him.

"Tell me that again – once again, just for him to hear," said the Jew, pointing to Sikes as he spoke.

"Tell yer what?" asked the sleepy Noah, shaking himself pettishly.

"That about – NANCY," said Fagin, clutching Sikes by the wrist, as if to prevent his leaving the house before he had heard enough. "You followed her?"

"Yes."

"To London Bridge?"

"Yes."

"Where she met two people?"

"So she did."

"A gentleman and a lady that she had gone to of her own accord before, who asked her to give up all her pals, and Monks first, which she did – and to describe him, which she did – and to tell her what house it was that we meet at, and go to, which she did – and where it could be best watched from, which she did – and what time the people went there, which she did. She did all this. She told it all every word without a threat, without a murmur – she did – did she not?" cried Fagin, half mad with fury.

"All right," replied Noah, scratching his head. "That's just what it was!"

"What did they say, about last Sunday?"

"About last Sunday!" replied Noah, considering. "Why I told yer that before."

"Again. Tell it again!" cried Fagin, tightening his grasp on Sikes, and brandishing his other hand aloft, as the foam flew from his lips.

"They asked her," said Noah, who, as he grew more wakeful, seemed to have a dawning perception who Sikes was, "they asked her why she didn't come, last Sunday, as she promised. She said she couldn't."

"Why – why? Tell him that."

"Because she was forcibly kept at home by Bill, the man she had told them of before," replied Noah.

"What more of him?" cried Fagin. "What more of the man she had told them of before? Tell him that, tell him that."

"Why, that she couldn't very easily get out of doors unless he knew where she was going to," said Noah; "and so the first time she went to see the lady, she – ha! ha! ha! it made me laugh when she said it, that it did – she gave him a drink of laudanum."

"Hell's fire!" cried Sikes, breaking fiercely from the Jew. "Let me go!"

Flinging the old man from him, he rushed from the room, and darted, wildly and furiously, up the stairs.

"Bill, Bill!" cried Fagin, following him hastily. "A word. Only a word."

The word would not have been exchanged, but that the housebreaker was unable to open the door: on which he was expending fruitless oaths and violence, when the Jew came panting up.

"Let me out," said Sikes. "Don't speak to me; it's not safe. Let me out, I say!"

"Hear me speak a word," rejoined Fagin, laying his hand upon the lock. "You won't be – "

"Well," replied the other.

"You won't be – too – violent, Bill?"

The day was breaking, and there was light enough for the men to see each other's faces. They exchanged one brief glance; there was a fire in the eyes of both, which could not be mistaken.

"I mean," said Fagin, showing that he felt all disguise was now useless, "not too violent for safety. Be crafty, Bill, and not too bold."

Sikes made no reply; but, pulling open the door, of which Fagin had turned the lock, dashed into the silent streets.

Without one pause, or moment's consideration; without once turning his head to the right or left, or raising his eyes to the sky, or lowering them to the ground, but looking straight before him with savage resolution: his teeth so tightly compressed that the strained jaw seemed starting through his skin; the robber held on his headlong course, nor muttered a word, nor relaxed a muscle, until he reached his own door. He opened it, softly, with a key; strode lightly up the stairs; and entering his own room, double-locked the door, and lifting a heavy table against it, drew back the curtain of the bed.

The girl was lying, half-dressed, upon it. He had roused her from her sleep, for she raised herself with a hurried and startled look.

"Get up!" said the man.

"It *is* you, Bill!" said the girl, with an expression of pleasure at his return.

"It is," was the reply. "Get up."

There was a candle burning, but the man hastily drew it from the candlestick, and hurled it under the grate. Seeing the faint light of early day without, the girl rose to undraw the curtain.

"Let it be," said Sikes, thrusting his hand before her. "There's light enough for wot I've got to do."

"Bill," said the girl, in the low voice of alarm, "why do you look like that at me!"

The robber sat regarding her, for a few seconds, with dilated nostrils and heaving breast; and then, grasping her by the head and throat, dragged her into the middle of the room, and looking once towards the door, placed his heavy hand upon her mouth.

"Bill, Bill!" gasped the girl, wrestling with the strength of mortal fear, – "I – I won't scream or cry – not once – hear me – speak to me – tell me what I have done!"

"You know, you she devil!" returned the robber, suppressing his breath. "You were watched to-night; every word you said was heard."

"Then spare my life for the love of Heaven, as I spared yours," rejoined the girl, clinging to him. "Bill, dear Bill, you cannot have the heart to kill me. Oh! think of all I have given up, only this one night, for you. You *shall* have time to think, and save yourself this crime; I will not loose my hold, you cannot throw me off. Bill, Bill, for dear God's sake, for your own, for mine, stop before you spill my blood! I have been true to you, upon my guilty soul I have!"

The man struggled violently, to release his arms; but those of the girl were clasped round his, and tear her as he would, he could not tear them away.

"Bill," cried the girl, striving to lay her head upon his breast, "the gentleman and that dear lady, told me to-night of a home in some foreign country where I could end my days in solitude and peace. Let me see them again, and beg them, on my knees, to show the same mercy and goodness to you; and let us both leave this dreadful place, and far apart lead better lives, and forget how we have lived, except in prayers, and never see each other more. It is never too late to repent. They told me so – I feel it now – but we must have time – a little, little time!"

The housebreaker freed one arm, and grasped his pistol. The certainty of immediate detection if he fired, flashed across his mind even in the midst of his fury; and he beat it twice with all the force he could summon, upon the upturned face that almost touched his own.

She staggered and fell: nearly blinded with the blood that rained down from a deep gash in her forehead; but raising herself, with difficulty, on her knees, drew from her bosom a white handkerchief – Rose Maylie's own – and holding it up, in her folded hands, as high towards Heaven as her feeble strength would allow, breathed one prayer for mercy to her Maker.

It was a ghastly figure to look upon. The murderer staggering backward to the wall, and shutting out the sight with his hand, seized a heavy club and struck her down.

Chapter XLVIII

The Flight of Sikes

Of all bad deeds that, under cover of the darkness, had been committed within wide London's bounds since night hung over it, that was the worst. Of all the horrors that rose with an ill scent upon the morning air, that was the foulest and most cruel.

The sun – the bright sun, that brings back, not light alone, but new life, and hope, and freshness to man – burst upon the crowded city in clear and radiant glory. Through costly-coloured glass and paper-mended window, through cathedral dome and rotten crevice, it shed its equal ray. It lighted up the room where the murdered woman lay. It did. He tried to shut it out, but it would stream in. If the sight had been a ghastly one in the dull morning, what was it, now, in all that brilliant light!

He had not moved; he had been afraid to stir. There had been a moan and motion of the hand; and, with terror added to rage, he had struck and struck again. Once he threw a rug over it; but it was worse to fancy the eyes, and imagine them moving towards him, than to see them glaring upward, as if watching the reflection of the pool of gore that quivered and danced in the sunlight on the ceiling. He had plucked it off again. And there was the body – mere flesh and blood, no more – but such flesh, and so much blood.

He struck a light, kindled a fire, and thrust the club into it. There was hair upon the end, which blazed and shrunk into a light cinder, and, caught by the air, whirled up the chimney. Even that frightened him, sturdy as he was; but he held the weapon till it broke, and then piled it on the coals to burn away, and smoulder into ashes. He washed himself, and rubbed his clothes; there were spots that would not be removed, but he cut the pieces out, and burnt them. How those stains were dispersed about the room! The very feet of the dog were bloody.

All this time he had, never once, turned his back upon the corpse; no, not for a moment. Such preparations completed, he moved, backward, towards the door: dragging the dog with him, lest he should soil his feet anew and carry out new evidences of the crime into the streets. He shut the door softly, locked it, took the key, and left the house.

He crossed over, and glanced up at the window, to be sure that nothing was visible from the outside. There was the curtain still drawn, which she would have opened to admit the light she never saw again. It lay nearly under there. *He* knew that. God, how the sun poured down upon the very spot!

The glance was instantaneous. It was a relief to have got free of the room. He whistled on the dog, and walked rapidly away.

He went through Islington; strode up the hill at Highgate on which stands the stone in honour of Whittington; turned down to Highgate Hill, unsteady of purpose, and uncertain where to go; struck off to the right again, almost as soon as he began to descend it; and taking the foot-path across the fields, skirted Caen Wood, and so came out on Hampstead Heath. Traversing the hollow by the Vale of Health, he mounted the opposite bank, and crossing the road which joins the villages of Hampstead and Highgate, made along the remaining portion of the Heath to the fields at North End, in one of which he laid himself down under a hedge, and slept.

Soon he was up again, and away, – not far into the country, but back towards London by the high-road – then back again – then over another part of the same ground as he already traversed – then wandering up and down in fields, and lying on ditches'' brinks to rest, and starting up to make for some other spot, and do the same, and ramble on again.

Where could he go, that was near and not too public, to get some meat and drink? Hendon. That was a good place, not far off, and out of most people's way. Thither he directed his steps, – running sometimes, and sometimes, with a strange perversity, loitering at a snail's pace, or stopping altogether and idly breaking the hedges with his stick. But when he got there, all the people he met – the very children at the doors – seemed to view him with suspicion. Back he turned again, without the courage to purchase bite or drop, though he had tasted no food for many hours; and once more he lingered on the Heath, uncertain where to go.

He wandered over miles and miles of ground, and still came back to the old place. Morning and noon had passed, and the day was on the wane, and still he rambled to and fro, and up and down, and round and round, and still lingered about the same spot. At last he got away, and shaped his course for Hatfield.

It was nine o'clock at night, when the man, quite tired out, and the dog, limping and lame from the unaccustomed exercise, turned down the hill by the church of the quiet village, and plodding along the little street, crept into a small public-house, whose scanty light had guided them to the spot. There was a fire in the tap-room, and some country-labourers were drinking before it. They made room for the stranger, but he sat down in the furthest corner, and ate and drank alone, or rather with his dog: to whom he cast a morsel of food from time to time.

The conversation of the men assembled here, turned upon the neighbouring land, and farmers; and when those topics were exhausted, upon the age of some old man who had been buried on the previous Sunday; the young men present considering him very old, and the old men present declaring him to have been quite young – not older, one white-haired grandfather said, than he was – with ten or fifteen year of life in him at least – if he had taken care; if he had taken care.

There was nothing to attract attention, or excite alarm in this. The robber, after paying his reckoning, sat silent and unnoticed in his corner, and had almost dropped asleep, when he was half wakened by the noisy entrance of a new-comer.

This was an antic fellow, half pedlar and half mountebank, who travelled about the country on foot to vend hones, strops, razors, washballs, harness-paste, medicine for dogs and horses, cheap perfumery, cosmetics, and such-like wares, which he carried in a case slung to his back. His entrance was the signal for various homely jokes with the countrymen, which slackened not until he had made his supper, and opened his box of treasures, when he ingeniously contrived to unite business with amusement.

"And what be that stoof? Good to eat, Harry?" asked a grinning countryman, pointing to some composition-cakes in one corner.

"This," said the fellow, producing one, "this is the infallible and invaluable composition for removing all sorts of stain, rust, dirt, mildew, spick, speck, spot, or spatter, from silk, satin, linen, cambric, cloth, crape, stuff, carpet, merino, muslin, bombazeen, or woollen stuff. Wine-stains, fruit-stains, beer-stains, water-stains, paint-stains, pitch-stains, any stains, all come out at one rub with the infallible and invaluable composition. If a lady stains her honour, she has only need to swallow one cake and she's cured at once – for it's poison. If a gentleman wants to prove this, he has only need to bolt one little square, and he has put it beyond question – for it's quite as satisfactory as a pistol-bullet, and a great deal nastier in the flavour, consequently the more credit in taking it. One penny a square. With all these virtues, one penny a square!"

There were two buyers directly, and more of the listeners plainly hesitated. The vendor observing this, increased in loquacity.

"It's all bought up as fast as it can be made," said the fellow. "There are fourteen water-mills, six steam-engines, and a galvanic battery, always a-working upon it, and they can't make it fast enough, though the men work so hard that they die off, and the windows is pensioned directly, with twenty pound a-year for each of the children, and a premium of fifty for twins. One penny a square! Two halfpence is all the same, and four farthings is received with joy. One penny a square! Wine-stains, fruit-stains, beer-stains, water-stains, paint-stains, pitch-stains, mud-stains, blood-stains! Here is a stain upon the hat of a gentleman in company, that I'll take clean out, before he can order me a pint of ale."

"Hah!" cried Sikes starting up. "Give that back."

"I'll take it clean out, sir," replied the man, winking to the company, "before you can come across the room to get it. Gentlemen all, observe the dark stain upon this gentleman's hat, no wider than a shilling, but thicker than a half-crown. Whether it is a wine-stain, fruit-stain, beer-stain, water-stain, paint-stain, pitch-stain, mud-stain, or blood-stain – "

The man got no further, for Sikes with a hideous imprecation overthrew the table, and tearing the hat from him, burst out of the house.

With the same perversity of feeling and irresolution that had fastened upon him, despite himself, all day, the murderer, finding that he was not followed, and that they most probably considered him some drunken sullen fellow, turned back up the town, and getting out of the glare of the lamps of a stage-coach that was standing in the street, was walking past, when he recognised the mail from London, and saw that it was standing at the little post-office. He almost knew what was to come; but he crossed over, and listened.

The guard was standing at the door, waiting for the letter-bag. A man, dressed like a gamekeeper, came up at the moment, and he handed him a basket which lay ready on the pavement.

"That's for your people," said the guard. "Now, look alive in there, will you. Damn that 'ere bag, it warn't ready night afore last; this won't do, you know!"

"Anything new up in town, Ben?" asked the gamekeeper, drawing back to the window-shutters, the better to admire the horses.

"No, nothing that I knows on," replied the man, pulling on his gloves. "Corn's up a little. I heerd talk of a murder, too, down Spitalfields way, but I don't reckon much upon it."

"Oh, that's quite true," said a gentleman inside, who was looking out of the window. "And a dreadful murder it was."

"Was it, sir?" rejoined the guard, touching his hat. "Man or woman, pray, sir?"

"A woman," replied the gentleman. "It is supposed – "

"Now, Ben," replied the coachman impatiently.

"Damn that 'ere bag," said the guard; "are you gone to sleep in there?"

"Coming!" cried the office keeper, running out.

"Coming," growled the guard. "Ah, and so's the young "ooman of property that's going to take a fancy to me, but I don't know when. Here, give hold. All ri-ight!"

The horn sounded a few cheerful notes, and the coach was gone.

Sikes remained standing in the street, apparently unmoved by what he had just heard, and agitated by no stronger feeling than a doubt where to go. At length he went back again, and took the road which leads from Hatfield to St Albans.

He went on doggedly; but as he left the town behind him, and plunged into the solitude and darkness of the road, he felt a dread and awe creeping upon him which shook him to the core. Every object before him, substance or shadow, still or moving, took the semblance of some fearful thing; but these fears were nothing compared to the sense that haunted him of that morning's ghastly figure following at his heels. He could trace its shadow in the gloom, supply the smallest item of the outline, and note how stiff and solemn it seemed to stalk along. He could hear its garments rustling in the leaves, and every breath of wind came laden with that last low cry. If he stopped it did the same. If he ran, it followed – not running too: that would have been a relief: but like a corpse endowed with the mere machinery of life, and borne on one slow melancholy wind that never rose or fell.

At times, he turned, with desperate determination, resolved to beat this phantom off, though it should look him dead; but the hair rose on his head, and his blood stood still, for it had turned with him and was behind him then. He had kept it before him that morning, but it was behind now – always. He leaned his back against a bank, and felt that it stood above him, visibly out against the cold night-sky. He threw himself upon the road – on his back upon the road. At his head it stood, silent, erect, and still – a living gravestone, with its epitaph in blood.

Let no man talk of murderers escaping justice, and hint that Providence must sleep. There were twenty score of violent deaths in one long minute of that agony of fear.

There was a shed in a field he passed, that offered shelter for the night. Before the door, were three tall poplar trees, which made it very dark within; and the wind moaned through them with a dismal wail. He *could not* walk on, till daylight came again; and here he stretched himself close to the wall – to undergo new torture.

For now, a vision came before him, as constant and more terrible than that from which he had escaped. Those widely staring eyes, so lustreless and so glassy, that he had better borne to see them than think upon them, appeared in the midst of the darkness; light in themselves, but giving light to nothing. There were but two, but they were everywhere. If he shut out the sight, there came the room with every well-known object – some, indeed, that he would have forgotten, if he had gone over its contents from memory – each in its accustomed place. The body was in *its* place, and its eyes were as he saw them when he stole away. He got up, and rushed into the field without. The figure was behind him. He re-entered the shed, and shrunk down once more. The eyes were there, before he had laid himself along.

And here he remained in such terror as none but he can know, trembling in every limb, and the cold sweat starting from every pore, when suddenly there arose upon the night-wind the noise of distant shouting, and the roar of voices mingled in alarm and wonder. Any sound of men in that lonely place, even though it conveyed a real cause of alarm, was something to him. He regained his strength and energy at the prospect of personal danger; and springing to his feet, rushed into the open air.

The broad sky seemed on fire. Rising into the air with showers of sparks, and rolling one above the other, were sheets of flame, lighting the atmosphere for miles round, and driving clouds of smoke in the direction where he stood. The shouts grew louder as new voices swelled the roar, and he could hear the cry of Fire! mingled with the ringing of an alarm-bell, the fall of heavy bodies, and the crackling of flames as they twined round some new obstacle, and shot aloft as though refreshed by food. The noise increased as he looked. There were people there – men and women – light, bustle. It was like new life to him. He darted onward – straight, headlong – dashing through brier and brake, and leaping gate and fence as madly as his dog, who careered with loud and sounding bark before him.

He came upon the spot. There were half-dressed figures tearing to and fro, some endeavouring to drag the frightened horses from the stables, others driving the cattle from the yard and out-houses, and others coming laden from the burning pile, amidst a shower of falling sparks, and the tumbling down of red-hot beams. The apertures, where doors and windows stood an hour ago, disclosed a mass of raging fire; walls rocked and crumbled into the burning well; the molten lead and iron poured down, white hot, upon the ground. Women and children shrieked, and men encouraged each other with noisy shouts and cheers. The clanking of the engine-pumps, and the spirting and hissing of the water as it fell upon the blazing wood, added to the tremendous roar. He shouted, too, till he was hoarse; and flying from memory and himself, plunged into the thickest of the throng.

Hither and thither he dived that night: now working at the pumps, and now hurrying through the smoke and flame, but never ceasing to engage himself wherever noise and men were thickest. Up and down the ladders, upon the roofs of buildings, over floors that quaked and trembled with his weight, under the lee of falling bricks and stones, in every part of that great fire was he; but he bore a charmed life, and had neither scratch nor bruise, nor weariness nor thought, till morning dawned again, and only smoke and blackened ruins remained.

This mad excitement over, there returned, with tenfold force, the dreadful consciousness of his crime. He looked suspiciously about him, for the men were conversing in groups, and he feared to be the subject of their talk. The dog obeyed the significant beck of his finger, and they drew off, stealthily, together. He passed near an engine where some men were seated, and they called to him to share in their refreshment. He took some bread and meat; and as he drank a draught of beer, heard the firemen, who were from London, talking about the murder. "He has gone to Birmingham, they say," said one: "but they'll have him yet, for the scouts are out, and by to-morrow night there'll be a cry all through the country."

He hurried off, and walked till he almost dropped upon the ground; then lay down in a lane, and had a long, but broken and uneasy sleep. He wandered on again, irresolute and undecided, and oppressed with the fear of another solitary night.

Suddenly, he took the desperate resolution of going back to London.

"There's somebody to speak to there, at all events," he thought. "A good hiding-place, too. They'll never expect to nab me there, after this country scent. Why can't I lie by for a week or so, and, forcing blunt from Fagin, get abroad to France? Damme, I'll risk it."

He acted upon this impulse without delay, and choosing the least frequented roads began his journey back, resolved to lie concealed within a short distance of the metropolis, and, entering it at dusk by a circuitous route, to proceed straight to that part of it which he had fixed on for his destination.

The dog, though. If any descriptions of him were out, it would not be forgotten that the dog was missing, and had probably gone with him. This might lead to his apprehension as he passed along the streets. He resolved to drown him, and walked on, looking about for a pond: picking up a heavy stone and tying it to his handkerchief as he went.

The animal looked up into his master's face while these preparations were making; whether his instinct apprehended something of their purpose, or the robber's sidelong look at him was sterner than ordinary, he skulked a little farther in the rear than usual, and cowered as he came more slowly along. When his master halted at the brink of a pool, and looked round to call him, he stopped outright.

"Do you hear me call? Come here!" cried Sikes.

The animal came up from the very force of habit; but as Sikes stooped to attach the handkerchief to his throat, he uttered a low growl and started back.

"Come back!" said the robber.

The dog wagged his tail, but moved not. Sikes made a running noose and called him again.

The dog advanced, retreated, paused an instant, turned, and scoured away at his hardest speed.

The man whistled again and again, and sat down and waited in the expectation that he would return. But no dog appeared, and at length he resumed his journey.

Chapter XLIX

Monks and Mr Brownlow at length meet. Their Conversation, and the Intelligence that interrupts it

THE twilight was beginning to close in, when Mr Brownlow alighted from a hackney-coach at his own door, and knocked softly. The door being opened, a sturdy man got out of the coach and stationed himself on one side of the steps, while another man, who had been seated on the box, dismounted too, and stood upon the other side. At a sign from Mr Brownlow, they helped out a third man, and taking him between them, hurried him into the house. This man was Monks.

They walked in the same manner up the stairs without speaking, and Mr Brownlow, preceding them, led the way into a back-room. At the door of this apartment, Monks, who had ascended with evident reluctance, stopped. The two men looked to the old gentleman as if for instructions.

"He knows the alternative," said Mr Brownlow. "If he hesitates or moves a finger but as you bid him, drag him into the street, call for the aid of the police, and impeach him as a felon in my name."

"How dare you say this of me?" asked Monks.

"How dare you urge me to it, young man?" replied Mr Brownlow, confronting him with a steady look. "Are you mad enough to leave this house? Unhand him. There, sir. You are free to go, and we to follow. But I warn you, by all I hold most solemn and most sacred, that the instant you set foot in the street, that instant will I have you apprehended on a charge of fraud and robbery. I am resolute and immoveable. If you are determined to be the same, your blood be upon your own head!"

"By what authority am I kidnapped in the street, and brought here by these dogs?" asked Monks, looking from one to the other of the men who stood beside him.

"By mine," replied Mr Brownlow. "Those persons are indemnified by me. If you complain of being deprived of your liberty – you had power and opportunity to retrieve it as you came along, but you deemed it advisable to remain quiet – I say again, throw yourself for protection on the law. I will appeal to the law too; but when you have gone too far to recede, do not sue to me for leniency, when the power will have passed into other hands; and do not say I plunged you down the gulf into which you rushed, yourself."

Monks was plainly disconcerted, and alarmed besides. He hesitated.

"You will decide quickly," said Mr Brownlow, with perfect firmness and composure. "If you wish me to prefer my charges publicly, and consign you to a punishment the extent of which, although I can, with a shudder, foresee, I cannot control, once more, I say, you know the way. If not, and you appeal to my forbearance, and the mercy of those you have deeply injured, seat yourself, without a word, in that chair. It has waited for you two whole days."

Monks muttered some unintelligible words, but wavered still.

"You will be prompt," said Mr Brownlow. "A word from me, and the alternative has gone for ever."

Still the man hesitated.

"I have not the inclination to parley," said Mr Brownlow, "and, as I advocate the dearest interests of others, I have not the right."

"Is there – " demanded Monks with a faltering tongue, – "is there – no middle course?"

"None."

Monks looked at the old gentleman, with an anxious eye; but, reading in his countenance nothing but severity and determination, walked into the room, and, shrugging his shoulders, sat down.

"Lock the door on the outside," said Mr Brownlow to the attendants, "and come when I ring."

The men obeyed, and the two were left alone together.

"This is pretty treatment, sir," said Monks, throwing down his hat and cloak, "from my father's oldest friend."

"It is because I was your father's oldest friend, young man," returned Mr Brownlow; "it is because the hopes and wishes of young and happy years were bound up with him, and that fair creature of his blood and kindred who rejoined her God in youth, and left me here a solitary, lonely man: it is because he knelt with me beside his only sister's deathbed when he was yet a boy, on the morning that would – but Heaven willed otherwise – have made her my young wife; it is because my seared heart clung to him, from that time forth, through all his trials and errors, till he died; it is because old recollections and associations filled my heart, and even the sight of you brings with it old thoughts of him; it is because of all these things that I am moved to treat you gently now – yes, Edward Leeford, even now – and blush for your unworthiness who bear the name."

"What has the name to do with it?" asked the other, after contemplating, half in silence, and half in dogged wonder, the agitation of his companion. "What is the name to me?"

"Nothing," replied Mr Brownlow, "nothing to you. But it was *hers*, and even at this distance of time brings back to me, an old man, the glow and thrill which I once felt, only to hear it repeated by a stranger. I am very glad you have changed it – very – very."

"This is all mighty fine," said Monks (to retain his assumed designation) after a long silence, during which he had jerked himself in sullen defiance to and fro, and Mr Brownlow had sat, shading his face with his hand. "But what do you want with me?"

"You have a brother," said Mr Brownlow, rousing himself: "a brother, the whisper of whose name in your ear when I came behind you in the street, was, in itself, almost enough to make you accompany me hither, in wonder and alarm."

"I have no brother," replied Monks. "You know I was an only child. Why do you talk to me of brothers? You know that, as well as I."

"Attend to what I do know, and you may not," said Mr Brownlow. "I shall interest you by and by. I know that of the wretched marriage, into which family pride, and the most sordid and narrowest of all ambition, forced your unhappy father when a mere boy, you were the sole and most unnatural issue."

"I don't care for hard names," interrupted Monks with a jeering laugh. "You know the fact, and that's enough for me."

"But I also know," pursued the old gentleman, "the misery, the slow torture, the protracted anguish of that ill-assorted union. I know how listlessly and wearily each of that wretched pair dragged on their heavy chain through a world that was poisoned to them both. I know how cold formalities were succeeded by open taunts; how indifference gave place to dislike, dislike to hate, and hate to loathing, until at last they wrenched the clanking bond asunder, and retiring a wide space apart, carried each a galling fragment, of which nothing but death could break the rivets, to hide it in new society beneath the gayest looks they could assume. Your mother succeeded; she forgot it soon. But it rusted and cankered at your father's heart for years."

"Well, they were separated," said Monks, "and what of that?"

"When they had been separated for some time," returned Mr Brownlow, "and your mother, wholly given up to continental frivolities, had utterly forgotten the young husband ten good years her junior, who, with prospects blighted, lingered on at home, he fell among new friends. *This* circumstance, at least, you know already."

"Not I," said Monks, turning away his eyes and beating his foot upon the ground, as a man who is determined to deny everything. "Not I."

"Your manner, no less than your actions, assures me that you have never forgotten it, or ceased to think of it with bitterness," returned Mr Brownlow. "I speak of fifteen years ago, when you were not more than eleven years old, and your father but one-and-thirty – for he was, I repeat, a boy, when *his* father ordered him to marry. Must I go back to events which cast a shade upon the memory of your parent, or will you spare it, and disclose to me the truth?"

"I have nothing to disclose," rejoined Monks. "You must talk on if you will."

"These new friends, then," said Mr Brownlow, "were a naval officer retired from active service, whose wife had died some half-a-year before, and left him with two children – there had been more, but, of all their family, happily but two survived. They were both daughters; one a beautiful creature of nineteen, and the other a mere child of two or three years old."

"What's this to me?" asked Monks.

"They resided," said Mr Brownlow, without seeming to hear the interruption, "in a part of the country to which your father in his wandering had repaired, and where he had taken up his abode. Acquaintance, intimacy, friendship, fast followed on each other. Your father was gifted as few men are. He had his sister's soul and person. As the old officer knew him more and more, he grew to love him. I would that it had ended there. His daughter did the same."

The old gentleman paused; Monks was biting his lips, with his eyes fixed upon the floor; seeing this, he immediately resumed:

"The end of a year found him contracted, solemnly contracted, to that daughter; the object of the first, true, ardent, only passion of a guileless girl."

"Your tale is of the longest," observed Monks, moving restlessly in his chair.

"It is a true tale of grief and trial, and sorrow, young man," returned Mr Brownlow, "and such tales usually are; if it were one of unmixed joy and happiness, it would be very brief. At length one of those rich relations to strengthen whose interest and importance your father had been sacrificed, as others are often – it is no uncommon case – died, and to repair the misery he had been instrumental in occasioning, left him *his* panacea for all griefs – Money. It was necessary that he should immediately repair to Rome, whither this man had sped for health, and where he had died, leaving his affairs in great confusion. He went; was seized with mortal illness there; was followed, the moment the intelligence reached Paris, by your mother who carried you with her; he died the day after her arrival, leaving no will – *no will* – so that the whole property fell to her and you."

At this part of the recital Monks held his breath, and listened with a face of intense eagerness, though his eyes were not directed towards the speaker. As Mr Brownlow paused, he changed his position with the air of one who has experienced a sudden relief, and wiped his hot face and hands.

"Before he went abroad, and as he passed through London on his way," said Mr Brownlow, slowly, and fixing his eyes upon the other's face, "he came to me."

"I never heard of that," interrupted Monks in a tone intended to appear incredulous, but savouring more of disagreeable surprise.

"He came to me, and left with me, among some other things, a picture – a portrait painted by himself – a likeness of this poor girl – which he did not wish to leave behind, and could not carry forward on his hasty journey. He was worn by anxiety and remorse almost to a shadow; talked in a wild, distracted way, of ruin and dishonour worked by himself; confided to me his intention to convert his whole property, at any loss, into money, and, having settled on his wife and you a portion of his recent acquisition, to fly the country – I guessed too well he would not fly alone – and never see it more. Even from me, his old and early friend, whose strong attachment had taken root in the earth that covered one most dear to both – even from me he withheld any more particular confession, promising to write and tell me all, and after that to see me once again, for the last time on earth. Alas! *That* was the last time. I had no letter, and I never saw him more.

"I went," said Mr Brownlow, after a short pause, "I went, when all was over, to the scene of his – I will use the term the world would freely use, for worldly harshness or favour are now alike to him – of his guilty love, resolved that if my fears were realised that erring child should find one heart and home to shelter and compassionate her. The family had left that part a week before; they had called in such trifling debts as were outstanding, discharged them, and left the place by night. Why, or whither, none can tell."

Monks drew his breath yet more freely, and looked round with a smile of triumph.

"When your brother," said Mr Brownlow, drawing nearer to the other's chair, "When your brother: a feeble, ragged, neglected child: was cast in my way by a stronger hand than chance, and rescued by me from a life of vice and infamy – "

"What?" cried Monks.

"By me," said Mr Brownlow. "I told you I should interest you before long. I say by me – I see that your cunning associate suppressed my name, although for aught he knew, it would be quite strange to your ears. When he was rescued by me, then, and lay recovering from sickness in my house, his strong resemblance to this picture I have spoken of, struck me with astonishment. Even when I first saw him in all his dirt and misery, there was a lingering expression in his face that came upon me like a glimpse of some old friend flashing on one in a vivid dream. I need not tell you he was snared away before I knew his history – "

"Why not?" asked Monks hastily.

"Because you know it well."

"I!"

"Denial to me is vain," replied Mr Brownlow. "I shall show you that I know more than that."

"You – you – can't prove anything against me," stammered Monks. "I defy you to do it!"

"We shall see," returned the old gentleman with a searching glance. "I lost the boy, and no efforts of mine could recover him. Your mother being dead, I knew that you alone could solve the mystery if anybody could, and as when I had last heard of you you were on your own estate in the West Indies – whither, as you well know, you retired upon your mother's death to escape the consequences of vicious courses here – I made the voyage. You had left it, months before, and were supposed to be in London, but no one could tell where. I returned. Your agents had no clue to your residence. You came and went, they said, as strangely as you had ever done: sometimes for days together and sometimes not for months: keeping to all appearance the same low haunts and mingling with the same infamous herd who had been your associates when a fierce ungovernable boy. I wearied them with new applications. I paced the streets by night and day, but until two hours ago, all my efforts were fruitless, and I never saw you for an instant."

"And now you do see me," said Monks, rising boldly, "what then? Fraud and robbery are high-sounding words – justified, you think, by a fancied resemblance in some young imp to an idle daub of a dead man's. Brother! You don't even know that a child was born of this maudlin pair; you don't even know that."

"I *did not*," replied Mr Brownlow, rising too; "but within the last fortnight I have learnt it all. You have a brother; you know it, and him. There was a will, which your mother destroyed, leaving the secret and the gain to you at her own death. It contained a reference to some child likely to be the result of this sad connection, which child was born, and accidentally encountered by you, when your suspicions were first awakened by his resemblance to his father. You repaired to the place of his birth. There existed proofs – proofs long suppressed – of his birth and parentage. Those proofs were destroyed by you, and now, in your own words to your accomplice the Jew, "*the only proofs of the boy's identity lie at the bottom of the river, and the old hag that received them from the mother is rotting in her coffin.*" Unworthy son, coward, liar, – you, who hold your councils with thieves and murderers in dark rooms at night, – you, whose plots and wiles have brought a violent death upon the head of one worth millions such as you, – you, who from your cradle were gall and bitterness to your own father's heart, and in whom all evil passions, vice, and profligacy, festered, till they found a vent in a hideous disease which has made your face an index even to your mind – you, Edward Leeford, do you still brave me!"

"No, no, no!" returned the coward, overwhelmed by these accumulated charges.

"Every word!" cried the old gentleman, "every word that has passed between you and this detested villain, is known to me. Shadows on the wall have caught your whispers, and brought them to my ear; the sight of the persecuted child has turned vice itself, and given it the courage and almost the attributes of virtue. Murder has been done, to which you were morally if not really a party."

"No, no," interposed Monks. "I – I – know nothing of that; I was going to inquire the truth of the story when you overtook me. I didn't know the cause. I thought it was a common quarrel."

"It was the partial disclosure of your secrets," replied Mr Brownlow. "Will you disclose the whole?"

"Yes, I will."

"Set your hand to a statement of truth and facts, and repeat it before witnesses?"

"That I promise too."

"Remain quietly here, until such a document is drawn up, and proceed with me to such a place as I may deem most advisable, for the purpose of attesting it?"

"If you insist upon that, I'll do that also," replied Monks.

"You must do more than that," said Mr Brownlow. "Make restitution to an innocent and unoffending child, for such he is, although the offspring of a guilty and most miserable love. You have not forgotten the provisions of the will. Carry them into execution so far as your brother is concerned, and then go where you please. In this world you need meet no more."

While Monks was pacing up and down, meditating with dark and evil looks on this proposal and the possibilities of evading it: torn by his fears on the one hand and his hatred on the other: the door was hurriedly unlocked, and a gentleman (Mr Losberne) entered the room in violent agitation.

"The man will be taken," he cried. "He will be taken to-night!"

"The murderer?" asked Mr Brownlow.

"Yes, yes," replied the other. "His dog has been seen lurking about some old haunt, and there seems little doubt that his master either is, or will be, there, under cover of the darkness. Spies are hovering about in every direction. I have spoken to the men who are charged with his capture, and they tell me he cannot escape. A reward of a hundred pounds is proclaimed by Government to-night."

"I will give fifty more," said Mr Brownlow, "and proclaim it with my own lips upon the spot, if I can reach it. Where is Mr Maylie?"

"Harry? As soon as he had seen your friend here, safe in a coach with you, he hurried off to where he heard this," replied the doctor, "and mounting his horse sallied forth to join the first party at some place in the outskirts agreed upon between them."

"Fagin," said Mr Brownlow; "what of him?"

"When I last heard, he had not been taken, but he will be, or is by this time. They're sure of him."

"Have you made up your mind?" asked Mr Brownlow, in a low voice, of Monks.

"Yes," he replied. "You – you – will be secret with me?"

"I will. Remain here till I return. It is your only hope of safety."

They left the room, and the door was again locked.

"What have you done?" asked the doctor in a whisper.

"All that I could hope to do, and even more. Coupling the poor girl's intelligence with my previous knowledge, and the result of our good friend's inquiries on the spot, I left him no loophole of escape, and laid bare the whole villany which by these lights became plain as day. Write and appoint the evening after to-morrow, at seven, for the meeting. We shall be down there, a few hours before, but shall require rest: especially the young lady, who *may* have greater need of firmness than either you or I can quite foresee just now. But my blood boils to avenge this poor murdered creature. Which way have they taken?"

"Drive straight to the office and you will be in time," replied Mr Losberne. "I will remain here."

The two gentlemen hastily separated; each in a fever of excitement wholly uncontrollable.

Chapter L

The Pursuit and Escape

NEAR to that part of the Thames on which the church at Rotherhithe abuts, where the buildings on the banks are dirtiest and the vessels on the river blackest with the dust of colliers and the smoke of close-built low-roofed houses, there exists the filthiest, the strangest, the most extraordinary of the many localities that are hidden in London, wholly unknown, even by name, to the great mass of its inhabitants.

To reach this place, the visitor has to penetrate through a maze of close, narrow, and muddy streets, thronged by the roughest and poorest of waterside people, and devoted to the traffic they may be supposed to occasion. The cheapest and least delicate provisions are heaped in the shops; the coarsest and commonest articles of wearing apparel dangle at the salesman's door, and stream from the house-parapet and windows. Jostling with unemployed labourers of the lowest class, ballast-heavers, coal-whippers, brazen women, ragged children, and the raff and refuse of the river, he makes his way with difficulty along, assailed by offensive sights and smells from the narrow alleys which branch off on the right and left, and deafened by the clash of ponderous waggons that bear great piles of merchandise from the stacks of warehouses that rise from every corner. Arriving, at length, in streets remoter and less-frequented than those through which he has passed, he walks beneath tottering house-fronts projecting over the pavement, dismantled walls that seem to totter as he passes, chimneys half crushed half hesitating to fall, windows guarded by rusty iron bars that time and dirt have almost eaten away, every imaginable sign of desolation and neglect.

In such a neighbourhood, beyond Dockhead in the Borough of Southwark, stands Jacob's Island, surrounded by a muddy ditch, six or eight feet deep and fifteen or twenty wide when the tide is in, once called Mill Pond, but known in the days of this story as Folly Ditch. It is a creek or inlet from the Thames, and can always be filled at high water by opening the sluices at the Lead Mills from which it took its old name. At such times, a stranger, looking from one of the wooden bridges thrown across it at Mill Lane, will see the inhabitants of the houses on either side lowering from their back doors and windows, buckets, pails, domestic utensils of all kinds, in which to haul the water up; and when his eye is turned from these operations to the houses themselves, his utmost astonishment will be excited by the scene before him. Crazy wooden galleries common to the backs of half-a-dozen houses, with holes from which to look upon the slime beneath; windows, broken and patched, with poles thrust out, on which to dry the linen that is never there; rooms so small, so filthy, so confined, that the air would seem too tainted even for the dirt and squalor which they shelter; wooden chambers thrusting themselves out above the mud, and threatening to fall into it – as some have done; dirt-besmeared walls and decaying foundations; every repulsive lineament of poverty, every loathsome indication of filth, rot, and garbage; all these ornament the banks of Folly Ditch.

In Jacob's Island, the warehouses are roofless and empty; the walls are crumbling down; the windows are windows no more; the doors are falling into the streets; the chimneys are blackened, but they yield no smoke. Thirty or forty years ago, before losses and chancery suits came upon it, it was a thriving place; but now it is a desolate island indeed. The houses have no owners; they are broken open, and entered upon by those who have the courage; and there they live, and there they die. They must have powerful motives for a secret residence, or be reduced to a destitute condition indeed, who seek a refuge in Jacob's Island.

In an upper room of one of these houses – a detached house of fair size, ruinous in other respects, but strongly defended at door and window: of which house the back commanded the ditch in manner already described – there were assembled three men, who, regarding each other every now and then with looks expressive of perplexity and expectation, sat for some time in profound and gloomy silence. One of these was Toby Crackit, another Mr Chitling, and the third a robber of fifty years, whose nose had been almost beaten in, in some old scuffle, and whose face bore a frightful scar which might probably be traced to the same occasion. This man was a returned transport, and his name was Kags.

"I wish," said Toby turning to Mr Chitling, "that you had picked out some other crib when the two old ones got too warm, and had not come here, my fine feller."

"Why didn't you, blunder-head!" said Kags.

"Well, I thought you'd have been a little more glad to see me than this," replied Mr Chitling, with a melancholy air.

"Why look'e, young gentleman," said Toby, "when a man keeps himself so very ex-clusive as I have done, and by that means has a snug house over his head with nobody a prying and smelling about it, it's rather a startling thing to have the honour of a wisit from a young gentleman (however respectable and pleasant a person he may be to play cards with at conweniency) circumstanced as you are."

"Especially, when the exclusive young man has got a friend stopping with him, that's arrived sooner than was expected from foreign parts, and is too modest to want to be presented to the Judges on his return," added Mr Kags.

There was a short silence, after which Toby Crackit, seeming to abandon as hopeless any further effort to maintain his usual devil-may-care swagger, turned to Chitling and said,

"When was Fagin took then?"

"Just at dinner-time – two o'clock this afternoon. Charley and I made our lucky up the wash"us chimney, and Bolter got into the empty water-butt, head downwards; but his legs were so precious long that they stuck out at the top, and so they took him too."

"And Bet?"

"Poor Bet! She went to see the Body, to speak to who it was," replied Chitling, his countenance falling more and more, "and went off mad, screaming and raving, and beating her head against the boards; so they put a strait-weskut on her and took her to the hospital – and there she is."

"Wot's come of young Bates?" demanded Kags.

"He hung about, not to come over here afore dark, but he'll be here soon," replied Chitling. "There's nowhere else to go to now, for the people at the Cripples are all in custody, and the bar of the ken – I went up there and see it with my own eyes – is filled with traps."

"This is a smash," observed Toby biting his lips. "There's more than one will go with this."

"The sessions are on," said Kags: "if they get the inquest over, and Bolter turns King's evidence: as of course he will, from what he's said already: they can prove Fagin an accessory before the fact, and get the trial on on Friday, and he'll swing in six days from this, by G—!"

"You should have heard the people groan," said Chitling; "the officers fought like devils, or they'd have torn him away. He was down once, but they made a ring round him, and fought their way along. You should have seen how he looked about him, all muddy and bleeding, and clung to them as if they were his dearest friends. I can see 'em now, not able to stand upright with the pressing of the mob, and dragging him along amongst 'em; I can see the people jumping up, one behind another, and snarling with their teeth and making at him; I can see the blood upon his hair and beard, and hear the cries with which the women worked themselves into the centre of the crowd at the street corner, and swore they'd tear his heart out!"

The horror-stricken witness of this scene pressed his hands upon his ears, and with his eyes closed got up and paced violently to and fro, like one distracted.

While he was thus engaged, and the two men sat by in silence with their eyes fixed upon the floor, a pattering noise was heard upon the stairs, and Sikes's dog bounded into the room. They ran to the window, down stairs, and into the street. The dog had jumped in at an open window; he made no attempt to follow them, nor was his master to be seen.

"What's the meaning of this?" said Toby when they had returned. "He can't be coming here. I – I – hope not."

"If he was coming here, he'd have come with the dog," said Kags, stooping down to examine the animal, who lay panting on the floor. "Here! Give us some water for him; he has run himself faint."

"He's drunk it all up, every drop," said Chitling after watching the dog some time in silence. "Covered with mud – lame – half-blind – he must have come a long way."

"Where can he have come from!" exclaimed Toby. "He's been to the other kens of course, and finding them filled with strangers come on here, where he's been many a time and often. But where can he have come from first, and how comes he here alone without the other!"

"He" – (none of them called the murderer by his old name) – "He can't have made away with himself. What do you think?" said Chitling.

Toby shook his head.

"If he had," said Kags, "the dog "ud want to lead us away to where he did it. No. I think he's got out of the country, and left the dog behind. He must have given him the slip somehow, or he wouldn't be so easy."

This solution, appearing the most probable one, was adopted as the right; the dog, creeping under a chair, coiled himself up to sleep, without more notice from anybody.

It being now dark, the shutter was closed, and a candle lighted and placed upon the table. The terrible events of the last two days had made a deep impression on all three, increased by the danger and uncertainty of their own position. They drew their chairs closer together, starting at every sound. They spoke little, and that in whispers, and were as silent and awe-stricken as if the remains of the murdered woman lay in the next room.

They had sat thus, some time, when suddenly was heard a hurried knocking at the door below.

"Young Bates," said Kags, looking angrily round, to check the fear he felt himself.

The knocking came again. No, it wasn't he. He never knocked like that.

Crackit went to the window, and shaking all over, drew in his head. There was no need to tell them who it was; his pale face was enough. The dog too was on the alert in an instant, and ran whining to the door.

"We must let him in," he said, taking up the candle.

"Isn't there any help for it?" asked the other man in a hoarse voice.

"None. He *must* come in."

"Don't leave us in the dark," said Kags, taking down a candle from the chimney-piece, and lighting it, with such a trembling hand that the knocking was twice repeated before he had finished.

Crackit went down to the door, and returned followed by a man with the lower part of his face buried in a handkerchief, and another tied over his head under his hat. He drew them slowly off. Blanched face, sunken eyes, hollow cheeks, beard of three days" growth, wasted flesh, short thick breath; it was the very ghost of Sikes.

He laid his hand upon a chair which stood in the middle of the room, but shuddering as he was about to drop into it, and seeming to glance over his shoulder, dragged it back close to the wall – as close as it would go – ground it against it – and sat down.

Not a word had been exchanged. He looked from one to another in silence. If an eye were furtively raised and met his, it was instantly averted. When his hollow voice broke silence, they all three started. They seemed never to have heard its tones before.

"How came that dog here?" he asked.

"Alone. Three hours ago."

"To-night's paper says that Fagin's took. Is it true, or a lie?"

"True."

They were silent again.

"Damn you all!" said Sikes, passing his hand across his forehead. "Have you nothing to say to me?"

There was an uneasy movement among them, but nobody spoke.

"You that keep this house," said Sikes, turning his face to Crackit, "do you mean to sell me, or to let me lie here till this hunt is over?"

"You may stop here, if you think it safe," returned the person addressed, after some hesitation.

Sikes carried his eyes slowly up the wall behind him: rather trying to turn his head than actually doing it: and said, "Is – it – the body – is it buried?"

They shook their heads.

"Why isn't it!" he retorted with the same glance behind him. "Wot do they keep such ugly things above the ground for? – Who's that knocking?"

Crackit intimated, by a motion of his hand as he left the room, that there was nothing to fear; and directly came back with Charley Bates behind him. Sikes sat opposite the door, so that the moment the boy entered the room he encountered his figure.

"Toby," said the boy falling back, as Sikes turned his eyes towards him, "why didn't you tell me this, down stairs?"

There had been something so tremendous in the shrinking off of the three, that the wretched man was willing to propitiate even this lad. Accordingly he nodded, and made as though he would shake hands with him.

"Let me go into some other room," said the boy, retreating still farther.

"Charley!" said Sikes, stepping forward. "Don't you – don't you know me?"

"Don't come nearer me," answered the boy, still retreating, and looking, with horror in his eyes, upon the murderer's face. "You monster!"

The man stopped half-way, and they looked at each other; but Sikes's eyes sunk gradually to the ground.

"Witness you three," cried the boy shaking his clenched fist, and becoming more and more excited as he spoke. "Witness you three – I'm not afraid of him – if they come here after him, I'll give him up; I will. I tell you out at once. He may kill me for it if he likes, or if he dares, but if I am here I'll give him up. I'd give him up if he was to be boiled alive. Murder! Help! If there's the pluck of a man among you three, you'll help me. Murder! Help! Down with him!"

Pouring out these cries, and accompanying them with violent gesticulation, the boy actually threw himself, single-handed, upon the strong man, and in the intensity of his energy and the suddenness of his surprise, brought him heavily to the ground.

The three spectators seemed quite stupefied. They offered no interference, and the boy and man rolled on the ground together; the former, heedless of the blows that showered upon him, wrenching his hands tighter and tighter in the garments about the murderer's breast and never ceasing to call for help with all his might.

The contest, however, was too unequal to last long. Sikes had him down, and his knee was on his throat, when Crackit pulled him back with a look of alarm, and pointed to the window. There were lights gleaming below, voices in loud and earnest conversation, the tramp of hurried footsteps – endless they seemed in number – crossing the nearest wooden bridge. One man on horseback seemed to be among the crowd; for there was the noise of hoofs rattling on the uneven pavement. The gleam of lights increased; the footsteps came more thickly and noisily on. Then, came a loud knocking at the door, and then a hoarse murmur from such a multitude of angry voices as would have made the boldest quail.

"Help!" shrieked the boy in a voice that rent the air.

"He's here! Break down the door!"

"In the King's name," cried the voices without; and the hoarse cry arose again, but louder.

"Break down the door!" screamed the boy. "I tell you they'll never open it. Run straight to the room where the light is. Break down the door!"

Strokes, thick and heavy, rattled upon the door and lower window-shutters as he ceased to speak, and a loud huzzah burst from the crowd; giving the listener, for the first time, some adequate idea of its immense extent.

"Open the door of some place where I can lock this screeching Hell-babe," cried Sikes fiercely; running to and fro, and dragging the boy, now, as easily as if he were an empty sack. "That door. Quick!" He flung him in, bolted it, and turned the key. "Is the down-stairs door fast?"

"Double-locked and chained," replied Crackit, who, with the other two men, still remained quite helpless and bewildered.

"The panels – are they strong?"

"Lined with sheet-iron."

"And the windows too?"

"Yes, and the windows."

"Damn you!" cried the desperate ruffian, throwing up the sash and menacing the crowd. "Do your worst! I'll cheat you yet!"

Of all the terrific yells that ever fell on mortal ears, none could exceed the cry of the infuriated throng. Some shouted to those who were nearest to set the house on fire; others roared to the officers to shoot him dead. Among them all, none showed such fury as the man on horseback, who, throwing himself out of the saddle, and bursting through the crowd as if he were parting water, cried, beneath the window, in a voice that rose above all others, "Twenty guineas to the man who brings a ladder!"

The nearest voices took up the cry, and hundreds echoed it. Some called for ladders, some for sledge-hammers; some ran with torches to and fro as if to seek them, and still came back and roared again; some spent their breath in impotent curses and execrations; some pressed forward with the ecstasy of madmen, and thus impeded the progress of those below; some among the boldest attempted to climb up by the water-spout and crevices in the wall; and all waved to and fro, in the darkness beneath, like a field of corn moved by an angry wind: and joined from time to time in one loud furious roar.

"The tide," cried the murderer, as he staggered back into the room, and shut the faces out, "the tide was in as I came up. Give me a rope, a long rope. They're all in front. I may drop into the Folly Ditch, and clear off that way. Give me a rope, or I shall do three more murders and kill myself."

The panic-stricken men pointed to where such articles were kept; the murderer, hastily selecting the longest and strongest cord, hurried up to the house-top.

All the windows in the rear of the house had been long ago bricked up, except one small trap in the room where the boy was locked, and that was too small even for the passage of his body. But, from this aperture, he had never ceased to call on those without, to guard the back; and thus, when the murderer emerged at last on the house-top by the door in the roof, a loud shout proclaimed the fact to those in front, who immediately began to pour round, pressing upon each other in an unbroken stream.

He planted a board, which he had carried up with him for the purpose, so firmly against the door that it must be matter of great difficulty to open it from the inside; and creeping over the tiles, looked over the low parapet.

The water was out, and the ditch a bed of mud.

The crowd had been hushed during these few moments, watching his motions and doubtful of his purpose, but the instant they perceived it and knew it was defeated, they raised a cry of triumphant execration to which all their previous shouting had been whispers. Again and again it rose. Those who were at too great a distance to know its meaning, took up the sound; it echoed and re-echoed; it seemed as though the whole city had poured its population out to curse him.

On pressed the people from the front – on, on, on, in a strong struggling current of angry faces, with here and there a glaring torch to light them up, and show them out in all their wrath and passion. The houses on the opposite side of the ditch had been entered by the mob; sashes were thrown up, or torn bodily out; there were tiers and tiers of faces in every window; cluster upon cluster of people clinging to every house-top. Each little bridge (and there were three in sight) bent beneath the weight of the crowd upon it. Still the current poured on to find some nook or hole from which to vent their shouts, and only for an instant see the wretch.

"They have him now," cried a man on the nearest bridge. "Hurrah!"

The crowd grew light with uncovered heads; and again the shout uprose.

"I will give fifty pounds," cried an old gentleman from the same quarter, "to the man who takes him alive. I will remain here, till he comes to ask me for it."

There was another roar. At this moment the word was passed among the crowd that the door was forced at last, and that he who had first called for the ladder had mounted into the room. The stream abruptly turned, as this intelligence ran from mouth to mouth; and the people at the windows, seeing those upon the bridges pouring back, quitted their stations, and running into the street, joined the concourse that now thronged pell-mell to the spot they had left: each man crushing and striving with his neighbour, and all panting with impatience to get near the door, and look upon the criminal as the officers brought him out. The cries and shrieks of those who were pressed almost to suffocation, or trampled down and trodden under foot in the confusion, were dreadful; the narrow ways were completely blocked up; and at this time, between the rush of some to regain the space in front of the house, and the unavailing struggles of others to extricate themselves from the mass, the immediate attention was distracted from the murderer, although the universal eagerness for his capture was, if possible, increased.

The man had shrunk down, thoroughly quelled by the ferocity of the crowd, and the impossibility of escape; but seeing this sudden change with no less rapidity than it had occurred, he sprang upon his feet, determined to make one last effort for his life by dropping into the ditch, and, at the risk of being stifled, endeavouring to creep away in the darkness and confusion.

Roused into new strength and energy, and stimulated by the noise within the house which announced that an entrance had really been effected, he set his foot against the stack of chimneys, fastened one end of the rope tightly and firmly round it, and with the other made a strong running noose by the aid of his hands and teeth almost in a second. He could let himself down by the cord to within a less distance of the ground than his own height, and had his knife ready in his hand to cut it then and drop.

At the very instant when he brought the loop over his head previous to slipping it beneath his arm-pits, and when the old gentleman before-mentioned (who had clung so tight to the railing of the bridge as to resist the force of the crowd, and retain his position) earnestly warned those about him that the man was about to lower himself down – at that very instant the murderer, looking behind him on the roof, threw his arms above his head, and uttered a yell of terror.

"The eyes again!" he cried in an unearthly screech.

Staggering as if struck by lightning, he lost his balance and tumbled over the parapet. The noose was on his neck. It ran up with his weight, tight as a bowstring, and swift as the arrow it speeds. He fell for five-and-thirty feet. There was a sudden jerk, a terrific convulsion of the limbs; and there he hung, with the open knife clenched in his stiffening hand.

The old chimney quivered with the shock, but stood it bravely. The murderer swung lifeless against the wall; and the boy, thrusting aside the dangling body which obscured his view, called to the people to come and take him out, for God's sake.

A dog, which had lain concealed till now, ran backwards and forwards on the parapet with a dismal howl, and collecting himself for a spring, jumped for the dead man's shoulders. Missing his aim, he fell into the ditch, turning completely over as he went; and striking his head against a stone, dashed out his brains.

Chapter LI

Affording an Explanation of more Mysteries than one, and comprehending a Proposal of Marriage with no Word of Settlement or Pin-money

THE events narrated in the last chapter were yet but two days old, when Oliver found himself, at three o'clock in the afternoon, in a travelling-carriage rolling fast towards his native town. Mrs Maylie, and Rose, and Mrs Bedwin, and the good doctor, were with him: and Mr Brownlow followed in a post-chaise, accompanied by one other person whose name had not been mentioned.

They had not talked much upon the way; for Oliver was in a flutter of agitation and uncertainty which deprived him of the power of collecting his thoughts, and almost of speech, and appeared to have scarcely less effect on his companions, who shared it, in at least an equal degree. He and the two ladies had been very carefully made acquainted by Mr Brownlow with the nature of the admissions which had been forced from Monks; and although they knew that the object of their present journey was to complete the work which had been so well begun, still the whole matter was enveloped in enough of doubt and mystery to leave them in endurance of the most intense suspense.

The same kind friend had, with Mr Losberne's assistance, cautiously stopped all channels of communication through which they could receive intelligence of the dreadful occurrences that had so recently taken place. "It was quite true," he said, "that they must know them before long, but it might be at a better time than the present, and it could not be at a worse." So, they travelled on in silence: each busied with reflections on the object which had brought them together: and no one disposed to give utterance to the thoughts which crowded upon all.

But if Oliver, under these influences, had remained silent while they journeyed towards his birth-place by a road he had never seen, how the whole current of his recollections ran back to old times, and what a crowd of emotions were wakened up in his breast, when they turned into that which he had traversed on foot: a poor houseless, wandering boy, without a friend to help him, or a roof to shelter his head.

"See there, there!" cried Oliver, eagerly clasping the hand of Rose, and pointing out at the carriage window; "that's the stile I came over; there are the hedges I crept behind, for fear any one should overtake me and force me back! Yonder is the path across the fields, leading to the old house where I was a little child! Oh Dick, Dick, my dear old friend, if I could only see you now!"

"You will see him soon," replied Rose, gently taking his folded hands between her own. "You shall tell him how happy you are, and how rich you have grown, and that in all your happiness you have none so great as the coming back to make him happy too."

"Yes, yes," said Oliver, "and we'll – we'll take him away from here, and have him clothed and taught, and send him to some quiet country place where he may grow strong and well, – shall we?"

Rose nodded "yes," for the boy was smiling through such happy tears that she could not speak.

"You will be kind and good to him, for you are to every one," said Oliver. "It will make you cry, I know, to hear what he can tell; but never mind, never mind, it will be all over, and you will smile again – I know that too – to think how changed he is; you did the same with me. He said "God bless you" to me when I ran away," cried the boy with a burst of affectionate emotion; "and I will say "God bless *you*" now, and show him how I love him for it!"

As they approached the town, and at length drove through its narrow streets, it became matter of no small difficulty to restrain the boy within reasonable bounds. There was Sowerberry's the undertaker's just as it used to be, only smaller and less imposing in appearance than he remembered it – there were all the well-known shops and houses, with almost every one of which he had some slight incident connected – there was Gamfield's cart, the very cart he used to have, standing at the old public-house door – there was the workhouse, the dreary prison of his youthful days, with its dismal windows frowning on the street – there was the same lean porter standing at the gate, at sight of whom Oliver involuntarily shrunk back, and then laughed again – there were scores of faces at the doors and windows that he knew quite well – there was nearly everything as if he had left it but yesterday, and all his recent life had been but a happy dream.

But it was pure, earnest, joyful reality. They drove straight to the door of the chief hotel (which Oliver used to stare up at, with awe, and think a mighty place, but which had somehow fallen off in grandeur and size); and here was Mr Grimwig all ready to receive them, kissing the young lady, and the old one too, when they got out of the coach, as if he were the grandfather of the whole party, all smiles and kindness, and not offering to eat his head – no, not once; not even when he contradicted a very old postboy about the nearest road to London, and maintained he knew it best, though he had only come that way once, and that time fast asleep. There was dinner prepared, and there were bed-rooms ready, and everything was arranged as if by magic.

Notwithstanding all this, when the hurry of the first half-hour was over, the same silence and constraint prevailed that had marked their journey down. Mr Brownlow did not join them at dinner, but remained in a separate room. The two other gentlemen hurried in and out with anxious faces, and, during the short intervals when they were present, conversed apart. Once, Mrs Maylie was called away, and after being absent for nearly an hour, returned with eyes swollen with weeping. All these things made Rose and Oliver, who were not in any new secrets, nervous and uncomfortable. They sat wondering, in silence; or, if they exchanged a few words, spoke in whispers, as if they were afraid to hear the sound of their own voices.

At length, when nine o'clock had come, and they began to think they were to hear no more that night, Mr Losberne and Mr Grimwig entered the room, followed by Mr Brownlow and a man whom Oliver almost shrieked with surprise to see; for they told him it was his brother, and it was the same man he had met at the market-town, and seen looking in with Fagin at the window of his little room. Monks cast a look of hate, which, even then, he could not dissemble, at the astonished boy, and sat down near the door. Mr Brownlow, who had papers in his hand, walked to a table near which Rose and Oliver were seated.

"This is a painful task," said he, "but these declarations, which have been signed in London before many gentlemen, must be in substance repeated here. I would have spared you the degradation, but we must hear them from your own lips before we part, and you know why."

"Go on," said the person addressed, turning away his face. "Quick. I have almost done enough, I think. Don't keep me here."

"This child," said Mr Brownlow, drawing Oliver to him, and laying his hand upon his head, "is your half-brother; the illegitimate son of your father, my dear friend Edwin Leeford, by poor young Agnes Fleming, who died in giving him birth."

"Yes," said Monks, scowling at the trembling boy: the beating of whose heart he might have heard. "That is their bastard child."

"The term you use," said Mr Brownlow, sternly, "is a reproach to those who long since passed beyond the feeble censure of the world. It reflects disgrace on no one living, except you who use it. Let that pass. He was born in this town."

"In the workhouse of this town," was the sullen reply. "You have the story there." He pointed impatiently to the papers as he spoke.

"I must have it here, too," said Mr Brownlow, looking round upon the listeners.

"Listen then! You!" returned Monks. "His father being taken ill at Rome, was joined by his wife, my mother, from whom he had been long separated, who went from Paris and took me with her – to look after his property, for what I know, for she had no great affection for him, nor he for her. He knew nothing of us, for his senses were gone, and he slumbered on till next day, when he died. Among the papers in his desk, were two, dated on the night his illness first came on, directed to yourself;" he addressed himself to Mr Brownlow; "and enclosed in a few short lines to you, with an intimation on the cover of the package that it was not to be forwarded till after he was dead. One of these papers was a letter to this girl Agnes; the other a will."

"What of the letter?" asked Mr Brownlow.

"The letter? – A sheet of paper crossed and crossed again, with a penitent confession, and prayers to God to help her. He had palmed a tale on the girl that some secret mystery – to be explained one day – prevented his marrying her just then; and so she had gone on, trusting patiently to him, until she trusted too far, and lost what none could ever give her back. She was, at that time, within a few months of her confinement. He told her all he had meant to do, to hide her shame, if he had lived, and prayed her, if he died, not to curse his memory, or think the consequences of their sin would be visited on her or their young child; for all the guilt was his. He reminded her of the day he had given her the little locket and the ring with her christian name engraved upon it, and a blank left for that which he hoped one day to have bestowed upon her – prayed her yet to keep it, and wear it next her heart, as she had done before – and then ran on, wildly, in the same words, over and over again, as if he had gone distracted. I believed he had."

"The will," said Mr Brownlow, as Oliver's tears fell fast.

Monks was silent.

"The will," said Mr Brownlow, speaking for him, "was in the same spirit as the letter. He talked of miseries which his wife had brought upon him; of the rebellious disposition, vice, malice, and premature bad passions of you his only son, who had been trained to hate him; and left you, and your mother, each an annuity of eight hundred pounds. The bulk of his property he divided into two equal portions – one for Agnes Fleming, and the other for their child, if it should be born alive, and ever come of age. If it were a girl, it was to inherit the money unconditionally; but if a boy, only on the stipulation that in his minority he should never have stained his name with any public act of dishonour, meanness, cowardice, or wrong. He did this, he said, to mark his confidence in the mother, and his conviction – only strengthened by approaching death – that the child would share her gentle heart, and noble nature. If he were disappointed in this expectation, then the money was to come to you: for then, and not till then, when both children were equal, would he recognise your prior claim upon his purse, who had none upon his heart, but had, from an infant, repulsed him with coldness and aversion."

"My mother," said Monks, in a louder tone, "did what a woman should have done. She burnt this will. The letter never reached its destination; but that, and other proofs, she kept, in case they ever tried to lie away the blot. The girl's father had the truth from her with every aggravation that her violent hate – I love her for it now – could add. Goaded by shame and dishonour he fled with his children into a remote corner of Wales, changing his very name that his friends might never know of his retreat; and here, no great while afterwards, he was found dead in his bed. The girl had left her home, in secret, some weeks before; he had searched for her, on foot, in every town and village near; it was on the night when he returned home, assured that she had destroyed herself, to hide her shame and his, that his old heart broke."

There was a short silence here, until Mr Brownlow took up the thread of the narrative.

"Years after this," he said, "this man's – Edward Leeford's – mother came to me. He had left her, when only eighteen; robbed her of jewels and money; gambled, squandered, forged, and fled to London: where for two years he had associated with the lowest outcasts. She was sinking under a painful and incurable disease, and wished to recover him before she died.

Inquiries were set on foot, and strict searches made. They were unavailing for a long time, but ultimately successful; and he went back with her to France."

"There she died," said Monks, "after a lingering illness; and, on her death-bed, she bequeathed these secrets to me, together with her unquenchable and deadly hatred of all whom they involved – though she need not have left me that, for I had inherited it long before. She would not believe that the girl had destroyed herself, and the child too, but was filled with the impression that a male child had been born, and was alive. I swore to her, if ever it crossed my path, to hunt it down; never to let it rest; to pursue it with the bitterest and most unrelenting animosity; to vent upon it the hatred that I deeply felt, and to spit upon the empty vaunt of that insulting will by dragging it, if I could, to the very gallows-foot. She was right. He came in my way at last. I began well; and, but for babbling drabs, I would have finished as I began!"

As the villain folded his arms tight together, and muttered curses on himself in the impotence of baffled malice, Mr Brownlow turned to the terrified group beside him, and explained that the Jew, who had been his old accomplice and confidant, had a large reward for keeping Oliver ensnared: of which some part was to be given up, in the event of his being rescued: and that a dispute on this head had led to their visit to the country house for the purpose of identifying him.

"The locket and ring?" said Mr Brownlow, turning to Monks.

"I bought them from the man and woman I told you of, who stole them from the nurse, who stole them from the corpse," answered Monks without raising his eyes. "You know what became of them."

Mr Brownlow merely nodded to Mr Grimwig, who disappearing with great alacrity, shortly returned, pushing in Mrs Bumble, and dragging her unwilling consort after him.

"Do my hi's deceive me!" cried Mr Bumble, with ill-feigned enthusiasm, "or is that little Oliver? Oh O-li-ver, if you know'd how I've been a-grieving for you – "

"Hold your tongue, fool," murmured Mrs Bumble.

"Isn't natur, natur, Mrs Bumble?" remonstrated the workhouse master. "Can't I be supposed to feel – *I* as brought him up porochially – when I see him a-setting here among ladies and gentlemen of the very affablest description! I always loved that boy as if he'd been my – my – my own grandfather," said Mr Bumble, halting for an appropriate comparison. "Master Oliver, my dear, you remember the blessed gentleman in the white waistcoat? Ah! he went to heaven last week, in a oak coffin with plated handles, Oliver."

"Come, sir," said Mr Grimwig, tartly; "suppress your feelings."

"I will do my endeavours, sir," replied Mr Bumble. "How do you do, sir? I hope you are very well."

This salutation was addressed to Mr Brownlow, who had stepped up to within a short distance of the respectable couple. He inquired, as he pointed to Monks,

"Do you know that person?"

"No," replied Mrs Bumble flatly.

"Perhaps *you* don't?" said Mr Brownlow, addressing her spouse.

"I never saw him in all my life," said Mr Bumble.

"Nor sold him anything, perhaps?"

"No," replied Mrs Bumble.

"You never had, perhaps, a certain gold locket and ring?" said Mr Brownlow.

"Certainly not," replied the matron. "Why are we brought here to answer to such nonsense as this?"

Again Mr Brownlow nodded to Mr Grimwig; and again that gentleman limped away with extraordinary readiness. But not again did he return with a stout man and wife; for this time, he led in two palsied women, who shook and tottered as they walked.

"You shut the door the night old Sally died," said the foremost one, raising her shrivelled hand, "but you couldn't shut out the sound, nor stop the chinks."

"No, no," said the other, looking round her and wagging her toothless jaws. "No, no, no."

"We heard her try to tell you what she'd done, and saw you take a paper from her hand, and watched you too, next day, to the pawnbroker's shop," said the first.

"Yes," added the second, "and it was a "locket and gold ring." We found out that, and saw it given you. We were by. Oh! we were by."

"And we know more than that," resumed the first, "for she told us often, long ago, that the young mother had told her that, feeling she should never get over it, she was on her way, at the time that she was taken ill, to die near the grave of the father of the child."

"Would you like to see the pawnbroker himself?" asked Mr Grimwig with a motion towards the door.

"No," replied the woman; "If he" – she pointed to Monks – "has been coward enough to confess, as I see he has, and you have sounded all these hags till you have found the right ones, I have nothing more to say. I *did* sell them, and they're where you'll never get them. What then?"

"Nothing," replied Mr Brownlow, "except that it remains for us to take care that neither of you is employed in a situation of trust again. You may leave the room."

"I hope," said Mr Bumble, looking about him with great ruefulness, as Mr Grimwig disappeared with the two old women: "I hope that this unfortunate little circumstance will not deprive me of my porochial office?"

"Indeed it will," replied Mr Brownlow. "You may make up your mind to that, and think yourself well off besides."

"It was all Mrs Bumble. She *would* do it," urged Mr Bumble; first looking round to ascertain that his partner had left the room.

"That is no excuse," replied Mr Brownlow. "You were present on the occasion of the destruction of these trinkets, and indeed are the more guilty of the two, in the eye of the law; for the law supposes that your wife acts under your direction."

"If the law supposes that," said Mr Bumble, squeezing his hat emphatically in both hands, "the law is a ass – a idiot. If that's the eye of the law, the law is a bachelor; and the worst I wish the law is, that his eye may be opened by experience – by experience."

Laying great stress on the repetition of these two words, Mr Bumble fixed his hat on very tight, and putting his hands in his pockets, followed his helpmate down stairs.

"Young lady," said Mr Brownlow, turning to Rose, "give me your hand. Do not tremble. You need not fear to hear the few remaining words we have to say."

"If they have – I do not know how they can, but if they have – any reference to me," said Rose, "pray let me hear them at some other time. I have not strength or spirits now."

"Nay," returned the old gentleman, drawing her arm through his; "you have more fortitude than this, I am sure. Do you know this young lady, sir?"

"Yes," replied Monks.

"I never saw you before," said Rose faintly.

"I have seen you often," returned Monks.

"The father of the unhappy Agnes had *two* daughters," said Mr Brownlow. "What was the fate of the other – the child?"

"The child," replied Monks, "when her father died in a strange place, in a strange name, without a letter, book, or scrap of paper that yielded the faintest clue by which his friends or relatives could be traced – the child was taken by some wretched cottagers, who reared it as their own."

"Go on," said Mr Brownlow, signing to Mrs Maylie to approach. "Go on!"

"You couldn't find the spot to which these people had repaired," said Monks, "but where friendship fails, hatred will often force a way. My mother found it, after a year of cunning search – ay, and found the child."

"She took it, did she?"

"No. The people were poor and began to sicken – at least the man did – of their fine humanity; so she left it with them, giving them a small present of money which would not last long, and promised more, which she never meant to send. She didn't quite rely, however, on their discontent and poverty for the child's unhappiness, but told the history of the sister's shame, with such alterations as suited her; bade them take good heed of the child, for she came of bad blood; and told them she was illegitimate, and sure to go wrong at one time or other. The circumstances countenanced all this; the people believed it; and there the child dragged on an existence, miserable enough even to satisfy us, until a widow lady, residing, then, at Chester, saw the girl by chance, pitied her, and took her home. There was some cursed spell, I think, against us; for in spite of all our efforts she remained there and was happy. I lost sight of her, two or three years ago, and saw her no more until a few months back."

"Do you see her now?"

"Yes. Leaning on your arm."

"But not the less my niece," cried Mrs Maylie, folding the fainting girl in her arms; "not the less my dearest child. I would not lose her now, for all the treasures of the world. My sweet companion, my own dear girl!"

"The only friend I ever had," cried Rose, clinging to her. "The kindest, best of friends. My heart will burst. I cannot bear all this."

"You have borne more, and have been, through all, the best and gentlest creature that ever shed happiness on every one she knew," said Mrs Maylie, embracing her tenderly. "Come, come, my love, remember who this is who waits to clasp you in his arms, poor child! See here – look, look, my dear!"

"Not aunt," cried Oliver, throwing his arms about her neck; "I'll never call her aunt – sister, my own dear sister, that something taught my heart to love so dearly from the first! Rose, dear, darling Rose!"

Let the tears which fell, and the broken words which were exchanged in the long close embrace between the orphans, be sacred. A father, sister, and mother, were gained, and lost, in that one moment. Joy and grief were mingled in the cup; but there were no bitter tears: for even grief itself arose so softened, and clothed in such sweet and tender recollections, that it became a solemn pleasure, and lost all character of pain.

They were a long, long time alone. A soft tap at the door, at length announced that some one was without. Oliver opened it, glided away, and gave place to Harry Maylie.

"I know it all," he said, taking a seat beside the lovely girl. "Dear Rose, I know it all."

"I am not here by accident," he added after a lengthened silence; "nor have I heard all this to-night, for I knew it yesterday – only yesterday. Do you guess that I have come to remind you of a promise?"

"Stay," said Rose. "You *do* know all."

"All. You gave me leave, at any time within a year, to renew the subject of our last discourse."

"I did."

"Not to press you to alter your determination," pursued the young man, "but to hear you repeat it, if you would. I was to lay whatever of station or fortune I might possess at your feet, and if you still adhered to your former determination, I pledged myself, by no word or act, to seek to change it."

"The same reasons which influenced me then, will influence me now," said Rose firmly. "If I ever owed a strict and rigid duty to her, whose goodness saved me from a life of indigence and suffering, when should I ever feel it, as I should to-night? It is a struggle," said Rose, "but one I am proud to make; it is a pang, but one my heart shall bear."

"The disclosure of to-night, – " Harry began.

"The disclosure of to-night," replied Rose softly, "leaves me in the same position, with reference to you, as that in which I stood before."

"You harden your heart against me, Rose," urged her lover.

"Oh, Harry, Harry," said the young lady, bursting into tears; "I wish I could, and spare myself this pain."

"Then why inflict it on yourself?" said Harry, taking her hand. "Think, dear Rose, think what you have heard to-night."

"And what have I heard! What have I heard!" cried Rose. "That a sense of his deep disgrace so worked upon my own father that he shunned all – there, we have said enough, Harry, we have said enough."

"Not yet, not yet," said the young man, detaining her as she rose. "My hopes, my wishes, prospects, feeling: every thought in life except my love for you: have undergone a change. I offer you, now, no distinction among a bustling crowd; no mingling with a world of malice and detraction, where the blood is called into honest cheeks by aught but real disgrace and shame; but a home – a heart and home – yes, dearest Rose, and those, and those alone, are all I have to offer."

"What do you mean!" she faltered.

"I mean but this – that when I left you last, I left you with a firm determination to level all fancied barriers between yourself and me; resolved that if my world could not be yours, I would make yours mine; that no pride of birth should curl the lip at you, for I would turn from it. This I have done. Those who have shrunk from me because of this, have shrunk from you, and proved you so far right. Such power and patronage: such relatives of influence and rank: as smiled upon me then, look coldly now; but there are smiling fields and waving trees in England's richest county; and by one village church – mine, Rose, my own! – there stands a rustic dwelling which you can make me prouder of, than all the hopes I have renounced, measured a thousandfold. This is *my* rank and station now, and here I lay it down!"

* * *

"It's a trying thing waiting supper for lovers," said Mr Grimwig, waking up, and pulling his pocket-handkerchief from over his head.

Truth to tell, the supper had been waiting a most unreasonable time. Neither Mrs Maylie, nor Harry, nor Rose (who all came in together), could offer a word in extenuation.

"I had serious thoughts of eating my head to-night," said Mr Grimwig, "for I began to think I should get nothing else. I'll take the liberty, if you'll allow me, of saluting the bride that is to be."

Mr Grimwig lost no time in carrying this notice into effect upon the blushing girl; and the example, being contagious, was followed both by the doctor and Mr Brownlow: some people affirm that Harry Maylie had been observed to set it, originally, in a dark room adjoining; but the best authorities consider this downright scandal: he being young and a clergyman.

"Oliver, my child," said Mrs Maylie, "where have you been, and why do you look so sad? There are tears stealing down your face at this moment. What is the matter?"

It is a world of disappointment; often to the hopes we most cherish, and hopes that do our nature the greatest honour.

Poor Dick was dead!

Chapter LII

Fagin's Last Night alive

THE court was paved, from floor to roof, with human faces. Inquisitive and eager eyes peered from every inch of space. From the rail before the dock, away into the sharpest angle of the smallest corner in the galleries, all looks were fixed upon one man – Fagin. Before him and behind: above, below, on the right and on the left: he seemed to stand surrounded by a firmament, all bright with gleaming eyes.

He stood there, in all this glare of living light, with one hand resting on the wooden slab before him, the other held to his ear, and his head thrust forward to enable him to catch with greater distinctness every word that fell from the presiding judge, who was delivering his charge to the jury. At times, he turned his eyes sharply upon them to observe the effect of the slightest featherweight in his favour; and when the points against him were stated with terrible distinctness, looked towards his counsel, in mute appeal that he would, even then, urge something in his behalf. Beyond these manifestations of anxiety, he stirred not hand or foot. He had scarcely moved since the trial began; and now that the judge ceased to speak, he still remained in the same strained attitude of close attention, with his gaze bent on him, as though he listened still.

A slight bustle in the court, recalled him to himself. Looking round, he saw that the jurymen had turned together, to consider of their verdict. As his eyes wandered to the gallery, he could see the people rising above each other to see his face: some hastily applying their glasses to their eyes: and others whispering their neighbours with looks expressive of abhorrence. A few there were, who seemed unmindful of him, and looked only to the jury, in impatient wonder how they could delay. But in no one face – not even among the women, of whom there were many there – could he read the faintest sympathy with himself, or any feeling but one of all-absorbing interest that he should be condemned.

As he saw all this in one bewildered glance, the death-like stillness came again, and looking back, he saw that the jurymen had turned towards the judge. Hush!

They only sought permission to retire.

He looked, wistfully, into their faces, one by one, when they passed out, as though to see which way the greater number leant; but that was fruitless. The jailer touched him on the shoulder. He followed mechanically to the end of the dock, and sat down on a chair. The man pointed it out, or he would not have seen it.

He looked up into the gallery again. Some of the people were eating, and some fanning themselves with handkerchiefs; for the crowded place was very hot. There was one young man sketching his face in a little note-book. He wondered whether it was like, and looked on when the artist broke his pencil-point, and made another with his knife, as any idle spectator might have done.

In the same way, when he turned his eyes towards the judge, his mind began to busy itself with the fashion of his dress, and what it cost, and how he put it on. There was an old fat gentleman on the bench, too, who had gone out, some half an hour before, and now come back. He wondered within himself whether this man had been to get his dinner, what he had had, and where he had had it; and pursued this train of careless thought until some new object caught his eye and roused another.

Not that, all this time, his mind was, for an instant, free from one oppressive overwhelming sense of the grave that opened at his feet; it was ever present to him, but in a vague and general way, and he could not fix his thoughts upon it. Thus, even while he trembled, and turned burning hot at the idea of speedy death, he fell to counting the iron spikes before him, and wondering how the head of one had been broken off, and whether they would mend it, or leave it as it was. Then, he thought of all the horrors of the gallows and the scaffold – and stopped to watch a man sprinkling the floor to cool it – and then went on to think again.

At length there was a cry of silence, and a breathless look from all towards the door. The jury returned, and passed him close. He could glean nothing from their faces; they might as well have been of stone. Perfect stillness ensued – not a rustle – not a breath – Guilty.

The building rang with a tremendous shout, and another, and another, and then it echoed loud groans, that gathered strength as they swelled out, like angry thunder. It was a peal of joy from the populace outside, greeting the news that he would die on Monday.

The noise subsided, and he was asked if he had anything to say why sentence of death should not be passed upon him. He had resumed his listening attitude, and looked intently at his questioner while the demand was made; but it was twice repeated before he seemed to hear it, and then he only muttered that he was an old man – an old man – an old man – and so, dropping into a whisper, was silent again.

The judge assumed the black cap, and the prisoner still stood with the same air and gesture. A woman in the gallery uttered some exclamation, called forth by this dread solemnity; he looked hastily up as if angry at the interruption, and bent forward yet more attentively. The address was solemn and impressive; the sentence fearful to hear. But he stood, like a marble figure, without the motion of a nerve. His haggard face was still thrust forward, his under-jaw hanging down, and his eyes staring out before him, when the jailer put his hand upon his arm, and beckoned him away. He gazed stupidly about him for an instant, and obeyed.

They led him through a paved room under the court, where some prisoners were waiting till their turns came, and others were talking to their friends, who crowded round a grate which looked into the open yard. There was nobody there, to speak to *him*; but, as he passed, the prisoners fell back to render him more visible to the people who were clinging to the bars: and they assailed him with opprobrious names, and screeched and hissed. He shook his fist, and would have spat upon them; but his conductors hurried him on, through a gloomy passage lighted by a few dim lamps, into the interior of the prison.

Here, he was searched, that he might not have about him the means of anticipating the law; this ceremony performed, they led him to one of the condemned cells, and left him there – alone.

He sat down on a stone bench opposite the door, which served for seat and bedstead; and casting his blood-shot eyes upon the ground, tried to collect his thoughts. After a while, he began to remember a few disjointed fragments of what the judge had said: though it had seemed to him, at the time, that he could not hear a word. These gradually fell into their proper places, and by degrees suggested more: so that in a little time he had the whole, almost as it was delivered. To be hanged by the neck, till he was dead – that was the end. To be hanged by the neck till he was dead.

As it came on very dark, he began to think of all the men he had known who had died upon the scaffold; some of them through his means. They rose up, in such quick succession, that he could hardly count them. He had seen some of them die, – and had joked too, because they died with prayers upon their lips. With what a rattling noise the drop went down; and how suddenly they changed, from strong and vigorous men to dangling heaps of clothes!

Some of them might have inhabited that very cell – sat upon that very spot. It was very dark; why didn't they bring a light? The cell had been built for many years. Scores of men must have passed their last hours there. It was like sitting in a vault strewn with dead bodies – the cap, the noose, the pinioned arms, the faces that he knew, even beneath that hideous veil. – Light, light!

At length, when his hands were raw with beating against the heavy door and walls, two men appeared: one bearing a candle, which he thrust into an iron candlestick fixed against the wall: the other dragging in a mattress on which to pass the night; for the prisoner was to be left alone no more.

Then came night – dark, dismal, silent night. Other watchers are glad to hear the church-clocks strike, for they tell of life and coming day. To him they brought despair. The boom of every iron bell came laden with the one, deep, hollow sound – Death. What availed the noise and bustle of cheerful morning, which penetrated even there, to him? It was another form of knell, with mockery added to the warning.

The day passed off. Day? There was no day; it was gone as soon as come – and night came on again; night so long, and yet so short; long in its dreadful silence, and short in its fleeting hours. At one time he raved and blasphemed; and at another howled and tore his hair. Venerable men of his own persuasion had come to pray beside him, but he had driven them away with curses. They renewed their charitable efforts, and he beat them off.

Saturday night. He had only one night more to live. And as he thought of this, the day broke – Sunday.

It was not until the night of this last awful day, that a withering sense of his helpless, desperate state came in its full intensity upon his blighted soul; not that he had ever held any defined or positive hope of mercy, but that he had never been able to consider more than the dim probability of dying so soon. He had spoken little to either of the two men, who relieved each other in their attendance upon him; and they, for their parts, made no effort to rouse his attention. He had sat there, awake, but dreaming. Now, he started up, every minute, and with gasping mouth and burning skin, hurried to and fro, in such a paroxysm of fear and wrath that even they – used to such sights – recoiled from him with horror. He grew so terrible, at last, in all the tortures of his evil conscience, that one man could not bear to sit there, eyeing him alone; and so the two kept watch together.

He cowered down upon his stone bed, and thought of the past. He had been wounded with some missiles from the crowd on the day of his capture, and his head was bandaged with a linen cloth. His red hair hung down upon his bloodless face; his beard was torn, and twisted into knots; his eyes shone with a terrible light; his unwashed flesh crackled with the fever that burnt him up. Eight – nine – ten. If it was not a trick to frighten him, and those were the real hours treading on each other's heels, where would he be, when they came round again! Eleven! Another struck, before the voice of the previous hour had ceased to vibrate. At eight, he would be the only mourner in his own funeral train; at eleven –

Those dreadful walls of Newgate, which have hidden so much misery and such unspeakable anguish, not only from the eyes, but, too often, and too long, from the thoughts, of men, never held so dread a spectacle as that. The few who lingered as they passed, and wondered what the man was doing who was to be hanged to-morrow, would have slept but ill that night, if they could have seen him.

From early in the evening until nearly midnight, little groups of two and three presented themselves at the lodge-gate, and inquired, with anxious faces, whether any reprieve had been received. These being answered in the negative, communicated the welcome intelligence to clusters in the street, who pointed out to one another the door from which he must come out, and showed where the scaffold would be built, and, walking with unwilling steps away, turned back to conjure up the scene. By degrees they fell off, one by one; and, for an hour, in the dead of night, the street was left to solitude and darkness.

The space before the prison was cleared, and a few strong barriers, painted black, had been already thrown across the road to break the pressure of the expected crowd, when Mr Brownlow and Oliver appeared at the wicket, and presented an order of admission to the prisoner, signed by one of the sheriffs. They were immediately admitted into the lodge.

"Is the young gentleman to come too, sir?" said the man whose duty it was to conduct them. "It's not a sight for children, sir."

"It is not indeed, my friend," rejoined Mr Brownlow; "but my business with this man is intimately connected with him; and as this child has seen him in the full career of his success and villany, I think it as well – even at the cost of some pain and fear – that he should see him now."

These few words had been said apart, so as to be inaudible to Oliver. The man touched his hat; and glancing at Oliver with some curiosity, opened another gate, opposite to that by which they had entered, and led them on, through dark and winding ways, towards the cells.

"This," said the man, stopping in a gloomy passage where a couple of workmen were making some preparations in profound silence – "this is the place he passes through. If you step this way, you can see the door he goes out at."

He led them into a stone kitchen, fitted with coppers for dressing the prison food, and pointed to a door. There was an open grating above it, through which came the sound of men's voices, mingled with the noise of hammering, and the throwing down of boards. They were putting up the scaffold.

From this place, they passed through several strong gates, opened by other turnkeys from the inner side; and, having entered an open yard, ascended a flight of narrow steps, and came into a passage with a row of strong doors on the left hand. Motioning them to remain where they were, the turnkey knocked at one of these with his bunch of keys. The two attendants, after a little whispering, came out into the passage, stretching themselves as if glad of the temporary relief, and motioned the visitors to follow the jailer into the cell. They did so.

The condemned criminal was seated on his bed, rocking himself from side to side, with a countenance more like that of a snared beast than the face of a man. His mind was evidently wandering to his old life, for he continued to mutter, without appearing conscious of their presence otherwise than as a part of his vision.

"Good boy, Charley – well done – " he mumbled. "Oliver, too, ha! ha! ha! Oliver too – quite the gentleman now – quite the – take that boy away to bed!"

The jailer took the disengaged hand of Oliver; and, whispering him not to be alarmed, looked on without speaking.

"Take him away to bed!" cried Fagin. "Do you hear me, some of you? He has been the – the – somehow the cause of all this. It's worth the money to bring him up to it – Bolter's throat, Bill; never mind the girl – Bolter's throat as deep as you can cut. Saw his head off!"

"Fagin," said the jailer.

"That's me!" cried the Jew, falling, instantly, into the attitude of listening he had assumed upon his trial. "An old man, my Lord; a very old, old man!"

"Here," said the turnkey, laying his hand upon his breast to keep him down. "Here's somebody wants to see you, to ask you some questions, I suppose. Fagin, Fagin! Are you a man?"

"I shan't be one long," he replied, looking up with a face retaining no human expression but rage and terror. "Strike them all dead! What right have they to butcher me?"

As he spoke he caught sight of Oliver and Mr Brownlow. Shrinking to the furthest corner of the seat, he demanded to know what they wanted there.

"Steady," said the turnkey, still holding him down. "Now, sir, tell him what you want. Quick, if you please, for he grows worse as the time gets on."

"You have some papers," said Mr Brownlow advancing, "which were placed in your hands, for better security, by a man called Monks."

"It's all a lie together," replied Fagin. "I haven't one – not one."

"For the love of God," said Mr Brownlow solemnly, "do not say that now, upon the very verge of death; but tell me where they are. You know that Sikes is dead; that Monks has confessed; that there is no hope of any further gain. Where are those papers?"

"Oliver," cried Fagin, beckoning to him. "Here, here! Let me whisper to you."

"I am not afraid," said Oliver in a low voice, as he relinquished Mr Brownlow's hand.

"The papers," said Fagin, drawing Oliver towards him, "are in a canvas bag, in a hole a little way up the chimney in the top front-room. I want to talk to you, my dear. I want to talk to you."

"Yes, yes," returned Oliver. "Let me say a prayer. Do! Let me say one prayer. Say only one, upon your knees, with me, and we will talk till morning."

"Outside, outside," replied Fagin, pushing the boy before him towards the door, and looking vacantly over his head. "Say I've gone to sleep – they'll believe *you*. You can get me out, if you take me so. Now then, now then!"

"Oh! God forgive this wretched man!" cried the boy with a burst of tears.

"That's right, that's right," said Fagin. "That'll help us on. This door first. If I shake and tremble, as we pass the gallows, don't you mind, but hurry on. Now, now, now!"

"Have you nothing else to ask him, sir?" inquired the turnkey.

"No other question," replied Mr Brownlow. "If I hoped we could recall him to a sense of his position – "

"Nothing will do that, sir," replied the man, shaking his head. "You had better leave him."

The door of the cell opened, and the attendants returned.

"Press on, press on," cried Fagin. "Softly, but not so slow. Faster, faster!"

The men laid hands upon him, and disengaging Oliver from his grasp, held him back. He struggled with the power of desperation, for an instant; and, then sent up cry upon cry that penetrated even those massive walls, and rang in their ears until they reached the open yard.

It was some time before they left the prison. Oliver nearly swooned after this frightful scene, and was so weak that for an hour or more, he had not the strength to walk.

Day was dawning when they again emerged. A great multitude had already assembled; the windows were filled with people, smoking and playing cards to beguile the time; the crowd were pushing, quarrelling, joking. Everything told of life and animation, but one dark cluster of objects in the centre of all – the black stage, the cross-beam, the rope, and all the hideous apparatus of death.

Chapter LIII

And Last

THE fortunes of those who have figured in this tale are nearly closed. The little that remains to their historian to relate, is told in few and simple words.

Before three months had passed, Rose Fleming and Harry Maylie were married in the village church which was henceforth to be the scene of the young clergyman's labours; on the same day they entered into possession of their new and happy home.

Mrs Maylie took up her abode with her son and daughter-in-law, to enjoy, during the tranquil remainder of her days, the greatest felicity that age and worth can know – the contemplation of the happiness of those on whom the warmest affections and tenderest cares of a well-spent life, have been unceasingly bestowed.

It appeared, on full and careful investigation, that if the wreck of property remaining in the custody of Monks (which had never prospered either in his hands or in those of his mother) were equally divided between himself and Oliver, it would yield, to each, little more than three thousand pounds. By the provisions of his father's will, Oliver would have been entitled to the whole; but Mr Brownlow, unwilling to deprive the elder son of the opportunity of retrieving his former vices and pursuing an honest career, proposed this mode of distribution, to which his young charge joyfully acceded.

Monks, still bearing that assumed name, retired with his portion to a distant part of the New World; where, having quickly squandered it, he once more fell into his old courses, and, after undergoing a long confinement for some fresh act of fraud and knavery, at length sunk under an attack of his old disorder, and died in prison. As far from home, died the chief remaining members of his friend Fagin's gang.

Mr Brownlow adopted Oliver as his son. Removing with him and the old housekeeper to within a mile of the parsonage-house, where his dear friends resided, he gratified the only remaining wish of Oliver's warm and earnest heart, and thus linked together a little society, whose condition approached as nearly to one of perfect happiness as can ever be known in this changing world.

Soon after the marriage of the young people, the worthy doctor returned to Chertsey, where, bereft of the presence of his old friends, he would have been discontented if his temperament had admitted of such a feeling; and would have turned quite peevish if he had known how. For two or three months, he contented himself with hinting that he feared the air began to disagree with him; then, finding that the place really no longer was, to him, what it had been, he settled his business on his assistant, took a bachelor's cottage outside the village of which his young friend was pastor, and instantaneously recovered. Here, he took to gardening, planting, fishing, carpentering, and various other pursuits of a similar kind: all undertaken with his characteristic impetuosity. In each and all, he has since become famous throughout the neighbourhood, as a most profound authority.

Before his removal, he had managed to contract a strong friendship for Mr Grimwig, which that eccentric gentleman cordially reciprocated. He is accordingly visited by Mr Grimwig a great many times in the course of the year. On all such occasions, Mr Grimwig plants, fishes, and carpenters, with great ardour; doing everything in a very singular and unprecedented manner, but always maintaining with his favourite asseveration, that his mode is the right one. On Sundays, he never fails to criticise the sermon to the young clergyman's face: always informing Mr Losberne, in strict confidence afterwards, that he considers it an excellent performance, but deems it as well not to say so. It is a standing and very favourite joke, for Mr Brownlow to rally him on his old prophecy concerning Oliver, and to remind him of the night on which they sat with the watch between them, waiting his return; but Mr Grimwig contends that he was right in the main, and, in proof thereof, remarks that Oliver *did not come back*, after all; which always calls forth a laugh on his side, and increases his good humour.

Mr Noah Claypole: receiving a free pardon from the Crown in consequence of being admitted approver against Fagin: and considering his profession not altogether as safe a one as he could wish: was, for some little time, at a loss for the means of a livelihood, not burthened with too much work. After some consideration, he went into business as an Informer, in which calling he realises a genteel subsistence. His plan is, to walk out once a week during church time attended by Charlotte in respectable attire. The lady faints away at the doors of charitable publicans, and the gentleman being accommodated with threepennyworth of brandy to restore her, lays an information next day, and pockets half the penalty. Sometimes Mr Claypole faints himself, but the result is the same.

Mr and Mrs Bumble, deprived of their situations, were gradually reduced to great indigence and misery, and finally became paupers in that very same workhouse in which they had once lorded it over others. Mr Bumble has been heard to say, that in this reverse and degradation, he has not even spirits to be thankful for being separated from his wife.

As to Mr Giles and Brittles, they still remain in their old posts, although the former is bald, and the last-named boy quite grey. They sleep at the parsonage, but divide their attentions so equally among its inmates, and Oliver, and Mr Brownlow, and Mr Losberne, that to this day the villagers have never been able to discover to which establishment they properly belong.

Master Charles Bates, appalled by Sikes's crime, fell into a train of reflection whether an honest life was not, after all, the best. Arriving at the conclusion that it certainly was, he turned his back upon the scenes of the past, resolved to amend it in some new sphere of action. He struggled hard, and suffered much, for some time; but, having a contented disposition, and a good purpose, succeeded in the end; and, from being a farmer's drudge, and a carrier's lad, he is now the merriest young grazier in all Northamptonshire.

And now, the hand that traces these words, falters, as it approaches the conclusion of its task; and would weave, for a little longer space, the thread of these adventures.

I would fain linger yet with a few of those among whom I have so long moved, and share their happiness by endeavouring to depict it. I would show Rose Maylie in all the bloom and grace of early womanhood, shedding on her secluded path in life soft and gentle light, that fell on all who trod it with her, and shone into their hearts. I would paint her the life and joy of the fire-side circle and the lively summer group; I would follow her through the sultry fields at noon, and hear the low tones of her sweet voice in the moonlit evening walk; I would watch her in all her goodness and charity abroad, and the smiling untiring discharge of domestic duties at home; I would paint her and her dead sister's child happy in their love for one another, and passing whole hours together in picturing the friends whom they had so sadly lost; I would summon before me, once again, those joyous little faces that clustered round her knee, and listen to their merry prattle; I would recall the tones of that clear laugh, and conjure up the sympathising tear that glistened in the soft blue eye. These, and a thousand looks and smiles, and turns of thought and speech – I would fain recall them every one.

How Mr Brownlow went on, from day to day, filling the mind of his adopted child with stores of knowledge, and becoming attached to him, more and more, as his nature developed itself, and showed the thriving seeds of all he wished him to become – how he traced in him new traits of his early friend, that awakened in his own bosom old remembrances, melancholy and yet sweet and soothing – how the two orphans, tried by adversity, remembered its lessons in mercy to others, and mutual love, and fervent thanks to Him who had protected and preserved them – these are all matters which need not to be told. I have said that they were truly happy; and without strong affection and humanity of heart, and gratitude to that Being whose code is Mercy, and whose great attribute is Benevolence to all things that breathe, happiness can never be attained.

Within the altar of the old village church there stands a white marble tablet, which bears as yet but one word: "AGNES." There is no coffin in that tomb; and may it be many, many years, before another name is placed above it! But, if the spirits of the Dead ever come back to earth, to visit spots hallowed by the love – the love beyond the grave – of those whom they knew in life, I believe that the shade of Agnes sometimes hovers round that solemn nook. I believe it none the less because that nook is in a Church, and she was weak and erring.

Hard Times

BOOK THE FIRST

SOWING

Chapter I

THE ONE THING NEEDFUL

"NOW, what I want is, Facts. Teach these boys and girls nothing but Facts. Facts alone are wanted in life. Plant nothing else, and root out every thing else. You can only form the minds of reasoning animals upon Facts: nothing else will ever be of any service to them. This is the principle on which I bring up my own children, and this is the principle on which I bring up these children. Stick to Facts, sir!"

The scene was a plain, bare, monotonous vault of a school-room, and the speaker's square forefinger emphasized his observations by underscoring every sentence with a line on the schoolmaster's sleeve. The emphasis was helped by the speaker's square wall of a forehead, which had his eyebrows for its base, while his eyes found commodious cellarage in two dark caves, overshadowed by the wall. The emphasis was helped by the speaker's mouth, which was wide, thin, and hard set. The emphasis was helped by the speaker's voice, which was inflexible, dry, and dictatorial. The emphasis was helped by the speaker's hair, which bristled on the skirts of his bald head, a plantation of firs to keep the wind from its shining surface, all covered with knobs, like the crust of a plum pie, as if the head had scarcely warehouse-room for the hard facts stored inside. The speaker's obstinate carriage, square coat, square legs, square shoulders—nay, his very neckcloth, trained to take him by the throat with an unaccommodating grasp, like a stubborn fact, as it was—all helped the emphasis.

"In this life, we want nothing but Facts, sir; nothing but Facts!"

The speaker, and the schoolmaster, and the third grown person present, all backed a little, and swept with their eyes the inclined plane of little vessels then and there arranged in order, ready to have imperial gallons of facts poured into them until they were full to the brim.

Chapter II

MURDERING THE INNOCENTS

THOMAS GRADGRIND, sir. A man of realities. A man of facts and calculations. A man who proceeds upon the principle that two and two are four, and nothing over, and who is not to be talked into allowing for any thing over. Thomas Gradgrind, sir—peremptorily Thomas—Thomas Gradgrind. With a rule and a pair of scales, and the multiplication table always in his pocket, sir, ready to weigh and measure any parcel of human nature, and tell you exactly what it comes to. It is a mere question of figures, a case of simple arithmetic. You might hope to get some other nonsensical belief into the head of George Gradgrind, or Augustus Gradgrind, or John Gradgrind, or Joseph Gradgrind (all suppositions, non-existent persons), but into the head of Thomas Gradgrind—no, sir!

In such terms Mr. Gradgrind always mentally introduced himself, whether to his private circle of acquaintance, or to the public in general. In such terms, no doubt, substituting the words "boys and girls," for "sir," Thomas Gradgrind now presented Thomas Gradgrind to the little pitchers before him, who were to be filled so full of facts.

Indeed, as he eagerly sparkled at them from the cellarage before mentioned, he seemed a kind of cannon loaded to the muzzle with facts, and prepared to blow them clean out of the regions of childhood at one discharge. He seemed a galvanizing apparatus, too, charged with a grim mechanical substitute for the tender young imaginations that were to be stormed away.

"Girl number twenty," said Mr. Gradgrind, squarely pointing with his square forefinger, "I don't know that girl. Who is that girl?"

"Sissy Jupe, sir," explained number twenty, blushing, standing up, and courtesying.

"Sissy is not a name," said Mr. Gradgrind. "Don't call yourself Sissy. Call yourself Cecilia."

"It's father as calls me Sissy, sir," returned the young girl in a trembling voice, and with another courtesy.

"Then he has no business to do it," said Mr. Gradgrind. "Tell him he mustn't. Cecilia Jupe. Let me see. What is your father?"

"He belongs to the horse-riding, if you please, sir."

Mr. Gradgrind frowned, and waved off the objectionable calling with his hand.

"We don't want to know any thing about that, here. You mustn't tell us about that, here. Your father breaks horses, don't he?"

"If you please, sir, when they can get any to break, they do break horses in the ring, sir."

"You mustn't tell us about the ring, here. Very well, then. Describe your father as a horsebreaker. He doctors sick horses, I dare say?"

"Oh yes, sir."

"Very well, then. He is a veterinary surgeon, a farrier and horsebreaker. Give me your definition of a horse."

(Sissy Jupe thrown into the greatest alarm by this demand.)

"Girl number twenty unable to define a horse!" said Mr. Gradgrind, for the general behoof of all the little pitchers. "Girl number twenty possessed of no facts, in reference to one of the commonest of animals! Some boy's definition of a horse. Bitzer, yours."

The square finger, moving here and there, lighted suddenly on Bitzer, perhaps because he chanced to sit in the same ray of sunlight which, darting in at one of the bare windows of the intensely whitewashed room, irradiated Sissy. For the boys and girls sat on the face of the inclined plane in two compact bodies, divided up the centre by a narrow interval; and Sissy, being at the corner of a row on the sunny side, came in for the beginning of a sunbeam, of which Bitzer, being at the corner of a row on the other side, a few rows in advance, caught the end. But, whereas the girl was so dark-eyed and dark-haired, that she seemed to receive a deeper and more lustrous color from the sun when it shone upon her, the boy was so light-eyed and light-haired that the self-same rays appeared to draw out of him what little color he ever possessed. His cold eyes would hardly have been eyes, but for the short ends of lashes which, by bringing them into immediate contrast with something paler than themselves, expressed their form. His short-cropped hair might have been a mere continuation of the sandy freckles on his forehead and face. His skin was so unwholesomely deficient in the natural tinge, that he looked as though, if he were cut, he would bleed white.

"Bitzer," said Thomas Gradgrind. "Your definition of a horse."

"Quadruped. Graminivorous. Forty teeth, namely twenty-four grinders, four eye-teeth, and twelve incisive. Sheds coat in the spring; in marshy countries, sheds hoofs, too. Hoofs hard, but requiring to be shod with iron. Age known by marks in mouth." Thus (and much more) Bitzer.

"Now girl number twenty," said Mr. Gradgrind. "You know what a horse is."

She courtesied again, and would have blushed deeper, if she could have blushed deeper than she had blushed all this time. Bitzer, after rapidly blinking at Thomas Gradgrind with both eyes at once, and so catching the light upon his quivering ends of lashes that they looked like the antennae of busy insects, put his knuckles to his freckled forehead, and sat down again.

The third gentleman now stepped forth. A mighty man at cutting and drying, he was; a government officer; in his way (and in most other people's too), a professed pugilist; always in training, always with a system to force down the general throat like a bolus, always to be heard of at the bar of his little Public-office, ready to fight all England. To continue in fistic phraseology, he had a genius for coming up to the scratch, wherever and whatever it was, and proving himself an ugly customer. He would go in and damage any subject whatever with his right, follow up with his left, stop, exchange, counter, bore his opponent (he always fought All England) to the ropes, and fall upon him neatly. He was certain to knock the wind out of common-sense, and render that unlucky adversary deaf to the call of time. And he had it in charge from high authority to bring about the great public-office Millennium, when Commissioners should reign upon earth.

"Very well," said this gentleman, briskly smiling, and folding his arms. "That's a horse. Now, let me ask you, girls and boys, Would you paper a room with representations of horses?"

After a pause, one half of the children cried in chorus, "Yes, sir!" Upon which the other half, seeing in the gentleman's face that Yes was wrong, cried out in chorus, "No, sir!"—as the custom is in these examinations.

"Of course, No. Why wouldn't you?"

A pause. One corpulent slow boy, with a wheezy manner of breathing, ventured the answer, Because he wouldn't paper a room at all, but would paint it.

"You *must* paper it," said the gentleman, rather warmly.

"You must paper it," said Thomas Gradgrind, "whether you like it or not. Don't tell *us* you wouldn't paper it. What do you mean, boy?"

"I'll explain to you, then," said the gentleman, after another and a dismal pause, "why you wouldn't paper a room with representations of horses. Do you ever see horses walking up and down the sides of rooms in reality—in fact? Do you?"

"Yes, sir!" from one half. "No, sir!" from the other.

"Of course, no," said the gentleman, with an indignant look at the wrong half. "Why, then, you are not to see any where, what you don't see in fact; you are not to have any where, what you don't have in fact. What is called Taste, is only another name for Fact."

Thomas Gradgrind nodded his approbation.

"This is a new principle, a discovery, a great discovery," said the gentleman. "Now, I'll try you again. Suppose you were going to carpet a room. Would you use a carpet having a representation of flowers upon it?"

There being a general conviction by this time that "No, sir!" was always the right answer to this gentleman, the chorus of No was very strong. Only a few feeble stragglers said Yes; among them Sissy Jupe.

"Girl number twenty," said the gentleman, smiling in the calm strength of knowledge.

Sissy blushed, and stood up.

"So you would carpet your room—or your husband's room, if you were a grown woman, and had a husband—with representations of flowers, would you?" said the gentleman. "Why would you?"

"If you please, sir, I am very fond of flowers," returned the girl.

"And is that why you would put tables and chairs upon them, and have people walking over them with heavy boots?"

"It wouldn't hurt them, sir. They wouldn't crush and wither, if you please, sir. They would be the pictures of what was very pretty and pleasant, and I would fancy—"

"Ay, ay, ay! But you mustn't fancy," cried the gentleman, quite elated by coming so happily to his point. "That's it! You are never to fancy."

"You are not, Mary Jupe," Thomas Gradgrind solemnly repeated, "to do anything of that kind."

"Fact, fact, fact!" said the gentleman. And "Fact, fact, fact!" repeated Thomas Gradgrind.

"You are to be in all things regulated and governed," said the gentleman, "by fact. We hope to have, before long, a board of fact, composed of commissioners of fact, who will force the people to be a people of fact, and of nothing but fact. You must discard the word Fancy altogether. You have nothing to do with it. You are not to have, in any object of use or ornament, what would be a contradiction in fact. You don't walk upon flowers in fact; you can not be allowed to walk upon flowers in carpets. You don't find that foreign birds and butterflies come and perch upon your crockery; you can not be permitted to paint foreign birds and butterflies upon your crockery. You never meet with quadrupeds going up and down walls; you must not have quadrupeds represented upon walls. You must see," said the gentleman, "for all these purposes, combinations and modifications (in primary colors) of mathematical figures which are susceptible of proof and demonstration. This is the new discovery. This is fact. This is taste."

The girl courtesied, and sat down. She was very young, and she looked as if she were frightened by the matter of fact prospect the world afforded.

"Now, if Mr. M'Choakumchild," said the gentleman, "will proceed to give his first lesson here, Mr. Gradgrind, I shall be happy, at your request, to observe his mode of procedure."

Mr. Gradgrind was much obliged. "Mr. M'Choakumchild, we only wait for you."

So Mr. M'Choakumchild began in his best manner. He and some one hundred and forty other school-masters, had been lately turned at the same time, in the same factory, on the same principles, like so many pianoforte legs. He had been put through an immense variety of paces, and had answered volumes of head-breaking questions. Orthography, etymology, syntax, and prosody, biography, astronomy, geography, and general cosmography, the sciences of compound proportion, algebra, land surveying and leveling, vocal music, and drawing from models, were all at the ends of his ten chilled fingers. He had worked his stony way into Her Majesty's most Honorable Privy Council's Schedule B, and had taken the bloom off the higher branches of mathematics and physical science, French, German, Latin, and Greek. He knew all about all the Water Sheds of all the world (whatever they are), and all the histories of all the peoples, and all the names of all the rivers and mountains, and all the productions, manners, and customs of all the countries, and all their boundaries and bearings on the two-and-thirty points of the compass. Ah, rather overdone, M'Choakumchild. If he had only learnt a little less, how infinitely better he might have taught much more!

He went to work in this preparatory lesson, not unlike Morgiana in the Forty Thieves: looking into all the vessels ranged before him, one after another, to see what they contained. Say, good M'Choakumchild. When from thy boiling store, thou shalt fill each jar brim full by-and-by, dost thou think that thou wilt always kill outright the robber Fancy lurking within—or sometimes only maim him and distort him!

Chapter III

A LOOPHOLE

MR. GRADGRIND walked homeward from the school, in a state of considerable satisfaction. It was his school, and he intended it to be a model. He intended every child in it to be a model—just as the young Gradgrinds were all models.

There were five young Gradgrinds, and they were models every one. They had been lectured at, from their tenderest years; coursed, like little hares. Almost as soon as they could run alone, they had been made to run to the lecture-room. The first object with which they had an association, or of which they had a remembrance, was a large black board with a dry Ogre chalking ghastly white figures on it.

Not that they knew, by name or nature, any thing about an Ogre. Fact forbid! I only use the word to express a monster in a lecturing castle, with Heaven knows how many heads manipulated into one, taking childhood captive, and dragging it into gloomy statistical dens by the hair.

No little Gradgrind had ever seen a face in the moon; it was up in the moon before it could speak distinctly. No little Grndgrind had ever learnt the silly jingle, Twinkle, twinkle, little star; how I wonder what you are; it had never known wonder on the subject, having at five years old dissected the Great Bear like a Professor Owen, and driven Charles's Wain like a locomotive engine-driver. No little Gradgrind had ever associated a cow in a field with that famous cow with the crumpled horn who tossed the dog who worried the cat who killed the rat who ate the malt, or with that yet more famous cow who swallowed Tom Thumb; it had never heard of those celebrities, and had only been introduced to a cow as a graminivorous ruminating quadruped with several stomachs.

To his matter of fact home, which was called Stone Lodge, Mr. Gradgrind directed his steps. He had virtually retired from the wholesale hardware trade before he built Stone Lodge, and was now looking about for a suitable opportunity of making an arithmetical figure in Parliament. Stone Lodge was situated on a moor within a mile or two of a great town—called Coketown in the present faithful guide-book.

A very regular feature on the face of the country, Stone Lodge was. Not the least disguise toned down or shaded off that uncompromising fact in the landscape. A great square house, with a heavy portico darkening the principal windows, as its master's heavy brows overshadowed his eyes. A calculated, cast up, balanced, and proved house. Six windows on this side of the door, six on that side; a total of twelve in this wing, a total of twelve in the other wing; four and twenty carried over to the back. A lawn and garden and an infant avenue, all ruled straight like a botanical account-book. Gas and ventilation, drainage and water-service, all of the primest quality. Iron clamps and girders, fireproof from top to bottom; mechanical lifts for the housemaids, with all their brushes and brooms; every thing, that heart could desire.

Every thing? Well, I suppose so. The little Gradgrinds had cabinets in various departments of science too. They had a little conchological cabinet, and a little metallurgical cabinet, and a little mineralogical cabinet; and the specimens were all arranged and labeled, and the bits of stone and ore looked as though they might have been broken from the parent substances by those tremendously hard instruments their own names; and, to paraphrase the idle legend of Peter Piper, who had never found his way into *their* nursery. If the greedy little Gradgrinds grasped at more than this, what was it for, good gracious goodness sake, that the greedy little Gradgrinds grasped at!

Their father walked on in a hopeful and satisfied frame of mind. He was an affectionate father, after his manner; but he would probably have described himself (if he had been put, like Sissy Jupe, upon a definition) as "an eminently practical" father. He had a particular pride in the phrase eminently practical, which was considered to have a special application to him. Whatsoever the public meeting held in Coketown, and whatsoever the subject of such meeting, some Coketowner was sure to seize the occasion of alluding to his eminently practical friend Gradgrind. This always pleased the eminently practical friend. He knew it to be his due, but his due was acceptable.

He had reached the neutral ground upon the outskirts of the town, which was neither town nor country, and yet was either spoiled, when his ears were invaded by the sound of music. The clashing and banging band attached to the horse-riding establishment which had there set up its rest in a wooden pavilion, was in full bray. A flag, floating from the summit of the temple, proclaimed to mankind that it was "Sleary's Horse-riding" which claimed their suffrages. Sleary himself, a stout modern statue with a money-box at its elbow, in an ecclesiastical niche of early Gothic architecture, took the money. Miss Josephine Sleary, as some very long and very narrow strips of printed bill announced, was then inaugurating the entertainments with her graceful equestrian Tyrolean flower-act. Among the other pleasing but always strictly moral wonders which must be seen to be believed, Signor Jupe was that afternoon to "elucidate the diverting accomplishments of his highly trained performing dog Merrylegs." He was also to exhibit "his astounding feat of throwing seventy-five hundred weight in rapid succession backhanded over his head, thus forming a fountain of solid iron in mid air, a feat never before attempted in this or any other country, and which having elicited such rapturous plaudits from enthusiastic throngs, it can not be withdrawn." The same Signor Jupe was to "enliven the varied performances at frequent intervals with his chaste Shakespearean quips and retorts." Lastly, he has to wind them up by appearing in his favorite character of Mr. William Button, of Tooley Street, in "the highly novel and laughable hippocomedietta of The Tailor's Journey to Brentford."

Thomas Gradgrind took no heed of these trivialities of course, but passed on as a practical man ought to pass on, either brushing the noisy insects from his thoughts, or consigning them to the House of Correction. But, the turning of the road took him by the back of the booth, and at the back of the booth a number of children were congregated in a number of stealthy attitudes, striving to peep in at the hidden glories of the place.

This brought him to a stop. "Now, to think of these vagabonds," said he, "attracting the young rabble from a model school!"

A space of stunted grass and dry rubbish being between him and the young rabble, he took his eye-glass out of his waistcoat to look for any child he knew by name, and might order off. Phenomenon almost incredible though distinctly seen, what did he then behold but his own metallurgical Louisa peeping with all her might through a hole in a deal board, and his own mathematical Thomas abasing himself on the ground to catch but a hoof of the graceful equestrian Tyrolean flower-act!

Dumb with amazement, Mr. Gradgrind crossed to the spot where his family was thus disgraced, laid his hand upon each erring child, and said:

"Louisa!! Thomas!!"

Both rose, red and disconcerted. But Louisa looked at her father with more boldness than Thomas did. Indeed, Thomas did not look at him, but gave himself up to be taken home like a machine.

"In the name of wonder, idleness, and folly!" said Mr. Gradgrind, leading each away by a hand; "what do you do here?"

"Wanted to see what it was like," returned Louisa shortly.

"What it was like?"

"Yes, father."

There was an air of jaded sullenness in them both, and particularly in the girl: yet, struggling through the dissatisfaction of her face, there was a light with nothing to rest upon, a fire with nothing to burn, a starved imagination keeping life in itself somehow, which brightened its expression. Not with the brightness natural to cheerful youth, but with uncertain, eager, doubtful flashes, which had something painful in them, analogous to the changes on a blind face groping its way.

She was a child now, of fifteen or sixteen; but at no distant day would seem to become a woman all at once. Her father thought so as he looked at her. She was pretty. Would have been self-willed (he thought in his eminently practical way) but for her bringing-up.

"Thomas, though I have the fact before me, I find it difficult to believe that you, with your education and resources, should have brought your sister to a scene like this."

"I brought *him,* father," said Louisa, quickly. "I asked him to come."

"I am sorry to hear it. I am very sorry indeed to hear it. It makes Thomas no better, and it makes you worse, Louisa."

She looked at her father again, but no tear fell down her cheek.

"You! Thomas and you, to whom the circle of the sciences is open, Thomas and you who may be said to be replete with facts, Thomas and you who have been trained to mathematical exactness, Thomas and you, here!" cried Mr. Gradgrind. "In this degraded position! I am amazed."

"I was tired, father. I have been tired a long time," said Louisa.

"Tired? Of what?" asked the astonished father.

"I don't know of what—of every thing, I think."

"Say not another word," returned Mr. Gradgrind. "You are childish. I will hear no more." He did not speak again until they had walked some half-a-mile in silence, when he gravely broke out with: "What would your best friends say, Louisa? Do you attach no value to their good opinion? What would Mr. Bounderby say?"

At the mention of this name, his daughter stole a look at him, remarkable for its intense and searching character. He saw nothing of it, for before he looked at her she had again cast down her eyes!

"What," he repeated presently, "would Mr. Bounderby say?" All the way to Stone Lodge, as with grave indignation he led the two delinquents home, he repeated at intervals "What would Mr. Bounderby say?"—as if Mr. Bounderby had been Mrs. Grundy.

Chapter IV

MR. BOUNDERBY

NOT being Mrs. Grundy, who *was* Mr. Bounderby?

Why, Mr. Bounderby was as near being Mr. Gradgrind's bosom friend, as a man perfectly devoid of sentiment can approach that spiritual relationship toward another man perfectly devoid of sentiment. So near was Mr. Bounderby—or, if the reader should prefer it, so far off.

He was a rich man: banker, merchant, manufacturer, and what not. A big, loud man, with a stare and a metallic laugh. A man made out of a coarse material, which seemed to have been stretched to make so much of him. A man with a great puffed head and forehead, swelled veins in his temples, and such a strained skin to his face that it seemed to hold his eyes open and lift his eyebrows up. A man with a pervading appearance on him of being inflated like a balloon, and ready to start. A man who could never sufficiently vaunt himself a self-made man. A man who was always proclaiming, through that brassy speaking-trumpet of a voice of his, his old ignorance and his old poverty. A man who was the Bully of humility.

A year or two younger than his eminently practical friend, Mr. Bounderby looked older; his seven or eight and forty might have had the seven or eight added to it again, without surprising any body. He had not much hair. One might have fancied he had talked it off; and that what was left, all standing up in disorder, was in that condition from being constantly blown about by his windy boastfulness.

In the formal drawing-room of Stone Lodge, standing on the hearth-rug, warming himself before the fire, Mr. Bounderby delivered some observations to Mrs. Gradgrind on the circumstance of its being his birth-day. He stood before the fire, partly because it was a cool spring afternoon, though the sun shone; partly because the shade of Stone Lodge was always haunted by the ghost of damp mortar; partly because he thus took up a commanding position, from which to subdue Mrs. Gradgrind.

"I hadn't a shoe to my foot. As to a stocking, I didn't know such a thing by name. I passed the day in a ditch, and the night in a pig-sty. That's the way I spent my tenth birth-day. Not that a ditch was new to me, for I was born in a ditch."

Mrs. Gradgrind, a little, thin, white, pink-eyed bundle of shawls, of surpassing feebleness, mental and bodily; who was always taking physic without any effect, and who, whenever she showed a symptom of coming to life, was invariably stunned by some weighty piece of fact tumbling on her; Mrs. Gradgrind hoped it was a dry ditch?

"No! As wet as a sop. A foot of water in it," said Mr. Bounderby.

"Enough to give a baby cold," Mrs. Gradgrind considered.

"Cold? I was born with inflammation of the lungs, and of every thing else, I believe, that was capable of inflammation," returned Mr. Bounderby. "For years, ma'am, I was one of the most miserable little wretches ever seen. I was so sickly, that I was always moaning and groaning. I was so ragged and dirty, that you wouldn't have touched me with a pair of tongs."

Mrs. Gradgrind faintly looked at the tongs, as the most appropriate thing her imbecility could think of doing.

"How I fought through it, *I* don't know," said Bounderby. "I was determined, I suppose. I have been a determined character in later life, and I suppose I was then. Here I am, Mrs. Gradgrind, any how, and nobody to thank for my being here but myself."

Mrs. Gradgrind meekly and weakly hoped that his mother—

"*My* mother? Bolted, ma'am!" said Bounderby.

Mrs. Gradgrind, stunned as usual, collapsed and gave it up.

"My mother left me to my grandmother," said Bounderby; "and, according to the best of my remembrance, my grandmother was the wickedest and the worst old woman that ever lived. If I got a little pair of shoes by any chance, she would take 'em off and sell 'em for drink. Why, I have known that grandmother of mine lie in her bed and drink her four-teen glasses of liquor before breakfast!"

Mrs. Gradgrind, weakly smiling, and giving no other sign of vitality, looked (as she always did) like an indifferently executed transparency of a small female figure, without enough light behind it.

"She kept a chandler's shop," pursued Bounderby, "and kept me in an egg-box. That was the cot of *my* infancy; an old egg-box. As soon as I was big enough to run away, of course I ran away. Then I became a young vagabond; and instead of one old woman knocking me about and starving me, every body of all ages knocked me about and starved me. They were right; they had no business to do any thing else. I was a nuisance, an incumbrance, and a pest. I know that very well."

His pride in having at any time of his life achieved such a great social distinction as to be a nuisance, an incumbrance, and a pest, was only to be satisfied by three sonorous repetitions of the boast.

"I was to pull through it, I suppose, Mrs. Gradgrind. Whether I was to do it or not, ma'am, I did it. I pulled through it, though nobody threw me out a rope. Vagabond, errand-boy, vagabond, laborer, porter, clerk, chief manager, small partner, Josiah Bounderby of Coketown. Those are the antecedents, and the culmination. Josiah Bounderby of Coketown learnt his letters from the outsides of the shops, Mrs. Gradgrind, and was first able to tell the time upon a dial-plate, from studying the steeple clock of St. Giles's Church, London, under the direction of a drunken cripple, who was a convicted thief and an incorrigible vagrant. Tell Josiah Bounderby, of Coketown of your district schools, and your model schools, and your training schools, and your whole kettle-of-fish of schools; and

Josiah Bounderby of Coketown tells you plainly, all right, all correct—he hadn't such advantages—but let us have hard-headed, solid-fisted people—the education that made him won't do for every body, he knows well—such and such his education was, however, and you may force him to swallow boiling fat, but you shall never force him to suppress the facts of his life."

Being heated when he arrived at this climax, Josiah Bounderby of Coketown stopped. He stopped just as his eminently practical friend, still accompanied by the two young culprits, entered the room. His eminently practical friend, on seeing him, stopped also, and gave Louisa a reproachful look that plainly said, "Behold your Bounderby!"

"Well!" blustered Mr. Bounderby, "what's the matter? What is young Thomas in the dumps about?"

He spoke of young Thomas, but he looked at Louisa.

"We were peeping at the circus," muttered Louisa haughtily, without lifting up her eyes, "and Father caught us."

"And Mrs. Gradgrind," said her husband in a lofty manner, "I should as soon have expected to find my children reading poetry."

"Dear me," whimpered Mrs. Gradgrind. "How can you, Louisa and Thomas! I wonder at you. I declare you're enough to make one regret ever having had a family at all. I have a great mind to say I wish I hadn't. *Then* what would you have done, I should like to know?"

Mr. Gradgrind did not seem favorably impressed by these cogent remarks. He frowned impatiently.

"As if, with my head in its present throbbing state, you couldn't go and look at the shells and minerals and things provided for you, instead of circuses!" said Mrs. Gradgrind. "You know, as well as I do, no young people have circus masters, or keep circuses in cabinets, or attend lectures about circuses. What can you possibly want to know of circuses then? I am sure you have enough to do, if that's what you want. With my head in its present state, I couldn't remember the mere names of half the facts you have got to attend to."

"That's the reason!" pouted Louisa.

"Don't tell me that's the reason, because it can be nothing of the sort," said Mrs. Gradgrind. "Go and be somethingological directly." Mrs. Gradgrind was not a scientific character, and usually dismissed her children to their studies with this general injunction to choose their pursuits.

In truth, Mrs. Gradgrind's stock of facts in general was woefully defective, but Mr. Gradgrind in raising her to her high matrimonial position had been influenced by two reasons. Firstly, she was most satisfactory as a question of figures; and, secondly, she had "no nonsense" about her. By nonsense he meant fancy; and truly it is probable she was as free from any alloy of that nature, as any human being not arrived at the perfection of an absolute idiot, ever was.

The simple circumstance of being left alone with her husband and Mr. Bounderby, was sufficient to stun this admirable lady again, without collision between herself and any other fact. So, she once more died away, and nobody minded her.

"Bounderby," said Mr. Gradgrind, drawing a chair to the fireside, "you are always so interested in my young people—particularly in Louisa—

that I make no apology for saying to you, I am very much vexed by this discovery. I have systematically devoted myself (as you know) to the education of the reason of my family. The reason is (as you know) the only faculty to which education should be addessed. And yet, Bounderby, it would appear from this unexpected circumstance of to-day, though in itself a trifling one, as if something had crept into Thomas's and Louisa's minds which is—or rather, which is not—I don't know that I can express myself better than by saying—which has never been intended to be developed, and in which their reason has no part."

"There certainly is no reason in looking with interest at a parcel of vagabonds," returned Bounderby. "When I was a vagabond myself, nobody looked with any interest at *me*; I know that."

"Then comes the question," said the eminently practical father, with his eyes on the fire, "in what has this vulgar curiosity its rise?"

"I'll tell you in what. In idle imagination."

"I hope not," said the eminently practical; "I confess, however, that the misgiving *has* crossed me on my way home."

"In idle imagination, Gradgrind," repeated Bounderby. "A very bad thing for any body, but a cursed bad thing for a girl like Louisa. I should ask Mrs. Gradgrind's pardon for strong expressions, but that she knows very well I am not a refined character. Whoever expects refinement in *me* will be disappointed. I hadn't a refined bringing up."

"Whether," said Gradgrind, pondering with his hands in his pockets, and his cavernous eyes on the fire, "whether any instructor or servant can have suggested any thing? Whether Louisa or Thomas can have been reading any thing? Whether, in spite of all precautions, any idle story-book can have got into the house? Because, in minds that have been practically formed by rule and line, from the cradle upwards, this is so curious, so incomprehensible."

"Stop a bit!" cried Bounderby, who all this time had been standing, as before, on the hearth, bursting at the very furniture of the room with explosive humility. "You have one of those strollers' children in the school."

"Cecilia Jupe, by name," said Mr. Gradgrind, with something of a stricken look at his friend.

"Now, stop a bit!" cried Bounderby again. "How did she come there?"

"Why, the fact is, I saw the girl myself for the first time, only just now. She specially applied here at the house to be admitted, as not regularly belonging to our town, and—yes, you are right, Bounderby, you are right."

"Now, stop a bit!" cried Bounderby, once more. "Louisa saw her when she came?"

"Louisa certainly did see her, for she mentioned the application to me. But Louisa saw her, I have no doubt, in Mrs. Gradgrind's presence."

"Pray, Mrs. Gradgrind," said Bounderby, "what passed?"

"Oh, my poor health!" returned Mrs. Gradgrind. "The girl wanted to come to the school, and Mr. Gradgrind wanted girls to come to the school, and Louisa and Thomas both said that the girl wanted to come, and that Mr. Gradgrind wanted girls to come, and how was it possible to contradict them when such was the fact!"

"Now I tell you what, Gradgrind!" said Mr. Bounderby. "Turn this girl to the right about, and there's an end of it."

"I am much of your opinion."

"Do it at once," said Bounderby, "has always been my motto from a child. When I thought I would run away from my egg-box and my grandmother, I did it at once. Do you the same. Do this at once!"

"Are you walking?" asked his friend. "I have the father's address. Perhaps you would not mind walking to town with me?"

"Not the least in the world," said Mr. Bounderby, "as long as you do it at once!"

So Mr. Bounderby threw on his hat—he always threw it on, as expressing a man who had been far too busily employed in making himself, to acquire any fashion of wearing his hat—and with his hands in his pockets sauntered out into the hall. "I never wear gloves," it was his custom to say. "I didn't climb up the ladder in *them.* Shouldn't be so high up if I had."

Being left to saunter in the hall a minute or two while Mr. Gradgrind went up-stairs for the address, he opened the door of the children's study and looked into that serene floor-clothed apartment, which, notwithstanding its bookcases and its cabinets and its variety of learned and philosophical appliances, had much of the genial aspect of a room devoted to hair-cutting. Louisa languidly leaned upon the window looking out, without looking at any-thing, while young Thomas stood sniffing revengefully at the fire. Adam Smith and Malthus, two younger Gradgrinds, were out at lecture in custody; and little Jane, after manufacturing a good deal of moist pipe-clay on her face with slate-pencil and tears, had fallen asleep over vulgar fractions.

"It's all right now, Louisa; it's all right, young Thomas," said Mr. Bounderby; "you won't do so any more. I'll answer for its being all over with father. Well, Louisa, that's worth a kiss, isn't it?"

"You can take one, Mr. Bounderby," returned Louisa, when she had coldly paused, and slowly walked across the room, and ungraciously raised her cheek towards him, with her face turned away.

"Always my pet; ain't you, Louisa?" said Mr. Bounderby. "Good-bye, Lousia!"

He went his way, but she stood on the same spot, rubbing the cheek he had kissed, with her handkerchief, until it was burning red. She was still doing this five minutes afterward.

"What are you about, Loo?" her brother sulkily remonstrated. "You'll rub a hole in your face."

"You may cut the piece out with your penknife if you like, Tom. I wouldn't cry!"

Chapter V

THE KEY-NOTE

COKETOWN, to which Messrs. Bounderby and Gradgrind now walked, was a triumph of fact; it had no greater taint of fancy in it than Mrs.

Gradgrind herself. Let us strike the key-note, Coketown, before pursuing our tune.

It was a town of red brick, or of brick that would have been red if the smoke and ashes had allowed it; but, as matters stood, it was a town of unnatural red and black, like the painted face of a savage. It was a town of machinery and tall chimneys, out of which interminable serpents of smoke trailed themselves forever and ever, and never got uncoiled. It had a black canal in it, and a river that ran purple with ill-smelling dye, and vast piles of building full of windows where there was a rattling and a trembling all day long, and where the piston of the steam-engine worked monotonously up and down, like the head of an elephant in a state of melancholy madness. It contained several large streets all very like one another, and many small streets still more like one another, inhabited by people equally like one another, who all went in and out at the same hours, with the same sound upon the same pavements, to do the same work, and to whom every day was the same as yesterday and to-morrow, and every year the counterpart of the last and the next.

These attributes of Coketown were in the main inseparable from the work by which it was sustained; against them were to be set off, comforts of life which found their way all over the world, and elegancies of life which made we will not ask how much of the fine lady, who could scarcely bear to hear the place mentioned. The rest of its features were voluntary, and they were these.

You saw nothing in Coketown but what was severely workful. If the members of a religious persuasion built a chapel there—as the members of eighteen religious persuasions had done—they made it a pious warehouse, of red brick, with sometimes (but this only in highly ornamented examples) a bell in a birdcage on the top of it. The solitary exception was the New Church; a stuccoed edifice with a square steeple over the door, terminating in four short pinnacles like florid wooden legs. All the public inscriptions in the town were painted alike, in severe characters of black and white. The jail might have been the infirmary, the infirmary might have been the jail, the town-hall might have been either, or both, or any thing else, for any thing that appeared to the contrary in the graces of their construction. Fact, fact, fact, every where in the material aspect of the town; fact, fact, fact, every where in the immaterial. The M'Choakumchild school was all fact, and the school of design was all fact, and the relations between master and man were all fact, and every thing was fact between the lying-in hospital and the cemetery, and what you couldn't state in figures, or show to be purchasable in the cheapest market and saleable in the dearest, was not, and never should be, world without end, Amen.

A town so sacred to fact, and so triumphant in its assertion, of course got on well? Why no, not quite well. No? Dear me!

No. Coketown did not come out of its own furnaces, in all respects like gold that had stood the fire. First, the perplexing mystery of the place was, Who belonged to the eighteen denominations? Because, whoever did, the laboring people did not. It was very strange to walk through the streets on a Sunday morning, and note how few of *them* the barbarous jangling of bells that was driving the sick and nervous mad, called away from their own quarter, from their own close rooms, from the corners of their own streets, where they lounged listlessly, gazing at all the churc-hand chapel-going, as at a thing with which they had no manner of concern. Nor was it merely the stranger who noticed this, because there was a native organization in Coketown itself, whose members were to be heard of in the House of Commons every session, indignantly petitioning for acts of parliament that should make these people religious by main force. Then, came the Teetotal Society, who complained that these same people *would* get drunk, and showed in tabular statements that they did get drunk, and proved at tea-parties that no inducement, human or Divine (except a medal), would induce them to forgo their custom of getting drunk. Then, came the chemist and druggist, with other tabular statements, showing that when they didn't get drunk, they took opium. Then, came the experienced chaplain of the jail, with more tabular statements, outdoing all the previous tabular statements, and showing that the same people *would* resort to low haunts, hidden from the public eye, where they heard low singing and saw low dancing, and mayhap joined in it; and where A. B., aged twenty-four next birthday, and committed for eighteen months' solitary, had himself said (not that he had ever shown himself particularly worthy of belief) his ruin began, as he was perfectly sure and confident that otherwise he would have been a tip-top moral specimen. Then, came Mr. Gradgrind and Mr. Bounderby, the two gentlemen at this present moment walking through Coketown, and both eminently practical, who could, on occasion, furnish more tabular statements derived from their own personal experience, and illustrated by cases they had known and seen, from which it clearly appeared—in short it was the only clear thing in the case—that these same people were a bad lot altogether, gentlemen; that do what you would for them they were never thankful for it, gentlemen; that they were restless, gentlemen; that they never knew what they wanted; that they lived upon the best, and bought fresh butter, and insisted on Mocha coffee, and rejected all but prime parts of meat, and yet were eternally dissatisfied and unmanageable. In short it was the moral of the old nursery fable:

> There was an old woman, and what do you think?
> She lived upon nothing but victuals and drink;
> Victuals and drink were the whole of her diet,
> And yet this old woman would NEVER be quiet.

Is it possible, I wonder, that there was any analogy between the case of the Coketown population and the case of the little Gradgrinds? Surely, none of us in our sober senses and acquainted with figures, are to be told at this time of day that one of the foremost elements in the existence of the Coketown working people had been for scores of years deliberately set at nought? That there was any Fancy in them demanding to be brought into healthy existence, instead of struggling on in convulsions?

That exactly in the ratio as they worked long and monotonously, the craving grew within them for some physical relief—some relaxation, encouraging good humor and good spirits, and giving them a vent—some recognized holiday, though it were but for an honest dance to a stirring band of music—some occasional light pie in which even M'Choakumchild had no finger—which craving must and would be satisfied aright, or must and would inevitably go wrong, until the laws of the Creation were repealed?

"This man lives at Pod's End, and I don't quite know Pod's End," said Mr. Gradgrind. "Which is it, Bounderby?"

Mr. Bounderby knew it was somewhere down town, but knew no more respecting it. So they stopped for a moment, looking about.

Almost as they did so, there came running round the corner of the street at a quick pace and with a frightened look, a girl whom Mr. Gradgrind recognized. "Halloo!" said he. "Stop! Where are you going! Stop!" Girl number twenty stopped then, palpitating, and made him a courtesy.

"Why are you tearing about the streets," said Mr. Gradgrind, "in this improper manner?"

"I was—I was run after, sir," the girl panted, "and I wanted to get away."

"Run after?" repeated Mr. Gradgrind. "Who would run after *you?*"

The question was unexpectedly and suddenly answered for her, by the colorless boy, Bitzer, who came round the corner with such blind speed and so littie anticipating a stoppage on the pavement, that he brought himself up against Mr. Gradgrind's waistcoat, and rebounded into the road.

"What do you mean, boy?" said Mr. Gradgrind. "What are you doing? How dare you dash against—every body—in this manner?"

Bitzer picked up his cap, which the concussion had knocked off, and backing, and knuckling his forehead, pleaded that it was an accident.

"Was this boy running after you, Jupe?" asked Mr. Gradgrind.

"Yes, sir," said the girl reluctantly.

"No, I wasn't, sir!" cried Bitzer. "Not till she ran away from me. But the horse-riders never mind what they say, sir; they're famous for it. You know the horse-riders are famous for never minding what they say," addressing Sissy. "It's as well known in the town as—please, sir, as the multiplication table isn't known to the horse-riders." Bitzer tried Mr. Bounderby with this.

"He frightened me so," said the girl, "with his cruel faces!"

"Oh!" cried Bitzer. "Oh! An't you one of the rest! An't you a horse-rider! I never looked at her, sir. I asked her if she would know how to define a horse to-morrow, and offered to tell her again, and she ran away, and I ran after her, sir, that she might know how to answer when she was asked. You wouldn't have thought of saying such mischief if you hadn't been a horse-rider!"

"Her calling seems to be pretty well known among 'em," observed Mr. Bounderby. "You'd have had the whole school peeping in a row, in a week."

"Truly, I think so," returned his friend. "Bitzer, turn you about and take yourself home. Jupe, stay here a moment. Let me hear of your running in this manner any more, boy, and you will hear of me through the master of the school. You understand what I mean. Go along."

The boy stopped in his rapid blinking, knuckled his forehead again, glanced at Sissy, turned about, and retreated.

"Now, girl," said Mr. Gradgrind, "take this gentleman and me to your father's; we are going there. What have you got in that bottle you are carrying?"

"Gin," said Mr. Bounderby.

"Dear, no, sir! It's the nine oils."

"The what?" cried Mr. Bounderby.

"The nine oils, sir. To rub father with."

"Then," said Mr. Bounderby, with a loud, short laugh, "What the devil do you rub your father with nine oils for?"

"It's what our people always use, sir, when they get any hurts in the ring," replied the girl, looking over her shoulder, to assure herself that her pursuer was gone. "They bruise themselves very bad sometimes."

"Serve 'em right," said Mr. Bounderby, "for being idle." She glanced up at his face, with mingled astonishment and dread.

"By George!" said Mr. Bounderby, "when I was four or five years younger than you, I had worse bruises upon me than ten oils, twenty oils, forty oils, would have rubbed off. I didn't get 'em by posture-making, but by being banged about. There was no rope-dancing for me; I danced on the bare ground and was larruped with the rope."

Mr. Gradgrind, though hard enough, was by no means so rough a man as Mr. Bounderby. His character was not unkind, all things considered; it might have been a very kind one indeed if he had only made some round mistake in the arithmatic that balanced it, years ago. He said, in what he meant for a re-assuring tone, as they turned down a narrow road, "And this is Pod's End; is it, Jupe?"

"This is it, sir, and—if you wouldn't mind, sir—this is the house."

She stopped, at twilight, at the door of a mean little public house, with dim red lights in it. As haggard and as shabby, as if, for want of custom, it had itself taken to drinking, and had gone the way all drunkards go, and was very near the end of it.

"It's only crossing the bar, sir, and up the stairs, if you would'nt mind, and waiting there for a moment till I get a candle. If you should hear a dog, sir, it's only Merrylegs, and he only barks."

"Merrylegs and nine oils, eh!" said Mr. Bounderby, entering last with his metallic laugh. "Pretty well this, for a self-made man!"

Chapter VI

SLEARY'S HORSEMANSHIP

THE name of the public house was the Pegasus's Arms. The Pegasus's legs might have been more to the purpose; but, underneath the winged horse upon the sign-board, The Pegasus's Arms was inscribed in Roman letters. Beneath that inscription again, in a flowing scroll, the painter had touched off the lines:

Good malt makes good beer,
Walk in, and they'll draw it here,
Good wine makes good brandy,
Give us a call, and you'll find it handy.

Framed and glazed upon the wall behind the dingy little bar, was another Pegasus—a theatrical one—with real gauze let in for his wings, golden stars stuck on all over him, and his ethereal harness made of red silk.

As it had grown too dusky without, to see the sign, and as it had not grown light enough within to see the picture, Mr. Gradgrind and Mr. Bounderby received no offence from these idealities. They followed the girl up some steep corner-stairs without meeting any one, and stopped in the dark while she went on for a candle. They expected every moment to hear Merrylegs give tongue, but the highly-trained performing dog had not barked when the girl and the candle appeared together.

"Father is not in our room, sir," she said, with a face of great surprise. "If you wouldn't mind walking in, I'll find him directly."

They walked in; and Sissy, having set two chairs for them, sped away with a quick light step. It was a mean, shabbily-furnished room, with a bed in it. The white nightcap, embellished with two peacock's feathers and a pigtail bolt upright, in which Signor Jupe had that very afternoon enlivened the varied performances with his chaste Shakespearean quips and retorts, hung upon a nail; but no other portion of his wardrobe, or other token of himself or his pursuits, was to be seen any where. As to Merrylegs, that respectable ancestor of the highly-trained animal who went aboard the ark, might have been accidentally shut out of it, for any sign of a dog that was manifest to eye or ear in the Pegasus's Arms.

They heard the doors of rooms above, opening and shutting as Sissy went from one to another in quest of her father; and presently they heard voices expressing surprise. She came bounding down again in a great hurry, opened a battered and mangey old hair-trunk, found it empty, and looked round with her hands clasped and her face full of terror.

"Father must have gone down to the Booth, sir. I don't know why he should go there, but he must be there; I'll bring him in a minute!" She was gone directly, without her bonnet; with her long, dark, childish hair streaming behind her.

"What does she mean!" said Mr. Gradgrind. "Back in a minute? It's more than a mile off."

Before Mr. Bounderby could reply, a young man appeared at the door, and introducing himself with the words, "By your leaves, gentlemen!" walked in with his hands in his pockets. His face, close-shaven, thin, and sallow, was shaded by a great quantity of dark hair brushed into a roll all round his head, and parted up the centre. His legs were very robust, but shorter than legs of good proportions should have been. His chest and back were as much too broad, as his legs were too short. He was dressed in a Newmarket coat and tight-fitting trowsers; wore a shawl round his neck; smelt of lamp-oil, straw, orange-peel, horses' provender, and sawdust; and looked a most remarkable sort of Centaur, compounded of the stable and the play-house. Where the one began, and the other ended, nobody could have told with any precision. This gentleman was mentioned in the bills of the day as Mr. E. W. B. Childers, so justly celebrated for his daring vaulting act as the Wild Huntsman of the North American Prairies; in which popular performance, a diminutive boy with an old face, who now accompanied him, assisted as his infant son: being carried upside down over his father's shoulder, by one foot, and held by the crown of his head, heels upward, in the palm of his father's hand, according to the violent paternal manner in which wild huntsmen may be observed to fondle their offspring. Made up with curls, wreaths, wings, white bismuth, and carmine, this hopeful young person soared into so pleasing a Cupid as to constitute the chief delight of the maternal part of the spectators; but, in private, where his characteristics were a precocious cutaway coat and an extremely gruff voice, he became of the Turf, turfy.

"By your leaves, gentlemen," said Mr. E. W. B. Childers, glancing round the room. "It was you, I believe, that were wishing to see Jupe?"

"It was," said Mr. Gradgrind. "His daughter has gone to fetch him, but I can't wait; therefore, if you please, I will leave a message for him with you."

"You see, my friend," Mr. Bounderby put in, "we are the kind of people who know the value of time, and you are the kind of people who don't know the value of time."

"I have not," retorted Mr. Childers, after surveying him from head to foot, "the honor of knowing *you;*—but if you mean that you can make more money of your time than I can of mine, I should judge from your appearance, that you are about right."

"And when you have made it, you can keep it too, I should think," said Cupid.

"Kidderminster, stow that!" said Mr. Childers (Master Kidderminster was Cupid's mortal name.)

"What does he come here cheeking us for, then?" cried Master Kidderminster, showing a very irascible temperament. "If you want to cheek us, pay your ochre at the doors and take it out."

"Kidderminster," said Mr. Childers, raising his voice, "stow that!—Sir," to Mr. Gradgrind, "I was addressing myself to you. You may or you may not be aware (for perhaps you have not been much in the audience), that Jupe has missed his tip very often, lately."

"Has—what has he missed?" asked Mr. Gradgrind, glancing at the potent Bounderby for assistance.

"Missed his tip."

"Offered at the Garters four times last night, and never done 'em once," said Master Kidderminster. "Missed his tip at the banners, too, and was loose in his ponging."

"Didn't do what he ought to do. Was short in his leaps and bad in his tumbling," Mr. Childers interpreted.

"Oh!" said Mr. Gradgrind, "that is tip, is it?"

"In a general way that's missing his tip," Mr. E. W. B. Childers answered.

"Nine-oils, Merrylegs, missing tips, garters, banners, and Ponging, eh!" ejaculated Bounderby with his laugh of laughs. "Queer sort of company, too, for a man who has raised himself."

"Lower yourself, then," retorted Cupid. "Oh Lord! If you've raised yourself so high as all that comes to, let yourself down a bit."

"This is a very obtrusive lad!" said Mr. Gradgrind, turning, and knitting his brows on him.

"We'd have have had a young gentleman to meet you, if we had known you were coming," retorted Master Kidderminster, nothing abashed. "It's a pity you don't have a bespeak, being so particular. You're on the Tight-Jeff, ain't you?"

"What does this unmannerly boy mean," asked Mr. Gradgrind, eying him in a sort of desperation, "by Tight-Jeff?"

"There! Get out, get out!" said Mr. Childers, thrusting his young friend from the room, rather in the prairie manner. "Tight-Jeff or Slack-Jeff, it don't much signify; it's only tight-rope and slack-rope. You were going to give me a message for Jupe?"

"Yes, I was."

"Then," continued Mr. Childers, quickly, "my opinion is, he will never receive it. Do you know much of him?"

"I never saw the man in my life."

"I doubt if you ever *will* see him now. It's pretty plain to me, he is off."

"Do you mean that he has deserted his daughter?"

"Ay! I mean," said Mr. Childers, with a nod, "that he has cut. He was goosed last night, he was goosed the night before last, he was goosed to-day. He has lately got in the way of being always goosed, and he can't stand it."

"Why has he been—so very much—Goosed?" asked Mr. Gradgrind, forcing the word out of himself, with great solemnity and reluctance.

"His joints are turning stiff, and he is getting used up," said Childers. "He has his points as a Cackler still, but he can't get a living out of *them.*"

"A Cackler!" Bounderby repeated. "Here we go again!"

"A speaker, if the gentleman likes it better," said Mr. E. W. B. Childers, superciliously throwing the interpretation over his shoulder, and accompanying it with a shake of his long hair—which all shook at once. "Now, it's a remarkable fact, sir, that it cut that man deeper, to know that his daughter knew of his being goosed, than to go through with it."

"Good!" interrupted Mr. Bounderby. "This is good, Gradgrind! A man so fond of his daughter, that he runs away from her! This is devilish good! Ha! ha! Now, I'll tell you what, young man. I haven't always occupied my present station in life. I know what these things are. You may be astonished to hear it, but my mother ran away from *me.*"

E. W. B. Childers replied pointedly, that he was not at all astonished to hear it.

"Very well," said Bounderby. "I was born in a ditch, and my mother ran away from me. Do I excuse her for it? No. Have I ever excused her for it? Not I. What do I call her for it? I call her probably the very worst woman that ever lived in the world, except my drunken grandmother.

There's no family pride about me, there's no imaginative sentimental humbug about me. I call a spade a spade; and I call the mother of Josiah Bounderby of Coketown, without any fear or any favor, what I should call her if she had been the mother of Dick Jones of Wapping. So, with this man. He is a runaway rogue and a vagabond, that's what he is, in English."

"It's all the same to me what he is or what he is not, whether in English or whether in French," retorted Mr. E. W. B. Childers, facing about. "I am telling your friend what's the fact; if you don't like to hear it, you can avail yourself of the open air. You give it mouth enough, you do; but give it mouth in your own building at least," remonstrated E. W. B. with stern irony. "Don't give it mouth in this building, till you're called upon. You have got some building of your own, I dare say now?"

"Perhaps so," replied Mr. Bounderby, rattling his money and laughing.

"Then give it mouth in your own building, will you, if you please?" said Childers. "Because this isn't a strong building, and too much of you might bring it down!"

Eying Mr. Bounderby from head to foot again, he turned from him, as from a man finally disposed of, to Mr. Gradgrind.

"Jupe sent his daughter out on an errand not an hour ago, and then was seen to slip out himself, with his hat over his eyes and a bundle tied up in a handkerchief under his arm. She will never believe it of him; but he has cut away and left her."

"Pray," said Mr. Gradgrind, "why will she never believe it of him?"

"Because those two were one. Because they were never asunder. Because, up to this time, he seemed to dote upon her," said Childers, taking a step or two to look into the empty trunk. Both Mr. Childers and Master Kidderminster walked in a curious manner; with their legs wider apart than the general run of men, and with a very knowing assumption of being stiff in the knees. This walk was common to all the male members of Sleary's company, and was understood to express that they were always on horseback.

"Poor Sissy! He had better have apprenticed her," said Childers, giving his hair another shake, as he looked up from the empty box. "Now, he leaves her without anything to take to."

"It is creditable to you who have never been apprenticed, to express that opinion," returned Mr. Gradgrind, approvingly.

"*I* never apprenticed? I was apprenticed when I was seven year old."

"Oh! Indeed?" said Mr. Gradgrind, rather resentfully, as having been defrauded of his good opinion. "I was not aware of its being the custom to apprentice young persons to—"

"Idleness," Mr. Bounderby put in with a loud laugh. "No, by the Lord Harry! Nor I!"

"Her father always had it in his head," resumed Childers, feigning unconsciousness of Mr. Bounderby's existence, "that she was to be taught the deuce-and-all of education. How it got into his head, I can't say; I can only say that it never got out. He has been picking up a bit of reading for her, here—and a bit of writing for her, there—and a bit of ciphering for her, somewhere else—these seven years."

Mr. E. W. B. Childers took one of his hands out of his pockets, stroked his face and chin, and looked, with a good deal of doubt and a little hope, at Mr. Gradgrind. From the first he had sought to conciliate that gentleman, for the sake of the deserted girl.

"When Sissy got into the school here," he pursued, "her father was as pleased as Punch. I couldn't altogether make out why, myself, as we were not stationary here, being but comers and goers any where. I suppose, however, he had this move in his mind—he was always half cracked—and then considered her provided for. If you should happen to have looked in to-night, for the purpose of telling him that you were going to do her any little service," said Mr. Childers, stroking his face again, and repeating his look, "it would be very fortunate and well timed; *very* fortunate and well timed."

"On the contrary," returned Mr. Gradgrind. "I came to tell him that her connections made her not an object for the school, and that she must not attend any more. Still, if her father really has left her, without any connivance on her part—Bounderby, let me have a word with you."

Upon this, Mr. Childers politely betook himself, with his equestrian walk, to the landing outside the door, and there stood stroking his face and softly whistling. While thus engaged, he overheard such phrases in Mr. Bounderby's voice, as "No. *I* say no. I advise you not. I say by no means." While, from Mr. Gradgrind, he heard in his much lower tone the words, "But even as an example to Louisa, of what this pursuit which has been the subject of a vulgar curiosity, leads to and ends in. Think of it, Bounderby, in that point of view."

Meanwhile, the various members of Sleary's company gradually gathered together from the upper regions, where they were quartered, and, from standing about, talking in low voices to one another and to Mr. Childers, gradually insinuated themselves and him into the room. There were two or three handsome young women among them, with their two or three husbands, and their two or three mothers, and their eight or nine little children, who did the fairy business when required. The father of one of the families was in the habit of balancing the father of another of the families on the top of a great pole; the father of a third family often made a pyramid of both those fathers, with Master Kidderminister for the apex, and himself for the base; all the fathers could dance upon rolling casks, stand upon bottles, catch knives and balls, twirl hand-basins, ride upon any thing, jump over every thing, and stick at nothing. All the mothers could (and did) dance, upon the slack wire and the tight rope, and perform rapid acts on bare-backed steeds; none of them were at all particular in respect of showing their legs; and one of them, alone in a Greek chariot, drove six in hand into every town they came to. They all assumed to be mighty rakish and knowing, they were not very tidy in their private dresses, they were not at all orderly in their domestic arrangements, and the combined literature of the whole company would have produced but a poor letter on any subject. Yet there was a remarkable gentleness and childishness about these people, a special inaptitude for any kind of sharp practice, and an untiring readiness to help and pity one another, deserving, often, of as much respect, and always of as much generous construction, as the everyday virtues of any class of people in the world.

Last of all appeared Mr. Sleary: a stout man as already mentioned, with one fixed eye and one loose eye, a voice (if it can be called so) like the efforts of a broken old pair of bellows, a flabby surface, and a muddled head which was never sober and never drunk.

"Thquire!" said Mr. Sleary, who was troubled with asthma, and whose breath came far too thick and heavy for the letter s, "your thervant! Thith ith a bad piethe of bithnith, thith ith. You've heard of my Clown and hith dog being thuppothed to have morrithed?"

He addressed Mr. Gradgrind, who answered "Yes."

"Well, Thquire," he returned, taking off his hat, and rubbing the lining with his pocket handkerchief, which he kept inside for the purpose. "Ith it your intenthionth to do any thing for the poor girl, Thquire?"

"I shall have something to propose to her when she comes back," said Mr. Gradgrind.

"Glad to hear it, Thquire. Not that I want to get rid of the child, any more than I want to thtand in her way. I'm willing to take her prentith, though at her age ith late. My voithe ith a little huthky, Thquire, and not eathy heard by them ath don't know me; but if you'd been chilled and heated, heated and chilled, chilled and heated, in the ring when you wath young, ath often ath I have been, *your* voithe wouldn't have lathted out, Thquire, no more than mine."

"I dare say not," said Mr. Gradgrind.

"What thall it be, Thquire, while you wait? Thall it be Therry? Give it a name, Thquire!" said Mr. Sleary, with hospitable ease.

"Nothing for me, I thank you," said Mr. Gradgrind.

"Don't thay nothing, Thquire. What doth your friend thay? If you haven't took your feed yet, have a glath of bitterth."

Here his daughter Josephine—a pretty fair-haired girl of eighteen, who had been tied on a horse at two years old, and had made a will at twelve, which she always carried about with her, expressive of her dying desire to be drawn to the grave by the two piebald ponies—cried "Father, hush! she has come back!" Then came Sissy Jupe, running into the room as she had run out of it. And when she saw them all assembled, and saw their looks, and saw no father there, she broke into a most deplorable cry, and took refuge on the bosom of the most accomplished tight-rope lady (herself in the family way), who knelt down to the floor to nurse her, and to weep over her.

"Ith an infernal thame, upon my thoul it ith," said Sleary.

"O my dear father, my good kind father, where are you gone? You are gone to try to do me some good, I know! You are gone away for my sake, I am sure. And how miserable and helpless you will be without me, poor, poor father, until you come back!" It was so pathetic to hear her saying many things of this kind, with her face turned upward, and her arms stretched out as if she were trying to stop his departing shadow and embrace it, that no one spoke a word until Mr. Bounderby (growing impatient) took the case in hand.

"Now, good people all," said he, "this is wanton waste of time. Let the girl understand the fact. Let her take it from me, if you like, who have been run away from, myself. Here, what's your name! Your father has absconded—deserted you—and you mustn't expect to see him again as long as you live."

They cared so little for plain Fact, these people, and were in that advanced state of degeneracy on the subject, that instead of being impressed by the speaker's strong common sense, they took it in extraordinary dudgeon. The men muttered "Shame!" and the women "Brute!" and Sleary, in some haste, communicated the following hint, apart to Mr. Bounderby.

"I tell you what, Thquire. To thpeak plain to you, my opinion ith that you had better cut it thort and drop it. They're a very good-natur'd people, my people, but they're accuthtomed to be quick in their movementh; and if you don't act upon my advithe, I'm damned if I don't believe they'll pith you out o' winder."

Mr. Bounderby being restrained by this mild suggestion, Mr. Gradgrind found an opening for his eminently practical exposition of the subject.

"It is of no moment," said he, "whether this person is to be expected back at any time, or the contrary. He is gone away, and there is no present expectation of his return. That, I believe, is agreed on all hands."

"Thath agreed, Thquire. Thtick to that!" From Sleary.

"Well then. I, who came here to inform the father of the poor girl, Jupe, that she could not be received at the school any more in consequence of there being practical objections, into which I need not enter, to the reception there of the children of persons so employed, am prepared in these altered circumstances to make a proposal. I am willing to take charge of you, Jupe, and to educate you, and provide for you. The only condition (over and above your good behaviour) I make is, that you decide now, at once, whether to accompany me or remain here. Also, that if you accompany me now, it is understood that you communicate no more with any of your friends, who are here present. These observations comprise the whole of the case."

"At the thame time," said Sleary, "I mutht put in my word, Thquire, tho that both thides of the banner may be equally theen. If you like, Thethilia, to be prentitht, you know the natur of the work and you know your companionth. Emma Gordon, in whothe lap you're a-lyin' at prethent, would be a mother to you, and Joth'phine would be a thithter to you. I don't pretend to be of the angel breed mythelf, and I don't thay but what, when you mith'd your tip, you'd find me cut up rough, and thwear a oath or two at you. But what I thay, Thquire, ith, that good- tempered or bad-tempered, I never did a horthe a injury yet, no more than thwearing at him went, and that I don't expect I thall begin otherwithe at my time of life, with a rider. I never wath muth of a Cackler, Thquire, and I have thed my thay."

The latter part of this speech was addressed to Mr. Gradgrind, who received it with a grave inclination of his head, and then remarked.

"The only observation I will make to you, Jupe, in the way of influencing your decision, is, that it is highly desirable to have a sound practical education, and that even your father himself (from what I understand) appears, on your behalf, to have known and felt that much."

The last words had a visible effect upon her. She stopped in her wild crying, a little detached herself from Emma Gordon, and turned her face full upon her patron. The whole company perceived the force of the change, and drew a long breath together, that plainly said, "She will go!"

"Be sure you know your own mind, Jupe," Mr. Gradgrind cautioned her; "I say no more. Be sure you know your own mind!"

"When father comes back," cried the girl, bursting into tears again after a minute's silence, "how will he ever find me if I go away?"

"You may be quite at ease," said Mr. Gradgrind, calmly; he worked out the whole matter like a sum; "you may be quite at ease, Jupe, on that score. In such a case, your father, I apprehend, must find out Mr.—"

"Thleary. Thath my name, Thquire. Not athamed of it. Known all over England, and alwayth paythe ith way."

"Must find out Mr. Sleary, who would then let him know where you went. I should have no power of keeping you against his wish, and he would have no difficulty at any time in finding Mr. Thomas Gradgrind of Coketown. I am well known."

"Well known," assented Mr. Sleary, rolling his loose eye. "You're one of the thort, Thquire, that keepth a prethious thight of money out of the houthe. But never mind that at prethent."

There was another silence; and then she exclaimed, sobbing with her hands before her face, "Oh, give me my clothes, give me my clothes, and let me go away before I break my heart!"

The women sadly bestirred themselves to get the clothes together—it was soon done, for they were not many—and to pack them in a basket which had often traveled with them. Sissy sat all the time, upon the ground, still sobbing and covering her eyes. Mr. Gradgrind and his friend Bounderby stood near the door, ready to take her away. Mr. Sleary stood in the middle of the room, with the male members of the company about him, exactly as he would have stood in the centre of the ring during his daughter Josephine's performance. He wanted nothing but his whip.

The basket packed in silence, they brought her bonnet to her, and smoothed her disordered hair, and put it on. Then they pressed about her, and bent over her in very natural attitudes, kissing and embracing her; and brought the children to take leave of her; and were a tender-hearted, simple, foolish set of women altogether.

"Now, Jupe," said Mr. Gradgrind, "if you are quite determined, come!"

But she had to take her farewell of the male part of the company yet, and every one of them had to unfold his arms (for they all assumed the professional attitude when they found themselves near Sleary), and give her a parting kiss—Master Kidderminster excepted, in whose young nature there was an original flavor of the misanthrope, who was also known to have harbored matrimonial views, and who moodily withdrew. Mr. Sleary was reserved until the last. Opening his arms wide he took her by both her hands, and would have sprung her up and down, after the riding-master manner of congratulating young ladies on their dismounting from a rapid act; but there was no rebound in Sissy, and she only stood before him crying.

"Good-by, my dear!" said Sleary. "You'll make your fortun, I hope, and none of our poor folkth will ever trouble you, I'll pound it. I with your father hadn't taken hith dog with him; ith a ill-conwenienth to have the dog out of the billth. But on thecond thoughth, he wouldn't have performed without hith mathter, tho ith ath broad ath ith long!"

With that, he regarded her attentively with his fixed eye, surveyed his company with his loose one, kissed her, shook his head, and handed her to Mr. Gradgrind as to a horse.

"There the ith, Thquire," he said, sweeping her with a professional glance as if she were being adjusted in her seat, "and the'll do you juthtithe. Good-by, Thethilia!"

"Good-by, Cecilia!" "Good-by, Sissy!" "God bless you, dear!" In a variety of voices from all the room.

But the riding-master's eye had observed the bottle of the nine-oils in her bosom, and he now interposed with, "Leave the bottle, my dear; ith large to carry, it will be of no uthe to you now. Give it to me!"

"No, no!" she said, in another burst of tears. "Oh, no! Pray let me keep it for father till he comes back! He will want it, when he comes back. He had never thought of going away, when he sent me for it. I must keep it for him, if you please!"

"Tho be it, my dear. (You thee how it ith, Thquire!) Farewell, Thethilia! My latht wordth to you ith thith, Thtick to the termth of your engagement, be obedient to the Thquire, and forget uth. But if, when you're grown up and married and well off, you come upon any horthe-riding ever, don't be hard upon it, don't be croth with it, give it a Bethpeak if you can, and think you might do wurth. People must be amuthed, Thquire, thomehow," continued Sleary, rendered more pursy than ever, by so much talking; "they can't be alwayth a-working, nor yet they can't be alwayth a-learning. Make the betht of uth: not the wurtht. I've got my living out of the horthe-riding all my life, I know; but I conthider that I lay down the philothophy of the thubject when I thay to you, Thquire, make the betht of uth: not the wurtht!"

The Sleary philosophy was propounded as they went down stairs; and the fixed eye of Philosophy—and its rolling eye, too—soon lost the three figures and the basket in the darkness of the street.

Chapter VII

MRS. SPARSIT

MR. BOUNDERBY being a bachelor, an elderly lady presided over his establishment, in consideration of a certain annual stipend. Mrs. Sparsit was this lady's name; and she was a prominent figure in attendance on Mr. Bounderby's car, as it rolled along in triumph with the Bully of humility inside.

For Mrs. Sparsit had not only seen different days, but was highly connected. She had a great aunt living in these very times called Lady Scadgers. Mr. Sparsit, deceased, of whom she was the relict, had been by the mother's side what Mrs. Sparsit still called "a Powler." Strangers of limited information and dull apprehension were sometimes observed not to know what a Powler was, and even to appear uncertain whether it might be a business, or a political party, or a profession of faith. The better class of minds, however, did not need to be informed that the Powlers were an ancient stock, who could trace themselves so exceedingly far back that it was not surprising if they sometimes lost themselves—which they had rather frequently done, as respected horse-flesh, blind-hookey, Hebrew monetary transactions, and the Insolvent Debtors Court.

The late Mr. Sparsit, being by the mother's side a Powler, married this lady, being by the father's side a Scadgers. Lady Scadgers (an immensely fat old woman, with an inordinate appetite for butcher's meat, and a mysterious leg, which had now refused to get out of bed for fourteen years) contrived the marriage, at a period when Sparsit was just of age, and chiefly noticeable for a slender body, weakly supported on two long slim props, and surmounted by no head worth mentioning. He inherited a fair fortune from his uncle, but owed it all before he came into it, and spent it twice over immediately afterward. Thus, when he died, at twenty-four (the scene of his decease Calais, and the cause brandy), he did not leave his widow, from whom he had been separated soon after the honeymoon, in affluent circumstances. That bereaved lady, fifteen years older than he, fell presently at deadly feud with her only relative, Lady Scadgers; and, partly to spite her ladyship, and partly to maintain herself, went out at a salary. And here she was now, in her elderly days, with the Coriolanian style of nose and the dense black eyebrows which had captivated Sparsit, making Mr. Bounderby's tea as he took his breakfast.

If Bounderby had been a Conqueror, and Mrs. Sparsit a captive Princess whom he took about as a feature in his state-processions, he could not have made a greater flourish with her than he habitually did. Just as it belonged to his boastfulness to depreciate his own extraction, so it belonged to it to exalt Mrs. Sparsit's. In the measure that he would not allow his own youth to have been attended by a single favorable circumstance, he brightened Mrs. Sparsit's juvenile career with every possible advantage, and showered wagon-loads of early roses all over that lady's path. "And yet, sir," he would say, "how does it turn out after all? Why here she is at a hundred a year (I give her a hundred, which she is pleased to term handsome), keeping the house of Josiah Bounderby of Coketown!"

Nay, he made this foil of his so very widely known that third parties took it up, and handled it on some occasions with considerable briskness. It was one of the most exasperating attributes of Bounderby, that he not only sang his own praises, but stimulated other men to sing them. There was a moral infection of claptrap in him. Strangers, modest enough elsewhere, started up at dinners in Coketown, and boasted, in quite a rampant way, of Bounderby. They made him out to be the Royal Arms, the Union-Jack, Magna Charta, John Bull, Habeas Corpus, the Bill of Rights, An Englishman's house is his castle, Church and State, and God save the Queen, all put together. And as often (and it was very often) as an orator of this kind brought into his peroration,

"Princes and Lords may floursh or may fade,
A breath can make them, as a breath has made:"

—it was, for certain, more or less understood among the company that he had heard of Mrs. Sparsit.

"Mr. Bounderby," said Mrs. Sparsit, "you are unusually slow, sir, with your breakfast this morning."

"Why, ma'am," he returned, "I am thinking about Tom Gradgrind's whim;" Tom Gradgrind, for a bluff independent manner of speaking —as if somebody were always endeavoring to bribe him with immense sums to say Thomas, and he wouldn't; "Tom Gradgrind's whim, ma'am, of bringing up the tumbling-girl."

"The girl is now waiting to know," said Mrs. Sparsit, "whether she is to go straight to the school, or up to the Lodge."

"She must wait, ma'am," answered Bounderby, "till I know myself. We shall have Tom Gradgrind down here presently, I suppose. If he should wish her to remain here a day or two longer, of course she can, ma'am."

"Of course she can if you wish it, Mr. Bounderby."

"I told him I would give her a shake-down here, last night, in order that he might sleep on it, before he decided to let her have any association with Louisa."

"Indeed, Mr. Bounderby? Very thoughtful of you!"

Mrs. Sparsit's Coriolanian nose underwent a slight expansion of the nostrils, and her black eyebrows contracted as she took a sip of tea.

"It's tolerably clear to *me*," said Bounderby, "that the little puss can get small good out of such companionship."

"Are you speaking of young Miss Gradgrind, Mr. Bounderby?"

"Yes, ma'am, I am speaking of Louisa."

"Your observation being limited to 'little puss,'" said Mrs. Sparsit, "and there being two little girls in question, I did not know which might be indicated by that expression."

"Louisa," repeated Mr. Bounderby. "Louisa, Louisa."

"You are quite another father to Louisa, sir." Mrs. Sparsit took a little more tea; and, as she bent her again contracted eyebrows over her steaming cup, rather looked as if her classical countenance were invoking the infernal gods.

"If you had said I was another father to Tom—young Tom, I mean, not my friend Tom Gradgrind—you might have been nearer the mark. I am going to take young Tom into my office. Going to have him under my wing, ma'am."

"Indeed? Rather young for that, is he not, sir?" Mrs. Sparsit's "sir," in addressing Mr. Bounderby, was a word of ceremony, rather exacting consideration for herself in the use, than honoring him.

"I'm not going to take him at once; he is to finish his educational cramming before then," said Bounderby. "By the Lord Harry, he'll have enough of it, first and last! He'd open his eyes, that boy would, if he knew how empty of learning *my* young maw was, at his time of life." Which, by-the-by, he probably did know, for he had heard of it often enough. "But it's extraordinary the difficulty I have on scores of such subjects, in speaking to any one on equal terms. Here, for example, I have been speaking to you this morning about Tumblers. Why, what do *you* know about tumblers? At the time when, to have been a tumbler in the mud of the streets, would have been a godsend to me, a prize in the lottery to me, you were at the Italian Opera. You were coming out of the Italian Opera, ma'am, in white satin and jewels, a blaze of splendor, when I hadn't a penny to buy a link to light you."

"I certainiy, sir," returned Mrs. Sparsit, with a dignity serenely mournful, "was familiar with the Italian Opera at a very early age."

"Egad, ma'am, so was I," said Bounderby "—with the wrong side of it. A hard bed the pavement of its Arcade used to make, I assure you. People like you, ma'am, accustomed from infancy to lie on Down feathers, have no idea *how* hard a paving-stone is, without trying it. No, no, it's of no use my talking to *you* about tumblers. I should speak of foreign dancers, and the West End of London, and May Fair, and lords and ladies and honorables."

"I trust, sir," rejoined Mrs. Sparsit, with decent resignation, "it is not necessary that you should do any thing of that kind. I hope I have learned how to accommodate myself to the changes of life. If I have acquired an interest in hearing of your instructive experiences, and can scarcely hear enough of them, I claim no merit for that, since I believe it is a general sentiment."

"Well, ma'am," said her patron, "perhaps some people may be pleased to say that they do like to hear, in his own unpolished way, what Josiah Bounderby of Coketown has gone through. But you must confess that you were born in the lap of luxury, yourself. Come, ma'am, you know you were born in the lap of luxury."

"I do not, sir," returned Mrs. Sparsit with a shake of her head, "deny it."

Mr. Bounderby was obliged to get up from the table, and stand with his back to the fire, looking at her; she was such an enhancement of his merits.

"And you were in crack society. Devilish high society," he said, warming his legs.

"It is true, sir," returned Mrs. Sparsit, with an affectation of humility the very opposite of his, and therefore in no danger of josting it.

"You were in the tiptop fashion, and all the rest of it," said Mr. Bounderby.

"Yes, sir," returned Mrs. Sparsit, with a kind of social widowhood upon her. "It is unquestionably true."

Mr. Bounderby, bending himself at the knees, literally embraced his legs in his great satisfaction, and laughed aloud. Mr. and Miss Gradgrind being then announced, he received the former with a shake of the hand, and the latter with a kiss.

"Can Jupe be sent here, Bounderby?" asked Mr. Gradgrind.

Certainly. So Jupe was sent there. On coming in, she courtesied to Mr. Bounderby, and to his friend Tom Gradgrind, and also to Louisa, but in her confusion unluckily omitted Mrs. Sparsit. Observing this, the blustrous Bounderby had the following remarks to make:

"Now, I tell you what, my girl. The name of that lady by the teapot is Mrs. Sparsit. That lady acts as mistress of this house, and she is a highly connected lady. Consequently, if ever you come again into any room in this house, you will make a short stay in it if you don't behave toward that lady in your most respecful manner. Now, I don't care a button what you do to *me*, because I don't affect to be any body. So far from having high connections, I have no connections at all, and I come of the scum of the earth. But toward that lady, I do care what you do; and you shall do what is deferential and respectful, or you shall not come here."

"I hope, Bounderby," said Mr. Gradgrind, in a conciliatory voice, "that this was merely an oversight."

"My friend Tom Gradgrind suggests, Mrs. Sparsit," said Bounderby, "that this was merely an oversight. Very likely. However, as you are aware, ma'am, I don't allow of even oversights toward you."

"You are very good indeed, sir," returned Mrs. Sparsit, shaking her head with her State humility. "It is not worth speaking of."

Sissy, who all this time had been faintly excusing herself with tears in her eyes, was now waved over by the master of the house to Mr. Gradgrind. She stood, looking intently at him, and Louisa stood coldly by, with her eyes upon the ground, while he proceeded thus:

"Jupe, I have made up my mind to take you into my house; and, when you are not in attendance at the school, to employ you about Mrs. Gradgrind, who is rather an invalid. I have explained to Miss Louisa—this is Miss Louisa—the miserable but natural end of your late career; and you are to expressly understand that the whole of that subject is past, and is not to be referred to any more. From this time you begin your history. You are, at present, ignorant, I know."

"Yes, sir, very," she answered, courtesying.

"I shall have the satisfaction of causing you to be strictly educated; and you will be a living proof to all who come into communication with you, of the advantages of the training you will receive. You will be reclaimed and formed. You have been in the habit, now, of reading to your father, and those people I found you among, I dare say?" said Mr. Gradgrind, beckoning her nearer to him before he said so, and dropping his voice.

"Only to father and Merrylegs, sir. At least I mean to father, when Merrylegs was always there."

"Never mind Merrylegs, Jupe," said Mr. Gradgrind, with a passing frown. "I don't ask about him. I understand you to have been in the habit of reading to your father?"

"O yes, sir, thousands of times. They were the happiest—O, of all the happy times we had together, sir!"

It was only now, when her sorrow broke out, that Louisa looked at her.

"And what," asked Mr. Gradgrind, in a still lower voice, "did you read to your father, Jupe?"

"About the Fairies, sir, and the Dwarf, and the Hunchback, and the Genies," she sobbed out.

"There!" said Mr. Gradgrind, "that is enough. Never breathe a word of such destructive nonsense any more. Bounderby, this is a case for rigid training, and I shall observe it with interest."

"Well," returned Mr. Bounderby, "I have given you my opinion already, and I shouldn't do as you do. But, very well, very well. Since you are bent upon it, *very* well!"

So Mr. Gradgrind and his daughter took Cecilia Jupe off with them to Stone Lodge, and on the way Louisa never spoke one word, good or bad. And Mr. Bounderby went about his daily pursuits. And Mrs. Sparsit got behind her eyebrows and meditated in the gloom of that retreat, all the morning.

Chapter VIII

NEVER WONDER

LET us strike the keynote again, before pursuing the tune.

When she was half a dozen years younger, Louisa had been overheard to begin a conversation with her brother one day, by saying, "Tom, I wonder—"upon which Mr. Gradgrind, who was the person overhearing, stepped forth into the light and said, "Louisa, never wonder!"

Herein lay the spring of the mechanical art and mystery of educating the reason without stooping to the cultivation of the sentiments and affections. Never wonder. By means of addition, subtraction, multiplication, and division, settle every thing somehow, and never wonder. Bring to me, says M'Choakumchild, yonder baby just able to walk, and I will engage that it shall never wonder.

Now, besides very many babies just able to walk, there happened to be in Coketown a considerable population of babies who had been walking against time toward the infinite world, twenty, thirty, forty, fifty years and more. These portentous infants being alarming creatures to stalk about in any human society, the eighteen denominations incessantly scratched one another's faces and pulled one another's hair, by way of agreeing on the steps to be taken for their improvement—which they never did; a surprising circumstance, when the happy adaptation of the means to the end is considered. Still, although they differed in every other particular, conceivable and inconceivable (especially inconceivable), they were pretty well united on the point that these unlucky infants were never to wonder. Body number one, said they must take every thing on trust. Body number two, said they must take every thing on political economy. Body number three, wrote leaden little books for them, showing how the good grown-up baby invariably got to the Savings' Bank, and the bad grown-up baby invariably got transported. Body number four, under dreary pretences of being droll (when it was very melancholy indeed), made the shallowest pretences of concealing pitfalls of knowledge, into which it was the duty of these babies to be smuggled and inveigled. But all the bodies agreed that they were never to wonder.

There was a library in Coketown, to which general access was easy. Mr. Gradgrind greatly tormented his mind about what the people read in this library: a point whereon little rivers of tabular statements periodically flowed into the howling ocean of tabular statements, which no diver ever got to any depth in and came up sane. It was a disheartening circumstance, but a melancholy fact, that even these readers persisted in wondering.

They wondered about human nature, human passions, human hopes and fears, the struggles, triumphs and defeats, the cares and joys and sorrows, the lives and deaths, of common men and women. They sometimes, after fifteen hours' work, sat down to read mere fables about men and women, more or less like themselves, and children, more or less like their own. They took De Foe to their bosoms, instead of Euclid, and seemed to be on the whole more comforted by Goldsmith than by Cocker. Mr. Gradgrind was forever working, in print and out of print, at this eccentric sum, and he never could make out how it yielded this unaccountable product.

"I am sick of my life, Loo. I hate it altogether, and I hate every body except you," said the unnatural young Thomas Gradgrind in the hair-cutting chamber at twilight.

"You don't hate Sissy, Tom."

"I hate to be obliged to call her Jupe. And she hates me," said Tom moodily.

"No she does not, Tom, I am sure."

"She must," said Tom. "She must just hate and detest the whole set-out of us. They'll bother her head off, I think, before they have done with her. Already she's getting as pale as wax, and as heavy as—I am."

Young Thomas expressed these sentiments, sitting astride of a chair before the fire, with his arms on the back, and his sulky face on his arms. His sister sat in the darker corner by the fireside, now looking at him, now looking at the bright sparks as they dropped upon the hearth.

"As to me," said Tom, tumbling his hair all manner of ways with his sulky hands, "I am a Donkey, that's what *I* am. I am as obstinate as one, I am more stupid than one, I get as much pleasure as one, and I should like to kick like one."

"Not me, I hope, Tom."

"No, Loo, I wouldn't hurt *you.* I made an exception of you at first. I don't know what this—jolly old—Jaundiced Jail—" Tom had paused to find a sufficiently complimentary and expressive name for the parental roof, and seemed to relieve his mind for a moment by the strong alliteration of this one, "would be without you."

"Indeed, Tom? Do you really and truly say so?"

"Why, of course I do. What's the use of talking about it!" returned Tom, chafing his face on his coat-sleeve as if to mortify his flesh, and have it in unison with his spirit.

"Because, Tom," said his sister, after silently watching the sparks awhile, "as I get older, and nearer growing up, I often sit wondering here, and think how unfortunate it is for me that I can't reconcile you to home better than I am able to do. I don't know what other girls know. I can't play to you, or sing to you. I can't talk to you so as to lighten your mind, for I never see any amusing sights or read any amusing books that it would be a pleasure or a relief to you to talk about, when you are tired."

"Well, no more do I. I am as bad as you in that respect; and I am a Mule too, which you're not. If father was determined to make me either a Prig or a Mule, and I am not a Prig, why, it stands to reason, I must be a Mule. And so I am," said Tom, desperately.

"It's a great pity," said Lousia, after another pause, and speaking thoughtfully out of her dark corner; "it's a great pity, Tom. It's very unfortunate for both of us."

"Oh! You," said Tom, "you are a girl, Loo, and a girl comes out of it better than a boy does. I don't miss any thing in you. You are the only pleasure I have—you can brighten even this place—and you can always lead me as you like."

"You are a dear brother, Tom; and while you think I can do such things, I don't so much mind knowing better. Though I do know better, Tom, and am very sorry for it." She came and kissed him, and went back into her corner again.

"I wish I could collect all the Facts we hear so much about," said Tom, spitefully setting his teeth, "and all the Figures, and all the people who found them out; and I wish I could put a thousand barrels of gunpowder under them, and blow them all up together! However, when I go to live with old Bounderby, I'll have my revenge."

"Your revenge, Tom?"

"I mean, I'll enjoy myself a little, and go about and see something, and hear something. I'll recompense myself for the way in which I have been brought up."

"But don't disappoint yourself beforehand, Tom. Mr. Bounderby thinks as father thinks, and is a great deal rougher, and not half so kind."

"Oh!" said Tom, laughing; "I don't mind that. I shall very well know how to manage and smooth old Bounderby!"

Their shadows were defined upon the wall, but those of the high presses in the room were all blended together on the wall and on the ceiling, as if the brother and sister were overhung by a dark cavern. Or, a fanciful imagination—if such treason could have been there—might have made it out to be the shadow of their subject, and of its lowering association with their future.

"What is your great mode of smoothing and managing, Tom? Is it a secret?"

"Oh!" said Tom, "if it is a secret, it's not far off. It's you. You are his little pet, you are his favorite; he'll do anything for you. When he says to me what I don't like, I shall say to him, 'My sister Loo will be hurt and disappointed, Mr. Bounderby. She always used to tell me she was sure you would be easier with me than this.' That'll bring him about, or nothing will."

After waiting for some answering remark, and getting none, Tom wearily relapsed into the present time, and twined himself yawning round and about the rails of his chair, and rumpled his head more and more, until he suddenly looked up, and asked:

"Have you gone to sleep, Loo?"

"No, Tom. I am looking at the fire."

"You seem to find more to look at in it than ever I could find," said Tom. "Another of the advantages, I suppose, of being a girl."

"Tom," inquired his sister, slowly, and in a curious tone, as if she were reading what she asked, in the fire, and it were not quite plainly written there, "do you look forward with any satisfaction to this change to Mr. Bounderby's?"

"Why, there's one thing to be said of it;" returned Tom, pushing his chair from him, and standing up; "it will be getting away from home."

"There is one thing to be said of it," Louisa repeated in her former curious tone; "it will be getting away from home. Yes."

"Not but what I shall be very unwilling, both to leave you, Loo, and to leave you here. But I must go, you know, whether I like it or not; and I had better go where I can take with me some advantage of your influence, than where I should lose it altogether. Don't you see?"

"Yes, Tom."

The answer was so long in coming, though there was no indecision in it, that Tom went and leaned on the back of her chair, to contemplate the fire which so engrossed her, from her point of view, and see what he could make of it.

"Except that it is a fire," said Tom, "it looks to me as stupid and blank as every thing else looks. What do you see in it? Not a circus?"

"I don't see anything in it, Tom, particularly. But since I have been looking at it, I have been wondering about you and me, grown up."

"Wondering again!" said Tom.

"I have such unmanageable thoughts," returned his sister, "that they *will* wonder."

"Then I beg of you, Louisa," said Mrs. Gradgrind, who had opened the door without being heard, "to do nothing of that description, for goodness sake, you inconsiderate girl, or I shall never hear the last of it from your father. And Thomas, it is really shameful, with my poor head continually wearing me out, that a boy brought up as you have been, and whose education has cost what yours has, should be found encouraging his sister to wonder, when he knows his father has expressly said that she is not to do it."

Louisa denied Tom's participation in the offence; but her mother stopped her with the conclusive answer, "Louisa, don't tell me, in my state of health; for unless you had been encouraged, it is morally and physically impossible that you could have done it."

"I was encouraged by nothing, mother, but by looking at the red sparks dropping out of the fire, and whitening and dying. It made me think, after all, how short my life would be, and how little I could hope to do in it."

"Nonsense!" said Mrs. Gradgrind, rendered almost energetic. "Nonsense! Don't stand there and tell me such stuff, Louisa, to my face, when you know very well that if it was ever to reach your father's ears I should never hear the last of it. After all the trouble that has been taken with you! After the lectures you have attended, and the experiments you have seen! After I have heard you myself, when the whole of my right side has been benumbed, going on with your master about combustion, and calcination, and calorification, and I may say every kind of ation that could drive a poor invalid distracted, to hear you talking in this absurd way about sparks and ashes! I wish," whimpered Mrs. Gradgrind, taking a chair, and discharging her strongest point before succumbing under these mere shadows of facts, "yes, I really *do* wish that I had never had a family, and then you would have known what it was to do without me!"

Chapter IX
SISSY'S PROGRESS

SISSY JUPE had not an easy time of it, between Mr. M'Choakumchild and Mrs. Gradgrind, and was not without strong impulses, in the first months of her probation, to run away. It hailed facts all day long so very hard, and life in general was opened to her as such a closely-ruled ciphering-book, that assuredly she would have run away, but for only one restraint.

It is lamentable to think of; but this restraint was the result of no arithmetical process, was self-imposed in defiance of all calculation, and went dead against any table of probabilities that any Actuary would have drawn up from the premises. The girl believed that her father had not deserted her; she lived in the hope that he would come back, and in the faith that he would be made the happier by her remaining where she was.

The wretched ignorance with which Jupe clung to this consolation, rejecting the superior comfort of knowing, on a sound arithmetical basis, that her father was an unnatural vagabond, filled Mr. Gradgrind with pity. Yet, what was to be done? M'Choakumchild reported that she had a very dense head for figures; that, once possessed with a general idea of the globe, she took the smallest conceivable interest in its exact measurements; that she was extremely slow in the acquisition of dates, unless some pitiful incident happened to be connected therewith; that she would burst into tears on being required (by the mental process) immediately to name the cost of two hundred and forty-seven muslin caps at fourteen-pence halfpenny; that she was as low down, in the school, as low could be; that after eight weeks of induction into the elements of Political Economy, she had only yesterday been set right by a prattler three feet high, for returning to the question, "What is the first principle of this science?" the absurd answer, "To do unto others as I would that they should do unto me."

Mr. Gradgrind observed, shaking his head, that all this was very bad; that it showed the necessity of infinite grinding at the mill of knowledge as per system, schedule, blue book, report, and tabular statements A to Z; and that Jupe "must be kept to it." So Jupe was kept to it, and became very low-spirited, but no wiser.

"It would be a fine thing to be you, Miss Louisa!" she said, one night, when Louisa had endeavored to make her perplexities for next day something clearer to her.

"Do you think so?"

"I should know so much, Miss Louisa. All that is difficult to me now would be so easy then."

"You might not be the better for it, Sissy."

Sissy submitted, after a little hesitation, "I should not be the worse, Miss Louisa." To which Miss Louisa answered, "I don't know that."

There had been so little communication between these two—both because life at Stone Lodge went monotonously round like a piece of machinery which discouraged human interference, and because of the prohibition relative to Sissy's past career—that they were still almost strangers. Sissy, with her dark eyes wonderingly directed to Louisa's face, was uncertain whether to say more or to remain silent.

"You are more useful to my mother, and more pleasant with her than I can ever be," Louisa resumed. "You are pleasanter to yourself, than *I* am to *my*self."

"But, if you please, Miss Louisa," Sissy pleaded, "I am—O so stupid!"

Louisa, with a brighter laugh than usual, told her she would be wiser by-and-by.

"You don't know," said Sissy, half crying, "what a stupid girl I am. All through school hours I make mistakes. Mr. and Mrs. M'Choakumchild call me up, over and over again, regularly to make mistakes. I can't help them. They seem to come natural to me."

"Mr. and Mrs. M'Choakumchild never make any mistakes themselves, I suppose, Sissy?"

"O no!" she eagerly returned. "They know everything."

"Tell me some of your mistakes."

"I am almost ashamed," said Sissy, with reluctance. "But to-day, for instance, Mr. M'Choakumchild was explaining to us about Natural Prosperity."

"National, I think it must have been," observed Louisa.

"Yes, it was.—But isn't it the same?" she timidly asked.

"You had better say, National, as he said so," returned Louisa, with her dry reserve.

"National Prosperity. And he said, Now, this schoolroom is a Nation. And in this nation, there are fifty millions of money. Isn't this a prosperous nation? Girl number twenty, isn't this a prosperous nation, and a'n't you in a thriving state?"

"What did you say?" asked Louisa.

"Miss Louisa, I said I didn't know. I thought I couldn't know whether it was a prosperous nation or not, and whether I was in a thriving state or not, unless I knew who had got the money, and whether any of it was mine. But that had nothing to do with it. It was not in the figures at all," said Sissy, wiping her eyes.

"That was a great mistake of yours," observed Louisa.

"Yes, Miss Louisa, I know it was, now. Then Mr. M'Choakumchild said he would try me again. And he said, This schoolroom is an immense town, and in it there are a million of inhabitants, and only five-and-twenty are starved to death in the streets, in the course of a year. What is your remark on that proportion? And my remark was—for I couldn't think of a better one—that I thought it must be just as hard upon those who were starved, whether the others were a million, or a million million. And that was wrong, too."

"Of course it was."

"Then Mr. M'Choakumchild said he would try me once more. And he said, Here are the stutterings—"

"Statistics," said Louisa.

"Yes, Miss Louisa—they always remind me of stutterings, and that's another of my mistakes—of accidents upon the sea. And I find (Mr.

M'Choakumchild said) that in a given time a hundred thousand persons went to sea on long voyages, and only five hundred of them were drowned or burned to death. What is the percentage? And I said, Miss;" here Sissy fairly sobbed as confessing with extreme contrition to her greatest error;"I said it was nothing."

"Nothing, Sissy?"

"Nothing, Miss—to the relations and friends of the people who were killed. I shall never learn," said Sissy. "And the worst of all is, that although my poor father wished me so much to learn, and although I am so anxious to learn because he wished me to, I am afraid I don't like it."

Louisa stood looking at the pretty modest head, as it drooped abashed before her, until it was raised again to glance at her face. Then she asked:

"Did your father know so much himself, that he wished you to be well taught too, Sissy?"

Sissy hesitated before replying, and so plainly showed her sense that they were entering on forbidden ground, that Louisa added, "No one hears us; and if any one did, I am sure no harm could be found in such an innocent question."

"No, Miss Louisa," answered Sissy, upon this encouragement, shaking her head; "father knows very little indeed. It's as much as he can do to write; and it's more than people in general can do to read his writing. Though it's plain to *me.*"

"Your mother?"

"Father says she was quite a scholar. She died when I was born. She was;" Sissy made the terrible communication nervously; "she was a dancer."

"Did your father love her?" Louisa asked these questions with a strong, wild, wandering interest peculiar to her; an interest gone astray like a banished creature, and hiding in solitary places.

"O yes! As dearly as he loves me. Father loved me, first, for her sake. He carried me about with him when I was quite a baby. We have never been asunder from that time."

"Yet he leaves you now, Sissy?"

"Only for my good. Nobody understands him as I do; nobody knows him as I do. When he left me for my good—he never would have left me for his own—I know he was almost broken-hearted with the trial. He will not be happy for a single minute, till he comes back."

"Tell me more about him," said Louisa, "I will never ask you again. Where did you live?"

"We traveled about the country, and had no fixed place to live in. Father's a—" Sissy whispered the awful word; "a clown."

"To make the people laugh?" said Louisa, with a nod of intelligence.

"Yes. But they wouldn't laugh sometimes, and then father cried. Lately, they very often wouldn't laugh, and he used to come home despairing. Father's not like most. Those who didn't know him as well as I do, and didn't love him as dearly as I do, might believe he was not quite right. Sometimes they played tricks upon him; but they never knew how he felt them, and shrunk up, when he was alone with me. He was far, far timider than they thought!"

"And you were his comfort through every thing?"

She nodded, with the tears rolling down her face. "I hope so, and father said I was. It was because he grew so scared and trembling, and because he felt himself to be a poor, weak, ignorant, helpless man (those used to be his words), that he wanted me so much to know a great deal and be different from him. I used to read to him to cheer his courage, and he was very fond of that. They were wrong books—I am never to speak of them here—but we didn't know there was any harm in them."

"And he liked them?" said Lousia, with a searching gaze on Sissy all this time.

"O very much! They kept him, many times, from what did him real harm. And often and often of a night, he used to forget all his troubles in wondering whether the Sultan would let the lady go on with the story,or would have her head cut off before it was finished."

"And your father was always kind? To the last?" asked Louisa; contravening the great principle, and wondering very much.

"Always, always!" returned Sissy, clasping her hands. "Kinder and kinder than I can tell. He was angry only one night, and that was not to me, but Merrylegs. Merrylegs;" she whispered the awful fact; "is his performing dog."

"Why was he angry with the dog?" Louisa demanded.

"Father, soon after they came home from performing, told Merrylegs to jump up on the backs of the two chairs and stand across them—which is one of his tricks. He looked at father, and didn't do it at once. Every thing of father's had gone wrong that night, and he hadn't pleased the public at all. He cried out that the very dog knew he was failing, and had no compassion on him. Then he beat the dog, and I was frightened, and said, 'Father, father! Pray don't hurt the creature who is so fond of you! O Heaven forgive you, father, stop!' And he stopped, and the dog was bloody, and father lay down crying on the floor with the dog in his arms, and the dog licked his face."

Louisa saw that she was sobbing; and going to her, kissed her, took her hand, and sat down beside her.

"Finish by telling me how your father left you, Sissy. Now that I have asked you so much, tell me the end. The blame, if there is any blame, is mine: not yours."

"Dear Miss Louisa," said Sissy, covering her eyes, and sobbing yet; "I came home from the school that afternoon, and found poor father just come home too, from the booth. And he sat rocking himself over the fire, as if he was in pain. And I said, 'Have you hurt yourself, father?' (as he did sometimes, like they all did), and he said, 'A little, my darling.' And when I came to stoop down and look up at his face, I saw that he was crying. The more I spoke to him, the more he hid his face; and at first he shook all over, and said nothing but 'My darling!' and 'My love!' "

Here Tom came lounging in, and stared at the two with a coolness not particularly savoring of interest in any thing but himself, and not much of that at present.

"I am asking Sissy a few questions, Tom," observed his sister. "You have no occasion to go away; but don't interrupt us for a moment, Tom dear."

"Oh! very well!" returned Tom. "Only father has brought old Bounderby home, and I want you to come into the drawing-room. Because if you come, there's a good chance of old Bounderby's asking me to dinner; and if you don't, there's none."

"I'll come directly."

"I'll wait for you," said Tom, "to make sure."

Sissy resumed in a lower voice. "At last poor father said that he had given no satisfaction again, and never did give any satisfaction now, and that he was a shame and disgrace, and I should have done better without him all along. I said all the affectionate things to him that came into my heart, and presently he was quiet and I sat down by him, and told him all about the school and every thing that had been said and done there. When I had no more left to tell, he put his arms round my neck, and kissed me a great many times. Then he asked me to fetch some of the stuff he used, for the little hurt he had had, and to get it at the best place, which was at the other end of town from there; and then, after kissing me again, he let me go. When I had gone down stairs, I turned back that I might be a little bit more company to him yet, and looked in at the door, and said, 'Father dear, shall I take Merrylegs?' Father shook his head and said, 'No, Sissy, no; take nothing that's known to be mine, my darling;' and I left him sitting by the fire. Then the thought must have come upon him, poor, poor father! of going away to try something for my sake; for, when I came back, he was gone."

"I say! Look sharp for old Bounderby, Loo!" Tom remonstrated,

"There's no more to tell, Miss Louisa. I keep the nine-oils ready for him, and I know he will come back. Every letter that I see in Mr. Gradgrind's hand takes my breath away and blinds my eyes, for I think it comes from father, or from Mr. Sleary about father. Mr. Sleary promised to write as soon as ever father should be heard of, and I trust to him to keep his word."

"Do look sharp for old Bounderby, Loo!" said Tom, with an impatient whistle. "He'll be off if you don't look sharp!"

After this, whenever Sissy dropped a courtesy to Mr. Gradgrind in the presence of his family, and said in a faltering way, "I beg your pardon, sir, for being troublesome—but—have you had any letter yet about me?" Louisa would suspend the occupation of the moment, whatever it was, and look for the reply as earnestly as Sissy did. And when Mr. Gradgrind regularly answered, "No, Jupe, nothing of the sort," the trembling of Sissy's lip would be repeated in Louisa's face, and her eyes would follow Sissy with compassion to the door. Mr. Gradgrind usually improved these occasions by remarking, when she was gone, that if Jupe had been properly trained from an early age she would have demonstrated to herself on sound principles the baselessness of these fantastic hopes. Yet it did seem (though not to him, for he saw nothing of it) as if fantastic hope could take as strong a hold as Fact.

This observation must be limited exclusively to his daughter. As to Tom, he was becoming that not unprecedented triumph of calculation which is usually at work on number one. As to Mrs. Gradgrind, if she said any thing on the subject, she would come a little way out of her wrappers, like a feminine dormouse, and say:

"Good gracious bless me, how my poor head is vexed and worried by that girl Jupe's so perseveringly asking, over and over again, about her tiresome letters! Upon my word and honor I seem to be fated, and destined, and ordained, to live in the midst of things that I am never to hear the last of. It really is a most extraordinary circumstance that it appears as if I never was to hear the last of any thing!"

At about this point, Mr. Gradgrind's eye would fall upon her; and under the influence of that wintry piece of fact, she would become torpid again.

Chapter X

STEPHEN BLACKPOOL

I ENTERTAIN a weak idea that the English people are as hard-worked as any people upon whom the sun shines. I acknowledge to this ridiculous idiosyncrasy, as a reason why I would give them a little more play.

In the hardest working part of Coketown; in the innermost fortifications of that ugly citadel, where Nature was as strongly bricked out as killing airs and gases were bricked in; at the heart of the labyrinth of narrow courts upon courts, and close streets upon streets, which had come into existence piecemeal, every piece in a violent hurry for some one man's purpose, and the whole an unnatural family, shouldering, and trampling, and pressing one another to death; in the last close nook of this great exhausted receiver, where the chimneys, for want of air to make a draught, were built in an immense variety of stunted and crooked shapes, as though every house put out a sign of the kind of people who might be expected to be born in it; among the multitude of Coketown, generically called "the Hands"—a race who would have found more favor with some people, if Providence had seen fit to make them only hands, or, like the lower creatures of the sea-shore, only hands and stomachs—lived a certain Stephen Blackpool, forty years of age.

Stephen looked older, but he had had a hard life. It is said that every life has its roses and thorns; there seemed, however, to have been a misadventure or mistake in Stephen's case, whereby somebody else had become possessed of his roses, and he had become possessed of the same somebody else's thorns in addition to his own. He had known, to use his words, a peck of trouble. He was usually called Old Stephen, in a kind of rough homage to the fact.

A rather stooping man, with a knitted brow, a pondering expression of face, and a hard-looking head sufficiently capacious, on which his iron-gray hair lay long and thin, Old Stephen might have passed for a particularly intelligent man in his condition. Yet he was not. He took no place among those remarkable "Hands," who, piecing together their broken intervals of leisure through many years, had mastered difficult sciences, and acquired a knowledge of most unlikely things. He held no station among the Hands who could make speeches and carry on debates.

Thousands of his compeers could talk much better than he, at any time. He was a good power-loom weaver, and a man of perfect integrity. What more he was, or what else he had in him, if any thing, let him show for himself.

The lights in the great factories, which looked, when they were illuminated, like Fairy palaces—or the travelers by express-train said so—were all extinguished; and the bells had rung for knocking off for the night, and had ceased again; and the Hands, men and women, boy and girl, were clattering home. Old Stephen was standing in the street, with the odd sensation upon him which the stoppage of the machinery always produced—the sensation of its having worked and stopped in his own head.

"Yet I don't see Rachael, still!" said he.

It was a wet night, and many groups of young women passed him, with their shawls drawn over their bare heads and held close under their chins to keep the rain out. He knew Rachael well, for a glance at any one of these groups was sufficient to show him that she was not there. At last, there were no more to come; and then he turned away, saying in a tone of disappointment, "Why, then, I ha' missed her!"

But he had not gone the length of three streets, when he saw another of the shawled figures in advance of him, at which he looked so keenly that perhaps its mere shadow indistinctly reflected on the wet pavement—if he could have seen it without the figure itself moving along from lamp to lamp, brightening and fading as it went—would have been enough to tell him who was there. Making his pace at once much quicker and much softer, he darted on until he was very near this figure, then fell into his former walk, and called "Rachael!"

She turned, being then in the brightness of a lamp; and raising her hood a little, showed a quiet oval face, dark and rather delicate, irradiated by a pair of very gentle eyes, and further set off by the perfect order of her shining black hair. It was not a face in its first bloom; she was a woman five-and-thirty years of age.

"Ah, lad! 'Tis thou?" When she had said this, with a smile which would have been quite expressed, though nothing of her had been seen but her pleasant eyes, she replaced her hood again, and they went on together.

"I thought thou wast ahind me, Rachael?"

"No."

"Early t'night, lass?"

"'Times I'm a little early, Stephen; 'times a little late. I'm never to be counted on, going home."

"Nor going t'other way, neither, 't seems to me, Rachael?"

"No, Stephen."

He looked at her with some disappointment in his face, but with a respectful and patient conviction that she must be right in whatever she did. The expression was not lost upon her; she laid her hand lightly on his arm a moment, as if to thank him for it.

"We are such true friends, lad, and such old friends, and getting to be such old folk, now."

"No, Rachael, thou'rt as young as ever thou wast."

"One of us would be puzzled how to get old, Stephen, without t'other getting so too, both being alive," she answered, laughing; "but, any ways, we're such old friends, that t' hide a word of honest truth fra' one another would be a sin and a pity. 'Tis better not to walk too much together. 'Times, yes! 'Twould be hard, indeed, if 'twas not to be at all," she said, with a cheerfulness she sought to communicate to him.

"'Tis hard, any ways, Rachael."

"Try to think not; and 'twill seem better."

"I've tried a long time, and 't a'nt got better. But thou'rt right; 't might make folk talk, even of thee. Thou hast been that to me, Rachael, through so many year: thou hast done me so much good, and heartened of me in that cheering way: that thy word is a law to me. Ah lass, and a bright good law! Better than some real ones."

"Never fret about them, Stephen," she answered quickly, and not without an anxious glance at his face. "Let the laws be."

"Yes," he said, with a slow nod or two. "Let 'em be. Let every thing be. Let all sorts alone. 'Tis a muddle, and that's all."

"Always a muddle?" said Rachael, with another gentle touch upon his arm, as if to recall him out of the thoughtfulness, in which he was biting the long ends of his loose neckerchief as he walked along. The touch had its instantaneous effect. He let them fall, turned a smiling face upon her, and said, as he broke into a good-humored laugh, "Ay, Rachael, lass, awlus a muddle. That's where I stick. I come to the muddle many times and agen, and I never get beyond it."

They had walked some distance, and were near their own homes. The woman's was the first reached. It was in one of the many small streets for which the favorite undertaker (who turned a handsome sum out of the one poor ghastly pomp of the neighborhood) kept a black ladder, in order that those who had done their daily groping up and down the narrow stairs might slide out of this working world by the windows. She stopped at the orner, and putting her hand in his, wished him good-night.

"Good-night, dear lass; good-night!"

She went, with her neat figure and her sober womanly step, down the dark street, and he stood looking after her until she turned into one of the small houses. There was not a flutter of her coarse shawl, perhaps, but had its interest in this man's eyes; not a tone of her voice but had its echo in his innermost heart.

When she was lost to his view, he pursued his homeward way, glancing up sometimes at the sky, where the clouds were sailing fast and wildly. But they were broken now, and the rain had ceased, and the moon shone—looking down the high chimneys of Coketown on the deep furnaces below, and casting Titanic shadows of the steam engines at rest, upon the walls where they were lodged. The man seemed to have brightened with the night, as he went on.

His home, in such another street as the first, saving that it was narrower, was over a little shop. How it came to pass that any people found it worth their while to sell or buy the wretched little toys, mixed up in its window with cheap newspapers and pork (there was a leg to be raffled for to-morrow night), matters not here. He took his end of candle from a shelf, lighted it at another end of candle on the counter, without disturbing the mistress of the shop who was asleep in her little room, and went up-stairs into his lodging.

It was a room, not unacquainted with the black ladder under various tenants, but as neat, at present, as such a room could be. A few books and writings were on an old bureau in a corner, the furniture was decent and sufficient, and, though the atmosphere was tainted, the room was clean.

Going to the hearth to set the candle down upon a round three-legged table standing there, he stumbled against something. As he recoiled, looking down at it, it raised itself up into the form of a woman in a sitting attitude.

"Heaven's mercy, woman!" he cried, falling farther off from the figure. "Hast thou come back again?"

Such a woman! A disabled, drunken creature, barely able to preserve her sitting posture by steadying herself with one begrimed hand on the floor, while the other was so purposeless in trying to push away her tangled hair from her face, that it only blinded her the more with the dirt upon it. A creature so foul to look at, in her tatters, stains, and splashes, but so much fouler than that in her moral infamy, that it was a shameful thing even to see her.

After an impatient oath or two, and some stupid clawing of herself with the hand not necessary to her support, she got her hair away from her eyes sufficiently to obtain a sight of him. Then she sat swaying her body to and fro, and making gestures with her unnerved arm, which seemed intended as the accompaniment to a fit of laughter, though her face was stolid and drowsy.

"Eigh lad? What, yo'r there?" Some hoarse sounds meant for this, came mockingly out of her at last; and her head dropped forward on her breast.

"Back agen?" she screeched, after some minutes, as if he had that moment said it. "Yes! And back agen. Back agen ever and ever so often. Back? Yes, back. Why not?"

Roused by the unmeaning violence with which she cried it out, she scrambled up, and stood supporting herself with her shoulders against the wall; dangling in one hand by the string a dunghill-fragment of a bonnet, and trying to look scornfully at him.

"I'll sell thee off again, and I'll sell thee off again, and I'll sell thee off a score of times!" she cried, with something between a furious menace and an effort at a defiant dance. "Come awa' from th' bed!" He was sitting on the side of it, with his face hidden in his hands. "Come awa' from 't. 'Tis mine, and I've a right to 't!"

As she staggered to it, he avoided her with a shudder, and passed—his face still hidden—to the opposite end of the room. She threw herself upon the bed heavily, and soon was snoring hard. He sunk into a chair, and moved but once all that night. It was to throw a covering over her; as if his hands were not enough to hide her, even in the darkness.

Chapter XI

NO WAY OUT

THE Fairy palaces burst into illumination, before pale morning, showed the monstrous serpents of smoke trailing themselves over Coketown. A clattering of clogs upon the pavement; a rapid ringing of bells; and all the melancholy-mad elephants, polished and oiled up for the day's monotony, were at their heavy exercise again.

Stephen bent over his loom, quiet, watchful, and steady. A special contrast, as every man was in the forest of looms where Stephen worked, to the crashing, smashing, tearing piece of mechanism at which he labored. Never fear, good people of an anxious turn of mind, that Art will consign Nature to oblivion. Set any where, side by side, the work of God and the work of man; and the former, even though it be a troop of Hands of very small account, will gain in dignity from the comparison.

Four hundred and more Hands in this Mill; Two hundred and fifty horse Steam Power. It is known, to the force of a single pound weight, what the engine will do; but, not all the calculators of the National Debt can tell me the capacity for good or evil, for love or hatred, for patriotism or discontent, for the decomposition of virtue into vice, or the reverse, at any single moment in the soul of one of these its quiet servants, with the composed faces and the regulated actions. There is no mystery in it; there is an unfathomable mystery in the meanest of them, forever.—Supposing we were to reverse our arithmetic for material objects, and to govern these awful unknown quantities by other means!

The day grew strong, and showed itself outside, even against the flaming lights within. The lights were turned out, and the work went on. The rain fell, and the Smoke-serpents, submissive to the curse of all that tribe, trailed themselves upon the earth. In the waste-yard outside, the steam from the escape-pipe, the litter of barrels and old iron, the shining heaps of coals, the ashes every where, were shrouded in a veil of mist and rain.

The work went on, until the noon-bell rang. More clattering upon the pavements. The looms, and wheels, and Hands, all out of gear for an hour.

Stephen came out of the hot mill into the damp wind and cold wet streets, haggard and worn. He turned from his own class and his own quarter, taking nothing but a little bread as he walked along, toward the hill on which his principal employer lived, in a red house with black outside shutters, green inside blinds, a black street door, up two white steps, BOUNDERBY (in letters very like himself) upon a brazen plate, and a round brazen door-handle underneath it like a brazen full-stop.

Mr. Bounderby was at his lunch. So Stephen had expected. Would his servant say that one of the Hands begged leave to speak to him? Message in return, requiring name of such Hand. Stephen Blackpool. There was nothing troublesome against Stephen Blackpool; yes, he might come in.

Stephen Blackpool in the parlor. Mr. Bounderby (whom he just knew by sight) at lunch on chop and sherry. Mrs. Sparsit netting at the fireside, in a side-saddle attitude, with one foot in a cotton stirrup. It was a part, at once of Mrs. Sparsit's dignity and service, not to lunch. She supervised the meal officially, but implied that in her own stately person she considered lunch a weakness.

"Now, Stephen," said Mr. Bounderby, "what's the matter with *you?*"

Stephen made a bow. Not a servile one—these Hands will never do that! Lord bless you, sir, you'll never catch them at that, if they have been with you twenty years!—and, as a complimentary toilet for Mrs. Sparsit, tucked his neckerchief ends into his waistcoat.

"Now, you know," said Mr. Bounderby, taking some sherry, "we have never had any difficulty with you, and you have never been one of the unreasonable ones. You don't expect to be set up in a coach and six, and to be fed on turtle-soup and venison, with a gold spoon, as a good many of 'em do;"Mr. Bounderby always represented this to be the sole, immediate, and direct object of any Hand who was not entirely satisfied, "and therefore I know already that you have not come here to make a complaint. Now, you know, I am certain of that, beforehand."

"No, sir, sure I ha' not coom for nowt o' th' kind."

Mr. Bounderby seemed agreeably surprised, notwithstanding his previous strong conviction. "Very well," he returned. "You're a steady Hand, and I was not mistaken. Now, let me hear what it's all about. As it's not that, let me hear what it is. What have you got to say? Out with it, lad!"

Stephen happened to glance towards Mrs. Sparsit. "I can go, Mr. Bounderby, if you wish it," said that self-sacrificing lady, making a feint of taking her foot out of the stirrup.

Mr. Bounderby stayed her, by holding a mouthful of chop in suspension before swallowing it, and putting out his left hand. Then, withdrawing his hand and swallowing his mouthful of chop, he said to Stephen:

"Now, you know, this good lady is a born lady, a high lady. You are not to suppose because she keeps my house for me, that she hasn't been very high up the tree—ah, up at the top of the tree! Now, if you have got any thing to say that can't be said before a born lady, this lady will leave the room. If what you have got to say *can* be said before a born lady, this lady will stay where she is."

"Sir, I hope I never had nowt to say, not fitten for a born lady to hear, sin' I were born mysen'," was the reply, accompained with a slight flush.

"Very well," said Mr. Bounderby, pushing away his plate, and leaning back. "Fire away!"

"I ha' coom," Stephen began, raising his eyes from the floor, after a moment's consideration, "to ask yo yor advice. I need 't overmuch. I were married on Eas'r Monday nineteen year sin, long and dree. She were a young lass—pretty enow—wi' good accounts of hersen.' Well! She went bad—soon. Not along of me. Gonnows I were not a unkind husband to her."

"I have heard all this before," said Mr. Bounderby. "She found other companions, took to drinking, left off working, sold the furniture, pawned the clothes, and played old Gooseberry."

"I were patient wi' her."

("The more fool you, I think," said Mr. Bounderby, in confidence to his wine-glass.)

"I were very patient wi' her. I tried to wean her fra't ower and ower agen. I tried this, I tried that, I tried t'oother. I ha' gone home, many's the time, and found all vanished as I had in the world, and her without a sense left to bless hersen' lying on bare ground. I ha' dun't not once, not twice—twenty time!"

Every line in his face deepened as he said it, and put in its affecting evidence of the suffering he had undergone.

"From bad to worse, from worse to worse. She left me. She disgraced hersen' every ways, bitter and bad. She coom back, she coom back, she coom back. What could I do t' hinder her? I ha' walked the streets nights long, ere ever I'd go home. I ha' gone t' th' brigg, minded to fling mysen' ower, and ha' no more on 't. I ha' bore that much that I were owd when I were young."

Mrs. Sparsit, easily ambling along with her netting-needles, raised the Coriolanian eye-brows and shook her head, as much as to say, "The great know trouble as well as the small. Please to turn your humble eye in My direction."

"I ha' paid her to keep awa' fra' me. These five year I ha' paid her. I ha' gotten decent fewtrils about me agen. I ha' lived hard and sad, but not ashamed and fearfo' a' the minnits o' my life. Last night I went home. There she lay upun my harston! There she IS!"

In the strength of his misfortune, and the energy of his distress, he fired for the moment like a proud man. In another moment, he stood as he had stood all the time—his usual stoop upon him; his pondering face addressed to Mr. Bounderby, with a curious expression on it, half-shrewd, half-perplexed, as if his mind were set upon unraveling something very difficult; his hat held tight in his left hand, which rested on his hip; his right arm, with a rugged propriety and force of action, very earnestly emphasizing what he said: not least so when it always paused, a little bent, but not withdrawn, as he paused.

"I was acquainted with all this, you know," said Mr. Bounderby, "except the last clause, long ago. It's a bad job; that's what it is. You had better have been satisfied as you were, and not have got married. However, it's too late to say that."

"Was it an unequal marriage, sir, in point of years?" asked Mrs. Sparsit.

"You hear what this lady asks. Was it an unequal marriage in point of years, this unlucky job of yours?" said Mr. Bounderby.

"Not e'en so. I were one-and-twenty mysen'; she were twenty nighbout."

"Indeed, sir?" said Mrs. Sparsit to her Chief, with great placidity. "I inferred, from its being so miserable a marriage, that it was probably an unequal one in point of years."

Mr. Bounderby looked very hard at the good lady in a sidelong way that had an odd sheepishness about it. He fortified himself with a littie more sherry.

"Well? Why don't you go on?" he then asked, turning rather irritably on Stephen Blackpool.

"I ha' coom to ask yo, sir, how I am to be ridden o' this woman." Stephen infused a yet deeper gravity into the mixed expression of his attentive face. Mrs. Sparsit uttered a gentle ejaculation, as having received a moral shock.

"What do you mean?" said Bounderby, getting up to lean his back against the chimney-piece. "What are you talking about? You took her, for better for worse."

"I mun' be ridden o' her. I cannot bear't nommore. I ha' lived under 't so long, for that I ha' had'n the pity and the comforting words o' th' best lass living or dead. Haply, but for her, I should ha' gone hottering mad."

"He wishes to be free, to marry the female of whom he speaks, I fear, sir," observed Mrs. Sparsit in an under-tone, and much dejected by the immorality of the people.

"I do. The lady says what's right. I do. I were a coming to't. I ha' read i' th' papers that great fo'lk (fair faw 'em a'! I wishes 'em no hurt!) are not bonded together for better for worse so fast, but that they can be set free fra' *their* misfortnet marriages, and marry ower agen. When they dunnot agree, for that their tempers is ill-sorted, they have rooms of one kind an' another in their houses, and they can live asunders. We fok ha' only one room, and we can't. When that won't do, they ha' gowd an' other cash, and they can say 'This for yo', an' that for me,' and they can go their separate ways. We can't. Spite o' all that, they can be set free for smaller wrongs than is suffered by hundreds an' hundreds of us—by women fur more than men—they can be set free for smaller wrongs than mine. So, I mun be ridden o' this wife o' mine, and I want t' know how?"

"No how," returned Mr. Bounderby.

"If I do her any hurt, sir, there's a law to punish me?"

"Of course there is."

"If I flee from her, there's a law to punish me?"

"Of course there is."

"If I marry t'oother dear lass, there's a law to punish me?"

"Of course there is.'

"If I was to live wi' her an' not marry her—saying such a thing could be, which it never could or would, an' her so good—there's a law to punish me, in every innocent chilt belonging to me?"

"Of course there is."

"Now, a' God's name," said Stephen Blackpool, "show me the law to help me!"

"There's a sanctity in this relation of life," said Mr. Bounderby, "and—and—it must be kept up."

"No, no, dunnot say that, sir. 'Tan't kep' up that way. Not that way. 'Tis kep' down that way. I'm a weaver, I were in a fact'ry when a chilt, but I ha' gotten een to see wi' and eern to hear wi'. I read in th' papers, every 'Sizes, every Sessions—and you read too—I know it!—with dismay—how th' unpossibility o' ever getting unchained from one another, at any price, on any terms, brings blood upon this land, and brings many common married fok (agen I say, women fur of'ener than men) to battle, murder, and sudden death. Let us ha' this, right understood. Mine's a grievous case, an' I want—if yo will be so good—t' know the law that helps me."

"Now, I tell you what!" said Mr. Bounderby, putting his hands in his pockets. "There *is* such a law."

Stephen, subsiding into his quiet manner, and never wandering in his attention, gave a nod.

"But it's not for you at all. It costs money. It costs a mint of money."

"How much might that be?" Stephen calmly asked.

"Why, you'd have to go to Doctors' Commons with a suit, and you'd have to go to a court of Common Law with a suit, and you'd have to go to the House of Lords with a suit, and you'd have to get an Act of Parliament to enable you to marry again, and it would cost you (if it was a case of very plain-sailing) , I suppose from a thousand to fifteen hundred pound" said Mr. Bounderby. "Perhaps twice the money."

"There's no other law?"

"Certanly not."

"Why then, sir," said Stephen, turning white, and motioning with that right hand of his, as if he gave every thing to the four winds, "*'tis a* muddle. 'Tis just a muddle a'toogether, an' the sooner I am dead, the better."

(Mrs. Sparsit again dejected by the impiety of the people.)

"Pooh, pooh! Don't you talk nonsense, my good fellow," said Mr. Bounderby, "about things you don't understand; and don't you call the Institutions of your country a muddle, or you'll get yourself into a real muddle one of these fine mornings. The institutions of your country are not your piece-work, and the only thing you have got to do, is, to mind your piece-work. You didn't take your wife for fast and for loose; but for better for worse. If she has turned out worse—why, all we have got to say is, she might have turned out better."

"'Tis a muddle," said Stephen, shaking his head as he moved to the door. "'Tis a' a muddle!"

"Now, I'll tell you what!" Mr. Bounderby resumed, as a valedictory address. "With what I shall call your unhallowed opinions, you have been quite shocking this lady: who, as I have already told you, is a born lady, and who, as I have not already told you, has had her own marriage misfortunes to the tune of tens of thousands of pounds—tens of Thousands of Pounds!" (he repeated it with great relish). "Now, you have always been a steady Hand hitherto; but my opinion is, and so I tell you plainly, that you are turning into the wrong road. You have been listening to some mischievous stranger or other—they're always about—and the best thing you can do is, to come out of that. Now, you understand; "—here his countenance expressed marvelous acuteness;"I can see as far into a grindstone as another man; further than a good many, perhaps, because I had my nose well kept to it when I was young. I see traces of the turtle soup, and venison, and gold spoon in this. Yes, I do!" cried Mr. Bounderby, shaking his head with obstinate cunning. "By the Lord Harry, I do!"

With a very different shake of the head a and deep sigh, Stephen said, "Thank you, sir, I wish you good-day." So, he left Mr. Bounderby swelling at his own portrait on the wall, as if he were going to explode himself into it; and Mrs. Sparsit still ambling on with her foot in her stirrup, looking quite cast down by the popular vices.

Chapter XII

THE OLD WOMAN

OLD STEPHEN descended the two white steps, shutting the black door with the brazen door-plate, by the aid of the brazen full-stop, to which he gave a parting polish with the sleeve of his coat, observing that his hot hand clouded it. He crossed the street with his eyes bent upon the ground, and thus was walking sorrowfully away, when he felt a touch upon his arm.

It was not the touch he needed most at such a moment—the touch that could calm the wild waters of his soul, as the uplifted hand of the sublimest love and patience could abate the raging of the sea—yet it was a woman's hand too. It was an old woman, tall and shapely still, though withered by time, on whom his eyes fell when he stopped and turned. She was very cleanly and plainly dressed, had country mud upon her shoes, and was newly come from a journey. The flutter of her manner, in the unwonted noise of the streets; the spare shawl, carrried unfolded on her arm; the heavy umbrella, and little basket; the loose long-fingered gloves, to which her hands were unused; all bespoke an old woman from the country, in her plain holiday clothes, come into Coketown on an expedition of rare occurrence. Remarking this at a glance, with the quick observation of his class, Stephen Blackpool bent his attentive face—his face, which, like the faces of many of his order, by dint of long working with eyes and hands in the midst of a prodigious noise, had acquired the concentrated look with which we are familiar in the countenances of the deaf—the better to hear what she asked him.

"Pray, sir," said the old woman, "didn't I see you come out of that gentleman's house?" pointing back to Mr. Bounderby's. "I believe it was you, unless I have had the bad luck to mistake the person in following?"

"Yes, missus," returned Stephen, "it were me."

"Have you—you'll excuse an old woman's curiosity—have you seen the gentleman?"

"Yes, missus."

"And how did he look, sir? Was he portly, bold, outspoken, hearty?" As she straightened her own figure, and held up her head in adapting her action to her words, the idea crossed Stephen that he had seen this old woman before, and had not quite liked her.

"O yes," he returned, observing her more attentively, "he were all that."

"And healthy," said the old woman, "as the fresh wind?"

"Yes," returned Stephen. "He were ett'n and drinking—as large and as loud as a Hummobee."

"Thank you!" said the old woman with infinite content. "Thank you!"

He certainly never had seen this old woman before. Yet there was a vague remembrance in his mind, as if he had more than once dreamed of some old woman like her.

She walked along at his side, and, gently accommodating himself to her humor, he said Coketown was a busy place, was it not? To which she answered "Eigh sure! Dreadful busy!" Then he said, she came from the country, he saw? To which she answered in the affirmative.

"By Parliamentary, this morning. I came forty mile by Parliamentary this morning, and am going back the same forty mile this afternoon. I walked nine mile to the station this morning, and if I find nobody on the road to give me a lift, I shall walk the nine mile back to-night. That's pretty well, sir, at my age!" said the chatty old woman, her eyes brightening with exultation.

"Deed 'tis. Don't do 't too often, missus."

"No, no. Once a year," she answered, shaking her head. "I spend my savings so, once every year. I come, regular, to tramp about the streets, and see the gentlemen."

"Only to see 'em?" returned Stephen.

"That's enough for me," she replied, with great earnestness and interest of manner. "I ask no more! I have been standing about, on this side of the way, to see that gentleman," turning her head back towards Mr. Bounderby's again, "come out. But he's late this year, and I have not seen him. You came out, instead. Now, if I am obliged to go back without a glimpse of him—I only want a glimpse—well! I have seen you, and you have seen him, and I must make that do." Saying this, she looked at Stephen as if to fix his features in her mind, and her eyes were not so bright as they had been.

With a large allowance for difference of tastes, and with all submission to the patricians of Coketown, this seemed so extraordinary a source of interest to take so much trouble about, that it perplexed him. But they were passing the church now, and as his eye caught the clock, he quickened his pace.

He was going to his work? the old woman said, quickening hers, too, quite easily. Yes, time was nearly out. On his telling her where he worked, the old woman became a more singular old woman than before.

"An't you happy?" she asked him.

"Why—there's—awmost nobody but has their troubles, missus." He answered evasively, because the old woman appeared to take it for granted that he would be very happy indeed, and he had not the heart to disappoint her. He knew that there was trouble enough in the world; and if the old woman had lived so long, and could count upon his having so little, why so much the better for her, and none the worse for him.

"Aye, aye! You have your troubles at home, you mean?" she said.

"Times. Just now and then," he answered, slightly.

"But, working under such a gentleman, they don't follow you to the Factory?"

No, no; they didn't follow him there, said Stephen. All correct there. Every thing accordant there. (He did not go so far as to say, for her pleasure, that there was a sort of Divine Right there; but, I have heard claims almost as magnificent of late years.)

They were now in the black by-road near the place, and the Hands were crowding in. The bell was ringing, and the Serpent was a Serpent of many coils, and the Elephant was getting ready. The strange old woman was delighted with the very bell. It was the beautifulest bell she had ever heard, she said, and sounded grand!

She asked him, when he stopped good-naturedly to shake hands with her before going in, how long he had worked there?

"A dozen year," he told her.

"I must kiss the hand," said she, "that has worked in this fine factory for a dozen year!" And she lifted it, though he would have prevented her, and put it to her lips. What harmony, besides her age and her simplicity, surrounded her, he did not know, but even in this fantastic action there was a something neither out of time nor place: a something which it seemed as if nobody else could have made as serious, or done with such a natural and touching air.

He had been at his loom full half an hour, thinking about this old woman, when, having occasion to move round the loom, for its adjustment, he glanced through a window which was in his corner, and saw her still looking up at the pile of building, lost in admiration. Heedless of the smoke and mud and wet, and of her two long journeys, she was gazing at it, as if the heavy thrum that issued from its many stories were proud music to her.

She was gone by and by, and the day went after her, and the lights sprung up again, and the Express whirled in full sight of the Fairy Palace over the arches near: little felt amid the jarring of the machinery, and scarcely heard above its crash and rattle. Long before then, his thoughts had gone back to the dreary room above the little shop, and to the shameful figure heavy on the bed, but heavier on his heart.

Machinery slackened; throbbing feebly like a fainting pulse; stopped. The bell again; the glare of light and heat dispelled; the factories, looming heavy in the black wet night—their tall chimneys rising up into the air like competing Towers of Babel.

He had spoken to Rachael only last night, it was true, and had walked with her a little way; but he had his new misfortune on him, in which no one else could give him a moment's relief, and, for the sake of it, and because he knew himself to want that softening of his anger which no voice but hers could effect, he felt he might so far disregard what she had said as to wait for her again. He waited, but she had eluded him. She was gone. On no other night in the year, could he so ill have spared her patient face.

O! Better to have no home in which to lay his head, than to have a home and dread to go to it, through such a cause. He ate and drank, for he was exhausted—but, he little knew or cared what; and he wandered about in the chill rain, thinking and thinking, and brooding and brooding.

No word of a new marriage had ever passed between them; but Rachael had taken great pity on him years ago, and to her alone he had opened his closed heart all this time, on the subject of his miseries; and he knew very well that if he were free to ask her, she would take him. He thought of the home he might at that moment have been seeking with pleasure and pride; of the different man he might have been that night; of the lightness then in his now heavy-laden breast; of the then restored honor, self-respect, and tranquility, now all torn to pieces. He thought of the waste of the best part of his life, of the change it made in his character for the worse every way, of the dreadful nature of his existence, bound hand and foot to a dead woman, and tormented by a demon in her shape. He thought of Rachael, how young when they were first brought together in these circumstances, how mature now, how soon to grow old. He thought of the number of girls and women she had seen marry, how many homes with children in them she had seen grow up around her, how she had contentedly pursued her own lone quiet path—for him—and how he had sometimes seen a shade of melancholy on her blessed face, that smote him with remorse and despair. He set the picture of her up, beside the infamous image of last night; and thought, could it be, that the whole earthly course of one so gentle, good, and self-denying was subjugate to such a wretch as that!

Filled with these thoughts—so filled that he had an unwholesome sense of growing larger, of being placed in some new and diseased relation toward the objects among which he passed, of seeing the iris round every misty light turn red—he went home for shelter.

Chapter XIII

RACHAEL

A CANDLE faintly burned in the window, to which the black ladder had often been raised for the sliding away of all that was most precious in this world to a striving wife and a brood of hungry babies; and Stephen added to his other thoughts the stern reflection, that of all the casualties of this existence upon earth, not one was dealt out with so unequal a hand as Death. The inequality of Birth was nothing to it. For, say that the child of a King and the child of a Weaver were born to-night in the same moment, what was that disparity, to the death of any human creature who was serviceable to, or beloved by, another, while this abandoned woman lived on!

From the outside of his home he gloomily passed to the inside, with suspended breath and with a slow footstep. He went up to his door, opened it, and so into the room.

Quiet and peace were there. Rachael was there, sitting by the bed.

She turned her head, and the light of her face shone in upon the midnight of his mind. She sat by the bed, watching and tending his wife. That is to say, he saw that some one lay there, and he knew too well it must be she; but Rachael's hands had put a curtain up, so that she was screened from his eyes. Her disgraceful garments were removed, and some of Rachael's were in the room. Every thing was in its place and order as he had always kept it, the little fire was newly trimmed, and the hearth was freshly swept. It appeared to him that he saw all this in Rachael's face, and looked at nothing besides. While looking at it, it was shut out from his view by the softened tears that filled his eyes; but, not before he had seen how earnestly she looked at him, and how her own eyes were filled too.

She turned again towards the bed, and satisfying herself that all was quiet there, spoke in a low, calm, cheerful voice.

"I am glad you have come at last, Stephen. You are very late."

"I ha' been walking up an' down."

"I thought so. But 'tis too bad a night for that. The rain falls very heavy, and the wind has risen."

The wind? True. It was blowing hard. Hark to the thundering in the chimney, and the surging noise! To have been out in such a wind, and not to have known it was blowing!

"I have been here once before to-day, Stephen. Landlady came round for me at dinner-time. There was someone here that needed looking to, she said. And 'deed she was right. All wandering and lost, Stephen. Wounded too, and bruised."

He slowly moved to a chair and sat down, drooping his head before her.

"I came to do what little I could, Stephen; first, for that she worked with me when we were girls both, and for that you courted her and married her when I was her friend—"

He laid his furrowed forehead on his hand, with a low groan.

"And next, for that I know your heart, and am right sure and certain that 'tis far too merciful to let her die, or even so much as suffer, for want of aid. Thou knowest who said, 'Let him who is without sin among you, cast the first stone at her!' There have been plenty to do that. Thou art not the man to cast the last stone, Stephen, when she is brought so low."

"O Rachael, Rachael!"

"Thou hast been a cruel sufferer, Heaven reward thee!" she said, in compassionate accents. "I am thy poor friend, with all my heart and mind."

The wounds of which she had spoken seemed to be about the neck of the self-made outcast. She dressed them now, still without showing her. She steeped a piece of linen in a basin, into which she poured some liquid from a bottle, and laid it with a gentle hand upon the sore. The three-legged table had been drawn close to the bedside, and on it there were two bottles. This was one.

It was not so far off, but that Stephen, following her hands with his eyes, could read what was printed on it, in large letters. He turned of a deadly hue, and a sudden horror seemed to fall upon him.

"I will stay here, Stephen," said Rachael, quietly resuming her seat, "till the bells go Three. 'Tis to be done again at three, and then she may be left till morning."

"But thy rest agen to-morrow's work, my dear."

"I slept sound, last night. I can wake many nights, when I am put to it. 'Tis thou who art in need of rest—so white and tired. Try to sleep in the chair there, while I watch. Thou hadst no sleep last night, I can well believe. To-morrow's work is far harder for thee than for me."

He heard the thundering and surging out of doors, and it seemed to him as if his late angry mood were going about trying to get at him. She had cast it out; she would keep it out; he trusted to her to defend him from himself.

"She don't know me, Stephen; she just drowsily mutters and stares. I have spoken to her times and again, but she don't notice! 'Tis as well so. When she comes to her right mind once more, I shall have done what I can, and she never the wiser."

"How long, Rachael, is't looked for, that she'll be so?"

"Doctor said she would haply come to her mind to-morrow."

His eyes fell again on the bottle, and a tremble passed over him, causing him to shiver in every limb. She thought he was chilled with the wet. "No," he said; "it was not that. He had had a fright."

"A fright?"

"Ay, ay! coming in. When I were walking. When I were thinking. When I—" It seized him again; and he stood up, holding by the mantel-shelf, as he pressed his dank cold hair down with a hand that shook as if it were palsied.

"Stephen!"

She was coming to him, but he stretched out his arm to stop her.

"No! Don't, please; don't! Let me see thee setten by the bed. Let me see thee, a' so good, and so forgiving. Let me see thee as I see thee when I coom in. I can never see thee better than so. Never, never, never!"

He had a violent fit of trembling, and then sunk into his chair. After a time he controlled himself, and, resting with an elbow on one knee, and his head upon that hand, could look toward Rachael. Seen across the dim candle with his moistened eyes, she looked as if she had a glory shining round her head. He could have believed she had. He did believe it, as the noise without shook the window, rattled at the door below, and went about the house clamoring and lamenting.

"When she gets better, Stephen, 'tis to be hoped she'll leave thee to thyself again, and do thee no more hurt. Any ways we will hope so now. And now I shall keep silence, for I want thee to sleep."

He closed his eyes, more to please her than to rest his weary head; but, by slow degrees, as he listened to the great noise of the wind, he ceased to hear it, or it changed into the working of his loom, or even into the voices of the day (his own included) saying what had been really said. Even this imperfect consciousness faded away at last, and he deamed a long, troubled dream.

He thought that he, and someone on whom his heart had long been set—but she was not Rachael, and that surprised him, even in the midst of his imaginary happiness—stood in the church being married. While the ceremony was performing, and while he recognized among the witnesses some whom he knew to be living, and many whom he knew to be dead, darkness came on, succeeded by the shining of a tremendous light. It broke from one line in the table of commandments at the altar, and illuminated the building with the words. They were sounded through the church too, as if there were voices in the fiery letters. Upon this, the whole appearance before him and around him changed, and nothing was left as it had been, but himself and the clergyman. They stood in the daylight before a crowd so vast, that if all the people in the world could have been brought together into one space, they could not have looked, he thought, more numerous; and they all abhorred him, and there was not one pitying or friendly eye among the millions that were fastened on his face. He stood on a raised stage, under his own loom; and, looking up at the shape the loom took, and hearing the burial service distinctly read, he knew that he was there to suffer death. In an instant what he stood on fell below him, and he was gone.

Out of what mystery he came back to his usual life, and to places that he knew, he was unable to consider; but he was back in those places by some means, and with this condemnation upon him, that he was never, in this world or the next, through all the unimaginable ages of eternity, to look on Rachael's face or hear her voice. Wandering to and fro, unceasingly, without hope, and in search of he knew not what (he only knew that he was doomed to seek it), he was the subject of a nameless, horrible dread, a mortal fear of one particular shape which every thing took. Whatsoever he looked at, grew into that form sooner or later. The object of his miserable existence was to prevent its recognition by any one among the various people he encountered. Hopeless labor! If he led them out of rooms where it was, if he shut up drawers and closets where it stood, if he drew the curious from places where he knew it to be secreted, and got them out into the streets, the very chimneys of the mills assumed that shape, and round them was the printed word.

The wind was blowing again, the rain was beating on the house-tops, and the larger spaces through which he had strayed contracted to the four walls of his room. Saving that the fire had died out, it was as his eyes had closed upon it. Rachael seemed to have fallen into a doze, in the chair by the bed. She sat wrapped in her shawl, perfectly still. The table stood in the same place, close by the bedside, and on it, in its real proportions and appearance, was the shape so often repeated.

He thought he saw the curtain move. He looked again, and he was sure it moved. He saw a hand come forth, and grope about a little. Then the curtain moved more perceptibly, and the woman in the bed put it back, and sat up.

With her woeful eyes, so haggard and wild, so heavy and large, she looked all round the room, and passed the corner where he slept in his chair. Her eyes returned to that corner, and she put her hand over them as a shade, while she looked into it. Again they went all round the room, scarcely heeding Rachael, if at all, and returned to that corner. He thought, as she once more shaded them—not so much looking at him, as looking for him with a brutish instinct that he was there—that no single trace was left in those debauched features, or in the mind that went along with them, of the woman he had married eighteen years before. But that he had seen her come to this by inches, he never could have believed her to be the same.

All this time, as if a spell were on him, he was motionless and powerless, except to watch her.

Stupidly dozing, or communing with her incapable self about nothing, she sat for a little while with her hands at her ears, and her head resting on them. Presently, she resumed her staring round the room. And now, for the first time, her eyes stopped at the table with the bottles on it.

Straightway she turned her eyes back to his corner, with the defiance of last night, and, moving very cautiously and softly, stretched out her greedy hand. She drew a mug into the bed, and sat for a while considering which of the two bottles she should choose. Finally, she laid her insensate grasp upon the bottle that had swift and certain death in it, and, before his eyes, pulled out the cork with her teeth.

Dream or reality, he had no voice, nor had he power to stir. If this be real, and her allotted time be not yet come, wake, Rachael, wake!

She thought of that, too. She looked at Rachael, and very slowly, very cautiously, poured out the contents. The draught was at her lips. A moment and she would be past all help, let the whole world wake and come about her with its utmost power. But, in that moment Rachael started up with a suppressed cry. The creature struggled, struck her, seized her by the hair; but Rachael had the cup.

Stephen broke out of his chair. "Rachael, am I wakin' or dreamin' this dreadfo' night?"

"'Tis all well, Stephen. I have been asleep myself. 'Tis near three. Hush! I hear the bells."

The wind brought the sounds of the church clock to the window. They listened, and it struck three. Stephen looked at her, saw how pale she was, noted the disorder of her hair, and the red marks of fingers on her forehead, and felt assured that his senses of sight and hearing had been awake. She held the cup in her hand even now.

"I thought it must be near three," she said, calmly pouring from the cup into the basin, and steeping the linen as before. "I am thankful I staied! 'Tis done now, when I have put this on. There! And now she's quiet again. The few drops in the basin I'll pour away, for 'tis bad stuff to leave about, though ever so little of it." As she spoke, she drained the basin into the ashes of the fire, and broke the bottle on the hearth.

She had nothing to do, then, but to cover herself with her shawl before going out into the wind and rain.

"Thou'lt let me walk wi' thee at this hour, Rachael?"

"No, Stephen. 'Tis but a minute and I'm home."

"Thou'rt not fearfo';" he said it in a low voice, as they went out at the door; "to leave me alone wi' her!"

As she looked at him, saying, "Stephen?" he went down on his knee before her, on the poor mean stairs, and put an end of her shawl to his lips.

"Thou art an Angel. Bless thee, bless thee!"

"I am, as I have told thee, Stephen, thy poor friend. Angels are not like me. Between them, and a working woman fu' of faults, there is a deep gulf set. My little sister is among them, but she is changed."

She raised her eyes for a moment as she said the words; and then they fell again, in all their gentleness and mildness, on his face.

"Thou changest me from bad to good. Thou mak'st me humbly wishfo' to be more like thee, and fearfo' to lose thee when this life is ower, an' a' the muddle cleared awa'. Thou'rt an Angel; it may be, thou hast saved my soul alive!"

She looked at him, on his knee at her feet, with her shawl still in his hand, and the reproof on her lips died away when she saw the working of his face.

"I coom home desp'rate. I coom home wi'out a hope, and mad wi' thinking that when I said a word o' complaint, I was reckoned a onreasonable Hand. I told thee I had had a fright. It were the Poison-bottle on table. I never hurt a livin' creetur; but happenin' so suddenly upon 't, I thowt, 'How can *I* say what I might ha' done to mysen, or her, or both!' "

She put her two hands on his mouth, with a face of terror, to stop him from saying more. He caught them in his unoccupied hand, and holding them, and still clasping the border of her shawl, said hurriedly:

"But I see thee, Rachael, setten by the bed. I ha' seen thee, a' this night. In my troublous sleep I ha' known thee still to be there. Evermore I will see thee there. I nevermore will see her or think o' her, but thou shalt be beside her. I nevermore will see or think o' any thing that angers me, but thou, so much better than me, shalt be by th' side on't. And so I will try t' look t' th' time, and so I will try t' trust t' th' time, when thou and me at last shall walk together far awa', beyond the deep gulf, in th' country where thy little sister is."

He kissed the border of her shawl again, and let her go. She bade him good night in a broken voice, and went out into the street.

The wind blew from the quarter where the day would soon appear, and still blew strongly. It had cleared the sky before it, and the rain had spent itself or traveled elsewhere, and the stars were bright. He stood bareheaded in the road, watching her quick disappearance. As the shining stars were to the heavy candle in the window, so was Rachael, in the rugged fancy of this man, to the common experiences of his life.

Chapter XIV

THE GREAT MANUFACTURER

TIME went on in Coketown like its own machinery: so much material wrought up, so much fuel consumed, so many powers worn out, so much money made. But, less inexorable than iron, steel, and brass, it brought its varying seasons even into that wilderness of smoke and brick, and made the only stand that ever *was* made in the place against its direful uniformity.

"Louisa is becoming," said Mr. Gradgrind, "almost a young woman."

Time, with his innumerable horse-power, worked away, not minding what any body said, and presently turned out young Thomas a foot taller than when his father had last taken particular notice of him.

"Thomas is becoming," said Mr. Gradgrind, "almost a young man."

Time passed Thomas on in the mill, while his father was thinking about it, and there he stood in a long tail-coat and a stiff shirt-collar.

"Really," said Mr. Gradgrind, "the period has arrived when Thomas ought to go to Bounderby."

Time, sticking to him, passed him on into Bounderby's Bank, made him an inmate of Bounderby's house, necessitated the purchase of his first razor, and exercised him diligently in his calculations relative to number one.

The same great manufacturer, always with an immense variety of work on hand, in every stage of development, passed Sissy onward in his mill, and worked her up into a very pretty article indeed.

"I fear, Jupe," said Mr. Gradgrind, "that your continuance at the school any longer, would be useless."

"I am afraid it would, sir," Sissy answered with a courtesy.

"I can not disguise from you, Jupe," said Mr. Gradgrind, knitting his brow, "that the result of your probation there has disappointed me; has greatly disappointed me. You have not acquired, under Mr. and Mrs. M'Choakumchild, any thing like that amount of exact knowledge which I looked for. You are extremely deficient in your facts. Your acquaintance with figures is very limited. You are altogether backward, and below the mark."

"I am sorry, sir," she returned; "but I know it is quite true. Yet I have tried hard, sir."

"Yes," said Mr. Gradgrind, "yes, I believe you have tried hard; I have observed you, and I can find no fault in that respect."

"Thank you, sir. I have thought sometimes;" Sissy very timid here; "that perhaps I tried to learn too much, and that if I had asked to be allowed to try a little less, I might have—"

"No, Jupe, no," said Mr. Gradgrind, shaking his head in his profoundest and most eminently practical way. "No. The course you pursued, you pursued according to the system—the system—and there is no more to be said about it. I can only suppose that the circumstances of your early life were too unfavorable to the development of your reasoning powers, and that we began too late. Still, as I have said already, I am disappointed."

"I wish I could have made a better acknowledgment, sir, of your kindness to a poor forlorn girl who had no claim upon you, and of your protection of her."

"Don't shed tears," said Mr. Gradgrind. "Don't shed tears. I don't complain of you. You are an affectionate, earnest, good young woman, and—and we must make that do."

"Thank you, sir, very much," said Sissy, with a grateful courtesy.

"You are useful to Mrs. Gradgrind, and (in a generally pervading way) you are serviceable in the family also; so I understand from Miss Louisa, and, indeed, so I have observed myself. I therefore hope," said Mr. Gradgrind, "that you can make yourself happy in those relations."

"I should have nothing to wish, sir, if—"

"I understand you," said Mr. Gradgrind; "you still refer to your father. I have heard from Miss Louisa that you still preserve that bottle. Well! If your training in the science of arriving at exact results had been more successful, you would have been wiser on these points. I will say no more."

He really liked Sissy too well to have a contempt for her; otherwise he held her calculating powers in such very slight estimation, that he must have fallen upon that conclusion. Somehow or other, he had become possessed by an idea that there was something in this girl which could hardly be set forth in a tabular form. Her capacity of definition might be easily stated at a very low figure, her mathematical knowledge at nothing; yet he was not sure that if he had been required, for example, to tick her off into columns in a parliamentary return, he would have quite known how to divide her.

In some stages of his manufacture of the human fabric, the processes of Time are very rapid. Young Thomas and Sissy being both at such a stage of their working up, these changes were effected in a year or two; while Mr. Gradgrind himself seemed stationary in his course, and underwent no alteration.

Except one, which was apart from his necessary progress through the mill. Time hustled him into a little noisy and rather dirty machinery, in a by-corner, and made him Member of Parliament for Coketown: one of the respected members for ounce weights and measures, one of the representatives of the multiplication table, one of the deaf honorable gentlemen, dumb honorable gentlemen, blind honorable gentlemen, lame honorable gentlemen, dead honorable gentlemen, to every other consideration. Else wherefore live we in a Christian land, eighteen hundred and odd years after our Master?

All this while, Louisa had been passing on, so quiet and reserved, and so much given to watching the bright ashes at twilight as they fell into the grate and became extinct, that from the period when her father had said she was almost a young woman—which seemed but yesterday—she had scarcely attracted his notice again, when he found her quite a young woman.

"Quite a young woman," said Mr. Gradgrind, musing. "Dear me!"

Soon after this discovery, he became more thoughful than usual for several days, and seemed much engrossed by one subject. On a certain night, when he was going out, and Louisa came to bid him good-by before his departure—as he was not to be home until late, and she would not see him again until the morning—he held her in his arms, looking at her in his kindest manner, and said:

"My dear Louisa, you are a woman!"

She answered with the old, quick, searching look of the night when she was found at the Circus; then cast down her eyes. "Yes, father."

"My dear," said Mr. Gradgrind, "I must speak with you alone and seriously. Come to me in my room after breakfast to-morrow, will you?"

"Yes, father."

"Your hands are rather cold, Louisa. Are you not well?"

"Quite well, father."

"And cheerful?"

She looked at him again, and smiled in her peculiar manner. "I am as cheerful, father, as I usually am, or usually have been."

"That's well," said Mr. Gradgrind. So he kissed her and went away; and Louisa returned to the serene apartment of the hair-cutting character, and leaning her elbow on her hand, looked again at the short-lived sparks that so soon subsided into ashes.

"Are you there, Loo?" said her brother, looking in at the door. He was quite a young gentleman of pleasure now, and not quite a prepossessing one.

"Dear Tom," she answered, rising and embracing him, "how long it is since you have been to see me!"

"Why, I have been otherwise engaged, Loo, in the evenings; and in the daytime old Bounderby has been keeping me at it rather. But I touch him up with you, when he comes it too strong, and so we preserve an understanding. I say! Has father said any thing particular to you to-day or yesterday, Loo?"

"No, Tom. But he told me to-night that he wished to do so in the morning."

"Ah! That's what I mean," said Tom. "Do you know where he is to-night?"—with a very deep expression.

"No."

"Then I'll tell you. He's with old Bounderby. They are having a regular confab together, up at the Bank. Why at the Bank, do you think? Well, I'll tell you again. To keep Mrs. Sparsit's ears as far off as possible, I expect."

With her hand upon her brother's shoulder, Louisa still stood looking at the fire. Her brother glanced at her face with greater interest than usual, and, encircling her waist with his arm, drew her coaxingly to him.

"You are very fond of me, ain't you, Loo?"

"Indeed I am, Tom, though you do let such long intervals go by without coming to see me."

"Well, sister of mine," said Tom, "when you say that, you are near my thoughts. We might be so much oftener together—mightn't we? Always together, almost—mightn't we? It would do me a great deal of good if you were to make up your mind to I know what, Loo. It would be a splendid thing for me. It would be uncommonly jolly!"

Her thoughtfulness baffled his cunning scrutiny. He could make nothing of her face. He pressed her in his arm, and kissed her cheek. She returned the kiss, but still looked at the fire.

"I say, Loo! I thought I'd come and just hint to you what was going on: though I supposed you'd most likely guess, even if you didn't know. I can't stay, because I'm engaged to some fellows to-night. You won't forget how fond you are of me?"

"No, dear Tom, I won't forget."

"That's a capital girl," said Tom. "Good-by, Loo."

She gave him an affectionate good-night, and went out with him to the door, whence the fires of Coketown could be seen, making the distance lurid. She stood there, looking steadfastly toward them, and listening to his departing steps. They retreated quickly, as glad to get away from Stone Lodge; and she stood there yet, when he was gone and all was quiet. It seemed as if, first in her own fire within the house, and then in the fiery haze without, she tried to discover what kind of woof Old Time, that greatest and longest-established Spinner of all, would weave from the threads he had already spun into a woman. But his factory is a secret place, his work is noiseless, and his Hands are mutes.

Chapter XV

FATHER AND DAUGHTER

ALTHOUGH Mr. Gradgrind did not take after Blue Beard, his room was quite a Blue chamber in its abundance of blue books. Whatever they could prove (which is usually any thing you like), they proved there, in an army constantly strengthening by the arrival of new recruits. In that charmed apartment, the most complicated social questions were cast up, got into exact totals, and finally settled—if those concerned could only have been brought to know it. As if an astronomical observatory should be made without any windows, and the astronomer within should arrange the starry universe solely by pen, ink, and paper, so Mr. Gradgrind, in *his* Observatory (and there are many like it), had no need to cast an eye upon the teeming myriads of human beings around him, but could settle all their destinies on a slate, and wipe out all their tears with one dirty little bit of sponge.

To this Observatory, then: a stern room with a deadly-statistical clock in it, which measured every second with a beat like a rap upon a coffin-lid: Louisa repaired on the appointed morning. The window looked toward Coketown; and when she sat down near her father's table, she saw the high chimneys and the long tracts of smoke looming in the heavy distance gloomily.

"My dear Louisa," said her father, "I prepared you last night to give me your serious attention in the conversation we are now going to have together. You have been so well trained, and you do, I am happy to say, so much justice to the education you have received, that I have perfect confidence in your good sense. You are not impulsive, you are not romantic, you are accustomed to view every thing from the strong dispassionate ground of reason and calculation. From that ground alone, I know you will view and consider what I am going to communicate."

He waited, as if he would have been glad that she said something. But she said never a word.

"Louisa, my dear, you are the subject of a proposal of marriage that has been made to me."

Again he waited, and again she answered not one word. This so far surprised him, as to induce him gently to repeat, "a proposal of marriage, my dear." To which she returned, without any visible emotion whatever:

"I hear you, father. I am attending, I assure you."

"Well!" said Mr. Gradgrind, breaking into a smile, after being for the moment at a loss, "you are even more dispassionate than I expected, Louisa. Or perhaps you are not unprepared for the announcement I have it in charge to make?"

"I can not say that, father, until I hear it. Prepared or unprepared, I wish to hear it all from you. I wish to hear you state it to me, father."

Strange to relate, Mr. Gradgrind was not so collected at this moment as his daughter was. He took a paper-knife in his hand, turned it over, laid it down, took it up again, and even then had to look along the blade of it, considering how to go on.

"What you say, my dear Louisa, is perfectly reasonable. I have undertaken then to let you know that—that Mr. Bounderby has informed me that he has long watched your progress with particular interest and pleasure, and has long hoped that the time might ultimately arrive when he should offer you his hand in marriage. That time, to which he has so long, and certainly with great constancy, looked forward, is now come. Mr. Bounderby has made his proposal of marriage to me, and has entreated me to make it known to you, and to express his hope that you will take it into your favorable consideration."

Silence between them. The deadly-statistical clock very hollow. The distant smoke very black and heavy.

"Father," said Lousia, "do you think I love Mr. Bounderby?"

Mr. Gradgrind was extremely discomfited by this unexpected question. "Well, my child," he returned, "I—really—can not take upon myself to say."

"Father," pursued Louisa in exactiy the same voice as before, "do you ask me to love Mr. Bounderby?"

"My dear Louisa, no. No. I ask nothing."

"Father," she still pursued, "does Mr. Bounderby ask me to love him?"

"Really, my dear," said Mr. Gradgrind, "it is difficult to answer your question—"

"Difficult to answer it, Yes or No, father?"

"Certainly, my dear. Because"—here was something to demonstrate, and it set him up again—"because the reply depends so materially, Louisa, on the sense in which we use the expression. Now, Mr. Bounderby does not do you the injustice, and does not do himself the injustice, of pretending to any thing fanciful, fantastic, or (I am using synonymous terms) sentimental. Mr. Bounderby would have seen you grow up under his eyes, to very little purpose, if he could so far forget what is due to your good sense, not to say to his, as to address you from any such ground. Therefore, perhaps the expression itself—I merely suggest this to you, my dear—may be a little misplaced."

"What would you advise me to use in its stead, father?"

"Why, my dear Louisa," said Mr. Gradgrind, completely recovered by this time, "I would advise you (since you ask me) to consider this question, as you have been accustomed to consider every other question, simply as one of tangible Fact. The ignorant and the giddy may embarrass such subjects with irrelevant fancies, and other absurdities that have no existence, properly viewed—really no existence—but it is no compliment to you to say that you know better. Now, what are the Facts of this case? You are, we will say in round numbers, twenty years of age; Mr. Bounderby is, we will say in round numbers, fifty. There is some disparity in your respective years, but in your means and positions there is none; on the contrary, there is a great suitability. Then the question arises, Is this one disparity sufficient to operate as a bar to such a marriage? In considering this question, it is not unimportant to take into account the statistics of marriage, so far as they have yet been obtained, in England and Wales. I find, on reference to the figures, that a large proportion of these marriages are contracted between parties of very unequal ages, and that the elder of these contracting parties is, in rather more than three-fourths of these instances, the bridegroom. It is remarkable as showing the wide prevalence of this law, that among the natives of the British possessions in India, also in a considerable part of China, and among the Calmucks of Tartary, the best means of computation yet furnished us by travelers, yield similar results. The disparity I have mentioned, therefore, almost ceases to be disparity, and (virtually) all but disappears."

"What do you recommend, father," asked Louisa, her reserved composure not in the least affected by these gratifying results, "that I should substitute for the term I used just now?—for the misplaced expression?"

"Louisa," returned her father, "it appears to me that nothing can be plainer. Confining yourself rigidly to Fact, the question of Fact you state to yourself is: Does Mr. Bounderby ask me to marry him? Yes, he does. The sole remaining question then is: Shall I marry him? I think nothing can be plainer than that."

"Shall I marry him?" repeated Louisa, with great deliberation.

"Precisely. And it is satisfactory to me, as your father, my dear Louisa, to know that you do not come to the consideration of that question with the previous habits of mind, and habits of life, that belong to many young women."

"No, father," she returned, "I do not."

"I now leave you to judge for yourself," said Mr. Gradgrind. "I have stated the case, as such cases are usually stated among practical minds; I have stated it, as the case of your mother and myself was stated in its time. The rest, my dear Louisa, is for you to decide."

From the beginning, she had sat looking at him fixedly. As he now leaned back in his chair, and bent his deep-set eyes upon her in his turn, perhaps he might have seen one wavering moment in her, when she was impelled to throw herself upon his breast, and give him the pent-up confidences of her heart. But, to see it, he must have overleaped at a bound the artificial barriers he had for many years been erecting between himself and all those subtle essences of humanity which will elude the utmost cunning of algebra until the last trumpet ever to be sounded shall blow even algebra to wreck. The barriers were too many and too high for such a leap. He did *not* see it. With his unbending, utilitarian, matter-of-fact face, he hardened her again; and the moment shot away into the plumbless depths of the past, to mingle with all the lost opportunities that are drowned there.

Removing her eyes from him, she sat so long looking silently toward the town, that he said at length: "Are you consulting the chimneys of the Coketown works, Louisa?"

"There seems to be nothing there but languid and monotonous smoke. Yet when the night comes, Fire bursts out, father!" she answered, turning quickly.

"Of course I know that, Louisa. I do not see the application of the remark." To do him justice, he did not at all.

She passed it away with a slight motion of her hand, and concentrating her attention upon him again, said, "Father, I have often thought that life is very short—" This was so distinctly one of his subjects that he interposed.

"It is short, no doubt, my dear. Still, the average duration of human life is proved to have increased of late years. The calculations of various life assurance and annuity offices, among other figures which cannot go wrong, have established the fact."

"I speak of my own life, father."

"O indeed? Still," said Mr. Gradgrind, "I need not point out to you, Louisa, that it is governed by the laws which govern lives in the aggregate."

"While it lasts, I would wish to do the little I can, and the little I am fit for. What does it matter?"

Mr. Gradgrind seemed rather at a loss to understand the last four words; replying, "How, matter? What, matter, my dear?"

"Mr. Bounderby," she went on in a steady, straight way, without regarding this, "asks me to marry him. The question I have to ask myself is, shall I marry him? That is so, father, is it not? You have told me so, father. Have you not?"

"Certainly, my dear."

"Let it be so. Since Mr. Bounderby likes to take me thus, I am satisfied to accept his proposal. Tell him, father, as soon as you please, that this was my answer. Repeat it, word for word, if you can, because I should wish him to know what I said."

"It is quite right, my dear," retorted her father, approvingly, "to be exact. I will observe your very proper request. Have you any wish, in reference to the period of your marriage, my child?"

"None, father. What does it matter?"

Mr. Gradgrind had drawn his chair a little nearer to her, and taken her hand. But, her repetition of these words seemed to strike with some little discord on his ear. He paused to look at her, and, still holding her hand, said:

"Louisa, I have not considered it essential to ask you one question, because the possibility implied in it appeared to me to be too remote. But, perhaps I ought to do so. You have never entertained in secret any other proposal?"

"Father," she returned, almost scornfully, "what other proposal can have been made to *me*? Whom have I seen? Where have I been? What are my heart's experiences?"

"My dear Louisa," returned Mr. Gradgrind, reassured and satisfied, "you correct me justly. I merely wished to discharge my duty."

"What do *I* know, father," said Louisa in her quiet manner, "of tastes and fancies; of aspirations and affections; of all that part of my nature in which such light things might have been nourished? What escape have I had from problems that could be demonstrated, and realities that could be grasped?" As she said it, she unconsciously closed her hand, as if upon a solid object, and slowly opened it as though she were releasing dust or ash.

"My dear," assented her eminently practical parent, "quite true, quite true."

"Why, father," she pursued, "what a strange question to ask *me!* The baby-preference that even I have heard of as common among children, has never had its innocent resting-place in my breast. You have been so careful of me, that I never had a child's heart. You have trained me so well, that I never dreamed a child's dream. You have dealt so wisely with me, father, from my cradle to this hour, that I never had a child's belief or a child's fear."

Mr. Gradgrind was quite moved by his success, and by this testimony to it. "My dear Louisa," said he, "you abundantly repay my care. Kiss me, my dear girl."

So, his daughter kissed him. Detaining her in his embrace, he said, "I may assure you now, my favourite child, that I am made happy by the sound decision at which you have arrived. Mr. Bounderby is a very remarkable man; and what ittle disparity can be said to exist between you—if any—is more than counterbalanced by the tone your mind has acquired. It has always been my object so to educate you, as that you might, while still in your early youth, be (if I may so express myself) almost any age. Kiss me once more, Louisa. Now, let us go and find your mother."

Accordingly, they went down to the drawing-room, where the esteemed lady with no nonsense about her was recumbent as usual, while Sissy worked beside her. She gave some feeble signs of returning animation when they entered, and presently the faint transparency was presented in a sitting attitude.

"Mrs. Gradgrind," said her husband, who had waited for the achievement of this feat with some impatience, "allow me to present to you Mrs. Bounderby."

"Oh!" said Mrs. Gradgrind, "so you have settled it! Well, I'm sure I hope your health may be good, Louisa; for, if your head begins to split as soon as you are married, which was the case with mine, I can not consider that you are to be envied, though I have no doubt you think you are, as all girls do. However, I give you joy, my dear—and I hope you may now turn all your ological studies to good account, I am sure I do! I must give you a kiss of congratulation, Louisa; but don't touch my right shoulder, for there's something running down it all day long. And now you see," whimpered Mrs. Gradgrind, adjusting her shawls after the affectionate ceremony, "I shall be worrying myself, morning, noon, and night, to know what I am to call him!"

"Mrs. Gradgrind," said her husband, solemnly, "what do you mean?"

"Whatever I am to call him, Mr. Gradgrind, when he is married to Louisa! I must call him something. It's impossible," said Mrs. Gradgrind, with a mingled sense of politeness and injury, "to be constantly addressing him, and never giving him a name. I can not call him Josiah, for the name is insupportable to me. You yourself wouldn't hear of Joe, you very well know. Am I to call my own son-in-law, Mister? Not, I believe, unless the time has arrived when, as an invalid, I am to be trampled upon by my relations. Then, what am I to call him?"

Nobody present having any suggestion to offer in the remarkable emergency, Mrs. Gradgrind departed this life for the time being, after delivering the following codicil to her remarks already executed:

"As to the wedding, all I ask, Louisa, is—and I ask it with a fluttering in my chest, which actually extends to the soles of my feet—that it may take place soon. Otherwise, I know it is one of those subjects I shall never hear the last of."

When Mr. Gradgrind had presented Mrs. Bounderby, Sissy had suddenly turned her head, and looked, in wonder, in pity, in sorrow, in doubt, in a multitude of emotions, toward Louisa. Louisa had known it, and seen it, without looking at her. From that moment she was impassive, proud, and cold—held Sissy at a distance—changed to her altogether.

Chapter XVI

HUSBAND AND WIFE

MR. BOUNDERBY'S first disquietude, on hearing of his happiness, was occasioned by the necessity of imparting it to Mrs. Sparsit. He could not make up his mind how to do that, or what the consequences of the step might be. Whether she would instantly depart, bag and baggage, to Lady Scadgers, or would positively refuse to budge from the premises; whether she would be plaintive or abusive, tearful or tearing; whether she would break her heart, or break the looking-glass; Mr. Bounderby could not at all foresee. However, as it must be done, he had no choice but to do it; so, after attempting several letters, and failing in them all, he resolved to do it by word of mouth.

On his way home, on the evening he set aside for this momentous purpose, he took the precaution of stepping into a chemist's shop and buying a bottle of the very strongest smelling-salts. "By George!" said Mr. Bounderby, "if she takes it in the fainting way, I'll have the skin off her nose, at all events!" But, in spite of being thus forearmed, he entered his own house with any thing but a courageous air; and appeared before the object of his misgivings, like a dog who was conscious of coming direct from the pantry.

"Good-evening, Mr. Bounderby!"

"Good-evening, ma'am, good-evening." He drew up his chair, and Mrs. Sparsit drew back hers, as who should say, "Your fire-side, sir. I freely admit it. It is for you to occupy it all, if you think proper."

"Don't go to the North Pole, ma'am!" said Mr. Bounderby.

"Thank you, sir," said Mrs. Sparsit, and returned, though short of her former position.

Mr. Bounderby sat looking at her, as, with the points of a stiff, sharp pair of scissors, she picked out holes for some inscrutable ornamental purpose, in a piece of cambric. An operation which, taken in connection with the bushy eyebrows and the Roman nose, suggested with some liveliness the idea of a hawk engaged upon the eyes of a tough little bird. She was so steadfastly occupied, that many minutes elapsed before she looked up from her work; when she did so, Mr. Bounderby bespoke her attention with a hitch of his head.

"Mrs. Sparsit, ma'am," said Mr. Bounderby, putting his hands in his pockets, and assuring himself with his right hand that the cork of the little bottle was ready for use, "I have no occasion to say to you, that you are not only a lady born and bred, but a devilish sensible woman."

"Sir," returned the lady, "this is indeed not the first time that you have honored me with similar expressions of your good opinion."

"Mrs. Sparsit, ma'am," said Mr. Bounderby, "I am going to astonish you."

"Yes, sir?" returned Mrs. Sparsit, interrogatively, and in the most tranquil manner possible. She generally wore mittens, and she now laid down her work, and smoothed those mittens.

"I am going, ma'am," said Bounderby, "to marry Tom Gradgrind's daughter."

"Yes, sir?" returned Mrs. Sparsit. "I hope you may be happy, Mr. Bounderby. Oh, indeed I hope you may be happy, sir!" And she said it with such great condescension, as well as with such great compassion for him, that Bounderby—far more disconcerted than if she had thrown her work-box at the mirror, or swooned on the hearth-rug—corked up the smelling-salts tight in his pocket, and thought, "Now con-found this woman, who could have even guessed that she would take it in this way!"

"I wish with all my heart, sir," said Mrs. Sparsit, in a highly superior manner; somehow she seemed, in a moment to have established a right to pity him ever afterwards; "that you may be in all respects very happy."

"Well, ma'am," returned Bounderby, with some resentment in his tone: which was clearly lowered, though in spite of himself, "I am obliged to you. I hope I shall be."

"*Do* you, sir!" said Mrs. Sparsit, with great affability. "But naturally you do; of course you do."

A very awkward pause on Mr. Bounderby's part succeeded. Mrs. Sparsit sedately resumed her work, and occasionally gave a small cough, which sounded like the cough of conscious strength and forbearance.

"Well, ma'am," resumed Bounderby, "under these circumstances, I imagine it would not be agreeable to a character like yours to remain here, though you would be very welcome here?"

"Oh dear no, sir, I could on no account think ofthat!" Mrs. Sparsit shook her head, still in her highly superior manner, and a little changed the small cough—coughing now, as if the spirit of prophecy rose within her, but had better be coughed down.

"However, ma'am," said Bounderby, "there are apartments at the Bank, where a born and bred lady, as keeper of the place, would be rather a catch than otherwise; and if the same terms—"

"I beg your pardon, sir. You were so good as to promise that you would always substitute the phrase, annual compliment."

"Well, ma'am, annual compliment. If the same annual compliment would be acceptable there, why, I see nothing to part us unless you do."

"Sir," returned Mrs. Sparsit. "The proposal is like yourself, and if the position I should assume at the Bank is one that I could occupy without descending lower in the social scale—"

"Why, of course it is," said Bounderby. "If it was not, ma'am, you don't suppose that I should offer it to a lady who has moved in the society you have moved in. Not that *I* care for such society, you know! But *you* do."

"Mr. Bounderby, you are very considerate."

"You'll have your own private apartments, and you'll have your coals and your candles and all the rest of it, and you'll have your maid to attend upon you, and you'll have your light porter to protect you, and you'll be what I take the liberty of considering precious comfortable," said Bounderby.

"Sir," rejoined Mrs. Sparsit, "say no more. In yielding up my trust here, I shall not be freed from the necessity of eating the bread of dependence:" she might have said the sweetbread, for that delicate article in a savory brown sauce was her favorite supper: "and I would rather receive it from your hand, than from any other. Therefore, sir, I accept your offer gratefully, and with many sincere acknowledgments for past favors. And I hope, sir," said Mrs. Sparsit, concluding in an impressively compassionate manner, "I fondly hope that Miss Gradgrind may be all you desire, and deserve!"

Nothing moved Mrs. Sparsit from that position any more. It was in vain for Bounderby to bluster, or to assert himself in any of his explosive ways; Mrs. Sparsit was resolved to have compassion on him, as a Victim. She was polite, obliging, cheerful, hopeful; but, the more polite, the more obliging, the more cheerful, the more hopeful, the more exemplary altogether, she; the forlorner Sacrifice and Victim, he. She had that tenderness for his melancholy fate that his great red countenance used to break out into cold perspirations when she looked at him.

Meanwhile the marriage was appointed to be solemnized in eight weeks' time, and Mr. Bounderby went every evening to Stone Lodge as an accepted wooer. Love was made on these occasions in the fom of bracelets; and, on all occasions during the period of betrothal, took a manufacturing aspect. Dresses were made, jewelery was made, cakes and gloves were made, settlements were made, and an extensive assortment of Facts did appropriate honor to the contract. The business was all Facts, from first to last. The Hours did not go through any of those rosy performances, which foolish poets have ascribed to them at such times; neither did the clocks go any faster, or any slower, than at other seasons. The deadly-statistical recorder in the Gradgrind observatory knocked every second on the head as it was born, and buried it with his accustomed regularity.

So the day came, as all other days come to people who will only stick to reason; and when it came, there were married in the church of the florid wooden legs—that popular order of architecture—Josiah Bounderby Esquire of Coketown, to Louisa eldest daughter of Thomas Gradgrind Esquire of Stone Lodge, M.P. for that borough. And when they were united in holy matrimony, they went home to breakfast at Stone Lodge aforesaid.

There was an improving party assembled on the auspicious occasion, who knew what every thing they had to eat and drink was made of, and how it was imported or exported, and in what quantities, and in what bottoms, whether native or foreign, and all about it. The bridesmaids, down to little Jane Gradgrind, were, in an intellectual point of view, fit helpmates for the calculating boy; and there was no nonsense about any of the company.

After breakfast, the bridegroom addressed them in the following terms:

"Ladies and gentlemen, I am Josiah Bounderby of Coketown. Since you have done my wife and myself the honor of drinking our healths and happiness, I suppose I must acknowledge the same; though, as you all know me, and know what I am, and what my extraction was, you won't expect a speech from a man who, when he sees a Post, says, 'that's a Post,' and when he sees a Pump, says, 'that's a Pump,' and is not to be got to call a Post a Pump, or a Pump a Post, or either of them a Toothpick. If you want a speech this morning, my friend and father-in-law, Tom Gradgrind, is a Member of Parliament, and you know where to get it.

I am not your man. However, if I feel a little independent when I look around this table to-day, and reflect how little I thought of marrying Tom Gradgrind's daughter when I was a ragged street-boy, who never washed his face unless it was at a pump, and that not oftener than once a fortnight, I hope I may be excused. So, I hope you like my feeling independent; if you don't, I can't help it. I *do* feel independent. Now, I have mentioned, and you have mentioned, that I am this day married to Tom Gradrind's daughter. I am very glad to be so. It has long been my wish to be so. I have watched her bringing-up, and I believe she is worthy of me. At the same time—not to deceive you—I believe I am worthy of her. So, I thank you, on both our parts, for the good-will you have shown toward us; and the best wish I can give the unmarried part of the present company, is this: I hope every bachelor may find as good a wife as I have found. And I hope every spinster may find as good a husband as my wife has found."

Shortly after which oration, as they were going on a nuptial trip to Lyons, in order that Mr. Bounderby might take the opportunity of seeing how the Hands got on in those parts, and whether they, too, required to be fed with gold spoons; the happy pair departed for the railroad. The bride, in passing down stairs, dressed for her journey, found Tom waiting for her—flushed, either with his feelings or the vinous part of the breakfast.

"What a game girl you are, to be such a first-rate sister, Loo!" whispered Tom.

She clung to him, as she would have clung to some far better nature that day, and was a little shaken in her reserved composure for the first time.

"Old Bounderby's quite ready," said Tom. "Time's up. Good-by! I shall be on the look-out for you, when you come back. I say, my dear Loo! *An't* it uncommonly jolly now!"

BOOK THE SECOND

REAPING

Chapter XVII

EFFECTS IN THE BANK

A SUNNY midsummer day. There was such a thing sometimes, even in Coketown.

Seen from a distance in such weather, Coketown lay shrouded in a haze of its own, which appeared impervious to the sun's rays. You only knew the town was there, because you knew there could have been no such sulky blotch upon the prospect without a town. A blur of soot and smoke, now confusedly tending this way, now that way, now aspiring to the vault of heaven, now murkily creeping along the earth, as the wind rose and fell, or changed its quarter: a dense formless jumble, with sheets of cross light in it, that showed nothing but masses of darkness:—Coketown in the distance was suggestive of itself, though not a brick of it could be seen.

The wonder was, it was there at all. It had been ruined so often, that it was amazing how it had borne so many shocks. Surely there never was such fragile china-ware as that of which the millers of Coketown were made. Handle them never so lightly, and they fell to pieces with such ease that you might suspect them of having been flawed before. They were ruined when they were required to send laboring children to school; they were ruined, when inspectors were appointed to look into their works; they were ruined, when such inspectors considered it doubtful whether they were quite justified in chopping people up with their machinery; they were utterly undone, when it was hinted that perhaps they need not always make quite so much smoke. Besides Mr. Bounderby's gold spoon which was generally received in Coketown, another prevalent fiction was very popular there. It took the form of a threat. Whenever a Coketowner felt he was ill-used—that is to say, whenever he was not left entirely alone, and it was proposed to hold him accountable for the consequences of any of his acts—he was sure to come out with the awful menace, that he would "sooner pitch his property into the Atlantic." This had terrified the Home Secretary within an inch of his life, on several occasions.

However, the Coketowners were so patriotic after all, that they never had pitched their property into the Atlantic yet, but on the contrary, had been kind enough to take mighty good care of it. So there it was, in the haze yonder; and it increased and multiplied.

The streets were hot and dusty on the summer day, and the sun was so bright that it even shone through the heavy vapor drooping over Coketown, and could not be looked at steadily. Stokers emerged from low underground doorways into factory yards; and sat on steps, and posts, and palings, wiping their swarthy visages, and contemplating coals. The whole town seemed to be frying in oil. There was a stifling smell of hot oil every where. The steam-engines shone with it, the dresses of the Hands were soiled with it, the mills throughout their many stories oozed and trickled it. The atmosphere of those Fairy palaces was like the breath of the simoom; and their inhabitants, wasting with heat, toiled languidly in the desert. But no temperature made the melancholy mad elephants more mad or more sane. Their wearisome heads went up and down at the same rate, in hot weather and cold, wet weather and dry, fair weather and foul. The measured motion of their shadows on the walls, was the substitute Coketown had to show for the shadows of rustling woods; while, for the summer hum of insects, it could offer, all the year round, from the dawn of Monday to the night of Saturday, the whirr of shafts and wheels.

Drowsily they whirred all through this sunny day, making the passenger more sleepy and more hot as he passed the humming walls of the mills. Sun-blinds, and sprinklings of water, a little cooled the main streets and the shops; but the mills, and the courts and alleys, baked at a fierce heat. Down upon the river that was black and thick with dye, some Coketown boys who were at large—a rare sight there —rowed a crazy boat, which made a spumous track upon the water as it jogged along, while every dip of an oar stirred up vile smells. But the sun itself, however beneficent generally, was less kind to Coketown than hard frost, and rarely looked intently into any of its closer regions without engendering more death than life. So does the eye of Heaven itself become an evil eye, when incapable or sordid hands are interposed between it and the things it looks upon to bless.

Mrs. Sparsit sat in her afternoon apartment at the Bank, on the shadier side of the frying street. Office-hours were over; and at that period of the day, in warm weather, she usually embellished with her genteel presence, a managerial board-room over the public office. Her own private sitting-room was a story higher, at the window of which post of observation she was ready, every morning, to greet Mr. Bounderby as he came across the road, with the sympathizing recognition appropriate to a Victim. He had been married now, a year; and Mrs. Sparsit had never released him from her determined pity a moment.

The Bank offered no violence to the wholesome monotony of the town. It was another red brick house, with black outside shutters, green inside blinds, a black street-door up two white steps, a brazen door-plate, and a brazen door-handle full stop. It was a size larger than Mr. Bounderby's house, as other houses were from a size to half-a-dozen sizes smaller; in all other particulars, it was strictly according to pattern.

Mrs. Sparsit was conscious that by coming in the evening-tide among the desks and writing implements, she shed a feminine, not to say also aristocratic, grace upon the office. Seated, with her needlework or netting apparatus, at the window, she had a self-laudatory sense of correcting, by her ladylike deportment, the rude business aspect of the place. With this impression of her interesting character upon her, Mrs. Sparsit considered herself, in some sort, the Bank Fairy. The townspeople, who, in their passing and repassing, saw her there, regarded her as the Bank Dragon, keeping watch over the treasures of the mine.

What those treasures were, Mrs. Sparsit knew as little as they did. Gold and silver coin, precious paper, secrets that if divulged would bring vague destruction upon vague persons (generally, however, people whom she disliked), were the chief items in her ideal catalogue thereof. For the rest, she knew that after office-hours, she reigned supreme over all the office furniture, and over a locked-up iron room with three locks, against the door of which strong chamber the light porter laid his head every night, on a truckle-bed that disappeared at cockcrow. Further, she was lady paramount over certain vaults in the basement, sharply spiked off from communication with the predatory world; and over the relics of the current day's work, consisting of blots of ink, worn-out pens, fragments of wafers, and scraps of paper torn so small, that nothing interesting could ever be deciphered on them when Mrs. Sparsit tried. Lastly, she was guardian over a little armory of cutlasses and carbines, arrayed in vengeful order above one of the official chimney-pieces; and over that respectable tradition never to be separated from a place of business claiming to be wealthy—a row of fire-buckets—vessels calculated to be of no physical utility on any occasion, but observed to exercise a fine moral influence, almost equal to bullion, on most beholders.

A deaf serving-woman and the light porter completed Mrs. Sparsit's empire. The deaf serving-woman was rumored to be wealthy; and a saying had for years gone about among the lower orders of Coketown, that she would be murdered some night when the Bank was shut, for the sake of her money. It was generally considered, indeed, that she had been due some time, and ought to have fallen long ago; but she had kept her life, and her situation, with an ill-conditioned tenacity that occasioned much offense and disappointment.

Mrs. Sparsit's tea was just set for her on a pert little table, with its tripod of legs in an attitude, which she insinuated after office-hours into, the company of the stern, leathern-topped, long board-table that bestrode the middle of the room. The light porter placed the tea-tray on it, knuckling his forehead as a form of homage.

"Thank you, Bitzer," said Mrs. Sparsit.

"Thank *you,* ma'am," returned the light porter. He was a very light porter indeed; as light as in the days when he blinkingly defined a horse, for girl number twenty.

"All is shut up, Bitzer?" said Mrs. Sparsit.

"All is shut up, ma'am."

"And what," said Mrs. Sparsit, pouring out her tea, "is the news of the day? Any thing?"

"Well, ma'am, I can't say that I have heard any thing particular. Our people are a bad lot, ma'am; but that is no news, unfortunately."

"What are the restless wretches doing now?" asked Mrs. Sparsit.

"Merely going on in the old way, ma'am. Uniting, and leaguing, and engaging to stand by one another."

"It is much to be regretted," said Mrs. Sparsit, making her nose more Roman and her eyebrows more Coriolanian in the strength of her severity, "that the united masters allow of any such class-combinations."

"Yes, ma'am," said Bitzer.

"Being united themselves, they ought one and all to set their faces against employing any man who is united with any other man," said Mrs. Sparsit.

"They have done that, ma'am," returned Bitzer; "but—it rather fell through, ma'am."

"I do not pretend to understand these things," said Mrs. Sparsit, with dignity, "my lot having been originally cast in a widely different sphere, and Mr. Sparsit, as a Powler, being also quite out of the pale of any such dissensions. I only know that these people must be conquered, and that it's high time it was done, once for all."

"Yes, ma'am," returned Bitzer, with a demonstration of great respect for Mrs. Sparsit's oracular authority. "You couldn't put it clearer, I am sure, ma'am."

As this was his usual hour for having a little confidential chat with Mrs. Sparsit, and as he had already caught her eye and seen that she was going to ask him something, he made a pretence of arranging the rulers, inkstands, and so forth, while that lady went on with her tea, glancing through the open window down into the street.

"Has it been a busy day, Bitzer?" asked Mrs. Sparsit.

"Not a very busy day, my lady. About an average day." He now and then slided into my lady, instead of ma'am, as an involuntary acknowledgment of Mrs. Sparsit's personal dignity and claims to reverence.

"The clerks," said Mrs. Sparsit, carefully brushing an imperceptible crumb of bread and butter from her left-hand mitten, "are trustworthy, punctual, and industrious, of course?"

"Yes, ma'am, pretty fair, ma'am. With the usual exception."

He held the respectable office of general spy and informer in the establishment, for which volunteer service he received a present at Christmas, over and above his weekly wage. He had grown into an extremely clear-headed, cautious, prudent young man, who was safe to rise in the world. His mind was so exactly regulated, that he had no affections or passions. All his proceedings were the result of the nicest and coldest calculation; and it was not without cause that Mrs. Sparsit habitually observed of him, that he was a young man of the steadiest principle she had ever known. Having satisfied himself, on his father's death, that his mother had a right of settlement in Coketown, this excellent young economist had asserted that right for her with such a steadfast adherence to the principle of the case, that she had been shut up in the workhouse ever since. It must be admitted that he allowed her half a pound of tea a year, which was weak in him: first, because all gifts have an inevitable tendency to pauperise the recipient, and secondly, because his only reasonable transaction in that commodity would have been to buy it for as little as he could possibly give, and sell it for as much as he could possibly get; it having been clearly ascertained by philosophers that in this is comprised the whole duty of man—not a part of man's duty, but the whole.

"Pretty fair, ma'am. With the usual exception, ma'am," repeated Bitzer.

"Ah—h!" said Mrs. Sparsit, shaking her head over her tea-cup, and taking a long gulp.

"Mr. Thomas, ma'am, I doubt Mr. Thomas very much, ma'am, I don't like his ways at all."

"Bitzer," said Mrs. Sparsit, in a very impressive manner, "do you recollect my having said any thing to you respecting names?"

"I beg your pardon, ma'am. It's quite true that you did object to names being used, and they're always best avoided."

"Please to remember that I have a charge here," said Mrs. Sparsit, with her air of state. "I hold a trust here, Bitzer, under Mr. Bounderby. However improbable both Mr. Bounderby and myself might have deemed it years ago, that he would ever become my patron, making me an annual compliment, I can not but regard him in that light. From Mr. Bounderby I have received every acknowledgement of my social station, and every recognition of my family descent, that I could possibly expect. More, far more. Therefore, to my patron I will be scrupulously true. And I do not consider, I will not consider, I can not consider," said Mrs. Sparsit, with a most extensive stock on hand of honor and morality, "that I *should* be scrupulously true, if I allowed names to be mentioned under this roof, that are unfortunately—most unfortunately—no doubt of that — connected with his."

Bitzer knuckled his forehead again, and again begged pardon.

"No, Bitzer," continued Mrs. Sparsit, "say an individual, and I will hear you; say Mr. Thomas, and you must excuse me."

"With the usual exception, ma'am," said Bitzer, trying back, "of an individual."

"Ah—h!" Mrs. Sparsit repeated the ejaculation, the shake of the head over her tea-cup, and the long gulp, as taking up the conversation again at the point where it had been interrupted.

"An individual, ma'am," said Bitzer, "has never been what he ought to have been, since he first came into the place. He is a dissipated, extravagant idler. He is not worth his salt, ma'am. He wouldn't get it either, if he hadn't a friend and relation at court, ma'am!"

"Ah—h!" said Mrs. Sparsit, with another melancholy shake of her head.

"I only hope, ma'am," pursued Bitzer, "that his friend and relation may not supply him with the means of carrying on. Otherwise, ma'am, we know out of whose pocket *that* money comes."

"Ah—h!" sighed Mrs. Sparsit again, with another melancholy shake of her head.

"He is to be pitied, ma'am. The last party I have alluded to, is to be pitied, ma'am," said Bitzer.

"Yes, Bitzer," said Mrs. Sparsit. "I have always pitied the delusion, always."

"As to an individual, ma'am," said Bitzer, dropping his voice and drawing nearer, "he is as improvident as any of the people in this town.

And you know what *their* improvidence is, ma'am. No one could wish to know it better than a lady of your eminence does."

"They would do well," returned Mrs. Sparsit, "to take example by you, Bitzer."

"Thank you, ma'am. But, since you do refer to me, now look at me, ma'am. I have put by a little, ma'am, already. That gratuity which I receive at Christmas, ma'am: I never touch it. I don't even go the length of my wages, though they're not high, ma'am. Why can't they do as I have done, ma'am? What one person can do, another can do."

This, again, was among the fictions of Coketown. Any capitalist there, who had made sixty thousand pounds out of sixpence, always professed to wonder why the sixty thousand nearest Hands didn't each make sixty thousand pounds out of sixpence, and more or less reproached them every one for not accomplishing the little feat. What I did, you can do. Why don't you go and do it?

"As to their wanting recreations, ma'am," said Bitzer, "it's stuff and nonsense. *I* don't want recreations. I never did, and I never shall; I don't like 'em. As to their combining together; there are many of them, I have no doubt, that by watching and informing upon one another could earn a trifle now and then, whether in money or good-will, and improve their livelihood. Then, why don't they improve it, ma'am? It's the first consideration of a rational creature, and it's what they pretend to want."

"Pretend indeed!" said Mrs. Sparsit.

"I am sure we are constantly hearing, ma'am, till it becomes quite nauseous, concerning their wives and families," said Bitzer. "Why look at me, ma'am! *I* don't want a wife and family. Why should they?"

"Because they are improvident," said Mrs. Sparsit.

"Yes, ma'am," returned Bitzer, "that's where it is. If they were more provident, and less perverse, ma'am, what would they do? They would say, 'While my hat covers my family,' or 'while my bonnet covers my family'—as the case might be, ma'am—'I have only one to feed, and that's the person I most like to feed.'"

"To be sure," assented Mrs. Sparsit, eating muffin.

"Thank you, ma'am," said Bitzer, knuckling his forehead again, in return for the favor of Mrs. Sparsit's improving conversation. "Would you wish a little more hot water, ma'am, or is there anything else that I could fetch you?"

"Nothing just now, Bitzer."

"Thank you, ma'am. I shouldn't wish to disturb you at your meals, ma'am, particularly tea, knowing your partiality for it," said Bitzer, craning a little to look over into the street from where he stood; "but there's a gentleman been looking up here for a minute or so, ma'am, and he has come across as if he was going to knock. That *is* his knock, ma'am, no doubt."

He stepped to the window; and looking out, and drawing in his head again, confirmed himself with, "Yes, ma'am. Would you wish the gentleman to be shown in, ma'am?"

"I don't know who it can be," said Mrs. Sparsit, wiping her mouth and arranging her mittens.

"A stranger, ma'am, evidently."

"What a stranger can want at the Bank at this time of the evening, unless he comes upon some business for which he is too late, I don't know," said Mrs. Sparsit; "but I hold a charge in this establishment from Mr. Bounderby, and I will never shrink from it. If to see him is any part of the duty I have accepted, I will see him. Use your own discretion, Bitzer."

Here the visitor, all unconscious of Mrs. Sparsit's magnanimous words, repeated his knock so loudly that the light porter hastened down to open the door; while Mrs. Sparsit took the precaution of concealing her little table, with all its appliances upon it, in a cupboard, and then decamped up-stairs, that she might appear, if needful, with the greater dignity.

"If you please, ma'am, the gentleman would wish to see you," said Bitzer, with his light eye at Mrs. Sparsit's keyhole. So, Mrs. Sparsit, who had improved the interval by touching up her cap, took her classical features down-stairs again, and entered the board room in the manner of a Roman matron going outside the city walls to treat with an invading general.

The visitor having strolled to the window, and being then engaged in looking carelessly out, was as unmoved by this impressive entry as man could possibly be. He stood whistling to himself with all imaginable coolness, with his hat still on, and a certain air of exhaustion upon him, in part arising from excessive summer, and in part from excessive gentility. For, it was to be seen with half an eye that he was a thorough gentleman, made to the model of the time; weary of every thing, and putting no more faith in any thing than Lucifer.

"I believe, sir," quoth Mrs. Sparsit, "you wished to see me."

"I beg your pardon," he said, turning and removing his hat; "pray excuse me."

"Humph!" thought Mrs. Sparsit, as she made a stately bend. "Five-and-thirty, good-looking, good figure, good teeth, good voice, good breeding, well dressed, dark hair, bold eyes." All which Mrs. Sparsit observed in her womanly way—like the Sultan who put his head in the pail of water—merely in dipping down and coming up again.

"Please to be seated, sir," said Mrs. Sparsit.

"Thank you. Allow me." He placed a chair for her, but remained himself carelessly lounging against the table. "I left my servant at the railway looking after the luggage—very heavy train and vast quantity of it in the van—and strolled on, looking about me. Exceedingly odd place. Will you allow me to ask you if it's *always* as black as this?"

"In general much blacker," returned Mrs. Sparsit, in her uncompromising way.

"Is it possible! Excuse me: you are not a native, I think?"

"No, sir," returned Mrs. Sparsit. "It was once my good or ill fortune, as it may be—before I became a widow—to move in a very different sphere. My husband was a Powler."

"Beg your pardon, really!" said the stranger. "Was—?"

Mrs. Sparsit repeated "A Powler." "Powler Family," said the stranger, after reflecting a few moments. Mrs. Sparsit signified assent. The stranger seemed a little more fatigued than before.

"You must be very much bored here?" was the inference he drew from the communication.

"I am the servant of circumstances, sir," said Mrs. Sparsit, "and I have long adapted myself to the governing power of my life."

"Very philosophical," returned the stranger, "and very exemplary and laudable, and—" It seemed to be scarcely worth his while to finish the sentence, so he played with his watch-chain wearily.

"May I be permitted to ask, sir," said Mrs. Sparsit, "to what I am indebted for the favor of—"

"Assuredly," said the stranger. "Much obliged to you for reminding me. I am the bearer of a letter of introduction to Mr. Bounderby the Banker. Walking through this extraordinarily black town, while they were getting dinner ready at the hotel, I asked a fellow whom I met; one of the working people; who appeared to have been taking a shower-bath of something fluffy, which I assume to be the raw material—"

Mrs. Sparsit inclined her head.

"—Raw material—where Mr. Bounderby the banker, might reside. Upon which, misled no doubt by the word Banker, he directed me to the Bank. Fact being, I presume, that Mr. Bounderby the Banker does *not* reside in the edifice in which I have the honor of offering this explanation?"

"No, sir," returned Mrs. Sparsit, "he does not."

"Thank you. I had no intention of delivering my letter at the present moment, nor have I. But, strolling on to the Bank to kill time, and having the good fortune to observe at the window," toward which he languidly waved his hand, then slightly bowed, "a lady of a very superior and agreeable appearance, I considered that I could not do better than take the liberty of asking that lady where Mr. Bounderby the Banker, *does* live. Which I accordingly venture, with all suitable apologies, to do."

The inattention and indolence of his manner were sufficiently relieved, to Mrs. Sparsit's thinking, by a certain gallantry at ease, which offered her homage too. Here he was, for instance, at this moment, all but sitting on the table, and yet lazily bending over her as if he acknowledged an attraction in her that made her charming—in her way.

"Banks, I know, are always suspicious, and officially must be," said the stranger, whose lightness and smoothness of speech were pleasant likewise; suggesting matter far more sensible and humorous than it ever contained—which was perhaps a shrewd device of the founder of this numerous sect, whosoever may have been that great man; "therefore I may observe that my letter—here it is—is from the member for this place—Gradgrind—whom I have had the pleasure of knowing in London."

Mrs. Sparsit recognized the hand, intimated that such confirmation was quite unnecessary, and gave Mr. Bounderby's address, with all needful clews and directions in aid.

"Thousand thanks," said the stranger. "Of course you know the Banker well?"

"Yes, sir," rejoined Mrs. Sparsit. "In my dependent relation towards him, I have known him ten years."

"Quite an eternity! I think he married Gradgrind's daughter?"

"Yes," said Mrs. Sparsit, suddenly compressing her mouth, "he had that—honor."

"The lady is quite a philosopher, I am told?"

"Indeed, sir," said Mrs. Sparsit. "*Is* she?"

"Excuse my impertinent curiosity," pursued the stranger, fluttering over Mrs. Sparsit's eyebrows, with a propitiatory air, "but you know the family, and know the world. I am about to know the family, and may have much to do with them. Is the lady so very alarming? Her father gives her such a portentously hard-headed reputation, that I have a burning desire to know. Is she absolutely unapproachable? Repellently and stunningly clever? I see, by your meaning smile, you think not. You have poured balm into my anxious soul. As to age, now. Forty? Five-and-thirty?"

Mrs. Sparsit laughed outright. "A chit," said she. "Not twenty when she was married."

"I give you my honor, Mrs. Powler," returned the stranger, detaching himself from the table, "that I never was so astonished in my life!"

It really did seem to impress him, to the utmost extent of his capacity of being impressed. He looked at his informant for full a quarter of a minute, and appeared to have the surprise in his mind all the time. "I assure you, Mrs. Powler," he then said, much exhausted, "that the father's manner prepared me for a grim and stony maturity. I am obliged to you, of all things, for correcting so absurd a mistake. Pray excuse my intrusion. Many thanks. Good-day!"

He bowed himself out; and Mrs. Sparsit, hiding in the window-curtain, saw him languishing down the street on the shady side of the way, observed of all the town.

"What do you think of the gentleman, Bitzer?" she asked the light porter, when he came to take away.

"Spends a deal of money on his dress, ma'am."

"It must be adimtted," said Mrs. Sparsit, "that it's very tasteful."

"Yes, ma'am," returned Bitzer, "if that's worth the money."

"Besides which, ma'am," resumed Bitzer, while he was polishing the table, "he looks to me as if he gamed."

"It's immoral to game," said Mrs. Sparsit.

"It's ridiculous, ma'am," said Bitzer, "because the chances are against the players."

Whether it was that the heat prevented Mrs. Sparsit from working, or whether it was that her hand was out, she did not work that night. She sat at the window, when the sun began to sink behind the smoke; she sat there, when the smoke was burning red, when the color faded from it, when darkness seemed to rise slowly out of the ground, and creep upward, upward, up to the house-tops, up the church steeple, up to the summits of the factory chimneys, up to the sky. Without a candle in her room, Mrs. Sparsit sat at the window, with her hands before her, not thinking much of the sounds of evening: the whooping of boys, the barking of dogs, the rumbling of wheels, the steps and voices of passengers, the shrill street cries, the clogs upon the pavement when it was their hour for going by, the shutting-up of shop-shutters. Not until the light porter announced that her nocturnal sweetbread was ready, did Mrs.

Sparsit arouse herself from her reverie, and convey her dense black eyebrows—by that time creased with meditation, as if they needed ironing out—up stairs.

"O, you Fool!" said Mrs. Sparsit, when she was alone at her supper. Whom she meant, she did not say; but she could scarcely have meant the sweetbread.

Chapter XVIII

MR. JAMES HARTHOUSE

THE Gradgrind party wanted assistace in murdering the Graces. They went about recruiting; and where could they enlist recruits more readily, than among the fine gentlemen who, having found out every thing to be worth nothing, were equally ready for any thing?

Moreover, the healthy spirits who had mounted to this sublime height were attractive to many of the Gradgrind school. They liked fine gentlemen; they pretended that they did not, but they did. They became exhausted in imitation of them; and they yaw-yawed in their speech like them; and they served out, with an enervated air, the little mouldy rations of political economy, on which they regaled their disciples. There never before was seen on earth such a wonderful hybrid race as was thus produced.

Among the fine gentlemen not regularly belonging to the Gradgrind school, there was one of a good family and a better appearance, with a happy turn of humor which had told immensely with the House of Commons on the occasion of his entertaining it with his (and the Board of Directors') view of a railway accident, in which the most careful officers ever known, employed by the most liberal managers ever heard of, assisted by the finest mechanical contrivances ever devised, the whole in action on the best line ever constructed, had killed five people and wounded thirty-two, by a casualty without which the excellence of the whole system would have been positively incomplete. Among the slain was a cow, and among the scattered articles unowned, a widow's cap. And the honorable member had so tickled the House (which has a delicate sense of humor) by putting the cap on the cow, that it became impatient of any serious reference to the Coroner's Inquest, and brought the railway off with Cheers and Laughter.

Now, this gentleman had a younger brother of still better appearance than himself, who had tried life as a Cornet of Dragoons, and found it a bore; and had afterward tried it in the train of an English minister abroad, and found it a bore; and had then strolled to Jerusalem, and got bored there; and had then gone yachting about the world, and got bored every where. To whom this honorable and jocular member fraternally said one day, "Jem, there's a good opening among the hard Fact fellows, and they want men. I wonder you don't go in for statistics." Jem, rather taken by the novelty of the idea, and very hard up for a change, was as ready to "go in" for statistics as for any thing else. So, he went in. He coached himself up with a blue book or two; and his brother put it about among the hard Fact fellows, and said, "If you want to bring in, for any place, a handsome dog who can make you a devilish good speech, look after my brother Jem, for he's your man." After a few dashes in the public meeting way, Mr. Gradgrind and a council of political sages approved of Jem, and it was resolved to send him down to Coketown, to become known there and in the neighborhood. Hence the letter Jem had last night shown to Mrs. Sparsit, which Mr. Bounderby now held in his hand; superscribed, "Josiah Bounderby, Esquire, Banker, Coketown. Specially to introduce James Harthouse, Esquire. Thomas Gradgrind."

Within an hour of the receipt of this dispatch and Mr. James Harthouse's card, Mr. Bounderby put on his hat and went down to the Hotel. There he found Mr. James Harthouse looking out of window, in a state of mind so disconsolate that he was already half disposed to "go in" for something else.

"My name, sir," said his visitor, "is Josiah Bounderby of Coketown."

Mr. James Harthouse was very happy indeed (though he scarcely looked so), to have a pleasure he had long expected.

"Coketown, sir," said Bounderby, obstinately taking a chair, "is not the kind of place you have been accustomed to. Therefore, if you'll allow me—or whether you will or not, for I am a plain man—I'll tell you something about it before we go any further."

Mr. Harthouse would be charmed.

"Don't be too sure of that," said Bounderby. "I don't promise it. First of all, you see our smoke. That's meat and drink to us. It's the healthiest thing in the world in all respects, and particularly for the lungs. If you are one of those who want us to consume it, I differ from you. We are not going to wear the bottoms of our boilers out any faster than we wear'em out now, for all the humbugging sentiment in Great Britain and Ireland."

By way of "going in" to the fullest extent, Mr. Harthouse rejoined, "Mr. Bounderby, I assure you I am entirely and completely of your way of thinking. On conviction."

"I am glad to hear it," said Bounderby. "Now, you have heard a lot of talk about the work in our mills, no doubt. You have? Very good. I'll state the fact of it to you. It's the pleasantest work there is, and it's the lightest work there is, and it's the best paid work there is. More than that, we couldn't improve the mills themselves, unless we laid down Turkey carpets on the floors, which we're not a-going to do."

"Mr. Bounderby, perfectly right."

"Lastly," said Bounderby, "as to our Hands. There's not a Hand in this town, sir, man, woman, or child, but has one ultimate object in life. That object is, to be fed on turtle soup and venison with a gold spoon. Now, they're not a-going—none of 'em—ever to be fed on turtle soup and venison with a gold spoon. And now you know the place."

Mr. Harthouse professed himself in the highest degree instructed and refreshed by this condensed epitome of the whole Coketown question.

"Why, you see," replied Mr. Bounderby, "it suits my disposition to have a full understanding with a man, particularly with a public man, when I make his acquaintance. I have only one thing more to say to you, Mr. Harthouse, before assuring you of the pleasure with which I shall respond, to the utmost of my poor ability, to my friend Tom Gradgrind's letter of introduction. You are a man of family. Don't you deceive yourself by supposing for a moment that *I* am a man of family. I am a bit of dirty riff-raff, and a genuine scrap of tag, rag, and bobtail."

If anything could have exalted Jem's interest in Mr. Bounderby, it would have been this very circumstance. Or, so he told him.

"So now," said Bounderby, "we may shake hands on equal terms. I say, equal terms, because although I know what I am, and the exact depth of the gutter I have lifted myself out of, better than any man does, I am as proud as you are. I am just as proud as you are. Having now asserted my independence in a proper manner, I may come to how do you find yourself, and I hope you're pretty well."

The better, Mr. Harthouse gave him to understand as they shook hands, for the salubrious air of Coketown. Mr. Bounderby received the answer with favor.

"Perhaps you know," said he, "or perhaps you don't know, I married Tom Gradgrind's daughter. If you have nothing better to do than to walk up town with me, I shall be glad to introduce you to Tom Gradgrind's daughter."

"Mr. Bounderby," said Jem, "you anticipate my dearest wishes."

They went out without further discourse; and Mr. Bounderby piloted the new acquaintance who so strongly contrasted with him, to the private red brick dwelling, with the black outside shutters, the green inside blinds, and the black street-door up the two white steps. In the drawingroom of which mansion, there presently entered to them the most remarkable girl Mr. James Harthouse had ever seen. She was so constrained, and yet so careless; so reserved, and yet so watchful; so cold and proud, and yet so sensitively ashamed of her husband's braggart humility—from which she shrunk as if every example of it were a cut or a blow; that it was quite a new sensation to observe her. In face she was no less remarkable than in manner. Her features were handsome; but their natural play was so suppressed and locked up, that it seemed impossible to guess at their genuine expression. Utterly indifferent, perfectly self-reliant, never at a loss, and yet never at her ease, with her figure in company with them there, and her mind apparently quite alone—it was of no use "going in" yet awhile to comprehend this girl, for she baffled all penetration.

From the mistress of the house, the visitor glanced to the house itself. There was no mute sign of a woman in the room. No graceful little adornment, no fanciful little device, however trivial, any where expressed her influence. Cheerless and comfortless, boastfully and doggedly rich, there the room stared at its present occupants, unsoftened and unrelieved by the least trace of any womanly occupation. As Mr. Bounderby stood in the midst of his household gods, so those unrelenting divinities occupied their places around Mr. Bounderby, and they were worthy of one another and well matched.

"This, sir," said Bounderby, "is my wife, Mrs. Bounderby: Tom Gradgrind's eldest daughter. Loo, Mr. James Harthouse. Mr. Harthouse has joined your father's muster-roll. If he is not Tom Gradgrind's colleague before long, I believe we shall at least hear of him in connection with one of our neighboring towns. You observe, Mr. Harthouse, that my wife is my junior. I don't know what she saw in me to marry me, but she saw something in me, I suppose, or she wouldn't have married me. She has lots of expensive knowledge, sir, political and otherwise. If you want to cram for any thing, I should be troubled to recommend you to a better adviser than Loo Bounderby."

To a more agreeable adviser, or one from whom he would be more likely to learn, Mr. Harthouse could never be recommended.

"Come!" said his host. "If you're in the complimentary line, you'll get on here, for you'll meet with no competition. I have never been in the way of learning compliments myself, and I don't profess to understand the art of paying 'em. In fact, I despise 'em. But, your bringing-up was different from mine; mine was a real thing, by George! You're a gentleman, and I don't pretend to be one. I am Josiah Bounderby of Coketown, and that's enough for me. However, though *I* am not influenced by manners and station, Loo Bounderby may be. She hadn't my advantages—disadvantages you would call 'em, but I call 'em advantages —so you'll not waste your power, I dare say."

"Mr. Bounderby," said Jem, turning with a smile to Louisa, "is a noble animal in a comparatively natural state, quite free from the harness in which a conventional hack like myself works."

"You respect Mr. Bounderby very much," she quietly returned. "It is natural that you should."

He was disgracefully thrown out, for a gentleman who had seen so much of the world, and thought, "Now, how am I to take this?"

"You are going to devote yourself, as I gather from what Mr. Bounderby has said, to the service of your country. You have made up your mind," said Louisa, still standing before him where she had first stopped—in all the singular contrariety of her self-possession, and her being obviously so very ill at ease—"to show the nation the way out of all its difficulties."

"Mrs. Bounderby," he returned, laughing, 'upon my honor, no. I will make no such pretence to you. I have seen a little, here and there, up and down; I have found it all to be very worthless, as every body has, and as some confess they have, and some do not; and I am going in for your respected father's opinions—really because I have no choice of opinions, and may as well back them as any thing else."

"Have you none of your own?" asked Louisa.

"I have not so much as the slightest predilection left. I assure you I attach not the least importance to any opinions. The result of the varieties of boredom I have undergone, is a conviction (unless conviction is too industrious a word for the lazy sentiment I entertain on the subject), that any set of ideas will do just as much good as any other set, and just as much harm as any other set. There's an English family with a capital Italian motto: What will be, will be. It's the only truth going!"

This vicious assumption of honesty in dishonesty—a vice so dangerous, so deadly, and so common—seemed, he observed, a little to impress her in his favor. He followed up the advantage, by saying in his pleasantest manner—a manner to which she might attach as much or as little meaning as she pleased—"The side that can prove any thing in a line of units, tens, hundreds, and thousands, Mrs. Bounderby, seems to me to afford the most fun, and to give a man the best chance. I am quite as much attached to it as if I believed it. I am quite ready to go in for it, to the same extent as if I believed it. And what more could I possibly do, if I did believe it!"

"You are a singular politician," said Louisa.

"Pardon me; I have not even that merit. We are the largest party in the state, I assure you, Mrs. Bounderby, if we all fell out of our adopted ranks and were reviewed together."

Mr. Bounderby, who had been in danger of bursting in silence, interposed here with a project for postponing the family dinner to half-past six, and taking Mr. James Harthouse in the mean time on a round of visits to the voting and interesting notabilities of Coketown and its vicinity. The round of visits was made; and Mr. James Harthouse, with a discreet use of his blue coaching, came off triumphantly, though with a considerable accession of boredom.

In the evening, he found the dinner-table laid for four, but they sat down only three. It was an appropriate occasion for Mr. Bounderby to discuss the flavor of the hap'orth of stewed eels he had purchased in the streets at eight years old, and also of the inferior water, specially used for laying the dust, with which he had washed down that repast. He likewise entertained his guest, over the soup and fish, with the calculation that he (Bounderby) had eaten in his youth at least three horses under the guise of polonies and saveloys. These recitals, Jem, in a languid manner, received with "charming!" every now and then; and they probably would have decided him to go in for Jerusalem again to-morrow morning, had he been less curious respecting Louisa.

"Is there nothing," he thought, glancing at her as she sat at the head of the table, where her youthful figure, small and slight, but very graceful, looked as pretty as it looked misplaced; "is there nothing that will move that face?"

Yes! By Jupiter, there was something, and here it was, in an unexpected shape! Tom appeared. She changed as the door opened, and broke into a beaming smile.

A beautiful smile. Mr. James Harthouse might not have thought so much of it, but that he had wondered so long at her impassive face. She put out her hand—a pretty little soft hand; and her fingers closed upon her brother's, as if she would have carried them to her lips.

"Ay, ay?" thought the visitor. "This whelp is the only creature she cares for. So, so!"

The whelp was presented, and took his chair. The appellation was not flattering, but not unmerited.

"When I was your age, young Tom," said Bounderby, "I was punctual, or I got no dinner!"

"When you were my age," returned Tom, "you hadn't a wrong balance to get right, and hadn't to dress afterward."

"Never mind that now," said Bounderby.

"Well, then," grumbled Tom. "Don't begin with me."

"Mrs. Bounderby," said Harthouse, perfectly hearing this under-strain as it went on; "your brother's face is quite familiar to me. Can I have seen him abroad? Or at some public school, perhaps?"

"No," she returned, quite interested, "he has never been abroad yet, and was educated here, at home. Tom, love, I am telling Mr. Harthouse that he never saw you abroad."

"No such luck, sir," said Tom.

There was little enough in him to brighten her face, for he was a sullen young fellow, and ungracious in his manner even to her. So much the greater must have been the solitude of her heart, and her need of some one on whom to bestow it. "So much the more is this whelp the only creature she has ever cared for," thought Mr. James Harthouse, turning it over and over. "So much the more. So much the more."

Both in his sister's presence, and after she had left the room, the whelp took no pains to hide his contempt for Mr. Bounderby, whenever he could indulge it without the observation of that independent man, by making wry faces, or shutting one eye. Without responding to these telegraphic communications, Mr. Harthouse encouraged him much in the course of the evening, and showed an unusual liking for him. At last, when he rose to return to his hotel, and was a little doubtful whether he knew the way by night, the whelp immediately proffered his services as guide, and turned out with him to escort him thither.

Chapter XIX

THE WHELP

It was very remarkable that a young gentleman who had been brought up under one continuous system of unnatural restraint, should be a hypocrite; but it was certainly the case with Tom. It was very strange that a young gentleman who had never been left to his own guidance for five consecutive minutes, should be incapable at last of governing himself; but so it was with Tom. It was altogether unaccountable that a young gentleman whose imagination had been strangled in his cradle, should be still inconvenienced by its ghost in the form of groveling sensualities; but such a monster, beyond all doubt, was Tom.

"Do you smoke?" asked Mr. James Harthouse, when they came to the hotel.

"I believe you!" said Tom.

He could do no less than ask Tom up; and Tom could do no less than go up. What with a cooling drink adapted to the weather, but not so weak as cool; and what with a rarer tobacco than was to be bought in those parts; Tom was soon in a highly free and easy state at his end of the sofa, and more than ever disposed to admire his new friend at the other end.

Tom blew his smoke aside, after he had been smoking a little while, and took an observation of his friend. "He don't seem to care about his dress," thought Tom, "and yet how capitally he does it. What an easy swell he is!."

Mr. James Harthouse, happening to catch Tom's eye, remarked that he drank nothing, and filled his glass with his own negligent hand.

"Thank'ee," said Tom. "Thank'ee. Well, Mr. Harthouse, I hope you have had about a dose of old Bounderby to-night." Tom said this with one eye shut up again, and looking over his glass knowingly, at his entertainer.

"A very good fellow indeed!" returned Mr. James Harthouse.

"You think so, don't you?" said Tom. And shut up his eye again.

Mr. James Harthouse smiled; and rising from his end of the sofa, and lounging with his back against the chimney-piece, so that he stood before the empty fire-grate as he smoked, in front of Tom, and looking down at him, observed:

"What a comical brother-in-law you are!"

"What a comical brother-in-law old Bounderby is, I think you mean," said Tom.

"You are a piece of caustic, Tom," retorted Mr. James Harthouse.

There was something so very agreeable in being so intimate with such a waistcoat; in being called Tom, by such a voice; in being on such off-hand terms so soon, with such a pair of whiskers; that Tom was uncommonly pleased with himself.

"Oh! I don't care for old Bounderby," said he, "if you mean that. I have always called old Bounderby by the same name when I have talked about him, and I have always thought of him in the same way. I am not going to begin to be polite now, about old Bounderby. It would be rather late in the day."

"Don't mind me," returned James; "but take care when his wife is by, you know."

"His wife?" said Tom. "My sister Loo? O yes!" And he laughed, and took a little more of the cooling drink.

James Harthouse continued to lounge in the same place and attitude, smoking his cigar in his own easy way, and looking pleasantly at the whelp, as if he knew himself to be a kind of agreeable demon who had only to hover over him, and he must give up his whole soul if required. It certainly did seem that the whelp yielded to this influence. He looked at his companion sneakingly, he looked at him admiringly, he looked at him boldly, and put up one leg on the sofa.

"My sister Loo?" said Tom. "*She* never cared for old Bounderby."

"That's the past tense, Tom," returned Mr. James Harthouse, striking the ash from his cigar with his little finger. "We are in the present tense, now."

"Verb neuter, not to care. Indicative mood, present tense. First person singular, I do not care; second person singular, thou dost not care; third person singular, she does not care," returned Tom.

"Good! Very quaint!" said his friend, "Though you don't mean it."

"But I *do* mean it," cried Tom. "Upon my honor! Why, you won't tell me, Mr. Harthouse, that you really suppose my sister Loo does care for old Bounderby."

"My dear fellow," returned the other, "what am I bound to suppose, when I find two married people living in harmony and happiness?"

Tom had by this time got both his legs on the sofa. If his second leg had not been already there when he was called a dear fellow, he would have put it up at that great stage of the conversation. Feeling it necessary to do something then, he stretched himself out at greater length, and, reclining with the back of his head on the end of the sofa, and smoking with an infinite assumption of negligence, turned his common face, and not too sober eyes, toward the face looking down upon him so carelessly yet so potently.

"You know our governor, Mr. Harthouse," said Tom, "and therefore you needn't be surprised that Loo married old Bounderby. She never had a lover, and the governor proposed old Bounderby, and she took him."

"Very dutiful in your interesting sister," said Mr. James Harthouse.

"Yes, but she wouldn't have been as dutiful, and it would not have come off as easily," returned the whelp, "if it hadn't been for me."

The tempter merely lifted his eyebrows; but the whelp was obliged to go on.

"*I* persuaded her," he said, with an edifying air of superiority. "I was stuck into old Bounderby's bank (where I never wanted to be), and I knew I should get into scrapes there, if she put old Bounderby's pipe out; so I told her my wishes, and she came into them. She would do any thing for me. It was very game of her, wasn't it?"

"It was charming, Tom!"

"Not that it was altogether so important to her as it was to me," continued Tom coolly, "because my liberty and comfort, and perhaps my getting on, depended on it; and she had no other lover, and staying at home was like staying in jail—especially when I was gone. It wasn't as if she gave up another lover for old Bounderby; but still it was a good thing in her."

"Perfectly delightful. And she gets on so placidly."

"Oh," returned Tom, with contemptuous patronage, "she's a regular girl. A girl can get on any where. She has settled down to the life, and *she* don't mind. The life does just as well for her, as another. Besides, though Loo is a girl, she's not a common sort of girl. She can shut herself up within herself, and think—as I have often known her sit and watch the fire—for an hour at a stretch."

"Ay, ay? Has resources of her own," said Harthouse, smoking quietly.

"Not so much of that as you may suppose," returned Tom; "for our governor had her crammed with all sorts of dry bones and sawdust. It's his system."

"Formed his daughter on his own model?" suggested Harthouse.

"His daughter? Ah! and every body else. Why, he formed Me that way," said Tom.

"Impossible!"

"He did though," said Tom, shaking his head. "I mean to say, Mr. Harthouse, that when I first left home and went to old Bounderby's, I was as flat as a warming-pan, and knew no more about life, than any oyster does."

"Come, Tom! I can hardly believe that. A joke's a joke."

"Upon my soul!" said the whelp. "I am serious; I am, indeed!" He smoked with great gravity and dignity for a little while, and then added, in a highly complacent tone, "Oh! I have picked up a little, since. I don't deny that. But I have done it myself; no thanks to the governor."

"And your intelligent sister?"

"My intelligent sister is about where she was. She used to complain to me that she had nothing to fall back upon, that girls usually fall back upon; and I don't see how she is to have got over that since. But *she* don't mind," he sagaciously added, puffing at his cigar again. "Girls can always get on, somehow."

"Calling at the Bank yesterday evening, for Mr. Bounderby's address, I found an ancient lady there, who seems to entertain great admiration for your sister," observed Mr. James Harthouse, throwing away the last small remnant of the cigar he had now smoked out.

"Mother Sparsit!" said Tom. "What! you have seen her already, have you?"

His friend nodded. Tom took his cigar out of his mouth, to shut up his eye (which had grown rather unmanageable) with the greater expression, and to tap his nose several times with his finger.

"Mother Sparsit's feeling for Loo is more than admiration, I should think," said Tom. "Say affection and devotion. Mother Sparsit never set her cap at Bounderby when he was a bachelor. Oh no!"

These were the last words spoken by the whelp, before a giddy drowsiness came upon him, followed by complete oblivion. He was roused from the latter state by an uneasy dream of being stirred up with a boot, and also of a voice saying: "Come, it's late. Be off!"

"Well!" he said, scrambling from the sofa. "I must take my leave of you though. I say. Yours is very good tobacco. But it's too mild."

"Yes, it's too mild," returned his entertainer.

"It's—it's ridiculously mild," said Tom. "Where's the door? Good night!"

He had another odd dream of being taken by a waiter through a mist, which, after giving him some trouble and difficulty, resolved itself into the main street, in which he stood alone. He then walked home pretty easily, though not yet free from an impression of the presence and influence of his new friend—as if he were lounging somewhere in the air, in the same negligent attitude, regarding him with the same look.

The whelp went home, and went to bed. If he had had any sense of what he had done that night, and had been less of a whelp and more of a brother, he might have turned short on the road, might have gone down to the ill-smelling river that was dyed black, might have gone to bed in it for good and all, and have curtained his head forever with its filthy waters.

Chapter XX

MEN AND BROTHERS

"OH my friends, the down-trodden operatives of Coketown! Oh my friends and fellow-countrymen, the slaves of an iron-handed and a grinding despotism! Oh my friends and fellow-sufferers, and fellow-workmen, and fellow-men! I tell you that the hour is come, when we must rally round one another as One united power, and crumble into dust the oppressors that too long have battened upon the plunder of our families, upon the sweat of our brows, upon the labor of our hands, upon the strength of our sinews, upon the God-created glorious rights of Humanity, and upon the holy and eternal privileges of Brotherhood!"

"Good!" "Hear, hear, hear!" "Hurrah!" and other cries, arose in many voices from various parts of the densely crowded and suffocatingly close Hall, in which the orator, perched on a stage, delivered himself of this and what other froth and fume he had in him. He had declaimed himself into a violent heat, and was as hoarse as he was hot. By dint of roaring at the top of his voice under a flaring gaslight, clenching his fists, knitting his brows, setting his teeth, and pounding with his arms, he had taken so much out of himself by this time, that he was brought to a stop, and called for a glass of water.

As he stood there, trying to quench his fiery face with his drink of water, the comparison between the orator and the crowd of attentive faces turned toward him, was extremely to his disadvantage. Judging him by Nature's evidence, he was above the mass in very little but the stage on which he stood. In many great respects, he was essentially below them. He was not so honest, he was not so manly, he was not so good-humored; he substituted cunning for their simplicity, and passion for their safe solid sense. An ill-made, high-shouldered man, with lowering brows, and his features crushed into an habitually sour expression, he contrasted most unfavorably, even in his mongrel dress, with the great body of his hearers in their plain working clothes. Strange as it always is to consider any assembly in the act of submissively resigning itself to the dreariness of some complacent person, lord or commoner, whom three-fourths of it could, by no human means, raise out of the slough of inanity to their own intellectual level, it was particularly strange, and it was even particularly affecting, to see this crowd of earnest faces, whose honesty in the main no competent observer free from bias could doubt, so agitated by such a leader.

Good! Hear, hear! Hurrah! The eagerness, both of attention and intention, exhibited in all the countenances, made them a most impressive sight. There was no carelessness, no languor, no idle curiosity; none of the many shades of indifference to be seen in all other assemblies, visible for one moment there. That every man felt his condition to be, somehow or other, worse than it might be; that every man considered it incumbent on him to join the rest, toward the making of it better; that every man felt his only hope to be in his allying himself to the comrades by whom he was surrounded; and that in this belief, right or wrong (unhappily wrong then), the whole of that crowd were gravely, deeply, faithfully in earnest; must have been as plain to any one who chose to see what was there as the bare beams of the roof, and the whitened brick walls. Nor could any such spectator fail to know in his own breast, that these men, through their very delusions, showed great qualities, susceptible of being turned to the happiest and best account; and that to pretend (on the strength of sweeping axioms, howsoever cut and dried) that they went astray wholly without cause, and of their own irrational wills, was to pretend that there could be smoke without fire, death without birth, harvest without seed, any thing or every thing produced from nothing.

The orator having refreshed himself, wiped his corrugated forehead from left to right several times with his handkerchief folded into a pad, and concentrated all his revived forces in a sneer of great disdain and bitterness.

"But, oh my friends and brothers! Oh men and Englishmen, the down-trodden operatives of Coketown! What shall we say of that man— that working-man, that I should find it necessary so to libel the glorious name—who, being practically and well acquainted with the grievances and wrongs of you, the injured pith and marrow of this land, and having heard you, with a noble and majestic unanimity that will make Tyrants tremble, resolve for to subscribe to the funds of the United Aggregate Tribunal, and to abide by the injunctions issued by that body for your benefit, whatever they may be—what, I ask you, will you say of that working man, since such I must acknowledge him to be, who, at such a time, deserts his post, and sells his flag; who, at such a time, turns a traitor and a craven and a recreant; who, at such a time, is not ashamed to make to you the dastardly and humiliating avowal that he will hold himself aloof, and will *not* be one of those associated in the gallant stand for Freedom and for Right?"

The assembly was divided at this point. There were some groans and hisses, but the general sense of honor was much too strong for the condemnation of a man unheard. "Be sure you're right, Slackbridge!" "Put him up!" "Let's hear him!" Such things were said on many sides. Finally, one strong voice called out, "Is the man heer? If the man's heer, Slackbridge, let's hear the man himseln, 'stead o' yo." Which was received with a round of applause.

Slackbridge, the orator, looked about him with a withering smile; and, holding out his right hand at arm's length (as the manner of all Slackbridges is), to still the thundering sea, waited until there was a profound silence.

"Oh my friends and fellow-men!" said Slackbridge then, shaking his head with violent scorn, "I do not wonder that you, the prostrate sons of labor, are incredulous of the existence of such a man. But he who sold his birth-right for a mess of pottage existed, and Judas Iscariot existed, and Castlereagh existed, and this man exists!"

Here, a brief press and confusion near the stage-ended in the man himself standing at the orator's side before the concourse. He was pale and a little moved in the face—his lips especially showed it; but he stood quiet, with his left hand at his chin, waiting to be heard. There was a chairman to regulate the proceedings, and this functionary now took the case into his own hands.

"My friends," said he, "by virtue o' my office as your president, I ashes o' our friend Slackbridge, who may be a little over hetter in this business, to take his seat, whiles this man Stephen Blackpool is heern. You all know this man Stephen Blackpool. You know him awlung o' his misfort'ns, and his good name."

With that, the chairman shook him frankly by the hand, and sat down again. Slackbridge likewise sat down, wiping his hot forehead—always from left to right, and never the reverse way.

"My friends," Stephen began, in the midst of a dead calm; "I ha' hed what's been spok'n o' me, and 'tis lickly that I shan't mend it. But I'd liefer you'd hearn the truth concernin myseln, fro my lips than fro-onny other man's, though I never cud'n speak afore so monny, wi'out bein moydert and muddled."

Slackbridge shook his head as if he would shake it off, in his bitterness.

"I'm th' one single Hand in Bounderby's mill, o' a' the men theer, as don't coom in wi' th' proposed reg'lations. I canna' coom in wi' 'em. My friends, I doubt their doin' yo onny good. Licker they'll do yo hurt."

Slackbridge laughed, folded his arms, and frowned sarcastically.

"But 't ant sommuch for that as I stands out. If that were aw, I'd coom in wi' th' rest. But I ha' my reasons—mine, yo see—for being hindered; not on'y now, but awlus —awlus—life long!"

Slackbridge jumped up and stood beside him, gnashing and tearing. "Oh my friends, what but this did I tell you? Oh my fellow-countrymen, what warning but this did I give you? And how shows this recreant conduct in a man on whom unequal laws are known to have fallen heavy? Oh you Engilshmen, I ask you how does this subornation show in one of yourselves, who is thus consenting to his own undoing and to yours, and to your children's and your children's children's?"

There was some applause, and some crying of Shame upon the man; but the greater part of the audience were quiet. They looked at Stephen's worn face, rendered more pathetic by the homely emotions it evinced; and, in the kindness of their nature, they were more sorry than indignant.

"'Tis this delegate's trade for t' speak," said Stephen, "an he's paid for 't, an he knows his work. Let him keep to 't. Let him give no heed to what I ha had'n to bear. That's not for him. That's not for nobbody but me."

There was a propriety, not to say a dignity in these words, that made the hearers yet more quiet and attentive. The same strong voice called out, "Slackbridge, let the man be heern, and howd thee tongue!" Then the place was wonderfully still.

"My brothers," said Stephen, whose low voice was distinctly heard, "and my fellow-workmen—for that yo are to me, though not, as I knows on, to this delegate heer—I ha but a word to sen, and I could sen nommore if I was to speak till Strike o' day. I know weel aw, what's afore me. I know weel that yo are aw resolved to ha nommore ado wi' a man who is not wi' yo in this matther. I know weel that if I was alyin parisht i' th' road, yo'd feel it right to pass me by as a forrenner and stranger. What I ha getn, I mun mak th' best on."

"Stephen Blackpool," said the chairman, rising, "think ont agen. Think ont once agen, lad, afore thou'rt shunned by aw owd friends."

There was an universal murmur to the same effect, though no man articulated a word. Every eye was fixed on Stephen's face. To repent of his determination would be to take a load from all their minds. He looked around him and knew that it was so. Not a grain of anger with them was in his heart; he knew them, far below their surface weaknesses and misconceptions, as no one but their fellow-laborer could.

"I ha thowt ont, above a bit, sir. I simply canna coom in. I mun go th way as lays afore me. I mun tak my leave o' aw heer."

He made a sort of reverence to them by holding up his arms, and stood for the moment in that attitude—not speaking until they slowly dropped at his sides.

"Monny's the pleasant word as soom heer has spok'n wi' me; monny's the face I see heer, as I first seen when I were yoong and lighter heart'n than now. I ha never had no fratch afore, sin ever I were born, wi' any o' my like; Gonnows I ha none now that's o' my makin'. Yo'll ca' me traitor and that—yo I mean t' say," addressing Slackbridge, "but 'tis easier to ca' than mak' out. So let be."

He had moved away a pace or two to come down from the platform, when he remembered something he had not said, and returned again.

"Haply," he said, turning his furrowed face slowly about, that he might as it were individually address the whole audience, those both near and distant; "haply, when this question has been tak'n up and discoosed, there'll be a threat to turn out if I'm let to work among yo. I hope I shall die ere ever such a time cooms, and I shall work solitary among yo unless it cooms—truly, I mun do't, my friends; not to brave yo, but to live. I ha nobbut work to live by; and wheerever can I go, I who ha worked sin I were no heighth at aw, in Coketown heer? I mak' no complaints o' bein turned to the wa', o' being outcasten and overlooken fro this time forrard, but hope I shall be let to work. If there is any right for me at aw, my friends, I think 'tis that."

Not a word was spoken. Not a sound was audible in the building, but the slight rustle of men moving a little apart, all along the centre of the room, to open a means of passing out, to the man with whom they had all bound themselves to renounce companionship. Looking at no one, and going his way with a lowly steadiness upon him that asserted nothing and sought nothing, Old Stephen, with all his troubles on his head, left the scene.

Then Slackbridge, who had kept his oratorical arm extended during the going out, as if he were repressing with infinite solicitude and by a wonderful moral power the vehement passions of the multitude, applied himself to raising their spirits. "Had not the Roman Brutus, oh my British countrymen, condemned his son to death; and had not the Spartan mothers, oh my soon to be victorious friends, driven their flying children on the points of their enemies' swords? Then was it not the sacred duty of the men of Coketown, with forefathers before them, an admiring world in company with them, and a posterity to come after them, to hurl out traitors from the tents they had pitched in a sacred and a God-like cause? The winds of Heaven answered, Yes; and bore Yes, east, west, north, and south. And consequently three cheers for the United Aggregate Tribunal!"

Slackbridge acted as fugleman, and gave the time. The multitude of doubtful faces (a little conscience-stricken) brightened at the sound, and took it up. Private feeling must yield to the common cause. Hurrah! The roof yet vibrated with the cheering, when the assembly dispersed.

Thus easily did Stephen Blackpool fall into the loneliest of lives, the life of solitude among a familiar crowd. The stranger in the land who looks into ten thousand faces for some answering look and never finds it, is in cheering society as compared with him who passes ten averted faces daily, that were once the countenances of friends. Such experience was to be Stephen's now, in every waking moment of his life; at his work, on his way to it and from it, at his door, at his window, every where. By general consent they even avoided that side of the street on which he habitually walked; and left it, of all the working men, to him only.

He had been, for many years, a quiet silent man, associating but little with other men, and used to companionship with his own thoughts. He had never known before, the strength of the want in his heart for the frequent recognition of a nod, a look, a word; or the immense amount of relief that had been poured into it by drops, through such small means. It was even harder than he could have believed possible, to separate in his own conscience his abandonment by all his fellows from a baseless sense of shame and disgrace.

The first four days of his endurance were days so long and heavy, that he began to be appalled by the prospect before him. Not only did he see no Rachael all the time, but he avoided every chance of seeing her; for, although he knew that the prohibition did not yet formally extend to the women working in the factories, he found that some of them with whom he was acquainted were changed to him, and he feared to try others, and dreaded that Rachael might be even singled out from the rest if she were seen in his company. So he had been quite alone during the four days, and had spoken to no one, when, as he was leaving his work at night, a young man of a very light complexion accosted him in the street.

"Your name's Blackpool, ain't it?" said the young man.

Stephen colored to find himself with his hat in his hand, in his gratitude for being spoken to, or in the suddenness of it, or both. He made a feint of adjusting the lining, and said, "Yes."

"You are the Hand they have sent to Coventry, I mean?" said Bitzer, the very light young man in question.

Stephen answered, "Yes," again.

"I supposed so, from their all appearing to keep away from you. Mr. Bounderby wants to speak to you. You know his house, don't you?"

Stephen said, "Yes," again.

"Then go straight up there, will you?" said Bitzer. "You're expected, and have only to tell the servant it's you. I belong to the Bank; so, if you go straight up without me (I was sent to fetch you), you'll save me a walk."

Stephen, whose way had been in the contrary direction, turned about and betook himself, as in duty bound, to the red brick castle of the giant Bounderby.

Chapter XXI

MEN AND MASTERS

"WELL Stephen," said Bounderby, in his windy manner, "what's this I hear? What have these pests of the earth been doing to *you*? Come in, and speak up."

It was into the drawing-room that he was thus bidden. A tea-table was set out; and Mr. Bounderby's young wife, and her brother, and a great gentleman from London, were present. To whom Stephen made his obeisance, closing the door and standing near it, with his hat in his hand.

"This is the man I was telling you about, Harthouse," said Mr. Bounderby. The gentleman he addressed, who was talking to Mrs. Bounderby on the sofa, got up, saying in an indolent way, "Oh really?" and dawdled to the hearth-rug, where Mr. Bounderby stood.

"Now," said Bounderby, "speak up!"

After the four days he had passed, this address fell rudely and discordantly on Stephen's ear. Besides being a rough handling of his wounded mind, it seemed to assume that he really was the self-interested deserter he had been called.

"What were it, sir," said Stephen, "as yo were pleased to want wi' me?"

"Why, I have told you," returned Bounderby. "Speak up like a man, since you are a man, and tell us about yourself and this Combination."

"Wi' yor pardon, sir," said Stephen Blackpool, "I ha' nowt to sen about it."

Mr. Bounderby, who was always more or less like a Wind, finding something in his way here, began to blow at it directly.

"Now, look here, Harthouse," said he, "here's a specimen of 'em. When this man was here once before, I warned this man against the mischievous strangers who are always about—and who ought to be hanged wherever they are found—and I told this man that he was going in the wrong direction. Now, would you believe it, that although they have put this mark upon him, he is such a slave to them still, that he's afraid to open his lips about them?"

"I sed as I had nowt to sen, sir; not as I was fearfo' o' openin' my lips."

"You said. Ah! *I* know what you said; more than that, I know what you mean, you see. Not always the same thing, by the Lord Harry! Quite different things. You had better tell us at once that that fellow Slackbridge is not in the town, stirring up the people to mutiny; and that he is not a regular qualified leader of the people; that is, a most confounded scoundrel. You had better tell us so at once; you can't deceive me. You want to tell us so. Why don't you?"

"I'm as sooary as yo, sir, when the people's leaders is bad," said Stephen, shaking his head. "They taks such as offers. Haply 'tis na' the sma'est o' their misfortuns when they can get no better."

The wind began to get boisterous.

"Now, you'll think this pretty well, Harthouse," said Mr. Bounderby. "You'll think this tolerably strong. You'll say, upon my soul this is a tidy specimen of what my friends have to deal with; but this is nothing, sir! You shall hear me ask this man a question. Pray, Mr. Blackpool"—wind springing up very fast—"may I take the liberty of asking you how it happens that you refused to be in this Combination?"

"How 't happens?"

"Ah!" said Mr. Bounderby, with his thumbs in the arms of his coat, and jerking his head and shutting his eyes in confidence with the opposite wall: "how it happens."

"I'd leefer not coom to't, sir; but sin you put th' question—an not want'n t' be ill-manner'n—I'll answer. I ha passed a promess." "Not to me, you know," said Bounderby. (Gusty weather, with deceitful calms. One now prevailing.)

"Oh, no, sir. Not to yo."

"As for me, any consideration for me has had just nothing at all to do with it," said Bounderby, still in confidence with the wall. "If only Josiah Bounderby of Coketown had been in question, you would have joined and made no bones about it?"

"Why yes, sir. 'Tis true."

"Though he knows," said Mr. Bounderby, now blowing a gale, "that there are a set of rascals and rebels whom transportation is too good for! Now, Mr. Harthouse, you have been knocking about in the world some time. Did you ever meet with any thing like that man out of this blessed country?" And Mr. Bounderby pointed him out for inspection, with an angry finger.

"Nay, ma'am," said Stephen Blackpool, stanchly protesting against the words that had been used, and instinctively addressing himself to Louisa, after glancing at her face. "Not rebels, nor yet rascals. Nowt o' th' kind, ma'am, nowt o' th' kind. They've not doon me a kindness, ma'am, as I know and feel. But there's not a dozen men amoong 'em, ma'am—a dozen? Not six—but what believes as he has doon his duty by the rest and by himseln. God forbid as I, that ha known and had'n experience o' these men aw my life—I, that ha' ett'n an droonken wi' 'em, an seet'n wi' 'em, and toil'n wi' 'em, and lov'n 'em, should fail fur to stan by 'em wi' the truth, let 'em ha doon to me what they may!"

He spoke with the rugged earnestness of his place and character—deepened perhaps by a proud consciousness that he was faithful to his class under all their mistrust; but he fully remembered where he was, and did not even raise his voice.

"No, ma'am, no. They're true to one another, faithfo' to one another, fectionate to one another, e'en to death. Be poor amoong 'em, be sick amoong 'em, grieve amoong 'em for onny o' th' monny causes that carries grief to the poor man's door, an' they'll be tender wi' yo, gentle wi' yo, comfortable wi' yo, Chrisen wi' yo. Be sure o' that, ma'am. They'd be riven to bits, ere ever they'd be different."

"In short," said Mr. Bounderby, "it's because they are so full of virtues that they have turned you adrift. Go through with it while you are about it. Out with it."

"How 'tis, ma'am," resumed Stephen, appearing still to find his natural refuge in Louisa's face, "that what is best in us fok seems to turn us most to trouble an misfort'n an mistake, I dunno. But 'tis so. I know 'tis, as I know the heavens is over me ahint the smoke. We're patient too, an wants in general to do right. An' I canna think the fawt is aw wi' us."

"No, my friend," said Mr. Bounderby, whom he could not have exasperated more, quite unconscious of it though he was, than by seeming to appeal to anyone else, "if you will favor me with your attention for half a minute, I should like to have a word or two with you. You said just now, that you had nothing to tell us about this business. You are quite sure of that, before we go any further?"

"Sir, I am sure on't."

"Here's a gentleman from London present," Mr. Bounderby made a back-handed point at Mr. James Harthouse with his thumb, "a Parliament gentleman. I should like him to hear a short bit of dialogue between you and me, instead of taking the substance of it—for I know precious well, beforehand, what it will be; nobody knows better than I do, take notice!—instead of receiving it on trust, from my mouth."

Stephen bent his head to the gentleman from London, and showed a rather more troubled mind than usual. He turned his eyes involuntarily to his former refuge, but at a look from that quarter (expressive though instantaneous) he settled them on Mr. Bounderby's face.

"Now, what do you complain of?" asked Mr. Bounderby.

"I ha' not coom here, sir," Stephen reminded him, "to complain. I coom for that I were sent for."

"What," repeated Mr. Bounderby, folding his arms, "do you people, in a general way, complain of?"

Stephen looked at him with some little irresolution for a moment, and then seemed to make up his mind.

"Sir, I were never good at showin' o't, though I ha' had'n my share in feeling o't. 'Deed we are in a muddle, sir. Look round town—so rich as 'tis—and see the numbers o' people as has been broughten into bein heer, fur to weave, an to card, an to piece out a livin, aw the same one way, somehows, 'twixt their cradles an their graves. Look how we live, an wheer we live, an' in what numbers, an' by what chances, and wi' what sameness; and look how the mills is awlus agoin, and how they never works us no nigher to onny dis'ant object—ceptin awlus, Death. Look how you considers of us, an writes of us, an talks of us, and goes up wi' yor deputations to Secretaries o' State 'bout us, and how yo are awlus right, and how we are awlus wrong, and never had'n no reason in us sin ever we were born. Look how this ha growen an growen, sir, bigger an bigger, broader an broader, harder an harder, fro year to year, fro generation unto generation. Who can look on't, sir, and fairly tell a man 'tis not a muddle?"

"Of course," said Mr. Bounderby. "Now perhaps you'll let the gentleman know, how you would set this muddle (as you're so fond of calling it) to rights."

"I donno, sir. I canna be expecten to't. 'Tis not me as should be looken to for that, sir. 'Tis them as is put ower me, and ower aw the rest of us. What do they tak upon themsen, sir, if not to do't?"

"I'll tell you something towards it, at any rate," returned Mr. Bounderby. "We will make an example of half a dozen Slackbridges. We'll indict the blackguards for felony, and get 'em shipped off to penal settlements."

Stephen gravely shook his head.

"Don't tell me we won't, man," said Mr. Bounderby, by this time blowing a hurricane, "because we will, I tell you!"

"Sir," returned Stephen, with a quiet confidence of absolute certainty, "if yo was t' tak a hundred Slackbridges—aw as there is, an aw the number ten times towd—an was t' sew 'em up in separate sacks, an sink 'em in the deepest ocean as were made ere ever dry land coom to be, yo'd leave the muddle just wheer 'tis. Mischeevous strangers!" said Stephen, with an anxious smile; "when ha we not heern, I am sure, sin ever we can call to mind, o' th' mischeevous strangers! 'Tis not by *them* the trouble's made, sir. 'Tis not wi' *them* 't commences. I ha no favor for 'em—I ha no reason to favor 'em—but 'tis hopeless and useless to dream o' takin them fro their trade, 'stead o' takin their trade fro them! Aw that's now about me in this room were heer afore I coom, an will be heer when I am gone. Put that clock aboard a ship an pack it off to Norfolk Island, an the time will go on just the same. So 'tis wi' Slackbridge every bit."

Reverting for a moment to his former refuge, he observed a cautionary movement of her eyes toward the door. Stepping back, he put his hand upon the lock. But he had not spoken out of his own will and desire; and he felt it in his heart a noble return for his late injurious treatment to be faithful to the last to those who had repudiated him. He staid to finish what was in his mind.

"Sir, I canna, wi' my little learning an my common way, tell the genelman what will better aw this—though some working-men o' this town could, above my powers—but I can tell him what I know will never do't. The strong hand will never do't. Vict'ry and triumph will never do't. Agreein fur to mak one side unnat'rally awlus and forever right, and toother side unnat'rally awlus and forever wrong, will never, never do't. Nor yet lettin alone will never do't. Let thousands upon thousands alone, aw leadin the like lives and aw faw'en into the like muddle, and they will be as one, and yo will be as anoother, wi' a black unpassable world betwixt yo, just as long or short a time as sitch like misery can last. Not drawin' nigh to fok, wi' kindness an patience an cherey ways, that so draws nigh to one another in their monny troubles, and so cherishes one another in their distresses wi' what they need themseln—like, I humbly believe, as no people the genelman ha seen in aw his travels can beat—will never do't till th' sun turns t' ice. Most o' aw, ratin 'em as so much Power, and reg'latin 'em as if they was figures in a soom, or machines: wi'out loves and likeins, wi'out memories and inclinations, wi'out souls to weary an souls to hope—when aw goes quiet, draggin on wi' 'em as if they'd nowt o' th' kind, an when aw goes onquiet, reproaching 'em fur their want o' sitch humanly feelins in their dealin's wi' yo—this will never do't, sir, till God's work is onmade."

Stephen stood with the open door in his hand, waiting to know if any thing more were expected of him.

"Just stop a moment," said Mr. Bounderby, excessively red in the face. "I told you, the last time you were here with a grievance, that you had better turn about and come out of that. And I also told you, if you remember, that I was up to the gold spoon look-out."

"I were not up to't myseln, sir; I do assure yo."

"Now it's clear to me," said Mr. Bounderby, "that you are one of those chaps who have always got a grievance. And you go about, sowing it and raising crops. That's the business of *your* life, my friend."

Stephen shook his head, mutely protesting that indeed he had other business to do for his life.

"You are such a waspish, raspish, ill-conditioned chap, you see," said Mr. Bounderby, "that even your own Union, the men who know you best, will have nothing to do with you. I never thought those fellows could be right in any thing; but I tell you what! I so far go along with them for a novelty, that *I'll* have nothing to do with you either."

Stephen raised his eyes quickly to his face.

"You can finish off what you are at," said Mr. Bounderby, with a meaning nod, "and then go elsewhere."

"Sir, yo know weel," said Stephen expressively, "that if I canna get work wi' yo, I canna get it elsewheer."

The reply was, "What I know, I know; and what you know, you know. I have no more to say about it."

Stephen glanced at Louisa again, but her eyes were raised to his no more; therefore, with a sigh, and saying, barely above his breath, "Heaven help us aw in this world!" he departed.

Chapter XXII

FADING AWAY

It was falling dark when Stephen came out of Mr. Bounderby's house. The shadows of night had gathered so fast that he did not look about him when he closed the door, but plodded straight along the street. Nothing was further from his thoughts than the curious old woman he had encountered on his previous visit to the same house, when he heard a step behind him that he knew, and, turning, saw her in Rachael's company.

He saw Rachael first, as he had heard her only.

"Ah, Rachael, my dear! Missus, thou wi' her!"

"Well, and now you are surprised to be sure, and with reason I must say," the old woman returned. "Here I am again, you see."

"But how wi' Rachael?" said Stephen, falling into their step, walking between them, and looking from the one to the other.

"Why, I come to be with this good lass pretty much as I came to be with you," said the old woman, cheerfully, taking the reply upon herself. "My visiting time is later this year than usual, for I have been rather troubled with shortness of breath, and so put it off till the weather was fine and warm. For the same reason I don't make all my journey in one day, but divide it into two days, and get a bed to-night at the Travelers' Coffee House down by the railroad (a nice clean house), and go back parliamentary, at six in the morning. Well, but what has this to do with this good lass, says you? I'm going to tell you. I have heard of Mr. Bounderby being married. I read it in the paper, where it looked grand—oh, it looked fine!" the old woman dwelt on it with strange enthusiasm; "and I want to see his wife. I have never seen her yet. Now, if you'll believe me, she has'nt come out of that house since noon today. So, not to give her up too easily, I was waiting about, a little last bit more, when I passed close to this good lass two or three times; and her face being so friendly I spoke to her, and she spoke to me. There!" said the old woman to Stephen, "you can make all the rest out for yourself now, a deal shorter than I can, I dare say!"

Once again, Stephen had to conquer an instinctive propensity to dislike this old woman, though her manner was as honest and simple as a manner possibly could be. With a gentleness that was as natural to him as he knew it to be to Rachael, he pursued the subject that interested her in her old age.

"Well, missus," said he, "I ha seen the lady, and she were yoong and hansom. Wi' fine dark thinkin eyes, and a still way, Rachael, as I ha never seen the like on."

"Young and handsome. Yes!" cried the old woman, quite delighted. "As bonny as a rose! And what a happy wife!"

"Aye, missus, I suppose she be," said Stephen. But with a doubtful glance at Rachael.

"Suppose she be? She must be. She's your master's wife," returned the old woman.

Stephen nodded assent. "Though as to master," said he, glancing again at Rachael, "not master onny more. That's aw enden 'twixt him and me."

"Have you left his work, Stephen?" asked Rachael, anxiously and quickly.

"Why, Rachael," he replied, "whether I ha lef'n his work, or whether his work ha lef'n me, cooms t' th' same. His work and me are parted. 'Tis as weel so—better, I were thinkin when yo coom up wi' me. It would ha brought'n trouble upon trouble if I had stayed theer. Haply 'tis a kindness to monny that I go; haply 'tis a kindness to myseln; anyways it mun be done. I mun turn my face fro Coketown fur th' time, and seek a fort'n, dear, by beginnin fresh."

"Where will you go, Stephen?"

"I dunno t'night," said he, lifting off his hat, and smoothing his thin hair with the flat of his hand. "But I'm not goin' t'night, Rachael nor yet t' morrow. Tan't easy overmuch, t'know wheer t' turn, but a good heart will coom to me."

Herein, too, the sense of even thinking unselfishly aided him. Before he had so much as closed Mr. Bounderby's door, he had reflected that at least his being obliged to go away was good for her, as it would save her from the chance of being brought into question for not withdrawing from him. Though it would cost him a hard pang to leave her, and though he could think of no similar place in which his condemnation would not pursue him, perhaps it was almost a relief to be forced away from the endurance of the last four days, even to unknown difficulties and distresses.

So he said, with truth, "I'm more leetsome, Rachael, under 't, than I couldn ha believed." It was not her part to make his burden heavier. She answered with her comforting smile, and the three walked on together.

Age, especially when it strives to be self-reliant and cheerful, finds much consideration among the poor. The old woman was so decent and contented, and made so light of her infirmities, though they had increased upon her since her former interview with Stephen, that they both took an interest in her. She was too sprightly to allow of their walking at a slow pace on her account, but she was very grateful to be talked to, and very willing to talk to any extent: so, when they came to their part of the town, she was more brisk and vivacious than ever.

"Coom to my poor place, missus," said Stephen, "and tak a coop o tea. Rachael will coom then, and arterward I'll see thee safe t' thy Travelers' lodgin. 'T may be long, Rachael, ere ever I ha th' chance o' thy coompany agen."

They complied, and the three went on to the house where he lodged. When they turned into a narrow street, Stephen glanced at his window with a dread that always haunted his desolate home; but it was open as he had left it, and no one was there. The evil spirit of his life had flitted away again, months ago, and he had heard no more of her since. The only evidence of her last return now, were the scantier movables in his room, and the grayer hair upon his head.

He lighted a candle, set out his little tea-board, got hot water from below, and brought in small portions of tea and sugar, a loaf, and some butter, from the nearest shop. The bread was new and crusty, the butter fresh, and the sugar lump, of course—in fulfillment of the standard testimony of the Coketown magnates, that these people lived like princes, sir. Rachael made the tea (so large a party necessitated the borrowing of a cup), and the visitor enjoyed it mightily. It was the first glimpse of sociality the host had had for many days. He too, with the world a wide heath before him, enjoyed the meal—again in corroboration of the magnates, as exemplifying the utter want of calculation on the part of these people, sir.

"I ha never thowt yet, missus," said Stephen, "o' askin thy name."

The old lady announced herself as "Mrs. Pegler."

"A widder, I think?" said Stephen.

"Oh, many long years!" Mrs. Pegler's husband (one of the best on record) was already dead, by Mrs. Pegler's calculation, when Stephen was born.

" 'Twere a bad job, too, to lose so good a one," said Stephen. "Onny children?"

Mrs. Pegler's cup, rattling against her saucer as she held it, denoted some nervousness on her part. "No," she said. "Not now, not now."

"Dead, Stephen," Rachael softly hinted.

"I'm sooary I ha spok'n on't," said Stephen, "I ought t' ha hadn in my mind as I might touch a sore place. I—I blame myseln."

While he excused himself, the old lady's cup rattled more and more. "I had a son," she said, curiously distressed, and not by any of the usual appearances of sorrow; "and he did well, wonderfully well. But he is not to be spoken of if you please. He is—" Putting down her cup, she moved her hands as if she would have added, by her action, "dead!" Then, she said, aloud, "I have lost him."

Stephen had not yet got the better of his having given the old lady pain, when his landlady came stumbling up the narrow stairs, and calling him to the door, whispered in his ear. Mrs. Pegler was by no means deaf, for she caught a word as it was uttered.

"Bounderby!" she cried, in a suppressed voice, starting up from the table, "Oh, hide me! Don't let me be seen for the world. Don't let him come up till I've got away. Pray, pray!" She trembled, and was excessively agitated; getting behind Rachael, when Rachael tried to reassure her; and not seeming to know what she was about.

"But hearken, missus, hearken;" said Stephen, astonished. " 'Tisn't Mr. Bounderby, 'tis his wife. Yor not fearfo' o' her. Yo was hey-go-mad about her, but an hour sin."

"But are you sure it's the lady and not the gentleman?" she asked, still trembling.

"Certain sure!"

"Well then, pray don't speak to me, nor yet take any notice of me," said the old woman. "Let me be quite to myself in this corner."

Stephen nodded; looking to Rachael for an explanation, which she was quite unable to give him; took the candle, went down stairs, and in a few moments returned, lighting Louisa into the room. She was followed by the whelp.

Rachael had risen, and stood apart with her shawl and bonnet in her hand, when Stephen, himself profoundly astonished by this visit, put the candle on the table. Then he too stood, with his doubled hand upon the table near it, waiting to be addressed.

For the first time in her life, Louisa had come into one of the dwellings of the Coketown Hands; for the first time in her life, she was face to face with any thing like individuality in connection with them. She knew of their existence by hundreds and by thousands. She knew what results in work a given number of them would produce, in a given space of time. She knew them in crowds passing to and from their nests, like ants or beetles. But she knew from her reading infinitely more of the ways of toiling insects, than of these toiling men and women.

Something to be worked so much and paid so much, and there ended; something to be infallibly settled by laws of supply and demand; something that blundered against those laws, and floundered into difficulty; something that was a little pinched when wheat was dear, and over-ate itself when wheat was cheap; something that increased at such a rate of percentage, and yielded such another percentage of crime, and such another percentage of pauperism; something wholesale, of which vast fortunes were made; something that occasionally rose like a sea, and did some harm and waste (chiefly to itself), and fell again; this she knew the Coketown Hands to be. But she had scarcely thought more of separating them into units, than of separating the sea itself into its component drops.

She stood for some moments looking round the room. From the few chairs, the few books, the common prints, and the bed, she glanced to the two women, and to Stephen.

"I have come to speak to you, in consequence of what passed just now. I should like to be serviceable to you, if you will let me. Is this your wife?"

Rachael raised her eyes, and they sufficiently answered no, and dropped again.

"I remember," said Louisa, reddening at her mistake; "I recollect, now, to have heard your domestic misfortunes spoken of, though I was not attending to the particulars at the time. It was not my meaning to ask a question that would give pain to anyone here. If I should ask any other question that may happen to have that result, give me credit, if you please, for being in ignorance how to speak to you as I ought."

As Stephen had but a little while ago instinctively addressed himself to her, so she now instinctively addressed herself to Rachael. Her manner was short and abrupt, yet faltering and timid.

"He has told you what has passed between himself and my husband? You would be his first resource, I think."

"I have heard the end of it, young lady," said Rachael.

"Did I understand, that, being rejected by one employer, he would probably be rejected by all? I thought he said as much?"

"The chances are very small, young lady—next to nothing—for a man who gets a bad name among them."

"What shall I understand that you mean by a bad name?"

"The name of being troublesome."

"Then, by the prejudices of his own class, and by the prejudices of the other, he is sacrificed alike? Are the two so deeply separated in this town, that there is no place whatever, for an honest workman between them?"

Rachael shook her head in silence.

"He fell into suspicion," said Louisa, "with his fellow-weavers because he had made a promise not to be one of them. I think it must have been to you that he made that promise. Might I ask you why he made it?"

Rachael burst into tears. "I did'nt seek it of him, poor lad. I prayed him to avoid trouble for his own good, little thinking he'd come to it through me. But I know he'd die a hundred deaths, ere ever he'd break his word. I know that of him well."

Stephen had remained quietly attentive, in his usual thoughtful attitude, with his hand at his chin. He now spoke in a voice rather less steady than usual.

"No one, excepting myseln, can ever know what honor, an what love, an respect, I bear to Rachael, or wi' what cause. When I passed that promess, I towd her true, she were th' Angel o' my life. 'Twere a solemn promess. 'Tis gone fro me, fur ever."

Louisa turned her head to him, and bent it with a deference that was new in her. She looked from him to Rachael, and her features softened. "What will you do?" she asked him. And her voice had softened too.

"Weel, ma'am," said Stephen, making the best of it, with a smile; "when I ha finished off, I mun quit this part and try another. Fortnet or misfortnet, a man can but try; there's nowt to be done wi'out tryin'—cept laying down and dying."

"How will you travel?"

"Afoot, my kind ledy, afoot."

Louisa colored, and a purse appeared in her hand. The rustling of a bank-note was audible, as she unfolded one and laid it on the table.

"Rachael, will you tell him—for you know how, without offence—that this is freely his, to help him on his way? Will you entreat him to take it?"

"I canna do that, young lady," she answered, turning her head aside; "bless you for thinking o' the poor lad wi' such tenderness. But 'tis for him to know his heart, and what is right according to it."

Louisa looked, in part incredulous, in part frightened, in part overcome with quick sympathy, when this man of so much self-command who had been so plain and steady through the late interview, lost his composure in a moment, and now stood with his hand before his face. She stretched out hers, as if she would have touched him; then checked herself, and remained still.

"Not e'en Rachael," said Stephen, when he stood again with his face uncovered, "could mak sitch a kind offerin, by onny words, kinder. T' show that I'm not a man wi'out reason and gratitude, I'll tak two pound. I'll borrow't for t' pay't back. 'Twill be the sweetest work as ever I ha done, that puts it in my power t' acknowledge once more my lastin thankfulness for this present action."

She was fain to take up the note again, and to substitute the much smaller sum he had named. He was neither courtly, nor handsome, nor picturesque, in any respect; and yet his manner of accepting it, and of expressing his thanks without more words, had a grace in it that Lord Chesterfield could not have taught his son in a century.

Tom had sat upon the bed, swinging one leg and sucking his walking-stick with sufficient unconcern, until the visit had attained this stage. Seeing his sister ready to depart, he got up, rather hurriedly, and put in a word.

"Just wait a moment, Loo! Before we go, I should like to speak to him a moment. Something comes into my head. If you'll step out on the stairs, Blackpool, I'll mention it. Never mind a light, man!" Tom was remarkably impatient of his moving toward the cupboard, to get one. "It don't want a light."

Stephen followed him out, and Tom closed the room door, and held the lock in his hand.

"I say!" he whispered. "I think I can do you a good turn. Don't ask me what it is, because it may not come to any thing. But there's no harm in my trying."

His breath fell like a flame of fire on Stephen's ear; it was so hot.

"That was our light porter at the Bank," said Tom, "who brought you the message to-night. I call him our light porter, because I belong to the Bank too."

Stephen thought, "What a hurry he is in!" He spoke so confusedly.

"Well!" said Tom. "Now look here! When are you off?"

"T'day's Monday," replied Stephen, considering. "Why, sir, Friday or Saturday, nigh 'bout."

"Friday or Saturday," said Tom. "Now, look here! I am not sure that I can do you the good turn I want to do you— that's my sister, you know, in your room—but I may be able to, and if I should not be able to, there's no harm done. So I tell you what. You'll know our light porter again?"

"Yes sure," said Stephen.

"Very well," returned Tom. "When you leave work of a night, between this and your going away, just hang about the Bank an hour or so, will you? Don't take on as if you meant any thing, if he should see you hanging about there; because I shan't put him up to speak to you, unless I find I can do you the service I want to do you. In that case he'll have a note or a message for you, but not else. Now look here! You are sure you understand."

He had wormed a finger, in the darkness, through a button-hole of

Stephen's coat, and was screwing that corner of the garment tight up, round and round, in an extraordinary manner.

"I understan, sir," said Stephen.

"Now look here!" repeated Tom. "Be sure you don't make any mistake then, and don't forget. I shall tell my sister as we go home, what I have in view, and she'll approve, I know. Now look here! You're all right, are you? You understand all about it? Very well then. Come along, Loo!"

He pushed the door open as he called to her, but did not return into the room, or wait to be lighted down the narrow stairs. He was at the bottom when she began to descend, and was in the street before she could take his arm.

Mrs. Pegler remained in her corner until the brother and sister were gone, and until Stephen came back with the candle in his hand. She was in a state of inexpressible admiration of Mrs. Bounderby, and, like an unaccountable old woman, wept, "because she was such a pretty dear." Yet Mrs. Pegler was so flurried lest the object of her admiration should return by any chance, or any body else should come, that her cheerfulness was ended for that night. It was late, too, to people who rose early and worked hard; therefore the party broke up; and Stephen and Rachael escorted their mysterious acquaintance to the door of the Travelers' Coffee House, where they parted from her.

They walked back together to the corner of the street where Rachael lived, and as they drew nearer and nearer to it, silence crept upon them. When they came to the dark corner where their unfrequent meetings always ended, they stopped, still silent, as if both were afraid to speak.

"I shall strive t'see thee agen, Rachael, afore I go, but if not—"

"Thou wilt not, Stephen, I know. 'Tis better that we make up our minds to be open wi' one another."

"Thou'rt awlus right. 'Tis bolder and better. I ha been thinkin then, Rachael, that as 'tis but a day or two that remains, 'twere better for thee, my dear, not t' be seen wi' me. 'T might bring thee into trouble, fur no good."

"'Tis not for that, Stephen, that I mind. But thou know'st our old agreement. 'Tis for that."

"Well, well," said he. "'Tis better, onnyways."

"Thou'lt write to me, and tell me all that happens, Stephen?"

"Yes. What can I say now, but Heaven be wi' thee, Heaven bless thee, Heaven thank thee and reward thee!"

"May it bless thee, Stephen, too, in all thy wanderings, and send thee peace and rest at last!"

"I towd thee, my dear," said Stephen Blackpool—"that night—that I would never see or think o' onnything that angered me, but thou, so much better than me, should'st be beside it. Thou'rt beside it now. Thou mak'st me see it wi' a better eye. Bless thee. Good-night. Good-bye!"

It was but a hurried parting in a common street, yet it was a sacred remembrance to these two common people. Utilitarian economists, skeletons of schoolmasters, Commissioners of Fact, genteel and used-up infidels, gabblers of many little dog's-eared creeds, the poor you will have always with you. Cultivate in them, while there is yet time, the utmost graces of the fancies and affections, to adorn their lives so much in need of ornament; or, in the day of your triumph, when romance is utterly driven out of their souls, and they and a bare existence stand face to face, Reality will take a wolfish turn, and make an end of you!

Stephen worked the next day, and the next, uncheered by a word from any one, and shunned in all his comings and goings as before. At the end of the second day, he saw land; at the end of the third, his loom stood empty.

He had overstayed his hour in the street outside the Bank, on each of the two first evenings; and nothing had happened there, good or bad. That he might not be remiss in his part of the engagement, he resolved to wait full two hours, on this third and last night.

There was the lady who had once kept Mr. Bounderby's house, sitting at the first floor window as he had seen her before; and there was the light porter, sometimes talking with her there, and sometimes looking over the blind below which had BANK upon it, and sometimes coming to the door and standing on the steps for a breath of air. When he first came out, Stephen thought he might be looking for him, and passed near; but the light porter only cast his winking eyes upon him slightly, and said nothing.

Two hours were a long stretch of lounging about, after a long day's labor. Stephen sat upon the step of a door, leaned against a wall under an archway, strolled up and down, listened for the church clock, stopped and watched children playing in the street. Some purpose or other is so natural to every one, that a mere loiterer always looks and feels remarkable. When the first hour was out, Stephen even began to have an uncomfortable sensation upon him of being for the time a disreputable character.

Then came the lamplighter, and two lengthening lines of light all down the long perspective of the street, until they were blended and lost in the distance. Mrs. Sparsit closed the first floor window, drew down the blind, and went up stairs. Presently, a light went up-stairs after her, passing first the fanlight of the door, and afterward the two staircase windows, on its way up. By-and-by, one corner of the second floor blind was disturbed, as if Mrs. Sparsit's eye were there; also the other corner, as if the light porter's eye were on that side. Still, no communication was made to Stephen. Much relieved when the two hours were at last accomplished, he went away at a quick pace, as a recompense for so much loitering.

He had only to take leave of his landlady, and lie down on his temporary bed upon the floor; for his bundle was made up for tomorrow, and all was arranged for his departure. He meant to be clear of the town very early: before the Hands were in the streets.

It was barely daybreak, when with a parting look around his room, mournfully wondering whether he should ever see it again, he went out. The town was as entirely deserted as if the inhabitants had abandoned it, rather than hold communication with him. Every thing looked wan at that hour. Even the coming sun made but a pale waste in the sky, like a sad sea.

By the place where Rachael lived, though it was not in his way; by the red brick streets; by the great silent factories, not trembling yet; by the railway, where the danger-lights were waning in the strengthening day;

by the railway's crazy neighborhood, half pulled down and half built up; by scattered red brick villas, where the besmoked evergreens were sprinkled with a dirty powder, like untidy snuff-takers; by coal-dust paths and many varieties of ugliness; Stephen got to the top of the hill and looked back.

Day was shining radiantly upon the town then, and the bells were going for the morning work. Domestic fires were not yet lighted, and the high chimneys had the sky to themselves. Puffing out their poisonous volumes, they would not be long in hiding it; but, for half a hour, some of the many windows were golden, which showed the Coketown people a sun eternally in eclipse, through a medium of smoked glass.

So strange to turn from the chimneys to the birds. So strange to have the road-dust on his feet instead of the coal-grit. So strange to have lived to his time of life, and yet to be beginning like a boy this summer morning! With these musings in his mind, and his bundle under his arm, Stephen took his attentive face along the high road. And the trees arched over him, whispering that he left a true and loving heart behind.

Chapter XXIII
GUNPOWDER

MR. JAMES HARTHOUSE, "going in" for his adopted party, soon began to score. With the aid of a little more coaching for the political sages, a little more genteel listlessness for the general society, and a tolerable management of the assumed honesty in dishonesty, most effective and most patronized of the polite deadly sins, he speedily came to be considered of much promise. The not being troubled with earnestness was a grand point in his favor, enabling him to take to the hard Fact fellows with as good a grace as if he had been born one of the tribe, and to throw all other tribes overboard, as conscious impostors.

"Whom none of us believe, my dear Mrs. Bounderby, and who do not believe themselves. The only difference between us and the professors of virtue or benevolence, or philanthropy—never mind the name—is that we know it is all meaningless, and say so; while they know it equally and will never say so."

Why should she be shocked or warned by this reiteration? It was not so unlike her father's principles, and her early training, that it need startle her. Where was the great difference between the two schools, when each chained her down to material realities, and inspired her with no faith in any thing else? What was there in her soul for James Harthouse to destroy, which Thomas Gradgrind had nurtured there in its state of innocence!

It was even the worse for her at this pass, that in her mind—implanted there before her eminently practical father began to form it—a struggling disposition to believe in a wider and higher humanity than she had ever heard of, constantly strove with doubts and resentments. With doubts, because the aspiration had been so laid waste in her youth. With resentments, because of the wrong that had been done her, if it were indeed a whisper of the truth. Upon a nature long accustomed to self-suppression, thus torn and divided, the Harthouse philosophy came as a relief and justification. Every thing being hollow, and worthless, she had missed nothing and sacrificed nothing. What did it matter, she had said to her father, when he proposed her husband. What did it matter, she said still. With a scornful self-reliance, she asked herself, What did any thing matter—and went on.

Toward what? Step by step, onward and downward, toward some end, yet so gradually that she believed herself to remain motionless. As to Mr. Harthouse, whither *he* tended, he neither considered nor cared. He had no particular design or plan before him: no energetic wickedness ruffled his lassitude. He was as much amused and interested, at present, as it became so fine a gentleman to be; perhaps even more than it would have been consistent with his reputation to confess. Soon after his arrival he languidly wrote to his brother, the honorable and jocular member, that the Bounderbys were "great fun;" and further, that the female Bounderby, instead of being the Gorgon he had expected, was young and remarkably pretty. After that, he wrote no more about them, and devoted his leisure chiefly to their house. He was very often in their house, in his flittings and visitings about the Coketown district; and was much encouraged by Mr. Bounderby. It was quite in Mr. Bounderby's gusty way to boast to all his world that *he* didn't care about your highly-connected people, but that if his wife Tom Gradgrind's daughter did, she was welcome to their company.

Mr. James Harthouse began to think it would be a new sensation if the face which changed so beautifully for the whelp, would change for him.

He was quick enough to observe; he had a good memory, and did not forget a word of the brother's revelations. He interwove them with every thing he saw of the sister, and he began to understand her. To be sure, the better and profounder part of her character was not within his scope of perception, for in natures, as in seas, depth answers unto depth; but he soon began to read the rest with a student's eye.

Mr. Bounderby had taken possession of a house and grounds, about fifteen miles from the town, and accessible within a mile or two by a railway striding on many arches over a wild country, undermined by deserted coal-pits, and spotted at night by fires and black shapes of engines. This country, gradually softening toward the neighborhood of Mr. Bounderby's retreat, there mellowed into a rustic landscape, golden with heath and snowy with hawthorn in the spring of the year, and tremulous with leaves and their shadows all the summer time. The bank had foreclosed a mortgage on the property thus pleasantly situated: effected by one of the Coketown magnates: who, in his determination to make a shorter cut than usual to an enormous fortune, overspeculated himself by about two hundred thousand pounds. These accidents did sometimes happen in the best-regulated families of Coketown, through the bankrupts had no connection whatever with the improvident classes.

It afforded Mr. Bounderby supreme satisfaction to install himself in this snug little estate, and with demonstrative humility to grow cabbages in the flower-garden. He delighted to live, barrack-fashion, among the elegant furniture, and he bullied the very pictures with his origin. "Why, sir," he would say to a visitor, "I am told that Nickits," the late owner, "gave seven hundred pound for that Sea-beach. Now, to be plain with you, if I ever, in the whole course of my life, take seven looks at it, at a hundred pound a look, it will be as much as I shall do. No, by George! I don't forget that I am Josiah Bounderby of Coketown. For years upon years, the only pictures in my possession, or that I could have got into my possession by any means, unless I stole 'em, were the engravings of a man shaving himself in a boot, on the blacking bottles that I was overjoyed to use in cleaning boots with, and that I sold when they were empty for a farthing apiece, and glad to get it!"

Then he would address Mr. Harthouse in the same style.

"Harthouse, you have a couple of horses down here. Bring half a dozen more if you like, and we'll find room for 'em. There's stabling in this place for a dozen horses; and unless Nickits is belied, he kept the full number. A round dozen of 'em, sir. When that man was a boy, he went to Westminster School. Went to Westminster School as a King's Scholar, when I was principally living on garbage, and sleeping in market baskets. Why, if I wanted to keep a dozen horses—which I don't, for one's enough for me—I couldn't bear to see 'em in their stalls here, and think what my own lodging used to be. I couldn't look at 'em, sir, and not order 'em out. Yet so things come round. You see this place; you know what sort of a place it is; you are aware that there's not a completer place of its size in this kingdom or elsewhere—I don't care where—and here, got into the middle of it, like a maggot into a nut, is Josiah Bounderby. While Nickits (as a man came into my office, and told me yesterday), Nickits, who used to act in Latin, in the Westminster School plays, with the chief-justices and nobility of this country applauding him till they were black in the face, is driveling at this minute—driveling, sir!—in a fifth floor, up a narrow dark back street in Antwerp."

It was among the leafy shadows of this retirement, in the long sultry summer days, that Mr. Harthouse began to prove the face which had set him wondering when he first saw it, and to try if it would change for him.

"Mrs. Bounderby, I esteem it a most fortunate accident that I find you alone here. I have for some time had a particular wish to speak to you."

It was not by any wonderful accident that he found her, the time of day being that at which she was always alone, and the place being her favorite resort. It was an opening in a dark wood, where some felled trees lay, and where she would sit watching the fallen leaves of last year, as she had watched the falling ashes at home.

He sat down beside her, with a glance at her face.

"Your brother. My young friend Tom—"

Her color brightened, and she turned to him with a look of interest. "I never in my life," he thought, "saw anything so remarkable and so captivating as the lighting of those features!" His face betrayed his thoughts—perhaps without betraying him, for it might have been according to its instructions so to do.

"Pardon me. The expression of your sisterly interest is so beautiful—

Tom should be so proud of it—I know this is inexcusable, but I am so compelled to admire."

"Being so impulsive," she said composedly.

"Mrs. Bounderby, no; you know I make no pretence with you. You know I am a sordid piece of human nature, ready to sell myself at any time for any reasonable sum, and altogether incapable of any Arcadian proceeding whatever."

"I am waiting," she returned, "for your further reference to my brother."

"You are rigid with me, and I deserve it. I am as worthless a dog as you will find, except that I am not false—not false. But you surprised and started me from my subject, which was your brother. I have an interest in him."

"Have you an interest in any thing, Mr. Harthouse?" she asked, half incredulously and half gratefully.

"If you had asked me when I first came here, I should have said no. I must say now—even at the hazard of appearing to make a pretence, and of justly awakening your incredulity—yes."

She made a slight movement, as if she were trying to speak, but could not find voice; at length she said, "Mr. Harthouse, I give you credit for being interested in my brother."

"Thank you. I claim to deserve it. You know how little I do claim, but I will go that length. You have done so much for him, you are so fond of him; your whole life, Mrs. Bounderby, expresses such charming self-forgetfulness on his account—pardon me again—I am running wide of the subject. I am interested in him for his own sake."

She had made the slightest action possible, as if she would have risen in a hurry and gone away. He had turned the course of what he said at that instant, and she remained.

"Mrs. Bounderby," he resumed, in a lighter manner, and yet with a show of effort in assuming it, which was even more expressive than the manner he dismissed; "it is no irrevocable offence in a young fellow of your brother's years, if he is heedless, inconsiderate, and expensive—a little dissipated, in the common phrase. Is he?"

"Yes."

"Allow me to be frank. Do you think he games at all?"

"I think he makes bets." Mr. Harthouse waiting, as if that were not her whole answer, she added, "I know he does."

"Of course he loses?"

"Yes."

"Every body does lose who bets. May I hint at the probability of your sometimes supplying him with money for these purposes?"

She sat, looking down, but, at this question, raised her eyes searchingly and a little resentfully.

"Acquit me of impertinent curiosity, my dear Mrs. Bounderby. I think Tom may be gradually falling into trouble, and I wish to stretch out a helping hand to him from the depths of my wicked experience. Shall I say again, for his sake? Is that necessary?"

She seemed to try to answer, but nothing came of it.

"Candidly to confess every thing that has occurred to me," said James Harthouse, again gliding with the same appearance of effort into his more airy manner; "I will confide to you my doubt whether he has had many advantages. Whether—forgive my plainness—whether any great amount of confidence is likely to have been established between himself and his most worthy father."

"I do not," said Louisa, flushing with her own great remembrance in that wise, "think it likely."

"Or, between himself, and—I may trust to your perfect understanding of my meaning I am sure—and his highly esteemed brother-in-law."

She flushed deeper and deeper, and was burning red when she replied in a fainter voice, "I do not think that likely either."

"Mrs. Bounderby," said Harthouse, after short silence, "may there be a better confidence between yourself and me? Tom has borrowed a considerable sum of you?"

"You will understand, Mr. Harthouse," she returned, after some indecision: she had been more or less uncertain, and troubled throughout the conversation, and yet had in the main preserved her self-contained manner: "you will understand that if I tell you what you press to know, it is not by way of complaint or regret. I would never complain of any thing, and what I have done, I do not in the least regret."

"So spirited, too!" thought James Harthouse.

"When I married, I found that my brother was even at that time heavily in debt. Heavily for him, I mean. Heavily enough to oblige me to sell some trinkets. They were no sacrifice. I sold them very willingly. I attached no value to them. They were quite worthless to me."

Either she saw in his face that he knew, or she only feared in her conscience that he knew, that she spoke of some of her husband's gifts. She stopped, and reddened again. If he had not known it before, he would have known it then, though he had been a much duller man than he was.

"Since then, I have given my brother, at various times, what money I could spare: in short, what money I have had. Confiding in you at all, on the faith of the interest you profess for him, I will not do so by halves. Since you have been in the habit of visiting here, he has wanted in one sum as much as a hundred pounds. I have not been able to give it to him. I have felt uneasy for the consequences of his being so involved, but I have kept these secrets until now, when I trust them to your honor. I have held no confidence with any one, because—you anticipated my reason just now." She abruptly broke off.

He was a ready man, and he saw, and seized, an opportunity here of presenting her own image to her, slightly disguised as her brother.

"Mrs. Bounderby, though a graceless person, of the world worldly, I feel the utmost interest, I assure you, in what you tell me. I can not possibly be hard upon your brother. I understand and share the wise consideration with which you regard his errors. With all possible respect both for Mr. Gradgrind and for Mr. Bounderby, I think I perceive that he has not been fortunate in his training. Bred at a disadvantage toward the society in which he has his part to play, he rushes into these extremes for himself, from opposite extremes that have long been forced—with the very best intentions we have no doubt—upon him. Mr. Bounderby's fine bluff English independence, though a most charming characteristic, does not—as we have agreed—invite confidence. If I might venture to remark that it is the least in the world deficient in that delicacy to which a youth mistaken, a character misconceived, and abilities misdirected, would turn for relief and guidance, I should express what it presents to my own view."

As she sat looking straight before her, across the changing lights upon the grass into the darkness of the wood beyond, he saw in her face her application of his very distinctly uttered words.

"All allowance," he continued, "must be made. I have one great fault to find with Tom however, which I cannot forgive and for which I take him heaviy to account."

Louisa turned her eyes to his face, and asked him what fault was that?

"Perhaps," he returned, "I have said enough. Perhaps it would have been better, on the whole, if no allusion to it had escaped me."

"You alarm me, Mr. Harthouse. Pray let me know it."

"To relieve you from needless apprehension—and as this confidence regarding your brother, which I prize I am sure above all possible things, has been established between us—I obey. I cannot forgive him for not being more sensible, in every word, look, and act of his life, of the affection of his best friend; of the devotion of his best friend; of her unselfishness; of her sacrifice. The return he makes her, within my observation, is a very poor one. What she has done for him demands his constant love and gratitude, not his ill-humor and caprice. Careless fellow as I am, I am nor so indifferent, Mrs. Bounderby, as to be regardless of this vice in your brother, or inclined to consider it a venial offence."

The wood floated before her, for her eyes were suffused with tears. They rose from a deep well, long concealed, and her heart was filled with acute pain that found no relief in them.

"In a word, it is to correct your brother in this, Mrs. Bounderby, that I must aspire. My better knowledge of his circumstances, and my direction and advice in extricating them—rather valuable, I hope, as coming from a scapegace on a much larger scale—will give me some influence over him, and all I gain I shall certainly use toward this end. I have said enough, and more than enough. I seem to be protesting that I am a sort of good fellow, when, upon my honor, I have not the least intention to make any protestation to that effect, and openly announce that I am nothing of the sort. Yonder, among the trees," he added, having lifted up his eyes and looked about; for he had watched her closely until now "is your brother himself; no doubt, just come down. As he seems to be loitering in this direction, it may be as well, perhaps, to walk towards him and throw ourselves in his way. He has been very silent and doleful of late. Perhaps his brotherly conscience is touched—if there are such things as consciences. Though, upon my honor, I hear of them much too often to believe in them."

He assisted her to rise, and she took his arm, and they advanced to meet the whelp. He was idly beating the branches as he lounged along: or he stooped viciously to rip the moss from the trees with his stick. He was startled when they came upon him while he was engaged in this latter pastime, and his color changed.

"Halloa!" he stammered, "I didn't know you were here."

"Whose name, Tom," said Mr. Harthouse, putting his hand upon his shoulder and turning him, so that they all three walked toward the house together, "have you been carving on the trees?"

"Whose name?" returned Tom. "Oh! You mean what girl's name?"

"You have a suspicious appearance of inscribing some fair creature's on the bark, Tom."

"Not much of that, Mr. Harthouse, unless some fair creature with a slashing fortune at her own disposal would take a fancy to me. Or she might be as ugly as she was rich, without any fear of losing me. I'd carve her name as often as she liked."

"I'm afraid you are mercenary, Tom."

"Mercenary," repeated Tom. "Who is not mercenary? Ask my sister."

"Have you so proved it to be a failing of mine, Tom?" said Louisa, showing no other sense of his discontent and ill-nature.

"You know whether the cap fits you, Loo," returned her brother sulkily. "If it does, you can wear it."

"Tom is misanthropical to-day, as all bored people are now and then," said Mr. Harthouse. "Don't believe him, Mrs. Bounderby. He knows much better. I shall disclose some of his opinions of you, privately expressed to me, unless he relents a little."

"At all events, Mr. Harthouse," said Tom, softening in his admiration of his patron, but shaking his head sullenly too, "you can't tell her that I ever praised her for being mercenary. I may have praised her for being the contrary, and I should do it again if I had as good reason. However, never mind this now; it's not very interesting to you, and I am sick of the subject."

They walked on to the house, where Louisa quitted her visitor's arm and went in. He stood looking after her, as she ascended the steps and passed into the shadow of the door; then put his hand upon her brother's shoulder again, and invited him with a confidential nod to a walk in the garden.

"Tom, my fine fellow, I want to have a word with you."

They had stopped among a disorder of roses—it was part of Mr. Bounderby's humility to keep Nickits's roses on a reduced scale—and Tom sat down on a terrace-parapet, plucking buds and picking them to pieces; while his powerful Familiar stood over him, with a foot upon the parapet, and his figure easily resting on the arm suported by that knee. They were just visible from her window. Perhaps she saw them.

"Tom, what's the matter?"

"Oh! Mr. Harthouse," said Tom with a groan, "I am hard up, and bothered out of my life."

"My good fellow, so am I."

"You!" returned Tom. "You are the picture of independence. Mr. Harthouse, I am in a horrible mess. You have no idea what a state I have got myself into—what a state my sister might have got me out of, if she would only have done it."

He took to biting the rose-buds now, and tearing them away from his teeth with a hand that trembled like an infirm old man's. After one exceedingly observant look at him, his companion relapsed into his lightest air.

"Tom, you are inconsiderate: you expect too much of your sister. You have had money of her, you dog, you know you have."

"Well, Mr. Harthouse, I know I have. How else was I to get it? Here's old Bounderby always boasting that at my age he lived upon two-pence a month, or something of that sort. Here's my father drawing what he calls a line, and tying me down to it from a baby, neck and heels. Here's my mother who never has anything of her own, except her complaints. What *is* a fellow to do for money, and where *am* I to look for it, if not to my sister?"

He was almost crying, and scattered the buds about by dozens. Mr. Harthouse took him persuasively by the coat.

"But, my dear Tom, if your sister has not got it—"

"Not got it, Mr. Harthouse? I don't say she has got it. I may have wanted more than she was likely to have got. But then she ought to get it. She could get it. It's no use pretending to make a secret of matters now, after what I have told you already; you know she didn't marry old Bounderby for her own sake, or for his sake, but for my sake. Then why doesn't she get what I want, out of him, for my sake? She is not obliged to say what she is going to do with it; she is sharp enough; she could manage to coax it out of him, if she chose. Then why doesn't she choose, when I tell her of what consequence it is? But no. There she sits in his company like a stone, instead of making herself agreeable and getting it easily. I don't know what you may call this, but *I* call it unnatural conduct."

There was a piece of ornamental water immediately below the parapet, on the other side, into which Mr. James Harthouse had a very strong inclination to pitch Mr. Thomas Gradgrind Junior, as the injured men of Coketown threatened to pitch their property into the Atlantic. But he preserved his easy attitude; and nothing more solid went over the stone balustrades than the accumulated rose-buds now floating about, a little surface-island.

"My dear Tom," said Harthouse, "let me try to be your banker."

"For God's sake," replied Tom, suddenly, "don't talk about bankers!" And very white he looked, in contrast with the roses. Very white.

Mr. Harthouse, as a thoroughly well-bred man, accustomed to the best society, was not to be surprised—he could as soon have been affected—but he raised his eyelids a little more, as if they were lifted by a feeble touch of wonder. Albeit it was as much against the precepts of his school to wonder, as it was against the doctrines of the Gradgrind College.

"What is the present need, Tom? Three figures? Out with them. Say what they are."

"Mr. Harthouse," returned Tom, now actually crying; and his tears were better than his injuries, however pitiful a figure he made; "it's too late; the money is of no use to me at present. I should have had it before, to be of use to me. But I am very much obliged to you; you're a true friend."

A true friend! "Whelp, whelp!" thought Mr. Harthouse, lazily; "what an Ass you are!"

"And I take your offer as a great kindness," said Tom, grasping his hand. "As a geat kindness, Mr. Harthouse."

"Well," returned the other, "it may be of more use by and by. And, my good fellow, if you will open your bedevilments to me when they come thick upon you, I may show you better ways out of them than you can find for yourself."

"Thank you," said Tom, shaking his head dismally, and chewing rose-buds. "I wish I had known you sooner, Mr. Harthouse."

"Now, you see, Tom," said Mr. Harthouse in conclusion; himself tossing over a rose or two, as a contribution to the island, which was always drifting to the wall as if it wanted to become a part of the mainland; "every man is selfish in every thing he does, and I am exactly like the rest of my fellow-creatures. I am desperately intent;" the languor of his desperation being quite tropical "on your softening toward your sister—which you ought to do; and on your being a more loving and agreeable sort of brother—which you ought to be."

"I will be, Mr. Harthouse."

"No time like the present, Tom. Begin at once."

"Certainly I will. And my sister Loo shall say so."

"Having made which bargain, Tom," said Harthouse, clapping him on the shoulder again, with an air which left him at liberty to infer—as he did, poor fool—that this condition was imposed upon him in mere careless good-nature, to lessen his sense of obligation, "we will tear ourselves asunder until dinner-time."

When Tom appeared before dinner, though his mind seemed heavy enough, his body was on the alert; and he appeared before Mr. Bounderby came in. "I didn't mean to be cross, Loo," he said, giving her his hand, and kissing her. "I know you are fond of me, and you know I am fond of you."

After this, there was a smile upon Louisa's face that day, for some one else. Alas, for some one else!

"So much the less is the whelp the only creature that she cares for," thought James Harthouse, reversing the reflection of his first day's knowledge of her pretty face. "So much the less, so much the less."

Chapter XXIV
EXPLOSION

THE next morning was too bright a morning for sleep, and James Harthouse rose early and sat in the pleasant bay window of his dressing-room, smoking the rare tobacco that had had so wholesome an influence on his young friend. Reposing in the sunlight, with the fragrance of his Eastern pipe about him, and the dreamy smoke vanishing into the air, so rich and soft with summer odors, he reckoned up his advantages as an idle winner might count his gains. He was not at all bored for the time, and could give his mind to it.

He had established a confidence with her, from which her husband was excluded. He had established a confidence with her, that absolutely turned upon her indifference toward her husband, and the absence, now and at all times, of any congeniality between them. He had artfully, but plainly, assured her, that he knew her heart in its last most delicate recesses; he had come so near to her through its tenderest sentiment; he had associated himself with that feeling; and the barrier behind which she lived, had melted away. All very odd, and very satisfactory!

And yet he had not, even now, any earnest wickedness of purpose in him. Publicly and privately, it were much better for the age in which he lived, that he and the legion of whom he was one were designedly bad, than indifferent and purposeless. It is the drifting icebergs, setting with any current any where, that wreck the ships.

When the Devil goeth about like a roaring lion, he goeth about in a shape by which few but savages and hunters are attracted. But, when he is trimmed, varnished, and polished according to the mode; when he is aweary of vice, and aweary of virtue, used up as to brimstone, and used up as to bliss; then, whether he take to the serving out of red tape, or to the kindling of red fire, he is the very Devil.

So, James Harthouse reclined in the window, indolently smoking, and reckoning up the steps he had taken on the road by which he happened to be traveling. The end to which it led was before him, pretty plainly; but he troubled himself with no calculations about it. What will be, will be.

As he had rather a long ride to take that day—for there was a public occasion "to do" at some distance, which afforded a tolerable opportunity of going in for the Gradgrind men—he dressed early, and went down to breakfast. He was anxious to see if she had relapsed since the previous evening. No. He resumed where he had left off. There was a look of interest for him again.

He got through the day as much (or as little) to his own satisfaction, as was to be expected under the fatiguing circumstances; and came riding back at six o'clock. There was a sweep of some half mile between the lodge and the house, and he was riding along at a foot pace over the smooth gravel, once Nickits's, when Mr. Bounderby burst out of the shrubbery with such violence as to make his horse shy across the road.

"Harthouse!" cried Mr. Bounderby. "Have you heard?"

"Heard what?" said Harthouse, soothing his horse, and inwardly favoring Mr. Bounderby with no good wishes.

"Then you *haven't* heard?"

"I have heard you, and so has this brute. I have heard nothing else."

Mr. Bounderby, red and hot, planted himself in the centre of the path before the horse's head, to explode his bombshell with more effect.

"The Bank's robbed!"

"You don't mean it!"

"Robbed last night, sir. Robbed in an extraordinary manner. Robbed with a false key."

"Of much?"

Mr. Bounderby, in his desire to make the most of it, really seemed mortified by being obliged to reply, "Why, no, not of very much. But it might have been."

"Of how much?"

"Oh! as a sum—if you stick to a sum—of not more than a hundred and fifty pound," said Bounderby, with impatience. "But it's not the sum; it's the fact. It's the fact of the Bank being robbed, that's the important circumstance. I am surprised you don't see it."

"My dear Bounderby," said James, dismounting, and giving his bridle to his servant, "I *do* see it; and am as overcome as you can possibly desire me to be, by the spectacle afforded to my mental view. Nevertheless, I may be allowed, I hope, to congratulate you—which I do with all my soul, I assure you—on your not having sustained a greater loss."

"Thank'ee," replied Bounderby, in a short, ungracious manner. "But I tell you what. It might have been twenty thousand pound."

"I suppose it might."

"Suppose it might? By the Lord, you *may* suppose so. By George!" said Mr. Bounderby, with sundry menacing nods and shakes of his head. "It might have been twice twenty. There's no knowing what it would have been, or wouldn't have been, as it was, but for the fellows' being disturbed."

Louisa had come up now, and Mrs. Sparsit, and Bitzer.

"Here's Tom Gradgrind's daughter knows pretty well what it might have been, if you don't," blustered Bounderby. "Dropped, sir, as if she was shot when I told her! Never knew her do such a thing before. Does her credit, under the circumstances, in my opinion!"

She still looked faint and pale. James Harthouse begged her to take his arm, and, as they moved on very slowly, asked how the robbery had been committed.

"Why, I am going to tell you," said Bounderby, irritably giving his arm to Mrs. Sparsit. "If you hadn't been so mighty particular about the sum, I should have begun to tell you before. You know this lady (for she *is* a lady), Mrs. Sparsit?"

"I have already had the honour—"

"Very well. And this young man, Bitzer, you saw him too on the same occasion?" Mr. Harthouse inclined his head in assent, and Bitzer knuckled his forehead.

"Very well. They live at the Bank. You know they live at the Bank perhaps? Very well. Yesterday afternoon, at the close of business hours, every thing was put away as usual. In the iron room that this young fellow sleeps outside of, there was never mind how much. In the little safe in young Tom's closet, the safe used for petty purposes, there was a hundred and fifty odd pound."

"A hundred and fifty-four, seven, one," said Bitzer.

"Come!" retorted Bounderby, stopping to wheel round upon him, "let's have none of *your* interruptions. It's enough to be robbed while you're snoring because you're too comfortable, without being put right with *your* four seven ones. I didn't snore, myself, when I was your age, let me tell you. I hadn't victuals enough to snore. And I didn't four seven one. Not if I knew it."

Bitzer knuckled his forehead again, in a sneaking manner, and seemed at once particularly impressed and depressed by the instance last given of Mr. Bounderby's moral abstinence.

"A hundred and fifty odd pound," resumed Mr. Bounderby. "That sum of money, young Tom locked in his safe; not a very strong safe, but that's no matter now. Every thing was left, all right. Some time in the night, while this young fellow snored—Mrs. Sparsit, ma'am, you say you have heard him snore?"

"Sir," returned Mrs. Sparsit, "I can not say that I have heard him precisely snore, and therefore must not make that statement. But on winter evenings, when he has fallen asleep at his table, I have heard him, what I should prefer to describe as partially choke. I have heard him on such occasions produce sounds of a nature similar to what may be sometimes heard in Dutch clocks. Not," said Mrs. Sparsit, with a lofty sense of giving strict evidence, "that I would convey any imputation on his moral character. Far from it. I have always considered Bitzer a young man of the most upright principle; and to that I beg to bear my testimony."

"Well!" said the exasperated Bounderby, "while he was snoring, *or* choking, *or* Dutch clocking, *or* something or other—being asleep—some fellows, somehow, whether previously concealed in the house or not remains to be seen, got to young Tom's safe, forced it, and abstracted the contents. Being then disturbed, they made off; letting themselves out at the main door, and double-locking it again (it was double-locked, and the key under Mrs. Sparsit's pillow) with a false key, which was picked up in the street near the Bank, about twelve o'clock today. No alarm takes place, till this chap, Bitzer, turns out this morning and begins to open and prepare the offices for business. Then, looking at Tom's safe, he sees the door ajar, and finds the lock forced, and the money gone."

"Where is Tom, by-the-by?" asked Harthouse, glancing round.

"He has been helping the police," said Bounderby, "and stays behind at the Bank. I wish these fellows had tried to rob me when I was at his time of life. They would have been out of pocket, if they had invested eighteenpence in the job; I can tell 'em that."

"Is any body suspected?"

"Suspected? I should think there was somebody suspected. Egod!" said Bounderby, relinquishing Mrs. Sparsit's arm to wipe his heated head. "Josiah Bounderby of Coketown is not to be plundered and nobody suspected. No, thank you!"

Might Mr. Harthouse inquire Who was suspected?

"Well," said Bounderby, stopping and facing about to confront them all, "I'll tell you. It's not to be mentioned every where; it's not to be mentioned any where—in order that the scoundrels concerned (there's a gang of 'em) may be thrown off their guard. So take this in confidence. Now wait a bit." Mr. Bounderby wiped his head again. "What should you say to;" here he violently exploded; "to a Hand being in it?"

"I hope," said Harthouse, lazily, "not our friend Blackpot?"

"Say Pool instead of Pot, sir," returned Bounderby, "and that's the man."

Louisa faintly uttered some word of incredulity and surprise.

"Oh, yes! I know!" said Bounderby, immediately catching at the sound. "I know! I am used to that. I know all about it. They are the finest people in the world, these fellows are. They have got the gift of gab, they have. They only want to have their rights explained to them, they do. But I tell you what. Show me a dissatisfied Hand, and I'll show you a man that's fit for any thing bad, I don't care what it is."

Another of the popular fictions of Coketown, which some pains had been taken to disseminate—and which some people really believed.

"But I am acquainted with these chaps," said Bounderby. "I can read 'em off, like books. Mrs. Sparsit, ma'am, I appeal to you. What warning did I give that fellow, the first time he set foot in the house, when the express object of his visit was to know how he could knock Religion over, and floor the Established Church? Mrs. Sparsit, in point of high connections, you are on a level with the aristocracy—did I say, or did I not say, to that fellow, 'you can't hide the truth from me; you are not the kind of fellow I like; you'll come to no good?' "

"Assuredly, sir," returned Mrs. Sparsit, "you did, in a highly impressive manner, give him such an admonition."

"When he shocked you, ma'am," said Bounderby; "when he shocked your feelings?"

"Yes, sir," returned Mrs. Sparsit, with a meek shake of her head, "he certainly did so. Though I do not mean to say but that my feelings may be weaker on such points—more foolish, if the term is preferred—than they might have been, if I had always occupied my present position."

Mr. Bounderby stared with a bursting pride at Mr. Harthouse, as much as to say, "I am the proprietor of this female, and she's worth your attention, I think." Then, resumed his discourse.

"You can recall for yourself, Harthouse, what I said to him when you saw him. I didn't mince the matter with him. I am never mealy with 'em. I KNOW 'em. Very well, sir. Three days after that, he bolted. Went off, nobody knows where: as my mother did in my infancy—only with this difference, that he is a worse subject than my mother, if possible. What did he do before he went? What do you say;" Mr. Bounderby, with his hat in his hand, gave a beat upon the crown at every little division of his sentences, as if it were a tambourine; "to his being seen—night after night—watching the Bank?—to his lurking about there—after dark?—To its striking Mrs. Sparsit—that he could be lurking for no good? To her calling Bitzer's attention to him, and their both taking notice of him? And to its appearing on inquiry to-day—that he was also noticed by the neighbors?" Having come to the chimax, Mr. Bounderby, like an Oriental dancer, put his tambourine on his head.

"Suspicious," said James Harthouse, "certainly."

"I think so, sir," said Bounderby, with a defiant nod. "I think so. But there are more of 'em in it. There's an old woman. One never hears of these things till the mischief's done; all sorts of defects are found out in the stable door after the horse is stolen; there's an old woman turns up now. An old woman who seems to have been flying into town on a broomstick, every now and then. *She* watches the place a whole day before this fellow begins, and, on the night when you saw him, she steals away with him and holds a council with him—I suppose, to make her report on going off duty, and be damned to her."

There was such a person in the room that night, and she shrunk from observation, thought Louisa.

"This is not all of 'em, even as we already know 'em," said Bounderby, with many nods of hidden meaning. "But I have said enough for the present. You'll have the goodness to keep it quiet and mention it to no one. It may take time, but we shall have 'em. It's policy to give 'em line enough, and there's no objection to that."

"Of course, they will be punished with the utmost rigor of the law, as notice-boards observe," replied James Harthouse, "and serve them right. Fellows who go in for Banks must take the consequences. If there were no consequences, we should all go in for Banks." He had gently taken Louisa's parasol from her hand, and had put it up for her; and she walked under its shade, though the sun did not shine there.

"For the present, Loo Bounderby," said her husband, "here's Mrs. Sparsit to look after. Mrs. Sparsit's nerves have been acted upon by this business, and she'll stay here a day or two. So, make her comfortable."

"Thank you very much, sir," that discreet lady observed, "but pray do not let My comfort be a consideration. Any thing will do for Me."

It soon appeared that if Mrs. Sparsit had a failing in her association with that domestic establishment, it was that she was so excessively regardless of herself and regardful of others, as to be a nuisance. On being shown her chamber, she was so dreadfully sensible of its comforts as to suggest the inference that she would have preferred to pass the night on the mangle in the laundry. True, the Powlers and the Scadgerses were accustomed to splendor, "but it is my duty to remember," Mrs. Sparsit was fond of observing with a lofty grace: particularly when any of the domestics were present, "that what I was, I am no longer. Indeed," said she, "if I could altogether cancel the remembrance that Mr. Sparsit was a Powler, or that I myself am related to the Scadgers family; or if I could even revoke the fact, and make myself a person of common descent and ordinary connections; I would gladly do so. I should think it, under existing circumstances, right to do so." The same hermitical state of mind led to her renunciation of made dishes and wines at dinner, until fairly commanded by Mr. Bounderby to take them; when she said, "Indeed you are very good, sir;" and departed from a resolution of which she had made rather formal and public announcement, to "wait for the simple mutton." She was likewise deeply apologetic for wanting the salt; and, feeling amiably bound to bear out Mr. Bounderby to the fullest extent in the testimony he had borne to her nerves, occasionally sat back in her chair and silently wept; at which periods a tear of large dimensions, like a crystal earring, might be observed (or rather, must be, for it insisted on public notice) sliding down her Roman nose.

But Mrs. Sparsit's greatest point, first and last, was her determination to pity Mr. Bounderby. There were occasions when in looking at him she was involuntarily moved to shake her head, as who would say, "Alas, poor Yorick!" After allowing herself to be betrayed into these evidences of emotion, she would force a lambent brightness, and would be fitfully cheeful, and would say, "You have still good spirits, sir, I am thankful to find;" and would appear to hail it as a blessed dispensation that Mr. Bounderby bore up as he did. One idiosyncrasy for which she often apologized, she found it excessively difficult to conquer. She had a curious propensity to call Mrs. Bounderby "Miss Gradgrind," and yielded to it some three or four score times in the course of the evening. Her repetition of this mistake covered Mrs. Sparsit with modest confusion; but indeed, she said, it seemed so natural to say Miss Gradgrind: whereas, to persuade herself that the young lady whom she had had the happiness of knowing from a child could be really and truly Mrs. Bounderby, she found almost impossible. It was a further singularity of this remarkable case, that the more she thought about it, the more impossible it appeared; "the differences," she observed, "being such—"

In the drawing-room after dinner, Mr. Bounderby tried the case of the robbery, examined the witnesses, made notes of the evidence, found the suspected persons guilty, and sentenced them to the extreme punishment of the law. That done, Bitzer was dismissed to town with instructions to recommend Tom to come home by the mail-train.

When candles were brought, Mrs. Sparsit murmured, "Don't be low, sir. Pray let me see you cheerful, sir, as I used to do." Mr. Bounderby, upon whom these consolations had begun to produce the effect of making him, in a bull-headed blundering way, sentimental, sighed like some large sea-animal. "I cannot bear to see you so, sir," said Mrs Sparsit. "Try a hand at backgammon, sir, as you used to do when I had the honor of living under your roof." "I haven't played backgammon, ma'am," said Mr. Bounderby, "since that time." "No, sir," said Mrs. Sparsit, soothingly, "I am aware that you have not. I remember that Miss Gradgrind takes no interest in the game. But I shall be happy, sir, if you will condescend."

They played near a window, opening on the garden. It was a fine night: not moonlight, but sultry and fragrant. Louisa and Mr. Harthouse strolled out into the garden, where their voices could be heard in the stillness, though not what they said. Mrs. Sparsit, from her place at the backgammon board, was constantly straining her eyes to pierce the shadows without. "What's the matter, ma'am?" said Mr. Bounderby; "you don't see a Fire, do you?"

"Oh dear no, sir," returned Mrs. Sparsit, "I was thinking of the dew?" "What have you got to do with the dew, ma'am?" said Mr. Bounderby. "It's not myself, sir," returned Mrs. Sparsit, "I am fearful of Miss Gradgrind's taking cold." "She never takes cold," said Mr. Bounderby. "Really, sir?" said Mrs. Sparsit. And was affected with a cough in her throat.

When the time drew near for retiring, Mr. Bounderby took a glass of water. "Oh, sir!" said Mrs. Sparsit. "Not your sherry warm, with lemon-peel and nutmeg?" "Why, I have got out of the habit of taking it now, ma'am," said Mr. Bounderby. "The more's the pity, sir," returned Mrs. Sparsit; "you are losing all your good old habits. Cheer up, sir! If Miss Gradgrind will permit me, I will offer to make it for you, as I have often done."

Miss Gradgrind readily permitting Mrs. Sparsit to do any thing she pleased, that considerate lady made the beverage, and handed it to Mr. Bounderby. "It will do you good, sir. It will warm your heart. It is the sort of thing you want, and ought to take, sir." And when Mr. Bounderby said, "Your health, ma'am!" she answered with great feeling, "Thank you, sir. The same to you, and happiness also." Finally, she wished him good-night, with great pathos; and Mr. Bounderby went to bed, with a maudlin persuasion that he had been crossed in something tender, though he could not, for his life, have mentioned what it was.

Long after Louisa had undressed and lain down, she watched and waited for her brother's coming home. That could hardly be, she knew, until an hour past midnight; but in the country silence, which did any thing but calm the trouble of her thoughts, time lagged wearily. At last, when the darkness and stilless had seemed for hours to thicken one another, she heard the bell at the gate. She felt as though she would have been glad that it rang on until daylight; but it ceased, and the circles of its last sound spread out fainter and wider in the air, and all was dead again.

She waited yet some quarter of an hour, as she judged. Then she arose, put on a loose robe, and went out of her room in the dark, and up the staircase to her brother's room. His door being shut, she softly opened it and spoke to him, approaching his bed with a noiseless step.

She kneeled down beside it, passed her arm over his neck, and drew his face to hers. She knew that he only feigned to be asleep, but she said nothing to him.

He started by-and-by as if he were just then awakened, and asked who that was, and what was the matter?

"Tom, have you any thing to tell me? If ever you loved me in your life, and have any thing concealed from every one besides, tell it to me."

"I don't know what you mean, Loo. You have been dreaming."

"My dear brother:" she laid her head down on his pillow, and her hair flowed over him as if she would hide him from every one but herself: "is there nothing that you have to tell me? Is there nothing you can tell me, if you will? You can tell me nothing that will change me. O Tom, tell me the truth!"

"I don't know what you mean, Loo!"

"As you lie here alone, my dear, in the melancholy night, so you must lie somewhere one night, when even I, if I am living then, shall have left you. As I am here beside you, barefoot, unclothed, undistinguishable in darkness, so must I lie through all the night of my decay, until I am dust. In the name of that time, Tom, tell me the truth now!"

"What is it you want to know?"

"You may be certain;" in the energy of her love she took him to her bosom as if he were a child; "that I will not reproach you. You may be certain that I will be compassionate and true to you. You may be certain that I will save you at whatever cost. O Tom, have you nothing to tell me? Whisper very softly. Say only 'yes,' and I shall understand you!"

She turned her ear to his lips, but he remained doggedly silent.

"Not a word, Tom?"

"How can I say, Yes, or how can I say, No, when I don't know what you mean? Loo, you are a brave, kind girl, worthy I begin to think of a better brother than I am. But I have nothing more to say. Go to bed, go to bed."

"You are tired," she whispered presently, more in her usual way.

"Yes, I am quite tired out."

"You have been so hurried and disturbed to day. Have any fresh discoveries been made?"

"Only those you have heard of, from—him."

"Tom, have you said to any one that we made a visit to those people, and that we saw those three together?"

"No. Didn't you yourself particularly ask me to keep it quiet, when you asked me to go there with you?"

"Yes. But I did not know then what was going to happen."

"Nor I neither. How could I?"

He was very quick upon her with the retort.

"Ought I to say, after what has happened," said his sister, standing by the bed—she had gradually withdrawn herself and risen, "that I made that visit? Should I say so? Must I say so?"

"Good Heavens, Loo," returned her brother, "you are not in the habit of asking my advice. Say what you like. If you keep it to yourself, I shall keep it to *my*self. If you disclose it, there's an end of it."

It was too dark for either to see the other's face; but each seemed very attentive, and to consider before speaking.

"Tom, do you believe the man I gave the money to, is really implicated in this crime?"

"I don't know. I don't see why he shouldn't be."

"He seemed to me an honest man."

"Another person may seem to you dishonest, and yet not be so."

There was a pause, for he had hesitated and stopped.

"In short," resumed Tom, as if he had made up his mind, "if you come to that, perhaps I was so far from being altogether in his favor that I took him outside the door to tell him quietly, that I thought he might consider himself very well off to get such a windfall as he had got from my sister, and that I hoped he would make good use of it. You remember whether I took him out or not. I say nothing against the man; he may be a very good fellow, for any thing I know; I hope he is."

"Was he offended by what you said?"

"No, he took it pretty well; he was civil enough. Where are you, Loo?" he sat up in bed and kissed her. "Good-night, my dear, good-night."

"You have nothing more to tell me?"

"No. What should I have? You wouldn't have me tell you a lie?"

"I wouldn't have you do that tonight, Tom, of all the nights in your life; many and much happier as I hope they will be."

"Thank you, my dear Loo. I am so tired, that I am sure I wonder I don't say any thing, to get to sleep. Go to bed, go to bed."

Kissing her again, he turned round, drew the coverlet over his head, and lay as still as if that time had come by which she had adjured him. She stood for some time at the bedside before she slowly moved away. She stopped at the door, looked back when she had opened it, and asked him if he had called her? But he lay still, and she softly closed the door and returned to her room.

Then the wretched boy looked cautiously up and found her gone, crept out of bed, fastened his door, and threw himself upon his pillow again: tearing his hair, morosely crying, grudgingly loving her, hatefully but impenitently spurning himself, and no less hatefully and unprofitably spurning all the good in the world.

Chapter XXV

HEARING THE LAST OF IT

MRS. SPARSIT, lying by to recover the tone of her nerves in Mr. Bounderby's retreat, kept such a sharp look-out, night and day, under her Coriolanian eyebrows, that her eyes, like a couple of lighthouses on an iron-bound coast, might have warned all prudent mariners from that bold rock her Roman nose and the dark and craggy region in its neighborhood, but for the placidity of her manner. Although it was hard to believe that her retiring for the night could be any thing but a form, so severely wide awake were those classical eyes of hers, and so impossible did it seem that her rigid nose could yield to any relaxing influence, yet her manner of sitting, smoothing her uncomfortable, not to say, gritty mittens (they were constructed of a cool fabric like a meat-safe), or of ambling to unknown places of destination with her foot in her cotton stirrup, was so perfectly serene, that most observers would have been constrained to suppose her a dove, embodied by some freak of nature, in the earthly tabernacle of a bird of the hook-beaked order.

She was a most wonderful woman for prowling about the house. How she got from story to story, was a mystery beyond solution. A lady so decorous in herself, and so highly connected, was not to be suspected of dropping over the banisters or sliding down them, yet her extraordinary facility of locomotion suggested the wild idea. Another noticeable circumstance in Mrs. Sparsit was, that she was never hurried. She would shoot with consummate velocity from the roof to the hall, yet would be in full possession of her breath and dignity on the moment of her arrival there. Neither was she ever seen by human vision to go at a great pace.

She took very kindly to Mr. Harthouse, and had some pleasant conversation with him soon after her arrival. She made him her stately courtsey in the garden, one morning before breakfast.

"It appears but yesterday, sir," said Mrs. Sparsit, "that I had the honor of receiving you at the Bank, when you were so good as to wish to be made acquainted with Mr. Bounderby's address."

"An occasion, I am sure, not to be forgotten by myself in the course of Ages," said Mr. Harthouse, inclining his head to Mrs. Sparsit with the most indolent of all possible airs.

"We live in a singular world, sir," said Mrs. Sparsit.

"I have had the honor, by a coincidence of which I am proud, to have made a remark, similar in effect, though not so epigrammatically expressed."

"A singular world, I would say, sir," pursued Mrs. Sparsit; after acknowledging the compliment with a drooping of her dark eyebrows, not altogether so mild in its expression as her voice was in its dulcet tones; "as regards the intimacies we form at one time, with individuals we were quite ignorant of, at another. I recall, sir, that on that occasion you went so far as to say you were actually apprehensive of Miss Gradgrind."

"Your memory does me more honor than my insignificance deserves. I availed myself of your obliging hints to correct my timidity, and it is unnecessary to add that they were perfectly accurate. Mrs. Sparsit's talent for—in fact for any thing requiring accuracy—with a combination of strength of mind—and Family—is too habitually developed to admit of any question." He was almost falling asleep over this compliment; it took him so long to get through, and his mind wandered so much in the course of its execution.

"You found Miss Gradgrind—I really cannot call her Mrs. Bounderby; it's very absurd of me—as youthful as I described her?" asked Mrs. Sparsit, sweetly.

"You drew her portrait perfectly," said Mr. Harthouse. "Presented her dead image."

"Very engaging, sir," said Mrs. Sparsit, causing her mittens slowly to revolve over one another.

"Highly so."

"It used to be considered," said Mrs. Sparsit, "that Miss Gradgrind was wanting in animation, but I confess she appears to me considerably and strikingly improved in that respect. Ay, and indeed here *is* Mr. Bounderby!" cried Mrs. Sparsit, nodding her head a great many times, as if she had been talking and thinking of no one else. "How do you find yourself this morning, sir? Pray let us see you cheerful, sir."

Now, these persistent assuagements of his misery, and lightenings of his load, had by this time begun to have the effect of making Mr. Bounderby softer than usual toward Mrs. Sparsit, and harder than usual to most other people from his wife downward. So, when Mrs. Sparsit said with forced lightness of heart, "You want your breakfast, sir, but I dare say Miss Gradgrind will soon be here to preside at the table," Mr. Bounderby replied, "If I waited to be taken care of by my wife, ma'am, I believe you know pretty well I should wait till Doomsday, so I'll trouble *you* to take charge of the tea pot." Mrs. Sparsit complied, and assumed her old position at table.

This again made the excellent woman vastly sentimental. She was so humble withal, that when Louisa appeared, she rose, protesting she never could think of sitting in that place under existing circumstances, often as she had had the honor of making Mr. Bounderby's breakfast before Mrs. Gradgrind—she begged pardon, she meant to say, Miss Bounderby—she hoped to be excused, but she really could not get it right yet, though she trusted to become familiar with it by-and-by—had assumed her present position. It was only (she observed) because Miss Gradgrind happened to be a little late, and Mr. Bounderby's time was so very precious, and she knew it of old to be so essential that he should breakfast to the moment, that she had taken the liberty of complying with his request: long as his will had been a law to her.

"There! Stop where you are, ma'am," said Mr. Bounderby, "stop where you are! Mrs. Bounderby will be very glad to be relieved of the trouble, I believe."

"Don't say that, sir," returned Mrs. Sparsit, almost with severity, "because that is very unkind to Mrs. Bounderby. And to be unkind is not to be you, sir."

"You may set your mind at rest, ma'am. You can take it very quietly, can't you, Loo?" said Mr. Bounderby, in a blustering way to his wife.

"Of course. It is of no moment. Why should it be of any importance to me?"

"Why should it be of any importance to any one, Mrs. Sparsit, ma'am?" said Mr. Bounderby, swelling with a sense of slight. "You attach too much importance to these things, ma'am. By George, you'll be corrupted in some of your notions here. You are old-fashioned, ma'am. You are behind Tom Gradgrind's children's time."

"What is the matter with you?" asked Louisa, coldly surprised. "What has given you offence?"

"Offence!" repeated Bounderby. "Do you suppose if there was any offence given me, I shouldn't name it, and request to have it corrected? I am a straightforward man, I believe. I don't go beating about for sidewinds."

"I suppose no one ever had occasion to think you too diffident, or too delicate," Louisa answered him composedly: "I have never made that objection to you, either as a child or as a woman. I don't understand what you would have."

"Have?" returned Mr. Bounderby. "Nothing. Otherwise, don't you, Loo Bounderby, know thoroughly well that I, Josiah Bounderby of Coketown, would have it?"

She looked at him, as he struck the table and made the tea cups ring, with a proud color in her face that was a new change, Mr. Harthouse thought. "You are incomprehensible this morning," said Louisa. "Pray take no further trouble to explain yourself. I am not curious to know your meaning. What does it matter!"

Nothing more was said on this theme, and Mr. Harthouse was soon idly gay on indifferent subjects. But, from this day, the Sparsit action upon Mr. Bounderby threw Louisa and James Harthouse more together, and strengthened the dangerous alienation from her husband and confidence against him with another, into which she had fallen by degrees so fine that she could not retrace them if she tried. But, whether she ever tried or no, lay hidden in her own closed heart.

Mrs. Sparsit was so much affected on this particular occasion, that, assisting Mr. Bounderby to his hat after breakfast, and being then alone with him in the hall, she imprinted a chaste kiss upon his hand, murmured "my benefactor!" and retired, overwhelmed with grief. Yet it is an indubitable fact, within the cognizance of this history, that five minutes after he had left the house in the self-same hat, the same descendant of the Scadgerses and connection by matrimony of the Powlers, shook her right-hand mitten at his portrait, made a contemptuous grimace at that work of art, and said "Serve you right, you Noodle, and I am glad of it!"

Mr. Bounderby had not been long gone, when Bitzer appeared. Bitzer had come down by train, shrieking and rattling over the long line of arches that bestrode the wild country of past and present coal-pits, with an express from Stone Lodge. It was a hasty note to inform Louisa, that Mrs. Gradgrind lay very ill. She had never been well within her daughter's knowledge; but she had declined within the last few days, had continued sinking all through the night, and was now as nearly dead, as her limited capacity of being in any state that implied the ghost of an intention to get out of it, allowed.

Accompanied by the lightest of porters, fit colorless servitor at Death's door when Mrs. Gradgrind knocked, Louisa rumbled to Coketown, over the coal-pits past and present, and was whirled into its smoky jaws. She dismissed the messenger to his own devices, and rode away to her old home.

She had seldom been there since her marriage. Her father was usually sifting and sifting at his parliamentary cinder-heap in London (without being observed to turn up many precious articles among the rubbish), and was still hard at it in the national dust-yard. Her mother had taken it rather as a disturbance than otherwise, to be visited, as she reclined upon her sofa; young people, Louisa felt herself all unfit for; Sissy she had never softened to again, since the night when the stroller's child had raised her eyes to look at Mr. Bounderby's intended wife. She had no inducements to go back, and had rarely gone.

Neither, as she approached her old home now, did any of the best influences of old home descend upon her. The dreams of childhood—its airy fables; its graceful, beautiful, humane, impossible adornments of the world beyond; so good to be believed in once, so good to be remembered when outgrown, for then the least among them rises to the stature of a great Charity in the heart, suffering little children to come into the midst of it, and to keep with their pure hands a garden in the stony ways of this world, wherein it were better for all the children of Adam that they should oftener sun themselves, simple and trustful, and not worldly-wise—what had she to do with these? Remembrances of how she had journeyed to the little that she knew, by the enchanted roads of what she and millions of innocent creatures had hoped and imagined; of how, first coming upon Reason through the tender light of Fancy, she had seen it a beneficent god, deferring to gods as great as itself: not a grim Idol, cruel and cold, with its victims bound hand to foot, and its big dumb shape set up with a sightless stare, never to be moved by any thing but so many calculated tons of leverage—what had she to do with these? Her remembrances of home and childhood, were remembrances of the drying up of every spring and fountain in her young heart as it gushed out. The golden waters were not there. They were flowing for the fertilization of the land where grapes are gathered from thorns, and figs from thistles.

She went, with a heavy, hardened kind of sorrow upon her, into the house and into her mother's room. Since the time of her leaving home, Sissy had lived with the rest of the family on equal terms. Sissy was at her mother's side; and Jane, her sister, now ten or twelve years old, was in the room.

There was great trouble before it could be made known to Mrs. Gradgrind that her eldest child was there. She reclined, propped up, from mere habit, on a couch—as nearly in her old usual attitude, as any thing so helpless could be kept in. She had positively refused to take to her bed; on the ground that if she did, she would never hear the last of it.

Her feeble voice sounded so far away in her bundle of shawls, and the sound of another voice addressing her seemed to take such a long time in getting down to her ears, that she might have been lying at the bottom of a well. The poor lady was nearer Truth than she ever had been: which had much to do with it.

On being told that Mrs. Bounderby was there, she replied, at cross-purposes, that she had never called him by that name since he married Louisa; that pending her choice of an objectionable name, she had called him J; and that she could not at present depart from that regulation, not being yet provided with a permanent substitute. Lousia had sat by her for some minutes, and had spoken to her often, before she arrived at a clear understanding who it was. She then seemed to come to it all at once.

"Well, my dear," said Mrs. Gradgrind, "and I hope you are going on satisfactorily to yourself. It was all your father's doing. He set his heart upon it. And he ought to know."

"I want to hear of you, mother, not of myself."

"You want to hear of me, my dear? That's something new, I am sure, when any body wants to hear of me. Not at all well, Louisa. Very faint and giddy."

"Are you in pain, dear Mother?"

"I think there's a pain somewhere in the room," said Mrs. Gradgrind, "but I couldn't positively say that I have got it."

After this strange speech, she lay silent for some time. Louisa, holding her hand, could feel no pulse; but, kissing it, could see a slight thin thread of life in fluttering motion.

"You very seldom see your sister," said Mrs. Gradgrind. "She grows like you. I wish you would look at her. Sissy, bring her here."

She was brought, and stood with her hand in her sister's. Louisa had observed her with her arm round Sissy's neck, and she felt the difference of this approach.

"Do you see the likeness, Louisa?"

"Yes, Mother. I should think her like me. But—"

"Eh? Yes, I always say so," Mrs. Gradgrind cried, with unexpected quickness. "And that reminds me. I want to speak to you, my dear. Sissy, my good girl, leave us alone a minute."

Louisa had relinquished the hand; had thought that her sister's was a better and brighter face than hers had ever been; had seen in it, not without a rising feeling of resentment, even in that place and at that time, something of the gentleness of the other face in the room: the sweet face with the trusting eyes, made paler than watching and sympathy made it, by the rich dark hair.

Left alone with her mother, Louisa saw her lying with an awful lull upon her face, like one who was floating away upon some great water, all resistance over, content to be carried down the stream. She put the shadow of a hand to her lips again, and recalled her.

"You were going to speak to me, mother."

"Eh? Yes, to be sure, my dear. You know your father is almost always away now, and therefore I must write to him about it."

"About what, mother? Don't be troubled. About what?"

"You must remember, my dear, that whenever I have said any thing, on any subject, I have never heard the last of it; and consequently, that I have long left off saying any thing."

"I can hear you, mother." But it was only by dint of bending down to her ear, and at the same time attentively watching the lips as they moved, that she could link such faint and broken sounds into any chain of connection.

"You learned a great deal, Louisa, and so did your brother. Ologies of all kinds, from morning to night. If there is any Ology left, of any description, that has not been worn to rags in this house, all I can say is, I hope I shall never hear its name."

"I can hear you, mother, when you have strength to go on." This, to keep her from floating away:

"But there's something—not an Ology at all—that your father has missed, or forgotten, Louisa. I don't know what it is. I have often sat with Sissy near me, and thought about it. I shall never get its name now. But your father may. It makes me restless. I want to write to him, to find out for God's sake, what it is. Give me a pen, give me a pen."

Even the power of restlessness was gone, except from the poor head, which could just turn from side to side.

She fancied, however, that her request had been complied with, and that the pen she could not have held was in her hand. It matters little what figures of wonderful no-meaning she began to trace upon her wrappers. The hand soon stopped in the midst of them; the light that had always been feeble and dim behind the weak transparency, went out; and even Mrs. Gradgrind, emerged from the shadow in which man walketh and disquieteth himself in vain. took upon her the dread solemnity of the sages and patriarchs.

Chapter XXVI

MRS. SPARSIT'S STAIRCASE

MRS. SPARSIT'S nerves being slow to recover their tone, the worthy woman made a stay of some weeks in duration at Mr. Bounderby's retreat, where, notwithstanding her anchorite turn of mind based upon her becoming consciousness of her altered station, she resigned herself, with noble fortitude, to lodging, as one may say, in clover, and feeding on the fat of the land. During the whole term of this recess from the guardianship of the Bank, Mrs. Sparsit was a pattern of consistency; continuing to take such pity on Mr. Bounderby to his face, as is rarely taken on man, and to call his portrait a Noodle to *its* face, with the greatest acrimony and contempt.

Mr. Bounderby, having got it into his explosive composition that Mrs. Sparsit was a highly superior woman to perceive that he had that general cross upon him in his deserts (for he had not yet settled what it was), and further that Louisa would have objected to her as a frequent visitor if it had comported with his greatness that she should object to any thing he chose to do, resolved not to lose sight of Mrs. Sparsit easily. So when her nerves were strung up to the pitch of again consuming sweetbreads in solitude, he said to her at the dinner-table, on the day before her departure, "I tell you what, ma'am; you shall come down here of a Saturday while the fine weather lasts, and stay till Monday." To which Mrs. Sparsit returned, in effect, though not of the Mohammedan persuasion: "To hear is to obey."

Now, Mrs. Sparsit was not a poetical woman; but she took an idea, in the nature of an allegorical fancy, into her head. Much watching of Louisa, and much consequent observation of her impenetrable demeanor, which keenly whetted and sharpened Mrs. Sparsit's edge, must have given her as it were, a lift in the way of inspiration. She erected in her mind a mighty Staircase, with a dark pit of shame and ruin at the bottom; and down those stairs, from day to day and hour to hour, she saw Louisa coming.

It became the business of Mrs. Sparsit's life, to look up at the staircase, and to watch Louisa coming down. Sometimes slowly, sometimes quickly, sometimes several steps at one bout, sometimes stopping, never turning back. If she had once turned back, it might have been the death of Mrs. Sparsit in spleen and grief.

She had been descending steadily, to the day, and on the day, when Mr. Bounderby issued the weekly invitation recorded above. Mrs. Sparsit was in good spirits, and inclined to be conversational.

"And pray, sir," said she, "if I may venture to ask a question appertaining to any subject on which you show reserve—which is indeed hardy in me, for I well know you have a reason for every thing you do—have you received intelligence respecting the robbery?"

"Why, ma'am, no; not yet. Under the circumstances, I didn't expect it yet. Rome wasn't built in a day, ma'am."

"Very true, sir," said Mrs. Sparsit, shaking her head.

"Nor yet in a week, ma'am."

"No, indeed, sir," returned Mrs. Sparsit, with an air of melancholy.

"In a similar manner," said Bounderby, "I can wait, you know. If Romulus and Remus could wait, Josiah Bounderby can wait. They were better off in their youth than I was, however. They had a she-wolf for a nurse; *I* had only a she-wolf for a grandmother. She didn't give any milk, ma'am; she gave bruises. She was a regular Alderney at that."

"Ah!" Mrs. Sparsit sighed and shuddered.

"No, ma'am," continued Bounderby, "I have not heard any thing more about it. It's in hand, though; and young Tom, who rather sticks to business at present—something new for him; he hadn't the schooling *I* had—is helping. My injunction is, Keep it quiet, and let it seem to blow over. Do what you like under the rose, but don't give a sign of what you're about; or half a hundred of 'em will combine together and get this fellow, who has bolted, out of reach for good. Keep it quiet, and the thieves will grow in confidence by little and little, and we shall have 'em."

"Very sagacious indeed, sir," said Mrs. Sparsit. "Very interesting. The old woman you mentioned, sir—"

"The old woman I mentioned, ma'am," said Bounderby, cutting the matter short, as it was nothing to boast about, "is not laid hold of; but she may take her oath she will be, if that is any satisfaction to her villainous old mind. In the mean time, ma'am, I am of opinion, if you ask me my opinion, that the less she is talked about, the better."

That same evening, Mrs. Sparsit, in her chamber window, resting from her packing operations, looked toward her great staircase and saw Louisa still descending.

She sat by Mr. Harthouse, in an alcove in the garden, talking very low. He stood leaning over her, as they whispered together, and his face almost touched her hair. "If not quite!" said Mrs. Sparsit, straining her hawk's eyes to the utmost. Mrs. Sparsit was too distant to hear a word of their discourse, or even to know that they were speaking softly, otherwise than from the expression of their figures; but what they said was this:

"You recollect the man, Mr. Harthouse?"

"Oh, perfectly!"

"His face, and his manner, and what he said?"

"Perfectly. And an infinitely dreary person he appeared to me to be. Lengthy and prosy in the extreme. It was knowing to hold forth, in the humble-virtue school of eloquence, but I assure you I thought at the time, 'My good fellow, you are overdoing this!'"

"It has been very difficult to me to think ill of that man."

"My dear Louisa—as Tom says" Which he never did say. "You know no good of the fellow?"

"No, certainly."

"Nor of any other such person?"

"How can I," she returned, with more of her first manner on her than he had lately seen, "when I know nothing of them, men or women?"

"My dear Mrs. Bounderby! Then consent to receive the submissive representation of your devoted friend, who knows something of several varieties of his excellent fellow-creatures—for excellent they are, I have no doubt, in spite of such little foibles as always helping themselves to what they can get hold of. This fellow talks. Well; every fellow talks. His professing morality only deserves a moment's consideration, as being a very suspicious circumstance. All sorts of humbugs profess morality, from the House of Commons to the House of Correction, except our people; it really is that exception which makes our people quite reviving. You saw and heard the case. Here was a common man, pulled up extremely short by my esteemed friend Mr. Bounderby—who, as we know, is not possessed of that delicacy which would soften so tight a hand. The common man was injured, exasperated, left the house grumbling, met somebody who proposed to him to go in for some share in this Bank business, went in, put something in his pocket which had nothing in it before, and relieved his mind extremely. Really he would have been an uncommon, instead of a common man, if he had not availed himself of such an opportunity. Or he may have made it altogether, if he had the cleverness. Equally probable!"

"I almost feel as though it must be bad in me," returned Louisa, after sitting thoughtful awhile, "to be so ready to agree with you, and to be so lightened in my heart by what you say."

"I only say what is reasonable; nothing worse. I have talked it over with my friend Tom more than once—of course I remain on terms of perfect confidence with Tom—and he is quite of my opinion, and I am quite of his. Will you walk?"

They strolled away, among the lanes beginning to be indistinct in the twilight—she leaning on his arm—and she little thought how she was going down, down, down, Mrs. Sparsit's staircase.

Night and day, Mrs. Sparsit kept it standing. When Louisa had arrived at the bottom and disappeared in the gulf, it might fall in upon her if it would; but, until then, there it was to be, a Building, before Mrs. Sparsit's eyes. And thzre Louisa always was, upon it. Always gliding down, down, down.

Mrs. Sparsit saw James Harthouse come and go; she heard of him here and there; she saw the changes of the face he had studied; she, too, remarked to a nicety how and when it clouded, how and when it cleared; she kept her black eyes wide open, with no touch of pity, with no touch of compunction, all absorbed in interest, but, in the interest of seeing her, ever drawing, with no hand to stay her, nearer and nearer to the bottom of this new Giant's Staircase.

With all her deference for Mr. Bounderby as contradistinguished from his portrait, Mrs. Sparsit had not the smallest intention of interrupting the descent. Eager to see it accomplished, and yet patient, she waited for the last fall, as for the ripeness and fullness of the harvest of her hopes. Hushed in expectancy, she kept her wary gaze upon the stairs; and seldom so much as darkly shook her right mitten (with her fist in it), at the figure coming down.

Chapter XXVII

LOWER AND LOWER

THE figure descended the great stairs, steadily; steadily, always verging, like a weight in deep water, to the black gulf at the bottom.

Mr. Gradgrind, apprised of his wife's decease, made an expedition from London, and buried her in a business-like manner. He then returned with promptitude to the national cinder-heap, and resumed his sifting for the odds and ends he wanted, and his throwing of the dust about into the eyes of other people who wanted other odds and ends—in fact, resumed his parliamentary duties.

In the mean time, Mrs. Sparsit kept unwinking watch and ward. Separated from her staircase, all the week, by the length of iron road dividing Coketown from the country house, she yet maintained her cat-like observation of Louisa, through her husband, through her brother, through James Harthouse, through the outsides of letters and packets, through every thing animate and inanimate that at any time went near the stairs. "Your foot on the last step, my lady," said Mrs. Sparsit, apostrophizing the descending figure, with the aid of her threatening mitten, "and all your art shall never blind me."

Art or nature though, the original stock of Louisa's character or the graft of circumstances upon it—her curious reserve did baffle, while it stimulated, one as sagacious as Mrs. Sparsit. There were times when Mr.

James Harthouse was not sure of her. There were times when he could not read the face he had studied so long and when this lonely girl was a greater mystery to him than any woman of the world with a ring of satellites to help her.

So the time went on; until it happened that Mr. Bounderby was called away from home by business which required his presence elsewhere, for three or four days. It was on a Friday that he intimated this to Mrs. Sparsit at the Bank, adding: "But you'll go down to-morrow, ma'am, all the same. You'll go down just as if I was there. It will make no difference to you."

"Pray, sir," returned Mrs. Sparsit, reproachfully, "let me beg you not to say that. Your absence will make a vast difference to me, sir, as I think you very well know."

"Well, ma'am, then you must get on in my absence as well as you can," said Mr. Bounderby, not displeased.

"Mr. Bounderby," retorted Mrs. Sparsit, "your will is to me a law, sir; otherwise, it might be my inclination to dispute your kind commands, not feeling sure that it will be quite so agreeable to Miss Gradgrind to receive me, as it ever is to your own munificent hospitality. But you shall say no more, sir. I will go, upon your invitation."

"Why, when I invite you to my house, ma'am," said Bounderby, opening his eyes, "I should hope you want no other invitation."

"No indeed, sir," returned Mrs. Sparsit, "I should hope not. Say no more, sir. I would, sir, I could see you gay again!"

"What do you mean, ma'am?" blustered Bounderby.

"Sir," rejoined Mrs. Sparsit, "there was wont to be an elasticity in you which I sadly miss. Be buoyant, sir!"

Mr. Bounderby, under the influence of this difficult adjuration, backed up by her compassionate eye, could only scratch his head in a feeble and ridiculous manner, and afterward assert himself at a distance by being heard to bully the small-fry of business all the morning.

"Bitzer," said Mrs. Sparsit that afternoon, when her patron was gone on his journey, and the Bank was closing, "present my compliments to young Mr. Thomas, and ask him if he would step up and partake of a lamb chop and walnut ketchup, with a glass of India ale?" Young Mr. Thomas, being usually ready for any thing in that way, returned a gracious answer, and followed on its heels. "Mr. Thomas," said Mrs. Sparsit, "these plain viands being on table, I thought you might be tempted."

"Thankee, Mrs. Sparsit," said the whelp. And gloomily fell to.

"How is Mr. Harthouse, Mr. Tom?" asked Mrs. Sparsit.

"Oh he's all right," said Tom.

"Where may he be at present?" Mrs. Sparsit asked in a light conversational manner, after mentally devoting the whelp to the Furies for being so uncommunicative.

"He is shooting in Yorkshire," said Tom. "Sent Loo a basket half as big as a church, yesterday."

"The kind of gentleman now," said Mrs. Sparsit, sweetly, "whom one might wager to be a good shot!"

"Crack," said Tom.

He had long been a down-looking young fellow, but this characteristic had so increased of late that he never raised his eyes to any face for three seconds together. Mrs. Sparsit consequently had ample means of watching his looks, if she were so inclined.

"Mr. Harthouse is a great favorite of mine," said Mrs. Sparsit, "as indeed he is of most people. May we expect to see him again shortly, Mr. Tom?"

"Why, *I* expect to see him tomorrow," returned the whelp.

"Good news!" cried Mrs. Sparsit, blandly.

"I have got an appointment with him to meet him in the evening at the station here," said Tom, "and I am going to dine with him afterward, I believe. He is not coming down to Nickits's for a week or so, being due somewhere else. At least, he says so; but I shouldn't wonder if he was to stop here over Sunday, and stray that way."

"Which reminds me!" said Mrs. Sparsit. "Would you remember a message to your sister, Mr. Tom, if I was to charge you with one?"

"Well! I'll try," returned the reluctant whelp, "if it isn't a long un."

"It is merely my respectful compliments," said Mrs. Sparsit, "and I fear I may not trouble her with my society this week; being still a little nervous, and better perhaps by my poor self."

"Oh! If that's all," observed Tom, "it wouldn't much matter even if I was to forget it, for Loo's not likely to think of you unless she sees you."

Having paid for his entertainment with this agreeable compliment, he relapsed into a hang-dog silence until there was no more India ale left, when he said, "Well, Mrs. Sparsit, I must be off!" and went off.

Next day, Saturday, Mrs. Sparsit sat at her window all day long: looking at the customers coming in and out, watching the postmen, keeping an eye on the general traffic of the street, revolving many things in her mind, but, above all, keeping her attention on her staircase. The evening come, she put on her bonnet and shawl, and went quietly out: having her reasons for hovering in a furtive way about the station by which a passenger would arrive from Yorkshire, and for preferring to peep into it round pillars and corners, and out of ladies' waiting-room windows, to appearing in its precincts openly.

Tom was in attendance, and loitered about until the expected train came in. It brought no Mr. Harthouse. Tom waited until the crowd had dispersed, and the bustle was over; and then referred to a posted list of trains, and took counsel with porters. That done, he strolled away idly, stopping in the street and looking up it and down it, and lifting his hat off and putting it on again, and yawning and stretching himself, and exhibiting all the symptoms of mortal weariness to be expected in one who had still to wait until the next train should come in, an hour and forty minutes hence.

"This is a device to keep him out of the way," said Mrs. Sparsit, starting from the dull office window whence she had watched him last. "Harthouse is with his sister now!"

It was the conception of an inspired moment, and she shot off with her utmost swiftness to work it out. The station for the country house was at the opposite end of the town, the time was short, the road not easy; but she was so quick in pouncing on a disengaged coach, so quick in darting out of it, producing her money, seizing her ticket, and diving into the train, that she was borne along the arches spanning the land of coal-pits past and present, as if she had been caught up in a cloud and whirled away.

All the journey, immovable in the air though never left behind; plain to the dark eyes of her mind, as the electric wires which ruled a colossal strip of music-paper out of the evening sky, were plain to the dark eyes of her body; Mrs. Sparsit saw her staircase, with the figure coming down. Very near the bottom now. Upon the brink of the abyss.

An overcast September evening, just at nightfall, saw beneath its drooping eyelids Mrs. Sparsit glide out of her carriage, pass down the wooden steps of the little station into a stony road, cross it into a green lane, and become hidden in a summer-growth of leaves and branches. One or two late birds sleepily chirping in their nests, and a bat heavily crossing and recrossing her, and the reek of her own tread in the thick dust that felt like velvet, were all Mrs. Sparsit heard or saw until she very softly closed a gate.

She went up to the house, keeping within the shrubbery, and went round it, peeping between the leaves at the lower windows. Most of them were open, as they usually were in such warm weather, but there were no lights yet, and all was sllent. She tried the garden with no better effect. She thought of the wood, and stole toward it, heedless of long grass and briers of worms, snails, and slugs, and all the creeping things that be. With her dark eyes and her hook nose warily in advance of her, Mrs. Sparsit softly crushed her way through the thick undergrowth, so intent upon her object that she probably would have done no less, if the wood had been a wood of adders.

Hark!

The smaller birds might have tumbled out of their nests, fascinated by the glittering of Mrs. Sparsit's eyes in the gloom, as she stopped and listened.

Low voices close at hand. His voice, and hers. The appointment *was* a device to keep the brother away! There they were yonder, by the felled tree.

Bending low among the dewy grass, Mrs. Sparsit advanced closer to them. She drew herself up, and stood behind a tree, like Robinson Crusoe in his ambuscade against the savages; so near to them that at a spring, and that no great one, she could have touched them both. He was there secretly, and had not shown himself at the house. He had come on horseback, and must have passed through the neighboring fields; for his horse was tied to the meadow side of the fence, within a few paces.

"My dearest love," said he, "what could I do? Knowing you were alone, was it possible that I could stay away?"

"You may hang your head, to make yourself the more attractive; *I* don't know what they see in you when you hold it up," thought Mrs. Sparsit; "but you little think, my dearest love, whose eyes are on you!"

That she hung her head, was certain. She urged him to go away, she commanded him to go away; but she neither turned her face to him, nor raised it. Yet it was remarkable that she sat as still, as ever the amiable woman in ambuscade had seen her sit, at any period in her life. Her hands rested in one another, like the hands of a statue; and even her manner of speaking was not hurried.

"My dear child," said Harthouse; Mrs. Sparsit saw with delight that his arm embraced her; "will you not bear with my society for a little while?"

"Not here."

"Where, Lousia?"

"Not here."

"But we have so little time to make so much of, and I have come so far, and am altogether so devoted, and distracted. There never was a slave at once so devoted and ill-used by his mistress. To look for your sunny welcome that has warmed me into life, and to be received in your frozen manner, is heart-rending."

"Am I to say again, that I must be left to myself here?"

"But we must meet, my dear Louisa. Where shall we meet?"

They both started. The listener started guiltily, too; for she thought there was another listener among the trees. It was only rain, beginning to fall fast, in heavy drops.

"Shall I ride up to the house a few minutes hence, innocently supposing that its master is at home and will be charmed to receive me?"

"No!"

"Your cruel commands are implicitly to be obeyed; though I am the most unfortunate fellow in the world, I believe, to have been insensible to all other women, and to have fallen prostrate at last under the foot of the most beautiful, and the most engaging, and the most imperious. My dearest Louisa, I cannot go myself, or let you go, in this hard abuse of your power."

Mrs. Sparsit saw him detain her with his encircling arm, and heard him then and there, within her (Mrs. Sparsit's) greedy hearing, tell her how he loved her, and how she was the stake for which he ardently desired to play away all that he had in life. The objects he had lately pursued turned worthless beside her; such success as was almost in his grasp, he flung away from him like the dirt it was, compared with her. Its pursuit, nevertheless, if it kept him near her, or its renunciation if it took him from her, or flight if she shared it, or secrecy if she commanded it, or any fate, or every fate, all was alike to him, so that she was true to him—the man who had seen how cast away she was, whom she had inspired at their first meeting with an admiration and interest of which he had thought himself incapable, whom she had received into her confidence, who was devoted to her and adored her. All this, and more, in his hurry, and in hers, in the whirl of her own gratified malice, in the dread of being discovered, in the rapidly increasing noise of heavy rain among the leaves, and a thunder-storm rolling up—Mrs. Sparsit received into her mind; set off with such an unavoidable halo of confusion and indistinctness, that when at length he climbed the fence and led his horse away, she was not sure where they were to meet, or when, except that they had said it was to be that night.

But one of them yet remained in the darkness before her; and while she tracked that one, she must be right. "Oh, my dearest love," thought Mrs. Sparsit, "you little think how well attended you are."

Mrs. Sparsit saw her out of the wood, and saw her enter the house. What to do next? It rained now, in a sheet of water. Mrs. Sparsit's white stockings were of many colors, green predominating; prickly things were in her shoes; caterpillars slung themselves, in hammocks of their own making, from various parts of her dress; rills ran from her bonnet, and her Roman nose. In such condition Mrs. Sparsit stood hidden in the density of the shrubbery, considering what next?

Lo, Louisa coming out of the house! Hastily cloaked and muffled, and stealing away. She elopes! She falls from the lowermost stair, and is swallowed up in the gulf!

Indifferent to the rain, and moving with a quick determined step, she struck into a side-path parallel with the ride. Mrs. Sparsit followed in the shadow of the trees, at but a short distance; for it was not easy to keep a figure in view going quickly through the umbrageous darkness.

When she stopped to close the side-gate without noise, Mrs. Sparsit stopped. When she went on, Mrs. Sparsit went on. She went by the way Mrs. Sparsit had come, emerged from the green lane, crossed the stony road, and ascended the wooden steps to the railroad. A train for Coketown would come through presently, Mrs. Sparsit knew; so she understood Coketown to be her first place of destination.

In Mrs. Sparsit's limp and streaming state, no extensive precautions were necessary to change her usual appearance; but, she stopped under the lee of the station wall, tumbled her shawl into a new shape, and put it on over her bonnet. So disguised, she had no fear of being recognized when she followed up the railroad steps, and paid her money in the small office. Louisa sat waiting in a corner. Mrs. Sparsit sat waiting in another corner. Both listened to the thunder, which was loud, and to the rain, as it washed off the roof, and pattered on the parapets of the arches. Two or three lamps were rained and blown out; so both saw the lightning to advantage as it quivered and zigzaged on the iron tracks.

The seizure of the station with a fit of trembling, gradually deepening to a complaint of the heart, announced the train. Fire and steam, and smoke, and red light; a hiss, a crash, a bell, and a shriek; Louisa put into one carriage, Mrs. Sparsit put into another; the little station a desert speck in the thunder-storm.

Though her teeth chattered in her head from wet and cold, Mrs. Sparsit exulted hugely. The figure had plunged down the precipice, and she felt herself, as it were, attending on the body. Could she, who had been so active in the getting up of the funeral triumph, do less than exult? "She will be at Coketown long before him," thought Mrs. Sparsit, "though his horse is never so good. Where will she wait for him? And where will they go together? Patience. We shall see."

The tremendous rain occasioned infinite confusion, when the train stopped at its destination. Gutters and pipes had burst, drains had overflowed, and streets were under water. In the first instant of alighting, Mrs. Sparsit turned her distracted eyes toward the waiting coaches, which were in great request. "She will get into one," she considered, "and will be away before I can follow in another. At all risks of being run over, I must see the number, and hear the order given to the coachman."

But Mrs. Sparsit was wrong in her calculation. Louisa got into no coach, and was already gone. The black eyes kept upon the railroad-carriage in which she had traveled, settled upon it a moment too late. The door not being opened after several minutes, Mrs. Sparsit passed it and repassed it, saw nothing, looked in, and found it empty. Wet through and through; with her feet squelching and squashing in her shoes whenever she moved; with a rush of rain upon her classical visage; with a bonnet like an over-ripe fig; with all her clothes spoiled; with damp impressions of every button, string, and hook-and-eye she wore; printed off upon her highly connected back, with a stagnant verdure on her general exterior, such as accumulates on an old park fence in a mouldy lane; Mrs. Sparsit had no resource but to burst into tears of bitterness and say, "I have lost her!"

Chapter XXVIII

DOWN

THE national dustmen, after entertaining one another with a great many noisy little fights among themselves, had dispersed for the present, and Mr. Gradgrind was at home for the vacation.

He sat writing in the room with the deadly statistical clock, proving something no doubt—probably, in the main, that the Good Samaritan was a Bad Economist. The noise of the rain did not disturb him much; but it attracted his attention sufficiently to make him raise his head sometimes, as if he were rather remonstrating with the elements. When it thundered very loudly, he glanced toward Coketown, having it in his mind that some of the tall chimneys might be struck by lightning.

The thunder was rolling into distance, and the rain was pouring down like a deluge, when the door of his room opened. He looked round the lamp upon his table, and saw with amazement, his eldest daughter.

"Louisa!"

"Father, I want to speak to you."

"What is the matter? How strange you look! And good Heaven," said Mr. Gradgrind, wondering more and more, "have you come here exposed to this storm?"

She put her hands to her dress, as if she hardly knew. "Yes." Then she uncovered her head, and, letting her cloak and hood fall where they might, stood looking at him: so colorless, so disheveled, so defiant and despairing, that he was afraid of her.

"What is it? I conjure you, Louisa, tell me what is the matter."

She dropped into a chair before him, and put her cold hand on his arm.

"Father, you have trained me from my cradle."

"Yes, Louisa."

"I curse the hour in which I was born to such a destiny."

He looked at her in doubt and dread, vacantly repeating, "Curse the hour! Curse the hour!"

"How could you give me life, and take from me all the inappreciable things that raise it from the state of conscious death? Where are the graces of my soul? Where are the sentiments of my heart? What have you done, O father what have you done, with the garden that should have bloomed once, in this great wilderness here!"

She struck herself with both her hands upon her bosom.

"If it had ever been here, its ashes alone would save me from the void in which my whole life sinks. I did not mean to say this; but father, you remember the last time we conversed in this room?"

He had been so wholly unprepared for what he heard now, that it was with difficulty he answered, "Yes, Louisa."

"What has risen to my lips now, would have risen to my lips then, if you had given me a moment's help. I don't reproach you, father. What you have never nurtured in me, you have never nurtured in yourself; but O! if you had only done so long ago, or if you had only neglected me, what a much better and much happier creature I should have been this day!"

On hearing this, after all his care, he bowed his head upon his hand and groaned aloud.

"Father, if you had known, when we were last together here, what even I feared while I strove against it—as it has been my task from infancy to strive against every natural prompting that has arisen in my heart; if you had known that there lingered in my breast, sensibilities, affections, weaknesses capable of being cherished into strength, defying all the calculations ever made by man, and no more known to his arithmetic than his Creator is—would you have given me to the husband whom I am now sure that I hate?"

He said, "No. No, my poor child."

"Would you have doomed me, at any time, to the frost and blight that have hardened and spoiled me? Would you have robbed me—for no one's enrichment—only for the greater desolation of this world—of the immaterial part of my life, the spring and summer of my belief, my refuge from what is sordid and bad in the real things around me, my school in which I should have learned to be more humble and more trusting with them, and to hope in my little sphere to make them better?"

"O no, no. No, Louisa."

"Yet, father, if I had been stone blind; if I had groped my way by my sense of touch, and had been free, while I knew the shapes and surfaces of things, to exercise my fancy somewhat, in regard to them; I should have been a million times wiser, happier, more loving, more contented, more innocent and human in all good respects, than I am with the eyes I have. Now, hear what I have come to say."

He moved, to support her with his arm. She rising as he did so, they stood close together—she with a hand upon his shoulder, looking fixedly in his face.

"With a hunger and thirst upon me, father, which have never been for a moment appeased; with an ardent impulse toward some region where rules, and figures, and defintions were not quite absolute; I have grown up, battling every inch of my way."

"I never knew you were unhappy, my child."

"Father, I always knew it. In this strife I have almost repulsed and crushed my better angel into a demon. What I have learned has left me doubting, misbelieving, despising, regretting, what I have not learned, and my dismal resource has been to think that life would soon go by, and that nothing in it could be worth the pain and trouble of a contest."

"And you so young, Louisa!" he said with pity.

"And I so young. In this condition, father—for I show you now, without fear or favor, the ordinary deadened state of my mind as I know it—you proposed my husband to me. I took him. I never made a pretence to him or you that I loved him. I knew, and father, you knew, and he knew, that I never did. I was not wholly indifferent, for I had a hope of being pleasant and useful to Tom. I made that wild escape into something visionary, and have gradually found out how wild it was. But Tom had been the subject of all the little tenderness of my life; perhaps he became so because I knew so well how to pity him. It matters little now, except as it may dispose you to think more leniently of his errors."

As her father held her in his arms, she put her other hand upon his other shoulder, and still looking fixedly in his face, went on:

"When I was irrevocably married, there rose up into rebellion against the tie, the old strife, made fiercer by all those causes of disparity which arise out of our two individual natures, and which no general laws shall ever rule or state for me, father, until they shall be able to direct the anatomist where to strike his knife into the secrets of my soul."

"Louisa!" he said, and said imploringly; for he well remembered what had passed between them in their former interview.

"I do not reproach you, father; I make no complaint. I am here with another object."

"What can I do, child? Ask me what you will."

"I am coming to it. Father, chance then threw into my way a new acquaintance; a man such as I had had no experience of; used to the world; light, polished, easy; making no pretences; avowing the low estimate of every thing, that I was half afraid to form in secret; conveying to me almost immediately, though I don't know how or by what degrees, that he understood me, and read my thoughts. I could not find that he was worse than I. There seemed to be a near affinity between us. I only wondered it should be worth his while, who cared for nothing else, to care so much for me."

"For you, Louisa!"

Her father might instinctively have loosened his hold, but that he felt her strength departing from her, and saw a wild dilating fire in the eyes steadfastly regarding him.

"I say nothing of his plea for claiming my confidence. It matters very little how he gained it. Father, he did gain it. What you know of the story of my marriage, he soon knew just as well."

Her father's face was ashy white, and he held her in both his arms.

"I have done no worse, I have not disgraced you. But if you ask me whether I have loved him, or do love him, I tell you plainly, father, that it may be so. I don't know."

She took her hands suddenly from his shoulders and pressed them both upon her side; while in her face, not like itself—and in her figure, drawn up, resolute to finish by a last effort what she had to say—the feelings long suppressed broke loose.

"This night, my husband being away, he has been with me, declaring himself my lover. This minute he expects me, for I could release myself of his presence by no other means. I do not know that I am sorry, I do not know that I am ashamed, I do not know that I am degraded in my own esteem. All that I know is, your philosophy and your teaching will not save me. Now, father, you have brought me to this. Save me by some other means!"

He tightened his hold in time to prevent her sinking on the floor, but she cried out in a terrible voice, "I shall die if you hold me! Let me fall upon the ground!" And he laid her down there, and saw the pride of his heart and the triumph of his system, lying, an insensible heap, at his feet.

BOOK THE THIRD

GARNERING

Chapter XXIX
ANOTHER THING NEEDFUL

LOUISA awoke from a torpor, and her eyes languidly opened on her old bed at home, and her old room. It seemed, at first, as if all that had happened since the days when these objects were familiar to her were the shadows of a dream; but gradually, as the objects became more real to her sight, the events became more real to her mind.

She could scarcely move her head for pain and heaviness; her eyes were strained and sore, and she was very weak. A curious passive inattention had such possession of her, that the presence of her little sister in the room did not attract her notice for some time. Even when their eyes had met, and her sister had approached the bed, Louisa lay for minutes looking at her in silence, and suffering her timidly to hold her passive hand, before she asked:

"When was I brought to this room?"

"Last night, Louisa."

"Who brought me here?"

"Sissy, I believe."

"Why do you believe so?"

"Because I found her here this morning. She didn't come to my bedside to wake me, as she always does; and I went to look for her. She was not in her own room either; and I went looking for her all over the house, until I found her here, taking care of you and cooling your head. Will you see father? Sissy said I was to tell him when you woke."

"What a beaming face you have, Jane!" said Louisa, as her young sister—timidly still—bent down to kiss her.

"Have I? I am very glad you think so. I am sure it must be Sissy's doing."

The arm Louisa had begun to twine around her neck, unbent itself. "You can tell father if you will." Then, staying her for a moment, she said, "It was you who made my room so cheerful, and gave it this look of welcome?"

"Oh, no, Lousia, it was done before I came. It was—"

Louisa turned upon her pillow, and heard no more. When her sister had withdawn, she turned her head back again, and lay with her face toward the door, until it opened and her father entered.

He had a jaded anxious look upon him, and his hand, usually steady, trembled in hers. He sat down at the side of the bed, tenderly asking how she was, and dwelling on the necessity of her keeping very quiet after her agitation and exposure to the weather last night. He spoke in a subdued and troubled voice, very different from his usual dictatorial manner; and was often at a loss for words.

"My dear Louisa. My poor daughter." He was so much at a loss at that place, that he stopped altogether. He tried again.

"My unfortunate child." The place was so difficult to get over, that he tried again.

"It would be hopeless for me, Louisa, to endeavor to tell you how overwhelmed I have been, and still am, by what broke upon me last night. The ground on which I stand has ceased to be solid under my feet. The only support on which I leaned, and the strength of which it seemed, and still does seem, impossible to question, has given way in an instant. I am stunned by these discoveries. I have no selfish meaning in what I say; but I find the shock of what broke upon me last night to be very heavy indeed."

She could give him no comfort herein. She had suffered the wreck of her whole life upon the rock.

"I will not say, Lousia, that if you had by any happy chance undeceived me some time ago, it would have been better for us both; better for your peace, and better for mine. For I am sensible that it may not have been a part of my system to invite any confidence of that kind. I had proved my—my system to myself, and I have rigidly administered it; and I must bear the responsibility of its failures. I only entreat you to believe, my favorite child, that I have meant to do right."

He said it earnestly, and to do him justice he had. In gauging fathomless deeps with his little mean excise-rod, and in staggering over the universe with his rusty stiff-legged compasses, he had meant to do great things. Within the limits of his short tether he had tumbled about, annihilating the flowers of existence with greater singleness of purpose than many of the blatant personages whose company he kept.

"I am well assured of what you say, father. I know I have been your favorite child. I know you have intended to make me happy. I have never blamed you, and I never shall."

He took her outstretched hand, and retained it in his.

"My dear, I have remained all night at my table, pondering again and again on what has so painfully passed between us. When I consider your character, when I consider that what has been known to me for hours has been concealed by you for years; when I consider under what immediate pressure it has been forced from you at last; I come to the conclusion that I can not but mistrust myself."

He might have added more than all, when he saw the face now looking at him. He did add it in effect perhaps, as he softly moved her scattered hair from her forehead with his hand. Such little actions, slight in another man, were very noticeable in him; and his daughter received them as if they had been words of contrition.

"But," said Mr. Gradgrind slowly, and with hesitation, as well as with a wretched sense of helplessness, "if I see reason to mistrust myself for the past, Louisa, I should also mistrust myself for the present and the future. To speak unreservedly to you, I do. I am far from feeling convinced now, however differently I might have felt only this time yesterday, that I am fit for the trust you repose in me; that I know how to respond to the appeal you have come home to make to me; that I have the right instinct—supposing it for the moment to be some quality of that nature—how to help you, and to set you right, my child."

She had turned upon her pillow, and lay with her face upon her arm, so that he could not see it. All her wildness and passion had subsided; but, though softened, she was not in tears. Her father was changed in nothing so much as in the respect that he would have been glad to see her in tears.

"Some persons hold," he pursued, still hesitating, "that there is a wisdom of the Head, and that there is a wisdom of the Heart. I have not supposed so; but, as I have said, I mistrust myself now. I have supposed the Head to be all-sufficient. It may not be all-sufficient; how can I venture this morning to say it is! If that other kind of wisdom should be what I have neglected, and should be the instinct that is wanted, Louisa—"

He suggested it very doubtfully, as if he were half unwilling to admit it even now. She made him no answer; lying before him on her bed, still half-dressed, much as he had seen her lying on the floor of his room last night.

"Louisa," and his hand rested on her hair again, "I have been absent from here, my dear, a good deal of late; and though your sister's training has been pursued according to—the system," he appeared to come to that word with great reluctance always, "it has necessarily been modified by daily associations begun, in her case, at an early age. I ask you—ignorantly and humbly, my daughter—for the better, do you think?"

"Father," she replied, without stirring, "if any harmony has been awakened in her young breast that was mute in mine until it turned to discord, let her thank Heaven for it, and go upon her happier way, taking it as her greatest blessing that she has avoided my way."

"O my child, my child!" he said, in a forlorn manner, "I am an unhappy man to see you thus! What avails it to me that you do not reproach me, if I so bitterly reproach myself!" He bent his head, and spoke low to her. "Louisa, I have a misgiving that some change may have been slowly working about me in this house, by mere love and gratitude; that what the Head had left undone and could not do, the Heart may have been doing silently. Can it be so?"

She made him no reply.

"I am not too proud to believe it, Louisa. How could I be arrogant, and you before me! Can it be so? Is it so, my dear?"

He looked upon her once more, lying cast away there; and without another word went out of the room. He had not been long gone, when she heard a light tread near the door, and knew that some one stood beside her.

She did not raise her head. A dull anger that she should be seen in her distress, and that the involuntary look she had so resented should come to this fulfillment, smouldered within her like an unwholesome fire. All closely imprisoned forces rend and destroy. The air that would be healtful to the earth, the water that would enrich it, the heat that would ripen it, tear it when caged up. So in her bosom even now; the strongest qualities she possessed, long turned upon themselves, became a heap of obduracy, that rose against a friend.

It was well that soft touch came upon her neck, and that she understood herself to be supposed to have fallen asleep. The sympathetic hand did not claim her resentment. Let it lie there, let it lie.

It lay there, warming into life a crowd of gentler thoughts; and she rested. As she softened with the quiet, and the consciousness of being so watched, some tears made their way into her eyes. The face touched hers, and she knew that there were tears upon it too, and she the cause of them.

As Louisa feigned to rouse herself, and sat up, Sissy retired, so that she stood placidly near the bedside.

"I hope I have not disturbed you. I have come to ask if you would let me stay with you?"

"Why should you stay with me? My sister will miss you. You are everything to her."

"Am I?" returned Sissy, shaking her head. "I would be something to you, if I might."

"What?" said Louisa, almost sternly.

"Whatever you want most, if I could be that. At all events, I would like to try to be as near it as I can. And however far off that may be, I will never tire of trying. Will you let me?"

"My father sent you to ask me?"

"No indeed," replied Sissy. "He told me that I might come in now, but he sent me away from the room this morning—or at least—" She hesitated and stopped.

"At least, what?" said Louisa, with her searching eyes upon her.

"I thought it best myself that I should be sent away, for I felt very uncertain whether you would like to find me here."

"Have I always hated you so much?"

"I hope not, for I have always loved you, and have always wished that you should know it. But you changed to me a little, shortly before you left home. Not that I wondered at it. You knew so much, and I knew so little, and it was so natural in many ways, going as you were among other friends, that I had nothing to complain of, and was not at all hurt."

Her color rose as she said it modestly and hurriedly. Louisa understood the loving pretence, and her heart smote her.

"May I try?" said Sissy, emboldened to raise her hand to the neck that was insensibly drooping toward her.

Louisa, taking down the hand that would have embraced her in another moment, held it in one of hers, and answered:

"First, Sissy, do you know what I am? I am so proud and so hardened, so confused and troubled, so resentful and unjust to every one and to myself, that every thing is stormy, dark, and wicked to me. Does not that repel you?"

"No!"

"I am so unhappy, and all that should have made me otherwise is so laid waste, that if I had been bereft of sense to this hour, and instead of being as learned as you think me, had to begin to acquire the simplest truths, I could not want a guide to peace, contentment, honor, all the good of which I am quite devoid, more abjectly than I do. Does not that repel you?"

"No!"

In the innocence of her brave affection, and the brimming up of her old devoted spirit, the once deserted girl shone like a beautiful light upon the darkness of the other.

Louisa raised the hand that it might clasp her neck, and join its fellow there. She fell upon her knees, and clinging to this stroller's child looked up at her almost with veneration.

"Forgive me, pity me, help me! Have compassion on my great need, and let me lay this head of mine upon a loving heart!"

"O lay it here!" cried Sissy. "Lay it here, my dear."

Chapter XXX

VERY RIDICULOUS

MR. JAMES HARTHOUSE passed a whole night and a day in a state of so much hurry, that the World, with its best glass in its eye, would scarcely have recognized him during that insane interval, as the brother Jem of the honorable and jocular member. He was positively agitated. He several times spoke with an emphasis, similar to the vulgar manner. He went in and went out in an unaccountable way, like a man without an object. He rode like a highwayman. In a word, he was so horribly bored by existing circumstances, that he forgot to go in for boredom in the manner prescribed by the authorities.

After putting his horse at Coketown through the storm, as if it were a leap, he waited up all night; from time to time ringing his bell with the greatest fury, charging the porter who kept watch with delinquency in withholding letters or messages that could not fail to have been entrusted to him, and demanding restitution on the spot. The dawn coming, the morning coming, and the day coming, and neither message nor letter coming with either, he went down to the country house. There the report was, Mr. Bounderby away, and Mrs. Bounderby in town. Left for town suddenly last evening. Not even known to be gone until receipt of message, importing that her return was not to be expected for the present.

In these circumstances he had nothing for it but to follow her to town. He went to the house in town. Mrs. Bounderby not there. He looked in at the Bank. Mr. Bounderby away, and Mrs. Sparsit away. Mrs. Sparsit away? Who could have been reduced to sudden extremity for the company of that griffin!

"Well! I don't know," said Tom, who had his own reasons for being uneasy about it. "She was off somewhere at daybreak this morning. She's always full of mystery; I hate her. So I do that white chap; he's always got his blinking eyes upon a fellow."

"Where were you last night, Tom?"

"Where was I last night!" said Tom. "Come! I like that. I was waiting for you, Mr. Harthouse, till it came down as *I* never saw it come down before. Where was I too! Where were you, you mean."

"I was prevented from coming—detained."

"Detained!" murmured Tom. "Two of us were detained. I was detained looking for you, till I lost every train but the mail. It would have been a pleasant job to go down by that on such a night, and have to walk home through a pond. I was obliged to sleep in town after all."

"Where?"

"Where? Why, in my own bed at Bounderby's."

"Did you see your sister?"

"How the deuce," returned Tom, staring, "could I see my sister when she was fifteen miles off?"

Cursing these quick retorts of the young gentleman to whom he was so true a friend, Mr. Harthouse disembarrassed himself of that interview with the smallest conceivable amount of ceremony, and debated for the hundredth time what all this could mean? He made only one thing clear. It was, that whether she was in town or out of town, whether he had been premature with her who was so hard to comprehend, or she had lost courage, or they were discovered, or some mischance or mistake, at present incomprehensible had occurred, he must remain to confront his fortune, whatever it was. The hotel where he was known to live when condemned to that region of blackness, was the stake to which he was tied. As to all the rest—what will be, will be.

"So, whether I am waiting for a hostile message, or an assignation, or a penitent remonstrance, or an impromptu wrestle with my friend Bounderby in the Lancashire manner—which would seem as likely as any thing else in the present state of affairs—I'll dine," said Mr. James Harthouse. "Bounderby has the advantage in point of weight; and if any thing of a British nature is to come off between us, it may be as well to be in training."

Therefore he rang the bell, and, tossing himself negligently on a sofa, ordered "Some dinner at six—with a beefsteak in it," and got through the intervening time as well as he could. That was not particularly well; for he remained in the greatest perplexity, and, as the hours went on, and no kind of explanation offered itself, his perplexity augmented at compound interest.

However, he took affairs as coolly as it was in human nature to do, and entertained himself with the facetious idea of the training more than once. "It wouldn't be bad," he yawned at one time, "to give the waiter five shillings, and throw him." At another time it occurred to him, "Or a fellow of about thirteen or fourteen stone might be hired by the hour." But these jests did not tell materially on the afternoon, or his suspense, and, sooth to say, they both lagged fearfully.

It was impossible, even before dinner, to avoid often walking about in the pattern of the carpet, looking out of the window, listening at the door for footsteps, and occasionally becoming rather hot when any steps approached that room. But, after dinner, when the day turned to twilight, and the twilight turned to night, and still no communication was made to him, it began to be, as he expressed it, "like the Holy Office and slow torture." However, still true to his conviction that indifference was the genuine high-breeding (the only conviction he had), he seized this crisis as the opportuntiy for ordering candles and a newspaper.

He had been trying in vain, for half an hour, to read this newspaper, when the waiter appeared and said, at once mysteriously and apologetically:

"Beg your pardon, sir. You're wanted, sir, if you please."

A general recollection that this was the kind of thing the Police said to the swell mob, caused Mr. Harthouse to ask the waiter in return, with bristling indignation, what the Devil he meant by "wanted?"

"Beg your pardon, sir. Young lady outside, sir, wishes to see you."

"Outside? Where?"

"Outside this door, sir."

Giving the waiter to the personage before-mentioned, as a blockhead duly qualified for that consignment, Mr. Harthouse hurried into the gallery. A young woman whom he had never seen stood there. Plainly dressed, very quiet, very pretty. As he conducted her into the room and placed a chair for her, he observed, by the light of the candles, that she was even prettier than he had at first believed. Her face was innocent and youthful, and its expression remarkably pleasant. She was not afraid of him, or in any way disconcerted; she seemed to have her mind entirely preoccupied with the occasion of her visit, and to have substituted that consideration for herself.

"I speak to Mr. Harthouse?" she said, when they were alone.

"To Mr. Harthouse." He added in his mind, "And you speak to him with the most confiding eyes I ever saw, and the most earnest voice (though so quiet) I ever heard."

"If I do not understand—and I do not, sir"—said Sissy, "what your honor as a gentleman binds you to, in other matters:" the blood really rose in his face as she began in these words—"I am sure I may rely upon it to keep my visit secret, and to keep secret what I am going to say. I will rely upon it, if you will tell me I may so far trust you."

"You may, I assure you."

"I am young, as you see; I am alone, as you see. In coming to you, sir, I have no advice or encouragement beyond my own hope."

He thought, "But that is very strong," as he followed the momentary upward glance of her eyes. He thought besides, "This is a very odd beginning. I don't see where we are going."

"I think," said Sissy, "you have already guessed whom I left just now?"

"I have been in the greatest concern and uneasiness during the last four-and-twenty hours (which have appeared as many years)," he returned, "on a lady's account. The hopes I have been encouraged to form that you come from that lady, do not deceive me, I trust."

"I left her within an hour."

"At—?"

"At her father's."

Mr. Harthouse's face lengthened in spite of his coolness, and his perplexity increased. "Then I certainly," he thought, "do *not* see where we are going."

"She hurried there last night. She arrived there in great agitation, and was insensible all through the night. I live at her father's, and was with her. You may be sure, sir, you will never see her again as long as you live."

Mr. Harthouse drew a long breath; and, if ever man found himself in the position of not knowing what to say, made the discovery beyond all question that he was so circumstanced. The child-like ingenuousness with which his visitor spoke, her modest fearlessness, her truthfulness which put all artifice aside, her entire forgetfulness of herself in her earnest quiet holding to the object with which she had come; all this, together with her reliance on his easily-given promise—which in itself shamed him—presented something in which he was so inexperienced, and against which he knew any of his usual weapons would fall so powerless; that not a word could he rally to his relief.

At last he said:

"So startling an announcement, so confidently made, and by such lips, is really disconcerting in the last degree. May I be permitted to inquire, if you are charged to convey that information to me in those hopeless words, by the lady of whom we speak?"

"I have no charge from her."

"The drowning man catches at the straw. With no disrespect for your judgment, and with no doubt of your sincerity, excuse my saying that I cling to the belief that there is yet hope that I am not condemned to perpetual exile from that lady's presence."

"There is not the least hope. The first object of my coming here, sir, is to assure you that you must believe that there is no more hope of your ever speaking with her again, than there would be if she had died when she came home last night."

"Must believe? But if I can't—or if I should by infirmity of nature, be obstinate—and won't—"

"It is still true. There is no hope."

James Harthouse looked at her with an incredulous smile upon his lips; but her mind looked over and beyond him, and the smile was quite thrown away.

He bit his lip, and took a lltle time for consideration.

"Well! If it should unhappily appear," he said, "after due pains and duty on my part, that I am brought to a position so desolate as this banishment, I shall not become the lady's persecutor. But you said you had no commission from her?"

"I have only the commission of my love for her, and her love for me. I have no other trust, than that I have been with her since she came home, and that she has given me her confidence. I have no further trust, than that I know something of her character and her marriage. O Mr. Harthouse, I think you had that trust too!"

He was touched in the cavity where his heart should have been—in that nest of addled eggs, where the birds of heaven would have lived if they had not been whistled away—by the fervor of this reproach.

"I am not a moral sort of fellow," he said, "and I never make any pretensions to the character of a moral sort of fellow. I am as immoral as need be. At the same time, in bringing any distress upon the lady who is the subject of the present conversation, or in unfortunately compromising her in any way, or in committing myself by any expression of sentiments toward her, not perfectly reconcilable with—in fact with—the domestic hearth; or in taking any advantage of her father's being a machine, or of her brother's being a whelp, or of her husband's being a bear; I beg to be allowed to assure you that I have had no particularly evil intentions, but have glided on from one step to another with a smoothness so perfectly irresistible, that I had not the slightest idea the catalogue was half so long until I began to turn it over. Whereas I find," said Mr. James Harthouse in conclusion, "that it is really in several volumes."

Though he said all this in his frivolous way, the way seemed, for that once, a conscious polishing of but an ugly surface. He was silent for a moment; and then proceeded with a more self-possessed air, though with traces of vexation and disappointment that would not be polished out.

"After what has been just now represented to me, in a manner I find it impossible to doubt—I know of hardly any other source from which I could have accepted it so readily—I feel bound to say to you, in whom the confidence you have mentioned has been reposed, that I can not refuse to contemplate the possibility (however unexpected) of my seeing the lady no more. I am solely to blame for the thing having come to this—and—and, I can not say," he added, rather hard up for a general peroration, "that I have any sanguine expectation of ever becoming a moral sort of fellow, or that I have any belief in any moral sort of fellow whatever."

Sissy's face sufficiently showed that her appeal to him was not finished.

"You spoke," he resumed, as she raised her eyes to him again, "of your first object. I may assume that there is a second to be mentioned?"

"Yes."

"Will you oblige me by confiding it?"

"Mr. Harthouse," returned Sissy, with a blending of gentleness and steadiness that quite defeated him, and with a simple confidence in his being bound to do what she required, that held him at a singular disadvantage, "the only reparation that remains with you is to leave here immediately and finally. I am quite sure that you can mitigate in no other way the wrong and harm you have done. I am quite sure that it is the only compensation you have left it in your power to make. I do not say that it is much, or that it is enough; but it is something, and it is necessary. Therefore, though without any other authority than I have given you, and even without the knowledge of any other person than yourself and myself, I ask you to depart from this place to-night, under an obligation never to return to it."

If she had asserted any influence over him beyond her plain faith in the truth and right of what she said; if she had concealed the least doubt or irresolution, or had harbored for the best purpose any reserve or pretence; if she had shown, or felt, the lightest trace of any sensitiveness to his ridicule or his astonishment, or any remonstrance he might offer; he would have carried it against her at this point. But he could as easily have changed a clear sky by looking at it in surprise, as affect her.

"But do you know," he asked, quite at a loss, "the extent of what you ask? You probably are not aware that I am here on a public kind of business, preposterous enough in itself, but which I have gone in for, and sworn by, and am supposed to be devoted to in quite a desperate manner? You probably are not aware of that, but I assure you it's the fact."

It had no effect on Sissy, fact or no fact.

"Besides which," said Mr. Harthouse, taking a turn or two across the room, dubiously, "it's so alarmingly absurd. It would make a man so ridiculous, after going in for these fellows, to back out in such an incomprehensible way."

"I am quite sure," repeated Sissy, "that it is the only reparation in your power, sir. I am quite sure, or I would not have come here."

He glanced at her face, and walked about again. "Upon my soul, I don't know what to say. So immensely absurd!"

It fell to his lot now to stipulate for secrecy.

"If I were to do such a very ridiculous thing," he said, stopping again presently, and leaning against the chimney-piece, "it could only be in the most inviolable confidence."

"I will trust to you, sir," returned Sissy, "and you will trust to me."

His leaning against the chimney-piece reminded him of the night with the whelp. It was the self-same chimney-piece, and somehow he felt as if *he* were the whelp tonight. He could make no way at all.

"I suppose a man never was placed in a more ridiculous position," he said, after looking down, and looking up, and laughing, and frowning, and walking off, and walking back again. "But I see no way out of it. What will be, will be. *This* will be, I suppose. I must take off myself, I imagine—in short, I engage to do it."

Sissy rose. She was not surprised by the result, but she was happy in it, and her face beamed brightly.

"You will permit me to say," continued Mr. James Harthouse, "that I doubt if any other embassador, or embassadress, could have addressed me with the same success. I must not only regard myself as being in a very ridiculous position, but as being vanquished at all points. Will you allow me the privilege of remembering my enemy's name?"

"*My* name?" said the embassadress.

"The only name I could possibly care to know to-night."

"Sissy Jupe."

"Pardon my curiosity at parting. Related to the family?"

"I am only a poor girl," returned Sissy. "I was separated from my father—he was only a stroller—and taken pity on by Mr. Gradgrind. I have lived in the house ever since."

She was gone.

"It wanted this to complete the defeat," said Mr. James Harthouse, sinking, with a resigned air, on the sofa, after standing transfixed a little while. "The defeat may now be considered perfectly accomplished. Only a poor girl—only a stroller—only James Harthouse made nothing of—only James Harthouse a Great Pyramid of failure."

The Great Pyramid put it into his head to go up the Nile. He took a pen upon the instant, and wrote the following note (in appropriate hieroglyphics) to his brother:

"DEAR JACK—All up at Coketown. Bored out of the place, and going in for camels. Affectionately, JEM."

He rang the bell.

"Send my fellow here."

"Gone to bed, sir."

"Tell him to get up, and pack up."

He wrote two more notes. One, to Mr. Bounderby, announcing his retirement from that part of the country, and showing where he would be found for the next fortnight. The other, similar in effect, to Mr. Gradgrind. Almost as soon as the ink was dry upon their superscriptions, he had left the tall chimneys of Coketown behind, and was in a railway carriage, tearing and glaring over the dark landscape.

The moral sort of fellows might suppose that Mr. James Harthouse derived some comfortable reflections afterward, from this prompt retreat, as one of his few actions that made any amends for any thing, and as a token to himself that he had escaped the climax of a very bad business. But it was not so, at all. A secret sense of having failed and been ridiculous—a dread of what other fellows who went in for similar sorts of things, would say at his expense if they knew it—so oppressed him that what was about the very best passage in his life was the one of all others he would not have owned to on any account, and the only one that made him ashamed of himself.

Chapter XXXI

VERY DECIDED

THE indefatigable Mrs. Sparsit, with a violent cold upon her, her voice reduced to a whisper, and her stately frame so racked by continual sneezes that it seemed in danger of dismemberment, gave chase to her patron until she found him in the metropolis; and there sweeping in upon him at his hotel in St. James's Street, exploded the combustibles with which she was charged, and blew up. Having executed her mission with infinite relish, this high-minded woman then fainted away on Mr. Bounderby's coat-collar.

Mr. Bounderby's first procedure was to shake Mrs. Sparsit off, and leave her to progress as she might through various stages of suffering on the floor. He next had recourse to the administration of potent restoratives, such as screwing the patient's thumbs, smiting her hands, abundantly watering her face, and inserting salt in her mouth. When these attentions had recovered her (which they speedily did), he hustled her into a fast train without offering any other refreshment, and carried her back to Coketown more dead than alive.

Regarded as a classical ruin, Mrs. Sparsit was an interesting spectacle on her arrival at her journey's end; but considered in any other light, the amount of damage she had by that time sustained was excessive, and impaired her claims to admiration. Utterly heedless of the wear and tear of her clothes and constitution, and adamant to her pathetic sneezes,

Mr. Bounderby immediately crammed her into a coach, and bore her off to Stone Lodge.

"Now, Tom Gradgrind," said Bounderby, bursting into his father-in-law's room late at night, "here's a lady here—Mrs. Sparsit—you know Mrs. Sparsit—who has something to say to you that will strike you dumb."

"You have missed my letter!" exclaimed Mr. Gradgrind, surprised by the apparition.

"Missed your letter, sir!" bawled Bounderby. "The present time is no time for letters. No man shall talk to Josiah Bounderby of Coketown about letters with his mind in the state it's in now."

"Bounderby," said Mr. Gradgrind, in a tone of temperate remonstrance, "I speak of a very special letter I have written to you, in reference to Louisa."

"Tom Gradgrind," replied Bounderby, knocking the flat of his hand several times with great vehemence on the table, "I speak of a very special messenger that has come to me in reference to Louisa. Mrs. Sparsit, ma'am, stand forward."

That unfortunate lady hereupon essaying to offer testimony without any voice, and with painful gestures expressive of an inflamed throat, became so aggravating and underwent so many facial contortions, that Mr. Bounderby, unable to bear it, seized her by the arm, and shook her.

"If you can't get it out, ma'am," said Bounderby, "leave *me* to get it out. This is not a time for a lady, however highly connected, to be totally inaudible and seemingly swallowing marbles. Tom Gradgrind, Mrs. Sparsit latterly found herself by accident in a situation to overhear a conversation out of doors between your daughter and your precious gentleman-friend, Mr. James Harthouse."

"Indeed?" said Mr. Gradgrind.

"Ah! Indeed!" cried Bounderby. "And in that conversation—"

"It is not necessary to repeat its tenor, Bounderby. I know what passed."

"You do? Perhaps," said Bounderby, staring with all his might at his so quiet and assuasive father-in-law, "you know where your daughter is at the present time?"

"Undoubtedly. She is here."

"Here?"

"My dear Bounderby, let me beg you to restrain these loud outbreaks, on all accounts. Louisa is here. The moment she could detach herself from that interview with the person of whom you speak, and whom I deeply regret to have been the means of introducing to you, Louisa hurried here, for protection. I myself had not been at home many hours, when I received her—here, in this room. She hurried by the train to town, she ran from town to this house through a raging storm, and presented herself before me in a state of distraction. Of course, she has remained here ever since. Let me entreat you, for your own sake, and for hers too, to be more quiet."

Mr. Bounderby silently gazed about him for some moments in every direction except Mrs. Sparsit's direction, and then abruptly turning upon the niece of Lady Scadgers, said to that wretched woman:

"Now, ma'am! We shall be happy to hear any little apology you may think proper to offer, for going about the country at express pace, with no other luggage than a Cock and a Bull, ma'am!"

"Sir," whispered Mrs. Sparsit, "my nerves are at present too much shaken, and my health is at present too much impaired, in your service, to admit of my doing more than taking refuge in tears."

Which she did.

"Well, ma'am," said Bounderby, "without making any observation to you that may not be made with propriety to a woman of good family, what I have got to add to that, is, that there's something else in which it appears to me you may take refuge, namely, a coach. And the coach in which we came here, being at the door, you'll allow me to hand you down to it and pack you home to the Bank: where the best course for you to pursue, will be to put your feet into the hottest water you can bear, and take a glass of scalding rum and butter after you get into bed." With these words Mr. Bounderby extended his right hand to the weeping lady and escorted her to the conveyance in question, shedding many plaintive sneezes by the way. He soon returned alone.

"Now, as you showed me in your face, Tom Gradgrind, that you wanted to speak to me," he resumed, "here I am. But I am not in a very agreeable state, I tell you plainly, not relishing this business even as it is, and not considering that I am at any time as dutifully and submissively treated by your daughter, as Josiah Bounderby of Coketown ought to be treated by his wife. You have your opinion, I dare say; and I have mine, I know. If you mean to say any thing to me to-night that goes against this candid remark, you had better leave it alone."

Mr. Gradgrind, it will be observed, being much softened, Mr. Bounderby took particular pains to harden himself at all points. It was his amiable nature.

"My dear Bounderby," Mr. Gradgrind began in reply.

"Now, you'll excuse me," said Bounderby, "but I don't want to be too dear. That to start with. When I begin to be dear to a man, I generally find that his intention is to come over me. I am not speaking to you politely; but, as you are aware, I am *not* polite. If you like politeness, you know where to get it. You have your gentleman friends you know, and they'll serve you with as much of the article as you want. I don't keep it myself."

"Bounderby," urged Mr. Gradgrind, "we are all liable to mistakes—"

"I thought you couldn't make 'em," interrupted Bounderby.

"Perhaps I thought so. But, I say we are all liable to mistakes; and I should feel sensible of your delicacy, and grateful for it, if you would spare me these references to Harthouse. I shall not associate him in our conversation with your intimacy and encouragement; pray do not persist in connecting him with mine."

"I never mentioned his name!" said Bounderby.

"Well, well!" returned Mr. Gradgrind, with a patient, even a submissive air. And he sat for a little while pondering. "Bounderby, I see reason to doubt whether we have ever quite understood Louisa."

"Who do you mean by We?"

"Let me say I, then," he returned, in answer to the coarsely blurted question; "I doubt whether I have understood Louisa. I doubt whether I have been quite right in the manner of her education."

"There you hit it," returned Bounderby. "There I agree with you. You have found it out at last, have you? Education! I'll tell you what education is—To be tumbled out of doors, neck and crop, and put upon the shortest allowance of every thing except blows. That's what *I* call education."

"I think your good sense will perceive," Mr. Gradgrind remonstrated in all humility, "that whatever the merits of such a system may be, it would be difficult of general application to girls."

"I don't see it at all, sir," returned the obstinate Bounderby.

"Well," sighed Mr. Gradgrind, "we will not enter into the question. I assure you I have no desire to be controversial. I seek to repair what is amiss, if I possibly can, and I hope you will assist me in a good spirit, Bounderby, for I have been very much distressed."

"I don't understand you, yet," said Bounderby, with determined obstinacy, "and therefore I won't make any promises."

"In the course of a few hours, my dear Bounderby," Mr. Gradgrind proceeded, in the same depressed and propitiatory manner, "I appear to myself to have become better informed as to Louisa's character than in previous years. The enlightenment has been painfully forced upon me, and the discovery is not mine. I think there are—Bounderby you will be surprised to hear me say this—I think there are imaginative qualities in Louisa, which—which have been hardly dealt with, and—and a little perverted. And—and I would suggest to you, that—that if you would kindly meet me in a timely endeavor to leave her to her better nature for awhile—and to encourage it to develop itself by tenderness and consideration—it—it would be the better for the happiness of all of us. Louisa," said Mr. Gradgrind, shading his face with his hand, "has always been my favorite child."

The blustrous Bounderby crimsoned and swelled to such an extent on hearing these words, that he seemed to be, and probably was on the brink of a fit. With his very ears a bright purple shot with crimson, he pent up his indignation, however, and said:

"You'd like to keep her here for a time?"

"I—I had intended to recommend, my dear Bounderby, that you should allow Louisa to remain here on a visit, and be attended by Sissy (I mean of course Cecilia Jupe), who understands her, and in whom she trusts."

"I gather from all this, Tom Gradgrind," said Bounderby, standing up with his hands in his pockets, "that you are of opinion that there's what people call some incompatibility between Loo Bounderby and myself."

"I fear there is at present a general incompatibility between Louisa, and—and—and almost all the relations in which I have placed her," was her father's sorrowful reply.

"Now, look you here, Tom Gradgrind," said Bounderby the flushed, confronting him with his legs wide apart, his hands deeper in his pockets, and his hair like a hay field wherein his windy anger was boisterous. "You have said your say; I am going to say mine. I am a Coketown man. I am Josiah Bounderby of Coketown. I know the bricks of this town, and I know the works of this town, and I know the chimneys of this town, and I know the smoke of this town, and I know the Hands of this town. I know 'em all pretty well. They're real. When a man tells me anything about imaginative qualities, I always tell that man, whoever he is, that I know what he means. He means turtle soup and venison, with a gold spoon, and that he wants to be set up with a coach and six. That's what your daughter wants. Since you are of opinion that she ought to have what she wants, I recommend you to provide it for her. Because, Tom Gradgrind, she will never have it from me."

"Bounderby," said Mr. Gradgrind, "I hoped, after my entreaty, you would have taken a different tone."

"Just wait a bit," retorted Bounderby; "you have said your say, I believe. I heard you out; hear me out, if you please. Don't make yourself a spectacle of unfairness as well as inconsistency, because, although I am sorry to see Tom Gradgrind reduced to his present position, I should be doubly sorry to see him brought so low as that. Now, there's an incompatibility of some sort or another, I am given to understand by you, between your daughter and me. I'll give you to understand, in reply to that, that there unquestionably is an incompatibility of the first magnitude to be summed up in this—that your daughter don't properly know her husband's merits, and is not impressed with such a sense as would become her, by George! of the honor of his alliance. That's plain speaking, I hope."

"Bounderby," urged Mr. Gradgrind, "this is unreasonable."

"Is it?" said Bounderby. "I am glad to hear you say so. Because when Tom Gradgrind, with his new lights, tells me that what I say is unreasonable, I am convinced at once it must be devilish sensible. With your permission I am going on. You know my origin, and you know that for a good many years of my life I didn't want a shoeing-horn in consequence of not having a shoe. Yet you may believe or not, as you think proper, that there are ladies—born ladies—belonging to families—families!—who next to worship the ground I walk on."

He discharged this, like a rocket, at his father-in-law's head.

"Whereas your daughter," proceeded Bounderby, "is far from being a born lady. That you know, yourself. Not that I care a pinch of candle-snuff about such things, for you are very well aware I don't; but that such is the fact, and you, Tom Gradgrind, can't change it. Why do I say this?"

"Not, I fear," observed Mr. Gradgrind, in a low voice, "to spare me."

"Hear me out," said Bounderby, "and refrain from cutting in till your turn comes round. I say this because highly-connected females have been astonished to see the way in which your daughter has conducted herself, and to witness her insensibility. They have wondered how I have suffered it. And I wonder myself now, and I won't suffer it."

"Bounderby," returned Mr. Gradgrind, rising, "the less we say to-night the better, I think."

"On the contrary, Tom Gradgrind, the more we say to-night, the better, I think. That is," the consideration checked him, "till I have said all I mean to say, and then I don't care how soon we stop. I come to a question that may shorten the business. What do you mean by the proposal you made just now?"

"What do I mean, Bounderby?"

"By your visiting proposition," said Bounderby, with an inflexible jerk of the hay field.

"I mean that I hope you may be induced to arrange, in a friendly manner, for allowing Louisa a period of repose and reflection here, which may tend to a gradual alteration for the better in many respects."

"To a softening down of your ideas of the incompatibility," said Bounderby.

"If you put it in those terms."

"What made you think of this?" said Bounderby.

"I have already said, I fear Louisa has not been understood. Is it asking too much, Bounderby, that you, so far her elder, should aid in trying to set her right? You have accepted a great charge of her; you took her for better for worse.

Mr. Bounderby may have been annoyed by the repetition of his own words to Stephen Blackpool, but he cut the quotation short with an angry start.

"Come!" said he, "I don't want to be told about that. I know what I took her for, as well as you do. Never you mind what I took her for; that's my look-out."

"I was merely going on to remark, Bounderby, that we may all be more or less in the wrong, not even excepting you; and that some yielding on your part, remembering the trust you have accepted, may not only be an act of true kindness, but perhaps a debt incurred toward Louisa."

"I think differently," blustered Bounderby; "I am going to finish this business according to my own opinions. I don't want to make a quarrel of it with you, Tom Gradgrind. To tell you the truth, I don't think it would be worthy of my reputation to quarrel on such a poor subject. As to your gentleman friend, he may take himself off, wherever he likes best. If he falls in my way, I shall tell him my mind; if he don't fall in my way, I shan't, for it won't be worth my while to do it. As to your daughter, whom I made Loo Bounderby, and might have done better by leaving Loo Gradgrind, if she don't come home to-morrow, by twelve o'clock at noon, I shall understand that she prefers to stay away, and I shall send her wearing apparel and so forth over here, and you'll take charge of her for the future. What I shall say to people in general, of the incompatibility that led to my so laying down the law, will be this. I am Josiah Bounderby, and I had my bringing-up. She's the daughter of Tom Gradgrind, and she had her bringing-up; and the two horses wouldn't pull together! I am pretty well known to be rather an uncommon man, I believe; and most people will understand fast enough that it must be a woman rather out of the common, also, who, in the long run, would come up to my mark."

"Let me seriously entreat you to re-onsider this, Bounderby," urged Mr. Gradgrind, "before you commit yourself to such a decision."

"I always come to a decision," said Bounderby, tossing his hat on, "and whatever I do, I do at once. I should be surprised at Tom Gradgrind's addressing such a remark to Josiah Bounderby of Coketown, knowing what he knows of him, if I could be surprised by any thing Tom Gradgrind did after his making himself a party to sentimental humbug. I have given you my decision and I have got no more to say. Good-night!"

So Mr. Bounderby went home to his town-house to bed. At five minutes past twelve o'clock next day, he directed Mrs. Bounderby's property to be carefully packed up and sent to Tom Gradgrind's, advertised Nickits's retreat for sale by private contract; and resumed a bachelor's life.

Chapter XXXII
LOST

THE robbery at the bank had not languished before, and did not cease to occupy a front place in the attention of the principal of that establishment now. In trustful proof of his promptitude and activity, as a remarkable man, and a self-made man, and a commercial wonder, more admirable than Venus, who had risen out of the mud instead of the sea, he liked to show how little his domestic affairs abated his business ardor. Consequently in the first few weeks of his resumed bachelorhood, he even advanced upon his usual display of lustre, and every day made such a rout in renewing his investigations into the robbery, that the professional persons who had it in hand almost wished it had never been committed.

They were at fault too, and off the scent. Although they had been so quiet since the first outbreak of the matter, that most people really did suppose it to have been abandoned as hopeless, nothing new occurred. No implicated man or woman took untimely courage or made a self-betraying step. More remarkable yet, Stephen Blackpool was not found, and the mysterious old woman remained a mystery.

Things having come to this pass, and showing no latent signs of stirring beyond it, the upshot of Mr. Bounderby's investigations was, that he resolved to hazard a bold burst. He drew up a placard offering Twenty Pounds' reward for the apprehension of Stephen Blackpool, suspected of complicity in the robbery of Coketown Bank on such a night; he described the said Stephen Blackpool by dress, complexion, estimated height, and manner, as minutely as he could; he recited how he had left the town, and in what direction he had been last seen going; he had the whole printed in great black letters on a staring broadsheet, and caused the walls to be posted with it in the dead of night, so that it should strike upon the sight of the whole population at one blow.

The factory-bells had need to ring their loudest that morning to disperse the groups of workers who stood in the tardy daybreak, collected round the placards, devouring them with eager eyes. Not the least eager of the eyes assembled were the eyes of those who could not read. These people, as they listened to the friendly voice that read aloud—there was always some such ready to help them—started at the characters which meant so much with a vague awe and respect that would have been half ludicrous if such a picture of a Country as a suicidal Idiot with its sword of state at its own heart could ever be otherwise than wholly shocking. Many ears and eyes were busy with a vision of the matter of these placards, among turning spindles, rattling looms, and whirring wheels, for hours afterwards; and when the Hands cleared out again into the streets, there were still as many readers as before.

Slackbridge, the delegate, had to address his audience too that night, and Slackbridge had obtained a clean bill from the printer, and had brought it in his pocket. Oh my friends and fellow-countrymen, the down-trodden operatives of Coketown, oh my fellow-brothers and fellow-workmen and fellow-citizens and fellow-men, what a stir was there when Slackbridge unfolded what he called "that damning document," and held it up to the gaze, and for the execration, of the working-man community! "Oh, my fellow-men, behold of what a traitor in the camp of those great spirits who are enrolled upon the holy scroll of Justice and of Union, is appropriately capable! Oh my prostrate friends, with the galling yoke of tyrants on your necks, and the iron foot of despotism treading down your fallen forms into the dust of the earth, upon which right glad would your oppressors be to see you creeping on your bellies all the days of your lives, like the serpent in the garden—oh my brothers, and shall I as a man not add my sisters too, what do you say, *now,* of Stephen Blackpool, with a slight stoop in his shoulders and about five foot seven in height, as set forth in this degrading and disgusting document, this blighting bill, this pernicious placard, this abominable advertisement; and with what majesty of denouncement, will you crush the viper who would bring this stain and shame upon the Godlike race that happily has cast him out forever! Yes, my compatriots, happily cast him out and sent him forth! For you remember how he stood here before you on this platform; you remember how, face to face and foot to foot, I pursued him though all his intricate windings; you remember how he sneaked, and slunked, and sidled, and splitted of straws, until with not an inch of ground to which to cling, I hurled him out from among us: an object for the undying finger of scorn to point at, and for the avenging fire of every free and thinking mind to scorch and slunk! And now, my friends, my laboring friends, for I rejoice and triumph in that stigma, my friends; whose hard but honest beds are made in toil, and whose scanty but independent pots are boiled in hardship; and, now I say, my friends, what appellation has that dastard craven taken to himself, when, with the mask torn from his features, he stands before us in all his native deformity, a What? a thief! a plunderer! a proscribed fugitive, with a price upon his head: a fester and a wound upon the noble character of the Coketown operative! Therefore, my band of brothers in a sacred bond, to which your children and your children's children yet unborn have set their infant hands and seals, I propose to you, on the part of the United Aggregate Tribunal, ever watchful for your welfare, ever zealous for your benefit, that this meeting does Resolve: That Stephen Blackpool, weaver, referred to in this placard, having been already solemnly disowned by the community of Coketown Hands, he same are free from the shame of his misdeeds, and cannot as a class be reproached with his dishonest actions."

Thus Slackbridge, gnashing and perspiring after a prodigious sort. A few stern voices called out "No!" and a score or two hailed with assenting cries of "Hear, hear!" the caution from one man, "Slackbridge, y'or over hetter int; y'or a goen too fast!" But these were pigmies against an army; the general assemblage subscribed to the gospel according to Slackbridge, and gave three cheers for him, as he sat demonstratively panting at them.

These men and women were yet in the streets, passing quietly to their homes, when Sissy, who had been called away frorn Louisa some minutes before, returned.

"Who is it?" asked Louisa.

"It is Mr. Bounderby," said Sissy, timid of the name, "and your brother Mr. Tom, and a young woman who says her name is Rachael, and that you know her."

"What do they want, Sissy dear?"

"They want to see you. Rachael has been crying and seems angry."

"Father," said Louisa, for he was present, "I cannot refuse to see them, for a reason you will soon understand. Shall they come in here?"

As he answered in the affirmative, Sissy went away to bring them. She reappeared with them directly. Tom was last, and remained standing in the obscurest part of the room, near the door.

"Mrs. Bounderby," said her husband, entering with a cool nod, "I don't disturb you, I hope. This is an unseasonable hour, but here is a young woman who has been making statements which render my visit necessary. Tom Gradgrind, as your son, young Tom, refuses for some obstinate reason or other to say anything at all about those statements good or bad, I am obliged to confront her with your daughter."

"You have seen me once before, young lady," said Rachael standing in front of Lousia.

Tom coughed.

"You have seen me, young lady," repeated Rachael, as she did not answer, "once before."

Tom couged again.

"I have."

Rachael cast her eyes proudly towards Mr. Bounderby, and said, "Will you make it known where, and who was there?"

"I went to the house where Stephen Blackpool lodged, on the night of his discharge from his work, and I saw you there. He was there too; and an old woman who did not speak, and whom I could scarcely see, stood in a dark corner. My brother went with me."

"Why couldn't you say so, young Tom?" demanded Bounderby.

"I promised my sister I wouldn't." Which Louisa hastily confirmed. "And besides," said the whelp bitterly, "she tells her own story so precious well—and so full—that what business had I to take it out of her mouth!"

"Say, young lady, if you please," pursued Rachael, "why, in an evil hour, you ever came to Stephen's that night."

"I felt compassion for him," sald Louisa, her color deepening, "and I wished to know what he was going to do, and wished to offer him assistance."

"Thank you, ma'am," said Bounderby. "Much flattered and obliged."

"Did you offer him," asked Rachael, "a bank-note?"

"Yes; but he refused it, and would only take two pounds in gold."

Rachael cast her eyes toward Mr. Bounderby again.

"Oh, certainly!" said Bounderby. "If you put the question whether your ridiculous and improbable account was true or not, I am bound to say it's confirmed."

"Young lady," said Rachael, "Stephen Blackpool is now named as a robber in public print all over this town and everywhere else! There have been a meeting to-night where he have been spoken of in the same shameful way. Stephen! The honestest lad, the truest lad, the best!" Her indignation failed her, and she broke off, sobbing.

"I am very, very sorry," said Louisa.

"O young lady, young lady," returned Rachael, "I hope you may be, but I don't know! I can't say what you may ha' done! The like of you don't feel for us, don't care for us, don't belong to us. I am not sure why you may ha' come that night. I can't tell but what you may ha' come wi' some aim of your own, not mindin' to what trouble you brought such as the poor lad. I said then, Bless you for coming, and I said it of my heart, you seemed to take so pitifully to him, but I don't know now, I don't know!"

Louisa could not reproach her for her unjust suspicions; she was so faithful to her idea of the man, and so unhappy.

"And when I think," said Rachael through her sobs, "that the poor lad was so grateful, thinkin' you so good to him—when I mind that he put his hand over his hard-worken face to hide the tears that you brought up there—Oh I hope you may be sorry, and ha' no bad cause to be it, but I don't know, I don't know!"

"You're a pretty article," growled the whelp, moving uneasily in his dark corner, "to come here with these precious imputations! You ought to be bundled out for not knowing how to behave yourself, and you would be by rights."

She said nothing in reply, and her low weeping was the only sound that was heard, until Mr. Bounderby spoke.

"Come!" said he, "you know what you have engaged to do. You had better give your mind to that; not this."

"'Deed, I am loath," returned Rachael, drying her eyes, "that any here should see me greet; but I won't be seen so again. Young lady, when I had read what's put in print of Stephen—and what has just as much truth in it as if it had been put in print of you, and no more—I went straight to the Bank to say I knew where Stephen was, and to give a sure and certain promise that he should be here in two days. I couldn't meet wi' Mr. Bounderby then, and your brother sent me away, and I tried to find you, but you was not to be found, and I went back to work. Soon as I come out of the Mill to-night I hastened to hear what was said of Stephen—for I know wi' pride he will come back to shame it! —and then I went again to seek Mr. Bounderby, and I found him, and I told him every word I knew, and he believed no word I said, and brought me here."

"So far that's true enough," assented Mr. Bounderby, with his hands in his pockets and his hat on. "But I have known you people before to-day, you'll observe, and I know you never die for want of talking. Now, I recommend you not so much to mind talking just now, as doing. You have undertaken to do something; all I remark upon that at present is, do it!"

"I have written to Stephen by the post that went out this afternoon, as I have written to him once before sin' he went away," said Rachael; "and he will be here at furthest, in two days."

"Then I'll tell you something. You are not aware, perhaps," retorted Mr. Bounderby, "that you yourself have been looked after now and then, not being considered quite free from suspicion in this business, on account of most people being judged according to the company they keep. The post-office hasn't been forgotten either. What I'll tell you is, that no letter to Stephen Blackpool has ever got into it. Therefore, what has become of yours, I leave you to guess. Perhaps you're mistaken, and never wrote any."

"He hadn't been gone from here, young lady," said Rachael, turning appealingly to Louisa, "as much as a week, when he sent me the only letter I have had, saying that he was forced to seek work in another name."

"Oh, by George!" cried Bounderby, with a whistle, "he changes his name, does he! That's rather unlucky, too, for such an immaculate lad. It's considered a little suspicious in Courts of Justice, I believe, when an Innocent happens to have many names."

"What," said Rachael, with the tears in her eyes again—"what, young lady, in the name of Mercy, was left the poor lad to do! The masters against him on one hand, the men against him on the other, he only wantin' to work hard in peace, and do what he felt right. Can a man have no soul of his own, no mind of his own? Must he go wrong all through wi' this side, or must he go wrong all through wi' that, or else be hunted like a hare?"

"Indeed, indeed, I pity him from my heart," returned Louisa; "and I hope that he will clear himself."

"You need have no fear of it, young lady. He is sure!"

"All the surer, I suppose," said Mr. Bounderby, "for your refusing to tell me where he is? Eh, lass?"

"He shall not, through any act of mine, come back wi' the unmerited reproach of being brought back. He shall come back of his own accord to clear himself, and put all those that have injured his good character, and he not here for its defence, to shame. I have told him what has been done against him," said Rachael, throwing off all distrust as a rock throws off the sea, "and he will be here, at furthest, in two days."

"Notwithstanding which," added Mr. Bounderby, "if he can be laid hold of any sooner, he shall have an earlier opportunity of clearing himself. As to you, I have nothing against you; what you came and told me turns out to be true, and I have given you the means of proving it to be true, and there's an end of it. I wish you Good night all! I must be off to look a little further into this."

Tom came out of his corner when Mr. Bounderby moved, moved with him, kept close to him, and went away with him. The only parting salutation of which he delivered himself was a sulky "Good night, father!" With a brief speech, and a scowl at his sister, he left the house.

Since his sheet-anchor had come home, Mr. Gradgrind had been sparing of speech. He still sat silent, when Lousia mildly said:

"Rachael, you will not mistrust me one day, when you know me better."

"It goes against me," Rachael answered, in a gentle manner, "to mistrust anyone; but when I am so mistrusted—when we all are—I can not keep such things quite out of my mind. I ask your pardon for having done you an injury. I don't think what I said, now. Yet I might come to think it again, wi' the poor lad so belied."

"Did you tell him in your letter," inquired Sissy, "that suspicion seemed to have fallen upon him, because he had been seen about the Bank at night? He would then know what he would have to explain on coming back, and would be ready."

"Yes, dear," she returned; "but I can't guess what can have ever taken him there. He never used to go there. It was never in his way. His way was the same as mine, and not near it."

Sissy had already been at her side asking her where she lived, and whether she might come to-morrow night, to inquire if there were news.

"I doubt," said Rachael, "if he can be here till next day."

"Then I will come next night too," said Sissy.

When Rachael, assenting to this, was gone, Mr. Gradgrind lifted up his head, and said to his daughter:

"Louisa, my dear, I have never, that I know of, seen this man. Do you believe him to be implicated?"

"I think I have believed it, father, though with great difficulty. I do not believe it now."

"That is to say, you once persuaded yourself to believe it, from knowing him to be suspected. His appearance and manner; are they so honest?"

"Very honest."

"And her confidence not to be shaken. I ask myself, then," said Mr. Gradgrind, musing, "does the real culprit know of these accusations? Where is he? Who is he?"

His hair had latterly began to change its color. As he leaned upon his hand again, looking grey and old, Louisa, with a face of fear and pity, hurriedly went over to him, and sat close at his side. Her eyes by accident met Sissy's at this moment. Sissy flushed and started, and Louisa put her finger on her lip.

Next night when Sissy returned home and told Louisa that Stephen was not come, she told it in a whisper. Next night again, when she came home with the same account, and added that he had not been heard of, she spoke in the same low frightened tone. From the moment of that interchange of looks, they never uttered his name, or any reference to him aloud; nor ever pursued the subject of the robbery when Mr. Gradgrind spoke of it.

The two appointed days ran out, three days and nights ran out, and Stephen Blackpool was not come, and remained unheard of. On the fourth day, Rachael, with unabated confidence, but considering her dispatch to have miscarried, went up to the Bank, and showed her letter from him with his address, at a working colony, one of many, not upon the main road, some sixty miles away. Messengers were sent to that place, and the whole town looked for Stephen to be brought in next day.

All this time the whelp moved about with Mr. Bounderby like his shadow, assisting in all the proceedings. He was greatly excited, horribly fevered, bit his nails down to the quick, spoke in a hard rattling voice, and with lips that were black and burnt up. At the time when the suspected man was looked for, the whelp was at the station, offering to wager that he had made off before the arrival of those who were sent in quest of him, and that he would not appear.

The whelp was right. The messengers returned alone. Rachael's letter had gone, Rachael's letter had been delivered, Stephen Blackpool had decamped in that same hour; and no soul knew more of him. The only doubt in Coketown was, whether Rachael had written in good faith, believing that he really would come back; or warning him to fly. On this point opinion was divided.

Six days, seven, far on into another week. The wretched whelp plucked up a ghastly courage, and began to grow defiant. "*Was* the suspected fellow the thief? A pretty question! If not, where was the man, and why did he not come back?"

Where was the man, and why did he not come back? In the dead of night the echoes of his own words, which had rolled Heaven knows how far away in the daytime, came back instead, and abided by him until morning.

Chapter XXXIII

FOUND

DAY and night again, day and night again. No Stephen Blackpool. Where was the man, and why did he not come back?

Every night Sissy went to Rachael's lodging, and sat with her in her small neat room. All day, Rachael toiled as such people must toil, whatever their anxieties. The smoke-serpents were indifferent who was lost or found, who turned out bad or good; the melancholy mad elephants, like the Hard Fact men, abated nothing of their set routine, whatever happened. Day and night again, day and night again, the monotony was unskaken. Even Stephen Blackpool's disappearance was falling into the general way, and becoming as monotonous a wonder as any piece of machinery in Coketown.

"I misdoubt," said Rachael, "if there is as many as twenty left in all this place who have any trust in the poor dear lad now."

She said it to Sissy as they sat in her lodging, lighted only by the lamp at the street corner. Sissy had come there when it was already dark, to wait for her return from work; and they had since sat at the window where Rachael had found her, wanting no brighter light to shine on their sorrowful talk.

"If it hadn't been mercifully brought about that I was to have you to speak to," pursued Rachael, "times are when I think my mind would not have kept right. But I get hope and strength through you, and you believe that though appearances may rise against him, he will be proved clear, living or dead."

"I do believe so," returned Sissy, "with my whole heart. I feel so certain, Rachael, that the confidence you hold in yours against all discouragement, is not like to be wrong, that I have no more doubt of him than if I had known him through as many years of trial as you have."

"And I, my dear," said Rachael, with a tremble in her voice, "have known him through them all, to be, according to his quiet ways, so faithful to everything honest and good, that if he was never to be heard of more, and I was to live to be a hundred years old, I would say with my last breath, God knows my heart, I have never once left trusting Stephen Blackpool!"

"We all belleve, up at the lodge, Rachael, that he will be freed from suspicion, sooner or later."

"The better I know it to be so believed there, my dear," said Rachael, "and the kinder I feel it that you come away from there purposely to comfort me, and keep me company, and be seen wi' me when I am not yet free from all suspicion myself, the more grieved I am that I should ever have spoken those mistrusting words to the young lady. And yet—"

"You don't mistrust her now, Rachael?"

"Now that you have brought us more together, no; not her. But I can't at all times keep out of my mind—"

Her voice so sunk into a low and slow communing with herself; that Sissy, sitting by her side, was obliged to listen with attention.

"I can't at all times keep out of my mind, mistrustings of some one. I can't think who 'tis, I can't think how or why it may be done, but I mistrust that someone has put Stephen out of the way. I mistrust that by his coming back of his own accord, and showing himself innocent before them all, some one would be confounded, who—to prevent that—has stopped him and put him out of the way."

"That is a dreadful thought," said Sissy, turning pale.

"It *is* a dreadful thought to think he may be murdered."

Sissy shuddered, and turned paler yet.

"When it makes its way into my mind, dear," said Rachael, "and it will come sometimes, though I do all I can to keep it out, wi' counting on to high numbers as I work, and saying over and over again pieces that I knew when I were a child, I fall into such a wild hot hurry, that, however tired I am, I want to walk fast, miles and miles. I must get the better of this before bed-time. I'll walk home wi' you now."

"He might fall ill upon the journey," said Sissy, faintly offering a worn-out scrap of hope; "and in such a case there are many places on the road where he might stop."

"But he is in none of them. He has been sought for in all, and he's not there."

"True," was Sissy's reluctant admission.

"He'd walk the journey in two days. If he was footsore and couldn't walk, I sent him, in the letter he got, the money to ride, lest he should have none of his own to spare."

"Let us hope that to-morrow will bring something better Rachael. Come into the air!"

Her gentle hand adjusted Rachael's shawl upon her shining black hair in the usual manner of her wearing it, and they went out. The night being fine, little knots of Hands were here and there lingering at street-corners; but it was supper-time with the greater part of them, and there were but few people in the streets.

"You're not so hurried now, Rachael, and your hand is cooler."

"I get better dear, if I can only walk and breathe a little fresh. Times when I can't, I turn weak and confused."

"But you must not begin to fail, Rachael, for you may be wanted at any time to stand by Stephen. To-morrow is Saturday. If no news comes to-morrow, let us walk in the country on Sunday morning, and strengthen you for another week. Will you go?"

"Yes, dear."

They were by this time in the street where Mr. Bounderby's house stood. The way to Sissy's destination led them past the door, and they were going straight towards it. Some train had newly arrived in Coketown, which had put a number of vehicles in motion, and scattered a considerable bustle about the town. Several coaches were rattling before them and behind them as they approached Mr. Bounderby's, and one of the latter drew up with such briskness as they were in the act of passing the house, that they looked round involuntarily. The bright gas-light over Mr. Bounderby's steps showed them Mrs. Sparsit in the coach in an ecstasy of excitement, struggling to open the door; Mrs. Sparsit seeing them at the same moment, called to them to stop.

"It's a coincidence," exclaimed Mrs. Sparsit, as she was released by the coachman. "It's a Providence! Come out, ma'am!" then said Mrs. Sparsit, to someone inside, "come out, or we'll have you dragged out!"

Hereupon, no other than the mysterious old woman descended; whom Mrs. Sparsit incontinently collared.

"Leave her alone, everybody!" cried Mrs. Sparsit, with great energy. "Let nobody touch her. She belongs to me. Come in, ma'am!" then said Mrs. Sparsit, reversing her former word of command. "Come in, ma'am, or we'll have you dragged in!"

The spectacle of a Roman-nosed matron of classical deportment seizing an ancient woman by the throat, and hauling her into a dwelling house, would have been, under any circumstances, sufficient temptation to all true English stragglers so blest as to witness it, to force a way into that dwelling-house and see the matter out. But when the phenomenon was enhanced by the notoriety and mystery by this time associated all over the town, with the Bank robbery, it would have lured the stragglers in with an irresistible attraction, though the roof had been expected to fall upon their heads. Accordingly, the chance witnesses on the ground, consisting of the busiest of the neighbors, to the number of some five-and-twenty, closed in after Sissy and Rachael, as they closed in after Mrs. Sparsit and her prize; and the whole body made a disorderly irruption into Mr. Bounderby's dining room, where the people behind lost not a moment's time in mounting on the chairs to get the better of the people in front.

"Fetch Mr. Bounderby down!" cried Mrs. Sparsit. "Rachael, young woman; you know who this is?"

"It's Mrs. Pegler," said Rachael.

"I should think it is!" cried Mrs. Sparsit, exulting. "Fetch Mr. Bounderby. Stand away everybody!" Here old Mrs. Pegler, muffling herself up, and shrinking from observation, whispered a word of entreaty. "Don't tell me," said Mrs. Sparsit aloud; "I have told you twenty times, coming along, that I will *not* leave you till I have handed you over to him myself."

Mr. Bounderby now appeared, accompanied by Mr. Gradgrind and the whelp, with whom he had been holding conference upstairs. Mr. Bounderby looked more astonished than hospitable at sight of this uninvited party in his dining-room.

"Why, what's the matter now!" said he. "Mrs. Sparsit, ma'am?"

"Sir," explained that worthy woman, "I trust it is my good fortune to produce a person you have much desired to find. Stimulated by my wish to relieve your mind, sir, and connecting together such imperfect clews to the part of the country in which that person might be supposed to reside, as have been afforded by the young woman Rachael, fortunately now present to identify, I have had the happiness to succeed, and to bring that person with me—I need not say most unwillingly on her part. It has not been, sir, without some trouble that I have effected this; but trouble in your service is to me a pleasure, and hunger, thirst, and cold, a real gratification."

Here Mrs. Sparsit ceased, for Mr. Bounderby's visage exhibited an extraordinary combination of all possible colors and expressions of discomfiture as old Mrs. Pegler was disclosed to his view.

"Why, what do you mean by this!" was his highly unexpected demand, in great wrath. "I ask you what do you mean by this, Mrs. Sparsit, ma'am?"

"Sir!" exclaimed Mrs. Sparsit, faintly.

"Why don't you mind your own business, ma'am?" roared Bounderby. "How dare you go and poke your officious nose into my family affairs?"

This allusion to her favorite feature overpowered Mrs. Sparsit. She sat down stiffly in a chair, as if she were frozen, and with a fixed stare at Mr. Bounderby, slowly grated her mittens against one another, as if they were frozen.

"My dear Josiah," cried Mrs. Pegler, trembling, "my darling boy! I am not to blame. It's not my fault, Josiah. I told this lady over and over again, that I knew she was doing what would not be agreeable, but she would do it."

"What did you let her bring you for? Couldn't you knock her cap off, or her tooth out, or scratch her, or do something to her?" asked Bounderby.

"My own boy! She threatened me that if I resisted her I should be brought by constables, and it was better to come quietly than make that stir in such a—" Mrs. Pegler glanced timidly but proudly round the walls—"such a fine house as this. Indeed, indeed, it is not my fault; my dear, noble, stately boy. I have always lived quiet and secret, Josiah, my dear. I have never broken the condition once. I have never said I was your mother. I have admired you at a distance; and if I have come to town sometimes, with long times between, to take a proud peep at you, I have done it unbeknown, my love, and gone away again."

Mr. Bounderby, with his hands in his pockets, walked in impatient mortification up and down at the side of the long dining-table, while the spectators greedily took in every syllable of Mrs. Pegler's appeal, and at each succeeding syllable became more and more round-eyed. Mr. Bounderby still walking up and down when Mrs. Pegler had done, Mr. Gradgrind addressed that maligned old lady:

"I am surprised, madam," he observed with severity, "that in your old age you have the face to claim Mr. Bounderby for your son after your unnatural and inhuman treatment of him."

"*Me* unnatural!" cried poor old Mrs. Pegler. "*Me* inhuman! To my dear boy?"

"Dear!" repeated Mr. Gradgrind. "Yes; dear in his self-made prosperity, madam, I dare say. Not very dear, however, when you deserted him in his infancy, and left him to the brutality of a drunken grandmother."

"*I* deserted my Josiah!" cried Mrs. Pegler, clasping her hands. "Lord forgive you, sir, for your wicked imaginations, and for your scandal against the memory of my poor mother, who died in my arms before Josiah was born. May you repent of it, sir, and live to know better."

She was so very earnest and injured that Mr. Gradgrind, shocked by the possibility which dawned upon him, said in a gentler tone,

"Do you deny, then, madam, that you left your son to be brought up in the gutter?"

"Josiah in the gutter!" exclaimed Mrs. Pegler. "No such a thing, sir. Never! For shame on you! My dear boy knows, and will give *you* to know, that though he come of humble parents, he come of parents that loved him as dear as the best could, and never thought it hardship on themselves to pinch a bit that he might write and cipher beautiful, and I've his books at home to show it! Aye, have I!" said Mrs. Pegier, with indignant pride. "And my dear boy knows, and wlll give *you* to know, sir, that after his beloved father died when he was eight years old, his mother, too, could pinch a bit, as it was her duty and her pleasure and her pride to do it, to help him out in life, and put him 'prentice. And a steady lad he was, and a kind master he had to lend him a hand, and well he worked his own way forward to be rich and thriving. And *I*'ll give you to know, sir—for this my dear boy won't—that though his mother kept but a little village shop, he never forgot her, but pensioned me on thirty pound a year—more than I want, for I put by out of it—only making the condition that I was to keep down in my own part, and make no boasts about him, and not trouble him. And I never have, except with looking at him once a year, when he has never knowed it. And it's right," said poor old Mrs. Pegler, in affectionate championship, "that I *should* keep down in my own part, and I have no doubts that if I was here I should do a many unbefitting things, and I am well contented, and I can keep my pride in my Josiah to myself, and I can love for love's own sake. And I am ashamed of you, sir," said Mrs. Pegler, lastly, "for your slanders and suspicions. And for I never stood here afore, or wanted to stand here when my dear son said no. And I shouldn't be here now, if it hadn't been for being brought. And for shame upon you, for shame, to accuse me of being a bad mother to my son, with my son standing here to tell you so different!"

The bystanders, on and off the dining-room chairs, raised a murmur of sympathy with Mrs. Pegler, and Mr. Gradgrind felt himself innocently placed in a very distressing predicament, when Mr. Bounderby, who had never ceased walking up and down, and had every moment swelled larger and larger and grown redder and redder, stopped short.

"I don't exactly know," said Mr. Bounderby, "how I come to be favored with the attendance of the present company, but I don't inquire. When they're quite satisfied, perhaps they'll be so good as to disperse; whether they're satisfied or not, perhaps they'll be so good as to disperse. I'm not bound to deliver a lecture on my family affairs! I have not undertaken to do it, and I'm not going to do it. Therefore those who expect any explanation whatever upon that branch of the subject will be disappointed—particularly Tom Gradgrind, and he can't know it too soon. In reference to the Bank robbery, there has been a mistake made, concerning my mother. If there hadn't been over-officiousness it wouldn't have been made, and I hate over-officiousness at all times, whether or no. Good-evening!"

Although Mr. Bounderby carried it off in these terms, holding the door open for the company to depart, there was a blustering sheepishness about him, at once extremely crest-fallen and superlatively absurd. Detected as the bully of humanity, who had built his windy reputation upon lies, and in his boastfulness had put the honest truth as far away from him as if he had advanced the mean claim (there is no meaner) to tack himself on to a pedigree, he cut a most ridiculous figure. With the people filing off at the door he held, who he knew would carry what had passed to the whole town, to be given to the four winds, he could not have looked a Bully more shorn and forlorn, if he had had his ears cropped. Even that unlucky female Mrs. Sparsit, fallen from her pinnacle of exultation into the Slough of Despond, was not in so bad a plight as that remarkable man and self-made Humbug, Josiah Bounderby of Coketown.

Rachael and Sissy, leaving Mrs. Pegler to occupy a bed at her son's for that night, walked together to the gate of Stone Lodge, and there parted. Mr. Gradgrind joined them before they had gone very far and spoke with much interest of Stephen Blackpool, for whom he thought this signal failure of the suspicions against Mrs. Pegler was likely to work well.

As to the whelp, throughout this scene, as on all other late occasions, he had stuck close to Bounderby. He seemed to feel that as long as Bounderby could make no discovery without his knowledge he was so far safe. He never visited his sister, and had only seen her once since she went home, that is to say on the night when he still stuck close to Bounderby as already related.

There was one dim unformed fear lingering about his sister's mind, to which she never gave utterance, which surrounded the graceless and ungrateful boy with a dreadful mystery. The same dark possibility had presented itself in the same shapeless guise, this very day to Sissy when Rachael spoke of someone who would be counfounded by Stephen's return, having put him out of the way. Louisa had never spoken of harbouring any suspicion of her brother in connexion with the robbery, she and Sissy had held no confidence on the subject save in that one interchange of looks when the unconscious father rested his grey head on his hand, but it was understood between them, and they both knew it. This other fear was so awful that it hovered about each of them like a ghostly shadow, neither daring to think of its being near herself, far less of its being near the other.

And still the forced spirit which the whelp had plucked up throve with them. If Stephen Blackpool was not the thief, let him show himself. Why didn't he!

Another night. Another day and night. No Stephen Blackpool! Where was the man, and why did he not come back?

Chapter XXXIV

THE STARLIGHT

THE Sunday was a bright Sunday in autumn, clear and cool, when early in the morning Sissy and Rachael met, to walk in the country.

As Coketown cast ashes not only on its own head but on the neighborhood's too—after the manner of those pious persons who do penance for their own sins by putting other people into sackcloth—it was customary for those who now and then thirsted for a draught of pure air, which is not absolutely the most wicked among the vanities of life, to get a few miles away by the railroad, and then begin their walk, or their lounge in the fields. Sissy and Rachael helped themselves out of the smoke by the usual means, and were put down at a station about midway between the town and Mr. Bounderby's retreat.

Though the green landscape was blotted here and there with heaps of coal, it was green, and there were trees to see, and there were larks singing (though it was Sunday), and there were pleasant scents in the air, and all was overarched by a bright blue sky. In the distance one way, Coketown showed as a black mist; in another distance, hills began to rise; in a third, there was a faint change in the light of the horizon, where it shone upon the far-off sea. Under their feet, the grass was fresh; beautiful shadows of branches flickered upon it and speckled it; hedgerows were luxuriant; every thing was at peace. Engines at pits' mouths, and lean old horses that had worn the circle of their daily labor into the ground, were alike quiet; wheels had ceased for a short space to turn; and the great wheel of earth seemed to revolve without the shocks and noises of another time.

They walked on across the fields and down the shady lanes, sometimes getting over a fragment of a fence so rotten that it dropped at a touch of the foot, sometimes passing near a wreck of bricks and beams overgrown with grass, marking the site of some deserted works. They followed paths and tracks, however slight. Mounds where the grass was rank and high, and where brambles, dock-weeds, and such-like vegetation were confusedly heaped together, they always avoided for dismal stories were told in that country of the old pits hidden beneath such indications.

The sun was high when they sat down to rest. They had seen no one, near or distant, for a long time, and the solitude remained unbroken. "It is so still here, Rachael, and the way is so untrodden, that I think we must be the first who have been here all the summer."

As Sissy said it, her eyes were attracted by another of those rotten fragments of fence upon the ground. She got up to look at it. "And yet I don't know. This has not been broken very long. The wood is quite fresh where it gave way. Here are footsteps too. O Rachael!"

She ran back and caught her round the neck. Rachael had already started up.

"What is the matter?"

"I don't know. There is a hat lying in the grass."

They went forward together. Rachael took it up, shaking from head to foot. She broke into a passion of tears and lamentations; Stephen Blackpool was written in his own hand on the inside.

"O, the poor lad, the poor lad! He has been made away with. He is lying murdered here!"

"Is there—has the hat any blood upon it?" Sissy faltered.

They were afraid to look, but they did examine it, and found no mark of violence, inside or out. It had been lying there some days, for rain and dew had stained it, and it left the mark of its shape was on the grass where it had fallen. They looked fearfully about them, without moving, but could see nothing more. "Rachael," Sissy whispered, "I will go on a little by myself."

She had unclasped her hand, and was in the act of stepping forward, when Rachael caught her in both arms with a scream that resounded over the wide landscape. Before them, at their very feet, was the brink of a black raged chasm hidden by the thick grass. They sprang back, and fell upon their knees, each hiding her face upon the other's neck.

"O my good God! He's down there! Down there!" At first this and her terrific screams, were all that could be got from Rachael by any tears, by any prayers, by any representations, by any means. It was impossible to hush her and it was deadly necessary to hold her, or she would have distractedly flung herself down the shaft.

"Rachael, dear Rachael, good Rachael, for the love of Heaven, not these dreadful cries! Think of Stephen, think of Stephen, think of Stephen!"

By an earnest repetition of this entreaty, poured out in all the agony of such a time, Sissy at last brought her to be silent, and to look at her with a tearless face of stone.

"Rachael, Stephen may be living. You wouldn't leave him lying maimed at the bottom of this dreadful place a moment if you could bring help to him?"

"No no no!"

"Don't stir from here, for his sake! Let me go and listen."

She shuddered to approach the pit, but she crept toward it on her hands and knees, and called to him as loud as she could call. She listened, but no sound replied. She called again and listened; still no answering sound. She did this twenty, thirty times. She took a little clod of earth from the broken ground where he had stumbled, and threw it in. She could not hear it fall.

The wide prospect, so beautiful in its stillness but a few minutes ago, almost carried despair to her brave heart, as she rose and looked all round her seeing no help. "Rachael, we must lose not a moment. We must go in different directions, seeking aid. You shall go by the way we have come, and I will go forward by the path. Tell any one you see and every one, what has happened. Think of Stephen, think of Stephen!"

She knew by Rachael's face that she might trust her now. And after standing for a moment to see her running wringing her hands as she went, she turned and went upon her own search; she stopped at the hedge to tie her shawl there as a guide to the place, then threw her bonnet aside, and ran as she had never run before.

Run, Sissy, run, in Heaven's name! Don't stop for breath. Run, run! Quickening herself by carrying such entreaties in her thoughts, she ran from field, to field and lane to lane, and place to place, as she had never run before, until she came to a shed by an engine-house, where two men lay in the shade asleep on straw.

First to wake them, and next to tell them, all so wild and breathless as she was, what had brought her there, were difficulties but they no sooner understood her than their spirits were on fire like hers. One of the men was in a drunken slumber, but on his comrade's shouting to him that a man had fallen down the OLD HELL SHAFT, he started out to a pool of dirty water, put his head in it, and came back sober.

With these two men she ran to another half-a-mile further, and with that one to another, while they ran elsewhere. Then a horse was found, and she got another man to ride for life or death to the railroad, and send a message to Louisa, which she wrote and gave him. By this time a whole village was up; and windlasses, ropes, poles, buckets, candles, lanterns, all things necessary, were fast collecting and being brought into one place to be carried to the Old Hell Shaft.

It seemed now hours and hours since she had left the lost man lying in the grave where he had been buried alive. She could not bear to remain away from it any longer—it was like deserting him—and she hurried swiftly back, accompained by half-a-dozen laborers, including the drunken man whom the news had sobered, and who was the best man of all. When they came to the Old Hell Shaft they found it as lonely as she had left it. The men called and listened as she had done, and examined the edge of the chasm, and settled how it had happened, and then sat down to wait until the implements they wanted should come up.

Every sound of insects in the air, every stirring of the leaves, every whisper among these men, made Sissy tremble, for she thought it was a cry at the bottom of the pit. But the wind blew idly over it, and no sound arose to the surface, and they sat upon the grass, waiting and waiting. After they had waited some time, straggling people who had heard of the accident began to come up; then the real help of implements began to arrive. In the midst of this, Rachael returned; and with her party there was a surgeon, who brought some wine and medicines. But the expectation among the working pitmen that the man would be found alive, was very slight indeed.

There being now people enough present to impede the work; the sobered man put himself at the head of the rest, or was put there by the general consent, and made a large ring round the Old Hell Shaft, and appointed men to keep it. Besides such volunteers as were accepted to work, only Sissy and Rachael were at first permitted within this ring; but later in the day, when the message brought an express from Coketown, Mr. Gradgrind and Louisa, and Mr. Bounderby, and the whelp, were also there.

The sun was four hours lower than when Sissy and Rachael had first sat down upon the grass, before a means of enabling two men to descend securely was rigged with poles and ropes. Difficulties had arisen in the construction of this machine, simple as it was; requisites had been found wanting, and messages had had to go and return. It was five o'clock in the afternoon of the bright autumnal Sunday, before a candle was sent down to try the air, while three or four rough faces stood crowded close together, actively watching it: the men at the windlass lowering as they were told. The candle was brought up again, feebly burning, and then some water was cast in. Then the bucket was hooked on, and the sobered man and another got in with lights, giving the word, "Lower away!"

As the rope went out, tight and strained, and the windlass creaked, there was not a breath among the one or two hundred men and women looking on that came as it was wont to come. The signal was given and the windlass stopped, with abundant rope to spare. Apparently so long an interval ensued, with the men at the windlass standing idle, that some women shrieked that another accident had happened. But the surgeon who held the watch, declared five minutes not to have elapsed yet, and sternly admonished them to keep silence. He had not well done speaking when the windlass was reversed and worked again. Practiced eyes knew that it did not go as heavily as it would if both workmen had been coming up, and that only one was returning.

The rope came in tight and strained, and ring after ring was coiled upon the barrel of the windlass, and all eyes were fastened on the pit.

The sobered man was brought up, and leaped out briskly on the grass. There was an universal cry of "Alive or dead?" and then a deep profound hush.

When he said, "Alive," a great shout arose, and many eyes had tears in them.

"But he's hurt very bad," he added, as soon as he could make himself heard again. "Where's doctor? He's hurt so very bad, sir, that we donno how to get him up."

They all consulted together, and looked anxiously at the surgeon, as he asked some questions and shook his head on receiving the replies. The sun was setting now, and the red light in the evening sky touched every face there, and caused it to be distinctly seen in all its rapt suspense.

The consultation ended in the men returning to the windlass, and the pitman going down again, carrying the wine and some other small matters with him. Then the other man came up. In the mean time, under the surgeon's directions, some men brought a bundle, on which others made a thick bed of spare clothes covered with straw, while he himself contrived some bandages and slings from shawls and handkerchiefs. As these were made, they were hung upon an arm of the pitman who had last come up, with instructions how to use them and as he stood, shown by the light he carried, leaning his powerful loose hand upon one of the poles, and sometimes glancing down the pit and sometimes glancing round upon the people, he was not the least conspicuous figure in the scene. It was dark now, and torches were kindled.

It appeared from the little this man had said to those about him, which was quickly repeated all over the circle, that the lost man had fallen upon a mass of crumbled rubbish with which the pit was half choked up, and that his fall had been further broken by some jagged earth at the side. He lay upon his back with one arm doubled under him, and according to his own belief had hardly stirred since he fell, except that he had moved his free hand to a side pocket, in which he remembered to have some bread and meat (of which he had swallowed crumbs), and had likewise scooped up a little water in it now and then. He had come straight away from his work on being written to; and had walked the whole journey; and was on his way to Mr. Bounderby's country-house after dark, when he fell. He was crossing that dangerous country at such a dangerous time because he was innocent of what was laid to his charge, and couldn't rest from coming the nearest way to deliver himself up. The Old Hell Shaft, the pitman said, with a curse upon it, was worthy of its bad name to the last, for though Stephen could speak now, he believed it would soon be found to have mangled the life out of him.

When all was ready, this man still taking his last hurried charges from his comrades and the surgeon after the windlass had begun to lower him, disappeared into the pit. The rope went out as before, the signal was made as before, and the windlass stopped. No man removed his hand from it now. Every one waited with his grasp set, and his body bent down to the work, ready to reverse and wind in. At length the signal was given, and all the ring leaned forward.

For now the rope came in tightened and strained to its utmost as it appeared, and the men turned heavily, and the windlass complained. It was scarcely endurable to look at the rope, and think of its giving way. But ring after ring was coiled upon the barrel of the windlass safely, and the connecting chains appeared, and finally the bucket with the two men holding on at the sides—a sight to make the head swim, and oppress the heart—and tenderly supporting between them, slung and tied within, the figure of a poor crushed human creature.

A low murmur of pity went round the throng, and the women wept aloud, as this form, almost without form, was moved very slowly from its iron deliverance, and laid upon the bed of straw. At first none but the surgeon went close to it. He did what he could in its adjustment on the couch, but the best that he could do was to cover it. That gently done, he called to him Rachael and Sissy, and at that time the pale, worn, patient face was seen looking up at the sky, with the broken right hand lying bare on the outside of the covering garments, as if waiting to be taken by another hand.

They gave him drink, moistened his face with water, and administered some drops of cordial and wine. Though he lay quite motionless looking up at the sky, he smiled and said, "Rachael."

She stooped down on the grass at his side, and bent over him until her eyes were between his and the sky, for he could not so much as turn them to look at her.

"Rachael my dear."

She took his hand. He smiled again and said, "Don't let it go."

"Thou'rt in great pain, my own dear Stephen?"

"I ha' been, but not now. I ha' been—dreadful, and dree, and long, my dear—but 'tis ower now. Ah Rachael, aw a muddle! Fro' first to last, a muddle!"

The spectre of his old look seemed to pass as he said the word.

"I ha' fell into th' pit, my dear, as have cost wi'n the knowledge o' old folk now livin' hundreds and hundreds o' men's lives—fathers, sons, brothers, dear to thousands an' thousands, and keepin' 'em fro' want and hunger. I ha' fell into a pit that ha' been wi' th' fire-damp crueller than battle. I ha' read on 't in the public petition, as onny one may read, fro' the men that works in pits, in which they ha' pray'n and pray'n the law-makers for Christ's sake not to let their work be murder to 'em, but to spare 'em for th' wives and children that they loves as well as gentlefolk loves theirs. When it were in work, it killed wi'out need; when 'tis let alone, it kills wi'out need. See how we die, an' no need, one way an' another—in a muddle, every day!"

He faintly said it, without any anger against anyone. Merely as the truth.

"Thy little sister, Rachael, thou hast not forgot her. Thou'rt not like to forget her now, and me so nigh her. Thou know'st, poor, patient, suff'rin' dear, how she died, young and misshapen; awlung o' sickly air as had'n no need to be, an' awlung o' working people's miserable homes. A muddle! Aw a muddle!"

Louisa approached him, but he could not see her, lying with his face turned up to the night sky.

"If aw th' things that touches us, my dear, was not so muddled, I should'n ha' had'n need to coom heer. If we was not in a muddle among ourseln, I should'n ha' been by my own fellow weavers and workin' brothers, so mistook. If Mr. Bounderby had ever know'd me right—rather if he'd ever know'd me at aw—he would'n ha' took'n offence wi' me. He would'n ha' suspect'n me. But look up yonder, Rachael! Look aboove!"

Following his eyes, she saw that he was gazing at a star.

"It ha' shined upon me," he said reverently, "in my pain and trouble down below. It ha' shined into my mind. I ha' look'n an 't thowt o' thee, Rachael, till the muddle in my mind have cleared away above a bit, I hope. If soom ha' been wantin' in unnerstannin' me better, I, too, ha' been wantin' in unnerstannin' them better. When I got thy letter, I easily believed that what the yoong lady sen an' done to me, and what her brother sen an' done to me were one, an' that there were a wicked plot betwixt um. When I fell, I were in anger wi' her, an' hurryin' on t' be as onjust t' her as others was t' me. But in our judgements like as in our doins, we mun bear and forbear. In my pain an' trouble, lookin' up yonder—wi' it shinin' on me—I ha' seen more clear, and ha' made it my dyin' prayer that aw th' world may on'y come toogether more, an' get a better unnerstanin' o' one another, than when I were in 't my own weak seln."

Louisa hearing what he said, bent over him on the opposite side to Rachael, so that he could see her.

"You ha' heard?" he said after a few moment's silence. "I ha' not forgot yo', ledy."

"Yes, Stephen, I have heard you. And your prayer is mine."

"You ha' a father. Will yo' tak a message to him?"

"He is here," said Louisa, with dread. "Shall I bring him to you?"

"If yo' please."

Louisa returned with her father. Standing hand-in-hand, they both looked down upon the solemn countenance.

"Sir, yo' will clear me an' mak' my name good wi' aw men. This I leave to yo'."

Mr. Gradgrind was troubled and asked how?

"Sir," was the reply, "your son will tell yo' how. Ask him. I mak' no charges. I leave none ahint me, not a single word. I ha' seen an' spok'n wi' yor son, one night. I ask no more o' yo' than that, to clear me—an' I trust to yo' to do 't."

The bearers being now ready to carry him away, and the surgeon being anxious for his removal, those who had torches or lanterns, prepared to go in front of the litter. Before it was raised, and while they were arranging how to go, he said to Rachael, looking upward at the star—

"Often as I coom to myseln, and found it shinin' on me down there in my trouble, I thowt it were the star as guided to Our Saviour's home, I awmust think it be the very star!"

They lifted him up, and he was overjoyed to find that they were about to take him in the direction whither the star seemed to him to lead.

"Rachael, beloved lass! Don't let go my hand. We may walk together t'night, my dear!"

"I will hold thy hand, and keep beside thee, Stephen, all the way."

"Bless thee! Will soombody be pleased to coover my face!"

They carried him very gently along the fields, and down the lanes, and over the wide landscape; Rachael always holding the hand in hers. Very few whispers broke the mournful silence. It was soon a funeral procession. The star had shown him where to find the God of the poor; and through humility, and sorrow, and forgiveness, he had gone to his Redeemer's rest.

Chapter XXXV

WHELP-HUNTING

BEFORE the ring formed round the Old Hell Shaft was broken, one figure had disappeared from within it. Mr. Bounderby and his shadow had not stood near Louisa, who held her father's arm, but in a retired place by themselves. When Mr. Gradgrind was summoned to the couch, Sissy, attentive to all that happened, slipped behind that wicked shadow—a sight in the horror of his face, if there had been eyes there for any sight but one—and whispered in his ear. Without turning his head, for she had begun by telling him not to even look round, he conferred with her a few moments, and vanished. Thus the whelp had gone out of the circle before the people moved.

When the father reached home, he sent a message to Mr. Bounderby's desiring his son to come to him directly. The reply was, that Mr. Bounderby having missed him in the crowd, and seen nothing of him since, had supposed him to be at Stone Lodge.

"I believe, father," said Louisa, "he will not come back to town to-night." Mr. Gradgrind turned away, and said no more.

In the morning, he went down to the Bank himself as soon as it was opened, and seeing his son's place empty (he had not the courage to look in at first), went back along the street to meet Mr. Bounderby on his way there. To whom he said that, for reasons he would soon explain, but entreated not then to be asked for, he had found it necessary to employ his son at a distance for a little while. Also, that he was charged with the duty of vindicating Stephen Blackpool's memory, and declaring the thief. Mr. Bounderby, quite confounded, stood stock still in the street after his father-in-law had left him, swelling like an immense soap-bubble, without its beauty.

Mr. Gradgrind went home, locked himself in his room, and kept it all that day. When Sissy and Louisa tapped at his door, he said, without opening it, "Not now, my dears; in the evening." On their return in the evening, he said, "I am not able yet—tomorrow." He ate nothing all day, and had no candle after dark, and they heard him walking to and fro late at night.

But in the morning he appeared at breakfast at the usual hour, and took his usual place at the table. Aged and bent, he looked, and quite bowed down; and yet he looked a wiser man, and a better man, than in the days when in this life he wanted nothing but Facts. Before he left the room, he appointed a time for them to come to him, and so, with his grey head drooping, went away.

"Dear father," said Louisa, when they kept their appointment, "you have three young children left. They will be different. *I* will be different yet, with Heaven's help."

She gave her hand to Sissy, as if she meant with her help of her loving heart.

"Your wretched brother," said Mr. Gradgrind. "Do you think he had planned this robbery when he went with you to the lodging?"

"I fear so, father. I know he had wanted money very much, and had spent a great deal."

"The poor man being about to leave the town, it came into his evil brain to cast suspicion on him?"

"I think it must have flashed upon him while he sat there, father. For I asked him to go there with me. The visit did not originate with him."

"He had some conversation with the poor man. Did he take him aside?"

"He took him out of the room. I asked him afterwards, why he had done so, and he made a plausible excuse; but since last night, father, and when I remembered the circumstances by its light, I am afraid I can imagine too truly what passed between them."

"Let me know," said her father, "if your thoughts present your guilty brother in the same dark view as mine do."

"I am afraid, father," hesitated Louisa, "that he must have made some representation to Stephen Blackpool—perhaps in my name, perhaps in his own—which induced him to do in good faith and honesty, what he had never done before, and to wait about the Bank those two or three nights before he left the town."

"Too plain!" returned the father. "Too plain!"

He shaded his face, and remained silent for some moments. Recovering himself, he said:

"And now, how is he to be found? How is he to be saved from justice? In the few hours that I can possibly allow to elapse before I publish the truth, how is he to be found by us and only by us? Ten thousand pounds could not effect it."

"Sissy has effected it, father."

He raised his eyes to where she stood, like a good fairy in his house, and said in a tone of softened gratitude and grateful kindness, "It is always you, my child."

"We had our fears," Sissy explained, glancing at Louisa, "before yesterday; and when I saw you brought to the side of the litter last night, and heard what passed (being close to Rachael all the time), I went to him when no one saw, and said to him, 'Don't look at me! See where your father is. Escape at once, for his sake and your own!' He was in a tremble before I whispered to him, and he started and trembled more, and said, 'Where can I go? I have very little money, and I don't know who will hide me!' I thought of father's old circus. I have not forgotten where Mr. Sleary goes at this time of year, and I read of him in a paper only the other day. I told him to hurry there, and tell his name, and ask Mr. Sleary to hide him till I came. 'I'll get to him before the morning,' he said. And I saw him shrink away among the people."

"Thank Heaven!" exclaimed his father. "He may be got abroad yet."

It was the more hopeful as the town to which Sissy had directed him was within three hours' journey of Liverpool, whence he could be swiftly dispatched to any part of the world but, caution being necessary in communicating with him—for there was a greater danger every moment of his being suspected now, and nobody could be sure at heart but that Mr. Bounderby himself, in a bullying view of public zeal, might play a Roman part—it was consented that Sissy and Louisa should repair to the place in question, by a circuitous course, alone; and that the unhappy father, setting forth at another time, and leaving the town by an opposite direction, should get round to the same bourne by another and wider route. It was further agreed that he should not present himself to Mr. Sleary, lest his intentions should be mistrusted, or the intelligence of his arrival should cause his son to take flight anew; but that the communication should be left to Sissy and Louisa to open, and that they should inform the cause of so much misery and disgrace of his father's being at hand, and of the purpose for which they had come. When these arrangements had been well considered and were fully understood by all three, it was time to begin to carry them into execution. Early in the afternoon Mr. Gradgrind walked direct from his own house into the country, to be taken up on the line by which he was to travel; and at night the remaining two set forth upon their different course, encouraged by not seeing any face they knew.

The two travelled all night, except when they were left for odd numbers of minutes at branch-places up illimitable flights of steps or down wells—which was the only variety of those branches—and, early in the morning, were turned out on a swamp, a mile or two from the town they sought. From this dismal spot they were rescued by a savage old postillon, who happened to be up early, kicking a horse in a fly, and so were smuggled into the town by all the back lanes where the pigs lived; which, although not a magnificent or even savory approach, was, as is usual in such cases, the legitimate highway.

The first thing they saw on entering the town was the skeleton of Sleary's Circus. The company had departed for another town more than twenty miles off, and had opened there last night. The connection between the two places was by a hilly turn-pike road, and the traveling on that road was very slow. Though they took but a hasty breakfast, and no rest (which it would have been in vain to seek under such anxious circumstances), it was noon before they began to find the bills of Sleary's Horse-riding on barns and walls, and one o'clock when they stopped in the market-place.

A Grand Morning Performance by the Riders commencing at that very hour, was in course of announcement by the bell man as they set their feet upon the stones of the street. Sissy recommended that, to avoid making inquiries and attracting attention in the town, they should present themselves to pay at the door. If Mr. Sleary were taking the money, he would be sure to know her, and would proceed with discretion. If he were not, he would be sure to see them inside, and knowing what he had done with the fugitive, would proceed with discretion still.

Therefore they repaired with fluttering hearts, to the well-remembered booth. The flag with the inscription—SLEARY'S HORSE RIDING, was there, and the Gothic niche was there, but Mr. Sleary was not there. Master Kidderminster, grown too maturely turfy to be received by the wildest credulity as Cupid any more, had yielded to the invincible force of circumstances (and his beard), and, in the capacity of a man who made himself generally useful, presided on this occasion over the exchequer—having also a drum in reserve, on which to expend his leisure moments and superfluous forces. In the extreme sharpness of his look-out for base coin, Mr. Kidderminster, as at present situated, never saw anything but money; so Sissy passed him unrecognized, and they went in.

The Emperor of Japan on a steady old white horse stenciled with black spots, was twirling five wash-hand-basins at once, as it is the favorite recreation of that monarch to do. Sissy, though well acquainted with his royal line, had no personal knowledge of the present Emperor, and his reign was peaceful. Miss Josephine Sleary in her celebrated graceful Equestrian Tyrolean Flower-Act, was then announced by a new clown (who humorously said Cauliflower-Act), and Mr. Sleary appeared, leading her in.

Mr. Sleary had only made one cut at the Clown with his long whip-lash, and the Clown had only said, "If you do it again, I'll throw the horse at you!" when Sissy was recognized both by father and daughter. But they got through the Act with great self-possession, and Mr. Sleary, saving for the first instant, conveyed no more expression into his locomotive eye than into his fixed one. The performance seemed a little long to

Sissy and Louisa in their suspense, particularly when it stopped to afford the Clown an opportunity of telling Mr. Sleary (who said "Indeed, sir?" to all his observations in the calmest way, and with his eye on the house) about two legs sitting on three legs looking at one leg, when in came four legs, and laid hold of one leg, and up got two legs, caught hold of three legs, and threw 'em at four legs, who ran away with one leg. For although an ingenious Allegory relating to a butcher, a three-legged stool, a dog, and a leg of mutton, this narrative consumed time and they were painfully anxious. At last, however, little fair-haired Josephine made her courtsey amid great applause; and the Clown, left alone in the ring, had just warmed himself, and said, "Now *I*'ll have a turn!" when Sissy was touched on the shoulder and beckoned out.

She took Louisa with her, and they were received by Mr. Sleary in a very little private apartment with canvas sides, a grass floor, and a wooden ceiling all aslant, on which the box company stamped their approbation as if they were coming through. "Thethilia," said Mr. Sleary, who had brandy and water at hand, "it doth me good to thee you. You wath alwayth a favorite with uth, and you've done uth credith thinth the old timeth I'm thure. You muth thee our people, my dear, afore we thpeak of bithnith, or they'll break their hearth—ethpethially the women. Here'th Joth-phine hath been and got married to E. W. B. Childerth, and thee hath got a boy, and though he'th only three yearth old, he stickth on to any pony you can bring againtht him. He'th named The Little Wonder of Thcolathtic Equitation; and if you don't hear of that boy at Athley'th you'll hear of him at Parith. And you recollect Kidderminthter, that wath thought to be rather thweet upon yourthelf? Well. Heth married too. Married a widder. Old enough to be hith mother. Thee wath Tightrope, thee wath, and now thee'th nothing—on account of fat. They've got two children, tho we're thtrong in the Fairy bithnith and the Nurthery dodge. If you wath to thee our Children in the Wood, with their father and mother both a dyin' on a horthe—their uncle a retheiving of 'em ath hith wardth, upon a horthe—the the both a goin' a black-berryin' on a horthe—and the Robinth a coming in to cover 'em with leavth, upon a horthe—you'd thay it wath the completeth thing ath ever you thet your eyeth on! And you remember Emma Gordon, my dear, ath wath a'motht a mother to you? Of courthe you do; I needn't athk. Well Emma, thee loth her huthband. He wath throw'd a heavy backfall off a Elephant in a thort of a Pagoda thing ath the Thultan of the Indieth, and he never got the better of it, and thee married a thecond time; married a Cheeth-emonger ath fell in love with her from the front, and he'th a Overtheer and makin' a fortun!"

These various changes Mr. Sleary, very short of breath now, related with great heartiness, and with a wonderful kind of innocence, considering what a bleary and brandy-and-watery old veteran he was. Afterwards he brought in Josephine, and E. W. B. Childers (rather deeply-lined in the jaws by daylight) , and The Little Wonder of Scholastic Equitation, and, in a word, all the company. Amazing creatures they were in Louisa's eyes, so white and pink of complexion, so scant of dress, and so demonstrative of leg; but it was very pleasant, for all that, to see them crowding about Sissy, and very natural in Sissy to be unable to refrain from tears.

"There! Now Thethilia hath kitht all the children, and hugged all the women, and thaken handth all round with all the men, clear, every one of you, and ring in the band for the thecond part!" said Sleary.

As soon as they were gone, he continued in a low tone. "Now, Thethilia, I don't athk to know any thecreth, but I thuppothe I may conthider thith to be Mith Thquire."

"This is his sister. Yes."

"And t'other one'th daughter. That'h what I mean. Hope I thee you well, mith. And I hope the Thquire'th well?"

"My father will be here soon," said Louisa, anxious to bring him to the point. "Is my brother safe?"

"Thafe and thound!" he replied. "I want you jutht to take a peep at the ring, mith, through here. Thethilia, you know the dodgeth; find a thpy-hole for yourthelf."

They each looked through a chink in the boards.

"That'th Jack the Giant Killer—piethe of comic infant bithnith," said Sleary. "There'th a property-houthe, you thee, for Jack to hide in; there'th my Clown with a thauthepan-lid and a thpit for Jack'th thervant; there'th little Jack himself in a thplendid thoot of armor; there'th two comic black thervanth twithe ath big ath the houthe, to thtand by it and bring it in and clear it; and the Giant (a very expenthive bathket one), he an't on yet. Now, do you thee 'em all?"

"Yes," they both said.

"Look at 'em again," said Sleary, "look at 'em well. You thee 'em all? Very good. Now, mith;" he put a form for them to sit on; "I have my opinionth, and the Thquire your father hath hith. I don't want to know what your brother'th been up to; ith better for me not to know. All I thay ith, the Thquire hath thood by Thethilia, and I'll thtand by the Thquire. Your brother ith one o' them black thervanth."

Louisa uttered an exclamation, partly of distress, partly of satisfaction.

"Ith a fact," said Sleary, "and even knowin' that, you couldn't put your finger on him. Let the Thquire come. I shall keep your brother here after the performanth. I thant undreth him, nor yet wath hith paint off. Let the Thquire come here after the performanth, or come here yourthelf after the performanth, and you shall find your brother, and have the whole plathe to talk to him in. Never mind the lookth of him long ath he'th well hid."

Louisa with many thanks and with a lightened load, detained Mr. Sleary no longer then. She left her love for her brother, with her eyes full of tears, and she and Sissy went away until later in the afternoon.

Mr. Gradgrind arrived within an hour afterwards. He too had encountered no one whom he knew, and was now sanguine, with Sleary's assistance, of getting his disgraced son to Liverpool in the night. As neither of the three could be his companion without almost identifying him under any disguise, he prepared a letter to a correspondent whom he could trust, beseeching him to ship the bearer off at any cost, to North or South America, or any distant part of the world to which he could be the most speedily and privately dispatched. This done, they walked about, waiting for the Circus to be quite vacated: not only by the audience, but by the company and by the horses. After watching it a long time, they saw Mr. Sleary bring out a chair and sit down by the side-door, smoking, as if that were his signal that they might approach.

"Your thervant, Thquire," was his cautious salutation as they passed in. "If you want me you'll find me here. You muthn't mind your thon having a comic livery on."

They all three went in, and Mr. Gradgrind sat down, forlorn, on the Clown's performing chair in the middle of the ring. On one of the back benches, remote in the subdued light and the strangeness of the place, sat the villainous whelp, sulky to the last, whom he had the misery to call his son.

In a preposterous coat, like a beadle's, with cuffs and flaps exaggerated to an unspeakable extent; in an immense waistcoat, knee-breeches, buckled shoes, and a mad cocked hat, with nothing fitting him, and everything of coarse material, moth-eaten, and full of holes; with seams in his black face, where fear and heat had started through the greasy composition daubed all over it, any thing so grimly, detestably, ridiculously shameful as the whelp in his comic livery Mr. Gradgrind never could by any other means have believed in, weighable and measureable fact though it was. And one of his model children had come to this!

At first the whelp would not draw any nearer, but persisted in remaining up there by himself. Yielding at length, if any concession so sullenly made can be called yielding, to the entreaties of Sissy—for Louisa he disowned altogether—he came down bench by bench until he stood in the sawdust, on the verge of the circle, as far as possible, within its limits, from where his father sat.

"How was this done?" asked the father.

"How was what done?" moodily answered the son.

"This robbery," said the father, raising his voice upon the word.

"I forced the safe myself overnight, and shut it up ajar before I went away. I had had the key that was found made long before. I dropped it that morning, that it might be supposed to have been used. I didn't take the money all at once. I pretended to put my balance away every night, but I didn't. Now you know all about it."

"If a thunderbolt had fallen on me," said his father, "it would have shocked me less than this."

"I don't see why," grumbled the son. "So many people are employed in situations of trust; so many people out of so many will be dishonest. I have heard you talk, a hundred times, of its being a law. How can *I* help laws? You have comforted others with such things, father. Comfort yourself!"

The father buried his face in his hands, and the son stood in his disgaceful grotesqueness, biting straw. His hands, with the black partly worn away inside, looking like the hands of a monkey. The evening was fast closing in, and from time to time, he turned the whites of his eyes restlessly and impatiently towards his father. They were the only parts of his face that showed any life or expression, the pigment upon it was so thick.

"You must be got to Liverpool, and sent on board."

"I suppose I must. I can't be more miserable any where," whimpered the whelp, "than I have been here, ever since I can remember. That's one thing."

Mr. Gradgrind went to the door, and returned with Sleary, to whom he submitted the question—How to get this deplorable object away.

"Why, I've been thinking of it, Thquire. There'th not much time to lothe, tho you muth thay yeth, or no. Ith over twenty mileth to the rail. There'th a coath in half an hour that goeth *to* the rail, purpothe to cath the mail train. That train will take him right to Liverpool."

"But look at him," groaned Mr. Gradgrind. "Will any coach—"

"I don't mean that he thould go in the comic livery," said Sleary. "Thay the word, and I'll make a Jothkin of him out of the wardrobe in five minutes."

"I don't understand," said Mr. Gradgrind.

"A Jothkin—a Carter. Make up your mind quick, Thquire. There'll be beer to feth. I've never met with nothing but beer ath'll ever clean a comic blackamoor."

Mr. Gradgrind rapidly assented; Mr. Sleary rapidly turned out from a box a smock frock, a felt hat, and other essentials; the whelp rapidly changed clothes behind a screen of baize; Mr. Sleary rapidly brought beer, and washed him white again.

"Now," said Sleary, "come along to the coath, and jump up behind; I'll go with you there, and they'll thuppothe you one of my people. Thay farewell to your family, and tharp'th the word!" With which he delicately retired.

"Here is your letter," said Mr. Gradgrind. "All necessary means will be provided for you. Atone by repentance and better conduct for this shocking act of dishonesty, and the dreadful consequences to which it has led. Give me your hand, my poor boy, and may God forgive you as I do!"

The culprit was moved to a few abject tears by these words, and their pathetic tone. But when Louisa opened her arms, he repulsed her afresh.

"Not you. No. I don't want to have anything to say to you!"

"O Tom, Tom, do we end so, after all my love!"

"After all your love!" he returned, obdurately. "Pretty love! Leaving old Bounderby to himself, and packing my best friend Mr. Harthouse off, and going home just when I was in the greatest danger. Pretty love that! Coming out with every word about our having gone to that place, when you saw the net was gathering round me. Pretty love that! You have regularly given me up. You never cared for me."

"Tharp'th the word!" said Sleary at the door.

They all confusedly went out, Louisa crying to him that she forgave him his ingratitude, and loved him still, and that he would one day be sorry to have left her so, and glad to think of those her last words, far away; when some one ran against them. Mr. Gradgrind and Sissy, who were both before him while his sister yet clung to his shoulder, stopped and recoiled.

For there was Bitzer, out of breath, his thin lips parted, his thin nostrils distended, his white eyelashes quivering, his colorless face more colorless than ever, as if he ran himself into a white heat, when other people ran themselves into a glow. There he stood, panting and heaving, as if he had never stopped since the night, now long ago, when he had run them down before.

"I'm sorry to interfere with your plans," said Bitzer, shaking his head, "but I can't allow myself to be done by horseriders. I must have young Mr. Tom; he mustn't be got away by horseriders; here he is in a smock frock, and I must have him!"

By the collar too, it seemed. For so he took possession of him.

Chapter XXXVI

PHILOSOPHICAL

THEY went back into the booth, Sleary shutting the door to keep intruders out. Bitzer, still holding the paralysed culprit by the collar, stood in the Ring blinking at his old patron through the darkness of the twilight.

"Bitzer," said Mr. Gradgrind, broken down, and miserably submissive to him, "have you a heart?"

"The circulation, sir," returned Bitzer, smiling at the oddity of the question, "couldn't be carried on without one. No man, sir, acquainted with the facts established by Harvey relating to the circulation of the blood, can doubt that I have a heart."

"Is it accessible," cried Mr. Gradgrind, "to any compassionate influence?"

"It is accessible to Reason, sir," returned the excellent young man. "And to nothing else."

They stood looking at each other; Mr. Gradgrind's face as white as the pursuer's.

"What motive—even what motive in Reason—can you have for preventing the escape of this wretched youth," said Mr. Gradgind, "and crushing his miserable father? See his sister here. Pity us!"

"Sir," returned Bitzer, in a very business-like and logical manner, "since you ask me what motive I have in reason, for taking young Mr. Tom back to Coketown, it is only reasonable to let you know. I have suspected young Mr. Tom of this bank robbery from the first. I had had my eye upon him before that time, and I knew his ways. I have kept my observations to myself, but I have made them, and I have got ample proofs against him now, besides his running away, and besides his own confession, which I was just in time to overhear. I had the pleasure of watching your house yesterday morning, and following you here. I am going to take young Mr. Tom back to Coketown, in order to deliver him over to Mr. Bounderby. Sir, I have no doubt whatever that Mr. Bounderby will then promote me to young Mr. Tom's situation. And I wish to have his situation, sir, for it will be a rise to me and will do me good."

"If this is solely a question of self-interest with you—" Mr. Gradgrind began.

"I beg your pardon for interrupting you, sir," returned Bitzer; "but I am sure you know that the whole social system is a question of self-interest. What you must always appeal to, is a person's self-interest. It's your only hold. We are so constituted. I was brought up in that catechism when I was very young, sir, as you are aware."

"What sum of money," said Mr. Gradgrind, "will you set against your expected promotion?"

"Thank you, sir," returned Bitzer, "for hinting at the proposal; but I will not set any sum against it. Knowing that your clear head would propose that alternative, I have gone over the calculations in my mind; and I find that to compound a felony, even on very high terms indeed, would not be as safe and good for me as my improved prospects in the Bank."

"Bitzer," said Mr. Gradgrind, stretching out his hands as though he would have said, See how miserable I am! "Bitzer, I have but one chance left to soften you. You were many years at my school. If, in remembrance of the pains bestowed upon you, you can persuade yourself in any degree to disregard your present interest and release my son, I entreat and pray you to give him the benefit of that remembrance."

"I really wonder, sir," rejoined the old pupil in an argumentative manner, "to find you taking a position so untenable. My schooling was paid for;—it was a bargain; and when I came away the bargain ended."

It was a fundamental principle of the Gradgrind philosophy, that every thing was to be paid for. Nobody was ever on any account to give any body any thing, or render any body help without return. Gratitude was to be abolished, and the virtues springing from it were not to be. The whole existence of mankind, from birth to death, was to be a bargain across a counter. And if we didn't get to Heaven that way it was not a politico-economical place, and we had no business there.

"I don't deny," added Bitzer, "that my schooling was cheap. But that comes right. I was made in the cheapest market, and have to dispose of myself in the dearest."

He was a little troubled here by, Louisa and Sissy crying.

"Pray don't do that," said he, "it's of no use doing that; it only worries. You seem to think that I have some animosity against young Mr. Tom; whereas I have none at all. I am only going, on the reasonable grounds I have mentioned, to take him back to Coketown. If he was to resist, I should set up the cry of Stop Thief! But he won't resist, you may depend upon it."

Mr. Sleary, who, with his mouth open and his rolling eye as immovably jammed in his head as his fixed one, had listened to these doctrines with profound attention, here stepped forward.

"Thquire, you know perfectly well, and your daughter knowth perfectly well (better than you, becauthe I thed it to her) that I didn't know what your thon had done, and that I didn't want to know—that I thed it wath better not, though I only thought it wath thome thylarking. However, thith young man having made it known to be a robbery of a bank, why, that'th a theriouth thing; muth too theriouth a thing for me to compound, ath thith young man hath very properly called it; conthequently, Thquire, you muthn't quarrel with me if I take thith young man'th thide, and thay he'th right and there'th no help for it. But I tell you what I'll do, Thquire; I'll drive your thon and thith young man over to the rail, and prevent expothure here. I can't conthent to do more, but I'll do that."

Fresh lamentations from Louisa, and deeper affliction on Mr. Gradgrind's part followed this desertion of them by their last friend. But Sissy glanced at him with great attention; nor did she in her own breast misunderstand him, as they were all going out again, he favored her with one slight roll of his moveable eye, desiring her to linger behind. As he locked the door, he said excitedly:

"The Thquire thtood by you, Thethilia, and I'll thtand by the Thquire. More than that; thith ith a prethiouth rathcal and belongth to that bluthtering Cove that my people nearly pitht out o' winder. It'll be a dark night; I've got a horthe that'll do anything but thpeak; I've got a pony that'll go fifteen mile an hour with Childerth driving of him; I've got a dog that'll keep a man to one plathe four-and-twenty hourth. Get a word with the young Thquire. Tell him when he theeth our horthe begin to danthe, not to be afraid of being thpilt. but to look out for a pony-gig coming up. Tell him when he theeth that gig clothe by, to jump down, and it'll take him off at a rattling pathe. If my dog leth thith young man thtir a peg or foot, I give him leave to go. And if my horthe ever thtirth from that thpot where he beginth a danthing, till the morning—I don't know him!—Tharp'th the word!"

The word was so sharp that in ten minutes Mr. Childers, sauntering about the market place in a pair of slippers, had his cue, and Mr. Sleary's equipage was ready. It was a fine sight, to behold the learned dog barking round it, and Mr. Sleary instructing him with his one practicable eye, that Bitzer was the object of his particular attentions. Soon after dark they all three got in and started; the learned dog (a formidable creature) already pinning Bitzer with his eye, and sticking close to the wheel on his side, that he might be ready for him in the event of his showing the slightest disposition to alight.

The three sat up at the inn all night in great suspense; at eight o'clock in the morning Mr. Sleary and the dog reappeared: both in high spirits.

"All right, Thquire!" said Mr. Sleary; "your thon may be aboard athip, by thith time. Childerth took him off, an hour and a half after we left here latht night. The horthe danthed the Polka till he wath dead beat (he would have walthed if he hadn't been in harneth), and then I gave him the word and he went to thleep comfortable. Bitther thed he'd go for'ard and the dog hung on to hith neck-hankercher with all four legth in the air and pulled him down and rolled him over. Tho he come back into the drag, and there he that till I got the better of the acthident and turned the horthe'th head, at half patht thixth thith morning."

Mr. Gradgrind overwhelmed him with thanks, of course, and hinted, as delicately as he could, at a handsome remuneration in money.

"Well! I don't want money myself, Thquire; but Childerth ith a family man, and if you wath to like to offer him a five-pound note, it mightn't be unactheptable. Likewithe if you wath to thtand a collar for the dog, or a thet of bellth for the horthe, I thould be very giad to take 'em. Brandy and water I alwayth take." He had already called for a glass, and now called for another. "If you wouldn't think it going too far, Thquire, to make a little thpread for the company at about three and thixth a head, not reckoning Luth, it would make 'em happy."

All these little tokens of his gratitude Mr. Gradgrind very willingly undertook to render. Though he thought them far too sllght, he said, for such a service.

"Very well, Thquire; then, if you'll only give a Horthe-riding a bethpeak, whenever you can, you'll more than balanthe the account. Now, Thquire, if your daughter will ethcuthe me, I thould like one parting word with you."

Louisa and Sissy withdrew into an adjoining room; Mr. Sleary, stirring and drinking his brandy and water as he stood, went on:

"Thquire, you don't need to be told that dodgth ith wonderful animalth."

"Their instinct," said Mr. Gradgrind, "is surprising."

"Whatever you call it—and I'm bletht if I know what to call it," said Sleary, "it ith no doubt athtonithing. The way in whith a dog'll find you—the dithtanthe he'll come!"

"His scent," said Mr. Gradgrind, "being so fine."

"I'm bletht if I know what to call it," repeated Sleary, shaking his head. "But I have had dogth find me, Thquire, in a way that made me think whether that dog hadn't gone to another dog and thed, 'You don't happen to know a perthon of the name of Thleary, do you? Perthon of the name of Thleary, in the Horthe-Riding way—thtout man—game eye?' And whether that dog mightn't have thed, 'Well, I can't thay I know him mythelf, but I know a dog that I think would be likely to be acquainted with him.' And whether that dog mightn't have thought it over, and thed, 'Thleary, Thleary? O yeth, to be thure! A friend of mine lived with him at one time. I can get you hith addreth directly.' In conthequenth of my being afore the public, and going about tho muth, you thee, there mutht be a number of dogth acquainted with me, Thquire, that I don't know."

Mr. Gradgrind seemed to be quite confounded by his speculation.

"Any way," said Sleary, after putting his lips to his brandy and water, "ith fourteen month ago, Thquire, thinthe we wath at Chethter—and very good bithnith we wath doing. We wath getting up our Children in the Wood one morning when there cometh into our Ring, by the thtage door, a dog. He had travelled a long way, he wath in very bad condithon, he wath lame, and pretty well blind. He went round to our children, one after another, as if he wath looking for a child he know'd; and then he come to me, and throwd hithelf up behind, and thood on hith two fore-legth, weak ath he wath, and then he wagged hith tail and died. Thquire, that dog wath Merrylegth."

"Sissy's father's dog!"

"Thethilia'th father'th old dog. Now, Thquire, I can take my oath, from my knowledge of that dog, that that man wath dead—and buried—afore that dog came back to me. Joth'phine and Childerth and me talked it over a long time, whether I should write or not. But we agreed, 'No. There'th nothing comfortable to tell; why, unthettle her mind, and make her unhappy?' Tho, whether her father detherted her, or whether he broke hith own heart alone, rather than pull her down along with him, never will be known, now, Thquire, till—not till we know how the dogth findth uth out."

"She keeps the bottle that he sent her for, to this hour: and she will believe in his affection to the last moment of her life," said Mr. Gradgrind.

"It theemth to prethent two thingth to a perthon, don't it, Thquire?" said Mr. Sleary, musing as he looked down into the depths of his brandy and water: "one, that there ith a love in the world, not all Thelf-interetht after all, but thomething very different; t'other, that it hath a way of ith own of calculating or not calculating, whith thomehow or another ith at leatht ath hard to give a name to, ath the wayth of the dogth ith!"

Mr. Gradgrind looked out of window, and made no reply. Mr. Sleary emptied his glass and recalled the ladies.

"Thethilia, my dear, kith me and good-bye! Mith Thquire, to thee you treating of her like a thithter, and a thithter that you trutht and honor with all your heart and more, ith a very pretty thight to me. I hope your brother may live to be better detherving of you, and a greater comfort to you. Thquire, thake handth firtht and latht! Don't be croth with uth poor vagabonth. People mutht be amuthed. They can't be alwayth a learning, nor yet they can't be alwayth a working; they a'n't made for it. You *mutht* have uth, Thquire. Do the withe thing and the kind thing too, and make the betht of uth; not the wortht!"

"And I never thought before," said Mr. Sleary, putting his head in at the door again to say it, "that I wath tho muth of a Cackler!"

Chapter XXXVII

FINAL

It is a dangerous thing to see anything in the sphere of a vain blusterer, before the vain blusterer sees it himself. Mr. Bounderby felt that Mrs. Sparsit had audaciously anticipated him, and presumed to be wiser than he. Inappeasably indignant with her for her triumphant discovery of Mrs. Pegler, he turned this presumption on the part of a woman in her dependent position over and over in his mind, until it accumulated with turning like a great snowball. At last he made the discovery that to discharge this highly-connected female—to have it in his power to say, "She was a woman of family, and wanted to stick to me, but I wouldn't have it, and got rid of her"—would be to get the utmost possible amount of crowning glory out of the connection, and at the same time to punish Mrs. Sparsit according to her deserts.

Filled fuller than ever, with this great idea, Mr. Bounderby came in to lunch, and sat himself down in the dining-room of former days, where his portrait was. Mrs. Sparsit sat by the fire, with her foot in her cotton stirrup, little thinking whither she was posting.

Since the Pegler affair, this gentlewoman had covered her pity for Mr. Bounderby with a vail of quiet melancholy and contrition. In virtue thereof, it had become her habit to assume a woeful look, which woeful look she now bestowed upon her patron.

"What's the matter with you, ma'am?" said Mr. Bounderby, in a very short rough way.

"Pray, sir," returned Mrs. Sparsit, "do not bite my nose off."

"Bite your nose off, ma'am!" repeated Mr. Bounderby. "*Your* nose." meaning, as Mrs. Sparsit conceived, that it was too developed a nose for the purpose. After which offensive implication he cut himself a crust of bread, and threw the knife down with a noise.

Mrs. Sparsit took her foot out of her stirrup, and said, "Mr. Bounderby, sir!"

"Well, ma'am?" retorted Mr. Bounderby. "What are you staring at?"

"May I ask, sir," said Mrs. Sparsit, "have you been ruffled this morning?"

"Yes, ma'am."

"May I inquire, sir," pursued the injured woman, "whether *I* am the unfortunate cause of your having lost your temper?"

"Now, I'll tell you what, ma'am," said Bounderby, "I am not come here to be bullied. A female may be highly connected, but she can't be permitted to bother and badger a man in my position, and I am not going to put up with it." (Mr. Bounderby felt it necessary to get on, foreseeing that if he allowed of details he would be beaten.)

Mrs. Sparsit, first elevated, then knitted, her Coriolanian eyebrows; gathered up her work into its proper basket, and rose.

"Sir," said she, majestically, "it is apparent to me that I am in your way at present. I will retire to my own apartment."

"Allow me to open the door, ma'am."

"Thank you, sir; I can do it for myself."

"You had better allow me, ma'am," said Bounderby, passing her, and getting his hand upon the lock, "because I can take the opportunity of saying a word to you before you go. Mrs. Sparsit, ma'am, I rather think you are cramped here, do you know? It appears to me that under my humble roof there's hardly opening enough for a lady of your genius in other people's affairs."

Mrs. Sparsit gave him a look of the darkest scorn, and said with great politeness, "Really, sir?"

"I have been thinking it over, you see, since the late affairs have happened, ma'am," said Bounderby, "and it appears to my poor judgement—"

"Oh! Pray sir," Mrs. Sparsit interposed with sprightly cheerfulness, "don't disparage your judgement. Every body knows how unerring Mr. Bounderby's judgement is. Every body has had proofs of it. It must be the theme of general conversation. Disparage any thing in yourself but your judgement, sir," said Mrs. Sparsit, laughing.

Mr. Bounderby, very red and uncomfortable, resumed:

"It appears to me, ma'am, I say, that a different sort of establishment altogether, would bring out a lady of your powers. Such an establishment as your relation, Lady Scadgers's, now. Don't you think you might find some affairs there, ma'am, to interfere with?"

"It never occurred to me before, sir," returned Mrs. Sparsit, in a light, social style of conversation, "but now you mention it, I should think it highly probable."

"Then suppose you try, ma'am," said Bounderby, laying an envelope with a check in it, in her little basket. "You can take your own time for going, ma'am, but perhaps, in the mean while, it will be more agreeable to a lady of your powers of mind, to eat her meals by herself, and not to be intruded upon. I really ought to apologize to you—being only Josiah Bounderby of Coketown—for having stood in your light so long."

"Pray don't name it, sir," returned Mrs. Sparsit. "If that portrait could speak, sir—but it has the advantage over the original of not possessing the power of committing itself and disgusting others—it would testify that a long period has elapsed since I first habitually addressed it as the picture of a Noodle. Nothing that a Noodle does can awaken surprise or indignation: the proceedings of a Noodle can only inspire contempt."

Thus saying, Mrs. Sparsit, with her Roman features like a medal, struck to commemorate her scorn of Mr. Bounderby, surveyed him fixedly from head to foot, swept disdainfully past him, and ascended the staircase. Mr. Bounderby closed the door, and stood before the fire, projecting himself after his old explosive manner into his portrait—and into futurity.

Into how much of futurity? He saw Mrs. Sparsit fighting out a daily fight at the points of all the weapons in the female armory, with the grudging, smarting, peevish, tormenting Lady Scadgers, still laid up in bed with her mysterious leg, and gobbling her insufficient income down by about the middle of every quarter, in a mean little airless lodging, a mere closet for one, a mere crib for two; but did he see more? Did he catch any glimpse of himself making a show of Bitzer to strangers as the rising young man so devoted to his master's great merits, who had now young Tom's place, and had almost captured young Tom himself, in the times when by various rascals he was spirited away? Did he see any faint reflection of his own image making a vain-glorious will, whereby five-and-twenty self-made men past fifty years of age, each taking upon himself the name, Josiah Bounderby of Coketown, should forever dine in Bounderby Hall, forever lodge in Bounderby Buildings, forever attend a Bounderby chapel, forever go to sleep under a Bounderby chaplain, forever be supported out of a Bounderby estate, and forever nauseate all healthy stomachs with a vast amount of Bounderby balderdash and bluster? Had he any prescience of the day, five years to come, when Josiah Bounderby of Coketown was to die of a fit in the Coketown street, and this same precious will was to begin its long career of quibble, plunder, false pretences, meanness, little service and much care? Probably not. Yet the portrait was to see it all out.

Here was Mr. Gradgrind on the same day, and in the same hour, sitting thoughtful in his own room. How much of futurity did *he* see? Did he see himself, a white-haired, decrepit man, bending his hitherto inflexible theories to appointed circumstances: making his facts and figures subservient to Faith, Hope, and Charity, and no longer trying to grind that heavenly trio in his dusty little mills? Did he catch sight of himself therefore much despised by his late political associates? Did he see them, in the era of its being quite settled that the national dustmen have only to do with one another, and owe no duty to an abstraction called a People, "taunting the honorable gentleman" with this and with that, and with what not, five nights a week, until the small hours of the morning? Probably he had that much fore-knowledge, knowing his men.

Here was Louisa on the night of the same day, watching the fire as in days of yore; though with a gentler and a humbler face. How much of the future might arise before *her* vision? Broadsides in the streets signed with her father's name, exonerating the late Stephen Blackpool, weaver, from misplaced suspicion, and publishing the guilt of his own unhappy son, with such extenuation as his years and temptation (he could not bring himself to add, his education) might beseech; were of the Present. So Stephen Blackpool's tombstone, with her father's record of his death, was almost of the Present, for she knew it was to be. These things she could plainly see. But how much of the Future?

A working woman christened Rachael, after a long illness, once again appearing at the ringing of the factory bell, and passing to and fro at the set hours, among the Coketown Hands; a woman of pensive beauty, always dressed in black, but sweet-tempered and serene, and even cheerful; a woman who, of all the people in the place, alone appeared to have compassion on a degraded, drunken wretch of her own sex, who was sometimes seen in the town secretly begging of her, and crying to her; a woman working, ever working, but content to do it, and prefering to do it as her natural lot, until she should be too old to labor any more? Did Louisa see this? Such a thing was to be.

A lonely brother, many thousands of miles away, writing on paper blotted with tears, that her words had too soon come true, and that all the treasures in the world would be cheaply bartered for a sight of her dear face? At length, this brother coming nearer home, with hope of seeing her, and being delayed by illness; and then a letter in a strange hand, saying, he died in hospital, of fever, such a day, and died in penitence and love of you; his last word being your name! Did Louisa see these things? Such things were to be.

Herself again a wife—a mother—lovingly watchful of her children, ever careful that they should have a childhood of the mind no less than a childhood of the body, as knowing it to be even a more beautiful thing, and, any hoarded scrap of the former a blessing and happiness to the wisest? Did Louisa see this? Such a thing was never to be.

But happy Sissy's happy children loving her; all childen loving her; she, grown learned in childish lore; thinking no innocent and pretty fancy ever to be despised; trying hard to know her humbler fellow-creatures, and to beautify their lives of machinery and reality with those imaginative graces and delights, without which the heart of infancy will wither up, the sturdiest physical manhood will be morally stark death, and the plainest national prosperity figures can show will be the Writing on the Wall; she holding this course as part of no fantastic vow, or bond, or brotherhood, or sisterhood, or pledge, or covenant, or fancy dress or fancy fair; but as a duty to be done—did Louisa see these things of herself? These things were to be!

Dear reader! It rests with you and me, whether, in our two fields of action, similar things shall be or not. Let them be! We shall sit with lighter bosoms on the hearth, to see the ashes of our fires turn gray and cold.

THE END.

A Christmas Carol

Stave One

MARLEY'S GHOST

MARLEY was dead: to begin with. There is no doubt whatever about that. The register of his burial was signed by the clergyman, the clerk, the undertaker, and the chief mourner. Scrooge signed it: and Scrooge's name was good upon 'Change, for anything he chose to put his hand to. Old Marley was as dead as a door-nail.

Mind! I don't mean to say that I know, of my own knowledge, what there is particularly dead about a door-nail. I might have been inclined, myself, to regard a coffin-nail as the deadest piece of ironmongery in the trade. But the wisdom of our ancestors is in the simile; and my unhallowed hands shall not disturb it, or the Country's done for. You will therefore permit me to repeat, emphatically, that Marley was as dead as a door-nail.

Scrooge knew he was dead? Of course he did. How could it be otherwise? Scrooge and he were partners for I don't know how many years. Scrooge was his sole executor, his sole administrator, his sole assign, his sole residuary legatee, his sole friend, and sole mourner. And even Scrooge was not so dreadfully cut up by the sad event, but that he was an excellent man of business on the very day of the funeral, and solemnized it with an undoubted bargain.

The mention of Marley's funeral brings me back to the point I started from. There is no doubt that Marley was dead. This must be distinctly understood, or nothing wonderful can come of the story I am going to relate. If we were not perfectly convinced that Hamlet's Father died before the play began, there would be nothing more remarkable in his taking a stroll at night, in an easterly wind, upon his own ramparts, than there would be in any other middle-aged gentleman rashly turning out after dark in a breezy spot—say Saint Paul's Churchyard for instance—literally to astonish his son's weak mind.

Scrooge never painted out Old Marley's name. There it stood, years afterwards, above the warehouse door: Scrooge and Marley. The firm was known as Scrooge and Marley. Sometimes people new to the business called Scrooge Scrooge, and sometimes Marley, but he answered to both names: it was all the same to him.

Oh! But he was a tight-fisted hand at the grindstone, Scrooge! a squeezing, wrenching, grasping, scraping, clutching, covetous old sinner! Hard and sharp as flint, from which no steel had ever struck out generous fire; secret and self-contained, and solitary as an oyster. The cold within him froze his old features, nipped his pointed nose, shrivelled his cheek, stiffened his gait; made his eyes red, his thin lips blue; and spoke out shrewdly in his grating voice. A frosty rime was on his head, and on his eyebrows, and his wiry chin. He carried his own low temperature always about with him; he iced his office in the dog-days; and didn't thaw it one degree at Christmas.

External heat and cold had little influence on Scrooge. No warmth could warm, nor wintry weather chill him. No wind that blew was bitterer than he, no falling snow was more intent upon its purpose, no pelting rain less open to entreaty. Foul weather didn't know where to have him. The heaviest rain, and snow, and hail, and sleet, could boast of the advantage over him in only one respect. They often "came down" handsomely and Scrooge never did.

Nobody ever stopped him in the street to say, with gladsome looks, "My dear Scrooge, how are you? when will you come to see me?" No beggars implored him to bestow a trifle, no children asked him what it was o'clock, no man or woman ever once in all his life inquired the way to such and such a place, of Scrooge. Even the blindmen's dogs appeared to know him; and when they saw him coming on, would tug their owners into doorways and up courts; and then would wag their tails as though they said, "no eye at all is better than an evil eye, dark master!"

But what did Scrooge care? It was the very thing he liked. To edge his way along the crowded paths of life, warning all human sympathy to keep its distance, was what the knowing ones call "nuts" to Scrooge.

Once upon a time—of all the good days in the year, on Christmas Eve—old Scrooge sat busy in his counting-house. It was cold, bleak, biting weather: foggy withal: and he could hear the people in the court outside go wheezing up and down, beating their hands upon their breasts, and stamping their feet upon the pavement-stones to warm them. The city clocks had only just gone three, but it was quite dark already: it had not been light all day: and candles were flaring in the windows of the neighboring offices, like ruddy smears upon the palpable brown air. The fog came pouring in at every chink and keyhole, and was so dense without, that although the court was of the narrowest, the houses opposite were mere phantoms. To see the dingy cloud come drooping down, obscuring everything, one might have thought that Nature lived hard by, and was brewing on a large scale.

The door of Scrooge's counting-house was open that he might keep his eye upon his clerk who in a dismal little cell beyond a sort of tank, was copying letters. Scrooge had a very small fire, but the clerk's fire was so very much smaller, that it looked like one coal. But he couldn't replenish it, for Scrooge kept the coal-box in his own room; and so surely as the clerk came in with the shovel, the master predicted that it would be necessary for them to part. Wherefore the clerk put on his white comforter, and tried to warm himself at the candle; in which effort, not being a man of a strong imagination, he failed.

"A merry Christmas, uncle! God save you!" cried a cheerful voice. It was the voice of Scrooge's nephew, who came upon him so quickly, that this was the first intimation he had of his approach.

"Bah!" said Scrooge, "Humbug!"

He had so heated himself with rapid walking in the fog and frost, this nephew of Scrooge's, that he was all in a glow; his face was ruddy and handsome; his eyes sparkled, and his breath smoked again.

"Christmas a humbug, uncle!" said Scrooge's nephew. "You don't mean that, I am sure."

"I do," said Scrooge. "Merry Christmas! what right have you to be merry? what reason have you to be merry? You're poor enough."

"Come then," returned the nephew gaily. "What right have you to be dismal? what reason have you to be morose? You're rich enough."

Scrooge having no better answer ready on the spur of the moment, said "Bah!" again; and followed it up with "Humbug."

"Don't be cross, uncle," said the nephew.

"What else can I be," returned the uncle, "when I live in such a world of fools as this? Merry Christmas! Out upon merry Christmas! What's Christmas time to you but a time for paying bills without money; a time for finding yourself a year older, and not an hour richer; a time for balancing your books, and having every item in 'em through a round dozen of months presented dead against you? If I could work my will," said Scrooge indignantly, "every idiot who goes about with 'Merry Christmas' on his lips, should be boiled with his own pudding, and buried with a stake of holly through his heart. He should!"

"Uncle!" repeated the nephew.

"Nephew!" returned the uncle, sternly, "keep Christmas in your own way, and let me keep it in mine."

"Keep it!" repeated Scrooge's nephew. "But you don't keep it."

"Let me leave it alone, then," said Scrooge. "Much good may it do you! Much good it has ever done you!"

"There are many things from which I might have derived good, by which I have not profited, I dare say," returned the nephew: "Christmas among the rest. But I am sure I have always thought of Christmas time, when it has come round—apart from the veneration due to its sacred name and origin, if anything belonging to it can be apart from that—as a good time: a kind, forgiving, charitable, pleasant time; the only time I know of, in the long calendar of the year, when men and women seem by one consent to open their shut-up hearts freely, and to think of people below them as if they really were fellow-passengers to the grave, and not another race of creatures bound on other journeys. And therefore, uncle, though it has never put a scrap of gold or silver in my pocket, I believe that it *has* done me good, and *will* do me good; and I say, God bless it!"

The clerk in the tank involuntarily applauded: becoming immediately sensible of the impropriety, he poked the fire, and extinguished the last frail spark for ever.

"Let me hear another sound from *you*," said Scrooge, "and you'll keep your Christmas by losing your situation. You're quite a powerful speaker, sir," he added, turning to his nephew. "I wonder you don't go into Parliament."

"Don't be angry, uncle. Come! Dine with us to-morrow."

Scrooge said that he would see him—yes, indeed, he did. He went the whole length of the expression, and said that he would see him in that extremity first.

"But why?" cried Scrooge's nephew. "Why?"

"Why did you get married?" said Scrooge.

"Because I fell in love."

"Because you fell in love!" growled Scrooge, as if that were the only one thing in the world more ridiculous than a merry Christmas. "Good afternoon."

"Nay, uncle, but you never came to see me before that happened. Why give it as a reason for not coming now?"

"Good afternoon!" said Scrooge.

"I want nothing from you; I ask nothing of you; why cannot we be friends?"

"Good afternoon!" said Scrooge.

"I am sorry with all my heart to find you so resolute. We have never had a quarrel to which I have been a party. But I have made the trial in homage to Christmas, and I'll keep my Christmas humor to the last. So A Merry Christmas, uncle!"

"Good afternoon!" said Scrooge.

"And A Happy New Year!"

"Good afternoon!" said Scrooge.

His nephew left the room without an angry word, notwithstanding. He stopped at the outer door to bestow the greetings of the season on the clerk, who, cold as he was, was warmer than Scrooge; for he returned them cordially.

"There's another fellow," muttered Scrooge, who overheard him: "my clerk, with fifteen shillings a-week, and a wife and family, talking about a merry Christmas. I'll retire to Bedlam."

This lunatic, in letting Scrooge's nephew out, had let two other people in. They were portly gentlemen, pleasant to behold, and now stood, with their hats off, in Scrooge's office. They had books and papers in their hands, and bowed to him.

"Scrooge and Marley's, I believe," said one of the gentlemen, referring to his list. "Have I the pleasure of addressing Mr. Scrooge, or Mr. Marley?"

"Mr. Marley has been dead these seven years," Scrooge replied. "He died seven years ago this very night."

"We have no doubt his liberality is well represented by his surviving partner," said the gentleman, presenting his credentials.

It certainly was; for they had been two kindred spirits. At the ominous word "liberality," Scrooge frowned, and shook his head, and handed the credentials back.

"At this festive season of the year, Mr. Scrooge," said the gentleman, taking up a pen, "it is more than usually desirable that we should make some slight provision for the poor and destitute, who suffer greatly at the present time. Many thousands are in want of common necessaries; hundreds of thousands are in want of common comforts, sir."

"Are there no prisons?" asked Scrooge.

"Plenty of prisons," said the gentleman, laying down the pen again.

"And the Union workhouses!" demanded Scrooge. "Are they still in operation?"

"They are. Still," returned the gentleman, "I wish I could say they were not."

"The Treadmill and the Poor Law are in full vigor, then!" said Scrooge.

"Both very busy, sir."

"Oh! I was afraid, from what you said at first, that something had occurred to stop them in their useful course," said Scrooge. "I'm very glad to hear it."

"Under the impression that they scarcely furnish Christian cheer of mind or body to the multitude," returned the gentleman, "a few of us are endeavoring to raise a fund to buy the Poor some meat and drink, and means of warmth. We choose this time, because it is a time, of all others, when Want is keenly felt, and Abundance rejoices. What shall I put you down for?"

"Nothing!" Scrooge replied.

"You wish to be anonymous!"

"I wish to be left alone," said Scrooge. "Since you ask me what I wish, gentlemen, that is my answer. I don't make merry myself at Christmas, and I can't afford to make idle people merry. I help to support the establishments I have mentioned: they cost enough: and those who are badly off must go there."

"Many can't go there; and many would rather die."

"If they would rather die," said Scrooge, "they had better do it, and decrease the surplus population. Besides—excuse me—I don't know that."

"But you might know it," observed the gentleman.

"It's not my business," Scrooge returned. "It's enough for a man to understand his own business, and not to interfere with other people's. Mine occupies me constantly. Good afternoon, gentlemen!"

Seeing clearly that it would be useless to pursue their point, the gentlemen withdrew. Scrooge resumed his labors with an improved opinion of himself, and in a more facetious temper than was usual with him.

Meanwhile the fog and darkness thickened so, that people ran about with flaring links, proffering their services to go before horses in carriages, and conduct them on their way. The ancient tower of a church, whose gruff old bell as always peeping slily down at Scrooge out of a Gothic window in the wall, became invisible, and struck the hours and quarters in the clouds, with tremulous vibrations afterwards, as if its teeth were chattering in its frozen head up there. The cold became intense. In the main street, at the corner of the court, some laborers were repairing the gas-pipes, and had lighted a great fire in a brazier round which a party of ragged men and boys were gathered, warming their hands and winking their eyes before the blaze in rapture. The water-plug being left in solitude, its overflowings sullenly congealed, and turned to misanthropic ice. The brightness of the shops, where holly sprigs and berries crackled in the lamp-heat of the windows, made pale faces ruddy as they passed. Poulterers' and grocers' trades became a splendid joke: a glorious pageant, with which it was next to impossible to believe that such dull principles as bargain and sale had anything to do. The Lord Mayor, in the stronghold of the mighty Mansion House, gave orders to his fifty cooks and butlers to keep Christmas as a Lord Mayor's household should; and even the little tailor, whom he had fined five shillings on the previous Monday for being drunk and blood-thirsty in the streets, stirred up to-morrow's pudding in his garret, while his lean wife and the baby sallied out to buy the beef.

Foggier yet and colder! Piercing, searching, biting cold. If the good Saint Dunstan had but nipped the Evil Spirit's nose with a touch of such weather as that, instead of using his familiar weapons, then indeed he would have roared to lusty purpose. The owner of one scant young nose, gnawed and mumbled by the hungry cold as bones are gnawed by dogs, stooped down at Scrooge's keyhole to regale him with a Christmas carol: but at the first sound of—

> "God bless you, merry gentleman!
> May nothing you dismay!"

Scrooge seized the ruler with such energy of action, that the singer fled in terror, leaving the keyhole to the fog and even more congenial frost.

At length the hour of shutting up the counting-house arrived. With an ill-will Scrooge dismounted from his stool, and tacitly admitted the fact to the expectant clerk in the Tank, who instantly snuffed his candle out, and put on his hat.

"You'll want all day to-morrow, I suppose?" said Scrooge.

"If quite convenient, sir."

"It's not convenient," said Scrooge, "and it's not fair. If I was to stop half-a-crown for it, you'd think yourself ill-used, I'll be bound?"

The clerk smiled faintly.

"And yet," said Scrooge, "you don't think *me* ill-used, when I pay a day's wages for no work."

The clerk observed that it was only once a year.

"A poor excuse for picking a man's pocket every twenty-fifth of December!" said Scrooge, buttoning his great-coat to the chin. "But I suppose you must have the whole day. Be here all the earlier next morning."

The clerk promised that he would; and Scrooge walked out with a growl. The office was closed in a twinkling, and the clerk, with the long ends of his white comforter dangling below his waist (for he boasted no great-coat), went down a slide on Cornhill, at the end of a lane of boys, twenty times in honor of its being Christmas-eve, and then ran home to Camden Town as hard as he could pelt, to play at blindman's-buff.

Scrooge took his melancholy dinner in his usual melancholy tavern; and having read all the newspapers, and beguiled the rest of the evening with his banker's-book, went home to bed. He lived in chambers which had once belonged to his deceased partner. They were a gloomy suite of rooms, in a lowering pile of building up a yard, where it had so little business to be, that one could scarcely help fancying it must have run there when it was a young house, playing at hide-and-seek with other houses, and have forgotten the way out again. It was old enough now, and dreary enough, for nobody lived in it but Scrooge, the other rooms being all let out as offices. The yard was so dark that even Scrooge, who knew its every stone, was fain to grope with his hands. The fog and frost so hung about the black old gateway of the house, that it seemed as if the Genius of the Weather sat in mournful meditation on the threshold.

Now, it is a fact, that there was nothing at all particular about the knocker on the door, except that it was very large. It is also a fact, that Scrooge had seen it night and morning during his whole residence in that place; also that Scrooge had as little of what is called fancy about him as any man in the City of London, even including—which is a bold word—the corporation, aldermen, and livery. Let it also be borne in mind that Scrooge had not bestowed one thought on Marley, since his last mention of his seven-years' dead partner that afternoon. And then let any man explain to me, if he can, how it happened that Scrooge, having his key in the lock of the door, saw in the knocker, without its undergoing any intermediate process of change: not a knocker, but Marley's face.

Marley's face. It was not in impenetrable shadow as the other objects in the yard were, but had a dismal light about it, like a bad lobster in a dark cellar. It was not angry or ferocious, but looked at Scrooge as Marley used to look: with ghostly spectacles turned up on its ghostly forehead. The hair was curiously stirred, as if by breath or hot-air; and though the eyes were wide open, they were perfectly motionless. That and its livid color made it horrible; but its horror seemed to be in spite of the face and beyond its control, rather than a part of its own expression.

As Scrooge looked fixedly at this phenomenon, it was a knocker again.

To say that he was not startled, or that his blood was not conscious of a terrible sensation to which it had been a stranger from infancy, would be untrue. But he put his hand upon the key he had relinquished, turned it sturdily, walked in, and lighted his candle.

He *did* pause, with a moment's irresolution, before he shut the door; and he *did* look cautiously behind at first, as if he half-expected to be terrified with the sight of Marley's pigtail sticking out into the hall. But there was nothing on the back of the door, except the screws and nuts that held the knocker on; so he said, "Pooh, pooh!" and closed it with a bang.

The sound resounded through the house like thunder. Every room above, and every cask in the wine merchant's cellars below, appeared to have a separate peal of echoes of its own. Scrooge was not a man to be frightened by echoes. He fastened the door, and walked across the hall and up the stairs: slowly too: trimming his candle as he went.

You may talk vaguely about driving a coach-and-six up a good old flight of stairs, or through a bad young Act of Parliament; but I mean to say you might have got a hearse up that staircase, and taken it broadwise, with the splinter-bar towards the wall, and the door towards the balustrades: and done it easy. There was plenty of width for that, and room to spare, which is perhaps the reason why Scrooge thought he saw a locomotive hearse going on before him in the gloom. Half a dozen gas-lamps out of the street wouldn't have lighted the entry too well, so you may suppose that it was pretty dark with Scrooge's dip.

Up Scrooge went, not caring a button for that: darkness is cheap, and Scrooge liked it. But before he shut his heavy door, he walked through his rooms to see that all was right. He had just enough recollection of the face to desire to do that.

Sitting-room, bed-room, lumber-room. All as they should be. Nobody under the table, nobody under the sofa; a small fire in the grate; spoon and basin ready; and the little saucepan of gruel (Scrooge had a cold in his head) upon the hob. Nobody under the bed: nobody in the closet; nobody in his dressing-gown, which was hanging up in a suspicious attitude against the wall. Lumber-room as usual. Old fire-guard, old shoes, two fish-baskets, washing-stand on three legs, and a poker.

Quite satisfied, he closed his door, and locked himself in; double-locked himself in, which was not his custom. Thus secured against surprise, he took off his cravat, put on his dressing-gown and slippers, and his night-cap, and sat down before the fire to take his gruel.

It was a very low fire indeed; nothing on such a bitter night. He was obliged to sit close to it, and brood over it, before he could extract the least sensation of warmth from such a handful of fuel. The fire-place was an old one, built by some Dutch merchant long ago, and paved all round with quaint Dutch tiles, designed to illustrate the Scriptures. There were Cains and Abels; Pharaoh's daughters, Queens of Sheba, Angelic messengers descending through the air on clouds like feather-beds, Abrahams, Belshazzars, Apostles putting off to sea in butter-boats, hundreds of figures to attract his thoughts; and yet that face of Marley, seven years dead, came like the ancient Prophet's rod, and swallowed up the whole. If each smooth tile had been a blank at first, with power to shape some picture on its surface from the disjointed fragments of his thoughts, there would have been a copy of old Marley's head on every one.

"Humbug!" said Scrooge, and walked across the room.

After several turns, he sat down again. As he threw his head back in the chair, his glance happened to rest upon a bell, a disused bell, that hung in the room, and communicated for some purpose now forgotten with a chamber in the highest story of the building. It was with great astonishment, and with a strange, inexplicable dread, that as he looked he saw this bell begin to swing. It swung so softly in the outset that it scarcely made a sound; but soon it rang out loudly, and so did every bell in the house.

This might have lasted half a minute, or a minute, but it seemed an hour. The bells ceased as they had begun, together. They were succeeded by a clanking noise, deep down below, as if some person were dragging a heavy chain over the casks in the wine-merchant's cellar. Scrooge then remembered to have heard that ghosts in haunted houses were described as dragging chains.

The cellar-door flew open with a booming sound, and then he heard the noise much louder, on the floors below; then coming up the stairs; then coming straight towards his door.

"It's humbug still!" said Scrooge. "I won't believe it."

His color changed though, when, without a pause, it came on through the heavy door, and passed into the room before his eyes. Upon its coming in, the dying flame leaped up, as though it cried, "I know him! Marley's Ghost!" and fell again.

The same face; the very same. Marley in his pig-tail, usual waistcoat, tights and boots; the tassels on the latter bristling, like his pig-tail, and his coat-skirts, and the hair upon his head. The chain he drew was clasped about his middle. It was long, and wound about him like a tail; and it was made (for Scrooge observed it closely) of cash-boxes, keys, padlocks, ledgers, deeds, and heavy purses wrought in steel. His body was transparent: so that Scrooge, observing him, and looking through his waistcoat, could see the two buttons on his coat behind.

Scrooge had often heard it said that Marley had no bowels, but he had never believed it until now.

No, nor did he believe it even now. Though he looked the phantom through and through, and saw it standing before him; though he felt the chilling influence of its death-cold eyes; and marked the very texture of the folded kerchief bound about its head and chin, which wrapper he had not observed before; he was still incredulous, and fought against his senses.

"How now!" said Scrooge, caustic and cold as ever. "What do you want with me?"

"Much!"—Marley's voice, no doubt about it.

"Who are you?"

"Ask me who I *was*."

"Who *were* you then?" said Scrooge, raising his voice. "You're particular—for a shade." He was going to say "*to* a shade," but substituted this, as more appropriate.

"In life I was your partner, Jacob Marley."

"Can you—can you sit down?" asked Scrooge, looking doubtfully at him.

"I can."

"Do it, then."

Scrooge asked the question, because he didn't know whether a ghost so transparent might find himself in a condition to take a chair; and felt that in the event of its being impossible, it might involve the necessity of an embarrassing explanation. But the ghost sat down on the opposite side of the fireplace, as if he were quite used to it.

"You don't believe in me," observed the Ghost.

"I don't," said Scrooge.

"What evidence would you have of my reality, beyond that of your senses?"

"I don't know," said Scrooge.

"Why do you doubt your senses?"

"Because," said Scrooge, "a little thing affects them. A slight disorder of the stomach makes them cheats. You may be an undigested bit of beef, a blot of mustard, a crumb of cheese, a fragment of an underdone potato. There's more of gravy than of grave about you, whatever you are!"

Scrooge was not much in the habit of cracking jokes, nor did he feel, in his heart, by any means waggish then. The truth is, that he tried to be smart, as a means of distracting his own attention, and keeping down his terror; for the spectre's voice disturbed the very marrow in his bones.

To sit, staring at those fixed, glazed eyes, in silence for a moment, would play, Scrooge felt, the very deuce with him. There was something very awful, too, in the spectre's being provided with an infernal atmosphere of its own. Scrooge could not feel it himself, but this was clearly the case; for though the Ghost sat perfectly motionless, its hair, and skirts, and tassels, were still agitated as by the hot vapor from an oven.

"You see this toothpick?" said Scrooge, returning quickly to the charge, for the reason just assigned; and wishing, though it were only for a second, to divert the vision's stony gaze from himself.

"I do," replied the Ghost.

"You are not looking at it," said Scrooge.

"But I see it," said the Ghost, "notwithstanding."

"Well!" returned Scrooge. "I have but to swallow this, and be for the rest of my days persecuted by a legion of goblins, all of my own creation. Humbug, I tell you—humbug!"

At this the spirit raised a frightful cry, and shook its chain with such a dismal and appalling noise, that Scrooge held on tight to his chair, to save himself from falling in a swoon. But how much greater was his horror, when the phantom taking off the bandage round its head, as if it were too warm to wear in-doors, its lower jaw dropped down upon its breast!

Scrooge fell upon his knees, and clasped his hands before his face.

"Mercy!" he said. "Dreadful apparition, why do you trouble me?"

"Man of the worldly mind!" replied the Ghost, "do you believe in me or not?"

"I do," said Scrooge. "I must. But why do spirits walk the earth, and why do they come to me?"

"It is required of every man," the Ghost returned, "that the spirit within him should walk abroad among his fellow-men, and travel far and wide; and if that spirit goes not forth in life, it is condemned to do so after death. It is doomed to wander through the world—oh, woe is me! and witness what it cannot share, but might have shared on earth, and turned to happiness!"

Again the spectre raised a cry, and shook its chain; and wrung its shadowy hands.

"You are fettered," said Scrooge, trembling. "Tell me why?"

"I wear the chain I forged in life," replied the Ghost. "I made it, link by link, and yard by yard; I girded it on of my own free will, and of my own free will I wore it. Is its pattern strange to *you?*"

Scrooge trembled more and more.

"Or would you know," pursued the Ghost, "the weight and length of the strong coil you bear yourself? It was full as heavy and as long as this, seven Christmas Eves ago. You have labored on it, since. It's a ponderous chain!"

Scrooge glanced about him on the floor, in the expectation of finding himself surrounded by some fifty or sixty fathoms of iron cable; but he could see nothing.

"Jacob," he said, imploringly. "Old Jacob Marley, tell me more. Speak comfort to me, Jacob."

"I have none to give," the Ghost replied. "It comes from other regions, Ebenezer Scrooge, and is conveyed by other ministers to other kinds of men. Nor can I tell you what I would. A very little more is all permitted to me. I cannot rest, I cannot stay, I cannot linger anywhere. My spirit never walked beyond our counting-house—mark me! in life my spirit never roved beyond the narrow limits of our money-changing hole; and weary journeys lie before me!"

It was a habit with Scrooge, whenever he became thoughtful, to put his hands in his breeches pockets. Pondering on what the Ghost had said, he did so now, but without lifting up his eyes, or getting off his knees.

"You must have been very slow about it, Jacob," Scrooge observed, in a business-like manner, though with humility and deference.

"Slow!" the Ghost repeated.

"Seven years dead," mused Scrooge. "And travelling all the time?"

"The whole time," said the Ghost. "No rest, no peace. Incessant torture of remorse."

"You travel fast?" said Scrooge.

"On the wings of the wind," replied the Ghost.

"You might have got over a great quantity of ground in seven years," said Scrooge.

The Ghost, on hearing this, set up another cry, and clanked its chain so hideously in the dead silence of the night, that the Ward would have been justified in indicting it for a nuisance.

"Oh! captive, bound, and double-ironed," cried the phantom, "not to know, that ages of incessant labor by immortal creatures, for this earth, must pass into eternity before the good of which it is susceptible is all developed. Not to know that any Christian spirit working kindly in its little sphere, whatever it may be, will find its mortal life too short for its vast means of usefulness. Not to know that no space of regret can make amends for one life's opportunities misused! Yet such was I! Oh! such was I!"

"But you were always a good man of business, Jacob," faltered Scrooge, who now began to apply this to himself.

"Business!" cried the Ghost, wringing its hands again. "Mankind was my business. The common welfare was my business; charity, mercy, forbearance, and benevolence were all my business. The dealings of my trade were but a drop of water in the comprehensive ocean of my business!"

It held up its chain at arm's length, as if that were the cause of all its unavailing grief, and flung it heavily upon the ground again.

"At this time of the rolling year," the spectre said, "I suffer most. Why did I walk through crowds of fellow-beings with my eyes turned down, and never raise them to that blessed Star which led the Wise Men to a poor abode? Were there no poor homes to which its light would have conducted *me!*"

Scrooge was very much dismayed to hear the spectre going on at this rate, and began to quake exceedingly.

"Hear me!" cried the Ghost. "My time is nearly gone."

"I will," said Scrooge. "But don't be hard upon me! Don't be flowery, Jacob! Pray!"

"How it is that I appear before you in a shape that you can see, I may not tell. I have sat invisible beside you many and many a day."

It was not an agreeable idea. Scrooge shivered, and wiped the perspiration from his brow.

"That is no light part of my penance," pursued the Ghost. "I am here to-night to warn you, that you may have yet a chance and hope of escaping my fate. A chance and hope of my procuring, Ebenezer."

"You were always a good friend to me," said Scrooge. "Thank'ee!"

"You will be haunted," resumed the Ghost, "by Three Spirits."

Scrooge's countenance fell almost as low as the Ghost's had done.

"Is that the chance and hope you mentioned, Jacob?" he demanded, in a faltering voice.

"It is."

"I—I think I'd rather not," said Scrooge.

"Without their visits," said the Ghost, "you cannot hope to shun the path I tread. Expect the first to-morrow, when the bell tolls one."

"Couldn't I take 'em all at once, and have it over, Jacob?" hinted Scrooge.

"Expect the second on the next night at the same hour. The third upon the next night, when the last stroke of twelve has ceased to vibrate. Look to see me no more; and look that, for your own sake, you remember what has passed between us!"

When it had said these words, the spectre took its wrapper from the table, and bound it round its head, as before. Scrooge knew this, by the smart sound its teeth made, when the jaws were brought together by the bandage. He ventured to raise his eyes again, and found his supernatural visitor confronting him in an erect attitude, with its chain wound over and about its arm.

The apparition walked backward from him; and at every step it took, the window raised itself a little, so that when the spectre reached it, it was wide open. It beckoned Scrooge to approach, which he did. When they were within two paces of each other, Marley's Ghost held up its hand, warning him to come no nearer. Scrooge stopped.

Not so much in obedience as in surprise and fear: for, on the raising of the hand, he became sensible of confused noises in the air; incoherent sounds of lamentation and regret; wailings inexpressibly sorrowful and self-accusatory. The spectre, after listening for a moment, joined in the mournful dirge; and floated out upon the bleak, dark night.

Scrooge followed to the window: desperate in his curiosity. He looked out.

The air was filled with phantoms, wandering hither and thither in restless haste, and moaning as they went. Every one of them wore chains like Marley's Ghost; some few (they might be guilty governments) were linked together; none were free. Many had been personally known to Scrooge in their lives. He had been quite familiar with one old ghost in a white waistcoat, with a monstrous iron safe attached to its ankle, who cried piteously at being unable to assist a wretched woman with an infant, whom it saw below, upon a door-step. The misery with them all was, clearly, that they sought to interfere, for good, in human matters, and had lost the power for ever.

Whether these creatures faded into mist, or mist enshrouded them, he could not tell. But they and their spirit voices faded together; and the night became as it had been when he walked home.

Scrooge closed the window, and examined the door by which the Ghost had entered. It was double-locked, as he had locked it with his own hands, and the bolts were undisturbed. He tried to say "Humbug!" but stopped at the first syllable. And being, from the emotion he had undergone, or the fatigues of the day, or his glimpse of the Invisible World, or the dull conversation of the Ghost, or the lateness of the hour, much in need of repose, went straight to bed, without undressing, and fell asleep upon the instant.

Stave Two

THE FIRST OF THE THREE SPIRITS

WHEN Scrooge awoke, it was so dark, that looking out of bed, he could scarcely distinguish the transparent window from the opaque walls of his chamber. He was endeavoring to pierce the darkness with his ferret eyes, when the chimes of a neighboring church struck the four quarters. So he listened for the hour.

To his great astonishment the heavy bell went on from six to seven, and from seven to eight, and regularly up to twelve; then stopped. Twelve! It was past two when he went to bed. The clock was wrong. An icicle must have got into the works. Twelve!

He touched the spring of his repeater, to correct this most preposterous clock. Its rapid little pulse beat twelve; and stopped.

"Why, it isn't possible," said Scrooge, "that I can have slept through a whole day and far into another night! It isn't possible that anything has happened to the sun, and this is twelve at noon!"

The idea being an alarming one, he scrambled out of bed, and groped his way to the window. He was obliged to rub the frost off with the sleeve of his dressing-gown before he could see anything; and could see very little then. All he could make out was, that it was still very foggy and extremely cold, and that there was no noise of people running to and fro, and making a great stir, as there unquestionably would have been if night had beaten off bright day, and taken possession of the world. This was a great relief, because "three days after sight of this First of Exchange pay to Mr. Ebenezer Scrooge or his order," and so forth, would have become a mere United States' security if there were no days to count by.

Scrooge went to bed again, and thought, and thought, and thought it over and over, and could make nothing of it. The more he thought, the more perplexed he was; and the more he endeavored not to think, the more he thought. Marley's Ghost bothered him exceedingly. Every time he resolved within himself, after mature inquiry, that it was all a dream, his mind flew back again, like a strong spring released, to its first position, and presented the same problem to be worked all through, "Was it a dream or not?"

Scrooge lay in this state until the chime had gone three quarters more, when he remembered, on a sudden, that the Ghost had warned him of a visitation when the bell tolled one. He resolved to lie awake until the hour was passed; and, considering that he could no more go to sleep than go to Heaven, this was perhaps the wisest resolution in his power.

The quarter was so long, that he was more than once convinced he must have sunk into a doze unconsciously, and missed the clock. At length it broke upon his listening ear.

"Ding, dong!"

"A quarter past," said Scrooge, counting.

"Ding, dong!"

"Half past," said Scrooge.

"Ding, dong!"

"A quarter to it," said Scrooge.

"Ding, dong!"

"The hour itself," said Scrooge, triumphantly, "and nothing else!"

He spoke before the hour bell sounded, which it now did with a deep, dull, hollow, melancholy ONE. Light flashed up in the room upon the instant and the curtains of his bed were drawn.

The curtains of his bed were drawn aside, I tell you, by a hand. Not the curtains at his feet, nor the curtains at his back, but those to which his face was addressed. The curtains of his bed were drawn aside; and Scrooge, starting up into a half-recumbent attitude, found himself face to face with the unearthly visitor who drew them: as close to it as I am now to you, and I am standing in the spirit at your elbow.

It was a strange figure—like a child: yet not so like a child as like an old man, viewed through some supernatural medium, which gave him the appearance of having receded from the view, and being diminished to a child's proportions. Its hair, which hung about its neck and down its back, was white as if with age; and yet the face had not a wrinkle in it, and the tenderest bloom was on the skin. The arms were very long and muscular; the hands the same, as if its hold were of uncommon strength. Its legs and feet, most delicately formed, were, like those upper members, bare. It wore a tunic of the purest white; and round its waist was bound a lustrous belt, the sheen of which was beautiful. It held a branch of fresh green holly in its hand; and, in singular contradiction of that wintry emblem, had its dress trimmed with summer flowers. But the strangest thing about it was, that from the crown of its head there sprung a bright clear jet of light, by which all this was visible; and which was doubtless the occasion of its using, in its duller moments, a great extinguisher for a cap, which it now held under its arm.

Even this, though, when Scrooge looked at it with increasing steadiness, was *not* its strangest quality. For as its belt sparkled and glittered now in one part and now in another, and what was light one instant, at another time was dark, so the figure itself fluctuated in its distinctness: being now a thing with one arm, now with one leg, now with twenty legs, now a pair of legs without a head, now a head without a body: of which dissolving parts, no outline could be visible in the dense gloom wherein they melted away. And in the very wonder of this, it would be itself again; distinct and clear as ever.

"Are you the Spirit, sir, whose coming was foretold to me?" asked Scrooge.

"I am!"

The voice was soft and gentle. Singularly low, as if instead of being so close beside him, it were at a distance.

"Who, and what are you?" Scrooge demanded.

"I am the Ghost of Christmas Past."

"Long past?" inquired Scrooge: observant of its dwarfish stature.

"No. Your past."

Perhaps, Scrooge could not have told anybody why, if anybody could have asked him; but he had a special desire to see the Spirit in his cap; and begged him to be covered.

"What!" exclaimed the Ghost, "would you so soon put out, with worldly hands, the light I give? Is it not enough that you are one of those whose passions made this cap, and force me through whole trains of years to wear it low upon my brow!"

Scrooge reverently disclaimed all intention to offend, or any knowledge of having wilfully "bonneted" the Spirit at any period of his life. He then made bold to inquire what business brought him there.

"Your welfare!" said the Ghost.

Scrooge expressed himself much obliged, but could not help thinking that a night of unbroken rest would have been more conducive to that end. The Spirit must have heard him thinking, for it said immediately:

"Your reclamation, then. Take heed!"

It put out its strong hand as it spoke, and clasped him gently by the arm.

"Rise! and walk with me!"

It would have been in vain for Scrooge to plead that the weather and the hour were not adapted to pedestrian purposes; that bed was warm, and the thermometer a long way below freezing; that he was clad but lightly in his slippers, dressing-gown, and nightcap; and that he had a cold upon him at that time. The grasp, though gentle as a woman's hand, was not to be resisted. He rose: but finding that the Spirit made towards the window, clasped its robe in supplication.

"I am a mortal," Scrooge remonstrated, "and liable to fall."

"Bear but a touch of my hand *there,*" said the Spirit, laying it upon his heart, "and you shall be upheld in more than this!"

As the words were spoken, they passed through the wall, and stood upon an open country road, with fields on either hand. The city had entirely vanished. Not a vestige of it was to be seen. The darkness and the mist had vanished with it, for it was a clear, cold, winter day, with snow upon the ground.

"Good Heaven!" said Scrooge, clasping his hands together, as he looked about him. "I was bred in this place. I was a boy here!"

The Spirit gazed upon him mildly. Its gentle touch, though it had been light and instantaneous, appeared still present to the old man's sense of feeling. He was conscious of a thousand odors floating in the air, each one connected with a thousand thoughts, and hopes, and joys, and cares long, long, forgotten!

"Your lip is trembling," said the Ghost. "And what is that upon your cheek?"

Scrooge muttered, with an unusual catching in his voice, that it was a pimple; and begged the Ghost to lead him where he would.

"You recollect the way!" inquired the Spirit.

"Remember it!" cried Scrooge with fervor—"I could walk it blindfold."

"Strange to have forgotten it for so many years!" observed the Ghost. "Let us go on."

They walked along the road; Scrooge recognizing every gate, and post, and tree; until a little market-town appeared in the distance, with its bridge, its church, and winding river. Some shaggy ponies now were seen trotting towards them with boys upon their backs, who called to other boys in country gigs and carts, driven by farmers. All these boys were in great spirits, and shouted to each other, until the broad fields were so full of merry music, that the crisp air laughed to hear it.

"These are but shadows of the things that have been," said the Ghost. "They have no consciousness of us."

The jocund travellers came on; and as they came, Scrooge knew and named them every one. Why was he rejoiced beyond all bounds to see them! Why did his cold eye glisten, and his heart leap up as they went past! Why was he filled with gladness when he heard them give each other Merry Christmas, as they parted at cross-roads and bye ways, for their several homes! What was merry Christmas to Scrooge? Out upon merry Christmas! What good had it ever done to him?

"The school is not quite deserted," said the Ghost. "A solitary child, neglected by his friends, is left there still."

Scrooge said he knew it. And he sobbed.

They left the high-road, by a well remembered lane, and soon approached a mansion of dull red brick, with a little weathercock-surmounted cupola, on the roof, and a bell hanging in it. It was a large house, but one of broken fortunes; for the spacious offices were little used, their walls were damp and mossy, their windows broken, and their gates decayed. Fowls clucked and strutted in the stables; and the coach-houses and sheds were overrun with grass. Nor was it more retentive of its ancient state, within; for entering the dreary hall, and glancing through the open doors of many rooms, they found them poorly furnished, cold, and vast. There was an earthly savor in the air, a chilly bareness in the place, which associated itself somehow with too much getting up by candle-light, and not too much to eat.

They went, the Ghost and Scrooge, across the hall, to a door at the back of the house. It opened before them, and disclosed a long, bare, melancholy room, made barer still by lines of plain deal forms and desks. At one of these a lonely boy was reading near a feeble fire; and Scrooge sat down upon a form, and wept to see his poor forgotten self as he used to be.

Not a latent echo in the house, not a squeak and scuffle from the mice behind the panelling, not a drip from the half-thawed water-spout in the dull yard behind, not a sigh among the leafless boughs of one despondent poplar, not the idle swinging of an empty store-house door, no, not a clicking in the fire, but fell upon the heart of Scrooge with a softening influence, and gave a freer passage to his tears.

The Spirit touched him on the arm, and pointed to his younger self, intent upon his reading. Suddenly a man, in foreign garments: wonderfully real and distinct to look at: stood outside the window, with an axe stuck in his belt, and leading an ass laden with wood by the bridle.

"Why, it's Ali Baba!" Scrooge exclaimed in ecstasy. "It's dear old honest Ali Baba! Yes, yes, I know! One Christmas time, when yonder solitary child was left here all alone, he *did* come, for the first time, just like that. Poor boy! And Valentine," said Scrooge, "and his wild brother, Orson; there they go! And what's his name, who was put down in his drawers, asleep, at the Gate of Damascus; don't you see him! And the Sultan's Groom turned upside down by the Genii; there he is upon his head! Serve him right! I'm glad of it. What business had *he* to be married to the Princess!"

To hear Scrooge expending all the earnestness of his nature on such subjects, in a most extraordinary voice between laughing and crying; and to see his heightened and excited face, would have been a surprise to his business friends in the city, indeed.

"There's the Parrot!" cried Scrooge. "Green body and yellow tail, with a thing like a lettuce growing out of the top of his head; there he is! Poor Robin Crusoe, he called him, when he came home again after sailing round the island. 'Poor Robin Crusoe, where have you been, Robin Crusoe?' The man thought he was dreaming, but he wasn't. It was the Parrot, you know. There goes Friday, running for his life to the little creek! Halloa! Hoop! Halloa!"

Then, with a rapidity of transition very foreign to his usual character, he said, in pity for his former self, "Poor boy!" and cried again.

"I wish," Scrooge muttered, putting his hand in his pocket, and looking about him, after drying his eyes with his cuff: "but it's too late now."

"What is the matter?" asked the Spirit.

"Nothing," said Scrooge. "Nothing. There was a boy singing a Christmas Carol at my door last night. I should like to have given him something: that's all."

The Ghost smiled thoughtfully, and waved its hand: saying as it did so, "Let us see another Christmas!"

Scrooge's former self grew larger at the words, and the room became a little darker and more dirty. The panels shrunk, the windows cracked; fragments of plaster fell out of the ceiling, and the naked laths were shown instead; but how all this was brought about, Scrooge knew no more than you do. He only knew that it was quite correct; that everything had happened so; that there he was, alone again, when all the other boys had gone home for the jolly holidays.

He was not reading now, but walking up and down despairingly. Scrooge looked at the Ghost, and with a mournful shaking of his head, glanced anxiously towards the door.

It opened; and a little girl, much younger than the boy, came darting in, and putting her arms about his neck, and often kissing him, addressed him as her "Dear, dear brother."

"I have come to bring you home, dear brother!" said the child, clapping her tiny hands, and bending down to laugh. "To bring you home, home, home!"

"Home, little Fan?" returned the boy.

"Yes!" said the child, brimful of glee. "Home, for good and all. Home, for ever and ever. Father is so much kinder than he used to be, that home's like Heaven! He spoke so gently to me one dear night when I was going to bed, that I was not afraid to ask him once more if you might come home; and he said, Yes, you should; and sent me in a coach to bring you. And you're to be a man!" said the child, opening her eyes, "and are never to come back here; but first, we're to be together all the Christmas long, and have the merriest time in all the world."

"You are quite a woman, little Fan!" exclaimed the boy.

She clapped her hands and laughed, and tried to touch his head; but being too little, laughed again, and stood on tiptoe to embrace him. Then she began to drag him, in her childish eagerness, towards the door; and he, nothing loth to go, accompanied her.

A terrible voice in the hall cried, "Bring down Master Scrooge's box, there!" and in the hall appeared the schoolmaster himself, who glared on Master Scrooge with a ferocious condescension, and threw him into a dreadful state of mind by shaking hands with him. He then conveyed him and his sister into the veriest old well of a shivering best-parlor that ever was seen, where the maps upon the wall, and the celestial and terrestrial globes in the windows, were waxy with cold. Here he produced a decanter of curiously light wine, and a block of curiously heavy cake, and administered instalments of those dainties to the young people: at the same time, sending out a meagre servant to offer a glass of "something" to the postboy, who answered that he thanked the gentleman, but if it was the same tap as he had tasted before, he had rather not. Master Scrooge's trunk being by this time tied on to the top of the chaise, the children bade the schoolmaster good-bye right willingly; and getting into it, drove gaily down the garden-sweep, the quick wheels dashing the hoarfrost and snow from off the dark leaves of the evergreens like spray.

"Always a delicate creature, whom a breath might have withered," said the Ghost. "But she had a large heart!"

"So she had," cried Scrooge. "You're right. I will not gainsay it, Spirit. God forbid!"

"She died a woman," said the Ghost, "and had, as I think, children."

"One child," Scrooge returned.

"True," said the Ghost. "Your nephew."

Scrooge seemed uneasy in his mind, and answered briefly, "Yes."

Although they had but that moment left the school behind them, they were now in the busy thoroughfares of the city, where shadowy passengers passed and repassed; where shadowy carts and coaches battled for the way, and all the strife and tumult of a real city were. It was made plain enough, by the dressing of the shops, that here too it was Christmas time again; but it was evening, and the streets were lighted up.

The Ghost stopped at a certain warehouse door, and asked Scrooge if he knew it.

"Know it!" said Scrooge. "Was I apprenticed here!"

They went in. At sight of an old gentleman in a Welsh wig, sitting behind such a high desk, that if he had been two inches taller he must have knocked his head against the ceiling, Scrooge cried in great excitement:

"Why, it's old Fezziwig! Bless his heart; it's Fezziwig alive again!"

Old Fezziwig laid down his pen, and looked up at the clock, which pointed to the hour of seven. He rubbed his hands; adjusted his capacious waistcoat; laughed all over himself, from his shoes to his organ of benevolence; and called out in a comfortable, oily, rich, fat, jovial voice:

"Yo ho, there! Ebenezer! Dick!"

Scrooge's former self, now grown a young man, came briskly in, accompanied by his fellow-'prentice.

"Dick Wilkins, to be sure!" said Scrooge to the Ghost. "Bless me, yes. There he is. He was very much attached to me, was Dick. Poor Dick! Dear, dear!"

"Yo ho, my boys!" said Fezziwig. "No more work to-night. Christmas Eve, Dick. Christmas, Ebenezer! Let's have the shutters up," cried old Fezziwig, with a sharp clap of his hands, "before a man can say Jack Robinson!"

You wouldn't believe how those two fellows went at it! They charged into the street with the shutters—one, two, three—had 'em up in their places—four, five, six—barred 'em and pinned 'em—seven, eight, nine—and came back before you could have got to twelve, panting like race-horses.

"Hilli-ho!" cried old Fezziwig, skipping down from the high desk, with wonderful agility. "Clear away, my lads, and let's have lots of room here! Hilli-ho, Dick! Chirrup, Ebenezer!"

Clear away! There was nothing they wouldn't have cleared away, or couldn't have cleared away, with old Fezziwig looking on. It was done in a minute. Every moveable was packed off, as if it were dismissed from public life for evermore; the floor was swept and watered, the lamps were trimmed, fuel was heaped upon the fire; and the warehouse was as snug, and warm, and bright a ball-room, as you would desire to see upon a winter's night.

In came a fiddler with a music-book, and went up to the lofty desk, and made an orchestra of it, and tuned like fifty stomach-aches. In came Mrs. Fezziwig, one vast substantial smile. In came the three Miss Fezziwigs, beaming and loveable. In came the six young followers whose hearts they broke. In came all the young men and women employed in the business. In came the housemaid, with her cousin, the baker. In came the cook, with her brother's particular friend, the milkman. In came the boy from over the way, who was suspected of not having board enough from his master; trying to hide himself behind the girl from next door but one, who was proved to have had her ears pulled by her mistress. In they all came, one after another; some shyly, some boldly, some gracefully, some awkwardly, some pushing, some pulling; in they all came, anyhow and everyhow. Away they all went, twenty couples at once, hands half round and back again the other way; down the middle and up again; round and round in various stages of affectionate grouping; old top couple always turning up in the wrong place; new top couple starting off again as soon as they got there; all top couples at last, and not a bottom one to help them. When this result was brought about, old Fezziwig, clapping his hands to stop the dance, cried out, "well done!" and the fiddler plunged his hot face into a pot of porter, especially provided for that purpose. But, scorning rest upon his reappearance, he instantly began again, though there were no dancers yet, as if the other fiddler had been carried home, exhausted, on a shutter, and he were a bran-new man resolved to beat him out of sight or perish.

There were more dances, and there were forfeits, and more dances; and there was cake, and there was negus, and there was a great piece of cold roast, and there was a great piece of cold boiled, and there were mince pies, and plenty of beer. But the great effect of the evening came after the roast and boiled, when the fiddler (an artful dog, mind! the sort of man who knew his business better than you or I could have told it him) struck up "Sir Roger de Coverley." Then old Fezziwig stood out to dance with Mrs. Fezziwig. Top couple, too; with a good stiff piece of work cut out for them; three or four and twenty pair of partners; people who were not to be trifled with; people who *would* dance, and had no notion of walking.

But if they had been twice as many, ah! four times, old Fezziwig would have been a match for them, and so would Mrs. Fezziwig. As to *her,* she was worthy to be his partner in every sense of the term. If that's not high praise, tell me higher, and I'll use it. A positive light appeared to issue from Fezziwig's calves. They shone in every part of the dance like moons. You couldn't have predicted, at any given time, what would become of 'em next. And when old Fezziwig and Mrs. Fezziwig had gone all through the dance—advance and retire, hold hands with your partner, bow and courtsey, corkscrew, thread-the-needle, and back again to your place—Fezziwig "cut," cut so deftly, that he appeared to wink with his legs, and came upon his feet again without a stagger.

When the clock struck eleven, this domestic ball broke up. Mr. and Mrs. Fezziwig took their stations, one on either side the door, and, shaking hands with every person individually as he or she went out, wished him or her a merry Christmas. When everybody had retired but the two 'prentices, they did the same to them; and thus the cheerful voices died away, and the lads were left to their beds, which were under a counter in the back shop.

During the whole of this time, Scrooge had acted like a man out of his wits. His heart and soul were in the scene, and with his former self. He corroborated everything, remembered everything, enjoyed everything, and underwent the strangest agitation. It was not until now, when the bright faces of his former self and Dick were turned from them, that he remembered the Ghost, and became conscious that it was looking full upon him, while the light upon its head burned very clear.

"A small matter," said the Ghost, "to make these silly folks so full of gratitude."

"Small?" echoed Scrooge.

The Spirit signed to him to listen to the two apprentices, who were pouring out their hearts in praise of Fezziwig: and when he had done so, said,

"Why! Is it not? He has spent but a few pounds of your mortal money: three or four, perhaps. Is that so much that he deserves this praise?"

"It isn't that," said Scrooge, heated by the remark, and speaking unconsciously like his former, not his latter, self. "It isn't that, Spirit. He has the power to render us happy or unhappy: to make our service light or burdensome: a pleasure or a toil. Say that his power lies in words and looks; in things so slight and insignificant that it is impossible to add and count 'em up: what then! The happiness he gives, is quite as great as if it cost a fortune."

He felt the Spirit's glance, and stopped.

"What is the matter?" asked the Ghost.

"Nothing particular," said Scrooge.

"Something, I think?" the Ghost insisted.

"No," said Scrooge, "No. I should like to be able to say a word or two to my clerk just now! That's all!"

His former self turned down the lamps as he gave utterance to the wish: and Scrooge and the Ghost again stood side by side in the open air.

"My time grows short," observed the Spirit. "Quick."

This was not addressed to Scrooge, or to any one whom he could see, but it produced an immediate effect. For again Scrooge saw himself. He was older now; a man in the prime of life. His face had not the harsh and rigid lines of later years; but it had begun to wear the signs of care and avarice. There was an eager, greedy, restless motion in the eye, which showed the passion that had taken root, and where the shadow of the growing tree would fall.

He was not alone, but sat by the side of a fair young girl in a morning-dress: in whose eyes there were tears, which sparkled in the light that shone out of the Ghost of Christmas Past.

"It matters little," she said, softly. "To you, very little. Another idol has displaced me; and if it can cheer and comfort you in time to come, as I would have tried to do, I have no just cause to grieve."

"What Idol has displaced you?" he rejoined.

"A golden one."

"This is the even-handed dealing of the world!" he said. "There is nothing on which it is so hard as poverty; and there is nothing it professes to condemn with such severity as the pursuit of wealth!"

"You fear the world too much," she answered, gently. "All your other hopes have merged into the hope of being beyond the chance of its sordid reproach. I have seen your nobler aspirations fall off one by one, until the master-passion, Gain, engrosses you. Have I not?"

"What then?" he retorted. "Even if I have grown so much wiser, what then? I am not changed towards you."

She shook her head.

"Am I?"

"Our contract is an old one. It was made when we were both poor and content to be so, until, in good season, we could improve our wordly fortune by our patient industry. You *are* changed. When it was made, you were another man."

"I was a boy," he said impatiently.

"Your own feeling tells you that you were not what you are," she returned. "I am. That which promised happiness when we were one in heart, is fraught with misery now that we are two. How often and how keenly I have thought of this, I will not say. It is enough that I *have* thought of it, and can release you."

"Have I ever sought release?"

"In words. No. Never."

"In what, then?"

"In a changed nature: in an altered spirit; in another atmosphere of life; another Hope as its great end. In everything that made my love of any worth or value in your sight. If this had never been between us," said the girl, looking mildly, but with steadiness, upon him; "tell me, would you seek me out and try to win me now? Ah, no?"

He seemed to yield to the justice of this supposition, in spite of himself. But he said with a struggle, "You think not."

"I would gladly think otherwise if I could," she answered, "Heaven knows! When *I* have learned a Truth like this, I know how strong and irresistible it must be. But if you were free to-day, to-morrow, yesterday, can even I believe that you would choose a dowerless girl—you who, in your very confidence with her, weigh everything with Gain: or, choosing her, if for a moment you were false enough to your one guiding principle to do so, do I not know that your repentance and regret would surely follow? I do; and I release you. With a full heart, for the love of him you once were."

He was about to speak; but with her head turned from him she resumed,

"You may—the memory of what is past half makes me hope you will—have pain in this. A very, very, brief time, and you will dismiss the recollection of it, gladly, as an unprofitable dream, from which it happened well that you awoke. May you be happy in the life you have chosen!"

She left him; and they parted.

"Spirit," said Scrooge, "show me no more! Conduct me home. Why do you delight to torture me?"

"One shadow more!" exclaimed the Ghost.

"No more!" cried Scrooge. "No more, I don't wish to see it. Show me no more!"

But the relentless Ghost pinioned him in both his arms, and forced him to observe what happened next.

They were in another scene and place: a room, not very large or handsome, but full of comfort. Near to the winter fire sat a beautiful young girl, so like the last that Scrooge believed it was the same, until he saw *her*, now a comely matron, sitting opposite her daughter. The noise in this room was perfectly tumultuous, for there were more children there, than Scrooge in his agitated state of mind could count; and, unlike the celebrated herd in the poem, they were not forty children conducting themselves like one, but every child was conducting itself like forty. The consequences were uproarious beyond belief; but no one seemed to care; on the contrary, the mother and daughter laughed heartily, and enjoyed it very much; and the latter, soon beginning to mingle in the sports, got pillaged by the young brigands most ruthlessly. What would I not have given to be one of them! Though I never could have been so rude, no, no! I wouldn't for the wealth of all the world have crushed that braided hair, and torn it down; and for the precious little shoe, I wouldn't have plucked it off, God bless my soul! to save my life. As to measuring her waist in sport, as they did, bold young brood, I couldn't have done it; I should have expected my arm to have grown round it for a punishment, and never come straight again. And yet I should have dearly liked, I own, to have touched her lips; to have questioned her, that she might have opened them; to have looked upon the lashes of her downcast eyes, and never raised a blush; to have let loose waves of hair, an inch of which would be a keepsake beyond price: in short, I should have liked, I do confess, to have had the lightest licence of a child, and yet been man enough to know its value.

But now a knocking at the door was heard, and such a rush immediately ensued that she with laughing face and plundered dress was borne towards it, the centre of a flushed and boisterous group, just in time to greet the father, who came home attended by a man laden with Christmas toys and presents. Then the shouting and the struggling, and the onslaught that was made on the defenceless porter! The scaling him, with chairs for ladders, to dive into his pockets, despoil him of brown-paper parcels, hold on tight by his cravat, hug him round neck, pommel his back, and kick his legs in irrepressible affection! The shouts of wonder and delight with which the development of every package was received! The terrible announcement that the baby had been taken in the act of putting a doll's frying-pan into his mouth, and was more than suspected of having swallowed a fictitious turkey, glued on a wooden platter! The immense relief of finding this a false alarm! The joy, and gratitude, and ecstasy! They are all indescribable alike. It is enough that by degrees the children and their emotions got out of the parlor and, by one stair at a time, up to the top of the house; where they went to bed, and so subsided.

And now Scrooge looked on more attentively than ever, when the master of the house, having his daughter leaning fondly on him, sat down with her and her mother at his own fireside; and when he thought that such another creature, quite as graceful and as full of promise, might have called him father, and been a spring-time in the haggard winter of his life, his sight grew very dim indeed.

"Belle," said the husband, turning to his wife with a smile, "I saw an old friend of yours this afternoon."

"Who was it?"

"Guess!"

"How can I? Tut, don't I know," she added in the same breath, laughing as he laughed. "Mr. Scrooge."

"Mr. Scrooge it was. I passed his office-window: and as it was not shut up, and he had a candle inside, I could scarcely help seeing him. His partner lies upon the point of death, I hear; and there he sat, alone. Quite alone in the world, I do believe."

"Spirit," said Scrooge, in a broken voice, "remove me from this place."

"I told you these were shadows of the things that have been," said the Ghost. "That they are what they are, do not blame me."

"Remove me!" Scrooge exclaimed. "I cannot bear it!"

He turned upon the Ghost, and, seeing that it looked upon him with a face in which, in some strange way, there were fragments of all the faces it had shown him, wrestled with it.

"Leave me! Take me back! Haunt me no longer!"

In the struggle, if that can be called a struggle in which the Ghost, with no visible resistance on its own part, was undisturbed by any effort of its adversary, Scrooge observed that its light was burning high and bright; and dimly connecting that with its influence over him, he seized the extinguisher-cap, and by a sudden action pressed it down upon its head.

The Spirit dropped beneath it, so that the extinguisher covered its whole form; but though Scrooge pressed it down with all his force, he could not hide the light, which streamed from under it, in an unbroken flood, upon the ground.

He was conscious of being exhausted, and overcome by an irresistible drowsiness; and, farther, of being in his own bedroom. He gave the cap a parting squeeze, in which his hand relaxed; and had barely time to reel to bed, before he sank into a heavy sleep.

Stave Three

THE SECOND OF THE THREE SPIRITS

AWAKING in the middle of a prodigiously tough snore, and sitting up in bed to get his thoughts together, Scrooge had no occasion to be told that the bell was again upon the stroke of One. He felt that he was restored to consciousness in the right nick of time, for the especial purpose of holding a conference with the second messenger despatched to him through Jacob Marley's intervention. But, finding that he turned uncomfortably cold when he began to wonder which of his curtains this new spectre would draw back, he put them every one aside with his own hands; and, lying down again, established a sharp look-out all round the bed. For he wished to challenge the Spirit on the moment of its appearance, and did not wish to be taken by surprise and made nervous.

Gentlemen of the free-and-easy sort, who plume themselves on being acquainted with a move or two, and being usually equal to the time-of-day, express the wide range of their capacity for adventure by observing that they are good for anything from pitch-and-toss to manslaughter; between which opposite extremes, no doubt, there lies a tolerably wide and comprehensive range of subjects. Without venturing for Scrooge quite as hardily as this, I don't mind calling on you to believe that he was ready for a good broad field of strange appearances, and that nothing between a baby and a rhinoceros would have astonished him very much.

Now, being prepared for almost anything, he was not by any means prepared for nothing; and, consequently, when the Bell struck One, and no shape appeared, he was taken with a violent fit of trembling. Five minutes, ten minutes, a quarter of an hour went by, yet nothing came. All this time, he lay upon his bed, the very core and centre of a blaze of ruddy light, which streamed upon it when the clock proclaimed the hour; and which being only light, was more alarming than a dozen ghosts, as he was powerless to make out what it meant, or would be at; and was sometimes apprehensive that he might be at that very moment an interesting case of spontaneous combustion, without having the consolation of knowing it. At last, however, he began to think—as you or I would have thought at first; for it is always the person not in the predicament who knows what ought to have been done in it, and would unquestionably have done it too—at last, I say, he began to think that the source and secret of this ghostly light might be in the adjoining room; from whence, on further tracing it, it seemed to shine. This idea taking full possession of his mind, he got up softly and shuffled in his slippers to the door.

The moment Scrooge's hand was on the lock, a strange voice called him by his name, and bade him enter. He obeyed.

It was his own room. There was no doubt about that. But it had undergone a surprising transformation. The walls and ceiling were so hung with living green, that it looked a perfect grove, from every part of which bright gleaming berries glistened. The crisp leaves of holly, mistletoe, and ivy reflected back the light, as if so many little mirrors had been scattered there; and such a mighty blaze went roaring up the chimney, as that dull petrifaction of a chimney had not known in Scrooge's time, or Marley's, or for many and many a winter season gone. Heaped up upon the floor, to form a kind of throne, were turkeys, geese, game, poultry, brawn, great joints of meat, suckling-pigs, long wreaths of sausages, mince-pies, plum-puddings, barrels of oysters, red-hot chestnuts, cherry-cheeked apples, juicy oranges, luscious pears, immense twelfth-cakes, and seething bowls of punch, that made the chamber dim with their delicious steam. In easy state upon this couch, there sat a jolly Giant, glorious to see; who bore a glowing torch, in shape not unlike Plenty's horn, and held it up, high up, to shed its light on Scrooge, as he came peeping round the door.

"Come in!" exclaimed the Ghost. "Come in! and know me better, man!"

Scrooge entered timidly, and hung his head before this Spirit. He was not the dogged Scrooge he had been; and though its eyes were clear and kind, he did not like to meet them.

"I am the Ghost of Christmas Present," said the Spirit. "Look upon me!"

Scrooge reverently did so. It was clothed in one simple deep green robe, or mantle, bordered with white fur. This garment hung so loosely on the figure, that its capacious breast was bare, as if disdaining to be warded or concealed by any artifice. Its feet, observable beneath the ample folds of the garment, were also bare; and on its head it wore no other covering than a holly wreath set here and there with shining icicles. Its dark brown curls were long and free; free as its genial face, its sparkling eye, its open hand, its cheery voice, its unconstrained demeanor, and its joyful air. Girded round its middle was an antique scabbard; but no sword was in it, and the ancient sheath was eaten up with rust.

"You have never seen the like of me before!" exclaimed the Spirit.

"Never," Scrooge made answer to it.

"Have never walked forth with the younger members of my family; meaning (for I am very young) my elder brothers born in these later years?" pursued the Phantom.

"I don't think I have," said Scrooge. "I am afraid I have not. Have you had many brothers, Spirit?"

"More than eighteen hundred," said the Ghost.

"A tremendous family to provide for!" muttered Scrooge.

The Ghost of Christmas Present rose.

"Spirit," said Scrooge, submissively, "conduct me where you will. I went forth last night on compulsion, and I learnt a lesson which is working now. To-night, if you have aught to teach me, let me profit by it."

"Touch my robe!"

Scrooge did as he was told, and held it fast.

Holly, mistletoe, red berries, ivy, turkeys, geese, game, poultry, brawn, meat, pigs, sausages, oysters, pies, puddings, fruit, and punch, all vanished instantly. So did the room, the fire, the ruddy glow, the hour of night, and they stood in the city streets on Christmas morning, where (for the weather was severe) the people made a rough, but brisk, and not unpleasant kind of music, in scraping the snow from the pavement in front of their dwellings, and from the tops of their houses: whence it was mad delight to the boys to see it come plumping down into the road below, and splitting into artificial little snow-storms.

The house fronts looked black enough, and the windows blacker, contrasting with the smooth white sheet of snow upon the ground; which last deposit had been ploughed up in deep furrows by the heavy wheels of carts and wagons; furrows that crossed and re-crossed each other hundreds of times where the great streets branched off, and made intricate channels, hard to trace, in the thick yellow mud and icy water. The sky was gloomy, and the shortest streets were choked up with a dingy mist, half-thawed, half-frozen, whose heavier particles descended in a shower of sooty atoms, as if all the chimneys in Great Britain had, by one consent, caught fire, and were blazing away to their dear heart's content. There was nothing very cheerful in the climate or the town, and yet was there an air of cheerfulness abroad that the clearest summer air and brightest summer sun might have endeavored to diffuse in vain.

For the people who were shovelling away on the house-tops were jovial and full of glee, calling out to one another from the parapets, and now and then exchanging a facetious snowball—better natured missile far than many a wordy jest—laughing heartily if it went right, and not less heartily if it went wrong. The poulterers' shops were still half-open, and the fruiterers' were radiant in their glory. There were great, round, pot-bellied baskets of chestnuts, shaped like the waistcoats of jolly old gentlemen, lolling at the doors, and tumbling out into the street in their apoplectic opulence. There were ruddy, brown-faced, broad-girthed Spanish Onions, shining in the fatness of their growth like Spanish Friars: and winking from their shelves in wanton slyness at the girls as they went by, and glanced demurely at the hung-up mistletoe. There were pears and apples, clustered high in blooming pyramids; there were bunches of grapes, made in the shopkeepers' benevolence, to dangle from conspicuous hooks, that people's mouths might water gratis as they passed; there were piles of filberts, mossy and brown, recalling, in their fragrance, ancient walks among the woods, and pleasant shufflings ankle-deep through withered leaves; there were Norfolk Biffins, squab and swarthy, setting off the yellow of the oranges and lemons, and, in the great compactness of their juicy persons, urgently entreating and beseeching to be carried home in paper bags and eaten after dinner. The very gold and silver fish, set forth among these choice fruits in a bowl, though members of a dull and stagnant-blooded race, appeared to know that there was something going on; and, to a fish, went gasping round and round their little world in slow and passionless excitement.

The Grocers'! oh the Grocers'! nearly closed, with perhaps two shutters down, or one; but through those gaps such glimpses! It was not alone that the scales descending on the counter made a merry sound, or that the twine and roller parted company so briskly, or that the canisters were rattled up and down like juggling tricks, or even that the blended scents of tea and coffee were so grateful to the nose, or even that the raisins were so plentiful and rare, the almonds so extremely white, the sticks of cinnamon so long and straight, the other spices so delicious, the candied fruits so caked and spotted with molten sugar as to make the coldest lookers-on feel faint and subsequently bilious. Nor was it that the figs were moist and pulpy, or that the French plums blushed in modest tartness from their highly-decorated boxes, or that everything was good to eat and in its Christmas dress: but the customers were all so hurried and so eager in the hopeful promise of the day, that they tumbled up against each other at the door, clashing their wicker baskets wildly, and left their purchases upon the counter, and came running back to fetch them, and committed hundreds of the like mistakes in the best humor possible; while the Grocer and his people were so frank and fresh that the polished hearts with which they fastened their aprons behind might have been their own, worn outside for general inspection, and for Christmas daws to peck at if they chose.

But soon the steeples called good people all, to church and chapel, and away they came, flocking through the streets in their best clothes, and with their gayest faces. And at the same time there emerged from scores of bye-streets, lanes, and nameless turnings, innumerable people, carrying their dinners to the bakers' shops. The sight of these poor revellers appeared to interest the Spirit very much, for he stood with Scrooge beside him in a baker's doorway, and taking off the covers as their bearers passed, sprinkled incense on their dinners from his torch. And it was a very uncommon kind of torch, for once or twice when there were angry words between some dinner-carriers who had jostled each other, he shed a few drops of water on them from it, and their good humor was restored directly. For they said, it was a shame to quarrel upon Christmas Day. And so it was! God love it, so it was!

In time the Bells ceased, and the bakers were shut up; and yet there was a genial shadowing forth of all these dinners and the progress of their cooking, in the thawed blotch of wet above each baker's oven; where the pavement smoked as if its stones were cooking too.

"Is there a peculiar flavor in what you sprinkle from your torch?" asked Scrooge.

"There is. My own."

"Would it apply to any kind of dinner on this day?" asked Scrooge.

"To any kindly given. To a poor one most."

"Why to a poor one most?" asked Scrooge.

"Because it needs it most."

"Spirit," said Scrooge, after a moment's thought, "I wonder you, of all the beings in the many worlds about us, should desire to cramp these people's opportunities of innocent enjoyment!"

"I!" cried the Spirit.

"You would deprive them of their means of dining every seventh day, often the only day on which they can be said to dine at all," said Scrooge. "Wouldn't you?"

"I!" cried the Spirit.

"You seek to close these places on the Seventh Day?" said Scrooge. "And it comes to the same thing."

"*I* seek!" exclaimed the Spirit.

"Forgive me if I am wrong. It has been done in your name, or, at least, in that of your family," said Scrooge.

"There are some upon this earth of yours," returned the Spirit, "who lay claim to know us, and who do their deeds of passion, pride, ill-will, hatred, envy, bigotry, and selfishness in our name; who are as strange to us and all our kith and kin, as if they had never lived. Remember that, and charge their doings on themselves, not us."

Scrooge promised that he would; and they went on, invisible, as they had been before, into the suburbs of the town. It was a remarkable quality of the Ghost (which Scrooge had observed at the baker's), that, notwithstanding his gigantic size, he could accommodate himself to any place with ease; and that he stood beneath a low roof quite as gracefully and like a supernatural creature, as it was possible he could have done in any lofty hall.

And perhaps it was the pleasure the good Spirit had in showing off this power of his, or else it was his own kind, generous, hearty nature, and his sympathy with all poor men, that led him straight to Scrooge's clerk's; for there he went, and took Scrooge with him, holding to his robe; and on the threshold of the door the Spirit smiled, and stopped to bless Bob Cratchit's dwelling with the sprinklings of his torch. Think of that! Bob had but fifteen "Bob" a week himself; he pocketed on Saturdays but fifteen copies of his Christian name; and yet the Ghost of Christmas Present blessed his four-roomed house!

Then up rose Mrs. Cratchit, Cratchit's wife, dressed out but poorly in a twice-turned gown, but brave in ribands, which are cheap and make a goodly show for sixpence; and she laid the cloth, assisted by Belinda Cratchit, second of her daughters, also brave in ribands; while Master Peter Cratchit plunged a fork into the saucepan of potatoes, and getting the corners of his monstrous shirt collar (Bob's private property, conferred upon his son and heir in honor of the day) into his mouth, rejoiced to find himself so gallantly attired, and yearned to show his linen in the fashionable Parks. And now two smaller Cratchits, boy and girl, came tearing in, screaming that outside the baker's they had smelt the goose, and known it for their own; and basking in luxurious thoughts of sage-and-onions, these young Cratchits danced about the table, and exalted Master Peter Cratchit to the skies, while he (not proud, although his collars nearly choked him) blew the fire, until the slow potatoes, bubbling up, knocked loudly at the saucepan-lid, to be let out and peeled.

"What has ever got your precious father, then?" said Mrs. Cratchit. "And your brother, Tiny Tim; and Martha warn't as late last Christmas Day by half-an-hour!"

"Here's Martha, mother!" said a girl, appearing as she spoke.

"Here's Martha, mother!" cried the two young Cratchits. "Hurrah! There's *such* a goose, Martha!"

"Why, bless your heart alive, my dear, how late you are!" said Mrs. Cratchit, kissing her a dozen times, and taking off her shawl and bonnet for her, with officious zeal.

"We'd a deal of work to finish up last night," replied the girl, "and had to clear away this morning, mother!"

"Well! Never mind, so long as you are come," said Mrs. Cratchit. "Sit ye down before the fire, my dear, and have a warm, Lord bless ye!"

"No, no! There's father coming," cried the two young Cratchits, who were everywhere at once. "Hide, Martha, hide!"

So Martha hid herself, and in came little Bob, the father, with at least three feet of comforter, exclusive of the fringe, hanging down before him; and his thread-bare clothes darned up and brushed, to look seasonable; and Tiny Tim upon his shoulder. Alas for Tiny Tim, he bore a little crutch, and had his limbs supported by an iron frame!

"Why, where's our Martha?" cried Bob Cratchit, looking round.

"Not coming!" said Mrs. Cratchit.

"Not coming!" said Bob, with a sudden declension in his high spirits; for he had been Tim's blood horse all the way from church, and had come home rampant. "Not coming upon Christmas Day!"

Martha didn't like to see him disappointed, if it were only in a joke; so she came out prematurely from behind the closet door, and ran into his arms, while the two young Cratchits hustled Tiny Tim, and bore him off into the wash-house, that he might hear the pudding singing in the copper!

"And how did little Tim behave?" asked Mrs. Cratchit, when she had rallied Bob on his credulity, and Bob had hugged his daughter to his heart's content.

"As good as gold," said Bob, "and better. Somehow he gets thoughtful sitting by himself so much, and thinks the strangest things you ever heard. He told me, coming home, that he hoped the people saw him in the church, because he was a cripple, and it might be pleasant to them to remember upon Christmas Day, who made lame beggars walk, and blind men see."

Bob's voice was tremulous when he told them this, and trembled more when he said that Tiny Tim was growing strong and hearty.

His active little crutch was heard upon the floor, and back came Tiny Tim before another word was spoken, escorted by his brother and sister to his stool beside the fire; and while Bob, turning up his cuffs, as if, poor fellow, they were capable of being made more shabby—compounded some hot mixture in a jug with gin and lemons, and stirred it round and round, and put it on the hob to simmer; Master Peter and the two ubiquitous young Cratchits went to fetch the goose, with which they soon returned in high procession.

Such a bustle ensued that you might have thought a goose the rarest of all birds; a feathered phenomenon, to which a black swan was a matter of course: and, in truth, it was something very like it in that house. Mrs. Cratchit made the gravy (ready before-hand in a little saucepan) hissing hot; Master Peter mashed the potatoes with incredible vigor; Miss Belinda sweetened up the apple-sauce; Martha dusted the hot plates; Bob took Tiny Tim beside him in a tiny corner, at the table, the two young Cratchits set chairs for everybody, not forgetting themselves, and mounting guard upon their posts, crammed spoons into their mouths, lest they should shriek for goose before their turn came to be helped. At last the dishes were set on, and grace was said. It was succeeded by a breathless pause, as Mrs. Cratchit, looking slowly all along the carving-knife, prepared to plunge it in the breast; but when she did and when the long-expected gush of stuffing issued forth, one murmur of delight arose all round the board, and even Tiny Tim, excited by the two young Cratchits, beat on the table with the handle of his knife, and feebly cried Hurrah!

There never was such a goose. Bob said he didn't believe there ever was such a goose cooked. Its tenderness and flavor, size and cheapness, were the themes of universal admiration. Eked out by the apple-sauce and mashed potatoes, it was a sufficient dinner for the whole family; indeed, as Mrs. Cratchit said with great delight (surveying one small atom of a bone on the dish), they hadn't ate it all at last! Yet every one had had enough, and the youngest Cratchits in particular were steeped in sage and onion to the eyebrows! But now, the plates being changed by Miss Belinda, Mrs. Cratchit left the room alone—too nervous to bear witnesses—to take the pudding up, and bring it in.

Suppose it should not be done enough! Suppose it should break in turning out! Suppose somebody should have got over the wall of the back-yard, and stolen it, while they were merry with the goose: a supposition at which the two young Cratchits became livid! All sorts of horrors were supposed.

Hallo! A great deal of steam! The pudding was out of the copper. A smell like a washing-day! That was the cloth. A smell like an eating-house and a pastry cook's next door to each other, with a laundress's next door to that? That was the pudding. In half a minute Mrs. Cratchit entered: flushed, but smiling proudly: with the pudding like a speckled cannon-ball, so hard and firm, blazing in half of half-a-quartern of ignited brandy, and bedight with Christmas holly stuck into the top.

Oh, a wonderful pudding! Bob Cratchit said, and calmly too, that he regarded it as the greatest success achieved by Mrs. Cratchit since their marriage. Mrs. Cratchit said that now the weight was off her mind, she would confess she had had her doubts about the quantity of flour. Everybody had something to say about it, but nobody said or thought it was at all a small pudding for so large a family. It would have been flat heresy to do so. Any Cratchit would have blushed to hint at such a thing.

At last the dinner was all done, the cloth was cleared, the hearth swept, and the fire made up. The compound in the jug being tasted and considered perfect, apples and oranges were put upon the table, and a shovel-full of chestnuts on the fire. Then all the Cratchit family drew round the hearth, in what Bob Cratchit called a circle, meaning half a one; and at Bob Cratchit's elbow stood the family display of glass; two tumblers, and a custard-cup without a handle.

These held the hot stuff from the jug, however, as well as golden goblets would have done; and Bob served it out with beaming looks, while the chesnuts on the fire sputtered and cracked noisily. Then Bob proposed:

"A Merry Christmas to us all, my dears. God bless us!"

Which all the family re-echoed.

"God bless us every one!" said Tiny Tim, the last of all.

He sat very close to his father's side, upon his little stool. Bob held his withered little hand in his, as if he loved the child, and wished to keep him by his side, and dreaded that he might be taken from him.

"Spirit," said Scrooge, with an interest he had never felt before, "tell me if Tiny Tim will live."

"I see a vacant seat," replied the Ghost, "in the poor chimney corner, and a crutch without an owner, carefully preserved. If these shadows remain unaltered by the Future, the child will die."

"No, no," said Scrooge. "Oh no, kind Spirit! say he will be spared."

"If these shadows remain unaltered by the future, none other of my race," returned the Ghost, "will find him here. When then? If he be like to die, he had better do it, and decrease the surplus population."

Scrooge hung his head to hear his own words quoted by the Spirit, and was overcome with penitence and grief.

"Man," said the Ghost, "if man you be in heart, not adamant, forbear that wicked cant until you have discovered what the surplus is, and where it is. Will you decide what men shall live, what men shall die? It may be that in the sight of Heaven you are more worthless and less fit to live than millions like this poor man's child. Oh God! to hear the Insect on the leaf pronouncing on the too much life among his hungry brothers in the dust!"

Scrooge bent before the Ghost's rebuke, and trembling cast his eyes upon the ground. But he raised them speedily, on hearing his own name.

"Mr. Scrooge!" said Bob; "I'll give you Mr. Scrooge, the Founder of the Feast!"

"The Founder of the Feast indeed!" cried Mrs. Cratchit, reddening. "I wish I had him here. I'd give him a piece of my mind to feast upon, and I hope he'd have a good appetite for it."

"My dear," said Bob, "the children; Christmas Day."

"It should be Christmas Day, I am sure," said she, "on which one drinks the health of such an odious, stingy, hard, unfeeling man as Mr. Scrooge. You know he is, Robert! Nobody knows it better than you do, poor fellow!"

"My dear," was Bob's mild answer, "Christmas Day."

"I'll drink his health for your sake, and the Day's," said Mrs. Cratchit, "not for his. Long life to him! A merry Christmas and a happy New Year!—he'll be very merry and very happy, I have no doubt!"

The children drank the toast after her. It was the first of their proceedings which had no heartiness in it. Tiny Tim drank it last of all, but he didn't care twopence for it. Scrooge was the Ogre of the family. The mention of his name cast a dark shadow on the party which was not dispelled for full five minutes.

After it had passed away, they were ten times merrier than before, from the mere relief of Scrooge the Baleful being done with. Bob Cratchit told them how he had a situation in his eye for Master Peter, which would bring in, if obtained, full five-and-sixpence weekly. The two young Cratchits laughed tremendously at the idea of Peter's being a man of business; and Peter himself looked thoughtfully at the fire from between his collars, as if he were deliberating what particular investments he should favor when he came into the receipt of that bewildering income. Martha, who was a poor apprentice at a milliner's, then told them what kind of work she had to do, and how many hours she worked at a stretch, and how she meant to lie abed to-morrow morning for a good long rest; to-morrow being a holiday, she passed at home. Also how she had seen a countess and a lord some days before, and how the lord was much about as tall as Peter; at which Peter pulled up his collars so high that you couldn't have seen his head if you had been there. All this time the chestnuts and the jug went round and round; and by and bye they had a song, about a lost child travelling in the snow, from Tiny Tim; who had a plaintive little voice, and sang it very well indeed.

There was nothing of high mark in this. They were not a handsome family; they were not well dressed; their shoes were far from being water-proof; their clothes were scanty; and Peter might have known, and very likely did, the inside of a pawn broker's. But they were happy, grateful, pleased with one another, and contented with the time; and when they faded, and looked happier yet in the bright sprinklings of the Spirit's torch at parting, Scrooge had his eye upon them, and especially on Tiny Tim, until the last.

By this time it was getting dark, and snowing pretty heavily; and as Scrooge and the Spirit went along the streets, the brightness of the roaring fires in kitchens, parlors, and all sorts of rooms, was wonderful. Here, the flickering of the blaze showed preparations for a cosy dinner, with hot plates baking through and through before the fire, and deep red curtains, ready to be drawn, to shut out cold and darkness. There, all the children of the house were running out into the snow to meet their married sisters, brothers, cousins, uncles, aunts, and be the first to greet them. Here, again, were shadows on the window-blind of guests assembling; and there a group of handsome girls, all hooded and fur-booted, and all chattering at once, tripped lightly off to some near neighbor's house; where, woe upon the single man who saw them enter—artful witches: well they knew it—in a glow.

But if you had judged from the numbers of people on their way to friendly gatherings, you might have thought that no one was at home to give them welcome when they got there, instead of every house expecting company, and piling up its fires half-chimney high. Blessings on it, how the Ghost exulted! How it bared its breadth of breast, and opened its capacious palm, and floated on, outpouring, with a generous hand, its bright and harmless mirth on everything within its reach! The very lamplighter, who ran on before, dotting the dusky street with specks of light, and who was dressed to spend the evening somewhere, laughed out loudly as the Spirit passed: though little kenned the lamplighter that he had any company but Christmas!

And now, without a word of warning from the Ghost, they stood upon a bleak and desert moor, where monstrous masses of rude stone were cast about, as though it were the burial-place of giants; and water spread itself wheresoever it listed—or would have done so, but for the frost that held it prisoner; and nothing grew but moss and furze, and coarse, rank grass. Down in the west the setting sun had left a streak of fiery red, which glared upon the desolation for an instant, like a sullen eye, and frowning lower, lower, lower yet, was lost in the thick gloom of darkest night.

"What place is this?" asked Scrooge.

"A place where Miners live, who labor in the bowels of the earth," returned the Spirit. "But they know me. See!"

A light shone from the window of a hut, and swiftly they advanced towards it. Passing through the wall of mud and stone, they found a cheerful company assembled round a glowing fire. An old, old man and woman, with their children and their children's children, and another generation beyond that, all decked out gaily in their holiday attire. The old man, in a voice that seldom rose above the howling of the wind upon the barren waste, was singing them a Christmas song; it had been a very old song when he was a boy; and from time to time they all joined in the chorus. So surely as they raised their voices, the old man got quite blithe and loud; and so surely as they stopped, his vigor sank again.

The Spirit did not tarry here, but bade Scrooge hold his robe, and passing on above the moor, sped whither? Not to sea? To sea. To Scrooge's horror, looking back, he saw the last of the land, a frightful range of rocks, behind them; and his ears were deafened by the thundering of water, as it rolled, and roared, and raged among the dreadful caverns it had worn, and fiercely tried to undermine the earth.

Built upon a dismal reef of sunken rocks, some league or so from shore, on which the waters chafed and dashed the wild year through, there stood a solitary lighthouse. Great heaps of sea-weed clung to its base, and storm-birds—born of the wind one might suppose, as sea-weed of the water—rose and fell about it, like the waves they skimmed.

But even here, two men who watched the light had made a fire, that through the loophole in the thick stone wall shed out a ray of brightness on the awful sea. Joining their horny hands over the rough table at which they sat, they wished each other a Merry Christmas in their can of grog; and one of them: the elder, too, with his face all damaged and scarred with hard weather, as the figure-head of an old ship might be: struck up a sturdy song that was like a gale in itself.

Again the Ghost sped on, above the black and heaving sea—on, on—until, being far away, as he told Scrooge, from any shore, they lighted on a ship. They stood beside the helmsman at the wheel, the look-out in the bow, the officers who had the watch; dark, ghostly figures in their several stations; but every man among them hummed a Christmas tune, or had a Christmas thought, or spoke below his breath to his companion of some bygone Christmas Day, with homeward hopes belonging to it.

And every man on board, waking or sleeping, good or bad, had had a kinder word for another on that day than on any day in the year; and had shared to some extent in its festivities; and had remembered those he cared for at a distance, and had known that they delighted to remember him.

It was a great surprise to Scrooge, while listening to the moaning of the wind, and thinking what a solemn thing it was to move on through the lonely darkness over an unknown abyss, whose depths were secrets as profound as Death: it was a great surprise to Scrooge, while thus engaged, to hear a hearty laugh. It was a much greater surprise to Scrooge to recognize it as his own nephew's, and to find himself in a bright, dry, gleaming room, with the Spirit standing smiling by his side, and looking at that same nephew with approving affability.

"Ha, ha!" laughed Scrooge's nephew. "Ha, ha, ha!"

If you should happen, by any unlikely chance, to know a man more blest in a laugh than Scrooge's nephew, all I can say is, I should like to know him, too. Introduce him to me, and I'll cultivate his acquaintance.

It is a fair, even handed, noble adjustment of things, that while there is infection in disease and sorrow, there is nothing in the world so irresistibly contagious as laughter and good-humor. When Scrooge's nephew laughed in this way; holding his sides, rolling his head, and twisting his face into the most extravagant contortions: Scrooge's niece, by marriage, laughed as heartily as he. And their assembled friends being not a bit behindhand, roared out, lustily.

"Ha, ha! Ha, ha, ha, ha!"

"He said that Christmas was a humbug, as I live!" cried Scrooge's nephew. "He believed it, too!"

"More shame for him, Fred!" said Scrooge's niece, indignantly. Bless those women; they never do anything by halves. They are always in earnest.

She was very pretty: exceedingly pretty. With a dimpled, surprised-looking, capital face; a ripe little mouth, that seemed made to be kissed—as no doubt it was; all kinds of good little dots about her chin, that melted into one another when she laughed; and the sunniest pair of eyes you ever saw in any little creature's head. Altogether she was what you would have called provoking, you know; but satisfactory, too. Oh, perfectly satisfactory!

"He's a comical old fellow," said Scrooge's nephew, "that's the truth; and not so pleasant as he might be. However, his offences carry their own punishment, and I have nothing to say against him."

"I'm sure he is very rich, Fred," hinted Scrooge's niece. "At least you always tell *me* so."

"What of that, my dear," said Scrooge's nephew. "His wealth is of no use to him. He don't do any good with it. He don't made himself comfortable with it. He hasn't the satisfaction of thinking—ha, ha, ha!—that he is ever going to benefit Us with it."

"I have no patience with him," observed Scrooge's niece. Scrooge's niece's sisters, and all the other ladies, expressed the same opinion.

"Oh, I have!" said Scrooge's nephew. "I am sorry for him; I couldn't be angry with him if I tried. Who suffers by his ill whims? Himself, always. Here, he takes it into his head to dislike us, and he won't come and dine with us. What's the consequence? He don't lose much of a dinner."

"Indeed, I think he loses a very good dinner," interrupted Scrooge's niece. Everybody said the same, and they must be allowed to have been competent judges, because they had just had dinner; and, with the dessert upon the table, were clustered round the fire, by lamplight.

"Well! I am very glad to hear it," said Scrooge's nephew, "because I haven't any great faith in these young housekeepers. What do *you* say, Topper?"

Topper had clearly got his eye upon one of Scrooge's niece's sisters, for he answered that a bachelor was a wretched outcast, who had no right to express an opinion on the subject. Whereat Scrooge's niece's sister—the plump one with the lace tucker: not the one with the roses—blushed.

"Do go on, Fred," said Scrooge's niece, clapping her hands. "He never finishes what he begins to say! He is such a ridiculous fellow!"

Scrooge's nephew revelled in another laugh, and as it was impossible to keep the infection off; though the plump sister tried hard to do it with aromatic vinegar; his example was unanimously followed.

"I was only going to say," said Scrooge's nephew, "that the consequence of his taking a dislike to us, and not making merry with us, is, as I think, that he loses some pleasant moments, which could do him no harm. I am sure he loses pleasanter companions than he can find in his own thoughts, either in his mouldy old office, or his dusty chambers. I mean to give him the same chance every year, whether he likes it or not, for I pity him. He may rail at Christmas till he dies, but he can't help thinking better of it—I defy him—if he finds me going there, in good temper, year after year, and saying Uncle Scrooge, how are you? If it only puts him in the vein to leave his poor clerk fifty pounds, *that's* something; and I think I shook him yesterday."

It was their turn to laugh now, at the notion of his shaking Scrooge. But being thoroughly good-natured, and not much caring what they laughed at, so that they laughed at any rate, he encouraged them in their merriment, and passed the bottle, joyously.

After tea, they had some music. For they were a musical family, and knew what they were about, when they sung a Glee or Catch, I can assure you: especially Topper, who could growl away in the bass like a good one, and never swell the large veins in his forehead, or get red in the face over it. Scrooge's niece played well upon the harp; and played among other tunes a simple little air (a mere nothing; you might learn to whistle it in two minutes), which had been familiar to the child who fetched Scrooge from the boarding-school, as he had been reminded by the Ghost of Christmas Past. When this strain of music sounded, all the things that Ghost had shown him, came upon his mind; he softened more and more; and thought that if he could have listened to it often, years ago, he might have cultivated the kindness of life for his own happiness with his own hands, without resorting to the sexton's spade that buried Jacob Marley.

But they didn't devote the whole evening to music. After a while they played at forfeits, for it is good to be children sometimes, and never better than at Christmas, when its mighty Founder was a child himself. Stop! There was first a game at blindman's buff. Of course there was. And I no more believe Topper was really blind than I believe he had eyes in his boots. My opinion is, that it was a done thing between him and Scrooge's nephew; and that the Ghost of Christmas Present knew it. The way he went after that plump sister in the lace tucker, was an outrage on the credulity of human nature. Knocking down the fire-irons, tumbling over the chairs, bumping against the piano, smothering himself among the curtains, wherever she went, there went he. He always knew where the plump sister was. He wouldn't catch anybody else. If you had fallen up against him, as some of them did, and stood there; he would have made a feint of endeavoring to seize you, which would have been an affront to your understanding; and would instantly have sidled off in the direction of the plump sister. She often cried out that it wasn't fair; and it really was not. But when, at last, he caught her; when, in spite of all her silken rustlings, and her rapid flutterings past him, he got her into a corner whence there was no escape; then his conduct was the most execrable. For his pretending not to know her; his pretending that it was necessary to touch her head-dress, and further to assure himself of her identity by pressing a certain ring upon her finger, and a certain chain about her neck; was vile, monstrous! No doubt she told him her opinion of it, when, another blindman being in office, they were so very confidential together, behind the curtains.

Scrooge's niece was not one of the blindman's buff party, but was made comfortable with a large chair and a footstool, in a snug corner, where the Ghost and Scrooge were close behind her. But she joined in the forfeits, and loved her love to admiration with all the letters of the alphabet. Likewise at the game of How, When, and Where, she was very great, and to the secret joy of Scrooge's nephew, beat her sisters hollow: though they were sharp girls too, as Topper could have told you. There might have been twenty people there, young and old, but they all played and so did Scrooge; for, wholly forgetting, in the interest he had in what was going on, that his voice made no sound in their ears, he sometimes came out with his guess quite loud, and very often guessed right, too; for the sharpest needle, best Whitechapel, warranted not to cut in the eye, was not sharper than Scrooge: blunt as he took it in his head to be.

The Ghost was greatly pleased to find him in this mood, and looked upon him with such favor that he begged like a boy to be allowed to stay until the guests departed. But this the Spirit said could not be done.

"Here's a new game," said Scrooge. "One half hour, Spirit, only one!"

It was a Game called Yes and No, where Scrooge's nephew had to think of something, the rest must find out what; he only answering to their questions yes or no, as the case was. The brisk fire of questioning to which he was exposed, elicited from him that he was thinking of an animal, a live animal, rather a disagreeable animal, a savage animal, an animal that growled and grunted sometimes, and talked sometimes, and lived in London, and walked about the streets, and wasn't made a show of, and wasn't led by anybody, and didn't live in a menagerie, and was never killed in a market, and was not a horse, or an ass, or a cow, or a bull, or a tiger, or a dog, or a pig, or a cat, or a bear. At every fresh question that was put to him, this nephew burst into a fresh roar of laughter; and was so inexpressibly tickled, that he was obliged to get up off the sofa and stamp. At last the plump sister, falling into a similar state, cried out:

"I have found it out! I know what it is, Fred! I know what it is!"

"What is it?" cried Fred.

"It's your Uncle Scro-o-o-o-oge!"

Which it certainly was. Admiration was the universal sentiment, though some objected that the reply to "Is it a bear?" ought to have been "Yes"; inasmuch as an answer in the negative was sufficient to have diverted their thoughts from Mr. Scrooge, supposing they had ever had any tendency that way.

"He has given us plenty of merriment, I am sure," said Fred, "and it would be ungrateful not to drink his health. Here is a glass of mulled wine ready to our hand at the moment; and I say, 'Uncle Scrooge!'"

"Well! Uncle Scrooge!" they cried.

"A Merry Christmas and a Happy New Year to the old man, whatever he is!" said Scrooge's nephew. "He wouldn't take it from me, but may he have it, nevertheless! Uncle Scrooge!"

Uncle Scrooge had imperceptibly become so gay and light of heart, that he would have pledged the unconscious company in return, and thanked them in an inaudible speech, if the Ghost had given him time. But the whole scene passed off in the breath of the last word spoken by his nephew: and he and the Spirit were again upon their travels.

Much they saw, and far they went, and many homes they visited, but always with a happy end. The Spirit stood beside sick beds, and they were cheerful; on foreign lands, and they were close at home; by struggling men, and they were patient in their greater hope; by poverty, and it was rich. In almshouse, hospital, and jail, in misery's every refuge, where vain man in his little brief authority had not made fast the door, and barred the Spirit out, he left his blessing, and taught Scrooge his precepts.

It was a long night, if it were only a night; but Scrooge had his doubts of this, because the Christmas holidays appeared to be condensed into the space of time they passed together. It was strange, too, that while Scrooge remained unaltered in his outward form, the Ghost grew older, clearly older. Scrooge had observed this change, but never spoke of it, until they left a children's Twelfth Night party, when, looking at the Spirit as they stood together in an open place, he noticed that its hair was grey.

"Are spirits' lives short?" asked Scrooge.

"My life upon this globe is very brief," replied the Ghost. "It ends to-night."

"To-night! cried Scrooge.

"To-night at midnight. Hark! The time is drawing near."

The chimes were ringing the three quarters past eleven at that moment.

"Forgive me if I am not justified in what I ask," said Scrooge, looking intently at the Spirit's robe, "but I see something strange, and not belonging to yourself, protruding from your skirts. Is it a foot or a claw?"

"It might be a claw, for the flesh there is upon it," was the Spirit's sorrowful reply. "Look here."

From the foldings of its robe it brought two children; wretched, abject, frightful, hideous, miserable. They knelt down at its feet, and clung upon the outside of its garment.

"Oh. Man! look here. Look, look down here!" exclaimed the Ghost.

They were a boy and a girl. Yellow, meagre, ragged, scowling, wolfish; but prostrate, too, in their humility. Where graceful youth should have filled their features out, and touched them with its freshest tints, a stale and shrivelled hand, like that of age, had pinched, and twisted them, and pulled them into shreds. Where angels might have sat enthroned, devils lurked, and glared out menacing. No change, no degradation, no perversion of humanity, in any grade, through all the mysteries of wonderful creation, has monsters half so horrible and dread.

Scrooge started back, appalled. Having them shown to him in this way, he tried to say they were fine children, but the words choked themselves, rather than be parties to a lie of such enormous magnitude.

"Spirit! Are they yours?" Scrooge could say no more.

"They are Man's," said the Spirit, looking down upon them. "And they cling to me, appealing from their fathers. This boy is Ignorance. This girl is Want. Beware them both, and all of their degree, but most of all beware this boy, for on his brow I see that written which is Doom, unless the writing be erased. Deny it!" cried the Spirit, stretching out its hand towards the city. "Slander those who tell it ye! Admit it for your factious purposes, and make it worse! And bide the end!"

"Have they no refuge or resources?" cried Scrooge.

"Are there no prisons?" said the Spirit, turning on him for the last time with his own words. "Are there no workhouses?"

The bell struck twelve.

Scrooge looked about him for the Ghost, and saw it not. As the last stroke ceased to vibrate, he remembered the prediction of old Jacob Marley, and lifting up his eyes, beheld a solemn Phantom, draped and hooded, coming, like a mist along the ground, towards him.

Stave Four

THE LAST OF THE SPIRITS

THE Phantom slowly, gravely, silently approached. When it came near him, Scrooge bent down upon his knee, for in the very air through which this Spirit moved it seemed to scatter gloom and mystery.

It was shrouded in a deep black garment, which concealed its head, its face, its form, and left nothing of it visible save one outstretched hand. But for this it would have been difficult to detach its figure from the night, and separate it from the darkness by which it was surrounded.

He felt that it was tall and stately when it came beside him, and that its mysterious presence filled him with a solemn dread. He knew no more, for the Spirit neither spoke nor moved.

"I am in the presence of the Ghost of Christmas Yet to Come?" said Scrooge.

The Spirit answered not, but pointed onward with its hand.

"You are about to show me shadows of the things that have not happened, but will happen in the time before us," Scrooge pursued. "Is that so, Spirit?"

The upper portion of the garment was contracted for an instant in its folds, as if the Spirit had inclined its head. That was the only answer he received.

Although well used to ghostly company by this time, Scrooge feared the silent shape so much that his legs trembled beneath him, and he found that he could hardly stand when he prepared to follow it. The Spirit paused a moment, as observing his condition, and giving him time to recover.

But Scrooge was all the worse for this. It thrilled him with a vague uncertain horror, to know that behind the dusky shroud there were ghostly eyes intently fixed upon him, while he, though he stretched his own to the utmost, could see nothing but a spectral hand and one great heap of black.

"Ghost of the Future!" he exclaimed, "I fear you more than any Spectre I have seen. But, as I know your purpose is to do me good, and as I hope to live to be another man from what I was, I am prepared to bear you company, and do it with a thankful heart. Will you not speak to me?"

It gave him no reply. The hand was pointed straight before them.

"Lead on!" said Scrooge. "Lead on! The night is waning fast, and it is precious time to me, I know. Lead on, Spirit!"

The Phantom moved away as it had come towards him. Scrooge followed in the shadow of its dress, which bore him up, he thought, and carried him along.

They scarcely seemed to enter the city; for the city rather seemed to spring up about them, and encompass them of its own act. But there they were, in the heart of it; on 'Change, amongst the merchants; who hurried up and down, and chinked the money in their pockets, and conversed in groups, and looked at their watches, and trifled thoughtfully with their great gold seals, and so forth, as Scrooge had seen them often.

The Spirit stopped beside one little knot of business men. Observing that the hand was pointed to them, Scrooge advanced to listen to their talk.

"No," said a great fat man with a monstrous chin, "I don't know much about it either way, I only know he's dead."

"When did he die?" inquired another.

"Last night, I believe."

"Why, what was the matter with him?" asked a third, taking a vast quantity of snuff out of a very large snuff-box. "I thought he'd never die."

"God knows," said the first, with a yawn.

"What has he done with his money?" asked a red-faced gentleman, with a pendulous excrescence on the end of his nose, that shook like the gills of a turkey-cock.

"I haven't heard," said the man with the large chin, yawning again. "Left it to his Company, perhaps. He hasn't left it to *me*. That's all I know."

This pleasantry was received with a general laugh.

"It's likely to be a very cheap funeral," said the same speaker; "for upon my life I don't know of anybody to go to it. Suppose we make up a party and volunteer?"

"I don't mind going if a lunch is provided," observed the gentleman with the excrescence on his nose. "But I must be fed, if I make one."

Another laugh.

"Well, I am the most disinterested among you, after all," said the first speaker, "for I never wear black gloves, and I never eat lunch. But I'll offer to go, if anybody else will. When I come to think of it, I'm not at all sure that I wasn't his most particular friend; for we used to stop and speak whenever we met. Bye, bye!"

Speakers and listeners strolled away, and mixed with other groups. Scrooge knew the men, and looked towards the Spirit for an explanation.

The Phantom glided on into a street. Its finger pointed to two persons meeting. Scrooge listened again, thinking that the explanation might lie here.

He knew these men, also, perfectly. They were men of business: very wealthy, and of great importance. He had made a point always of standing well in their esteem: in a business point of view, that is; strictly in a business point of view.

"How are you?" said one.

"How are you?" returned the other.

"Well!" said the first. "Old Scratch has got his own at last, hey?"

"So I am told," returned the second. "Cold, isn't it?"

"Seasonable for Christmas time. You're not a skater, I suppose?"

"No. No. Something else to think of. Good morning!"

Not another word. That was their meeting, their conversation, and their parting.

Scrooge was at first inclined to be surprised that the Spirit should attach importance to conversations apparently so trivial; but feeling assured that they must have some hidden purpose, he set himself to consider what it was likely to be. They could scarcely be supposed to have any bearing on the death of Jacob, his old partner, for that was Past, and this Ghost's province was the Future. Nor could he think of any one immediately connected with himself, to whom he could apply them. But nothing doubting that to whomsoever they applied they had some latent moral for his own improvement, he resolved to treasure up every word he heard, and everything he saw; and especially to observe the shadow of himself when it appeared. For he had an expectation that the conduct of his future self would give him the clue he missed, and would render the solution of these riddles easy.

He looked about in that very place for his own image; but another man stood in his accustomed corner, and though the clock pointed to his usual time of day for being there, he saw no likeness of himself among the multitudes that poured in through the Porch. It gave him little surprise, however, for he had been revolving in his mind a change of life, and thought and hoped he saw his new-born resolutions carried out in this.

Quiet and dark, beside him stood the Phantom, with its out-stretched hand. When he roused himself from his thoughtful quest, he fancied from the turn of the hand, and its situation in reference to himself, that the Unseen Eyes were looking at him keenly. It made him shudder, and feel very cold.

They left the busy scene, and went into an obscure part of the town, where Scrooge had never penetrated before, although he recognized its situation, and its bad repute. The ways were foul and narrow; the shops and houses wretched; the people half-naked, drunken, slipshod, ugly. Alleys and archways, like so many cesspools, disgorged their offences of smell, and dirt, and life, upon the straggling streets, and the whole quarter reeked with crime, with filth, and misery.

Far in this den of infamous resort, there was a low-browed beetling shop, below a pent-house roof, where iron, old rags, bottles, and bones, and greasy offal were bought. Upon the floor within, were piled up heaps of rusty keys, nails, chains, hinges, files, scales, weights, and refuse iron of all kinds. Secrets that few would like to scrutinize were bred and hidden in mountains of unseemly rags, masses of corrupted fat, and sepulchres of bones. Sitting in among the wares he dealt in, by a charcoal-stove, made of old bricks, was a grey-haired rascal, nearly seventy years of age, who had screened himself from the cold air without by a frowsy curtaining of miscellaneous tatters, hung upon a line, and smoked his pipe in all the luxury of calm retirement.

Scrooge and the Phantom came into the presence of this man just as a woman with a heavy bundle slunk into the shop. But she had scarcely entered, when another woman, similarly laden, came in too; and she was closely followed by a man in faded black, who was no less startled by the sight of them than they had been upon the recognition of each other. After a short period of blank astonishment, in which the old man with the pipe had joined them, they all three burst into a laugh.

"Let the charwoman alone to be the first!" cried she who had entered first. "Let the laundress alone to be the second; and let the undertaker's man alone to be the third. Look here, old Joe, here's a chance. If we haven't all three met here without meaning it!"

"You couldn't have met in a better place," said old Joe, removing his pipe from his mouth. "Come into the parlor. You were made free of it long ago, you know; and the other two an't strangers. Stop till I shut the door of the shop. Ah! How it skreeks! There an't such a rusty bit of metal in the place as its own hinges, I believe, and I'm sure there's no such old bones here as mine. Ha, ha! We're all suitable to our calling, we're well matched. Come into the parlor. Come into the parlor."

The parlor was the space behind the screen of rags. The old man raked the fire together with an old stair-rod, and having trimmed his smoky lamp (for it was night) with the stem of his pipe, put it in his mouth again.

While he did this the woman who had already spoken threw her bundle on the floor and sat down in a flaunting manner on a stool; crossing her elbows on her knees, and looking with a bold defiance at the other two.

"What odds, then! What odds, Mrs. Dilber?" said the woman. "Every person has a right to take care of themselves. *He* always did!"

"That's true, indeed!" said the laundress. "No man more so."

"Why, then, don't stand staring as if you was afraid, woman; who's the wiser? We're not going to pick holes in each other's coats, I suppose?"

"No, indeed!" said Mrs. Dilber and the man together. "We should hope not."

"Very well, then!" cried the woman. "That's enough. Who's the worse for the loss of a few things like these? Not a dead man, I suppose."

"No, indeed," said Mrs. Dilber, laughing.

"If he wanted to keep 'em after he was dead, a wicked old screw," pursued the woman, "why wasn't he natural in his lifetime? If he had been, he'd have had somebody to look after him when he was struck with Death, instead of lying gasping out his last there, alone by himself."

"It's the truest word that ever was spoke," said Mrs. Dilber. "It's a judgment on him."

"I wish it was a little heavier judgment," replied the woman; "and it should have been, you may depend upon it, if I could have laid my hands on anything else. Open that bundle, old Joe, and let me know the value of it. Speak out plain. I'm not afraid to be the first, nor afraid for them to see it. We knew pretty well that we were helping ourselves, before we met here, I believe. It's no sin. Open the bundle, Joe."

But the gallantry of her friends would not allow of this; and the man in faded black, mounting the breach first, produced *his* plunder. It was not extensive. A seal or two, a pencil-case, a pair of sleeve-buttons, and a brooch of no great value, were all. They were severally examined and appraised by old Joe, who chalked the sums he was disposed to give for each upon the wall, and added them up in a total when he found that there was nothing more to come.

"That's your account," said Joe, "and I wouldn't give another sixpence, if I was to be boiled for not doing it. Who's next?"

Mrs. Dilber was next. Sheets and towels, a little wearing apparel, two old-fashioned silver teaspoons, a pair of sugar-tongs, and a few boots. Her account was stated on the wall in the same manner.

"I always give too much to ladies. It's a weakness of mine, and that's the way I ruin myself," said old Joe. "That's your account. If you asked me for another penny, and made it an open question, I'd repent of being so liberal and knock off half-a-crown."

"And now undo *my* bundle, Joe," said the first woman.

Joe went down on his knees for the greater convenience of opening it, and having unfastened a great many knots, dragged out a large and heavy roll of some dark stuff.

"What do you call this?" said Joe. "Bedcurtains?"

"Ah!" returned the woman, laughing and leaning forward on her crossed arms. "Bedcurtains!"

"You don't mean to say you took 'em down, rings and all, with him lying there?" said Joe.

"Yes, I do," replied the woman. "Why not?"

"You were born to make your fortune," said Joe, "and you'll certainly do it."

"I certainly shan't hold my hand, when I can get anything in it by reaching it out, for the sake of such a man as He was, I promise you, Joe," returned the woman coolly. "Don't drop that oil upon the blankets, now."

"His blankets?" asked Joe.

"Whose else's do you think?" replied the woman. "He isn't likely to take cold without 'em, I dare say."

"I hope he didn't die of anything catching? Eh?" said old Joe, stopping in his work, and looking up.

"Don't you be afraid of that," returned the woman. "I an't so fond of his company that I'd loiter about him for such things, if he did. Ah! You may look through that shirt till your eyes ache; but you won't find a hole in it, nor a threadbare place. It's the best he had, and a fine one too. They'd have wasted it, if it hadn't been for me."

"What do you call wasting of it?" asked old Joe.

"Putting it on him to be buried in, to be sure," replied the woman with a laugh. "Somebody was fool enough to do it, but I took it off again. If calico an't enough for such a purpose, it isn't good enough for anything. It's quite as becoming to the body. He can't look uglier than he did in that one."

Scrooge listened to this dialogue in horror. As they sat grouped about their spoil, in the scanty light afforded by the old man's lamp, he viewed them with a detestation and disgust, which could hardly have been greater, though they had been obscene demons, marketing the corpse itself.

"Ha, ha!" laughed the same woman, when old Joe, producing a flannel bag with money in it, told out their several gains upon the ground. "This is the end of it, you see! He frightened every one away from him when he was alive, to profit us when he was dead! Ha, ha, ha!"

"Spirit!" said Scrooge, shuddering from head to foot. "I see, I see. The case of this unhappy man might be my own. My life tends that way, now. Merciful Heaven, what is this!"

He recoiled in terror, for the scene had changed, and now he almost touched a bed: a bare, uncurtained bed: on which, beneath a ragged sheet, there lay a something covered up, which, though it was dumb, announced itself in awful language.

The room was very dark, too dark to be observed with any accuracy, though Scrooge glanced round it in obedience to a secret impulse, anxious to know what kind of room it was. A pale light, rising in the outer air, fell straight upon the bed; and on it, plundered and bereft, unwatched, unwept, uncared for, was the body of this man.

Scrooge glanced towards the phantom. Its steady hand was pointed to the head. The cover was so carelessly adjusted that the slightest raising of it, the motion of a finger upon Scrooge's part, would have disclosed the face. He thought of it, felt how easy it would be to do, and longed to do it; but had no more power to withdraw the veil than to dismiss the spectre at his side.

Oh cold, cold, rigid, dreadful Death, set up thine altar here, and dress it with such terrors as thou hast at thy command: for this is thy dominion!

But of the loved, revered, and honored head, thou canst not turn one hair to thy dread purposes, or make one feature odious. It is not that the hand is heavy and will fall down when released; it is not that the heart and pulse are still; but that the hand was open, generous and true; the heart brave, warm, and tender; and the pulse a man's. Strike, Shadow, strike! And see his good deeds springing from the wound, to sow the world with life immortal!

No voice pronounced these words in Scrooge's ears, and yet he heard them when he looked upon the bed. He thought if this man could be raised up now, what would be his foremost thoughts? Avarice, hard-dealing, griping cares; They have brought him into a rich end, truly!

He lay, in the dark empty house, with not a man, a woman, or a child, to say he was kind to me in this or that, and for the memory of one kind word I will be kind to him. A cat was tearing at the door, and there was a sound of gnawing rats beneath the hearth-stone. What *they* wanted in the room of death, and why they were so restless and disturbed, Scrooge did not dare to think.

"Spirit!" he said, "this is a fearful place. In leaving it, I shall not leave its lesson, trust me. Let us go!"

Still the ghost pointed with an unmoved finger to the head.

"I understand you," Scrooge returned, "and I would do it, if I could. But I have not the power, Spirit. I have not the power."

Again it seemed to look upon him.

"If there is any person in the town who feels emotion caused by this man's death," said Scrooge, quite agonized, "show that person to me, Spirit, I beseech you!"

The phantom spread its dark robe before him for a moment, like a wing; and withdrawing it, revealed a room by daylight, where a mother and her children were.

She was expecting some one, and with anxious eagerness; for she walked up and down the room; started at every sound; looked out from the window; glanced at the clock; tried, but in vain, to work with her needle; and could hardly bear the voices of the children in their play.

At length the long-expected knock was heard. She hurried to the door, and met her husband; a man whose face was careworn and depressed, though he was young. There was a remarkable expression in it now; a kind of serious delight of which he felt ashamed, and which he struggled to repress.

He sat down to the dinner that had been hoarding for him by the fire; and when she asked him faintly what news (which was not until after a long silence), he appeared embarrassed how to answer.

"Is it good," she said, "or bad?" to help him.

"Bad," he answered.

"We are quite ruined?"

"No. There is hope yet, Caroline."

"If *he* relents," she said, amazed, "there is! Nothing is past hope, if such a miracle has happened."

"He is past relenting," said her husband. "He is dead."

She was a mild and patient creature, if her face spoke truth; but she was thankful in her soul to hear it, and she said so, with clasped hands.

She prayed forgiveness the next moment, and was sorry; but the first was the emotion of her heart.

"What the half-drunken woman, whom I told you of last night, said to me when I tried to see him and obtain a week's delay; and what I thought was a mere excuse to avoid me; turns out to have been quite true. He was not only very ill, but dying, then."

"To whom will our debt be transferred?"

"I don't know. But before that time we shall be ready with the money; and even though we were not, it would be a bad fortune, indeed, to find so merciless a creditor in his successor. We may sleep to-night with light hearts, Caroline!"

Yes. Soften it as they would, their hearts were lighter. The children's faces hushed, and clustered round to hear what they so little understood, were brighter; and it was a happier house for this man's death! The only emotion that the Ghost could show him, caused by the event, was one of pleasure.

"Let me see some tenderness connected with a death," said Scrooge; "or that dark chamber, Spirit, which we left just now, will be for ever present to me."

The Ghost conducted him through several streets familiar to his feet; and as they went along, Scrooge looked here and there to find himself, but nowhere was he to be seen. They entered poor Bob Cratchit's house; the dwelling he had visited before; and found the mother and the children seated round the fire.

Quiet. Very quiet. The noisy little Cratchits were as still as statues in one corner, and sat looking up at Peter, who had a book before him. The mother and her daughters were engaged in sewing. But surely they were very quiet!

"'And he took a child and set him in the midst of them.'"

Where had Scrooge heard those words? He had not dreamed them. The boy must have read them out, as he and the Spirit crossed the threshold. Why did he not go on?

The mother laid her work upon the table, and put her hand up to her face.

"The color hurts my eyes," she said.

The color? Ah, poor Tiny Tim!

"They're better now again," said Cratchit's wife. "It makes them weak by candle-light; and I wouldn't show weak eyes to your father when he comes home, for the world. It must be near his time."

"Past it, rather," Peter answered, shutting up his book. "But, I think he's walked a little slower than he used, these few last evenings, mother."

They were very quiet again. At last she said, and in a steady, cheerful voice, that only faltered once:

"I have known him walk with—I have known him walk with Tiny Tim upon his shoulder, very fast, indeed."

"And so have I," cried Peter. "Often."

"And so have I!" exclaimed another. So had all.

"But he was very light to carry," she resumed, intent upon her work, "and his father loved him so, that it was no trouble—no trouble. And there is your father at the door!"

She hurried out to meet him; and little Bob in his comforter—he had need of it, poor fellow—came in. His tea was ready for him on the hob, and they all tried who should help him to it most. Then the two young Cratchits got upon his knees and laid, each child, a little cheek, against his face, as if they said, "Don't mind it, father. Don't be grieved!"

Bob was very cheeful with them, and spoke pleasantly to all the family. He looked at the work upon the table, and praised the industry and speed of Mrs. Cratchit and the girls. They would be done long before Sunday, he said.

"Sunday! You went to-day, then, Robert?" said his wife.

"Yes, my dear," returned Bob. "I wish you could have gone. It would have done you good to see how green a place it is. But you'll see it often. I promised him that I would walk there on a Sunday. My little, little child!" cried Bob. "My little child!"

He broke down all at once. He couldn't help it. If he could have helped it, he and his child would have been farther apart, perhaps, than they were.

He left the room, and went upstairs into the room above, which was lighted cheerfully, and hung with Christmas. There was a chair set close beside the child, and there were signs of some one having been there lately. Poor Bob sat down in it, and when he had thought a little and composed himself, he kissed the little face. He was reconciled to what had happened, and went down again quite happy.

They drew about the fire and talked; the girls and mother working still. Bob told them of the extraordinary kindness of Mr. Scrooge's nephew, whom he had scarcely seen but once, and who, meeting him in the street that day, and seeing that he looked a little—"just a little down, you know," said Bob, inquired what had happened to distress him. "On which," said Bob, "for he is the pleasantest-spoken gentleman you ever heard, I told him. 'I am heartily sorry for it, Mr. Cratchit,' he said, 'and heartily sorry for your good wife.' By the bye, how he ever knew *that,* I don't know."

"Knew what, my dear?"

"Why, that you were a good wife," replied Bob.

"Everybody knows that!" said Peter.

"Very well observed, my boy!" cried Bob. "I hope they do. 'Heartily sorry,' he said, 'for your good wife. If I can be of service in any way,' he said, giving me his card, 'that's where I live. Pray come to me.' Now, it wasn't," cried Bob, "for the sake of anything he might be able to do for us, so much as for his kind way, that this was quite delightful. It really seemed as if he had known our Tiny Tim, and felt with us."

"I'm sure he's a good soul!" said Mrs. Cratchit.

"You would be surer of it, my dear," returned Bob, "if you saw and spoke to him. I shouldn't be at all surprised, mark what I say, if he got Peter a better situation."

"Only hear that, Peter," said Mrs. Cratchit.

"And then," cried one of the girls, "Peter will be keeping company with some one, and setting up for himself."

"Get along with you!" retorted Peter, grinning.

"It's just as likely as not," said Bob, "one of these days; though there's plenty of time for that, my dear. But however and whenever we part from one another, I am sure we shall none of us forget poor Tiny Tim—shall we—or this first parting that there was among us?"

"Never, father!" cried they all.

"And I know," said Bob, "I know, my dears, that when we recollect how patient and how mild he was; although he was a little, little child; we shall not quarrel easily among ourselves, and forget poor Tiny Tim in doing it."

"No, never, father!" they all cried again.

"I am very happy," said little Bob, "I am very happy!"

Mrs. Cratchit kissed him, his daughters kissed him, the two young Cratchits kissed him, and Peter and himself shook hands. Spirit of Tiny Tim, thy childish essence was from God!

"Spectre," said Scrooge, "something informs me that our parting moment is at hand. I know it, but I know not how. Tell me what man that was whom we saw lying dead?"

The Ghost of Christmas Yet To Come conveyed him, as before—though at a different time, he thought: indeed, there seemed no order in these latter visions, save that they were in the Future—into the resorts of business men, but showed him not himself. Indeed, the Spirit did not stay for anything, but went straight on, as to the end just now desired, until besought by Scrooge to tarry for a moment.

"This court," said Scrooge, "through which we hurry now, is where my place of occupation is, and has been for a length of time. I see the house. Let me behold what I shall be in days to come."

The Spirit stopped; the hand was pointed elsewhere.

"The house is yonder," Scrooge exclaimed. "Why do you point away!"

The inexorable finger underwent no change.

Scrooge hastened to the window of his office, and looked in. It was an office still, but not his. The furniture was not the same, and the figure in the chair was not himself. The Phantom pointed as before.

He joined it once again, and wondering why and whither he had gone, accompanied it until they reached an iron gate. He paused to look round before entering.

A churchyard. Here, then, the wretched man whose name he had now to learn, lay underneath the ground. It was a worthy place. Walled in by houses; overrun by grass and weeds, the growth of vegetation's death, not life; choked up with too much burying; fat with repleted appetite. A worthy place!

The Spirit stood among the graves, and pointed down to One. He advanced towards it trembling. The Phantom was exactly as it had been, but he dreaded that he saw new meaning in its solemn shape.

"Before I draw nearer to that stone to which you point," said Scrooge, "answer me one question. Are these the shadows of the things that Will be, or are they shadows of things that May be, only?"

Still the Ghost pointed downward to the grave by which it stood.

"Men's courses will foreshadow certain ends, to which, if persevered in, they must lead," said Scrooge. "But if the courses be departed from, the ends will change. Say it is thus with what you show me!"

The Spirit was immovable as ever.

Scrooge crept towards it, trembling as he went; and following the finger, read upon the stone of the neglected grave his own name, EBENEZER SCROOGE.

"Am *I* that man who lay upon the bed?" he cried, upon his knees.

The finger pointed from the grave to him, and back again.

"No, Spirit! Oh no, no!"

The finger still was there.

"Spirit!" he cried, tight clutching at its robe, "hear me! I am not the man I was. I will not be the man I must have been but for this intercourse. Why show me this, if I am past all hope?"

For the first time the hand appeared to shake.

"Good Spirit," he pursued, as down upon the ground he fell before it: "your nature intercedes for me, and pities me. Assure me that I yet may change these shadows you have shown me, by an altered life!"

The kind hand trembled.

"I will honor Christmas in my heart, and try to keep it all the year. I will live in the Past, the Present, and the Future. The Spirits of all three shall strive within me. I will not shut out the lessons that they teach. Oh, tell me I may sponge away the writing on this stone!"

In his agony, he caught the spectral hand. It sought to free itself, but he was strong in his entreaty, and detained it. The Spirit, stronger yet, repulsed him.

Holding up his hands in a last prayer to have his fate reversed, he saw an alteration in the phantom's hood and dress. It shrunk, collapsed, and dwindled down into a bedpost.

Stave Five

THE END OF IT

YES! and the bedpost was his own. The bed was his own, the room was his own. Best and happiest of all, the Time before him was his own to make amends in!

"I will live in the Past, the Present, and the Future!" Scrooge repeated, as he scrambled out of bed. "The spirits of all Three shall strive within me. Oh Jacob Marley! Heaven, and the Christmas Time be praised for this! I say it on my knees, old Jacob; on my knees!"

He was so fluttered and so glowing with his good intentions, that his broken voice would scarcely answer to his call. He had been sobbing violently in his conflict with the Spirit, and his face was wet with tears.

"They are not torn down," cried Scrooge, folding one of his bed-curtains in his arms, "they are not torn down, rings and all. They are here: I am here: the shadows of the things that would have been, may be dispelled. They will be. I know they will!"

His hands were busy with his garments all this time: turning them inside out, putting them on upside down, tearing them, mislaying them, making them parties to every kind of extravagance.

"I don't know what to do!" cried Scrooge, laughing and crying in the same breath; and making a perfect Laocöon of himself with his stocking. "I am as light as a feather, I am as happy as an angel, I am as merry as a school-boy. I am as giddy as a drunken man. A merry Christmas to everybody. A happy New Year to all the world. Hallo here! Whoop! Hallo!"

He had frisked into the sitting-room, and was now standing there perfectly winded.

"There's the saucepan that the gruel was in!" cried Scrooge, starting off again, and going round the fire-place. "There's the door by which the Ghost of Jacob Marley entered! There's the corner where the Ghost of Christmas Present sat! There's the window where I saw the wandering Spirits! It's all right, it's all true, it all happened. Ha, ha, ha!"

Really, for a man who had been out of practice for so many years, it was a splendid laugh, a most illustrious laugh. The father of a long, long line of brilliant laughs!

"I don't know what day of the month it is!" said Scrooge. "I don't know how long I've been among the Spirits. I don't know anything. I'm quite a baby. Never mind. I don't care. I'd rather be a baby. Hallo! Whoop! Hallo here!"

He was checked in his transports by the churches ringing out the lustiest peals he had ever heard. Clash, clang, hammer, ding, dong, bell. Bell, dong, ding, hammer, clang, clash! Oh, glorious, glorious!

Running to the window, he opened it, and put out his head. No fog, no mist; clear, bright, jovial, stirring, cold; cold; cold, piping for the blood to dance to; Golden sunlight; Heavenly sky; sweet fresh air; merry bells. Oh, glorious, glorious!

"What's to-day?" cried Scrooge, calling down to a boy in Sunday clothes, who perhaps had loitered in to look about him.

"EH?" returned the boy with all his might of wonder.

"What's to-day, my fine fellow?" said Scrooge.

"To-day!" replied the boy. "Why, CHRISTMAS DAY."

"It's Christmas Day!" said Scrooge to himself. "I haven't missed it. The Spirits have done it all in one night. They can do anything they like. Of course they can. Of course they can. Hallo, my fine fellow!"

"Hallo!" returned the boy.

"Do you know the Poulterer's, in the next street but one, at the corner?" Scrooge inquired.

"I should hope I did," replied the lad.

"An intelligent boy!" said Scrooge. "A remarkable boy! Do you know whether they've sold the prize Turkey that was hanging up there? Not the little prize Turkey: the big one?"

"What, the one as big as me?" returned the boy.

"What a delightful boy!" said Scrooge. "It's a pleasure to talk to him. Yes, my buck!"

"It's hanging there now," replied the boy.

"Is it?" said Scrooge. "Go and buy it."

"Walk-ER!" exclaimed the boy.

"No, no," said Scrooge, "I am in earnest. Go and buy it, and tell 'em to bring it here, that I may give them the direction where to take it. Come back with the man, and I'll give you a shilling. Come back with him in less than five minutes, and I'll give you half-a-crown!"

The boy was off like a shot. He must have had a steady hand at a trigger who could have got a shot off half so fast.

"I'll send it to Bob Cratchit's!" whispered Scrooge, rubbing his hands, and splitting with a laugh. "He shan't know who sends it. It's twice the size of Tiny Tim. Joe Miller never made such a joke as sending it to Bob's will be!"

The hand in which he wrote the address was not a steady one, but write it he did, somehow, and went down stairs to open the street door, ready for the coming of the poulterer's man. As he stood there, waiting his arrival, the knocker caught his eye.

"I shall love it as long as I live!" cried Scrooge, patting it with his hand. "I scarcely ever looked at it before. What an honest expression it has in its face! It's a wonderful knocker!—Here's the Turkey. Hallo! Whoop! How are you! Merry Christmas!"

It *was* a Turkey! He never could have stood upon his legs, that bird. He would have snapped 'em short off in a minute, like sticks of sealing-wax.

"Why, it's impossible to carry that to Camden Town," said Scrooge. "You must have a cab."

The chuckle with which he said this, and the chuckle with which he paid for the Turkey, and the chuckle with which he paid for the cab, and the chuckle with which he recompensed the boy, were only to be exceeded by the chuckle with which he sat down breathless in his chair again, and chuckled till he cried.

Shaving was not an easy task, for his hand continued to shake very much; and shaving requires attention, even when you don't dance while you are at it. But if he had cut the end of his nose off, he would have put a piece of sticking-plaister over it, and been quite satisfied.

He dressed himself "all in his best," and at last got out into the streets. The people were by this time pouring forth, as he had seen them with the Ghost of Christmas Present; and walking with his hands behind him, Scrooge regarded every one with a delightful smile. He looked so irresistibly pleasant, in a word, that three of four good-humored fellows said, "Good morning, sir! A merry Christmas to you!" And Scrooge said often afterwards, that of all the blithe sounds he had ever heard, those were the blithest in his ears.

He had not gone far, when coming on towards him he beheld the portly gentleman, who had walked into his counting-house the day before and said, "Scrooge and Marley's, I believe?" It sent a pang across his heart to think how this old gentleman would look upon him when they met; but he knew what path lay straight before him, and he took it.

"My dear sir," said Scrooge, quickening his pace, and taking the old gentleman by both his hands. "How do you do? I hope you succeeded yesterday. It was very kind of you. A merry Christmas to you, sir!"

"Mr. Scrooge?"

"Yes," said Scrooge. "That is my name, and I fear it may not be pleasant to you. Allow me to ask your pardon. And will you have the goodness"—here Scrooge whispered in his ear.

"Lord bless me!" cried the gentleman, as if his breath were taken away. "My dear Mr. Scrooge, are you serious?"

"If you please," said Scrooge. "Not a farthing less. A great many back-payments are included in it, I assure you. Will you do me that favor?"

"My dear sir," said the other, shaking hands with him. "I don't know what to say to such munifi—"

"Don't say anything, please," retorted Scrooge. "Come and see me. Will you come and see me?"

"I will!" cried the old gentleman. And it was clear he meant to do it.

"Thank'ee," said Scrooge. "I am much obliged to you. I thank you fifty times. Bless you!"

He went to church, and walked about the streets, and watched the people hurrying to and fro, and patted children on the head, and questioned beggars, and looked down into the kitchens of houses, and up to the windows; and found that everything could yield him pleasure. He had never dreamed that any walk—that anything—could give him so much happiness. In the afternoon he turned his steps towards his nephew's house.

He passed the door a dozen times before he had the courage to go up and knock. But he made a dash, and did it.

"Is your master at home, my dear?" said Scrooge to the girl. Nice girl! Very.

"Yes, sir."

"Where is he, my love?" said Scrooge.

"He's in the dining-room, sir, along with mistress. I'll show you up stairs, if you please."

"Thank'ee. He knows me," said Scrooge, with his hand already on the dining-room lock. "I'll go in here, my dear."

He turned it gently, and sidled his face in, round the door. They were looking at the table (which was spread out in great array); for these young housekeepers are always nervous on such points, and like to see that everything is right.

"Fred!" said Scrooge.

Dear heart alive, how his niece by marriage started! Scrooge had forgotten, for the moment, about her sitting in the corner with the footstool, or he wouldn't have done it, on any account.

"Why bless my soul!" cried Fred, "who's that?"

"It's I. Your uncle Scrooge. I have come to dinner. Will you let me in, Fred?"

Let him in! It is a mercy he didn't shake his arm off. He was at home in five minutes. Nothing could be heartier. His niece looked just the same. So did Topper when *he* came. So did the plump sister when *she* came. So did every one when *they* came. Wonderful party, wonderful games, wonderful unanimity, won-der-ful happiness!

But he was early at the office next morning. Oh! he was early there. If he could only be there first, and catch Bob Cratchit coming late! That was the thing he had set his heart upon.

And he did it; yes, he did! The clock struck nine. No Bob. A quarter past. No Bob. He was full eighteen minutes and a half behind his time. Scrooge sat with his door wide open, that he might see him come into the Tank.

His hat was off, before he opened the door; his comforter too. He was on his stool in a jiffy; driving away with his pen, as if he were trying to overtake nine o'clock.

"Hallo!" growled Scrooge, in his accustomed voice as near as he could feign it. "What do you mean by coming here at this time of day?"

"I am very sorry, sir," said Bob. "I *am* behind my time."

"You are!" repeated Scrooge. "Yes. I think you are. Step this way, if you please."

"It's only once a year, sir," pleaded Bob, appearing from the Tank. "It shall not be repeated. I was making rather merry yesterday, sir."

"Now, I'll tell you what, my friend," said Scrooge, "I am not going to stand this sort of thing any longer. And therefore," he continued, leaping from his stool, and giving Bob such a dig in the waistcoat that he staggered back into the Tank again, "and therefore I am about to raise your salary!"

Bob trembled, and got a little nearer to the ruler. He had a momentary idea of knocking Scrooge down with it; holding him; and calling to the people in the court for help and a strait-waistcoat.

"A merry Christmas, Bob!" said Scrooge, with an earnestness that could not be mistaken, as he clapped him on the back. "A merrier Christmas, Bob, my good fellow, than I have given you for many a year! I'll raise your salary, and endeavour to assist your struggling family, and we will discuss your affairs this very afternoon, over a Christmas bowl of smoking bishop, Bob! Make up the fires, and buy another coal-scuttle before you dot another i, Bob Cratchit!"

Scrooge was better than his word. He did it all, and infinitely more; and to Tiny Tim, who did NOT die, he was a second father. He became as good a friend, as good a master, and as good a man, as the good old city knew, or any other good old city, town, or borough, in the good old world. Some people laughed to see the alteration in him, but he let them laugh, and little heeded them; for he was wise enough to know that nothing ever happened on this globe, for good, at which some people did not have their fill of laughter in the outset; and knowing that such as these would be blind any way, he thought it quite as well that they should wrinkle up their eyes in grins, as have the malady in less attractive forms. His own heart laughed: and that was quite enough for him.

He had no farther intercourse with Spirits, but lived upon the Total Abstinence Principle, ever afterward; and it was always said of him, that he knew how to keep Christmas well, if any man alive possessed the knowledge. May that be truly said of us, and all of us! And so, as Tiny Tim observed, God Bless Us, Every One!

was on his stool in a jiffy; driving away with his pen, as if he were trying to overtake nine o'clock.

"Hallo!" growled Scrooge, in his accustomed voice, as near as he could feign it. "What do you mean by coming here at this time of day?"

"I am very sorry, sir," said Bob. "I am behind my time."

"You are?" repeated Scrooge. "Yes. I think you are. Step this way, if you please."

"It's only once a year, sir," pleaded Bob, appearing from the Tank. "It shall not be repeated. I was making rather merry yesterday, sir."

"Now, I'll tell you what, my friend," said Scrooge, "I am not going to stand this sort of thing any longer. And therefore," he continued, leaping from his stool, and giving Bob such a dig in the waistcoat that he staggered back into the Tank again; "and therefore I am about to raise your salary!"

Bob trembled, and got a little nearer to the ruler. He had a momentary idea of knocking Scrooge down with it, holding him, and calling to the people in the court for help and a strait-waistcoat.

"A merry Christmas, Bob!" said Scrooge, with an earnestness that could not be mistaken, as he clapped him on the back. "A merrier Christmas, Bob, my good fellow, than I have given you for many a year! I'll raise your salary, and endeavour to assist your struggling family, and we will discuss your affairs this very afternoon, over a Christmas bowl of smoking bishop, Bob! Make up the fires, and buy another coal-scuttle before you dot another i, Bob Cratchit!"

Scrooge was better than his word. He did it all, and infinitely more; and to Tiny Tim, who did NOT die, he was a second father. He became as good a friend, as good a master, and as good a man, as the good old city knew, or any other good old city, town, or borough, in the good old world. Some people laughed to see the alteration in him, but he let them laugh, and little heeded them; for he was wise enough to know that nothing ever happened on this globe, for good, at which some people did not have their fill of laughter in the outset; and knowing that such as these would be blind anyway, he thought it quite as well that they should wrinkle up their eyes in grins, as have the malady in less attractive forms. His own heart laughed: and that was quite enough for him.

He had no further intercourse with Spirits, but lived upon the Total Abstinence Principle, ever afterwards; and it was always said of him, that he knew how to keep Christmas well, if any man alive possessed the knowledge. May that be truly said of us, and all of us! And so, as Tiny Tim observed, God bless Us, Every One!

A Tale of Two Cities

BOOK THE FIRST

RECALLED TO LIFE

Chapter I

THE PERIOD

IT was the best of times, it was the worst of times, it was the age of wisdom, it was the age of foolishness, it was the epoch of belief, it was the epoch of incredulity, it was the season of Light, it was the season of Darkness, it was the spring of hope, it was the winter of despair, we had everything before us, we had nothing before us, we were all going direct to Heaven, we were all going direct the other way—in short, the period was so far like the present period, that some of its noisiest authorities insisted on its being received, for good or for evil, in the superlative degree of comparison only.

There were a king with a large jaw, and a queen with a plain face, on the throne of England; there were a king with a large jaw and a queen with a fair face, on the throne of France. In both countries it was clearer than crystal to the Lords of the State preserves of loaves and fishes, that things in general were settled forever.

It was the year of Our Lord one thousand seven hundred and seventy-five. Spiritual revelations were conceded to England at that favored period, as at this. Mrs. Southcott had recently attained her five-and-twentieth blessed birth-day, of whom a prophetic private in the Life Guards had heralded the sublime appearance by announcing that arrangements were made for the swallowing up of London and Westminster. Even the Cock-lane ghost had been laid only a round dozen of years, after rapping out its messages, as the spirits of this very year last past (supernaturally deficient in originality) rapped out theirs. Mere messages in the earthly order of events had lately come to the English Crown and People, from a congress of British subjects in America; which, strange to relate, have proved more important to the human race than any communications yet received through any of the chickens of the Cock-lane brood.

France, less favored on the whole as to matters spiritual than her sister of the shield and trident, rolled with exceeding smoothness down hill, making paper-money and spending it. Under the guidance of her Christian pastors, she entertained herself, besides, with such humane achievements as sentencing a youth to have his hands cut off, his tongue torn out with pincers, and his body burned alive, because he had not kneeled down in the rain to do honor to a dirty procession of monks which passed within his view, at a distance of some fifty or sixty yards. It is likely enough that, rooted in the woods of France and Norway, there were growing trees, when that sufferer was put to death, already marked by the Woodman, Fate, to come down and be sawn into boards, to make a certain movable frame-work with a sack and a knife in it, terrible in history. It is likely enough that in the rough outhouses of some tillers of the heavy lands adjacent to Paris, there were sheltered from the weather that very day, rude carts, bespattered with rustic mire, snuffed about by pigs, and roosted in by poultry, which the Farmer, Death, had already set apart to be his tumbrils of the Revolution. But, that Woodman and that Farmer, though they work unceasingly, work silently, and no one heard them as they went about with muffled tread: the rather, forasmuch as to entertain any suspicion that they were awake, was to be atheistical and traitorous.

In England, there was scarcely an amount of order and protection to justify much national boasting. Daring burglaries by armed men, and highway robberies, took place in the capital itself every night; families were publicly cautioned not to go out of town without removing their furniture to upholsterers' warehouses for security; the highwayman in the dark was a City tradesman in the light, and, being recognized and challenged by his fellow-tradesman whom he stopped in his character of "the Captain," gallantly shot him through the head and rode away; the mail was waylaid by seven robbers, and the guard shot three dead, and then got shot dead himself by the other four, "in consequence of the failure of his ammunition;" after which the mail was robbed in peace; that magnificent potentate, the Lord Mayor of London, was made to stand and deliver on Turnham Green by one highwayman, who despoiled the illustrious creature in sight of all his retinue; prisoners in London gaols fought battles with their turnkeys, and the majesty of the law fired blunderbusses in among them, loaded with rounds of shot and ball; thieves snipped off diamond crosses from the necks of noble lords at Court drawing-rooms; musketeers went into St. Giles's to search for contraband goods, and the mob fired on the musketeers, and the musketeers fired on the mob, and nobody thought any of these occurrences much out of the common way. In the midst of them, the hangman, ever busy and ever worse than useless, was in constant requisition; now, stringing up long rows of miscellaneous criminals; now, hanging a housebreaker on Saturday who had been taken on Tuesday; now, burning people in the hand at Newgate by the dozen, and now burning pamphlets at the door of Westminster Hall; to-day, taking the life of an atrocious murderer, and to-morrow of a wretched pilferer who had robbed a farmer's boy of sixpence.

All these things, and a thousand like them, came to pass in and close upon the dear old year one thousand seven hundred and seventy-five. Environed by them, while the Woodman and the Farmer worked unheeded, those two of the large jaws, and those other two of the plain and the fair faces, trod with stir enough, and carried their divine rights with a high hand. Thus did the year one thousand seven hundred and seventy-five conduct their Greatness, and myriads of small creatures—

the creatures of this chronicle among the rest—along the roads that lay before them.

Chapter II

THE MAIL

It was the Dover road that lay, on a Friday night late in November, before the first of the persons with whom this history has business. The Dover road lay, as to him, beyond the Dover mail, as it lumbered up Shooter's Hill. He walked uphill in the mire by the side of the mail, as the rest of the passengers did; not because they had the least relish for walking exercise, under the circumstances, but because the hill, and the harness, and the mud, and the mail, were all so heavy, that the horses had three times already come to a stop, besides once drawing the coach across the road, with the mutinous intent of taking it back to Blackheath. Reins and whip and coachman and guard, however, in combination, had read that article of war which forbade a purpose otherwise strongly in favor of the argument, that some brute animals are endued with reason; and the team had capitulated and returned to their duty.

With drooping heads and tremulous tails, they mashed their way through the thick mud, floundering and stumbling between whiles, as if they were falling to pieces at the larger joints. As often as the driver rested them and brought them to a stand, with a wary "Wo-ho! so-ho then!" the near leader violently shook his head and everything upon it—like an unusually emphatic horse, denying that the coach could be got up the hill. Whenever the leader made this rattle, the passenger started, as a nervous passenger might, and was disturbed in mind.

There was a steaming mist in all the hollows, and it had roamed in its forlornness up the hill, like an evil spirit, seeking rest and finding none. A clammy and intensely cold mist, it made its slow way through the air in ripples that visibly followed and overspread one another, as the waves of an unwholesome sea might do. It was dense enough to shut out every thing from the light of the coach-lamps but these its own workings, and a few yards of road; and the reek of the laboring horses steamed into it, as if they had made it all.

Two other passengers, besides the one, were plodding up the hill by the side of the mail. All three were wrapped to the cheek-bones and over the ears, and wore jack-boots. Not one of the three could have said, from any thing he saw, what either of the other two was like; and each was hidden under almost as many wrappers from the eyes of the mind, as from the eyes of the body, of his two companions. In those days, travelers were very shy of being confidential on a short notice, for any body on the road might be a robber or in league with robbers. As to the latter, when every posting-house and ale-house could produce somebody in "the Captain's" pay, ranging from the landlord to the lowest stable nondescript, it was the likeliest thing upon the cards. So the guard of the Dover mail thought to himself, that Friday night in November, one thousand seven hundred and seventy-five, lumbering up Shooter's Hill, as he stood on his own particular perch behind the mail, beating his feet, and keeping an eye and a hand on the arm-chest before him, where a loaded blunderbuss lay at the top of six or eight loaded horse-pistols, deposited on a substratum of cutlass.

The Dover mail was in its usual genial position that the guard suspected the passengers, the passengers suspected one another and the guard, they all suspected everybody else, and the coachman was sure of nothing but the horses; as to which cattle he could with a clear conscience have taken his oath on the two Testaments that they were not fit for the journey.

"Wo-ho!" said the coachman. "So then! One more pull and you're at the top and be damned to you, for I have had trouble enough to get you to it!—Joe!"

"Halloa!" the guard replied.

"What o'clock do you make it, Joe?"

"Ten minutes good, past eleven."

"My blood!" ejaculated the vexed coachman, "and not atop of Shooter's yet! Tst! Yah! Get on with you!"

The emphatic horse, cut short by the whip in a most decided negative, made a scramble for it, and the three other horses followed suit. Once more, the Dover mail struggled on, with the jack-boots of its passengers squashing along by its side. They had stopped when the coach stopped, and they kept close company with it. If any one of the three had had the hardihood to propose to another to walk on a little ahead into the mist and darkness, he would have put himself in a fair way of getting shot instantly as a highwayman.

The last burst carried the mail to the summit of the hill. The horses stopped to breathe again, and the guard got down to skid the wheel for the descent, and open the coach door to let the passengers in.

"Tst! Joe!" cried the coachman in a warning voice, looking down from his box.

"What do you say, Tom?"

They both listened.

"I say a horse at a canter coming up, Joe."

"*I* say a horse at a gallop, Tom," returned the guard, leaving his hold of the door, and mounting nimbly to his place. "Gentlemen! In the king's name, all of you!"

With this hurried adjuration, he cocked his blunderbuss, and stood on the offensive.

The passenger booked by this history was on the coach-step, getting in; the two other passengers were close behind him, and about to follow. He remained on the step, half in the coach and half out of it; they remained in the road below him. They all looked from the coachman to the guard, and from the guard to the coachman, and listened. The coachman looked back and the guard looked back, and even the emphatic leader pricked up his ears and looked back, without contradicting.

The stillness consequent on the cessation of the rumbling and laboring of the coach, added to the stillness of the night, made it very quiet indeed. The panting of the horses communicated a tremulous motion to the coach, as if it were in a state of agitation. The hearts of the passengers beat loud enough perhaps to be heard; but at any rate, the quiet pause was audibly expressive of people out of breath, and holding the breath, and having the pulses quickened by expectation.

The sound of a horse at a gallop came fast and furiously up the hill.

"So-ho!" the guard sang out, as loud as he could roar. "Yo there! Stand! I shall fire!"

The pace was suddenly checked, and, with much splashing and floundering, a man's voice called from the mist, "Is that the Dover mail?"

"Never you mind what it is!" the guard retorted. "What are you?"

"*Is* that the Dover mail?"

"Why do you want to know?"

"I want a passenger, if it is."

"What passenger?"

"Mr. Jarvis Lorry."

Our booked passenger showed in a moment that it was his name. The guard, the coachman, and the two other passengers eyed him distrustfully.

"Keep where you are," the guard called to the voice in the mist, "because, if I should make a mistake, it could never be set right in your lifetime. Gentleman of the name of Lorry answer straight."

"What is the matter?" asked the passenger, then, with mildly quavering speech. "Who wants me? Is it Jerry?"

("I don't like Jerry's voice, if it is Jerry," growled the guard to himself. "He's hoarser than suits me, is Jerry.")

"Yes, Mr. Lorry."

"What is the matter?"

"A dispatch sent after you from over yonder. T. and Co."

"I know this messenger, guard," said Mr. Lorry, getting down into the road—assisted from behind more swiftly than politely by the other two passengers, who immediately scrambled into the coach, shut the door, and pulled up the window.

"He may come close; there's nothing wrong."

"I hope there ain't, but I can't make so 'nation sure of that," said the guard, in gruff soliloquy. "Hallo you!"

"Well! And hallo you!" said Jerry, more hoarsely than before.

"Come on at a footpace; d'ye mind me? And if you've got holsters to that saddle o' yourn, don't let me see your hand go nigh 'em. For I'm a devil at a quick mistake, and when I make one it takes the form of Lead. So now let's look at you."

The figures of a horse and rider came slowly through the eddying mist, and came to the side of the mail, where the passenger stood. The rider stooped, and, casting up his eyes at the guard, handed the passenger a small folded paper. The rider's horse was blown, and both horse and rider were covered with mud, from the hoofs of the horse to the hat of the man.

"Guard!" said the passenger, in a tone of quiet business confidence.

The watchful guard, with his right hand at the stock of his raised blunderbuss, his left at the barrel, and his eye on the horseman, answered curtly, "Sir."

"There is nothing to apprehend. I belong to Tellson's Bank. You must know Tellson's Bank in London. I am going to Paris on business. A crown to drink. I may read this?"

"If so be as you're quick, sir."

He opened it in the light of the coach-lamp on that side, and read—first to himself and then aloud: " 'Wait at Dover for Ma'amselle.' It's not long, you see, guard. Jerry, say that my answer was, RECALLED TO LIFE."

Jerry started in his saddle. "That's a blazing strange answer, too," said he, at his hoarsest.

"Take that message back, and they will know that I received this, as well as if I wrote. Make the best of your way. Good-night."

With those words the passenger opened the coach door and got in; not at all assisted by his fellow-passengers, who had expeditiously secreted their watches and purses in their boots, and were now making a general pretense of being asleep, with no more definite purpose than to escape the hazard of originating any other kind of action.

The coach lumbered on again, with heavier wreaths of mist closing round it as it began the descent. The guard soon replaced his blunderbuss in his arm-chest, and having looked to the rest of its contents, and having looked to the supplementary pistols that he wore in his belt, looked to a smaller chest beneath his seat, in which there were a few smith's tools, a couple of torches, and a tinder-box. For he was furnished with that completeness, that if the coach-lamps had been blown and stormed out, which did occasionally happen, he had only to shut himself up inside, keep the flint and steel sparks well off the straw, and get a light with tolerable safety and ease (if he were lucky) in five minutes.

"Tom!" softly over the coach-roof.

"Hallo, Joe."

"Did you hear the message?"

"I did, Joe."

"What did you make of it, Tom?"

"Nothing at all, Joe."

"That's coin*cid*ence, too," the guard mused, "for I made the same of it myself."

Jerry, left alone in the mist and darkness, dismounted meanwhile, not only to ease his spent horse, but to wipe the mud from his face, and shake the wet out of his hat-brim, which might be capable of holding about half a gallon. After standing with the bridle over his heavily-splashed arm, until the wheels of the mail were no longer within hearing, and the night was quite still again, he turned to walk down the hill.

"After that there gallop from Temple-bar, old lady, I won't trust your fore-legs till I get you on the level," said this hoarse messenger, glancing at his mare. " 'Recalled to life.' That's a blazing strange message. Much of that wouldn't do for you, Jerry! I say, Jerry! You'd be in a blazing bad way if recalling to life was to come into fashion, Jerry!"

Chapter III

THE NIGHT SHADOWS

A WONDERFUL fact to reflect upon, that every human creature is constituted to be that profound secret and mystery to every other. A solemn consideration, when I enter a great city by night, that every one of those darkly clustered houses encloses its own secret; that every room in every one of them encloses its own secret; that every beating heart in the hundreds of thousands of breasts there, is, in some of its imaginings, a secret to the heart nearest it! Something of the awfulness, even of Death itself, is referable to this. No more can I turn the leaves of this dear book that I loved, and vainly hope in time to read it all. No more can I look into the depths of this unfathomable water, wherein, as momentary lights glanced into it, I have had glimpses of buried treasure and other things submerged. It was appointed that the book should shut with a spring, forever and forever, when I had read but a page. It was appointed that the water should be locked in an eternal frost, when the light was playing on its surface, and I stood in ignorance on the shore. My friend is dead, my neighbor is dead, my love, the darling of my soul, is dead; it is the inexorable consolidation and perpetuation of the secret that was always in that individuality, and which I shall carry in mine to my life's end. In any of the burial-places of this city through which I pass, is there a sleeper more inscrutable than its busy inhabitants are, in their innermost personality, to me, or than I am to them?

As to this, his natural and not to be alienated inheritance, the messenger on horseback had exactly the same possessions as the King, the first Minister of State, or the richest merchant in London. So with the three passengers shut up in the narrow compass of one lumbering old mail coach; they were mysteries to one another, as complete as if each had been in his own coach and six, or his own coach and sixty, with the breadth of a county between him and the next.

The messenger rode back at an easy trot, stopping pretty often at ale-houses by the way to drink, but evincing a tendency to keep his own counsel, and to keep his hat cocked over his eyes. He had eyes that assorted very well with that decoration, being of a surface black, with no depth in the color or form, and much too near together—as if they were afraid of being found out in something, singly, if they kept too far apart. They had a sinister expression, under an old cocked-hat like a three-cornered spittoon, and over a great muffler for the chin and throat, which descended nearly to the wearer's knees. When he stopped for drink, he moved this muffler with his left hand, only while he poured his liquor in with his right; as soon as that was done, he muffled again.

"No, Jerry, no!" said the messenger, harping on one theme as he rode. "It wouldn't do for you, Jerry. Jerry, you honest tradesman, it wouldn't suit *your* line of business! Recalled—! Bust me, if I don't think he'd been a drinking!"

His message perplexed his mind to that degree that he was fain, several times, to take off his hat to scratch his head. Except on the crown, which was raggedly bald, he had stiff, black hair standing jaggedly all over it, and growing downhill almost to his broad, blunt nose. It was so like smith's work, so much more like the top of a strongly spiked wall than a head of hair, that the best of players at leap-frog might have declined him, as the most dangerous man in the world to go over.

While he trotted back with the message he was to deliver to the night watchman in his box at the door of Tellson's Bank, by Temple-bar, who was to deliver it to greater authorities within, the shadows of the night took such shapes to him as arose out of the message, and took such shapes to the mare as arose out of *her* private topics of uneasiness. They seemed to be numerous, for she shied at every shadow on the road.

What time, the mail-coach lumbered, jolted, rattled, and bumped upon its tedious way, with its three fellow inscrutables inside. To whom, likewise, the shadows of the night revealed themselves, in the forms their dozing eyes and wandering thoughts suggested.

Tellson's Bank had a run upon it in the mail. As the bank passenger—with an arm drawn through the leathern strap, which did what lay in it to keep him from pounding against the next passenger, and driving him into his corner, whenever the coach got a special jolt—nodded in his place, with half-shut eyes, the little coach windows, and the coach-lamp dimly gleaming through them, and the bulky bundle of opposite passenger, became the bank, and did a great stroke of business. The rattle of the harness was the chink of money, and more drafts were honored in five minutes than even Tellson's, with all its foreign and home connection, ever paid in thrice the time. Then, the strong-rooms underground, at Tellson's, with such of their valuable stores and secrets as were known to the passenger (and it was not a little that he knew about them), opened before him, and he went in among them with the great keys and the feebly-burning candle, and found them safe, and strong, and sound, and still, just as he had last seen them.

But, though the bank was almost always with him, and though the coach (in a confused way, like the presence of pain under an opiate), was always with him, there was another current of impression that never ceased to run, all through the night. He was on his way to dig some one out of a grave.

Now, which of the multitude of faces that showed themselves before him was the true face of the buried person, the shadows of the night did not indicate; but they were all the faces of a man of five-and-forty by years, and they differed principally in the passions they expressed, and in the ghastliness of their worn and wasted state. Pride, contempt, defiance, stubbornness, submission, lamentation, succeeded one another; so did varieties of sunken cheek, cadaverous color, emaciated hands and figures. But the face was, in the main, one face, and every head was prematurely white. A hundred times the dozing passenger inquired of this spectre:

"Buried how long?"

The answer was always the same; "Almost eighteen years."

"You had abandoned all hope of being dug out?"

"Long ago."

"You know that you are recalled to life?"

"They tell me so."

"I hope you care to live?"

"I can't say."

"Shall I show her to you? Will you come and see her?"

The answers to this question were various and contradictory. Sometimes the broken reply was, "Wait! It would kill me if I saw her too soon." Sometimes, it was given in a tender rain of tears, and then it was, "Take me to her." Sometimes, it was staring and bewildered, and then it was, "I don't know her. I don't understand."

After such imaginary discourse, the passenger in his fancy would dig, dig, dig—,now, with a spade, now with a great key, now with his hands—to dig this wretched creature out. Got out at last, with earth hanging about his face and hair, he would suddenly fall away to dust. The passenger would then start to himself, and lower the window, to get the reality of mist and rain on his cheek.

Yet even when his eyes were opened on the mist and rain, on the moving patch of light from the lamps, and the hedge at the roadside retreating by jerks, the night-shadows outside the coach would fall into the train of the night shadows within. The real Banking-house by Temple-bar, the real business of the past day, the real strong-rooms, the real express sent after him, and the real message returned, would all be there. Out of the midst of them, the ghostly face would rise, and he would accost it again.

"Buried how long?"

"Almost eighteen years."

"I hope you care to live?"

"I can't say."

Dig—dig—dig—until an impatient movement from one of the two passengers would admonish him to pull up the window, draw his arm securely through the leathern strap, and speculate upon the two slumbering forms, until his mind lost its hold of them, and then again slid away into the bank and the grave.

"Buried how long?"

"Almost eighteen years."

"You had abandoned all hope of being dug out?"

"Long ago."

The words were still in his hearing as just spoken—distinctly in his hearing as ever words had been in his life—when the weary passenger started to the consciousness of daylight, and found that the shadows of the night were gone.

He lowered the window, and looked out at the rising sun. There was a ridge of plowed land, with a plow upon it where it had been left last night when the horses were unyoked; beyond, a quiet coppice-wood, in which many leaves of burning red and golden yellow still remained upon the trees. Though the earth was cold and wet, the sky was clear, and the sun rose bright, placid, and beautiful.

"Eighteen years!" said the passenger, looking at the sun. "Gracious Creator of Day! To be buried alive for eighteen years!"

Chapter IV

THE PREPARATION

WHEN the mail got successfully to Dover, in the course of the forenoon, the head-drawer at the Royal George Hotel opened the coach-door, as his custom was. He did it with some flourish of ceremony, for a mail journey from London in winter, was an achievement to congratulate an adventurous traveler upon.

By that time, there was only one adventurous traveler left to be congratulated; for, the two others had been set down at their respective roadside destinations. The mildewy inside of the coach, with its damp and dirty straw, its disagreeable smell, and its obscurity, was rather like a larger dog-kennel. Mr. Lorry, the passenger, shaking himself out of it, in chains of straw, a tangle of shaggy wrapper, flapping hat, and muddy legs, was rather like a larger sort of dog.

"There will be a packet to Calais to-morrow, drawer?"

"Yes, sir, if the weather holds and the wind sets tolerable fair. The tide will serve pretty nicely at about two in the afternoon, sir. Bed, sir?"

"I shall not go to bed till night; but I want a bedroom and a barber."

"And then breakfast, sir? Yes, sir. That way, sir, if you please. Show Concord! Gentleman's valise and hot water to Concord. Pull off gentleman's boots in Concord. (You will find a fine sea-coal fire, sir.) Fetch barber to Concord. Stir about there, now, for Concord!"

The Concord bed-chamber being always assigned to a passenger by the mail, and passengers by the mail being always heavily wrapped up from head to foot, the room had the odd interest for the establishment of the Royal George, that although but one kind of man was seen to go into it, all kinds and varieties of men came out of it. Consequently another drawer, and two porters, and several maids, and the landlady, were all loitering by accident at various points of the road between the Concord and the coffee-room, when a gentleman of sixty, formally dressed in a brown suit of clothes, pretty well worn, but very well kept, with large square cuffs, and large flaps to the pockets, passed along on his way to his breakfast.

The coffee-room had no other occupant, that forenoon, than the gentleman in brown. His breakfast-table was drawn before the fire, and as he sat, with the light shining on him, waiting for the meal, he sat so still, that he might have been sitting for his portrait.

Very orderly and methodical he looked, with a hand on each knee, and a loud watch ticking a sonorous sermon under his flapped waistcoat, as though it pitted its gravity and longevity against the levity and evanescence of the brisk fire. He had a good leg, and was a little vain of it, for his brown stockings fitted sleek and close, and were of a fine texture; his shoes and buckles, too, though plain, were trim. He wore an odd little sleek crisp flaxen wig, setting very close to his head: which wig, it is to be presumed, was made of hair, but which looked far more as though it were spun from filaments of silk or glass. His linen, though not of a fineness in accordance with his stockings, was as white as the tops of the waves that broke upon the neighboring beach, or the specks of sail that glinted in the sunlight far at sea. A face, habitually suppressed and quieted was still lighted up under the quaint wig by a pair of moist bright eyes that must have cost their owner, in years gone by, some pains to drill to the composed and reserved expression of Tellson's Bank. He had a healthy color in his cheeks, and his face, though lined, bore few traces of anxiety. But, perhaps the confidential bachelor clerks in Tellson's Bank were principally occupied with the cares of other people; and perhaps second-hand cares, like second-hand clothes, come easily off and on.

Completing his resemblance to a man who was sitting for his portrait, Mr. Lorry dropped off asleep. The arrival of his breakfast roused him, and he said to the drawer, as he moved his chair to it:

"I wish accommodation prepared for a young lady who may come here at any time to-day. She may ask for Mr. Jarvis Lorry, or she may only ask for a gentleman from Tellson's Bank. Please to let me know."

"Yes, sir. Tellson's Bank in London, sir?"

"Yes."

"Yes, sir. We have oftentimes the honor to entertain your gentlemen in their traveling backward and forward betwixt London and Paris, sir. A vast deal of traveling, sir, in Tellson and Company's house."

"Yes, we are quite a French house, as well as an English one."

"Yes, sir. Not much in the habit of such traveling yourself, I think, sir?"

"Not of late years. It is fifteen years since we—since I—came last from France."

"Indeed, sir? That was before my time here, sir. Before our people's time here, sir. The George was in other hands at that time, sir."

"I believe so."

"But I would hold a pretty wager, sir, that a house like Tellson and Company was flourishing, a matter of fifty, not to speak of fifteen years ago?"

"You might treble that, and say a hundred and fifty, yet not be far from the truth."

"Indeed, sir!"

Rounding his mouth and both his eyes, as he stepped backward from the table, the waiter shifted his napkin from his right arm to his left, dropped into a comfortable attitude, and stood surveying the guest while he ate and drank, as from an observatory or watch-tower. According to the immemorial usage of waiters in all ages.

When Mr. Lorry had finished his breakfast, he went out for a stroll on the beach. The little, narrow, crooked town of Dover hid itself away from the beach, and ran its head into the chalk-cliffs, like a marine ostrich. The beach was a desert of heaps of sea and stones tumbling wildly about, aud the sea did what it liked, and what it liked was destruction. It thundered at the town, and thundered at the cliffs, and brought the coast down, madly. The air among the houses was of so strong a piscatory flavor that one might have supposed sick fish went up to be dipped in it, as sick people went down to be dipped in the sea. A little fishing was done in the port, and a quantity of strolling about by night and looking seaward: particularly at those times when the tide made and was near flood. Small tradesmen, who did no business whatever, sometimes unaccountably realized large fortunes, and it was remarkable that nobody in the neighborhood could endure a lamplighter.

As the day declined into the afternoon, and the air, which had been at intervals clear enough to allow the French coast to be seen, became again charged with mist and vapor, Mr. Lorry's thoughts seemed to cloud too. When it was dark, and he sat before the coffee-room fire, awaiting his dinner as he had awaited his breakfast, his mind was busily digging, digging, digging, in the live red coals.

A bottle of good claret after dinner does a digger in the red coals no harm, otherwise than as it has a tendency to throw him out of work. Mr. Lorry had been idle a long time, and had just poured out his last glassful of wine with as complete an appearance of satisfaction as is ever to be found in an elderly gentleman of a fresh complexion who has got to the end of a bottle, when a rattling of wheels came up the narrow street, and rumbled into the inn-yard.

He set down his glass untouched. "This is Mam'selle!" said he.

In a very few minutes the waiter came in, to announce that Miss Manette had arrived from London, and would be happy to see the gentleman from Tellson's.

"So soon?"

Miss Manette had taken some refreshment on the road, and required none then, and was extremely anxious to see the gentleman from Tellson's immediately, if it suited his pleasure and convenience.

The gentleman from Tellson's had nothing left for it but to empty his glass with an air of stolid desperation, settle his odd, little flaxen wig at the ears, and follow the waiter to Miss Manette's apartment. It was a large, dark room, furnished in a funereal manner with black horse-hair, and loaded with heavy dark tables. These had been oiled and oiled, until the two tall candles on the table in the middle of the room were gloomily reflected on every leaf; as if *they* were buried in deep graves of black mahogany, and no light to speak of could be expected from them until they were dug out.

The obscurity was so difficult to penetrate that Mr. Lorry, picking his way over the well-worn Turkey carpet, supposed Miss Manette to be, for the moment, in some adjacent room, until, having got past the two tall candles, he saw standing to receive him by the table between them and the fire, a young lady of not more than seventeen, in a riding-cloak, and still holding her straw traveling-hat by its ribbon, in her hand. As his eyes rested on a short, slight-pretty figure, a quantity of golden hair, a pair of blue eyes that met his own with an inquiring look, and a forehead with a singular capacity (remembering how young and smooth it was), of lifting and knitting itself into an expression that was not quite one of perplexity, or wonder, or alarm, or merely of a bright fixed attention, though it included all the four expressions—as his eyes rested on these things, a sudden vivid likeness passed before him, of a child whom he had held in his arms on the passage across that very Channel, one cold time, when the hail drifted heavily and the sea ran high. The likeness passed away, say, like a breath along the surface of the gaunt pier-glass behind her, on the frame of which, a hospital procession of negro cupids, several headless and all cripples, were offering black baskets of Dead-Sea fruit to black divinities of the feminine gender—and he made his formal bow to Miss Manette.

"Pray take a seat, sir." In a very clear and pleasant young voice: a little foreign in its accent, but a very little indeed.

"I kiss your hand, Miss," said Mr. Lorry, with the manners of an earlier date, as he made his formal bow again, and took his seat.

"I received a letter from the Bank, sir, yesterday, informing me that some new intelligence—or discovery—"

"The word is not material, Miss; either word will do."

"—respecting the small property of my poor father whom I never saw—so long dead—"

Mr. Lorry moved in his chair, and cast a troubled look toward the hospital procession of negro cupids. As if *they* had any help for anybody in their absurd baskets!

"—rendered it necessary that I should go to Paris, there to communicate with a gentleman of the Bank, so good as to be dispatched to Paris for the purpose."

"Myself."

"As I was prepared to hear, sir."

She courtesied to him (young ladies made courtesies in those days), with a pretty desire to convey to him that she felt how much older and wiser he was than she. He made her another bow.

"I replied to the Bank, sir, that as it was considered necessary, by those who know, and who are so kind as to advise me, that I should go to France, and that as I am an orphan and have no friend who could go with me, I should esteem it highly if I might be permitted to place myself, during the journey, under that worthy gentleman's protection. This gentleman had left London, but I think a messenger was sent after him to beg the favor of his waiting for me here."

"I was happy," said Mr. Lorry, "to be entrusted with the charge. I shall be more happy to execute it."

"Sir, I thank you indeed. I thank you very gratefully. It was told me by the Bank that the gentleman would explain to me the details of the business, and that I must prepare myself to find them of a surprising nature. I have done my best to prepare myself, and I naturally have a strong and eager interest to know what they are."

"Naturally," said Mr. Lorry. "Yes—I—"

After a pause, he added, again settling the crisp, flaxen wig at the ears:

"It is very difficult to begin."

He did not begin, but, in his indecision, met her glance. The young forehead lifted itself into that singular expression—but it was pretty and characteristic, besides being singular—and she raised her hand, as if with an involuntary action she caught at, or stayed some passing shadow.

"Are you quite a stranger to me, sir?"

"Am I not?" Mr. Lorry opened his hands, and extended them outward with an argumentative smile.

Between the eyebrows and just over the little feminine nose, the line of which was as delicate and fine as it was possible to be, the expression deepened itself as she took her seat thoughtfully in the chair by which she had hitherto remained standing. He watched her as she mused, and, the moment she raised her eyes again, went on:

"In your adopted country, I presume, I cannot do better than address you as a young English lady, Miss Manette?"

"If you please, sir."

"Miss Manette, I am a man of business. I have a business charge to acquit myself of. In your reception of it, don't heed me any more than if I was a speaking machine—truly, I am not much else. I will, with your leave, relate to you, miss, the story of one of our customers."

"Story!"

He seemed willfully to mistake the word she had repeated, when he added, in a hurry, "Yes, customers; in the banking business we usually call our connection our customers. He was a French gentleman; a scientific gentleman; a man of great acquirements—a Doctor."

"Not of Beauvais?"

"Why, yes, of Beauvais. Like Monsieur Manette, your father, the gentleman was of Beauvais. Like Monsieur Manette, your father, the gentleman was of repute in Paris. I had the honor of knowing him there. Our relations were business relations, but confidential. I was at that time in our French House, and, had been—oh! twenty years."

"At that time—I may ask, at what time, sir?"

"I speak, miss, of twenty years ago. He married—an English lady—and I was one of the trustees. His affairs, like the affairs of many other French gentlemen and French families, were entirely in Tellson's hands. In a similar way, I am, or I have been, trustee of one kind or other for scores of our customers. These are mere business relations, Miss; there is no friendship in them, no particular interest, nothing like sentiment. I have passed from one to another, in the course of my business life, just as I pass from one of our customers to another, in the course of my business day; in short, I have no feelings; I am a mere machine. To go on—"

"But this is my father's story, sir; and I begin to think"—the curiously roughened forehead was very intent upon him—"that when I was left an orphan, through my mother's surviving my father only two years, it was you who brought me to England. I am almost sure it was you."

Mr. Lorry took the hesitating little hand that confidingly advanced to take his, and he put it with some ceremony to his lips. He then conducted the young lady straightway to her chair again, and, holding the chair-back with his left hand, and using his right by turns to rub his chin, pull his wig at the ears, or point what he said, stood looking down into her face while she sat looking up into his.

"Miss Manette, it *was* I. And you will see how truly I spoke of myself just now, in saying I had no feelings, and that all the relations I hold with my fellow-creatures are mere business relations, when you reflect that I have never seen you since. No; you have been the ward of Tellson's House since, and I have been busy with the other business of Tellson's House since. Feelings! I have no time for them, no chance of them. I pass my whole life, Miss, in turning an immense pecuniary Mangle."

After this odd description of his daily routine of employment, Mr. Lorry flattened his flaxen wig upon his head with both hands (which was most unnecessary, for nothing could be flatter than its shining surface was before), and resumed his former attitude.

"So far, Miss (as you have remarked), this is the story of your regretted father. Now comes the difference. If your father had not died when he did— Don't be frightened! How you start!"

She did indeed, start. And she caught his wrist with both her hands.

"Pray," said Mr. Lorry, in a soothing tone, bringing his left hand from the back of the chair to lay it on the supplicatory fingers that clasped him in so violent a tremble: "pray control your agitation—a matter of business. As I was saying—"

Her look so discomposed him that he stopped, wandered, and began anew:

"As I was saying: if Monsieur Manette had not died; if he had suddenly and silently disappeared; if he had been spirited away; if it had not been difficult to guess to what dreadful place, though no art could trace him; if he had an enemy in some compatriot who could exercise a privilege that I in my own time have known the boldest people afraid to speak of in a whisper, across the water, there; for instance, the privilege of filling up blank forms for the consignment of any one to the oblivion of a prison for any length of time; if his wife had implored the king, the queen, the court, the clergy, for any tidings of him, and all quite in vain;—then the history of your father would have been the history of this unfortunate gentleman, the Doctor of Beauvais."

"I entreat you to tell me more, sir."

"I will. I am going to. You can bear it?"

"I can bear anything but the uncertinty you leave me in at this moment."

"You speak collectedly, and you—*are* collected. That's good!" (Though his manner was less satisfied than his words.) "A matter of business. Regard it as a matter of business—business that must be done. Now, if this Doctor's wife, though a lady of great courage and spirit, had suffered so intensely from this cause before her little child was born—"

"The little child was a daughter, sir?"

"A daughter. A—a—matter of business—don't be distressed. Miss, if the poor lady had suffered so intensely before her little child was born, that she came to the determination of sparing the poor child the inheritance of any part of the agony she had known the pains of, by rearing her in the belief, that her father was dead— No, don't kneel! In Heaven's name why should you kneel to me!"

"For the truth. O dear, good, compassionate sir, for the truth!"

"A—a matter of business. You confuse me, and how can I transact business if I am confused? Let us be clear-headed. If you could kindly mention now, for instance, what nine times ninepence are, or how many shillings in twenty guineas, it would be so encouraging. I should be so much more at my ease about your state of mind."

Without directly answering to this appeal, she sat so still when he had very gently raised her, and the hands that had not ceased to clasp his wrists were so much more steady than they had been, that she communicated some reassurance to Mr. Jarvis Lorry.

"That's right, that's right. Courage! Business! You have business before you; useful business. Miss Manette, your mother took this course with you. And when she died—I believe broken-hearted—having never slackened her unavailing search for your father, she left you, at two years old, to grow to be blooming, beautiful, and happy, without the dark cloud upon you of living in uncertainty whether your father soon wore his heart out in prison, or wasted there through many lingering years."

As he said the words, he looked down, with admiring pity, on the flowing golden hair; as if he pictured to himself that it might have been already tinged with gray.

"You know that your parents had no great possession, and that what they had was secured to your mother and to you. There has been no new discovery of money, or of any other property; but—"

He felt his wrist held closer, and he stopped. The expression of the forehead, which had so particularly attracted his notice, and which was now immovable, had deepened into one of pain and horror.

"But he has been—been found. He is alive. Greatly changed, it is too probable; almost a wreck, it is possible; though we will hope the best. Still, alive. Your father has been taken to the house of an old servant in Paris, and we are going there: I, to identify him if I can: you, to restore him to life, love, duty, rest, comfort."

A shiver ran through her frame, and from it through his. She said, in a low distinct, awe-stricken voice, as if she were saying it in a dream,"I am going to see his Ghost! It will be his Ghost—not him!"

Mr. Lorry quietly chafed the hands that held his arm. "There, there, there! See now, see now! The best and the worst are known to you now. You are well on your way to the poor wronged gentleman, and, with a fair sea voyage, and a fair land journey, you will be soon at his dear side."

She repeated in the same tone, sunk to a whisper, "I have been free, I have been happy, yet his ghost has never haunted me!"

"Only one thing more," said Mr. Lorry, laying stress upon it as a wholesome means of enforcing her attention: "he has been found under another name; his own, long forgotten or long concealed. It would be worse than useless now to inquire which; worse than useless to seek to know whether he has been for years overlooked, or always designedly held prisoner. It would be worse than useless now to make any inquiries, because it would be dangerous. Better not to mention the subject, anywhere or in any way, and to remove him—for a while at all events—out of France. Even I, safe as an Englishman, and even Tellson's, important as they are to French credit, avoid all naming of the matter. I carry about me, not a scrap of writing openly referring to it. This is a secret service altogether. My credentials, entries, and memoranda, are all comprehended in the one line, 'Recalled to Life;' which may mean any thing. But what is the matter! She doesn't notice a word! Miss Manette!"

Perfectly still and silent, and not even fallen back in her chair, she sat under his hand, utterly insensible, with her eyes open and fixed upon him, and with that last expression looking as if it were carved or branded into her forehead. So close was her hold upon his arm, that he feared to detach himself lest he should hurt her; therefore he called out loudly for assistance without moving.

A wild-looking woman, whom, even in his agitation, Mr. Lorry observed to be all of a red color, and to have red hair, and to be dressed in some extraordinary tight-fitting fashion, and to have on her head a most wonderful bonnet like a Grenadier wooden measure, and good measure too, or a great Stilton cheese, came running into the room in advance of the inn servants, and soon settled the question of his detachment from the poor young lady, by laying a brawny hand upon his chest, and sending him flying back against the nearest wall.

("I really think this must be a man!" was Mr. Lorry's breathless reflection, simultaneously with his coming against the wall.)

"Why look at you all!" bawled this figure, addressing the inn servants. "Why don't you go and fetch things, instead of standing there staring at me? I am not so much to look at, am I? Why don't you go and fetch things? I'll let you know, if you don't bring smelling salts, cold water, and vinegar, quick, I will."

There was an immediate dispersal for these restoratives, and she softly laid the patient on a sofa, and tended her with great skill and gentleness: calling her "my precious!" and "my bird!" and spreading her golden hair aside over her shoulders with great pride and care.

"And you in brown!" she said, indignantly turning on Mr. Lorry; "couldn't you tell her what you had to tell her, without frightening her to death? Look at her, with her pretty pale face and her cold hands. Do you call *that* being a banker?"

Mr. Lorry was so exceedingly disconcerted by a question so hard to answer, that he could only look on, at a distance, with much feebler sympathy and humility, while the strong woman, having banished the inn servants under the mysterious penalty of "letting them know" something not mentioned if they stayed there, staring, recovered her charge by a regular series of gradations, and coaxed her to lay her drooping head upon her shoulder.

"I hope she will do well now," said Mr. Lorry.

"No thanks to you in brown, if she does. My darling pretty!"

"I hope," said Mr. Lorry, after another pause of feeble sympathy and humility, "that you accompany Miss Manette to France?"

"A likely thing, too!" replied the strong woman. "If it was ever intended that I should go across salt water, do you suppose Providence would have cast my lot in an island?"

This being another question hard to answer, Mr. Jarvis Lorry withdrew to consider it.

Chapter V

THE WINE-SHOP

A LARGE cask of wine had been dropped and broken, in the street. The accident had happened in getting it out of a cart; the cask had tumbled out with a run, the hoops had burst, and it lay on the stones just outside the door of the wine-shop, shattered like a walnut-shell.

All the people within reach had suspended their business, or their idleness, to run to the spot and drink the wine. The rough, irregular stones of the street, pointing every way, and designed, one might have thought, expressly to lame all living creatures that approached them, had dammed it into little pools; these were surrounded, each by its own jostling group or crowd, according to its size. Some men kneeled down, made scoops of their two hands joined, and sipped, or tried to help women, who bent over their shoulders, to sip, before the wine had all run out between their fingers. Others, men and women, dipped in the puddles with little mugs of mutilated earthenware, or even with handkerchiefs from women's heads, which were squeezed dry into infants' mouths; others made small mud-embankments, to stem the wine as it ran; others, directed by lookers-on up at high windows, darted here and there, to cut off little streams of wine that started away in new directions; others, devoted themselves to the sodden and lee-dyed pieces of the cask, licking, and even champing the moister wine-rotted fragments with eager relish. There was no drainage to carry off the wine, and not only did it all get taken up, but so much mud got taken up along with it, that there might have been a scavenger in the street, if anybody acquainted with it could have believed in such a miraculous presence.

A shrill sound of laughter and of amused voices—voices of men, women, and children—resounded in the street while this wine-game lasted. There was little roughness in the sport, and much playfulness. There was a special companionship in it, an observable inclination on the part of every one to join some other one, which led, especially among the luckier or lighter-hearted, to frolicsome embraces, drinking of healths, shaking of hands, and even joining of hands and dancing, a dozen together. When the wine was gone, and the places where it had been most abundant were raked into a gridiron-pattern by fingers, these demonstrations ceased, as suddenly as they had broken out. The man who had left his saw sticking in the firewood he was cutting, set it in motion again; the woman who had left on a door-step the little pot of hot ashes, at which she had been trying to soften the pain in her own starved fingers and toes, or in those of her child, returned to it; men with bare arms, matted locks, and cadaverous faces, who had emerged into the winter light from cellars, moved away to descend again; and a gloom gathered on the scene that appeared more natural to it than sunshine.

The wine was red wine, and had stained the ground of the narrow street in the suburb of Saint Antoine, in Paris, where it was spilled. It had stained many hands, too, and many faces, and many naked feet, and many wooden shoes. The hands of the man who sawed the wood, left red marks on the billets; and the forehead of the woman who nursed her baby was stained with the stain of the old rag she wound about her head again. Those who had been greedy with the staves of the cask, had acquired a tigerish smear about the mouth; and one tall joker so besmirched, his head more out of a long squalid bag of a nightcap than in it, scrawled upon a wall with his finger dipped in muddy wine lees—BLOOD.

The time was to come, when that wine too would be spilled on the street-stones, and when the stain of it would be red upon many there.

And now that the cloud settled on Saint Antoine, which a momentary gleam had driven from his sacred countenance, the darkness of it was heavy—cold, dirt, sickness, ignorance, and want, were the lords in waiting on the saintly presence—nobles of great power all of them; but, most especially the last. Samples of a people that had undergone a terrible grinding and regrinding in the mill, and certainly not in the fabulous mill which ground old people young, shivered at every corner, passed in and out at every doorway, looked from every window, fluttered in every vestige of a garment that the wind shook. The mill which had worked them down, was the mill that grinds young people old; the children had ancient faces and grave voices; and upon them, and upon the grown faces, and plowed into every furrow of age and coming up afresh, was the sign, Hunger. It was prevalent everywhere. Hunger was pushed out of the tall houses, in the wretched clothing that hung upon poles and lines; Hunger was patched into them with straw and rag and wood and paper; Hunger was repeated in every fragment of the small modicum of firewood that the man sawed off; Hunger stared down from the smokeless chimneys, and started up from the filthy street that had no offal, among its refuse, of anything to eat. Hunger was the inscription on the baker's shelves, written in every small loaf of his scanty stock of bad bread; at the sausage-shop, in every dead-dog preparation that was offered for sale. Hunger rattled its dry bones among the roasting chestnuts in the turned cylinder: Hunger was shred into atomies in every farthing porringer of husky chips of potato, fried with some reluctant drops of oil.

Its abiding-place was in all things fitted to it. A narrow winding street, full of offence and stench, with other narrow winding streets diverging, all peopled by rags and nightcaps, and all smelling of rags and nightcaps, and all visible things with a brooding look upon them that looked ill. In the hunted air of the people there was yet some wild-beast thought of the possibility of turning at bay. Depressed and slinking though they were, eyes of fire were not wanting among them; nor compressed lips, white with what they suppressed; nor foreheads knitted into the likeness of the gallows-rope they mused about enduring, or inflicting. The trade signs (and they were almost as many as the shops) were, all, grim illustrations of Want. The butcher and the porkman painted up, only the leanest scrags of meat; the baker, the coarsest of meagre loaves. The people rudely pictured as drinking in the wine-shops, croaked over their scanty measures of thin wine and beer, and were gloweringly confidential together. Nothing was represented in a flourishing condition, save tools aud weapons; but the cutler's knives and axes were sharp and bright, the smith's hammers were heavy, and the gunmaker's stock was murderous. The crippling stones of the pavement, with their many little reservoirs of mud and water, had no footways, but broke off abruptly at the doors. The kennel, to make amends, ran down the middle of the street—when it ran at all: which was only after heavy rains, and then it ran, by many eccentric fits, into the houses. Across the streets, at wide intervals, one clumsy lamp was slung by a rope and pulley; at night, when the lamplighter had let these down, and lighted, and hoisted them again, a feeble grove of dim wicks swung in a sickly manner overhead, as if they were at sea. Indeed they were at sea, and the ship and crew were in peril of tempest.

For, the time was to come, when the gaunt scarecrows of that region should have watched the lamplighter, in their idleness and hunger, so long, as to conceive the idea of improving on his method, and hauling up men by those ropes and pulleys, to flare upon the darkness of their condition. But, the time was not come yet; and every wind that blew over France shook the rags of the scarecrows in vain, for the birds, fine of song and feather, took no warning.

The wine-shop was a corner-shop, better than most others in its appearance and degree, and the master of the wine-shop had stood outside it, in a yellow waistcoat and green breeches, looking on at the struggle for the lost wine. "It's not my affair," said he, with a final shrug of his shoulders. "The people from the market did it. Let them bring another."

There, his eyes happening to catch the tall joker writing up his joke, he called to him across the way:

"Say then, my Gaspard, what do you do there?"

The fellow pointed to his joke with immense significance, as is often the way with his tribe. It missed its mark, and completely failed, as is often the way with his tribe too.

"What now? Are you a subject for the mad-hospital?" said the wine-shop keeper, crossing the road, and obliterating the jest with a handful of mud, picked up for the purpose, and smeared over it. "Why do you write in the public streets? Is there—tell me thou—is there no other place to write such words in?"

In his expostulation he dropped his cleaner hand (perhaps accidentally, perhaps not), upon the joker's heart. The joker rapped it with his own, took a nimble spring upward, and came down in a fantastic dancing attitude, with one of his stained shoes jerked off his foot into his hand, and held out. A joker of an extremely, not to say wolfishly, practical character, he looked, under those circumstances.

"Put it on, put it on," said the other. "Call wine, wine; and finish there." With that advice, he wiped his soiled hand upon the joker's dress, such as it was—quite deliberately, as having dirtied the hand on his account; and then recrossed the road and entered the wine-shop.

This wine-shop keeper was a bull-necked, martial-looking man of thirty, and he should have been of a hot temperament, for, although it was a bitter day, he wore no coat, but carried one slung over his shoulder. His shirt-sleeves were rolled up, too, and his brown arms were bare to the elbows. Neither did he wear anything more on his head than his own crisply-curling, short, dark hair. He was a dark man altogether, with good eyes and a good bold breadth between them. Good-humoured-looking on the whole, but implacable-looking, too; evidently a man of a strong resolution and a set purpose; a man not desirable to be met, rushing down a narrow pass with a gulf on either side, for nothing would turn the man.

Madame Defarge, his wife, sat in the shop behind the counter as he came in. Madame Defarge was a stout woman of about his own age, with a watchful eye that seldom seemed to look at any thing, a large hand heavily ringed, a steady face, strong features, and great composure of manner. There was a character about Madame Defarge, from which one might have predicated that she did not often make mistakes against herself in any of the reckonings over which she presided. Madame Defarge being sensitive to cold, was wrapped in fur, and had a quantity of bright shawl twined about her head, though not to the concealment of her large earrings. Her knitting was before her, but she had laid it down to pick her teeth with a toothpick. Thus engaged, with her right elbow supported by her left hand, Madame Defarge said nothing when her lord came in, but coughed just one grain of cough. This, in combination with the lifting of her dark, defined eyebrows over her toothpick by the breadth of a line, suggested to her husband that he would do well to look round the shop among the customers, for any new customer who had dropped in while he stepped over the way.

The wine-shop keeper accordingly rolled his eyes about, until they rested upon an elderly gentleman and a young lady, who were seated in a corner. Other company were there: two playing cards, two playing dominoes, three standing by the counter lengthening out a short supply of wine. As he passed behind the counter, he took notice that the elderly gentleman said in a look to the young lady, "This is our man."

"What the devil do *you* do in that galley there!" said Monsieur Defarge to himself; "I don't know you."

But he feigned not to notice the two strangers, and fell into discourse with the triumvirate of customers who were drinking at the counter.

"How goes it, Jacques?" said one of these three to Monsieur Defarge. "Is all the spilt wine swallowed?"

"Every drop, Jacques," answered Monsieur Defarge.

When this interchange of Christian name was effected, Madame Defarge, picking her teeth with her toothpick, coughed another grain of cough, and raised her eyebrows by the breadth of another line.

"It is not often," said the second of the three, addressing Monsieur Defarge, "that many of these miserable beasts know the taste of wine, or of anything but black bread and death. Is it not so, Jacques?"

"It is so, Jacques," Monsieur Defarge returned.

At this second interchange of the Christian name, Madame Defarge, still using her toothpick with profound composure, coughed another grain of cough, and raised her eyebrows by the breadth of another line.

The last of the three now said his say, as he put down his empty drinking vessel and smacked his lips.

"Ah! So much the worse! A bitter taste it is that such poor cattle always have in their mouths, and hard lives they live, Jacques. Am I right, Jacques?"

"You are right, Jacques," was the response of Monsieur Defarge.

This third interchange of the Christian name was completed at the moment when Madame Defarge put her toothpick by, kept her eyebrows up, and slightly rustled in her seat.

"Hold then! True!" muttered her husband. "Gentlemen—my wife!"

The three customers pulled off their hats to Madame Defarge, with three flourishes. She acknowledged their homage by bending her head, and giving them a quick look. Then she glanced in a casual manner round the wine-shop, took up her knitting with great apparent calmness and repose of spirit, and became absorbed in it.

"Gentlemen," said her husband, who had kept his bright eye observantly upon her, "good day. The chamber, furnished bachelor-fashion, that you wished to see, and were inquiring for when I stepped out, is on the fifth floor. The doorway of the staircase gives on the little court-yard close to the left here," pointing with his hand, "near to the window of my establishment. But, now that I remember, one of you has already been there, and can show the way. Gentlemen, adieu!"

They paid for their wine, and left the place. The eyes of Monsieur Defarge were studying his wife at her knitting, when the elderly gentleman advanced from his corner, and begged the favor of a word.

"Willingly, sir," said Monsieur Defarge, and quietly stepped with him to the door.

Their conference was very short, but very decided. Almost at the first word, Monsieur Defarge started and became deeply attentive. It had not lasted a minute, when he nodded and went out. The gentleman then beckoned to the young lady, and they, too, went out. Madame Defarge knitted with nimble fingers and steady eyebrows, and saw nothing.

Mr. Jarvis Lorry and Miss Manette, emerging from the wine-shop thus, joined Monsieur Defarge in the doorway to which he had directed his other company just before. It opened from a stinking little black court-yard, and was the general public entrance to a great pile of houses, inhabited by a great number of people. In the gloomy, tile-paved entry to the gloomy, tile-paved staircase, Monsieur Defarge bent down on one knee to the child of his old master, and put her hand to his lips. It was a gentle action, but not at all gently done; a very remarkable transformation had come over him in a few seconds. He had no good humor in his face, nor any openness of aspect left, but had become a secret, angry, dangerous man.

"It is very high; it is a little difficult. Better to begin slowly." Thus Monsieur Defarge, in a stern voice, to Mr. Lorry, as they began ascending the stairs.

"Is he alone?" the latter whispered.

"Alone! God help him, who should be with him!" said the other in the same voice.

"Is he always alone, then?"

"Yes."

"Of his own desire?"

"Of his own necessity. As he was, when I first saw him after they found me and demanded to know if I would take him, and, at my peril, be discreet—as he was then, so he is now."

"He is greatly changed?"

"Changed!"

The keeper of the wine-shop stopped to strike the wall with his hand, and muttered a tremendous curse. No direct answer could be half so forcible. Mr. Lorry's spirits grew heavier and heavier, as he and his two companions ascended higher and higher.

Such a staircase, with its accessories, in the older and more crowded parts of Paris, would be bad enough now; but, at that time, it was vile indeed to unaccustomed and unhardened senses. Every little habitation within the great foul nest of one high building—that is to say, the room or rooms within every door that opened on the general staircase—left its own heap of refuse on its own landing, besides flinging other refuse from its own windows. The uncontrollable and hopeless mass of decomposition so engendered would have polluted the air, even if poverty and deprivation had not loaded it with their intangible impurities; the two bad sources combined made it almost insupportable. Through such an atmosphere, by a steep dark shaft of dirt and poison, the way lay. Yielding to his own disturbance of mind, and to his young companion's agitation, which became greater every instant, Mr. Jarvis Lorry twice stopped to rest. Each of these stoppages was made at a doleful grating by which any languishing good airs that were left uncorrupted, seemed to escape, and spoilt and sickly vapors seemed to crawl in. Through the rusted bars, tastes, rather than glimpses, were caught of the jumbled neighborhood; and nothing within range, nearer or lower than the summits of the two great towers of Notre-Dame had any promise on it of healthy life or wholesome aspirations.

At last, the top of the staircase was gained, and they stopped for the third time. There was yet an upper staircase, of a steeper inclination and of contracted dimensions, to be ascended, before the garret story was reached. The keeper of the wine-shop, always going a little in advance, and always going on the side which Mr. Lorry took, as though he dreaded to be asked any questions by the young lady, turned himself about here, and, carefully feeling in the pockets of the coat he carried over his shoulder, took out a key.

"The door is locked then, my friend?" said Mr. Lorry, surprised.

"Ay. Yes," was the grim reply of Monsieur Defarge.

"You think it necessary to keep the unfortunate gentleman so retired?"

"I think it necessary to turn the key." Monsieur Defarge whispered it closer in his ear, and frowned heavily.

"Why?"

"Why! Because he has lived so long, locked up, that he would be frightened—rave—tear himself to pieces—die—come to I know not what harm—if his door was left open."

"Is it possible!" exclaimed Mr. Lorry.

"Is it possible?" repeated Defarge, bitterly. "Yes. And a beautiful world we live in, when it *is* possible, and when many other such things are possible, and not only possible, but done—done, see you!—under that sky there, every day. Long live the Devil. Let us go on."

This dialogue had been held in so very low a whisper, that not a word of it had reached the young lady's ears. But, by this time, she trembled under such strong emotion, and her face expressed such deep anxiety, and, above all, such dread and terror, that Mr. Lorry felt it incumbent on him to speak a word or two of reassurance.

"Courage, dear Miss! Courage! Business! The worst will be over in a moment; it is but passing the room door, and the worst is over. Then, all the good you bring to him, all the relief, all the happiness you bring to him, begin. Let our good friend here assist you on that side. That's well, friend Defarge. Come, now. Business, business!"

They went up slowly and softly. The staircase was short, and they were soon at the top. There, as it had an abrupt turn in it, they came all at once in sight of three men, whose heads were bent down close together at the side of a door, and who were intently looking into the room to which the door belonged, through some chinks or holes in the wall. On hearing footsteps close at hand, these three turned, and rose, and showed themselves to be the three of one name who had been drinking in the wine-shop.

"I forgot them in the surprise of your visit," exclaimed Monsieur Defarge. "Leave us, good boys; we have business here."

The three glided by, and went silently down.

There appearing to be no other door on that floor, and the keeper of the wine-shop going straight to this one when they were left alone, Mr. Lorry asked him in a whisper, with a little anger:

"Do you make a show of Monsieur Manette?"

"I show him in the way you have seen, to a chosen few."

"Is that well?"

"*I* think it is well."

"Who are the few? How do you choose them?"

"I choose them as real men, of my name—Jacques is my name—to whom the sight is likely to do good. Enough; you are English; that is another thing. Stay there, if you please, a little moment."

With an admonitory gesture to keep them back, he stooped and looked in through the crevice in the wall. Soon raising his head again, he struck twice or thrice upon the door—evidently with no other object than to make a noise there. With the same intention, he drew the key across it, three or four times, before he put it clumsily into the lock, and turned it as heavily as he could.

The door slowly opened inward under his hand, and he looked into the room and said something. A faint voice answered something. Little more than a single syllable could have been spoken on either side.

He looked back over his shoulder and beckoned them to enter. Mr. Lorry got his arm securely round the daughter's waist and held her; for he felt that she was sinking.

"A—a—a—business, business!" he urged, with a moisture that was not of business shining on his cheek. "Come in, come in!"

"I am afraid of it," she answered, shuddering.

"Of it? What?"

"I mean of him. Of my father."

Rendered in a manner desperate, by her state and by the beckoning of their conductor, he drew over his neck the arm that shook upon his shoulder, lifted her a little, and hurried her into the room. He set her down just within the door, and held her, clinging to him.

Defarge drew out the key, closed the door, locked it on the inside, took out the key again, and held it in his hand. All this he did methodically, and with as loud and harsh an accompaniment of noise as he could make. Finally, he walked across the room with a measured tread to where the window was. He stopped there, and faced around.

The garret, built to be a dry depository for firewood and the like, was dim and dark: for, the window of a dormer shape was in truth a door in the roof, with a lIttle crane over it for the hoisting up of stores from the street: unglazed, and closing up the middle in two pieces, like any other door of French construction. To exclude the cold, one half of this door was fast closed, and the other was opened but a very little way. Such a scanty portion of light was admitted through the seams, that it was difficult, on first coming in, to see anything; and long habit alone could have slowly formed in any one, the ability to do any work requiring nicety in such obscurity. Yet, work of that kind was being done in the garret; for, with his back toward the door, and his face toward the window where the keeper of the wine-shop stood looking at him, a white-haired man sat on a low bench, stooping forward and very busy, making shoes.

Chapter VI

THE SHOEMAKER

"GOOD-DAY!" said Monsieur Defarge, looking down at the white head that bent low over the shoemaking.

It was raised for a moment, and a very faint voice responded to the salutation, as if it were at a distance:

"Good-day!"

"You are still hard at work, I see?"

After a long silence, the head was lifted for another moment, and the voice replied, "Yes—I am working." This time, a pair of haggard eyes had looked at the questioner, before the face had dropped again.

The faintness of the voice was pitiable and dreadful. It was not the faintness of physical weakness, though confinement and hard fare no doubt had their part in it. Its deplorable peculiarity was, that it was the faintness of solitude and disuse. It was like the last feeble echo of a sound made long and long ago. So entirely had it lost the life and resonance of the human voice, that it affected the senses llke a once beautiful color faded away into a poor weak stain. So sunken and suppressed it was, that it was like a voice underground. So expressive it was, of a hopeless and lost creature, that a famished traveler, wearied out by lonely wandering in a wilderness, would have remembered home and friends in such a tone before lying down to die.

Some minutes of silent work had passed, and the haggard eyes had looked up again: not with any interest or curiosity, but with a dull, mechanical perception, beforehand, that the spot where the only visitor they were aware of had stood, was not yet empty.

"I want," said Defarge, who had not removed his gaze from the shoemaker, "to let in a little more light here. You can bear a little more?"

The shoemaker stopped his work; looked, with a vacant air of listening, at the floor on one side of him; then, similarly, at the floor on the other side of him; then, upward at the speaker.

"What did you say?"

"You can bear a little more light?"

"I must bear it, if you let it in." (Laying the palest shadow of a stress upon the second word.)

The opened half-door was opened a little further, and secured at that angle for the time. A broad ray of light fell into the garret, and showed the workman, with an unfinished shoe upon his lap, pausing in his labor. His few common tools and various scraps of leather were at his feet and on his bench. He had a white beard, raggedly cut, but not very long, a hollow face, and exceedingly bright eyes. The hollowness and thinness of his face would have caused them to look large, under his yet dark eyebrows and his confused white hair, though they had been really otherwise; but they were naturally large, and looked unnaturally so. His yellow rags of shirt lay open at the throat, and showed his body to be withered and worn. He, and his old canvas frock, and his loose stockings, and all his poor tatters of clothes, had, in a long seclusion from direct light and air, faded down to such a dull uniformity of parchment-yellow, that it would have been hard to say which was which.

He had put up a hand between his eyes and the light, and the very bones of it seemed transparent. So he sat, with a steadfastly vacant gaze, pausing in his work. He never looked at the figure before him, without first looking down on this side of himself, then on that, as if he had lost the habit of associating place with sound; he never spoke without first wandering in this manner, and forgetting to speak.

"Are you going to finish that pair of shoes to-day?" asked Defarge, motioning to Mr. Lorry to come forward.

"What did you say?"

"Do you mean to finish that pair of shoes to-day?"

"I can't say that I mean to. I suppose so. I don't know."

But the question reminded him of his work, and he bent over it again.

Mr. Lorry came silently forward, leaving the daughter by the door. When he had stood, for a minute or two, by the side of Defarge, the shoemaker looked up. He showed no surprise at seeing another figure, but the unsteady fingers of one of his hands strayed to his lips as he looked at it (his lips and his nails were of the same pale lead color), and then the hand dropped to his work, and he once more bent over the shoe. The look and the action had occupied but an instant.

"You have a visitor, you see," said Monsieur Defarge.

"What did you say?"

"Here is a visitor."

The shoemaker looked up as before, but without removing a hand from his work.

"Come!" said Defarge. "Here is monsieur, who knows a well-made shoe when he sees one. Show him that shoe you are working at. Take it, monsieur."

Mr. Lorry took it in his hand.

"Tell monsieur what kind of shoe it is, and the maker's name."

There was a longer pause than usual, before the shoemaker replied.

"I forget what it was you asked me. What did you say?"

"I said, couldn't you describe the kind of shoe, for monsieur's information?"

"It is a lady's shoe. It is a young lady's walking shoe. It is in the present mode. I never saw the mode. I have had a pattern in my hand." He glanced at the shoe, with some little passing touch of pride.

"And the maker's name?" said Defarge.

Now that he had no work to hold, he laid the knuckles of the right hand in the hollow of the left, and then the knuckles of the left hand in the hollow of the right, and then passed a hand across his bearded chin, and so on in regular changes, without a moment's intermission. The task of recalling him from the vacancy into which he always sank when he had spoken, was like recalling some very weak person from a swoon, or endeavoring, in the hope of some disclosure, to stay the spirit of a fast dying man.

"Did you ask me for my name?"

"Assuredly I did."

"One Hundred and Five, North Tower."

"Is that all?"

"One Hundred and Five, North Tower."

With a weary sound that was not a sigh, nor a groan, he went to work again, until the silence was again broken.

"You are not a shoemaker by trade?" said Mr. Lorry, looking steadfastly at him.

His haggard eyes turned to Defarge as if he would have transferred the question to him; but as no help came from that quarter, they turned back on the questioner when they had sought the ground.

"I am not a shoemaker by trade? No, I was not a shoemaker by trade. I—I learnt it here. I taught myself. I asked leave to—"

He lapsed away, even for minutes, ringing those measured changes on his hands the whole time. His eyes came slowly back, at last, to the face from which they had wandered; when they rested on it, he started, and resumed, in the manner of a sleeper that moment awake, reverting to a subject of last night.

"I asked leave to teach myself, and I got it with much difficulty after a long while, and I have made shoes ever since."

As he held out his hand for the shoe that had been taken from him, Mr. Lorry said, still looking steadfastly in his face:

"Monsieur Manette, do you remember nothing of me?"

The shoe dropped to the ground, and he sat looking fixedly at the questioner.

"Monsieur Manette;" Mr. Lorry laid his hand upon Defarge's arm; "do you remember nothing of this man? Look at him. Look at me. Is there no old banker, no old business, no old servant, no old time, rising in your mind, Monsieur Manette?"

As the captive of many years sat looking fixedly by turns at Mr. Lorry and Defarge, some long-obliterated marks of an actively intent intelligence in the middle of the forehead, gradually forced themselves through the black mist that had fallen on him. They were overclouded again, they were fainter, they were gone; but, they had been there. And so exactly was the expression repeated on the fair young face of her who had crept along the wall to a point where she could see him, and where she now stood looking at him, with hands which at first had been only raised in frightened compassion, if not even to keep him off and shut out the sight of him, but which were now extending toward him, trembling with eagerness to lay the spectral face upon her warm young breast, and love it back to life and hope—so exactly was the expression repeated (though in stronger characters) on her fair young face, that it looked as though it had passed, like a moving light, from him to her.

Darkness had fallen on him in its place. He looked at the two, less and less attentively, and his eyes in gloomy abstraction sought the ground and looked about him in the old way. Finally, with a deep, long sigh, he took the shoe up, and resumed his work.

"Have you recognized him, monsieur?" asked Defarge, in a whisper.

"Yes; for a moment. At first I thought it quite hopeless, but I have unquestionably seen, for a single moment, the face that I once knew well. Hush! Let us draw further back. Hush!"

She had moved from the wall of the garret, very near to the bench on which he sat. There was something awful in his unconsciousness of the figure that could have put out its hand and touched him as he stooped over his labor.

Not a word was spoken, not a sound was made. She stood, like a spirit, beside him, and he bent over his work.

It happened, at length, that he had occasion to change the instrument in his hand, for his shoemaker's knife. It lay on that side of him which was not the side on which she stood. He had taken it up, and was stooping to work again, when his eyes caught the skirt of her dress. He raised them, and saw her face. The two spectators started forward, but she stayed them with a motion of her hand. She had no fear of his striking at her with the knife, though they had.

He stared at her with a fearful look, and after a while his lips began to form some words, though no sound proceeded from them. By degrees, in the pauses of his quick and labored breathing, he was heard to say:

"What is this!"

With the tears streaming down her face, she put her two hands to her lips, and kissed them to him; then clasped them on her breast, as if she laid his ruined head there.

"You are not the gaoler's daughter?"

She signed "No."

"Who are you?"

Not yet trusting the tones of her voice, she sat down on the bench beside him. He recoiled, but she laid her hand upon his arm. A strange thrill struck him when she did so, and visibly passed over his frame; he laid the knife down softly, as he sat staring at her.

Her golden hair, which she wore in long curls, had been hurriedly pushed aside, and fell down over her neck. Advancing his hand by lIttle and little, he took it up and looked at it. In the midst of the action he went astray, and, with another deep sigh, fell to work at his shoemaking.

But, not for long. Releasing his arm, she laid her hand upon his shoulder. After looking doubtfully at it, two or three times, as if to be sure that it was really there, he laid down his work, put his hand to his neck, and took off a blackened string with a scrap of folded rag attached to it. He opened this, carefully, on his knee, and it contained a very lIttle quantity of hair: not more than one or two long, golden hairs, which he had, in some old day, wound off upon his finger.

He took her hair into his hand again, and looked closely at it. "It is the same. How can it be! When was it! How was it!"

As the concentrating expression returned to his forehead, he seemed to become conscious that it was in hers too. He turned her full to the light, and looked at her.

"She laid her head upon my shoulder, that night when I was summoned out—she had a fear of my going, though I had none—and when I was brought to the North Tower they found these upon my sleeve. 'You will leave me them? They can never help me to escape in the body, though they may in the spirit.' Those were the words I said. I remember them very well."

He formed this speech with his lips many times before he could utter it. But when he did find spoken words for it, they came to him coherently, though slowly.

"How was this—*Was it you?*"

Once more, the two spectators started, as he turned upon her with a frightful suddenness. But, she sat perfectly still in his grasp, and only said, in a low voice, "I entreat you, good gentlemen, do not come near us, do not speak, do not move!"

"Hark!" he exclaimed. "Whose voice was that?"

His hands released her as he uttered this cry, and went up to his white hair, which they tore in a frenzy. It died out, as every thing but his shoemaking did die out of him, and he refolded his little packet and tried to secure it in his breast; but, he still looked at her, and gloomily shook his head.

"No, no, no; you are too young, too blooming. It can't be. See what the prisoner is. These are not the hands she knew, this is not the face she knew, this is not a voice she ever heard. No, no. She was—and He was—before the slow years of the North Tower—ages ago. What is your name, my gentle angel?"

Hailing his softened tone and manner, his daughter fell upon her knees before him, with her appealing hands upon his breast.

"Oh, sir, at another time you shall know my name, and who my mother was, and who my father, and how I never knew their hard, hard history. But I cannot tell you at this time, and I cannot tell you here. All that I may tell you, here and now, is, that I pray to you to touch me and to bless me. Kiss me, kiss me! O my dear, my dear!"

His cold white head mingled with her radiant hair, which warmed and lighted it as though it were the light of Freedom shining on him.

"If you hear in my voice—I don't know that it is so, but I hope it is—if you hear in my voice any resemblance to a voice that once was sweet music in your ears, weep for it, weep for it! If you touch, in touching my hair, any thing that recalls a beloved head that lay in your breast when you were young and free, weep for it, weep for it! If, when I hint to you of a home there is before us, where I will be true to you with all my duty and with all my faithful service, I bring back the remembrance of a home long desolate, while your poor heart pined away, weep for it, weep for it!"

She held him closer round the neck, and rocked him on her breast like a child.

"If, when I tell you, dearest dear, that your agony is over, and that I have come here to take you from it, and that we go to England to be at peace and at rest, I cause you to think of your useful life laid waste, and of our native France so wicked to you, weep for it, weep for it! And if, when I shall tell you of my name, and of my father who is living, and of my mother who is dead, you learn that I have to kneel to my honored father, and implore his pardon for having never for his sake striven all day, and lain awake and wept all night, because the love of my poor mother hid his torture from me, weep for it, weep for it! Weep for her then, and for me! Good gentlemen, thank God! I feel his sacred tears upon my face, and his sobs strike against my heart. O, see! Thank God for us, thank God!"

He had sunk in her arms, with his face dropped on her breast: a sight so touching, yet so terrible in the tremendous wrong and suffering which had gone before it, that the two beholders covered their faces.

When the quiet of the garret had been long undisturbed, and his heaving breast and shaken form had long yielded to the calm that must follow all storms—emblem to humanity, of the rest and silence into which the storm called Life must hush at last—they came forward to raise the father and daughter from the ground. He had gradually dropped to the floor, and lay there in a lethargy, worn out. She had nestled down with him, that his head might lie upon her arm; and her hair drooping over him curtained him from the light.

"If, without disturbing him," she said, raising her hand to Mr. Lorry as he stooped over them, after repeated blowings of his nose, "all could be arranged for our leaving Paris at once, so that, from the very door, he could be taken away—"

"But, consider. Is he fit for the journey?" asked Mr. Lorry.

"More fit for that, I think, than to remain in this city, so dreadful to him."

"It is true," said Defarge, who was kneeling to look on and hear. "More than that; Monsieur Manette is, for all reasons, best out of France. Say, shall I hire a carriage and post-horses?"

"That's business," said Mr. Lorry, resuming on the shortest notice his methodical manners; "and if business is to be done, I had better do it."

"Then be so kind," urged Miss Manette, "as to leave us here. You see how composed he has become, and you cannot be afraid to leave him with me now. Why should you be? If you will lock the door, to secure us from interruption, I do not doubt that you will find him, when you come back, as quiet as you leave him. In any case, I will take care of him until you return, and then we will remove him straight."

Both Mr. Lorry and Defarge were rather disinclined to this course, and in favor of one of them remaining. But, as there were not only carriages and horses to be seen to, but traveling papers; and as time pressed, for the day was drawing to an end, it came at last to their hastily dividing the business that was necessary to be done, and hurrying away to do it.

Then, as the darkness closed in, the daughter laid her head down on the hard ground close at the father's side, and watched him. The darkness deepened and deepened, and they both lay quiet, until a light gleamed through the chinks in the wall.

Mr. Lorry and Monsieur Defarge had made all ready for the journey, and brought with them, besides traveling cloaks and wrappers, bread and meat, wine, and hot coffee. Monsieur Defarge put this provender, and the lamp he carried, on the shoemaker's bench (there was nothing else in the garret but a pallet bed), and he and Mr. Lorry roused the captive, and assisted him to his feet.

No human intelligence could have read the mysteries of his mind, in the scared blank wonder of his face. Whether he knew what had happened, whether he recollected what they had said to him, whether he knew that he was free, were questions which no sagacity could have solved. They tried speaking to him; but he was so confused, and so very slow to answer, that they took fright at his bewilderment, and agreed for the time to tamper with him no more. He had a wild, lost manner of occasionally clasping his head in his hands, that had not been seen in him before; yet, he had some pleasure in the mere sound of his daughter's voice, and invariably turned to it when she spoke.

In the submissive way of one long accustomed to obey under coercion, he ate and drank what they gave him to eat and drink, and put on the cloak and other wrappings that they gave him to wear. He readily responded to his daughter's drawing her arm through his, and took—and kept—her hand in both his own.

They began to descend; Monsieur Defarge going first with the lamp, Mr. Lorry closing the little procession. They had not traversed many steps of the long main staircase when he stopped, and stared at the roof and round at the walls.

"You remember the place, my father? You remember coming up here?"

"What did you say?"

But, before she could repeat the question, he murmured an answer as if she had repeated it.

"Remember? No, I don't remember. It was so very long ago."

That he had no recollection whatever of his having been brought from his prison to that house, was apparent to them. They heard him mutter, "One Hundred and Five, North Tower;" and when he looked about him, it evidently was for the strong fortress-walls which had long encompassed him. On their reaching the court-yard, he instinctively altered his tread, as being in expectation of a drawbridge; and when there was no drawbridge, and he saw the carriage waiting in the open street, he dropped his daughter's hand, and clasped his head again.

No crowd was about the door; no people were discernible at any of the many windows; not even a chance passer-by was in the street. An unnatural silence and desertion reigned there. Only one soul was to be seen, and that was Madame Defarge—who leaned against the door-post, kintting, and saw nothing.

The prisoner had got into the coach, and his daughter had followed him, when Mr. Lorry's feet were arrested on the step by his asking, miserably, for his shoemaking tools and the unfinished shoes. Madame Defarge immediately called to her husband that she would get them, and went, knitting, out of the lamplight, through the court-yard. She quickly brought them down and handed them in; and immediately afterward leaned against the door-post, knitting, and saw nothing.

Defarge got upon the box, and gave the word "To the Barrier!" The postilion cracked his whip, and they clattered away under the feeble over-swinging lamps.

Under the over-swinging lamps—swinging ever brighter in the better streets, and ever dimmer in the worse—and by lighted shops, gay crowds, illuminated coffee-houses, and theatre doors, to one of the city gates. Soldiers with lanterns, at the guard-house there. "Your papers, travelers!" "See here then, Monsieur the Officer," said Defarge, getting down, and taking him gravely apart, "these are the papers of monsieur inside, with the white head. They were consigned to me, with him, at the—." He dropped his voice, there was a flutter among the military lanterns, and one of them being handed into the coach by an arm in uniform, the eyes connected with the arm looked, not an every-day or an every-night look, at monsieur with the white head. "It is well. Forward!" from the uniform. "Adieu!" from Defarge. And so, under a short grove of feebler and feebler over-swinging lamps, out under the great grove of stars.

Beneath that arch of unmoved and eternal lights; some, so remote from this little earth, that the learned tell us it is doubtful whether their rays have even yet discovered it, as a point in space where any thing is suffered or done: the shadows of the night were broad and black. All through the cold and restless interval until dawn, they once more whispered in the ears of Mr. Jarvis Lorry—sitting opposite the buried man who had been dug out, and wondering what subtle powers were forever lost to him, and what were capable of restoration—the old inquiry:

"I hope you care to be recalled to life?"

And the old answer:

"I can't say."

BOOK THE SECOND

THE GOLDEN THREAD

Chapter I

FIVE YEARS LATER

TELLSON'S Bank by Temple-bar was an old-fashioned place, even in the year one thousand seven hundred and eighty. It was very small, very dark, very ugly, very incommodious. It was an old-fashioned place, moreover, in the moral attribute that the partners in the House were proud of its smallness, proud of its darkness, proud of its ugliness, proud of its incommodiousness. They were even boastful of its eminence in those particulars, and were fired by an express conviction that, if it were less objectionable, it would be less respectable. This was no passive belief, but an active weapon which they flashed at more convenient places of business. Tellson's (they said) wanted no elbow-room, Tellson's wanted no light, Tellson's wanted no embellishment. Noakes and Co.'s might, or Snooks Brothers' might; but Tellson's, thank Heaven!—

Any one of these partners would have disinherited his son on the question of rebuilding Tellson's. In this respect the house was much on a par with the country; which did very often disinherit its sons for suggesting improvements in laws and customs that had long been highly objectionable, but were only the more respectable.

Thus it had come to pass, that Tellson's was the triumphant perfection of inconvenience. After bursting open a door of idiotic obstinacy with a weak rattle in its throat, you fell into Tellson's down two steps, and came to your senses in a miserable little shop, with two little counters, where the oldest of men made your check shake as if the wind rustled it, while they examined the signature by the dingiest of windows, which were always under a shower-bath of mud from Fleet street, and which were made the dingier by their own iron bars proper, and the heavy shadow of Temple-bar. If your business necessitated your seeing "the House," you were put into a species of Condemned Hold at the Back, where you meditated on a misspent life, until the House came with its hands in its pockets, and you could hardly blink at it in the dismal twilight.

Your money came out of, or went into, wormy old wooden drawers, parricles of which flew up your nose and down your throat when they were opened and shut. Your bank-notes had a musty odor, as if they were fast decomposing into rags again. Your plate was stowed away among the neighboring cesspools, and evil communications corrupted its good polish in a day or two. Your deeds got into extemporised strong-rooms made of kitchen and sculleries, and fretted all the fat out of their parchments into the banking-house air. Your lighter boxes of family papers went up-stairs into a Barmecide room, that had always a great dining-table in it and never had a dinner, and where, even in the year one thousand seven hundred and eighty, the first letters written to you by your old love, or by your little children, were but newly released from the horror of being ogled through the windows by the heads exposed on Temple-bar with an insensate brutality and ferocity worthy of Abyssinia or Ashantee.

But, indeed, at that time, putting to Death was a recipe much in vogue with all trades and professions, and not least of all with Tellson's. Death is Nature's remedy for all things, and why not Legislation's? Accordingly the forger was put to Death; the utterer of a bad note was put to Death; the unlawful opener of a letter was put to Death; the purloiner of forty shillings and sixpence was put to Death; the holder of a horse at Tellson's door, who made off with it, was put to Death; the coiner of a bad shilling was put to Death; the sounders of three-fourths of the notes in the whole gamut of Crime, were put to Death. Not that it did the least good in the way of prevention—it might almost have been worth remarking that the fact was exactly the reverse—but, it cleared off (as to this world) the trouble of each particular case, and left nothing else connected with it to be looked after. Thus, Tellson's, in its day, like greater places of business, its contemporaries, had taken so many lives, that, if the heads laid low before it had been ranged on Temple-bar instead of being privately disposed of, they would probably have excluded what little light the ground floor had, in a rather significant manner.

Cramped in all kinds of dim cupboards and hutches at Tellson's the oldest of men carried on the business gravely. When they took a young man into Tellson's London house, they hid him somewhere till he was old. They kept him in a dark place, like a cheese, until he had the full Tellson flavor and blue-mould upon him. Then only was he permitted to be seen, spectacularly poring over large books, and casting his breeches and gaiters into the general weight of the establishment.

Outside Tellson's—never by any means in it, unless called in—was an odd-job-man, an occasional porter and messenger, who served as the live sign of the house. He was never absent during business hours, unless upon an errand, and then he was represented by his son; a grisly urchin of twelve, who was his express image. People understood that Tellson's, in a stately way, tolerated the odd-job-man. The house had always tolerated some person in that capacity, and time and tide had drifted this person to the post. His surname was Cruncher, and on the youthful occasion of his renouncing by proxy the works of darkness, in the easterly parish church of Hounsditch, he had received the added appellation of Jerry.

The scene was Mr. Cruncher's private lodging in Hangingsword-alley, Whitefriars; the time, half-past seven of the clock on a windy March morning, Anno Domini, seventeen hundred and eighty. (Mr. Cruncher himself always spoke of the year of our Lord as Anna Dominoes; apparently under the impression that the Christian era dated from the invention of a popular game, by a lady who had bestowed her name upon it.)

Mr. Cruncher's apartments were not in a savory neighborhood, and were but two in number, even if a closet with a single pane of glass in it might be accounted as one. But, they were very decently kept. Early as it was, on the windy March morning, the room in which he lay a-bed was already scrubbed throughout; and between the cups and saucers arranged for breakfast, and the lumbering deal table, a very clean, white cloth was spread.

Mr. Cruncher reposed under a patchwork counterpane, like a Harlequin at home. At first, he slept heavily, but by degrees, began to roll and surge in bed, until he rose above the surface, with his spiky hair looking as if it must tear the sheets to ribbons. At which juncture, he exclaimed, in a voice of dire exasperation:

"Bust me, if she ain't at it agin!"

A woman of orderly and industrious appearance rose from her knees in a corner, with sufficient haste and trepidation to show that she was the person referred to.

"What!" said Mr. Cruncher, looking out of bed for a boot. "You're at it agin, are you?"

After hailing the morn with this second salutation, he threw a boot at the woman as a third. It was a very muddy boot, and may introduce the old circumstance connected with Mr. Cruncher's domestic economy, that, whereas he often came home after banking hours with clean boots, he often got up next morning to find the same boots covered with clay.

"What," said Mr. Cruncher, varying his apostrophe after missing his mark— "what are you up to Aggerawayter?"

"I was only saying my prayers."

"Saying your prayers! You're a nice woman! What do you mean by flopping yourself down and praying agin me?"

"I was not praying against you; I was praying for you."

"You weren't. And if you were, I won't be took the liberty with. Here! your mother's a nice woman, young Jerry, going a praying agin your father's prosperity. You've got a dutiful mother, you have, my son. You've got a religious mother, you have, my boy: going and flopping herself down, and praying that the bread-and-butter may be snatched out of the mouth of her only child!"

Master Cruncher (who was in his shirt) took this very ill, and, turning to his mother, strongly deprecated any praying away of his personal board.

"And what do you suppose, you conceited female," said Mr. Cruncher, with unconscious inconsistency, "that the worth of *your* prayers may be? Name the price that you put *your* prayers at!"

"They only come from the heart, Jerry. They are worth no more than that."

"Worth no more than that," repeated Mr. Cruncher. "They ain't worth much, then. Whether or no, I won't be prayed agin, I tell you. I can't afford it. I'm not a going to be made unlucky by *your* sneaking. If you must go flopping yourself down, flop in favor of your husband and child, and not in opposition to 'em. If I had had any but a unnat'ral wife, and this poor boy had had any but a unnat'ral mother, I might have made some money last week, instead of being counterprayed and countermined and being religiously circumwented into the worst of luck. Bu-u-ust me!" said Mr. Cruncher, who all this time had been putting on his clothes, "if I ain't, what with piety and one blowed thing and another, been choused this last week into as bad luck as ever a poor devil of a honest tradesman met with! Young Jerry, dress yourself, my boy, and while I clean my boots keep a eye upon your mother now and then, and if you see any signs of more flopping, give me a call. For, I tell you," here he addressed his wife once more, "I won't be gone agin in this manner. I am as rickety as a hackney-coach. I'm as sleepy as laudanum, my lines is strained to that degree that I shouldn't know, if it wasn't for the pain in 'em, which was me and which somebody else, yet I'm none the better for it in pocket; and it's my suspicion that you've been at it from morning to night to prevent me from being the better for it in pocket; and I won't put up with it, Aggerawayter, and what do you say now!"

Growling, in addition, such phrases as "Ah! yes! You're religious, too. You wouldn't put yourself in opposition to the interests of your husband and child, would you? Not you!" and throwing off other sarcastic sparks from the whirling grindstone of his indignation, Mr. Cruncher betook himself to his boot-cleaning and his general preparations for business. In the mean-time, his son, whose head was garnished with tenderer spikes, and whose young eyes stood close by one another, as his father's did, kept the required watch upon his mother. He greatly disturbed that poor woman at intervals, by darting out of his sleeping-closet, where he made his toilet, with a suppressed cry of "You are going to flop, mother. Halloa, father!" and, after raising this fictitious alarm, darting in again with an undutiful grin.

Mr. Cruncher's temper was not at all improved when he came to his breakfast. He resented Mrs. Cruncher's saying grace with particular animosity.

"Now, Aggerawayter! What are you up to? At it agin?"

His wife explained that she had merely "asked a blessing."

"Don't do it!" said Mr. Cruncher, looking about, as if he rather expected to see the loaf disappear under the efficacy of his wife's petitions. "I ain't a going to be blest out of house and home. I won't have my wittles blest off my table. Keep still!"

Exceedingly red-eyed and grim, as if he had been up all night at a party which had taken any thing but a convivial turn, Jerry Cruncher worried his breakfast rather than ate it, growling over it like any four-footed inmate of a menagerie. Toward nine o'clock he smoothed his ruffled aspect, and, presenting as respectful and business-like an exterior as he could overlay his natural self with, issued forth to the occupation of the day.

It could scarcely be called a trade, in spite of his favorite description of himself as "a honest tradesman." His stock consisted of a wooden stool, made out of a broken-backed chair cut down, which stool Young Jerry, walking at his father's side, carried every morning to beneath the banking-house window that was nearest Temple-bar: where, with the addition of the first handful of straw that could be gleaned from any passing vehicle to keep the cold and wet from the odd-job-man's feet, it formed the encampment for the day. On this post of his, Mr. Cruncher was as well known to Fleet street and the Temple, as the Bar itself—and was almost as ill-looking.

Encamped at a quarter before nine, in good time to touch his three-cornered hat to the oldest of men as they passed in to Tellson's, Jerry took up his station on this windy March morning, with young Jerry standing by him, when not engaged in making forays through the Bar, to infiict bodily and mental injuries of an acute description on passing boys who were small enough for his amiable purpose. Father and son, extremely like each other, looking silently on at the morning traffic in Fleet street, with their two heads as near to one another as the two eyes of each were, bore a considerable resemblance to a pair of monkeys. The resemblance was not lessened by the accidental circumstance, that the mature Jerry bit and spat out straw, while the twinkling eyes of the youthful Jerry were as restlessly watchful of him as of every thing else in Fleet street.

The head of one of the regular in-door messengers attached to Tellson's establishment was put through the door, and the word was given:

"Porter wanted!"

"Hooray, father! Here's an early job to begin with!"

Having thus given his parent God speed, Young Jerry seated himself on the stool, entered on his reversionary interest in the straw his father had been chewing, and cogitated.

"Al-ways rusty! His fingers is al-ways rusty!" muttered young Jerry. "Where does my father get all that iron rust from? He don't get no iron rust here!"

Chapter II

A SIGHT

"YOU know the Old Bailey well, no doubt?" said one of the oldest of clerks to Jerry the messenger.

"Ye-es, sir," returned Jerry, in something of a dogged manner. "I *do* know the Bailey."

"Just so. And you know Mr. Lorry."

"I know Mr. Lorry, sir, much better than I know the Bailey. Much better," said Jerry, not unlike a reluctant witness at the establishment in question, "than I, as a honest tradesman, wish to know the Bailey."

"Very well. Find the door where the witnesses go in, and show the doorkeeper this note for Mr. Lorry. He will then let you in."

"Into the court, sir?"

"Into the court."

Mr. Cruncher's eyes seemed to get a little closer to one another, and to interchange the inquiry, "What do you think of this?"

"Am I to wait in the court, sir?" he asked, as the result of that conference.

"I am going to tell you. The doorkeeper will pass the note to Mr. Lorry, and do you make any gesture that will attract Mr. Lorry's attention, and show him where you stand. Then what you have to do, is, to remain there until he wants you."

"Is that all, sir?"

"That's all. He wishes to have a messenger at hand. This is to tell him you are there."

As the ancient clerk deliberately folded and superscribed the note, Mr. Cruncher, after surveying him in silence until he came to the blotting-paper stage, remarked:

"I suppose they'll be trying forgeries this morning?"

"Treason!"

"That's quartering," said Jerry. "Barbarous!"

"It is the law," remarked the ancient clerk, turning his surprised spectacles upon him. "It is the law!"

"It's hard in the law to spile a man, I think. It's hard enough to kill him, but it's very hard to spile him, sir."

"Not at all," returned the ancient clerk. "Speak well of the law. Take care of your chest and voice, my good friend, and leave the law to take care of itself. I give you that advice."

"It's the damp, sir, what settles on my chest and voice," said Jerry. "I leave you to judge what a damp way of earning a living mine is."

"Well, well," said the old clerk; "We all have our various ways of gaining a livelihood. Some of us have damp ways, and some of us have dry ways. Here is the letter. Go along."

Jerry took the letter, and, remarking to himself with less internal deference than he made an outward show of, "You are a lean old one, too," made his bow, informed his son in passing of his destination, and went his way.

They hanged at Tyburn, in those days, so the street outside Newgate had not obtained one infamous notoriety that has since attached to it. But the gaol was a vile place, in which most kinds of debauchery and villainy were practiced, and where dire diseases were bred, that came into court with the prisoners, and sometimes rushed straight from the dock at my Lord Chief Justice himself, and pulled him off the bench. It had more than once happened, that the Judge in the black cap pronounced his own doom as certainly as the prisoner's, and even died before him. For the rest, the Old Bailey was famous as a kind of deadly inn-yard, from which pale travelers set out continually, in carts and coaches, on a violent passage into the other world: traversing some two miles and a half of publlc street and road, and shaming few good citizens, if any. So powerful is use, and so desirable to be good use in the beginning. It was famous, too, for the pillory, a wise old institution, that inflicted a punishment of which no one could foresee the extent; also, for the whipping-post, another dear old institution, very humanizing and softening to behold in action; also, for extensive transactions in blood-money, another fragment of ancestral wisdom, systematically leading to the most frightful mercenary crimes that could be committed under Heaven. Altogether, the Old Bailey, at that date, was a choice illustration of the precept, that "Whatever is is right;" an aphorism that would be as final as it is lazy, did it not include the troublesome consequence, that nothing that ever was, was wrong.

Making his way through the tainted crowd, dispersed up and down this hideous scene of action, with the skill of a man accustomed to make his way quietly, the messenger found out the door he sought, and handed in his letter through a trap in it. For people then paid to see the play at the Old Bailey, just as they paid to see the play in Bedlam—only the former entertainment was much the dearer. Therefore, all the Old Bailey doors were well guarded—except, indeed, the social doors by which the criminals got there, and they were always left wide open.

After some delay and demur, the door grudgingly turned on its hinges a very little way, and allowed Mr. Jerry Cruncher so to squeeze himself into court.

"What's on?" he asked, in a whisper, of the man he found himself next to.

"Nothing yet."

"What's coming on?"

"The Treason case."

"The quartering one, eh?"

"Ah!" returned the man, with a relish; "he'll be drawn on a hurdle to be half-hanged, and then he'll be taken down and sliced before his own face, and then his inside will be taken out and burnt while he looks on, and then his head will be chopped off, and he'll be cut into quarters. That's the sentence."

"If he's found Guilty, you mean to say?" Jerry added, by way of proviso.

"Oh! they'll find him Guilty," said the other. "Don't you be afraid of that."

Mr. Cruncher's attention was here diverted to the doorkeeper, whom he saw making his way to Mr. Lorry, with the note in his hand. Mr. Lorry sat at a table, among the gentlemen in wigs: not far from a wigged gentleman, the prisoner's counsel, who had a great bundle of papers before him: and nearly opposite another wigged gentleman with his hands in his pockets, whose whole attention, when Mr. Cruncher looked at him then or afterward, seemed to be concentrated on the ceiling of the court. After some gruff coughing and rubbing of his chin and signing with his hand, Jerry attracted the notice of Mr. Lorry, who had stood up to look for him, and who quietly nodded, and sat down again.

"What's *he* got to do with this case?" asked the man he had spoken with.

"Blest if I know," said Jerry.

"What have *you* to do with it, then, if a person may inquire?"

"Blest if I know that either," said Jerry.

The entrance of the Judge, and a consequent great stir and settling-down in the court, stopped the dialogue. Presently, the dock became the central point of interest. Two gaolers, who had been standing there, went out, and the prisoner was brought in, and put to the bar.

Every body present, except the one-wigged gentleman who looked at the ceiling, stared at him. All the human breath in the place,rolled at him, like a sea, or a wind, or a fire. Eager faces strained round pillars and corners, to get a sight of him; spectators in back rows stood up, not to miss a hair of him; people on the floor of the court, laid their hands on the shoulders of the people before them, to help themselves, at any body's cost, to a view of him—stood a-tiptoe, got upon ledges, stood upon next to nothing, to see every inch of him. Conspicuous among these latter, like an animated bit of the spiked wall of Newgate, Jerry stood; aiming at the prisoner the beery breath of a whet he had taken as he came along, and discharging it to mingle with the waves of other beer, and gin, and tea, and coffee, and what not, that flowed at him, and already broke upon the great windows behind him in an impure mist and rain.

The object of all this staring and blaring, was a young man of about five-and-twenty, well-grown and well-looking, with a sunburnt cheek and a dark eye. His condition was that of a young gentleman. He was plainly dressed in black, or very dark gray, and his hair, which was long and dark, was gathered in a ribbon at the back of his neck: more to be out of his way than for ornament. As an emotion of the mind will express itself through any covering of the body, so the paleness which his situation engendered came through the brown upon his cheek, showing the soul to be stronger than the sun. He was otherwise quite self-possessed, bowed to the judge, and stood quiet.

The sort of interest with which this man was stared and breathed at,was not a sort that elevated humanity. Had he stood in peril of a less horrible sentence—had there been a chance of any one of its savage details being spared —by just so much would he have lost in his fascination. The form that was to be doomed to be so shamefully mangled, was the sight; the immortal creature that was to be so butchered and torn asunder, yielded the sensation. Whatever gloss the various spectators put upon the interest, according to their several arts and powers of self-deceit, the interest was, at the root of it, ogreish.

Silence in the court! Charles Darnay had yesterday pleaded Not Guilty to an indictment denouncing him (with infinite jingle and jangle) for that he was a false traitor to our serene, illustrious, excellent and so forth, prince, our Lord the King, by reason of his having, on divers occasions, and by divers means and ways, assisted Lewis, the French king, in his wars against our said serene, illustrious, excellent, and so forth; that was to say, by coming and going between the dominions of our said serene, illustrious, excellent, and so forth, and those of the said French Lewis, and wickedly, falsely, traitorously, and otherwise evil-adverbiously, revealing to the said French Lewis what forces our said serene, illustrious, excellent, and so forth, had in preparation to send to Canada and North America. This much, Jerry, with his head becoming more and more spiky as the law terms bristled it, made out with huge satisfaction, and so arrived circuitously at the understanding that the aforesaid, and over and over again aforesaid Charles Darnay, stood there before him upon his trial; that the jury were swearing in; and that Mr. Attorney-General was making ready to speak.

The accused, who was, (and who knew he was) being mentally hanged, beheaded, and quartered, by every body there, neither flinched from the situation, nor assumed any theatrical air in it. He was quiet and attentive; watched the opening proceedings with a grave interest; and stood with his hands resting on the slab of wood before him, so composedly, that they had not displaced a leaf of the herbs with which it was strewn.

The court was all bestrewn with herbs and sprinkled with vinegar, as a precaution against gaol air and gaol fever.

Over the prisoner's head, there was a mirror, to throw the light down upon him. Crowds of the wicked and the wretched had been reflected in it, and had passed from its surface and from the earth's together. Haunted in a most ghastly manner that abominable place would have been, if the glass could ever have rendered back its reflections, as the ocean is one day to give up its dead. Some passing thought of the infamy and disgrace for which it had been reserved, may have struck the prisoner's mind. Be that as it may, a change in his position, making him conscious of a bar of light across his face, he looked up; and when he saw the glass his face flushed, and his right hand pushed the herbs away.

It happened, that the action turned his face to that side of the court which was on his left. About on a level with his eyes, there sat, in that corner of the Judge's bench, two persons upon whom his look immediately rested; so immediately, and so much to the changing of his aspect, that all the eyes that were turned upon him, turned to them.

The spectators saw in the two figures, a young lady of little more than twenty, and a gentleman who was evidently her father; a man of a very remarkable appearance in respect of the absolute whiteness of his hair, and a certain indescribable intensity of face: not of an active kind, but pondering and self-communing. When this expression was upon him, he looked as if he were old; but, when it was stirred and broken up—as it was now, in a moment, on his speaking to his daughter—he became a handsome man, not past the prime of life.

His daughter had one of her hands drawn through his arm, as she sat by him, and the other pressed upon it. She had drawn close to him, in her dread of the scene, and in her pity for the prisoner. Her forehead had been strikingly expressive of an engrossing terror and compassion that saw nothing but the peril of the accused. This had been so very noticeable, so very powerfully and naturally shown, that starers who had had no pity for him were touched by her; and the whisper went about, "Who are they?"

Jerry, the messenger, who had made his own observations in his own manner, and who had been sucking the rust off his fingers in his absorption, stretched his neck to hear who they were. The crowd about him had pressed and passed the inquiry on to the nearest attendant, and from him it had been more slowly pressed and passed back; at last it got to Jerry.

"Witnesses."

"For which side?"

"Against."

"Against what side?"

"The prisoner's."

The Judge, whose eyes had gone in the general direction, recalled them, leaned back in his seat, and looked steadily at the man whose life was in his hand, as Mr. Attorney-General rose to spin the rope, grind the axe, and hammer the nails into the scaffold.

Chapter III

A DISAPPOINTMENT

MR. ATTORNEY-GENERAL had to inform the jury, that the prisoner before them, though young in years, was old in the treasonable practices which claimed the forfeit of his life. That this correspondence with the public enemy was not a correspondence of to-day, or of yesterday, or even of last year, or of the year before. That it was certain the prisoner had, for longer than that, been in the habit of passing and repassing between France and England, on secret business of which he could give no honest account. That, if it were in the nature of traitorous ways to thrive (which, happily, it never was), the real wickedness and guilt of his business might have remained undiscovered. That, Providence, however, had put it into the heart of a person who was beyond fear and beyond reproach, to ferret out the nature of the prisoner's schemes, and, struck with horror, to disclose them to his Majesty's Chief Secretary of State and most honorable Privy Council. That this patriot would be produced before them. That, his position and attitude were, on the whole, sublime. That, he had been the prisoner's friend, but, at once in an auspicious and an evil hour detecting his infamy, had resolved to immolate the traitor he could no longer cherish in his bosom, on the sacred altar of his country. That, if statues were decreed in Britain, as in ancient Greece and Rome, to public benefactors, this shining citizen would assuredly have had one. That, as they were not so decreed, he probably would not have one. That, Virtue, as had been observed by the poets (in many passages which he well knew the jury would have, word for word, at the tips of their tongues; whereat the jury's countenances displayed a guilty consciousness that they knew nothing about the passages), was in a manner contagious; more especially the bright virtue known as patriotism, or love of country. That, the lofty example of this immaculate and unimpeachable witness for the Crown, to refer to whom, however unworthily, was an honor, had communicated itself to the prisoner's servant, and had engendered in him a holy determination to examine his master's table-drawers and pockets, and secrete his papers. That, he (Mr. Attorney-General) was prepared to hear some disparagement attempted of this admirable servant; but that, in a general way, he preferred him to his (Mr. Attorney-General's) brothers and sisters, and honored him more than his (Mr. Attorney-General's) father and mother. That, he called with confidence on the jury to come and do likewise. That, the evidence of these two witnesses, coupled with the documents of their discovering that would be produced, would show the prisoner to have been furnished with lists of his Majesty's forces, and of their disposition and preparation, both by sea and land, and would leave no doubt that he had habitually conveyed such information to a hostile power. That, these lists could not be proved to be in the prisoner's handwriting; but that it was all the same; that, indeed, it was rather the better for the prosecution, as showing the prisoner to be artful in his precautions. That, the proof would go back five years, and would show the prisoner already engaged in these pernicious missions, within a few weeks before the date of the very first action fought between the British troops and the Americans. That, for these reasons, the jury, being a loyal jury (as he knew they were), and being a responsible jury (as *they* knew they were), must positively find the prisoner guilty, and make an end of him, whether they liked it or not. That, they never could lay their heads upon their pillows; that, they never could tolerate the idea of their wives laying their heads upon their pillows; that, they never could endure the notion of their children laying their heads upon their pillows; in short, that there never more could be, for them or theirs, any laying of heads upon pillows at all, unless the prisoner's head was taken off. That head Mr. Attorney-General concluded by demanding of them, in the name of every thing he could think of with a round turn in it, and on the faith of his solenm asseveration that he already considered the prisoner as good as dead and gone.

When the Attorney-General ceased, a buzz arose in the court as if a cloud of great blue-flies were swarming about the prisoner, in anticipation of what he was soon to become. When toned down again, the unimpeachable patriot appeared in the witness-box.

Mr. Solicitor-General then, following his leader's lead, examined the patriot: John Barsad, gentleman, by name. The story of his pure soul was exactly what Mr. Attorney-General had described it to be—perhaps, if it had a fault, a little too exactly. Having released his noble bosom of its burden, he would have modestly withdrawn himself, but that the wigged gentleman with the papers before him, sitting not far from Mr. Lorry, begged to ask him a few questions. The wigged gentleman sitting opposite, still looked at the ceiling of the court.

Had he ever been a spy himself? No, he scorned the base insinuation. What did he live upon? His property. Where was his property? He didn't precisely remember where it was. What was it? No business of anybody's. Had he inherited it? Yes, he had. From whom? Distant relation? Very distant? Rather. Ever been in prison? Certainly not. Never in a debtors' prison? Didn't see what that had to do with it. Never in a debtors' prison?Come, once again. Never? Yes. How many times? Two or three times. Not five or six? Perhaps. Of what profession? Gentleman. Ever been kicked? Might have been. Frequently? No. Ever kicked down stairs? Decidedly not; once received a kick on the top of a staircase, and fell down stairs of his own accord. Kicked on that occasion for cheating at dice? Something to that effect was said by the intoxicated liar who committed the assault, but it was not true. Swear it was not true? Positively. Ever live by cheating at play? Never. Ever live by play? Not more than other gentlemen do. Ever borrow money of the prisoner? Yes. Ever pay him? No. Was not this intimacy with the prisoner, in reality a very slight one, forced upon the prisoner in coaches, inns, and packets? No. Sure he saw the prisoner with these lists? Certain. Knew no more about the lists? No. Had not procured them himself, for instance? No. Expect to get any thing by this evidence? No. Not in regular government pay and employment, to lay traps? Oh dear, no. Or to do any thing? Oh dear, no. Swear that? Over and over again. No motives but motives of sheer patriotism? None whatever.

The virtuous servant, Roger Cly, swore his way through the case at a great rate. He had taken service with the prisoner, in good faith and simplicity, four years ago. He had asked the prisoner, aboard the Calais packet, if he wanted a handy fellow, and the prisoner had engaged him. He had not asked the prisoner to take the handy fellow as an act of charity—never thought of such a thing. He began to have suspicions of the prisoner, and to keep an eye upon him soon afterward. In arranging his clothes, while traveling, he had seen similar lists to these in the prisoner's pockets, over and over again. He had taken these lists from the drawer of the prisoner's desk. He had not put them there first. He had seen the prisoner show these identical lists to French gentlemen at Calais, and similar lists to French gentlemen, both at Calais and Boulogne. He loved his country, and couldn't bear it, and had given information. He had never been suspected of stealing a silver teapot; he had been maligned respecting a mustard-pot, but it turned out to be only a plated one. He had known the last witness seven or eight years; that was merely a coincidence. He didn't call it a particularly curious coincidence; most coincidences were curious. Neither did he call it a curious coincidence that true patriotism was *his* only motive too. He was a true Briton, and hoped there were many like him.

The blue-flies buzzed again, and Mr. Attorney-General called Mr. Jarvis Lorry.

"Mr. Jarvis Lorry, are you a clerk in Tellson's Bank?"

"I am."

"On a certain Friday night in November one thousand seven hundred and seventy-five, did business occasion you to travel between London and Dover by the mail?"

"It did."

"Were there any other passengers in the mail?"

"Two."

"Did they alight on the road in the course of the night?"

"They did."

"Mr. Lorry, look upon the prisoner. Was he one of those two passengers?"

"I cannot undertake to say that he was."

"Does he resemble either of these two passengers?"

"Both were so wrapped up, and the night was so dark, and we were all so reserved, that I cannot undertake to say even that."

"Mr. Lorry, look again upon the prisoner. Supposing him wrapped up as those two passengers were, is there any thing in his bulk and stature to render it unlikely that he was one of them?"

"No."

"You will not swear, Mr. Lorry, that he was not one of them?"

"No."

"So at least you say he may have been one of them?"

"Yes. Except that I remember them both to have been —like myself— timorous of highwaymen, and the prisoner has not a timorous air."

"Did you ever see a countefeit of timidity, Mr. Lorry?"

"I certainly have seen that."

"Mr. Lorry, look once more upon the prisoner. Have you seen him, to your certain knowledge, before?"

"I have."

"When?"

"I was returning from France a few days afterward, and, at Calais, the prisoner came on board the packet-ship in which I returned, and made the voyage with me."

"At what hour did he come on board?"

"At a little after midnight."

"In the dead of the night. Was he the only passenger who came on board at that untimely hour?"

"He happened to be the only one."

"Never mind about 'happening,' Mr. Lorry. He was the only passenger who came on board in the dead of the night?"

"He was."

"Were you traveling alone, Mr. Lorry, or with any companion?"

"With two companions. A gentleman and lady. They are here."

"They are here. Had you any conversation with the prisoner?"

"Hardly any. The weather was stormy, and the passage long and rough, and I lay on a sofa, almost from shore to shore."

"Miss Manette!"

The young lady, to whom all eyes had been turned before, and were now turned again, stood up where she had sat. Her father rose with her, and kept her hand drawn throug his arm.

"Miss Manette, look upon the prisoner."

To be confronted with such pity, and such earnest youth and beauty, was far more trying to the accused than to be confronted with all the crowd. Standing, as it were, apart with her on the edge of his grave, not all the staring curiosity that looked on, could, for the moment, nerve him to remain quite still. His hurried right hand parcelled out the herbs before him into imaginary beds of flowers in a garden; and his efforts to control and steady his breathing, shook the lips from which the color rushed to his heart. The buzz of the great flies was loud again.

"Miss Manette, have you seen the prisoner before?"

"Yes, sir."

"Where?"

"On board of the packet-ship just now referred to, sir, and on the same occasion."

"You are the young lady just now referred to?"

"O! most unhappily, I am!"

Thee plaintive tone of her compassion merged into the less musical voice of the Judge, as he said, something fiercely: "Answer the questions put to you, and make no remark upon them."

"Miss Manette, had you any conversation with the prisoner on that passage across the Channel?"

"Yes, sir."

"Recall it."

In the midst of a profound stillness, she faintly began.

"When the gentleman came on board—"

"Do you mean the prisoner?" inquired the Judge, knitting his brows.

"Yes, my Lord."

"Then say the prisoner."

"When the prisoner came on board, he noticed that my father," turning her eyes lovingly to him as he stood beside her, "was much fatigued and in a very weak state of health. My father was so reduced, that I was afraid to take him out of the air, and I had made a bed for him on the deck near the cabin steps, and I sat on the deck at his side to take care of him. There were no other passengers that night, but we four. The prisoner was so good as to beg permission to advise me how I could shelter my father from the wind and weather, better than I had done. I had not known how to do it well, not understanding how the wind would set when we were out of the harbor. He did it for me. He expressed great gentleness and kindness for my father's state, and I am sure he felt it. That was the manner of our beginning to speak together."

"Let me interrupt you for a moment. Had he come on board alone?"

"No."

"How many were with him?"

"Two French gentlemen."

"Had they conferred together?'

"They had conferred together until the last moment, when it was necessary for the French gentlemen to be landed in their boat."

"Had any papers been handed about among them, similar to these lists?"

"Some papers had been handed about among them, but I don't know what papers."

"Like these in shape and size?"

"Possibly, but indeed I don't know, although they stood whispering very near to me: because they stood at the top of the cabin steps to have the light of the lamp that was hanging there; it was a dull lamp, and they spoke very low, and I did not hear what they said, and saw only that they looked at papers."

"Now, to the prisoner's conversation, Miss Manette."

"The prisoner was as open in his confidence with me—which arose out of my helpless situation—as he was kind, and good, and useful to my father. I hope," bursting into tears, "I may not repay him by doing him harm to-day."

Buzzing from the blue-flies.

"Miss Manette, if the prisoner does not perfectly understand that you give the evidence which it is your duty to give—which you must give—and which you cannot escape from giving—with great unwillingness, he is the only person present in that condition. Please to go on."

"He told me that he was traveling on business of a delicate and difficult nature, which might get people into trouble, and that he was therefore traveling under an assumed name. He said, that this business had, within a few days, taken him to France, and might, at intervals, take him backward and forward between France and England, for a long time to come."

"Did he say anything about America, Miss Manette? Be particular."

"He tried to explain to me how that quarrel had arisen, and he said that, so far as he could judge, it was a wrong and foolish one on England's part. He added, in a jesting way, that perhaps George Washington might gain almost as great a name in history as George the Third. But there was no harm in his way of saying this: it was said laughingly, and to beguile the time."

Any strongly marked expression of face on the part of a chief actor in a scene of great interest to whom many eyes are directed, will be unconsciously imitated by the spectators. Her forehead was painfully anxious and intent as she gave this evidence, and, in the pauses when she stopped for the Judge to write it down, watched its effect upon the counsel for and against. Among the lookers-on there was the same expression in all quarters of the court; insomuch, that a great majority of the foreheads there, might have been mirrors reflecting the witness, when the Judge looked up from his notes to glare at that tremendous heresy about George Washington.

Mr. Attorney-General now signified to my Lord, that he deemed it necessary, as a matter of precaution and form, to call the young lady's father, Doctor Manette. Who was called accordingly.

"Doctor Manette, look upon the prisoner. Have you ever seen him before?"

"Once. When he called at my lodgings in London. Some three years, or three years and a half, ago."

"Can you identify him as your fellow-passenger on board the packet, or speak to his conversation with your daughter?"

"Sir, I can do neither."

"Is there any particular and special reason for your being unable to do either?"

He answered, in a low voice, "There is."

"Has it been your misfortune to undergo a long imprisonment without trial, or even accusation, in your native country, Dr. Manette?"

He answered, in a tone that went to every heart, "A long imprisonment."

"Were you newly released on the occasion in question?"

"They tell me so."

"Have you no remembrance of the occasion?"

"None. My mind is a blank, from some time—I cannot even say what time—when I employed myself in my captivity, in making shoes, to the time when I found myself living in London with my dear daughter here. She had become familiar to me, when a gracious God restored my faculties; but I am quite unable even to say how she had become familiar. I have no remembrance of the process."

Mr. Attorney-General sat down, and the father and daughter sat down together.

A singular circumstance then arose in the case. The object in hand, being, to show that the prisoner went down, with some fellow-plotter untracked, in the Dover mail on that Friday night in November five years ago, and got out of the mail in the night, as a blind, at a place where he did not remain, but from which he traveled back some dozen miles or more, to a garrison and dockyard, and there collected information; a witness was called to identify him as having been at the precise time required, in the coffee-room of an hotel in that garrison-and-dockyard town, waiting for another person. The prisoner's counsel was cross-examining this witness with no result, except that he had never seen the prisoner on any other occasion, when the wigged gentleman who had all this time been looking at the ceiling of the court, wrote a word or two on a little piece of paper, screwed it up, and tossed it to him. Opening this piece of paper in the next pause, the counsel looked with great attention and curiosity at the prisoner.

"You say again, you are quite sure that it *was* the prisoner?"

The witness was quite sure.

"Did you ever see any body very like the prisoner?"

Not so like (the witness said), as that he could be mistaken.

"Look well upon that gentleman, my learned friend there," pointing to him who had tossed the paper over, "and then look well upon the prisoner. How say you? Are they very like each other?"

Allowing for my learned friend's appearance being careless and slovenly, if not debauched, they were sufficiently like each other to surprise, not only the witness, but every body present, when they were thus brought into comparison. My Lord being prayed to bid my learned friend lay aside his wig, and giving no very gracious consent, the likeness became much more remarkable. My Lord inquired of Mr. Stryver, (the prisoner's counsel), whether they were next to try Mr. Carton (name of my learned friend) for treason? But, Mr. Stryver replied to my Lord, no; but he would ask the witness to tell him whether what happened once, might happen twice; whether he would have been so confident if he had seen this illustration of his rashness sooner; whether he would be so confident, having seen it; and more. The upshot of which, was, to smash this witness like a crockery vessel, and shiver his part of the case to useless lumber.

Mr. Cruncher had by this time taken quite a lunch of rust off his fingers, in his following of the evidence. He had now to attend while Mr. Stryver fitted the prisoner's case on the jury, like a compact suit of clothes; showing them how the patriot, Barsad, was a hired spy and traitor, an unblushing trafficker in blood, and one of the greatest scoundrels upon earth since accursed Judas—which he certainly did look rather like. How the virtuous servant, Cly, was his friend and partner, and was worthy to be; how the watchful eyes of those forgers and false swearers had rested on the prisoner as a victim, because some family affairs in France, he being of French extraction, did require his making those passages across the Channel—though what those affairs were, a consideration for others who were near and dear to him, forbade him, even for his life, to disclose. How the evidence that had been warped and wrested from the young lady, whose anguish in giving it they had witnessed, came to nothing, involving the mere little innocent gallantries and politenesses likely to pass between any young gentleman and young lady so thrown together:—with the exception of that reference to George Washington, which was altogether too extravagant and impossible, to be regarded in any other light than as a monstrous joke. How it would be a weakness in the government to break down in this attempt to practice for popularity on the lowest national antipathies and fears, and therefore Mr. Attorney-General had made the most of it; how, nevertheless, it rested upon nothing, save that vile and infamous character of evidence too often disfiguring such cases, and of which the State Trials of this country were full. But, there my Lord interposed (with as grave a face as if it had not been true), saying that he could not sit upon that Bench and suffer those allusions.

Mr. Stryver then called his few witnesses, and Mr. Cruncher had next to attend while Mr. Attorney-General turned the whole suit of clothes Mr. Stryver had fitted on the jury, inside out; showing how Barsad and Cly were even a hundred times better than he had thought them, and the prisoner a hundred times worse. Lastly, came My Lord himself, turning the suit of clothes, now inside out, now outside in, but on the whole decidedly trimming and shaping them into grave-clothes for the prisoner.

And now, the jury turned to consider, and the great flies swarmed again.

Mr. Carton, who had so long sat looking at the ceiling of the court, changed neither his place nor his attitude, even in this excitement. While his learned friend, Mr. Stryver, massing his papers before him, whispered with those who sat near, and from time to time glanced anxiously at the jury; while all the spectators moved more or less, and grouped themselves anew; while even My Lord himself arose from his seat, and slowly paced up and down his platform, not unattended by a suspicion in the minds of the audience that his state was feverish; this one man sat leaning back, with his torn gown half off him, his untidy wig put on just as it had happened to light on his head after its removal, his hands in his pockets, and his eyes on the ceiling as they had been all day. Something especially reckless in his demeanor, not only gave him a disreputable look, but so diminished the strong resemblance he undoubtedly bore to the prisoner (which his momentary earnestness, when they were compared together, had strengthened), that many of the lookers-on, taking note of him now, said to one another they would hardly have thought the two were so alike. Mr. Cruncher made the observation to his next neighbor, and added, "I'd hold half a guinea that *he* don't get no law-work to do. Don't look like the sort of one to get any, do he?"

Yet, this Mr. Carton took in more of the details of the scene than he appeared to take in; for now, when Miss Manette's head dropped upon her father's breast, he was the first to see it, and to say audibly: "Officer! look to that young lady. Help the gentleman to take her out. Don't you see she will fall!"

There was much commiseration for her as she was removed and much sympathy with her father. It had evidently been a great distress to him, to have the days of his imprisonment recalled. He had shown strong internal agitation when he was questioned, and that pondering or brooding look which made him old, had been upon him like a heavy cloud, ever since. As he passed out, the jury, who had turned back and paused a moment, spoke, through their foreman.

They were not agreed, and wished to retire. My Lord (perhaps with George Washington on his mind) showed some surprise that they were not agreed, but signified his pleasure that they should retire under watch and ward, and retired himself. The trial had lasted all day, and the lamps in the court were now being lighted. It began to be rumored that the jury would be out a long while. The spectators dropped off to get refreshment, and the prisoner withdrew to the back of the dock, and sat down.

Mr. Lorry, who had gone out when the young lady and her father went out, now reappeared, and beckoned to Jerry: who, in the slackened interest, could easily get near him.

"Jerry, if you wish to take something to eat, you can. But, keep in the way. You will be sure to hear when the jury come in. Don't be a moment behind them, for I want you to take the verdict back to the bank. You are the quickest messenger I know, and will get to Temple Bar long before I can."

Jerry had just enough forehead to knuckle, and he knuckled it in acknowledgment of this communication and a shillIng. Mr. Carton came up at the moment, and touched Mr. Lorry on the arm.

"How is the young lady?"

"She is greatly distressed; but her father is comforting her, and she feels the better for being out of court."

"I'll tell the prisoner so. It won't do for a respectable bank-gentleman like you, to be seen speaking to him publicly, you know."

Mr. Lorry reddened, as if he were conscious of having debated the point in his mind, and Mr. Carton made his way to the outside of the bar. The way out of court lay in that direction, and Jerry followed him, all eyes, ears, and spikes.

"Mr. Darnay!"

The prisoner came forward directly.

"You will naturally be anxious to hear of the witness, Miss Manette. She will do very well. You have seen the worst of her agitation."

"I am deeply sorry to have been the cause of it. Could you tell her so for me, with my fervent acknowledgments?"

"Yes, I could. I will, if you ask it."

Mr. Carton's manner was so careless as to be almost insolent. He stood, half turned from the prisoner, lounging with his elbow against the bar.

"I do ask it. Accept my cordial thanks."

"What," said Carton, still only half turned toward him, "do you expect, Mr. Darnay?"

"The worst."

"It's the wisest thing to expect, and the likeliest. But I think their withdrawing is in your favor."

Loitering on the way out of court not being allowed, Jerry heard no more; but left them—so like each other in feature, so unlike each other in manner—standing side by side, both reflected in the glass above them.

An hour and a half limped heavily away in the thief-and-rascal-crowded passages below, even though assisted off with mutton pies and ale. The hoarse messenger, uncomfortably seated on a form, after taking that refection, had dropped into a doze, when a loud murmur and a rapid tide of people setting up the stairs that led to the court, carried him along with them.

"Jerry! Jerry!" Mr. Lorry was already calling at the door when he got there.

"Here, sir! It's a fight to get back again. Here I am, sir!"

Mr. Lorry handed him a paper through the throng. "Quick! Have you got it?"

"Yes, sir."

Hastily written on the paper was the word "ACQUITTED."

"If you had sent the message, 'Recalled to Life,' again," muttered Jerry, as he turned, "I should have known what you meant, this time."

He had no opportunity of saying, or so much as thinking, any thing else, until he was clear of the Old Bailey; for, the crowd came pouring out with a vehemence that nearly took him off his legs, and a loud buzz swept into the street as if the baffled blue-flies were dispersing in search of other carrion.

Chapter IV
CONGRATULATORY

FROM the dimly-lighted passages of the court, the last sediment of the human stew that had been boiling there all day, was straining off, when Doctor Manette, Lucie Manette his daughter, Mr. Lorry, the solicitor for the defence, and its counsel, Mr. Stryver, stood gathered around Mr. Charles Darnay—just released—congratulating him on his escape from death.

It would have been difficult by a far brighter light, to recognize in Doctor Manette, intellectual of face and upright of bearing, the shoemaker of the garret in Paris. Yet, no one could have looked at him twice, without looking again: even though the opportunity of observation had not extended to the mournful cadence of his low, grave voice, and to the abstraction that overclouded him fitfully, without any apparent reason. While one external cause, and that a reference to his long, lingering agony, would always—as on the trial—evoke this condition from the depths of his soul, it was also in its nature to arise of itself, and to draw a gloom over him, as incomprehensible to those unacquainted with his story as if they had seen the shadow of the actual Bastille thrown upon him by a summer sun, when the substance was three hundred miles away.

Only his daughter had the power of charming this black brooding from his mind. She was the golden thread that united him to a Past beyond his misery, and to a Present beyond his misery: and the sound of her voice, the light of her face, the touch of her hand, had a strong beneficial influence with him almost always. Not absolutely always, for she could recall some occasions on which her power had failed; but, they were few and slight, and she believed them over.

Mr. Darnay had kissed her hand fervently and gratefully, and had turned to Mr. Stryver, whom he warmly thanked. Mr. Stryver was of little more than thirty, but looking twenty years older than he was, stout, loud, red, bluff, and free from any drawback of delicacy, had a pushing way of shouldering himself (morally and physicaily) into companies and conversations, that argued well for his shouldering his way up in life.

He still had his wig and gown on, and he said, squaring himself at his late client to that degree that he squeezed the innocent Mr. Lorry clean out of the group: "I am glad to have brought you off with honor, Mr. Darnay. It was an infamous prosecution, grossly infamous; but not the less likely to succeed, on that account."

"You have laid me under an obligation to you for life —in two senses," said his late client, taking his hand.

"I have done my best for you, Mr. Darnay; and my best is as good as another man's, I believe."

It clearly being incumbent on someone to say, "Much better," Mr. Lorry said it; perhaps not quite disinterestedly, but with the interested object of squeezing himself back again.

"You think so?" said Mr. Stryver. "Well! you have been present all day, and you ought to know. You are a man of business, too."

"And as such," quoth Mr. Lorry, whom the counsel learned in the law had now shouldered back into the group, just as he had previously shouldered him out of it—"as such, I will appeal to Doctor Manette, to break up this conference and order us all to our homes. Miss Lucie looks ill, Mr. Darnay has had a terrible day; we are worn out."

"Speak for yourself, Mr. Lorry," said Stryver; "I have a night's work to do yet. Speak for yourself."

"I speak for myself," answered Mr. Lorry, "and for Mr. Darnay, and for Miss Lucie, and—Miss Lucie, do you not think I may speak for us all?" He asked her the question pointedly, and with a glance at her father.

His face had become frozen, as it were, in a very curious look at Darnay: an intent look, deepening into a frown of dislike and distrust, not even unmixed with fear. With this strange expression on him, his thoughts had wandered away.

"My father," said Lucie, softly laying her hand on his.

He slowly shook the shadow off and turned to her.

"Shall we go home, my father?"

With a long breath, he answered, "Yes."

The friends of the acquitted prisoner had dispersed, under the impression—which he himself had originated—that he would not be released that night. The lights were nearly all extinguished in the passages, the iron gates were being closed with a jar and a rattle, and the dismal place was deserted until to-morrow morning's interest of gallows, pillory, whipping-post, and branding-iron, should repeople it. Walking between her father and Mr. Darnay, Lucie Manette passed into the open air. A hackney-coach was called, and the father and daughter departed in it.

Mr. Stryver had left them in the passages, to shoulder his way back to the robing-room. Another person who had not joined the group, or interchanged a word with any one of them, but who had been leaning against the wall where its shadow was darkest, had silently strolled out after the rest, and had looked on until the coach drove away. He now stepped up to where Mr. Lorry and Mr. Darnay stood upon the pavement.

"So, Mr. Lorry! Men of business may speak to Mr. Darnay now?"

Nobody had made any acknowledgment of Mr. Carton's part in the day's proceedings; nobody had known of it. He was unrobed, and was none the better for it in appearance.

"If you knew what a conflict goes on in the business mind, when the business mind is divided between good-natured impulse and business appearances, you would be amused, Mr. Darnay."

Mr. Lorry reddened, and said, warmly, "You have mentioned that before, sir. We men of business who serve a House, are not our own masters. We have to think of the House, more than ourselves."

"*I* know, *I* know," rejoined Mr. Carton, carelessly. "Don't be nettled, Mr. Lorry. You are as good as another, I have no doubt ; better, I dare say."

"And indeed, sir," pursued Mr. Lorry, not minding him, "I really don't know what you have to do with the matter. If you'll excuse me, as very much your elder, for saying so, I really don't know that it is your business."

"Business! Bless you, *I* have no business," said Mr. Carton.

"It is a pity you have not, sir."

"I think so too."

"If you had," pursued Mr. Lorry, "perhaps you would attend to it."

"Lord love you, no!—I shouldn't," said Mr. Carton.

"Well, sir" cried Mr. Lorry, thoroughly heated by his indifference, "business is a very good thing, and a very respectable thing. And, sir, if business imposes its restraints and its silences and impediments, Mr. Darnay, as a young gentleman of generosity, knows how to make allowance for that circumstance. Mr. Darnay, good-night, God bless you, sir! I hope you have been this day preserved for a prosperous and happy life. Chair there!"

Perhaps a little angry with himself, as well as with the barrister, Mr. Lorry bustled into the chair, and was carried off to Tellson's. Carton, who smelt of port wine, and did not appear to be quite sober, laughed then, and turned to Darnay:

"This is a strange chance that throws you and me together. This must be a strange night to you, standing alone here with your counterpart on these street-stones?"

"I hardly seem yet," returned Charles Darnay, "to belong to this world again."

"I don't wonder at it; it's not so long since you were pretty far advanced on your way to another. You speak faintly."

"I begin to think I *am* faint."

"Then why the devil don't you dine? I dined myself, while those numskulls were deliberating which world you should belong to—this, or some other. Let me show you the nearest tavern to dine well at."

Drawing his arm through his own, he took him down Ludgate-hill to Fleet street, and so, up a covered way, into a tavern. Here, they were shown into a little room, where Charles Darnay was soon recruiting his strength with a good, plain dinner and good wine: while Carton sat opposite to him at the same table, with his separate bottle of port before him, and his fully half-insolent manner upon him.

"Do you feel, yet, that you belong to this terrestrial scheme again, Mr. Darnay?"

"I am frightfully confused regarding time and place; but I am so far mended as to feel that."

"It must be an immense satisfaction!"

He said it bitterly, and filled up his glass again: which was a large one.

"As to me, the greatest desire I have, is to forget that I belong to it. It has no good in it for me—except wine like this—nor I for it. So we were not much alike in that particular. Indeed, I begin to think we are not much alike in any particular, you and I."

Confused by the emotion of the day, and feeling his being there with this Double of coarse deportment, to be like a dream, Charles Darnay was at a loss how to answer; finally, answered not at all.

"Now your dinner is done," Carton presently said, "why don't you call a health, Mr. Darnay? why don't you give your toast?"

"What health? What toast?"

"Why, it's on the tip of your tongue. It ought to be, it must be, I'll swear it's there."

"Miss Manette, then!"

"Miss Manette, then!"

Looking his companion full in the face while he drank the toast, Carton flung his glass over his shoulder against the wall, where it shivered to pieces; then, rang the bell, and ordered in another.

"That's a fair young lady to hand to a coach in the dark Mr. Darnay!" he said, filling his new goblet.

A light frown and a laconic "Yes," were the answer.

"That's a fair young lady to be pitied by and wept for by! How does it feel? Is it worth being tried for one's llfe, to be the object of such sympathy and compassion, Mr. Darnay?"

Again Darnay answered not a word.

"She was mightily pleased to have your message, when I gave it her. Not that she showed she was pleased, but I suppose she was."

The allusion served as a timely reminder to Darnay that this disagreeable companion had, of his own free will, assisted him in the strait of the day. He turned the dialogue to that point, and thanked him for it.

"I neither want any thanks, nor merit any," was the careless rejoinder. "It was nothing to do, in the first place; and I don't know why I did it, in the second. Mr. Darnay, let me ask you a question."

"Willingly, and a small return for your good offices."

"Do you think I particularly like you?"

"Really, Mr. Carton," returned the other, oddly disconcerted, "I have not asked myself the question."

"But ask yourself the question now."

"You have acted as if you do; but I don't think you do."

"*I* don't think I do," said Carton. "I begin to have a very good opinion of your understanding."

"Nevertheless," pursued Darnay, rising to ring the bell, "there is nothing in that, I hope, to prevent my calling the reckoning, and our parting without ill-blood on either side."

Carton rejoining, "Nothing in life!" Darnay rang. "Do you call the whole reckoning?" said Carton. On his answering in the affirmative, "Then bring me another pint of this same wine, drawer, and come and wake me at ten."

The bill being paid, Charles Darnay rose and wished him good-night. Without returning the wish, Carton rose too, with something of a threat or defiance in his manner, and said, "A last word, Mr. Darnay: you think I am drunk!"

"I think you have been drinking, Mr. Carton."

"Think? You know I have been drinking."

"Since I must say so, I know it."

"Then you shall likewise know why. I am a disappointed drudge, sir. I care for no man on earth, and no man on earth cares for me."

"Much to be regretted. You might have used your talents better."

"May be so, Mr. Darnay; may be not. Don't let your sober face elate you, however; you don't know what it may come to. Good-night!"

When he was left alone, this strange being took up a candle, went to a glass that hung against the wall, and surveyed himself minutely in it.

"Do you particularly like the man?" he muttered, at his own image; "why should you particularly like a man who resembles you? There is nothing in you to like; you know that. Ah, confound you! What a change you have made in yourself! A good reason for taking to a man, that he shows you what you have fallen away from and what you might have been! Change places with him, and would you have been looked at by those blue eyes as he was, and commiserated by that agitated face as he was? Come on, and have it out in plain words! You hate the fellow."

He resorted to his pint of wine for consolation, drank it all in a few minutes, and fell asleep on his arms, with his hair straggling over the table, and a long winding-sheet in the candle dripping down upon him.

Chapter V
THE JACKAL

THOSE were drinking days, and most men drank hard. So very great is the improvement Time has brought about in such habits, that a moderate statement of the quantity of wine and punch which one man would swallow in the course of a night, without any detriment to his reputation as a perfect gentleman, would seem, in these days, a ridiculous exaggeration. The learned profession of the Law was certainly not behind any other learned profession in its Bacchanalian propensities; neither was Mr. Stryver, already fast shouldering his way to a large and lucrative practice, behind his compeers in this particular, any more than in the drier parts of the legal race.

A favorite at the Old Bailey, and eke at the Sessions, Mr. Stryver had begun cautiously to hew away the lower staves of the ladder on which he mounted. Sessions and Old Bailey had now to summon their favorite, specially, to their longing arms; and shouldering itself toward the visage of the Lord Chief Justice in the Court of King's Bench, the florid countenance of Mr. Stryver might be daily seen, bursting out of the bed of wigs, like a great sunflower pushing its way at the sun from among a rank garden full of flaring companions.

It had once been noted at the Bar, that while Mr. Stryver was a glib man, and an unscrupulous, and a ready, and a bold, he had not that faculty of extracting the essence from a heap of statements, which is among the most striking and necessary of the advocate's accomplishments. But, a remarkable improvement came upon him as to this. The more business he got, the greater his power seemed to grow of getting at its pith and marrow; and however late at night he sat carousing with Sydney Carton, he always had his points at his fingers' ends in the morning.

Sydney Carton, idlest and most unpromising of men, was Stryver's great ally. What the two drank together, between Hilary Term and Michaelmas, might have floated a king's ship. Stryver never had a case in hand, anywhere, but Carton was there, with his hands in his pockets, staring at the ceiling of the court; they went the same Circuit, and even there they prolonged their usual orgies late into the night, and Carton was rumored to be seen at broad day, going home stealthily and unsteadily to his lodging, like a dissipated cat. At last, it began to get about, among such as were interested in the matter, that although Sydney Carton would never be a lion, he was an amazingly good jackal, and that he rendered suit and service to Stryver in that humble capacity.

"Ten o'clock, sir," said the man at the tavern, whom he had charged to wake him—"ten o'clock, sir."

"*What's* the matter?"

"Ten o'clock, sir."

"What do you mean? Ten o'clock at night?"

"Yes, sir. Your honor told me to call you."

"Oh! I remember. Very well, very well."

After a few dull efforts to get to sleep again, which the man dexterously combated by stirring the fire continuously for five minutes, he got up, tossed his hat on, and walked out. He turned into the Temple, and, having revived himself by twice pacing the pavements of King's Bench-walk and Paper-buildings, turned into the Stryver's chambers.

The Stryver clerk, who never assisted at these conferences, had gone home, and the Stryver principal opened the door. He had his slippers on, and a loose bedgown, and his throat was bare for his greater ease. He had that rather wild, strained, seared marking about the eyes, which may be observed in all free livers of his class, from the portrait of Jeffries downward, and which can be traced, under various disguises of Art, through the portraits of every Drinking Age.

"You are a little late, Memory," said Stryver.

"About the usual time; it may be a quarter of an hour later."

They went into a dingy room lined with books and littered with papers, where there was a blazing fire. A kettle steamed upon the hob, and in the midst of the wreck of papers a table shone, with plenty of wine upon it, and brandy, and rum, and sugar, and lemons.

"You have had your bottle, I perceive, Sydney."

"Two to-night, I think. I have been dining with the day's client; or seeing him dine—it's all one!"

"That was a rare point, Sydney, that you brought to bear upon the identification. How did you come by it? When did it strike you?"

"I thought he was rather a handsome fellow, and I thought I should have been much the same sort of fellow, if I had had any luck."

Mr. Stryver laughed, till he shook his precocious paunch.

"You and your luck, Sydney! Get to work, get to work."

Sullenly enough, the jackal loosened his dress, went into an adjoining room, and came back with a large jug of cold water, a basin, and a towel or two. Steeping the towels in the water, and partially wringing them out, he folded them on his head in a manner hideous to behold, sat down at the table, and said, "Now I am ready!"

"Not much boiling down to be done to-night, Memory," said Mr. Stryver, gayly, as he looked among his papers.

"How much?"

"Only two sets of them."

"Give me the worst first."

"There they are, Sydney. Fire away!"

The lion then composed himself on his back on a sofa on one side of the drinking-table, while the jackal sat at his own paper-bestrewn table proper, on the other side of it, with the bottles and glasses ready to his hand. Both resorted to the drinking-table without stint, but each in a different way; the lion for the most part reclining with his hands in his waistband, looking at the fire, or occasionally flirting with some lighter document; the jackal, with knitted brows and intent face, so deep in his task, that his eyes did not even follow the hand he stretched out for his glass—which often groped about, for a minute or more, before it found the glass for his lips. Two or three times, the matter in hand became so knotty, that the jackal found it imperative on him to get up, and steep his towels anew. From these pilgrimages to the jug and basin, he returned with such eccentricities of damp head-gear as no words can describe; which were made the more ludicrous by his anxious gravity.

At length the jackal had got together a compact repast for the lion, and proceeded to offer it to him. The lion took it with care and caution, made his selections from it, and his remarks upon it, and the jackal assisted both. When the repast was fully discussed, the lion put his hands in his waistband again, and lay down to meditate. The jackal then invigorated himself with a bumper for his throttle, and a fresh application for his head, and applied himself to the collection of a second meal; this was administered to the lion in the same manner, and was not disposed of until the clocks struck three in the morning.

"And now we have done, Sydney, fill a bumper of punch," said Mr. Stryver.

The jackal removed the towels from his head, which had been steaming again, shook himself, yawned, shivered, and complied,

"You were very sound, Sydney, in the matter of those crown witnesses to-day. Every question told."

"I always am sound; am I not?"

"I don't gainsay it. What has roughened your temper? Put some punch to it and smooth it again."

With a deprecatory grunt, the jackal again complied.

"The old Sydney Carton of old Shrewsbury School," said Stryver, nodding his head over him as he reviewed him in the present and the past, "the old seesaw Sydney. Up one minute and down the next; now in spirits and now in despondency!"

"Ah!" returned the other, sighing: "yes! The same Sydney, with the same luck. Even then, I did exercises for other boys, and seldom did my own."

"And why not?"

"God knows. It was my way; I suppose.'

He sat, with his hands in his pockets and his legs stretched out before him, looking at the fire.

"Carton," said his friend, squaring himself at him with a bullying air, as if the fire-grate had been the furnace in which sustained endeavor was forged, and the one delicate thing to be done for the old Sydney Carton of old Shrewsbury School was to shoulder him into it, "your way is, and always was, a lame way. You summon no energy and purpose. Look at me."

"Oh, botheration!" returned Sydney, with a lighter and more good-humored laugh, "don't *you* be moral!"

"How have I done what I have done?" said Stryver; "how do I do what I do?"

"Partly through paying me to help you, I suppose. But it's not worth your while to apostrophise me, or the air, about it; what you want to do, you do. You were always in the front rank, and I was always behind."

"I had to get into the front rank; I was not born there, was I?"

"I was not present at the ceremony; but my opinion is you were," said Carton. At this, he laughed again, and they both laughed.

"Before Shrewsbury, and at Shrewsbury, and ever since Shrewsbury," pursued Carton, "you have fallen into your rank, and I have fallen into mine. Even when we were fellow-students in the Quartier Latin ,picking up French, and French law, and other French crumbs that we didn't get much good of, you were always somewhere, and I was always—nowhere."

"And whose fault was that?"

"Upon my soul, I am not sure that it was not yours. You were always driving and riving and shouldering and pressing, to that restless degree that I had no chance for my life but in rust and repose. It's a gloomy thing, however, to talk about one's own past, with the day breaking. Turn me in some other direction before I go."

"Well then! Pledge me to the pretty witness," said Stryver, holding up his glass. "Are you turned in a pleasant direction?"

Apparently not, for he became gloomy again.

"Pretty witness," he muttered, looking down into his glass. "I have had enough of witnesses to-day and to-night; who's your pretty witness?"

"The picturesque doctor's daughter, Miss Manette."

"*She* pretty?"

"Is she not?"

"No."

"Why, man alive, she was the admiration of the whole Court."

"Rot the admiration of the whole Court! Who made the Old Bailey a judge of beauty? She was a golden-haired doll?"

"Do you know, Sydney," said Mr. Stryver, looking at him with sharp eyes, and slowly drawing a hand across his florid face: "do you know, I rather thought, at the time, that you sympathised with the golden-haired doll, and were quick to see what happened to the golden-haired doll?"

"Quick to see what happened! If a girl, doll or no doll, swoons within a yard or two of a man's nose, he can see it without a perspective-glass. I pledge you, but I deny the beauty. And now I'll have no more drink; I'll get to bed."

When his host followed him out on the staircase with a candle, to light him down the stairs, the day was coldly looking in through its grimy windows. When he got out of the house, the air was cold and sad, the dull sky overcast, the river dark and dim, the whole scene like a lifeless desert. And wreaths of dust were spinning round and round before the morning blast, as if the desert-sand had risen far away, and the first spray of it in its advance had begun to overwhelming the city.

Waste forces within him, and a desert all around, this man stood still on his way across a silent terrace, and saw for a moment, lying in the wilderness before him, a mirage of honorable ambition, self-denial, and perseverance. In the fair city of this vision, there were airy galleries from which the loves and graces looked upon him, gardens in which the fruits of life hung ripening, waters of Hope that sparkled in his sight. A moment, and it was gone. Climbing to a high chamber in a well of houses, he threw himself down in his clothes on a neglected bed, and its pillow was wet with wasted tears.

Sadly, sadly, the sun rose; it rose upon no sadder sight than the man of good abilities, and good emotions, incapable of their directed exercise, incapable of his own help and his own happiness, sensible of the blight on him, and resigning himself to let it eat him away.

Chapter VI

HUNDREDS OF PEOPLE

THE quiet lodgings of Doctor Manette were in a quiet street-corner not far from Soho-square. On the afternoon of a certain fine Sunday when the waves of four months had rolled over the trial for treason, and carried it, as to the public interest and memory, far out to sea, Mr. Jarvis Lorry walked along the sunny streets from Clerkenwell, where he lived, on his way to dine with the Doctor. After several relapses into business-absorption, Mr. Lorry had become the Doctor's friend, and the quiet street-corner was the sunny part of his life.

On this certain fine Sunday, Mr. Lorry walked toward Soho, early in the afternoon, for three reasons of habit. Firstly, because, on fine Sundays, he often walked out, before dinner, with the Doctor and Lucie; secondly, because, on unfavorable Sundays, he was accustomed to be with them as the family friend, talking, reading, looking out of window, and generally getting through the day; thirdly, because he happened to have his own little shrewd doubts to solve, and knew how the ways of the Doctor's household pointed to that time as a likely time for solving them.

A quainter corner than the corner where the Doctor lived, was not to be found in London. There was no way through it, and the front windows of the Doctor's lodgings commanded a pleasant little vista of street that had a congenial air of retirement on it. There were few buildings then, north of the Oxford road, and forest-trees floriurished, and wild-flowers grew, and the hawthorn blossomed, in the now vanished fields. As a consequence, country airs circulated in Soho with vigorous freedom, instead of languishing into the prarish like stray paupers without a settlement; and there was many a good south wall, not far off, on which the peaches ripened in their season.

The summer light struck into the corner brilliantly in the earlier part of the day; but, when the streets grew hot, the corner was in shadow, though not in shadow so remote but that you could see beyond it into a glare of brightness. It was a cool spot, staid but cheerful, a wonderful place for echoes, and a very harbor from the raging streets.

There ought to have been a tranquil bark in such an anchorage, and there was. The Doctor occupied two floors of a large still house, where several callings purported to be pursued by day, but whereof little was audible any day, and which was shunned by all of them at night. In a building at the back, attainable by a court-yard where a plane-tree rustled its green leaves, church-organs claimed to be made, and silver to be chased, and likewise gold to be beaten by some mysterious giant who had a golden arm starting out of the wall of the front hall—as if he had beaten himself precious, and menaced a similar conversion of all visitors. Very little of these trades, or of a lonely lodger rumored to live up stairs, or of a dim coach-timming maker asserted to have a counting-house below, was ever heard or seen. Occasionally, a stray workman putting his coat on, traversed the hall, or a stranger peered about there, or a distant clink was heard across the court-yard, or a thump from the golden giant. These, however, were only the exceptions required to prove the rule that the sparrows in the plane-tree behind the house, and the echoes in the corner before it, had their own way from Sunday morning unto Saturday night.

Doctor Manette received such patients here as his old reputation, and its revival in the floating whispers of his story, brought him. His scientific knowledge, and his vigilance and skill in conducting ingenious experiments, brought him otherwise into moderate request, and he earned as much as he wanted.

These things were within Mr. Jarvis Lorry's knowledge, thoughts, and notice, when he rang the door-bell of the tranquil house in the corner, on the fine Sunday afternoon.

"Doctor Manette at home?"

Expected home.

"Miss Lucie at home?"

Expected home.

"Miss Pross at home?"

Possibly at home, but of a certainty impossible for handmaid to anticipate intentions of Miss Pross, as to admission or denial of the fact.

"As I am at home myself," said Mr. Lorry, "I'll go upstairs."

Although the Doctor's daughter had known nothing of the country of her birth, she appeared to have innately derived from it that ability to make much of little means, which is one of its most useful and most agreeable characteristics. Simple as the furniture was, it was set off by so many little adornments, of no value but for their taste and fancy, that its effect was delightful. The disposition of every thing in the rooms, from the largest object to the least; the arrangement of colors, the elegant variety and contrast obtained by thrift in trifles, by delicate hands, clear eyes, and good sense; were at once so pleasant in themselves, and so expressive of their originator, that, as Mr. Lorry stood looking about him, the very chairs and tables seemed to ask him, with something of that peculiar expression which he knew so well by this time, whether he approved?

There were three rooms on a floor, and, the doors by which they communicated being put open that the air might pass freely through them all, Mr. Lorry, smilingly observant of that fanciful resemblance which he detected all around him, walked from one to another. The first was the best room, and in it were Lucie's birds, and flowers, and books, and desk, and work-table, and box of water-colors; the second was the Doctor's consulting-room, used also as the dining-room; the third, changingly speckled by the rustle of the plane-tree in the yard, was the Doctor's bedroom—and there, in a corner, stood the disused shoemaker's bench and tray of tools, much as it had stood on the fifth floor of the dismal house by the wine-shop, in the suburb of Saint Antoine in Paris.

"I wonder," said Mr. Lorry, pausing in his looking about, "that he keeps that reminder of his sufferings by him!"

"And why wonder at that?" was the abrupt inquiry that made him start.

It proceeded from Miss Pross, the wild red woman, strong of hand, whose acquaintance he had first made at the Royal George Hotel at Dover, and had since improved.

"I should have thought—" Mr. Lorry began.

"Pooh! You'd have thought!" said Miss Pross; and Mr. Lorry left off.

"How do you do?" inquired that lady then—sharply, and yet as if to express that she bore him no malice.

"I am pretty well, I thank you," answered Mr. Lorry, with meekness, "how are you?"

"Nothing to boast of," said Miss Pross.

"Indeed?"

"Ah! indeed!" said Miss Pross. "I am very much put out about my ladybird."

"Indeed?"

"For gracious sake say something else besides 'indeed,' or you'll fidget me to death," said Miss Pross: whose character (dissociated from stature) was shortness.

"Really, then?" said Mr. Lorry, as an amendment.

"Really, is bad enough," returned Miss Pross, "but better. Yes, I am very much put out."

"May I ask the cause?"

"I don't want dozens of people who are not at all worthy of ladybird, to come here looking after her," said Miss Pross.

"*Do* dozens come for that purpose?"

"Hundreds," said Miss Pross.

It was characteristic of this lady (as of some other people before her time and since) that whenever her original proposition was questioned, she exaggerated it.

"Dear me!" said Mr. Lorry, as the safest remark he could think of.

"I have lived with the darling—or the darling has lived with me, and paid me for it; which she certainly should never have done, you may take your affidavit, if I could have afforded to keep either myself or her for nothing—since she was ten years old. And it's really very hard," said Miss Pross.

Not seeing with precision what was very hard, Mr. Lorry shook his head; using that important part of himself as a sort of fairy cloak that would fit any thing.

"All sorts of people who are not in the least degree worthy of the pet, are always turning up," said Miss Pross. "When you began it—"

"*I* began it, Miss Pross?"

"Didn't you? Who brought her father to life?"

"Oh! If *that* was beginning it—" said Mr. Lorry.

"It wasn't ending it, I suppose? I say, when you began it, it was hard enough; not that I have any fault to find with Doctor Manette, except that he is not worthy of such a daughter, which is no imputation on him, for it was not to be expected that anybody should be, under any circumstances. But it really is doubly and trebly hard to have crowds and multitudes of people turning up after him (I could have forgiven him), to take ladybird's affections away from me."

Mr. Lorry knew Miss Pross to be very jealous, but he also knew her by this time to be, beneath the surface of her eccentricity, one of those unselfish creatures—found only among women—who will, for pure love and admiration, bind themselves willing slaves, to youth when they have lost it, to beauty that they never had, to accomplishments that they were never fortunate enough to gain, to bright hopes that never shone upon their own sombre lives. He knew enough of the world to know that there is nothing in it better than the faithful service of the heart; so rendered and so free from any mercenary taint, he had such an exalted respect for it, that in the retributive arrangements made by his own mind—we all make such arrangements, more or less—he stationed Miss Pross much nearer to the lower Angels than many ladies immeasurably better got up both by Nature and Art, who had balances at Tellson's.

"There never was, nor will be, but one man worthy of ladybird," said Miss Pross; "and that was my brother Solomon, if he hadn't made a mistake in life."

Here again: Mr. Lorry's inquiries into Miss Pross's personal history, had established the fact that her brother Solomon was a heartless scoundrel who had stripped her of every thing she possessed as a stake to speculate with, and had abandoned her in her poverty for evermore, with no touch of compunction. Miss Pross's fidelity of belief in Solomon (deducting a mere trifle for this slight mistake) was quite a serious matter with Mr. Lorry, and had its weight in his good opinion of her.

"As we happen to be alone for the moment, and are both people of business," he said, when they had got back to the drawing-room, and had sat down there in friendly relations, "let me ask you—does the Doctor, in talking with Lucie, never refer to the shoemaking time, yet?"

"Never."

"And yet keeps that bench and those tools beside him?"

"Ah!" returned Miss Pross, shaking her head. "But I don't say he don't refer to it within himself."

"Do you believe that he thinks of it much?"

"I do," said Miss Pross.

"Do you imagine—" Mr. Lorry had begun, when Miss Pross took him up short with:

"Never imagine any thing. Have no imagination at all."

"I stand corrected; do you suppose—you go so far as to suppose, sometimes?"

"Now and then," said Miss Pross.

"Do you suppose," Mr. Lorry went on, with a laughing twinkle in his bright eye, as it looked kindly at her, "that Doctor Manette has any theory of his own, preserved through all those years, relative to the cause of his being so oppressed; perhaps, even to the name of his oppressor?"

"I don't suppose any thing about it but what Ladybird tells me."

"And this is—?"

"That she thinks he has."

"Now don't be angry at my asking all these questions; because I am a mere dull man of business, and you are a woman of business."

"Dull?" Miss Pross inquired, with placidity.

Rather wishing his modest adjective away, Mr. Lorry replied, "No, no, no. Surely not. To return to business:—Is it not remarkable that Doctor Manette, unquestionably innocent of any crime, as we are well assured he is, should never touch upon that question? I will not say with me, though he had business relations with me many years ago, and we are now intimate; I will say with the fair daughter to whom he is so devotedly attached, and who is so devotedly attached to him? Believe me, Miss Pross, I don't approach the topic with you, out of curiosity, but out of zealous interest."

"Well! To the best of my understanding, and bad's the best you'll tell me," said Miss Pross, softened by the tone of the apology, "he is afraid of the whole subject."

"Afraid?"

"It's plain enough, I should think, why he may be. It's a dreadful remembrance. Besides that, his loss of himself grew out of it. Not knowing how he lost himself, or how he recovered himself, he may never feel certain of not losing himself again. That alone wouldn't make the subject pleasant, I should think."

It was a profounder remark than Mr. Lorry had looked for. "True," said he, "and fearful to reflect upon. Yet, a doubt lurks in my mind, Miss Pross, whether it is good for Doctor Manette to have that suppression always shut up within him. Indeed, it is this doubt and the uneasiness it sometimes causes me, that has led me to our present confidence."

"Can't be helped," said Miss Pross, shaking her head. "Touch that string, and he instantly changes for the worse. Better leave it alone. In short, must leave it alone, like or no like. Sometimes, he gets up in the dead of the night, and will be heard, by us overhead there, walking up and down, walking up and down, in his room. Ladybird has learnt to know then, that his mind is walking up and down, walking up and down, in his old prison. She hurries to him, and they go on together, walking up and down, walking up and down, until he is composed. But he never says a word of the true reason for his restlessness, to her, and she finds it best not to hint at it to him. In silence they go walking up and down together, walking up and down together, till her love and company have brought him to himself."

Notwithstanding Miss Pross's denial of her own imagination, there was a perception of the pain of being monotonously haunted by one sad idea, in her repetition of the phrase, walking up and down, which testified to her possessing such a thing.

The corner has been mentioned as a wondeful corner for echoes; it had begun to echo so resoundingly to the tread of coming feet, that it seemed as though the very mention of that weary pacing to and fro had set it a going.

"Here they are!" said Miss Pross, rising to break up the conference; "and now we shall have hundreds of people pretty soon!"

It was such a curious corner in its acoustical properties, such a peculiar ear of a place, that as Mr. Lorry stood at the open window, looking for the father and daughter whose steps he heard, he fancied they would never approach. Not only would the echoes die away, as though the steps had gone; but echoes of other steps that never came, would be heard in their stead, and would die away for good when they seemed close at hand. However, father and daughter did at last appear, and Miss Pross was ready at the street door to receive them.

Miss Pross was a pleasant sight, albeit wild, and red, and grim, taking off her darling's bonnet when she came up-stairs, and touching it up with the ends of her handkerchief, and blowing the dust off it, and folding her mantle ready for laying by, and smoothing her rich hair with as much pride as she could possibly have taken in her own hair if she had been the vainest and handsomest of women. Her darling was a pleasant sight too, embracing her and thanking her, and protesting against her taking so much trouble for her—which last she only dared to do playfully, or Miss Pross, sorely hurt, would have retired to her own chamber and cried. The Doctor was a pleasant sight too, lookng on at them, and telling Miss Pross how she spoilt Lucie, in accents and with eyes that had as much spoiling in them as Miss Pross had, and would have had more if it were possible. Mr. Lorry was a pleasant sight too, beaming at all this in his little wig, and thanking his bachelor stars for having lighted him in his declining years to a Home. But, no Hundreds of people came to see the sights, and Mr. Lorry looked in vain for the fulfullment of Miss Pross's prediction.

Dinner time, still no Hundreds of people. In the arrangements of the little household, Miss Pross took charge of the lower regions, and always acquitted herself marvelously. Her dinners, of a very modest quality, were so well cooked and so well served, and so neat in their contrivances, half English and half French, that nothing could be better. Miss Pross's friendship being of the thoroughly practical kind, she had ravaged Soho and the adjacent provinces, in search of impoverished French, who, tempted by shillings and half-crowns, would impart culinary mysteries to her. From these decayed sons and daughters of Gaul, she had acquired such wonderful arts, that the woman and girl who formed the staff of domestics regarded her as quite a Sorceress, or Cinderella's Godmother:

who would send out for a fowl, a rabbit, a vegetable or two from the garden, and change them into any thing she pleased.

On Sunday, Miss Pross dined at the Doctor's table, but on other days persisted in taking her meals, at unknown periods, either in the lower regions, or in her own room on the second floor—a blue chamber, to which no one but her Ladybird ever gained admittance. On this occasion Miss Pross, responding to Ladybird's pleasant face and pleasant efforts to please her, unbent exceedingly; so the dinner was very pleasant too.

It was an oppressive day, and, after dinner, Lucie proposed that the wine should be carried out under the plane-tree, and they should sit there in the air. As every thing turned upon her and revolved about her, they went out under the plane-tree, and she carried the wine down for the special benefit of Mr. Lorry. She had installed herself, some time before, as Mr. Lorry's cup-bearer; and while they sat under the plane-tree, talking, she kept his glass replenished. Mysterious backs and ends of houses peeped at them as they talked, and the plane-tree whispered to them, in its own way, above their heads.

Still, the Hundreds of people did not present themselves. Mr. Darnay presented himself while they were sitting under the plane-tree, but he was only One.

Doctor Manette received him kindly, and so did Lucie. But Miss Pross suddenly became afflicted with a twitching in the head and body, and retired into the house. She was not unfrequently the victim of this disorder, and she called it, in familiar conversation, "a fit of the jerks."

The Doctor was in his best condition, and looked specially young. The resemblance between him and Lucie was very strong at such times and as they sat side by side, she leaning on his shoulder, and he resting his arm on the back of her chair, it was very agreeable to trace the likeness.

He had been talking, all day, on many subjects and with unusual vivacity. "Pray, Doctor Manette," said Mr. Darnay, as they sat under the plane-tree—and he said it in the natural pursuit of the topic in hand, which happened to be the old buildings of London—"have you seen much of the Tower?"

"Lucie and I have been there; but only casually. We have seen enough of it, to know that it teems with interest; little more."

"*I* have been there, as you remember," said Darnay, with a smile, though reddening a little angrily, "in another character, and not in a character that gives facilities for seeing much of it. They told me a curious thing when I was there."

"What was that?" Lucie asked.

"In making some alterations, the workmen came upon an old dungeon, which had been, for many years, built up and forgotten. Every stone of its inner wall was covered by inscriptions which had been carved by prisoners—dates, names, complaints, and prayers. Upon a corner stone in an angle of the wall, one prisoner, who seemed to have gone to execution, had cut, as his last work, three letters. They were done with some very poor instrument, and hurriedly, with an unsteady hand. At first, they were read as D. I. C.; but, on being more carefully examined, the last letter was found to be G. There was no record or legend of any prisoner with those initials, and many fruitless guesses were made what the name could have been. At length it was suggested that the letters were not initials, but the complete word, DIG. The floor was examined very carefully under the inscription, and, in the earth, beneath a stone, or tile, or some fragment of paving were found the ashes of a paper, mingled with the ashes of a small leathern case or bag. What the unknown prisoner had written will never be read, but he had written something, and hidden it away to keep it from the gaoler."

"My father!" exclaimed Lucie, "you are ill!"

He had suddenly started up, with his hand to his head. His manner and his look quite terrified them all.

"No, my dear, not ill. There are large drops of rain falling, and they made me start. We had better go in."

He recovered himself almost instantly. Rain was really falling in large drops, and he showed the back of his hand with rain-drops on it. But, he said not a single word in reference to the discovery that had been told of, and, as they went into the house, the business eye of Mr. Lorry either detected, or fancied it detected, on his face, as it turned toward Charles Darnay, the same singular look, that had been upon it when it turned toward him in the passage of the Court House.

He recovered himself so quickly, however, that Mr. Lorry had doubts of his business eye. The arm of the golden giant in the hall was not more steady than he was, when he stopped under it to remark to them that he was not yet proof against slight surprises (if he ever would be) , and that the rain had startled him.

Tea-time, and Miss Pross making tea, with another fit of the jerks upon her, and yet no Hundreds of people. Mr. Carton had lounged in, but he made only Two.

The night was so very sultry, that although they sat with doors and windows open, they were overpowered by heat. When the tea-table was done with, they all moved to one of the windows, and looked out into the heavy twilight. Lucie sat by her father; Darnay sat beside her; Carton leaned against a window. The curtains were long and white, and some of the thunder-gusts that whirled into the corner, caught them up to the ceiling, and waved them like spectral wings.

"The rain-drops are still falling, large, heavy, and few," said Doctor Manette. "It comes slowly."

"It comes surely," said Carton.

They spoke low, as people watching and waiting mostly do; as people in a dark room, watching and waiting for Lightning, always do.

There was a great hurry in the streets, of people speeding away to get shelter before the storm broke; the wonderful corner for echoes resounded with the echoes of footsteps coming and going, yet not a footstep was there.

"A multitude of people, and yet a solitude!" said Darnay, when they had listened for a while.

"Is it not impressive, Mr. Darnay?" asked Lucie. "Sometimes, I have sat here of an evening, until I have fancied—but even the shade of a foolish fancy makes me shudder to-night, when all is so black and solemn—"

"Let us shudder, too. We may know what it is?"

"It will seem nothing to you. Such whims are only impressive as we originate them, I think; they are not to be communicated. I have sometimes sat alone here of an evening, listening, until I have made the echoes out to be the echoes of all the footsteps that are coming by-and-by into our lives."

"There is a great crowd coming one day into our lives, if that be so," Sydney Carton struck in, in his moody way.

The footsteps were incessant, and the hurry of them became more and more rapid. The corner echoed and re-echoed with the tread of feet; some, as it seemed, under the windows; some, as it seemed, in the room; some coming, some going, some breaking off, some stopping altogether; all in the distant streets, and not one within sight.

"Are all these footsteps destined to come to all of us, Miss Manette, or are we to divide them among us?"

"I don't know, Mr. Darnay; I told you it was a foolish fancy, but you asked for it. When I have yielded myself to it, I have been alone, and then I have imagined them the footsteps of the people who are to come into my life, and my father's."

"I take them into mine!" said Carton. "*I* ask no questions and make no stipulations. There is a great crowd bearing down upon us, Miss Manette, and I see them—by the lightning." He added the last words, after there had been a vivid flash which had shown him lounging in the window.

"And I hear them!" he added again, after a peal of thunder. "Here they come, fast, fierce, and furious!"

It was the rush and roar of rain that he typified, and it stopped him, for no voice could be heard in it. A memorable storm of thunder and lightning broke with that sweep of water, and there was not a moment's interval in crash, and fire, and rain until after the moon rose at midnight.

The great bell of Saint Paul's was striking One in the cleared air, when Mr. Lorry, escorted by Jerry, high-booted, and bearing a lantern, set forth on his return-passage to Clerkenwell. There were solitary patches of road on the way between Soho and Clerkenwell, and Mr. Lorry, mindful of footpads, always retained Jerry for this service: though it was usually performed a good two hours earlier.

"What a night it has been! Almost a night, Jerry," said Mr. Lorry, "to bring the dead out of their graves."

"I never see the night myself, master—nor yet I don't expect to it—what would do that," answered Jerry.

"Good-night, Mr. Carton," said the man of business. "Good-night, Mr. Darnay. Shall we ever see such a night again, together!"

Perhaps. Perhaps, see the great crowd of people with its rush and roar, bearing down upon them, too.

Chapter VII
MONSIEUR THE MARQUIS IN TOWN

MONSEIGNEUR, one of the great lords in power at the Court, held his fortnightly reception in his grand hotel in Paris. Monseigneur was in his inner room, his sanctuary of sanctuaries, the Holiest of Holiest to the crowd of worshipers in the suite of rooms without. Monseigneur was about to take his chocolate. Monseigneur could swallow a great many things with ease, and was by some few sullen minds supposed to be rather rapidly swallowing France; but, his morning's chocolate could not so much as get into the throat of Monseigneur, without the aid of four strong men besides the cook.

Yes. It took four men, all four ablaze with gorgeous decoration. And the Chief of them, unable to exist with fewer than two gold watches in his pocket, emulative of the noble and chaste fashion set by Monseigneur, to conduct the happy chocolate to Monseigneur's lips. One lacquey carried the chocolate-pot into the sacred presence; a second, milled and frothed the chocolate with the little instrument he bore for that function; a third, presented the favored napkin; a fourth, (he of the two gold watches) poured the chocolate out. It was impossible for Monseigneur to dispense with one of these attendants on the chocolate and hold his high place under the admiring Heavens. Deep would have been the blot upon his escutcheon if his chocolate had been ignobly waited on by only three men; he must have died of two.

Monseigneur had been out at a little supper last night, where the Comedy and the Grand Opera were charmingly represented. Monseigneur was out at a little supper most nights, with fascinating company. So polite and so impressible was Monseigneur, that the Comedy and the Grand Opera had far more influence with him in the tiresome articles of State affairs and State secrets, than the needs of all France. A happy circumstance for France, as the like always is for all countries similarly favored!—always was for England (by way of example), in the regretted days of the merry Stuart who sold it.

Monseigneur had one truly noble idea of general public business, which was, to let every thing go on in its own way; of particular public business, Monseigneur had the other truly noble idea that it must all go his way—tend to his own power and pocket. Of his pleasures, general and particular, Monseigneur had the other truly noble idea, that the world was made for them. The text of his order (altered from the original by only a pronoun, which is not much) ran: "The earth and the fullness thereof are mine, said Monseigneur."

Yet, Monseigeur had slowly found that vulgar embarrassments crept into his affairs, both private and public, and he had, as to both classes of affairs, allied himself per force with a Farmer-General. As to finances public, because Monseigneur could not make any thing at all of them, and must consequently let them out to somebody who could; as to finances private, because Farmer-Generals were rich, and Monseigneur, after generations of great luxury and expense, was growing poor. Hence,

Monseigneur had taken his sister from a convent, while there was yet time to ward off the impending vail, the cheapest garment she could wear, and had bestowed her as a prize upon a very rich Farmer-General, poor in family. Which Farmer-General, carrying an appropriate cane with a golden apple on the top of it, was now among the company in the outer rooms, much prostrated before by mankind—always excepting superior mankind of the blood of Monseigneur, who, his own wife included, looked down upon him with the loftiest contempt.

A sumptuous man was the Farmer-General. Thirty horses stood in his stables, twenty-four male domestics sat in his halls, six body-women waited on his wife. As one who pretended to do nothing but plunder and forage where he could, the Farmer-General—howsoever his matrimonial relations conduced to social morality—was at least the greatest reality among the personages who attended at the hotel of Monseigneur that day.

For, the rooms, though a beautiful scene to look at, and adorned with every device of decoration that the taste and skill of the time could achieve, were, in truth, not a sound business; considered with any reference to the scarecrows in the rags and nightcaps elsewhere (and not so far off either, but that the watching towers of Notre-Dame, almost equidistant from the two extremes, could see them both), they would have been an exceedingly uncomfortable business—if that could have been anybody's business, at the house of Monseigneur. Military officers destitute of military knowledge; naval officers with no idea of a ship; civil officers without a notion of affairs; brazen ecclesiastics, of the worst world worldly, with sensual eyes, loose tongues, and looser lives; all totally unfit for their several callings, all lying horribly in pretending to belong to them, but all nearly or remotely of the order of Monseigneur, and therefore foisted on all public employments from which any thing was to be got; these were to be told off by the score and the score. People not immediately connected with Monseigneur or the State, yet equally unconnected with any thing that was real, or with lives passed in traveling by any straight road to any true earthly end, were no less abundant. Doctors who made great fortunes out of dainty remedies for imaginary disorders that never existed, smiled upon their courtly patients in the ante-chambers of Monseigneur. Projectors who had discovered every kind of remedy for the little evils with which the State was touched, except the remedy of setting to work in earnest to root out a single sin, poured their distracting babble into any ears they could lay hold of, at the reception of Monseigueur. Unbelieving Philosophers who were remodelling the world with words, and making card-towers of Babel to scale the skies with, talked with Unbelieving Chemists who had an eye on the transmutation of metals, at this wonderful gathering accumulated by Monseigneur. Exquisite gentlemen of the finest breeding, which was at that remarkable time—and has been since—to be known by its fruits of indifference to every natural subject of human interest, were in the most exemplary state of exhaustion, at the hotel of Monseigneur. Such homes had these various notabilities left behind them in the fine world of Paris, that the Spies among the assembled devotees of Monseigneur—forming a goodly half of the polite company—would have found it hard to discover among the angels of that sphere, one solitary wife, who, in her manners and appearance, owned to being a mother. Indeed, except for the mere act of bringing a troublesome creature into this world—which does not go far toward the realization of the name of mother—there was no such thing known to the fashion. Peasant women kept the unfashionable babies close, and brought them up; and charming grandmammas of sixty dressed and supped as at twenty.

The leprosy of unreality disfigured every human creature in attendance upon Monseigneur. In the outermost room were half a dozen exceptional people who had had, for a few years, some vague misgiving in them that things in general were going rather wrong. As a promising way of setting them right, half of the half-dozen had become members of a fantastic sect of Convulsionists, and were even then considering within themselves whether they should foam, rage, roar, and turn cataleptic on the spot—thereby setting up a highly intelligible finger-post to the Future, for Monseigneur's guidance. Besides these Dervishes, were other three who had rushed into another sect, which mended matters with a jargon about "The Centre of truth:" holding that Man had got out of the Centre of truth—which did not need much demonstration—but had not got out of the Circumference, and that he was to be kept from flying out of the Circumference, and was even to be shoved back into the Centre, by fasting and seeing of spirits. Among these, accordingly, much discoursing with spirits went on—and it did a world of good which never became manifest.

But, the comfort was, that all the company at the grand hotel of Monseigeur were perfectly dressed. If the Day of Judgment had only been ascertained to be a dress day, every body there would have been eternally correct. Such frizzling and powdering and sticking up of hair, such delicate complexions artificially preserved and mended, such gallant swords to look at, and such delicate honor to the sense of smell, would surely keep any thing going, forever and ever. The exqusite gentlemen of the finest breeding wore little pendent trinkets that chinked as they languidly moved; these golden fetters rang like precious little bells; and what with that ringing, and with the rustle of silk and brocade and fine linen, there was a flutter in the air that fanned Saint Antoine and his devouring hunger far away.

Dress was the one unfailing talisman and charm used for keeping all things in their places. Every body was dressed for a Fancy Ball that was never to leave off. From the Palace of the Tuileries, through Monseigneur and the whole Court, through the Chambers, the Tribunals of Justice, and all society (except the scarecrows), the Fancy Ball descended to the Common Executioner; who, in pursuance of the charm, was required to officiate "frizzled, powdered, in a gold-laced coat, pumps, and white silk stockings." At the gallows and the wheel—the axe was a rarity—Monsieur Paris, as it was the episcopal mode among his brother Professors of the provinces, Monsieur Orleans, and the rest, to call him, presided in this dainty dress. And who among the company at Monseigneur's reception in that seventeen hundred and eightieth year of our Lord, could possibly doubt, that a system rooted in a frizzled hangman, powdered, gold-laced, pumped, and white-silk stockinged, would see the very stars out!

Monseigneur having eased his four men of their burdens and taken his chocolate, caused the doors of the Holiest of Holiests to be thrown open, and issued forth. Then, what submission, what cringing and fawning, what servility, what abject humiliation! As to bowing down in body and spirit, nothing in that way was left for Heaven—which may have been one among other reasons why the worshipers of Monseigneur never troubled it.

Bestowing a word of promise here and a smile there, a whisper on one happy slave and a wave of the hand on another, Monseigneur affably passed through his rooms to the remote region of the Circumference of Truth. There, Monseigneur turned, and came back again, and so in the due course of time got himself shut up in his sanctuary by the chocolate sprites, and was seen no more.

The show being over, the flutter in the air became quite a little storm, and the precious little bells went ringing down stairs. There was soon but one person left of all the crowd, and he, with his hat under his arm and his snuff-box in his hand, slowly passed among the mirrors on his way out.

"I devote you," said this person, stopping at the last door on his way, and turning in the direction of the sanctuary, "to the Devil!"

With that, he shook the snuff from his fingers as if he had shaken the dust from his feet, and quietly waked down stairs.

He was a man of about sixty, handsomely dressed, haughty in manner, and with a face like a fine mask. A face of a transparent paleness; every feature in it clearly defined; one set expression on it. The nose, beautifully formed otherwise, was very slightly pinched at the top of each nostril. In those two compressions, or dints, the only little change that the face ever showed, resided. They persisted in changing color sometimes, and they would be occasionally dilated and contracted by something like a faint pulsation; then, they gave a look of treachery, and cruelty, to the whole countenance. Examined with attention, its capacity of helping such a look was to be found in the line of the mouth, and the lines of the orbits of the eyes, being much too horizontal and thin; still, in the effect the face made, it was a handsome face, and a remarkable one.

Its owner went down stairs into the courtyard, got into his carriage, and drove away. Not many people had talked with him at the reception; he had stood in a little space apart, and Monseigneur might have been warmer in his manner. It appeared, under the circumstances, rather agreeable to him to see the common people dispersed before his horses, and often barely escaping from being run down. His man drove as if he were charging an enemy, and the furious recklessness of the man brought no check into the face, or to the lips, of the master. The complaint had sometimes made itself audible, even in that deaf city and dumb age, that, in the narrow streets without footways, the fierce patrician custom of hard driving endangered and maimed the mere vulgar in a barbarous manner. But, few cared enough for that to think of it a second time, and, in this matter, as in all others, the common wretches were left to get out of their difficulties as they could.

With a wild rattle and clatter, and an inhuman abandonment of consideration not easy to be understood in these days, the carriage dashed through streets and swept round corners, with women screaming before it, and men clutching each other and clutching children out of its way. At last, swooping at a street corner by a fountain, one of its wheels came to a sickening little jolt, and there was a loud cry from a number of voices, and the horses reared and plunged.

But for the latter inconvenience, the carriage probably would not have stopped; carriages were often known to drive on, and leave their wounded behind, and why not? But, the frightened valet had got down in a hurry, and there were twenty hands at the horses' bridles.

"What has gone wrong?" said Monsieur, calmly looking out.

A tall man in a nightcap had caught up a bundle from among the feet of the horses, and had laid it on the basement of the fountain, and was down in the mud and wet, howling over it like a wild animal.

"Pardon, Monsieur the Marquis!" said a ragged and submissive man, "it is a child."

"Why does he make that abominable noise? Is it his child?"

"Excuse me, Monsieur the Marquis—it is a pity—yes."

The fountain was a little removed; for the street opened, where it was, into a space some ten or twelve yards square. As the tall man suddenly got up from the gound, and came running at the carriage, Monsieur the Marquis clapped his hand for an instant on his sword-hilt.

"Killed!" shrieked the man, in wild desperation, extending both arms at their length above his head, and staring at him. "Dead!"

The people closed round, and looked at Monsieur the Marquis. There was nothing revealed by the many eyes that looked at him but watchfulness and eagerness; there was no visible menacing or anger. Neither did the people say any thing; after the first cry, they had been silent, and they remained so. The voice of the submissive man who had spoken, was flat and tame in its extreme submission. Monsieur the Marquis ran his eyes over them all, as if they had been mere rats come out of their holes.

He took out his purse.

"It is extraordinary to me," said he, "that you people cannot take care of yourselves and your children. One or the other of you is forever in the way. How do I know what injury you have done my horses? See! Give him that."

He threw out a gold coin for the valet to pick up, and all the heads craned forward that all the eyes might look down at it as it fell. The tall man called out again with a most unearthly cry, "Dead!"

He was arrested by the quick arrival of another man, for whom the rest made way. On seeing him, the miserable creature fell upon his shoulder, sobbing aud crying, and pointing to the fountain, where some women were stooping over the motioniess bundle, and moving gently about it. They were as silent, however, as the men.

"I know all, I know all," said the last comer. "Be a brave man, my Gaspard! It is better for the poor little plaything to die so, than to live. It has died in a moment without pain. Could it have lived an hour as happily?"

"You are a philosopher, you there," said the Marquis, smiling. "How do they call you?"

"They call me Defarge."

"Of what trade?"

"Monsieur the Marquis, vendor of wine."

"Pick up that, philosopher and vendor of wine," said the Marquis, throwing him another gold coin, "and spend it as you will. The horses there; are they right?"

Without deigning to look at the assemblage a second time, Monsieur the Marquis leaned back in his seat, and was just being driven away with the air of a gentleman who had accidentally broken some common thing, and had paid for it, and could afford to pay for it; when his ease was suddenly disturbed by a coin flying into his carriage and ringing on its floor.

"Hold!" said Monsieur the Marquis. "Hold the horses! Who threw that?"

He looked to the spot where Defarge the vendor of wine had stood, a moment before; but the wretched father was groveling on his face on the pavement in that spot, and the figure that stood beside him was the figure of a dark stout woman, knitting.

"You dogs!" said the Marquis, but smoothly, and with an unchanged front, except as to the spots on his nose: "I would ride over any of you very willingly, and exterminate you from the earth. If I knew which rascal threw at the carriage, and if that brigand were sufficiently near it, he should be crushed under the wheels."

So cowed was their condition, and so long and so hard their experience of what such a man could do to them, within the law and beyond it, that not a voice, or a hand, or even an eye, was raised. Among the men, not one. But, the woman who stood knitting looked up steadily, and looked the Marquis in the face. It was not for his dignity to notice it; his contemptuous eyes passed over her, and over all the other rats; and he leaned back in his seat again, and gave the word "Go on!"

He was driven on, and other carriages came whirling by in quick succession; the Minister, the State-Projector, the Farmer-General, the Doctor, the Lawyer, the Ecclesiastic, the Grand Opera, the Comedy, the whole Fancy Ball in a bright continuous flow, came whirling by. The rats had crept out of their holes to look on, and they remained looking on for hours; soldiers and police often passing between them and the spectacle, and making a barrier behind which they slunk, and through which they peeped. The father had long ago taken up his bundle and hidden himself away with it, when the woman who had tended the bundle while it lay on the base of the fountain, sat there watching the running of the water and the rolling of the Fancy Ball—when the one woman who had stood conspicuous, knitting, still knitted on with the steadfastness of Fate. The water of the fountain ran, the swift river ran, the day ran into evening, so much life in the city ran into death according to rule, time and tide waited for no man, the rats were sleeping close together in their dark holes again, the Fancy Ball was lighted up at supper, all things ran their course.

Chapter VIII

MONSIEUR THE MARQUIS IN THE COUNTRY

A BEAUTIFUL landscape, with the corn bright in it, but not abundant. Patches of poor rye where corn should have been, patches of poor peas and beans, patches of most coarse vegetable substitutes for wheat. On inanimate nature, as on the men and women who cultivated it, a prevalent tendency toward an appearance of vegetating unwillingly—a dejected disposition to give up, and wither away.

Monsieur the Marquis in his traveling carriage (which might have been lighter), conducted by four post-horses and two postilions, fagged up a steep hill. A blush on the countenance of Monsieur the Marquis was no impeachment of his high breeding; it was not from within; it was occasioned by an external circumstance beyond his control—the setting sun.

The sunset struck so brilliantly into the traveling carriage when it gained the hill-top, that its occupant was steeped in crimson. "It will die out," said Monsieur the Marquis, glancing at his hands, "directly."

In effect, the sun was so low that it dipped at the moment. When the heavy drag had been adjusted to the wheel, and the carriage slid down hill, with a cinderous smell, in a cloud of dust, the red glow departed quickly; the sun and the Marquis going down together, there was no glow left when the drag was taken off.

But, there remained a broken country, bold and open, a little village at the bottom of the hill, a broad sweep and rise beyond it, a church-tower, a windmill, a forest for the chase, and a crag with a fortress on it used as a prison. Round upon all these darkening objects as the night drew on, the Marquis looked, with the air of one who was coming near home.

The village had its one poor street, with its poor brewery, poor tannery, poor tavern, poor stable-yard for relays of post-horses, poor fountain, all usual poor appointments. It had its poor people too. All its people were poor, and many of them were sitting at their doors, shredding spare onions and the like for supper, while many were at the fountain, washing leaves, and grasses, and any such small yieldings of the earth that could be eaten. Expressive signs of what made them poor, were not wanting; the tax for the state, the tax for the church, the tax for the lord, tax local, and tax general, were to be paid here and to be paid there, according to solemn inscription in the little village, until the wonder was, that there was any village left unswallowed.

Few children were to be seen, and no dogs. As to the men and women, their choice on earth was stated in the prospect—Life on the lowest terms that could sustain it, down in the little village under the mill; or captivity and Death in the dominant prison on the crag.

Heralded by a courier in advance, and by the cracking of his postilions' whips, which twined snakelike about their heads in the evening air, as if he came attended by the Furies, Monsieur the Marquis drew up in his traveling carriage at the posting-house gate. It was hard by the fountain, and the peasants suspended their operations to look at him. He looked at them, and saw in them, without knowing it, the slow, sure filing down of misery-worn face and figure, that was to make the meagreness of Frenchmen an English superstition which should survive the truth through the best part of a hundred years.

Monsieur the Marquis cast his eyes over the submissive faces that drooped before him, as the like of himself had drooped before Monseigneur of the Court—only the difference was, that these faces drooped merely to suffer and not to propitiate—when a grizzled mender of the roads joined the group.

"Bring me hither that fellow!" said the Marquis to the courier.

The fellow was brought, cap in hand, and the other fellows closed round to look and listen, in the manner of the people at the Paris fountain.

"I passed you on the road?"

"Monseigneur, it is true. I had the honor of being passed on the road."

"Coming up the hill, and at the top of the hill, both?"

"Monseigneur, it is true."

"What did you look at, so fixedly?"

"Monseigneur, I looked at the man."

He stooped a little, and with his tattered blue cap pointed under the carriage. All his fellows stooped to look under the carriage.

"What man, pig? And why look there?"

"Pardon, Monseigneur; he swung by the chain of the shoe—the drag."

"Who?" demanded the traveler.

"Monseigneur, the man."

"May the Devil carry away these idiots! How do you call the man? You know all the men of this part of the country. Who was he?"

"Your clemency, Monseigneur! He was not of this part of the country. Of all the days of my life, I never saw him."

"Swinging by the chain? To be suffocated?"

"With your gracious permission, that was the wonder of it, Monseigneur. His head hanging over—like this!"

He turned himself sideways to the carriage, and leaned back, with his face thrown up to the sky, and his head hanging down; then recovered himself, fumbled with his cap, and made a bow.

"What was he like?"

"Monseigneur, he was whiter than the miller. All covered with dust, white as a spectre, tall as a spectre!"

The picture produced an immense sensation in the little crowd; but all eyes, without comparing notes with other eyes, looked at Monsieur the Marquis. Perhaps, to observe whether he had any spectre on his conscience.

"Truly, you did well," said the Marquis, felicitously sensible that such vermin were not to ruffle him, "to see a thief accompanying my carriage, and not open that great mouth of yours. Bah! Put him aside, Monsieur Gabelle!"

Monsieur Gabelle was the Postmaster, and some other taxing functionary, united; he had come out with great obsequiousness to assist at this examination, and had held the examined by the drapery of his arm in an official manner.

"Bah! Go aside!" said Monsieur Gabelle.

"Lay hands on this stranger if he seeks to lodge in your village to-night, and be sure that his business is honest, Gabelle."

"Monseigneur, I am flattered to devote myself to your orders."

"Did he run away, fellow?—where is that accursed?"

The accursed was already under the carriage with some half-dozen particular friends, pointing out the chain with his blue cap. Some half-dozen other particular friends promptly hauled him out, and presented him breathless to Monsieur the Marquis.

"Did the man run away, Dolt, when we stopped for the drag?"

"Monseigneur, he precipitated himself over the hill-side, head first, as a person plunges into the river."

"See to it, Gabelle. Go on!"

The half-dozen who were peering at the chain were still among the wheels, like sheep; the wheels turned so suddenly that they were lucky to save their skins and bones; they had very little else to save, or they might not have been so fortunate.

The burst with which the carriage started out of the village and up the rise beyond, was soon checked by the steepness of the hill. Gradually, it subsided to a foot-pace, swinging and lumbering upward among the many sweet scents of a summer night. The postilions, with a thousand gossamer gnats circling about them in lieu of the Furies, quietly mended the points to the lashes of their whips; the valet walked by the horses; the courier was audible, trotting on ahead into the dim distance.

At the steepest point of the hill there was a little burial-ground, with a cross, and a new, large figure of Our Saviour on it; it was a poor figure in wood, done by some inexperienced rustic carver, but he had studied the figure from the life—his own life, maybe—for it was dreadfully spare and thin.

To this distressful emblem of a great distress that had long been growing worse, and was not at its worst, a woman was kneeling. She turned her head as the carriage came up to her, rose quickly, and presented herself at the carriage door.

"It is you, Monseigneur! Monseigneur, a petition!"

With an exclamation of impatience, but with his unchangeable face, the Marquis looked out.

"How, then! What is it? Always petitions!"

"Monseigneur. For the love of the great God! My husband, the forester."

"What of your husband, the forester? Always the same with you people. He cannot pay something?"

"He has paid all, Monseigneur. He is dead."

"Well! He is quiet. Can I restore him to you?"

"Alas, no, Monseigneur! But he lies yonder, under a little heap of poor grass."

"Well?"

"Monseigneur, there are so many little heaps of poor grass."

"Again, well?"

She looked an old woman, but was young. Her manner was one of passionate gief; by turns she clasped her veinous and knotted hands together with wild energy, and laid one of them on the carriage-door—

tenderly, caressingly, as if it had been a human breast, and could be expected to feel the appealing touch.

"Monseigneur, hear me! Monseigneur, hear my petition! My husband died of want; so many die of want; so many more will die of want."

"Again, well? Can I feed them?"

"Monseigneur, the good God knows; but I don't ask it. My petition is, that a morsel of stone or wood, with my husband's name, may be placed over him to show where he lies. Otherwise, the place will be quickly forgotten, it will never be found when I am dead of the same malady. I shall be laid under some other heap of poor grass. Monseigneur, they are so many, they increase so fast, there is so much want. Monseigneur! Monseigneur!"

The valet had put her away from the door, the carriage had broken into a brisk trot, the postilions had quickened the pace, she was left far behind, and the Marquis, again escorted by the Furies, was rapidly diminishing the league or two of distance that remained between him and his chateau.

The sweet scents of the summer night rose all around him, and rose, as the rain falls, impartially, on the dusty, ragged, and toil-worn group at the fountain not far away; to whom the mender of roads, with the aid of the blue cap without which he was nothing, still enlarged upon his man like a spectre, as long as they could bear it. By degrees, as they could bear no more, they dropped off one by one, and the lights twinkled in little casements; which lights, as the casements darkened, and more stars came out, seemed to have shot up into the sky instead of having been extinguished.

The shadow of a large high-roofed house, and of many overhanging trees, was upon Monsieur the Marquis by that time; and the shadow was exchanged for the light of a flambeau, as his carriage stopped, and the great door of his chateau was opened to him.

"Monsieur Charles, whom I expect; is he arrived from England?"

"Monseigneur, not yet."

Chapter IX

THE GORGON'S HEAD

IT was a heavy mass of building, that chateau of Monsieur the Marquis, with a large stone court-yard before it, and two stone sweeps of staircase meeting in a stone terrace before the principal door. A stony business altogether, with heavy stone balustrades, and stone urns, and stone flowers, and stone faces of men, and stone heads of lions, in all directions. As if the Gorgon's head had surveyed it, when it was finished, two centuries ago.

Up the broad flight of shallow steps, Monsieur the Marquis, flambeau preceded, went from his carriage, sufficiently disturbing the darkness to elicit loud remonstrance from an owl in the roof of the great pile of stable-building away among the trees. All else was so quiet, that the flambeau carried up the steps, and the other flambeau held at the great door, burnt as if they were in a close room of state, instead of being in the open night-air. Other sound than the Owl's voice there was none, save the falling of a fountain into its stone basin; for, it was one of those dark nights that hold their breath by the hour together, and then heave a long, low sigh, and hold their breath again.

The great door clanged behind him, and Monsieur the Marquis crossed a hall grim with certain old boar spears, swords, and knives of the chase; grimmer with certain heavy riding-rods and riding-whips, of which many a peasant, gone to his benefactor, Death, had felt the weight when his lord was angry.

Avoiding the larger rooms, which were dark and made fast for the night, Monsieur the Marquis, with his flambeau-bearer going on before, went up the staircase to a door in a corridor. This thrown open, admitted him to his own private apartment of three rooms: his bedchamber and two others. High vaulted rooms, with cool uncarpeted floors, great dogs upon the hearths for the burning of wood in winter time, and all luxuries befitting the state of a marquis in a luxurious age and country. The fashion of the last Louis but one, of the line that was never to break—the fourteenth Louis—was conspicuous in their rich furniture; but, it was diversified by many objects that were illustrations of old pages in the history of France.

A supper-table was laid for two, in the third of the rooms; a round room, in one of the chateau's four extinguisher-topped towers; a small lofty room, with its window wide open, and the wooden jalousie-blinds closed, so that the dark night only showed in slight horizontal lines of black, alternating with their broad lines of stone color.

"My nephew," said the Marquis, glancing at the supper preparation; "they said he was not arrived."

Nor was he; but he had been expected with Monseigneur.

"Ah! It is not probable he will arrive to-night; nevertheless, leave the table as it is. I shall be ready in a quarter of an hour."

In a quarter of an hour, Monseigneur was ready, and sat down alone to his sumptuous and choice supper. His chair was opposite to the window, and he had taken his soup, and was raising his glass of Bordeaux to his lips, when he put it down.

"What is that?" he calmly asked, looking with attention at the horizontal lines of black and stone color.

"Monseigneur? That?"

"Outside the blinds. Open the blinds."

It was done.

"Well?"

"Monseigneur, it is nothing. The trees and the night are all that are here."

The servant who spoke, had thrown the blinds wide, had looked out into the vacant darkness, and stood, with that blank behind him, looking round for instructions.

"Good," said the imperturbable master. "Close them again."

That was done too, and the Marquis went on with his supper. He was half way through it, when he again stopped with his glass in his hand, hearing the sound of wheels. It came on briskly, and came up to the front of the chateau.

"Ask who is arrived."

It was the nephew of Monseigneur. He had been some few leagues behind Monseigneur, early in the afternoon. He had diminished the distance rapidly, but not so rapidly as to come up with Monseigneur on the road. He had heard of Monseigneur, at the posting houses, as being before him.

He was to be told (said Monseigneur) that supper awaited him then and there, and that he was prayed to come to it. In a little while, he came. He had been known in England as Charles Darnay.

Monseigneur received him in a courtly manner, but they did not shake hands.

"You left Paris yesterday, sir?" he said to Monseigneur, as he took his seat at table.

"Yesterday. And you?"

"I come direct."

"From London?"

"Yes."

"You have been a long time coming," said the Marquis, with a smile.

"On the contrary, I come direct."

"Pardon me! I mean, not a long time on the journey; a long time intending the journey."

"I have been detained by"—the nephew stopped a moment in his answer—"various business."

"Without doubt," said the polished uncle.

So long as a servant was present, no other words passed between them. When coffee had been served and they were alone together, the nephew, looking at the uncle and meeting the eyes of the face that was like a fine mask, opened a conversation.

"I have come back, sir, as you anticipate, pursuing the object that took me away. It carried me into great and unexpected peril; but it is a sacred object, and if it had carried me to death, I hope it would have sustained me."

"Not to death," said the uncle; "it is not necessary to say, to death."

"I doubt, sir," returned the nephew, "whether, if it had carried me to the utmost brink of death, you would have cared to stop me there."

The deepened marks in the nose, and the lengthening of the fine straight lines in the cruel face, looked ominous as to that; the uncle made a graceful gesture of protest, which was so clearly a slight form of good breeding that it was not reassuring.

"Indeed, sir," pursued the nephew, "for any thing I know, you may have expressly worked to give a more suspicious appearance to the suspicious circumstances that surrounded me."

"No, no, no," said the uncle, pleasantly.

"But, however that may be," resumed the nephew, glancing at him with deep distrust, "I know that your diplomacy would stop me by any means, and would know no scruple as to means."

"My friend, I told you so," said the uncle, with a fine pulsation in the two marks. "Do me the favor to recall that I told you so, long ago."

"I recall it."

"Thank you," said the Marquis—very sweetly indeed.

His tone lingered in the air, almost like the tone of a musical instrument.

"In effect, sir," pursued the nephew, "I believe it to be at once your bad fortune, and my good fortune, that has kept me out of a prison in France here."

"I do not quite understand," returned the uncle, sipping his coffee. "Dare I ask you to explain?"

"I believe that if you were not in disgrace with the court, and had not been overshadowed by that cloud for years past, a letter *de cachet* would have sent me to some fortress indefinitely."

"It is possible," said the uncle, with great calmness. "For the honor of the family, I could even resolve to incommode you to that extent. Pray excuse me!"

"I perceive that, happily for me, the reception of the day before yesterday was, as usual, a cold one," observed the nephew.

"I would not say happily, my friend," returned the uncle, with refined politeness; "I would not be sure of that. A good opportunity for consideration, surrounded by the advantages of solitude, might influence your destiny to far greater advantage than you influence it for yourself. But it is useless to discuss the question. I am, as you say, at a disadvantage. These little instruments of correction, these gentle aids to the power and honor of families, these slight favors that might so incommode you, are only to be obtained now by interest and importunity. They are sought by so many, and they are granted (comparatively) to so few! It used not to be so, but France in all such things is changed for the worse. Our not remote ancestors held the right of life and death over the surrounding vulgar. From this room, many such dogs have been taken out to be hanged; in the next room (my bedroom), one fellow, to our knowledge, was poniarded on the spot for professing some insolent delicacy respecting his daughter—*his* daughter! We have lost many privileges; a new philosophy has become the mode; and the assertion of our station, in these days, might (I do not go so far as to say would, but might) cause us real inconvenience. All very bad, very bad!"

The Marquis took a gentle little pinch of snuff, and shook his head; as elegantly despondent as he could becomingly be, of a country still containing himself, that great means of regeneration.

"We have so asserted our station, both in the old time and in the modern time also," said the nephew, gloomily, "that I believe our name to be more detested than any name in France."

"Let us hope so," said the uncle. "Detestation of the high, is the involuntary homage of the low."

"There is not," pursued the nephew in his former tone, "a face I can look at, in all this country round about us, which looks at me with any deference on it but the dark deference of fear and slavery."

"A compliment," said the Marquis, "to the grandeur of the family, merited by the manner in which the family has sustained its grandeur. Hah!" And he took another gentle little pinch of snuff, and lightly crossed his legs.

But, when his nephew, leaning an elbow on the table, covered his eyes thoughtfully and dejectedly with his hand, the fine mask looked at him sideways, with a stronger concentration of keenness, closeness, and dislike, than was comportable with its wearer's assumption of indifference.

"Repression is the only lasting philosophy. The dark deference of fear and slavery, my friend," observed the Marquis, "will keep the dogs obedient to the whip, as long as this roof," looking up to it, "shuts out the sky."

That might not be so long as the Marquis supposed. If a picture of the chateau as it was to be a very few years hence, and of fifty like it as they too were to be a very few years hence, could have been shown to him that night, he might have been at a loss to claim his own from the ghastly, fire-charred, plunder-wrecked ruins. As for the roof he vaunted, he might have found *that* shutting out the sky in a new way—to wit, forever, from the eyes of the bodies into which its lead was fired, out of the barrels of a hundred thousand muskets.

"Meanwhile," said the Marquis, "I will preserve the honor and repose of the family, if you will not. But you must be fatigued. Shall we terminate our conference for the night?"

"A moment more."

"An hour, if you please."

"Sir," said the nephew, "we have done wrong, and are reaping the fruits of wrong."

"*We* have done wrong?" repeated the Marquis, with an inquiring smile, and delicately pointing, first to the nephew, then to himself.

"Our family; our honorable family, whose honor is of so much account to both of us, in such different ways. Even in my father's time, we did a world of wrong, injuring every human creature who came between us and our pleasure, whatever it was. Why need I speak of my father's time, when it is equally yours? Can I separate my father's twin-brother, joint inheritor, and next successor, from himself?"

"Death has done that," said the Marquis.

"And has left me," answered the nephew, "bound to a system that is frightful to me, responsible for it, but powerless in it; seeking to execute the last request of my dear mother's lips, and obey the last look of my dear mother's eyes, which implored me to have mercy and to redress; and tortured by seeking assistance and power in vain."

"Seeking them from me, my nephew," said the Marquis, touching him on the breast with his forefinger—they were now standing by the hearth—"you will forever seek them in vain, be assured."

Every fine straight line in the clear whiteness of his face, was cruelly, craftily, and closely compressed, while he stood looking quietly at his nephew, with his snuff-box in his hand. Once again he touched him on the breast, as though his finger were the fine point of a small sword, with which, in delicate finesse, he ran him through the body, and said,

"My friend, I will die, perpetuating the system under which I have lived."

When he had said it, he took a culminating pinch of snuff, and put his box in his pocket.

"Better to be a rational creature," he added then, after ringing a small bell on the table, "and accept your natural destiny. But you are lost, Monsieur Charles, I see."

"This property and France are lost to me," said the nephew, sadly; "I renounce them."

"Are they both yours to renounce? France may be, but is the property? It is scarcely worth mentioning; but, is it yet?"

"I had no intention, in the words I used, to claim it yet. If it passed to me from you, to-morrow——"

"Which I have the vanity to hope is not probable."

"—or twenty years hence——"

"You do me too much honor," said the Marquis; "still, I prefer that supposition."

"—I would abandon it, and live otherwise and elsewhere. It is little to relinquish. What is it but a wilderness of misery and ruin!"

"Hah!" said the Marquis, glancing round the luxurious room.

"To the eye it is fair enough, here; but seen in its integrity, under the sky and by the daylight, it is a crumbling tower of waste, mismanagement, extortion, debt, mortgage, oppression, hunger, nakedness, and suffering."

"Hah!" said the Marquis again, in a well satisfied manner.

"If it ever becomes mine, it shall be put into some hands better qualified to free it slowly (if such a thing is possible) from the weight that drags it down, so that the miserable people who cannot leave it and who have been long wrung to the last point of endurance, may, in another generation, suffer less; but it is not for me. There is a curse on it, and on all this land."

"And you?" said the uncle. "Forgive my curiosity; do you, under your new philosophy, graciously intend to live?"

"I must do, to live, what others of my countrymen, even with nobility at their backs, may have to do some day—work."

"In England, for example?"

"Yes. The family honor, sir, is safe from me in this country. The family name can suffer from me in no other, for I bear it in no other."

The ringing of the bell had caused the adjoining bedchamber to be lighted. It now shone brightly, through the door of communication. The Marquis looked that way, and listened for the retreating step of his valet.

"England is very attractive to you, seeing how indifferently you have prospered there," he observed then, turning his calm face to his nephew with a smile.

"I have already said, that for my prospering there, I am sensible I may be indebted to you, sir. For the rest, it is my Refuge."

"They say, those boastful English, that it is the Refuge of many. You know a compatriot who has found a Refuge there? A Doctor?"

"Yes."

"With a daughter?"

"Yes."

"Yes," said the Marquis. "You are fatigued. Good-night!"

As he bent his head in his most courtly manner, there was a secrecy in his smiling face, and he conveyed an air of mystery to those words, which struck the eyes and ears of his nephew forcibly. At the same time, the thin straight lines of the setting of the eyes, and the thin straight lips, and the markings in the nose, curved with a sarcasm that looked handsomely diabolic.

"Yes," repeated the Marquis. "A Doctor with a daughter. Yes. So commences the new philosophy! You are fatigued. Good-night!"

It would have been of as much avail to interrogate any stone face outside the chateau, as to interrogate that face of his. The nephew looked at him, in vain, in passing on to the door.

"Good-night!" said the uncle. "I look to the pleasure of seeing you again in the morning. Good repose! Light Monsieur my nephew to his chamber there!—And burn Monsieur my nephew in his bed, if you will," he added to himself, before he rang his little bell again, and summoned his valet to his own bedroom.

The valet come and gone, Monsieur the Marquis walked to and fro in his loose chamber-robe, to prepare himself gently for sleep, that hot, still night. Rustling about the room, his softly-slippered feet making no noise on the floor, he moved like a refined tiger:—looked like some enchanted marquis of the impenitently wicked sort, in story, whose periodical change into tiger form was either just going off, or just coming on.

He moved from end to end of his voluptuous bedroom, looking again at the scraps of the day's journey that came unbidden into his mind; the slow toil up the hill at sunset, the setting sun, the descent, the mill, the prison on the crag, the little village in the hollow, the peasants at the fountain, and the mender of roads with his blue cap pointing out the chain under the carriage. That fountain suggested the Paris fountain, the little bundle lying on the step, the women bending over it, and the tall man with his arms up, crying, "Dead!"

"I am cool now," said Monsieur the Marquis, "and may go to bed."

So, leaving only one light burning on the large hearth, he let his thin gauze curtains fall around him, and heard the night break its silence with a long sigh as he composed himself to sleep.

The stone faces on the outer walls stared blindly at the black night for three heavy hours; for three heavy hours, the horses in the stables rattled at their racks, the dogs barked, and the owl made a noise with very little resemblance in it to the noise conventionally assigned to the owl by men-poets. But, it is the obstinate custom of such creatures hardly ever to say what is set down for them.

For three heavy hours, the stone faces of the chateau, lion and human, stared blindly at the night. Dead darkness lay on all the landscape, dead darkness added its own hush to the hushing dust on all the roads. The burial-place had got to the pass that its little heaps of poor grass were undistinguishable from one another; the figure on the Cross might have come down, for any thing that could be seen of it. In the village, taxers and taxed were fast asleep. Dreaming, perhaps, of banquets, as the starved usually do, and of ease and rest, as the driven slave and the yoked ox may, its lean inhabitants slept soundly, and were fed and freed.

The fountain in the village flowed unseen and unheard, and the fountain at the chateau dropped unseen and unheard—both melting away, like the minutes that were falling from the spring of Time—through three dark hours. Then, the gray water of both began to be ghostly in the light, and the eyes of the stone faces of the chateau were opened.

It grew lighter and lighter, until at last the sun touched the tops of the still trees, and poured its radiance over the hill. In the glow, the water of the chateau fountain seemed to turn to blood, and the stone faces crimsoned. The carol of the birds was loud and high, and, on the weather-beaten sill of the great window of the bedchamber of Monsieur the Marquis, one little bird sang its sweetest song with all its might. At this, the nearest stone face seemed to stare amazed, and, with open mouth and dropped under-jaw, looked awe-stricken.

Now, the sun was full up, and movement began in the village. Casement windows opened, crazy doors were unbarred, and people came forth shivering—chilled, as yet, by the new sweet air. Then began the rarely lightened toil of the day among the village population. Some, to the fountain; some, to the fields; men and women here, to dig and delve; men and women there, to see to the poor live stock, and lead the bony cows out, to such pasture as could be found by the roadside. In the church and at the Cross, a kneeling figure or two; attendant on the latter prayers, the led cow, trying for a breakfast among the weeds at the Cross-foot.

The chateau awoke later, as became its quality, but awoke gradually and surely. First, the lonely boar-spears and knives of the chase had been reddened as of old; then, had gleamed trenchant in the morning sunshine; now, doors and windows were thrown open, horses in their stables looked round over their shoulders at the light and freshness pouring in at doorways, leaves sparkled and rustled at iron-grated windows, dogs pulled hard at their chains, and reared impatient to be loosed.

All these trivial incidents belonged to the routine of life, and the return of morning. Surely, not so the ringing of the great bell of the chateau, nor the running up and down the stairs, nor the hurried figures on the terrace, nor the booting and tramping here and there and everywhere, nor the quick saddling of horses and riding away?

What winds conveyed this hurry to the grizzled mender of roads, already at work on the hill-top beyond the village, with his day's dinner (not much to carry) laying in a bundle that it was worth no crow's while to peck at, on a heap of stones? Had the birds, carrying some grains of it to a distance, dropped one over him as they sow chance seeds? Whether or no, the mender of roads ran, on the sultry morning, as if for his life, down the hill, knee-high in dust, and never stopped till he got to the fountain.

All the people of the village were at the fountain, standing about in their depressed manner, and whispering softly, but showing no other emotions than grim curiosity and surprise. The led cows, hastily brought in and tethered to any thing that would hold them, were looking stupidly on, or lying down chewing the cud of nothing particularly repaying their trouble, which they had picked up in their interrupted saunter. Some of the people of the chateau, and some of those of the posting-house, and all the taxing authorities, were armed more or less, and were crowded on the other side of the little street in a purposeless way, that was highly fraught with nothing. Already, the mender of roads had penetrated into the midst of a group of fifty particular friends, and was smiting himself in the breast with his blue cap. What did all this portend, and what portended the swift hoisting-up of Monsieur Gabelle behind a servant on horseback, and the conveying away of the said Gabelle (double-laden though the horse was), at a gallop, like a new version of the German ballad of Leonora?

It portended that there was one stone face too many, up at the chateau.

The Gorgon had surveyed the building again in the night, and had added the one stone face wanting; the stone face for which it had waited through about two hundred years.

It lay back on the pillow of Monsieur the Marquis. It was like a fine mask, suddenly startled, made angry, and petrified. Driven home into the heart of the stone figure attached to it, was a knife. Round its hilt was a frill of paper, on which was scrawled:

"*Drive him fast to his tomb. This, from* JACQUES."

Chapter X

TWO PROMISES

MORE months, to the number of twelve, had come and gone, and Mr. Charles Darnay was established in England as a higher teacher of the French language who was conversant with French literature. In this age, he would have been a Professor; in that age, he was a Tutor. He read with young men who could find any leisure and interest for the study of a living tongue spoken all over the world, and he cultivated a taste for its stores of knowledge and fancy. He could write of them, besides, in sound English, and render them into sound English. Such masters were not at that time easily found; Princes that had been, and Kings that were to be, were not yet of the Teacher class, and no ruined nobility had dropped out of Tellson's ledgers, to turn cooks and carpenters. As a tutor, whose attainments made the student's way unusually pleasant and profitable, and as an elegant translator, who brought something to his work besides mere dictionary knowledge, young Mr. Darnay soon became known and encouraged. He was well acquainted, moreover, with the circumstances of his country, and those were of ever-growing interest. So, with great perseverance and untiring industry, he prospered.

In London, he had expected neither to walk on pavements of gold, nor lie on beds of roses; if he had had any such exalted expectation, he would not have prospered. He had expected labor, and he found it, and did it, and made the best of it. In this, his prosperity consisted.

A certain portion of his time was passed at Cambridge, where he read with undergraduates as a sort of tolerated smuggler who drove a contraband trade in European languages, instead of conveying Greek and Latin through the Custom-house. The rest of his time he passed in London.

Now, from the days when it was always summer in Eden, to these days when it is mostly winter in fallen latitudes, the world of a man has invariably gone one way—Charles Darnay's way—the way of the love of a woman.

He had loved Lucie Manette from the hour of his danger. He had never heard a sound so sweet and dear as the sound of her compassionate voice; he had never seen a face so tenderly beautiful as hers, when it was confronted with his own on the edge of the grave that had been dug for him. But, he had not yet spoken to her on the subject; the assassination at the deserted chateau far away beyond the heaving water and the long, long, dusty roads—the solid stone chateau which had itself become the mere mist of a dream—had been done a year, and he had never yet, by so much as a single spoken word, disclosed to her the state of his heart.

That he had his reasons for this, he knew full well. It was again a summer day when, lately arrived in London from his college occupation, he turned into the quiet corner in the Soho, bent on seeking an opportunity of opening his mind to Doctor Manette. It was the close of the summer day, and he knew Lucie to be out with Miss Pross.

He found the Doctor reading in his arm-chair at a window. The energy which had at once supported him under his old sufferings and aggravated their sharpness, had been gradually restored to him. He was now a very energetic man indeed, with great firmness of purpose, strength of resolution, and vigor of action. In his recovered energy he was sometimes a little fitful and sudden, as he had at first been in the exercise of his other recovered faculties; but this had never been frequently observable, and had grown more and more rare.

He studied much, slept little, sustained a great deal of fatigue with ease, and was equably cheerful. To him, now entered Charles Darnay, at sight of whom he laid aside his book and held out his hand.

"Charles Darnay! I rejoice to see you. We have been counting on your return these three or four days past. Mr. Stryver and Sydney Carton were both here yesterday, and both made you out to be more than due."

"I am obliged to them for their interest in the matter," he answered, a little coldly as to them, though very warmly as to the Doctor. "Miss Manette—"

"Is well," said the Doctor, as he stopped short, "and your return will delight us all. She has gone out on some household matters, but will soon be home."

"Doctor Manette, I knew she was from home. I took the opportunity of her being from home, to beg to speak to you."

There was a blank silence.

"Yes;" said the Doctor, with evident constraint. "Bring your chair here, and speak on."

He complied as to the chair, but appeared to find the speaking on less easy.

"I have had the happiness, Doctor Manette, of being so intimate here," so he at length began, "for some year and a half, that I hope the topic on which I am about to touch may not——"

He was stayed by the Doctor's putting out his hand to stop him. When he had kept it so a little while, he said, drawing it back:

"Is Lucie the topic?"

"She is."

"It is hard for me to speak of her, at any time. It is very hard for me to hear her spoken of in that tone of yours, Charles Darnay."

"It is a tone of fervent admiration, true homage and deep love, Doctor Manette!" he said, deferentially.

There was another blank silence before her father rejoined:

"I believe it. I do you justice; I believe it."

His constraint was so manifest, and it was so manifest, too, that it originated in an unwillingness to approach the subject, that Charles Darnay hesitated.

"Shall I go on, sir?"

Another blank.

"Yes, go on."

"You anticipate what I would say, though you cannot know how earnestly I say it, how earnestly I feel it, without knowing my secret heart, and the hopes and fears and anxieties with which it has long been laden. Dear Doctor Manette, I love your daughter fondly, dearly, disinterestedly, devotedly. If ever there were love in the world, I love her. You have loved yourself; let your old love speak for me!"

The Doctor sat with his face turned away, and his eyes bent on the ground. At the last words, he stretched out his hand again, hurriedly, and cried:

"Not that, sir! Let that be! I adjure you, do not recall that!"

His cry was so like a cry of actual pain, that it rang in Charles Darnay's ears long after he had ceased. He motioned with the hand he had extended, and it seemed to be an appeal to Darnay to pause. The latter so received it, and remained silent.

"I ask your pardon," said the Doctor, in a subdued tone, after some moments. "I do not doubt your loving Lucie; you may be satisfied of it."

He turned toward him in his chair, but did not look at him, or raise his eyes. His chin dropped upon his hand, and his white hair overshadowed his face:

"Have you spoken to Lucie?"

"No."

"Nor written?"

"Never."

"It would be ungenerous to affect not to know that your self-denial is to be referred to your consideration for her father. Her father thanks you."

He offered his hand; but his eyes did not go with it.

"I know," said Darnay, respectfully, "how can I fail to know, Doctor Manette, I who have seen you together from day to day, that between you and Miss Manette there is an affection so unusual, so touching, so belonging to the circumstances in which it has been nurtured, that it can have few parallels, even in the tenderness between a father and child. I know, Doctor Manette—how can I fail to know—that, mingled with the affection and duty of a daughter who has become a woman, there is, in her heart toward you, all the love and reliance of infancy itself. I know that, as in her childhood she had no parent, so she is now devoted to you with all the constancy and fervor of her present years and character, united to the trustfulness and attachment of the early days in which you were lost to her. I know perfectly well that if you had been restored to her from the world beyond this life, you could hardly be invested, in her sight, with a more sacred character than that in which you are always with her. I know that when she is clinging to you, the hands of baby, girl, and woman, all in one, are round your neck. I know that in loving you she sees and loves her mother at her own age, sees and loves you at my age, loves her mother broken-hearted, loves you through your dreadful trial and in your blessed restoration. I have known this, night and day, since I have known you in your home."

Her father sat silent, with his face bent down. His breathing was a little quickened; but he repressed all other signs of agitation.

"Dear Doctor Manette, always knowing this, always seeing her and you with this hallowed light about you, I have forborne, and forborne, as long as it was in the nature of man to do it. I have felt, and do even now feel, that to bring my love—even mine—between you, is to touch your history with something not quite so good as itself. But I love her. Heaven is my witness that I love her!"

"I believe it," answered her father, mournfully. "I have thought so, before now. I believe it."

"But, do not believe," said Darnay, upon whose ear the mournful voice struck with a reproachful sound, "that if my fortune were so cast as that, being one day so happy as to make her my wife, I must at any time put any separation between her and you I could or would breathe a word of what I now say. Besides that I should know it to be hopeless, I should know it to be baseness. If I had any such possibility, even at a remote distance of years, harbored in my thoughts and hidden in my heart—if it ever had been there—if it ever could be there—I could not now touch this honored hand."

He laid his own upon it as he spoke.

"No, dear Doctor Manette. Like you, a voluntary exile from France; like you, driven from it by its distractions, oppressions, and miseries; like you, striving to live away from it by my own exertions, and trusting in a happier future; I look only to sharing your fortunes, sharing your life and home, and being faithful to you to the death. Not to divide with Lucie her privilege as your child, companion, and friend; but to come in aid of it, and bind her closer to you, if such a thing can be."

His touch still lingered on her father's hand. Answering the touch for a moment, but not coldly, her father rested his hands upon the arms of his chair, and looked up for the first time since the beginning of the conference. A struggle was evidently in his face; a struggle with that occasional look which had a tendency in it to dark doubt and dread.

"You speak so feelingly and so manfully, Charles Darnay, that I thank you with all my heart, and will open all my heart—or nearly so. Have you any reason to believe that Lucie loves you?"

"None. As yet, none."

"Is it the immediate object of this confidence, that you may at once ascertain that, with my knowledge?"

"Not even so. I might not have the hopefulness to do it for weeks; I might (mistaken or not mistaken) have that hopefulness to-morrow."

"Do you seek any guidance from me?"

"I ask none, sir. But I have thougt it possible that you might have it in your power, if you should deem it right, to give me some."

"Do you seek any promise from me?"

"I do seek that."

"What is it?"

"I well understand that, without you, I could have no hope. I well understand that, even if Miss Manette held me at this moment in her innocent heart—do not think I have the presumption to assume so much—I could retain no place in it against her love for her father."

"If that be so, do you see what, on the other hand, is involved in it?"

"I understand equally well, that a word from her father in any suitor's favor, would outweigh herself and all the world. For which reason, Doctor Manette," said Darnay, modestly but firmly, "I would not ask that word, to save my life."

"I am sure of it. Charles Darnay, mysteries arise out of close love, as well as out of wide division; in the former case, they are subtle and delicate, and difficult to penetrate. My daughter Lucie is, in this one respect, such a mystery to me; I can make no guess at the state of her heart."

"May I ask, sir, if you think she is——" As he hesitated, her father supplied the rest.

"Is sought by any other suitor?"

"It is what I meant to say."

Her father considered a little before he answered:

"You have seen Mr. Carton here, yourself. Mr. Stryver is here too, occasionally. If it be at all, it can only be by one of these."

"Or both," said Darnay.

"I had not thought of both; I should not think either, likely. You want a promise from me. Tell me what it is."

"It is, that if Miss Manette should bring to you at any time, on her own part, such a confidence as I have ventured to lay before you, you will bear testimony to what I have said, and to your belief in it. I hope you may be able to think so well of me, as to urge no influence against me. I say nothing more of my stake in this; this is what I ask. The condition on which I ask it, and which you have an undoubted right to require, I will observe immediately."

"I give the promise," said the Doctor, "without any condition. I believe your object to be, purely and truthfully, as you have stated it. I believe your intention is to perpetuate, and not to weaken, the ties between me and my other and far dearer self. If she should ever tell me that you are essential to her perfect happiness, I will give her to you. If there were—Charles Darnay, if there were—"

The young man had taken his hand gratefully; their hands were joined as the Doctor spoke:

"—any fancies, any reasons, any apprehensions, any thing whatsoever, new or old, against the man she really loved—the direct responsibility thereof not lying on his head—they should all be obliterated for her sake. She is everything to me; more to me than suffering, more to me than wrong, more to me—Well! This is idle talk."

So strange was the way in which he faded into silence, and so strange his fixed look when he had ceased to speak, that Darnay felt his own hand turn cold in the hand that slowly released and dropped it.

"You said something to me," said Doctor Manette, breaking into a smile. "What was it you said to me?"

He was at a loss how to answer, until he remembered having spoken of a condition. Relieved as his mind reverted to that, he answered:

"Your confidence in me ought to be returned with full confidence on my part. My present name, though but slightly changed from my mother's, is not, as you will remember, my own. I wish to tell you what that is, and why I am in England."

"Stop!" said the Doctor of Beauvais.

"I wish it, that I may the better deserve your confidence, and have no secret from you."

"Stop!"

For an instant, the Doctor even had his two hands at his ears; for another instant, even had his two hands laid on Darnay's lips.

"Tell me when I ask you, not now. If your suit should prosper, if Lucie should love you, you shall tell me on your marriage morning. Do you promise?"

"Willingly."

"Give me your hand. She will be home directly, and it is better she should not see us together to-night. Go! God bless you!"

It was dark when Charles Darnay left him, and it was an hour later and darker when Lucie came home; she hurried into the room alone—for Miss Pross had gone straight up stairs—and was surprised to find his reading chair empty.

"My father!" she called to him. "Father dear!"

Nothing was said in answer, but she heard a low hammering sound in his bedroom. Passing lightly across the intermediate room, she looked in at his door and came running back frightened, crying to herself, with her blood all chilled, "What shall I do! What shall I do!"

Her uncertainty lasted but a moment; she hurried back, and tapped at his door, and softly called to him. The noise ceased at the sound of her voice, and he presently came out to her, and they walked up and down together for a long time.

She came down from her bed, to look at him in his sleep that night. He slept heavily, and his tray of shoemaking tools, and his old unfinished work, were all as usual.

Chapter XI

A COMPANION PICTURE

"SYDNEY," said Mr. Stryver, on that self-same night, or morning, to his jackal; "mix another bowl of punch; I have something to say to you."

Sydney had been working double tides that night, and the night before, and the night before that, and a good many nights in succession, making a grand clearance among Mr. Stryver's papers before the setting in of the long vacation. The clearance was effected at last; the Stryver arrears were handsomely fetched up; everything was got rid of, until November should come with its fogs atmospheric and fogs legal, and bring grist to the mill again.

Sydney was none the livelier and none the soberer for so much application. It had taken a deal of extra wet-toweling to pull him through the night; a correspondingly extra quantity of wine had preceded the toweling; and he was in a very damaged condition, as he now pulled his turban off and threw it into the basin in which he had steeped it at intervals for the last six hours.

"Are you mixing that other bowl of punch?" said Stryver the portly, with his hands in his waistband, glancing round from the sofa where he lay on his back.

"I am."

"Now, look here! I am going to tell you something that will rather surprise you, and that perhaps will make you think me not quite as shrewd as you usually do think me. I intend to marry."

"*Do* you?"

"Yes. And not for money. What do you say now?"

"I don't feel disposed to say much. Who is she?"

"Guess."

"Do I know her?"

"Guess."

"I am not going to guess, at five o'clock in the morning, with my brains frying and sputtering in my head. If you want me to guess, you must ask me to dinner."

"Well, then, I'll tell you," said Stryver, coming slowly into a sitting posture. "Sydney, I rather despair of making myself intelligible to you, because you are such an insensible dog."

"And you," returned Sydney, busy concocting the punch, "are such a sensitive and poetical spirit."

"Come!" rejoined Stryver, laughing boastfully, "though I don't prefer any claim to being the soul of Romance (for I hope I know better), still I am a tenderer sort of fellow than *you*."

"You are a luckier, if you mean that."

"I don't mean that. I mean, I am a man of more——more——"

"Say gallantry, while you are about it," suggested Carton.

"Well! I'll say gallantry. My meaning is that, I am a man," said Stryver, inflating himself at his friend as he made the punch, "who cares more to be agreeable, who takes more pains to be agreeable, who knows better how to be agreeable, in a woman's society, than you do."

"Go on," said Sydney Carton.

"No; but before I go on," said Stryver shaking his head in his bullying way, "I'll have this out with you. You have been at Doctor Manette's house as much as I have, or more than I have. Why, I have been ashamed of your moroseness there! Your manners have been of that silent and sullen and hang-dog kind, that, upon my life and soul, I have been ashamed of you, Sydney!"

"It should be very beneficial to a man in your practice at the bar, to be ashamed of any thing," returned Sydney; "you ought to be much obliged to me."

"You shall not get off in that way," rejoined Stryver, shouldering the rejoinder at him; "no, Sydney, it's my duty to tell you—and I tell you to your face to do you good—that you are a de-vilish ill-conditioned fellow in that sort of society. You are a disagreeable fellow."

Sydney drank a bumper of the punch he had made, and laughed.

"Look at me!" said Stryver, squaring himself; "I have less need to make myself agreeable than you have, being more independent in circumstances. Why do I do it?"

"I never saw you do it yet," muttered Carton.

"I do it because it's politic; I do it on principle. And look at me! I get on."

"You don't get on with your account of your matrimonial intentions," answered Carton, with a careless air, "I wish you would keep to that. As to me—will you never understand that I am incorrigible?"

He asked the question with some appearance of scorn.

"You have no business to be incorrigible," was his friend's answer, delivered in no very soothing tone.

"I have no business to be, at all, that I know of," said Sydney Carton. "Who is the lady?"

"Now, don't let my announcement of the name make you uncomfortable, Sydney," said Mr. Stryver, preparing him with ostentatious friendliness for the disclosure he was about to make, "because I know you don't mean half you say; and if you meant it all, it would be of no importance. I make this little preface, because you once mentioned the young lady to me in slighting terms."

"I did?"

"Certainly; and in these chambers."

Sydney Carton looked at his punch and looked at his complacent friend; drank his punch and looked at his complacent friend.

"You made mention of the young lady as a golden-haired doll. The young lady is Miss Manette. If you had been a fellow of any sensitiveness or delicacy of feeling in that kind of way, Sydney, I might have been a little resentful of your employing such a designation; but you are not. You want that sense altogether; therefore, I am no more annoyed when I think of the expression, than I should be annoyed by a man's opinion of a picture of mine, who had no eye for pictures; or of a piece of music of mine, who had no ear for music."

Sydney Carton drank the punch at a great rate; drank it by bumpers, looking at his friend.

"Now you know all about it, Syd," said Mr. Stryver. "I don't care about fortune: she is a charming creature, and I have made up my mind to please myself: on the whole, I think I can afford to please myself. She will have in me a man already pretty well off, and a rapidly rising man, and a man of some distinction: it is a piece of good fortune for her, but she is worthy of good fortune. Are you astonished?"

Carton, still drinking the punch, rejoined, "Why should I be astonished?"

"You approve?"

Carton, still drinking the punch, rejoined, "Why should I not approve?"

"Well!" said his friend Stryver, "you take it more easily than I fancied you would, and are less mercenary on my behalf than I thought you would be; though, to be sure, you know well enough by this time that your ancient chum is a man of a pretty strong will. Yes, Sydney, I have had enough of this style of life, with no other as a change from it; I feel that it is a pleasant thing for a man to have a home when he feels inclined to go to it (when he doesn't, he can stay away), and I feel that Miss Manette will tell well in any station, and will always do me credit. So I have made up my mind. And now, Sydney, old boy, I want to say a word to *you* about *your* prospects. You are in a bad way, you know; you really are in a bad way. You don't know the value of money, you live hard, you'll knock up one of these days, and be ill and poor; you really ought to think about a nurse."

The prosperous patronage with which he said it, made him look twice as big as he was, and four times as offensive.

"Now, let me recommend you," pursued Stryver, "to look it in the face. I have looked it in the face, in my different way; look it in the face, you, in your different way. Marry. Provide somebody to take care of you. Never mind your having no enjoyment of women's society, nor understanding of it, nor tact for it. Find out somebody. Find out some respectable woman with a little property—somebody in the landlady way, or lodging-letting way—and marry her against a rainy day. That's the kind of thing for *you*. Now, think of it, Sydney."

"I'll think of it," said Sydney.

Chapter XII

THE FELLOW OF DELICACY

MR. STRYVER having made up his mind to that magnanimous bestowal of good fortune on the doctor's daughter, resolved to make her happiness known to her before he left town for the Long Vacation. After some mental debating of the point, he came to the conclusion that it would be as well to get all the preliminaries done with, and they could then arrange at their leisure whether he should give her his hand a week or two before Michaelmas Term, or in the little Christmas vacation between it and Hilary.

As to the strength of his case, he had not a doubt about it, but clearly saw his way to the verdict. Argued with the jury on substantial worldly grounds—the only grounds ever worth taking into account—it was a plain case, and had not a weak spot in it. He called himself for the plaintiff, there was no getting over his evidence. The counsel for the defendant threw up his brief, and the jury did not even turn to consider. After trying it, Stryver, C. J., was satisfied that no plainer case could be.

Accordingly, Mr. Stryver inaugurated the Long Vacation with a formal proposal to take Miss Manette to Vauxhall Gardens; that failing, to Ranelagh; that unaccountably failing too, it behooved him to present himself in Soho, and there declare his noble mind.

Toward Soho, therefore, Mr. Stryver shouldered his way from the

Temple, while the bloom of the Long Vacation's infancy was still upon it. Anybody who had seen him projecting himself into Soho while he was yet on Saint Dunstan's side of Temple Bar, bursting in his full-blown way along the pavement, to the jostlement of all weaker people, might have seen how safe and strong he was.

His way taking him past Tellson's, and he both banking at Tellson's and knowing Mr. Lorry as the intimate friend of the Manettes, it entered Mr. Stryver's mind to enter the bank, and reveal to Mr. Lorry the brightness of the Soho horizon. So, he pushed open the door with the weak rattle in its throat, stumbled down the two steps, got past the two ancient cashiers, and shouldered himself into the musty back closet where Mr. Lorry sat at great books ruled for figures, with perpendicular iron bars to his window, as if that were ruled for figures too, and every thing under the clouds were a sum.

"Halloa!" said Mr. Stryver. "How do you do? I hope you are well!"

It was Stryver's grand peculiarity that he always seemed too big for any place, or space. He was so much too big for Tellson's that old clerks in distant corners looked up with looks of remonstrance, as though he squeezed them against the wall.

The House itself, magnificently reading the paper quite in the far-off perspective, lowered displeased, as if the Stryver head had been butted into its responsible waistcoat.

The discreet Mr. Lorry said, in a sample tone of the voice he would recommend under the circumstances, "How do you do, Mr. Stryver? How do you do, sir?" and shook hands. There was a peculiarity in his manner of shaking hands, always to be seen in any clerk at Tellson's who shook hands with a customer when the House pervaded the air. He shook in a self-abnegating way, as for one who shook for Tellson and Co.

"Can I do any thing for you, Mr. Stryver?" asked Mr. Lorry, in his business character.

"Why, no thank you; this is a private visit to yourself, Mr. Lorry; I have come for a private word."

"Oh indeed!" said Mr. Lorry, bending down his ear, while his eyes strayed to the House afar off.

"I am going," said Mr. Stryver, leaning his arms confidentially on the desk: whereupon, although it was a large double one, there appeared to be not half desk enough for him: "I am going to make an offer of myself in marriage to your agreeable little friend Miss Manette, Mr. Lorry."

"Oh dear me!" cried Mr. Lorry, rubbing his chin, and looking at his visitor dubiously.

"Oh dear me, sir?" repeated Stryver, drawing back. "Oh dear you, sir? What may your meaning be, Mr. Lorry?"

"My meaning?" answered the man of business, "is, of course, friendly and appreciative, and that it does you the greatest credit, and, in short, my meaning is every thing you could desire. But—really, you know, Mr. Stryver——" Mr. Lorry paused, and shook his head at him in the oddest manner, as if he were compelled against his will to add, internally, "you know there really is so much too much of you!"

"Well!" said Stryver, slapping the desk with his contentious hand, opening his eyes wider, and taking a long breath, "if I understand you, Mr. Lorry, I'll be hanged!"

Mr. Lorry adjusted his little wig at both ears as a means toward that end, and bit the feather of a pen.

"D—n it all, sir!" said Stryver, staring at him, "am I not eligible?"

"Oh dear, yes! Yes. Oh yes, you're eligible!" said Mr. Lorry. "If you say eligible, you are eligible."

"Am I not prosperous?" asked Stryver.

"Oh! if you come to prosperous, you are prosperous," said Mr. Lorry.

"And advancing?"

"If you come to advancing, you know," said Mr. Lorry, delighted to be able to make another admission, "nobody can doubt that."

"Then what on earth is your meaning, Mr. Lorry?" demanded Stryver, perceptibly crest-fallen.

"Well! I——Were you going there now?" asked Mr. Lorry.

"Straight!" said Stryver, with a plump of his fist on the desk.

"Then I think I wouldn't, if I was you."

"Why?" said Stryver. "Now, I'll put you in a corner," forensically shaking a forefinger at him. "You are a man of business and bound to have a reason. State your reason. Why wouldn't you go?"

"Because," said Mr. Lorry, "I wouldn't go on such an object without having some cause to believe that I should succeed."

"D—n ME!" cried Stryver, "but this beats everything!"

Mr. Lorry glanced at the distant House, and glanced at the angry Stryver.

"Here's a man of business—a man of years—a man of experience—in a Bank," said Stryver; "and having summed up three leading reasons for complete success, he says there's no reason at all! Says it with his head on!" Mr. Stryver remarked upon the peculiarity as if it would have been infinitely less remarkable if he had said it with his head off.

"When I speak of success, I speak of success with the young lady; and when I speak of causes and reasons to make success probable, I speak of causes and reasons that will tell as such with the young lady. The young lady, my good sir," said Mr. Lorry, mildly tapping the Stryver arm, "the young lady. The young lady goes before all."

"Then you mean to tell me, Mr. Lorry," said Stryver, squaring his elbows, "that it is your deliberate opinion that the young lady at present in question is a mincing Fool?"

"Not exactly so. I mean to tell you, Mr. Stryver," said Mr. Lorry, reddening, "that I will hear no disrespectful word of that young lady from any lips; and that if I knew any man—which I hope I do not—whose taste was so coarse, and whose temper was so overbearing, that he could not restrain himself from speaking disrespectfully of that young lady at this desk, not even Tellson's should prevent my giving him a piece of my mind."

The necessity of being angry in a suppressed tone had put Mr. Stryver's blood-vessels into a dangerous state when it was his turn to be angry. Mr. Lorry's veins, methodical as their courses could usually be, were in no better state now it was his turn.

"That is what I mean to tell you, sir," said Mr. Lorry. "Pray let there be no mistake about it."

Mr. Stryver sucked the end of a ruler for a little while, and then stood hitting a tune out of his teeth with it, which probably gave him the toothache. He broke the awkward silence by saying:

"This is something new to me, Mr. Lorry. You deliberately advise me not to go up to Soho and offer myself—*my*self, Stryver of the King's Bench bar?"

"Do you ask me for my advice, Mr. Stryver?"

"Yes, I do."

"Very good. Then I give it, and you have repeated it correctly."

"And all I can say of it, is," laughed Stryver with a vexed laugh, "that this—ha, ha!—beats every thing past, present, and to come."

"Now understand me," pursued Mr. Lorry. "As a man of business, I am not justified in saying anything about this matter, for, as a man of business, I know nothing of it. But, as an old fellow, who has carried Miss Manette in his arms, who is the trusted friend of Miss Manette and of her father too, and who has a great affection for them both, I have spoken. The confidence is not of my seeking, recollect. Now, you think I may not be right?"

"Not I!" said Stryver, whistling. "I can't undertake to find third parties in common sense; I can only find it for myself. I suppose sense in certain quarters; you suppose mincing bread-and-butter nonsense. It's new to me, but you are right, I dare say."

"What I suppose, Mr. Stryver, I claim to characterize for myself. And understand me, sir," said Mr. Lorry, quickly flushing again. "I will not—not even at Tellson's—have it characterized for me by any gentleman breathing."

"There! I beg your pardon!" said Stryver.

"Granted. Thank you. Well, Mr. Stryver, I was about to say:—it might be painful to you to find yourself mistaken, it might be painful to Doctor Manette to have the task of being explicit with you, it might be very painful to Miss Manette to have the task of being explicit with you. You know the terms upon which I have the honor and happiness to stand with the family. If you please, committing you in no way, representing you in no way, I will undertake to correct my advice by the exercise of a little new observation and judgment expressly brought to bear upon it. If you should then be dissatisfied with it, you can but test its soundness for yourself; if, on the other hand, you should be satisfied with it, and it should be what it now is, it may spare all sides what is best spared. What do you say?"

"How long would you keep me in town?"

"Oh! It is only a question of a few hours. I could go to Soho this evening, and come to your chambers afterward."

"Then I say yes," said Stryver: "I won't go up there now. I am not so hot upon it as that comes to; I say yes, and I shall expect you to look in to-night. Good-morning."

Then Mr. Stryver turned and burst out of the Bank, causing such a concussion of air on his passage through, that to stand up against it, bowing behind the two counters, required the utmost remaining strength of the two ancient clerks. Those vulnerable and feeble persons were seen by the public in the act of bowing, and were popularly believed, when they had bowed a customer out, still to keep on bowing in the empty office until they bowed another customer in.

The barrister was keen enough to divine that the banker would not have gone so far in his expression of opinion on any less solid ground than moral certainty. Unprepared as he was for the large pill he had to swallow, he got it down. "And now," said Mr. Stryver, shaking his forensic forefinger at the Temple in general, when it was down, "my way out of this, is, to put you all in the wrong."

It was a bit of the art of an Old Bailey tactician, in which he found great relief. "You shall not put me in the wrong, young lady," said Mr. Stryver; "I'll do that for you."

Accordingly, when Mr. Lorry called that night as late as ten o'clock, Mr. Stryver, among a quantity of books and papers littered out for the purpose, seemed to have nothing less on his mind than the subject of the morning. He even showed surprise when he saw Mr. Lorry, and was altogether in an absent and preoccupied state.

"Well!" said that good-natured emissary, after a full half-hour of bootless attempts to bring him round to the question, "I have been to Soho."

"To Soho?" repeated Mr. Stryver, coldly. "Oh, to be sure! What am I thinking of!"

"And I have no doubt," said Mr. Lorry, "that I was right in the conversation we had. My opinion is confirmed, and I reiterate my advice."

"I assure you," returned Mr. Stryver, in the friendliest way, "that I am sorry for it on your account, and sorry for it on the poor father's account. I know this must always be a sore subject with the family; let us say no more about it."

"I don't understand you," said Mr. Lorry.

"I dare say not," rejoined Stryver, nodding his head in a smoothing and final way; "no matter, no matter."

"But it does matter," Mr. Lorry urged.

"No it doesn't; I assure you it doesn't. Having supposed that there was sense where there is no sense, and a laudable ambition where there is not a laudable ambition, I am well out of my mistake, and no harm is done. Young women have committed similar follies often before, and have repented them in poverty and obscurity often before. In an unselfish aspect, I am sorry that the thing has dropped, because it would have been a good thing for others in a worldly point of view; in a selfish aspect, I am glad that the thing has dropped, because it would have been a bad thing for me in a worldly point of view—it is hardly necessary to say I could have gained nothing by it. There is no harm at all done. I have not proposed to the young lady, and between ourselves, I am by no means certain, on reflection, that I ever should have committed myself to that extent. Mr. Lorry, you cannot control the mincing vanities and giddinesses of empty-headed girls; you must not expect to do it, or you will always be disappointed. Now, pray say no more about it. I tell you, I regret it on account of others, but I am satisfied on my own account. And I am really very much obliged to you for allowing me to sound you, and for giving me your advice; you know the young lady better than I do; you were right, it never would have done."

Mr. Lorry was so taken aback, that he looked quite stupidly at Mr. Stryver shouldering him toward the door, with an appearance of showering generosity, forbearance and good-will, on his erring head. "Make the best of it, my dear sir," said Stryver; "say no more about it; thank you again for allowing me to sound you; good-night!"

Mr. Lorry was out in the night, before he knew where he was. Mr. Stryver was lying back on his sofa, winking at his ceiling.

Chapter XIII

THE FELLOW OF NO DELICACY

If Sydney Carton ever shone anywhere, he certainly never shone in the house of Dr. Manette. He had been there often, during a whole year, and had always been the same moody and morose lounger there. When he cared to talk, he talked well; but, the cloud of caring for nothing, which overshadowed him with such a fatal darkness, was very rarely pierced by the light within him.

And yet he did care something for the streets that environed that house, and for the senseless stones that made their pavements. Many a night he vaguely and unhappily wandered there, when wine had brought no transitory gladness to him; many a dreary daybreak revealed his solitary figure lingering there, and still lingering there when the first beams of the sun brought into strong relief, removed beauties of architecture in spires of churches and lofty buildings, as perhaps the quiet time brought some sense of better things, else forgotten and unattainable, into his mind. Of late, the neglected bed in the Temple court had known him more scantily than ever; and often when he had thrown himself upon it no longer than a few minutes he had got up again, and haunted that neighborhood.

On a day in August, when Mr. Stryver (after notifying to his jackal that "he had thought better of that marrying matter") had carried his delicacy into Devonshire, and when the sight and scent of flowers in the city streets had some waifs of goodness in them for the worst, of health for the sickliest, and of youth for the oldest, Sydney's feet still trod those stones. From being irresolute and purposeless, his feet became animated by an intention, and in the working out of that intention, they took him to the Doctor's door.

He was shown up stairs, and found Lucie at her work, alone. She had never been quite at her ease with him, and received him with some little embarrassment as he seated himself near her table. But, looking up at his face in the interchange of the first few common-places, she observed a change in it.

"I fear you are not well, Mr. Carton!"

"No. But the life I lead, Miss Manette, is not conducive to health. What is to be expected of, or by, such profligates?"

"Is it not—forgive me; I have begun the question on my lips—a pity to live no better life?"

"God knows it is a shame!"

"Then why not change it?"

Looking gently at him again, she was surprised and saddened to see that there were tears in his eyes. There were tears in his voice too, as he answered:

"It is too late for that. I shall never be better than I am. I shall sink lower, and be worse."

He leaned an elbow on her table, and covered his eyes with his hand. The table trembled in the silence that followed.

She had never seen him softened, and was much distressed. He knew her to be so, without looking at her, and said:

"Pray forgive me, Miss Manette. I break down before the knowledge of what I want to say to you. Will you hear me?"

"If it will do you any good. Mr. Carton, if it would make you happier, it would make me very glad!"

"God bless you for your sweet compassion!"

He unshaded his face after a little while, and spoke steadily.

"Don't be afraid to hear me. Don't shrink from anything I say. I am like one who died young. All my life might have been."

"No, Mr. Carton. I am sure that the best part of it might still be; I am sure that you might be much, much worthier of yourself."

"Say of you, Miss Manette; and although I know better—although in the mystery of my own wretched heart I know better—I shall never forget it!"

She was pale and trembling. He came to her relief with a fixed despair of himself which made the interview unlike any other that could have been holden.

"If it had been possible, Miss Manette, that you could have returned the love of the man you see before you—self-flung away, wasted, drunken, poor creature of misuse as you know him to be—he would have been conscious this day and hour, in spite of his happiness, that he would bring you to misery, bring you to sorrow and repentance, blight you, disgrace you, pull you down with him. I know very well that you can have no tenderness for me; I ask for none; I am even thankful that it cannot be."

"Without it, can I not save you, Mr. Carton? Can I not recall you—forgive me again!—to a better course? Can I in no way repay your confidence? I know this is a confidence," she modestly said, after a little hesitation, and in earnest tears, "I know you would say this to no one else. Can I turn it to no good account for yourself, Mr. Carton?"

He shook his head.

"To none. No, Miss Manette, to none. If you will hear me through a very little more, all you can ever do for me is done. I wish you to know that you have been the last dream of my soul. In my degradation, I have not been so degraded but that the sight of you with your father, and of this home made such a home by you, has stirred old shadows that I thought had died out of me. Since I knew you, I have been troubled by a remorse that I thought would never reproach me again, and have heard whispers from old voices impelling me upward, that I thought were silent forever. I have had unformed ideas of striving afresh, beginning anew, shaking off sloth and sensuality, and fighting out the abandoned fight. A dream, all a dream, that ends in nothing, and leaves the sleeper where he lay down, but I wish you to know that you inspired it."

"Will nothing of it remain? O, Mr. Carton, think again! Try again!"

"No, Miss Manette; all through it, I have known myself to be quite undeserving. And yet I have had the weakness, and have still the weakness, to wish you to know, with what a sudden mastery you kindled me, heap of ashes that I am, into fire—a fire, however, inseparable in its nature from myself, quickening nothing, lighting nothing, doing no service, idly burning away."

"Since it is my misfortune, Mr. Carton, to have made you more unhappy than you were before you knew me——"

"Don't say that, Miss Manette, for you would have reclaimed me, if any thing could. You will not be the cause of my becoming worse."

"Since the state of your mind that you describe, is, at all events, attributable to some influence of mine—this is what I mean, if I can make it plain—can I use no influence to serve you? Have I no power for good, with you, at all?"

"The utmost good that I am capable of now, Miss Manette, I have come here to realize. Let me carry through the rest of my misdirected life, the remembrance that I opened my heart to you, last of all the world; and that there was something left in me at this time which you could deplore and pity."

"Which I entreated you to believe, again and again, most fervently, with all my heart, was capable of better things, Mr. Carton!"

"Entreat me to believe it no more, Miss Manette. I have proved myself, and I know better. I distress you; I draw fast to an end. Will you let me believe, when I recall this day, that the last confidence of my life was reposed in your pure and innocent breast, and that it lies there alone, and will be shared by no one?"

"If that will be a consolation to you, yes."

"Not even by the dearest one ever to be known to you?"

"Mr. Carton," she answered, after an agitated pause, "the secret is yours, not mine; and I promise to respect it."

"Thank you. And again, God bless you!"

He put her hand to his lips, and moved toward the door.

"Be under no apprehension, Miss Manette, of my ever resuming this conversation by so much as a passing word. I will never refer to it again. If I were dead, that could not be surer than it is henceforth. In the hour of my death, I shall hold sacred the one good remembrance—and shall thank and bless you for it—that my last avowal of myself was made to you, and that my name, and faults, and miseries, were gently carried in your heart. May it otherwise be light and happy!"

He was so unlike what he had ever shown himself to be, and it was so sad to think how much he had thrown away, and how much he every day kept down and perverted, that Lucie Manette wept mournfully for him as he stood looking back at her.

"Be comforted!" he said. "I am not worth such feeling, Miss Manette.

An hour or two hence, and the low companions and low habits that I scorn but yield to, will render me less worth such tears as those, than any wretch who creeps along the streets. Be comforted! But, within myself I shall always be, toward you, what I am now, though outwardly I shall be what you have heretofore seen me. The last supplication but one I make to you, is, that you will believe this of me."

"I will, Mr. Carton."

"My last supplication of all, is this; and with it, I will relieve you of a visitor with whom I well know you have nothing in unison, and between whom and you there is an impassable space. It is useless to say it, I know, but it rises out of my soul. For you, and for any dear to you, I would do any thing. If my career were of that better kind that there was any opportunity or capacity of sacrifice in it, I would embrace any sacrifice for you and for those dear to you. Try to hold me in your mind, at some quiet times, as ardent and sincere in this one thing. The time will come, the time will not be long in coming, when new ties will be formed about you—ties that will bind you yet more tenderly and strongly to the home you so adorn—the dearest ties that will ever grace and gladden you. O Miss Manette, when the little picture of a happy father's face looks up in yours, when you see your own bright beauty springing up anew at your feet, think now and then that there is a man who would give his life, to keep a life you love beside you!"

He said "Farewell!" and " A last God bless you!" and left her.

Chapter XIV
THE HONEST TRADESMAN

TO the eyes of Mr. Jeremiah Cruncher, sitting on his stool in Fleet-street with his grisly urchin beside him, a vast number and variety of objects in movement were every day presented. Who could sit upon any thing in Fleet-street during the busy hours of the day, and not be dazed and deafened by two immense processions, one ever tending westward with the sun, the other ever tending eastward from the sun, both ever tending to the plains beyond the range of red and purple where the sun goes down!

With his straw in his mouth, Mr. Cruncher sat watching the two streams, like the heathen rustic who has for several centuries been on duty watching one stream—saving that Jerry had no expectation of their ever running dry. Nor would it have been an expectation of a hopeful kind, since a small part of his income was derived from the pilotage of timid women (mostly of a full habit and past the middle term of life) from Tellson's side of the tides to the opposite shore. Brief as such companionship was in every separate instance, Mr. Cruncher never failed to become so interested in the lady as to express a strong desire to have the honor of drinking her very good health. And it was from the gifts bestowed upon him toward the execution of this benevolent purpose, that he recruited his finances, as just now observed.

Time was, when a poet sat upon a stool in a public place, and mused in the sight of men. Mr. Cruncher, sitting on a stool in a public place but not being a poet, mused as little as possible, and looked about him.

It fell out that he was thus engaged in a season when crowds were few, and belated women few, and when his affairs in general were so unprosperous as to awaken a strong suspicion in his breast that Mrs. Cruncher must have been "flopping" in some pointed manner, when an unusual concourse pouring down Fleet-street westward, attracted his attention. Looking that way, Mr. Cruncher made out that some kind of funeral was coming along, and that there was popular objection to this funeral, which engendered uproar.

"Young Jerry," said Mr. Cruncher, turning to his offspring, "it's a buryin'."

"Hooroar, father!" cried Young Jerry.

The young gentleman uttered this exultant sound with mysterious significance. The elder gentleman took the cry so ill, that he watched his opportunity, and smote the young gentleman on the ear.

"What d'ye mean? What are you hooroaring at? What do you want to conwey to your own father, you young Rip? This boy is a getting too many for *me!*" said Mr. Cruncher, surveying him. "Him and his hooroars! Don't let me hear no more of you, or you shall feel some more of me. D'ye hear?"

"I warn't doing no harm," Young Jerry protested, rubbing his cheek.

"Drop it then," said Mr. Cruncher; "I won't have none of *your* no harms. Get atop of that there seat, and look at the crowd."

His son obeyed, and the crowd approached; they were bawling and hissing round a dingy hearse and dingy mourning coach, in which mourning coach there was only one mourner, dressed in the dingy trappings that were considered essential to the dignity of the position. The position appeared by no means to please him, however, with an increasing rabble surrounding the coach, deriding him, making grimaces at him, and incessantly groaning and calling out: "Yah! Spies! Tst! Yaha! Spies!" with many compliments too numerous and forcible to repeat.

Funerals had at all times a remarkable attraction for Mr. Cruncher; he always pricked up his senses, and became excited, when a funeral passed Tellson's. Naturally, therefore, a funeral with this uncommon attendance excited him greatly, and he asked of the first man who ran against him:

"What is it, brother? What's it about?"

"*I* don't know," said the man. "Spies! Yaha! Tst! Spies!"

He asked another man. "Who is it?"

"*I* don't know," returned the man, clapping his hands to his mouth nevertheless, and vociferating in a surprising heat and with the greatest ardor, "Spies! Yaha! Tst, tst! Spi-ies!"

At length, a person better informed on the merits of the case, tumbled against him, and from this person he learned that the funeral was the funeral of one Roger Cly.

"Was he a spy?" asked Mr. Cruncher.

"Old Bailey spy," returned his informant. "Yaha! Tst! Yah! Old Bailey Spi-i-es!"

"Why, to be sure!" exclaimed Jerry, recalling the Trial at which he had assisted, "I've seen him. Dead, is he?"

"Dead as mutton," returned the other, "and can't be too dead. Have 'em out, there! Spies! Pull 'em out, there! Spies!"

The idea was so acceptable in the prevalent absence of any idea, that the crowd caught it up with eagerness, and loudly repeating the suggestion to have 'em out, and to pull 'em out, mobbed the two vehicles so closely that they came to a stop. On the crowd's opening the coach-doors, the one mourner scuffled out of himself and was in their hands for a moment; but he was so alert, and made such good use of his time, that in another moment he was scouring away up a by-street, after shedding his cloak, hat, long hatband, white pocket-handkerchief, and other symbolical tears.

These, the people tore to pieces and scattered far and wide with great enjoyment, while the tradesmen hurriedly shut up their shops; for a crowd in those times stopped at nothing, and was a monster much dreaded. They had already got the length of opening the hearse to take the coffin out, when some brighter genius proposed instead, its being escorted to its destination amidst general rejoicing. Practical suggestions being much needed, this suggestion, too, was received with acclamation, and the coach was immediately filled with eight inside and a dozen out, while as many people got on the roof of the hearse as could by any exercise of ingenuity stick upon it. Among the first of these volunteers was Jerry Cruncher himself, who modestly concealed his spiky head from the observation of Tellson's, in the further corner of the mourning coach.

The officiating undertakers made some protest against these changes in the ceremonies; but, the river being alarmingly near, and several voices remarking on the efficacy of cold immersion in bringing refractory members of the profession to reason, the protest was faint and brief. The remodelled procession started, with a chimney-sweep driving the hearse—advised by the regular driver, who was perched beside him, under close inspection for the purpose—and with a pieman, also attended by his cabinet minister, driving the mourning coach. A bear-leader, a popular street character of the time, was impressed as an additional ornament, before the cavalcade had gone far down the Strand; and his bear, who was black and very mangy, gave quite an Undertaking air to that part of the procession in which he walked.

Thus, with beer-drinking, pipe-smoking, song roaring, and infinite caricaturing of woe, the disorderly procession went its way, recruiting at every step, and all the shops shutting up before it. Its destination was the old church of Saint Pancras, far off in the fields. It got there in course of time; insisted on pouring into the burial-ground; finally, accomplished the interment of the deceased Roger Cly in its own way, and highly to its own satisfaction.

The dead man disposed of, and the crowd being under the necessity of providing some other entertainment for itself, another brighter genius (or perhaps the same) conceived the humor of impeaching casual passers-by, as Old Bailey spies, and wreaking vengeance on them. Chase was given to some scores of inoffensive persons who had never been near the Old Bailey in their lives, in the realization of this fancy, and they were roughly hustled and maltreated. The transition to the sport of window breaking, and thence to the plundering of public houses, was easy and natural. At last, after several hours, when sundry summer-houses had been pulled down, and some area railings had been torn up, to arm the more belligerent spirits, a rumor got about that the Guards were coming. Before this rumor, the crowd gradually melted away, and perhaps the Guards came, and perhaps they never came, and this was the usual progress of a mob.

Mr. Cruncher did not assist at the closing sports, but had remained behind in the churchyard, to confer and condole with the undertakers. The place had a soothing influence on him. He procured a pipe from a neighboring public-house, and smoked it, looking in at the railings, and maturely considering the spot.

"Jerry," said Mr. Cruncher, apostrophizing himself in his usual way, "you see that there Cly that day, and you see with your own eyes that he was a young 'un and a straight made 'un."

Having smoked his pipe out, and ruminated a little longer, he turned himself about, that he might appear, before the hour of closing, on his station at Tellson's. Whether his meditations on mortality had touched his liver, or whether his general health had been previously at all amiss, or whether he desired to show a little attention to an eminent man, is not so much to the purpose, as that he made a short call upon his medical adviser—a distinguished surgeon—on his way back.

Young Jerry relieved his father with dutiful interest, and reported No job in his absence. The bank closed, the ancient clerks came out, the usual watch was set, and Mr. Cruncher and his son went home to tea.

"Now, I tell you where it is!" said Mr. Cruncher to his wife, on entering. "If, as a honest tradesman, my wenturs goes wrong to-night, I shall make sure that you've been praying again me, and I shall work you for it the same as if I seen you do it."

The dejected Mrs. Cruncher shook her head.

"Why, you're at it afore my face!" said Mr. Cruncher, with signs of angry apprehension.

"I am saying nothing."

"Well, then; don't meditate nothing. You might as well flop as meditate. You may as well go again me one way as another. Drop it altogether."

"Yes, Jerry."

"Yes, Jerry," repeated Mr. Cruncher, sitting down to tea. "Ah! It *is* yes, Jerry. That's about it. You may say yes, Jerry."

Mr. Cruncher had no particular meaning in these sulky corroborations, but made use of them, as people not unfrequently do, to express general ironical dissatisfaction.

"You and your yes, Jerry," said Mr. Cruncher, taking a bite out of his bread and butter, and seeming to help it down with a large invisible oyster out of his saucer. "Ah! I think so. I believe you."

"You are going out to-night?" asked his decent wife, when he took another bite.

"Yes, I am."

"May I go with you, father?" asked his son, briskly.

"No, you mayn't. I'm a going—as your mother knows—a fishing. That's where I'm going to. Going a fishing."

"Your fishing-rod gets rather rusty; don't it, father?"

"Never you mind."

"Shall you bring any fish home, father?"

"If I don't, you'll have short commons to-morrow," returned that gentleman, shaking his head; "that's questions enough for you; I an't a going out, till you've been long a-bed."

He devoted himself during the remainder of the evening to keeping a most viligant watch on Mrs. Cruncher, and sullenly holding her in conversation that she might be prevented from meditating any petitions to his disadvantage. With this view, he urged his son to hold her in conversation also, and led the unfortunate woman a hard life by dwelling on any causes of complaint he could bring against her, rather than he would leave her for a moment to her own reflections. The devoutest person could have rendered no greater homage to the efficacy of an honest prayer than he did in this distrust of his wife. It was as if a professed unbeliever in ghosts should be frightened by a ghost story.

"And mind you!" said Mr. Cruncher. "No games to-morrow! If I, as a honest tradesman, succeed in providing a jinte of meat or two, none of your not touching of it, and sticking to bread. If I, as a honest tradesman, am able to provide a little beer, none of your declaring on water. When you go to Rome, do as Rome does. Rome will be a ugly customer to you, if you don't. *I*'m your Rome, you know."

Then he began grumbling again:

"With your flying into the face of your own wittles and drink! I don't know how scarce you mayn't make the wittles and drink here, by your flopping tricks and your unfeeling conduct. Look at your boy: he *is* your'n, ain't he? He's as thin as a lath. Do you call yourself a mother, and not know that a mother's first duty is to blow her boy out?"

This touched Young Jerry on a tender place; who adjured his mother to perform her first duty, and, whatever else she did or neglected, above all things to lay especial stress on the discharge of that maternal function so affectingly and delicately indicated by his other parent.

Thus the evening wore away with the Cruncher family, until Young Jerry was ordered to bed, and his mother laid under similar injunctions, obeyed them. Mr. Cruncher beguiled the earlier watches of the night with solitary pipes, and did not start upon his excursion until nearly one o'clock. Toward that small and ghostly hour, he rose up from his chair, took a key out of his pocket, opened a locked cupboard, and brought forth a sack, a crowbar of convenient size, a rope and chain, and other fishing tackle of that nature. Disposing these articles about him in a skillful manner, he bestowed a parting defiance on Mrs. Cruncher, extinguished the light, and went out.

Young Jerry, who had only made a feint of undressing when he went to bed, was not long after his father. Under cover of the darkness he followed out of the room, followed down the stairs, followed down the court, followed out into the streets. He was in no uneasiness concerning his getting into the house again, for it was full of lodgers, and the door stood ajar all night.

Impelled by a laudable ambition to study the art and mystery of his father's honest calling, Young Jerry, keeping as close to house-fronts, walls, and doorways, as his eyes were close to one another, held his honored parent in view. The honored parent steering northward, had not gone far, when he was joined by another disciple of Izaak Walton, and the two trudged on together.

Within half an hour from the first starting, they were beyond the winking lamps, and the more than winking watchmen, and were out upon a lonely road. Another fisherman was picked up here—and that so silently, that if Young Jerry had been superstitious, he might have supposed the second follower of the gentle craft to have, all of a sudden, split himself in two.

The three went on, and Young Jerry went on, until the three stopped under a bank overhanging the road. Upon the top of the bank was a low brick wall surmounted by an iron railing. In the shadow of bank and wall, the three turned out of the road, and up a blind lane, of which the wall—there, risen to some eight or ten feet high—formed one side. Crouching down in a corner, peeping up the lane, the next object that Young Jerry saw, was the form of his honored parent, pretty well defined against a watery and clouded moon, nimbly scaling an iron gate. He was soon over, and then the second fisherman got over, and then the third. They all dropped softly on the ground within the gate, and lay there a little—listening perhaps. Then, they moved away on their hands and knees.

It was now Young Jerry's turn to approach the gate: which he did, holding his breath. Crouching down again in a corner there, and looking in, he made out the three fishermen creeping through some rank grass; and all the gravestones in the churchyard—it was a large churchyard that they were in—looking on like ghosts in white, while the church, tower itself looked on like the ghost of a monstrous giant. They did not creep far, before they stopped and stood upright. And then they began to fish.

They fished with a spade, at first. Presently the honored parent appeared to be adjusting some instrument like a great corkscrew. Whatever tools they worked with, they worked hard, until the awful striking of the church-clock so terrified Young Jerry, that he made off, with his hair as stiff as his father's.

But, his long-cherished desire to know more about these matters, not only stopped him in his running away, but lured him back again. They were still fishing perseveringly, when he peeped in at the gate for the second time; but, now they seemed to have got a bite. There was a screwing and complaining sound down below, and their bent figures were strained, as if by a weight. By slow degrees the weight broke away the earth upon it, and came to the surface. Young Jerry very well knew what it would be; but, when he saw it, and saw his honored parent about to wrench it open, he was so frightened, being new to the sight, that he made off again, and never stopped until he had run a mile or more.

He would not have stopped then, for any thing less necessary than breath, it being a spectral sort of race that he ran, and one highly desirable to get to the end of. He had a strong idea that the coffin he had seen was running after him; and, pictured as hopping on behind him, bolt upright upon its narrow end, always on the point of overtaking him and hopping on at his side—perhaps taking his arm—it was a pursuer to shun. It was an inconsistent and ubiquitous fiend too, for, while it was making the whole night behind him dreadful, he darted out into the roadway to avoid dark alleys, fearful of its coming hopping out of them like a dropsical boy's-Kite without tail and wings. It hid in doorways too, rubbing its horrible shoulders against doors, and drawing them up to its ears as if it were laughing. It got into shadows on the road, and lay cunningly on its back to trip him up. All this time, it was incessantly hopping on behind and gaining on him, so that when the boy got to his own door he had reason for being half-dead. And even then it would not leave him, but followed him up stairs with a bump on every stair, scrambled into bed with him, and bumped down, dead and heavy, on his breast when he fell asleep.

From his oppressed slumber, Young Jerry in his closet was awakened, after daybreak and before sunrise, by the presence of his father in the family room. Something had gone wrong with him; at least, so Young Jerry inferred, from the circumstance of his holding Mrs. Cruncher by the ears, and knocking the back of her head against the headboard of the bed.

"I told you I would," said Mr. Cruncher, "and I did."

"Jerry, Jerry, Jerry!" his wife implored.

"You oppose yourself to the profit of the business," said Jerry, "and me and my partners suffer. You was to honor and obey; why the devil don't you?"

"I try to be a good wife, Jerry," the poor woman protested, with tears.

"Is it being a good wife to oppose your husband's business? Is it honoring your husband to dishonor his business? Is it obeying your husband to disobey him on the wital subject of his business?"

"You hadn't taken to the dreadful business then, Jerry?"

"It's enough for you," retorted Mr. Cruncher, "to be the wife of a honest tradesman, and not to occupy your female mind with calculations when he took to his trade or when he didn't. A honoring and obeying wife would let his trade alone altogether. Call yourself a religious woman? If you're a religious woman, give me a irreligious one! You have no more nat'ral sense of duty than the bed of this here Thames river has of a pile, and similarly it must be knocked into you."

The altercation was conducted in a low tone of voice, and terminated in the honest tradesman's kicking off his clay-soiled boots and lying down at his length on the floor. After taking a timid peep at him lying on his back, with his rusty hands under his head for a pillow, his son lay down too, and fell asleep again.

There was no fish for breakfast, and not much of any thing else. Mr. Cruncher was out of spirits, and out of temper, and kept an iron pot-lid by him as a projectile for the correction of Mrs. Cruncher, in case he should observe any symptoms of her saying Grace. He was brushed and washed at the usual hour, and set off with his son to pursue his ostensible calling.

Young Jerry walking with the stool under his arm at his father's side along sunny and crowded Fleet-street, was a very different Young Jerry from him of the previous night, running home through darkness and solitude from his grim pursuer. His cunning was fresh with the day, and his qualms were gone with the night—in which particulars it is not improbable that he had compeers in Fleet-street and the City of London, that fine morning.

"Father," said Young Jerry, as they walked along: taking care to keep at arm's length and to have the stool well between them: "what's a Resurrection-Man?"

Mr. Cruncher came to stop on the pavement before he answered, "How should I know?"

"I thought you knowed every thing, father," said the artless boy.

"Hem! Well," returned Mr. Cruncher, going on again, and lifting off his hat to give his spikes free play, "he's a tradesman."

"What's his goods, father?" asked the brisk Young Jerry.

"His goods," said Mr. Cruncher, after turning it over in his mind, "is a branch of Scientific goods."

"Persons' bodies, ain't it, father?" asked the lively boy.

"I believe it is something of that sort," said Mr. Cruncher.

"Oh, father, I should so like to be a Resurrection-Man when I'm quite growed up!"

Mr. Cruncher was soothed, but shook his head in a dubious and moral way. "It depends upon how you develop your talents. Be careful to develop your talents, and never to say no more than you can help to nobody, and there's no telling at the present time what you may not come to be fit for." As Young Jerry, thus encouraged, went on a few yards in advance, to plant the stool in the shadow of the Bar, Mr. Cruncher added to himself: "Jerry, you honest tradesman, there's hopes wot that boy will yet be a blessing to you, and a recompense to you for his mother!"

Chapter XV
KNITTING

THERE had been earlier drinking than usual in the wine-shop of Monsieur Defarge. As early as six o'clock in the morning, sallow faces peeping through its barred windows had descried other faces within, bending over measures of wine. Monsieur Defarge sold a very thin wine at the best of times, but it would seem to have been an unusually thin wine that he sold at this time. A sour wine, moreover, or a souring, for its influence on the mood of those who drank it was to make them gloomy. No vivacious bacchanalian flame leaped out of the pressed grape of Monsieur Defarge; but, a smoldering fire that burnt in the dark, lay hidden in the dregs of it.

This had been the third morning in succession, on which there had been early drinking at the wine-shop of Monsieur Defarge. It had begun on Monday, and here was Wednesday come. There had been more of early brooding than drinking; for many men had listened, and whispered, and slunk about there from the time of the opening of the door, who could not have laid a piece of money on the counter to save their souls. These were to the full as interested in the place, however, as if they could have commanded whole barrels of wine; and they glided from seat to seat, and from corner to corner, swallowing talk in lieu of drink, with greedy looks.

Notwithstanding an unusual flow of company, the master of the wine-shop was not visible. He was not missed; for nobody who crossed the threshold looked for him, nobody asked for him, nobody wondered to see only Madame Defarge in her seat, presiding over the distribution of wine, with a bowl of battered small coins before her, as much defaced and beaten out of their original impress as the small coinage of humanity from whose ragged pockets they had come.

A suspended interest and a prevalent absence of mind, were perhaps observed by the spies who looked in at the wine-shop, as they looked in at every place, high and low, from the king's palace to the criminal's jail. Games at cards languished, players at dominoes musingly built towers with them, drinkers drew figures on the tables with spilt drops of wine, Madame Defarge herself picked out the pattern on her sleeve with her toothpick, and saw and heard something inaudible and invisible a long way off.

Thus Saint Antoine in this vinous feature of his, until midday. It was high noontide, when two dusty men passed through his streets and under his swinging lamps; of whom, one was Monsieur Defarge, the other, a mender of roads in a blue cap. All adust and athirst, the two entered the wine-shop. Their arrival had lighted a kind of fire in the breast of Saint Antoine, fast spreading as they came along, which stirred and flickered in flames of faces at most doors and windows. Yet, no one had followed them, and no man spoke when they entered the wine-shop, though the eyes of every man there were turned upon them.

"Good-day, gentlemen!" said Monsieur Defarge.

It may have been a signal for loosening the general tongue. It elicited an answering chorus of "Good-day!"

"It is bad weather, gentlemen," said Defarge, shaking his head.

Upon which every man looked at his neighbor, and then all cast down their eyes and sat silent, except one man, who got up and went out.

"My wife," said Defarge aloud, addressing Madame Defarge; "I have traveled certain leagues with this good mender of roads, called Jacques. I met him—by accident—a day and a half's journey out of Paris. He is a good child, this mender of roads, called Jacques. Give him to drink, my wife."

A second man got up and went out. Madame Defarge set wine before the mender of roads called Jacques, who doffed his blue cap to the company, and drank. In the breast of his blouse he carried some coarse dark bread; he ate of this between whiles, and sat munching and drinking near Madame Defarge's counter. A third man got up and went out.

Defarge refreshed himself with a draught of wine—but he took less than was given to the stranger, as being himself a man to whom it was no rarity—and stood waiting until the countryman had made his breakfast. He looked at no one present, and no one now looked at him; not even Madame Defarge, who had taken up her knitting, and was at work.

"Have you finished your repast, friend?" he asked, in due season.

"Yes, thank you."

"Come then! You shall see the apartment that I told you you could occupy. It will suit you to a marvel."

Out of the wine-shop into the street, out of the street into a court-yard, out of the court-yard up a steep staircase, out of the staircase into a garret—formerly the garret where a white-haired man sat on a low bench, stooping forward, and very busy, making shoes.

No white-haired man was there now; but, the three men were there who had gone out of the wine-shop singly. And between them and the white-haired man afar off, was the one small link, that they had once looked in at him through the chinks in the wall.

Defarge closed the door carefully, and spoke in a subdued voice:

"Jacques One, Jacques Two, Jacques Three! This is the witness encountered by appointment, by me, Jacques Four. He will tell you all. Speak, Jacques Five!"

The mender of roads, blue cap in hand, wiped his swarthy forehead with it, and said, "Where shall I commence, Monsieur?"

"Commence," was Monsieur Defarge's not unreasonable reply, "at the commencement."

"I saw him then, messieurs," began the mender of roads, "a year ago this running summer, underneath the carriage of the Marquis, hanging by the chain. Behold the manner of it. I leaving my work on the road, the sun going to bed, the carriage of the Marquis slowly ascending the hill, he hanging by the chain—like this."

Again the mender of roads went through the whole performance; in which he ought to have been perfect by that time, seeing that it had been the infallible resource and indispensable entertainment of his village during a whole year.

Jacques One struck in, and asked if he had ever seen the man before?

"Never," answered the mender of roads, recovering his perpendicular.

Jacques Three demanded how he afterwards recognized him then?

"By his tall figure," said the mender of roads, softly, and with his finger at his nose. "When Monsieur the Marquis demands that evening, 'Say, what is he like?' I make response, 'Tall as a spectre.'"

"You should have said, short as a dwarf," returned Jacques Two.

"But what did I know? The deed was not then accomplished, neither did he confide in me. Observe! Under those circumstances, even, I do not offer my testimony. Monsieur the Marquis indicates me with his finger, standing near our little fountain, and says, 'To me! Bring that rascal!' My faith, messieurs, I offer nothing."

"He is right there, Jacques," murmured Defarge, to him who had interrupted. "Go on!"

"Good," said the mender of roads, with an air of mystery. "The tall man is lost, and he is sought—how many months? Nine, ten, eleven?"

"No matter, the number," said Defarge. "He is well hidden, but at last he is unluckily found. Go on!"

"I am again at work upon the hill-side, and the sun is again about to go to bed. I am collecting my tools to descend to my cottage down in the village below, where it is already dark, when I raise my eyes, and see coming over the hill, six soldiers. In the midst of them is a tall man with his arms bound—tied to his sides, like this!"

With the aid of his indispensable cap, he represented a man with his elbows bound fast at his hips, with cords that were knotted behind him.

"I stand aside, messieurs, by my heap of stones, to see the soldiers and their prisoner pass (for it is a solitary road, that, where any spectacle is well worth looking at), and at first, as they approach, I see no more than that they are six soldiers, with a tall man bound, and that they are almost black, to my sight—except on the side of the sun going to bed, where they have a red edge, messieurs. Also, I see that their long shadows are on the hollow ridge on the opposite side of the road, and are on the hill above it, and are like the shadows of giants. Also, I see that they are covered with dust, and that the dust moves with them as they come, tramp, tramp! But when they advance quite near to me, I recognize the tall man, and he recognizes me. Ah, but he would be well content to precipitate himself over the hill-side once again, as on the evening when he and I first encountered, close to the same spot!"

He described it as if he were there, and it was evident that he saw it vividly; perhaps he had not seen much in his life.

"I do not show the soldiers that I recogize the tall man; he does not show the soldiers that he recognizes me; we do it, and we know it, with our eyes. 'Come on!' says the chief of that company, pointing to the village, 'bring him fast to his tomb!' and they bring him faster. I follow. His arms are swelled because of being bound so tight, his wooden shoes are large and clumsy, and he is lame. Because he is lame, and consequently slow, they drive him with their guns—like this!"

He imitated the action of a man's being impelled forward by the butt-ends of muskets.

"As they descend the hill like madmen running a race, he falls. They laugh and pick him up again. His face is bleeding and covered with dust, but he cannot touch it; thereupon, they laugh again. They bring him into the village; all the village runs to look; they take him past the mill, and up to the prison; all the village sees the prison gate open in the darkness of night, and swallow him—like this!"

He opened his mouth as wide as he could, and shut it with a sounding snap of his teeth. Observant of his unwillingness to mar the effect by opening it again, Defarge said, "Go on, Jacques."

"All the village," pursued the mender of roads, on tiptoe and in a low voice, "withdraws; all the village whispers by the fountain; all the village sleeps; all the village dreams of that unhappy one, within the locks and bars of the prison on the crag, and never to come out of it, except to perish. In the morning, with my tools upon my shoulder, eating my morsel of black bread as I go, I make a circuit by the prison, on my way to my work. There, I see him, high up, behind the bars of a lofty iron cage, bloody and dusty as last night, looking through. He has no hand free, to wave to me; I dare not call to him; he regards me like a dead man."

Defarge and the three glanced darkly at one another. The looks of all of them were dark, repressed, and revengeful, as they listened to the countryman's story; the manner of all of them, while it was secret, was authoritative too. They had the air of a rough tribunal; Jacques One and Two sitting on the old pallet-bed, each with his chin resting on his hand, and his eyes intent on the road mender; Jacques Three, equally intent, on one knee behind them, with his agitated hand always gliding over the network of fine nerves about his mouth and nose; Defarge standing between them, and the narrator whom he had stationed in the light of the window, by turns looking from him to them and from them to him.

"Go on, Jacques," said Defarge.

"He remains up there in his iron cage, some days. The village looks at him by stealth, for it is afraid. But it always looks up, from a distance, at the prison on the crag; and in the evening when the work of the day is achieved, and it assembles to gossip at the fountain, all faces are turned toward the prison. Formerly, they were turned toward the posting-house; now, they are turned toward the prison. They whisper at the fountain, that although condemned to death he will not be executed; they say that petitions have been presented in Paris, showing that he was enraged and made mad by the death of his child; they say that a petition has been presented to the King himself. What do I know? It is possible. Perhaps yes, perhaps no."

"Listen then, Jacques," Number One of that name sternly interposed. "Know that a petition was presented to the King and Queen. All here, yourself excepted, saw the King take it, in his carriage in the street, sitting beside the Queen. It is Defarge whom you see here, who, at the hazard of his life, darted out before the horses, with the petition in his hand."

"And once again listen, Jacques!" said the kneeling Number Three: his fingers ever wandering over and over those fine nerves, with a strikingly greedy air, as if he hungered for something—that was neither food nor drink; "the guard, horse and foot, surrounded the petitioner, and struck him blows. You hear?"

"I hear, messieurs."

"Go on, then," said Defarge.

"Again; on the other hand, they whisper at the fountain," resumed the countryman, "that he is brought down into our country to be executed on the spot, and that he will very certainly be executed. They even whisper that because he has slain Monseigneur, and because Monseigneur was the father of his tenants—serfs—what you will—he will be executed as a parricide. One old man says at the fountain, that his right hand, armed with the knife, will be burnt off before his face; that, into wounds which will be made in his arms, his breast, and his legs, there will be poured boiling oil, melted lead, hot resin, wax, and sulphur; finally, that he will be torn limb from limb by four strong horses. That old man says, all this was actually done to a prisoner who made an attempt on the life of the last King, Louis Fifteen. But how do I know if he lies? I am not a scholar."

"Listen once again then, Jacques!" said the man with the restless hand and the craving air. "The name of that prisoner was Damiens, and it was all done in open day, in the open streets of this city of Paris; and nothing was more noticed in the vast concourse that saw it done, than the crowd of ladies of quality and fashion, who were full of eager attention to the last—to the last, Jacques, prolonged until nightfall, when he had lost two legs and an arm, and still breathed! And it was done—why; how old are you?"

"Thirty-five," said the mender of roads, who looked sixty.

"It was done when you were more than ten years old; you might have seen it."

"Enough!" said Defarge, with grim impatience. "Long live the Devil! Go on."

"Well. Some whisper this, some whisper that; they speak of nothing else: even the fountain appears to fall to that tune. At length, on Sunday night, when all the village is asleep, come soldiers, winding down from the prison, and their guns ring on the stones of the little street. Workmen dig, workmen hammer, soldiers laugh and sing; in the morning, by the fountain, there is raised a gallows forty feet high, poisoning the water."

The mender of roads looked *through* rather than *at* the low ceiling, and pointed as if he saw the gallows somewhere in the sky.

"All work is stopped, all assemble there, nobody leads the cows out, the cows are there with the rest. At mid-day, the roll of drums. Soldiers have marched into the prison in the night, and he is in the midst of many soldiers. He is bound as before, and in his mouth there is a gag—tied so, with a tight string, making him look almost as if he laughed." He suggested it, by creasing his face with his two thumbs, from the corners of his mouth to his ears. "On the top of the gallows is fixed the knife, blade upward, with its point in the air. He is hanged there forty feet high—and is left hanging, poisoning the water."

They looked at one another, as he used his blue cap to wipe his face, on which the perspiration had started afresh while he recalled the spectacle.

"It is frightful, messieurs. How can the women and the children draw water! Who can gossip of an evening, under that shadow! Under it, have I said? When I left the village, Monday evening as the sun was going to bed, and looked back from the hill, the shadow struck across the church, across the mill, across the prison—seemed to strike across the earth, messieurs, to where the sky rests upon it!"

The hungry man gnawed one of his fingers as he looked at the other three, and his finger quivered with the craving that was on him.

"That's all, messieurs. I left at sunset (as I had been warned to do), and I walked on, that night and half next day, until I met (as I was warned I should) this comrade. With him, I came on, now riding and now walking, through the rest of yesterday and through last night. And here you see me!"

After a gloomy silence, the first Jacques said, "Good! You have acted and recounted, faithfully. Will you wait for us a little, outside the door?"

"Very willingly," said the mender of roads. Whom Defarge escorted to the top of the stairs, and leaving seated there, returned.

The three had risen, and their heads were together when he came back to the garret.

"How say you, Jacques?" demanded Number One. "To be registered?"

"To be registered, as doomed to destruction," returned Defarge.

"Magnificent!" croaked the man with the craving.

"The chateau, and all the race?" inquired the first.

"The chateau and all the race," returned Defarge. "Extermination."

The hungry man repeated, in a rapturous croak, "Magnificent!" and began gnawing another finger.

"Are you sure," asked Jacques Two, of Defarge, "that no embarrassment can arise from our manner of keeping the register? Without doubt it is safe, for no one beyond ourselves can decipher it; but shall we always be able to decipher it—or, I ought to say, will she?"

"Jacques," returned Defarge, drawing himself up, "if madame my wife undertook to keep the register in her memory alone, she would not lose a word of it—not a syllable of it. Knitted, in her own stitches and her own symbols, it will always be as plain to her as the sun. Confide in Madame Defarge. It would be easier for the weakest poltroon that lives, to erase himself from existence, than to erase one letter of his name or crimes from the knitted register of Madame Defarge."

There was a murmur of confidence and approval, and then the man who hungered, asked: "Is this rustic to be sent back soon? I hope so. He is very simple; is he not a little dangerous?"

"He knows nothing," said Defarge; "at least nothing more than would easily elevate himself to a gallows of the same height. I charge myself with him; let him remain with me; I will take care of him, and set him on his road. He wishes to see the fine world—the King, the Queen, and Court; let him see them on Sunday."

"What?" exclaimed the hungry man, staring. "Is it a good sign, that he wishes to see Royalty and Nobility?"

"Jacques," said Defarge, "judiciously show a cat, milk, if you wish her to thirst for it. Judiciously show a dog his natural prey if you wish him to bring it down one day."

Nothing more was said, and the mender of roads, being found already dozing on the topmost stair, was advised to lay himself down on the pallet-bed and take some rest. He needed no persuasion, and was soon asleep.

Worse quarters than Defarge's wine-shop, could easily have been found in Paris for a provincial slave of that degree. Saving for a mysterious dread of madame, by which he was constantly haunted, his life was very new and agreeable. But, madame sat all day at her counter, so expressly unconscious of him, and so particularly determined not to perceive that his being there had any connection with any thing below the surface, that he shook in his wooden shoes whenever his eye lighted on her. For, he contended with himself that it was impossible to foresee what that lady might pretend next; and he felt assured that if she should take it into her brightly ornamented head to pretend that she had seen him do a murder and afterward flay the victim, she would infallibly go through with it until the play was played out.

Therefore, when Sunday came, the mender of roads was not enchanted (though he said he was) to find that madame was to accompany monseigneur and himself to Versailles. It was additionally disconcerting to have madame knitting all the way there, in a public conveyance; it was additionally disconcerting yet, to have madame in the crowd in the afternoon, still with her knitting in her hands as the crowd waited to see the carriage of the King and Queen.

"You work hard, madame," said a man near her.

"Yes," answered Madame Defarge; "I have a good deal to do."

"What do you make, madame?"

"Many things."

"For instance——"

"For instance," returned Madame Defarge, composedly, "shrouds."

The man moved a little further away, as soon as he could, and the mender of roads fanned himself with his blue cap: feeling it mightily close and oppressive. If he needed a King and Queen to restore him, he was fortunate in having his remedy at hand; for, soon the large-faced King and the fair-faced Queen came in their golden coach, attended by the shining Bull's Eye of their Court, a glittering multitude of laughing ladies and fine lords; and in jewels and silks and powder and splendor and elegantly spurning figures and handsomely disdainful faces of both sexes, the mender of roads bathed himself, so much to his temporary intoxication, that he cried Long live the King, Long live the Queen, Long live everybody and every thing! as if he had never heard of ubiquitous Jacques in his time. Then, there were gardens, court-yards, terraces, fountains, green banks, more King and Queen, more Bull's Eye, more lords and ladies, more Long live they all! until he absolutely wept with sentiment. During the whole of this scene, which lasted some three hours, he had plenty of shouting and weeping and sentimental company, and throughout Defarge held him by the collar, as if to restrain him from flying at the objects of his brief devotion and tearing them to pieces.

"Bravo!" said Defarge, clapping him on the back when it was over, like a patron; "you are a good boy!"

The mender of roads was now coming to himself, and was mistrustful of having made a mistake in his late demonstrations; but no.

"You are the fellow we want," said Defarge, in his ear; "you make these fools believe that it will last forever. Then, they are the more insolent, and it is the nearer ended."

"Hey!" cried the mender of roads, reflectively; "that's true."

"These fools know nothing. While they despise your breath, and would stop it forever and ever, in you or in a hundred like you rather than in one of their own horses or dogs, they only know what your breath tells them. Let it deceive them, then, a little longer; it cannot deceive them too much."

Madame Defarge looked superciliously at the client, and nodded in confirmation.

"As to you," said she, "you would shout and shed tears for any thing, if it made a show and a noise. Say! Would you not?"

"Truly, madame, I think so. For the moment."

"If you were shown a great heap of dolls, and were set upon them to pluck them to pieces and despoil them for your own advantage, you would pick out the richest and gayest. Say! Would you not?"

"Truly yes, madame."

"Yes. And if you were shown a flock of birds unable to fly, and were set upon them to strip them of their feathers for your own advantage, you would set upon the birds of the finest feathers; would you not?"

"It is true, madame."

"You have seen both dolls and birds to-day," said Madame Defarge, with a wave of her hand toward the place where they had last been apparent; "now, go home!"

Chapter XVI

STILL KNITTING

MADAME DEFARGE and monsieur her husband returned amicably to the bosom of Saint Antoine, while a speck in a blue cap toiled through the darkness, and through the dust, and down the weary miles of avenue by the wayside, slowly tending toward that point of the compass where the chateau of Monsieur the Marquis, now in his grave, listened to the whispering trees. Such ample leisure had the stone faces, now, for listening to the trees and to the fountain, that the few village scarecrows who, in their quest for herbs to eat and fragments of dead stick to burn, strayed within sight of the great stone court-yard and terrace staircase, had it borne in upon their starved fancy that the expression of the faces was altered. A rumour just lived in the village—had a faint and bare existence there, as its people had—that when the knife struck home, the faces changed, from faces of pride to faces of anger and pain; also, that when that dangling figure was hauled up forty feet above the fountain, they changed again, and bore a cruel look of being avenged, which they would henceforth bear forever. In the stone face over the great window of the bed-chamber where the murder was done, two fine dints were pointed out in the sculptured nose, which everybody recognised, and which nobody had seen of old; and on the scarce occasion when two or three ragged peasants emerged from the crowd to take a hurried peep at Monsieur the Marquis petrified, a skinny finger would not have pointed to it for a minute, before they all started away among the moss and leaves, like the more fortunate hares who could find a living there.

Chateau and hut, stone face and dangling figure, the red stain on the stone floor and the pure water in the village well—thousands of acres of land—a whole province of France—all France itself—lay under the night sky, concentrated into a faint hair-breadth line. So does a whole world with all its greatnesses and littlenesses, lie in a twinkling star. And as mere human knowledge can split a ray of light and analyse the manner of its composition, so, sublimer intelligences may read in the feeble shining of this earth of ours, every thought and act, every vice and virtue, of every responsible creature on it.

The Defarges, husband and wife, came lumbering under the starlight, in their public vehicle, to that gate of Paris whereunto their journey naturally tended. There was the usual stoppage at the barrier guard-house, and the usual lanterns came glancing forth for the usual examination and inquiry. Monsieur Defarge alighted: knowing one or two of the soldiery there, and one of the police. The latter he was intimate with, and affectionately embraced.

When Saint Antoine had again enfolded the Defarges in his dusky wings, and they, having finally alighted near the Saint's boundaries, were picking their way on foot through the black mud and offal of his streets, Madame Defarge spoke to her husband:

"Say then, my friend; what did Jacques of the police tell thee?"

"Very little to-night, but all he knows. There is another spy commissioned for our quarter. There may be many more, for all that he can say, but he knows of one."

"Eh well!" said Madame Defarge, raising her eyebrows with a cool business air. "It is necessary to register him. How do they call that man?"

"He is English."

"So much the better. His name?"

"Barsad," said Defarge, making it French by pronunciation. But, he had been so careful to get it accurately, that he then spelt it with perfect correctness.

"Barsad," repeated madame. "Good. Christian name?"

"John."

"John Barsad," repeated madame, after murmuring it once to herself. "Good. His appearance; is it known?"

"Age, about forty years; height, about five feet nine; black hair; complexion dark; generally, rather handsome visage; eyes dark, face thin, long, and sallow; nose aquiline, but not straight, having a peculiar inclination towards the left cheek; expression, therefore, sinister."

"Eh, my faith. It is a portrait!" said madame, laughing. "He shall be registered to-morrow."

They turned into the wine-shop, which was closed (for it was midnight), and where Madame Defarge immediately took her post at her desk, counted the small moneys that had been taken during her absence, examined the stock, went through the entries in the book, made other entries of her own, checked the serving man in every possible way, and finally dismissed him to bed. Then she turned out the contents of the bowl of money for the second time, and began knotting them up in her handkerchief, in a chain of separate knots, for safe keeping through the night. All this while, Defarge, with his pipe in his mouth, walked up and down, complacently admiring, but never interfering; in which condition, indeed, as to the business and his domestic affairs, he walked up and down through life.

The night was hot, and the shop, close shut and surrounded by so foul a neighbourhood, was ill-smelling. Monsieur Defarge's olfactory sense was by no means delicate, but the stock of wine smelt much stronger than it ever tasted, and so did the stock of rum and brandy and aniseed. He whiffed the compound of scents away, as he put down his smoked-out pipe.

"You are fatigued," said madame, raising her glance as she knotted the money. "There are only the usual odors."

"I am a little tired," her husband acknowledged.

"You are a little depressed, too," said madame, whose quick eyes had never been so intent on the accounts, but they had had a ray or two for him. "Oh, the men, the men!"

"But my dear," began Defarge.

"But my dear!" repeated madame, nodding firmly: "but my dear! You are faint of heart to-night, my dear!"

"Well, then," said Defarge, as if a thought were wrung out of his breast, "it *is* a long time."

"It is a long time," repeated his wife; "and when is it not a long time? Vengeance and retribution require a long time; it is the rule."

"It does not take a long time to strike a man with Lightning," said Defarge.

"How long," demanded madame, composedly, "does it take to make and store the lightning? Tell me?"

Defarge raised his forehead thoughtfully, as if there were something in that, too.

"It does not take a long time," said madame, "for an earthquake to swallow a town. Eh well! Tell me how long it takes to prepare the earthquake?"

"A long time, I suppose," said Defarge.

"But when it is ready, it takes place, and grinds to pieces everything before it. In the mean time, it is always preparing, though it is not seen or heard. That is your consolation. Keep it."

She tied a knot with flashing eyes, as if it throttled a foe.

"I tell thee," said madame, extending her right hand, for emphasis, "that although it is a long time on the road, it is on the road and coming. I tell thee it never retreats, and never stops. I tell thee it is always advancing. Look around and consider the lives of all the world that we know, consider the faces of all the world that we know, consider the rage and discontent to which the Jacquerie addresses itself with more and more of certainty every hour. Can such things last? Bah! I mock you."

"My brave wife," returned Defarge, standing before her with his head a little bent, and his hands clasped at his back, like a docile and attentive pupil before his catechist, "I do not question all this. But it has lasted a long time, and it is possible—you know well, my wife, it is possible—that it may not come, during our lives."

"Eh well! How then?" demanded madame, tying another knot, as if there were another enemy strangled.

"Well!" said Defarge, with a half complaining and half apologetic shrug. "We shall not see the triumph."

"We shall have helped it," returned madame, with her extended hand in strong action. "Nothing that we do, is done in vain. I believe, with all my soul, that we shall see the triumph. But even if not, even if I knew certainly not, show me the neck of an aristocrat and tyrant, and still I would—"

Then madame, with her teeth set, tied a very terrible knot indeed.

"Hold!" cried Defarge, reddening a little as if he felt charged with cowardice; "I too, my dear, will stop at nothing."

"Yes! But it is your weakness that you sometimes need to see your victim and your opportunity, to sustain you. Sustain yourself without that. When the time comes, let loose a tiger and a devil; but wait for the time with the tiger and the devil chained—not shown—yet always ready."

Madame enforced the conclusion of this piece of advice by striking her little counter with her chain of money as if she knocked its brains out, and then gathering the heavy handkerchief under her arm in a serene manner, and observing that it was time to go to bed.

Next noontide saw the admirable woman in her usual place in the wine-shop, knitting away assiduously. A rose lay beside her, and if she now and then glanced at the flower, it was with no infraction of her usual preoccupied air. There were a few customers, drinking or not drinking, standing or seated, sprinkled about. The day was very hot, and heaps of flies, who were extending their inquisitive and adventurous perquisitions into all the glutinous little glasses near madame, fell dead at the bottom. Their decease made no impression on the other files out promenading, who looked at them in the coolest manner (as if they themselves were elephants, or something as far removed), until they met the same fate. Curious to consider how heedless flies are!—perhaps they thought as much at Court that sunny summer day.

A figure entering at the door threw a shadow on Madame Defarge which she felt to be a new one. She laid down her knitting, and began to pin the rose in her head-dress, before she looked at the figure.

It was curious. The moment Madame Defarge took up the rose, the customers ceased talking, and began gradually to drop out of the wine-shop.

"Good day, madame," said the new comer.

"Good day, monsieur."

She said it aloud, but added to herself, as she resumed her knitting: "Hah! Good-day, age about forty, height about five feet nine, black hair, generally rather handsome visage, complexion dark, eyes dark, thin, long and sallow face, aquillne nose but not straight, having a peculiar inclination toward the left cheek, which imparts a sinister expression! Good day, one and all!"

"Have the goodness to give me a little glass of old cognac, and a mouthful of cool fresh water, madame."

Madame complied with a polite air.

"Marvelous cognac this, madame!"

It was the first time it had ever been so complimented, and Madame Defarge knew enough of its antecedents to know better. She said, however, that the cognac was flattered, and took up her knitting. The visitor watched her fingers for a few moments, and took the opportunity of observing the place in general.

"You knit with great skill, madame."

"I am accustomed to it."

"A pretty pattern, too!"

"*You* think so?" said madame, looking at him with a smile.

"Decidedly. May one ask what it is for?"

"Pastime," said madame, looking at him with a smile, while her fingers moved nimbly.

"Not for use?"

"That depends. I may find a use for it one day. If I do——well," said madame, drawing a breath and nodding her head with a stern kind of coquetry, "I'll use it!"

It was remarkable; but the taste of Saint Antoine seemed to be decidedly opposed to a rose on the head-dress of Madame Defarge. Two men had entered separately, and had been about to order drinks, when, catching sight of that novelty, they faltered, made a pretence of looking about as if for some friend who was not there, and went away. Nor, of those who had been there when this visitor entered, was there one left. They had all dropped off. The spy had kept his eyes open, but had been able to detect no sign. They had lounged away in a poverty-stricken, purposeless, accidental manner, quite natural and unimpeachable.

"JOHN," thought madame, checking off her work as her fingers knitted, and her eyes looked at the stranger. "Stay long enough, and I shall knit 'BARSAD' before you go."

"You have a husband, madame?"

"I have."

"Children?"

"No children."

"Business seems bad?"

"Business is very bad; the people are so poor."

"Ah, the unfortunate, miserable people! So oppressed, too—as you say."

"As *you* say," madame retorted, correcting him and deftly knitting an extra something into his name that boded him no good.

"Pardon me; certainly it was I who said so, but you naturally think so. Of course."

"*I* think?" returned madame, in a high voice. "I and my husband have enough to do to keep this wine-shop open, without thinking. All we think, here, is how to live. That is the subject *we* think of, and it gives us, from morning to night, enough to think about, without embarrassing our heads concerning others. *I* think for others? No, no."

The spy, who was there to pick up any crumbs he could find or make, did not allow his baffled state to express itself in his sinister face; but, stood with an air of gossiping gallantry, leaning his elbow on Madame Defarge's little counter, and occasionally sipping his cognac.

"A bad business this, madame, of Gaspard's execution. Ah! the poor Gaspard!" With a sigh of great compassion.

"My faith!" returned madame, coolly and lightly, "if people use knives for such purposes, they have to pay for it. He knew beforehand what the price of his luxury was; he has paid the price."

"I believe," said the spy, dropping his soft voice to a tone that invited confidence, and expressing an injured revolutionary susceptibility in every muscle of his wicked face: "I believe there is much compassion and anger in this neighborhood, touching the poor fellow? Between ourselves."

"Is there?" asked madame, vacantly.

"Is there not?"

"—Here is my husband!" said Madame Defarge.

As the keeper of the wine-shop entered at the door, the spy saluted him by touching his hat, and saying, with an engaging smile, "Good-day, Jacques!" Defarge stopped short, and stared at him.

"Good day, Jacques!" the spy repeated; with not quite so much confidence, or quite so easy a smile under the stare.

"You deceive yourself, monsieur," returned the keeper of the wine-shop. "You mistake me for another. That is not my name. I am Ernest Defarge."

"It is all the same," said the spy, airily, but discomfited too; "good-day!"

"Good day!" answered Defarge, drily.

"I was saying to madame, with whom I had the pleasure of chatting when you entered, that they tell me there is—and no wonder!—much sympathy and anger in Saint Antoine, touching the unhappy fate of poor Gaspard."

"No one has told me so," said Defarge, shaking his head; "I know nothing of it."

Having said it, he passed behind the little counter, and stood with his hand on the back of his wife's chair, looking over that barrier at the person to whom they were both opposed, and whom either of them would have shot with the greatest satisfaction.

The spy, well used to his business, did not change his unconscious attitude, but drained his little glass of cognac, took a sip of fresh water, and asked for another glass of cognac. Madame Defarge poured it out for him, took to her knitting again, and hummed a little song over it.

"You seem to know this quarter well; that is to say, better than I do?" observed Defarge.

"Not at all, but I hope to know it better. I am so profoundly interested in its miserable inhabitants."

"Hah!" muttered Defarge.

"The pleasure of conversing with you, Monsieur Defarge, recalls to me," pursued the spy, "that I have the honour of cherishing some interesting associations with your name."

"Indeed?" said Defarge, with much indifference.

"Yes, indeed. When Doctor Manette was released, you his old domestic had the charge of him, I know. He was delivered to you. You see I am informed of the circumstances?"

"Such is the fact, certainly," said Defarge. He had had it conveyed to him, in an accidental touch of his wife's elbow as she knitted and warbled, that he would do best to answer, but always with brevity.

"It was to you," said the spy, "that his daughter came; and it was from your care that his daughter took him, accompanied by a neat brown monsieur; how is he called?—in a little wig—Lorry—of the bank of Tellson and Company—over to England."

"Such is the fact," repeated Defarge.

"Very interesting remembrances!" said the spy. "I have known Doctor Manette and his daughter, in England."

"Yes?" said Defarge.

"You don't hear much about them now?" said the spy.

"No," said Defarge.

"In effect," madame struck in, looking up from her work and her little song, "we never hear about them. We received the news of their safe arrival, and perhaps another letter or perhaps two; but since then, they have gradually taken their road in life—we, ours—and we have held no correspondence."

"Perfectly so, madame," replied the spy. "She is going to be married."

"Going?" echoed madame. "She was pretty enough to have been married long ago. You English are cold, it seems to me."

"Oh! You know I am English."

"I perceive your tongue is," returned madame; "and what the tongue is, I suppose the man is."

He did not take the identification as a compliment; but he made the best of it, and turned it off with a laugh. After sipping his cognac to the end, he added:

"Yes, Miss Manette is going to be married. But not to an Englishman; to one who, like herself, is French by birth. And speaking of Gaspard (ah, poor Gaspard! It was cruel, cruel!), it is a curious thing that she is going to marry the nephew of Monsieur the Marquis, for whom Gaspard was exalted to that height of so many feet; in other words, the present Marquis. But he lives unknown in England, he is no Marquis there; he is Mr. Charles Darnay. D'Aulnais is the name of his mother's family."

Madame Defarge knitted steadily, but the intelligence had a palpable effect upon her husband. Do what he would behind the little counter, as to the striking of a light and the lighting of his pipe, he was troubled, and his hand was not trustworthy. The spy would have been no spy if he had failed to see it, or to record it in his mind.

Having made, at least, this one hit, whatever it might prove to be worth, and no customers coming in to help him to any other, Mr. Barsad paid for what he had drunk, and took his leave: taking occasion to say, in a genteel manner, before he departed, that he looked forward to the pleasure of seeing Monsieur and Madame Defarge again. For some minutes after he had emerged into the outer presence of Saint Antoine, the husband and wife remained exactly as he had left them, lest he should come back.

"Can it be true," said Defarge, in a low voice, looking down at his wife as he stood smoking with his hand on the back of her chair "what he has said of Ma'amselle Manette?"

"As he has said it," returned madame, lifting her eyebrows a little, "it is probably false. But it may be true."

"If it is——" Defarge began, and stopped.

"If it is?" repeated his wife.

"—And if it does come, while we live to see it triumph—I hope, for her sake, Destiny will keep her husband out of France."

"Her husband's destiny," said Madame Defarge, with her usual composure, "will take him where he is to go, and will lead him to the end that is to end him. That is all I know."

"But it is very strange—now, at least is it not very strange"—said Defarge, rather pleading with his wife to induce her to admit it, "that, after all our sympathy for Monsieur her father and herself, her husband's name should be proscribed under your hand at this moment, by the side of that infernal dog's who has just left us?"

"Stranger things than that, will happen when it does come," answered madame. "I have them both here, of a certainty; and they are both here for their merits; that is enough."

She rolled up her knitting when she had said those words, and presently took the rose out of the handkerchief that was wound about her head. Either Saint Antoine had an instinctive sense that the objectionable decoration was gone, or Saint Antoine was on the watch for its disappearance; howbeit, the Saint took courage to lounge in, very shortly afterward, and the wine-shop recovered its habitual aspect.

In the evening, at which season of all others, Saint Antoine turned himself inside out, and sat on door-steps and window-ledges, and came to the corners of vile streets and courts, for a breath of air, Madame Defarge with her work in her hand was accustomed to pass from place to place and from group to group: a missionary—there were many like her—such as the world will do well never to breed again. All the women knitted. They knitted worthless things; but, the mechanical work was a mechanical substitute for eating and drinking; the hands moved for the jaws and the digestive apparatus; if the bony fingers had been still, the stomachs would have been more famine-pinched.

But, as the fingers went, the eyes went, and the thoughts. And as Madame Defarge moved on from group to group, all three went quicker and fiercer among every little knot of women that she had spoken with, and left behind.

Her husband smoked at his door, looking after her with admiration. "A great woman," said he, "strong woman, a grand woman, a frightfully grand woman!"

Darkness closed around, and then came the ringing of church bells and the distant beating of the military drums of the Royal Guard, as the women sat knitting, knitting. Darkness encompassed them. Another darkness was closing in as surely, when the church bells, then ringing pleasantly in many an airy steeple over France, should be melted into thunder cannon; when the military drums should be beating to drown a wretched voice, that night all potent as the voice of Power and Plenty, Freedom and Life. So much was closing in about the women who sat knitting, knitting, that they their very selves were closing in around a structure yet unbuilt, where they were to sit knitting, knitting, counting dropping heads.

Chapter XVII

ONE NIGHT

NEVER did the sun go down with a brighter glory on the quiet corner of Soho, than one memorable evening when the Doctor and his daughter sat under the plane-tree together. Never did the moon rise with a milder radiance over great London, than on that night when it found them still seated under the tree, and shone upon their faces through its leaves.

Lucie was to be married to-morrow. She had reserved this last evening for her father, and they sat alone under the plane-tree.

"You are happy, my dear father?"

"Quite, my child."

They had said little, though they had been there a long time. When it was yet light enough to work and read, she had neither engaged herself in her usual work, nor had she read to him. She had employed herself in both ways, at his side under the tree, many and many a time; but, this time was not quite like any other, and nothing could make it so.

"And I am very happy to-night, dear father. I am deeply happy in the love that Heaven has so blessed—my love for Charles, and Charles's love for me. But, if my life were not to be still consecrated to you, or if my marriage were so arranged as that it would part us, even by the length of a few of these streets, I should be more unhappy and self-reproacful now, than I can tell you. Even as it is——"

Even as it was, she could not command her voice.

In the sad moonlight, she clasped him by the neck, and laid her face upon his breast. In the moonlight which is always sad, as the light of the sun itself is—as the light called human life is—as its coming and its going.

"Dearest dear! Can you tell me, this last time, that you feel quite, quite sure no new affections of mine, and no new duties of mine, will ever interpose between us? *I* know it well, but do you know it? In your own heart, do you feel quite certain?"

Her father answered with a cheerful firmness of conviction he could scarcely have assumed "Quite sure, my darling! More than that," he added, as he tenderly kissed her: "my future is far brighter, Lucie, seen through your marriage, than it could have been—nay, than it ever was—without it."

"If I could hope *that,* my father!——"

"Believe it, love! Indeed it is so. Consider how natural and how plain it is, my dear, that it should be so. You, devoted and young, cannot freely appreciate the anxiety I have felt that your life should not be wasted——"

She moved her hand toward his lips, but he took it in his, and repeated the word.

"—wasted, my child—should not be wasted, struck aside from the natural order of things,— for my sake. Your unselfishness cannot entirely comprehend how much my mind has gone on this; but, only ask yourself, how could my happiness be perfect, while yours was incomplete?"

"If I had never seen Charles, my father, I should have been quite happy with you."

He smiled at her unconscious admission that she would have been unhappy without Charles, having seen him, and replied:

"My child, you did see him, and it is Charles. If it had not been Charles, it would have been another. Or, if it had been no other, I should have been the cause, and then the dark part of my life would have cast its shadow beyond myself, and would have fallen on you."

It was the first time, except at the trial, of her ever hearing him refer to the period of his suffering. It gave her a strange and new sensation while his words were in her ears; and she remembered it long afterward.

"See!" said the Doctor of Beauvais, raising his hand toward the moon. "I have looked at her, from my prison-window, when I could not bear her light. I have looked at her when it has been such torture to me to think of her shining upon what I had lost, that I have beaten my head against my prison-walls. I have looked at her, in a state so dull and lethargic, that I have thought of nothing but the number of horizontal lines I could draw across her at the full, and the number of perpendicular lines with which I could intersect them." He added, in his inward and pondering manner, as he looked at the moon, "It was twenty either way, I remember, and the twentieth was difficult to squeeze in."

The strange thrill with which she heard him go back to that time, deepened as he dwelt upon it; but, there was nothing to shock her in the manner of his reference. He only seemed to contrast his present cheefulness and felicity with the dire endurance that was over.

"I have looked at her, speculating thousands of times upon the unborn child from whom I had been rent. Whether it was alive. Whether it had been born alive, or the poor mother's shock had killed it. Whether it was a son who would some day avenge his father. (There was a time in my imprisonment, when my desire for vengeance was unbearable.) Whether it was a son who would never know his father's story; who might even live to weigh the possibility of his father's having disappeared of his own will and act. Whether it was a daughter who would grow to be a woman."

She drew closer to him, and kissed his cheek and his hand.

"I have pictured my daughter, to myself, as perfectly forgetful of me—rather, altogether ignorant of me, and unconscious of me. I have cast up the years of her age, year after year. I have seen her married to a man who knew nothing of my fate. I have altogether perished from the remembrance of the living, and in the next generation my place was a blank."

"My father! Even to hear that you had such thoughts of a daughter who never existed, strikes to my heart as if I had been that child."

"You, Lucie? It is out of the consolation and restoration you have brought to me, that these remembrances arise, and pass between us and the moon on this last night.—What did I say just now?"

"She knew nothing of you. She cared nothing for you."

"So! But on other moonlight nights, when the sadness and the silence have touched me in a different way—have affected me with something as like a sorrowful sense of peace, as any emotion that had pain for its foundations could—I have imagined her as coming to me in my cell, and leading me out into the freedom beyond the fortress. I have seen her image in the moonlight, often, as I now see you; except that I never held her in my arms; it stood between the little grated window and the door. But, you understand that that was not the child I am speaking of?"

"The figure was not; the—the—image; the fancy?"

"No. That was another thing. It stood before my disturbed sense of sight, but it never moved. The phantom that my mind pursued was another and more real child. Of her outward appearance I know no more than that she was like her mother. The other had that likeness too—as you have—but was not the same. Can you follow me, Lucie? Hardly, I think. I doubt you must have been a solitary prisoner to understand these perplexed distinctions."

His collected and calm manner could not prevent her blood from running cold, as he thus tried to anatomize his old condition.

"In that more peaceful state, I have imagined her, in the moonlight, coming to me and taking me out to show me that the home of her married life was full of her loving remembrance of her lost father. My picture was in her room, and I was in her prayers. Her life was active, cheerful, useful; but my poor history pervaded it all."

"I was that child, my father. I was not half so good, but in my love that was I."

"And she showed me her children," said the Doctor of Beauvais, "and they had heard of me, and had been taught to pity me. When they passed a prison of the State, they kept far from its frowning walls, and looked up at its bars, and spoke in whispers. She could never deliver me; I imagined that she always brought me back after showing me such things. But then, blessed with the relief of tears, I fell upon my knees, and blessed her."

"I am that child, I hope, my father. O my dear, my dear, will you bless me as fervently to-morrow?"

"Lucie, I recall these old troubles in the reason that I have to-night for loving you better than words can tell, and thanking God for my great happiness. My thoughts, when they were wildest, never rose near the happiness that I have known with you, and that we have before us."

He embraced her, solemnly commended her to Heaven, and humbly thanked Heaven for having bestowed her on him. By-and-by, they went into the house.

There was no one bidden to the marriage but Mr. Lorry; there was even to be no bridesmaid but the gaunt Miss Pross. The marriage was to make no change in their place of residence; they had been able to extend it, by taking to themselves the upper rooms, formerly belonging to the apocryphal invisible lodger, and they desired nothing more.

Doctor Manette was very cheerful at the little supper. They were only three at table, and Miss Pross made the third. He regretted that Charles was not there; was more than half disposed to object to the loving little plot that kept him away; and drank to him affectionately.

So, the time came for him to bid Lucie good-night, and they separated. But, in the stillness of the third hour of the morning, Lucie came downstairs again, and stole into his room; not free from unshaped fears, beforehand.

All things, however, were in their places; all was quiet; and he lay asleep, his white hair picturesque on the untroubled pillow, and his hands lying quiet on the coverlet. She put her needless candle in the shadow at a distance, crept up to his bed, and put her lips to his; then, leaned over him, and looked at him.

Into his handsome face, the bitter waters of captivity had worn; but, he covered up their tracks with a determination so strong, that he held the mastery of them, even in his sleep. A more remarkable face in its quiet, resolute, and guarded struggle with an unseen assailant was not to be beheld in all the wide dominions of sleep, that night.

She timidly laid her hand on his dear breast, and put up a prayer that she might ever be as true to him as her love aspired to be, and as his sorrows deserved. Then, she withdrew her hand, and kissed his lips once more, and went away. So, the sunrise came, and the shadows of the leaves of the plane-tree moved upon his face, as softly as her lips had moved in praying for him.

Chapter XVIII

NINE DAYS

THE marriage day was shining brightly, and they were ready outside the closed door of the Doctor's room, where he was speaking with Charles Darnay. They were ready to go to church; the beautiful bride, Mr. Lorry, and Miss Pross—to whom the event, through a gradual process of reconcilement to the inevitable, would have been one of absolute bliss, but for the yet lingering consideration that her brother, Solomon should have been the bride groom.

"And so," said Mr. Lorry, who could not sufficiently admire the bride, and who had been moving round her to take in every point of her quiet pretty dress; "and so it was for this, my sweet Lucie, that I brought you across the Channel, such a baby! Lord bless me! How little I thought what I was doing. How lightly I valued the obligation I was conferring on my friend Mr. Charles!"

"You didn't mean it," remarked the matter-of-fact Miss Pross, "and therefore how could you know it? Nonsense!"

"Really? Well; but don't cry," said the gentle Mr. Lorry.

"I am not crying," said Miss Pross; "*you* are."

"I, my Pross?" (By this time Mr. Lorry dared to be pleasant with her, on occasion.)

"You were just now; I saw you do it, and I don't wonder at it. Such a present of plate as you have made 'em, is enough to bring tears into any body's eyes. There's not a fork or a spoon in the collection," said Miss Pross, "that I didn't cry over, last night after the box came, till I couldn't see it."

"I am highly gratified," said Mr. Lorry, "though, upon my honor, I had no intention of rendering those trifling articles of remembrance invisible to any one. Dear me! This is an occasion that makes a man speculate on all he has lost. Dear, dear, dear! To think that there might have been a Mrs. Lorry, any time these fifty years almost!"

"Not at all!" From Miss Pross.

"You think there never might have been a Mrs. Lorry?" asked the gentleman of that name.

"Pooh!" rejoined Miss Pross; "you were a bachelor in your cradle."

"Well!" observed Mr. Lorry, beamingly adjusting his little wig, "that seems probable, tóo."

"And you were cut out for a bachelor," pursued Miss Pross, "before you were put in your cradle."

"Then, I think," said Mr. Lorry, "that I was very unhandsomely dealt with, and that I ought to have had a voice in the selection of my pattern. Enough! Now, my dear Lucie," drawing his arm soothingly round her waist, "I hear them moving in the next room, and Miss Pross and I, as two formal folks of business, are anxious not to lose the final opportunity of saying something to you that you wish to hear. You leave your good father, my dear, in hands as earnest and as loving as your own; he shall be taken every conceivable care of: during the next fortnight, while you are in Warwickshire and thereabouts, even Tellson's shall go to the wall (comparatively speaking) before him. And when, at the fortnight's end, he comes to join you and your beloved husband, on your other fortnight's trip in Wales, you shall say that we have sent him to you in the best health and in the happiest frame. Now, I hear Somebody's step coming to the door. Let me kiss my dear girl with an old-fashioned bachelor blessing, before Somebody comes to claim his own."

For a moment, he held the fair face from him to look at the well-remembered expression on the forehead, and then laid the bright golden hair against his little brown wig, with a genuine tenderness and delicacy, which, if such things be old-fashioned, were as old as Adam.

The door of the Doctor's room opened, and he came out with Charles Darnay. He was so deadly pale—which had not been the case when they went in together—that no vestige of color was to be seen in his face. But, in the composure of his manner he was unaltered, except that to the shrewd glance of Mr. Lorry it disclosed some shadowy indication that the old air of avoidance and dread had lately passed over him, like a cold wind.

He gave his arm to his daughter, and took her down-stairs to the chariot which Mr. Lorry had hired in honor of the day. The rest followed in another carriage, and soon, in a neighboring church, where no strange eyes looked on, Charles Darnay and Lucie Manette were happily married.

Besides the glancing tears that shone among the smiles of the little group when it was done, some diamonds, very bright and sparkling, glanced on the bride's hand, which were newly released from the dark obscurity of one of Mr. Lorry's pockets. They returned home to breakfast, and all went well, and in due course the golden hair that had mingled with the poor shoemaker's white locks in the Paris garret, were mingled with them again in the morning sunlight, on the threshold of the door at parting.

It was a hard parting, though it was not for long. But her father cheered her, and said at last, gently disengaging himself from her enfolding arms, "Take her, Charles! She is yours!"

And her agitated hand waved to them from a chaise window, and she was gone.

The corner being out of the way of the idle and curious, and the preparations having been very simple and few, the Doctor, Mr. Lorry, and Miss Pross, were left quite alone. It was when they turned into the welcome shade of the cool, old hall, that Mr. Lorry observed a great change to have come over the Doctor; as if the golden arm uplifted there, had struck him a poisoned blow.

He had naturally repressed much, and some revulsion might have been expected in him when the occasion for repression was gone. But, it was the old, scared, lost look that troubled Mr. Lorry; and through his absent manner of clasping his head and drearily wandering away into his own room when they got upstairs, Mr. Lorry was reminded of Defarge the wine-shop keeper, and the starlight ride.

"I think," he whispered to Miss Pross, after anxious consideration, "I think we had best not speak to him just now, or at all disturb him. I must look in at Tellson's; so I will go there at once and come back presently. Then, we will take him a ride into the country, and dine there, and all will be well."

It was easier for Mr. Lorry to look in at Tellson's than to look out of Tellson's. He was detained two hours. When he came back, he ascended the old staircase alone, having asked no question of the servant; going thus into the Doctor's rooms, he was stopped by a low sound of knocking.

"Good God!" he said, with a start. "What's that?"

Miss Pross, with a terrified face, was at his ear. "O me, O me! All is lost!" cried she, wringing her hands. "What is to be told to Ladybird? He doesn't know me, and is making shoes!"

Mr. Lorry said what he could to calm her, and went himself into the Doctor's room. The bench was turned toward the light, as it had been when he had seen the shoemaker at his work before, and his head was bent down, and he was very busy.

"Doctor Manette. My dear friend, Doctor Manette!"

The Doctor looked at him for a moment—half inquiringly, half as if he were angry at being spoken to—and bent over his work again.

He had laid aside his coat and waistcoat; his shirt was open at the throat, as it used to be when he did that work; and even the old haggard, faded surface of face had come back to him. He worked hard—impatiently—as if in some sense of having been interrupted.

Mr. Lorry glanced at the work in his hand, and observed that it was a shoe of the old size and shape. He took up another that was lying by him, and asked what it was?

"A young lady's walking shoe," he muttered, without looking up. "It ought to have been finished long ago. Let it be."

"But, Doctor Manette. Look at me!"

He obeyed, in the old mechanically submissive manner, without pausing in his work.

"You know me, my dear friend? Think again. This is not your proper occupation. Think, dear friend!"

Nothing would induce him to speak more. He looked up, for an instant at a time, when he was requested to do so; but, no persuasion would extract a word from him. He worked, and worked, and worked in silence, and words fell on him as they would have fallen on an echoeless wall, or on the air. The only ray of hope that Mr. Lorry could discover, was, that he sometimes furtively looked up without being asked. In that there seemed a faint expression of curiosity or perplexity—as though he were trying to reconcile some doubts in his mind.

Two things at once impressed themselves on Mr. Lorry, as important above all others; the first, that this must be kept secret from Lucie; the second, that it must be kept secret from all who knew him. In conjunction with Miss Pross, he took immediate steps towards the latter precaution, by giving out that the Doctor was not well, and required a few days of complete rest. In aid of the kind deception to be practised on his daughter, Mss Pross was to write, describing his having been called away professionally, and referring to an imaginary letter of two or three hurried lines in his own hand, represented to have been addressed to her by the same post.

These measures, advisable to be taken in any case, Mr. Lorry took in the hope of his coming to himself. If that should happen soon, he kept another course in reserve; which was, to have a certain opinion that he thought the best, on the Doctor's case.

In the hope of his recovery, and of resort to this third course being thereby rendered practicable, Mr. Lorry resolved to watch him attentively, with as little appearance as possible of doing so. He therefore made arrangements to absent himself from Tellson's for the first time in his life, and took his post by the window in the same room.

He was not long in discovering that it was worse than useless to speak to him, since, on being pressed, he became worried. He abandoned that attempt in the first day, and resolved merely to keep himself always before him, as a silent protest against the delusion into which he had fallen, or was falling. He remained, therefore, in his seat near the window, reading and writing, and expressing in as many pleasant and natural ways as he could think of, that it was a free place.

Doctor Manette took what was given him to eat and drink, and worked on, that first day, until it was too dark to see—worked on, half an hour after Mr. Lorry could not have seen, for his life, to read or write. When he put his tools aside as useless, until morning, Mr. Lorry rose and said:

"Will you go out?"

He looked down at the floor on either side of him in the old manner, looked up in the old manner, and repeated in the old low voice,

"Out?"

"Yes; for a walk with me. Why not?"

He made no effort to say why not, and said not a word more. But, Mr. Lorry thought he saw, as he leaned forward on his bench in the dusk, with his elbows on his knees and his head in his hands, that he was in some misty way asking himself, "Why not?" The sagacity of the man of business perceived an advantage here, and determined to hold it.

Miss Pross and he divided the night into two watches, and observed him at intervals from the adjoining room. He paced up and down for a long time before he lay down; but, when he did finally lay himself down, he fell asleep. In the morning, he was up betimes, and went straight to his bench and to work.

On the second day, Mr. Lorry saluted him cheerfully by his name, and spoke to him on topics that had been of late familiar to them. He returned no reply, but it was evident that he heard what was said, and that he thought about it, however confusedly. This encouraged Mr. Lorry to have Miss Pross in with her work, several times during the day; at those times, they quietly spoke of Lucie, and of her father then present, precisely in the usual manner, and as if there were nothing amiss. This was done without any demonstrative accompaniment, not long enough or often enough to harass him; and it lightened Mr. Lorry's friendly heart to believe that he looked up oftener, and that he appeared to be stirred by some perception of inconsistencies surrounding him.

When it fell dark again, Mr. Lorry asked him as before:

"Dear Doctor, will you go out?"

As before, he repeated, "Out?"

"Yes; for a walk with me. Why not?"

This time, Mr. Lorry feigned to go out when he could extract no answer from him, and, after remaining absent for an hour, returned. In the meanwhile, the Doctor had removed to the seat in the window, and had sat there looking down at the plane-tree; but, on Mr. Lorry's return, he slipped away to his bench.

The time went very slowly on, and Mr. Lorry's hope darkened, and his heart grew heavier again, and grew yet heavier and heavier every day. The third day came and went, the fourth, the fifth. Five days, six days, seven days, eight days, nine days.

With a hope ever darkening, and with a heart always growing heavier and heavier, Mr. Lorry passed through this anxious time. The secret was well kept, and Lucie was unconscious and happy; but he could not fail to observe that the shoemaker, whose hand had been a little out at first, was growing dreadfully skillful, and that he had never been so intent on his work, and that his hands had never been so nimble and expert, as in the dusk of the ninth evening.

Chapter XIX

AN OPINION

WORN out by anxious watching, Mr. Lorry fell asleep at his post. On the tenth morning of his suspense, he was startled by the shining of the sun into the room where a heavy slumber had overtaken him when it was dark night.

He rubbed his eyes and roused himself; but he doubted, when he had done so, whether he was not still asleep. For, going to the door of the Doctor's room and looking in, he perceived that the shoemaker's bench and tools were put aside again, and that the Doctor himself sat reading at the window. He was in his usual morning dress, and his face (which Mr. Lorry could distinctly see), though still very pale, was calmly studious and attentive.

Even when he had satisfied himself that he was awake, Mr. Lorry felt giddily uncertain for some few moments whether the late shoemaking might not be a disturbed dream of his own; for, did not his eyes show him his friend before him in his accustomed clothing and aspect, and employed as usual; and was there any sign within their range, that the change of which he had so strong an impression had actually happened?

It was but the inquiry of his first confusion and astonishment, the answer being obvious. If the impression were not produced by a real corresponding, and sufficient cause, how came he, Jarvis Lorry, there? How came he to have fallen asleep, in his clothes, on the sofa in Doctor Manette's consulting-room, and to be debating these points outside the Doctor's bedroom door in the early morning?

Within a few minutes, Miss Pross stood whispering at his side. If he had had any particle of doubt left, her talk would of necessity have resolved it; but he was by that time clear-headed, and had none. He advised that they should let the time go by until the regular breakfast-hour, and should then meet the Doctor as if nothing unusual had occurred. If he appeared to be in his customary state of mind, Mr. Lorry would then cautiously proceed to seek direction and guidance from the opinion he had been, in his anxiety, so anxious to obtain.

Miss Pross submitting herself to his judgment, the scheme was worked out with care. Having abundance of time for his usual methodical toilette, Mr. Lorry presented himself at the breakfast-hour in his usual white linen and with his usual neat leg. The Doctor was summoned in the usual way, and came to breakfast.

So far as it was possible to comprehend him without overstepping those delicate and gradual approaches which Mr. Lorry felt to be the only safe advance, he at first supposed that his daughter's marriage had taken place yesterday. An incidental allusion, purposely thrown out, to the day of the week, and the day of the month, set him thinking and counting, and evidently made him uneasy. In all other respects, however, he was so composedly himself, that Mr. Lorry determined to have the aid he sought. And that aid was his own.

Therefore, when the breakfast was done and cleared away, and he and the Doctor were left together, Mr. Lorry said, feelingly:

"My dear Manette, I am anxious to have your opinion, in confidence, on a very curious case in which I am deeply interested; that is to say, it is very curious to me; perhaps, to your better information it may be less so."

Glancing at his hands, which were discoloured by his late work, the Doctor looked troubled, and listened attentively. He had already glanced at his hands more than once.

"Doctor Manette," said Mr. Lorry, touching him affectionately on the arm, "the case is the case of a particularly dear friend of mine. Pray give your mind to it, and advise me well for his sake—and above all, for his daughter's—his daughter's, my dear Manette."

"If I understand," said the Doctor, in a subdued tone, "some mental shock——?"

"Yes!"

"Be explicit," said the Doctor. "Spare no detail."

Mr. Lorry saw that they understood one another, and proceeded.

"My dear Manette, it is the case of an old and a prolonged shock, of great acuteness and severity, to the affections, the feelings, the—the—as you express it—the mind. The mind. It is the case of a shock under which the sufferer was borne down, one cannot say for how long, because I believe he cannot calculate the time himself, and there are no other means of getting at it. It is the case of a shock from which the sufferer recovered, by a process that he cannot trace himself—as I once heard him publicly relate in a striking manner. It is the case of a shock from which he has recovered, so completely, as to be a highly intelligent man, capable of close application of mind, and great exertion of body, and of constantly making fresh additions to his stock of knowledge, which was already very large. But, unfortunately, there has been," he paused, and took a deep breath—"a slight relapse."

The Doctor, in a low voice, asked, "Of how long duration?"

"Nine days and nights."

"How did it show itself? I infer," glancing at his hands again, "in the resumption of some old pursuit connected with the shock?"

"That is the fact."

"Now, did you ever see him," asked the Doctor, distinctly and collectedly, though in the same low voice, "engaged in that pursuit originally?"

"Once."

"And when the relapse fell on him, was he in most respects—or in all respects—as he was then?"

"I think in all respects."

"You spoke of his daughter. Does his daughter know of the relapse?"

"No. It has been kept from her, and I hope will always be kept from her. It is known only to myself, and to one other who may be trusted."

The Doctor grasped his hand, and murmured, "That was very kind. That was very thoughtful!" Mr. Lorry grasped his hand in return, and neither of the two spoke for a little while.

"Now, my dear Manette," said Mr. Lorry, at length, in his most considerate and most affectionate way, "I am a mere man of business, and unfit to cope with such intricate and difficult matters. I do not possess the kind of information necessary; I do not possess the kind of intelligence; I want guiding. There is no man in this world on whom I could so rely for right guidance, as on you. Tell me, how does this relapse come about? Is there danger of another? Could a repetition of it be prevented? How should a repetition of it be treated? How does it come about at all? What can I do for my friend? No man ever can have been more desirous in his heart to serve a friend, than I am to serve mine, if I knew how. But I don't know how to originate in such a case. If your sagacity, knowledge, and experience could put me on the right track, I might be able to do so much; unenlightened and undirected, I can do so little. Pray discuss it with me; pray enable me to see it a little more clearly, and teach me how to be a little more useful."

Doctor Manette sat meditating after these earnest words were spoken, and Mr. Lorry did not press him.

"I think it probable," said the Doctor, breaking silence with an effort, "that the relapse you have described, my dear friend, was not quite unforeseen by its subject."

"Was it dreaded by him?" Mr. Lorry ventured to ask.

"Very much." He said it with an involuntary shudder.

"You have no idea how such an apprehension weighs on the sufferer's mind, and how difficult—how almost impossible—it is, for him to force himself to utter a word upon the topic that oppresses him."

"Would he," asked Mr. Lorry, "be sensibly relieved if he could prevail upon himself to impart that secret brooding to any one, when it is on him?"

"I think so. But it is, as I have told you, next to impossible. I even believe it—in some cases—to be quite impossible."

"Now," said Mr. Lorry, gently laying his hand on the Doctor's arm again, after a short silence on both sides, "to what would you refer this attack?"

"I believe," returned Doctor Manette, "that there had been a strong and extraordinary revival of the train of thought and remembrance that was the first cause of the malady. Some intense associations of a most distressing nature were vividly recalled, I think. It is probable that there had long been a dread lurking in his mind, that those associations would be recalled—say, under certain circumstances—say, on a particular occasion. He tried to prepare himself in vain; perhaps the effort to prepare himself made him less able to bear it."

"Would e remember what took place in the relapse?" asked Mr. Lorry, with natural hesitation.

The Doctor looked desolately round the room, shook his head, and answered, in a low voice, "Not at all."

"Now, as to the future," hinted Mr. Lorry.

"As to the future," said the Doctor, recovering firmness, "I should have great hope. As it pleased heaven in its mercy to restore him so soon, I should have great hope. He, yielding under the pressure of a complicated something, long dreaded and long vaguely foreseen and contended against, and recovering after the cloud had burst and passed, I should hope that the worst was over."

"Well, well! That's good comfort. I am thankful!" said Mr. Lorry.

"I am thankful!" repeated the Doctor, bending his head with reverence.

"There are two other points," said Mr. Lorry, "on which I am anxious to be instructed. I may go on?"

"You cannot do your friend a better service." The Doctor gave him his hand.

"To the first, then. He is of a studious habit, and unusually energetic; he applies himself with great ardor to the acquisition of professional knowledge, to the conducting of experiments, to many things. Now, does he do too much?"

"I think not. It may be the character of his mind, to be always in singular need of occupation. That may be, in part, natural to it; in part, the result of affliction. The less it was occupied with healthy things, the more it would be in danger of turning in the unhealthy direction. He may have observed himself, and made the discovery."

"You are sure that he is not under too great a strain?"

"I think I am quite sure of it."

"My dear Manette, if he were overworked now——"

"My dear Lorry, I doubt if that could easily be. There has been a violent stress in one direction, and it needs a counter weight."

"Excuse me, as a persistent man of business. Assuming for a moment that he *was* overworked; it would show itself in some renewal of this disorder?"

"I do not think so. I do not think," said Doctor Manette, with the firmness of self-conviction, "that any thing but the one train of association would renew it. I think that, henceforth, nothing but some extraordinary jarring of that chord could renew it. After what has happened, and after his recovery, I find it difficult to imagine any such violent sounding of that string again. I trust, and I almost believe, that the circumstances likely to renew it are exhausted."

He spoke with the diffidence of a man who knew how slight a thing would overset the delicate organization of the mind, and yet with the confidence of a man who had slowly won his assurance out of personal endurance and distress. It was not for his friend to abate that confidence. He professed himself more relieved and encouraged than he really was, and approached his second and last point. He felt it to be the most difficult of all; but, remembering his old Sunday-morning conversation with Miss Pross, and remembering what he had seen in the last nine days, he knew that he must face it.

"The occupation resumed under the influence of this passing affliction so happily recovered from," said Mr. Lorry, clearing his throat, "we will call—Blacksmith's work, Blacksmith's work. We will say, to put a case and for the sake of illustration, that he had been used, in his bad time, to work at a little forge. We will say that he was unexpectedly found at his forge again. Is it not a pity that he should keep it by him?"

The Doctor shaded his forehead with his hand, and beat his foot nervously on the ground.

"He has always kept it by him," said Mr. Lorry, with an anxious look at his friend. "Now, would it not be better that he should let it go?"

Still, the Doctor, with shaded forehead, beat his foot nervously on the ground.

"You do not find it easy to advise me?" said Mr. Lorry. "I quite understand it to be a nice question. And yet I think——" And there he shook his head, and stopped.

"You see," said Doctor Manette, turning to him after an uneasy pause, "it is very hard to explain, consistently, the innermost workings of this poor man's mind. He once yearned so frightfully for that occupation, and it was so welcome when it came; no doubt it relieved his pain so much, by substituting the perplexity of the fingers for the perpleaxity of the brain, and by substituting, as he became more practised, the ingenuity of the hands for the ingenuity of the mental torture; that he has never been able to bear the thought of putting it quite out of his reach. Even now, when, I believe, he is more hopeful of himself than he has ever been, and even speaks of himself with a kind of confidence, the idea that he might need that old employment, and not find it, gives him a sudden sense of terror, like that which one may fancy strikes to the heart of a lost child."

He looked like his illustration, as he raised his eyes to Mr. Lorry's face.

"But may not—mind! I ask for information, as a plodding man of business who only deals with such material objects as guineas, shillings, and bank-notes—may not the retention of the thing involve the retention of the idea? If the thing were gone, my dear Manette, might not the fear go with it? In short, is it not a concession to the misgiving, to keep the forge?"

There was another silence.

"You see, too," said the Doctor, tremulously, "it is such an old companion."

"I would not keep it," said Mr. Lorry, shaking his head; for he gained in firmness as he saw the Doctor disquieted. "I would recommend him to sacrifice it. I only want your authority. I am sure it does no good.

Come! Give me your authority, like a dear good man. For his daughter's sake, my dear Manette!"

Very strange to see what a struggle there was within him!

"In her name, then, let it be done; I sanction it. But, I would not take it away while he was present. Let it be removed when he is not there; let him miss his old companion after an absence."

Mr. Lorry readily engaged for that, and the conference was ended. They passed the day in the country, and the Doctor was quite restored. On the three following days, he remained perfectly well, and on the fourteenth day, he went away to join Lucie and her husband. The precaution that had been taken to account for his silence, Mr. Lorry had previously explained to him, and he had written to Lucie in accordance with it, and she had no suspicions.

On the night of the day on which he had left the house, Mr. Lorry went into his room with a chopper, saw, chisel, and hammer, attended by Miss Pross carrying a light. There, with closed doors, and in a mysterious and guilty manner, Mr. Lorry hacked the shoemaker's bench to pieces, while Miss Pross held the candle as if she were assisting at a murder—for which, indeed, in her grimness, she was no unsuitable figure. The burning of the body (previously reduced to pieces convenient for the purpose), was commenced without delay in the kitchen fire; and the tools, shoes, and leather, were buried in the garden. So wicked do destruction and secrecy appear to honest minds, that Mr. Lorry and Miss Pross, while engaged in the commission of their deed and in the removal of its traces, almost felt, and almost looked, like accomplices in a horrible crime.

Chapter XX

A PLEA

WHEN the newly-married pair came home, the first person who appeared, to offer his congratulations, was Sydney Carton. They had not been at home many hours, when he presented himself. He was not improved in habits, or in looks, or in manner; but there was a certain rugged air of fidelity about him, which was new to the observation of Charles Darnay.

He watched his opportunity of taking Darnay aside into a window, and of speaking to him when no one overheard.

"Mr. Darnay," said Carton, "I wish we might be friends."

"We are already friends, I hope."

"You are good enough to say so, as a fashion of speech; but, I don't mean any fashion of speech. Indeed, when I say I wish we might be friends, I scarcely mean quite that, either."

Charles Darnay—as was natural—asked him, in all good-humor and good-fellowship, what he did mean?

"Upon my life," said Carton, smiling, "I find that easier to comprehend in my own mind, than to convey to yours. However, let me try. You remember a certain famous occasion when I was more drunk than—than usual?"

"I remember a certain famous occasion when you forced me to confess that you had been drinking."

"I remember it too. The curse of those occasions is heavy upon me, for I always remember them. I hope it may be taken into account one day, when all days are at an end for me! Don't be alarmed; I am not going to preach."

"I am not at all alarmed. Earnestness in you is anything but alarming to me."

"Ah!" said Carton, with a careless wave of his hand, as if he waved that away. "On the drunken occasion in question (one of a large number, as you know), I was insufferable about liking you, and not liking you. I wish you would forget it."

"I forgot it long ago."

"Fashion of speech again! But, Mr. Darnay, oblivion is not so easy to me, as you represent it to be to you. I have by no means forgotten it, and a light answer does not help me to forget it."

"If it was a light answer," returned Darnay, "I beg your forgiveness for it. I had no other object than to turn a slight thing, which, to my surprise, seems to trouble you too much, aside. I declare to you on the faith of a gentleman, that I have long dismissed it from my mind. Good Heaven, what was there to dismiss! Have I had nothing more important to remember, in the great service you rendered me that day?"

"As to the great service," said Carton, "I am bound to avow to you, when you speak of it in that way, that it was mere professional claptrap. I don't know that I cared what became of you, when I rendered it. Mind! I say when I rendered it; I am speaking of the past."

"You make light of the obligation," returned Darnay, "but I will not quarrel with *your* light answer."

"Genuine truth, Mr. Darnay, trust me! I have gone aside from my purpose; I was speaking about our being friends. Now, you know me; you know I am incapable of all the higher and better flights of men. If you doubt it, ask Stryver, and he'll tell you so."

"I prefer to form my own opinion, without the aid of his."

"Well! At any rate you know me as a dissolute dog, who has never done any good, and never will."

"I don't know that you 'never will.'"

"But I do, and you must take my word for it. Well! If you could endure to have such a worthless fellow, and a fellow of such indifferent reputation, coming and going at odd times, I should ask that I might be permitted to come and go as a privileged person here; that I might be regarded as a useless (and I would add, if it were not for the resemblance I detected between you and me), an unornamental, piece of furniture, tolerated for its old service and taken no notice of. I doubt if I should abuse the permission. It is a hundred to one if I should avail myself of it four times in a year. It would satisfy me, I dare say, to know that I had it."

"Will you try?"

"That is another way of saying that I am placed on the footing I have indicated. I thank you, Darnay. I may use that freedom with your name?"

"I think so, Carton, by this time."

They shook hands upon it, and Sydney turned away. Within a minute afterwards, he was, to all outward appearance, as unsubstantial as ever.

When he was gone, and in the course of an evening passed with Miss Pross, the Doctor, and Mr. Lorry, Charles Darnay made some mention of this conversation in general terms, and spoke of Sydney Carton as a problem of carelessness and recklessness. He spoke of him, in short, not bitterly or meaning to bear hard upon him, but as anybody might who saw him as he showed himself.

He had no idea that this could dwell in the thoughts of his fair young wife; but, when he afterwards joined her in their own room, he found her waiting for him with the old pretty lifting of the forehead strongly marked.

"We are thoughtful to-night!" said Darnay, drawing his arm about her.

"Yes, dearest Charles," with her hand on his breast, and the inquiring and attentive expression fixed upon him; "we are rather thoughtful to-night, for we have something on our mind to-night."

"What is it, my Lucie?"

"Will you promise not to press one question on me, if I beg you not to ask it?"

"Will I promise? What will I not promise to my Love?"

What, indeed, with his hand putting aside the golden hair from the cheek, and his other hand against the heart that beat for him!

"I think, Charles, poor Mr. Carton deserves more consideration and respect than you expressed for him to-night."

"Indeed, my own? Why so?"

"That is what you are not to ask me! But I think—I know—he does."

"If you know it, it is enough. What would you have me do, my Life?"

"I would ask you, dearest, to be very generous with him always, and very lenient on his faults, when he is not by. I would ask you to believe that he has a heart he very, very seldom reveals, and that there are deep wounds in it. My dear, I have seen it bleeding."

"It is a painful reflection to me," said Charles Darnay, quite astounded, "that I should have done him any wrong. I never thought this of him."

"My husband, it is so. I fear he is not to be reclaimed; there is scarcely a hope that anything in his character or fortunes is reparable now. But, I am sure that he is capable of good things, gentle things, even magnanimous things."

She looked so beautiful in the purity of her faith in this lost man, that her husband could have looked at her as she was for hours.

"And, O my dearest Love!" she urged, clinging nearer to him, laying her head upon his breast, and raising her eyes to his, "remember how strong we are in our happiness, and how weak he is in his misery!"

The supplication touched him home. "I will always remember it, dear Heart! I will remember it as long as I live."

He bent over the golden head, and put the rosy lips to his, and folded her in his arms. If one forlorn wanderer then pacing the dark streets, could have heard her innocent disclosure, and could have seen the drops of pity kissed away by her husband from the soft, blue eyes so loving of that husband, he might have cried to the night—and the words would not have parted from his lips for the first time—

"God bless her for her sweet compassion!"

Chapter XXI

ECHOING FOOTSTEPS

A WONDERFUL corner for echoes, it has been remarked, that corner where the Doctor lived. Ever busily winding the golden thread which bound her husband, and her father, and herself, and her old directress and companion, in a life of quiet bliss, Lucie sat in the still house in the tranquilly resounding corner, listening to the echoing footsteps of years.

At first, there were times, though she was a perfectly happy young wife, when her work would slowly fall from her hands, and her eyes would be dimmed. For, there was something coming in the echoes, something light, afar off, and scarcely audible yet, that stirred her heart too much. Fluttering hopes and doubts—hopes, of a love as yet unknown to her; doubts of her remaining upon earth, to enjoy that new delight—divided her breast. Among the echoes then, there would arise the sound of footsteps at her own early grave; and thoughts of the husband who would be left so desolate, and who would mourn for her so much, swelled to her eyes and broke like waves.

That time passed, and her little Lucie lay on her bosom. Then, among the advancing echoes, there was the tread of her tiny feet and the sound of her prattling words. Let greater echoes resound as they would, the young mother at the cradle side could always hear those coming. They came, and the shady house was sunny with a child's laugh, and the Divine friend of children, to whom in her trouble she had confided hers, seemed to take her child in His arms, as He took the child of old, and made it a sacred joy to her.

Ever busily winding the golden thread that bound them all together, weaving the service of her happy influence through the tissue of all their lives, and making it predominate nowhere, Lucie heard in the echoes of years none but friendly and soothing sounds. Her husband's step was strong and prosperous among them; her father's firm and equal. Lo, Miss Pross, in harness of string, awakening the echoes, as an unruly charger whip-corrected, snorting and pawing the earth under the plane-tree in the garden!

Even when there were sounds of sorrow among the rest, they were not harsh nor cruel. Even when golden hair, like her own, lay in a halo on a pillow round the worn face of a little boy, and he said, with a radiant smile, "Dear papa and mamma, I am very sorry to leave you both, and to leave my pretty sister; but I am called, and I must go!" those were not tears all of agony that wetted his young mother's cheek, as the spirit departed from her embrace that had been entrusted to it. Suffer them and forbid them not. They see my Father's face. 0 Father, blessed words!

Thus, the rustling of an Angel's wings got blended with the other echoes, and they were not wholly of earth, but had in them that breath of Heaven. Sighs of the winds that blew over a little garden-tomb were mingled with them also, and both were audible to Lucie, in a hushed murmur—like the breathing of a summer sea asleep upon a sandy shore—as the little Lucie, comically studious at the task of the morning, or dressing a doll at her mother's footstool, chattered in the tongues of the Two Cities that were blended in her life.

The echoes rarely answered to the actual tread of Sydney Carton. Some half-dozen times a year, at most, he claimed his privilege of coming in uninvited, and would sit among them through the evening as he had once done often. He never came there heated with wine. And one other thing regarding him was whispered in the echoes, which has been whispered by all true echoes for ages and ages.

No man ever really loved a woman, lost her, and knew her with a blameless though an unchanged mind, when she was a wife and a mother, but her children had a strange sympathy with him—an instinctive delicacy of pity for him. What fine hidden sensibilities are touched in such a case, no echoes tell; but, it is so, and it was so here. Carton was the first stranger to whom little Lucie held out her chubby arms and he kept his place with her as she grew. The little boy had spoken of him, almost at the last. "Poor Carton! Kiss him for me!"

Mr. Stryver shouldered his way through the law, like some great engine forcing itself through turbid waters, and dragged his useful friend in his wake, like a boat towed astern. As the boat so favored is usually in a rough plight and mostly under water, so, Sydney had a swamped life of it. But, easy and strong custom, unhappily so much easier and stronger in him than any stimulating sense of desert or disgrace, made it the life he was to lead; and he no more thought of emerging from his state of lion's jackal, than any real jackal may be supposed to think of rising to be a lion. Stryver was rich; had married a florid widow with property and three boys, who had nothing particularly shining about them but the straight hair of their dumpling heads.

These three young gentlemen, Mr. Stryver, exuding patronage of the most offensive quality from every pore, had walked before him like three sheep to the quiet corner in Soho, and had offered as pupils to Lucie's husband: delicately saying, "Halloa! here are three lumps of bread-and-cheese towards your matrimonial picnic, Darnay!" The polite rejection of the three lumps of bread-and-cheese had quite bloated Mr. Stryver with indignation, which he afterward turned to account in the training of the young gentlemen, by directing them to beware of the pride of beggars, like that tutor-fellow. He was also in the habit of declaiming to Mrs. Stryver, over his full-bodied wine, on the arts Mrs. Darnay had once put in practice to "catch" him, and on the diamond-cut-diamond arts in himself, madam, which had rendered him "not to be caught." Some of his King's Bench familiars, who were occasionally parties to the full-bodied wine and the lie, excused him for the latter by saying that he had told it so often, that he believed it himself—which is surely such an incorrigible aggravation of an originally bad offence, as to justify any such offender's being carried off to some suitably retired spot, and there hanged out of the way.

These were among the echoes to which Lucie, sometimes pensive, sometimes amused and laughing, listened in the echoing corner, until her little daughter was six years old. How near to her heart, the echoes of her child's tread came, and those of her own dear father's, always active and self-possessed, and those of her dear husband's, need not be told. Nor, how the slightest echo of their united home, directed by herself with such a wise and elegant thrift, that it was more abundant than any waste, was music to her. Nor, how there were echoes all about her, sweet in her ears, of the many times her father had told her that he found her more devoted to him married (if that could be) than single, and of the many times her husband had said to her that no cares and duties seemed to divide her love for him or her help to him, and asked her, "What is the magic secret, my darling, of your being everything to all of us, as if there were only one of us, yet never seeming to be hurried, or to have too much to do?"

But, there were other echoes, from a distance, that rumbled menacingly in the corner all through this space of time. And it was now, about little Lucie's sixth birthday, that they began to have an awful sound, as of a great storm in France with a dreadful sea rising.

On a night in mid-July, one thousand seven hundred and eighty-nine, Mr. Lorry came in late, from Tellson's, and sat himself down by Lucie and her husband in the dark window. It was a hot, wild night, and they were all three reminded of the old Sunday night when they had looked at the lighttning from the same place.

"I began to think," said Mr. Lorry, pushing his brown wig back, "that I should have to pass the night at Tellson's. We have been so full of business all day, that we have not known what to do first, or which way to turn. There is such an uneasiness in Paris, that we have actually a run of confidence upon us! Our customers over there seem not to be able to confide their property to us fast enough. There is positively a mania among some of them for sending it to England."

"That has a bad look," said Darnay.

"A bad look, you say, my dear Darnay? Yes, but we don't know what reason there is in it. People are so unreasonable! Some of us at Tellson's are getting old, and we really can't be troubled out of the ordinary course without due occasion."

"Still," said Darnay, "you know how gloomy and threatening the sky is."

"I know that, to be sure," assented Mr. Lorry, trying to persuade himself that his sweet temper was soured, and that he grumbled, "but I am determined to be peevish after my long day's botheration. Where is Manette?"

"Here he is," said the Doctor, entering the dark room at the moment.

"I am quite glad you are at home; for these hurries and foreboding, by which I have been surrounded all day long, have made me nervous without reason. You are not going out, I hope?"

"No; I am going to play backgammon with you, if you like," said the Doctor.

"I don't think I do like, if I may speak my mind. I am not fit to be pitted against you to-night. Is the tea-board still there, Lucie? I can't see."

"Of course, it has been kept for you."

"Thank ye, my dear. The precious child is safe in bed?"

"And sleeping soundly."

"That's right; all safe and well! I don't know why anything should be otherwise than safe and well here, thank God; but I have been so put out all day, and I am not as young as I was! My tea, my dear? Thank ye. Now, come and take your place in the circle, and let us sit quiet, and hear the echoes about which you have your theory."

"Not a theory; it was a fancy."

"A fancy, then, my wise pet," said Mr. Lorry, patting her hand. "They are very numerous and very loud, though, are they not? Only hear them!"

Headlong, mad, and dangerous footsteps to force their way into anybody's life, footsteps not easily made clean again if once stained red, the footsteps raging in Saint Antoine afar off, as the little circle sat in the dark London window.

Saint Antoine had been, that morning, a vast dusky mass of scarecrows heaving to and fro, with frequent gleams of light above the billowy heads, where steel blades and bayonets shone in the sun. A tremendous roar arose from the throat of Saint Antoine, and a forest of naked arms struggled in the air like shrivelled branches of trees in a winter wind: all the fingers convulsively clutching at every weapon or semblance of a weapon that was thrown up from the depths below, no matter how far off.

Who gave them out, whence they last came, where they began, through what agency they crookedly quivered and jerked, scores at a time, over the heads of the crowd, like a kind of lightning, no eye in the throng could have told; but, muskets were being distributed—so were cartridges, powder, and ball, bars of iron and wood, knives, axes, pikes, every weapon that distracted ingenuity could discover or devise. People who could lay hold of nothing else, set themselves with bleeding hands to force stones and bricks out of their places in walls. Every pulse and heart in Saint Antoine was on high fever strain and at high fever heat. Every living creature there, held life as of no account, and was demented with a passionate readiness to sacrifice it.

As a whirlpool of boiling waters has a centre point, so, all this raging circled round Defarge's wine-shop, and every human drop in the caldron had a tendency to be sucked toward the vortex where Defarge himself, already begrimed with gunpowder and sweat, issued orders, issued arms, thrust this man back, dragged this man forward, disarmed one to arm another, labored and strove in the thickest of the uproar.

"Keep near to me, Jacques Three," cried Defarge; "and do you, Jacques One and Two, separate and put yourselves at the head of as many of these patriots as you can. Where is my wife?"

"Eh, well! Here you see me!" said madame, composed as ever, but not knitting to-day. Madame's resolute right hand was occupied with an axe, in place of the usual softer implements, and in her girdle were a pistol and a cruel knife.

"Where do you go, my wife?"

"I go," said madame, "with you at present. You shall see me at the head of women, by-and-by."

"Come, then!" cried Defarge, in a resounding voice. "Patriots and friends, we are ready! The Bastille!"

With a roar that sounded as if all the breath in France had been shaped into the detested word, the living sea rose, wave on wave, depth on depth, and overflowed the city to that point. Alarm bells ringing, drums beating, the sea raging and thundering on its new beach, the attack begun.

Deep ditches, double drawbridge, massive stone walls, eight great towers, cannon, muskets, fire and smoke. Through the fire and through the smoke—in the fire and in the smoke, for the sea cast him up against a cannon, and on the instant he became a cannonier—Defarge of the wine-shop worked like a manful soldier, Two fierce hours.

Deep ditch, single drawbridge, massive stone walls, eight great towers, cannon, muskets, fire and smoke. One drawbridge down! "Work, comrades all, work! Work, Jacques One, Jacques Two, Jacques One Thousand, Jacques Two Thousand, Jacques Five-and-Twenty Thousand; in the name of all the Angels or the Devils—which you prefer—work!" Thus Defarge of the wine-shop, still at his gun, which had long grown hot.

"To me, women!" cried madame his wife. "What! We can kill as well as the men when the place is taken!" And to her, with a shrill, thirsty, cry, trooping women variously armed, but all armed alike in hunger and revenge.

Cannon, muskets, fire, and smoke; but, still the deep ditch, the single drawbridge, the massive stone walls, and the eight great towers. Slight displacements of the raging sea, made by the falling wounded. Flashing weapons, blazing torches, smoking wagon-loads of wet straw, hard work at neighboring barricades, in all directions, shrieks, volleys, execrations, bravery without stint, boom smash and rattle, and the furious sounding of the living sea; but, still the deep ditch, and the single drawbridge, and the massive stone walls, and the eight great towers, and still Defarge of the wine-shop at his gun, grown doubly hot by the service of Four fierce hours.

A white flag from within the fortress, and a parley—this dimly perceptible through the raging storm, nothing audible in it—suddenly the sea rose immeasurably wider and higher, and swept Defarge of the wine-shop over the lowered drawbridge, past the massive stone outer walls, in among the eight great towers surrendered!

So resistless was the force of the ocean bearing him on, that even to draw his breath or turn his head was as impracticable as if he had been struggling in the surf at the South Sea, until he was landed in the outer court-yard of the Bastille. There, against an angle of a wall, he made a struggle to look about him. Jacques Three was nearly at his side; Madame Defarge, still heading some of her women, was visible in the inner distance, and her knife was in her hand. Everywhere was tumult, exultation, deafening and maniacal bewilderment, astounding noise, yet furious dumb-show.

"The Prisoners!"

"The Records!"

"The secret cells!"

"The instruments of torture!"

"The Prisoners!"

Of all these cries, and ten thousand incoherencies, "The Prisoners!" was the cry most taken up by the sea that rushed in, as if there were an eternity of people, as well as of time and space. When the foremost billows rolled past, bearing the prison officers with them, and threatening them all with instant death if any secret nook remained undisclosed, Defarge laid his strong hand on the breast of one of these men—a man with a gray head who had a lighted torch in his hand—separated him from the rest, and got him between himself and the wall.

"Show me the North Tower!" said Defarge. "Quick!"

"I will, faithfully," replied the man, "if you will come with me. But there is no one there."

"What is the meaning of One Hundred and Five, North Tower?" asked Defarge. "Quick!"

"The meaning, monsieur?"

"Does it mean a captive, or a place of captivity? Or do you mean that I shall strike you dead?"

"Kill him!" croaked Jacques Three, who had come close up.

"Monsieur, it is a cell."

"Show it me!"

"Pass this way, then."

Jacques Three, with his usual craving on him, and evidently disappointed by the dialogue taking a turn that did not seem to promise bloodshed, held by Defarge's arm as he held by the turnkey's. Their three heads had been close together during this brief discourse, and it had been as much as they could do to hear one another, even then: so tremendous was the noise of the living ocean, in its irruption into the Fortress, and its inundation of the courts and passages and staircases. All around outside, too, it beat the walls with a deep, hoarse roar, from which, occasionally, some partial shouts of tumult broke and leaped into the air like spray.

Through gloomy vaults where the light of day had never shone, past hideous doors of dark dens and cages, down cavernous flights of steps, and again up steep rugged ascents of stone and brick, more like dry waterfalls than staircases, Defarge, the turnkey, and Jacques Three, linked hand and arm, went, with all the speed they could make. Here and there, especially at first, the innudation started on them and swept by; but, when they had done descending, and were winding and climbing up a tower, they were alone. Hemmed in here by the massive thickness of walls and arches, the storm within the fortress and without was only audible to them in a dull, subdued way, as if the noise out of which they had come had almost destroyed their sense of hearing.

The turnkey stopped at a low door, put a key in a clashing lock, swung the door slowly open, and said, as they all bent their heads and passed in:

"One Hundred and Five, North Tower!"

There was a small, heavily-grated, unglazed window high in the wall, with a stone screen before it, so that the sky could be only seen by stooping low and looking up. There was a small chimney, heavily barred across, a few feet within. There was a heap of old feathery wood ashes on the hearth. There were a stool, and table, and a straw bed. There were the four blackened walls, and a rusted iron ring in one of them.

"Pass that torch slowly along these walls, that I may see them," said Defarge to the Turnkey.

The man obeyed, and Defarge followed the light closely with his eyes.

"Stop! Look here, Jacques!"

"A. M. !" croaked Jacques Three, as he read greedily.

"Alexander Manette," said Defarge in his ear, following the letters with his swart fore-finger, deeply engrained with gunpowder. "And here he wrote 'a poor physician.' And it was he, without doubt, who scratched a calendar on this stone. What is that in your hand? A crowbar? Give it me!"

He had still the linstock of his gun in his own hand. He made a sudden exchange of the two instruments, and turning on the worm-eaten stool and table, beat them to pieces in a few blows.

"Hold the light higher!" he said, wrathfully, to the turnkey. "Look among those fragments with care, Jacques. And see! Here is my knife," throwing it to him; "rip open that bed, and search the straw. Hold the light higher, you!"

With a menacing look at the turnkey he crawled upon the hearth, and, peering up the chimney, struck and prised at its sides with the crowbar, and worked at the iron grating across it. In a few minutes, some mortar and dust came dropping down, which he averted his face to avoid; and in it, and in the old wood-ashes, and in a crevice in the chimney into which his weapon had slipped or wrought itself, he groped with a cautious touch.

"Nothing in the wood, and nothing in the straw, Jacques?"

"Nothing."

"Let us collect them together, in the middle of the cell. So! Light them, you!"

The turnkey fired the little pile, which blazed high and hot. Stooping again to come out at the low-arched door, they left it burning, and retraced their way to the court-yard; seeming to recover their sense of hearing as they came down, until they were in the raging flood once more.

They found it surging and tossing, in quest of Defarge himself. Saint Antoine was clamorous to have its wine-shop-keeper foremost in the guard upon the governor who had defended the Bastille and shot the people. Otherwise, the governor would not be marched to the Hotel de Ville for judgment. Otherwise, the governor would escape, and the people's blood (suddenly of some value, after many years of worthlessness) be unavenged.

In the howling universe of passion and contention that seemed to encompass this grim old officer, conspicuous in his gray coat and red decoration, there was but one quite steady figure, and that was a woman's. "See, there is my husband!" she cried, pointing him out. "See Defarge!" She stood immovable close to the grim old officer, and remained immovable close to him; remained immovable close to him through the streets, as

Defarge and the rest bore him along; remained immovable close to him when he got near his destination, and began to be struck at from behind; remained immovable close to him when the long-gathering rain of stabs and blows fell heavy; was so close to him when he dropped dead under it, that, suddenly animated, she put her foot upon his neck, and with her cruel knife—long ready—hewed off his head.

The hour was come, when Saint Antoine was to execute his horrible idea of hoisting up men for lamps to show what he could be and do. Saint Antoine's blood was up, and the blood of tyranny and domination by the iron hand was down—down on the steps of the Hotel de Ville where the governor's body lay—down on the sole of the shoe of Madame Defarge where she had trodden on the body to steady it for mutilation. "Lower the lamp yonder!" cried Saint Antoine, after glaring round for a new means of death; "here is one of his soldiers to be left on guard!" The swinging sentinel was posted, and the sea rushed on.

The sea of black and threatening waters, and of destructive upheaving of wave against wave, whose depths were yet unfathomed and whose forces were yet unknown. The remorseless sea of turbulently swaying shapes, voices of vengeance, and faces hardened in the furnaces of suffering until the touch of pity could make no mark on them.

But, in the ocean of faces, where every fierce and furious expression was in vivid life, there were two groups of faces—each seven in number—so fixedly contrasting with the rest, that never did sea roll which bore more memorable wrecks with it. Seven faces of prisoners, suddenly released by the storm that had burst their tomb, were carried high overhead: all scared, all lost, all wondering and amazed, as if the Last Day were come, and those who rejoiced around them were lost spirits. Other seven faces there were, carried higher, seven dead faces, whose drooping eyelids and half-seen eyes awaited the Last Day. Impassive faces, yet with a suspended—not an abolished—expression on them; faces, rather, in a fearful pause, as having yet to raise the dropped lids of the eyes, and bear witness with the bloodless lips, "THOU DIDST IT!"

Seven prisoners released, seven gory heads on pikes, the keys of the accursed fortress of the eight strong towers, some discovered letters and other memorials of prisoners of old time, long dead of broken hearts,—such, and such-like, the loudly echoing footsteps of Saint Antoine escort through the Paris streets in mid-July, one thousand seven hundred and eighty-nine. Now, Heaven defeat the fancy of Lucie Darnay, and keep these feet far out of her life! For, they are headlong, mad, and dangerous; and in the years so long after the breaking of the cask at Defarge's wine-shop door, they are not easily purified when once stained red.

Chapter XXII

THE SEA STILL RISES

HAGGARD Saint Antoine had had only one exultant week, in which to soften his modicum of hard and bitter bread to such extent as he could, with the relish of fraternal embraces and congratulations, when Madame Defarge sat at her counter, as usual, presiding over the customers. Madame Defarge wore no rose in her head, for the great brotherhood of Spies had become, even in one short week, extremely chary of trusting themselves to the saint's mercies. The lamps across his streets had a portentously elastic swing with them.

Madame Defarge, with her arms folded, sat in the morning light and heat, contemplating the wine-shop and the street. In both, there were several knots of loungers, squalid and miserable, but now with a manifest sense of power enthroned on their distress. The raggedest nightcap, awry on the wretchedest head, had this crooked significance in it: "I know how hard it has grown for me, the wearer of this, to support life in myself; but do you know how easy it has grown for me, the wearer of this, to destroy life in you?" Every lean bare arm, that had been without work before, had this work always ready for it now, that it could strike. The fingers of the knitting women were vicious, with the experience that they could tear. There was a change in the appearance of Saint Antoine; the image had been hammering into this for hundreds of years, and the last finishing blows had told mightily on the expression.

Madame Defarge sat observing it, with such suppressed approval as was to be desired in the leader of the Saint Antoine women. One of her sisterhood knitted beside her. The short, rather plump wife of a starved grocer, and the mother of two children withal, this lieutenant had already earned the complimentary name of The Vengeance.

"Hark!" said The Vengeance. "Listen, then! Who comes?"

As if a train of powder laid from the outermost bound of the Saint Antoine Quarter to the wine-shop door, had been suddenly fired, a fast-spreading murmur came rushing along.

"It is Defarge," said Madame. "Silence, patriots!"

Defarge came in breathless, pulled off a red cap he wore, and looked around him. "Listen, everywhere!" said Madame again. "Listen to him!" Defarge stood, panting, against a background of eager eyes and open mouths, formed outside the door; all those within the wine-shop had sprung to their feet.

"Say then, my husband. What is it?"

"News from the other world!"

"How, then?" cried Madame, contemptuously. "The other world?"

"Does everybody here recall old Foulon, who told the famished people that they might eat grass, and who died, and went to Hell?"

"Everybody!" from all throats.

"The news is of him. He is among us!"

"Among us!" from the universal throat again. "And dead?"

"Not dead! He feared us so much—and with reason—that he caused himself to be represented as dead, and had a grand mock-funeral. But they have found him alive, hiding in the country, and have brought him in. I have seen him but now, on his way to the Hôtel de Ville, a prisoner. I have said that he had reason to fear us. Say all! *Had* he reason?"

Wretched old sinner of more than threescore years and ten, if he had never known it yet, he would have known it in his heart of hearts if he could have heard the answering cry.

A moment of profound silence followed. Defarge and his wife looked steadfastly at one another. The Vengeance stooped, and the jar of a drum was heard as she moved it at her feet behind the counter.

"Patriots!" said Defarge, in a determined voice, "are we ready?"

Instantly Madame Defarge's knife was in her girdle; the drum was beating in the streets, as if it and a drummer had flown together by magic; and The Vengeance, uttering terrific shrieks, and flinging her arms about her head like all the forty Furies at once, was tearing from house to house, rousing the women.

The men were terrible, in the bloody-minded anger with which they looked from windows, caught up what arms they had, and came pouring down into the streets; but, the women were a sight to chill the boldest. From such household occupations as their bare poverty yielded, from their children, from their aged and their sick crouching on the bare ground famished and naked, they ran out with streaming hair, urging one another, and themselves, to madness with the wildest cries and actions. Villain Foulon taken, my sister! Old Foulon taken, my mother! Miscreant Foulon taken, my daughter! Then, a score of others ran into the midst of these, beating their breasts, tearing their hair, and screaming, Foulon alive! Foulon who told the starving people they might eat grass! Foulon who told my old father that he might eat grass, when I had no bread to give him! Foulon who told my baby it might suck grass, when these breasts were dry with want! O mother of God, this Foulon! O Heaven, our suffering! Hear me, my dead baby and my withered father: I swear on my knees, on these stones, to avenge you on Foulon! Husbands, and brothers, and young men, Give us the blood of Foulon, Give us the head of Foulon, Give us the heart of Foulon, Give us the body and soul of Foulon, Rend Foulon to pieces, and dig him into the ground, that grass may grow from him! With these cries, numbers of the women, lashed into blind frenzy, whirled about, striking and tearing at their own friends until they dropped into a passionate swoon, and were only saved by the men belonging to them from being trampled under foot.

Nevertheless, not a moment was lost; not a moment! This Foulon was at the Hôtel de Ville, and might be loosed. Never, if Saint Antoine knew his own sufferings, insults, and wrongs! Armed men and women flocked out of the Quarter so fast, and drew even these last dregs after them with such a force of suction, that within a quarter of an hour there was not a human creature in Saint Antoine's bosom but a few old crones and the wailing children.

No. They were all by that time choking the Hall of examination where this old man, ugly and wicked, was, and overflowing into the adjacent open space and streets. The Defarges, husband and wife, The Vengeance, and Jacques Three, were in the first press, and at no great distance from him in the Hall.

"See!" cried Madame, pointing with her knife. "See the old villain bound with ropes. That was well done to tie a bunch of grass upon his back. Ha, ha! That was well done. Let him eat it now!" Madame put her knife under her arm, and clapped her hands as at a play.

The people immediately behind Madame Defarge, explaining the cause of her satisfaction to those behind them, and those again explaining to others, and those to others, the neighboring streets resounded with the clapping of hands. Similarly, during two or three hours of drawl, and the winnowing of many bushels of words, Madame Defarge's frequent expressions of impatience were taken up, with marvelous quickness, at a distance; the more readily, because certain men who had by some wonderful exercise of agility climbed up the external architecture to look in from the windows, knew Madame Defarge well, and acted as a telegraph between her and the crowd outside the building.

At length, the sun rose so high that it struck a kindly ray as of hope or protection, directly down upon the old prisoner's head. The favor was too much to bear; in an instant the barrier of dust and chaff that had stood surprisingly long, went to the winds, and Saint Antoine had got him!

It was known directly, to the furthest confines of the crowd. Defarge had but sprung over a railing and a table, and folded the miserable wretch in a deadly embrace—Madame Defarge had but followed and turned her hand in one of the ropes with which he was tied—The Vengeance and Jacques Three were not yet up with them, and the men at the windows had not yet swooped into the Hall, like birds of prey from their high perches—when the cry seemed to go up, all over the city, "Bring him out! Bring him to the lamp!"

Down, and up, and head foremost on the steps of the building; now, on his knees; now, on his feet; now, on his back; dragged, and struck at, and stifled by the bunches of grass and straw that were thrust into his face by hundreds of hands; torn, bruised, panting, bleeding, yet always entreating and beseeching for mercy; now, full of vehement agony of action, with a small clear space about him as the people drew one another back that they might see; now, a log of dead wood drawn through a forest of legs; he was hauled to the nearest street corner where one of the fatal lamps swung, and there Madame Defarge let him go—as a cat might have done to a mouse—and silently and composedly looked at him while they made ready, and while he besought her: the women passionately screeching at him all the time, and the men sternly calling out to have him killed with grass in his mouth. Once, he went aloft, and the rope broke, and they caught him shrieking; twice, he went aloft, and the rope broke, and they caught him shrieking; then, the rope was merciful, and held him, and his head was soon upon a pike, with grass enough in the mouth for all Saint Antoine to dance at the sight of.

Nor was this the end of the day's bad work, for Saint Antoine so shouted and danced his angry blood up, that it boiled again, on hearing when the day closed in that the son-in-law of the dispatched, another of the people's enemies and insulters, was coming into Paris under a guard five hundred strong, in cavalry alone. Saint Antoine wrote his crimes on flaring sheets of paper, seized him—would have torn him out of the breast of an army to bear Foulon company—set his head and heart on pikes, and carried the three spoils of the day, in Wolf-procession, through the streets.

Not before dark night did the men and women come back to the children, wailing and breadless. Then, the miserable bakers' shops were beset by long files of them, patiently waiting to buy bad bread; and while they waited with stomachs faint and empty, they beguiled the time by embracing one another on the triumphs of the day, and achieving them again in gossip. Gradually, these strings of ragged people shortened and frayed away; and then poor lights began to shine in high windows, and slender fires were made in the streets, at which neighbors cooked in common, afterward supping at their doors.

Scanty and insufficient suppers those, and innocent of meat, as of most other sauce to wretched bread. Yet, human fellowship infused some nourishment into the flinty viands, and struck some sparks of cheerfulness out of them. Fathers and mothers who had had their full share in the worst of the day, played gently with their meagre children; and lovers, with such a world around them and before them, loved and hoped.

It was almost morning, when Defarge's wine-shop parted with its last knot of customers, and Monsieur Defarge said to Madame his wife, in husky tones, while fastening the door:

"At last it is come, my dear!"

"Eh well!" returned Madame. "Almost."

Saint Antoine slept, the Defarges slept: even The Vengeance slept with her starved grocer, and the drum was at rest. The drum's was the only voice in Saint Antoine, that blood and hurry had not changed. The Vengeance as custodian of the drum, could have wakened him up and had the same speech out of him as before the Bastille fell, or old Foulon was seized; not so with the hoarse tones of the men and women in Saint Antoine's bosom.

Chapter XXIII

FIRE RISES

THERE was a change on the village where the fountain fell, and where the mender of roads went forth daily to hammer out of the stones on the highway, such morsels of bread as might serve for patches to hold his poor ignorant soul and his poor reduced body, together. The prison on the crag was not so dominant as of yore; there were soldiers to guard it, but not many; there were officers to guard the soldiers, but not one of them knew what his men would do—beyond this: that it would probably not be what he was ordered.

Far and wide, lay a ruined country, yielding nothing but desolation. Every green leaf, every blade of grass and blade of grain, was as shrivelled and poor as the miserable people. Every thing was bowed down, dejected, oppressed, and broken. Habitations, fences, domesticated animals, men, women, children, and the soil that bore them—all worn out.

Monseigneur (often a most worthy individual gentleman) was a national blessing, gave a chivalrous tone to things, was a polite example of luxurious and shining life, and a great deal more to equal purpose; nevertheless, Monseigneur as a class had, somehow or other, brought things to this. Strange that creation, designed expressly for Monseigneur, should be so soon wrung dry and squeezed out! There must be something short-sighted in the eternal arrangements, surely! Thus it was, however; and the last drop of blood having been extracted from the flints, and the last screw of the rack having been turned so often that its purchase crumbled, and it now turned and turned with nothing to bite, Monseigneur began to run away from a phenomenon so low and unaccountable.

But, this was not the change on the village, and on many a village like it. For scores of years gone by, Monseigneur had squeezed it and wrung it, and had seldom graced it with his presence except for the pleasures of the chase—now, found in hunting the people; now, found in hunting the beasts, for whose preservation Monseigneur made edifying spaces of barbarous and barren wilderness. No. The change consisted in the appearance of strange faces of low caste, rather than in the disappearance of the high-caste, chiseled, and otherwise beatified and beatifying features of Monseigneur.

For, in these times, as the mender of roads worked, solitary, in the dust, not often troubling himself to reflect that dust he was and to dust he must return, being for the most part too much occupied in thinking how little he had for supper and how much more he would eat if he had it—in these times, as he raised his eyes from his lonely labor, and viewed the prospect, he would see some rough figure approaching on foot, the like of which was once a rarity in those parts, but was now a frequent presence. As it advanced, the mender of roads would discern without surprise, that it was a shaggy-haired man, of almost barbarian aspect, tall, in wooden shoes that were clumsy even to the eyes of a mender of roads, grim, rough, swart, steeped in the mud and dust of many highways, dank with the marshy moisture of many low grounds, sprinkled with the thorns and leaves and moss of many byways through woods.

Such a man came upon him, like a ghost, at noon in the July weather, as he sat on his heap of stones under a bank, taking such shelter as he could get from a shower of hail.

The man looked at him, looked at the village in the hollow at the mill, and at the prison on the crag. When he had identified these objects in what benighted mind he had, he said, in a dialect that was just intelligible:

"How goes it, Jacques?"

"All well, Jacques."

"Touch then!"

They joined hands, and the man sat down on the heap of stones.

"No dinner?"

"Nothing but supper now," said the mender of roads, with a hungry face.

"It is the fashion," growled the man. "I meet no dinner anywhere."

He took out a blackened pipe, filled it, lighted it with flint and steel, pulled at it until it was in a bright glow: then, suddenly held it from him and dropped something into it from between his finger and thumb, that blazed and went out in a puff of smoke.

"Touch then." It was the turn of the mender of roads to say it this time, after observing these operations. They again joined hands.

"To-night?" said the mender of roads.

"To-night," said the man, putting the pipe in his mouth.

"Where?"

"Here."

He and the mender of roads sat on the heap of stones looking silently at one another, with the hail driving in between them like a pigmy charge of bayonets, until the sky began to clear over the village.

"Show me!" said the traveller then, moving to the brow of the hill.

"See!" returned the mender of roads, with extended finger. "You go down here, and straight through the street, and past the fountain—"

"To the Devil with all that!" interrupted the other, rolling his eyes over the landscape. "*I* go through no streets and past no fountains. Well?"

"Well! About two leagues beyond the summit of that hill above the village."

"Good. When do you cease to work?"

"At sunset."

"Will you wake me, before departing? I have walked two nights without resting. Let me finish my pipe, and I shall sleep like a child. Will you wake me?"

"Surely."

The wayfarer smoked his pipe out, put it in his breast, slipped off his great wooden shoes, and lay down on his back on the heap of stones. He was fast asleep directly.

As the road-mender plied his dusty labor, and the hail-clouds, rolling away, revealed bright bars and streaks of sky which were responded to by silver gleams upon the landscape, the little man (who wore a red cap now, in place of his blue one) seemed fascinated by the figure on the heap of stones. His eyes were so often turned towards it, that he used his tools mechanically, and, one would have said, to very poor account. The bronze face, the shaggy black hair and beard, the coarse woollen red cap, the rough medley dress of homespun stuff and hairy skins of beasts, the powerful frame attenuated by spare living, and the sullen and desperate compression of the lips in sleep, inspired the mender of roads with awe. The traveller had travelled far, and his feet were footsore, and his ankles chafed and bleeding; his great shoes, stuffed with leaves and grass, had been heavy to drag over the many long leagues, and his clothes were chafed into holes, as he himself was into sores. Stooping down beside him, the road-mender tried to get a peep at secret weapons in his breast or where not; but in vain, for he slept with his arms crossed upon him, and set as resolutely as his lips. Fortified towns with their stockades, guard-houses, gates, trenches, and drawbridges, seemed, to the mender of roads, to be so much air as against this figure. And when he lifted his eyes from it to the horizon and looked around, he saw in his small fancy similar figures, stopped by no obstacle, tending to centres all over France.

The man slept on, indifferent to showers of hail and intervals of brightness, to sunshine on his face and shadow, to the pattering lumps of dull ice on his body and the diamonds into which the sun changed them, until the sun was low in the west, and the sky was glowing. Then the mender of roads having got his tools together and all things ready to go down into the village, roused him.

"Good!" said the sleeper, rising on his elbow. "Two leagues beyond the summit of the hill?"

"About."

"About. Good!"

The mender of roads went home, with the dust going on before him according to the set of the wind, and was soon at the fountain, squeezing himself in among the lean kine brought there to drink, and appearing even to whisper to them in his whispering to all the village. When the village had taken its poor supper, it did not creep to bed, as it usually did, but came out of doors again, and remained there. A curious contagion of whispering was upon it, and also, when it gathered together at the fountain in the dark, another curious contagion of looking expectantly at the sky in one direction only. Monsieur Gabelle, chief functionary of the place, became uneasy; went out on his house-top alone, and looked in that direction too; glanced down from behind his chimeys at the darkening faces by the fountain below, and sent word to the sacristan who kept the keys of the church, that there might be need to ring the tocsin by-and-by.

The night deepened. The trees environing the old chateau, keeping its solitary state apart, moved in a rising wind, as though they threatened the pile of building massive and dark in the gloom. Up the two terrace flights of steps the rain ran wildly, and beat at the great door, like a swift messenger rousing those within; uneasy rushes of wind went through the hall, among the old spears and knives, and passed lamenting up the stairs, and shook the curtains of the bed where the last Marquis had slept. East, West, North, and South, through the woods, four heavy-treading, unkempt figures crushed the high grass and cracked the branches, striding on cautiously to come together in the courtyard. Four lights broke out there, and moved away in different directions, and all was black again.

But, not for long. Presently, the chateau began to make itself strangely visible by some light of its own, as though it were growing luminous. Then, a flickering streak played behind the architecture of the front, picking out transparent places, and showing where balustrades, arches, and windows were. Then it soared higher, and grew broader and brighter. Soon, from a score of the great windows, flames burst forth, and the stone faces, awakened, stared out of fire.

A faint murmur arose about the house from the few people who were left there, and there was a saddling of a horse and riding away. There was spurring and splashing through the darkness, and bridle was drawn in the space by the village fountain, and the horse in a foam stood at Monsieur Gabelle's door. "Help, Gabelle! Help, every one!" The tocsin rang impatiently, but other help (if that were any) there was none. The mender of roads, and two hundred and fifty particular friends, stood with folded arms at the fountain, looking at the pillar of fire in the sky. "It must be forty feet high," said they, grimly; and never moved.

The rider from the chateau, and the horse in a foam, clattered away through the village, and galloped up the stony steep, to the prison on the crag. At the gate, a group of officers were looking at the fire; removed from them, a group of soldiers. "Help, gentlemen-officers! The chateau is on fire; valuable objects may be saved from the flames by timely aid! Help, help!" The officers looked toward the soldiers who looked at the fire; gave no orders; and answered, with shrugs and biting of lips, "It must burn."

As the rider rattled down the hill again and through the street, the village was illuminating. The mender of roads, and the two hundred and fifty particular friends, inspired as one man and woman by the idea of lighting up, had darted into their houses, and were putting candles in every dull little pane of glass. The general scarcity of every thing occasioned candles to be borrowed in a rather peremptory manner of Monsieur Gabelle; and in a moment of reluctance and hesitation on that functionary's part, the mender of roads, once so submissive to authority, had remarked that carriages were good to make bonfires with, and that post-horses would roast.

The chateau was left to itself to flame and burn. In the roaring and raging of the conflagration, a red-hot wind, driving straight from the infernal regions, seemed to be blowing the edifice away. With the rising and falling of the blaze, the stone faces showed as if they were in torment. When the great masses of stone and timber fell, the face with the two dints in the nose became obscured: anon struggled out of the smoke again, as if it were the face of the cruel Marquis, burning at the stake and contending with the fire.

The chateau burned; the nearest trees, laid hold of by the fire, scorched and shrivelled; trees at a distance, fired by the four fierce figures, begirt the blazing edifice with a new forest of smoke. Molten lead and iron boiled in the marble basin of the fountain; the water ran dry; the extinguisher tops of the towers vanished like ice before the heat, and trickled down into four rugged wells of flame. Great rents and splits branched out in the solid walls, like crystallization; stupefied birds wheeled about, and dropped into the furnace; four fierce figures trudged away, East, West, North, and South, along the night-enshrouded roads guided by the beacon they had lighted, toward their next destination. The illuminated village had seized hold of the tocsin, and, abolishing the lawful ringer, rang for joy.

Not only that; but the village, light-headed with famine, fire, and bell-ringing, and bethinking itself that Monsieur Gabelle had to do with the collection of rent and taxes—though it was but a small instalment of taxes, and no rent at all, that Gabelle had got in those latter days—became impatient for an interview with him, and, surrounding his house, summoned him to come forth for personal conference. Whereupon, Monsieur Gabelle did heavily bar his door, and retire to hold counsel with himself. The result of that conference was that Gabelle again withdrew himself to his housetop behind his stack of chimneys: this time resolved, if his door was broken in (he was a small Southern man of retaliative temperament), to pitch himself, head foremost over the parapet, and crush a man or two below.

Probably, Monsieur Gabelle passed a long night up there, with the distant chateau for fire and candle, and the beating at his door, combined with the joy-ringing, for music; not to mention his having an ill-omened lamp slung across the road before his posting-house gate, which the village showed a lively inclination to displace in his favor. A trying suspense, to be passing a whole summer night on the brink of the black ocean, ready to take that plunge into it upon which Monsieur Gabelle had resolved! But, the friendly dawn appearing at last, and the rush-candles of the village guttering out, the people happily dispersed, and Monsieur Gabelle came down, bringing his life with him for that while.

Within a hundred miles, and in the light of other fires, there were other functionaries less fortunate, that night and other nights, whom the rising sun found hanging across once-peaceful streets, where they had been born and bred; also, there were other villages and townspeople less fortunate than the mender of roads and his fellows, upon whom the functionaries and soldiery turned with success, and whom they strung up in their turn. But the fierce figures were steadily wending East, West, North, and South, be that as it would; and whosoever hung, fire burned. The altitude of the gallows that would turn to water and quench it, no functionary, by any stretch of mathematics, was able to calculate successfully.

Chapter XXIV

DRAWN TO THE LOADSTONE ROCK

In such risings of fire and risings of sea—the firm earth shaken by the rushes of an angry ocean which had now no ebb but was always on the flow, higher and higher, to the terror and wonder of the beholders on the shore—three years of tempest were consumed. Three more birthdays of little Lucie had been woven by the golden thread into the peaceful tissue of the life of her home.

Many a night and many a day had its inmates listened to the echoes in the corner, with hearts that failed them when they heard the thronging feet. For, the footsteps had become to their minds as the footsteps of a people, tumultuous under a red flag and with their country declared in danger, changed into wild beasts, by terrible enchantment long persisted in.

Monseigneur, as a class, had dissociated himself from the phenomenon of his not being appreciated: of his being so little wanted in France, as to incur considerable danger of receiving his dismissal from it, and this life together. Like the fabled rustic who raised the Devil with infinite pains, and was so terrified at the sight of him that he could ask the Enemy no question, but immediately fled; so, Monseigneur, after boldly reading the Lord's Prayer backward for a great number of years, and performing many other potent spells for compelling the Evil One, no sooner beheld him in his terrors than he took to his noble heels.

The shining Bull's Eye of the Court was gone, or it would have been the mark for a hurricane of national bullets. It had never been a good eye to see with—had long had the mote in it of Lucifer's pride, Sardanapalus's luxury, and a mole's blindness—but it had dropped out and was gone. The Court, from that exclusive inner circle to its outermost rotten ring of intrige, corruption, and dissimulation, was all gone together. Royalty was gone; had been besieged in its Palace and "suspended," when the last tidings came over.

The August of the year one thousand seven hundred and ninety-two was come, and Monseigneur was by this time scattered far and wide.

As was natural, the head-quarters and great gathering-place of Monseigneur, in London, was Tellson's Bank. Spirits are supposed to haunt the places where their bodies most resorted, and Monseigneur without a guinea haunted the spot where his guineas used to be. Moreover, it was the spot to which such French intelligence as was most to be relied upon came quickest. Again: Tellson's was a munificent house, and extended great liberality to old customers who had fallen from their high estate. Again: those nobles who had seen the coming storm in time, and, anticipating plunder or confiscation, had made provident remittances to Tellson's, were always to be heard of there by their needy brethren. To which must be added that every new comer from France reported himself and his tidings at Tellson's, almost as a matter of course. For such variety of reasons, Tellson's was at that time, as to French intelligence, a kind of High Exchange; and this was so well known to the publlc, and the inquiries made there were in consequence so numerous, that Tellson's sometimes wrote the latest news out in a line or so and posted it in the Bank windows, for all who ran through Temple Bar to read.

On a steaming, misty afternoon, Mr. Lorry sat at his desk, and Charles Darnay stood leaning on it, talking with him in a low voice. The penitential den once set apart for interviews with the House, was now the news-Exchange, and was filled to overflowing. It was within half an hour or so of the time of closing.

"But, although you are the youngest man that ever lived," said Charles Darnay, rather hesitating, "I must still suggest to you——"

"I understand. That I am too old?" said Mr. Lorry.

"Unsettled weather, a long journey, uncertain means of traveling, a disorganised country, a city that may not be even safe for you."

"My dear Charles," said Mr. Lorry, with cheerful confidence, "you touch some of the reasons for my going: not for my staying away. It is safe enough for me; nobody will care to interfere with an old fellow of hard upon fourscore when there are so many people there much better worth interfering with. As to its being a disorganised city, if it were not a disorganised city there would be no occasion to send somebody from our House here to our House there, who knows the city and the business, of old, and is in Tellson's confidence. As to the uncertain traveling, the long journey, and the winter weather, if I were not prepared to submit myself to a few inconveniences for the sake of Tellson's, after all these years, who ought to be?"

"I wish I were going myself," said Charles Darnay, somewhat restlessly, and like one thinking aloud..

"Indeed! You are a pretty fellow to object and advise!" exclaimed Mr. Lorry. "You wish you were going yourself? And you a Frenchman born? You are a wise counselor."

"My dear Mr. Lorry, it is because I am a Frenchman born, that the thought (which I did not mean to utter here, however) has passed through my mind often. One cannot help thinking, having had some sympathy for the miserable people, and having abandoned something to them," he spoke here in his former thoughtful manner, "that one might be listened to, and might have the power to persuade to some restraint. Only last night, after you had left us, when I was talking to Lucie—"

"When you were talking to Lucie," Mr. Lorry repeated. "Yes. I wonder you are not ashamed to mention the name of Lucie! Wishing you were going to France at this time of day!"

"However, I am not going," said Charles Darnay, with a smile. "It is more to the purpose that you say you are."

"And I am, in plain reality. The truth is, my dear Charles," Mr. Lorry glanced at the distant House, and lowered his voice, "you can have no conception of the difficulty with which our business is transacted, and of the peril in which our books and papers over yonder are involved. The Lord above knows what the compromising consequence would be to numbers of people, if some of our documents were seized or destroyed; and they might be, at any time, you know, for who can say that Paris is not set afire to-day, or sacked to-morrow! Now, a judicious selection from these with the least possible delay, and the burying of them, or otherwise getting them out of harm's way, is within the power (without loss of precious time) of scarcely any one but myself, if any one. And shall I hang back, when Tellson's knows this and says this—Tellson's, whose bread I have eaten these sixty years—because I am a little stiff about the joints? Why, I am a boy, sir, to half a dozen old codgers here!"

"How I admire the gallantry of your youthful spirit, Mr. Lorry."

"Tut! Nonsense, sir! And, my dear Charles," said Mr. Lorry, glancing at the House again, "you are to remember, that getting things out of Paris at this present time, no matter what things, is next to an impossibility. Papers and precious matters were this very day brought to us here (I speak in strict confidence; it is not business-like to whisper it, even to you), by the strangest bearers you can imagine, every one of whom had his head hanging on by a single hair as he passed the Barriers. At another time, our parcels would come and go, as easily as in business-like Old England; but now, everything is stopped."

"And do you really go to-night?"

"I really go to-night, for the case has become too pressing to admit of delay."

"And do you take no one with you?"

"All sorts of people have been proposed to me, but I will have nothing to say to any of them. I intend to take Jerry. Jerry has been my body-guard on Sunday nights for a long time past, and I am used to him. Nobody will suspect Jerry of being anything but an English bull-dog, or of having any design in his head but to fly at somebody who touches his master."

"I must say again that I heartily admire your gallantry and youthfulness."

"I must say again, nonsense, nonsense! When I have executed this little commission, I shall, perhaps, accept Tellson's proposal to retire and live at my ease. Time enough, then, to think about growing old."

This dialogue had taken place at Mr. Lorry's usual desk, with Monseigneur swarming within a yard or two of it, boastful of what he would do to avenge himself on the rascal-people before long. It was too much the way of Monseigneur under his reverses as a refugee, and it was much too much the way of native British orthodoxy, to talk of this terrible

Revolution as if it were the one only harvest ever known under the skies that had not been sown—as if nothing had ever been done, or omitted to be done, that had led to it—as if observers of the wretched millions in France, and of the misused and perverted resources that should have made them prosperous, had not seen it inevitably coming, years before, and had not in plain words recorded what they saw. Such vaporing, combined with the extravagant plots of Monseigneur for the restoration of a state of things that had utterly exhausted itself, and worn out Heaven and earth as well as itself, was hard to be endured without some remonstrance by any sane man who knew the truth. And it was such vaporing all about his ears, like a troublesome confusion of blood in his own head, added to a latent uneasiness in his mind, which had already made Charles Darnay restless, and which still kept him so.

Among the talkers was Stryver, of the King's Bench Bar, far on his way to state promotion, and, therefore, loud on the theme; broaching to Monseigneur his devices for blowing the people up and exterminating them from the face of the earth, and doing without them: and for accomplishing many similar objects akin in their nature to the abolition of eagles, by sprinkling salt on the tails of the race. Him, Darnay heard with a particular feeling of objection; and Darnay stood divided between going away that he might hear no more, and remaining to interpose his word, when the thing that was to be went on to shape itself out.

The House approached Mr. Lorry, and laying a soiled and unopened letter before him, asked if he had yet discovered any traces of the person to whom it was addressed? The House laid the letter down so close to Darnay that he saw the direction—the more quickly because it was his own right name. The address, turned into English, ran: "Very pressing. To Monsieur heretofore the Marquis St. Evrémonde, of France, Confided to the cares of Messrs. Tellson and Co., Bankers, London, England."

On the marriage morning, Doctor Manette had made it his one urgent and express request to Charles Darnay, that the secret of this name should be—unless he, the Doctor, dissolved the obligation—kept inviolate between them. Nobody else knew it to be his name; his own wife had no suspicion of the fact; Mr. Lorry could have none.

"No," said Mr. Lorry, in reply to the House; "I have referred it, I think, to everybody now here, and no one can tell me where this gentleman is to be found."

The hands of the clock verging upon the hour of closing the Bank, there was a general set of the current of talkers past Mr. Lorry's desk. He held the letter out inquiringly; and Monseigneur looked at it, in the person of this plotting and indignant refugee; and Monseigneur looked at it, in the person of that plotting and indignant refugee; and This, That, and The Other, all had something disparaging to say, in French or in English, concerning the Marquis who was not to be found.

"Nephew, I believe—but in any case degenerate successor—of the polished Marquis who was murdered," said one. "Happy to say, I never knew him."

"A craven who abandoned his post," said another—this Monseigneur had been got out of Paris, legs uppermost and half suffocated, in a load of hay—"some years ago."

"Infected with the new doctrines," said a third, eyeing the direction through his glass in passing; "set himself in opposition to the last Marquis, abandoned the estates when he inherited them, and left them to the ruffian herd. They will recompense him now, I hope, as he deserves."

"Hey?" cried the blatant Stryver. "Did he though? Is that the sort of fellow? Let us look at his infamous name. D—n the fellow!"

Darnay, unable to restrain himself any longer, touched Mr. Stryver on the shoulder, and said:

"I know the fellow."

"Do you, by Jupiter?" said Stryver. "I am sorry for it."

"Why?"

"Why, Mr. Darnay? D'ye hear what he did? Don't ask why, in these times."

"But I do ask why."

"Then I tell you again, Mr. Darnay, I am sorry for it. I am sorry to hear you putting any such extraordinary questions. Here is a fellow, who, infected by the most pestilent and blasphemous code of deviltry that ever was known, abandoned his property to the vilest scum of the earth that ever did murder by wholesale, and you ask me why I am sorry that a man who instructs youth knows him? Well, but I'll answer you. I am sorry, because I believe there is contamination in such a scoundrel. That's why."

Mindful of the secret, Darnay with great difficulty checked himself, and said: "You may not understand the gentleman."

"I understand how to put *you* in a corner, Mr. Darnay," said Bully Stryver, "and I'll do it. If this fellow is a gentleman, I *don't* understand him. You may tell him so, with my compliments. You may also tell him, from me, that after abandoning his worldly goods and position to this butcherly mob, I wonder he is not at the head of them. But, no, gentlemen," said Stryver, looking all round, and snapping his fingers, "I know something of human nature, and I tell you that you'll never find a fellow like this fellow, trusting himself to the mercies of such precious *protégés*. No, gentlemen; he'll always show 'em a clean pair of heels very early in the scuffle, and sneak away."

With those words, and a final snap of his fingers, Mr. Stryver shouldered himself into Fleet Street, amidst the general approbation of his hearers. Mr. Lorry and Charles Darnay were left alone at the desk, in the general departure from the Bank.

"Will you take charge of the letter?" said Mr. Lorry. "You know where to deliver it?"

"I do."

"Will you undertake to explain that we suppose it to have been addressed here, on the chance of our knowing where to forward it, and that it has been here some time?"

"I will do so. Do you start for Paris from here?"

"From here, at eight."

"I will come back, to see you off."

Very ill at ease with himself, and with Stryver and most other men, Darnay made the best of his way into the quiet of the Temple, opened the letter and read it. These were its contents:

"Prison of the Abbaye, Paris. June 21, 1792.

"MONSIEUR HERETOFORE THE MARQUIS,

"After having long been in danger of my life at the hands of the village, I have been seized, with great violence and indignity, and brought a long journey on foot to Paris. On the road I have suffered a great deal. Nor is that all; my house has been destroyed—razed to the ground.

"The crime for which I am imprisoned, Monsieur heretofore the Marquis, and for which I shall be summoned before the tribunal, and shall lose my life (without your so generous help), is, they tell me, treason against the majesty of the people, in that I have acted against them for an emigrant. It is in vain I represent that I have acted for them, and not against, according to your commands. It is in vain I represent that, before the sequestration of emigrant property, I had remitted the imposts they had ceased to pay; that I had collected no rent; that I had had recourse to no process. The only response is, that I have acted for an emigrant, and where is that emigrant?

"Ah! most gracious Monsieur heretofore the Marquis, where is that emigrant! I cry in my sleep where is he! I demand of Heaven will he not come to deliver me! No answer. Ah! Monsieur heretofore the Marquis, I send my desolate cry across the sea, hoping it may perhaps reach your ears through the great bank of Tellson known at Paris!

"For the love of Heaven, of justice, of generosity, of the honor of your noble name, I supplicate you, Monsieur heretofore the Marquis, to succor and release me. My fault is, that I have been true to you. O Monsieur heretofore the Marquis, I pray you be you true to me!

"From this prison here of horror, whence I every hour tend nearer and nearer to destruction, I send you, Monsieur heretofore the Marquis, the assurance of my dolorous and unhappy service.

"Your afflicted,

"GABELLE"

The latent uneasiness in Darnay's mind was roused to vigorous life by this letter. The peril of an old servant and a good one, whose only crime was fidelity to himself and his family, stared him so reproachfully in the face, that, as he walked to and fro in the Temple considering what to do, he almost hid his face from the passers-by.

He knew very well, that in his horror of the deed which had culminated the bad deeds and bad reputation of the old family house, in his resentful suspicions of his uncle, and in the aversion with which his conscience regarded the crumbling fabric that he was supposed to uphold, he had acted imperfectly. He knew very well that in his love for Lucie, his renunciation of his social place, though by no means new to his own mind, had been hurried and incomplete. He knew that he ought to have systematically worked it out and supervised it, and that he had meant to do it, and that it had never been done.

The happiness of his own chosen English home, the necessity of being always actively employed, the swift changes and troubles of the time which had followed on one another so fast, that the events of this week annihilated the immature plans of last week, and the events of the week following made all new again; he knew very well, that to the force of these circumstances he had yielded:—not without disquiet, but still without continuous and accumulating resistance. That he had watched the times for a time of action, and that they had shifted and struggled until the time had gone by, and the nobility were trooping from France by every highway and byway, and their property was in course of confiscation and destruction, and their very names were blotting out, was as well known to himself as it could be to any new authority in France that might impeach him for it.

But, he had oppressed no man, he had imprisoned no man; he was so far from having harshly exacted payment of his dues, that he had relinquished them of his own will, thrown himself on a world with no favor in it, won his own private place there, and earned his own bread. Monsieur Gabelle had held the impoverished and involved estate on written instructions to spare the people, to give them what little there was to give—such fuel as the heavy creditors would let them have in the winter, and such produce as could be saved from the same grip in the summer—and no doubt he had put the fact in plea and proof, for his own safety, so that it could not but appear now.

This favored the desperate resolution Charles Darnay had begun to make, that he would go to Paris.

Yes. Like the mariner in the old story, the winds and streams had driven him within the influence of the Loadstone Rock, and it was drawing him to itself, and he must go. Every thing that arose before his mind drifted him on, faster and faster, more and more steadily, to the terrible attraction. His latent uneasiness had been, that bad aims were being worked out in his own unhappy land by bad instruments, and that he who could not fail to know that he was better than they, was not there, trying to do something to stay bloodshed, and assert the claims of mercy and humanity. With this uneasiness half stifled, and half reproaching him, he had been brought to the pointed comparison of himself with the brave old gentleman in whom duty was so strong; upon that comparison (injurious to himself), had instantly followed the sneers of Monseigneur, which had stung him bitterly, and those of Stryver, which above all, were coarse and galling, for old reasons. Upon those, had followed Gabelle's letter: the appeal of an innocent prisoner, in danger of death, to his justice, honor, and good name.

His resolution was made. He must go to Paris.

Yes. The Loadstone Rock was drawing him, and he must sail on, until he struck. He knew of no rock; he saw hardly any danger. The intention with which he had done what he had done, even although he had left it incompleted, presented it before him in an aspect that would be gratefully acknowledged in France on his presenting himself to assert it. Then, that glorious vision of doing good, which is so often the sanguine mirage of so many good minds, arose before him, and he even saw himself in the illusion with some influence to guide this raging Revolution that was running so fearfully wild.

As he walked to and fro with his resolution made, he considered that neither Lucie nor her father must know of it until he was gone. Lucie should be spared the pain of separation; and her father, always reluctant to turn his thoughts toward the dangerous ground of old, should come to the knowledge of the step, as a step taken, and not in the balance of suspense and doubt. How much of the incompleteness of his situation was referable to her father, through the painful anxiety to avoid reviving old associations of France in his mind, he did not discuss with himself. But, that circumstance too, had its influence in his course.

He walked to and fro, with thoughts very busy, until it was time to return to Tellson's, and take leave of Mr. Lorry. As soon as he arrived in Paris he would present himself to this old friend, but he must say nothing of his intention now.

A carriage with post-horses was ready at the Bank door, and Jerry was booted and equipped.

"I have delivered that letter," said Charles Darnay to Mr. Lorry. "I would not consent to your being charged with any written answer, but perhaps you will take a verbal one?"

"That I will, and readily," said Mr. Lorry, "if it is not dangerous.

"Not at all. Though it is to a prisoner in the Abbaye."

"What is his name?" said Mr. Lorry, with his open pocket-book in his hand.

"Gabelle."

"Gabelle. And what is the message to the unfortunate Gabelle in prison?"

"Simply, 'that he has received the letter, and will come.'"

"Any time mentioned?"

"He will start upon his journey to-morrow night."

"Any person mentioned?"

"No."

He helped Mr. Lorry to wrap himself in a number of coats and cloaks, and went out with him from the warm atmosphere of the old bank, into the misty air of Fleet Street. "My love to Lucie, and to little Lucie," said Mr. Lorry at parting, "and take precious care of them till I come back." Charles Darnay shook his head and doubtfully smiled, as the carriage rolled away.

That night—it was the fourteenth of August—he sat up late, and wrote two fervent letters; one was to Lucie, explaining the strong obligation he was under to go to Paris, and showing her, at length, the reasons that he had, for feeling confident that he could become involved in no personal danger there; the other was to the Doctor, confiding Lucie and their dear child to his care, and dwelling on the same topics with the strongest assurances. To both, he wrote that he would despatch letters in proof of his safety, immediately after his arrival.

It was a hard day, that day of being among them, with the first reservation of their joint lives on his mind. It was a hard matter to preserve the innocent deceit of which they were profoundly unsuspicious. But, an affectionate glance at his wife, so happy and busy, made him resolute not to tell her what impended (he had been half moved to do it, so strange it was to him to act in anything without her quiet aid), and the day passed quickly. Early in the evening he embraced her, and her scarcely less dear namesake, pretending that he would return by-and-by (an imaginary engagement took him out, and he had secreted a valise of clothes ready), and so he emerged into the heavy mist of the heavy street, with a heavier heart.

The unseen force was drawing him fast to itself, now, and all the tides and winds were setting straight and strong toward it. He left his two letters with a trusty porter, to be delivered half an hour before midnight, and no sooner; took horse for Dover; and began his journey. "For the love of Heaven, justice, of generosity, of the honor of your noble name!" was the poor prisoner's cry with which he strengthened his sinking heart, as he left all that was dear on earth behind him, and floated away for the Loadstone Rock.

BOOK THE THIRD

THE TRACK OF A STORM

Chapter I

IN SECRET

THE traveler fared slowly on his way, who fared towards Paris from England in the autumn of the year one thousand seven hundred and ninety-two. More than enough of bad roads, bad equipages, and bad horses, he would have encountered to delay him, though the fallen and unfortunate King of France had been upon his throne in all his glory; but, the changed times were fraught with other obstacles than these. Every town gate and village taxing-house had its band of citizen-patriots, with their national muskets in a most explosive state of readiness, who stopped all comers and goers, cross-questioned them, inspected their papers, looked for their names in lists of their own, turned them back, or sent them on, or stopped them and laid them in hold, as their capricious judgment or fancy deemed best for the dawning Republic One and Indivisible, of Liberty, Equality, Fraternity, or Death.

A very few French leagues of his journey were accomplished, when Charles Darnay began to perceive that for him along these country roads there was no hope of return until he should have been declared a good citizen at Paris. Whatever might befall now, he must on to his journey's end. Not a mean village closed upon him, not a common barrier dropped across the road behind him, but he knew it to be another iron door in the series that was barred between him and England. The universal watchfulness so encompassed him, that if he had been taken in a net, or were being forwarded to his destination in a cage, he could not have felt his freedom more completely gone.

This universal watchfulness not only stopped him on the highway twenty times in a stage, but retarded his progress twenty times in a day, by riding after him and taking him back, riding before him and stopping him by anticipation, riding with him and keeping him in charge. He had been days upon his journey in France alone, when he went to bed tired out, in a little town on the high road, still a long way from Paris.

Nothing but the production of the afflicted Gabelle's letter from his prison of the Abbaye would have got him on so far. His difficulty at the guard-house in this small place had been such, that he felt his journey to have come to a crisis. And he was, therefore, as little surprised as a man could be, to find himself awakened at the small inn to which he had been remitted until morning, in the middle of the night.

Awakened by a timid local functionary and three armed patriots in rough red caps and with pipes in their mouths, who sat down on the bed.

"Emigrant," said the functionary, "I am going to send you on to Paris, under an escort."

"Citizen, I desire nothing more than to get to Paris, though I could dispense with the escort."

"Silence!" growled a red-cap, striking at the coverlet with the butt-end of his musket. "Peace, aristocrat!"

"It is as the good patriot says," observed the timid functionary. "You are an aristocrat, and must have an escort—and must pay for it."

"I have no choice," said Charles Darnay.

"Choice! Listen to him!" cried the same scowling red-cap. "As if it was not a favor to be protected from the lamp-iron!"

"It is always as the good patriot says," observed the functionary. "Rise and dress yourself, emigrant."

Darnay complied, and was taken back to the guard-house where other patriots in rough red caps were smoking, drinking, and sleeping, by a watch-fire. Here he paid a heavy price for his escort, and hence he started with it on the wet, wet roads at three o'clock in the morning.

The escort were two mounted patriots in red caps and tricolored cockades, armed with national muskets and sabres, who rode one on either side of him. The escorted governed his own horse, but a loose line was attached to his bridle, the end of which one of the patriots kept girded round his wrist. In this state they set forth, with the sharp rain driving in their faces: clattering at a heavy dragoon trot over the uneven town pavement, and out upon the mire-deep roads. In this state they traversed without change, except of horses and pace, all the mire-deep leagues that lay between them and the capital.

They traveled in the night, halting an hour or two after daybreak, and lying by until the twilight fell. The escort were so wretchedly clothed, that they twisted straw round their bare legs, and thatched their ragged shoulders to keep the wet off. Apart from personal discomfort of being so attended, and apart from such considerations of present danger as arose from one of the patriots being chronically drunk, and carrying his musket very recklessly, Charles Darnay did not allow the restraint that was laid upon him to awaken any serious fears in his breast; for, he reasoned with himself that it could have no reference to the merits of an individual case that was not yet stated, and of representations, confirmable by the prisoner in the Abbaye, that were not yet made.

But, when they came to the town of Beauvais—which they did at eventide, when the streets were filled with people—he could not conceal from himself that the aspect of affairs was very alarming. An ominous crowd gathered to see him dismount at the posting-yard, and many voices called out loudly, "Down with the emigrant!"

He stopped in the act of swinging himself out of his saddle, and, resuming it as his safest place, said:

"Emigrant, my friends! Do you not see me here, in France, of my own will?"

"You are a cursed emigrant," cried a farrier, making at him in a furious manner through the press, hammer in hand; "and you are a cursed aristocrat!"

The postmaster interposed himself between this man and the rider's bridle (at which he was evidently making), and soothingiy said, "Let him be; let him be! He will be judged at Paris."

"Judged!" repeated the farrier, swinging his hammer. "Ay! and condemned as a traitor." At this, the crowd roared approval.

Checking the postmaster, who was for turning his horse's head to the yard (the drunken patriot sat composedly in his saddle looking on, with the line round his wrist), Darnay said, as soon as he could make his voice heard:

"Friends, you deceive yourselves, or you are deceived. I am not a traitor."

"He lies!" cried the smith. "He is a traitor since the decree. His life is forfeit to the people. His cursed life is not his own!"

At the instant, when Darnay saw a rush in the eyes of the crowd, which another instant would have brought upon him, the postmaster turned his horse into the yard, the escort rode in close upon his horse's flanks, and the postmaster shut and barred the crazy double gates. The farrier struck a blow upon them with his hammer, and the crowd groaned; but, no more was done.

"What is this decree that the smith spoke of?" Darnay asked the postmaster, when he had thanked him, and stood beside him in the yard.

"Truly, a decree for selling the property of emigrants."

"When passed?"

"On the fourteenth."

"The day I left England!"

"Everybody says it is but one of several, and that there will be others—if there are not already—banishing all emigrants, and condemning all to death who return. That is what he meant when he said your life was not your own."

"But there are no such decrees yet?"

"What do I know!" said the postmaster, shrugging his shoulders; "there may be, or there will be. It is all the same. What would you have?"

They rested on some straw in a loft until the middle of the night, and then rode forward again when all the town was asleep. Among the many wild changes observable on familiar things which made this wild ride unreal, not the least was the seeming rarity of sleep. After long and lonely spurring over dreary roads, they would come to a cluster of poor cottages, not steeped in darkness, but all glittering with lights, and would find the people, in a ghostly manner in the dead of the night, circling hand in hand round a shriveled tree of Liberty, or all drawn up together singing a Liberty song. Happily, however, there was sleep in Beauvais that night to help them out of it, and they passed on once more into solitude and loneliness: jingling through the untimely cold and wet, among impoverished fields that had yielded no fruits of the earth that year, diversified by the blackened remains of burnt houses, and by the sudden emergence from ambuscade, and sharp reining up across their way, of patriot patrols on the watch on all the roads.

Daylight at last found them before the wall of Paris. The barrier was closed and strongly guarded when they rode up to it.

"Where are the papers of this prisoner?" demanded a resolute-looking man in authority, who was summoned out by the guard.

Naturally struck by the disagreeable word, Charles Darnay requested the speaker to take notice that he was a free traveller and French citizen, in charge of an escort which the disturbed state of the country had imposed upon him, and which he had paid for.

"Where," repeated the same personage, without taking any heed of him whatever, "are the papers of this prisoner?"

The drunken patriot had them in his cap, and produced them. Casting his eyes over Gabelle's letter, the same personage in authority showed some disorder and surprise, and looked at Darnay with a close attention.

He left escort and escorted without saying a word, however, and went into the guard-room; meanwhile, they sat upon their horses outside the gate. Looking about him while in this state of suspense, Charles Darnay observed that the gate was held by a mixed guard of soldiers and patriots, the latter far out-numbering the former; and that while ingress into the city for peasants' carts bringing in supplies, and for similar traffic and traffickers, was easy enough, egress, even for the homeliest people, was very difficult. A numerous medley of men and women, not to mention beasts and vehicles of various sorts, was waiting to issue forth; but, the previous identification was so strict that they filtered through the barrier very slowly. Some of these people knew their turn for examination to be so far off, that they lay down on the ground to sleep or smoke, while others talked together, or loitered about. The red cap and tricolor cockade were universal, both among men and women.

When he had sat in his saddle some half-hour, taking note of these things, Darnay found himself confronted by the same man in authority, who directed the gaurd to open the barrier. Then he delivered to the escort, drunk and sober, a receipt for the escorted, and requested him to dismount. He did so, and the two patriots, leading his tired horse, turned and rode away without entering the city.

He accompanied his conductor into a guard-room, smelling of common wine and tobacco, where certain soldiers and patriots, asleep and awake, drunk and sober, and in various neutral states between sleeping and waking, drunkenness and sobriety, were standing and lying about. The light in the guard-house, half derived from the waning oil-lamps of the night, and half from the overcast day, was in a correspondingly uncertain condition. Some registers were lying open on a desk, and an officer of a coarse, dark aspect presided over these.

"Citizen Defarge," said he to Darnay's conductor, as he took a slip of paper to write on. "Is this the emigrant Evremonde?"

"This is the man."

"Your age, Evremonde?"

"Thirty-seven."

"Married, Evremonde?"

"Yes."

"Where married?"

"In England."

"Without doubt. Where is your wife, Evremonde?"

"In England."

"Without doubt. You are consigned, Evremonde, to the prison of La Force."

"Just Heaven!" exclaimed Darnay. "Under what law, and for what offence?"

The officer looked up from his slip of paper for a moment.

"We have new laws, Evremonde, and new offences, since you were here." He said it with a hard smile, and went on writing.

"I entreat you to observe that I have come here voluntarily, in response to that written appeal of a fellow-citizen which lies before you. I have come here, to clear him and to clear myself. I demand no more than the opportunity to do so without delay. Is not that my right?"

"Emigrants have no rights, Evremonde," was the stolid reply. The officer wrote until he had finished, read over to himself what he had written, sanded it, and handed it to Defarge, with the words "In secret."

Defarge motioned with the paper to the prisoner that he must accompany him. The prisoner obeyed, and a guard of two armed patriots attended them.

"Is it you," said Defarge, in a low voice, as they went down the guard-house steps and turned into Paris, "who married the daughter of Doctor Manette, once a prisoner in the Bastille that is no more?"

"Yes," replied Darnay, looking at him with surprise.

"My name is Defarge, and I keep a wine-shop in the Quarter Saint Antoine. Possibly you have heard of me?"

"My wife came to your house to reclaim her father? Yes!"

The word "wife" seemed to serve as a gloomy reminder to Citizen Defarge, to say with sudden impatience, "In the name of that sharp female newly born and called La Guillotine, why did you come to France?"

"You heard me say why, a minute ago. Do you not believe it is the truth?"

"A bad truth for you," said Defarge, speaking with knitted brows, and looking straight before him.

"Indeed, I am lost here. All here is so unprecedented, so changed, so sudden and unfair, that I am absolutely lost. Will you render me a little help?"

"None." Defarge spoke, always looking straight before him.

"Will you answer me a single question?"

"Perhaps. According to its nature. You can say what it is."

"In this prison that I am going to so unjustly, shall I have some free communication with the world outside?"

"You will see."

"I am not to be buried there, prejudged, and without any means of presenting my case?"

"You will see. But, what then? Other people have been similarly buried in worse prisons, before now."

"But never by me, Citizen Defarge."

Citizen Defarge glanced darkly at him for answer, and walked on in a steady and set silence. The deeper he sank into this silence, the fainter hope there was—or so Darnay thought—of his softening in any slight degree. He, therefore, made haste to say:

"It is of the utmost importance to me (you know, Citizen, even better than I, of how much importance) that I should be able to communicate to Mr. Lorry of Tellson's Bank, an English gentleman who is now in Paris, the simple fact, without comment, that I have been thrown into the prison of La Force. Will you cause that to be done for me?"

"I will do," Defarge doggedly rejoined, "nothing for you. My duty is to my country and the people. I am the sworn servant of both, against you. I will do nothing for you."

Charles Darnay felt it hopeless to entreat him further, and his pride was touched besides. As they walked on in silence, he could not but see how used the people were to the spectacle of prisoners passing along the streets. The very children scarcely noticed him. A few passers turned their heads, and a few shook their fingers at him as an aristocrat; otherwise, that a man in good clothes should be going to prison was no more remarkable than that a laborer in working clothes should be going to work. In one narrow, dark, and dirty street through which they passed, an excited orator, mounted on a stool, was addressing an excited audience on the crimes against the people, of the king and the royal family. The few words that he caught from this man's lips, first made it known to Charles Darnay that the king was in prison, and that the foreign ambassadors had one and all left Paris. On the road (except at Beauvais) he had heard absolutely nothing. The escort and the universal watchfulness had completely isolated him.

That he had fallen among far greater dangers than those which had developed themselves when he left England, he of course knew now. That perils had thickened about him fast, and might thicken faster and faster yet, he of course knew now. He could not but admit to himself that he might not have made this journey, if he could have foreseen the events of a few days. And yet his misgivings were not so dark as, imagined by the light of this later time, they would appear. Troubled as the future was, it was the unknown future, and in its obscurity there was ignorant hope. The horrible massacre, days and nights long, which, within a few rounds of the clock, was to set a great mark of blood upon the blessed garnering time of harvest, was as far out of his knowledge as if it had been a hundred thousand years away. The "sharp female newly-born, and called La Guillotine," was hardly known to him, or to the generality of people, by name. The frightful deeds that were to be soon done were probably unimagined at that time in the brains of the doers. How could they have a place in the shadowy conceptions of a gentle mind?

Of unjust treatment in detention and hardship, and in cruel separation from his wife and child, he foreshadowed the likelihood, or the certainty; but, beyond this, he dreaded nothing distinctly. With this on his mind, which was enough to carry into a dreary prison courtyard, he arrived at the prison of La Force.

A man with a bloated face opened the strong wicket, to whom Defarge presented "The Emigrant Evremonde."

"What the Devil! How many more of them!" exclaimed the man with the bloated face.

Defarge took his receipt without noticing the exclamation, and withdrew, with his two fellow-patriots.

"What the Devil, I say again!" exclaimed the gaoler, left with his wife. "How many more!"

The gaoler's wife, being provided with no answer to the question, merely replied, "One must have patience, my dear!" Three turnkeys who entered responsive to a bell she rang, echoed the sentiment, and one added, "For the love of Liberty!" which sounded in that place like an inappropriate conclusion.

The prison of La Force was a gloomy prison, dark and filthy, and with a horrible smell of foul sleep in it. Extraordinary how soon the noisome flavour of imprisoned sleep becomes manifest in all such places that are ill cared for!

"In secret, too," grumbled the gaoler, looking at the written paper. "As if I was not already full to bursting!"

He stuck the paper on a file, in an ill-humor, and Charles Darnay awaited his further pleasure for half an hour: sometimes, pacing to and fro in the strong arched room; sometimes, resting on a stone seat: in either case detained to be imprinted on the memory of the chief and his subordinates.

"Come!" said the chief, at length taking up his keys, "come with me, emigrant."

Through the dismal prison twilight, his new charge accompanied him by corridor and staircase, many doors clanging and locking behind them, until they came into a large, low, vaulted chamber, crowded with prisoners of both sexes. The women were seated at a long table, reading and writing, knitting, sewing, and embroidering; the men were for the most part standing behind their chairs, or lingering up and down the room.

In the instinctive association of prisoners with shameful crime and disgrace, the new-comer recoiled from this company. But, the crowning unreality of his long unreal ride, was, their all at once rising to receive him, with every refinement of manner known to the time, and with all the engaging graces and courtesies of life.

So strangely clouded were these refinements by the prison manners and gloom, so spectral did they become in the inappropriate squalor and misery through which they were seen, that Charles Darnay seemed to stand in a company of the dead. Ghosts all! The ghost of beauty, the ghost of stateliness, the ghost of elegance, the ghost of pride, the ghost of frivolity, the ghost of wit, the ghost of youth, the ghost of age, all waiting their dismissal from the desolate shore, all turning on him eyes that were changed by the death they had died in coming there.

It struck him motionless. The gaoler standing at his side, and the other gaolers moving about, who would have been well enough as to appearance in the ordinary exercise of their functions, looked so extravagantly coarse contrasted with sorrowing mothers and blooming daughters who were there—with the apparitions of the coquette, the young beauty, and the mature woman delicately bred—that the inversion of all experience and likelihood which the scene of shadows presented, was heightened to its utmost. Surely, ghosts all. Surely, the long unreal ride some progress of disease that had brought him to these gloomy shades.

"In the name of the assembled companions in misfortune," said a gentleman of courtly appearance and address, coming forward, "I have the honor of giving you welcome to La Force, and of condoling with you on the calamity that has brought you among us. May it soon terminate happily! It would be an impertinence elsewhere, but it is not so here, to ask your name and condition?"

Charles Darnay roused himself, and gave the required information, in words as suitable as he could find.

"But I hope," said the gentleman, following the chief gaoler with his eyes, who moved across the room, "that you are not in secret?"

"I do not understand the meaning of the term, but I have heard them say so."

"Ah, what a pity! We so much regret it! But take courage; several members of our society have been in secret, at first, and it has lasted but a short time." Then he added, raising his voice, "I grieve to inform the society—in secret."

There was a murmur of commiseration as Charles Darnay crossed the room to a grated door where the gaoler awaited him, and many voices—among which, the soft and compassionate voices of women were conspicuous—gave him good wishes and encouragement. He turned at the grated door, to render the thanks of his heart; it closed under the gaoler's hand; and the apparitions vanished from his sight for ever.

The wicket opened on a stone staircase, leading upward. When they had ascended forty steps (the prisoner of half an hour already counted them), the gaoler opened a low black door, and they passed into a solitary cell. It struck cold and damp, but it was not dark.

"Yours," said the gaoler.

"Why am I confined alone?"

"How do I know!"

"I can buy pen, ink, and paper?"

"Such are not my orders. You will be visited, and can ask then. At present, you may buy your food, and nothing more."

There were in the cell, a chair, a table, and a straw mattress. As the gaoler made a general inspection of these objects, and of the four walls, before going out, a wandering fancy wandered through the mind of the prisoner leaning against the wall opposite to him, that this gaoler was so unwholesomely bloated, both in face and person, as to look like a man who had been drowned and filled with water. When the gaoler was gone, he thought, in the same wandering way, "Now am I left, as if I were dead." Stopping then, to look down at the mattress, he turned from it with a sick feeling, and thought, "And here in these crawling creatures is the first condition of the body after death.

"Five paces by four and a half, five paces by four and a half, five paces by four and a half." The prisoner walked to and fro in his cell, counting its measurement, and the roar of the city arose like muffled drums with a wild swell of voices added to them. "He made shoes, he made shoes, he made shoes." The prisoner counted the measurement again, and paced faster, to draw his mind with him from that latter repetition. "The ghosts that vanished when the wicket closed. There was one among them, the appearance of a lady dressed in black, who was leaning in the embrasure of a window, and she had a light shining upon her golden hair, and she looked like * * * * Let us ride on again, for God's sake, through the illuminated villages with the people all awake! * * * * He made shoes, he made shoes, he made shoes. * * * * Five paces by four and a half." With such scraps tossing and rolling upward from the depths of his mind, the prisoner walked faster and faster, obstinately counting and counting; and the roar of the city changed to this extent—that it still rolled in like muffled drums, but with the wail of voices that he knew, in the swell that rose above them.

Chapter II

THE GRINDSTONE

TELLSON'S Bank, established in the Saint Germain Quarter of Paris, was in a wing of a large house, approached by a courtyard and shut off from the street by a high wall and a strong gate. The house belonged to a great nobleman who had lived in it until he made a flight from the troubles, in his own cook's dress, and got across the borders. A mere beast of the chase flying from hunters, he was still in his metempsychosis no other than the same Monseigneur, the preparation of whose chocolate for whose lips had once occupied three strong men besides the cook in question.

Monseigneur gone, and the three strong men absolving themselves from the sin of having drawn his high wages, by being more than ready and willing to cut his throat on the altar of the dawning Republic one and indivisible of Liberty, Equality, Fraternity, or Death, Monseigneur's house had been first sequestrated, and then confiscated. For, all things moved so fast, and decree followed decree with that fierce precipitation, that now upon the third night of the autumn month of September, patriot emissaries of the law were in possession of Monseigneur's house, and had marked it with the tricolor, and were drinking brandy in its state apartments.

A place of business in London like Tellson's place of business in Paris, would soon have driven the House out of its mind and into the Gazette. For, what would staid British responsibility and respectability have said to orange-trees in boxes in a Bank courtyard, and even to a Cupid over the counter? Yet such things were. Tellson's had whitewashed the Cupid, but he was still to be seen on the ceiling, in the coolest linen, aiming (as he very often does) at money from morning to night. Bankruptcy must inevitably have come of this young Pagan, in Lombard-street, London, and also of a curtained alcove in the rear of the immortal boy, and also of a looking-glass let into the wall, and also of clerks not at all old who danced in public on the slightest provocation. Yet, a French Tellson's could get on with these things exceedingly well, and, as long as the times held together, no man had taken fright at them, and drawn out his money.

What money would be drawn out of Tellson's, henceforth, and what would lie there, lost and forgotten; what plate and jewels would tarnish in Tellson's hiding-places, while the depositors rusted in prisons, and when they should have violently perished; how many accounts with Tellson's, never to be balanced in this world, must be carried over into the next; no man could have said, that night, any more than Mr. Jarvis Lorry could, though he thought heavily of these questions. He sat by a newly lighted wood fire (the blighted and unfruitful year was prematurely cold), and on his honest and courageous face there was a deeper shade than the pendent lamp could throw, or any object in the room distortedly reflect—a shade of horror.

He occupied rooms in the Bank, in his fidelity to the house of which he had grown to be a part, like strong root-ivy. It chanced that they derived a kind of security from the patriotic occupation of the main building, but the true-hearted old gentleman never calculated about that. All such circumstances were indifferent to him, so that he did his duty. On the opposite side of the court-yard, under a colonnade, was extensive standing for carriages—where, indeed, some carriages of Monseigneur yet stood. Against two of the pillars were fastened two great flaring flambeaux, and, in the light of these, standing out in the open air, was a large grindstone: a roughly mounted thing which appeared to have hurriedly been brought there from some neighboring smithy, or other workshop. Rising and looking out of window at these harmless objects, Mr. Lorry shivered, and retired to his seat by the fire. He had opened, not only the glass window, but the lattice blind outside it, and he had closed both again, and he shivered through his frame.

From the street beyond the high wall and the strong gate, there came the usual night hum of the city, with now and then an indescribable ring to it, weird and unearthly, as if some unwonted sounds of a terrible nature were going up to heaven.

"Thank God," said Mr. Lorry, clasping his hands, "that no one near and dear to me is in this dreadful town to-night. May He have mercy on all who are in danger!"

Soon afterward, the bell at the great gate sounded, and he thought, "They have come back!" and sat listening. But, there was no loud irruption into the court-yard, as he had expected, and he heard the gate clash again, and all was quiet.

The nervousness and dread that were upon him inspired that vague uneasiness respecting the Bank which a great charge would naturally awaken, with such feelings roused. It was well guarded, and he got up to go among the trusty people who were watching it, when his door suddenly opened, and two figures rushed in, at sight of which he fell back in amazement.

Lucie and her father! Lucie with her arms stretched out to him, and with that old look of earnestness so concentrated and intensified, that it seemed as though it had been stamped upon her face expressly to give force and power to it in this one passage of her life.

"What is this!" cried Mr. Lorry, breathless and confused. "What is the matter? Lucie! Manette! What has happened? What has brought you here? What is it?"

With the look fixed upon him, in her paleness and wildness, she panted out in his arms, imploringly, "Oh my dear friend! My husband!"

"Your husband, Lucie?"

"Charles."

"What of Charles?"

"Here."

"Here, in Paris?"

"Has been here some days—three or four—I don't know how many—I can't collect my thoughts. An errand of generosity brought him here unknown to us; he was stopped at the barrier, and sent to prison."

The old man uttered an irrepressible cry. Almost at the same moment, the bell of the great gate rang again, and a loud noise of feet and voices came pouring into the court-yard.

"What is that noise?" said the Doctor, turning toward the window.

"Don't look!" cried Mr. Lorry. "Don't look out! Manette, for your life, don't touch the blind!"

The Doctor turned, with his hand upon the fastening of the window, and said, with a cool bold smile:

"My dear friend, I have a charmed life in this city. I have been a Bastille prisoner. There is no patriot in Paris—in Paris?—in France—who, knowing me to have been a prisoner in the Bastille would touch me, except to overwhelm me with embraces, or carry me in triumph. My old pain has given me a power that has brought us through the barrier, and gained us news of Charles there, and brought us here. I knew it would be so; I knew I could help Charles out of all danger; I told Lucie so.—What is that noise?" His hand was again upon the window.

"Don't look!" cried Mr. Lorry, absolutely desperate. "No, Lucie, my dear, nor you!" He got his arm around her, and held her. "Don't be so terrified, my love. I solemnly swear to you that I know of no harm having happened to Charles; that I had no suspicion even, of his being in this fatal place. What prison is he in?"

"La Force."

"La Force! Lucie, my child, if ever you were brave and serviceable in your life—and you were always both—you will compose yourself now, to do exactly as I bid you; for, more depends upon it than you can think, or I can say. There is no help for you in any action on your part to-night; you cannot possibly stir out. I say this, because what I must bid you to do for Charles's sake, is the hardest thing to do of all. You must instantly be obedient, still, and quiet. You must let me put you in a room at the back here. You must leave your father and me alone for two minutes, and as there are Life and Death in the world, you must not delay."

"I will be submissive to you. I see in your face that you know I can do nothing else than this. I know you are true."

The old man kissed her, and hurried her into his room, and turned the key; then, came hurrying back to the Doctor, and opened the window and partly opened the blind, and put his hand upon the Doctor's arm, and looked out with him into the court-yard.

Looked out upon a throng of men and women: not enough in number, or near enough, to fill the court-yard: not more than forty or fifty in all. The people in possession of the house had let them in at the gate, and they had rushed in to work at the grindstone; it had evidently been set up there for their purpose, as in a convenient and retired spot.

But, such awful workers, and such awful work!

The grindstone had a double handle, and, turning at it madly were two men, whose faces, as their long hair flapped back when the whirlings of the grindstone brought their faces up, were more horrible and cruel than the visages of the wildest savages in their most barbarous disguise. False eyebrows and false mustaches were stuck upon them, and their hideous countenances were all bloody and sweaty, and all awry with howling, and all staring and glaring with beastly excitement and want of sleep. As these ruffians turned and turned, their matted locks now flung forward over their eyes, now flung backward over their necks, some women held wine to their mouths that they might drink; and what with dropping blood, and what with dropping wine, and what with the stream of sparks struck out of the stone, all their wicked atmosphere seemed gore and fire. The eye could not detect one creature in the group free from the smear of blood. Shouldering one another to get next at the sharpening-stone were men stripped to the waist, with the stain all over their limbs and bodies; men in all sorts of rags, with the stain upon those rags; men devilishly set off with spoils of women's lace and silk and ribbon, with the stain dyeing those trifless through and through. Hatchets, knives, bayonets, swords, all brought to be sharpened, were all red with it. Some of the hacked swords were tied to the wrists of those who carried them, with strips of linen and fragments of dress: ligatures various in kind, but all deep of the one color. And as the frantic wielders of these weapons snatched them from the stream of sparks and tore away into the streets, the same red hue was red in their frenzied eyes;—eyes which any unbrutalized beholder would have given twenty years of life, to petrify with a well-directed gun.

All this was seen in a moment, as the vision of a drowning man, or of any human creature at any very great pass, could see a world if it were there. They drew back from the window, and the doctor looked for explanation in his friend's ashy face.

"They are," Mr. Lorry whispered the words glancing fearfully round at the locked room, "murdering the prisoners. If you are sure of what you say; if you really have the power you think you have—as I believe you have—make yourself known to these devils, and get taken to La Force. It may be too late, I don't know, but let it not be a minute later!"

Doctor Manette pressed his hand, hastened bareheaded out of the room, and was in the court-yard when Mr. Lorry regained the blind.

His streaming white hair, his remarkable face, and the impetuous confidence of his manner, as he put the weapons aside like water, carried him in an instant to the heart of the concourse at the stone. For a few moments there was a pause, and a hurry, and a murmur, and the unintelligible sound of his voice; and then Mr. Lorry saw him, surrounded by all, and in the midst of a line of twenty men long, all linked shoulder to shoulder, and hand to shoulder, hurried out with cries of—"Live the Bastille prisoner! Help for the Bastille prisoner's kindred in La Force!

Room for the Bastille prisoner in front there! Save the prisoner Evremonde at La Force!" and a thousand answering shouts.

He closed the lattice again with a fluttering heart, closed the window and the curtain, hastened to Lucie, and told her that her father was assisted by the people, and gone in search of her husband. He found her child and Miss Pross with her; but it never occurred to him to be surprised by their appearance until a long time afterward, when he sat watching them in such quiet as the night knew.

Lucie had, by that time, fallen into a stupor on the floor at his feet, clinging to his hand. Miss Pross had laid the child down on his own bed, and her head had gradually fallen on the pillow beside her pretty charge. O the long, long night, with the moans of the poor wife. And O the long, long night, with no return of her father and no tidings!

Twice more in the darkness the bell at the great gate sounded, and the irruption was repeated, and the grindstone whirled and spluttered. "What is it?" cried Lucie, affrighted. "Hush! The soldiers' swords are sharpened there," said Mr. Lorry. "The place is national property now, and used as a kind of armory, my love."

Twice more in all; but, the last spell of work was feeble and fitful. Soon afterward the day began to dawn, and he softly detached himself from the clasping hand, and cautiously looked out again. A man, so besmeared that he might have been a sorely wounded soldier creeping back to consciousness on a field of slain, was rising from the pavement by the side of the grindstone, and looking about him with a vacant air. Shortly, this worn-out murderer descried in the imperfect light one of the carriages of Monseigneur, and, staggering to that gorgeous vehicle, climbed in at the door, and shut himself up to take his rest on its dainty cushions.

The great grindstone, Earth, had turned when Mr. Lorry looked out again, and the sun was red on the court-yard. But, the lesser grindstone stood alone there in the calm morning air, with a red upon it that the sun had never given, and would never take away.

Chapter III

THE SHADOW

ONE of the first considerations which arose in the business mind of Mr. Lorry when business hours came round, was this:—that he had no right to imperil Tellson's by sheltering the wife of an emigrant prisoner under the bank roof. His own possessions, safety, life, he would have hazarded for Lucie and her child, without a moment's demur; but, the great trust he held was not his own, and as to that business charge he was a strict man of business.

At first, his mind reverted to Defarge, and he thought of finding out the wine-shop again and taking counsel with its master in reference to the safest dwelling-place in the distracted state of the city. But, the same consideration that suggested him, repudiated him; he lived in the most violent Quarter, and doubtless was influential there, and deep in its dangerous workings.

Noon coming, and the Doctor not returning, and every minute's delay tending to compromise Tellson's, Mr. Lorry advised with Lucie. She said that her father had spoken of hiring a lodging for a short term, in that Quarter, near the Banking-house. As there was no business objection to this, and as he foresaw that even if it were all well with Charles, and he were to be released, he could not hope to leave the city, Mr. Lorry went out in quest of such a lodging, and found a suitable one, high up in a removed by-street, where the closed blinds in all the other windows of a high melancholy square of buildings marked deserted homes.

To this lodging he at once removed Lucie and her child, and Miss Pross: giving them what comfort he could, and much more than he had himself. He left Jerry with them, as a figure to fill a doorway that would bear considerable knocking on the head, and returned to his own occupations. A disturbed and doleful mind he brought to bear upon them, and slowly and heavily the day lagged on with him.

It wore itself out, and wore him out with it, until the Bank closed. He was again alone in his room of the previous night, considering what to do next, when he heard a foot upon the stair. In a few moments, a man stood in his presence, who, with a keenly observant look at him, addressed him by his name.

"Your servant," said Mr. Lorry. "Do you know me?"

He was a strongly made man with dark curling hair, from forty-five to fifty years of age. For answer he repeated, without any change of emphasis, the words:

"Do you know me?"

"I have seen you somewhere."

"Perhaps at my wine-shop?"

Much interested and agitated, Mr. Lorry said: "You come from Doctor Manette?"

"Yes. I come from Doctor Manette."

"And what says he? What does he send me?"

Defarge gave into his anxious hand, an open scrap of paper. It bore the words in the Doctor's writing:

"Charles is safe, but I cannot safely leave this place yet. I have obtained the favor that the bearer has a short note from Charles to his wife. Let the bearer see his wife."

It was dated from La Force, within an hour.

"Will you accompany me," said Mr. Lorry, joyfully relieved after reading this note aloud, "to where his wife resides?"

"Yes," returned Defarge.

Scarcely noticing, as yet, in what a curiously reserved and mechanical way Defarge spoke, Mr. Lorry put on his hat and they went down into the court-yard. There, they found two women; one knitting.

"Madame Defarge, surely!" said Mr. Lorry, who had left her in exactly the same attitude some seventeen years ago.

"It is she," observed her husband.

"Does madame go with us?" inquired Mr. Lorry, seeing that she moved as they moved.

"Yes. That she may be able to recognise the faces and know the persons. It is for their safety."

Beginning to be struck by Defarge's manner, Mr. Lorry looked dubiously at him, and led the way. Both the women followed; the second woman being The Vengeance.

They passed through the intervening streets as quickly as they might, ascended the staircase of the new domicile, were admitted by Jerry, and found Lucie weeping, alone. She was thrown into a transport by the tidings Mr. Lorry gave her of her husband, and clasped the hand that delivered his note—little thinking what it had been doing near him in the night, and might, but for a chance, have done to him.

> "DEAREST,—Take courage. I am well, and your father has influence around me. You cannot answer this. Kiss our child for me."

That was all the writing. It was so much, however, to her who received it, that she turned from Defarge to his wife, and kissed one of the hands that knitted. It was a passionate, loving, thankful, womanly action, but the hand made no response—dropped cold and heavy, and took to its knitting again.

There was something in its touch that gave Lucie a check. She stopped in the act of putting the note in her bosom, and, with her hands yet at her neck, looked terrified at Madame Defarge. Madame Defarge met the lifted eyebrows and forehead with a cold, impassive stare.

"My dear," said Mr. Lorry, striking in to explain; "there are frequent risings in the streets; and, although it is not likely they will ever trouble you, Madame Defarge wishes to see those whom she has the power to protect at such times, to the end that she may know them—that she may identify them. I believe," said Mr. Lorry, rather halting in his reassuring words, as the stony manner of all the three impressed itself upon him more and more, "I state the case, Citizen Defarge?"

Defarge looked gloomily at his wife, and gave no other answer than a gruff sound of acquiescence.

"You had better, Lucie," said Mr. Lorry, doing all he could to propitiate, by tone and manner, "have the dear child here, and our good Pross. Our good Pross, Defarge, is an English lady and knows no French."

The lady in question, whose rooted conviction that she was more than a match for any foreigner, was not to be shaken by distress and danger, appeared with folded arms, and observed in English to The Vengeance whom her eyes first encountered, "Well, I am sure, Boldface! I hope *you* are pretty well!" She also bestowed a British cough on Madame Defarge; but, neither of the two took much heed of her.

"Is that his child?" said Madame Defarge, stopping in her work for the first time, and pointing her knitting-needle at little Lucie as if it were the finger of Fate.

"Yes, madame," answered Mr. Lorry; "this is our poor prisoner's darling daughter, and only child."

The shadow attendant on Madame Defarge and her party seemed to fall so threatening and dark on the child, that her mother instinctively kneeled on the ground beside her, and held her to her breast. The shadow attendant on Madame Defarge and her party seemed then to fall, threatening and dark, on both the mother and the child.

"It is enough, my husband," said Madame Defarge. "I have seen them. We may go."

But, the suppressed manner had enough of menace in it—not visible and presented, but indistinct and withheld—to alarm Lucie into saying, as she laid her appealing hand on Madame Defarge's dress:

"You will be good to my poor husband. You will do him no harm. You will help me to see him if you can?"

"Your husband is not my business here," returned Madame Defarge, looking down at her with perfect composure. "It is the daughter of your father who is my business here."

"For my sake, then, be merciful to my husband. For my child's sake! She will put her hands together and pray you to be merciful. We are more afraid of you than of these others."

Madame Defarge received it as a compliment, and looked at her husband. Defarge, who had been uneasily biting his thumb-nail and looking at her, collected his face into a sterner expression.

"What is it that your husband says in that little letter?" asked Madame Defarge, with a lowering smile. "Influence; he says something touching influence?"

"That my father," said Lucie, hurriedly taking the paper from her breast, but with her alarmed eyes on her questioner, and not on it, "has much influence around him."

"Surely it will release him!" said Madame Defarge. "Let it do so."

"As a wife and mother," cried Lucie, most earnestly, "I implore you to have pity on me, and not to exercise any power that you possess, against my innocent husband, but to use it in his behalf. Oh sister woman, think of me! As a wife and mother!"

Madame Defarge looked coldly as ever at the suppliant, and said, turning to her friend, The Vengeance:

"The wives and mothers we have been used to see, since we were as little as this child, and much less, have not been geatly considered? We have known *their* husbands and fathers laid in prison and kept from them, often enough? All our lives, we have seen our sister women suffer, in themselves and in their children, poverty, nakedness, hunger, thirst, sickness, misery, oppression and neglect of all kinds?"

"We have seen nothing else," returned The Vengeance.

"We have borne this a long time," said Madame Defarge, turning her eyes again upon Lucie. "Judge you! Is it likely that the trouble of one wife and mother would be much to us now?"

She resumed her knitting and went out. The Vengeance followed. Defarge went last, and closed the door.

"Courage, my dear Lucie," said Mr. Lorry, as he raised her. "Courage, courage! So far all goes well with us—much, much better than it has of late gone with many poor souls. Cheer up, and have a thankful heart."

"I am not thankless, I hope, but that dreadful woman seems to throw a shadow on me and on all my hopes."

"Tut, tut!" said Mr. Lorry; "what is this despondency in the brave little breast? A shadow, indeed! No substance in it, Lucie."

But the shadow of the manner of these Defarges was dark upon himself, for all that, and in his secret mind it troubled him greatly.

Chapter IV

CALM IN A STORM

DOCTOR MANETTE did not return until the morning of the fourth day of his absence. So much of what had happened in that dreadful time as could be kept from the knowledge of Lucie, was so well concealed from her, that not until long afterward, when France and she were far apart, did she know that eleven hundred defenceless prisoners of both sexes and all ages, had been killed by the populace; that four days and nights had been darkened by this deed of horror; and that the air around her had been tainted by the slain. She only knew that there had been an attack upon the prisons, that all political prisoners had been in danger, and that some had been dragged out by the crowd and murdered.

To Mr. Lorry, the Doctor communicated under an injunction of secrecy on which he had no need to dwell, that the crowd had taken him through a scene of carnage to the prison of La Force. That, in the prison he had found a self-appointed Tribunal sitting, before which the prisoners were brought singly, and by which they were rapidly ordered to be put forth to be massacred, or to be released, or (in a few cases) to be sent back to their cells. That, presented by his conductors to this Tribunal, he had announced himself by name and profession as having been for eighteen years a secret and unaccused prisoner in the Bastille; that one of the body so sitting in judgment had risen and identified him, and that this man was Defarge.

That, hereupon he had ascertained, through the registers on the table, that his son-in-law was among the living prisoners, and had pleaded hard to the tribunal—of whom some members were asleep and some awake, some dirty with murder and some clean, some sober and some not—for his life and liberty. That, in the first frantic greetings lavished on himself as a notable sufferer under the overthrown system, it had been accorded to him to have Charles Darnay brought before the lawless Court, and examined. That he seemed on the point of being at once released, when the tide in his favor met with some unexplained check (not intelligible to the Doctor), which led to a few words of secret conference. That, the man sitting as President had then informed Doctor Manette that the prisoner must remain in custody, but should, for his sake, be held inviolate in safe custody. That, immediately, on a signal, the prisoner was removed to the interior of the prison again; but that he, the Doctor, had then so strongly pleaded for permission to remain and assure himself that his son-in-law was, through no malice or mischance, delivered to the concourse whose murderous yells outside the gate had often drowned the proceedings; that he had obtained the permission, and had remained in that Hall of Blood until the danger was over.

The sights he had seen there, with brief snatches of food and sleep by intervals, shall remain untold. The mad joy over the prisoners who were saved, had astounded him scarcely less than the mad ferocity against those who were cut to pieces. One prisoner there was, he said, who had been discharged into the street free, but at whom a mistaken savage had thrust a pike as he passed out. Being besought to go to him and dress the wound, the Doctor had passed out at the same gate, and had found him in the arms of a company of Samaritans, who were seated on the bodies of their victims. With an inconsistency as monstrous as anything in this awful nightmare, they had helped the healer, and tended the wounded man with the gentlest solicitude—had made a litter for him and escorted him carefully from the spot—had then caught up their weapons and plunged anew into a butchery so dreadful, that the Doctor had covered his eyes with his hands, and swooned away in the midst of it.

As Mr. Lorry received these confidences, and as he watched the face of his friend now sixty-two years of age, a misgiving arose within him that such dread experiences would revive the old danger. But, he had never seen his friend in his present aspect; he had never at all known him in his present character. For the first time the Doctor felt, now, that his suffering was strength and power. For the first time, he felt that in that sharp fire, he had slowly forged the iron which could break the prison door of his daughter's husband, and deliver him. "It all tended to a good end, my friend; it was not mere waste and ruin. As my beloved child was helpful in restoring me to myself, I will be helpful now in restoring the dearest part of herself to her; by the aid of heaven I will do it!" Thus, Doctor Manette. And when Jarvis Lorry saw the kindled eyes, the resolute face, the calm strong look and bearing of the man whose life always seemed to him to have been stopped, like a clock, for so many years, and then set going again with an energy which had lain dormant during the cessation of its usefulness, he believed greater things than the Doctor had at that time to contend with, would have yielded before his persevering purpose.

While he kept himself in his place, as a physician whose business was with all degrees of mankind, bond and free, rich and poor, bad and good, he used his personal influence so wisely, that he was soon the inspecting physician of three prisons, and among them of La Force. He could now assure Lucie that her husband was no longer confined alone, but was mixed with the general body of prisoners; he saw her husband weekly, and brought sweet messages to her, straight from his lips; sometimes her husband himself sent a letter to her, (though never by the Doctor's hand), but she was not permitted to write to him: for, among the many wild suspicions of plots in the prisons, the wildest of all pointed at emigrants who were known to have made friends or permanent connections abroad.

This new life of the Doctor's was an anxious life, no doubt; still, the sagacious Mr. Lorry saw that there was a new sustaining pride in it. Nothing unbecoming tinged the pride; it was a natural and worthy one; but he observed it as a curiosity. The Doctor knew, that up to that time, his imprisonment had been associated in the minds of his daughter and his friend, with his personal affliction, deprivation, and weakness. Now that this was changed, and he knew himself to be invested through that old trial, with forces to which they both looked for Charles's ultimate safety and deliverance, he became so far exalted by the change, that he took the lead and direction, and required them as the weak, to trust to him as the strong. The preceding relative positions of himself and Lucie were reversed, yet only as the liveliest gratitude and affection could reverse them, for he could have had no pride but in rendering some service to her who had rendered so much to him. "All curious to see," thought Mr. Lorry, in his amiably shrewd way, "but all natural and right; so, take the lead, my dear friend, and keep it; it couldn't be in better hands."

But, though the Doctor tried hard, and never ceased trying to get Charles Darnay set at liberty, or at least to get him brought to trial, the public current of the time set too strong and fast for him. The new Era began; the king was tried, doomed, and beheaded; the Republic of Liberty, Equality, Fraternity, or Death, declared for victory or death against the world in arms; the black flag waved night and day from the great towers of Notre Dame; three hundred thousand men, summoned to rise against the tyrants of the earth, rose from all the varying soils of France, as if the dragon's teeth had been sown broadcast, and had yielded fruit equally on hill and plain, on rock, in gravel, and alluvial mud, under the bright sky of the South, and under the clouds of the North, in fell and forest, in the vineyards and the olive-grounds, and among the cropped grass and the stubble of the corn, along the fruitful banks of the broad rivers, and in the sand of the sea-shore. What private solicitude could rear itself against the deluge of the Year One of Liberty—the deluge rising from below, not falling from above, and with the windows of Heaven shut, not opened!

There was no pause, no pity, no peace, no interval of relenting rest, no measurement of time. Though days and nights circled as regularly as when time was young, and the evening and morning were the first day, other count of time there was none. Hold of it was lost in the raging fever of a nation, as it is in the fever of one patient. Now, breaking the unnatural silence of a whole city, the executioner showed the people the head of the king—and now, it seemed almost in the same breath, the head of his fair wife, which had had eight weary months of imprisoned widowhood and misery, to turn it gray.

And yet, observing the strange law of contradiction which obtains in all such cases, the time was long, while it flamed by so fast. A revolutionary tribunal in the capital, and forty or fifty thousand revolutionary committees all over the land; a law of the Suspected, which struck away all security for liberty or life, and delivered over any good and innocent person to any bad and guilty one; prisons gorged with people who had committed no offence, and could obtain no hearing; these things became the established order and nature of appointed things, and seemed to be ancient usage before they were many weeks old. Above all, one hideous figure grew as familiar as if it had been before the general gaze from the foundations of the world—the figure of the sharp female called La Guillotine.

It was the popular theme for jests; it was the best cure for headache; it infallibly prevented the hair from turning gray; it imparted a peculiar delicacy to the complexion; it was the National Razor which shaved close: who kissed La Guillotine, looked through the little window and sneezed into the sack. It was the sign of the regeneration of the human race. It superseded the Cross. Models of it were worn on breasts from which the Cross was discarded, and it was bowed down to and believed in where the Cross was denied.

It sheared off heads so many, that it, and the ground it most polluted, were a rotten red. It was taken to pieces, like a toy puzzle for a young Devil, and was put together again when the occasion wanted it. It hushed the eloquent, struck down the powerful, abolished the beautiful and good. Twenty-two friends of high public mark, twenty-one living and one dead, it had lopped the heads off, in one morning, in as many minutes. The name of the strong man of Old Scripture had descended to the chief functionary who worked it; but, so armed, he was stronger than his namesake, and blinder, and tore away the gates of God's own Temple every day.

Among these terrors, and the brood belonging to them, the Doctor walked with a steady head; confident in his power, cautiously persistent in his end, never doubting that he would save Lucie's husband at last. Yet the current of the time swept by, so strong and deep, and carried the time away so fiercely, that Charles had lain in prison one year and three months when the Doctor was thus steady and confident. So much more wicked and distracted had the Revolution grown in that December month, that the rivers of the South were encumbered with the bodies of the violently drowned by night, and prisoners were shot in lines and squares under the southern wintry sun. Still, the Doctor walked among the terrors with a steady hand. No man better known than he in Paris at that day; no man in a stranger situation. Silent, humane, indispensable in hospital and prison, using his art equally among assassins and victims, he was a man apart. In the exercise of his skill, the appearance and the story of the Bastille Captive removed him from all other men. He was not suspected or brought in question, any more than if he had indeed been recalled to life some eighteen years before, or were a Spirit moving among mortals.

Chapter V

THE WOOD-SAWYER

ONE year and three months. During all that time Lucie was never sure, from hour to hour, but that the Guillotine would strike off her husband's head next day. Every day, through the stony streets, the tumbrils now jolted heavily, filled with Condemned. Lovely girls; bright women, brown-haired, black-haired, and gray; youths; stalwart men and old; gentle born and peasant born; all red wine for La Guillotine, all daily brought into light from the dark cellars of the loathsome prisons, and carried to her through the streets to slake her devouring thirst. Liberty, equality, fraternity, or death; the last much the easiest to bestow, O Guillotine!

If the suddenness of her calamity, and the whirling wheels of the time, had stunned the Doctor's daughter into awaiting the result in idle despair, it would but have been with her as it was with many. But, from the hour when she had taken the white head to her fresh young bosom in the garret of Saint Antoine, she had been true to her duties. She was truest to them in the season of trial, as all the quietly loyal and good will always be.

As soon as they were established in their new residence, and her father had entered on the routine of his avocations, she arranged the little household as exactly as if her husband had been there. Every thing had its appointed place and its appointed time. Little Lucie she taught as regularly as if they had all been united in their English home. The slight devices with which she cheated herself in the show of a belief that they would soon be reunited—the little preparations for his speedy return, the setting aside of his chair and his books—these, and the solemn prayer at night for one dear prisoner especially, among the many unhappy souls in prison, and the shadow of death—were almost the only outspoken reliefs of her heavy mind.

She did not greatly alter in appearance. The plain dark dresses, akin to mourning dresses, which she and her child wore, were as neat and as well attended to as the brighter clothes of happy days. She lost her color, and the old and intent expression was a constant, not an occasional, thing: otherwise, she remained very pretty and comely. Sometimes, at night on kissing her father, she would burst into the grief she had repressed all day, and would say that her sole reliance, under Heaven, was on him. He always resolutely answered:?—"Nothing can happen to him without my knowledge, and I know that I can save him, Lucie."

They had not made the round of their changed life many weeks, when her father said to her, on coming home one evening:—

"My dear, there is an upper window in the prison, to which Charles can sometimes gain access at three in the afternoon. When he can get to it—which depends on many uncertainties and incidents—he might see you in the street, he thinks, if you stood in a certain place that I can show you. But you will not be able to see him, my poor child, and even if you could, it would be unsafe for you to make a sign of recogintion."

"O show me the place, my father, and I will go there every day."

From that time, in all weathers, she waited there two hours. As the clock struck two, she was there, and at four she turned resignedly away. When it was not too wet or inclement for her child to be with her, they went together; at other times she was alone; but she never missed a single day.

It was the dark and dirty corner of a small winding street. The hovel of a cutter of wood into lengths for burning, was the only house at that end; all else was wall. On the third day of her being there, he noticed her.

"Good-day, citizeness."

"Good-day, citizen."

This mode of address was now prescribed by decree. It had been established voluntarily some time ago, among the more thorough patriots; but, was now law for everybody.

"Walking here again, citizeness?"

"You see me, citizen!"

The wood-sawyer, who was a little man with a redundancy of gesture, (he had once been a mender of roads), cast a glance at the prison, pointed at the prison, and putting his ten fingers before his face to represent bars, peeped through them jocosely.

"But it's not my business," said he. And went on sawing his wood.

Next day, he was looking out for her, and accosted her the moment she appeared.

"What? Walking here again, citizeness?"

"Yes, citizen."

"Ah! A child too! Your mother, is it not, my little citizeness?"

"Do I say yes, mamma?" whispered little Lucie, drawing close to her.

"Yes, dearest."

"Yes, citizen."

"Ah! But it's not my business. My work is my business. See my saw! I call it my Little Guillotine. La, la, la! La, la, la! And off his head comes!"

The billet fell as he spoke, and he threw it into a basket.

"I call myself the Samson of the firewood guillotine. See here again! Loo, loo, loo! Loo, loo, loo! And off *her* head comes! Now, a child. Tickle, tickle; Pickle, pickle! And off *its* head comes! All the family!"

Lucie shuddered as he threw two more billets into his basket, but it was impossible to be there while the wood-sawyer was at work, and not be in his sight. Thenceforth, to secure his good-will, she always spoke to him first, and often gave him drink-money, which he readily received.

He was an inquisitive fellow, and sometimes when she had quite forgotten him in gazing at the prison roof and grates, and in lifting her heart up to her husband, she would come to herself to find him looking at her, with his knee on his bench and his saw stopped in its work. "But it's not my business!" he would generally say at those times, and briskly fall to his sawing again.

In all weathers, in the snow and frost of winter, in the bitter winds of spring, in the hot sunshine of summer, in the rain of autumn, again in the snow and frost of winter, Lucie passed two hours of every day at this place; and every day, on leaving it, she kissed the prison wall. Her husband saw her, (so she learned from her father), it might be once in five or six times: it might be twice or thrice running: it might be, not for a week or a fortnight together. It was enough that he could and did see her when the chances served, and on that possibility she would have waited out the day, seven days a week.

These occupations brought her round to the December month, wherein her father walked among the terrors with a steady head. On a lightly snowing afternoon she arrived at the usual corner. It was a day of some wild rejoicing, and a festival. She had seen the houses, as she came along, decorated with little pikes, and with little red caps stuck upon them; also, with tricolored ribbons; also, with the standard inscription, (tricolored letters were the favorite), Republic One and Indivisible. Liberty, Equality, Fraternity, or Death!

The miserable shop of the wood-sawyer was so small, that its whole surface furnished very indifferent space for this legend. He had got somebody to scrawl it up for him, however, who had squeezed Death in with most inappropriate difficulty. On his house-top, he displayed pike and cap, as a good citizen must, and in a window he had stationed his saw, inscribed as his "Little Saint Guillotine"—for the great sharp female was by that time popularly canonized. His shop was shut and he was not there, which was a relief to Lucie, and left her quite alone.

But, he was not far off, for presently she heard a troubled movement and a shouting coming along, which filled her with fear. A moment afterward, and a throng of people came pouring round the corner by the prison wall, in the midst of whom was the wood-sawyer, hand in hand with The Vengeance. There could not be fewer than five hundred people, and they were dancing like five thousand demons. There was no other music than their own singing. They danced to the popular Revolution song, keeping a ferocious time that was like a gnashing of teeth in unison. Men and women danced together, women danced together, men danced together, as hazard had brought them together. At first, they were a mere storm of coarse red caps and coarse woollen rags; but, as they filled the place, and stopped to dance about Lucie, some ghastly apparition of a dance-figure gone raving mad arose among them. They advanced, retreated, struck at one another's hands, clutched at one another's heads, spun round alone, caught one another and spun round in pairs, until many of them dropped. While those were down, the rest linked hand in hand, and all spun round together; then the ring broke, and in separate rings of two and four they turned and turned until they all stopped at once, began again, struck, clutched, and tore, and then reversed the spin, and all spun round another way. Suddenly they stopped again, paused, struck out the time afresh, formed into lines the width of the public way, and, with their heads low down and their hands high up, swooped screaming off. No fight could have been half so terrible as this dance. It was so emphatically a fallen sport—a something once innocent delivered over to all devilry—a healthy pastime changed into a means of angering the blood, bewildering the senses, and steeling the heart. Such grace as was visible in it, made it the uglier, showing how warped and perverted all things good by nature were become. The maidenly bosom bared to this, the pretty almost-child's head thus distracted, the delicate foot mincing in this slough of blood and dirt, were types of the disjointed time.

This was the Carmagnole. As it passed, leaving Lucie frightened and bewildered in the doorway of the wood-sawyer's house, the feathery snow fell as quietly and lay as white and soft, as if it had never been.

"O my father!" for he stood before her when she lifted up the eyes she had momentarily darkened with her hand; "such a cruel, bad sight!"

"I know, my dear, I know. I have seen it many times. Don't be frightened! Not one of them would harm you."

"I am not frightened for myself, my father. But when I think of my husband, and the mercies of these people—"

"We will set him above their mercies very soon. I left him climbing to the window, and I came to tell you. There is no one here to see. You may kiss your hand toward that highest shelving roof."

"I do so, Father, and I send my soul with it."

"You cannot see him, my poor dear?"

"No, father," said Lucie, yearning and weeping as she kissed her hand, "no."

A footstep in the snow. Madame Defarge. "I salute you, citizeness," from the Doctor. "I salute you, citizen." This in passing. Nothing more. Madame Defarge gone, like a shadow over the white road.

"Give me your arm, my love. Pass from here with an air of cheerfulness and courage, for his sake. That was well done"; they had left the spot; "it shall not be in vain. Charles is summoned for to-morrow."

"For to-morrow!"

"There is no time to lose. I am well prepared, but there are precautions to be taken, that could not be taken until he was actually summoned before the Tribunal. He has not received the notice yet, but I know that he will presently be summoned for to-morrow, and removed to the Conciergerie; I have timely information. You are not afraid?"

She could scarcely answer, "I trust in you."

"Do so, implicitly. Your suspense is nearly ended, my darling; he shall be restored to you within a few hours; I have encompassed him with every protection. I must see Lorry."

He stopped. There was a heavy lumbering of wheels within hearing. They both knew too well what it meant. One. Two. Three. Three tumbrils faring away with their dread loads over the hushing snow.

"I must see Lorry," the Doctor repeated, turning her another way.

The stanch old gentleman was still in his trust: had never left it. He and his books were in frequent requisition as to property confiscated and made national. What he could save for the owners, he saved. No better man living to hold fast by what Tellson's had in keeping, and to hold his peace.

A murky red and yellow sky, and a rising mist from the Seine, denoted the approach of darkness. It was almost dark when they arrived at the Bank. The stately residence of Monseigneur was altogether blighted and deserted. Above a heap of dust and ashes in the court, ran the letters: National Property. Republic One and Indivisible. Liberty, Equality, Fraternity, or Death.

Who could that be with Mr. Lorry—the owner of the riding-coat upon the chair—who must not be seen? From whom newly arrived, did he come out, agitated and surprised, to take his favorite in his arms? To whom did he appear to repeat her faltering words, when, raising his voice and turning his head toward the door of the room from which he had issued, he said: "Removed to the Conciergerie, and summoned for to-morrow?"

Chapter VI

TRIUMPH

THE dread Tribunal of five Judges, Public Prosecutor, and determined Jury, sat every day. Their lists went forth every evening, and were read out by the gaolers of the various prisons to their prisoners. The standard gaoler-joke was, "Come out and listen to the Evening Paper, you inside there!"

"Charles Evremonde, called Darnay!"

So, at last began, the Evening Paper at La Force.

When a name was called, its owner stepped apart into a spot reserved for those who were announced as being thus fatally recorded. Charles Evremonde, called Darnay, had reason to know the usage; he had seen hundreds pass away so.

His bloated gaoler, who wore spectacles to read with, glanced over them to assure himself that he had taken his place, and went through the list, making a similar short pause at each name. There were twenty-three names, but only twenty were responded to; for one of the prisoners so summoned had died in gaol and been forgotten, and two had already been guillotined and forgotten. The list was read, in the vaulted chamber where Darnay had seen the associated prisoners on the night of his arrival. Every one of those had perished in the massacre; every human creature he had since cared for and parted with, had died on the scaffold.

There were hurried words of farewell and kindness, but the parting was soon over. It was the incident of every day, and the society of La Force were engaged in the preparation of some games of forfeits and a little concert, for that evening. They crowded to the grates and shed tears there; but, twenty places in the projected entertainments had to be refilled, and the time was, at best, short to the lock-up hour, when the common rooms and corridors would be delivered over to the great dogs who kept watch there through the night. The prisoners were far from insensible or unfeeling; their ways arose out of a condition of the time. Similarly, though with a subtle difference, a species of fervor or intoxication, known, without doubt, to have led some persons to brave the guillotine unnecessarily, and to die by it, was not mere boastfulness, but a wild infection of the wildly shaken public mind. In seasons of pestilence, some of us will have a secret attraction to the disease—a terrible passing inclination to die of it. And all of us have like wonders hidden in our breasts, only needing circumstances to evoke them.

The passage to the Conciergerie was short and dark; the night in its vermin-haunted cells was long and cold. Next day, fifteen prisoners were put to the bar before Charles Darnay's name was called. All the fifteen were condenmed, and the trials of the whole occupied an hour and a half.

"Charles Evremonde, called Darnay," was at length arraigned.

His Judges sat upon the bench in feathered hats; but the rough red cap and tricolored cockade was the head-dress otherwise prevailing. Looking at the Jury and the turbulent audience he might have thought that the usual order of things was reversed, and that the felons were trying the honest men. The lowest, cruelest, and worst populace of a city, never without its quantity of low, cruel, and bad, were the directing spirits of the scene: noisily commenting, applauding, disapproving, anticipating, and precipitating the result, without a check. Of the men, the greater part were armed in various ways; of the women, some wore knives, some daggers, some ate and drank as they looked on, many knitted. Among these last, was one, with a spare piece of knitting under her arm as she worked. She was in a front row, by the side of a man whom he had never seen since his arrival at the Barrier, but whom he directly remembered as Defarge. He noticed that she once or twice whispered in his ear, and that she seemed to be his wife; but, what he most noticed in the two figures was, that although they were posted as close to himself as they could be, they never looked toward him. They seemed to be waiting for something with a dogged determination, and they looked at the Jury, but at nothing else. Under the President sat Doctor Manette, in his usual quiet dress. As well as the prisoner could see, he and Mr. Lorry were the only men there, unconnected with the Tribunal, who wore their usual clothes, and had not assumed the coarse garb of the Carmagnole.

Charles Evremonde, called Darnay, was accused by the public prosecutor as an emigrant, whose life was forfeit to the Republic, under the decree which banished all emigrants on pain of Death. It was nothing that the decree bore date since his return to France. There he was, and there was the decree; he had been taken in France, and his head was demanded.

"Take off his head!" cried the audience. "An enemy to the Republic!"

The President rang his bell to silence those cries, and asked the prisoner whether it was not true that he had lived many years in England?

Undoubtedly it was.

Was he not an emigrant then? What did he call himself?

Not an emigrant, he hoped, within the sense and spirit of the law.

"Why not?" the President desired to know.

Because he had voluntarily relinquished a title that was distasteful to him, and a station that was distasteful to him, and had left his country—he submitted before the word emigrant in the present acceptation by the Tribunal was in use—to live by his own industry in England, rather than on the industry of the overladen people of France.

What proof had he of this?

He handed in the names of two witnesses: Theophile Gabelle, and Alexandre Manette.

But he had married in England? the President reminded him.

True, but not an English woman.

A citizeness of France?

Yes. By birth.

Her name and family?

"Lucie Manette, only daughter of Doctor Manette, the good physician who sits there."

This answer had a happy effect upon the audience. Cries in exaltation of the well-known good physician rent the hall. So capriciously were the people moved, that tears immediately rolled down several ferocious countenances which had been glaring at the prisoner a moment before, as if with impatience to pluck him out into the streets and kill him.

On these few steps of his dangerous way, Charles Darnay had set his foot according to Doctor Manette's reiterated instructions. The same cautious counsel directed every step that lay before him, and had prepared every inch of his road.

The President asked why had he returned to France when he did, and not sooner?

He had not returned sooner, he replied, simply because he had no means of living in France, save those he had resigned; whereas, in England, he lived by giving instruction in the French langauge and literature. He had returned when he did, on the pressing and written entreaty of a French citizen, who represented that his life was endangered by his absence. He had come back, to save a citizen's life, and to bear his testimony, at whatever personal hazard, to the truth. Was that criminal in the eyes of the republic?

The populace cried enthusiastically, "No!" and the President rang his bell to quiet them. Which it did not, for they continued to cry "No!" until they left off, of their own will.

The President required the name of that citizen? The accused explained that the citizen was his first witness. He also referred with confidence to the citizen's letter, which had been taken from him at the Barrier, but which he did not doubt would be found among the papers then before the President.

The Doctor had taken care that it should be there—had assured him that it would be there—and at this stage of the proceedings it was produced and read. Citizen Gabelle was called to confirm it, and did so. Citizen Gabelle hinted, with infinite delicacy and politeness, that in the pressure of business imposed on the Tribunal by the multitudes of enemies of the Republic with which it had to deal, he had been slightly overlooked in his prison of the Abbaye—in fact, had rather passed out of the Tribunal's patriotic remembrance—until three days ago; when he had been summoned before it, and had been set at liberty on the jury's declaring themselves satisfied that the accusation against him was answered, as to himself, by the surrender of the citizen Evremonde, called Darnay.

Doctor Manette was next questioned. His high personal popularity, and the clearness of his answers, made a great impression; but, as he proceeded as he showed that the accused was his first friend on his release from his long imprisonment; that the accused had remained in England, always faithful and devoted to his daughter and himself in their exile; that, so far from being in favor with the aristocrat government there, he had actually been tried for his life by it, as the foe of England and friend of the United States—as he brought these circumstances into view, with the greatest discretion and with the straightforward force of truth and earnestness, the Jury and the populace became one. At last, when he appealed by name to Monsieur Lorry, an English gentleman then and there present, who, like himself, had been a witness on that English trial and could corroborate his account of it, the Jury declared that they had heard enough, and that they were ready with their votes if the President were content to receive them.

At every vote (the jurymen voted aloud and individually), the populace set up a shout of applause. All the voices were in the prisoner's favor, and the President declared him free.

Then, began one of those extraordinary scenes with which the populace sometimes gratified their fickleness, or their better impulses toward generosity and mercy, or which they regarded as some set-off against their swollen account of cruel rage. No man can decide now to which of these motives such extraordinary scenes were referable; it is probable, to a blending of all the three, with the second predominating. No sooner was the acquittal pronounced, than tears were shed as freely as blood at another time, and such fraternal embraces were bestowed upon the prisoner by as many of both sexes as could rush at him, that after his long and unwholesome confinement he was in danger of fainting from exhaustion; none the less he knew very well, that the very same people, carried by another current, would have rushed at him with the very same intensity, to rend him to pieces and strew him over the streets.

His removal, to make way for other accused persons who were to be tried, rescued him from these caresses for the moment. Five were to be tried together, next, as enemies of the Republic, forasmuch as they had not assisted it by word or deed. So quick was the Tribunal to compensate itself and the nation for a chance lost, that these five came down to him before he left the place, condenmed to die within twenty-four hours. The first of them told him so, with the customary prison sign of Death—a raised finger—and they all added in words, "Long live the Republic!"

The five had had, it is true, no audience to lengthen their proceedings, for when he and Doctor Manette emerged from the gate, there was a great crowd about it, in which there seemed to be every face he had seen in Court—except two, for which he looked in vain. On his coming out, the concourse made at him anew, weeping, embracing, and shouting, all by turns and all together, until the very tide of the river on the bank of which the mad scene was acted, seemed to run mad, like the people on the shore.

They put him into a great chair they had among them, and which they had taken either out of the court itself, or one of its rooms or passages. Over the chair they had thrown a red flag, and to the back of it they had bound a pike with a red cap on its top. In this car of triumph, not even the Doctor's entreaties could prevent his being carried to his home on men's shoulders, with a confused sea of red caps heaving about him, and casting up to sight from the stormy deep such wrecks of faces, that he more than once misdoubted his mind being in confusion, and that he was in the tumbril on his way to the Guillotine.

In wild, dreamlike procession, embracing whom they met, and pointing him out, they carried him on. Reddening the snowy streets with the prevailing Republican color, in winding and tramping through them, as they had reddened them below the snow with a deeper dye, they carried him thus into the courtyard of the building where he lived. Her father had gone on before, to prepare her, and when her husband stood upon his feet, she dropped insensible in his arms.

As he held her to his heart and turned her beautiful head between his face and the brawling crowd, so that his tears and her lips might come together unseen, a few of the people fell to dancing. Instantly, all the rest fell to dancing, and the courtyard overflowed with the Carmagnole. Then, they elevated into the vacant chair a young woman from the crowd to be carried as the Goddess of Liberty, and then swelling and overflowing out into the adjacent streets, and along the river's bank, and over the bridge, the Carmagnole absorbed them every one and whirled them away.

After grasping the Doctor's hand, as he stood victorious and proud before him; after grasping the hand of Mr. Lorry, who came panting in breathless from his struggle against the waterspout of the Carmagnole; after kissing little Lucie, who was lifted up to clasp her arms round his neck; and after embracing the ever zealous and faithful Pross who lifted her, he took his wife in his arms and carried her up to their rooms.

"Lucie! My own! I am safe."

"O dearest Charles! let me thank God for this on my knees as I have prayed to Him."

They all reverently bowed their heads and hearts. When she was again in his arms, he said to her:

"And now speak to your father, dearest. No other man in all this France could have done what he has done for me."

She laid her head upon her father's breast as she had lain his poor head on her own breast, long, long ago. He was happy in the return he had made her, he was recompensed for his suffering, he was proud of his strength. "You must not be weak, my darling," he remonstrated; "don't tremble so. I have saved him."

Chapter VII

A KNOCK AT THE DOOR

"I HAVE saved him." It was not another of the dreams in which he had often come back; he was really here. And yet his wife trembled, and a vague but heavy fear was upon her.

All the air around was so thick and dark, the people were so passionately revengeful and fitful, the innocent were so constantly put to death on vague suspicion and black malice, it was so impossible to forget that many as blameless as her husband, and as dear to others as he was to her, every day shared the fate from which he had been clutched, that her heart could not be as lightened of its load as she felt it ought to be. The shadows of the wintry afternoon were beginning to fall, and even now the dreadful carts were rolling through the streets. Her mind pursued them, looking for him among the Condemned; and then she clung to his real presence, and trembled more.

Her father, cheering her, showed a compassionate superiority to this woman's weakness, which was wonderful to see. No garret, no shoemaking, no One Hundred and Five, North Tower, now! He had accomplished the task he had set himself, his promise was redeemed he had saved Charles. Let them all lean upon him.

Their housekeeping was of a very frugal kind; not only because that was the safest way of life, involving the least offence to the people, but because they were not rich, and Charles, throughout his imprisonment, had had to pay heavily for his bad food, and for his guard, and toward the living of the poorer prisoners. Partly on this account, and partly to avoid a domestic spy, they kept no servant; the citizen and citizeness who acted as porters at the court-yard gate rendered them occasional service; and Jerry (almost wholly transferred to them by Mr. Lorry) had become their daily retainer, and had his bed there every night.

It was an ordinance of the Republic One and Indivisible of Liberty, Equality, Fraternity, or Death, that on the door or door-post of every house, the name of every inmate must be legibly inscribed in letters of a certain size, at a certain convenient height from the ground. Mr. Jerry Cruncher's name, therefore, duly embellished the doorpost down below; and, as the afternoon shadows deepened, the owner of that name himself appeared, from overlooking a painter whom Doctor Manette had employed to add to the list the name of Charles Evremonde, called Darnay.

In the universal fear and distrust that darkened the time, all the usual harmless ways of life were changed. In the Doctor's little household, as in very many others, the articles of daily consumption that were wanted were purchased every evening, in small quantities, and at various small shops. To avoid attracting notice, and to give as little occasion as possible for talk and envy, was the general desire.

For some months past, Miss Pross and Mr. Cruncher had discharged the office of purveyors: the former carrying the money; the latter the basket. Every afternoon, at about the time when the public lamps were lighted, they fared forth on this duty, and made and brought home such purchases as were needful. Although Miss Pross, through her long association with a French family, might have known as much of their language as of her own, if she had had a mind, she had no mind in that direction; consequently she knew no more of "that nonsense," (as she was pleased to call it,) than Mr. Cruncher did. So her manner of marketing was to plump a noun-substantive at the head of a shopkeeper without any introduction in the nature of an article, and, if it happened not to be the name of the thing she wanted, to look round for that thing, lay hold of it, and hold on by it until the bargain was concluded. She always made a bargain for it, by holding up, as a statement of its just price, one finger less than the merchant held up, whatever his number might be.

"Now, Mr. Cruncher," said Miss Pross, whose eyes were red with felicity; "if you are ready, I am."

Jerry hoarsely professed himself at Miss Pross's service. He had worn all his rust off long ago, but nothing would file his spiky head down.

"There's all manner of things wanted," said Miss Pross, "and we shall have a precious time of it. We want wine, among the rest. Nice toasts these Redheads will be drinking, wherever we buy it."

"It will be much the same to your knowledge, miss, I should think," retorted Jerry, "whether they drink your health or the Old Un's."

"Who's he?" said Miss Pross.

Mr. Cruncher, with some difference, explained himself as meaning "Old Nick's."

"Ha!" said Miss Pross, "it doesn't need an interpreter to explain the meaning of these creatures. They have but one, and it's Midnight Murder and Mischief!"

"Hush, dear! Pray, pray, be cautious!" cried Lucie.

"Yes, yes, yes, I'll be cautious," said Miss Pross; "but I may say among ourselves, that I do hope there will be no oniony and tobaccoey smotherings in the form of embracings going on in the streets. Now, Ladybird, never you stir from that fire till I come back! Take care of the dear husband you have recovered, and don't move your pretty head from his shoulder as you have it now, till you see me again! May I ask a question, Doctor Manette, before I go?"

"I think you may take that liberty," the Doctor answered, smiling.

"For gracious sake don't talk about liberty; we have quite enough of that," said Miss Pross.

"Hush, dear! Again?" Lucie remonstrated.

"Well, my sweet," said Miss Pross, nodding her head emphatically, "the short and the long of it is, that I am a subject of His Most Gracious Majesty King George the Third"; Miss Pross courtsied at the name; "and as such, my maxim is, Confound their politics, Frustrate their knavish tricks, On him our hopes we fix, God save the King!"

Mr. Cruncher, in an access of loyalty, growlingly repeated the words after Miss Pross, like somebody at church.

"I am glad you have so much of the Englishman in you, though I wish you had never taken that cold in your voice," said Miss Pross, approvingly. "But the question, Doctor Manette. Is there"—it was the good creature's way to affect to make light of any thing that was a great anxiety with them all, and to come at it in this chance manner—"is there any prospect, yet, of our getting out of this place?"

"I fear not yet. It would be dangerous for Charles yet."

"Heigh-ho-hum!" said Miss Pross, cheerfully repressing a sigh, as she glanced at her darling's golden hair in the light of the fire, "then we must have patience and wait: that's all. We must hold up our heads and fight low, as my brother Solomon used to say. Now, Mr. Cruncher!—Don't you move, Ladybird!"

They went out leaving Lucie, and her husband, her father and the child, by a bright fire. Mr. Lorry was expected back presently from the Banking House. Miss Pross had lighted the lamp, but had put it aside in a corner, that they might enjoy the firelight undisturbed. Little Lucie sat by her grandfather, with her hands clasped through his arm; and he, in a tone not rising much above a whisper, began to tell her a story of a great and powerful Fairy who had opened a prison wall and let out a captive who had once done the Fairy a service. All was subdued and quiet, and Lucie was more at ease than she had been.

"What is that" she cried, all at once.

"My dear!" said her father, stopping in his story, and laying his hand on hers, "command yourself. What a disordered state you are in! The least thing—nothing—startles you. *You*, your father's daughter?"

"I thought, my father," said Lucie, excusing herself, with a pale face and in a faltering voice, "that I heard strange feet upon the stairs."

"My love, the staircase is as still as Death."

As he said the word, a blow was struck upon the door.

"O Father, Father. What can this be! Hide, Charles. Save him!"

"My child," said the Doctor, rising and laying his hand upon her shoulder. "I have *saved* him. What weakness is this, my dear! Let me go to the door."

He took the lamp in his hand, crossed the two intervening outer rooms, and opened it. A rude clattering of feet over the floors, and four rough men in red caps, armed with sabres and pistols, entered the room.

"The Citizen Evremonde, called Darnay," said the first.

"Who seeks him?" answered Darnay.

"I seek him. We seek him. I know you, Evremonde; I saw you before the Tribunal to-day. You are again the prisoner of the Republic."

The four surrounded him, where he stood with his wife and child clinging to him.

"Tell me how and why am I again a prisoner?"

"It is enough that you return straight to the Conciergerie, and will know to-morrow. You are summoned for to-morrow."

Doctor Manette, whom this visitation had so turned into stone, that he stood with the lamp in his hand, as if he were a statue made to hold it, moved after these words were spoken, put the lamp down, and confronting the speaker, and taking him, not ungently, by the loose front of his red woollen shirt, said:—

"You know him, you have said. Do you know me?"

"Yes, I know you, Citizen Doctor."

"We all know you, Citizen Doctor," said the other three.

He looked abstractedly from one to another, and said, in a lower voice, after a pause:

"Will you answer his question to me? How does this happen?"

"Citizen Doctor," said the first, reluctantly, "he has been denounced to the section of Saint Antoine. This citizen," pointing out the second who had entered, "is from Saint Antoine."

The citizen here indicated nodded his head, and added:

"He is accused by Saint Antoine."

"Of what?" asked the Doctor.

"Citizen Doctor," said the first, with his former reluctance, "ask no more. If the Republic demands sacrifices from you, without doubt you, as a good patriot, will be happy to make them. The Republic goes before all. The people is supreme. Evremonde, we are pressed."

"One word," the Doctor entreated. "Will you tell me who denounced him?"

"It is against rule," answered the first; "but you can ask Him of Saint Antoine here."

The Doctor turned his eyes upon that man, who moved uneasily on his feet, pulled his beard a little, and at length said:—

"Well! Truly it is against rule. But he is denounced—and gravely—by the Citizen and Citizeness Defarge. And by one other."

"What other?"

"Do *you* ask, Citizen Doctor?"

"Yes!"

"Then," said he of Saint Antoine, with a strange look, "you will be answered to-morrow. Now, I am dumb!"

Chapter VIII

A HAND AT CARDS

HAPPILY unconscious of the new calamity at home, Miss Pross threaded her way along the narrow streets and crossed the river by the bridge of the Pont-Neuf, reckoning in her mind the number of indispensable purchases she had to make. Mr. Cruncher, with the basket, walked at her side. They both looked to the right and to the left into most of the shops they passed, had a wary eye for all gregarious assemblages of people, and turned out of their road to avoid any very excited group of talkers. It was a raw evening, and the misty river, blurred to the eye with blazing lights and to the ear with harsh noises, showed where the barges were stationed in which the smiths worked, making guns for the Army of the Republic. Woe to the man who played tricks with *that* Army, or got undeserved promotion in it! Better for him that his beard had never grown, for the National Razor shaved him close.

Having purchased a few small articles of grocery, and a measure of oil for the lamp, Miss Pross bethought herself of the wine they wanted. After peeping into several wine-shops, she stopped at the sign of The Good Republican Brutus of Antiquity, not far from the National Palace, once (and twice) the Tuileries, where the aspect of things rather took her fancy. It had a quieter look than any other place of the same description they had passed, and, though red with patriotic caps, was not so red as the rest. Sounding Mr. Cruncher and finding him of her opinion, Miss Pross resorted to The Good Republican Brutus of Antiquity, attended by her cavalier.

Slightly observant of the smoky lights; of the people, pipe in mouth, playing with limp cards and yellow dominoes; of the one bare-breasted, bare-armed, soot-begrimed workman, reading a journal aloud, and of the others listening to him; of the weapons worn, or laid aside to be resumed; of the two or three customers fallen forward asleep, who in the popular, high-shouldered shaggy black spencer, looked, in that attitude, like slumbering bears or dogs; the two outlandish customers approached the counter, and showed what they wanted.

As their wine was measuring out, a man parted from another man in a corner, and rose to depart. In going, he had to face Miss Pross. No sooner did he face her, than Miss Pross uttered a scream, and clapped her hands.

In a moment the whole company were on their feet. That somebody was assassinated by somebody vindicating a difference of opinion, was the likeliest occurrence. Everybody looked to see somebody fall, but only saw a man and a woman standing staring at each other; the man with all the outward aspect of a Frenchman and a thorough Republican; the woman, evidently English.

What was said in this disappointing anti-climax, by the disciples of The Good Republican Brutus of Antiquity, except that it was something very voluble and loud, would have been as so much Hebrew or Chaldean to Miss Pross and her protector, though they had been all ears. But, they had no ears for any thing in their surprise. For, it must be recorded, that not only was Miss Pross lost in amazement and agitation; but, Mr. Cruncher—though it seemed on his own separate and individual account—was in a state of the greatest wonder.

"What is the matter?" said the man who had caused Miss Pross to scream; speaking in a vexed, abrupt voice, (though in a low tone), and in English.

"Oh, Solomon, dear Solomon!" cried Miss Pross, clapping her hands again. "After not setting eyes upon you or hearing of you for so long a time, do I find you here!"

"Don't call me Solomon. Do you want to be the death of me?" asked the man, in a furtive, frightened way.

"Brother, brother!" cried Miss Pross, bursting into tears. "Have I ever been so hard with you that you ask me such a cruel question!"

"Then hold your meddlesome tongue," said Solomon, "and come out, if you want to speak to me. Pay for your wine, and come out. Who's this man?"

Miss Pross, shaking her loving and dejected head at her by no means affectionate brother, said, through her tears, "Mr. Cruncher."

"Let him come out, too," said Solomon. "Does he think me a ghost?"

Apparently, Mr. Cruncher did, to judge from his looks. He said not a word, however, and Miss Pross, exploring the depths of her reticule through her tears, with great difficulty, paid for her wine. As she did so, Solomon turned to the followers of The Good Republican Brutus of Antiquity, and offered a few words of explanation in the French language, which caused them all to relapse into their former places and pursuits.

"Now," said Solomon, stopping at the dark street corner, "what do you want?"

"How dreadfully unkind in a brother nothing has ever turned my love away from," cried Miss Pross, "to give me such a greeting, and show me no affection."

"There. Con-found it! There!" said Solomon, making a dab at Miss Pross's lips with his own. "Now are you content?"

Miss Pross only shook her head and wept in silence.

"If you expect me to be surprised," said her brother Solomon, "I am not surprised; I knew you were here; I know of most people who are here. If you really don't want to endanger my existence—which I half believe you do—go your ways as soon as possible, and let me go mine. I am busy. I am an official."

"My English brother Solomon," mourned Miss Pross, casting up her tear-fraught eyes, "that had the makings in him of one of the best and greatest of men in his native country, an official among foreigners, and such foreigners! I would almost sooner have seen the dear boy lying in his——"

"I said so!" cried her brother, interrupting. "I knew it! You want to be the death of me. I shall be rendered Suspected, by my own sister. Just as I am getting on!"

"The gracious and merciful Heavens forbid!" cried Miss Pross. "Far rather would I never see you again, dear Solomon, though I have ever loved you truly, and ever shall. Say but one affectionate word to me, and tell me there is nothing angry or estranged between us, and I will detain you no longer."

Good Miss Pross! As if the estrangement between them had come of any culpability of hers. As if Mr. Lorry had not known it for a fact, years ago, in the quiet corner in Soho, that this precious brother had spent her money and left her!

He was saying the affectionate word, however, with a far more grudging condescension and patronage than he could have shown if their relative merits and positions had been reversed (which is invariably the case, all the world over), when Mr. Cruncher, touching him on the shoulder, hoarsely and unexpectedly interposed with the following singular question:—

"I say! Might I ask the favor? As to whether your name is John Solomon, or Solomon John?"

The official turned towards him with sudden distrust. He had not previously uttered a word.

"Come!" said Mr. Cruncher. "Speak out, you know." (Which, by the way, was more than he could do himself.) "John Solomon, or Solomon John? She calls you Solomon, and she must know, being your sister. And *I* know you're John, you know. Which of the two goes first? And regarding that name of Pross, likewise? That warn't your name over the water."

"What do you mean?"

"Well, I don't know all I mean, for I can't call to mind what your name was over the water."

"No?"sneered Solomon.

"No. But I'll swear it was a name of two syllables."

"Indeed!"

"Yes. T'other one's was one syllable. I know you. You was a spy-witness at the Bailey. What in the name of the Father of Lies—own father to yourself—was you called at that time?"

"Barsad," said another voice, striking in.

"That's the name for a thousand pound!" cried Jerry.

The speaker who struck in was Sydney Carton. He had his hands behind him, under the skirts of his riding-coat, and he stood at Mr. Cruncher's elbow as negligently as he might have stood at the Old Bailey itself.

"Don't be alarmed, my dear Miss Pross. I arrived at Mr. Lorry's, to his surprise, yesterday evening; we agreed that I would not present myself elsewhere until all was well, or unless I could be useful; I present myself here, to beg a little talk with your brother. I wish you had a better employed brother than Mr. Barsad. I wish for your sake, Mr. Barsad was not a Sheep of the Prisons."

Sheep was a cant word of the time for a spy, under the gaolers. The spy, who was pale, turned paler, and asked him how he dared——

"I'll tell you," said Sydney. "I lighted on you, Mr. Barsad, coming out of the prison of the Conciergerie while I was contemplating the walls, an hour or more ago. You have a face to be remembered, and I remember faces well. Made curious by seeing you in that connection, and having a reason to which you are no stranger, for associating you with the misfortunes of a friend now very unfortunate, I walked in your direction.

I walked into the wine-shop here, close after you, and sat near you. I had no difficulty in deducing from your unreserved conversation, and the rumour openly going about among your admirers, the nature of your calling. And gradually, what I had done at random seemed to shape itself into a purpose, Mr. Barsad."

"What purpose?" the spy asked.

"It would be troublesome, and might be dangerous, to explain in the street. Could you favor me, in confidence, with some minutes of your company—at the office of Tellson's Bank, for instance?"

"Under a threat?"

"Oh! Did I say that?"

"Then, why should I go there?"

"Really, Mr. Barsad, I can't say, if you can't."

"Do you mean that you won't say, sir?" the spy irresolutely asked.

"You apprehend me very clearly, Mr. Barsad. I won't."

Carton's negligent recklessness of manner came powerfully in aid of his quickness and skill, in such a business as he had in his secret mind, and with such a man as he had to do with. His practiced eye saw it, and made the most of it.

"Now, I told you so," said the spy, casting a reproachful look at his sister; "if any trouble comes of this, it's your doing."

"Come, come, Mr. Barsad!" exclaimed Sydney. "Don't be ungrateful. But for my great respect for your sister, I might not have led up so pleasantly to a little proposal that I wish to make for our mutual satisfaction. Do you go with me to the Bank?"

"I'll hear what you have got to say. Yes, I'll go with you."

"I propose that we first conduct your sister safely to the corner of her own street. Let me take your arm, Miss Pross. This is not a good city, at this time, for you to be out in, unprotected; and as your escort knows Mr. Barsad, I will invite him to Mr. Lorry's with us. Are we ready? Come then!"

Miss Pross recalled soon afterward, and to the end of her life remembered, that as she pressed her hands on Sydney's arm and looked up in his face, imploring him to do no hurt to Solomon, there was a braced purpose in the arm and a kind of inspiration in the eyes, which not only contradicted his light manner, but changed and raised the man. She was too much occupied then, with fears for the brother who so little deserved her affection, and with Sydney's friendly reassurances, adequately to heed what she observed.

They left her at the corner of the street, and Carton led the way to Mr. Lorry's, which was within a few minutes' walk. John Barsad, or Solomon Pross, walked at his side.

Mr. Lorry had just finished his dinner, and was sitting before a cheery little log or two of fire—perhaps looking into their blaze for the picture of that younger elderly gentleman from Tellson's, who had looked into the red coals at the Royal George at Dover, now a good many years ago. He turned his head as they entered, and showed the surprise with which he saw a stranger.

"Miss Pross's brother, sir," said Sydney. "Mr. Barsad."

"Barsad?" repeated the old gentleman, "Barsad! I have an association with the name—and with the face."

"I told you, you had a remarkable face, Mr. Barsad," observed Carton, coolly. "Pray sit down."

As he took a chair himself, he supplied the link that Mr. Lorry wanted, by saying to him with a frown, "Witness at that trial." Mr. Lorry immediately remembered, and regarded his new visitor with an undisguised look of abhorrence.

"Mr. Barsad has been recognized by Miss Pross as the affectionate brother you have heard of," said Sydney, "and has acknowledged the relationship. I pass to worse news. Darnay has been arrested again."

Struck with consternation, the old gentleman exclaimed: "What do you tell me! I left him safe and free within these two hours, and am about to return to him!"

"Arrested for all that. When was it done, Mr. Barsad?"

"Just now, if at all."

"Mr. Barsad is the best authority possible, sir," said Sydney; "and I have it from Mr. Barsad's communication to a friend and brother sheep over a bottle of wine, that the arrest has taken place. He left the messengers at the gate, and saw them admitted by the porter. There is no earthly doubt that he is retaken."

Mr. Lorry's business eye read in the speaker's face that it was loss of time to dwell upon the point. Confused, but sensible that something might depend upon his presence of mind, he commanded himself, and was silently attentive.

"Now, I trust," said Sydney to him, "that the name and influence of Doctor Manette may stand him in as good stead to-morrow—you said he would be before the Tribunal again to-morrow, Mr. Barsad?——"

"Yes; I believe so."

"——In as good stead to-morrow as to-day. But it may not be so. I own to you, I am shaken, Mr. Lorry, by Doctor Manette's not having the power to prevent this arrest."

"He may not have known of it beforehand," said Mr. Lorry.

"But that very circumstance would be alarming, when we remember how identified he is with his son-in-law."

"That's true," Mr. Lorry acknowledged, with his troubled hand at his chin, and his troubled eyes on Carton.

"In short," said Sydney, "this is a desperate time, when desperate games are played for desperate stakes. Let the Doctor play the winning game; I will play the losing one. No man's life here is worth purchase. Any one carried home by the people to-day, may be condemned to-morrow. Now, the stake I have resolved to play for, in case of the worst, is a friend in the Conciergerie. And the friend I purpose to myself to win is Mr. Barsad."

"You need have good cards, sir," said the spy.

"I'll run them over. I'll see what I hold. Mr. Lorry, you know what a brute I am; I wish you'd give me a little brandy."

It was put before him, and he drank off a glassful—drank off another glassful—pushed the bottle thoughtfully away.

"Mr. Barsad," he went on, in the tone of one who really was looking over a hand at cards: "Sheep of the prisons, emisary of Republican committees, now turnkey, now prisoner, always spy and secret informer, so much the more valuable here for being English that an Englishman is less open to suspicion of subornation in those characters than a Frenchman, represents himself to his employers under a false name. That's a very good card. Mr. Barsad, now in the employ of the republican French government, was formerly in the employ of the aristocratic English government, the enemy of France and freedom. That's an excellent card. Inference clear as day in this region of suspicion, that Mr. Barsad, still in the pay of the aristocratic English government, is the spy of Pitt, the treacherous foe of the Republic, crouching in its bosom, the English traitor and agent of all mischief so much spoken of and so difficult to find. That's a card not to be beaten. Have you followed my hand, Mr. Barsad?"

"Not to understand your play," returned the spy, somewhat uneasily.

"I play my Ace, Denunciation of Mr. Barsad to the nearest Section Committee. Look over your hand, Mr. Barsad, and see what you have. Don't hurry."

He drew the bottle near, poured out another glassful of brandy, and drank it off. He saw that the spy was fearful of his drinking himself into a fit state for the immediate denunciation of him. Seeing it, he poured out and drank another glassful.

"Look over your hand carefully, Mr. Barsad. Take time."

It was a poorer hand than he suspected. Mr. Barsad saw losing cards in it that Sydney Carton knew nothing of. Thrown out of his honorable employment in England, through too much unsuccessful hard swearing there—not because he was wanted there: our English reasons for vaunting our superiority to secrecy and spies are of very modern date—he knew that he had crossed the Channel, and accepted service in France: first, as a tempter and an eavesdropper among his own countrymen there: gradually, as a tempter and an eavesdropper among the natives. He knew that under the overthrown government he had been a spy upon Saint Antoine and Defarge's wine-shop; had received from the watchful police such heads of information concerning Doctor Manette's imprisonment, release, and history, as should serve him for an introduction to familiar conversation with the Defarges; and tried them on Madame Defarge, and had broken down with them signally. He always remembered with fear and trembling, that that terrible woman had knitted when he talked with her, and had looked ominously at him as her fingers moved. He had since seen her, in the Section of Saint Antoine, over and over again produce her knitted registers, and denounce people whose lives the guillotine then surely swallowed up. He knew, as every one employed as he was, did, that he was never safe; that flight was impossible; that he was tied fast under the shadow of the axe; and that in spite of his utmost tergiversation and treachery in furtherance of the reigning terror, a word might bring it down upon him. Once denounced, and on such grave grounds as had just now been suggested to his mind, he foresaw that the dreadful woman of whose unrelenting character he had seen many proofs, would produce against him that fatal register, and would quash his last chance of life. Besides that all secret men are men soon terrified, here were surely cards enough of one black suit, to justify the holder in growing rather livid as he turned them over.

"You scarcely seem to like your hand," said Sydney, with the greatest composure. "Do you play?"

"I think, sir," said the spy, in the meanest manner, as he turned to Mr. Lorry, "I may appeal to a gentleman of your years and benevolence, to put it to this other gentleman, so much your junior, whether he can under any circumstances reconcile it to his station to play that Ace of which he has spoken. I admit that *I* am a spy, and that it is considered a discreditable station—though it must be filled by somebody; but this gentleman is no spy, and why should he so demean himself as to make himself one?"

"I play my Ace, Mr. Barsad," said Carton, taking the answer on himself, and looking at his watch, "without any scruple, in a very few minutes."

"I should have hoped, gentlemen both," said the spy, always striving to hook Mr. Lorry into the discussion, "that your respect for my sis ter——"

"I could not better testify my respect for your sister than by finally relieving her of her brother," said Sydney Carton.

"You think not, sir?"

"I have thoroughly made up my mind about it."

The smooth manner of the spy, curiously in dissonance with his ostentatiously rough dress, and probably with his usual demeanor, received such a check from the inscrutability of Carton,—who was a mystery to wiser and honester men than he—that it faltered here and failed him. While he was at a loss, Carton said, resuming his former air of contemplating cards:

"And indeed, now I think again, I have a strong impression that I have another good card here, not yet enumerated. That friend and fellow-sheep, who spoke of himself as pasturing in the country prisons; who was he?"

"French. You don't know him," said the spy, quickly.

"French, eh?" repeated Carton, musing, and not appearing to notice him at all, though he echoed the word. "Well; he may be."

"Is, I assure you," said the spy; "though it's not important."

"Though it's not important," repeated Carton in the same mechanical way—"though it's not important——No, it's not important—— No. Yet I know the face."

"I think not. I am sure not. It can't be," said the spy.

"It—can't—be," muttered Sydney Carton, retrospectively, and filling his glass (which fortunately was a small one) again. "Can't—be. Spoke good French. Yet like a foreigner, I thought?"

"Provincial," sald the spy.

"No. Foreign?" cried Carton, striking his open hand on the table, as a light broke clearly on his mind. "Cly! Disgised, but the same man. We had that man before us at the Old Bailey."

"Now, there you are hasty, sir," said Barsad, with a smile that gave his aquiline nose an extra inclination to one side; "there you really give me an advantage over you. Cly (who I will unreservedly admit, at this distance of time, was a partner of mine) has been dead several years. I attended him in his last illness. He was buried in London, at the church of Saint Pancras-in-the-fields. His unpopularity with the blackguard multitude at the moment prevented my following his remains, but I helped to lay him in his coffin."

Here Mr. Lorry became aware, from where he sat, of a most remarkable goblin shadow on the wall. Tracing it to its source, he discovered it to be caused by a sudden extraordinary rising and stiffening of all the risen and stiff hair on Mr. Cruncher's head.

"Let us be reasonable," said the spy, "and let us be fair. To show you how mistaken you are, and what an unfounded assumption yours is, I will lay before you a certificate of Cly's burial, which I happen to have carried in my pocket-book," (with a hurried hand he produced and opened it,) "ever since. There it is. Oh, look at it, look at it! You may take it in your hand; it's no forgery."

Here Mr. Lorry perceived the reflection on the wall to elongate, and Mr. Cruncher rose and stepped forward. His hair could not have been more violently on end, if it had been that moment dressed by the cow with the crumpled horn in the house that Jack built.

Unseen by the spy, Mr. Cruncher stood at his side, and touched him on the shoulder like a ghostly bailiff.

"That there Roger Cly, master," said Mr. Cruncher, with a taciturn and iron-bound visage. "So *you* put him in his coffin?"

"I did."

"Who took him out of it?"

Barsad leaned back in his chair, and stammered, "What do you mean?"

"I mean," said Mr. Cruncher, "that he warn't never in it. No! Not he! I'll have my head took off, if he was ever in it."

The spy looked round at the two gentlemen; they both looked in unspeakable astonishment at Jerry.

"I tell you," said Jerry, "that you buried paving-stones and earth in that there coffin. Don't go and tell *me* that you buried Cly. It was a take-in. Me and two more knows it."

"How do you know it?"

"What's that to you? Ecod!" growled Mr. Cruncher, "it's you I have got a old grudge again, is it, with your shameful impositions upon tradesmen! I'd catch hold of your throat and choke you for half a guinea." Sydney Carton, who, with Mr. Lorry, had been lost in amazement at this turn of the business, here requested Mr. Cruncher to moderate and explain himself.

"At another time, sir," he returned, evasively, "the present time is ill-convenient for explainin'. What I stand to, is, that he knows well wot that there Cly was never in that there coffin. Let him say he was, in so much as a word of one syllable, and I'll either catch hold of his throat and choke him for half a guinea;"—Mr. Cruncher dwelt upon this as quite a liberal offer; "or I'll out and announce him."

"Humph! I see one thing," said Carton. "I hold another card, Mr. Barsad. Impossible, here in raging Paris, with Suspicion filling the air, for you to outlive denunciation, when you are in communication with another aristocratic spy of the same antecedents as yourself, who, moreover, has the mystery about him of having feigned death and come to life again! A plot in the prisons, of the foreigners against the Republic. A strong card—a certain Guillotine card! Do you play?"

"No!" returned the spy. "I throw up. I confess that we were so unpopular with the outrageous mob, that I only got away from England at the risk of being ducked to death, and that Cly was so ferreted up and down that he never would have got away at all but for that sham. Though how this man knows it was a sham, is a wonder of wonders to me."

"Never you trouble your head about this man," retorted the contentious Mr. Cruncher; "you'll have trouble enough with giving your attention to that gentleman. And look here! Once more!"—Mr. Cruncher could not be restrained from making rather an ostentatious parade of his liberality—"I'd catch hold of your throat and choke you for half a guinea."

The Sheep of the prisons turned from him to Sydney Carton and said, with more decision, "It has come to a point. I go on duty soon, and can't overstay my time. You told me you had a proposal; what is it? Now, it is of no use asking too much of me. Ask me to do any thing in my office, putting my head in great extra danger, and I had better trust my life to the chances of a refusal than the chances of consent. In short, I should make that choice. You talk of desperation. We are all desperate here. Remember! I may denounce you if I think proper, and I can swear my way through stone walls, and so can others. Now, what do you want with me?"

"Not very much. You are a turnkey at the Conciergerie?"

"I tell you once for all, there is no such thing as an escape possible," said the spy, firmly.

"Why need you tell me what I have not asked? You are a turnkey at the Conciergerie?"

"I am sometimes."

"You can be when you choose?"

"I can pass in and out when I choose."

Sydney Carton filled another glass with brandy, poured it slowly out upon the hearth, and watched it as it dropped. It being all spent, he said, rising:

"So far, we have spoken before these two, because it was as well that the merits of the cards should not rest solely between you and me. Come into the dark room here and let us have one final word alone."

Chapter IX

THE GAME MADE

WHILE Sydney Carton and the Sheep of the prisons were in the adjoining dark room, speaking so low that not a sound was heard, Mr. Lorry looked at Jerry in considerable doubt and mistrust. That honest tradesman's manner of receiving the look, did not inspire confidence; he changed the leg on which he rested, as often as if he had fifty of those limbs, and were trying them all; he examined his finger-nails with a very questionable closeness of attention; and whenever Mr. Lorry's eye caught his, he was taken with that peculiar kind of short cough requiring the hollow of a hand before it, which is seldom, if ever, known to be an infirmity attendant on perfect openness of character.

"Jerry," said Mr. Lorry. "Come here."

Mr. Cruncher came forward sideways, with one of his shoulders in advance of him.

"What have you been besides a messenger?"

After some cogitation, accompanied with an intent look at his patron, Mr. Cruncher conceived the luminous idea of replying, "Agricultooral character."

"My mind misgives me much," said Mr. Lorry, angrily shaking his forefinger at him, "that you have used the respectable and great house of Tellson's as a blind, and that you have had an unlawful occupation of an infamous description. If you have, don't expect me to befriend you, when you get back to England. If you have, don't expect me to keep your secret. Tellson's shall not be imposed upon."

"I hope, sir," pleaded the abashed Mr. Cruncher, "that a gentleman like yourself, wot I've had the honour of odd-jobbing till I'm gray at it, would think twice about harming of me, even if it wos so—I don't say it is, but even if it wos. And which it is to be took into account that if it wos, it wouldn't, even then, be all o' one side. There'd be two sides to it. There might be medical doctors at the present hour, a picking up their guineas where a honest tradesman don't pick up his fardens—fardens! no, nor yet his half fardens—half fardens! no, nor yet his quarter—a banking away like smoke at Tellson's, and a cocking their medical eyes at that tradesman on the sly, a going in and going out to their own carriages—ah! equally like smoke, if not more so. Well, that 'ud be imposing, too, on Tellson's. For you cannot sarse the goose and not the gander. And here's Mrs. Cruncher, or leastways wos in the Old England times, and would be to-morrow, if cause given, a floppin' again the business to that degree as is ruinating—stark ruinating! Whereas them medical doctors' wives don't flop—catch 'em at it! Or, if they flop, their floppings goes in favor of more patients, and how can you rightly have one without t'other? Then, wot with undertakers, and wot with parish clerks, and wot with sextons, and wot with private watchmen (all awaricious, and all in it), a man wouldn't get much by it, even if it wos so. And wot little a man did get, would never prosper with him, Mr. Lorry. He'd never have no good of it; he'd want all along to be out of the line, if he could see his way out, being once in—even if it wos so."

"Ugh!" cried Mr. Lorry, rather relenting, nevertheless. "I am shocked at the sight of you."

"Now, what I would humbly offer to you, sir," pursued Mr. Cruncher, "even if it wos so, which I don't say it is——"

"Don't prevaricate," said Mr. Lorry.

"No, I will *not*, sir," returned Mr. Cruncher, as if nothing were further from his thoughts or practice—"which I don't say it is—wot I would humbly offer to you, sir, would be this. Upon that there stool, at that there Bar, sets that there boy of mine, brought up and growed up to be a man, wot will errand you, message you, general-light-job you, till your heels is where your head is, if such should be your wishes. If it wos so, which I still don't say it is (for I will not prewaricate to you, sir), let that there boy keep his father's place, and take care of his mother; don't blow upon that boy's father—do not do it, sir—and let that father go into the line of the reg'lar diggin', and make amends for what he would have un-dug—if it wos so—by diggin' of 'em in with a will, and with conwictions respectin' the future keepin' of 'em safe. That, Mr. Lorry," said Mr. Crucher, wiping his forehead with his arm, as an announcement that he had arrived at the peroration of his discourse, "is wot I would respectfully offer to you, sir. A man don't see all this here goin' on dreadful round him, in the way of subjects without heads, dear me, plentiful enough fur to bring the price down to porterage and hardly that without havin' his serious thoughts of things. And these here would be mine, if it wos so, entreatin' of you fur to bear in mind that wot I said just now, I up and said in the good cause when I might have kep' it back."

"That at least is true," said Mr. Lorry. "Say no more now. It may be that I shall yet stand your friend, if you deserve it, and repent in action—not in words. I want no more words."

Mr. Cruncher knuckled his forehead, as Sydney Carton and the spy returned from the dark room. "Adieu, Mr. Barsad!" said the former; "our arrangement thus made, you have nothing to fear from me."

He sat down in a chair on the hearth, over against Mr. Lorry. When they were alone, Mr. Lorry asked him what he had done?

"Not much. If it should go ill with the prisoner, I have ensured access to him, once."

Mr. Lorry's countenance fell.

"It is all I could do," said Carton. "To propose too much would be to put this man's head under the axe, and, as he himself said, nothing worse could happen to him if he were denounced. It was obviously the weakness of the position. There is no help for it."

"But access to him," said Mr. Lorry, "if it should go ill before the tribunal, will not save him."

"I never said it would."

Mr. Lorry's eyes gradually sought the fire; his sympathy with his darling, and the heavy disappointment of this second arrest, gradually weakened them; he was an old man now, overborne with anxiety of late, and his tears fell.

"You are a good man and a true friend," said Carton, in an altered voice. "Forgive me if I notice that you are affected. I could not see my father weep, and sit by, careless. And I could not respect your sorrow more, if you were my father. You are free from that misfortune, however."

Though he said the last words, with a slip into his usual manner, there was a true feeling and respect both in his tone and in his touch, that Mr. Lorry, who had never seen the better side of him, was wholly unprepared for. He gave him his hand, and Carton gently pressed it.

"To return to poor Darnay," said Carton. "Don't tell Her of this interview, or this arrangement. It would not enable Her to go to see him. She might think it was contrived, in case of the worst, to convey to him the means of anticipating the sentence."

Mr. Lorry had not thought of that, and he looked quickly at Carton to see if it were in his mind. It seemed to be; he returned the look, and evidently understood it.

"She might think a thousand things," he said, "and any of them would only add to her trouble. Don't speak of me to her. As I said to you when I first came, I had better not see her. I can put my hand out to do any little helpful work for her that my hand can find to do, without that. You are going to her, I hope? She must be very desolate to-night."

"I am going now, directly."

"I am glad of that. She has such a strong attachment to you and reliance on you. How does she look?"

"Anxious and unhappy, but very beautiful."

"Ah!"

It was a long, grieving sound, like a sigh—almost like a sob. It attracted Mr. Lorry's eyes to Carton's face, which was turned to the fire. A light, or a shade (the old gentleman could not have said which), passed from it as swiftly as a change would sweep over a hill-side on a wild, bright day, and he lifted his foot to put back one of the little flaming logs, which was tumbling forward. He wore the white riding-coat and top-boots, then in vogue, and the light of the fire touching their light surfaces made him look very pale, with his long brown hair, all untrimmed, hanging loose about him. His indifference to fire was sufficiently remarkable to elicit a word of remonstrance from Mr. Lorry; his boot was still upon the hot embers of the flaming log, when it had broken under the weight of his foot.

"I forgot it," he said.

Mr. Lorry's eyes were again attracted to his face. Taking note of the wasted air which clouded the naturally handsome features, and having the expression of prisoners' faces fresh in his mind, he was strongly reminded of that expression.

"And your duties here have drawn to an end, sir?" said Carton, turning to him.

"Yes. As I was telling you last night, when Lucie came in so unexpectedly, I have at length done all that I can do here. I hoped to have left them in perfect safety, and then to have quitted Paris. I have my Leave to Pass. I was ready to go."

They were both silent.

"Yours is a long life to look back upon, sir?" said Carton, wistfully.

"I am in my seventy-eighth year."

"You have been useful all your life; steadily and constantly occupied; trusted, respected, and looked up to?"

"I have been a man of business, ever since I have been a man. Indeed, I may say that I was a man of business when a boy."

"See what a place you fill at seventy-eight. How many people will miss you when you leave it empty!"

"A solitary old bachelor," answered Mr. Lorry, shaking his head. "There is nobody to weep for me."

"How can you say that? Wouldn't She weep for you? Wouldn't her child?"

"Yes, yes, thank God. I didn't quite mean what I said."

"It *is* a thing to thank God for; is it not?"

"Surely, surely."

"If you could say, with truth, to your own solitary heart, to-night, 'I have secured to myself the love and attachment, the gratitude or respect, of no human creature; I have won myself a tender place in no regard; I have done nothing good or serviceable to be remembered by!' your seventy-eight years would be seventy-eight heavy curses; would they not?"

"You say truly, Mr. Carton; I think they would be."

Sydney turned his eyes again upon the fire, and, after a silence of a few moments, said:

"I should like to ask you: Does your childhood seem far off? Do the days when you sat at your mother's knee, seem days of very long ago?"

Responding to his softened manner, Mr. Lorry answered:

"Twenty years back, yes; at this time of my life, no. For, as I draw closer and closer to the end, I travel in the circle, nearer and nearer to the beginning. It seems to be one of the kind smoothings and preparings of the way. My heart is touched now, by many remembrances that had long fallen asleep, of my pretty young mother (and I so old!), and by many associations of the days when what we call the World was not so real with me, and my faults were not confirmed in me."

"I understand the feeling!" exclaimed Carton, with a bright flush. "And you are the better for it?"

"I hope so."

Carton terminated the conversation here, by rising to help him on with his outer coat. "but you," said Mr. Lorry, reverting to the theme, "you are young."

"Yes," said Carton. "I am not old, but my young way was never the way to age. Enough of me."

"And of me, I am sure," said Mr. Lorry. "Are you going out?"

"I'll walk with you to her gate. You know my vagabond and restless habits. If I should prowl about the streets a long time, don't be uneasy; I shall reappear in the morning. You go to the Court to-morrow?"

"Yes, unhappily."

"I shall be there, but only as one of the crowd. My spy will find a place for me. Take my arm, sir."

Mr. Lorry did so, and they went down-stairs and out in the streets. A few minutes brought them to Mr. Lorry's destination. Carton left him there; but lingered at a little distance, and turned back to the gate again when it was shut, and touched it. He had heard of her going to the prison every day. "She came out here," he said, looking about him, "turned this way, must have trod on these stones often. Let me follow in her steps."

It was ten o'clock at night when he stood before the prison of La Force, where she had stood hundreds of times. A little wood-sawyer, having closed his shop, was smoking his pipe at his shop-door.

"Good-night, citizen," said Sydney Carton, pausing in going by; for, the man eyed him inquisitively.

"Good-night, citizen."

"How goes the Republic?"

"You mean the Guillotine. Not ill. Sixty-three to-day. We shall mount to a hundred soon. Samson and his men complain sometimes, of being exhausted. Ha, ha, ha! He is so droll, that Samson. Such a Barber!"

"Do you often go to see him——"

"Shave? Always. Every day. What a barber! You have seen him at work?"

"Never."

"Go and see him when he has a good batch. Figure this to yourself, citizen; he shaved the sixty-three to-day, in less than two pipes! Less than two pipes. Word of honor!"

As the grinning little man held out the pipe he was smoking, to explain how he timed the executioner, Carton was so sensible of a rising desire to strike the life out of him, that he turned away.

"But you are not English," said the wood-sawyer, "though you wear English dress?"

"Yes," said Carton, pausing again, and answering over his shoulder.

"You speak like a Frenchman."

"I am an old student here."

"Aha, a perfect Frenchman! Good-night, Englishman."

"Good-night, citizen."

"But go and see that droll dog," the little man persisted, calling after him. "And take a pipe with you!"

Sydney had not gone far out of sight, when he stopped in the middle of the street under a glimmering lamp, and wrote with his pencil on a scrap of paper. Then, traversing with the decided step of one who remembered the way well, several dark and dirty streets—much dirtier than usual, for the best public thoroughfares remained uncleansed in those times of terror—he stopped at a chemist's shop, which the owner was closing with his own hands. A small, dim, crooked shop, kept in a tortuous, up-hill thoroughfare, by a small, dim, crooked man.

Giving this citizen, too, good-night, as he confronted him at his counter, he laid the scrap of paper before him. "Whew!" the chemist whistled softly, as he read it. "Hi! hi! hi!"

Sydney Carton took no heed, and the chemist said:

"For you, citizen?"

"For me."

"You will be careful to keep them separate, citizen? You know the consequences of mixing them?"

"Perfectly."

Certain small packets were made and given to him. He put them, one by one, in the breast of his inner coat, counted out the money for them, and deliberately left the shop. "There is nothing more to do," said he, glancing upward at the moon, "until to-morrow. I can't sleep."

It was not a reckless manner, the manner in which he said these words aloud under the fast-sailing clouds, nor was it more expressive of negligence than defiance. It was the settled manner of a tired man, who had wandered and struggled and got lost, but who at length struck into his road and saw its end.

Long ago, when he had been famous among his earliest competitors as a youth of great promise, he had followed his father to the grave. His mother had died, years before. These solemn words, which had been read at his father's grave, arose in his mind as he went down the dark streets, among the heavy shadows, with the moon and the clouds sailing on high above him. "I am the resurrection and the life, saith the Lord: he that believeth in me, though he were dead, yet shall he live: and whosoever liveth and believeth in me, shall never die."

In a city dominated by the axe, alone at night, with natural sorrow rising in him for the sixty-three who had been that day put to death, and for to-morrow's victims then awaiting their doom in the prisons, and still of to-morrow's and to-morrow's, the chain of association that brought the words home, like a rusty old ship's anchor from the deep, might have been easily found. He did not seek it, but repeated them and went on.

With a solemn interest in the lighted windows where the people were going to rest, forgetful through a few calm hours of the horrors surrounding them; in the towers of the churches, where no prayers were said, for the popular revulsion had even traveled that length of self-destruction from years of priestly impostors, plunderers, and profligates; in the distant burial-places, reserved, as they wrote upon the gates, for Eternal Sleep; in the abounding gaols; and in the streets along which the sixties rolled to a death which had become so common and material, that no sorrowful story of a haunting Spirit ever arose among the people out of all the working of the Guillotine; with a solemn interest in the whole life and death of the city settling down to its short, nightly pause in fury; Sydney Carton crossed the Seine again for the lighter streets.

Few coaches were abroad, for riders in coaches were liable to be suspected, and gentility hid its head in red nightcaps, and put on heavy shoes, and trudged. But, the theatres were all well filled, and the people poured cheerfully out as he passed, and went chatting home. At one of the theatre doors, there was a little girl with a mother, looking for a way across the street through the mud. He carried the child over, and before the timid arm was loosed from his neck asked her for a kiss.

"I am the resurrection and the life, saith the Lord: he that believeth in me, though he were dead, yet shall he live: and whosoever liveth, and believeth in me, shall never die."

Now, that the streets were quiet, and the night wore on, the words were in the echoes of his feet, and were in the air. Perfectly calm and steady, he sometimes repeated them to himself as he walked; but, he heard them always.

The night wore out, and, as he stood upon the bridge listening to the water as it splashed the river-walls of the Island of Paris, where the picturesque confusion of houses and cathedral shone bright in the light of the moon, the day came coldly, looking like a dead face out of the sky. Then, the night, with the moon and the stars, turned pale and died, and for a little while it seemed as if Creation were delivered over to Death's dominion. But, the glorious sun, rising, seemed to strike those words, that burden of the night, straight and warm to his heart in its long bright rays. And looking along them, with reverently shaded eyes, a bridge of light appeared to span the air between him and the sun, while the river sparkled under it.

The strong tide, so swift, so deep, and certain, was like a congenial friend in the morning stillness. He walked by the stream, far from the houses, and in the light and warmth of the sun, fell asleep on the bank.

When he awoke and was afoot again, he lingered there yet a little longer, watching an eddy that turned and turned purposeless, until the stream absorbed it, and carried it on to the sea. "Like me!"

A trading-boat, with a sail of the softened color of a dead leaf, then glided into his view, floated by him, and died away. As its silent track in the water disappeared, the prayer that had broken up out of his heart for a merciful consideration of all his poor blindness and errors, ended in the words, "I am the resurrection and the life."

Mr. Lorry was aleady out when he got back, and it was easy to surmise where the good old man was gone. Sydney Carton drank nothing but a little coffee, ate some bread, and, having washed and changed to refresh himself, went out to the place of trial.

The court was all astir and abuzz, when the black sheep—whom many fell away from in dread—pressed him into an obscure corner among the crowd. Mr. Lorry was there, and Doctor Manette was there. She was there, sitting beside her father.

When her husband was brought in, she turned a look upon him, so sustaining, so encouraging, so full of admiring love and pitying tenderness, yet so courageous for his sake, that it called the healthy blood into his face, brightened his glance, and animated his heart. If there had been any eyes to notice the influence of her look on Sydney Carton, it would have been seen to be the same influence exactly.

Before that unjust Tribunal, there was little or no order of procedure, insuring to any accused person any reasonable hearing. There could have been no such Revolution, if all laws, forms, and ceremonies had not first been so monstrously abused, that the suicidal vengeance of the Revolution was to scatter them all to the winds.

Every eye was turned to the jury. The same determined patriots and good republicans as yesterday and the day before, and to-morrow and the day after. Eager and prominent among them, one man with a craving face, and his fingers perpetually hovering about his lips, whose appearance gave great satisfaction to the spectators. A life-thirsting, cannibal-looking, bloody-minded juryman, the Jacques Three of Saint Antoine. The whole jury, as a jury of dogs impanelled to try the deer.

Every eye then turned to the five judges and the public prosecutor. No favorable leaning in that quarter to-day. A fell, uncompromising, murderous business-meaning there. Every eye then sought some other eye in the crowd, and gleamed at it approvingly; and heads nodded at one another, before bending forward with a strained attention.

Charles Evremonde, called Darnay. Released yesterday. Reaccused and retaken yesterday. Indictment delivered to him last night. Suspected and denounced enemy of the Republic, Aristocrat, one of a family of tyrants, one of a race proscribed, for that they had used their abolished privileges to the infamous oppression of the people. Charles Evremonde, called Darnay, in right of such proscription absolutely Dead in law.

To this effect, in as few or fewer words, the Public Prosecutor.

The President asked, was the accused openly denounced or secretly?

"Openly, President."

"By whom?"

"Three voices. Ernest Defarge, wine-vendor of Saint Antoine."

"Good."

"Therese Defarge, his wife."

"Good."

"Alexandre Manette, physician."

A great uproar took place in the court, and in the midst of it, Doctor Manette was seen, pale and trembling, standing where he had been seated.

"President, I indignantly protest to you that this is a forgery and a fraud. You know the accused to be the husband of my daughter. My daughter, and those dear to her, are far dearer to me than my life. Who and where is the false conspirator who says that I denounce the husband of my child?"

"Citizen Manette, be tranquil. To fail in submission to the authority of the Tribunal, would be to put yourself out of Law. As to what is dearer to you than life, nothing can be so dear to a good citizen as the Republic."

Loud acclamations hailed this rebuke. The President rang his bell, and with warmth resumed.

"If the Republic should demand of you the sacrifice of your child herself, you would have no duty but to sacrifice her. Listen to what is to follow. In the meanwhile, be silent!"

Frantic acclamations were again raised. Doctor Manette sat down, with his eyes looking around, and his lips trembing; his daughter drew closer to him. The craving man on the jury rubbed his hands together, and restored the usual hand to his mouth.

Defarge was produced, when the Court was quiet enough to admit of his being heard, and rapidly expounded the story of the imprisonment, and of his having been a mere boy in the Doctor's service, and of the release, and of the state of the prisoner when released and delivered to him. This short examination followed, for the court was quick with its work.

"You did good service at the taking of the Bastille, citizen?"

"I believe so."

Here, an excited woman screeched from the crowd: "You were one of the best patriots there. Why not say so? You were a cannonier that day there, and you were among the first to enter the accursed fortress when it fell. Patriots, I speak the truth!"

It was The Vengeance who, amidst the warm commendations of the audience, thus assisted the proceedings. The President rang his bell; but, The Vengeance, warming with encouragement, shrieked, "I defy that bell!" wherein she was likewise much commended.

"Inform the Tribunal of what you did that day within the Bastille, citizen."

"I knew," said Defarge, looking down at his wife, who stood at the bottom of the steps on which he was raised, looking steadily up at him; "I knew that this prisoner, of whom I speak, had been confined in a cell known as One Hundred and Five, North Tower. I knew it from himself. He knew himself by no other name than One Hundred and Five, North Tower, when he made shoes under my care. As I serve my gun that day, I resolve, when the place shall fall, to examine that cell. It falls. I mount to the cell, with a fellow-citizen who is one of the Jury, directed by a gaoler. I examine it, very closely. In a hole in the chimney, where a stone has been worked out and replaced, I find a written paper. This is that written paper. I have made it my business to examine some specimens of the writing of Doctor Manette. This is the writing of Doctor Manette. I confide this paper, in the writing of Doctor Manette, to the hands of the President."

"Let it be read."

In a dead silence and stillness—the prisoner under trial looked lovingly at his wife, his wife only looking from him to look with solicitude at her father, Doctor Manette keeping his eyes fixed on the reader, Madame Defarge never taking hers from the prisoner, Defarge never taking his from his feasting wife, and all the other eyes there intent upon the Doctor, who saw none of them—the paper was read, as follows.

Chapter X

THE SUBSTANCE OF THE SHADOW

"I, Alexander Manette, unfortunate physician, native of Beauvais, and afterward resident in Paris, write this melancholy paper in my doleful cell in the Bastille, during the last month of the year 1767. I write it at stolen intervals, under every difficulty. I design to secrete it in the wall of the chimney, where I have slowly and laboriously made a place of concealment for it. Some pitying hand may find it there, when I and my sorrows are dust.

"These words are formed by the rusty iron point with which I write with difficulty in scrapings of soot and charcoal from the chimney, mixed with blood, in the last month of the tenth year of my captivity. Hope has quite departed from my breast. I know from terrible warnings I have noted in myself that my reason will not long remain unimpaired; but I solemnly declare that I am at this time in the possession of my right mind—that my memory is exact and circumstantial—and that I write the truth as I shall answer for these, my last recorded words, whether they be ever read by men or not, at the Eternal Judgment seat.

"One cloudy moonlight night, in the third week of December (I think the twenty-second of the month) in the year 1757, I was walking on a retired part of the quay by the Seine for the refreshment of the frosty air, at an hour's distance from my place of residence in the Street of the School of Medicine, when a carriage came along behind me, driven very fast. As I stood aside to let that carriage pass, apprehensive that it might otherwise run me down, a head was put out at the window, and a voice called to the driver to stop.

"The carriage stopped as soon as the driver could rein in his horses, and the same voice called to me by my name. I answered. The carriage was then so far in advance of me that the two gentlemen had time to open the door and alight before I came up with it. I observed that they were both wrapped in cloaks, and appeared to conceal themselves. As they stood side by side near the carriage-door, I also observed that they both looked of about my own age, or rather younger, and that they were greatly alike, in stature, manner, voice, and (as far as I could see) face too.

" 'You are Doctor Manette?' said one.

" 'I am.'

" 'Doctor Manette, formerly of Beauvais,' said the other; 'the young physician, originally an expert surgeon, who within the last year or two has made a rising reputation in Paris?'

" 'Gentlemen,' I returned, 'I am that Doctor Manette of whom you speak so graciously.'

" 'We have been to your residence,' said the first, 'and not being so fortunate as to find you there, and being informed that you were probably walking in this direction, we followed, in the hope of overtaking you. Will you please to enter the carriage?' "

"The manner of both was imperious, and they both moved, as these words were spoken, so as to place me between themselves and the carriage door. They were armed. I was not.

" 'Gentlemen,' said I, 'pardon me; but I usually inquire who does me the honour to seek my assistance, and what is the nature of the case to which I am summoned.'

"The reply to this was made by him who had spoken second. 'Doctor, your clients are people of condition. As to the nature of the case, our confidence in your skill assures us that you will ascertain it for yourself better than we can describe it. Enough. Will you please to enter the carriage?'

"I could do nothing but comply, and I entered it in silence. They both entered after me—the last springing in, after putting up the steps. The carriage turned about, and drove on at its former speed.

"I repeat this conversation exactly as it occurred. I have no doubt that it is, word for word, the same. I describe everything exactly as it took place, constraining my mind not to wander from the task. Where I make the broken marks that follow here, I leave off for the time, and put my paper in its hiding-place. . . .

"The carriage left the streets behind, passed the North Barrier, and emerged upon the country road. At two-thirds of a league from the Barrier—I did not estimate the distance at that time, but afterwards when I traversed it—it struck out of the main avenue, and presently stopped at a solitary house. We all three alighted, and walked, by a damp soft footpath in a garden where a neglected fountainhad overflowed, to the door of the housc. It was not opened immediately, in answer to the ringing of the bell, and one of my two conductors struck the man who opened it, with his heavy riding-glove, across the face.

"There was nothing in this action to attract my particular attention, for I had seen common people struck more commonly than dogs. But, the other of the two, being angry likewise, struck the man in like manner with his arm; the look and bearing of the brothers were then so exactly alike, that I then first perceived them to be twin brothers.

"From the time of our alighting at the outer gate (which we found locked, and which one of the brothers had opened to admit us, and had relocked), I had heard cries proceeding from an upper chamber. I was conducted to this chamber straight, the cries growing louder as we ascended the stairs, and I found a patient in a high fever of the brain, lying on a bed.

"The patient was a woman of great beauty, and young; assuredly not much past twenty. Her hair was torn and ragged, and her arms were bound to her sides with sashes and handkerchiefs. I noticed that these bonds were all portions of a gentleman's dress. On one of them, which was a fringed scarf for a dress of ceremony, I saw the armorial bearings of a noble, and the letter *E*.

"I saw this, within the first minute of my contemplation of the patient; for, in her restless strivings she had turned over on her face on the edge of the bed, had drawn the end of the scarf into her mouth, and was in danger of suffocation. My first act was to put out my hand to relieve her breathing; and in moving the scarf aside, the embroidery in the corner caught my sight.

"I turned her gently over, placed my hands upon her breast to calm her and keep her down, and looked into her face. Her eyes were dilated and wild, and she constantly uttered piercing shrieks, and repeated the words, 'My husband, my father, and my brother!' and then counted up to twelve, and said, 'Hush!' For an instant, and no more, she would pause to listen, and then the piercing shrieks would begin again, and she would repeat the cry, 'My husband, my father, and my brother!' and would count up to twelve, and say 'Hush!' There was no variation in the order, or the manner. There was no cessation, but the regular moment's pause, in the utterance of these sounds.

" 'How long,' I asked, 'has this lasted?'

"To distinguish the brothers, I will call them the elder and the younger; by the elder, I mean him who exercised the most authority. It was the elder who replied, 'Since about this hour last night.'

" 'She has a husband, a father, and a brother?'

" 'A brother.'

" 'I do not address her brother?'

"He answered with great contempt, 'No.'

" 'She has some recent association with the number twelve?'

"The younger brother impatiently rejoined, 'With twelve o'clock.'

" 'See, gentlemen,' said I, still keeping my hands upon her breast, 'how useless I am, as you have brought me! If I had known what I was coming to see, I could have come provided. As it is, time must be lost. There are no medicines to be obtained in this lonely place.'

"The elder brother looked to the younger, who said haughtily, 'There is a case of medicines here;' and brought it from a closet, and put it on the table. . . .

"I opened some of the bottles, smelled them, and put the stoppers to my lips. If I had wanted to use anything save narcotic medicines that were poisons in themselves, I would not have administered any of those.

" 'Do you doubt them?' asked the younger brother.

" 'You see, monsieur, I am going to use them,' I replied, and said no more.

"I made the patient swallow, with great difficulty, and after many efforts, the dose that I desired to give. As I intended to repeat it after a while, and as it was necessary to watch its influence, I then sat down by the side of the bed. There was a timid and suppressed woman in attendance (wife of the man downstairs), who had retreated into a corner. The house was damp and decayed, indifferently furnished—evidently, recently occupied and temporarily used. Some thick old hangings had been nailed up before the windows, to deaden the sound of the shrieks. They continued to be uttered in their regular succession, with the cry, 'My husband, my father, and my brother!' the counting up to twelve, and 'Hush!' The frenzy was so violent, that I had not unfastened the bandages restraining the arms; but I had looked to them to see that they were not painful. The only spark of encouragement in the case was that my hand upon the sufferer's breast had this much soothing influence, that for a few minutes at a time it tranquillized the figure. It had no effect upon the cries: no pendulum could be more regular.

"For the reason that my hand had this effect (I assume), I had sat by the side of the bed for half an hour, with the two brothers looking on, before the elder said:

"'There is another patient.'

"I was startled and asked, 'Is it a pressing case?'

"'You had better see,' he carelessly answered; and took up a light. . . .

"The other patient lay in a back room across a second staircase, which was a species of loft over a stable. There was a low plastered ceiling to a part of it; the rest was open, to the ridge of the tiled roof, and there were beams across. Hay and straw were stored in that portion of the place, fagots for firing, and a heap of apples in sand. I had to pass through that part, to get at the other. My memory is circumstantial and unshaken. I try it with these details, and I see them all, in this my cell in the Bastille, near the close of the tenth year of my captivity, as I saw them all that night.

"On some hay on the ground, with a cushion thrown under his head, lay a handsome peasant boy—a boy of not more than seventeen at the most. He lay on his back, with his teeth set, his right hand clenched on his breast, and his glaring eyes looking straight upward. I could not see where his wound was, as I kneeled on one knee over him; but I could see that he was dying of a wound from a sharp point.

"'I am a doctor, my poor fellow,' said I. 'Let me examine it.'

"'I do not want it examined,' he answered; 'let it be.'

"It was under his hand, and I soothed him to let me move his hand away. The wound was a sword-thrust, received from twenty to twenty-four hours before, but no skill could have saved him if it had been looked to without delay. He was then dying fast. As I turned my eyes to the elder brother, I saw him looking down at this handsome boy whose life was ebbing out, as if he were a wounded bird, or hare, or rabbit; not at all as if he were a fellow-creature.

"'How has this been done, monsieur?' said I.

"'A crazed young common dog! A serf! Forced my brother to draw upon him, and has fallen by my brother's sword—like a gentleman.'

"There was no touch of pity, sorrow, or kindred humanity in this answer. The speaker seemed to acknowledge that it was inconvenient to have that different order of creature dying there, and that it would have been better if he had died in the usual obscure routine of his vermin kind. He was quite incapable of any compassionate feeling about the boy, or about his fate.

"The boy's eyes had slowly moved to him as he had spoken, and they now slowly moved to me.

" 'Doctor, they are very proud, these Nobles; but we common dogs are proud too, sometimes. They plunder us, outrage us, beat us, kill us; but we have a little pride left, sometimes. She— Have you seen her?'

"The shrieks and the cries were audible there, though subdued by the distance. He referred to them, as if she were lying in our presence.

"I said, 'I have seen her.'

" 'She is my sister, Doctor. They have had their shameful rights, these Nobles, in the modesty and virtue of our sisters, many years, but we have had good girls among us. I know it, and have heard my father say so. She was a good girl. She was betrothed to a good young man, too; a tenant of his. We were all tenants of his—that man's who stands there. The other is his brother, the worst of a bad race.'

"It was with the greatest difficulty that the boy gathered bodily force to speak; but his spirit spoke with a dreadful emphasis.

" 'We were so robbed by that man who stands there, as all we common dogs are by those superior Beings—taxed by him without mercy, obliged to work for him without pay, obllged to grind our corn at his mill, obliged to feed scores of his tame birds on our wretched crops, and forbidden for our lives to keep a single tame bird of our own, pillaged and plundered to that degree that when we chanced to have a bit of meat, we ate it in fear, with the door barred and the shutters closed, that his people should not see it and take it from us—I say, we were so robbed, and hunted, and were made so poor, that our father told us it was a dreadful thing to bring a child into the world, and that what we should most pray for was that our women might be barren and our miserable race die out!'

"I had never before seen the sense of being oppressed—bursting forth like a fire. I had supposed that it must be latent in the people somewhere; but, I had never seen it break out, until I saw it in the dying boy.

" 'Nevertheless, Doctor, my sister married. He was ailing at that time, poor fellow, and she married her lover, that she might tend and comfort him in our cottage—our dog hut, as that man would call it. She had not been married many weeks, when that man's brother saw her and admired her, and asked that man to lend her to him—for what are husbands among us! He was willing enough, but my sister was good and virtuous, and hated his brother with a hatred as strong as mine. What did the two then, to persuade her husband to use his influence with her, to make her willing?'

"The boy's eyes, which had been fixed on mine, slowly turned to the looker-on, and I saw in the two faces that all he said was true. The two opposing kinds of pride confronting one another I can see even in this Bastille; the gentleman's all negligent indifference; the peasant's, all trodden-down sentiment and passionate revenge.

" 'You know, Doctor, that it is among the Rights of these Nobles to harness us common dogs to carts, and drive us. They so harnessed him and drove him. You know that it is among their Rights to keep us in their grounds all night, quieting the frogs, in order that their noble sleep may not be disturbed. They kept him out in the unwholesome mists at night, and ordered him back into his harness in the day. But he was not persuaded. No! Taken out of harness one day at noon, to feed—if he could find food—he sobbed twelve times, once for every stroke of the bell, and died on her bosom.'

" 'Nothing human could have held life in the boy but his determination to tell all his wrong. He forced back the gathering shadows of death, as he forced his clenched right hand to remain clenched, and to cover his wound.

" 'Then, with that man's permission and even with his aid, his brother took her away; in spite of what I know she must have told his brother—and what that is, will not be long unknown to you, Doctor, if it is now—his brother took her away—for his pleasure and diversion, for a little while. I saw her pass me on the road. When I took the tidings home our father's heart burst; he never spoke one of the words that filled it. I took my young sister (for I have another) to a place beyond the reach of this man, and where, at least, she will never be *his* vassal. Then I tracked the brother here, and last night climbed in—a common dog, but sword in hand.—Where is the loft window? It was somewhere here.'

"The room was darkening to his sight; the world was narrowing around him. I glanced about me, and saw that the hay and straw were trampled over the floor, as if there had been a struggle.

" 'She heard me, and ran in. I told her not to come near us till he was dead. He came in and first tossed me some pieces of money; then struck at me with a whip. But I, though a common dog, so struck at him as to make him draw. Let him break into as many pieces as he will the sword that he stained with my common blood; he drew to defend himself—thrust at me with all his skill for his life.'

"My glance had fallen, but a few moments before, on the fragments of a broken sword, lying among the hay. That weapon was a gentleman's. In another place lay an old sword that seemed to have been a soldier's.

" 'Now, lift me up, Doctor; lift me up. Where is he?'

" 'He is not here,' I said, supporting the boy, and thinking that he referred to the brother.

" 'He! Proud as these nobles are, he is afraid to see me. Where is the man who was here? Turn my face to him.'

"I did so, raising the boy's head against my knee. But, invested for the moment with extraordinary power, he raised himself completely: obliging me to rise too, or I could not have still supported him.

" 'Marquis,' said the boy, turning to him with his eyes opened wide, and his right hand raised, 'in the days when all these things are to be answered for, I summon you and yours, to the last of your bad race, to answer for them. I mark this cross of blood upon you, as a sign that I do it. In the days when all these things are to be answered for, I summon your brother, the worst of the bad race, to answer for them separately. I mark this cross of blood upon him, as a sign that I do it.' "Twice, he put his hand to the wound in his breast, and with his forefinger drew a cross in the air. He stood for an instant with the finger yet raised, and, as it dropped, he dropped with it, and I laid him down dead. . . .

"When I returned to the bedside of the young woman I found her raving in precisely the same order and contintuity. I knew that this might last for many, hours and that it would probably end in the silence of the grave.

"I repeated the medicines I had given her, and I sat at the side of the bed until the night was far advanced. She never abated the piercing quality of her shrieks, never stumbled in the distinctness or the order of her words. They were always 'My husband, my father, and my brother! One, two, three, four, five, six, seven, eight, nine, ten, eleven, twelve. Hush!'

"This lasted twenty-six hours from the time when I first saw her. I had come and gone twice, and was again sitting by her, when she began to falter. I did what little could be done to assist that opportunity, and by-and-by she sank into a lethargy, and lay like the dead.

"It was as if the wind and rain had lulled at last, after a long and fearful storm. I released her arms, and called the woman to assist me to compose her figure and the dress she had torn. It was then that I knew her condition to be that of one in whom the first expectations of being a mother have arisen; and it was then that I lost the little hope I had had of her.

"'Is she dead?' asked the Marquis, whom I will still describe as the elder brother, coming booted into the room from his horse.

"'Not dead,' said I; 'but like to die.'

"'What strength there is in these common bodies!' he said, looking down at her with some curiosity.

"'There is prodigious strength,' I answered him, 'in sorrow and despair.'

"He first laughed at my words, and then frowned at them. He moved a chair with his foot near to mine, ordered the woman away, and said in a subdued voice:

"'Doctor, finding my brother in this difficulty with these hinds, I recommended that your aid should be invited. Your reputation is high, and, as a young man with your fortune to make, you are probably mindful of your interest. The things that you see here are things to be seen, and not spoken of.'

"I listened to the patient's breathing, and avoided answering.

"'Do you honour me with your attention, Doctor?'

"'Monsieur,' said I, 'in my profession, the communications of patients are always received in confidence.' I was guarded in my answer, for I was troubled in my mind with what I had heard and seen.

"Her breathing was so difficult to trace, that I carefully tried the pulse and the heart. There was life, and no more. Looking round as I resumed my seat, I found both the brothers intent upon me. . . .

"I write with so much difficulty, the cold is so severe, I am so fearful of being detected and consigned to an under-ground cell and total darkness, that I must abridge this narrative. There is no confusion or failure in my memory; it can recall, and could detail, every word that was ever spoken between me and those brothers.

"She lingered for a week. Towards the last, I could understand some few syllables that she said to me, by placing my ear close to her lips. She asked me where she was, and I told her; who I was, and I told her. It was in vain that I asked her for her family name. She faintly shook her head upon the pillow, and kept her secret, as the boy had done.

"I had no opportunity of asking her any question, until I had told the brothers she was sinking fast, and could not live another day. Until then, though no one was ever presented to her consciousness save the woman and myself, one or other of them had always jealously sat behind the curtain at the head of the bed when I was there. But when it came to that, they seemed careless what communication I might hold with her; as if—the thought passed through my mind—I were dying too.

"I always observed that their pride bitterly resented the younger brother's (as I call him) having crossed swords with a peasant, and that peasant a boy. The only consideration that appeared to affect the mind of either of them was the consideration that this was highly degrading to the family, and was ridiculous. As often as I caught the younger brother's eyes, their expression reminded me that he disllked me deeply, for knowing what I knew from the boy. He was smoother and more polite to me than the elder; but I saw this. I also saw that I was an incumbrance in the mind of the elder too.

"My patient died, two hours before midnight—at a time, by my watch, answering almost to the minute when I had first seen her. I was alone with her, when her forlorn young head drooped gently on one side, and all her earthly wrongs and sorrows ended.

"The brothers were waiting in a room downstairs, impatient to ride away. I had heard them, alone at the bedside, striking their boots with their riding-whips, and loitering up and down.

" 'At last she is dead?' said the elder, when I went in.

" 'She is dead,' said I.

" 'I congratulate you, my brother,' were his words as he turned round.

"He had before offered me money, which I had postponed taking. He now gave me a rouleau of gold. I took it from his hand, but laid it on the table. I had considered the question, and had resolved to accept nothing.

" 'Pray excuse me,' said I. 'Under the circumstances, no.'

"They exchanged looks, but bent their heads to me as I bent mine to them, and we parted without another word on either side. . . .

"I am weary, weary, weary—worn down by misery. I cannot read what I have written with this gaunt hand.

"Early in the morning, the rouleau of gold was left at my door in a little box, with my name on the outside. From the first, I had curiously considered what I ought to do. I decided, that day, to write privately to the Minister, stating the nature of the two cases to which I had been summoned, and the place to which I had gone: in effect, stating all the circumstances. I knew what Court influence was, and what the immunities of the Nobles were, and I expected that the matter would never be heard of; but I wished to relieve my own mind. I had kept the matter a profound secret, even from my wife; and this, too, I resolved to state in my letter. I had no apprehension whatever of my real danger; but I was conscious that there might be danger for others, if others were compromised by possessing the knowledge that I possessed.

"I was much engaged that day, and could not complete my letter that night. I rose long before my usual time next morning to finish it. It was the last day of the year. The letter was lying before me just completed, when I was told that a lady waited, who wished to see me. . . .

"I am growing more and more unequal to the task I have set myself. It is so cold, so dark, my senses are so benumbed, and the gloom upon me is so dreadful.

"The lady was young, engaging, and handsome, but not marked for long life. She was in great agitation. She presented herself to me as the wife of the Marquis St. Evremonde. I connected the title by which the boy had addressed the elder brother, with the initial letter embroidered on the scarf, and had no difficulty in arriving at the conclusion that I had seen that nobleman very lately.

"My memory is still accurate, but I cannot write the words of our conversation. I suspect that I am watched more closely than I was, and I know not at what times I may be watched. She had in part suspected, and in part discovered, the main facts of the cruel story, of her husband's share in it, and my being resorted to. She did not know that the girl was dead. Her hope had been, she said in great distress, to show her, in secret, a woman's sympathy. Her hope had been to avert the wrath of Heaven from a House that had long been hateful to the suffering many.

"She had reasons for believing that there was a young sister living, and her greatest desire was to help that sister. I could tell her nothing but that there was such a sister; beyond that, I knew nothing. Her inducement to come to me, relying on my confidence, had been the hope that I could tell her the name and place of abode. Whereas, to this wretched hour I am ignorant of both. . . .

"These scraps of paper fail me. One was taken from me, with a warnmg, yesterday. I must finish my record to-day.

"She was a good, compassionate lady, and not happy in her marriage. How could she be! The brother distrusted and disllked her, and his influence was all opposed to her; she stood in dread of him, and in dread of her husband too. When I handed her down to the door, there was a child, a pretty boy from two to three years old, in her carriage.

" 'For his sake, Doctor,' she said, pointing to him in tears, 'I would do all I can to make what poor amends I can. He will never prosper in his inheritance otherwise. I have a presentiment that if no other innocent atonement is made for this, it will one day be required of him. What I have left to call my own—it is little beyond the worth of a few jewels—I will make it the first charge of his life to bestow, with the compassion and lamenting of his dead mother, on this injured family, if the sister can be discovered.'

"She kissed the boy, and said, caressing him, 'It is for thine own dear sake. Thou wilt be faithful, little Charles?' The child answered her bravely, 'Yes!' I kissed her hand, and she took him in her arms, and went away caressing him. I never saw her more.

"As she had mentioned her husband's name in the faith that I knew it, I added no mention of it to my letter. I sealed my letter, and, not trusting it out of my own hands, delivered it myself that day.

"That night, the last night of the year, towards nine o'clock, a man in a black dress rang at my gate, demanded to see me, and softly followed my servant, Ernest Defarge, a youth, upstairs. When my servant came into the room where I sat with my wife—Oh my wife, beloved of my heart! My fair, young, English wife!—we saw the man, who was supposed to be at the gate, standing silent behind him.

"An urgent case in the Rue St. Honoré, he said. It would not detain me, he had a coach in waiting.

"It brought me here, it brought me to my grave. When I was clear of the house, a black muffler was drawn tightly over my mouth from behind, and my arms were pinioned. The two brothers crossed the road from a dark corner, and identified me with a single gesture. The Marquis took from his pocket the letter I had written, showed it me, burnt it in the light of a lantern that was held, and extinguished the ashes with his foot. Not a word was spoken. I was brought here, I was brought to my living grave.

"If it had pleased God to put it in the hard heart of either of the brothers, in all these frightful years, to grant me any tidings of my dearest wife—so much as to let me know by a word whether alive or dead—I might have thought that He had not quite abandoned them. But, now I believe that the mark of the red cross is fatal to them, and that they have no part in His mercies. And them and their descendants, to the last of their race, I, Alexandre Manette, unhappy prisoner, do this last night of the year 1767, in my unbearable agony, denounce to the times when all these things shall be answered for. I denounce them to Heaven and to earth."

A terrible sound arose when the reading of this document was done. A sound of craving and eagerness that had nothing articulate in it but blood. The narrative called up the most revengeful passions of the time, and there was not a head in the nation but must have dropped before it.

Little need, in presence of that tribunal and that auditory, to show how the Defarges had not made the paper public, with the other captured Bastille memorials borne in procession, and had kept it, biding their time. Little need to show that this detested family name had long been anathematized by Saint Antoine, and was wrought into the fatal register. The man never trod ground whose virtues and services would have sustained him in that place that day, against such denunciation.

And all the worse for the doomed man, that the denouncer was a well-known citizen, his own attached friend, the father of his wife. One of the frenzied aspirations of the populace was for imitations of the questionable public virtues of antiquity, and for sacrifices and self-immolations on the people's altar. Therefore when the President said (else had his own head quivered on his shoulders), that the good physician of the Republic would deserve better still of the Republic by rooting out an obnoxious family of aristocrats, and would doubtless feel a sacred glow and joy in making his daughter a widow and her child an orphan, there was wild excitement, patriotic fervor, not a touch of human sympathy.

"Much influence around him, has that Doctor?" murmured Madame Defarge, smiling to The Vengeance. "Save him now, my Doctor, save him!"

At every juryman's vote, there was a roar. Another and another. Roar and roar.

Unanimously voted. At heart and by descent an Aristocrat, an enemy of the Republic, a notorious oppressor of the People. Back to the Conciergerie, and Death within four-and-twenty hours!

Chapter XI
DUSK

THE wretched wife of the innocent man thus doomed to die fell under the sentence as if she had been mortally stricken. But she uttered no sound; and so strong was the voice within her, representing that it was she of all the world who must uphold him in his misery and not augment it, that it quickly raised her, even from that shock.

The judges having to take part in a public demonstration out of doors, the tribunal adjourned. The quick noise and movement of the court's emptying itself by many passages had not ceased, when Lucie stood stretching out her arms toward her husband, with nothing in her face but love and consolation.

"If I might touch him! If I might embrace him once! Oh, good citizens, if you would have so much compassion for us!"

There was but a jailer left, along with two of the four men who had taken him last night, and Barsad. The people had all poured out to the show in the streets. Barsad proposed to the rest, "Let her embrace him then; it is but a moment." It was silently acquiesced in, and they passed her over the seats in the hall to a raised place, where he, by leaning over the dock, could fold her in his arms.

"Farewell, dear darling of my soul. My parting blessing on my love. We shall meet again, where the weary are at rest!"

They were her husband's words, as he held her to his bosom.

"I can bear it, dear Charles. I am supported from above : don't suffer for me. A parting blessing for our child."

"I send it to her by you. I kiss her by you. I say farewell to her by you."

"My husband. No! A moment!" He was tearing himself apart from her. "We shall not be separated long. I feel that this will break my heart by-and-by; but I will do my duty while I can, and when I leave her, God will raise up friends for her, as He did for me."

Her father had followed her, and would have fallen on his knees to both of them, but that Darnay put out a hand and seized him, crying :

"No, no! What have you done, what have you done, that you should kneel to us! We know now what a struggle you made of old. We know now what you underwent when you suspected my descent, and when you knew it. We know now the natural antipathy you strove against, and conquered, for her dear sake. We thank you with all our hearts, and all our love and duty. Heaven be with you!"

Her father's only answer was to draw his hands through his white hair, and wring them with a shriek of anguish.

"It could not be otherwise," said the prisoner. "All things have worked together as they have fallen out. It was the always vain endeavour to discharge my poor mother's trust that first brought my fatal presence near you. Good could never come of such evil, a happier end was not in nature to so unhappy a beginning. Be comforted, and forgive me. Heaven bless you!"

As he was drawn away, his wife released him, and stood looking after him with her hands touching one another in the attitude of prayer, and with a radiant look upon her face, in which there was even a comforting smile. As he went out at the prisoners' door, she turned, laid her head lovingly on her father's breast, tried to speak to him, and fell at his feet.

Then, issuing from the obscure corner from which he had never moved, Sydney Carton came and took her up. Only her father and Mr. Lorry were with her. His arm trembled as it raised her, and supported her head. Yet, there was an air about him that was not all pity—that had a flush of pride in it.

"Shall I take her to a coach? I shall never feel her weight."

He carried her lightly to the door, and laid her tenderly down in a coach. Her father and their old friend got into it, and he took his seat beside the driver.

When they arrived at the gateway where he had paused in the dark not many hours before, to picture to himself on which of the rough stones of the street her feet had trodden, he lifted her again, and carried her up the staircase to their rooms. There, he laid her down on a couch, where her child and Miss Pross wept over her.

"Don't recall her to herself," he said, softly, to the latter; "she is better so; don't revive her to consciousness, while she only faints."

"Oh, Carton, Carton, dear Carton!" cried little Lucie, springing up and throwing her arms passionately round him, in a burst of grief. "Now that you have come, I think you will do something to help mamma, something to save papa! Oh, look at her, dear Carton! Can you, of all the people who love her, bear to see her so?"

He bent over the child, and laid her blooming cheek against his face. He put her gently from him, and looked at her unconscious mother.

"Before I go," he said, and paused—"I may kiss her?"

It was remembered afterwards that when he bent down and touched her face with his lips, he murmured some words. The child, who was nearest to him, told them afterwards, and told her grandchildren when she was a handsome old lady, that she heard him say, "A life you love."

When he had gone out into the next room, he turned suddeniy on Mr. Lorry and her father, who were following, and said to the latter:

"You had great influence but yesterday, Doctor Manette; let it at least be tried. These judges, and all the men in power, are very friendly to you, and very recognizant of your services; are they not?"

"Nothing connected with Charles was concealed from me. I had the strongest assurances that I should save him; and I did." He returned the answer in great trouble, and very slowly.

"Try them again. The hours between this and to-morrow afternoon are few and short, but try."

"I intend to try. I will not rest a moment."

"That's well. I have known such energy as yours do great things before now—though never," he added, with a smile and a sigh together, "such great things as this. But try! Of littie worth as life is when we misuse it, it is worth that effort. It would cost nothing to lay down if it were not."

"I will go," said Doctor Manette, "to the Prosecutor and the President straight, and I will go to others whom it is better not to name. I will write too, and—But stay! There is a celebration in the streets, and no one will be accessible until dark."

"That's true. Well! It is a forlorn hope at the best, and not much the forlorner for being delayed till dark. I should like to know how you speed; though, mind! I expect nothing! When are you likely to have seen these dread powers, Doctor Manette?"

"Immediately after dark, I should hope, Within an hour or two from this."

"It will be dark soon after four. Let us stretch the hour or two. If I go to Mr. Lorry's at nine, shall I hear what you have done, either from our friend or from yourself?"

"Yes."

"May you prosper!"

Mr. Lorry followed Sydney to the outer door, and, touching him on the shoulder as he was going away, caused him to turn.

"I have no hope," said Mr. Lorry, in a sorrowful whisper.

"Nor have I."

"If any one of these men, or all of these men, were disposed to spare him—which is a large supposition; for what is his life, or any man's to them!—I doubt if they durst spare him after the demonstration in the court."

"And so do I. I heard the fall of the axe in that sound."

Mr. Lorry leaned his arm upon the doorpost, and bowed his face upon it.

"Don't despond," said Carton, very gently; "don't grieve. I encouraged Doctor Manette in this idea, because I felt that it might one day be consolatory to her. Otherwise, she might think 'his life was wantonly thrown away or wasted,' and that might trouble her."

"Yes, yes, yes," returned Mr. Lorry, drying his eyes, "you are right. But he will perish; there is no real hope."

"Yes. He will perish; there is no real hope," echoed Carton. And walked with a settled step, down stairs.

Chapter XII

DARKNESS

SYDNEY CARTON paused in the street, not quite decided where to go. "At Tellson's banking-house at nine," he said with a musing face. "Shall I do well, in the meantime, to show myself? I think so. It is best that these people should know there is such a man as I here; it is a sound precaution, and may be a necessary preparation. But care, care, care! Let me think it out!"

Checking his steps, which had begun to tend towards an object, he took a turn or two in the already darkening street, and traced the thought in his mind to its possible consequences. His first impression was confirmed. "It is best," he said, finally resolved, "that these people should know there is such a man as I here." And he turned his face towards Saint Antoine.

Defarge had described himself, that day, as the keeper of a wine-shop in the Saint Antoine suburb. It was not difficult, for one who knew the city well, to find his house without asking any question. Having ascertained its situation, Carton came out of those closer streets again, and dined at a place of refreshment and fell sound asleep after dinner. For the first time in many years, he had no strong drink. Since last night he had taken nothing but a little light thin wine, and last night he had dropped the brandy slowly down on Mr. Lorry's hearth like a man who had done with it.

It was as late as seven o'clock when he awoke refreshed, and went out into the streets again. As he passed along towards Saint Antoine, he stopped at a shop-window where there was a mirror, and slightly altered the disordered arrangement of his loose cravat, and his coat-collar, and his wild hair. This done he went on direct to Defarge's, and went in.

There happened to be no customer in the shop but Jacques Three, of the restless fingers and the croaking voice. This man, whom he had seen upon the Jury, stood drinking at the little counter, in conversation with the Defarges, man and wife. The Vengeance assisted in the conversation, like a regular member of the establishment.

As Carton walked in, took his seat and asked (in very indifferent French) for a small measure of wine, Madame Defarge cast a careless glance at him, and then a keener, and then a keener, and then advanced to him herself, and asked him what it was he had ordered.

He repeated what he had already said.

"English?" asked Madame Defarge, inquisitively raising her dark eyebrows.

After looking at her, as if the sound of even a single French word were slow to express itself to him, he answered, in his former strong foreign accent, "Yes, madame, yes. I am English!"

Madame Defarge returned to her counter to get the wine, and as he took up a Jacobin journal and feigned to pore over it puzzling out its meaning, he heard her say, "I swear to you, like Evremonde!"

Defarge brought him the wine, and gave him Good-evening.

"How?"

"Good evening."

"Oh! Good-evening, citizen," filling his glass. "Ah! and good wine. I drink to the Republic."

Defarge went back to the counter, and said, "Certainly, a little like." Madame sternly retorted, "I tell you a good deal like." Jacques Three pacifically remarked, "He is so much in your mind, see you, madame." The amiable Vengeance added, with a laugh, "Yes, my faith! And you are looking forward with so much pleasure to seeing him once more to-morrow!"

Carton followed the lines and words of his paper with a slow forefinger, and with a studious and absorbed face. They were all leaning their arms on the counter close together, speaking low. After a silence of a few moments, during which they all looked towards him without disturbing his outward attention from the Jacobin editor, they resumed their conversation.

"It is true what madame says," observed Jacques Three. "Why stop? There is great force in that. Why stop?"

"Well, well," reasoned Defarge, "but one must stop somewhere. After all, the question is still where?"

"At extermination" said madame.

"Magnifincent!" croaked Jacques Three. The Vengeance, also, highly approved.

"Extermination is good doctrine, my wife," said Defarge, rather troubled; "in general, I say nothing against it. But this Doctor has suffered much; you have seen him to-day; you have observed his face when the paper was read."

"I have observed his face!" repeated madame, contemptuously and angrily. "Yes. I have observed his face. I have observed his face to be not the face of a true friend of the Republic. Let him take care of his face!"

"And you have observed, my wife," said Defarge, in a deprecatory manner, "the anguish of his daughter, which must be dreadful anguish to him!"

"I have observed his daughter!" repeated madame; "yes, I have observed his daughter more times than one. I have observed her to-day, and I have observed her other days. I have observed her in the court, and I have observed her in the street by the prison. Let me but lift my finger—!" She seemed to raise it (the listener's eyes were always on his paper), and to let it fall with a rattle on the ledge before her, as if the axe had dropped.

"The citizeness is superb!" croaked the Juryman.

"She is an Angel!" said The Vengeance, and embraced her.

"As to thee," pursued madame, implacably, addressing her husband, "if it depended on thee—which, happily, it does not—thou wouldst rescue this man even now."

"No!" protested Defarge. "Not if to lift this glass would do it! But I would leave the matter there. I say, stop there."

"See you then, Jacques," said Madame Defarge, wrathfully; "and see you too, my little Vengeance; see you both! Listen! For other crimes as tyrants and oppressors, I have this race a long time on my register, doomed to destruction and extermination. Ask my husband, is that so."

"It is so," asserted Defarge, without being asked.

"In the beginning of the great days, when the Bastille falls, he finds this paper of to-day, and he brings it home, and in the middle of the night when this place is clear and shut, we read it, here on this spot, by the light of this lamp. Ask him, is that so."

"It is so," assented Defarge.

"That night I tell him, when the paper is read through, and the lamp is burned out, and the day is gleaming in above those shutters and between those iron bars, that I have now a secret to communicate. Ask him, is that so."

"It is so," assented Defarge again.

"I communicate to him that secret. I smite this bosom with these two hands as I smite it now, and I tell him, 'Defarge, I was brought up among the fishermen of the sea-shore, and that injured family is mine. Defarge, that sister was my sister, that husband was my sister's husband, that unborn child was their child, that brother was my brother, that father was my father, those dead are my dead, and that summons to answer for those things descends to me!' Ask him is that so."

"It is so," assented Defarge once more.

"Then tell Wind and Fire where to stop," returned madame; "but don't tell me."

Both her hearers derived a horrible enjoyment from the deadly nature of her wrath—the listener could feel how white she was, without seeing her—and both highly commended it. Defarge, a weak minority, interposed a few words for the memory of the compassionate wife of the Marquis; but only elicited from his own wife a repetition of her last reply. "Tell the Wind and the Fire where to stop; not me!"

Customers entered, and the group was broken up. The English customer paid for what he had had, perplexedly counted his change, and asked, as a stranger, to be directed toward the National Palace. Madame Defarge took him to the door, and put her arm on his in pointing out the road. The English customer was not without his reflections then, that it might be a good deed to seize that arm, lift it, and strike under it sharp and deep.

But, he went on his way, and was soon swallowed up in the shadow of the prison wall. At the appointed hour, he emerged from it to present himself in Mr. Lorry's room again, where he found the old gentleman walking to and fro in restless anxiety. He said he had been with Lucie until just now, and had only left her for a few minutes, to come and keep his appointment. Her father had not been seen, since he quitted the banking-house toward four o'clock. She had some faint hopes that his mediation might save Charles, but they were very slight. He had been more than five hours gone: where could he be?

Mr. Lorry waited until ten; but, Doctor Manette not returning, and he being unwilling to leave Lucie any longer, it was arranged that he should go back to her, and come to the banking-house again at midnight. In the meanwhile, Carton would wait alone by the fire for the Doctor.

He waited and waited, and the clock struck twelve; but Doctor Manette did not come back. Mr. Lorry returned, and found no tidings of him, and brought none. Where could he be?

They were discussing this question, and were almost building up some weak structure of hope on his prolonged absence, when they heard him on the stairs. The instant he entered the room, it was plain that all was lost.

Whether he had really been to any one, or whether he had been all that time traversing the streets, was never known. As he stood staring at them, they asked him no question, for his face told them every thing.

"I cannot find it," said he, "and I must have it. Where is it?"

His head and throat were bare, and as he spoke with a helpless look straying all around, he took his coat off and let it drop on the floor.

"Where is my bench? I have been looking everywhere for my bench, and I can't find it. What have they done with my work? Time presses: I must finish those shoes."

They looked at one another, and their hearts died within them.

"Come, come!" said he, in a whimpering miserable way; "let me get to work. Give me my work."

Receiving no answer, he tore his hair and beat his feet upon the ground like a distracted child.

"Don't torture a poor, forlorn wretch," he implored them, with a dreadful cry; "but give me my work! What is to become of us if those shoes are not done to-night?"

Lost, utterly lost!

It was so clearly beyond hope to reason with him or try to restore him, that—as if by agreement—they each put a hand upon his shoulder, and soothed him to sit down before the fire, with a promise that he should have his work presently. He sank into the chair, and brooded over the embers and shed tears. As if all that had happened since the garret time were a momentary fancy or a dream, Mr. Lorry saw him shrink into the exact figure that Defarge had had in keeping.

Affected, and impressed with terror as they both were, by this spectacle of ruin, it was not a time to yield to such emotions. His lonely daughter, bereft of her final hope and reliance, appealed to them both too strongly. Again, as if by agreement, they looked at one another with one meaning in their faces. Carton was the first to speak:

"The last chance is gone: it was not much. Yes; he had better be taken to her. But before you go, will you for a moment, steadily attend to me? Don't ask me why I make the stipulations I am going to make, and exact the promise I am going to exact; I have a reason—a good one."

"I do not doubt it," answered Mr. Lorry. "Say on."

The figure in the chair between them was all the time monotonously rocking itself to and fro, and moaning. They spoke in such a tone as they would have used if they had been watching by a sick bed in the night.

Carton stooped to pick up the coat which lay almost entangling his feet. As he did so, a small case in which the Doctor was accustomed to carry the list of his day's duties, fell lightly on the floor. Carton took it up, and there was a folded paper in it. "We should look at this!" he said. Mr. Lorry nodded his consent. He opened it, and exclaimed, "Thank God!"

"What is it?" asked Mr. Lorry, eagerly.

"A moment! Let me speak of it in its place. First," he put his hand in his coat, and took another paper from it, "that is the certificate which enables me to pass out of this city. Look at it. You see—Sydney Carton, an Englishman?"

Mr. Lorry held it open in his hand, gazing in his earnest face.

"Keep it for me until to-morrow. I shall see him to-morrow, you remember, and I had better not take it into the prison."

"Why not?"

"I don't know; I prefer not to do so. Now take this paper that Doctor Manette has carried about him. It is a similar certificate, enabling him and his daughter and her child, at any time to pass the barrier and the frontier. You see?"

"Yes!"

"Perhaps he obtained it as his last and utmost precaution against evil, yesterday. When is it dated? But no matter; don't stay to look; put it up carefully with mine and your own. Now, observe! I never doubted until within this hour or two, that he had or could have such a paper. It is good until recalled. But it may be soon recalled, and, I have reason to think will be."

"They are not in danger?"

"They are in great danger. They are in danger of denunciation by Madame Defarge. I know it from her own lips. I have overheard words of that woman's, to-night which have presented their danger to me in strong colors. I have lost no time, and since then I have seen the spy. He confirms me. He knows that a wood-sawyer, living by the prison-wall, is under the control of the Defarges, and has been rehearsed by Madame Defarge as to his having seen *Her*"—he never mentioned Lucie's name—"making signs and signals to prisoners. It is easy to foresee that the pretence will be the common one, a prison plot, and that it will involve her life—and perhaps her child's—and perhaps her father's—for both have been seen with her at that place. Don't look so horrified. You will save them all."

"Heaven grant I may, Carton! But how?"

"I am going to tell you how. It will depend on you, and it could depend on no better man. This new denunciation will certainly not take place until after to-morrow; probably not until two or three days afterward: more probably a week afterward. You know it is a capital crime to mourn for, or sympathize with, a victim of the guillotine. She and her father would unquestionably be guilty of this crime, and this woman (the inveteracy of whose pursuit cannot be described) would wait to add that strength to her case, and make herself doubly sure. You follow me?"

"So attentively, and with so much confidence in what you say, that for the moment I lose sight," touching the back of the Doctor's chair, "even of this distress."

"You have money, and can buy the means of traveling to the sea-coast as quickly as the journey can be made. Your preparations have been completed for some days to return to England. Early to-morrow have your horses ready, so that they may be in starting trim at two o'clock in the afternoon."

"It shall be done!"

His manner was so fervent and inspiring, that Mr. Lorry caught the flame, and was quick as youth.

"You are a noble heart. Did I say we could depend upon no better man? Tell her, to-night what you know of her danger as involving her child and her father. Dwell upon that, for she would lay her own fair head beside her husband's cheerfully." He faltered for an instant; then went on as before. "For the sake of her child and her father, press upon her the necessity of leaving Paris, with them and you, at that hour. Tell her that it was her husband's last arrangement. Tell her that more depends upon it than she dare believe, or hope. You think that her father, even in this sad state, will submit himself to her; do you not?"

"I am sure of it."

"I thought so. Quietly and steadily have all these arrangements made in the court-yard here, even to the taking of your own seat in the carriage. The moment I come to you take me in, and drive away."

"I understand that I wait for you under all circumstances?"

"You have my certificate in your hand with the rest, you know, and will reserve my place. Wait for nothing but to have my place occupied, and then for England!"

"Why, then," said Mr. Lorry, grasping his eager but so firm and steady hand, "it does not all depend on one old man, but I shall have a young and ardent man at my side."

"By the help of Heaven you shall! Promise me solemnly that nothing will influence you to alter the course on which we now stand pledged to one another."

"Nothing, Carton."

"Remember these words to-morrow: change the course, or delay in it—for any reason—and no life can possibly be saved, and many lives must inevitably be sacrificed."

"I will remember them. I hope to do my part faithfully."

"And I hope to do mine. Now, good-bye!"

Though he said it with a grave smile of earnestness, and though he even put the old man's hand to his lips, he did not part from him then. He helped him so far to arouse the rocking figure before the dying embers as to get a cloak and hat put upon it, and to tempt it forth to find where the bench and work were hidden that it still moaningly besought to have. He walked on the other side of, it and protected it to the court-yard of the house where the afflicted heart—so happy in the memorable time when he had revealed his own desolate heart to it—outwatched the awful night. He entered the courtyard and remained there for a few moments alone, looking up at the light in the window of her room. Before he went away, he breathed a blessing toward it, and a farewell.

Chapter XIII
FIFTY-TWO

In the black prison of the Conciergerie the doomed of the day awaited their fate. They were in number as the weeks of the year. Fifty-two were to roll that afternoon on the life-tide of the city to the boundless, everlasting sea. Before their cells were quit of them, new occupants were appointed; before their blood ran into the blood spilled yesterday, the blood that was to mingle with theirs to-morrow was already set apart.

Two score and twelve were told off. From the farmer-general of seventy, whose riches could not buy his life, to the seamstress of twenty, whose poverty and obscurity could not save her. Physical diseases, engendered in the vices and neglects of men, will seize on victims of all degrees; and the frightful moral disorder, born of unspeakable suffering, intolerable oppression, and heartless indifference, smote equally without distinction.

Charles Darnay, alone in a cell, had sustained himself with no flattering delusion since he came to it from the Tribunal. In every line of the narrative he had heard read, he had heard his condemnation. He had fully comprehended that no personal influence could possibly save him—that he was virtually sentenced by the millions, and that units could avail him nothing.

Nevertheless, it was not easy, with the face of his beloved wife fresh before him, to compose his mind to what it must bear. His hold on life was strong, and it was very, very hard to loosen; by gradual efforts and degrees unclosed a little here, it clenched the tighter there, and when he brought his strength to bear on that hand and it yielded, this was closed again. There was a hurry, too, in all his thoughts, a turbulent and heated working of his heart, that contended against resignation. If, for a moment, he did feel resigned, then his wife and child, who had to live after him, seemed to protest and to make it a selfish thing.

But all this was at first. Before long the consideration that there was no disgrace in the fate he must meet, and that numbers went the same road wrongfully, and trod it firmly, every day, sprang up to stimulate him. Next followed the thought that much of the future peace of mind enjoyable by the dear ones depended on his quiet fortitude. So, by degrees he calmed into the better state, when he could raise his thoughts much higher, and draw comfort down.

Before it had set in dark on the night of his condemnation he had travelled thus far on his last way. Being allowed to purchase the means of writing, and a light, he sat down to write until such time as the prison lamps should be extinguished.

He wrote a long letter to Lucie, showing her that he had known nothing of her father's imprisonment, until he had heard of it from herself, and that he had been as ignorant as she of his father's and uncle's responsibility for that misery until the paper had been read. He had already explained to her that his concealment from herself of the name he had relinquished was the one condition—fully intelligible now—that her father had attached to their betrothal, and was the one promise he had still exacted on the morning of their marriage. He entreated her, for her father's sake, never to seek to know whether her father had become oblivious of the existence of the paper, or had had it recalled to him (for the moment, or for good), by the story of the Tower, on that old Sunday under the dear old plane-tree in the garden. If he had preserved any definite remembrance of it, there could be no doubt that he had supposed it destroyed with the Bastille, when he had found no mention of it among the relics of prisoners which the populace had discovered there, and which had been described to all the world. He besought her—though he added that he knew it was needless—to console her father, by impressing him, through every tender means she could think of, with the truth that he had done nothing for which he could justly reproach himself, but had uniformly forgotten himself for their joint sakes. Next to her preservation of his own last grateful love and blessing, and her overcoming of her sorrow, to devote herself to their dear child, he adjured her, as they would meet in Heaven, to comfort her father.

To her father himself, he wrote in the same strain; but he told her father that he expressly confided his wife and child to his care. And he told him this, very strongly, with the hope of rousing him from any despondency or dangerous retrospect toward which he foresaw he might be tending.

To Mr. Lorry, he commended them all, and explained his worldly affairs. That done, with many added sentences of grateful friendship and warm attachment, all was done. He never thought of Carton. His mind was so full of the others, that he never once thought of him.

He had time to finish these letters before the lights were put out. When he lay down on his straw bed, he thought he had done with this world.

But it beckoned him back in his sleep, and showed itself in shining forms. Free and happy, back in the old house in Soho (though it had nothing in it like the real house), unaccountably released and light of heart, he was with Lucie again, and she told him it was all a dream, and he had never gone away. A pause of forgetfulness, and then he had even suffered, and had come back to her, dead and at peace, and yet there was no difference in him. Another pause of oblivion, and he awoke in the sombre morning, unconscious where he was or what had happened, until it flashed upon his mind, "This is the day of my death!"

Thus, had he come through the hours to the day when the fifty-two heads were to fall. And now, while he was composed and hoped that he could meet the end with quiet heroism, a new action began in his waking thoughts, which was very difficult to master.

He had never seen the instrument that was to terminate his life. How high it was from the ground, how many steps it had, where he would be stood, how he would be touched, whether the touching hands would be dyed red, which way his face would be turned, whether he would be the first, or might be the last: these and many similar questions, in no wise directed by his will, obtruded themselves over and over again, countless times. Neither were they connected with fear; he was conscious of no fear. Rather, they originated in a strange besetting desire to know what to do when the time came; a desire gigantically disproportionate to the few split moments to which it referred; a wondering that was more like the wondering of some other spirit within his than his own.

The hours went on as he walked to and fro, and the clocks struck the numbers he would never hear again. Nine gone forever, ten gone forever, eleven gone for ever, twelve coming on to pass away. After a hard contest with that eccentric action of thought which had last perplexed him, he had got the better of it. He walked up and down, softly repeating their names to himself. The worst of the strife was over. He could walk up and down, free from distracting fancies, praying for himself and for them.

Twelve gone forever.

He had been apprised that the final hour was Three, and he knew he would be summoned some time earlier, inasmuch as the tumbrils jolted heavily and slowly through the streets. Therefore, he resolved to keep Two before his mind as the hour, and so to strengthen himself in the interval that he might be able, after that time, to strengthen others.

Walking regularly to and fro with his arms folded on his breast, a very different man from the prisoner who had walked to and fro at La Force, he heard One struck away from him without surprise. The hour had measured like most other hours. Devoutly thankful to Heaven for his recovered self-possession, he thought, "There is but another now," and turned to walk again.

Footsteps in the stone passage outside the door. He stopped.

The key was put in the lock, and turned. Before the door was opened, or as it opened, a man said in a low voice, in English: "He has never seen me here; I have kept out of his way. Go you in alone; I wait near. Lose no time!"

The door was quickly opened and closed, and there stood before him face to face, quiet, intent upon him, with the light of a smile on his features, and a cautionary finger on his lip, Sydney Carton.

There was something so bright and remarkable in his look, that, for the first moment, the prisoner misdoubted him to be an apparition of his own imagining. But he spoke, and it was his voice; he took the prisoner's hand, and it was his real grasp.

"Of all the people upon earth, you least expected to see me!" he said.

"I could not believe it to be you. I can scarcely believe it now. You are not"—the apprehension came suddenly into his mind—"a prisoner?"

"No. I am accidentally possessed of a power over one of the keepers here, and in virtue of it I stand before you. I come from her—your wife, dear Darnay."

The prisoner wrung his hand.

"I bring you a request from her."

"What is it?"

"A most earnest, pressing, and emphatic entreaty, addressed to you in the most pathetic tones of the voice so dear to you, that you well remember."

The prisoner turned his face partly aside.

"You have no time to ask me why I bring it, or what it means; I have no time to tell you. You must comply with it—take off those boots you wear, and draw on these of mine."

There was a chair against the wall of the cell, behind the prisoner. Carton, pressing forward, had already, with the speed of lightning, got him down into it, and stood over him, barefoot.

"Draw on those boots of mine. Put your hands to them; put your will to them. Quick!"

"Carton, there is no escaping from this place; it never can be done. You will only die with me. It is madness."

"It would be madness if I asked you to escape; but do I? When I ask you to pass out at that door, tell me it is madness and remain here. Change that cravat for this of mine, that coat for this of mine. While you do it, let me take this ribbon from your hair, and shake out your hair like this of mine!"

With wonderful quickness, and with a strength both of will and action, that appeared quite supernatural, he forced all these changes upon him. The prisoner was like a young child in his hands.

"Carton! Dear Carton! It is madness. It cannot be accomplished, it never can be done, it has been attempted, and has always failed. I implore you not to add your death to the bitterness of mine."

"Do I ask you, my dear Darnay, to pass the door? When I ask that, refuse. There are pen and ink and paper on this table. Is your hand steady enough to write?"

"It was when you came in."

"Steady it again, and write what I shall dictate. Quick, friend, quick!"

Pressing his hand to his bewildered head, Darnay sat down at the table. Carton, with his right hand in his breast, stood close beside him.

"Write exactly as I speak."

"To whom do I address it?"

"To no one." Carton still had his hand in his breast.

"Do I date it?"

"No."

The prisoner looked up at each question. Carton, standing over him with his hand in his breast, looked down.

" 'If you remember,' " said Carton, dictating, " 'the words that passed between us, long ago, you will readily comprehend this when you see it. You do remember them, I know. It is not in your nature to forget them.' "

He was drawing his hand from his breast; the prisoner chancing to look up in his hurried wonder as he wrote, the hand stopped, closing upon something.

"Have you written 'forget them'?" Carton asked.

"I have. Is that a weapon in your hand?"

"No; I am not armed."

"What is it in your hand?"

"You shall know directly. Write on; there are but a few words more." He dictated again. " 'I am thankful that the time has come, when I can prove them. That I do so is no subject for regret or grief.' " As he said these words with his eyes fixed on the writer, his hand slowly and softly moved down close to the writer's face.

The pen dropped from Darnay's fingers on the table, and he looked about him vacantly.

"What vapour is that?" he asked.

"Vapour?"

"Something that crossed me?"

"I am conscious of nothing; there can be nothing here. Take up the pen and finish. Hurry, hurry!"

As if his memory were impaired, or his faculties disordered, the prisoner made an effort to rally his attention. As he looked at Carton with clouded eyes and with an altered manner of breathing, Carton—his hand again in his breast—looked steadily at him.

"Hurry, hurry!"

The prisoner bent over the paper once more.

" 'If it had been otherwise;' " Carton's hand was again watchfully and softly stealing down; " 'I never should have used the longer opportunity.

If it had been otherwise;'" the hand was at the prisoner's face; "'I should but have had so much the more to answer for. If it had been otherwise—'" Carton looked at the pen and saw it was trailing off into unintelligible signs.

Carton's hand moved back to his breast no more. The prisoner sprang up with a reproachful look, but Carton's hand was close and firm at his nostrils, and Carton's left arm caught him round the waist. For a few seconds he faintly struggled with the man who had come to lay down his life for him; but within a minute or so, he was stretched insensible on the ground.

Quickly, but with hands as true to the purpose as his heart was, Carton dressed himself in the clothes the prisoner had laid aside, combed back his hair, and tied it with the ribbon the prisoner had worn. Then, he softly called, "Enter there! Come in!" and the spy presented himself.

"You see?" said Carton, looking up at him as he kneeled on one knee beside the insensible figure, putting the paper in the breast: "is your hazard very great?"

"Mr. Carton," the Spy answered, with a timid snap of his fingers, "my hazard is not *that,* in the thick of business here, if you are true to the whole of your bargain."

"Don't fear me. I will be true to the death."

"You must be, Mr. Carton, if the tale of fifty-two is to be right. Being made right by you in that dress, I shall have no fear."

"Have no fear! I shall soon be out of the way of harming you, and the rest will soon be far from here, please God! Now, get assistance and take me to the coach."

"You?" said the Spy nervously.

"Him, man, with whom I have exchanged. You go out at the gate by which you brought me in?"

"Of course."

"I was weak and faint when you brought me in, and I am fainter now you take me out. The parting interview has overpowered me. Such a thing has happened here, often, and too often. Your life is in your own hands. Quick! Call assistance!"

"You swear not to betray me?" said the trembling Spy, as he paused for a last moment.

"Man, man!" returned Carton, stamping his foot; "have I sworn by no solemn vow already, to go through with this, that you waste the precious moments now? Take him yourself to the courtyard you know of, place him yourself in the carriage, show him yourself to Mr. Lorry, tell him yourself to give him no restorative but air, and to remember my words of last night, and his promise of last night, and drive away!"

The spy withdrew, and Carton seated himself at the table, resting his forehead on his hands. The spy returned immediately, with two men.

"How, then?" said one of them, contemplating the fallen figure. "So afflicted to find that his friend has drawn a prize in the lottery of Saint Guillotine?"

"A good patriot," said the other, "could hardly have been more afflicted if the Aristocrat had drawn a blank."

They raised the unconscious figure, placed it on a litter they had brought to the door, and bent to carry it away.

"The time is short, Evremonde," said the Spy, in a warning voice.

"I know it well," answered Carton. "Be careful of my friend, I entreat you, and leave me."

"Come, then, my children," said Barsad. "Lift him, and come away!"

The door closed, and Carton was left alone. Straining his powers of listening to the utmost, he listened for any sound that might denote suspicion or alarm. There was none. Keys turned, doors clashed, footsteps passed along distant passages: no cry was raised, or hurry made, that seemed unusual. Breathing more freely in a little while, he sat down at the table, and listened again until the clock struck Two.

Sounds that he was not afraid of, for he divined their meaning, then began to be audible. Several doors were opened in succession, and finally his own. A gaoler, with a list in his hand, looked in, merely saying, "Follow me, Evremonde!" and he followed into a large dark room at a distance. It was a dark winter day, and what with the shadows within, and what with the shadows without, he could but dimly discern the others who were brought there to have their arms bound. Some were standing; some seated. Some were lamenting, and in restless motion; but, these were few. The great majority were silent and still, looking fixedly at the ground.

As he stood by the wall in a dim corner, while some of the fifty-two were brought in after him, one man stopped in passing, to embrace him, as having a knowledge of him. It thrilled him with a great dread of discovery; but the man went on. A very few moments after that, a young woman, with a slight girlish form, a sweet spare face in which there was no vestige of color, and large widely-opened patient eyes, rose from the seat where he had observed her sitting, and came to speak to him.

"Citizen Evremonde," she said, touching him with her cold hand, "I am a poor little seamstress, who was with you in La Force."

He murmured for answer, "True. I forget what you were accused of?"

"Plots. Though the just Heaven knows I am innocent of any. Is it likely? Who would think of plotting with a poor little weak creature like me?"

The forlorn smile with which she said it so touched him, that tears started from his eyes.

"I am not afraid to die, Citizen Evremonde, but I have done nothing! I am not unwilling to die, if the Republic which is to do so much good for us poor, will profit by my death; but I do not know how that can be, Citizen Evremonde. Such a poor weak little creature!"

As the last thing on earth that his heart was to warm and soften to, it warmed and softened to this pitiable girl.

"I heard you were released, Citizen Evremonde. I hoped it was true?"

"It was. But, I was again taken and condemned."

"If I may ride with you, Citizen Evremonde, will you let me hold your hand? I am not afraid, but I am little and weak, and it will give me more courage."

As the patient eyes were lifted to his face, he saw a sudden doubt in them, and then astonisbment. He pressed the work-worn, hunger-worn young fingers, and touched his lips.

"Are you dying for him?" she whispered.

"And his wife and child. Hush! Yes."

"Oh, you will let me hold your brave hand, stranger?"

"Hush! Yes, my poor sister; to the last."

The same shadows that are falling on the prison are falling, in that same hour of the early afternoon, on the Barrier with the crowd about it, when a coach going out of Paris drives up to be examined.

"Who goes here? Whom have we within? Papers!"

The papers are handed out, and read.

"Alexandre Manette. Physician. French. Which is he?"

This is he; this helpless, inarticulately-murmuring, wandering old man pointed out.

"Apparently the Citizen-Doctor is not in his right mind? The Revolution-fever will have been too much for him?"

Greatly too much for him.

"Hah! Many suffer with it. Lucie. His daughter. English. Which is she?"

This is she.

"Apparently it must be. Lucie, the wife of Evremonde; is it not?"

It is.

"Hah! Evrémonde has an assignation elsewhere. Lucie, her child. English. This is she?"

She and no other.

"Kiss me, child of Evrémonde. Now, thou hast kissed a good Republican; something new in thy family; remember it! Sydney Carton. Advocate. English. Which is he?"

He lies here, in this corner of the carriage. He, too, is pointed out.

"Apparently the English advocate is in a swoon?"

It is hoped he will recover in the fresher air. It is represented that he is not in strong health, and has separated sadly from a friend who is under the displeasure of the Republic.

"Is that all? It is not a great deal, that! Many are under the displeasure of the Republic, and must look out at the little window. Jarvis Lorry. Banker. English. Which is he?"

"I am he. Necessarily, being the last."

It is Jarvis Lorry who has replied to all the previous questions. It is Jarvis Lorry who has alighted and stands with his hands on the coach-door, replying to a group of officials. They leisurely walk round the carriage and leisurely mount the box, to look at what little luggage it carries on the roof; the country-people hanging about press nearer to the coach-doors and greedily stare in; a little child, carried by its mother, has its short arm held out for it, that it may touch the wife of an aristocrat who has gone to the Guillotine.

"Behold your papers, Jarvis Lorry, countersigned."

"One can depart, citizen?"

"One can depart. Forward, my postillions! A good journey!"

"I salute you, citizens.—And the first danger passed!"

These are again the words of Jarvis Lorry, as he clasps his hands, and looks upward. There is terror in the carriage there is weeping, there is the heavy breathing of the insensible traveller.

"Are we not going too slowly? Can they not be induced to go faster?" asks Lucie, clinging to the old man.

"It would seem like flight, my darling. I must not urge them too much; it would rouse suspicion."

"Look back, look back, and see if we are pursued!"

"The road is clear, my dearest. So far, we are not pursued."

Houses in twos and threes pass by us, solitary farms, ruinous buildings, dye-works, tanneries, and the like, open country, avenues of leafless trees. The hard uneven pavement is under us, the soft deep mud is on either side. Sometimes we strike into the skirting mud, to avoid the stones that clatter us and shake us and sometimes we stick in ruts and sloughs there. The agony of our impatience is then so great, that in our wild alarm and hurry, we are for getting out and running—hiding—doing anything but stopping.

Out of the open country, in again among ruinous buildings, solitary farms, dye-works, tanneries, and the like, cottages in twos and threes, avenues of leafless trees. Have these men deceived us, and taken us back by another road? Is not this the same place twice over? Thank Heaven, no. A village. Look back, look back, and see if we are pursued! Hush; the posting-house.

Leisurely, our four horses are taken out; leisurely, the coach stands in the little street, bereft of horses, and with no likelihood upon it of ever moving again; leisurely, the new horses come into visible existence, one by one; leisurely, the new postillions follow, sucking and plaiting the lashes of their whips; leisurely, the old postillions count their money, make wrong additions, and arrive at dissatisfied results. All the time, our overfraught hearts are beating at a rate that would far outstrip the fastest gallop of the fastest horses ever foaled.

At length the new postillions are in their saddles, and the old are left behind. We are through the village, up the hill, and down the hill, and on the low watery grounds. Suddenly, the postillions exchange speech with animated gesticulation, and the horses are pulled up, almost on their haunches. We are pursued?

"Ho! Within the carriage there. Speak then!"

"What is it?" asks Mr. Lorry, looking out at window.

"How many did they say?"

"I do not understand you."

"—At the last post. How many to the Guillotine today?"

"Fifty-two."

"I said so! A brave number! My fellow-citizen here would have it forty-two; ten more heads are worth having. The Guillotine goes handsomely. I love it. Hi forward! Whoop then!"

The night comes on dark. He moves more; he is beginning to revive, and to speak intelligibly; he thinks they are still together; he asks him, by his name, what he has in his hand. O pity us, kind Heaven, and help us! Look out, look out, and see if we are pursued.

The wind is rushing after us, and the clouds are flying after us, and the moon is plunging after us, and the whole wild night is in pursuit of us; but, so far, we are pursued by nothing else.

Chapter XIV

THE KNITTING DONE

IN that same juncture of time when the Fifty-Two awaited their fate, Madame Defarge held darkly ominous council with The Vengeance and Jacques Three of the Revolutionary Jury. Not in the wine-shop did Madame Defarge confer with these ministers, but in the shed of the wood-sawyer, erst a mender of roads. The sawyer himself did not participate in the conference, but abided at a little distance, like an outer satellite who was not to speak until required, or to offer an opinion until invited.

"But our Defarge," said Jacques Three, "is undoubtedly a good Republican? Eh?"

"There is no better," the voluble Vengeance protested in her shrill notes, "in France."

"Peace, little Vengeance," said Madame Defarge, laying her hand with a slight frown on her lieutenant's llps, "hear me speak. My husband, fellow-citizen, is a good Republican and a bold man; he has deserved well of the Republic, and possesses its confidence. But my husband has his weaknesses, and he is so weak as to relent towards this Doctor."

"It is a great pity," croaked Jacques Three, dubiously shaking his head, with his cruel fingers at his hungry mouth; "it is not quite like a good citizen; it is a thing to regret."

"See you," said madame, "I care nothing for this Doctor, I. He may wear his head or lose it, for any interest I have in him; it is all one to me. But, the Evrémonde people are to be exterminated, and the wife and child must follow the husband and father."

"She has a fine head for it," croaked Jacques Three. 'I have seen blue eyes and golden hair there, an.d they looked charming when Samson held them up." Ogre that he was, he spoke like an epicure.

Madame Defarge cast down her eyes, and reflected a little.

"The child also," observed Jacques Three, with a meditative enjoyment of his words, "has golden hair and blue eyes. And we seldom have a child there. It is a pretty sight!"

"In a word," said Madame Defarge, coming out of her short abstraction, "I cannot trust my husband in this matter. Not only do I feel, since last night, that I dare not confide to him the details of my projects; but also I feel that if I delay, there is danger of his giving warning, and then they might escape."

"That must never be," croaked Jacques Three; "no one must escape. We have not half enough as it is: We ought to have six score a day."

"In a word," Madame Defarge went on, "my husband has not my reason for pursuing this family to annihilation, and I have not his reason for regarding this Doctor with any sensibility. I must act for myself, therefore. Come hither, little citizen."

The wood-sawyer, who held her in the respect, and himself in the submission, of mortal fear, advanced with his hand to his red cap.

"Touching those signals, little citizen," said Madame Defarge, sternly, "that she made to the prisoners; you are ready to bear witness to them this very day?"

"Ay, ay, why not?" cried the sawyer. "Every day, in all weathers, from two to four, always signalling, sometimes with the little one, sometimes without. I know what I know. I have seen with my eyes."

He made all manner of gestures while he spoke, as if in incidental imitation of some few of the great diversity of signals that he had never seen.

"Clearly plots," said Jacques Three. "Transparently!"

"There is no doubt of the Jury?" inquired Madame Defarge, letting her eyes turn to him with a gloomy smile.

"Rely upon the patriotic Jury, dear citizeness. I answer for my fellow-Jurymen."

"Now, let me see," said Madame Defarge, pondering again. "Yet once more! Can I spare this Doctor to my husband? I have no feeling either way. Can I spare him?"

"He would count as one head," observed Jacques Three, in a low voice. "We really have not heads enough; it would be a pity, I think."

"He was signalling with her when I saw her," argued Madame Defarge; "I cannot speak of one without the other; and I must not be silent, and trust the case wholly to him, this little citizen here. For, I am not a bad witness."

The Vengeance and Jacques Three vied with each other in their fervent protestations that she was the most admirable and marvellous of witnesses. The little citizen, not to be outdone, declared her to be a celestial witness.

"He must take his chance," said Madame Defarge. "No, I cannot spare him! You are engaged at three o'clock; you are going to see the batch of to-day executed.—You?"

The question was addressed to the wood-sawyer, who hurriedly replied in the affirmative: seizing the occasion to add that he was the most ardent of Republicans, and that he would be in effect the most desolate of Republicans, if anything prevented him from enjoying the pleasure of smoking his afternoon pipe in the contemplation of the droll national barber. He was so very demonstrative herein, that he might have been suspected (perhaps was, by the dark eyes that looked contemptuously at him out of Madame Defarge's head) of having his small individual fears for his own personal safety, every hour in the day.

"I," said madame, "am equally engaged at the same place. After it is over—say at eight to-night—come you to me, in Saint Antoine, and we will give information against these people at my Section."

The wood-sawyer said he would be proud and flattered to attend the citizeness. The citizeness looking at him, he became embarrassed, evaded her glance as a small dog would have done, retreated among his wood, and hid his confusion over the handle of the saw.

Madame Defarge beckoned the Juryman and The Vengeance a little nearer to the door, and there expounded her further views to them thus:

"She will now be at home, awaiting the moment of his death. She will be mourning and grieving. She will be in a state of mind to impeach the justice of the Republlc. She will be full of sympathy with its enemies. I will go to her."

"What an admirable woman; what an adorable woman!" exclaimed Jacques Three, rapturously. "Ah, my cherished!" cried The Vengeance; and embraced her.

"Take you my knitting," said Madame Defarge, placing it in her lieutenant's hands, "and have it ready for me in my usual seat. Keep me my usual chair. Go you there, straight, for there will probably be a greater concourse than usual, to-day."

"I willingly obey the orders of my chief," said The Vengeance with alacrity, and kissing her cheek. "You will not be late?"

"I shall be there before the commencement."

"And before the tumbrils arrive. Be sure you are there, my soul," said The Vengeance, calling after her, for she had already turned into the street, "before the tumbrils arrive!"

Madame Defarge slightly waved her hand, to imply that she heard, and might be relied upon to arrive in good time, and so went through the mud and round the corner of the prison wall. The Vengeance and the Juryman, looking after her as she walked away, were highly appreciative of her fine figure, and her superb moral endowments.

There were many women at that time, upon whom the time laid a dreadfully disfiguring hand; but, there was not one among them more to be dreaded than this ruthless woman, now taking her way along the streets. Of a strong and fearless character, and shrewd sense and readiness, of great determination, of that kind of beauty which not only seems to impart to its possessor firmness and animosity, but to strike into others an instinctive recognition of those qualities; the troubled time would have heaved her up under any circumstances. But imbued from her childhood with a brooding sense of wrong, and an inveterate hatred of a class, opportunity had developed her into a tigress. She was absolutely without pity. If she had ever had the virtue in her, it had quite gone out of her.

It was nothing to her that an innocent man was to die for the sins of his forefathers; she saw, not him, but them. It was nothing to her, that his wife was to be made a widow and his daughter an orphan; that was insufficient punishment, because they were her natural enemies and her prey, and as such had no right to live. To appeal to her was made hopeless by her having no sense of pity, even for herself. If she had been laid low in the streets, in any of the many encounters in which she had been engaged, she would not have pitied herself: nor, if she had been ordered to the axe to-morrow, would she have gone to it with any softer feeling than a fierce desire to change places with the man who sent her there.

Such a heart Madame Defarge carried under her rough robe. Carelessly worn, it was a becoming robe enough, in a certain weird way, and her dark hair looked rich under her coarse red cap. Lying hidden in her bosom was a loaded pistol. Lying hidden at her waist was a sharpened dagger. Thus accoutred, and walking with the confident tread of such a character, and with the supple freedom of a woman who had habitually walked in her girlhood, bare-foot and bare-legged, on the brown sea-sand, Madame Defarge took her way along the streets.

Now, when the journey of the travelling coach, at that very moment waiting for the completion of its load, had been planned out last night, the difficulty of taking Miss Pross in it had much engaged Mr. Lorry's attention. It was not merely desirable to avoid overloading the coach, but it was of the highest importance that the time occupied in examining it and its passengers, should be reduced to the utmost, since their escape might depend on the saving of only a few seconds here and there. Finally, he had proposed, after anxious consideration, that Miss Pross and Jerry, who were at liberty to leave the city, would leave it at three o'clock in the lightest-wheeled conveyance known to that period. Unencumbered with luggage, they would soon overtake the coach, and, passing it and preceding it on the road, would order its horses in advance, and greatly facilitate its progress during the precious hours of the night, when delay was the most to be dreaded.

Seeing in this arrangement the hope of rendering real service in that pressing emergency, Miss Pross hailed it with joy. She and Jerry had beheld the coach start, had known who it was that Solomon brought, had passed some ten minutes in tortures of suspense, and were now concluding their arrangements to follow the coach, even as Madame Defarge, taking her way through the streets, now drew nearer and nearer to the else-deserted lodging in which they held their consultation.

"Now what do you think, Mr. Cruncher," said Miss Pross, whose agitation was so great that she could hardly speak, or stand, or move, or live; "what do you think of our not starting from this court-yard? Another carriage having already gone from here to-day, it might awaken suspicion."

"My opinion, Miss," returned Mr. Cruncher, "is as you're right. Likewise wot. I'll stand by you, right or wrong."

"I am so distracted with fear and hope for our precious creatures," said Miss Pross, wildly crying, "that I am incapable of forming any plan. Are *you* capable of forming any plan, my dear, good Mr. Cruncher?"

"Respectin' a future spear o' life, miss," returned Mr. Cruncher, "I hope so. Respectin' any present use o' this here blessed old head o' mine, I think not. Would you do me the favor, miss, to take notice o' two promises and wows wot it is my wishes fur to record in this here crisis?"

"Oh, for gracious' sake!" cried Miss Pross, still wildly crying, "record them at once, and get them out of the way, like an excellent man."

"First," said Mr. Crucher, who was all in a tremble, and who spoke with an ashy and solemn visage, "them poor things well out o' this, never no more will I do it, never no more!"

"I am quite sure, Mr. Cruncher," returned Miss Pross, "that you never will do it again, whatever it is, and I beg you not to think it necessary to mention more particularly what it is."

"No, miss," returned Jerry, "it shall not be named to you. Second: them poor things well out o' this, and never no more will I interfere with Mrs. Cruncher's flopping, never no more!"

"Whatever housekeeping arrangement that may be," said Miss Pross, striving to dry her eyes and compose herself, "I have no doubt it is best that Mrs. Cruncher should have it entirely under her own superintendence.—O my poor darlings!"

"I go so far as to say, miss, moreover," proceeded Mr. Cruncher, with a most alarming tendency to hold forth as from a pulpit—"and let my words be took down and took to Mrs. Cruncher through yourself—that wot my opinions respectin' flopping has undergone a change, and that wot I only hope with all my heart as Mrs. Cruncher may be a flopping at the present time."

"There, there, there! I hope she is, my dear man," cried the distracted Miss Pross, "and I hope she finds it answering her expectations."

"Forbid it," proceeded Mr. Cruncher, with additional solemnity, additional slowness, and additional tendency to hold forth and hold out, "as anything wot I have ever said or done should be wisited on my earnest wishes for them poor creeturs now! Forbid it as we shouldn't all flop (if it was anyways conwenient) to get 'em out o' this here dismal risk! Forbid it, miss! Wot I say, for—BID it!" This was Mr. Cruncher's conclusion after a protracted but vain endeavor to find a better one.

And still Madame Defarge, pursuing her way along the streets, came nearer and nearer.

"If we ever get back to our native land," sald Miss Pross, "you may rely upon my telling Mrs. Cruncher as much as I may be able to remember and understand of what you have so impressively said; and at all events you may be sure that I shall bear witness to your being thoroughly in earnest at this dreadful time. Now, pray let us think! My esteemed Mr. Cruncher, let us think!"

Still, Madame Defarge, pursuing her way along the streets, came nearer and nearer.

"If you were to go before," said Miss Pross, "and stop the vehicle and horses from coming here, and were to wait somewhere for me, wouldn't that be best?"

Mr. Cruncher thought it might be best.

"Where could you wait for me?" asked Miss Pross.

Mr. Cruncher was so bewildered that he could think of no locality but Temple Bar. Alas! Temple Bar was hundreds of miles away, and Madame Defarge was drawing very near indeed.

"By the cathedral door," said Miss Pross. "Would it be much out of the way, to take me in, near the great cathedral door between the two towers?"

"No, miss," answered Mr. Cruncher.

"Then, like the best of men," said Miss Pross, "go to the post-house straight, and make that change."

"I am doubtful," said Mr. Cruncher, hesitating and shaking his head, "about leaving of you, you see. We don't know what may happen."

"Heaven knows we don't," returned Miss Pross, "but have no fear of me. Take me in at the cathedral, at Three o'clock, or as near it as you can, and I am sure it will be better than our going from here. I feel certain of it. There! Bless you, Mr. Cruncher! Think—not of me, but of the lives that may depend on both of us!"

This exordium, and Miss Pross's two hands in quite agonized entreaty clasping his, decided Mr. Cruncher. With an encouraging nod or two, he immediately went out to alter the arrangements, and left her by herself to follow as she had proposed.

The having originated a precaution which was already in course of execution was a great relief to Miss Pross. The necessity of composing her appearance so that it should attract no special notice in the streets was another relief. She looked at her watch, and it was twenty minutes past two. She had no time to lose, but must get ready at once.

Afraid, in her extreme perturbation, of the loneliness of the deserted rooms, and of half-imagined faces peeping from behind every open door in them, Miss Pross got a basin of cold water and began laving her eyes, which were swollen and red. Haunted by her feverish apprehensions, she could not bear to have her sight obscured for a minute at a time by the dripping water, but constantly paused and looked around to see that there was no one watching her. In one of those pauses she recoiled and cried out, for she saw a figure standing in the room.

The basin fell to the ground broken, and the water flowed to the feet of Madame Defarge. By wild, wild ways, and through much staining blood, those feet had come to meet that water.

Madame Defarge looked coldly at her, and said, "The wife of Evrémonde; where is she?"

It flashed upon Miss Pross's mind that the doors were all standing open, and would suggest the flight. Her first act was to shut them. There were four in the room, and she shut them all. She then placed herself before the door of the chamber which Lucie had occupied.

Madame Defarge's dark eyes followed her through this rapid movement, and rested on her when it was finished. Miss Pross had nothing beautiful about her; years had not tamed the wildness, or softened the grimness, of her appearance; but, she too, was a determined woman in her different way, and she measured Madame Defarge with her eyes, every inch.

"You might, from your appearance, be the wife of Lucifer," said Miss Pross, in her breathing. "Nevertheless, you shall not get the better of me. I am an Englishwoman."

Madame Defarge looked at her scornfully, but still with something of Miss Pross's own perception that they two were at bay. She saw a tight, hard, wiry woman before her, as Mr. Lorry had seen in the same figure a woman with a strong hand, in the years gone by. She knew full well that Miss Pross was the family's devoted friend; Miss Pross knew full well that Madame Defarge was the family's malevolent enemy.

"On my way yonder," said Madame Defarge, with a slight movement of her hand towards the fatal spot, "where they reserve my chair and my knitting for me, I am come to make my compliments to her in passing. I wish to see her."

"I know that your intentions are evil," said Miss Pross, "and you may depend upon it, I'll hold my own against them."

Each spoke in her own language; neither understood the other's words; both were very watchful, and intent to deduce, from look and manner, what the unintelligible words meant.

"It will do her no good to keep herself concealed from me at this moment," said Madame Defarge. "Good patriots will know what that means. Let me see her. Go tell her that I wish to see her. Do you hear?"

"If those eyes of yours were bed-winches," returned Miss Pross, "and I was an English four-poster, they shouldn't loose a splinter of me. No, you wicked foreign woman; I am your match."

Madame Defarge was not likely to follow these idiomatic remarks in detail; but she so far understood them as to perceive that she was set at naught.

"Woman imbecile and pig-like!" said Madame Defarge, frowning. "I take no answer from you. I demand to see her. Either tell her that I demand to see her, or stand out of the way of the door and let me go to her!" This, with an angry explanatory wave of her right arm.

"I little thought," said Miss Pross, "that I should ever want to understand your nonsensical language; but I would give all I have, to the very clothes I wear, to know whether you suspect the truth, or any part of it."

Neither of them for a single moment released the other's eyes. Madame Defarge had not moved from the spot where she stood when Miss Pross first became aware of her; but she now advanced one step.

"I am a Briton," said Miss Pross, "I am desperate. I don't care an English Twopence for myself. I know that the longer I keep you here, the greater hope there is for my Ladybird. I'll not leave a handful of that dark hair upon your head, if you lay a finger on me!"

Thus Miss Pross, with a shake of her head and a flash of her eyes between every rapid sentence, and every rapid sentence a whole breath. Thus Miss Pross, who had never struck a blow in her life.

But her courage was of that emotional nature that it brought the irrepressible tears into her eyes. This was a courage that Madame Defarge so little comprehended, as to mistake for weakness. "Ha, ha!" she laughed, "you poor wretch! What are you worth! I address myself to that Doctor." Then she raised her voice and called out, "Citizen Doctor! Wife of Evrémonde! Child of Evrémonde! Any person but this miserable fool, answer the Citizeness Defarge!"

Perhaps the following silence, perhaps some latent disclosure in the expression of Miss Pross's face, perhaps a sudden misgiving apart from either suggestion, whispered to Madame Defarge that they were gone. Three of the doors she opened swiftly, and looked in.

"Those rooms are all in disorder, there has been hurried packing, there are odds and ends upon the ground. There is no one in that room behind you! Let me look."

"Never!" said Miss Pross, who understood the request as perfectly as Madame Defarge understood the answer.

"If they are not in that room, they are gone, and can be pursued and brought back," said Madame Defarge to herself.

"As long as you don't know whether they are in that room or not, you are uncertain what to do," said Miss Pross to *herself*; "and you shall not know that, if I can prevent your knowing it; and know that, or not know that, you shall not leave here while I can hold you."

"I have been in the streets from the first, nothing has stopped me, I wiil tear you to pieces, but I will have you from that door," said Madame Defarge.

"We are alone at the top of a high house in a solitary courtyard, we are not likely to be heard, and I pray for bodily strength to keep you here, while every minute you are here is worth a hundred thousand guineas to my darling,"said Miss Pross.

Madame Defarge made at the door. Miss Pross, on the instinct of the moment, seized her round the waist in both her arms, and held her tight. It was in vain for Madame Defarge to struggle and to strike; Miss Pross, with the vigorous tenacity of love, always so much stronger than hate, clasped her tight, and even lifted her from the floor in the struggle that they had. The two hands of Madame Defarge buffeted and tore her face; but, Miss Pross, with her head down, held her round the waist, and clung to her with more than the hold of a drowning woman.

Soon, Madame Defarge's hands ceased to strike, and felt at her encircled waist. "It is under my arm," said Miss Pross, in smothered tones, "you shall not draw it. I am stronger than you, I bless Heaven for it. I'll hold you till one or other of us faints or dies!"

Madame Defarge's hands were at her bosom. Miss Pross looked up, saw what it was, struck at it, struck out a flash and a crash, and stood alone—blinded with smoke.

All this was in a second. As the smoke cleared, leaving an awful stillness, it passed out on the air, like the soul of the furious woman whose body lay lifeless on the ground.

In the first fright and horror of her situation, Miss Pross passed the body as far from it as she could, and ran down the stairs to call for fruitless help. Happily, she bethought herself of the consequences of what she did, in time to check herself and go back. It was dreadful to go in at the door again; but she did go in, and even went near it, to get the bonnet and other things that she must wear. These she put on, out on the staircase, first shutting and locking the door, and taking away the key. She then sat down on the stairs a few moments to breathe and to cry, and then got up and hurried away.

By good fortune she had a veil on her bonnet, or she could hardly have gone along the streets without being stopped. By good fortune, too, she was naturally so peculiar in appearance as not to show disfigurement like any other woman. She needed both advantages, for the marks of griping fingers were deep in her face, and her hair was torn, and her dress (hastily composed with unsteady hands) was clutched and dragged a hundred ways.

In crossing the bridge, she dropped the door key in the river. Arriving at the cathedral some few minutes before her escort, and waiting there, she thought, what if the key were already taken in a net, what if it were identified, what if the door were opened and the remains discovered, what if she were stopped at the gate, sent to prison, and charged with murder! In the midst of these fluttering thoughts, the escort appeared, took her in, and took her away.

"Is there any noise in the streets?" she asked him.

"The usual noises," Mr. Cruncher replied; and looked surprised by the question and by her aspect.

"I don't hear you," said Miss Pross. "What do you say?"

It was in vain for Mr. Cruncher to repeat what he said; Miss Pross could not hear him. "So I'll nod my head," thought Mr. Cruncher, amazed, "at all events she'll see that." And she did.

"Is there any noise in the streets now?" asked Miss Pross again, presently.

Again Mr. Cruncher nodded his head.

"I don't hear it."

"Gone deaf in a hour?" said Mr. Cruncher, ruminating, with his mind much disturbed; "wot's come to her?"

"I feel," said Miss Pross, "as if there had been a flash and a crash, and that crash was the last thing I should ever hear in this life."

"Blest if she ain't in a queer condition!" said Mr. Cruncher, more and more disturbed. "Wot can she have been a takin', to keep her courage up? Hark! There's the roll of them dreadful carts! You can hear that, miss?"

"I can hear," said Miss Pross, seeing that he spoke to her, "nothing. Oh, my good man, there was first a great crash, and then a great stillness, and that stillness seems to be fixed and unchangeable, never to be broken any more as long as my life lasts."

"If she don't hear the roll of those dreadful carts, now very nigh their journey's end," said Mr. Cruncher, glancing over his shoulder, "it's my opinion that indeed she never will hear anything else in this world."

And indeed she never did.

Chapter XV

THE FOOTSTEPS DIE OUT FOREVER

ALONG the Paris streets, the dead-carts rumble, hollow and harsh. Six tumbrils carry the day's wine to La Guillotine. All the devouring and insatiate monsters imagined since imagination could record itself, are fused in the one realisation, Guillotine. And yet there is not in France, with its rich variety of soil and climate, a blade, a leaf, a root, a sprig, a peppercorn, which will grow to maturity under conditions more certain than those that have produced this horror. Crush humanity out of shape once more, under similar hammers, and it will twist itself into the same tortured forms. Sow the same seed of rapacious license and oppression over again, and it will surely yield the same fruit according to its kind.

Six tumbrils roll along the streets. Change these back again to what they were, thou powerful enchanter, Time, and they shall be seen to be the carriages of absolute monarchs, the equipages of feudal nobles, the toilettes of flaring Jezebels, the churches that are not my father's house but dens of thieves, the huts of millions of starving peasants! No; the great magician who majestically works out the appointed order of the Creator never reverses his transformations. "If thou be changed into this shape by the will of God," say the seers to the enchanted, in the wise Arabian stories, "then remain so! But, if thou wear this form through mere passing conjuration, then resume thy former aspect!" Changeless and hopeless, the tumbrils roll along.

As the sombre wheels of the six carts go round, they seem to plow up a long crooked furrow among the populace in the streets. Ridges of faces are thrown to this side and to that, and the plows go steadily onward. So used are the regular inhabitants of the houses to the spectacle, that in many windows there are no people, and in some the occupation of the hands is not so much as suspended, while the eyes survey the faces in the tumbrils. Here and there, the inmate has visitors to see the sight; then he points his finger, with something of the complacency of a curator or authorized exponent, to this cart and to this, and seems to tell who sat here yesterday, and who sat there the day before.

Of the riders in the tumbrils, some observe these things, and all things on their last roadside, with an impassive stare; others, with a lingering interest in the ways of life and men. Some, seated with drooping heads, are sunk in silent despair; again, there are some so heedful of their looks that they cast upon the multitude such glances as they have seen in theatres, and in pictures. Several close their eyes, and think, or try to get their straying thoughts together. Only one, and he a miserable creature, of a crazed aspect, is so shattered and made drunk by horror, that he sings, and tries to dance. Not one of the whole number appeals, by look or gesture, to the pity of the people.

There is a guard of sundry horsemen riding abreast of the tumbrils, and faces are often turned up to some of them, and they are asked some questions. It would seem to be always the same question, for, it is always followed by a press of people towards the third cart. The horsemen abreast of that cart frequently point out one man in it with their swords. The leading curiosity is to know which is he; he stands at the back of the tumbril with his head bent down, to converse with a mere girl who sits on the side of the cart, and holds his hand. He has no curiosity or care for the scene about him, and always speaks to the girl. Here and there in the long street of St. Honoré, cries are raised against him. If they move him at all, it is only to a quiet smile, as he shakes his hair a little more loosely about his face. He cannot easily touch his face, his arms being bound.

On the steps of a church, awaiting the coming-up of the tumbrils, stands the Spy and prison-sheep. He looks into the first of them: not there. He looks into the second: not there. He already asks himself, "Has he sacrificed me?" when his face clears, as he looks into the third.

"Which is Evremonde?" says a man behind him.

"That. At the back there."

"With his hand in the girl's?"

"Yes."

The man cries, "Down, Evremonde! To the Guillotine all aristocrats; Down, Evremonde!"

"Hush, hush!" the Spy entreats him, timidly.

"And why not, citizen?"

"He is going to pay the forfeit; it will be paid in five minutes more. Let him be at peace."

But the man continuing to exclaim, "Down, Evremonde!" the face of Evremonde is for a moment turned towards him. Evremonde then sees the Spy, and looks attentively at him, and goes his way.

The clocks are on the stroke of three, and the furrow plowed among the populace is turning round, to come on into the place of execution, and end. The ridges thrown to this side and to that, now crumble in and close behind the last plow as it passes on, for all are following to the Guillotine. In front of it, seated in chairs, as in a garden of public diversion, are a number of women, busily knitting. On one of the foremost Chairs stands The Vengeance, looking about for her friend.

"Therese!" she cries, in her shrill tones. "Who has seen her? Therese Defarge!"

"She never missed before," says a knitting-woman of the sisterhood.

"No; nor will she miss now," cries The Vengeance, petulantly. "Therese!"

"Louder," the woman recommends.

Aye! Louder, Vengeance, much louder, and still she will scarcely hear thee. Louder yet, Vengeance, with a little oath or so added, and yet it will hardly bring her. Send other women up and down to seek her, lingering somewhere; and yet, although the messengers have done dread deeds, it is questionable whether of their own will they will go far enough to find her!

"Bad Fortune!" cries The Vengeance, stamping her foot in the chair, "and here are the tumbrils! And Evremonde will be dispatched in a wink, and she not here! See her knitting in my hand, and her empty chair ready for her. I cry with vexation and disappointment!"

As The Vengeance descends from her elevation to do it, the tumbrils begin to discharge their loads. The ministers of Saint Guillotine are robed and ready. Crash!—A head is held up, and the knitting-women who scarcely lifted their eyea to look at it a moment ago when it could think and speak, count One.

The second tumbril empties and moves on; the third comes up. Crash!—And the knitting-women, never faltering or pausing in their work, count Two.

The supposed Evremonde descends, and the seamstress is lifted out next after him. He has not relinquished her patient hand in getting out, but still holds it as he promised. He gently places her with her back to the crashing engine that constantly whirrs up and falls, and she looks into his face and thanks him.

"But for you, dear stranger, I should not be so composed, for I am naturally a poor littie thing, faint of heart; nor should I have been able to raise my thoughts to Him who was put to death, that we might have hope and comfort here to-day. I think you were sent to me by Heaven."

"Or you to me," says Sydney Carton. "Keep your eyes upon me, dear child, and mind no other object."

"I mind nothing while I hold your hand. I shall mind nothing when I let it go, if they are rapid."

"They will be rapid. Fear not!"

The two stand in the fast-thinning throng of victims, but they speak as if they were alone. Eye to eye, voice to voice, hand to hand, heart to heart, these two children of the Universal Mother, else so wide apart and differing, have come together on the dark highway, to repair home together, and to rest in her bosom.

"Brave and generous friend, will you let me ask you one last question? I am very ignorant, and it troubles me—just a little."

"Tell me what it is."

"I have a cousin, an only relative and an orphan like myself, whom I love very dearly. She is five years younger than I, and she lives in a farmer's house in the south country. Poverty parted us, and she knows nothing of my fate—for I cannot write—and if I could, how should I tell her! It is better as it is."

"Yes, yes; better as it is."

"What I have been thinking as we came along, and what I am still thinking now, as I look into your kind, strong face, which gives me much support, is this:—If the Republic really does good to the poor, and they come to be less hungry, and in all ways to suffer less, she may live a long time! she may even llve to be old."

"What then, my gentle sister?"

"Do you think"—the uncomplaining eyes in which there is so much endurance, fill with tears, and the lips part a little more and tremble—"that it will seem long to me, while I wait for her in the better land where I trust both you and I will be mercifully sheltered?"

"It cannot be, my child; there is no Time there, and no trouble there."

"You comfort me so much! I am so ignorant. Am I to kiss you now? Is the moment come?"

"Yes."

She kisses his lips; he kisses hers; they solemnly bless each other. The spare hand does not tremble as he releases it: nothing worse than a sweet, bright constancy is in the patient face. She goes next before him—is gone; the knitting-women count Twenty-two.

"I am the Resurrection and the Life, saith the Lord; he that believeth in me, though he were dead, yet shall he live: and whosoever liveth and believeth in me shall never die."

The murmuring of many voices, the upturning of many faces, the pressing on of many footsteps in the outskirts of the crowd, so that it swells forward in a mass, like one great heave of water, all flashes away. Twenty-three.

They said of him, about the city that night, that it was the peacefullest man's face ever beheld there. Many added that he looked sublime and prophetic.

One of the most remarkable sufferers by the same axe—a woman—had asked at the foot of the same scaffold, not long before, to be allowed to write down the thoughts that were inspiring her. If he had given an utterance to his, and they were prophetic, they would have been these:

"I see Barsad, and Cly, Defarge, The Vengeance, the Juryman, the Judge, long ranks of the new oppressors who have risen on the destruction of the old, perishing by this retributive instrument, before it shall cease out of its present use. I see a beautiful city and a brilliant people rising from this abyss, and, in their struggles to be truly free, in their triumphs and defeats through long, long years to come, I see the evil of this time and of the previous time of which this is the natural birth, gradually making expiation for itself and wearing out.

"I see the lives for which I lay down my life, peaceful, useful, prosperous and happy, in that England which I shall see no more. I see Her with a child upon her bosom, who bears my name. I see her father, aged and bent, but otherwise restored, and faithful to all men in his healing office, and at peace. I see the good old man, so long their friend, in ten years' time enriching them with all he has, and passing tranquilly to his reward.

"I see that I hold a sanctuary in their hearts, and in the hearts of their descendants, generations hence. I see her, an old woman, weeping for me on the anniversary of this day. I see her and her husband, their course done, living side by side in their last earthly bed, and I know that each was not more honored and held sacred in the other's soul, than I was in the souls of both.

"I see that child who lay upon her bosom and who bore my name, a man winning his way up in that path of life which once was mine. I see him winning it so well, that my name is made illustrious there by the light of his. I see the blots I threw upon it faded away. I see him, foremost of just judges and honored men, bringing a boy of my name, with a forehead that I know and golden hair, to this place—then fair to look upon, with not a trace of this day's disfigurement—and I hear him tell the child my story, with a tender and faltering voice.

"It is a far, far better thing that I do, than I have ever done; it is a far, far better rest that I go to, than I have ever known."